MMM– I'D SAY IT WAS ELLERMAN, OR ONE OF THE ROTHSCHILDS. PERHAPS...? MAYBE OPPENHEIMER. THE DIAMOND MAN
YES, SIR!

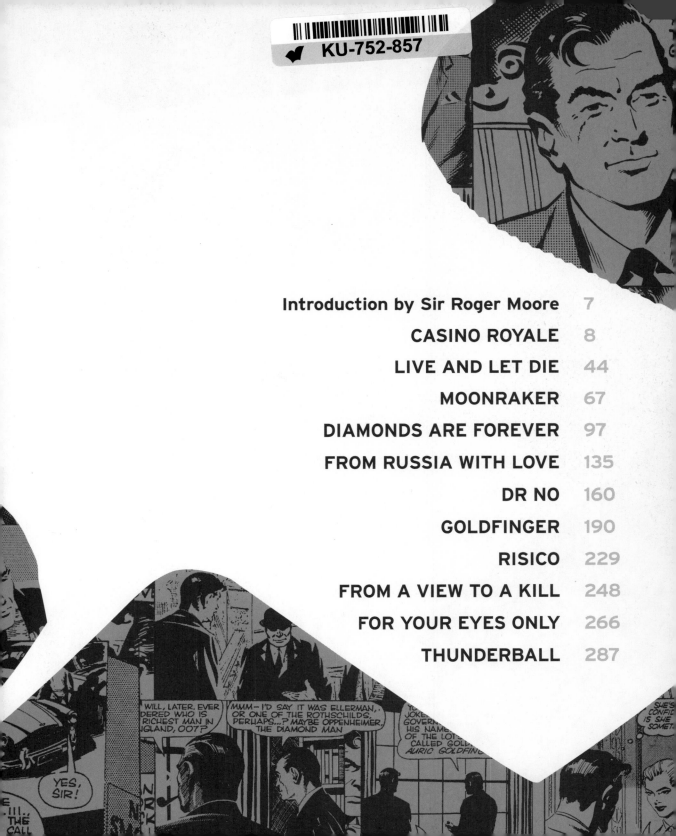

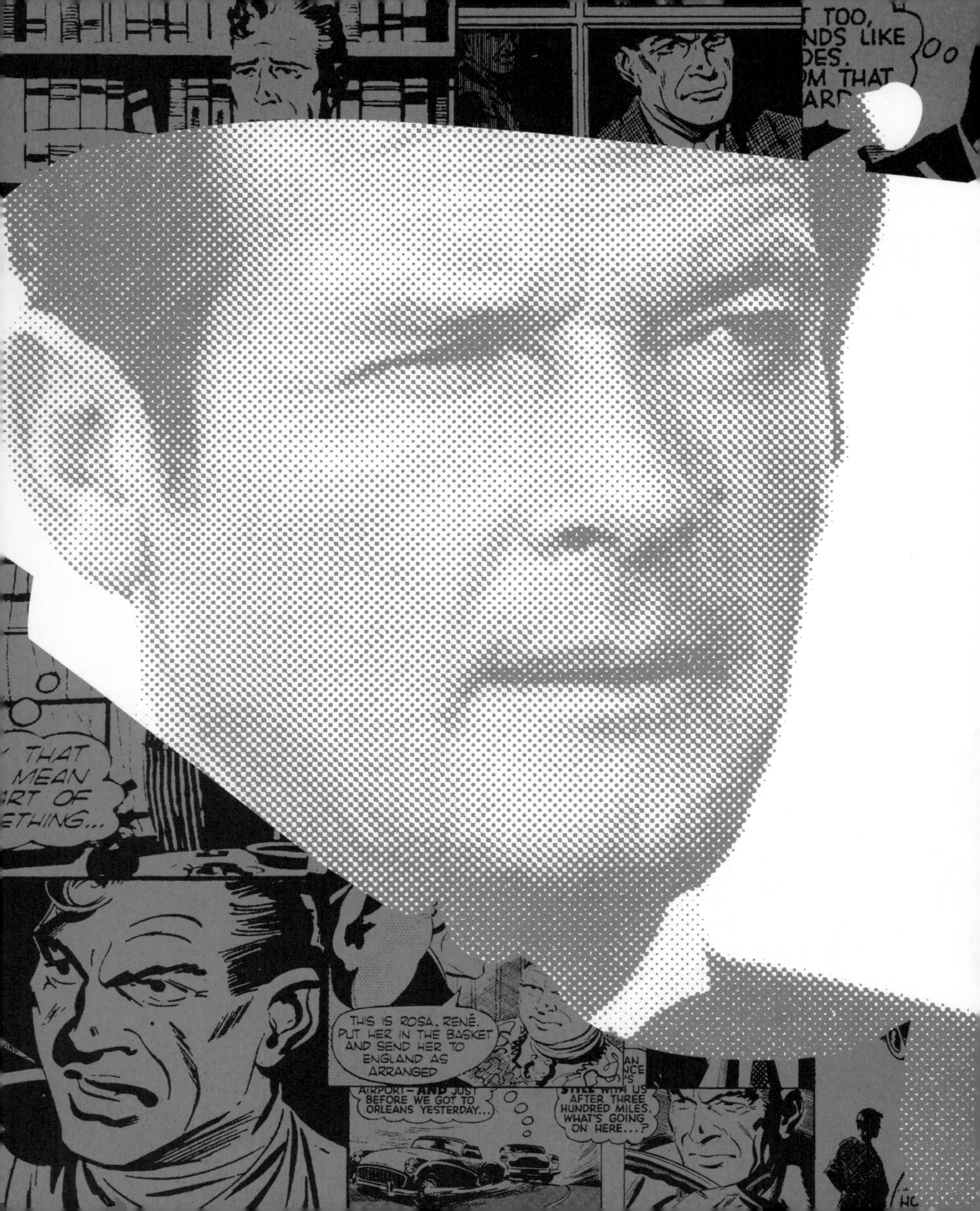
THIS IS ROSA, RENÉ. PUT HER IN THE BASKET AND SEND HER TO ENGLAND AS ARRANGED
AIRPORT — AND JUST BEFORE WE GOT TO ORLEANS YESTERDAY...
STILL WITH US AFTER THREE HUNDRED MILES. WHAT'S GOING ON HERE...?

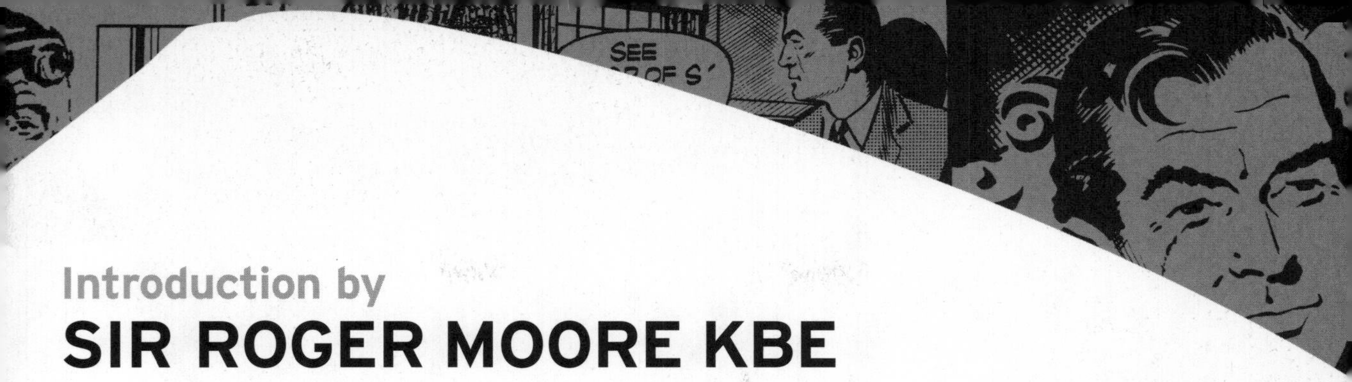
SEE

Introduction by

SIR ROGER MOORE KBE

BOND, JAMES BOND... was the name Ian Fleming chose for the hero in his first novel *Casino Royale* in 1953, because it was, he said, "the dullest name I could find". Yet we all recognise the character as one of the most exciting in the literary and film worlds.

It was Fleming's impending marriage to Anne Rothermere, at the age of forty-three, that was the catalyst in his writing the novel. The ensuing success of the book ensured a sequel, or rather a series of thirteen more volumes of adventure, womanising, hard drinking and espionage.

In 1954 the second of those thirteen, *Live and Let Die*, was published. It is a story for which I have a particular soft spot, as it was to become the basis of my first *James Bond* film – of the same name – nineteen years later. Fleming's second novel benefited from greater descriptive detail than his first, and it perhaps features one of his best plots. Its treatment of black people is extremely out of place in today's society, indeed as it was in 1973 too, but the story is perhaps more violent and hard-hitting than any other Fleming penned.

When gold coins from a seventeenth century pirate hoard turn up in pawn shops and banks in Harlem and further down the east coast in Florida, M suspects the treasure is being used to finance a Soviet spy ring, and that Mr Big – a powerful black businessman with reported links to SMERSH – is behind it. For the film, the central plot was changed to that of drugs, and the SMERSH links dropped. Whilst much of the film is centred around Fleming's wonderful characters and story, a couple of sequences from the novel – namely the shark attack on Felix Leiter and the coral dragging of Bond and the story's heroine Solitaire – were not used in the film, but did turn up in later ones.

Fortunately, I managed to get through the film pretty unscathed and must have done something right because they asked me to do another six – the biggest and most successful being *Moonraker* in 1979. It was in fact Fleming's third novel, and published in 1955. It had less action than his first two novels and tells of the main protagonist, Sir Hugo Drax, a respected and wealthy businessman, and his plans to donate £10 million to help Britain's defence... with a nuclear rocket called the Moonraker. However suspicions are aroused over Drax and Bond soon discovers that Drax is receiving backing from the USSR to turn his rocket on London – and destroy it!

Moonraker wasn't going to be my fourth film, but after *The Spy Who Loved Me*, films such as *Star Wars* and *Close Encounters* were dominating the box office charts; and so Cubby Broccoli said that the previously announced *For Yours Eyes Only* would become my fifth *Bond*, and *Moonraker* would be the *Bond* release for 1979. Of course the rather tame plot soon received an injection of high-tech hokum and the action dial was cranked up a few notches, thus launching Bond into space with a fiendish plot involving Drax wiping out the whole of mankind to create his own "perfect" race of humans. Thankfully Jimmy Bond was on hand to ensure he wouldn't succeed.

Bond has been a big part of my life – well, twelve years and seven movies would be a big part of anyone's life – and I for one am very grateful that fifty-odd years ago, Ian Fleming sat down at his Jamaican home and starting typing the first page of *Casino Royale*.

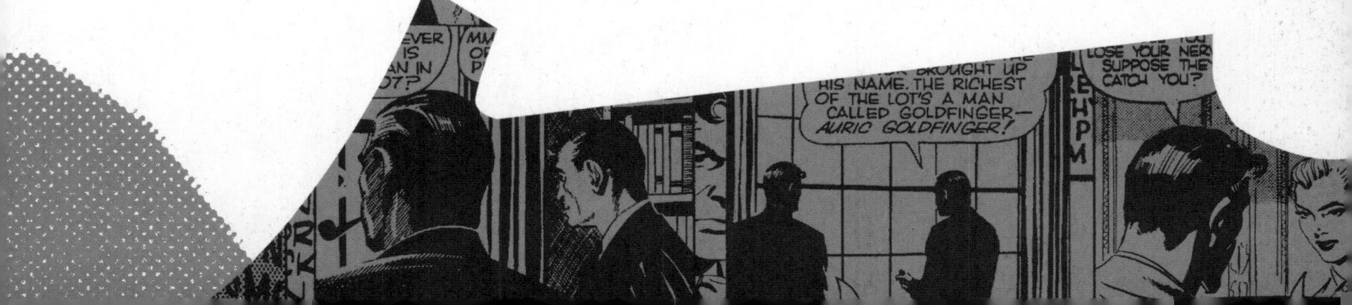
HIS NAME. THE RICHEST
OF THE LOT'S A MAN
CALLED GOLDFINGER—
AURIC GOLDFINGER!

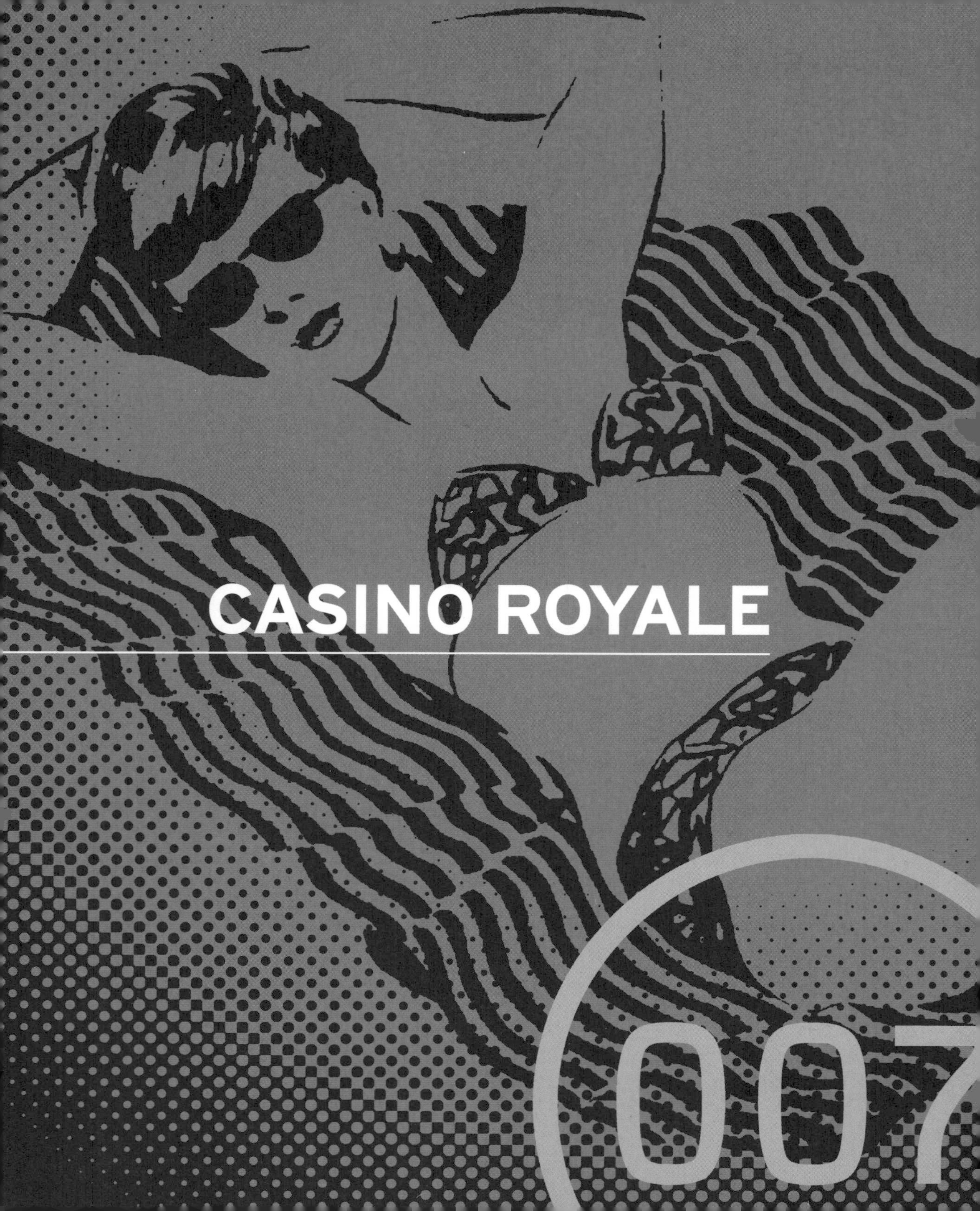
CASINO ROYALE
007

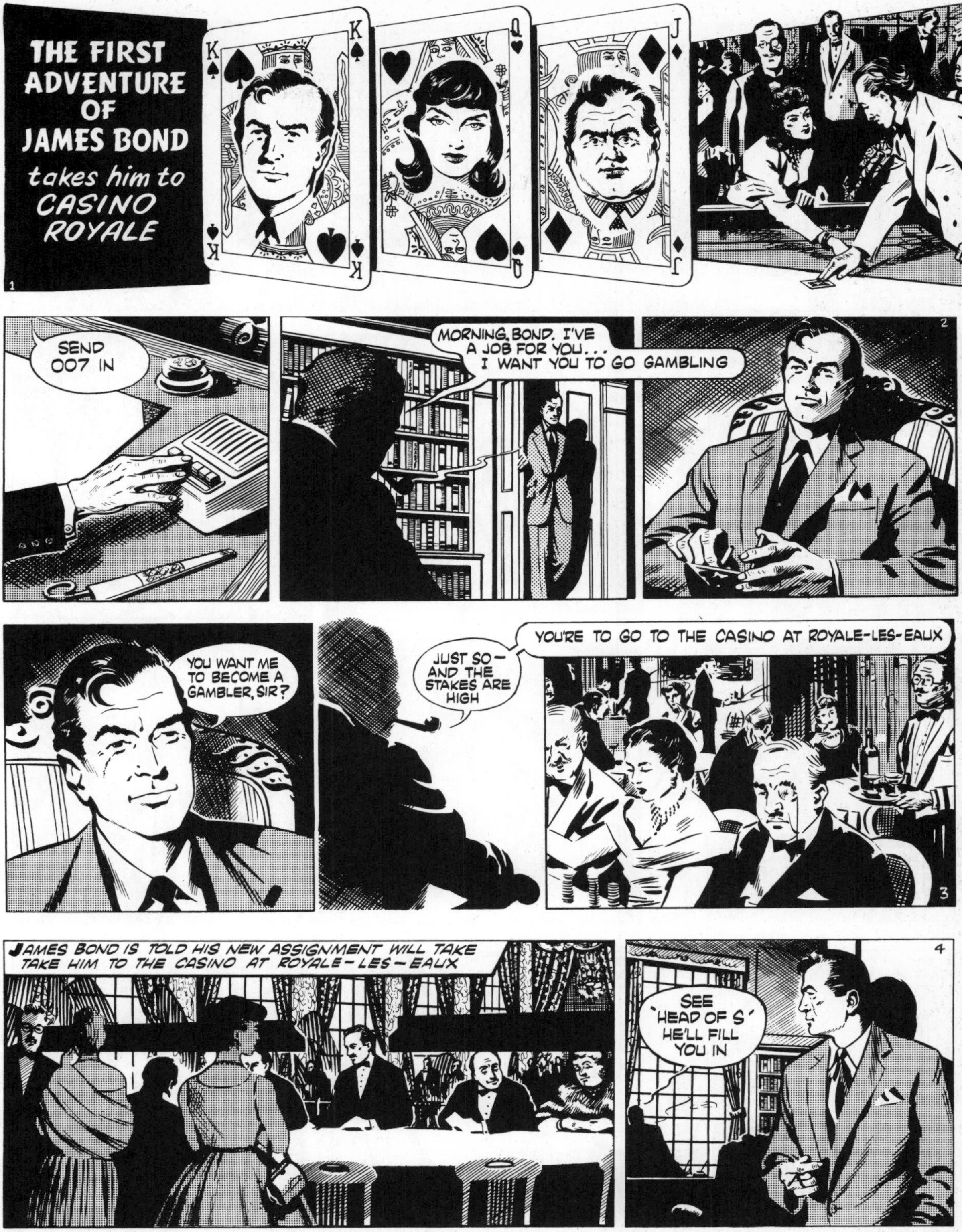
THE FIRST ADVENTURE OF JAMES BOND
takes him to CASINO ROYALE
1
SEND 007 IN
MORNING, BOND. I'VE A JOB FOR YOU... I WANT YOU TO GO GAMBLING
2
YOU WANT ME TO BECOME A GAMBLER, SIR?
JUST SO— AND THE STAKES ARE HIGH
YOU'RE TO GO TO THE CASINO AT ROYALE-LES-EAUX
3
JAMES BOND IS TOLD HIS NEW ASSIGNMENT WILL TAKE TAKE HIM TO THE CASINO AT ROYALE-LES-EAUX
4
SEE 'HEAD OF S' HE'LL FILL YOU IN

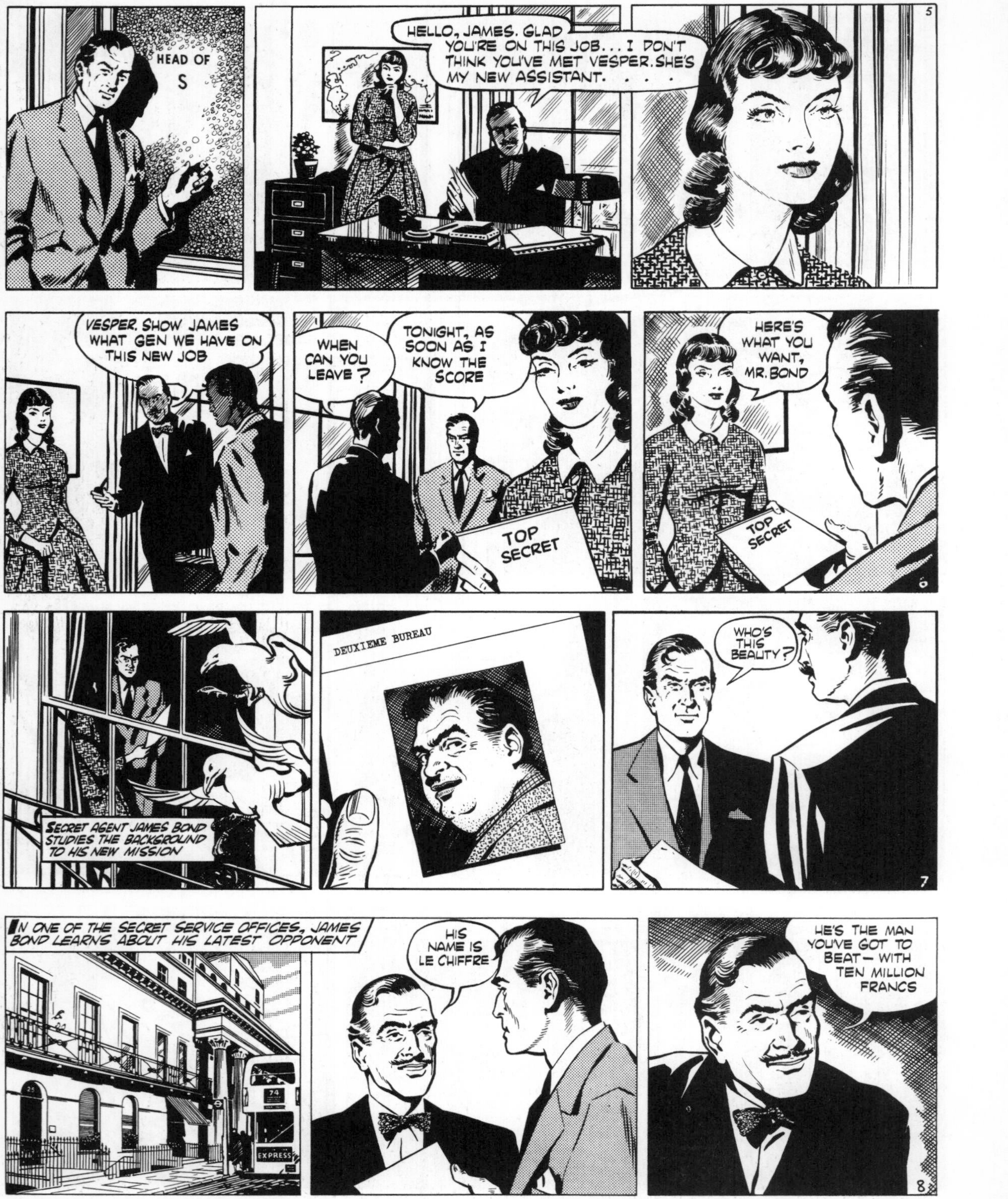
HEAD OF
S
HELLO, JAMES. GLAD YOU'RE ON THIS JOB... I DON'T THINK YOU'VE MET VESPER. SHE'S MY NEW ASSISTANT. . . .
5
VESPER. SHOW JAMES WHAT GEN WE HAVE ON THIS NEW JOB
WHEN CAN YOU LEAVE ?
TONIGHT, AS SOON AS I KNOW THE SCORE
TOP SECRET
HERE'S WHAT YOU WANT, MR. BOND
TOP SECRET
6
SECRET AGENT JAMES BOND STUDIES THE BACKGROUND TO HIS NEW MISSION
DEUXIEME BUREAU
WHO'S THIS BEAUTY?
7
IN ONE OF THE SECRET SERVICE OFFICES, JAMES BOND LEARNS ABOUT HIS LATEST OPPONENT
74
EXPRESS
HIS NAME IS LE CHIFFRE
HE'S THE MAN YOU'VE GOT TO BEAT— WITH TEN MILLION FRANCS
8

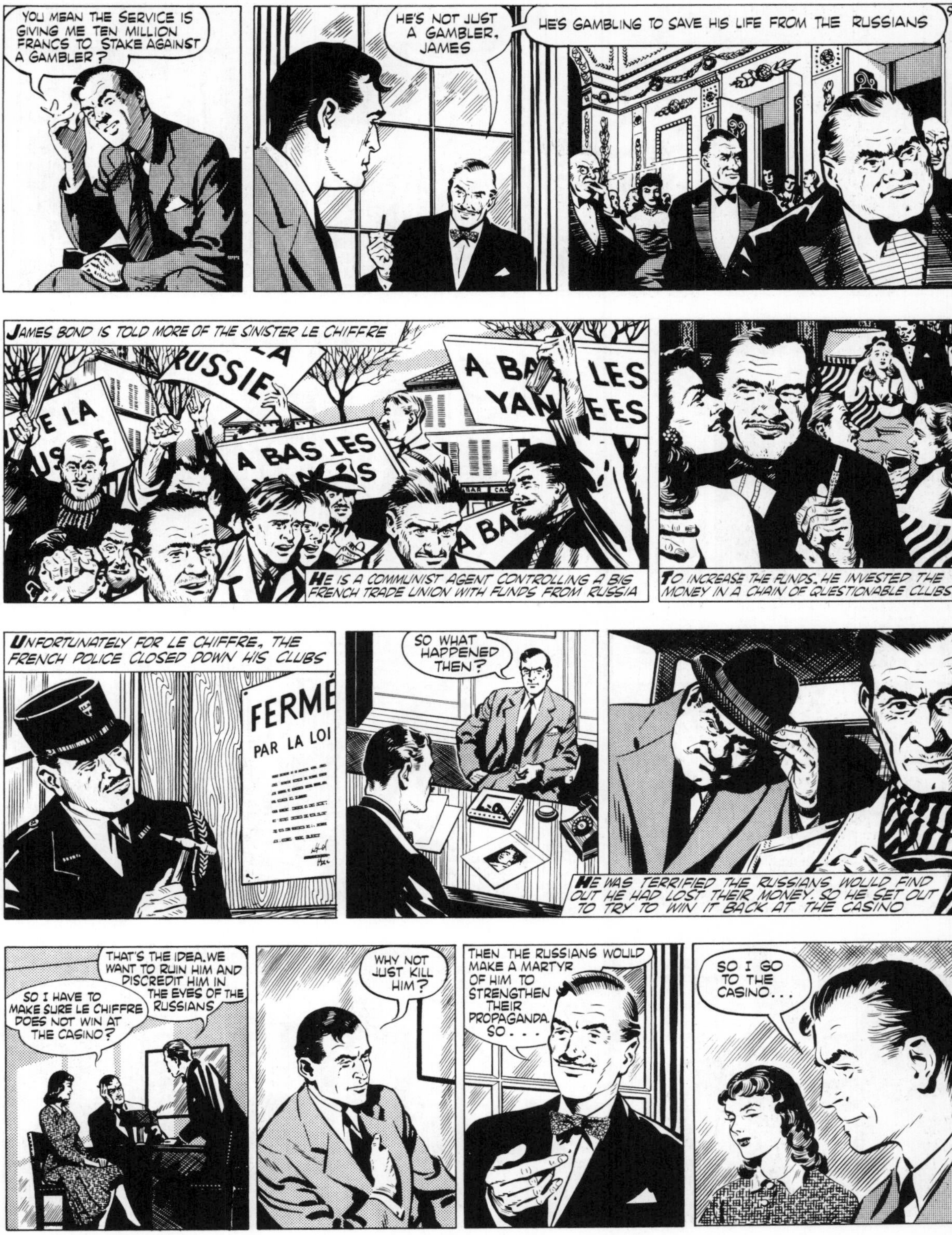
YOU MEAN THE SERVICE IS GIVING ME TEN MILLION FRANCS TO STAKE AGAINST A GAMBLER?
HE'S NOT JUST A GAMBLER, JAMES
HE'S GAMBLING TO SAVE HIS LIFE FROM THE RUSSIANS
9
JAMES BOND IS TOLD MORE OF THE SINISTER LE CHIFFRE
RUSSIE
A BAS LES
HE IS A COMMUNIST AGENT CONTROLLING A BIG FRENCH TRADE UNION WITH FUNDS FROM RUSSIA
10
TO INCREASE THE FUNDS, HE INVESTED THE MONEY IN A CHAIN OF QUESTIONABLE CLUBS
UNFORTUNATELY FOR LE CHIFFRE, THE FRENCH POLICE CLOSED DOWN HIS CLUBS
FERMÉ
PAR LA LOI
SO WHAT HAPPENED THEN?
HE WAS TERRIFIED THE RUSSIANS WOULD FIND OUT HE HAD LOST THEIR MONEY. SO HE SET OUT TO TRY TO WIN IT BACK AT THE CASINO
11
SO I HAVE TO MAKE SURE LE CHIFFRE DOES NOT WIN AT THE CASINO?
THAT'S THE IDEA. WE WANT TO RUIN HIM AND DISCREDIT HIM IN THE EYES OF THE RUSSIANS
WHY NOT JUST KILL HIM?
THEN THE RUSSIANS WOULD MAKE A MARTYR OF HIM TO STRENGTHEN THEIR PROPAGANDA. SO . . .
12
SO I GO TO THE CASINO . . .

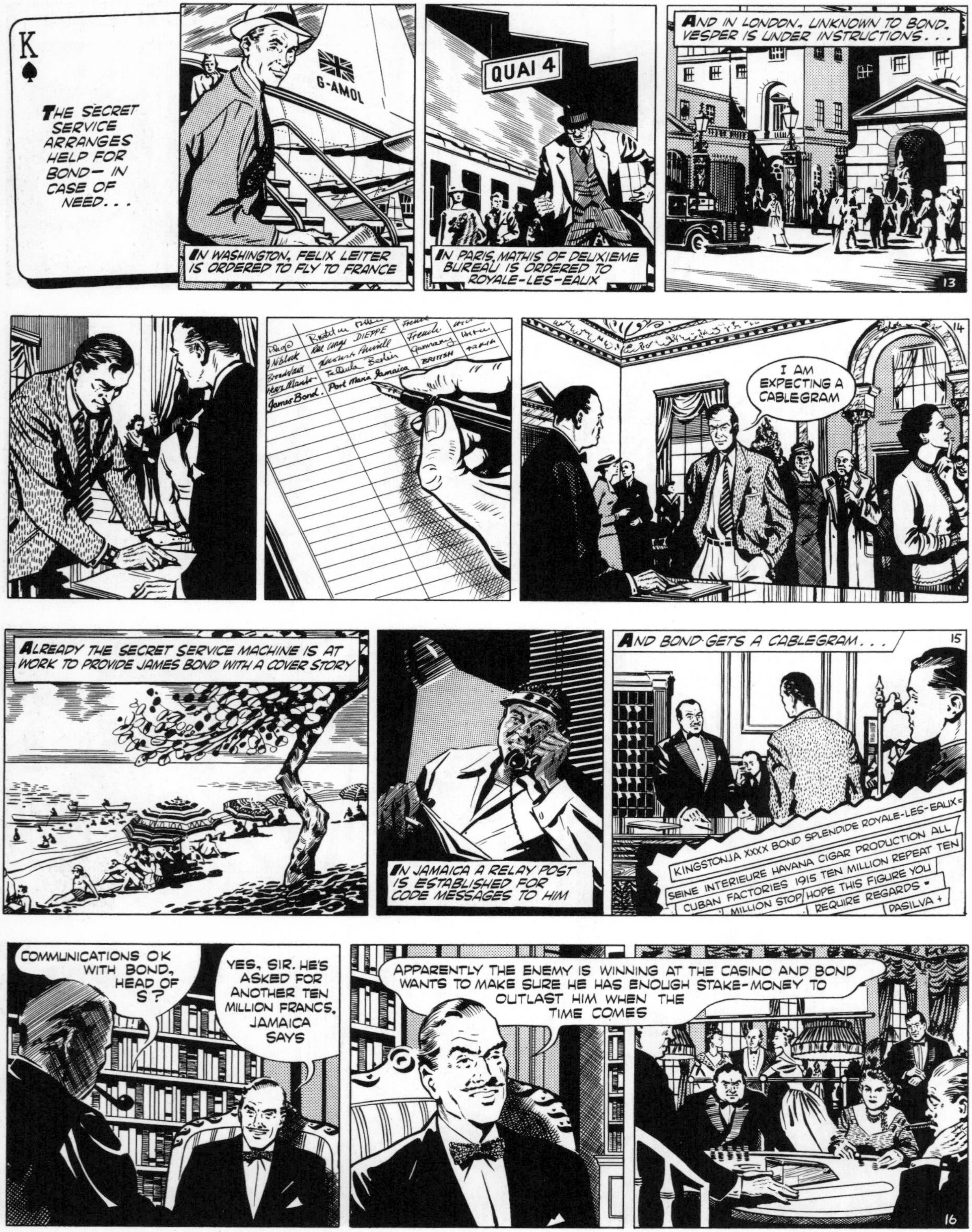

K
THE SECRET SERVICE ARRANGES HELP FOR BOND— IN CASE OF NEED...
G-AMOL
IN WASHINGTON, FELIX LEITER IS ORDERED TO FLY TO FRANCE
QUAI 4
IN PARIS, MATHIS OF DEUXIEME BUREAU IS ORDERED TO ROYALE-LES-EAUX
AND IN LONDON, UNKNOWN TO BOND, VESPER IS UNDER INSTRUCTIONS...
13
James Bond. Port Maria Jamaica
14
I AM EXPECTING A CABLEGRAM
ALREADY THE SECRET SERVICE MACHINE IS AT WORK TO PROVIDE JAMES BOND WITH A COVER STORY
IN JAMAICA A RELAY POST IS ESTABLISHED FOR CODE MESSAGES TO HIM
AND BOND GETS A CABLEGRAM...
15
KINGSTONJA XXXX BOND SPLENDIDE ROYALE-LES-EAUX=
SEINE INTERIEURE HAVANA CIGAR PRODUCTION ALL
CUBAN FACTORIES 1915 TEN MILLION REPEAT TEN
MILLION STOP HOPE THIS FIGURE YOU
REQUIRE REGARDS =
DASILVA +
COMMUNICATIONS OK WITH BOND, HEAD OF S?
YES, SIR. HE'S ASKED FOR ANOTHER TEN MILLION FRANCS, JAMAICA SAYS
APPARENTLY THE ENEMY IS WINNING AT THE CASINO AND BOND WANTS TO MAKE SURE HE HAS ENOUGH STAKE-MONEY TO OUTLAST HIM WHEN THE TIME COMES
16

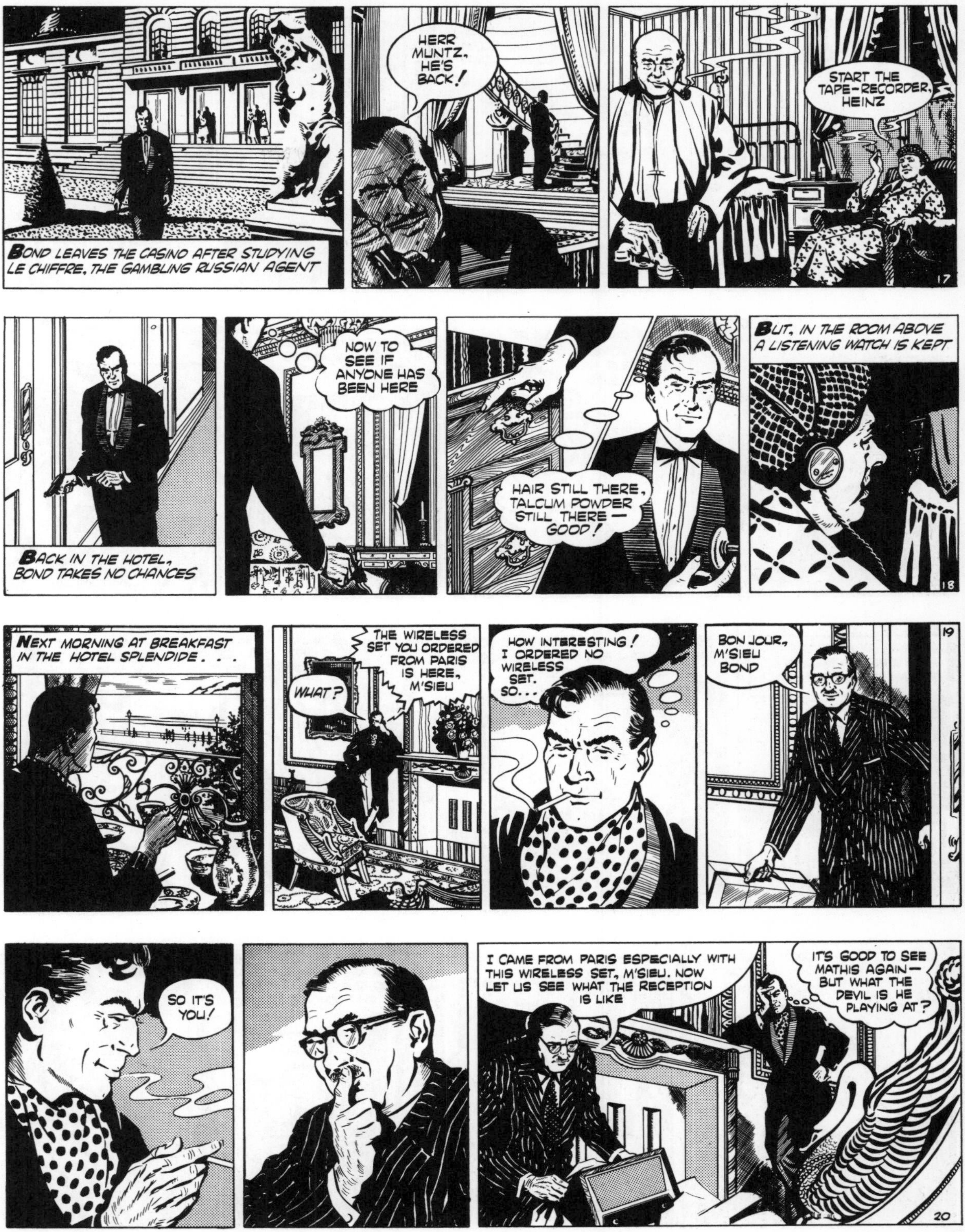
BOND LEAVES THE CASINO AFTER STUDYING LE CHIFFRE, THE GAMBLING RUSSIAN AGENT
HERR MUNTZ, HE'S BACK!
START THE TAPE-RECORDER, HEINZ
17
BACK IN THE HOTEL, BOND TAKES NO CHANCES
NOW TO SEE IF ANYONE HAS BEEN HERE
HAIR STILL THERE, TALCUM POWDER STILL THERE — GOOD!
BUT, IN THE ROOM ABOVE A LISTENING WATCH IS KEPT
18
NEXT MORNING AT BREAKFAST IN THE HOTEL SPLENDIDE . . .
THE WIRELESS SET YOU ORDERED FROM PARIS IS HERE, M'SIEU
WHAT?
HOW INTERESTING! I ORDERED NO WIRELESS SET. SO . . .
BON JOUR, M'SIEU BOND
19
SO IT'S YOU!
I CAME FROM PARIS ESPECIALLY WITH THIS WIRELESS SET, M'SIEU. NOW LET US SEE WHAT THE RECEPTION IS LIKE
IT'S GOOD TO SEE MATHIS AGAIN — BUT WHAT THE DEVIL IS HE PLAYING AT?
20

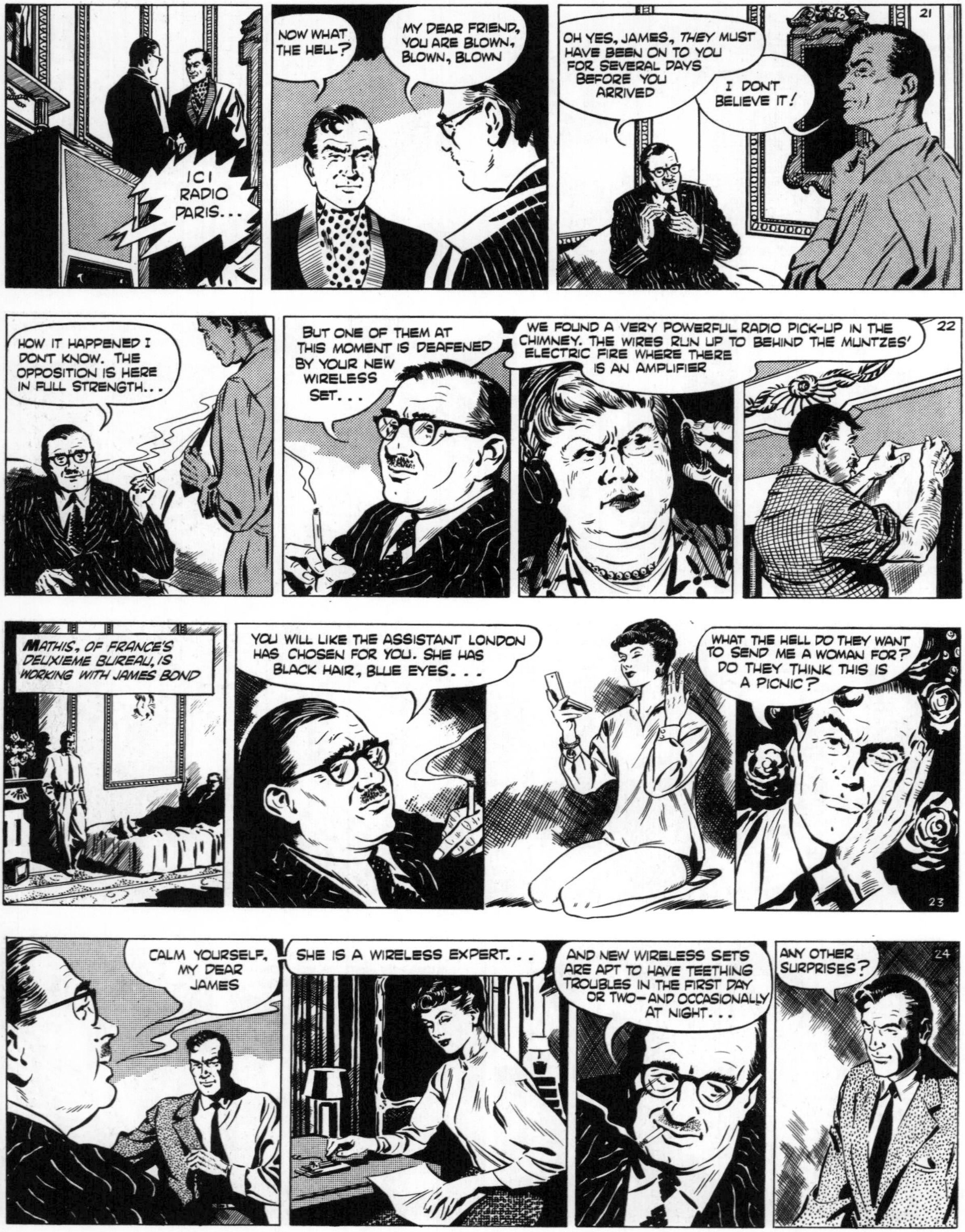
ICI RADIO PARIS...
NOW WHAT THE HELL?
MY DEAR FRIEND, YOU ARE BLOWN, BLOWN, BLOWN
21
OH YES, JAMES, *THEY* MUST HAVE BEEN ON TO YOU FOR SEVERAL DAYS BEFORE YOU ARRIVED
I DON'T BELIEVE IT!
HOW IT HAPPENED I DONT KNOW. THE OPPOSITION IS HERE IN FULL STRENGTH...
BUT ONE OF THEM AT THIS MOMENT IS DEAFENED BY YOUR NEW WIRELESS SET...
WE FOUND A VERY POWERFUL RADIO PICK-UP IN THE CHIMNEY. THE WIRES RUN UP TO BEHIND THE MUNTZES' ELECTRIC FIRE WHERE THERE IS AN AMPLIFIER
22
MATHIS, OF FRANCE'S DEUXIEME BUREAU, IS WORKING WITH JAMES BOND
YOU WILL LIKE THE ASSISTANT LONDON HAS CHOSEN FOR YOU. SHE HAS BLACK HAIR, BLUE EYES...
WHAT THE HELL DO THEY WANT TO SEND ME A WOMAN FOR? DO THEY THINK THIS IS A PICNIC?
23
CALM YOURSELF, MY DEAR JAMES
SHE IS A WIRELESS EXPERT...
AND NEW WIRELESS SETS ARE APT TO HAVE TEETHING TROUBLES IN THE FIRST DAY OR TWO—AND OCCASIONALLY AT NIGHT...
ANY OTHER SURPRISES?
24

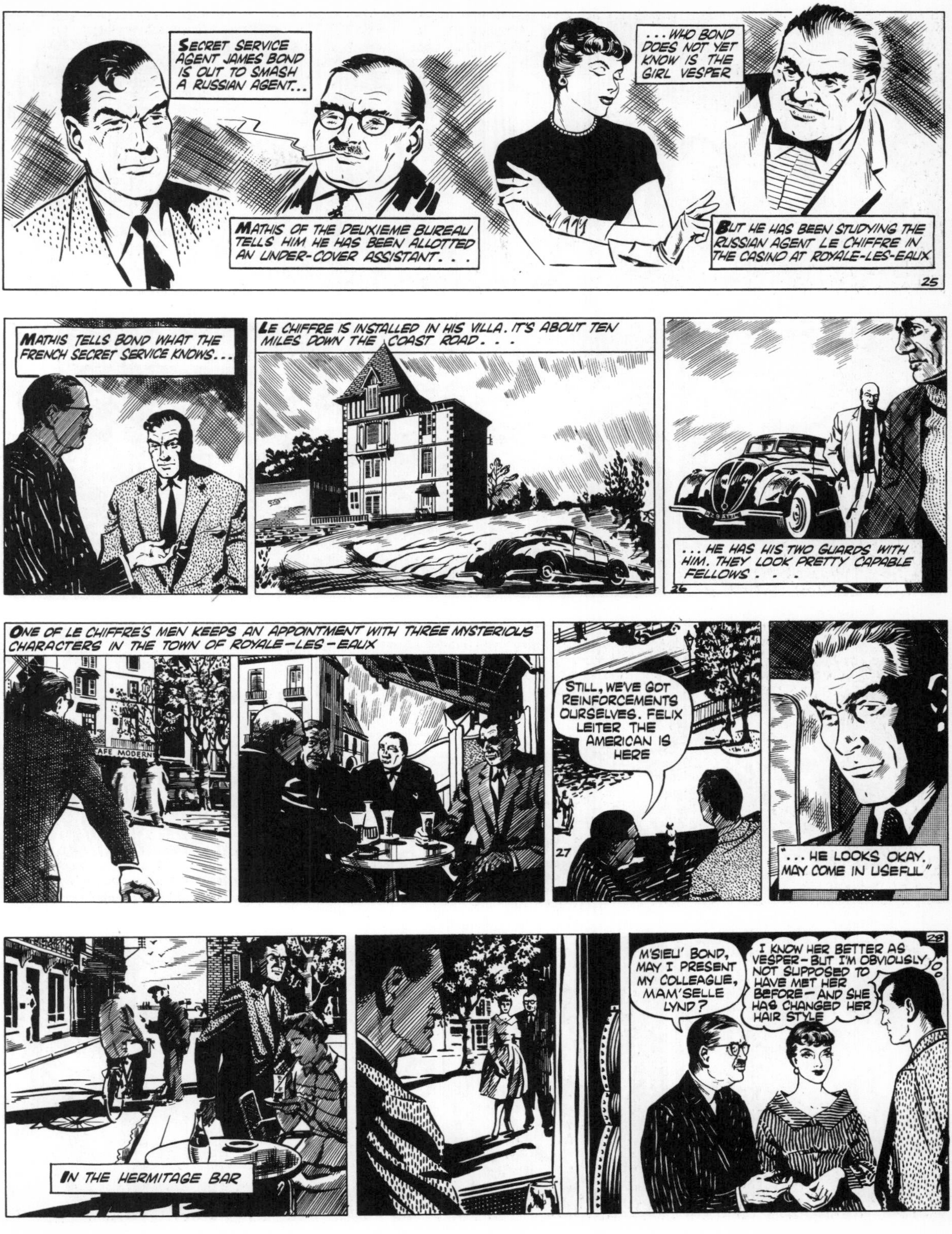
SECRET SERVICE AGENT JAMES BOND IS OUT TO SMASH A RUSSIAN AGENT...
MATHIS OF THE DEUXIEME BUREAU TELLS HIM HE HAS BEEN ALLOTTED AN UNDER-COVER ASSISTANT . . .
. . . WHO BOND DOES NOT YET KNOW IS THE GIRL VESPER
BUT HE HAS BEEN STUDYING THE RUSSIAN AGENT LE CHIFFRE IN THE CASINO AT ROYALE-LES-EAUX
25
MATHIS TELLS BOND WHAT THE FRENCH SECRET SERVICE KNOWS...
LE CHIFFRE IS INSTALLED IN HIS VILLA. IT'S ABOUT TEN MILES DOWN THE COAST ROAD . . .
. . . HE HAS HIS TWO GUARDS WITH HIM. THEY LOOK PRETTY CAPABLE FELLOWS . . .
26
ONE OF LE CHIFFRE'S MEN KEEPS AN APPOINTMENT WITH THREE MYSTERIOUS CHARACTERS IN THE TOWN OF ROYALE-LES-EAUX
CAFE MODERNE
STILL, WE'VE GOT REINFORCEMENTS OURSELVES. FELIX LEITER THE AMERICAN IS HERE
27
"... HE LOOKS OKAY. MAY COME IN USEFUL"
IN THE HERMITAGE BAR
M'SIEU' BOND, MAY I PRESENT MY COLLEAGUE, MAM'SELLE LYND?
I KNOW HER BETTER AS VESPER– BUT I'M OBVIOUSLY NOT SUPPOSED TO HAVE MET HER BEFORE– AND SHE HAS CHANGED HER HAIR STYLE
28

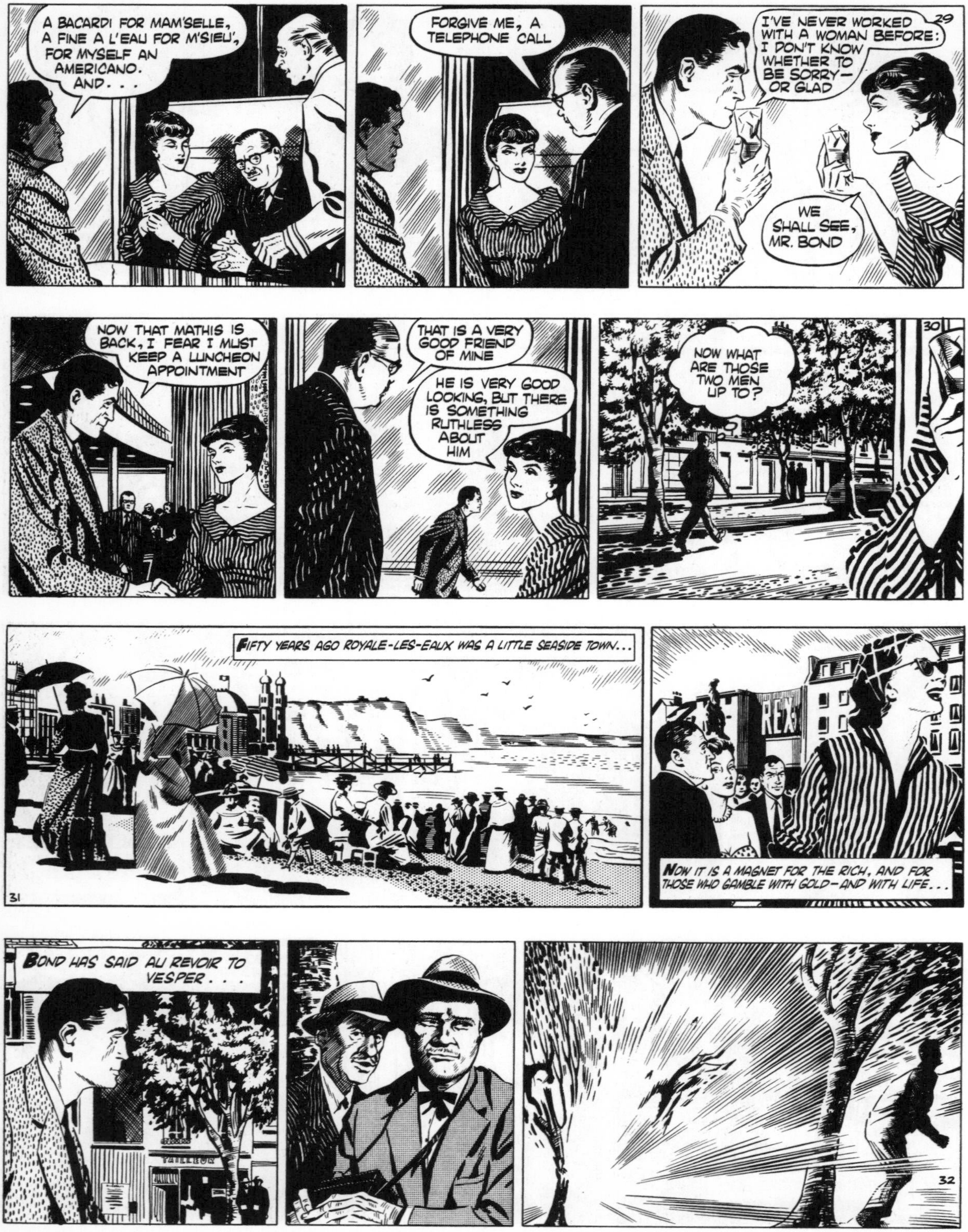
A BACARDI FOR MAM'SELLE, A FINE A L'EAU FOR M'SIEU', FOR MYSELF AN AMERICANO. AND . . .
FORGIVE ME, A TELEPHONE CALL
I'VE NEVER WORKED WITH A WOMAN BEFORE: I DON'T KNOW WHETHER TO BE SORRY— OR GLAD
WE SHALL SEE, MR. BOND
NOW THAT MATHIS IS BACK, I FEAR I MUST KEEP A LUNCHEON APPOINTMENT
THAT IS A VERY GOOD FRIEND OF MINE
HE IS VERY GOOD LOOKING, BUT THERE IS SOMETHING RUTHLESS ABOUT HIM
NOW WHAT ARE THOSE TWO MEN UP TO?
FIFTY YEARS AGO ROYALE-LES-EAUX WAS A LITTLE SEASIDE TOWN...
REX
NOW IT IS A MAGNET FOR THE RICH, AND FOR THOSE WHO GAMBLE WITH GOLD—AND WITH LIFE...
BOND HAS SAID AU REVOIR TO VESPER . . .

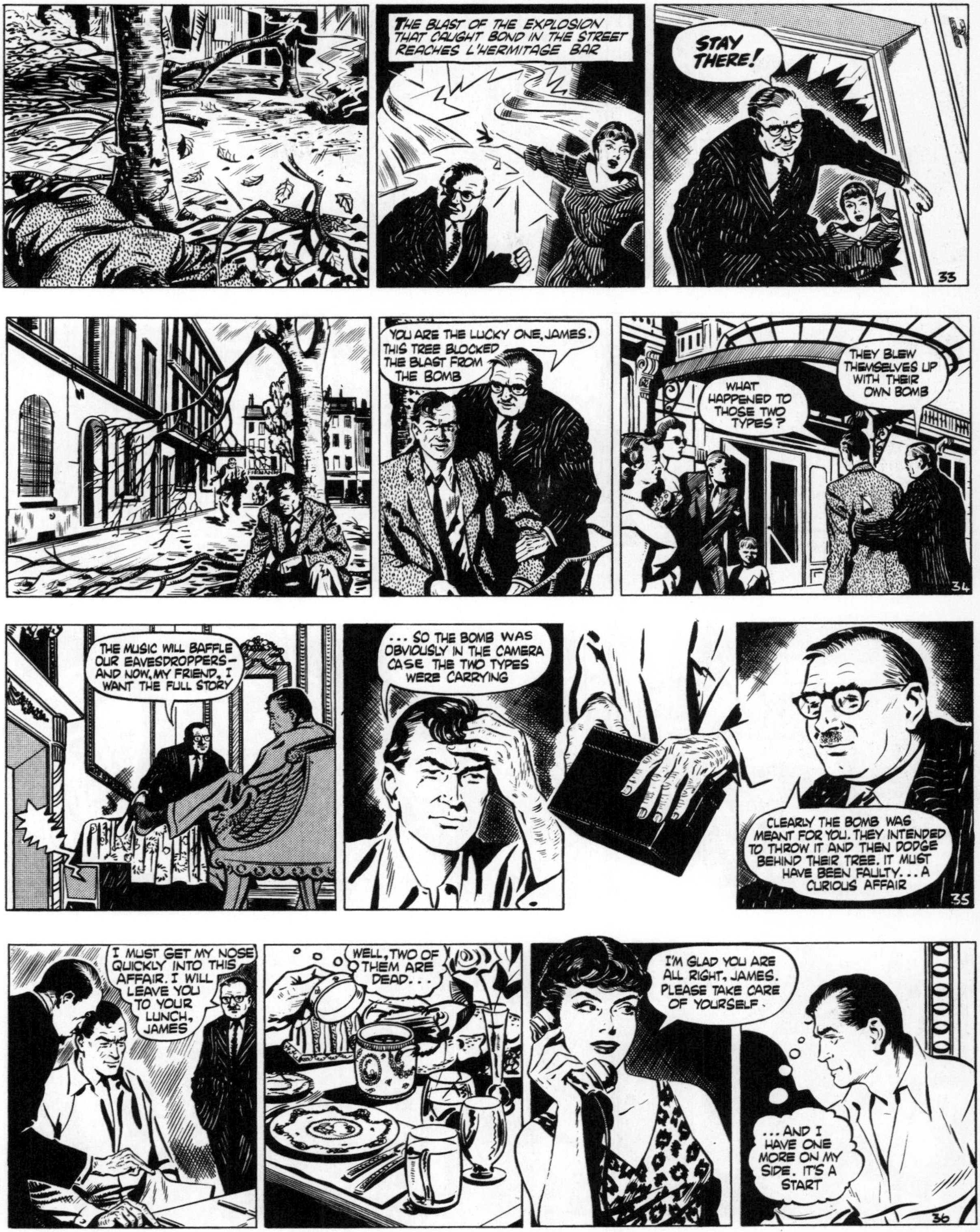

THE BLAST OF THE EXPLOSION THAT CAUGHT BOND IN THE STREET REACHES L'HERMITAGE BAR
STAY THERE!
33
YOU ARE THE LUCKY ONE, JAMES. THIS TREE BLOCKED THE BLAST FROM THE BOMB
WHAT HAPPENED TO THOSE TWO TYPES?
THEY BLEW THEMSELVES UP WITH THEIR OWN BOMB
34
THE MUSIC WILL BAFFLE OUR EAVESDROPPERS– AND NOW, MY FRIEND, I WANT THE FULL STORY
... SO THE BOMB WAS OBVIOUSLY IN THE CAMERA CASE THE TWO TYPES WERE CARRYING
CLEARLY THE BOMB WAS MEANT FOR YOU. THEY INTENDED TO THROW IT AND THEN DODGE BEHIND THEIR TREE. IT MUST HAVE BEEN FAULTY... A CURIOUS AFFAIR
35
I MUST GET MY NOSE QUICKLY INTO THIS AFFAIR. I WILL LEAVE YOU TO YOUR LUNCH, JAMES
WELL, TWO OF THEM ARE DEAD...
I'M GLAD YOU ARE ALL RIGHT, JAMES. PLEASE TAKE CARE OF YOURSELF.
... AND I HAVE ONE MORE ON MY SIDE. IT'S A START
36

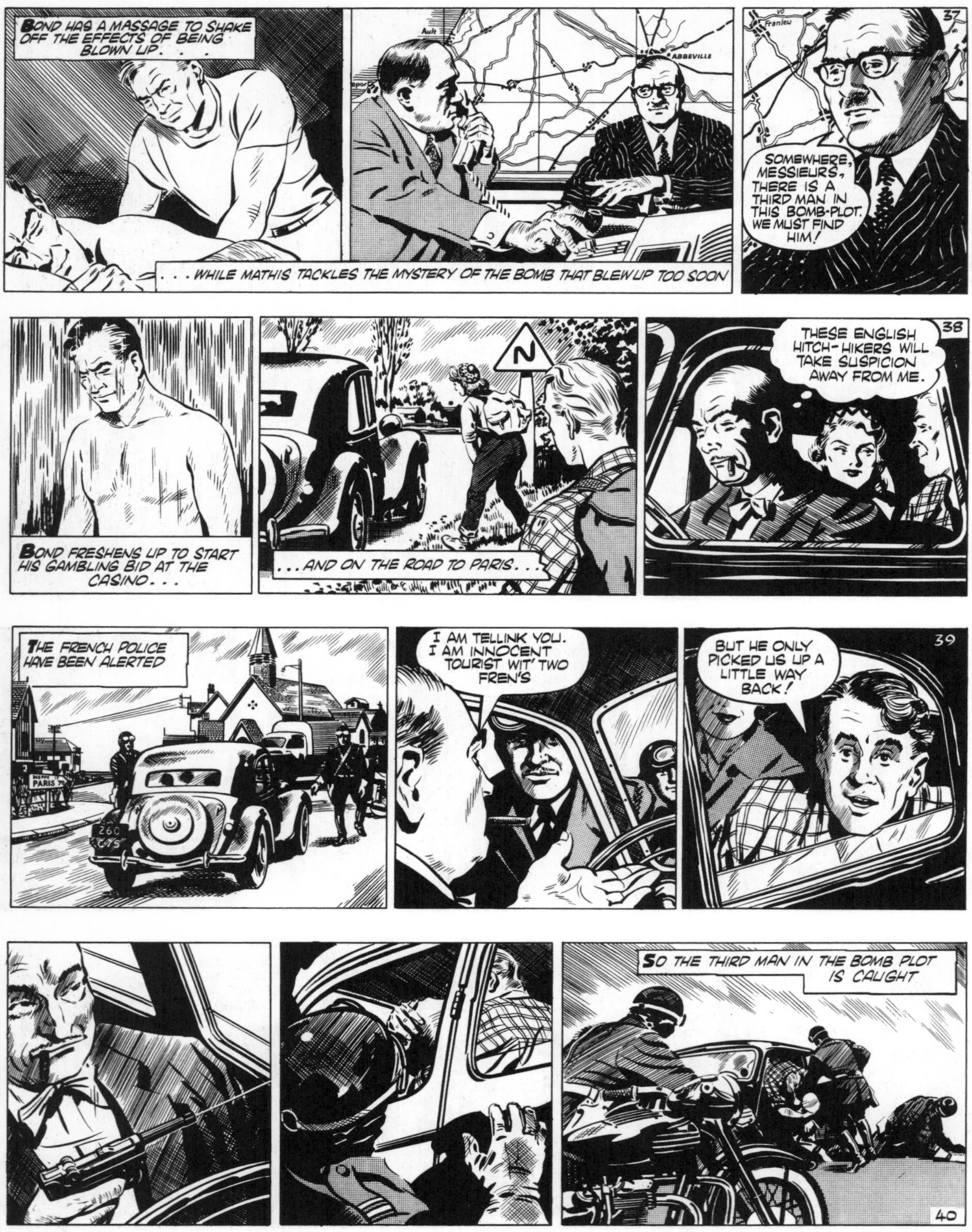
BOND HAS A MASSAGE TO SHAKE OFF THE EFFECTS OF BEING BLOWN UP. . .
Ault
ABBEVILLE
. . . WHILE MATHIS TACKLES THE MYSTERY OF THE BOMB THAT BLEW UP TOO SOON
Franleu
37
SOMEWHERE, MESSIEURS, THERE IS A THIRD MAN IN THIS BOMB-PLOT. WE MUST FIND HIM!
BOND FRESHENS UP TO START HIS GAMBLING BID AT THE CASINO . . .
N
. . . AND ON THE ROAD TO PARIS . . .
38
THESE ENGLISH HITCH-HIKERS WILL TAKE SUSPICION AWAY FROM ME.
THE FRENCH POLICE HAVE BEEN ALERTED
PARIS
I AM TELLINK YOU. I AM INNOCENT TOURIST WIT' TWO FREN'S
39
BUT HE ONLY PICKED US UP A LITTLE WAY BACK!
SO THE THIRD MAN IN THE BOMB PLOT IS CAUGHT
40

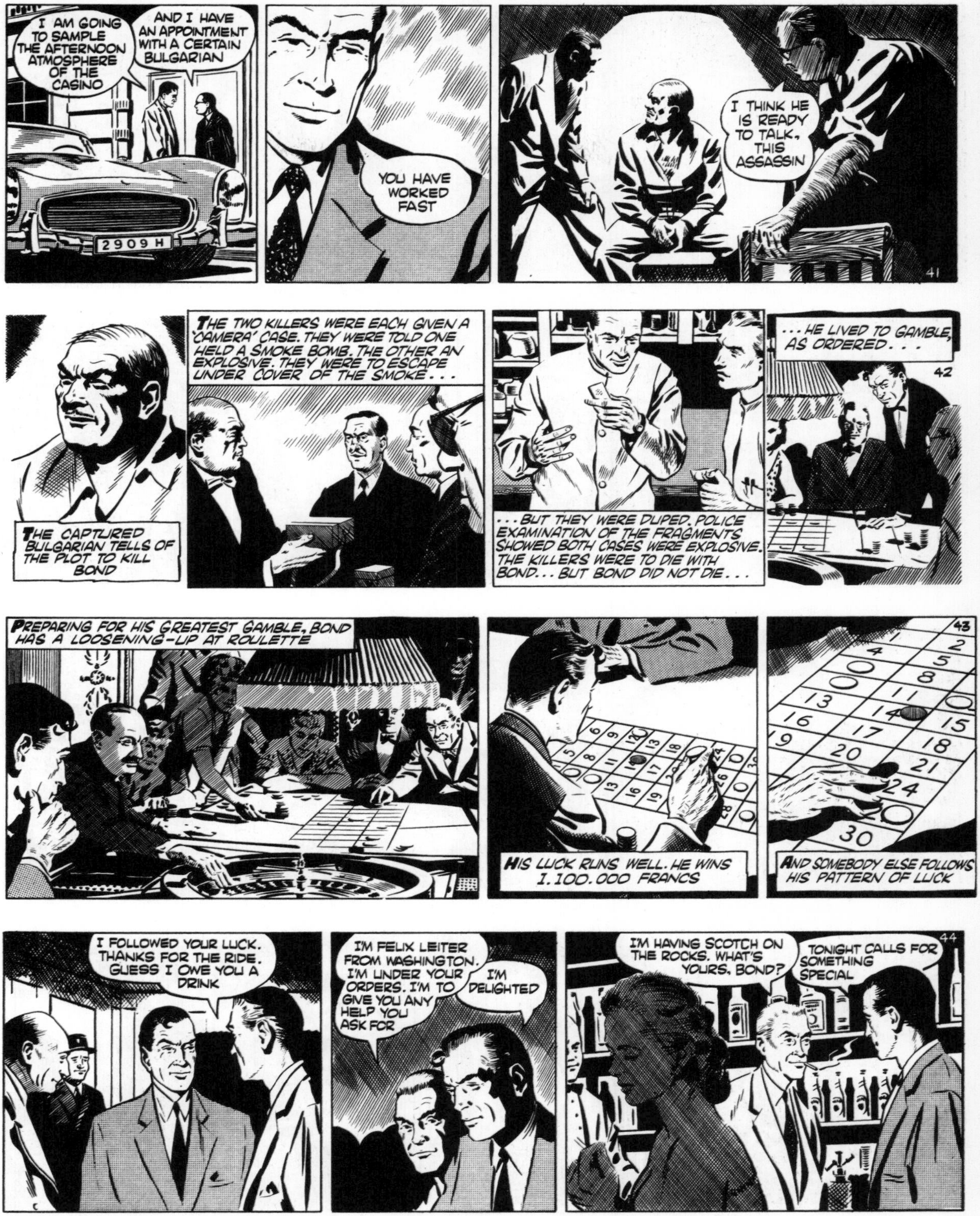
I AM GOING TO SAMPLE THE AFTERNOON ATMOSPHERE OF THE CASINO
AND I HAVE AN APPOINTMENT WITH A CERTAIN BULGARIAN
2909 H
YOU HAVE WORKED FAST
I THINK HE IS READY TO TALK, THIS ASSASSIN
41
THE CAPTURED BULGARIAN TELLS OF THE PLOT TO KILL BOND
THE TWO KILLERS WERE EACH GIVEN A 'CAMERA' CASE. THEY WERE TOLD ONE HELD A SMOKE BOMB. THE OTHER AN EXPLOSIVE. THEY WERE TO ESCAPE UNDER COVER OF THE SMOKE . . .
. . . BUT THEY WERE DUPED. POLICE EXAMINATION OF THE FRAGMENTS SHOWED BOTH CASES WERE EXPLOSIVE. THE KILLERS WERE TO DIE WITH BOND . . . BUT BOND DID NOT DIE . . .
. . . HE LIVED TO GAMBLE, AS ORDERED . . .
42
PREPARING FOR HIS GREATEST GAMBLE, BOND HAS A LOOSENING-UP AT ROULETTE
HIS LUCK RUNS WELL. HE WINS 1.100.000 FRANCS
43
AND SOMEBODY ELSE FOLLOWS HIS PATTERN OF LUCK
I FOLLOWED YOUR LUCK. THANKS FOR THE RIDE. GUESS I OWE YOU A DRINK
I'M FELIX LEITER FROM WASHINGTON. I'M UNDER YOUR ORDERS. I'M TO GIVE YOU ANY HELP YOU ASK FOR
I'M DELIGHTED
I'M HAVING SCOTCH ON THE ROCKS. WHAT'S YOURS, BOND?
TONIGHT CALLS FOR SOMETHING SPECIAL
44

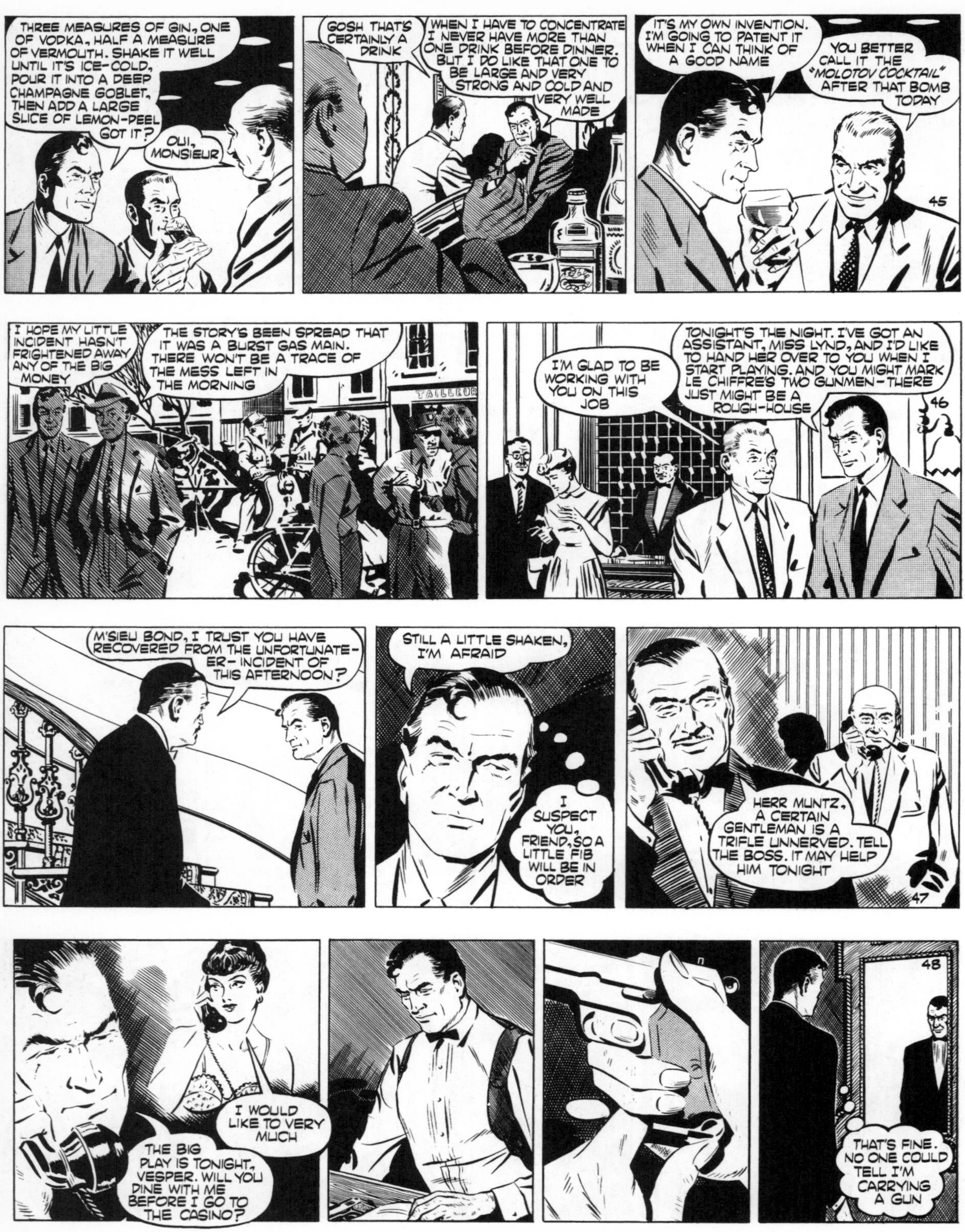
THREE MEASURES OF GIN, ONE OF VODKA, HALF A MEASURE OF VERMOUTH. SHAKE IT WELL UNTIL IT'S ICE-COLD, POUR IT INTO A DEEP CHAMPAGNE GOBLET, THEN ADD A LARGE SLICE OF LEMON-PEEL GOT IT?
OUI, MONSIEUR
GOSH THAT'S CERTAINLY A DRINK
WHEN I HAVE TO CONCENTRATE I NEVER HAVE MORE THAN ONE DRINK BEFORE DINNER. BUT I DO LIKE THAT ONE TO BE LARGE AND VERY STRONG AND COLD AND VERY WELL MADE
IT'S MY OWN INVENTION. I'M GOING TO PATENT IT WHEN I CAN THINK OF A GOOD NAME
YOU BETTER CALL IT THE "MOLOTOV COCKTAIL" AFTER THAT BOMB TODAY
45
I HOPE MY LITTLE INCIDENT HASN'T FRIGHTENED AWAY ANY OF THE BIG MONEY
THE STORY'S BEEN SPREAD THAT IT WAS A BURST GAS MAIN. THERE WON'T BE A TRACE OF THE MESS LEFT IN THE MORNING
TAILLEUR
I'M GLAD TO BE WORKING WITH YOU ON THIS JOB
TONIGHT'S THE NIGHT. I'VE GOT AN ASSISTANT, MISS LYND, AND I'D LIKE TO HAND HER OVER TO YOU WHEN I START PLAYING. AND YOU MIGHT MARK LE CHIFFRE'S TWO GUNMEN–THERE JUST MIGHT BE A ROUGH-HOUSE
46
M'SIEU BOND, I TRUST YOU HAVE RECOVERED FROM THE UNFORTUNATE–ER–INCIDENT OF THIS AFTERNOON?
STILL A LITTLE SHAKEN, I'M AFRAID
I SUSPECT YOU, FRIEND, SO A LITTLE FIB WILL BE IN ORDER
HERR MUNTZ, A CERTAIN GENTLEMAN IS A TRIFLE UNNERVED. TELL THE BOSS. IT MAY HELP HIM TONIGHT
47
THE BIG PLAY IS TONIGHT, VESPER. WILL YOU DINE WITH ME BEFORE I GO TO THE CASINO?
I WOULD LIKE TO VERY MUCH
48
THAT'S FINE. NO ONE COULD TELL I'M CARRYING A GUN

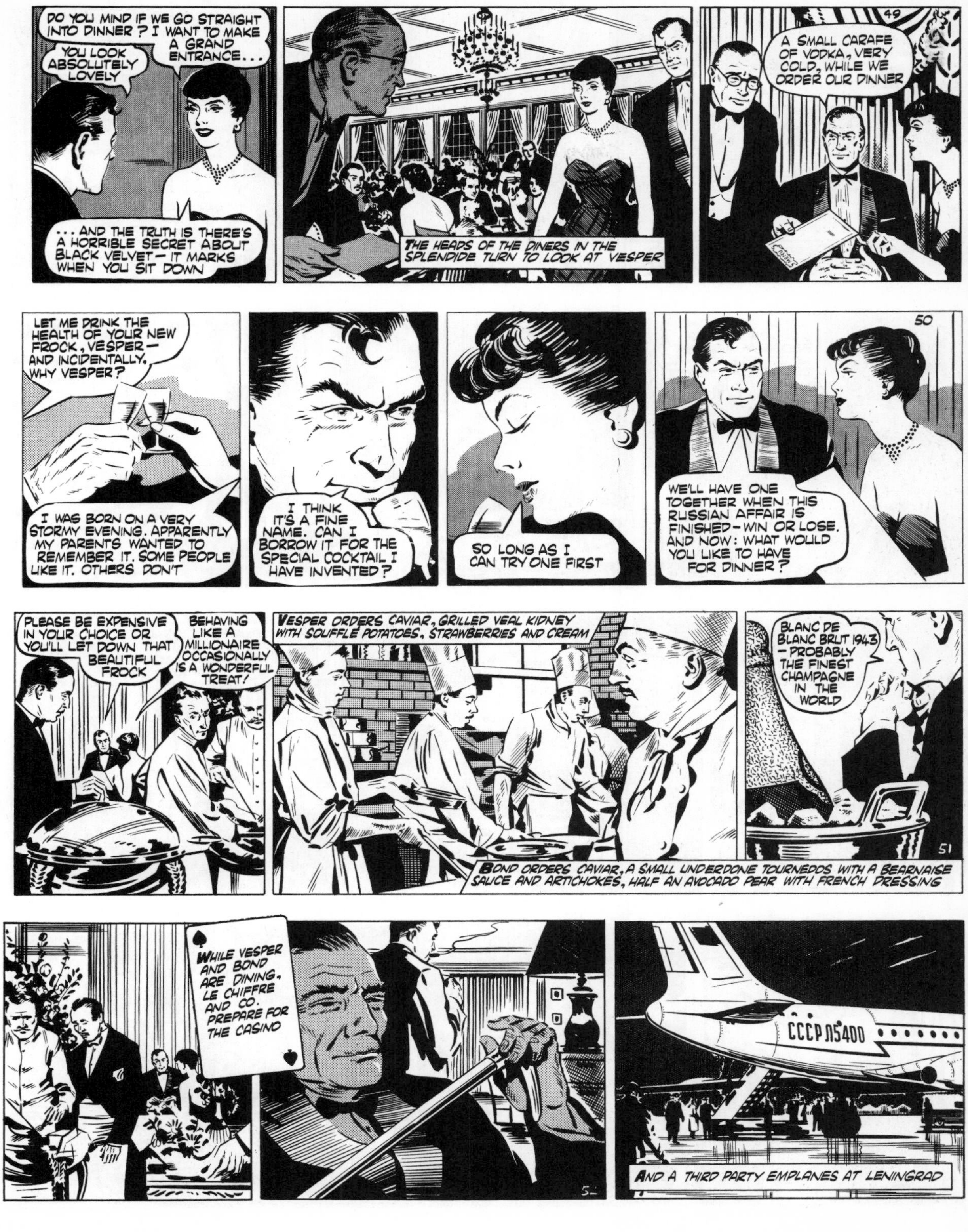
DO YOU MIND IF WE GO STRAIGHT INTO DINNER ? I WANT TO MAKE A GRAND ENTRANCE . . .
YOU LOOK ABSOLUTELY LOVELY
. . . AND THE TRUTH IS THERE'S A HORRIBLE SECRET ABOUT BLACK VELVET — IT MARKS WHEN YOU SIT DOWN
THE HEADS OF THE DINERS IN THE SPLENDIDE TURN TO LOOK AT VESPER
49
A SMALL CARAFE OF VODKA, VERY COLD, WHILE WE ORDER OUR DINNER
LET ME DRINK THE HEALTH OF YOUR NEW FROCK, VESPER — AND INCIDENTALLY, WHY VESPER ?
I WAS BORN ON A VERY STORMY EVENING. APPARENTLY MY PARENTS WANTED TO REMEMBER IT. SOME PEOPLE LIKE IT. OTHERS DON'T
I THINK IT'S A FINE NAME. CAN I BORROW IT FOR THE SPECIAL COCKTAIL I HAVE INVENTED ?
SO LONG AS I CAN TRY ONE FIRST
50
WE'LL HAVE ONE TOGETHER WHEN THIS RUSSIAN AFFAIR IS FINISHED — WIN OR LOSE. AND NOW : WHAT WOULD YOU LIKE TO HAVE FOR DINNER ?
PLEASE BE EXPENSIVE IN YOUR CHOICE OR YOU'LL LET DOWN THAT BEAUTIFUL FROCK
BEHAVING LIKE A MILLIONAIRE OCCASIONALLY IS A WONDERFUL TREAT !
VESPER ORDERS CAVIAR, GRILLED VEAL KIDNEY WITH SOUFFLÉ POTATOES, STRAWBERRIES AND CREAM
BLANC DE BLANC BRUT 1943 — PROBABLY THE FINEST CHAMPAGNE IN THE WORLD
51
BOND ORDERS CAVIAR, A SMALL UNDERDONE TOURNEDOS WITH A BEARNAISE SAUCE AND ARTICHOKES, HALF AN AVOCADO PEAR WITH FRENCH DRESSING
WHILE VESPER AND BOND ARE DINING, LE CHIFFRE AND CO. PREPARE FOR THE CASINO
CCCP Л5400
AND A THIRD PARTY EMPLANES AT LENINGRAD

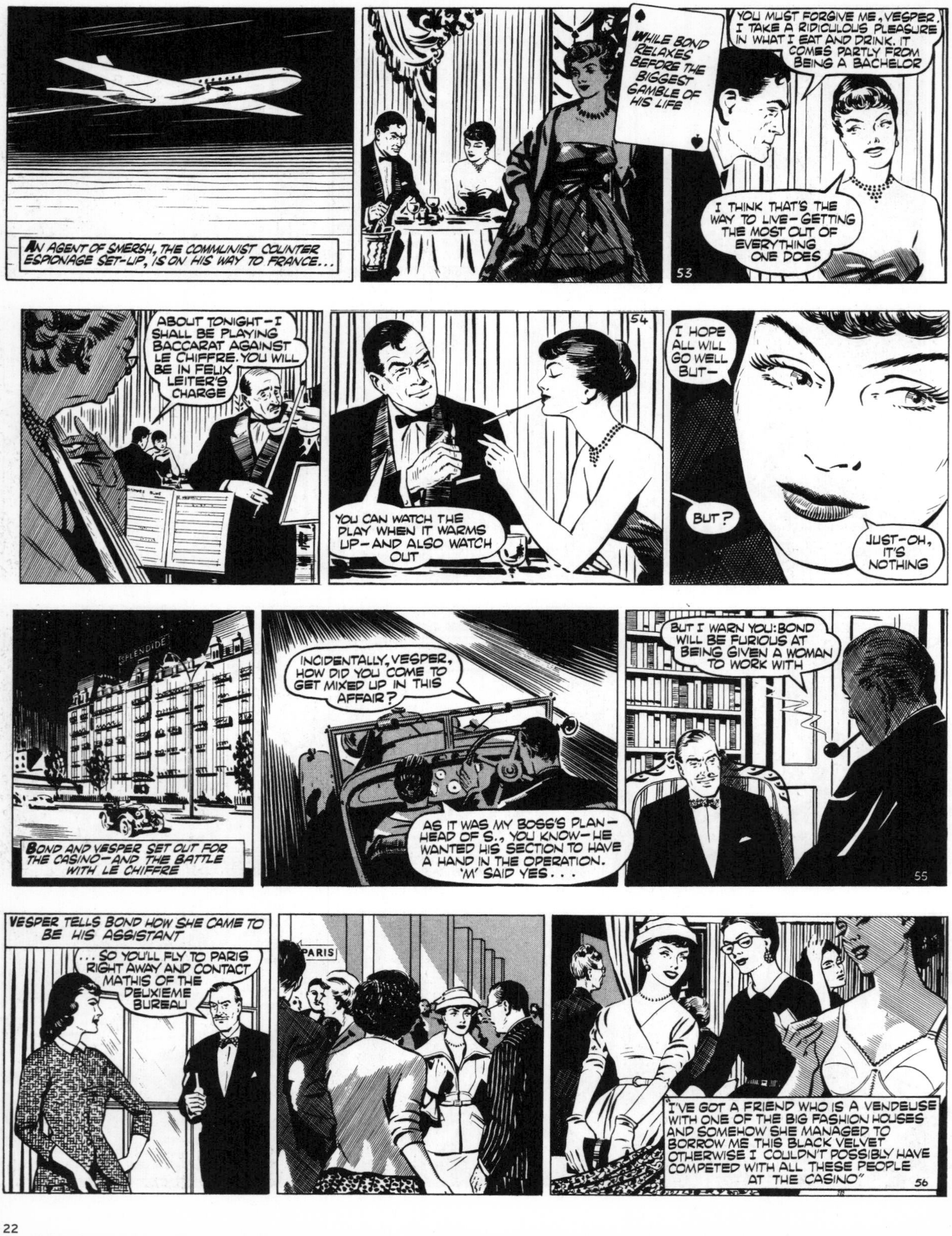
AN AGENT OF SMERSH, THE COMMUNIST COUNTER ESPIONAGE SET-UP, IS ON HIS WAY TO FRANCE...
WHILE BOND RELAXES BEFORE THE BIGGEST GAMBLE OF HIS LIFE
53
YOU MUST FORGIVE ME, VESPER. I TAKE A RIDICULOUS PLEASURE IN WHAT I EAT AND DRINK. IT COMES PARTLY FROM BEING A BACHELOR
I THINK THAT'S THE WAY TO LIVE—GETTING THE MOST OUT OF EVERYTHING ONE DOES
ABOUT TONIGHT—I SHALL BE PLAYING BACCARAT AGAINST LE CHIFFRE. YOU WILL BE IN FELIX LEITER'S CHARGE
54
YOU CAN WATCH THE PLAY WHEN IT WARMS UP—AND ALSO WATCH OUT
I HOPE ALL WILL GO WELL BUT—
BUT?
JUST—OH, IT'S NOTHING
SPLENDIDE
BOND AND VESPER SET OUT FOR THE CASINO—AND THE BATTLE WITH LE CHIFFRE
INCIDENTALLY, VESPER, HOW DID YOU COME TO GET MIXED UP IN THIS AFFAIR?
AS IT WAS MY BOSS'S PLAN—HEAD OF S., YOU KNOW—HE WANTED HIS SECTION TO HAVE A HAND IN THE OPERATION. 'M' SAID YES . . .
BUT I WARN YOU: BOND WILL BE FURIOUS AT BEING GIVEN A WOMAN TO WORK WITH
55
VESPER TELLS BOND HOW SHE CAME TO BE HIS ASSISTANT
. . . SO YOU'LL FLY TO PARIS RIGHT AWAY AND CONTACT MATHIS OF THE DEUXIEME BUREAU
PARIS
"I'VE GOT A FRIEND WHO IS A VENDEUSE WITH ONE OF THE BIG FASHION HOUSES AND SOMEHOW SHE MANAGED TO BORROW ME THIS BLACK VELVET OTHERWISE I COULDN'T POSSIBLY HAVE COMPETED WITH ALL THESE PEOPLE AT THE CASINO"
56

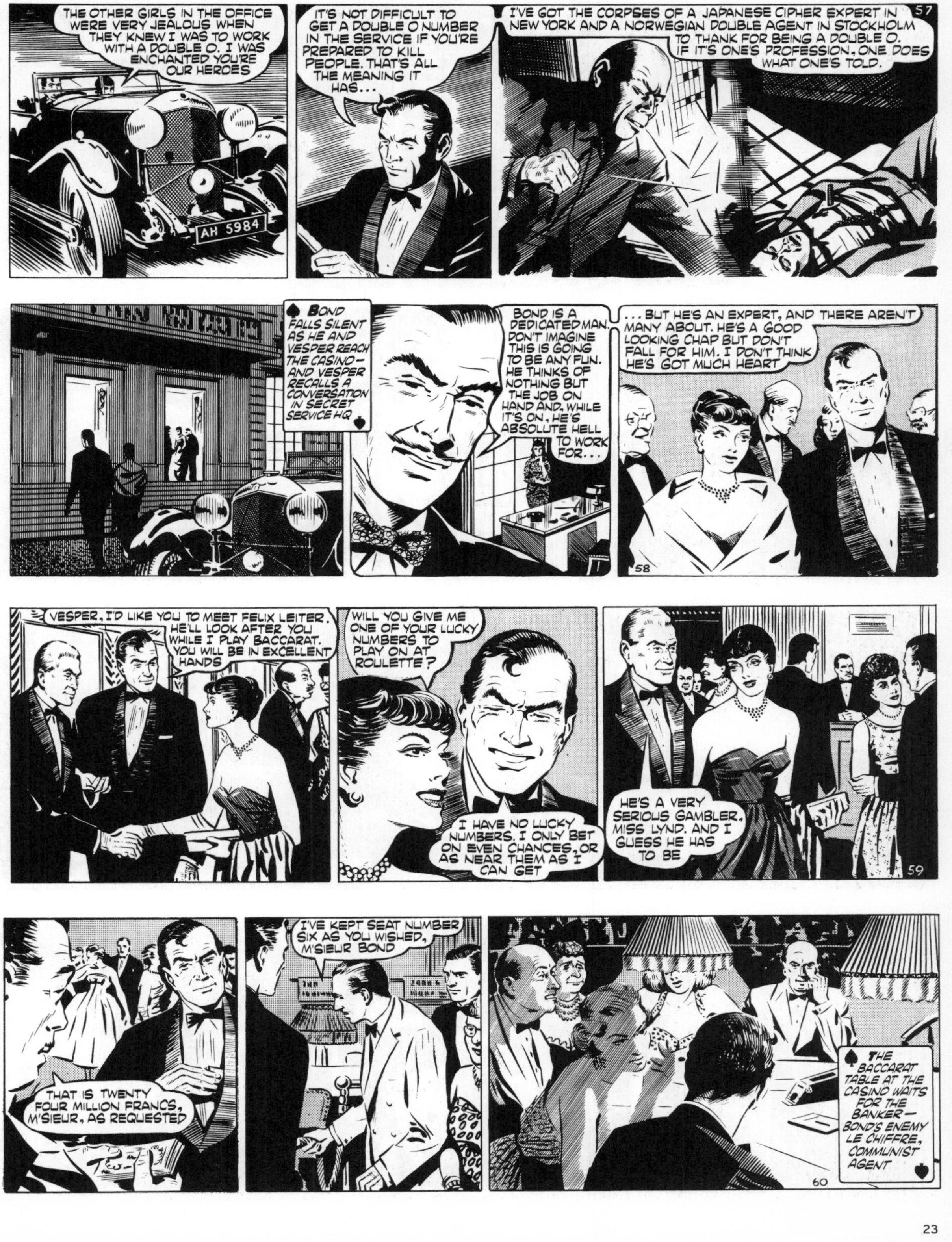
THE OTHER GIRLS IN THE OFFICE WERE VERY JEALOUS WHEN THEY KNEW I WAS TO WORK WITH A DOUBLE O. I WAS ENCHANTED YOU'RE OUR HEROES
AH 5984
IT'S NOT DIFFICULT TO GET A DOUBLE O NUMBER IN THE SERVICE IF YOU'RE PREPARED TO KILL PEOPLE. THAT'S ALL THE MEANING IT HAS...
I'VE GOT THE CORPSES OF A JAPANESE CIPHER EXPERT IN NEW YORK AND A NORWEGIAN DOUBLE AGENT IN STOCKHOLM TO THANK FOR BEING A DOUBLE O. IF IT'S ONE'S PROFESSION, ONE DOES WHAT ONE'S TOLD.
57
BOND FALLS SILENT AS HE AND VESPER REACH THE CASINO—AND VESPER RECALLS A CONVERSATION IN SECRET SERVICE HQ
BOND IS A DEDICATED MAN. DON'T IMAGINE THIS IS GOING TO BE ANY FUN. HE THINKS OF NOTHING BUT THE JOB ON HAND AND, WHILE IT'S ON, HE'S ABSOLUTE HELL TO WORK FOR...
...BUT HE'S AN EXPERT, AND THERE AREN'T MANY ABOUT. HE'S A GOOD LOOKING CHAP BUT DON'T FALL FOR HIM. I DON'T THINK HE'S GOT MUCH HEART
58
VESPER, I'D LIKE YOU TO MEET FELIX LEITER. HE'LL LOOK AFTER YOU WHILE I PLAY BACCARAT. YOU WILL BE IN EXCELLENT HANDS
WILL YOU GIVE ME ONE OF YOUR LUCKY NUMBERS TO PLAY ON AT ROULETTE?
I HAVE NO LUCKY NUMBERS. I ONLY BET ON EVEN CHANCES, OR AS NEAR THEM AS I CAN GET
HE'S A VERY SERIOUS GAMBLER, MISS LYND. AND I GUESS HE HAS TO BE
59
THAT IS TWENTY FOUR MILLION FRANCS, M'SIEUR, AS REQUESTED
I'VE KEPT SEAT NUMBER SIX AS YOU WISHED, M'SIEUR BOND
THE BACCARAT TABLE AT THE CASINO WAITS FOR THE BANKER—BOND'S ENEMY LE CHIFFRE, COMMUNIST AGENT
60

QUOTE by James Bond, Secret Service Agent No. 007 : "The object of the game of baccarat is to hold two or three cards which together count nine points, or as nearly nine as possible. Court cards and tens count nothing ; aces one each ; any other card its face value. It is only the last figure of your count that signifies. So nine plus seven equals six—not 16. "I get two cards and the banker gets two and, unless anyone wins outright, either or both of us can get one more card. The winner is the one whose count is nearest to nine."

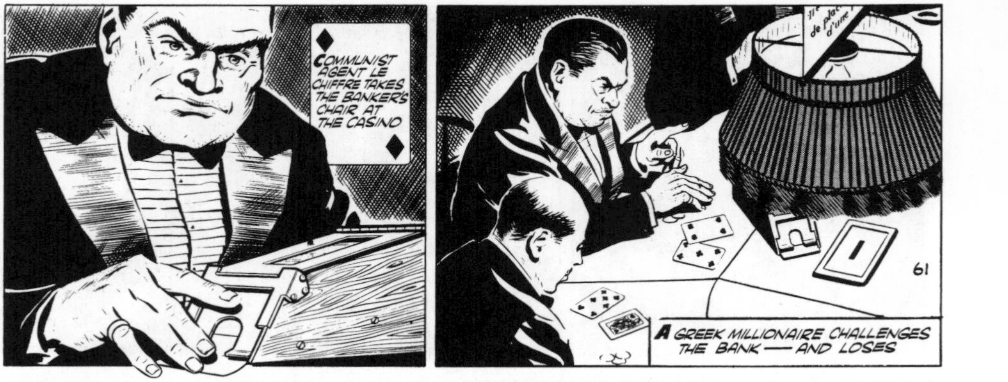
COMMUNIST AGENT LE CHIFFRE TAKES THE BANKER'S CHAIR AT THE CASINO
A GREEK MILLIONAIRE CHALLENGES THE BANK — AND LOSES
61

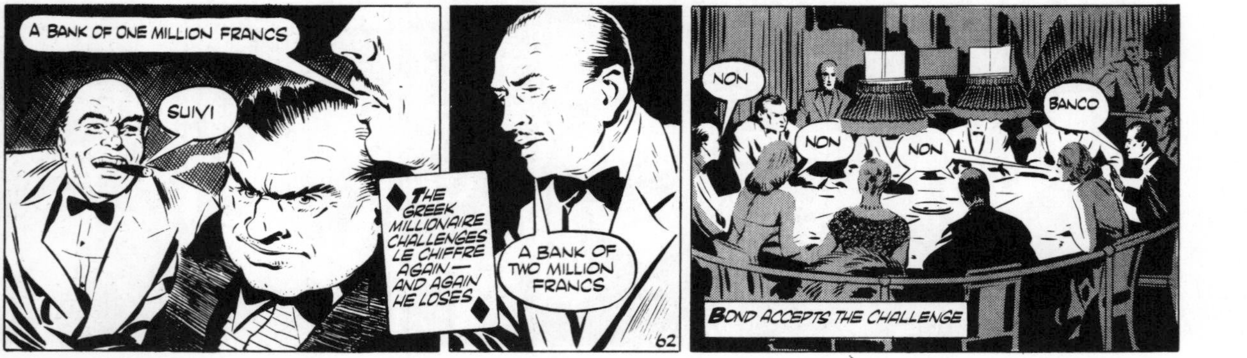
A BANK OF ONE MILLION FRANCS
SUIVI
THE GREEK MILLIONAIRE CHALLENGES LE CHIFFRE AGAIN — AND AGAIN HE LOSES
A BANK OF TWO MILLION FRANCS
62
NON
NON
NON
BANCO
BOND ACCEPTS THE CHALLENGE

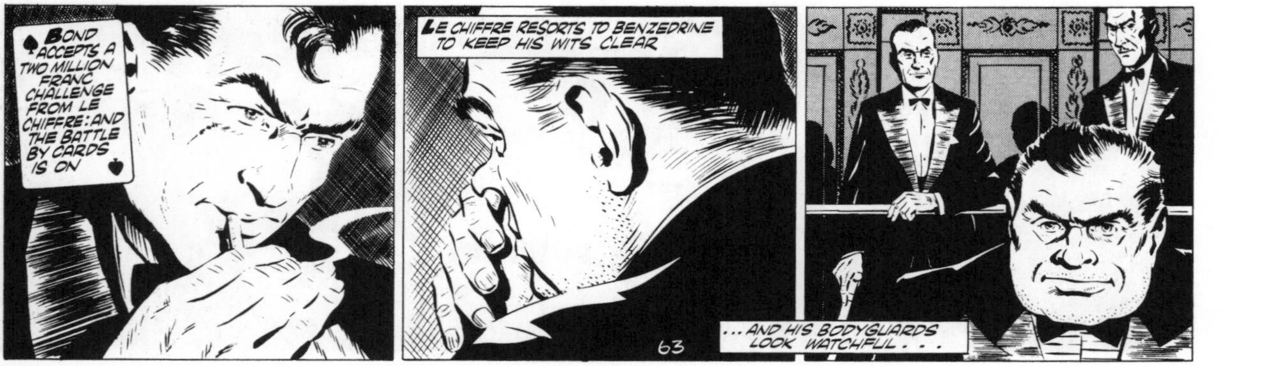
BOND ACCEPTS A TWO MILLION FRANC CHALLENGE FROM LE CHIFFRE: AND THE BATTLE BY CARDS IS ON
LE CHIFFRE RESORTS TO BENZEDRINE TO KEEP HIS WITS CLEAR
63
... AND HIS BODYGUARDS LOOK WATCHFUL . . .

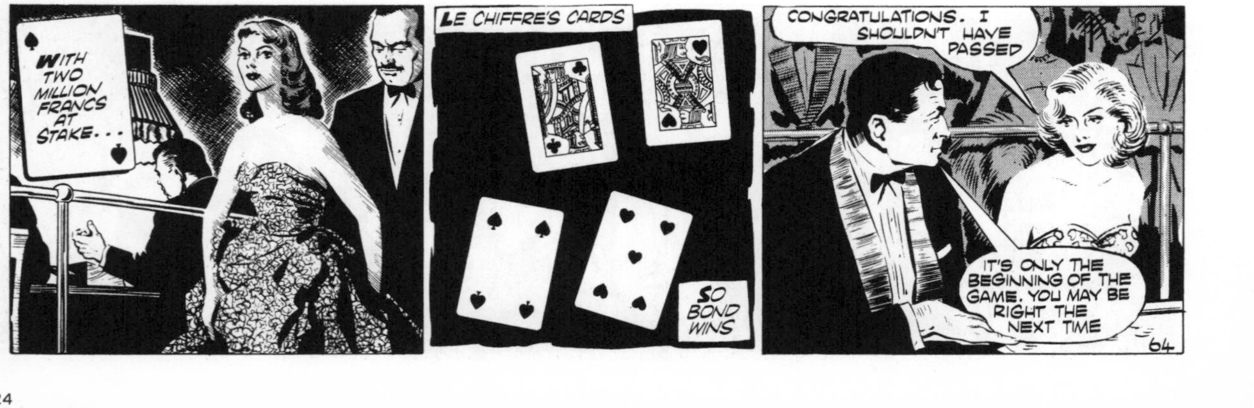
WITH TWO MILLION FRANCS AT STAKE . . .
LE CHIFFRE'S CARDS
SO BOND WINS
CONGRATULATIONS. I SHOULDN'T HAVE PASSED
IT'S ONLY THE BEGINNING OF THE GAME. YOU MAY BE RIGHT THE NEXT TIME
64

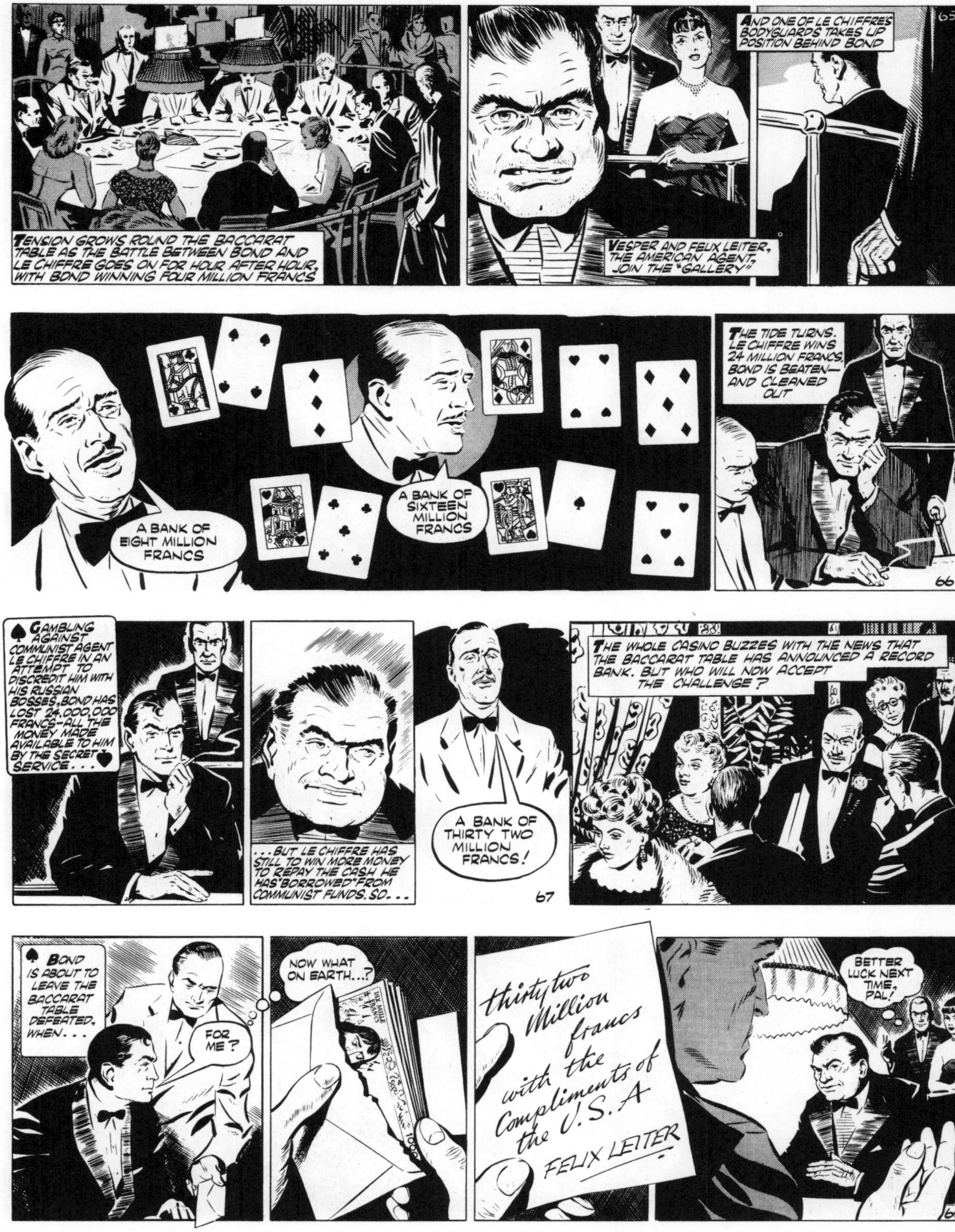
TENSION GROWS ROUND THE BACCARAT TABLE AS THE BATTLE BETWEEN BOND AND LE CHIFFRE GOES ON FOR HOUR AFTER HOUR, WITH BOND WINNING FOUR MILLION FRANCS
VESPER AND FELIX LEITER, THE AMERICAN AGENT, JOIN THE "GALLERY"
AND ONE OF LE CHIFFRE'S BODYGUARDS TAKES UP POSITION BEHIND BOND
65
A BANK OF EIGHT MILLION FRANCS
A BANK OF SIXTEEN MILLION FRANCS
THE TIDE TURNS. LE CHIFFRE WINS 24 MILLION FRANCS, BOND IS BEATEN— AND CLEANED OUT
66
GAMBLING AGAINST COMMUNIST AGENT LE CHIFFRE IN AN ATTEMPT TO DISCREDIT HIM WITH HIS RUSSIAN BOSSES, BOND HAS LOST 24,000,000 FRANCS—ALL THE MONEY MADE AVAILABLE TO HIM BY THE SECRET SERVICE . . .
. . . BUT LE CHIFFRE HAS STILL TO WIN MORE MONEY TO REPAY THE CASH HE HAS "BORROWED" FROM COMMUNIST FUNDS. SO . . .
A BANK OF THIRTY TWO MILLION FRANCS!
67
THE WHOLE CASINO BUZZES WITH THE NEWS THAT THE BACCARAT TABLE HAS ANNOUNCED A RECORD BANK. BUT WHO WILL NOW ACCEPT THE CHALLENGE?
BOND IS ABOUT TO LEAVE THE BACCARAT TABLE DEFEATED, WHEN . . .
FOR ME?
NOW WHAT ON EARTH...?
thirty two Million francs with the Compliments of the U.S.A
FELIX LEITER
BETTER LUCK NEXT TIME, PAL!
68

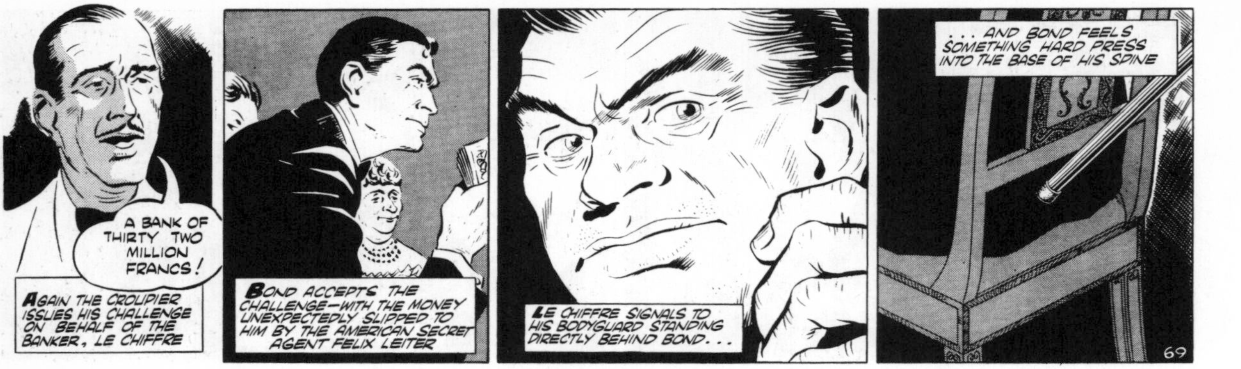
A BANK OF THIRTY TWO MILLION FRANCS!
AGAIN THE CROUPIER ISSUES HIS CHALLENGE ON BEHALF OF THE BANKER, LE CHIFFRE
BOND ACCEPTS THE CHALLENGE—WITH THE MONEY UNEXPECTEDLY SLIPPED TO HIM BY THE AMERICAN SECRET AGENT FELIX LEITER
LE CHIFFRE SIGNALS TO HIS BODYGUARD STANDING DIRECTLY BEHIND BOND...
... AND BOND FEELS SOMETHING HARD PRESS INTO THE BASE OF HIS SPINE
69

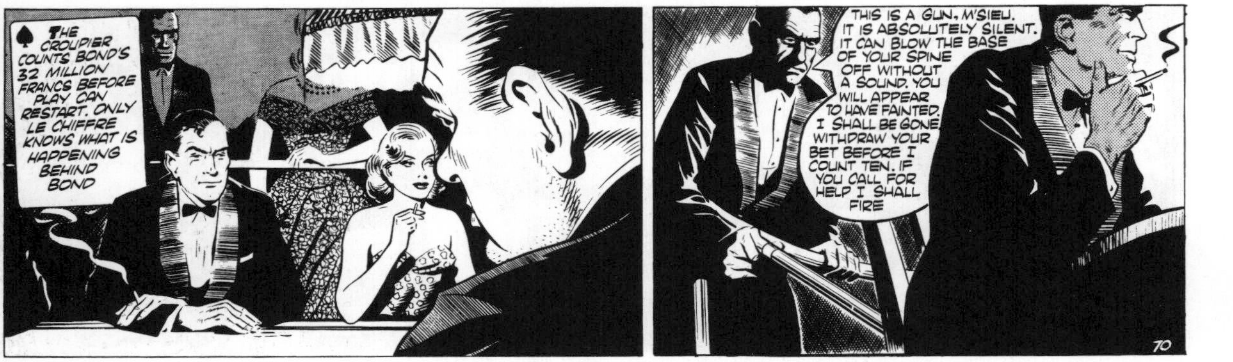
THE CROUPIER COUNTS BOND'S 32 MILLION FRANCS BEFORE PLAY CAN RESTART. ONLY LE CHIFFRE KNOWS WHAT IS HAPPENING BEHIND BOND
THIS IS A GUN, M'SIEU. IT IS ABSOLUTELY SILENT. IT CAN BLOW THE BASE OF YOUR SPINE OFF WITHOUT A SOUND. YOU WILL APPEAR TO HAVE FAINTED. I SHALL BE GONE. WITHDRAW YOUR BET BEFORE I COUNT TEN. IF YOU CALL FOR HELP I SHALL FIRE
70

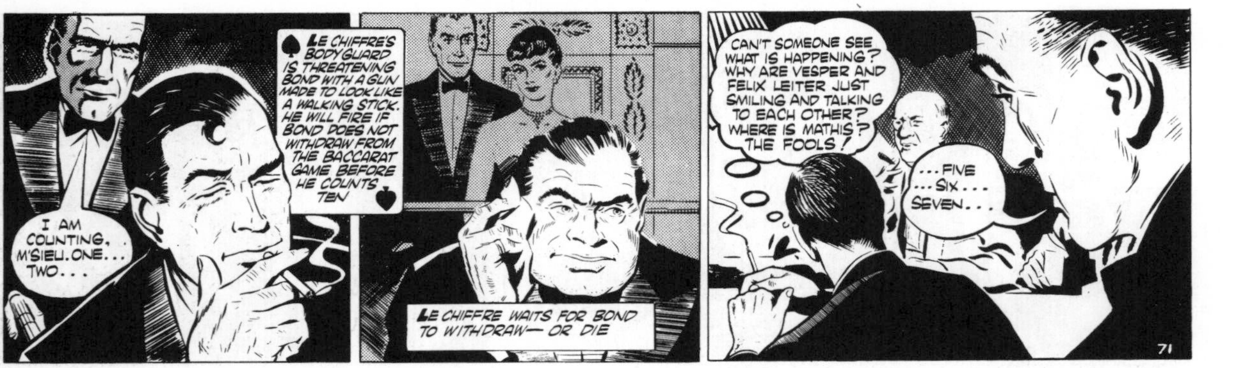
I AM COUNTING, M'SIEU. ONE... TWO...
LE CHIFFRE'S BODYGUARD IS THREATENING BOND WITH A GUN MADE TO LOOK LIKE A WALKING STICK. HE WILL FIRE IF BOND DOES NOT WITHDRAW FROM THE BACCARAT GAME BEFORE HE COUNTS TEN
LE CHIFFRE WAITS FOR BOND TO WITHDRAW— OR DIE
CAN'T SOMEONE SEE WHAT IS HAPPENING? WHY ARE VESPER AND FELIX LEITER JUST SMILING AND TALKING TO EACH OTHER? WHERE IS MATHIS? THE FOOLS!
...FIVE ...SIX ... SEVEN...
71

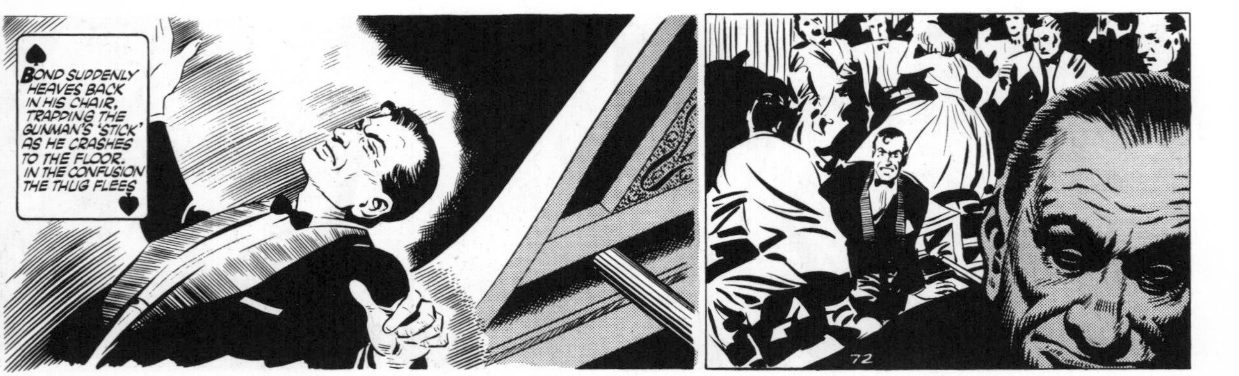
BOND SUDDENLY HEAVES BACK IN HIS CHAIR, TRAPPING THE GUNMAN'S 'STICK' AS HE CRASHES TO THE FLOOR. IN THE CONFUSION THE THUG FLEES
72

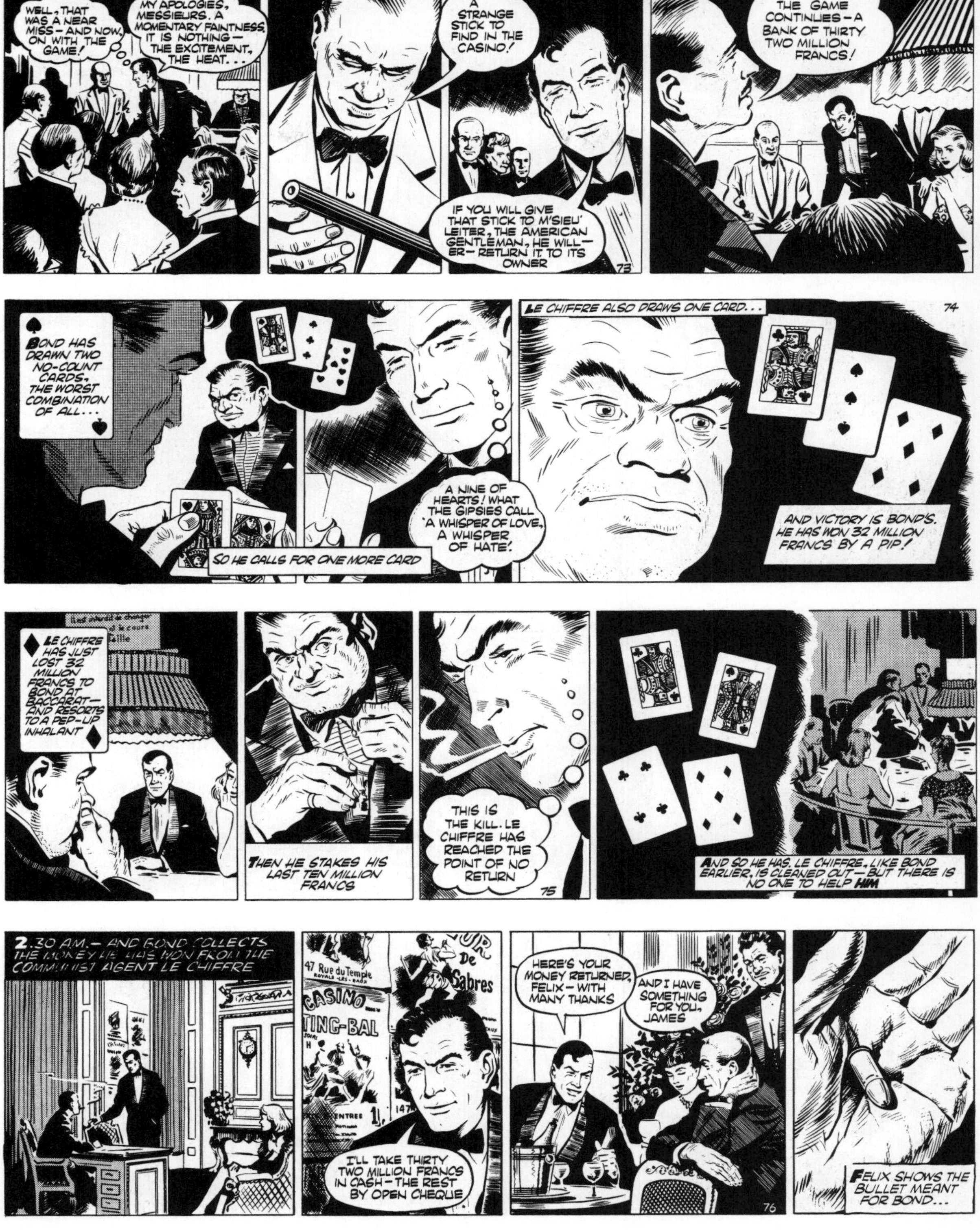
WELL, THAT WAS A NEAR MISS—AND NOW, ON WITH THE GAME!
MY APOLOGIES, MESSIEURS. A MOMENTARY FAINTNESS, IT IS NOTHING—THE EXCITEMENT, THE HEAT...
A STRANGE STICK TO FIND IN THE CASINO!
IF YOU WILL GIVE THAT STICK TO M'SIEU' LEITER, THE AMERICAN GENTLEMAN, HE WILL—ER—RETURN IT TO ITS OWNER
73
THE GAME CONTINUES—A BANK OF THIRTY TWO MILLION FRANCS!
BOND HAS DRAWN TWO NO-COUNT CARDS, THE WORST COMBINATION OF ALL...
SO HE CALLS FOR ONE MORE CARD
A NINE OF HEARTS! WHAT THE GIPSIES CALL 'A WHISPER OF LOVE, A WHISPER OF HATE'.
LE CHIFFRE ALSO DRAWS ONE CARD...
74
AND VICTORY IS BOND'S. HE HAS WON 32 MILLION FRANCS BY A PIP!
LE CHIFFRE HAS JUST LOST 32 MILLION FRANCS TO BOND AT BACCARAT—AND RESORTS TO A PEP-UP INHALANT
THEN HE STAKES HIS LAST TEN MILLION FRANCS
THIS IS THE KILL. LE CHIFFRE HAS REACHED THE POINT OF NO RETURN
75
AND SO HE HAS. LE CHIFFRE, LIKE BOND EARLIER, IS CLEANED OUT—BUT THERE IS NO ONE TO HELP HIM
2.30 AM.—AND BOND COLLECTS THE MONEY HE HAS WON FROM THE COMMUNIST AGENT LE CHIFFRE
47 Rue du Temple
CASINO
TING-BAL
De Sabres
I'LL TAKE THIRTY TWO MILLION FRANCS IN CASH—THE REST BY OPEN CHEQUE
HERE'S YOUR MONEY RETURNED, FELIX—WITH MANY THANKS
AND I HAVE SOMETHING FOR YOU, JAMES
76
FELIX SHOWS THE BULLET MEANT FOR BOND...

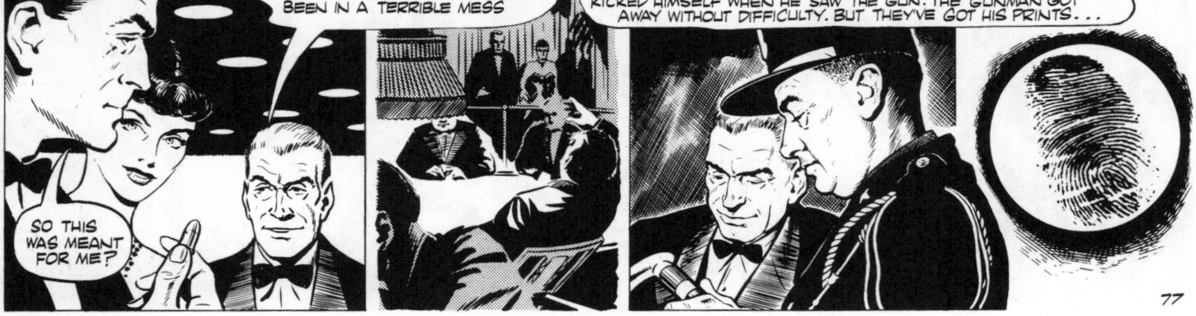
YEAH. THE NOSE HAS BEEN CUT WITH A DUM DUM CROSS. YOU'D HAVE BEEN IN A TERRIBLE MESS
SO THIS WAS MEANT FOR ME?
"I GAVE THE GUN TO MATHIS. HE WAS AS PUZZLED AS WE WERE BY THE SPILL YOU TOOK. YOU CAN IMAGINE HOW HE KICKED HIMSELF WHEN HE SAW THE GUN. THE GUNMAN GOT AWAY WITHOUT DIFFICULTY. BUT THEY'VE GOT HIS PRINTS...
77

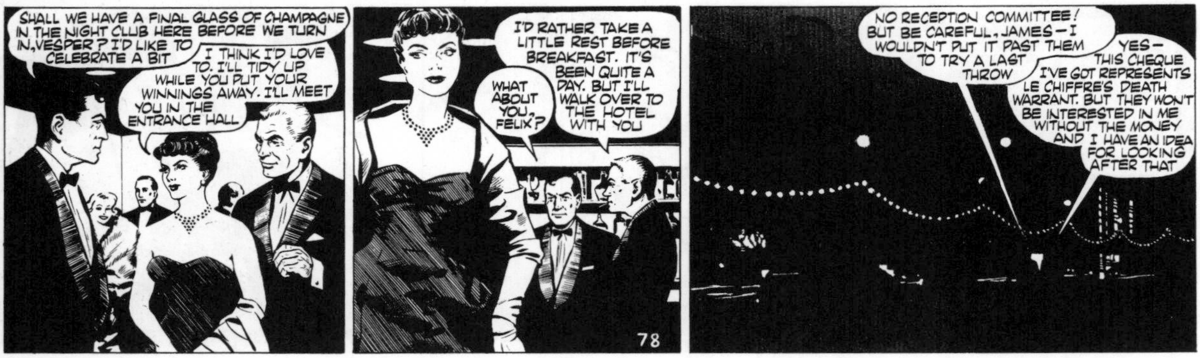
SHALL WE HAVE A FINAL GLASS OF CHAMPAGNE IN THE NIGHT CLUB HERE BEFORE WE TURN IN, VESPER? I'D LIKE TO CELEBRATE A BIT
I THINK I'D LOVE TO. I'LL TIDY UP WHILE YOU PUT YOUR WINNINGS AWAY. I'LL MEET YOU IN THE ENTRANCE HALL
I'D RATHER TAKE A LITTLE REST BEFORE BREAKFAST. IT'S BEEN QUITE A DAY. BUT I'LL WALK OVER TO THE HOTEL WITH YOU
WHAT ABOUT YOU, FELIX?
78
NO RECEPTION COMMITTEE! BUT BE CAREFUL, JAMES—I WOULDN'T PUT IT PAST THEM TO TRY A LAST THROW
YES—THIS CHEQUE I'VE GOT REPRESENTS LE CHIFFRE'S DEATH WARRANT. BUT THEY WON'T BE INTERESTED IN ME WITHOUT THE MONEY AND I HAVE AN IDEA FOR LOOKING AFTER THAT

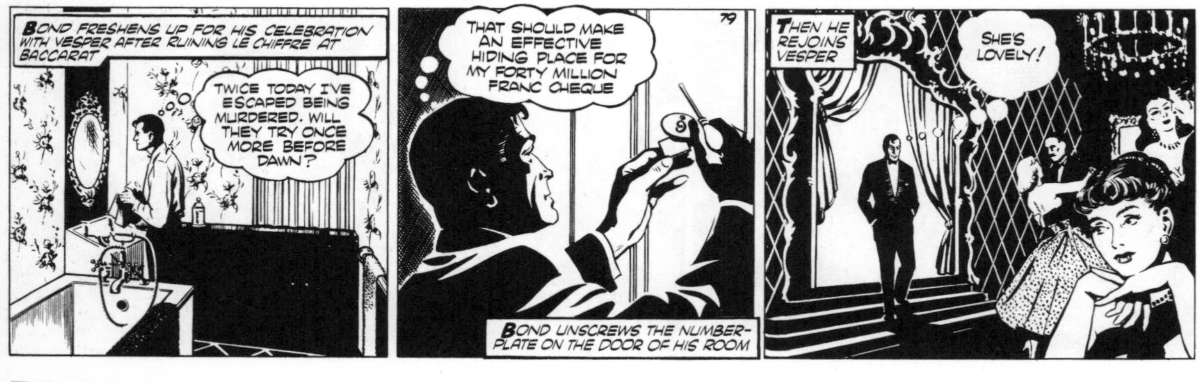
BOND FRESHENS UP FOR HIS CELEBRATION WITH VESPER AFTER RUINING LE CHIFFRE AT BACCARAT
TWICE TODAY I'VE ESCAPED BEING MURDERED. WILL THEY TRY ONCE MORE BEFORE DAWN?
THAT SHOULD MAKE AN EFFECTIVE HIDING PLACE FOR MY FORTY MILLION FRANC CHEQUE
79
BOND UNSCREWS THE NUMBER-PLATE ON THE DOOR OF HIS ROOM
THEN HE REJOINS VESPER
SHE'S LOVELY!

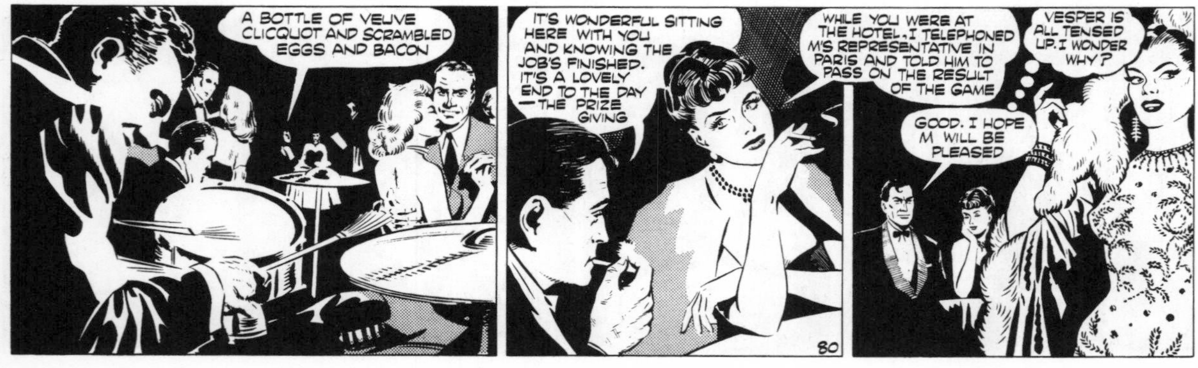
A BOTTLE OF VEUVE CLICQUOT AND SCRAMBLED EGGS AND BACON
IT'S WONDERFUL SITTING HERE WITH YOU AND KNOWING THE JOB'S FINISHED. IT'S A LOVELY END TO THE DAY—THE PRIZE GIVING
WHILE YOU WERE AT THE HOTEL, I TELEPHONED M'S REPRESENTATIVE IN PARIS AND TOLD HIM TO PASS ON THE RESULT OF THE GAME
80
VESPER IS ALL TENSED UP. I WONDER WHY?
GOOD. I HOPE M WILL BE PLEASED

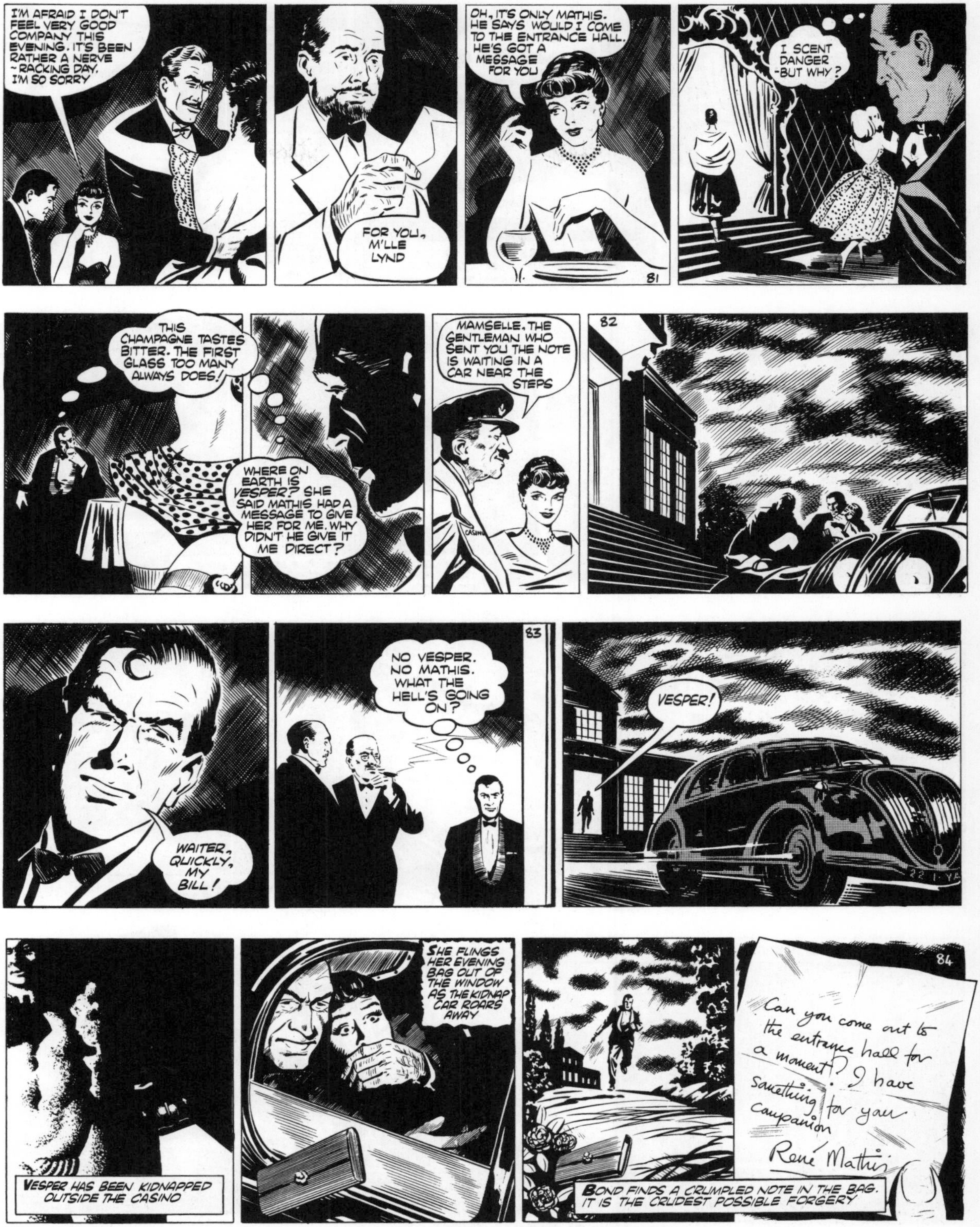
I'M AFRAID I DON'T FEEL VERY GOOD COMPANY THIS EVENING. IT'S BEEN RATHER A NERVE-RACKING DAY. I'M SO SORRY
FOR YOU, M'LLE LYND
OH, IT'S ONLY MATHIS. HE SAYS WOULD I COME TO THE ENTRANCE HALL. HE'S GOT A MESSAGE FOR YOU
81
I SCENT DANGER - BUT WHY?
THIS CHAMPAGNE TASTES BITTER. THE FIRST GLASS TOO MANY ALWAYS DOES!
WHERE ON EARTH IS VESPER? SHE SAID MATHIS HAD A MESSAGE TO GIVE HER FOR ME. WHY DIDN'T HE GIVE IT ME DIRECT?
MAMSELLE, THE GENTLEMAN WHO SENT YOU THE NOTE IS WAITING IN A CAR NEAR THE STEPS
82
WAITER, QUICKLY, MY BILL!
83
NO VESPER. NO MATHIS. WHAT THE HELL'S GOING ON?
VESPER!
VESPER HAS BEEN KIDNAPPED OUTSIDE THE CASINO
SHE FLINGS HER EVENING BAG OUT OF THE WINDOW AS THE KIDNAP CAR ROARS AWAY
84
Can you come out to the entrance hall for a moment? I have something for your companion
René Mathis
BOND FINDS A CRUMPLED NOTE IN THE BAG. IT IS THE CRUDEST POSSIBLE FORGERY

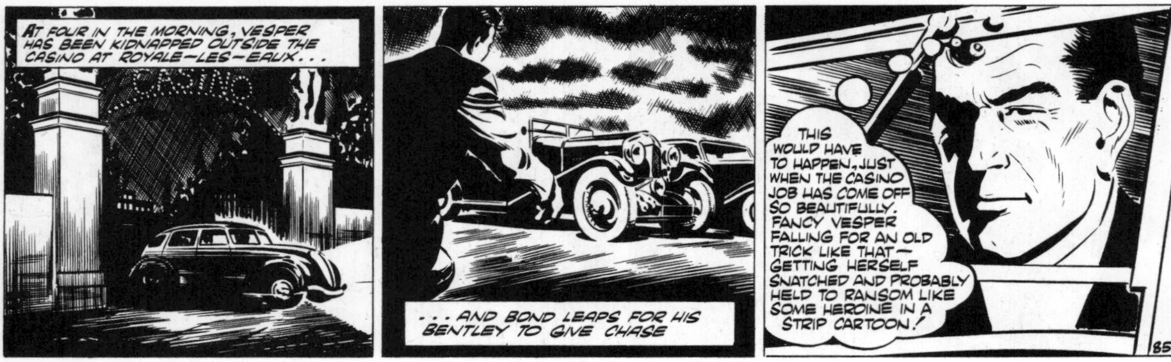
AT FOUR IN THE MORNING, VESPER HAS BEEN KIDNAPPED OUTSIDE THE CASINO AT ROYALE-LES-EAUX . . .
. . . AND BOND LEAPS FOR HIS BENTLEY TO GIVE CHASE
THIS WOULD HAVE TO HAPPEN, JUST WHEN THE CASINO JOB HAS COME OFF SO BEAUTIFULLY. FANCY VESPER FALLING FOR AN OLD TRICK LIKE THAT—GETTING HERSELF SNATCHED AND PROBABLY HELD TO RANSOM LIKE SOME HEROINE IN A STRIP CARTOON!
85

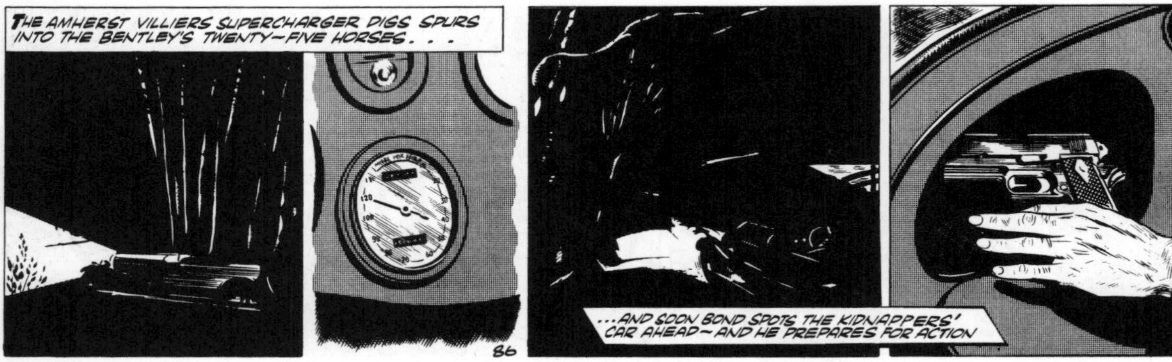
THE AMHERST VILLIERS SUPERCHARGER DIGS SPURS INTO THE BENTLEY'S TWENTY-FIVE HORSES . . .
. . . AND SOON BOND SPOTS THE KIDNAPPERS' CAR AHEAD—AND HE PREPARES FOR ACTION
86

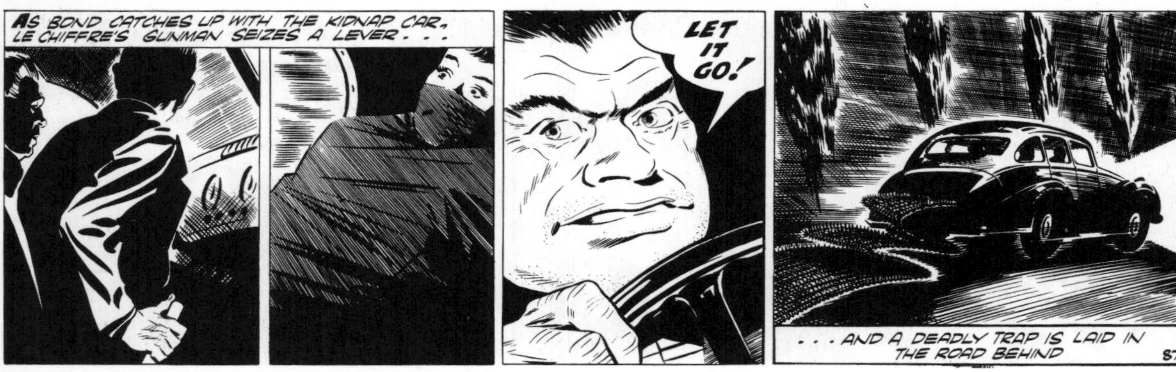
AS BOND CATCHES UP WITH THE KIDNAP CAR, LE CHIFFRE'S GUNMAN SEIZES A LEVER . . .
LET IT GO!
. . . AND A DEADLY TRAP IS LAID IN THE ROAD BEHIND
87

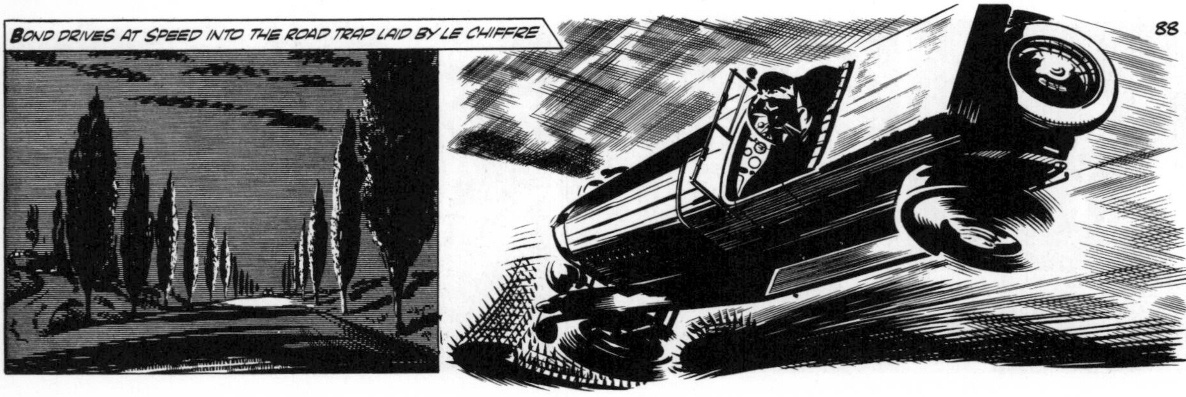
BOND DRIVES AT SPEED INTO THE ROAD TRAP LAID BY LE CHIFFRE
88

PUT YOUR GUNS AWAY AND GET BOND OUT. I'LL KEEP YOU COVERED. BE CAREFUL OF HIM. I DON'T WANT A CORPSE. AND HURRY UP. IT'S GETTING LIGHT

HE IS ALIVE ALL RIGHT. HE IS TOUGH THIS ONE

TAKE HIS GUN AND TIE HIM UP. THEN PUT HIM IN THE CAR — WITH THE GIRL

8-9

THE SHARP BITE OF THE WIRE FLEX INTO HIS WRISTS BRINGS BOND BACK TO CONSCIOUSNESS

VESPER! ARE YOU ALL RIGHT?

THE GUNMAN SILENCES BOND WITH A RABBIT PUNCH ON THE BACK OF THE NECK

I HOPE I'LL GET THE CHANCE OF KILLING YOU BEFORE LONG, MY FRIEND

QUIET!

90

AT THE LONDON HEADQUARTERS OF THE SECRET SERVICE, M" IS TOLD OF BOND'S SUCCESS AT THE CASINO IN BEGGARING THE COMMUNIST AGENT LE CHIFFRE

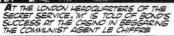

HE DOES NOT YET KNOW THAT, TWO HOURS AFTER THE VICTORY, LE CHIFFRE HAS CAPTURED BOTH BOND AND HIS ASSISTANT VESPER

BUT LE CHIFFRE IS UNAWARE THAT AN AGENT OF SMERSH, THE RUSSIAN COUNTER ESPIONAGE ORGANISATION, IS ON HIS WAY TO ROYALE - LES - EAUX

91

AS DAWN BREAKS, LE CHIFFRE AND HIS GUNMEN CONTINUE THEIR JOURNEY — WITH VESPER AND BOND AS THEIR PRISONERS

FOR THE FIRST TIME SINCE HIS CAPTURE, FEAR COMES TO BOND AND CRAWLS UP HIS SPINE

92

NO ONE KNOWS WHERE I AM, NO ONE WILL MISS ME FOR HOURS

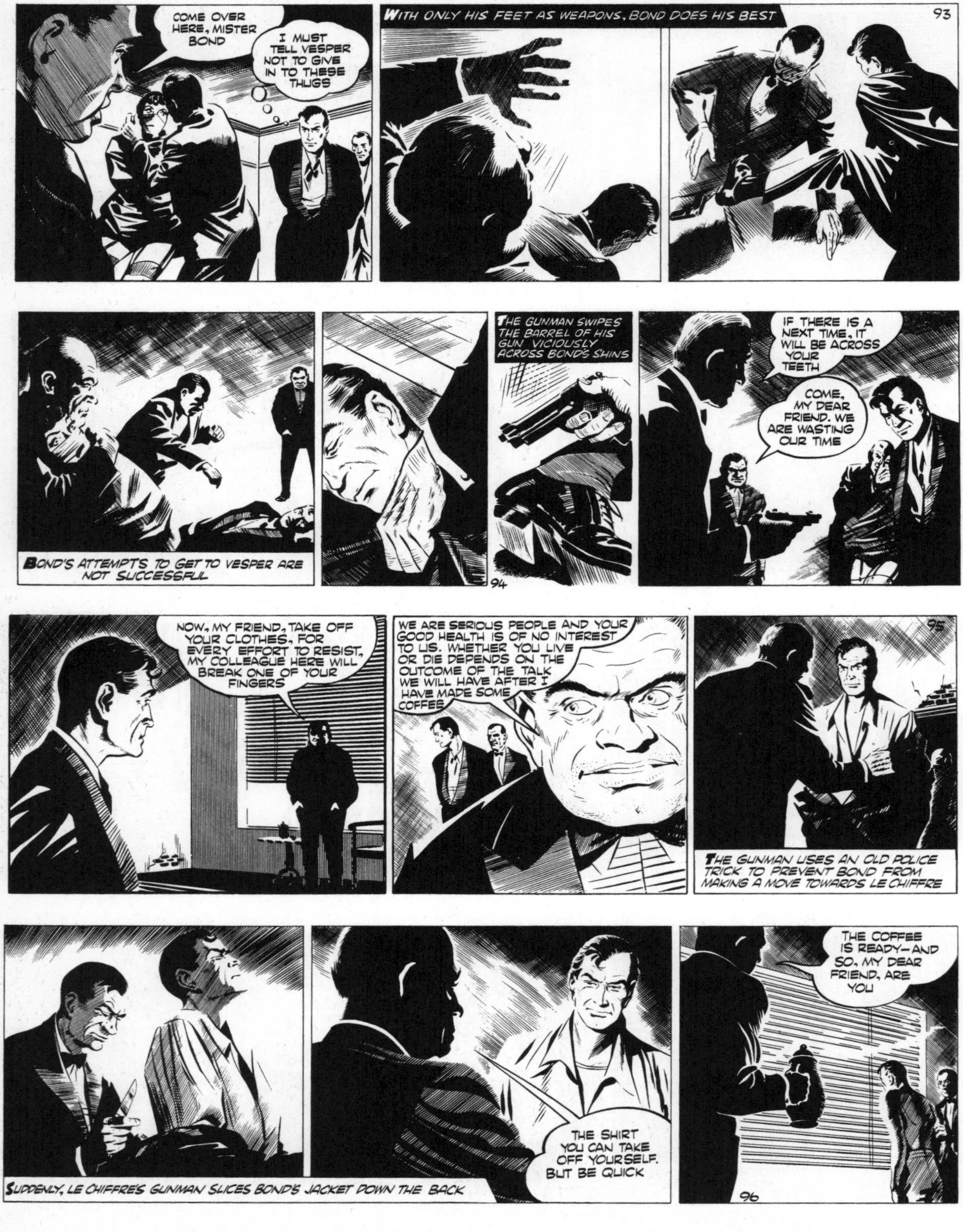
93
COME OVER HERE, MISTER BOND
I MUST TELL VESPER NOT TO GIVE IN TO THESE THUGS
WITH ONLY HIS FEET AS WEAPONS, BOND DOES HIS BEST
BOND'S ATTEMPTS TO GET TO VESPER ARE NOT SUCCESSFUL
THE GUNMAN SWIPES THE BARREL OF HIS GUN VICIOUSLY ACROSS BOND'S SHINS
IF THERE IS A NEXT TIME, IT WILL BE ACROSS YOUR TEETH
COME, MY DEAR FRIEND. WE ARE WASTING OUR TIME
94
NOW, MY FRIEND, TAKE OFF YOUR CLOTHES. FOR EVERY EFFORT TO RESIST, MY COLLEAGUE HERE WILL BREAK ONE OF YOUR FINGERS
WE ARE SERIOUS PEOPLE AND YOUR GOOD HEALTH IS OF NO INTEREST TO US. WHETHER YOU LIVE OR DIE DEPENDS ON THE OUTCOME OF THE TALK WE WILL HAVE AFTER I HAVE MADE SOME COFFEE
95
THE GUNMAN USES AN OLD POLICE TRICK TO PREVENT BOND FROM MAKING A MOVE TOWARDS LE CHIFFRE
SUDDENLY, LE CHIFFRE'S GUNMAN SLICES BOND'S JACKET DOWN THE BACK
THE SHIRT YOU CAN TAKE OFF YOURSELF. BUT BE QUICK
THE COFFEE IS READY—AND SO, MY DEAR FRIEND, ARE YOU
96

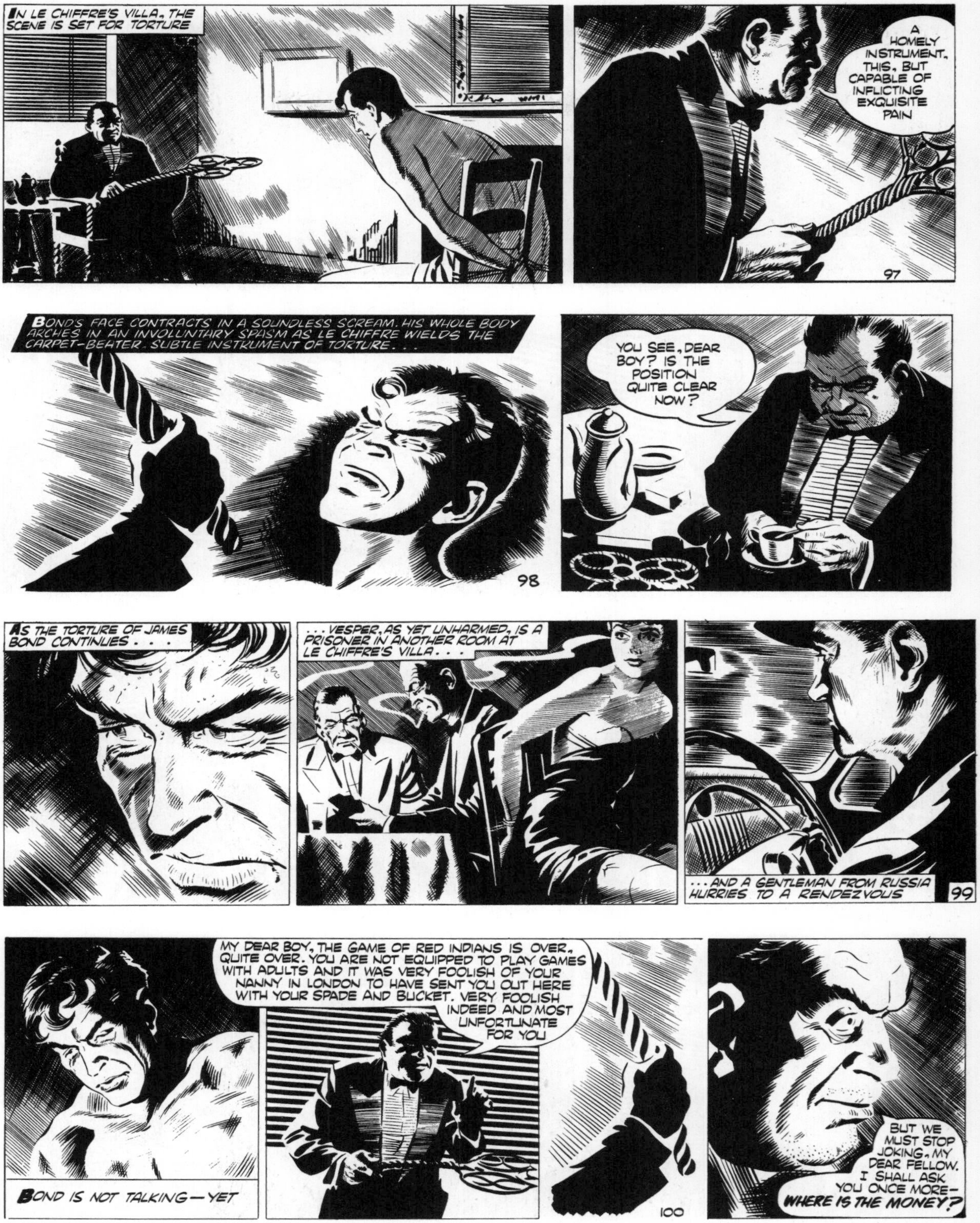
IN LE CHIFFRE'S VILLA, THE SCENE IS SET FOR TORTURE
A HOMELY INSTRUMENT, THIS, BUT CAPABLE OF INFLICTING EXQUISITE PAIN
97
BOND'S FACE CONTRACTS IN A SOUNDLESS SCREAM. HIS WHOLE BODY ARCHES IN AN INVOLUNTARY SPASM AS LE CHIFFRE WIELDS THE CARPET-BEATER, SUBTLE INSTRUMENT OF TORTURE . . .
98
YOU SEE, DEAR BOY? IS THE POSITION QUITE CLEAR NOW?
AS THE TORTURE OF JAMES BOND CONTINUES . . .
. . . VESPER, AS YET UNHARMED, IS A PRISONER IN ANOTHER ROOM AT LE CHIFFRE'S VILLA . . .
. . . AND A GENTLEMAN FROM RUSSIA HURRIES TO A RENDEZVOUS
99
BOND IS NOT TALKING—YET
MY DEAR BOY, THE GAME OF RED INDIANS IS OVER, QUITE OVER. YOU ARE NOT EQUIPPED TO PLAY GAMES WITH ADULTS AND IT WAS VERY FOOLISH OF YOUR NANNY IN LONDON TO HAVE SENT YOU OUT HERE WITH YOUR SPADE AND BUCKET. VERY FOOLISH INDEED AND MOST UNFORTUNATE FOR YOU
100
BUT WE MUST STOP JOKING, MY DEAR FELLOW. I SHALL ASK YOU ONCE MORE—WHERE IS THE MONEY?

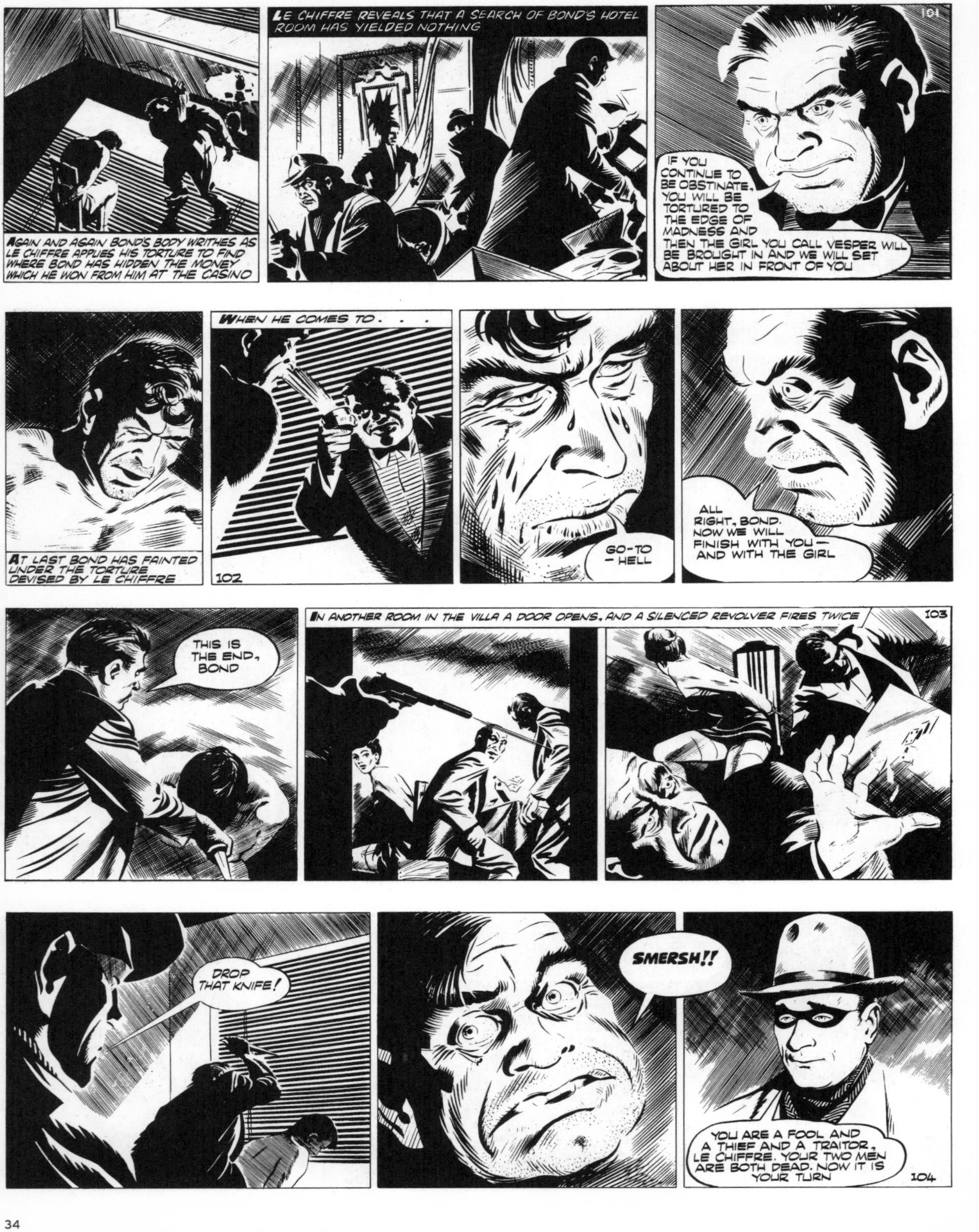
AGAIN AND AGAIN BOND'S BODY WRITHES AS LE CHIFFRE APPLIES HIS TORTURE TO FIND WHERE BOND HAS HIDDEN THE MONEY WHICH HE WON FROM HIM AT THE CASINO
LE CHIFFRE REVEALS THAT A SEARCH OF BOND'S HOTEL ROOM HAS YIELDED NOTHING
101
IF YOU CONTINUE TO BE OBSTINATE, YOU WILL BE TORTURED TO THE EDGE OF MADNESS AND THEN THE GIRL YOU CALL VESPER WILL BE BROUGHT IN AND WE WILL SET ABOUT HER IN FRONT OF YOU
AT LAST BOND HAS FAINTED UNDER THE TORTURE DEVISED BY LE CHIFFRE
WHEN HE COMES TO . . .
102
GO-TO -HELL
ALL RIGHT, BOND. NOW WE WILL FINISH WITH YOU— AND WITH THE GIRL
THIS IS THE END, BOND
IN ANOTHER ROOM IN THE VILLA A DOOR OPENS, AND A SILENCED REVOLVER FIRES TWICE
103
DROP THAT KNIFE!
SMERSH!!
YOU ARE A FOOL AND A THIEF AND A TRAITOR, LE CHIFFRE. YOUR TWO MEN ARE BOTH DEAD. NOW IT IS YOUR TURN
104

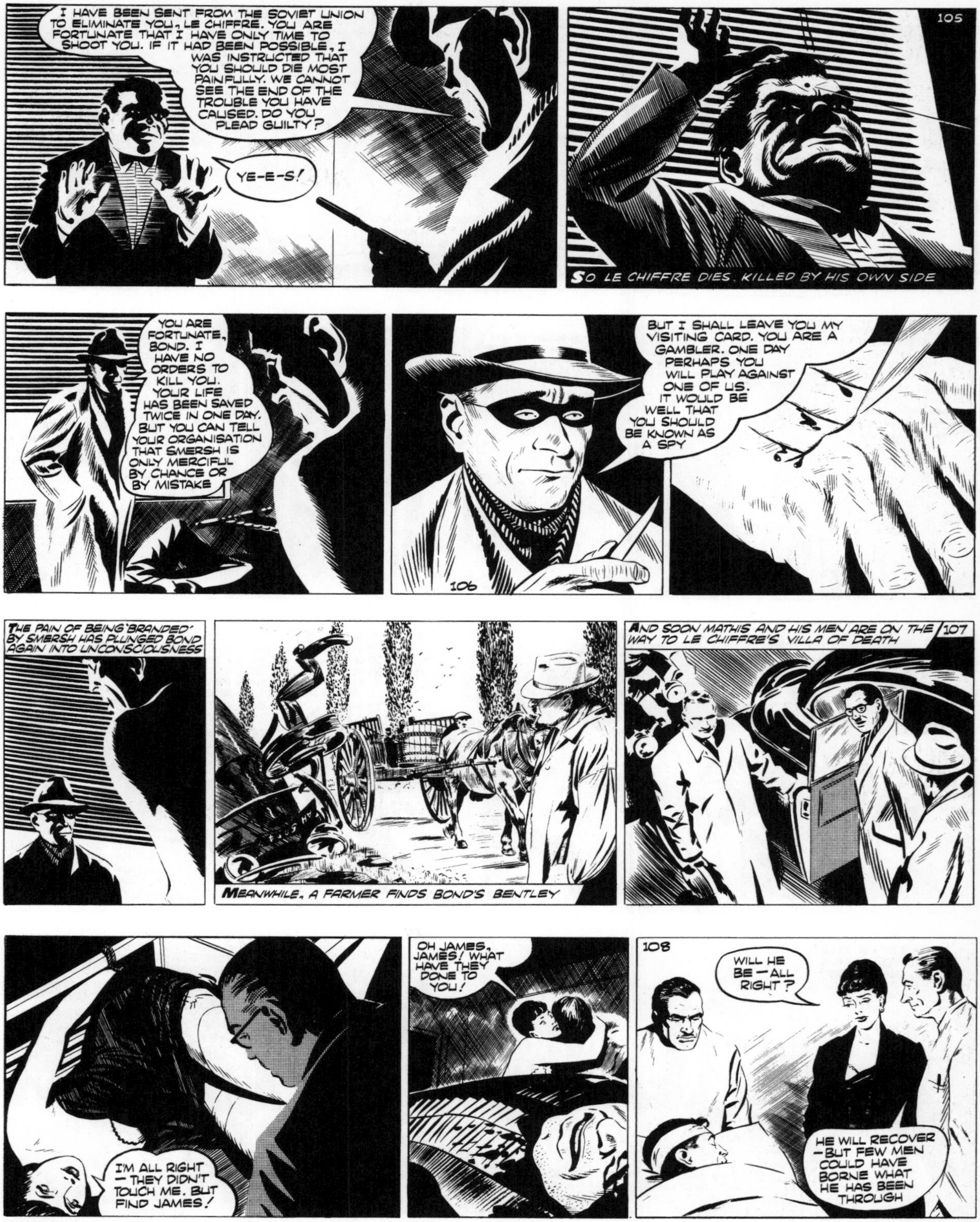
I HAVE BEEN SENT FROM THE SOVIET UNION TO ELIMINATE YOU, LE CHIFFRE. YOU ARE FORTUNATE THAT I HAVE ONLY TIME TO SHOOT YOU. IF IT HAD BEEN POSSIBLE, I WAS INSTRUCTED THAT YOU SHOULD DIE MOST PAINFULLY. WE CANNOT SEE THE END OF THE TROUBLE YOU HAVE CAUSED. DO YOU PLEAD GUILTY?
YE-E-S!
105
SO LE CHIFFRE DIES, KILLED BY HIS OWN SIDE
YOU ARE FORTUNATE, BOND. I HAVE NO ORDERS TO KILL YOU. YOUR LIFE HAS BEEN SAVED TWICE IN ONE DAY. BUT YOU CAN TELL YOUR ORGANISATION THAT SMERSH IS ONLY MERCIFUL BY CHANCE OR BY MISTAKE
106
BUT I SHALL LEAVE YOU MY VISITING CARD. YOU ARE A GAMBLER. ONE DAY PERHAPS YOU WILL PLAY AGAINST ONE OF US. IT WOULD BE WELL THAT YOU SHOULD BE KNOWN AS A SPY
THE PAIN OF BEING 'BRANDED' BY SMERSH HAS PLUNGED BOND AGAIN INTO UNCONSCIOUSNESS
MEANWHILE, A FARMER FINDS BOND'S BENTLEY
AND SOON MATHIS AND HIS MEN ARE ON THE WAY TO LE CHIFFRE'S VILLA OF DEATH
107
I'M ALL RIGHT — THEY DIDN'T TOUCH ME. BUT FIND JAMES!
OH JAMES, JAMES! WHAT HAVE THEY DONE TO YOU!
108
WILL HE BE — ALL RIGHT?
HE WILL RECOVER — BUT FEW MEN COULD HAVE BORNE WHAT HE HAS BEEN THROUGH

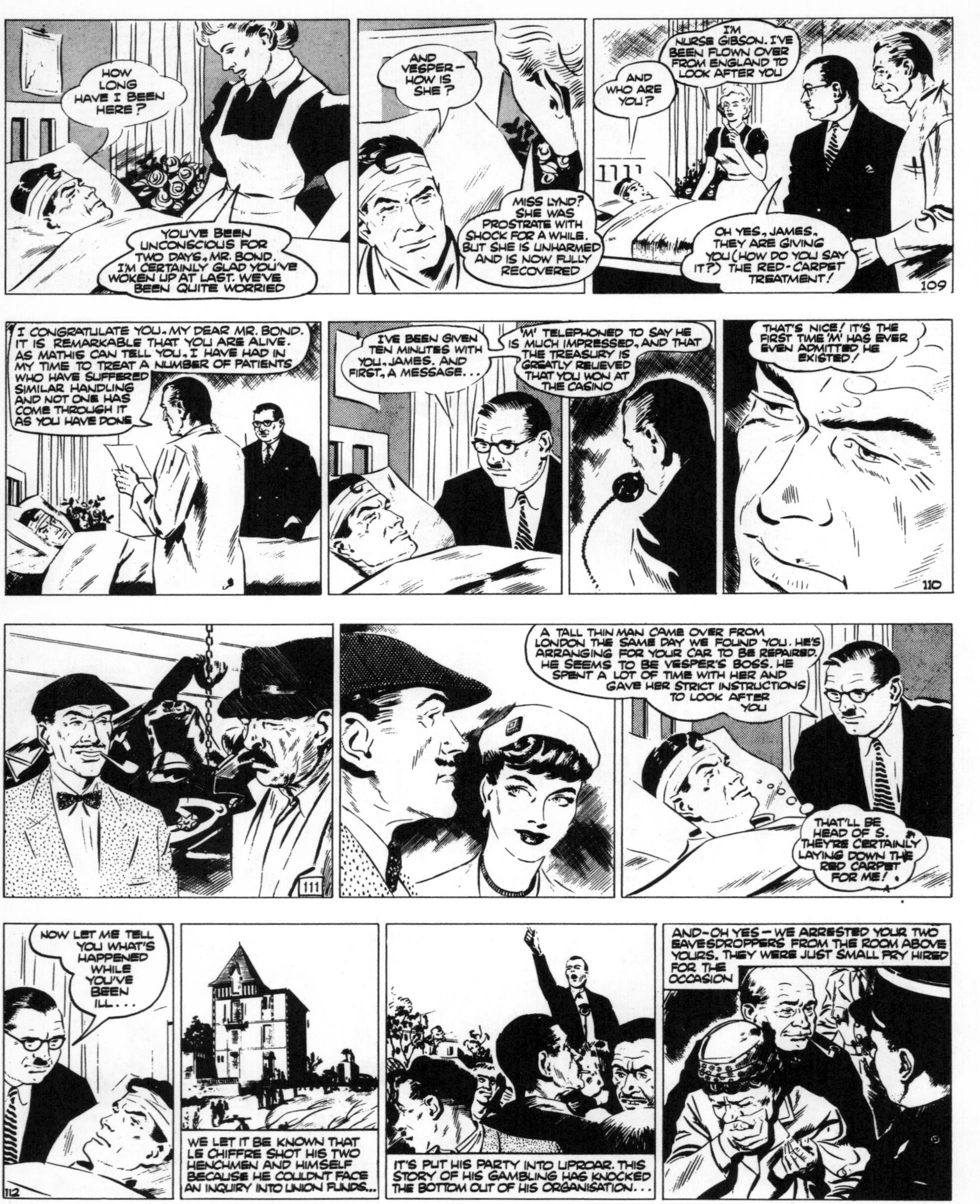

HOW LONG HAVE I BEEN HERE?
YOU'VE BEEN UNCONSCIOUS FOR TWO DAYS, MR. BOND. I'M CERTAINLY GLAD YOU'VE WOKEN UP AT LAST. WE'VE BEEN QUITE WORRIED
AND VESPER– HOW IS SHE?
MISS LYND? SHE WAS PROSTRATE WITH SHOCK FOR A WHILE. BUT SHE IS UNHARMED AND IS NOW FULLY RECOVERED
I'M NURSE GIBSON. I'VE BEEN FLOWN OVER FROM ENGLAND TO LOOK AFTER YOU
AND WHO ARE YOU?
OH YES, JAMES. THEY ARE GIVING YOU (HOW DO YOU SAY IT?) THE RED-CARPET TREATMENT!
109
I CONGRATULATE YOU, MY DEAR MR. BOND. IT IS REMARKABLE THAT YOU ARE ALIVE. AS MATHIS CAN TELL YOU, I HAVE HAD IN MY TIME TO TREAT A NUMBER OF PATIENTS WHO HAVE SUFFERED SIMILAR HANDLING AND NOT ONE HAS COME THROUGH IT AS YOU HAVE DONE
I'VE BEEN GIVEN TEN MINUTES WITH YOU, JAMES. AND FIRST, A MESSAGE...
'M' TELEPHONED TO SAY HE IS MUCH IMPRESSED, AND THAT THE TREASURY IS GREATLY RELIEVED THAT YOU WON AT THE CASINO
THAT'S NICE! IT'S THE FIRST TIME 'M' HAS EVER EVEN ADMITTED HE EXISTED!
110
111
A TALL THIN MAN CAME OVER FROM LONDON THE SAME DAY WE FOUND YOU. HE'S ARRANGING FOR YOUR CAR TO BE REPAIRED. HE SEEMS TO BE VESPER'S BOSS. HE SPENT A LOT OF TIME WITH HER AND GAVE HER STRICT INSTRUCTIONS TO LOOK AFTER YOU
THAT'LL BE HEAD OF S. THEY'RE CERTAINLY LAYING DOWN THE RED CARPET FOR ME!
NOW LET ME TELL YOU WHAT'S HAPPENED WHILE YOU'VE BEEN ILL...
112
WE LET IT BE KNOWN THAT LE CHIFFRE SHOT HIS TWO HENCHMEN AND HIMSELF BECAUSE HE COULDN'T FACE AN INQUIRY INTO UNION FUNDS...
IT'S PUT HIS PARTY INTO UPROAR. THIS STORY OF HIS GAMBLING HAS KNOCKED THE BOTTOM OUT OF HIS ORGANISATION...
AND–OH YES – WE ARRESTED YOUR TWO EAVESDROPPERS FROM THE ROOM ABOVE YOURS. THEY WERE JUST SMALL FRY HIRED FOR THE OCCASION

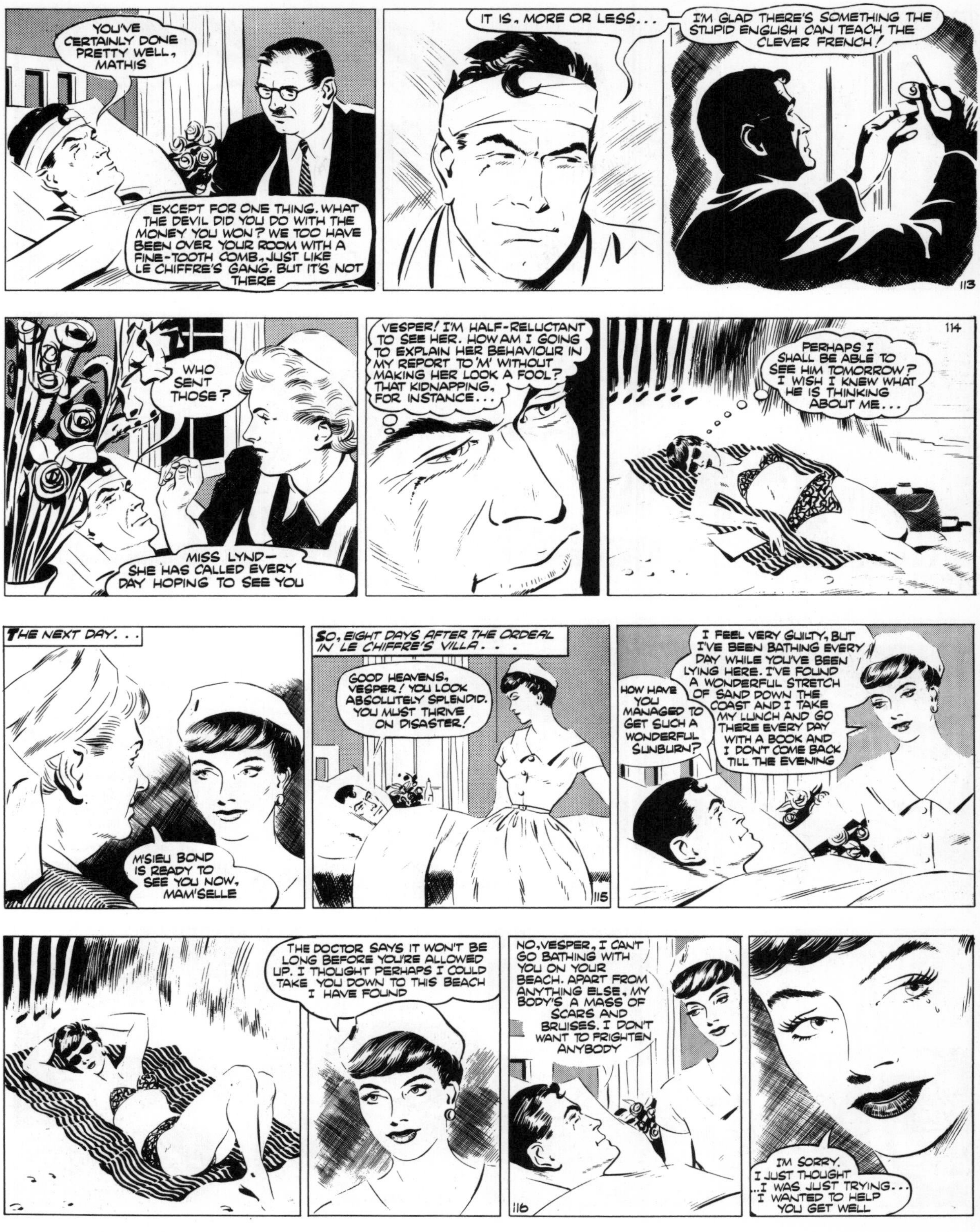
YOU'VE CERTAINLY DONE PRETTY WELL, MATHIS
EXCEPT FOR ONE THING. WHAT THE DEVIL DID YOU DO WITH THE MONEY YOU WON? WE TOO HAVE BEEN OVER YOUR ROOM WITH A FINE-TOOTH COMB, JUST LIKE LE CHIFFRE'S GANG. BUT IT'S NOT THERE
IT IS, MORE OR LESS...
I'M GLAD THERE'S SOMETHING THE STUPID ENGLISH CAN TEACH THE CLEVER FRENCH!
113
WHO SENT THOSE?
MISS LYND— SHE HAS CALLED EVERY DAY HOPING TO SEE YOU
VESPER! I'M HALF-RELUCTANT TO SEE HER. HOW AM I GOING TO EXPLAIN HER BEHAVIOUR IN MY REPORT TO 'M' WITHOUT MAKING HER LOOK A FOOL? THAT KIDNAPPING, FOR INSTANCE...
114
PERHAPS I SHALL BE ABLE TO SEE HIM TOMORROW? I WISH I KNEW WHAT HE IS THINKING ABOUT ME...
THE NEXT DAY...
M'SIEU BOND IS READY TO SEE YOU NOW, MAM'SELLE
SO, EIGHT DAYS AFTER THE ORDEAL IN LE CHIFFRE'S VILLA...
GOOD HEAVENS, VESPER! YOU LOOK ABSOLUTELY SPLENDID. YOU MUST THRIVE ON DISASTER!
115
HOW HAVE YOU MANAGED TO GET SUCH A WONDERFUL SUNBURN?
I FEEL VERY GUILTY, BUT I'VE BEEN BATHING EVERY DAY WHILE YOU'VE BEEN LYING HERE. I'VE FOUND A WONDERFUL STRETCH OF SAND DOWN THE COAST AND I TAKE MY LUNCH AND GO THERE EVERY DAY WITH A BOOK AND I DON'T COME BACK TILL THE EVENING
THE DOCTOR SAYS IT WON'T BE LONG BEFORE YOU'RE ALLOWED UP. I THOUGHT PERHAPS I COULD TAKE YOU DOWN TO THIS BEACH I HAVE FOUND
NO, VESPER, I CAN'T GO BATHING WITH YOU ON YOUR BEACH. APART FROM ANYTHING ELSE, MY BODY'S A MASS OF SCARS AND BRUISES. I DON'T WANT TO FRIGHTEN ANYBODY
116
I'M SORRY. I JUST THOUGHT ...I WAS JUST TRYING... ...I WANTED TO HELP YOU GET WELL

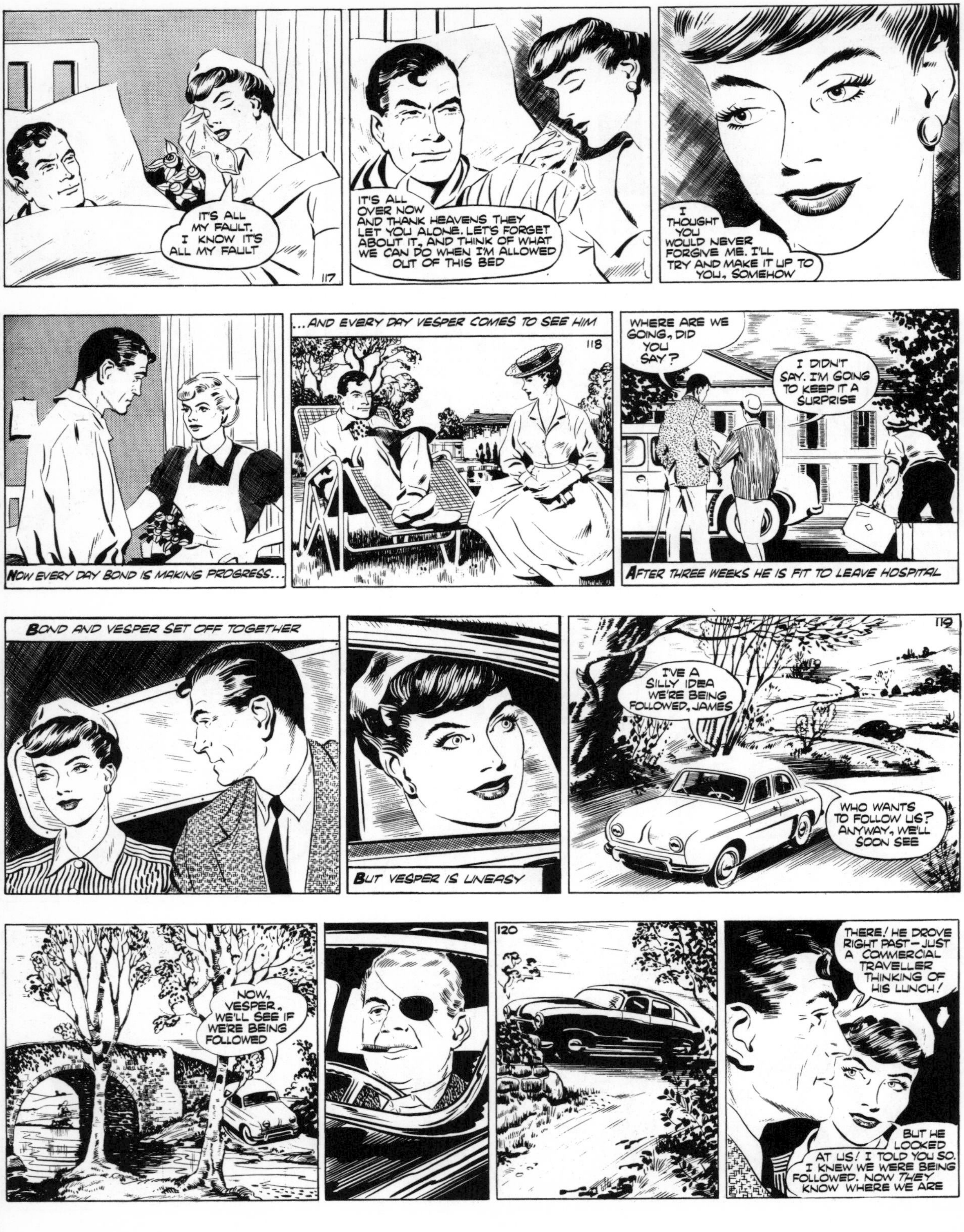
IT'S ALL MY FAULT. I KNOW IT'S ALL MY FAULT
117
IT'S ALL OVER NOW AND THANK HEAVENS THEY LET YOU ALONE. LET'S FORGET ABOUT IT, AND THINK OF WHAT WE CAN DO WHEN I'M ALLOWED OUT OF THIS BED
I THOUGHT YOU WOULD NEVER FORGIVE ME. I'LL TRY AND MAKE IT UP TO YOU, SOMEHOW
NOW EVERY DAY BOND IS MAKING PROGRESS...
...AND EVERY DAY VESPER COMES TO SEE HIM
118
WHERE ARE WE GOING, DID YOU SAY?
I DIDN'T SAY. I'M GOING TO KEEP IT A SURPRISE
AFTER THREE WEEKS HE IS FIT TO LEAVE HOSPITAL
BOND AND VESPER SET OFF TOGETHER
BUT VESPER IS UNEASY
119
I'VE A SILLY IDEA WE'RE BEING FOLLOWED, JAMES
WHO WANTS TO FOLLOW US? ANYWAY, WE'LL SOON SEE
NOW, VESPER, WE'LL SEE IF WE'RE BEING FOLLOWED
120
THERE! HE DROVE RIGHT PAST—JUST A COMMERCIAL TRAVELLER THINKING OF HIS LUNCH!
BUT HE LOOKED AT US! I TOLD YOU SO. I KNEW WE WERE BEING FOLLOWED. NOW THEY KNOW WHERE WE ARE

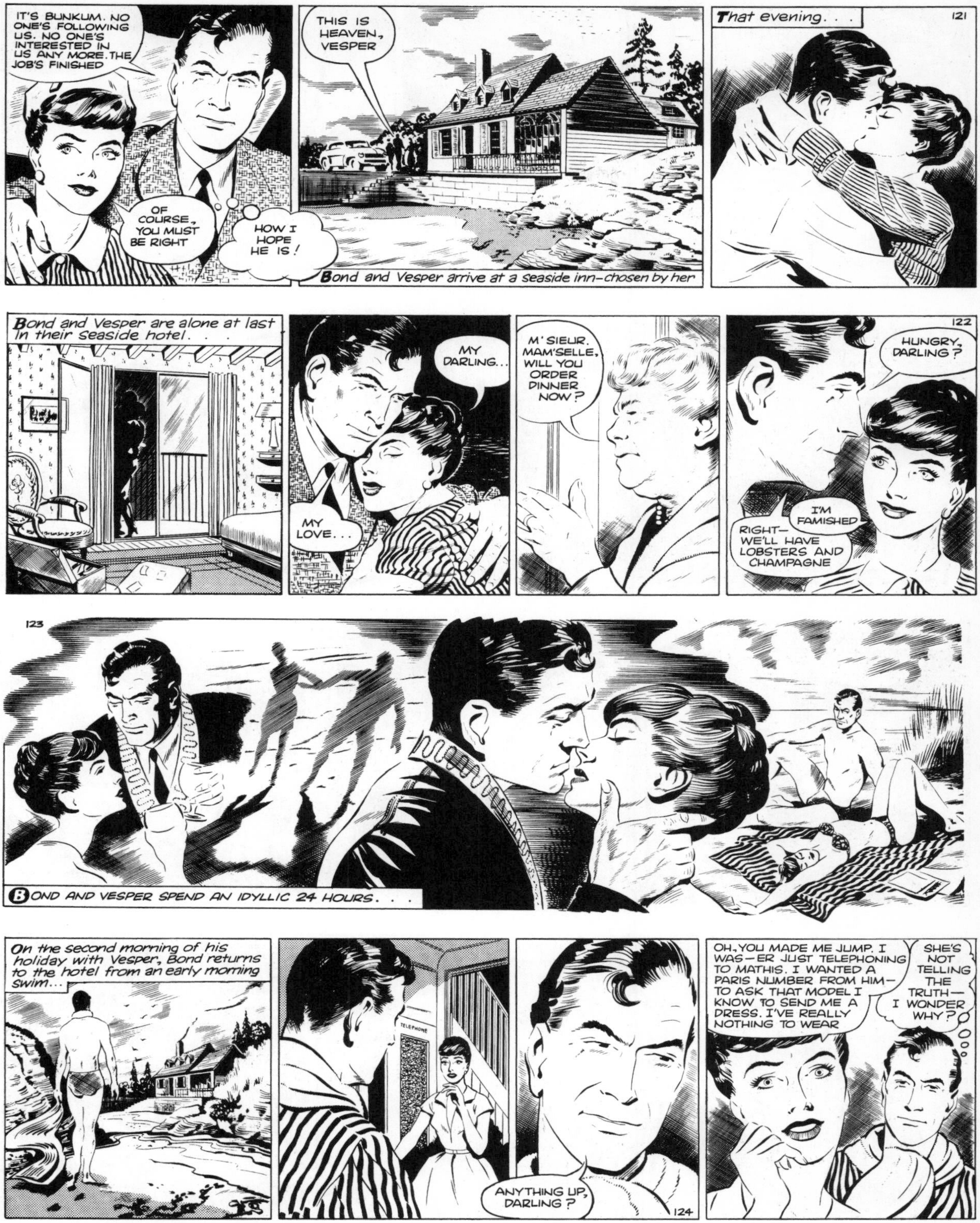
IT'S BUNKUM. NO ONE'S FOLLOWING US. NO ONE'S INTERESTED IN US ANY MORE. THE JOB'S FINISHED
OF COURSE, YOU MUST BE RIGHT
HOW I HOPE HE IS!
THIS IS HEAVEN, VESPER
Bond and Vesper arrive at a seaside inn—chosen by her
That evening. . .
121
Bond and Vesper are alone at last in their seaside hotel. . .
MY DARLING...
MY LOVE...
M'SIEUR. MAM'SELLE, WILL YOU ORDER DINNER NOW?
122
HUNGRY, DARLING?
I'M FAMISHED
RIGHT— WE'LL HAVE LOBSTERS AND CHAMPAGNE
123
BOND AND VESPER SPEND AN IDYLLIC 24 HOURS. . .
On the second morning of his holiday with Vesper, Bond returns to the hotel from an early morning swim...
TELEPHONE
ANYTHING UP, DARLING?
124
OH, YOU MADE ME JUMP. I WAS—ER JUST TELEPHONING TO MATHIS. I WANTED A PARIS NUMBER FROM HIM— TO ASK THAT MODEL I KNOW TO SEND ME A DRESS. I'VE REALLY NOTHING TO WEAR
SHE'S NOT TELLING THE TRUTH— I WONDER WHY?

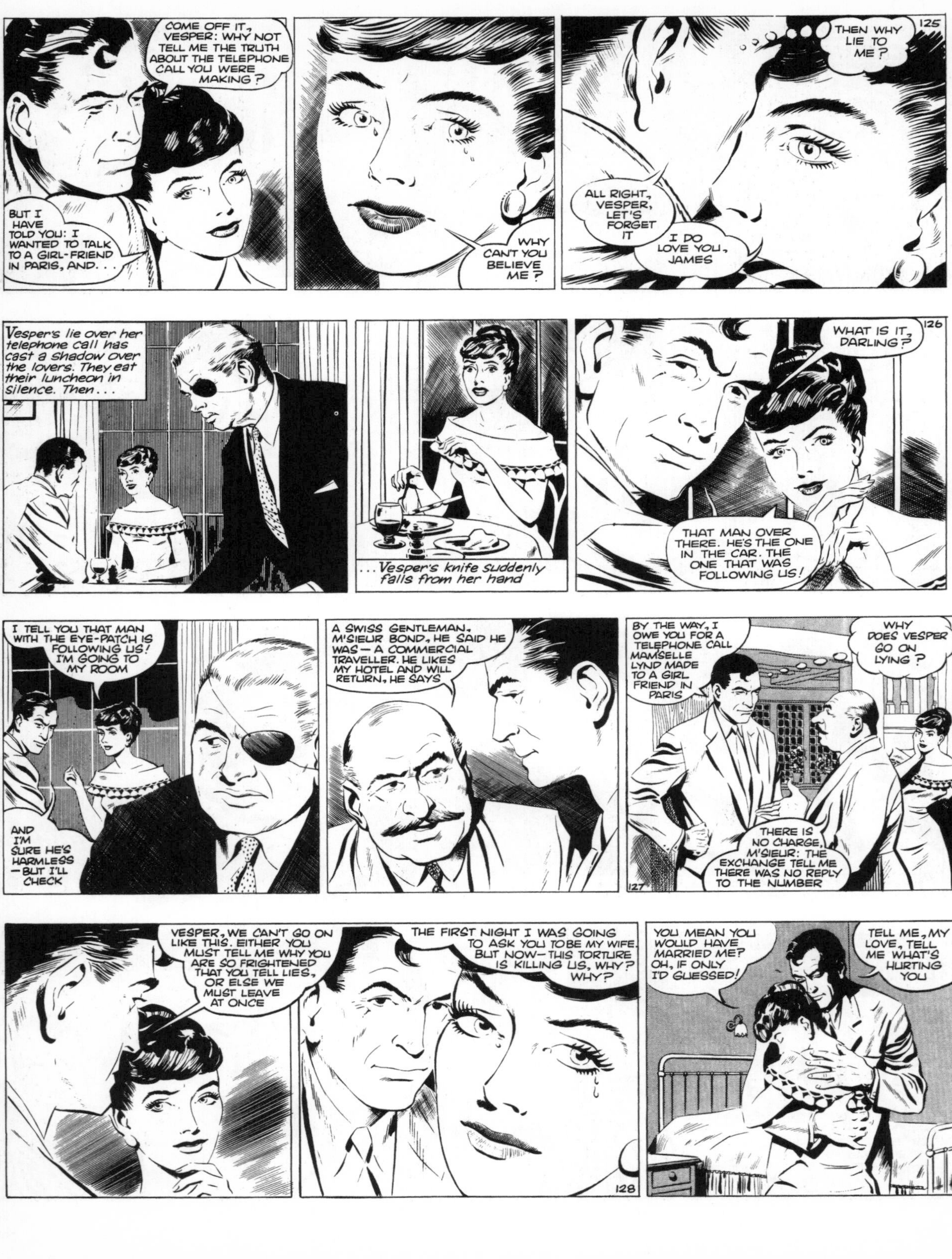
COME OFF IT, VESPER: WHY NOT TELL ME THE TRUTH ABOUT THE TELEPHONE CALL YOU WERE MAKING?
BUT I HAVE TOLD YOU: I WANTED TO TALK TO A GIRL-FRIEND IN PARIS, AND...
WHY CAN'T YOU BELIEVE ME?
125
THEN WHY LIE TO ME?
ALL RIGHT, VESPER, LET'S FORGET IT
I DO LOVE YOU, JAMES
Vesper's lie over her telephone call has cast a shadow over the lovers. They eat their luncheon in silence. Then...
...Vesper's knife suddenly falls from her hand
126
WHAT IS IT, DARLING?
THAT MAN OVER THERE. HE'S THE ONE IN THE CAR. THE ONE THAT WAS FOLLOWING US!
I TELL YOU THAT MAN WITH THE EYE-PATCH IS FOLLOWING US! I'M GOING TO MY ROOM
AND I'M SURE HE'S HARMLESS —BUT I'LL CHECK
A SWISS GENTLEMAN, M'SIEUR BOND, HE SAID HE WAS — A COMMERCIAL TRAVELLER. HE LIKES MY HOTEL AND WILL RETURN, HE SAYS
BY THE WAY, I OWE YOU FOR A TELEPHONE CALL MAMSELLE LYND MADE TO A GIRL FRIEND IN PARIS
WHY DOES VESPER GO ON LYING?
THERE IS NO CHARGE, M'SIEUR: THE EXCHANGE TELL ME THERE WAS NO REPLY TO THE NUMBER
127
VESPER, WE CAN'T GO ON LIKE THIS. EITHER YOU MUST TELL ME WHY YOU ARE SO FRIGHTENED THAT YOU TELL LIES, OR ELSE WE MUST LEAVE AT ONCE
THE FIRST NIGHT I WAS GOING TO ASK YOU TO BE MY WIFE. BUT NOW—THIS TORTURE IS KILLING US, WHY? WHY?
128
YOU MEAN YOU WOULD HAVE MARRIED ME? OH, IF ONLY I'D GUESSED!
TELL ME, MY LOVE, TELL ME WHAT'S HURTING YOU

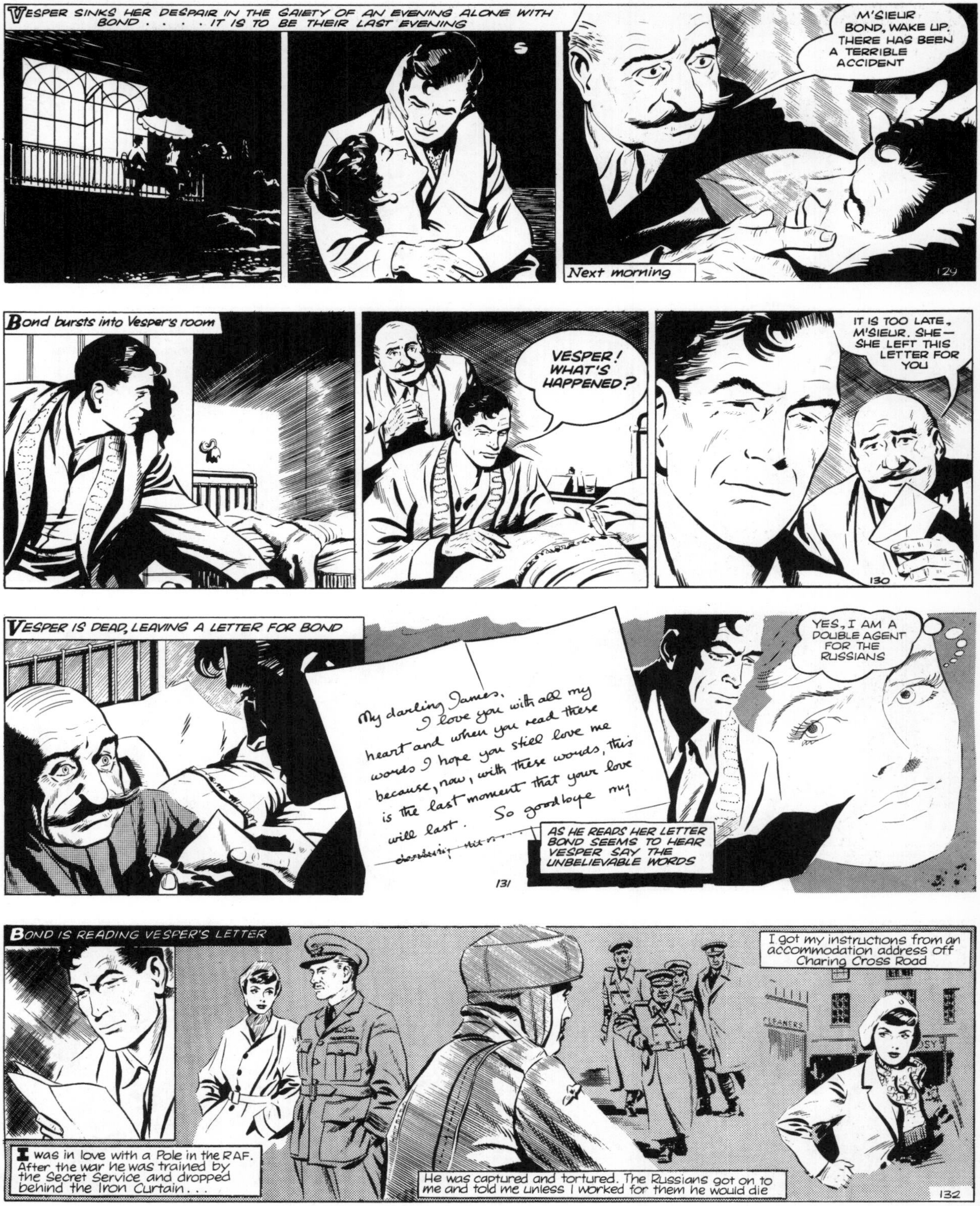
VESPER SINKS HER DESPAIR IN THE GAIETY OF AN EVENING ALONE WITH BOND . . . . IT IS TO BE THEIR LAST EVENING
M'SIEUR BOND, WAKE UP. THERE HAS BEEN A TERRIBLE ACCIDENT
Next morning
129
Bond bursts into Vesper's room
VESPER! WHAT'S HAPPENED?
IT IS TOO LATE, M'SIEUR. SHE— SHE LEFT THIS LETTER FOR YOU
130
VESPER IS DEAD, LEAVING A LETTER FOR BOND
My darling James,
I love you with all my heart and when you read these words I hope you still love me because, now, with these words, this is the last moment that your love will last. So goodbye my
AS HE READS HER LETTER BOND SEEMS TO HEAR VESPER SAY THE UNBELIEVABLE WORDS
YES, I AM A DOUBLE AGENT FOR THE RUSSIANS
131
BOND IS READING VESPER'S LETTER
I was in love with a Pole in the RAF. After the war he was trained by the Secret Service and dropped behind the Iron Curtain . . .
He was captured and tortured. The Russians got on to me and told me unless I worked for them he would die
I got my instructions from an accommodation address off Charing Cross Road
132

VESPER'S "LAST TESTAMENT" TELLS HER STARTLING STORY

133

So I was told not to stand behind you at the Casino, that was why the gunman was nearly able to shoot you. And then I had to stage the kidnapping to trap you

Even when I first met you I was spying on you

And then, I began to fall in love with you, and everything went wrong. The Russians traced me to our hotel, they will kill my Polish lover now, and there is nothing I can do

VESPER A RUSSIAN SPY! I STILL CAN'T BELIEVE IT!

I KNEW IT WOULD BE THE END OF OUR LOVE IF I TOLD YOU. I REALISED THAT I COULD EITHER WAIT TO BE KILLED BY THE RUSSIANS AND PERHAPS GET YOU KILLED, TOO, OR I COULD KILL MYSELF...

The words in her last letter still dance before Bond's eyes

I can't tell you much to help you. My contact in Paris was a telephone number: Invalides 55200

James, My Love, my love
Vesper

134

BOND'S DREAM OF HAPPINESS WITH VESPER HAS BEEN SHATTERED BY THE REVELATION OF HER DEATH AND DOUBLE LIFE

BUT AS A SECRET SERVICE AGENT, HIS JOB IS TO REPAIR THE DAMAGE — IF HE CAN

MY GOD! A SPY RIGHT BANG IN THE MIDDLE OF SECRET SERVICE HQ! I MUST WARN 'M'

135

WHO? 007? WHAT THE HELL D'YOU MEAN RINGING ME DIRECT? IT'S ABSOLUTELY AGAINST ORDERS. YOU'LL BE FIRED FOR THIS

I DON'T THINK SO, SIR— NOT WHEN YOU'VE HEARD WHAT I HAVE TO TELL YOU. THIS IS AN EMERGENCY

GET OFF THE LINE

THAT ASSISTANT YOU SENT ME, NO. 3030—

ONE MOMENT SIR. SHE WAS A "DOUBLE"

YES. SHE'S DEAD!

DID YOU SAY 'WAS'?

136

BOND'S WARNING THAT VESPER WAS A SPY STARTS THE SECRET SERVICE MACHINE WORKING

CODES HAVE TO BE CHANGED

FRIENDLY AGENCIES ARE WARNED AND BOND IS TOLD TO REPORT BACK TO LONDON

137

WELL, 007, WE'VE CLEARED UP THAT CASINO MESS. HOW'S THE HAND?

HAD A SKIN-GRAFT, SIR. SMERSH'S TRADEMARK IS FADING NICELY

GOOD. I'VE GOT ANOTHER JOB FOR YOU. YOU'RE DUE IN NEW YORK TOMORROW MORNING

SO—LIVE AND LET DIE

138

007

LIVE AND LET DIE

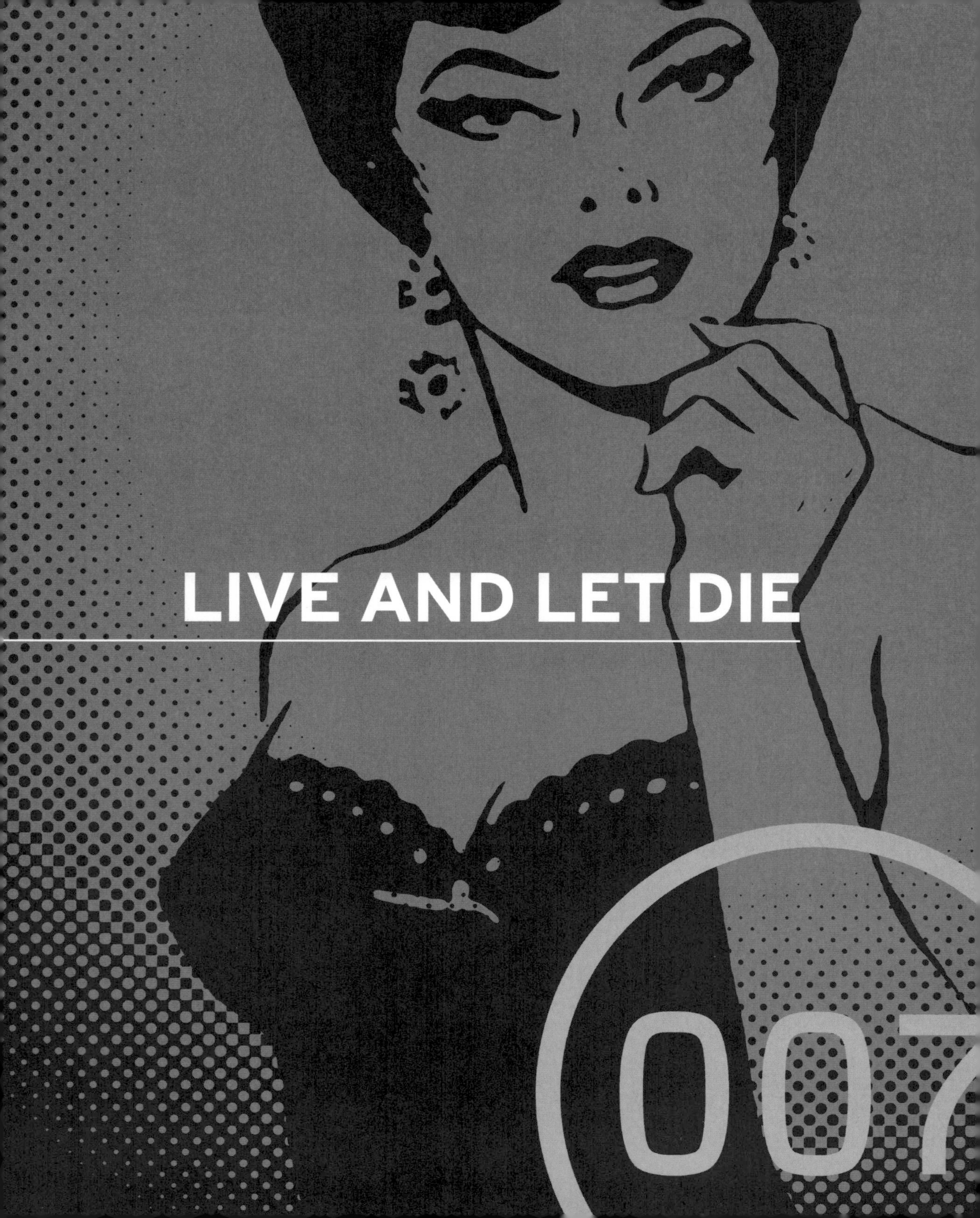
007

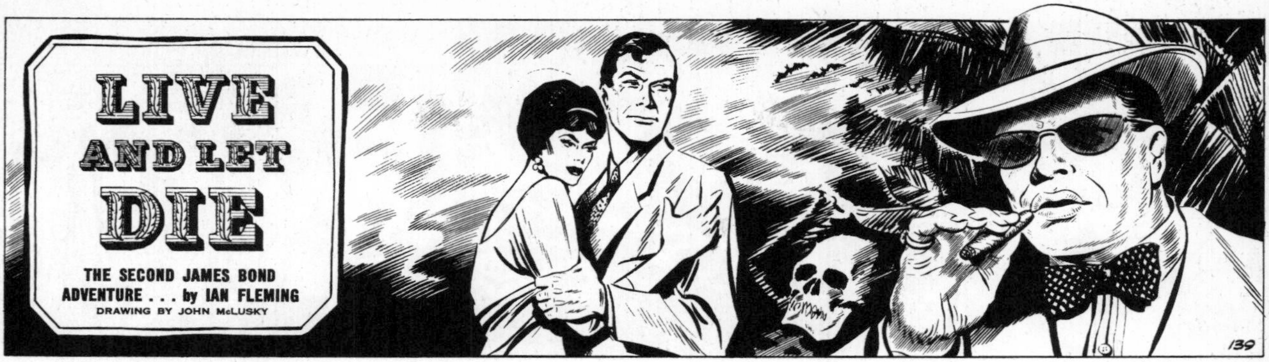
LIVE AND LET DIE
THE SECOND JAMES BOND ADVENTURE . . . by IAN FLEMING
DRAWING BY JOHN McLUSKY
139

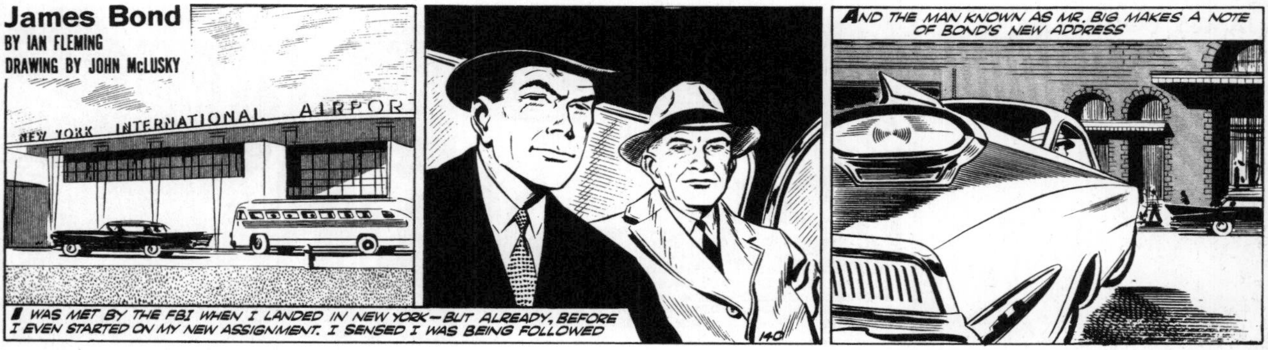
James Bond
BY IAN FLEMING
DRAWING BY JOHN McLUSKY
NEW YORK INTERNATIONAL AIRPORT
I WAS MET BY THE FBI WHEN I LANDED IN NEW YORK—BUT ALREADY, BEFORE I EVEN STARTED ON MY NEW ASSIGNMENT, I SENSED I WAS BEING FOLLOWED
140
AND THE MAN KNOWN AS MR. BIG MAKES A NOTE OF BOND'S NEW ADDRESS

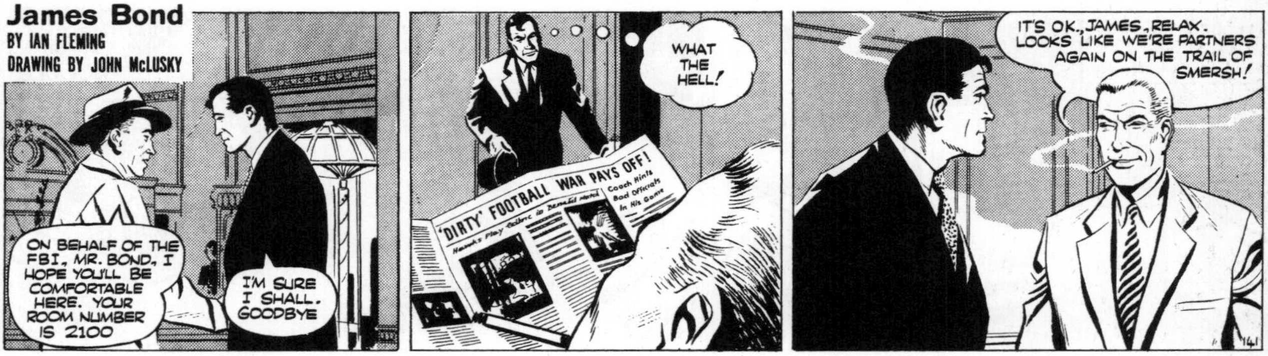
James Bond
BY IAN FLEMING
DRAWING BY JOHN McLUSKY
ON BEHALF OF THE FBI, MR. BOND, I HOPE YOU'LL BE COMFORTABLE HERE. YOUR ROOM NUMBER IS 2100
I'M SURE I SHALL. GOODBYE
'DIRTY' FOOTBALL WAR PAYS OFF!
Coach Hints Bad Officials In His Game
WHAT THE HELL!
IT'S OK., JAMES, RELAX. LOOKS LIKE WE'RE PARTNERS AGAIN ON THE TRAIL OF SMERSH!
141

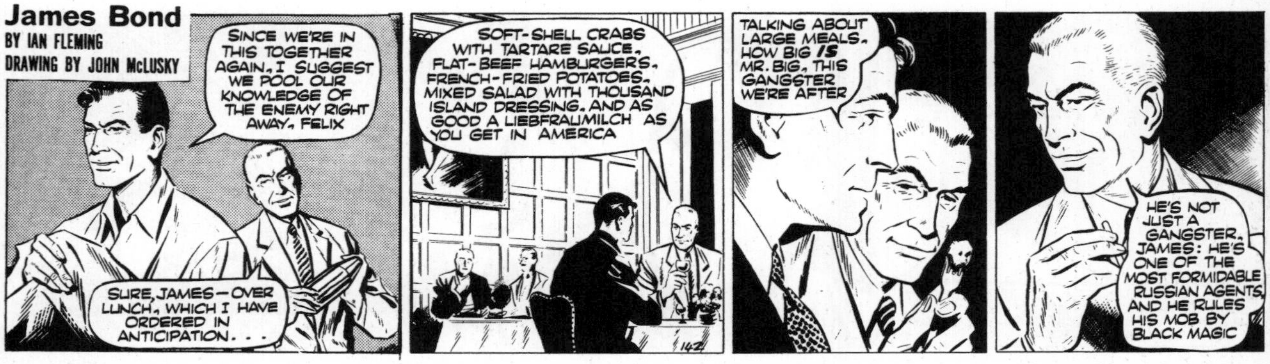
James Bond
BY IAN FLEMING
DRAWING BY JOHN McLUSKY
SINCE WE'RE IN THIS TOGETHER AGAIN, I SUGGEST WE POOL OUR KNOWLEDGE OF THE ENEMY RIGHT AWAY, FELIX
SURE, JAMES—OVER LUNCH, WHICH I HAVE ORDERED IN ANTICIPATION. . .
SOFT-SHELL CRABS WITH TARTARE SAUCE, FLAT-BEEF HAMBURGERS, FRENCH-FRIED POTATOES, MIXED SALAD WITH THOUSAND ISLAND DRESSING, AND AS GOOD A LIEBFRAUMILCH AS YOU GET IN AMERICA
142
TALKING ABOUT LARGE MEALS, HOW BIG IS MR. BIG, THIS GANGSTER WE'RE AFTER
HE'S NOT JUST A GANGSTER, JAMES: HE'S ONE OF THE MOST FORMIDABLE RUSSIAN AGENTS, AND HE RULES HIS MOB BY BLACK MAGIC

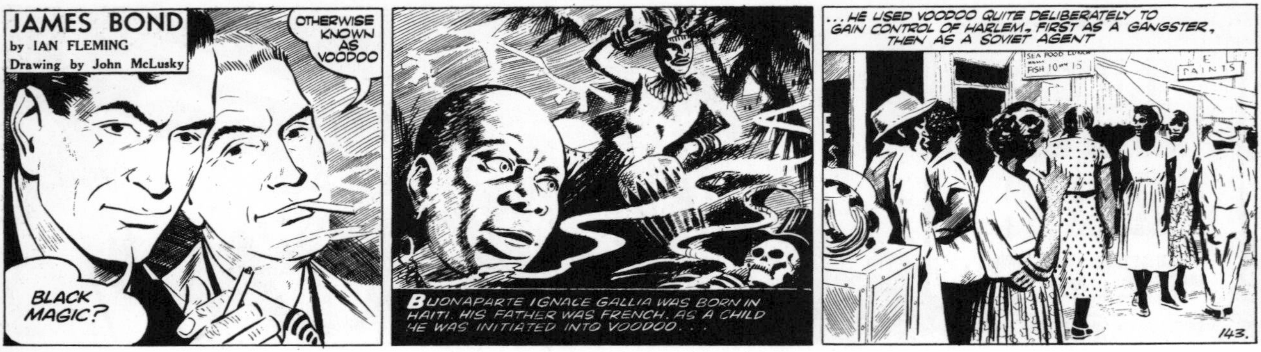
JAMES BOND
by IAN FLEMING
Drawing by John McLusky
BLACK MAGIC?
OTHERWISE KNOWN AS VOODOO
BUONAPARTE IGNACE GALLIA WAS BORN IN HAITI. HIS FATHER WAS FRENCH. AS A CHILD HE WAS INITIATED INTO VOODOO . . .
. . . HE USED VOODOO QUITE DELIBERATELY TO GAIN CONTROL OF HARLEM, FIRST AS A GANGSTER, THEN AS A SOVIET AGENT
PAINTS
143.

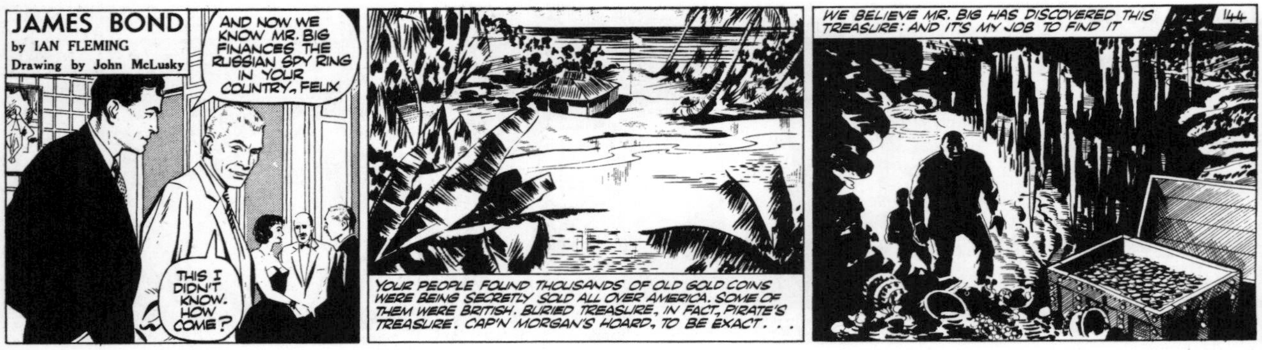
JAMES BOND
by IAN FLEMING
Drawing by John McLusky
AND NOW WE KNOW MR. BIG FINANCES THE RUSSIAN SPY RING IN YOUR COUNTRY, FELIX
THIS I DIDN'T KNOW. HOW COME?
YOUR PEOPLE FOUND THOUSANDS OF OLD GOLD COINS WERE BEING SECRETLY SOLD ALL OVER AMERICA. SOME OF THEM WERE BRITISH. BURIED TREASURE, IN FACT, PIRATE'S TREASURE. CAP'N MORGAN'S HOARD, TO BE EXACT . . .
WE BELIEVE MR. BIG HAS DISCOVERED THIS TREASURE: AND IT'S MY JOB TO FIND IT
144

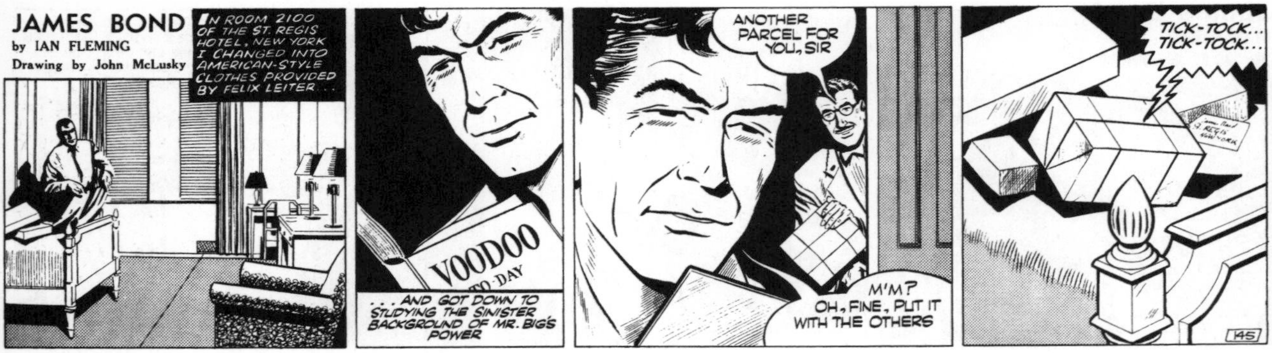
JAMES BOND
by IAN FLEMING
Drawing by John McLusky
IN ROOM 2100 OF THE ST. REGIS HOTEL, NEW YORK I CHANGED INTO AMERICAN-STYLE CLOTHES PROVIDED BY FELIX LEITER . . .
VOODOO
TO-DAY
. . . AND GOT DOWN TO STUDYING THE SINISTER BACKGROUND OF MR. BIG'S POWER
ANOTHER PARCEL FOR YOU, SIR
M'M? OH, FINE, PUT IT WITH THE OTHERS
TICK-TOCK . . .
TICK-TOCK . . .
145

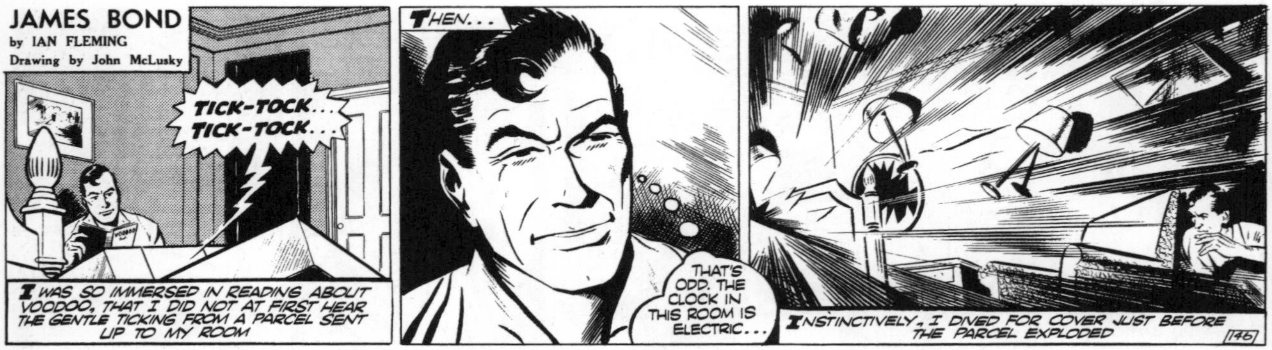
JAMES BOND
by IAN FLEMING
Drawing by John McLusky
TICK-TOCK . . .
TICK-TOCK . . .
I WAS SO IMMERSED IN READING ABOUT VOODOO, THAT I DID NOT AT FIRST HEAR THE GENTLE TICKING FROM A PARCEL SENT UP TO MY ROOM
THEN . . .
THAT'S ODD. THE CLOCK IN THIS ROOM IS ELECTRIC . . .
INSTINCTIVELY, I DIVED FOR COVER JUST BEFORE THE PARCEL EXPLODED
146

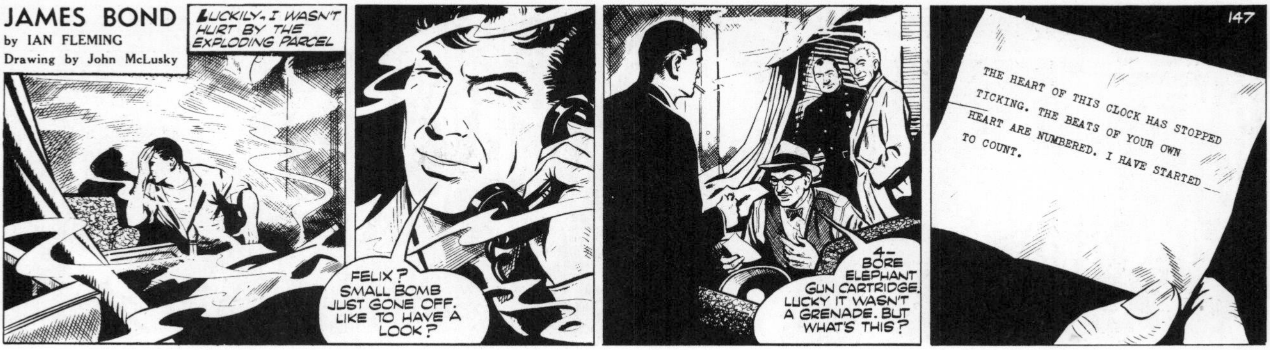
JAMES BOND
by IAN FLEMING
Drawing by John McLusky
LUCKILY, I WASN'T HURT BY THE EXPLODING PARCEL
FELIX? SMALL BOMB JUST GONE OFF. LIKE TO HAVE A LOOK?
4-BORE ELEPHANT GUN CARTRIDGE. LUCKY IT WASN'T A GRENADE. BUT WHAT'S THIS?
147
THE HEART OF THIS CLOCK HAS STOPPED TICKING. THE BEATS OF YOUR OWN HEART ARE NUMBERED. I HAVE STARTED TO COUNT.

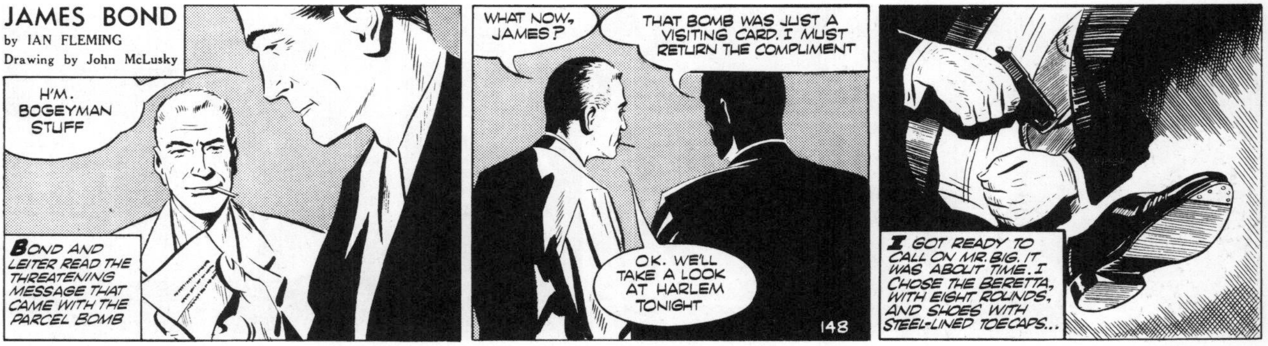
JAMES BOND
by IAN FLEMING
Drawing by John McLusky
H'M. BOGEYMAN STUFF
BOND AND LEITER READ THE THREATENING MESSAGE THAT CAME WITH THE PARCEL BOMB
WHAT NOW, JAMES?
THAT BOMB WAS JUST A VISITING CARD. I MUST RETURN THE COMPLIMENT
OK. WE'LL TAKE A LOOK AT HARLEM TONIGHT
148
I GOT READY TO CALL ON MR. BIG. IT WAS ABOUT TIME. I CHOSE THE BERETTA, WITH EIGHT ROUNDS, AND SHOES WITH STEEL-LINED TOECAPS...

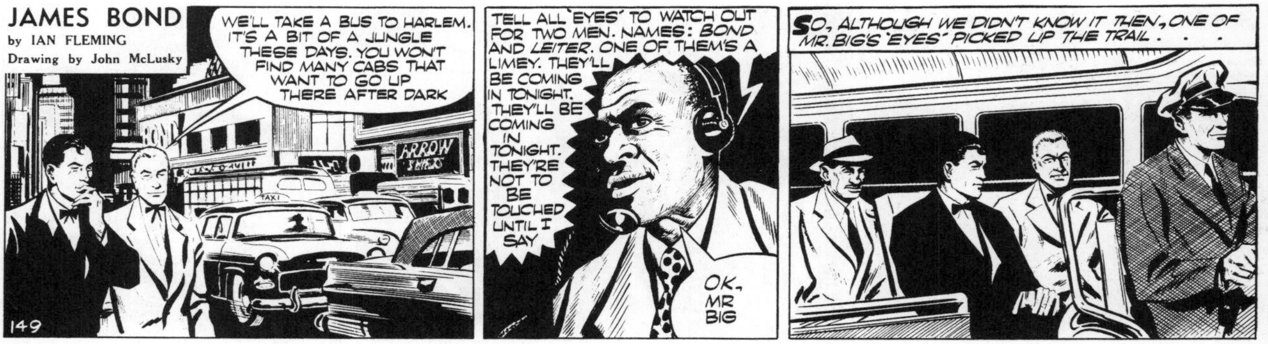
JAMES BOND
by IAN FLEMING
Drawing by John McLusky
WE'LL TAKE A BUS TO HARLEM. IT'S A BIT OF A JUNGLE THESE DAYS. YOU WON'T FIND MANY CABS THAT WANT TO GO UP THERE AFTER DARK
ARROW
TAXI
149
TELL ALL 'EYES' TO WATCH OUT FOR TWO MEN. NAMES: BOND AND LEITER. ONE OF THEM'S A LIMEY. THEY'LL BE COMING IN TONIGHT. THEY'LL BE COMING IN TONIGHT. THEY'RE NOT TO BE TOUCHED UNTIL I SAY
OK, MR BIG
SO, ALTHOUGH WE DIDN'T KNOW IT THEN, ONE OF MR. BIG'S 'EYES' PICKED UP THE TRAIL . . .

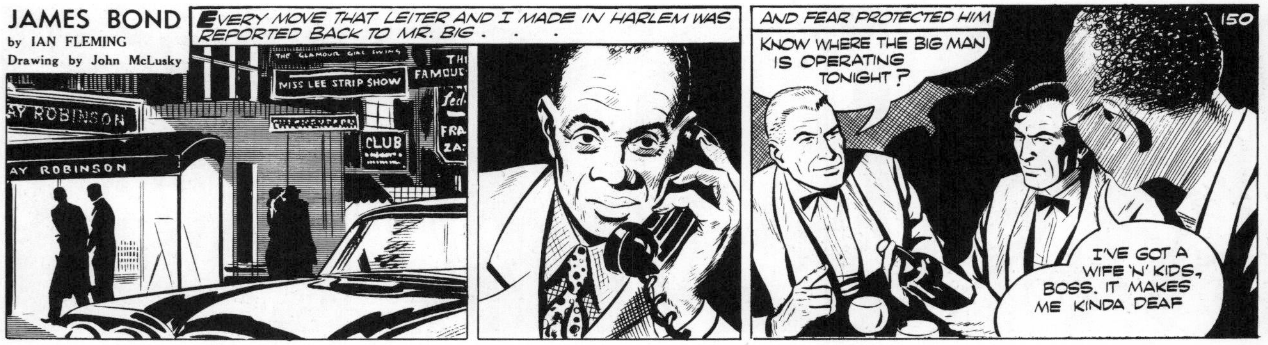
JAMES BOND
by IAN FLEMING
Drawing by John McLusky
EVERY MOVE THAT LEITER AND I MADE IN HARLEM WAS REPORTED BACK TO MR. BIG . . .
MISS LEE STRIP SHOW
CLUB
AY ROBINSON
AND FEAR PROTECTED HIM
150
KNOW WHERE THE BIG MAN IS OPERATING TONIGHT?
I'VE GOT A WIFE 'N' KIDS, BOSS. IT MAKES ME KINDA DEAF

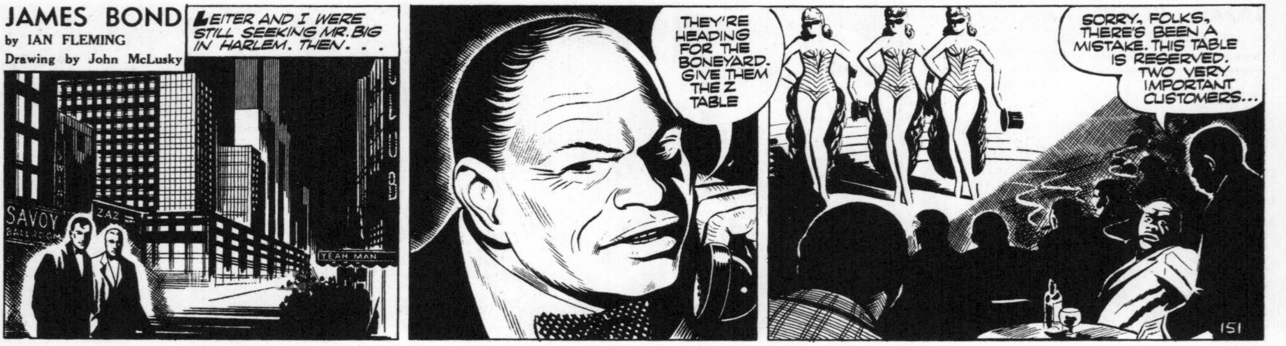
JAMES BOND
by IAN FLEMING
Drawing by John McLusky
LEITER AND I WERE STILL SEEKING MR. BIG IN HARLEM. THEN . . .
SAVOY
ZAZ
YEAH MAN
THEY'RE HEADING FOR THE BONEYARD. GIVE THEM THE Z TABLE
SORRY, FOLKS, THERE'S BEEN A MISTAKE. THIS TABLE IS RESERVED. TWO VERY IMPORTANT CUSTOMERS...
151

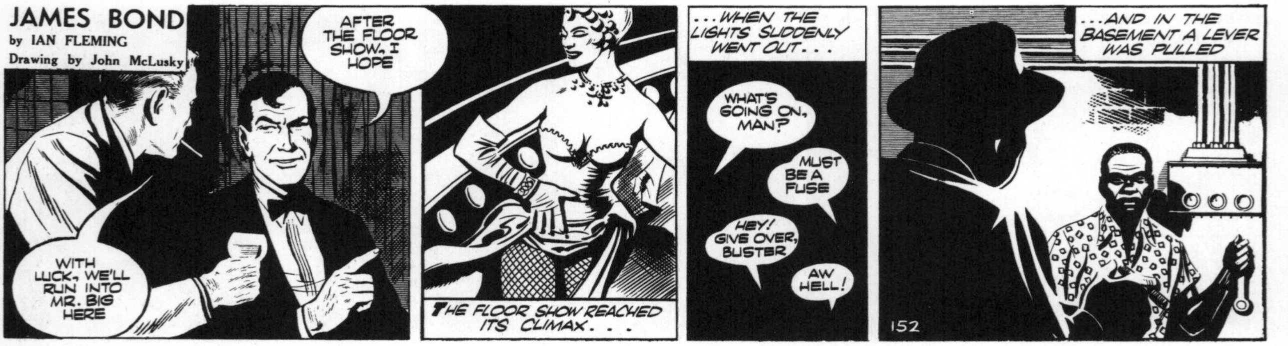
JAMES BOND
by IAN FLEMING
Drawing by John McLusky
WITH LUCK, WE'LL RUN INTO MR. BIG HERE
AFTER THE FLOOR SHOW, I HOPE
THE FLOOR SHOW REACHED ITS CLIMAX. . .
. . . WHEN THE LIGHTS SUDDENLY WENT OUT . . .
WHAT'S GOING ON, MAN?
MUST BE A FUSE
HEY! GIVE OVER, BUSTER
AW HELL!
152
. . . AND IN THE BASEMENT A LEVER WAS PULLED

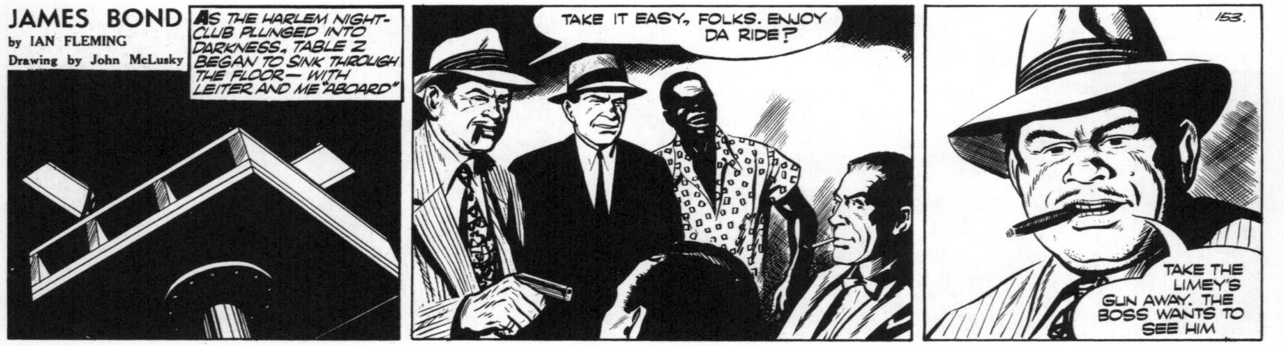
JAMES BOND
by IAN FLEMING
Drawing by John McLusky
AS THE HARLEM NIGHT-CLUB PLUNGED INTO DARKNESS, TABLE Z BEGAN TO SINK THROUGH THE FLOOR— WITH LEITER AND ME "ABOARD"
TAKE IT EASY, FOLKS. ENJOY DA RIDE?
153.
TAKE THE LIMEY'S GUN AWAY. THE BOSS WANTS TO SEE HIM

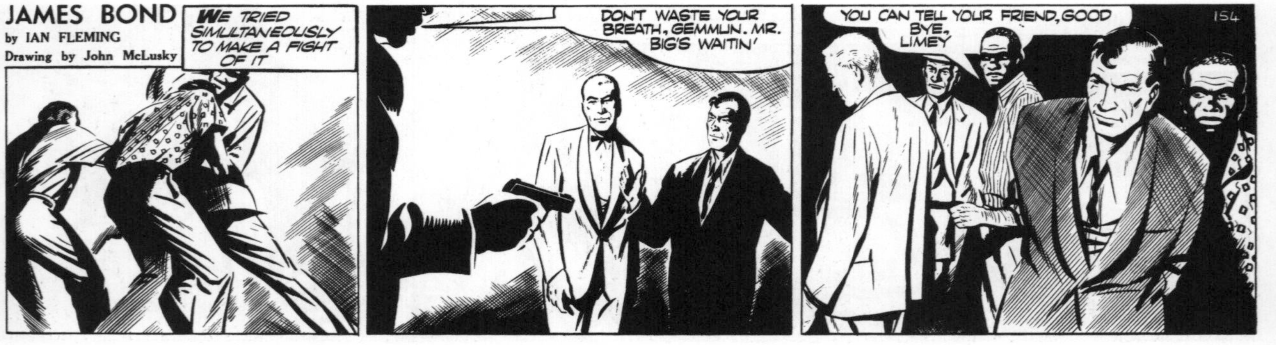
JAMES BOND
by IAN FLEMING
Drawing by John McLusky
WE TRIED SIMULTANEOUSLY TO MAKE A FIGHT OF IT
DON'T WASTE YOUR BREATH, GEMMUN. MR. BIG'S WAITIN'
YOU CAN TELL YOUR FRIEND, GOOD BYE, LIMEY
154

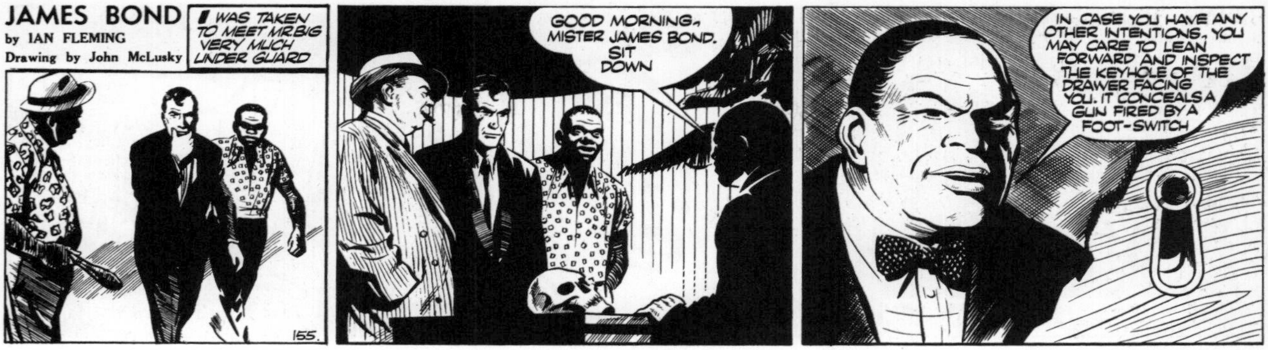
JAMES BOND
by IAN FLEMING
Drawing by John McLusky
I WAS TAKEN TO MEET MR.BIG VERY MUCH UNDER GUARD
155.
GOOD MORNING, MISTER JAMES BOND. SIT DOWN
IN CASE YOU HAVE ANY OTHER INTENTIONS, YOU MAY CARE TO LEAN FORWARD AND INSPECT THE KEYHOLE OF THE DRAWER FACING YOU. IT CONCEALS A GUN FIRED BY A FOOT-SWITCH

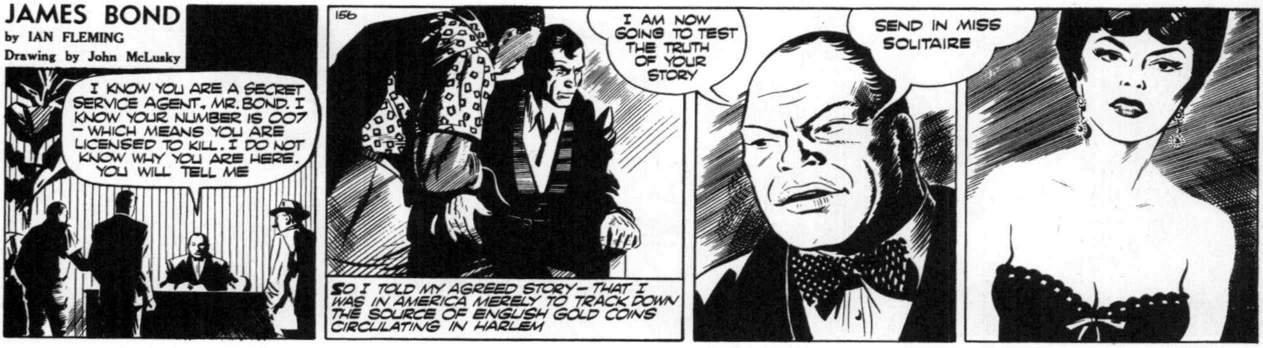
JAMES BOND
by IAN FLEMING
Drawing by John McLusky
I KNOW YOU ARE A SECRET SERVICE AGENT, MR. BOND. I KNOW YOUR NUMBER IS 007 - WHICH MEANS YOU ARE LICENSED TO KILL. I DO NOT KNOW WHY YOU ARE HERE. YOU WILL TELL ME
156
SO I TOLD MY AGREED STORY - THAT I WAS IN AMERICA MERELY TO TRACK DOWN THE SOURCE OF ENGLISH GOLD COINS CIRCULATING IN HARLEM
I AM NOW GOING TO TEST THE TRUTH OF YOUR STORY
SEND IN MISS SOLITAIRE

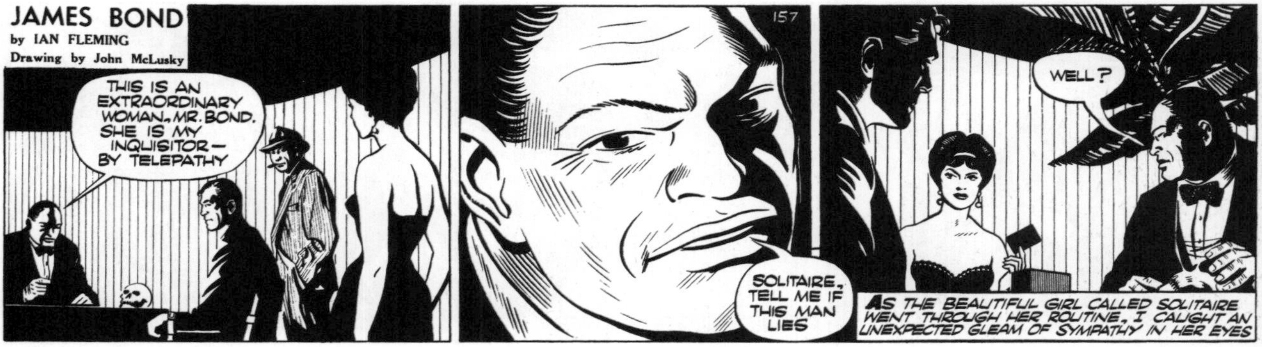
JAMES BOND
by IAN FLEMING
Drawing by John McLusky
THIS IS AN EXTRAORDINARY WOMAN, MR. BOND. SHE IS MY INQUISITOR - BY TELEPATHY
157
SOLITAIRE, TELL ME IF THIS MAN LIES
WELL?
AS THE BEAUTIFUL GIRL CALLED SOLITAIRE WENT THROUGH HER ROUTINE, I CAUGHT AN UNEXPECTED GLEAM OF SYMPATHY IN HER EYES

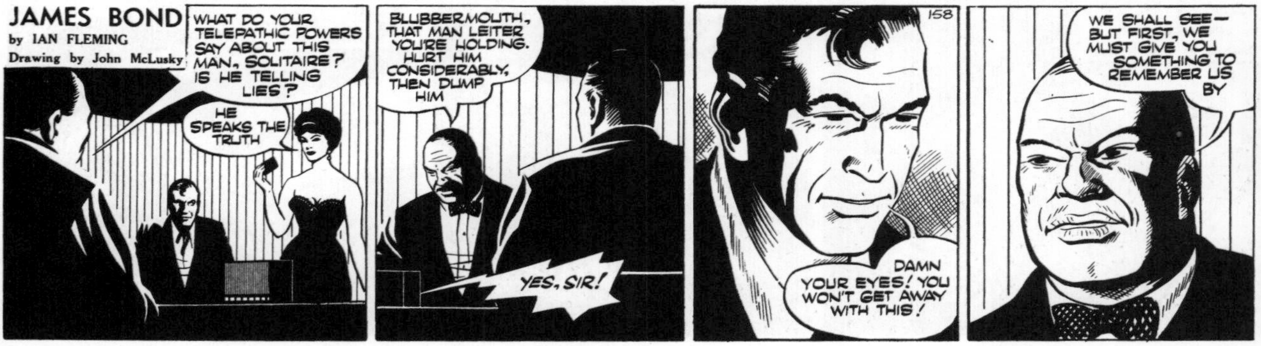
JAMES BOND
by IAN FLEMING
Drawing by John McLusky
WHAT DO YOUR TELEPATHIC POWERS SAY ABOUT THIS MAN, SOLITAIRE? IS HE TELLING LIES?
HE SPEAKS THE TRUTH
BLUBBERMOUTH, THAT MAN LEITER YOU'RE HOLDING. HURT HIM CONSIDERABLY, THEN DUMP HIM
YES, SIR!
158
DAMN YOUR EYES! YOU WON'T GET AWAY WITH THIS!
WE SHALL SEE - BUT FIRST, WE MUST GIVE YOU SOMETHING TO REMEMBER US BY

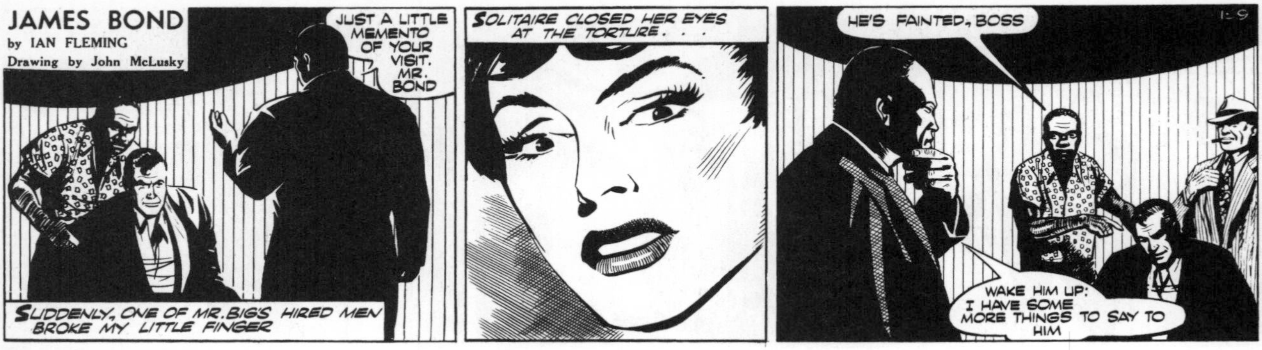
JAMES BOND
by IAN FLEMING
Drawing by John McLusky
JUST A LITTLE MEMENTO OF YOUR VISIT, MR. BOND
SUDDENLY, ONE OF MR. BIG'S HIRED MEN BROKE MY LITTLE FINGER
SOLITAIRE CLOSED HER EYES AT THE TORTURE . . .
HE'S FAINTED, BOSS
WAKE HIM UP: I HAVE SOME MORE THINGS TO SAY TO HIM

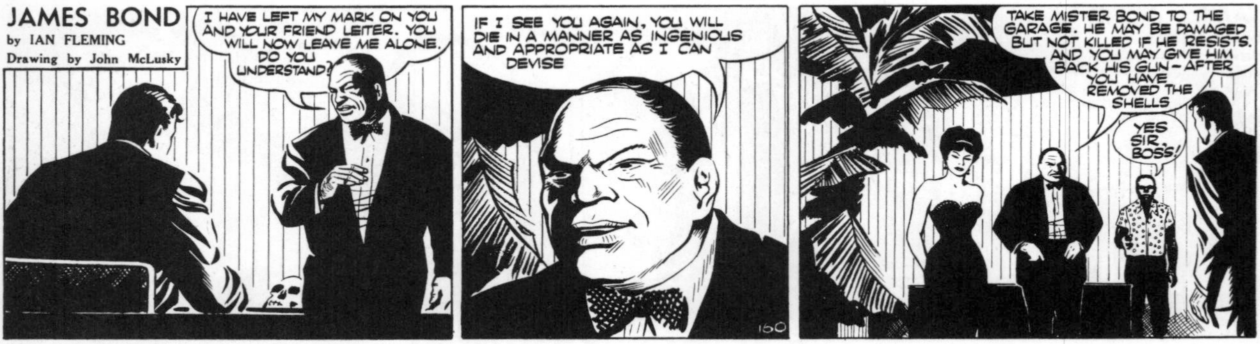
JAMES BOND
by IAN FLEMING
Drawing by John McLusky
I HAVE LEFT MY MARK ON YOU AND YOUR FRIEND LEITER. YOU WILL NOW LEAVE ME ALONE. DO YOU UNDERSTAND?
IF I SEE YOU AGAIN, YOU WILL DIE IN A MANNER AS INGENIOUS AND APPROPRIATE AS I CAN DEVISE
160
TAKE MISTER BOND TO THE GARAGE. HE MAY BE DAMAGED BUT NOT KILLED IF HE RESISTS. AND YOU MAY GIVE HIM BACK HIS GUN - AFTER YOU HAVE REMOVED THE SHELLS
YES SIR, BOSS!

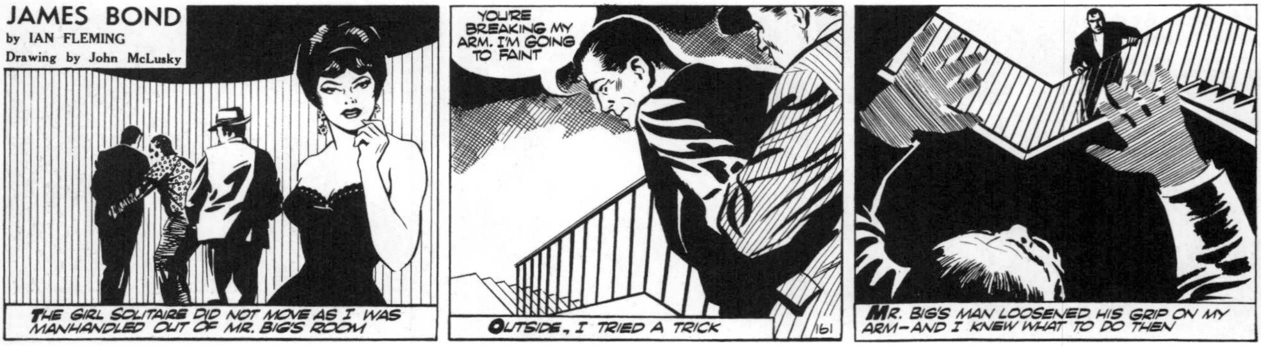
JAMES BOND
by IAN FLEMING
Drawing by John McLusky
THE GIRL SOLITAIRE DID NOT MOVE AS I WAS MANHANDLED OUT OF MR. BIG'S ROOM
YOU'RE BREAKING MY ARM. I'M GOING TO FAINT
OUTSIDE, I TRIED A TRICK
161
MR. BIG'S MAN LOOSENED HIS GRIP ON MY ARM - AND I KNEW WHAT TO DO THEN

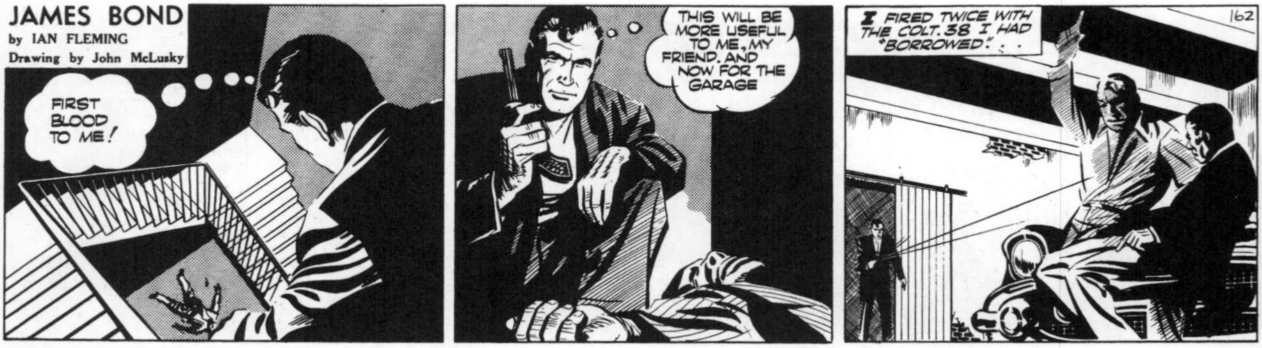
JAMES BOND
by IAN FLEMING
Drawing by John McLusky
FIRST BLOOD TO ME!
THIS WILL BE MORE USEFUL TO ME, MY FRIEND. AND NOW FOR THE GARAGE
I FIRED TWICE WITH THE COLT.38 I HAD "BORROWED" . .
162

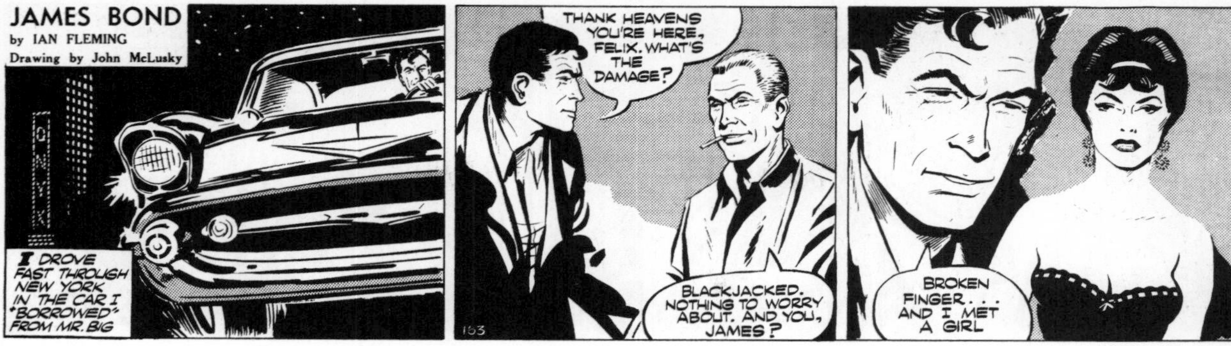
JAMES BOND
by IAN FLEMING
Drawing by John McLusky
I DROVE FAST THROUGH NEW YORK IN THE CAR I "BORROWED" FROM MR. BIG
THANK HEAVENS YOU'RE HERE, FELIX. WHAT'S THE DAMAGE?
BLACKJACKED. NOTHING TO WORRY ABOUT. AND YOU, JAMES?
BROKEN FINGER . . . AND I MET A GIRL

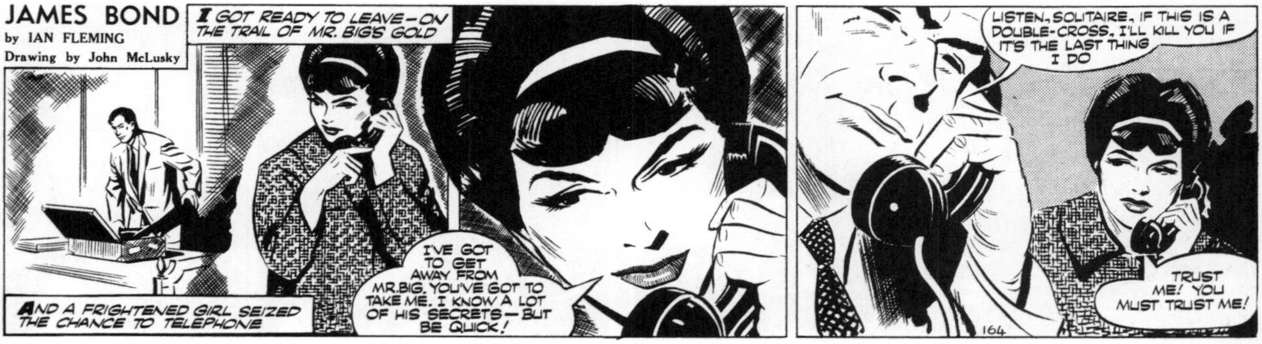
JAMES BOND
by IAN FLEMING
Drawing by John McLusky
I GOT READY TO LEAVE—ON THE TRAIL OF MR. BIG'S GOLD
AND A FRIGHTENED GIRL SEIZED THE CHANCE TO TELEPHONE
I'VE GOT TO GET AWAY FROM MR. BIG. YOU'VE GOT TO TAKE ME. I KNOW A LOT OF HIS SECRETS—BUT BE QUICK!
LISTEN, SOLITAIRE, IF THIS IS A DOUBLE-CROSS, I'LL KILL YOU IF IT'S THE LAST THING I DO
TRUST ME! YOU MUST TRUST ME!

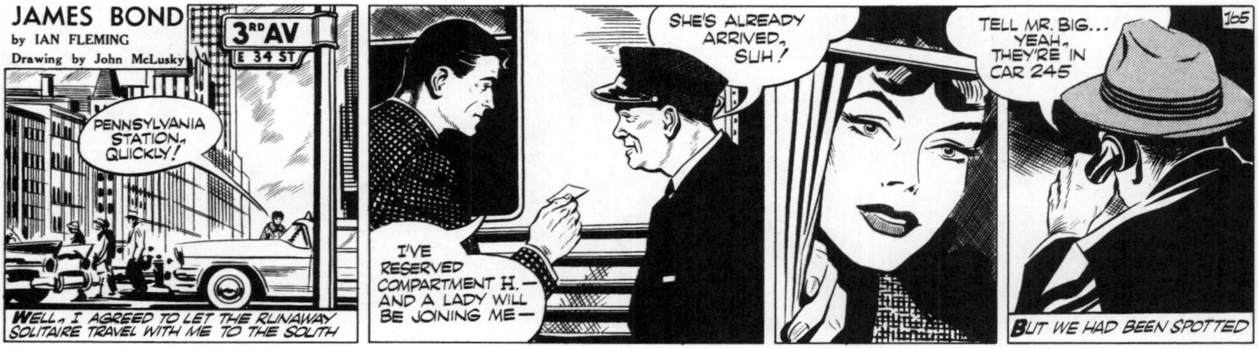
JAMES BOND
by IAN FLEMING
Drawing by John McLusky
3RD AV
E 34 ST
PENNSYLVANIA STATION, QUICKLY!
WELL, I AGREED TO LET THE RUNAWAY SOLITAIRE TRAVEL WITH ME TO THE SOUTH
I'VE RESERVED COMPARTMENT H.—AND A LADY WILL BE JOINING ME—
SHE'S ALREADY ARRIVED, SUH!
TELL MR. BIG... YEAH, THEY'RE IN CAR 245
BUT WE HAD BEEN SPOTTED

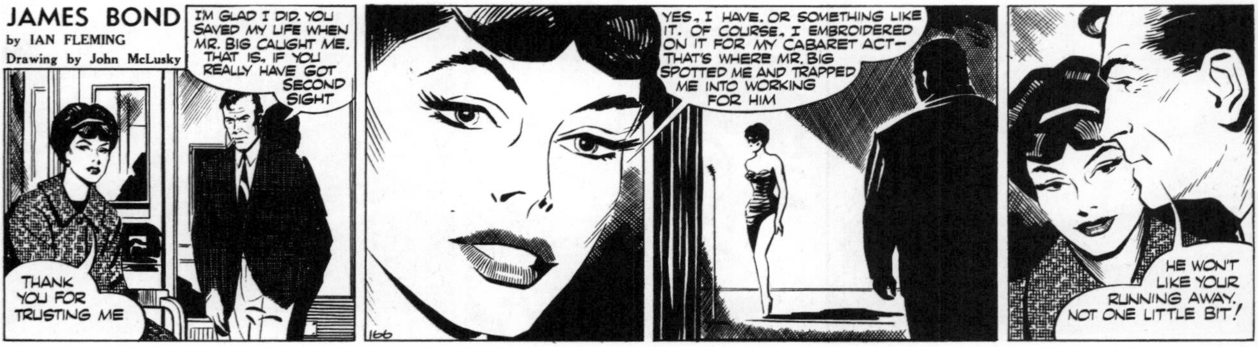
JAMES BOND
by IAN FLEMING
Drawing by John McLusky
I'M GLAD I DID. YOU SAVED MY LIFE WHEN MR. BIG CAUGHT ME. THAT IS, IF YOU REALLY HAVE GOT SECOND SIGHT
THANK YOU FOR TRUSTING ME
YES, I HAVE. OR SOMETHING LIKE IT. OF COURSE, I EMBROIDERED ON IT FOR MY CABARET ACT—THAT'S WHERE MR. BIG SPOTTED ME AND TRAPPED ME INTO WORKING FOR HIM
HE WON'T LIKE YOUR RUNNING AWAY. NOT ONE LITTLE BIT!

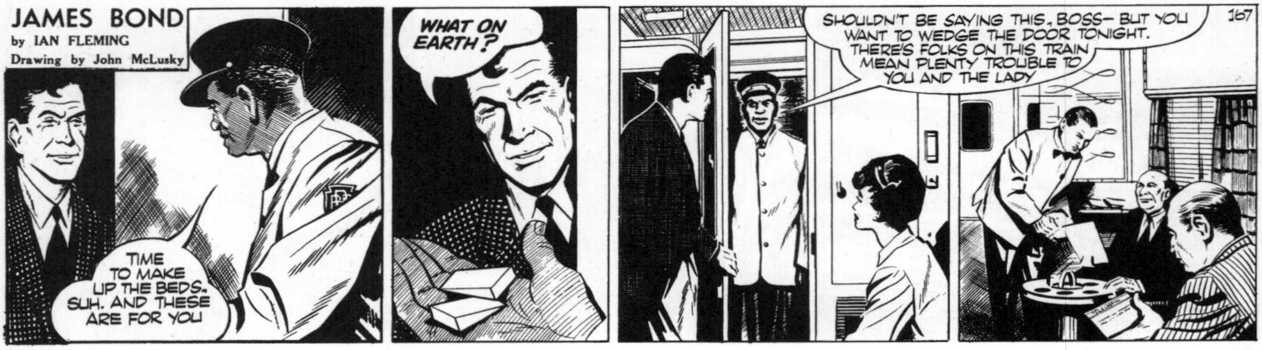
JAMES BOND
by IAN FLEMING
Drawing by John McLusky
TIME TO MAKE UP THE BEDS, SUH. AND THESE ARE FOR YOU
WHAT ON EARTH?
167
SHOULDN'T BE SAYING THIS, BOSS— BUT YOU WANT TO WEDGE THE DOOR TONIGHT. THERE'S FOLKS ON THIS TRAIN MEAN PLENTY TROUBLE TO YOU AND THE LADY

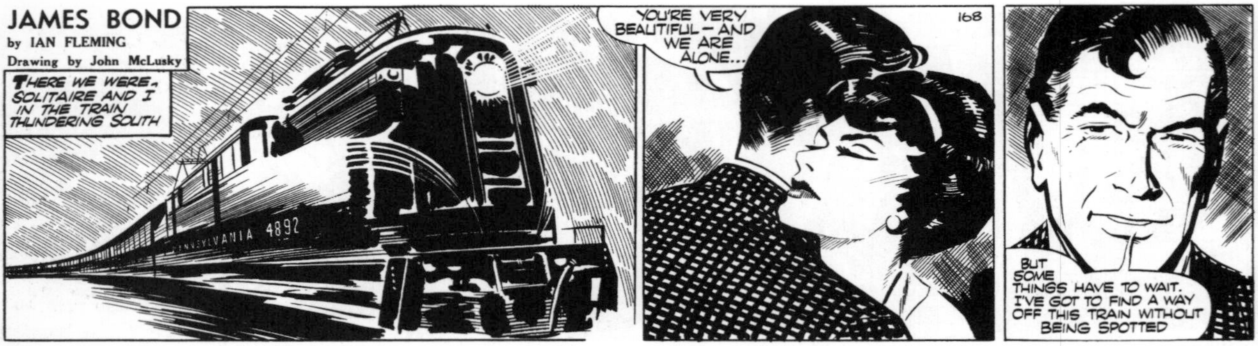
JAMES BOND
by IAN FLEMING
Drawing by John McLusky
THERE WE WERE, SOLITAIRE AND I IN THE TRAIN THUNDERING SOUTH
4892
YOU'RE VERY BEAUTIFUL— AND WE ARE ALONE...
168
BUT SOME THINGS HAVE TO WAIT. I'VE GOT TO FIND A WAY OFF THIS TRAIN WITHOUT BEING SPOTTED

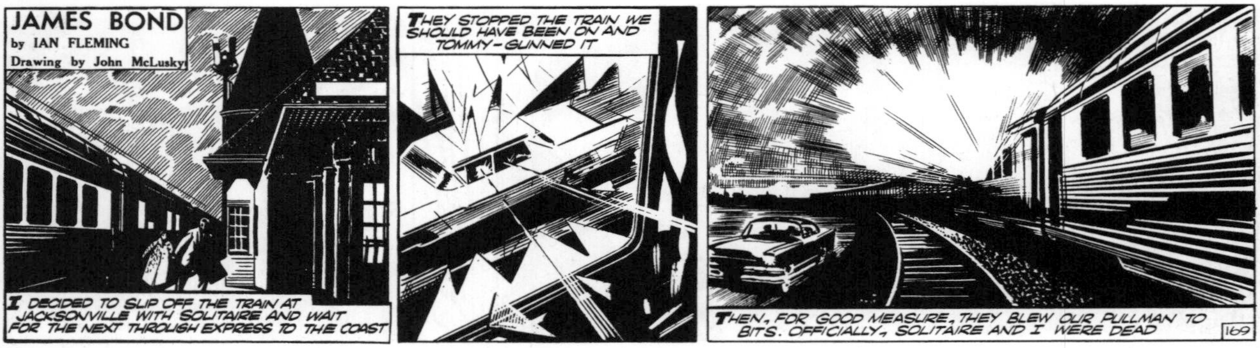
JAMES BOND
by IAN FLEMING
Drawing by John McLusky
I DECIDED TO SLIP OFF THE TRAIN AT JACKSONVILLE WITH SOLITAIRE AND WAIT FOR THE NEXT THROUGH EXPRESS TO THE COAST
THEY STOPPED THE TRAIN WE SHOULD HAVE BEEN ON AND TOMMY-GUNNED IT
THEN, FOR GOOD MEASURE, THEY BLEW OUR PULLMAN TO BITS. OFFICIALLY, SOLITAIRE AND I WERE DEAD
169

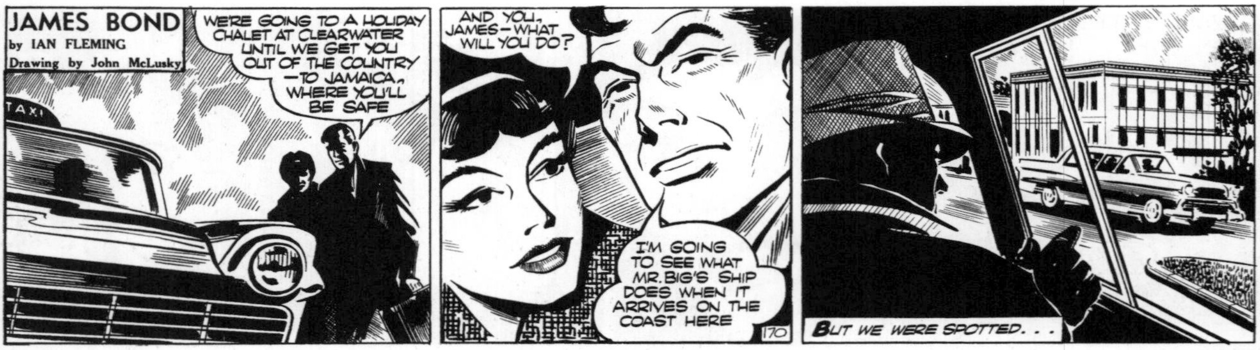
JAMES BOND
by IAN FLEMING
Drawing by John McLusky
WE'RE GOING TO A HOLIDAY CHALET AT CLEARWATER UNTIL WE GET YOU OUT OF THE COUNTRY —TO JAMAICA, WHERE YOU'LL BE SAFE
TAXI
AND YOU, JAMES—WHAT WILL YOU DO?
I'M GOING TO SEE WHAT MR. BIG'S SHIP DOES WHEN IT ARRIVES ON THE COAST HERE
170
BUT WE WERE SPOTTED...

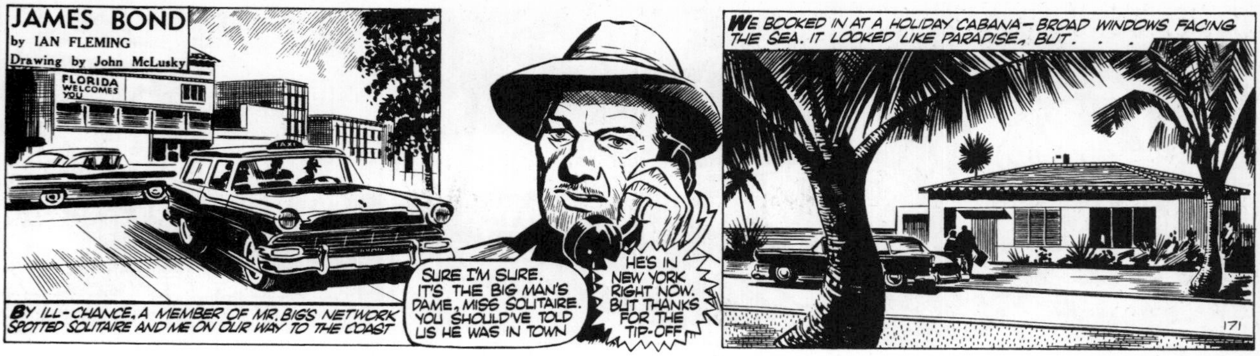
JAMES BOND
by IAN FLEMING
Drawing by John McLusky
FLORIDA WELCOMES YOU
TAXI
BY ILL-CHANCE, A MEMBER OF MR. BIG'S NETWORK SPOTTED SOLITAIRE AND ME ON OUR WAY TO THE COAST
SURE I'M SURE. IT'S THE BIG MAN'S DAME, MISS SOLITAIRE. YOU SHOULD'VE TOLD US HE WAS IN TOWN
HE'S IN NEW YORK RIGHT NOW. BUT THANKS FOR THE TIP-OFF
WE BOOKED IN AT A HOLIDAY CABANA—BROAD WINDOWS FACING THE SEA. IT LOOKED LIKE PARADISE, BUT . . .
171

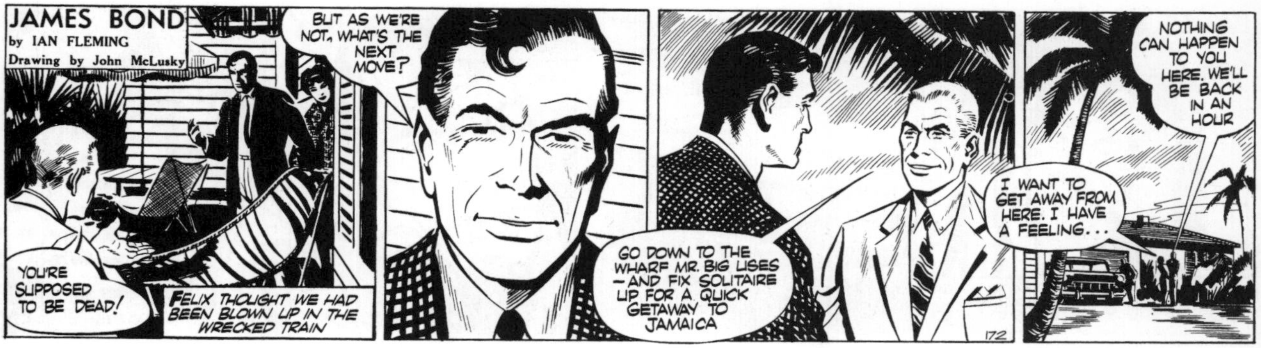
JAMES BOND
by IAN FLEMING
Drawing by John McLusky
YOU'RE SUPPOSED TO BE DEAD!
FELIX THOUGHT WE HAD BEEN BLOWN UP IN THE WRECKED TRAIN
BUT AS WE'RE NOT, WHAT'S THE NEXT MOVE?
GO DOWN TO THE WHARF MR. BIG USES —AND FIX SOLITAIRE UP FOR A QUICK GETAWAY TO JAMAICA
I WANT TO GET AWAY FROM HERE. I HAVE A FEELING...
NOTHING CAN HAPPEN TO YOU HERE. WE'LL BE BACK IN AN HOUR
172

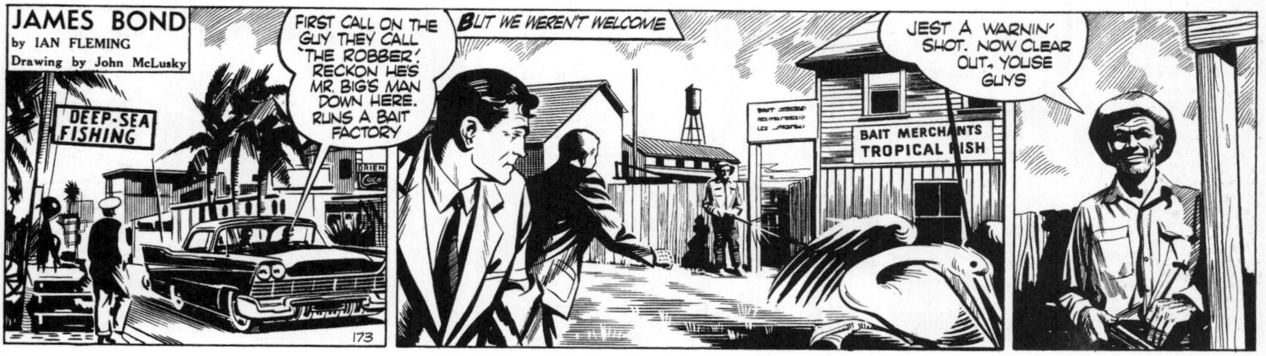
JAMES BOND
by IAN FLEMING
Drawing by John McLusky
DEEP-SEA FISHING
FIRST CALL ON THE GUY THEY CALL 'THE ROBBER'. RECKON HE'S MR. BIG'S MAN DOWN HERE. RUNS A BAIT FACTORY
173
BUT WE WEREN'T WELCOME
BAIT MERCHANTS TROPICAL FISH
JEST A WARNIN' SHOT. NOW CLEAR OUT, YOUSE GUYS

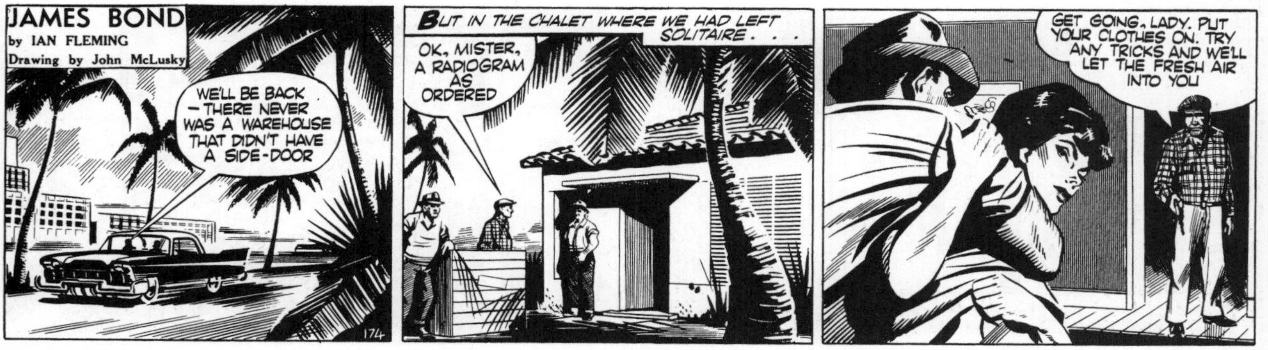
JAMES BOND
by IAN FLEMING
Drawing by John McLusky
WE'LL BE BACK —THERE NEVER WAS A WAREHOUSE THAT DIDN'T HAVE A SIDE-DOOR
BUT IN THE CHALET WHERE WE HAD LEFT SOLITAIRE . . .
OK, MISTER, A RADIOGRAM AS ORDERED
174
GET GOING, LADY. PUT YOUR CLOTHES ON. TRY ANY TRICKS AND WE'LL LET THE FRESH AIR INTO YOU

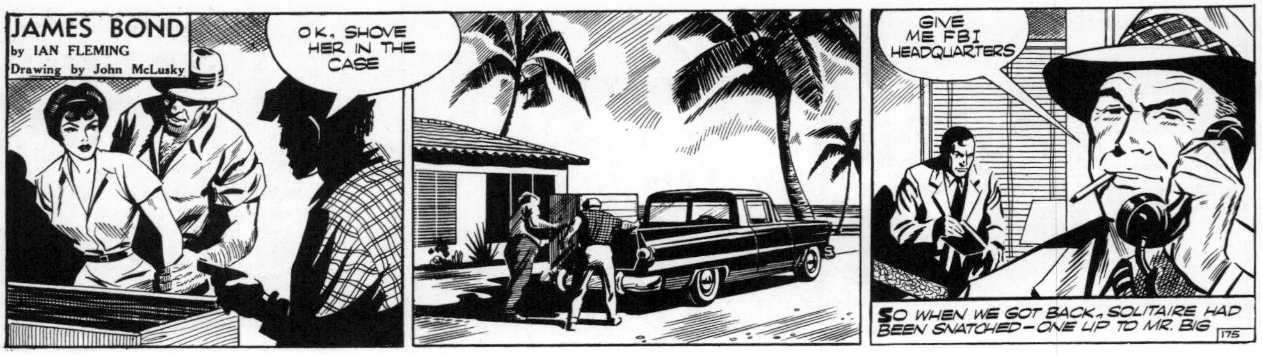
JAMES BOND
by IAN FLEMING
Drawing by John McLusky
O.K., SHOVE HER IN THE CASE
GIVE ME FBI HEADQUARTERS
SO WHEN WE GOT BACK, SOLITAIRE HAD BEEN SNATCHED—ONE UP TO MR. BIG
175

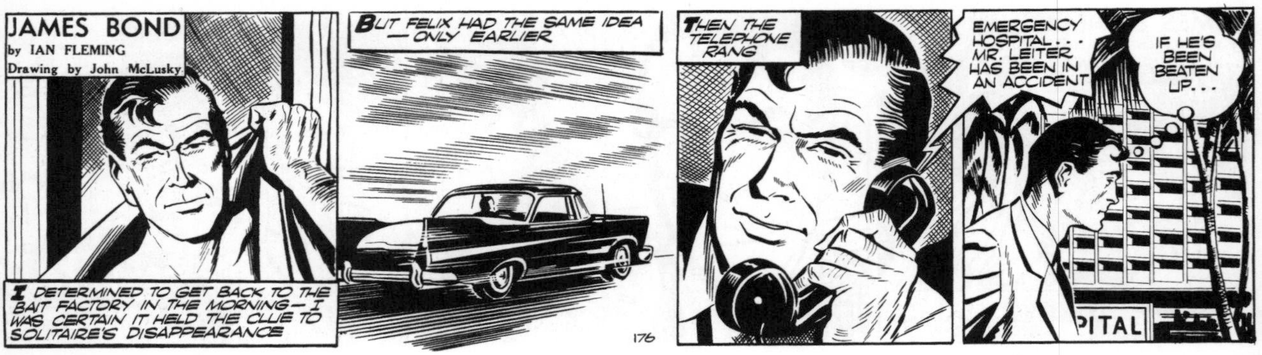
JAMES BOND
by IAN FLEMING
Drawing by John McLusky
I DETERMINED TO GET BACK TO THE BAIT FACTORY IN THE MORNING—I WAS CERTAIN IT HELD THE CLUE TO SOLITAIRE'S DISAPPEARANCE
BUT FELIX HAD THE SAME IDEA —ONLY EARLIER
176
THEN THE TELEPHONE RANG
EMERGENCY HOSPITAL... MR. LEITER HAS BEEN IN AN ACCIDENT
IF HE'S BEEN BEATEN UP...
PITAL

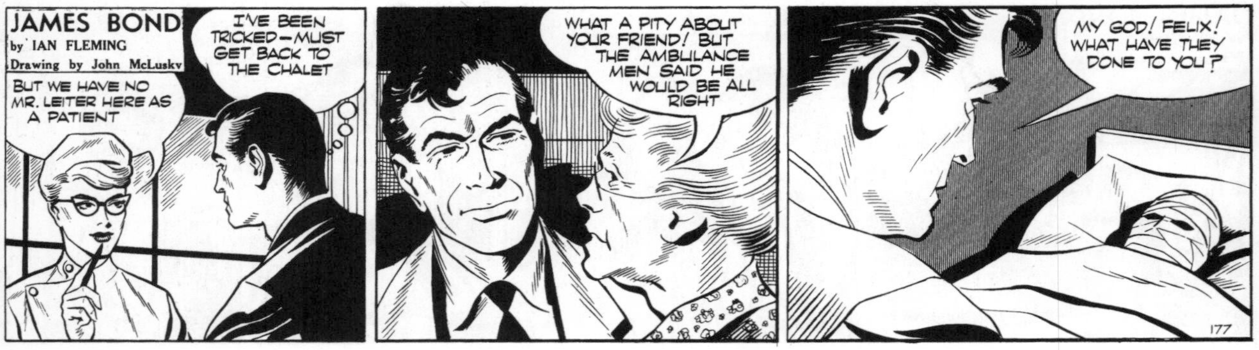
JAMES BOND
by IAN FLEMING
Drawing by John McLusky
BUT WE HAVE NO MR. LEITER HERE AS A PATIENT
I'VE BEEN TRICKED—MUST GET BACK TO THE CHALET
WHAT A PITY ABOUT YOUR FRIEND! BUT THE AMBULANCE MEN SAID HE WOULD BE ALL RIGHT
MY GOD! FELIX! WHAT HAVE THEY DONE TO YOU?
177

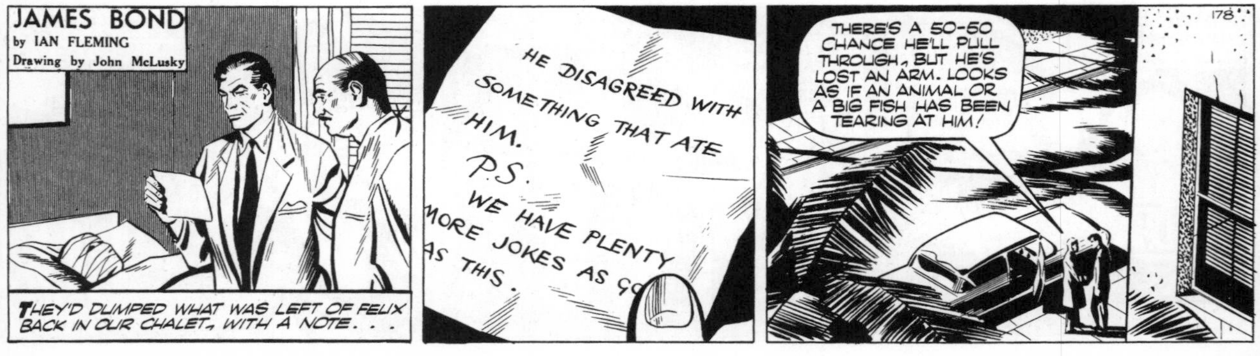
JAMES BOND
by IAN FLEMING
Drawing by John McLusky
THEY'D DUMPED WHAT WAS LEFT OF FELIX BACK IN OUR CHALET, WITH A NOTE...
HE DISAGREED WITH SOMETHING THAT ATE HIM.
P.S.
WE HAVE PLENTY MORE JOKES AS THIS.
178
THERE'S A 50-50 CHANCE HE'LL PULL THROUGH, BUT HE'S LOST AN ARM. LOOKS AS IF AN ANIMAL OR A BIG FISH HAS BEEN TEARING AT HIM!

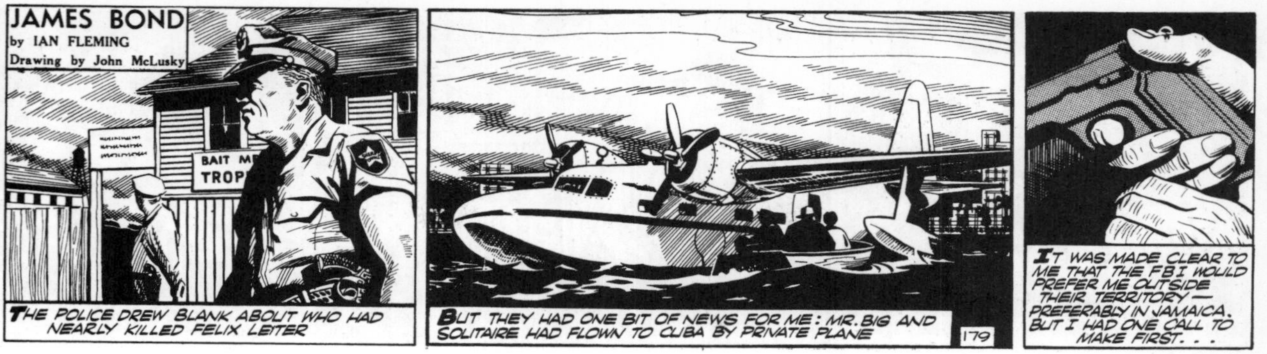
JAMES BOND
by IAN FLEMING
Drawing by John McLusky
THE POLICE DREW BLANK ABOUT WHO HAD NEARLY KILLED FELIX LEITER
BUT THEY HAD ONE BIT OF NEWS FOR ME: MR. BIG AND SOLITAIRE HAD FLOWN TO CUBA BY PRIVATE PLANE
179
IT WAS MADE CLEAR TO ME THAT THE FBI WOULD PREFER ME OUTSIDE THEIR TERRITORY— PREFERABLY IN JAMAICA. BUT I HAD ONE CALL TO MAKE FIRST. . .

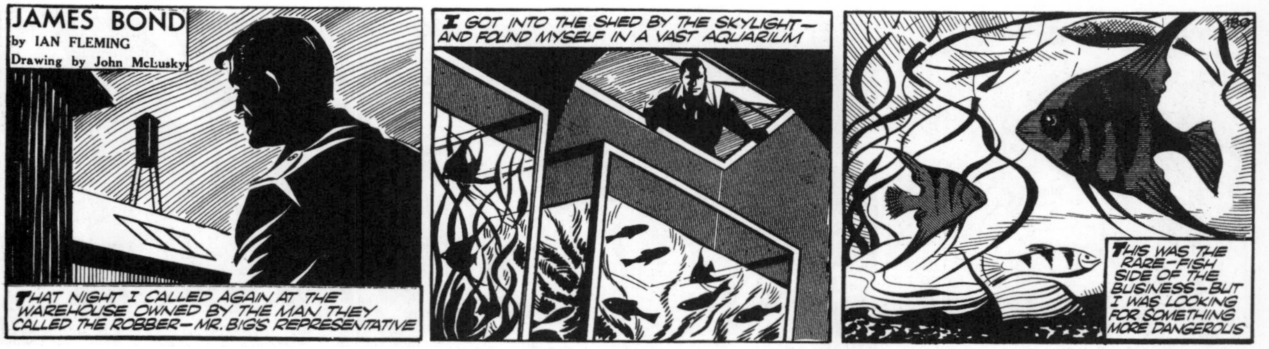
JAMES BOND
by IAN FLEMING
Drawing by John McLusky
THAT NIGHT I CALLED AGAIN AT THE WAREHOUSE OWNED BY THE MAN THEY CALLED THE ROBBER—MR. BIG'S REPRESENTATIVE
I GOT INTO THE SHED BY THE SKYLIGHT— AND FOUND MYSELF IN A VAST AQUARIUM
180
THIS WAS THE RARE-FISH SIDE OF THE BUSINESS—BUT I WAS LOOKING FOR SOMETHING MORE DANGEROUS

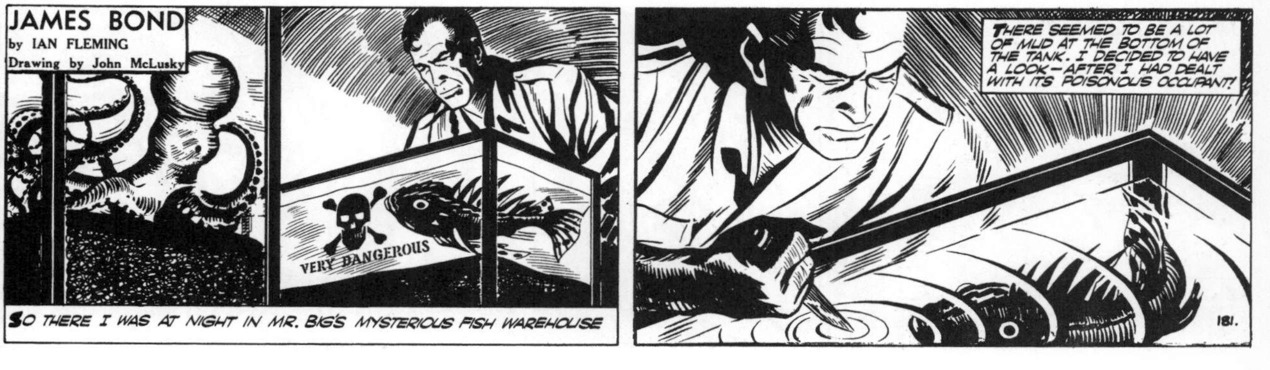
JAMES BOND
by IAN FLEMING
Drawing by John McLusky
VERY DANGEROUS
SO THERE I WAS AT NIGHT IN MR. BIG'S MYSTERIOUS FISH WAREHOUSE
THERE SEEMED TO BE A LOT OF MUD AT THE BOTTOM OF THE TANK. I DECIDED TO HAVE A LOOK—AFTER I HAD DEALT WITH ITS POISONOUS OCCUPANT!
181.

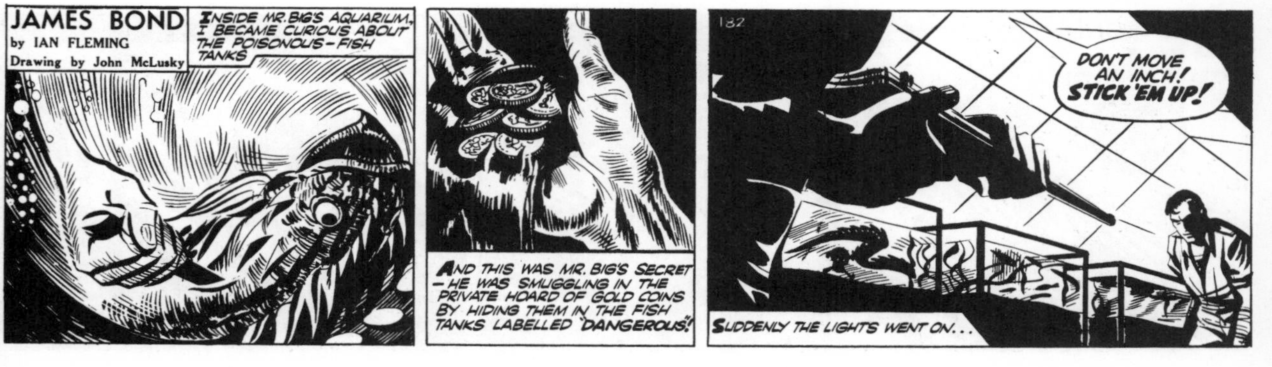
JAMES BOND
by IAN FLEMING
Drawing by John McLusky
INSIDE MR. BIG'S AQUARIUM, I BECAME CURIOUS ABOUT THE POISONOUS-FISH TANKS
AND THIS WAS MR. BIG'S SECRET—HE WAS SMUGGLING IN THE PRIVATE HOARD OF GOLD COINS BY HIDING THEM IN THE FISH TANKS LABELLED "DANGEROUS"!
182
DON'T MOVE AN INCH! STICK 'EM UP!
SUDDENLY THE LIGHTS WENT ON. . .

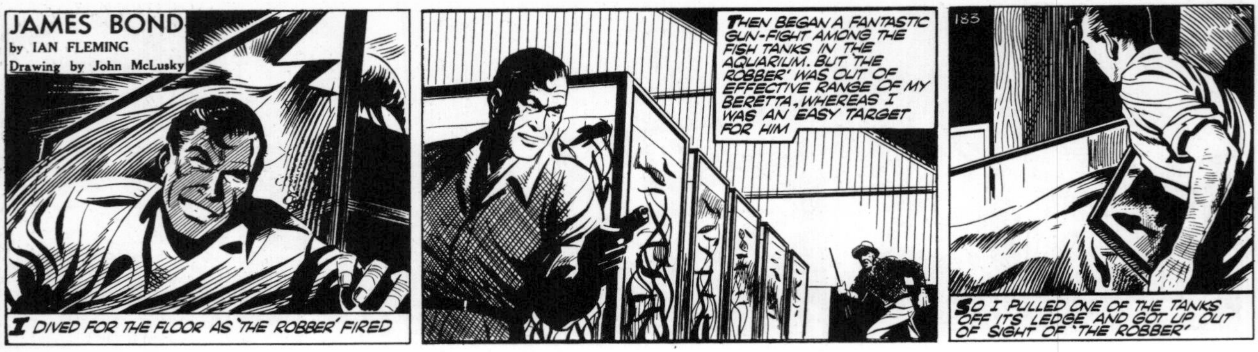
JAMES BOND
by IAN FLEMING
Drawing by John McLusky
I DIVED FOR THE FLOOR AS 'THE ROBBER' FIRED
THEN BEGAN A FANTASTIC GUN-FIGHT AMONG THE FISH TANKS IN THE AQUARIUM. BUT 'THE ROBBER' WAS OUT OF EFFECTIVE RANGE OF MY BERETTA, WHEREAS I WAS AN EASY TARGET FOR HIM
183
SO I PULLED ONE OF THE TANKS OFF ITS LEDGE AND GOT UP OUT OF SIGHT OF 'THE ROBBER'

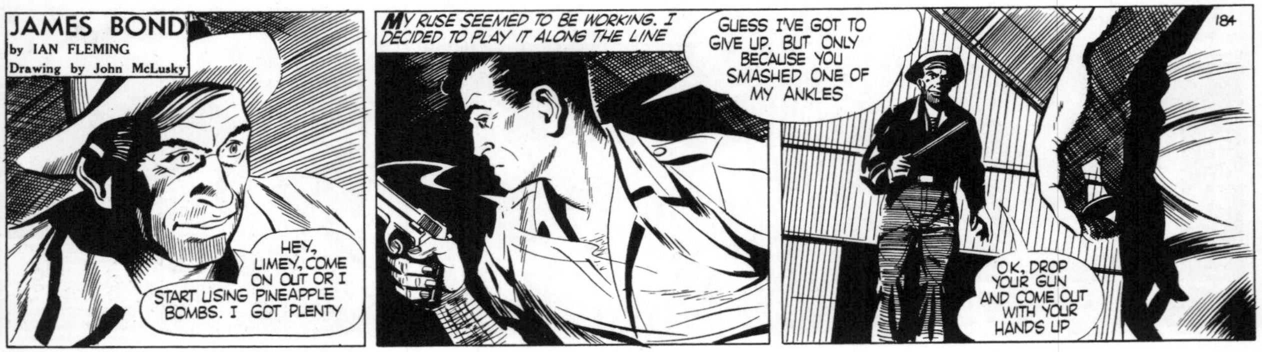
JAMES BOND
by IAN FLEMING
Drawing by John McLusky
HEY, LIMEY, COME ON OUT OR I START USING PINEAPPLE BOMBS. I GOT PLENTY
MY RUSE SEEMED TO BE WORKING. I DECIDED TO PLAY IT ALONG THE LINE
GUESS I'VE GOT TO GIVE UP. BUT ONLY BECAUSE YOU SMASHED ONE OF MY ANKLES
184
O.K. DROP YOUR GUN AND COME OUT WITH YOUR HANDS UP

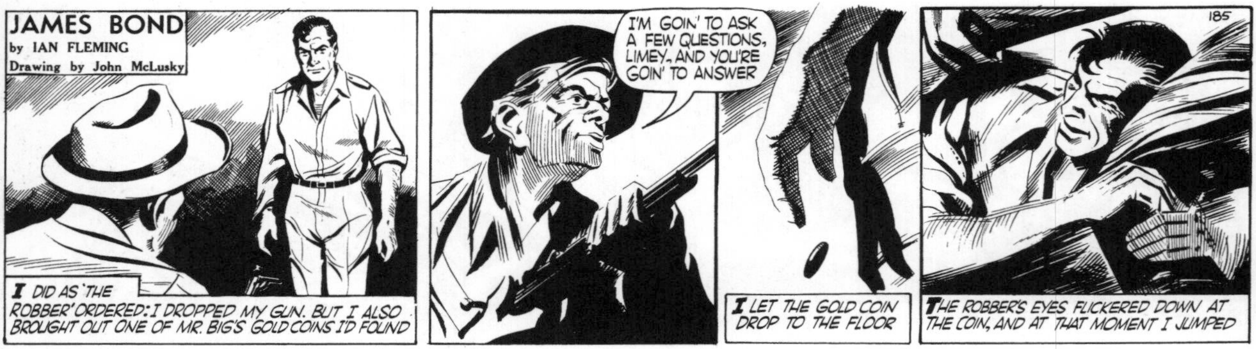
JAMES BOND
by IAN FLEMING
Drawing by John McLusky
I DID AS 'THE ROBBER' ORDERED: I DROPPED MY GUN. BUT I ALSO BROUGHT OUT ONE OF MR. BIG'S GOLD COINS I'D FOUND
I'M GOIN' TO ASK A FEW QUESTIONS, LIMEY, AND YOU'RE GOIN' TO ANSWER
I LET THE GOLD COIN DROP TO THE FLOOR
185
THE ROBBER'S EYES FLICKERED DOWN AT THE COIN, AND AT THAT MOMENT I JUMPED

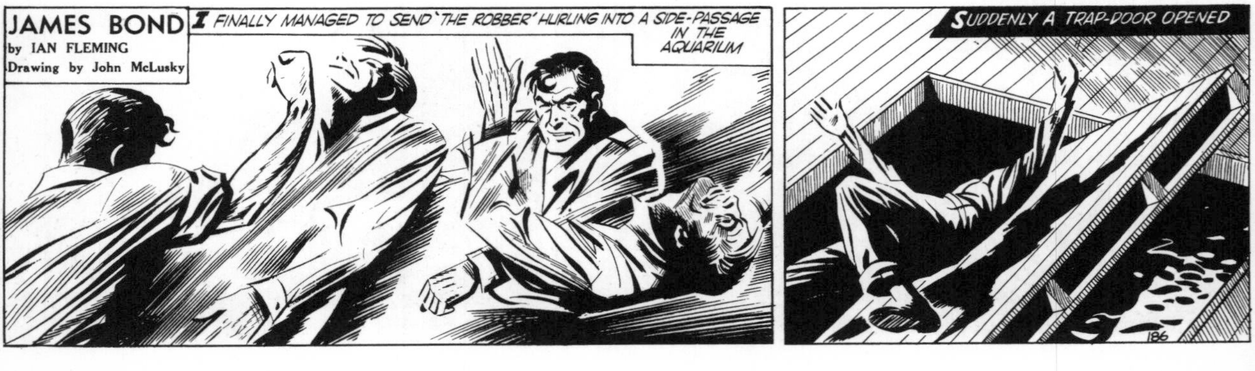
JAMES BOND
by IAN FLEMING
Drawing by John McLusky
I FINALLY MANAGED TO SEND 'THE ROBBER' HURLING INTO A SIDE-PASSAGE IN THE AQUARIUM
SUDDENLY A TRAP-DOOR OPENED
186

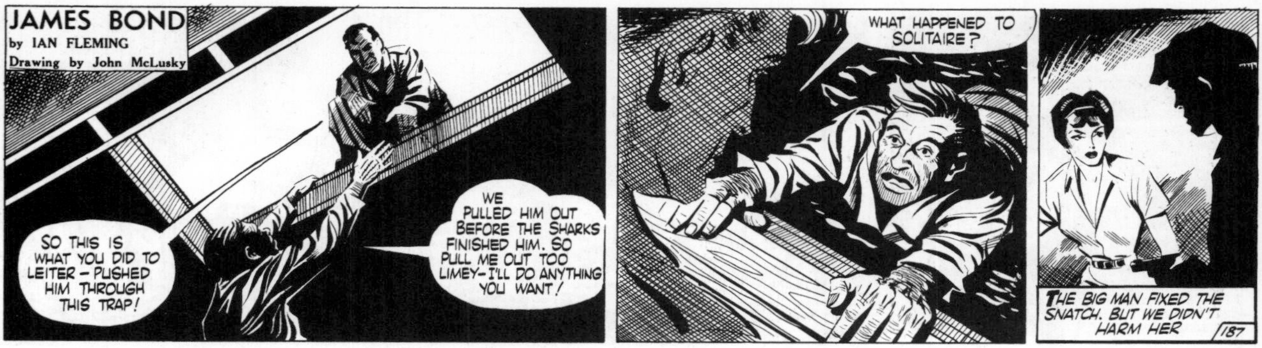
JAMES BOND
by IAN FLEMING
Drawing by John McLusky
SO THIS IS WHAT YOU DID TO LEITER – PUSHED HIM THROUGH THIS TRAP!
WE PULLED HIM OUT BEFORE THE SHARKS FINISHED HIM. SO PULL ME OUT TOO LIMEY– I'LL DO ANYTHING YOU WANT!
WHAT HAPPENED TO SOLITAIRE?
THE BIG MAN FIXED THE SNATCH. BUT WE DIDN'T HARM HER
187

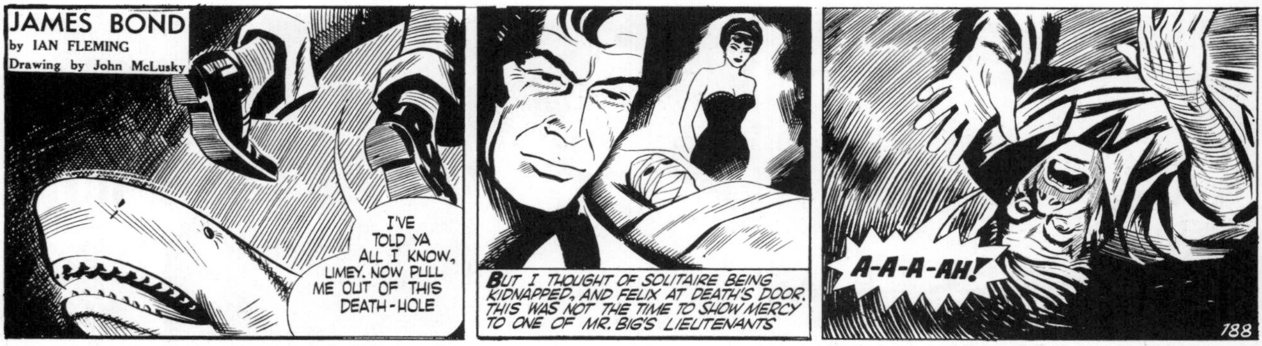
JAMES BOND
by IAN FLEMING
Drawing by John McLusky
I'VE TOLD YA ALL I KNOW, LIMEY. NOW PULL ME OUT OF THIS DEATH-HOLE
BUT I THOUGHT OF SOLITAIRE BEING KIDNAPPED, AND FELIX AT DEATH'S DOOR. THIS WAS NOT THE TIME TO SHOW MERCY TO ONE OF MR. BIG'S LIEUTENANTS
A-A-A-AH!
188

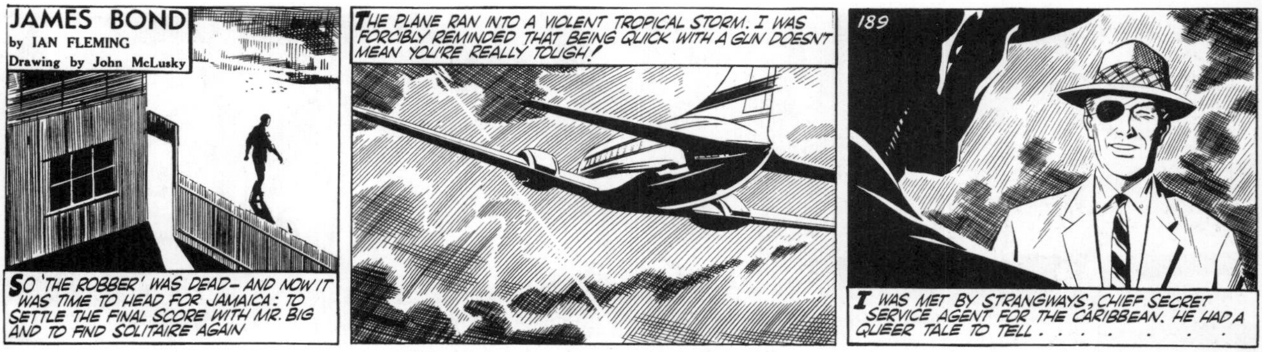
JAMES BOND
by IAN FLEMING
Drawing by John McLusky
SO 'THE ROBBER' WAS DEAD– AND NOW IT WAS TIME TO HEAD FOR JAMAICA: TO SETTLE THE FINAL SCORE WITH MR. BIG AND TO FIND SOLITAIRE AGAIN
THE PLANE RAN INTO A VIOLENT TROPICAL STORM. I WAS FORCIBLY REMINDED THAT BEING QUICK WITH A GUN DOESN'T MEAN YOU'RE REALLY TOUGH!
189
I WAS MET BY STRANGWAYS, CHIEF SECRET SERVICE AGENT FOR THE CARIBBEAN. HE HAD A QUEER TALE TO TELL . . . .

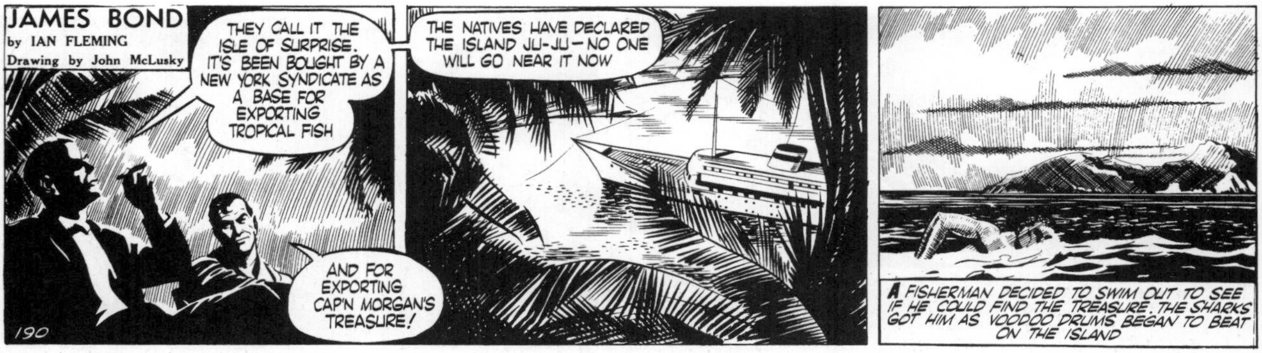
JAMES BOND
by IAN FLEMING
Drawing by John McLusky
THEY CALL IT THE ISLE OF SURPRISE. IT'S BEEN BOUGHT BY A NEW YORK SYNDICATE AS A BASE FOR EXPORTING TROPICAL FISH
AND FOR EXPORTING CAP'N MORGAN'S TREASURE!
190
THE NATIVES HAVE DECLARED THE ISLAND JU-JU – NO ONE WILL GO NEAR IT NOW
A FISHERMAN DECIDED TO SWIM OUT TO SEE IF HE COULD FIND THE TREASURE. THE SHARKS GOT HIM AS VOODOO DRUMS BEGAN TO BEAT ON THE ISLAND

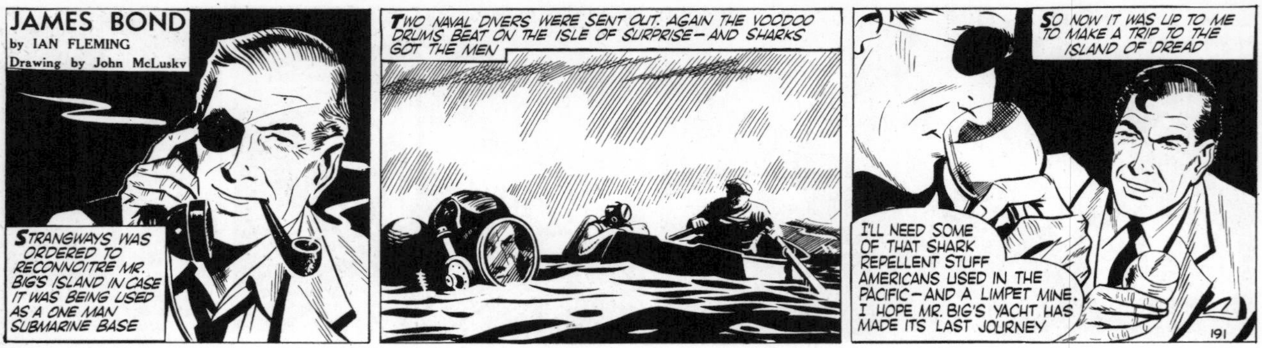
JAMES BOND
by IAN FLEMING
Drawing by John McLusky
STRANGWAYS WAS ORDERED TO RECONNOITRE MR. BIG'S ISLAND IN CASE IT WAS BEING USED AS A ONE MAN SUBMARINE BASE
TWO NAVAL DIVERS WERE SENT OUT. AGAIN THE VOODOO DRUMS BEAT ON THE ISLE OF SURPRISE—AND SHARKS GOT THE MEN
SO NOW IT WAS UP TO ME TO MAKE A TRIP TO THE ISLAND OF DREAD
I'LL NEED SOME OF THAT SHARK REPELLENT STUFF AMERICANS USED IN THE PACIFIC—AND A LIMPET MINE. I HOPE MR. BIG'S YACHT HAS MADE ITS LAST JOURNEY
191

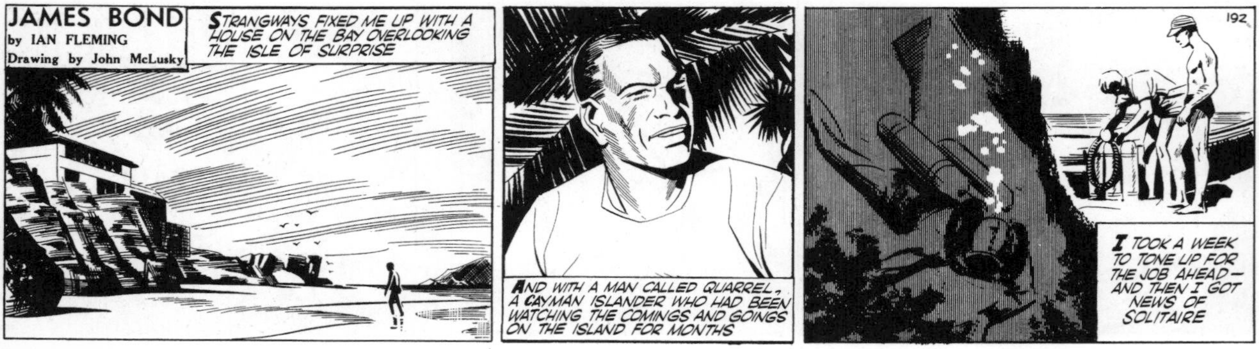
JAMES BOND
by IAN FLEMING
Drawing by John McLusky
STRANGWAYS FIXED ME UP WITH A HOUSE ON THE BAY OVERLOOKING THE ISLE OF SURPRISE
AND WITH A MAN CALLED QUARREL, A CAYMAN ISLANDER WHO HAD BEEN WATCHING THE COMINGS AND GOINGS ON THE ISLAND FOR MONTHS
192
I TOOK A WEEK TO TONE UP FOR THE JOB AHEAD—AND THEN I GOT NEWS OF SOLITAIRE

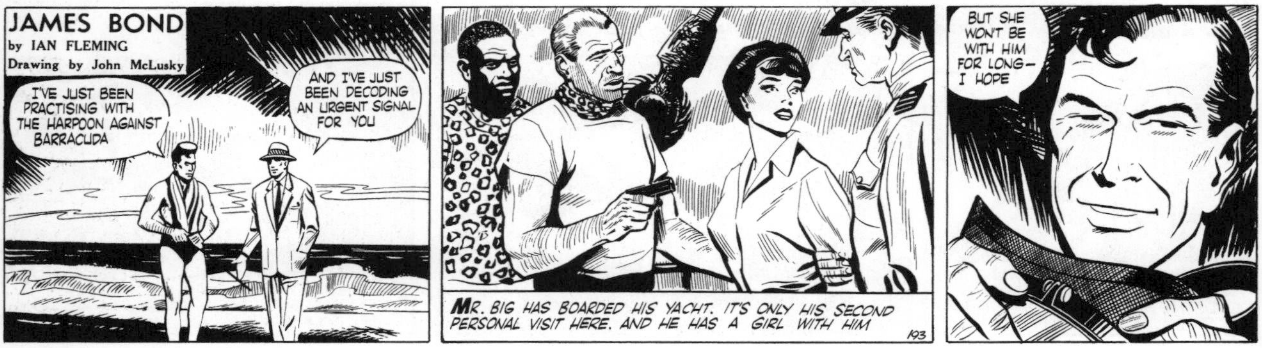
JAMES BOND
by IAN FLEMING
Drawing by John McLusky
I'VE JUST BEEN PRACTISING WITH THE HARPOON AGAINST BARRACUDA
AND I'VE JUST BEEN DECODING AN URGENT SIGNAL FOR YOU
MR. BIG HAS BOARDED HIS YACHT. IT'S ONLY HIS SECOND PERSONAL VISIT HERE. AND HE HAS A GIRL WITH HIM
193
BUT SHE WON'T BE WITH HIM FOR LONG—I HOPE

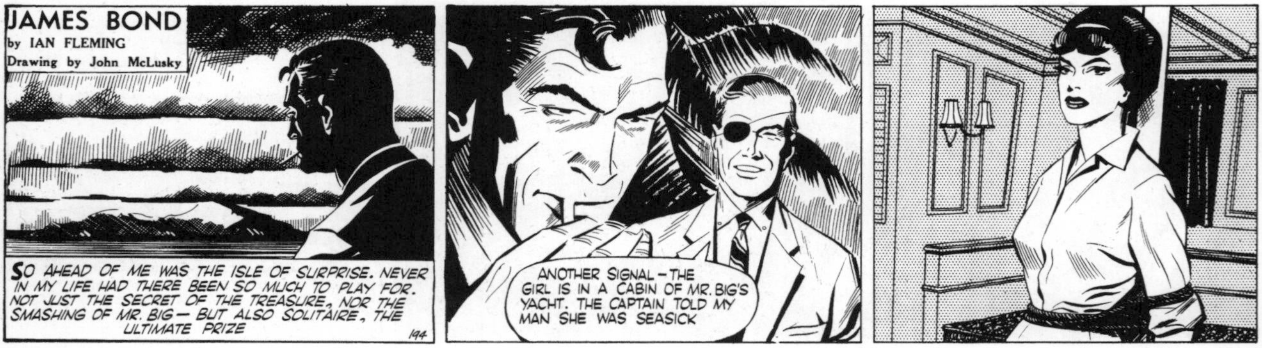
JAMES BOND
by IAN FLEMING
Drawing by John McLusky
SO AHEAD OF ME WAS THE ISLE OF SURPRISE. NEVER IN MY LIFE HAD THERE BEEN SO MUCH TO PLAY FOR. NOT JUST THE SECRET OF THE TREASURE, NOR THE SMASHING OF MR. BIG—BUT ALSO SOLITAIRE, THE ULTIMATE PRIZE
194
ANOTHER SIGNAL—THE GIRL IS IN A CABIN OF MR. BIG'S YACHT. THE CAPTAIN TOLD MY MAN SHE WAS SEASICK

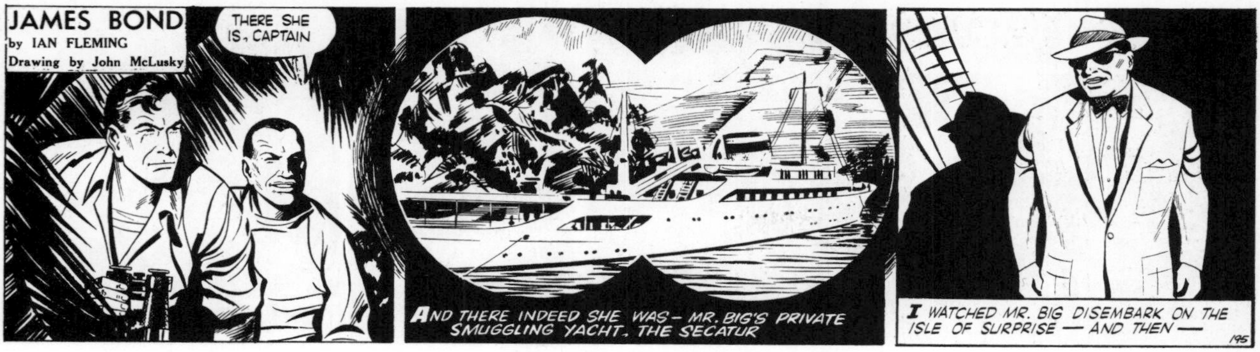
JAMES BOND
by IAN FLEMING
Drawing by John McLusky
THERE SHE IS, CAPTAIN
AND THERE INDEED SHE WAS— MR. BIG'S PRIVATE SMUGGLING YACHT, THE SECATUR
I WATCHED MR. BIG DISEMBARK ON THE ISLE OF SURPRISE — AND THEN —
195

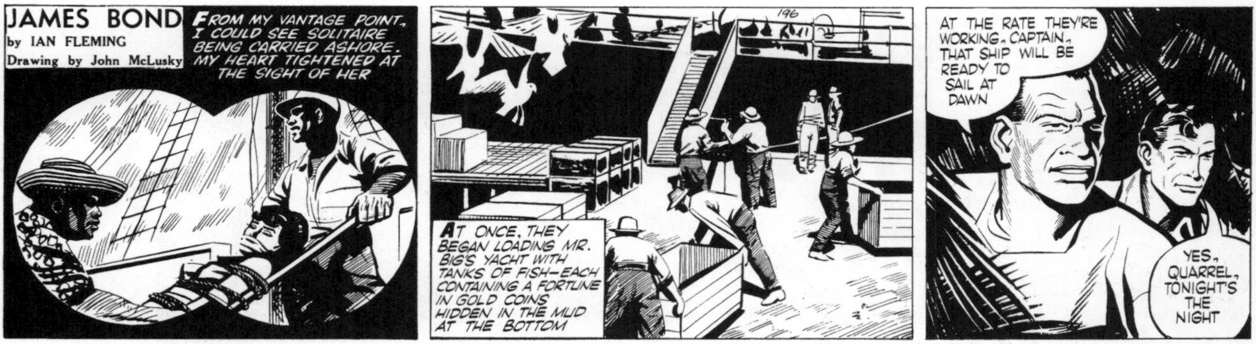
JAMES BOND
by IAN FLEMING
Drawing by John McLusky
FROM MY VANTAGE POINT, I COULD SEE SOLITAIRE BEING CARRIED ASHORE. MY HEART TIGHTENED AT THE SIGHT OF HER
196
AT ONCE, THEY BEGAN LOADING MR. BIG'S YACHT WITH TANKS OF FISH—EACH CONTAINING A FORTUNE IN GOLD COINS HIDDEN IN THE MUD AT THE BOTTOM
AT THE RATE THEY'RE WORKING, CAPTAIN, THAT SHIP WILL BE READY TO SAIL AT DAWN
YES, QUARREL, TONIGHT'S THE NIGHT

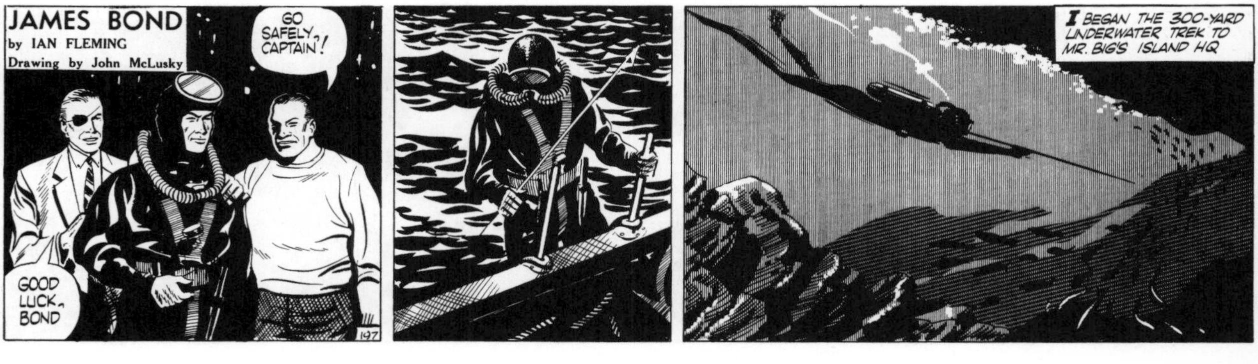
JAMES BOND
by IAN FLEMING
Drawing by John McLusky
GO SAFELY, CAPTAIN!
GOOD LUCK, BOND
197
I BEGAN THE 300-YARD UNDERWATER TREK TO MR. BIG'S ISLAND HQ

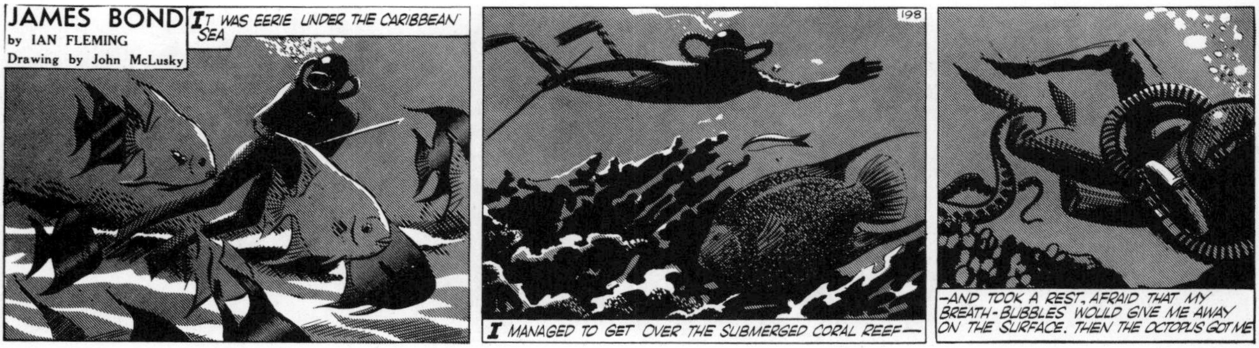
JAMES BOND
by IAN FLEMING
Drawing by John McLusky
IT WAS EERIE UNDER THE CARIBBEAN SEA
198
I MANAGED TO GET OVER THE SUBMERGED CORAL REEF—
—AND TOOK A REST, AFRAID THAT MY BREATH-BUBBLES WOULD GIVE ME AWAY ON THE SURFACE. THEN THE OCTOPUS GOT ME

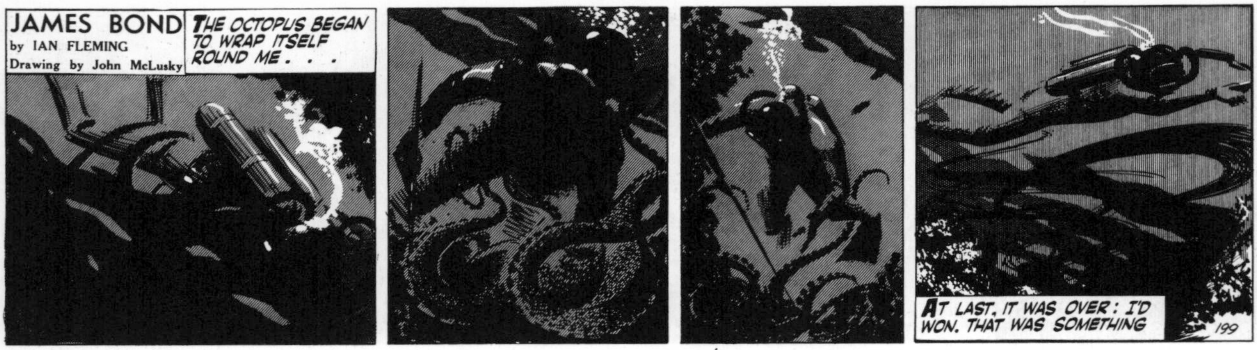
JAMES BOND
by IAN FLEMING
Drawing by John McLusky
THE OCTOPUS BEGAN TO WRAP ITSELF ROUND ME . . .
AT LAST, IT WAS OVER: I'D WON. THAT WAS SOMETHING
199

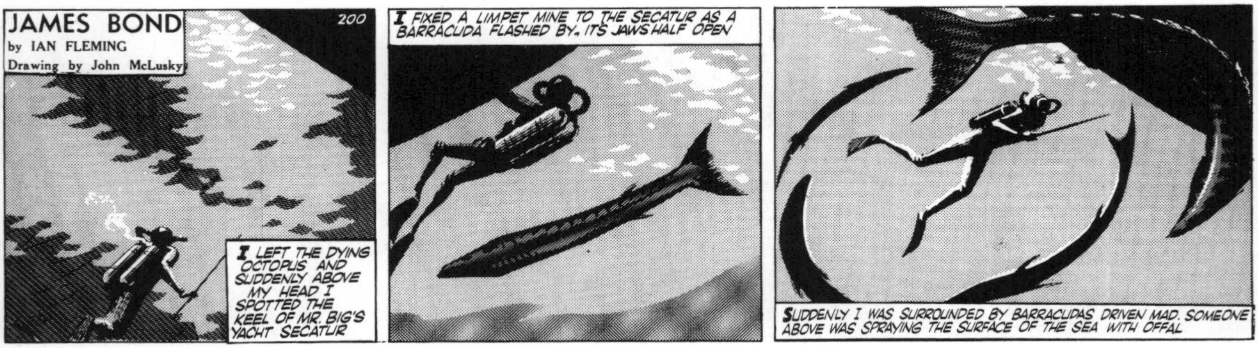
JAMES BOND
by IAN FLEMING
Drawing by John McLusky
200
I LEFT THE DYING OCTOPUS AND SUDDENLY ABOVE MY HEAD I SPOTTED THE KEEL OF MR. BIG'S YACHT SECATUR
I FIXED A LIMPET MINE TO THE SECATUR AS A BARRACUDA FLASHED BY, ITS JAWS HALF OPEN
SUDDENLY I WAS SURROUNDED BY BARRACUDAS DRIVEN MAD. SOMEONE ABOVE WAS SPRAYING THE SURFACE OF THE SEA WITH OFFAL

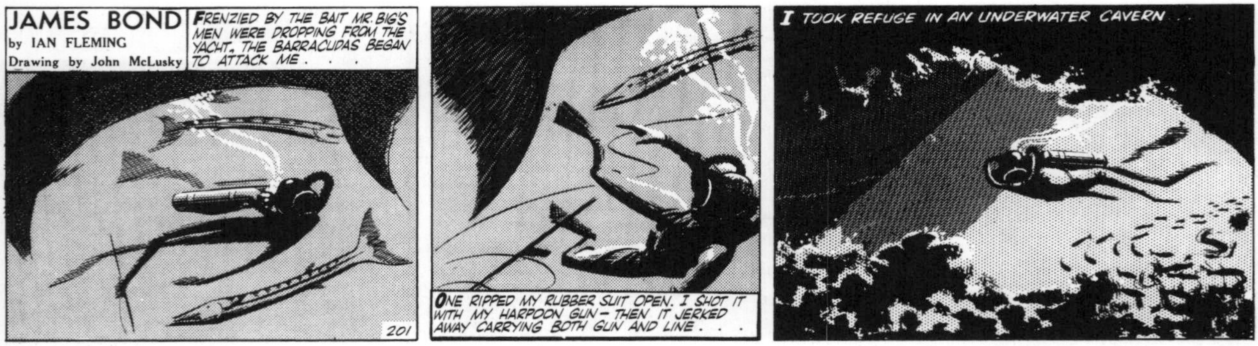
JAMES BOND
by IAN FLEMING
Drawing by John McLusky
FRENZIED BY THE BAIT MR. BIG'S MEN WERE DROPPING FROM THE YACHT, THE BARRACUDAS BEGAN TO ATTACK ME . . .
201
ONE RIPPED MY RUBBER SUIT OPEN. I SHOT IT WITH MY HARPOON GUN — THEN IT JERKED AWAY CARRYING BOTH GUN AND LINE . . .
I TOOK REFUGE IN AN UNDERWATER CAVERN . .

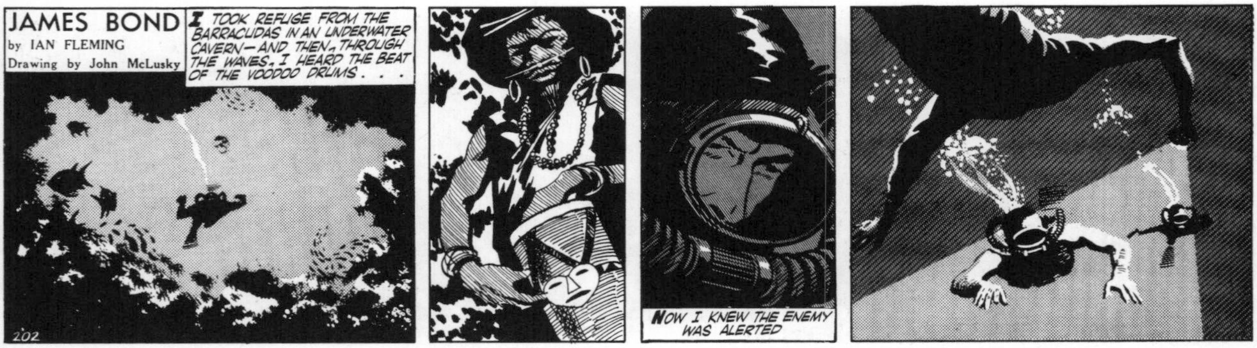
JAMES BOND
by IAN FLEMING
Drawing by John McLusky
I TOOK REFUGE FROM THE BARRACUDAS IN AN UNDERWATER CAVERN — AND THEN, THROUGH THE WAVES, I HEARD THE BEAT OF THE VOODOO DRUMS . . .
202
NOW I KNEW THE ENEMY WAS ALERTED

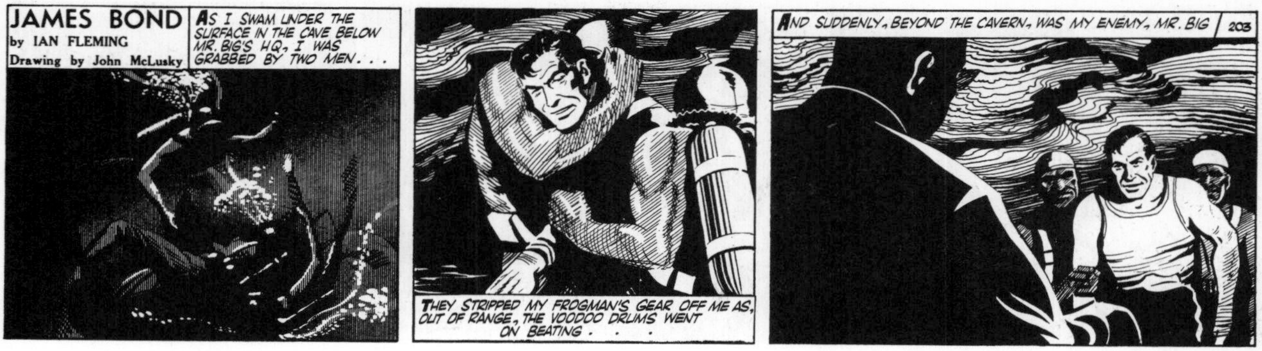
JAMES BOND
by IAN FLEMING
Drawing by John McLusky
AS I SWAM UNDER THE SURFACE IN THE CAVE BELOW MR. BIG'S HQ, I WAS GRABBED BY TWO MEN . . .
THEY STRIPPED MY FROGMAN'S GEAR OFF ME AS, OUT OF RANGE, THE VOODOO DRUMS WENT ON BEATING . . .
AND SUDDENLY, BEYOND THE CAVERN, WAS MY ENEMY, MR. BIG
203

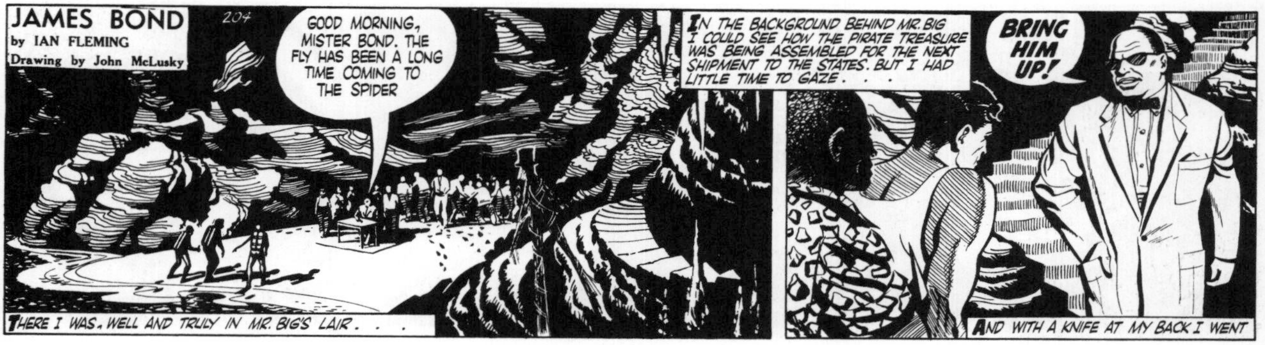
JAMES BOND
by IAN FLEMING
Drawing by John McLusky
204
GOOD MORNING, MISTER BOND. THE FLY HAS BEEN A LONG TIME COMING TO THE SPIDER
THERE I WAS, WELL AND TRULY IN MR. BIG'S LAIR . . .
IN THE BACKGROUND BEHIND MR. BIG I COULD SEE HOW THE PIRATE TREASURE WAS BEING ASSEMBLED FOR THE NEXT SHIPMENT TO THE STATES. BUT I HAD LITTLE TIME TO GAZE . . .
BRING HIM UP!
AND WITH A KNIFE AT MY BACK I WENT

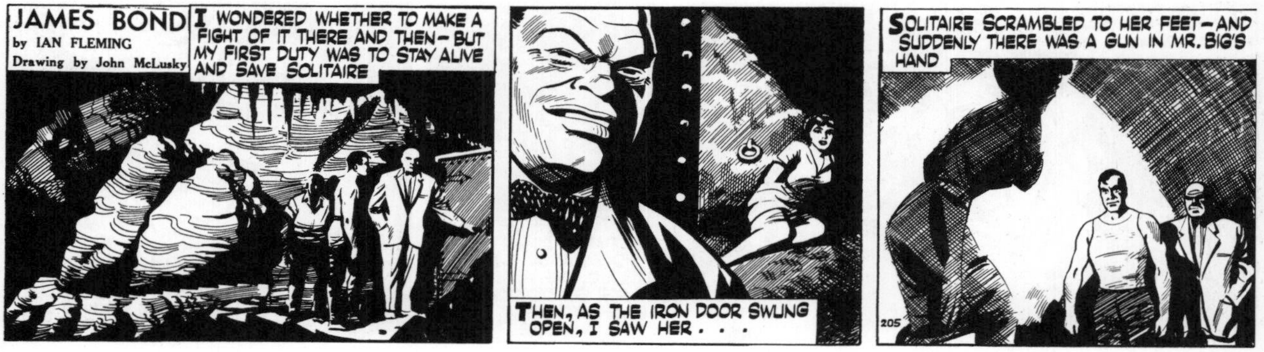
JAMES BOND
by IAN FLEMING
Drawing by John McLusky
I WONDERED WHETHER TO MAKE A FIGHT OF IT THERE AND THEN—BUT MY FIRST DUTY WAS TO STAY ALIVE AND SAVE SOLITAIRE
THEN, AS THE IRON DOOR SWUNG OPEN, I SAW HER . . .
SOLITAIRE SCRAMBLED TO HER FEET—AND SUDDENLY THERE WAS A GUN IN MR. BIG'S HAND
205

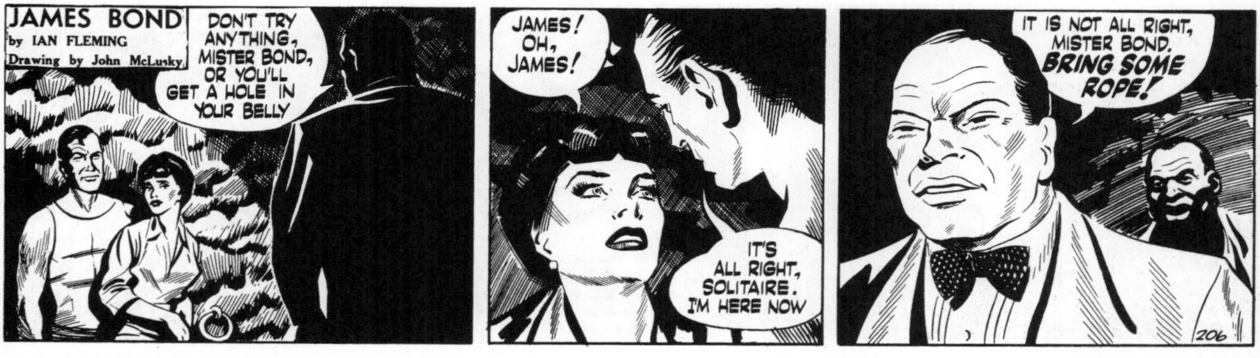
JAMES BOND
by IAN FLEMING
Drawing by John McLusky
DON'T TRY ANYTHING, MISTER BOND, OR YOU'LL GET A HOLE IN YOUR BELLY
JAMES! OH, JAMES!
IT'S ALL RIGHT, SOLITAIRE. I'M HERE NOW
IT IS NOT ALL RIGHT, MISTER BOND. BRING SOME ROPE!
206

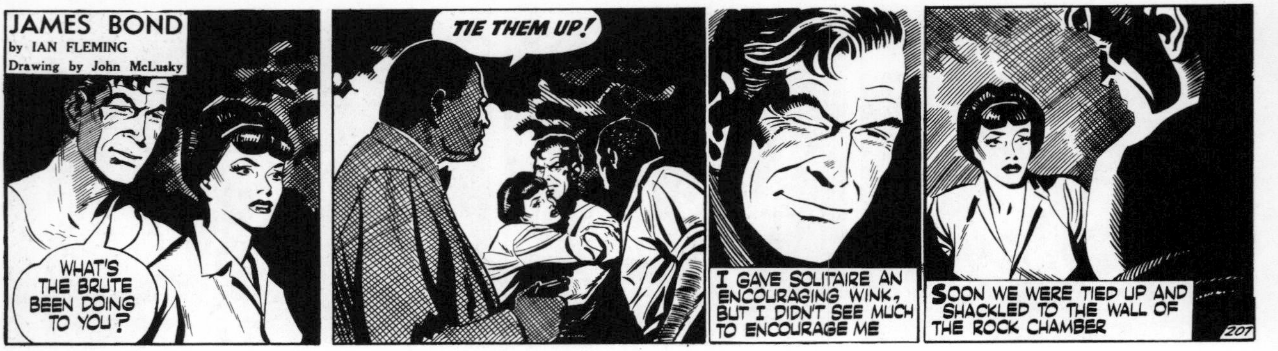
JAMES BOND
by IAN FLEMING
Drawing by John McLusky
WHAT'S THE BRUTE BEEN DOING TO YOU?
TIE THEM UP!
I GAVE SOLITAIRE AN ENCOURAGING WINK, BUT I DIDN'T SEE MUCH TO ENCOURAGE ME
SOON WE WERE TIED UP AND SHACKLED TO THE WALL OF THE ROCK CHAMBER
207

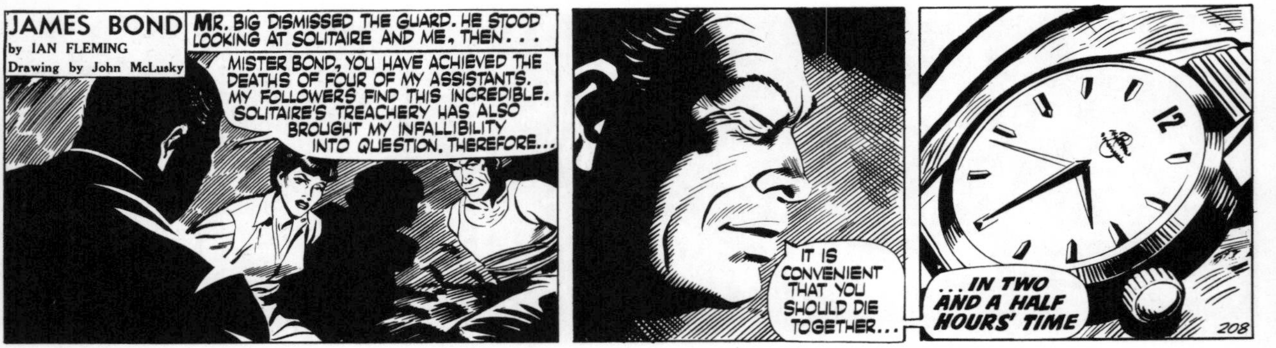
JAMES BOND
by IAN FLEMING
Drawing by John McLusky
MR. BIG DISMISSED THE GUARD. HE STOOD LOOKING AT SOLITAIRE AND ME, THEN . . .
MISTER BOND, YOU HAVE ACHIEVED THE DEATHS OF FOUR OF MY ASSISTANTS. MY FOLLOWERS FIND THIS INCREDIBLE. SOLITAIRE'S TREACHERY HAS ALSO BROUGHT MY INFALLIBILITY INTO QUESTION. THEREFORE...
IT IS CONVENIENT THAT YOU SHOULD DIE TOGETHER...
...IN TWO AND A HALF HOURS' TIME
208

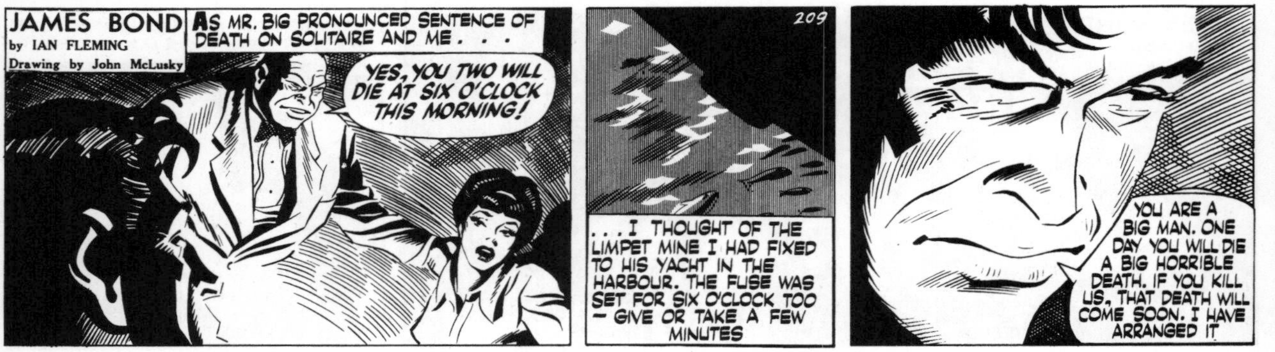
JAMES BOND
by IAN FLEMING
Drawing by John McLusky
AS MR. BIG PRONOUNCED SENTENCE OF DEATH ON SOLITAIRE AND ME . . .
YES, YOU TWO WILL DIE AT SIX O'CLOCK THIS MORNING!
209
. . . I THOUGHT OF THE LIMPET MINE I HAD FIXED TO HIS YACHT IN THE HARBOUR. THE FUSE WAS SET FOR SIX O'CLOCK TOO – GIVE OR TAKE A FEW MINUTES
YOU ARE A BIG MAN. ONE DAY YOU WILL DIE A BIG HORRIBLE DEATH. IF YOU KILL US, THAT DEATH WILL COME SOON. I HAVE ARRANGED IT

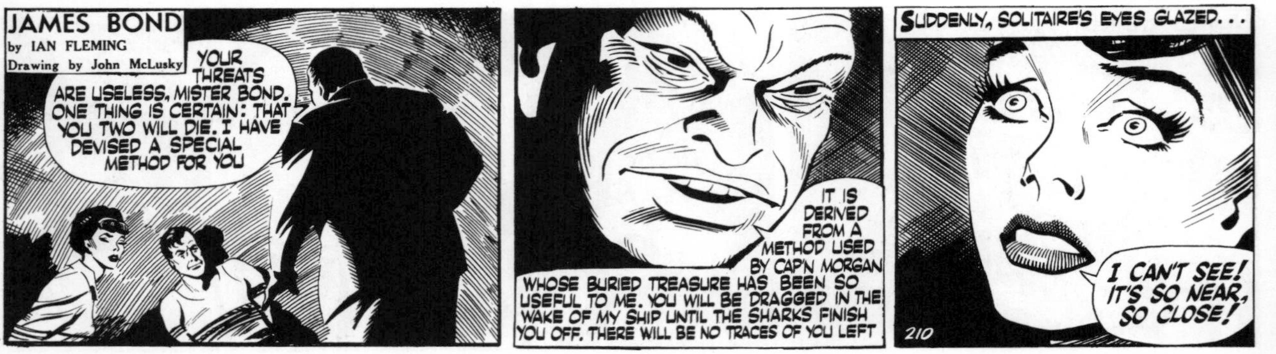
JAMES BOND
by IAN FLEMING
Drawing by John McLusky
YOUR THREATS ARE USELESS, MISTER BOND. ONE THING IS CERTAIN: THAT YOU TWO WILL DIE. I HAVE DEVISED A SPECIAL METHOD FOR YOU
IT IS DERIVED FROM A METHOD USED BY CAP'N MORGAN
WHOSE BURIED TREASURE HAS BEEN SO USEFUL TO ME. YOU WILL BE DRAGGED IN THE WAKE OF MY SHIP UNTIL THE SHARKS FINISH YOU OFF. THERE WILL BE NO TRACES OF YOU LEFT
SUDDENLY, SOLITAIRE'S EYES GLAZED...
I CAN'T SEE! IT'S SO NEAR, SO CLOSE!
210

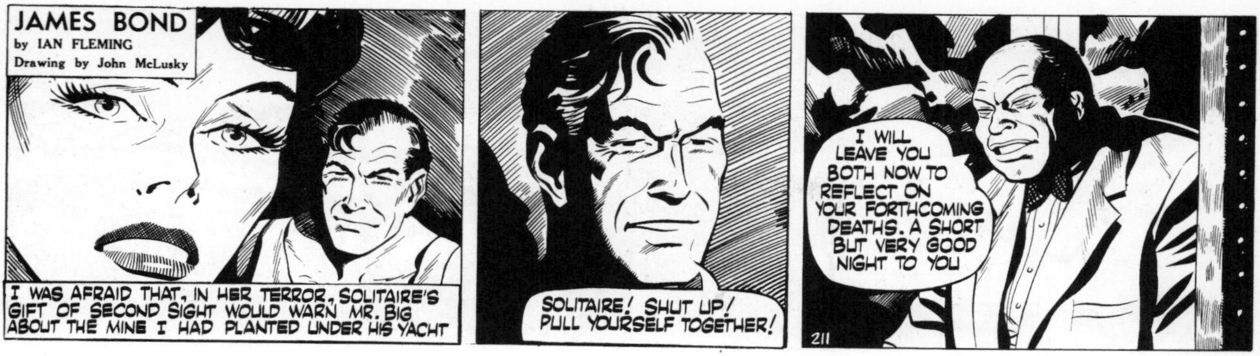
JAMES BOND
by IAN FLEMING
Drawing by John McLusky
I WAS AFRAID THAT, IN HER TERROR, SOLITAIRE'S GIFT OF SECOND SIGHT WOULD WARN MR. BIG ABOUT THE MINE I HAD PLANTED UNDER HIS YACHT
SOLITAIRE! SHUT UP! PULL YOURSELF TOGETHER!
I WILL LEAVE YOU BOTH NOW TO REFLECT ON YOUR FORTHCOMING DEATHS. A SHORT BUT VERY GOOD NIGHT TO YOU
211

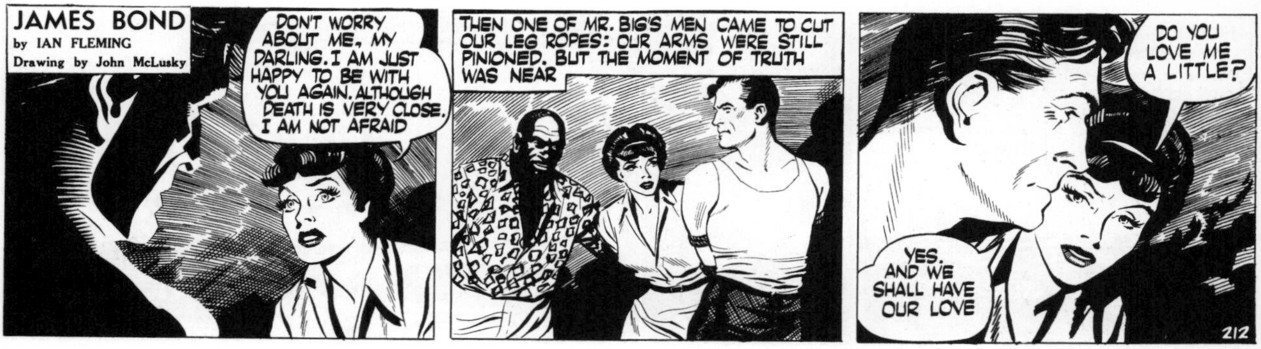
JAMES BOND
by IAN FLEMING
Drawing by John McLusky
DON'T WORRY ABOUT ME, MY DARLING. I AM JUST HAPPY TO BE WITH YOU AGAIN. ALTHOUGH DEATH IS VERY CLOSE, I AM NOT AFRAID
THEN ONE OF MR. BIG'S MEN CAME TO CUT OUR LEG ROPES: OUR ARMS WERE STILL PINIONED. BUT THE MOMENT OF TRUTH WAS NEAR
DO YOU LOVE ME A LITTLE?
YES. AND WE SHALL HAVE OUR LOVE
212

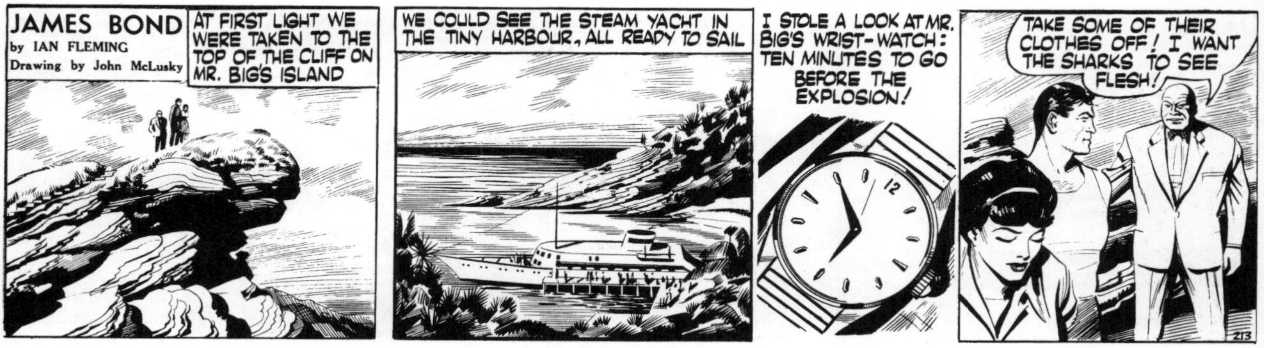
JAMES BOND
by IAN FLEMING
Drawing by John McLusky
AT FIRST LIGHT WE WERE TAKEN TO THE TOP OF THE CLIFF ON MR. BIG'S ISLAND
WE COULD SEE THE STEAM YACHT IN THE TINY HARBOUR, ALL READY TO SAIL
I STOLE A LOOK AT MR. BIG'S WRIST-WATCH: TEN MINUTES TO GO BEFORE THE EXPLOSION!
TAKE SOME OF THEIR CLOTHES OFF! I WANT THE SHARKS TO SEE FLESH!
213

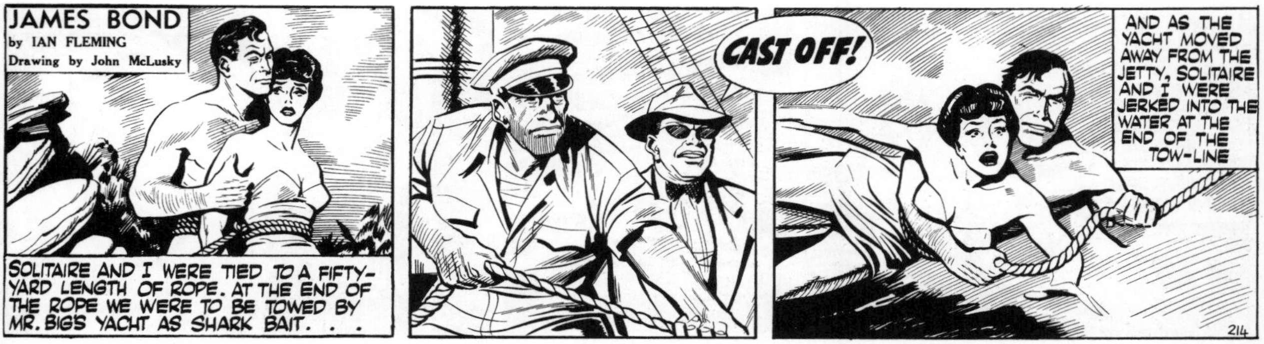
JAMES BOND
by IAN FLEMING
Drawing by John McLusky
SOLITAIRE AND I WERE TIED TO A FIFTY-YARD LENGTH OF ROPE. AT THE END OF THE ROPE WE WERE TO BE TOWED BY MR. BIG'S YACHT AS SHARK BAIT. . .
CAST OFF!
AND AS THE YACHT MOVED AWAY FROM THE JETTY, SOLITAIRE AND I WERE JERKED INTO THE WATER AT THE END OF THE TOW-LINE
214

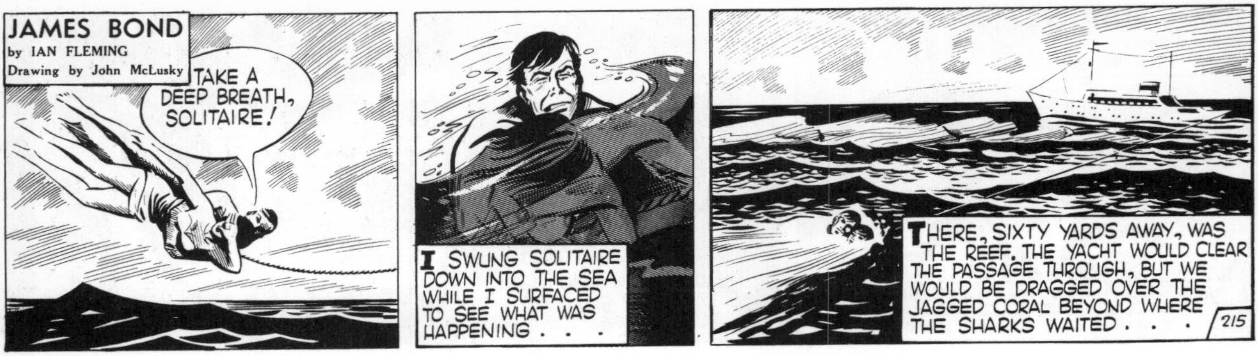
JAMES BOND
by IAN FLEMING
Drawing by John McLusky
TAKE A DEEP BREATH, SOLITAIRE!
I SWUNG SOLITAIRE DOWN INTO THE SEA WHILE I SURFACED TO SEE WHAT WAS HAPPENING . . .
THERE, SIXTY YARDS AWAY, WAS THE REEF. THE YACHT WOULD CLEAR THE PASSAGE THROUGH, BUT WE WOULD BE DRAGGED OVER THE JAGGED CORAL BEYOND WHERE THE SHARKS WAITED . . .
215

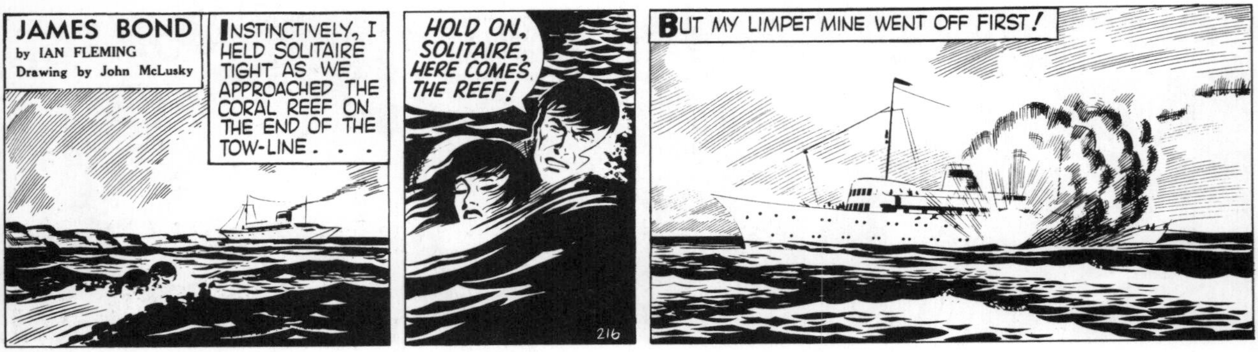
JAMES BOND
by IAN FLEMING
Drawing by John McLusky
INSTINCTIVELY, I HELD SOLITAIRE TIGHT AS WE APPROACHED THE CORAL REEF ON THE END OF THE TOW-LINE . . .
HOLD ON, SOLITAIRE, HERE COMES THE REEF!
216
BUT MY LIMPET MINE WENT OFF FIRST!

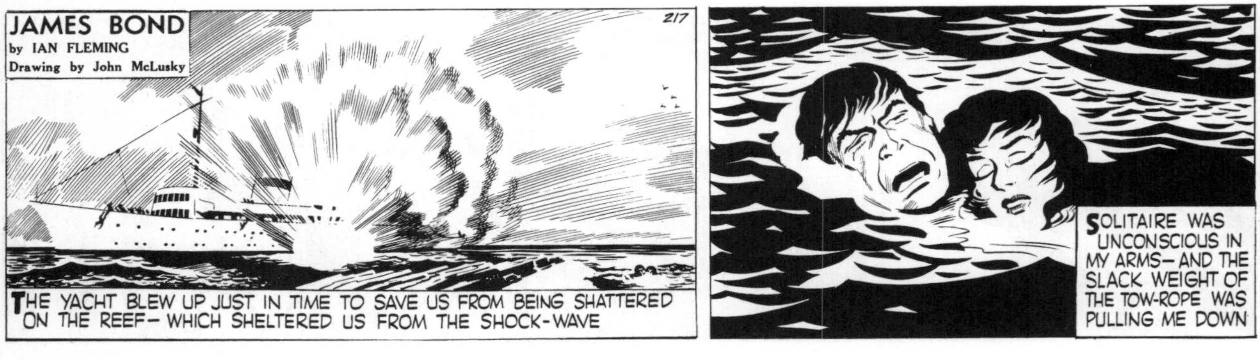
JAMES BOND
by IAN FLEMING
Drawing by John McLusky
217
THE YACHT BLEW UP JUST IN TIME TO SAVE US FROM BEING SHATTERED ON THE REEF— WHICH SHELTERED US FROM THE SHOCK-WAVE
SOLITAIRE WAS UNCONSCIOUS IN MY ARMS—AND THE SLACK WEIGHT OF THE TOW-ROPE WAS PULLING ME DOWN

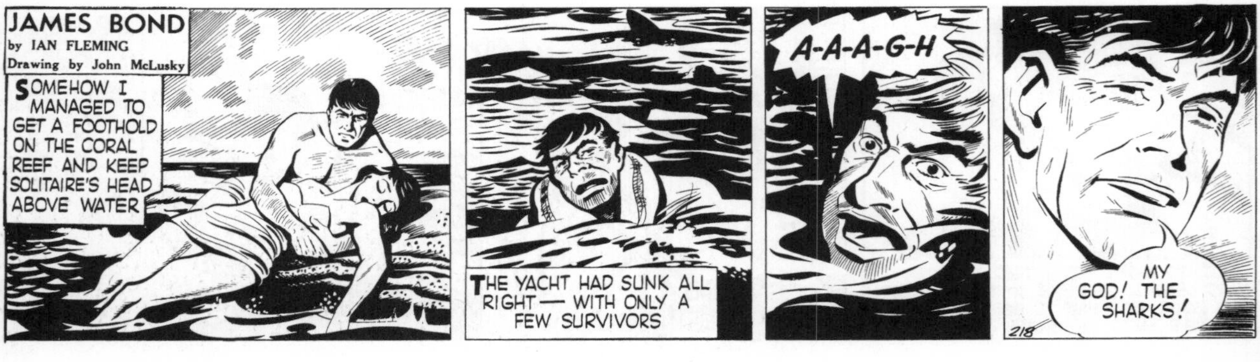
JAMES BOND
by IAN FLEMING
Drawing by John McLusky
SOMEHOW I MANAGED TO GET A FOOTHOLD ON THE CORAL REEF AND KEEP SOLITAIRE'S HEAD ABOVE WATER
THE YACHT HAD SUNK ALL RIGHT — WITH ONLY A FEW SURVIVORS
A-A-A-G-H
218
MY GOD! THE SHARKS!

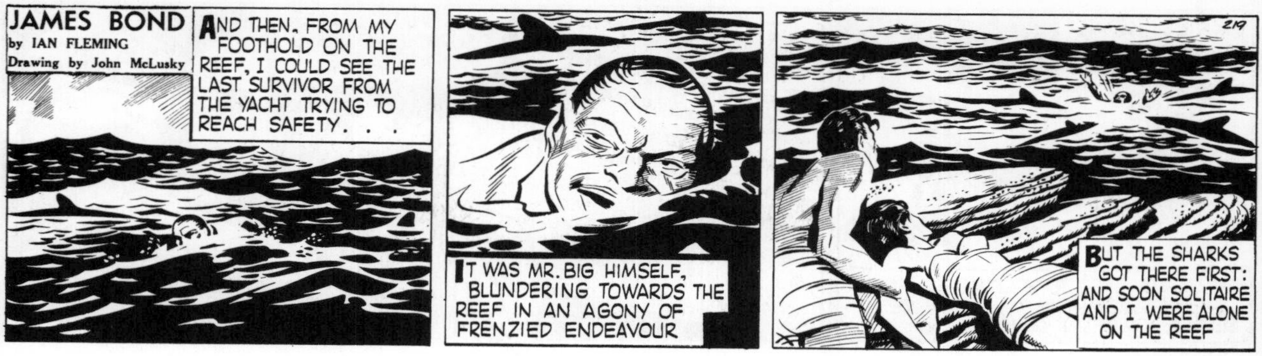

JAMES BOND
by IAN FLEMING
Drawing by John McLusky
AND THEN, FROM MY FOOTHOLD ON THE REEF, I COULD SEE THE LAST SURVIVOR FROM THE YACHT TRYING TO REACH SAFETY . . .
IT WAS MR. BIG HIMSELF, BLUNDERING TOWARDS THE REEF IN AN AGONY OF FRENZIED ENDEAVOUR
219
BUT THE SHARKS GOT THERE FIRST: AND SOON SOLITAIRE AND I WERE ALONE ON THE REEF

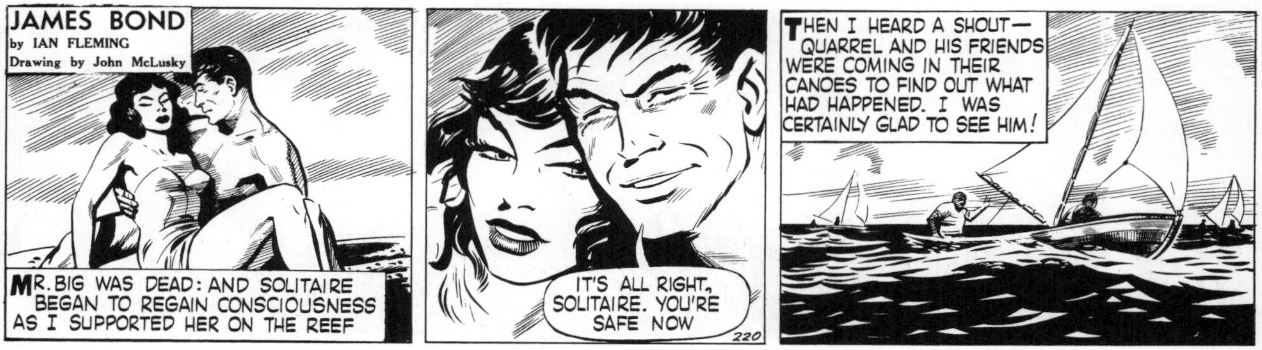

JAMES BOND
by IAN FLEMING
Drawing by John McLusky
MR. BIG WAS DEAD: AND SOLITAIRE BEGAN TO REGAIN CONSCIOUSNESS AS I SUPPORTED HER ON THE REEF
IT'S ALL RIGHT, SOLITAIRE. YOU'RE SAFE NOW
220
THEN I HEARD A SHOUT— QUARREL AND HIS FRIENDS WERE COMING IN THEIR CANOES TO FIND OUT WHAT HAD HAPPENED. I WAS CERTAINLY GLAD TO SEE HIM!

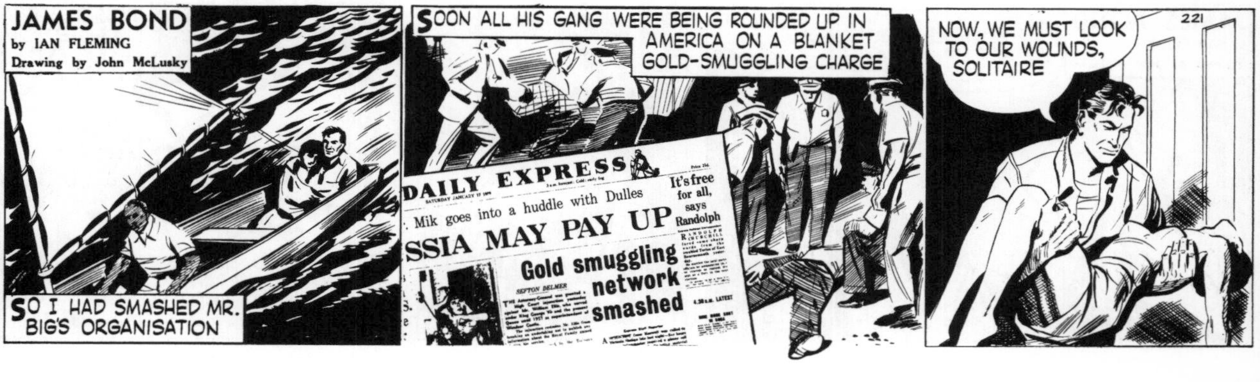

JAMES BOND
by IAN FLEMING
Drawing by John McLusky
SO I HAD SMASHED MR. BIG'S ORGANISATION
SOON ALL HIS GANG WERE BEING ROUNDED UP IN AMERICA ON A BLANKET GOLD-SMUGGLING CHARGE
DAILY EXPRESS
Mik goes into a huddle with Dulles
It's free for all, says Randolph
SSIA MAY PAY UP
Gold smuggling network smashed
SEFTON DELMER
221
NOW, WE MUST LOOK TO OUR WOUNDS, SOLITAIRE

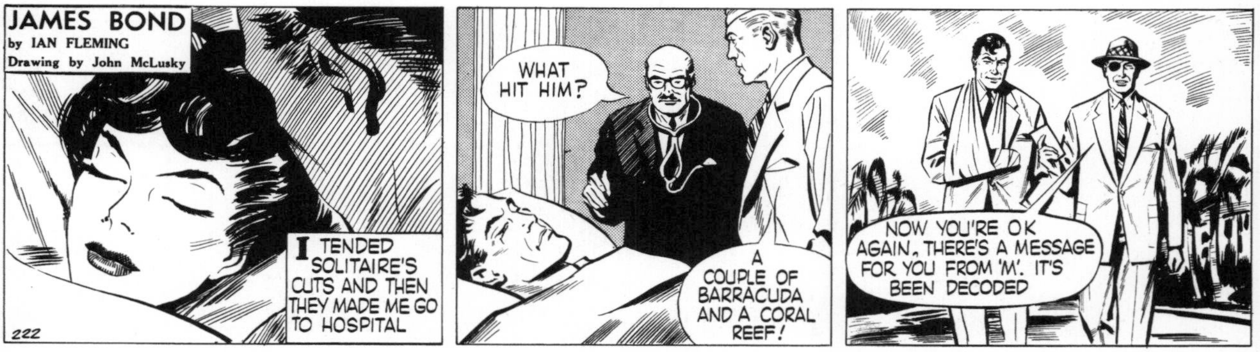

JAMES BOND
by IAN FLEMING
Drawing by John McLusky
I TENDED SOLITAIRE'S CUTS AND THEN THEY MADE ME GO TO HOSPITAL
222
WHAT HIT HIM?
A COUPLE OF BARRACUDA AND A CORAL REEF!
NOW YOU'RE OK AGAIN, THERE'S A MESSAGE FOR YOU FROM 'M'. IT'S BEEN DECODED

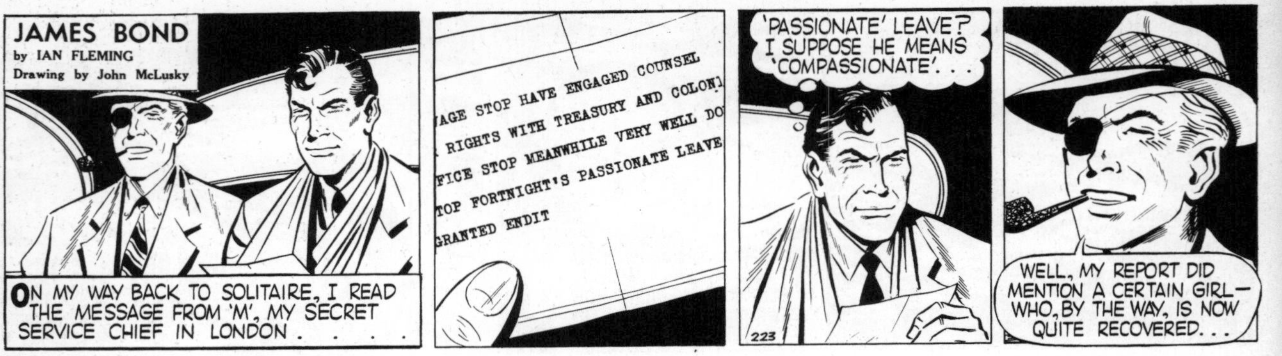
JAMES BOND
by IAN FLEMING
Drawing by John McLusky
ON MY WAY BACK TO SOLITAIRE, I READ THE MESSAGE FROM 'M', MY SECRET SERVICE CHIEF IN LONDON . . . .
AGE STOP HAVE ENGAGED COUNSEL
RIGHTS WITH TREASURY AND COLON
FICE STOP MEANWHILE VERY WELL DO
TOP FORTNIGHT'S PASSIONATE LEAVE
GRANTED ENDIT
'PASSIONATE' LEAVE? I SUPPOSE HE MEANS 'COMPASSIONATE'. . .
223
WELL, MY REPORT DID MENTION A CERTAIN GIRL– WHO, BY THE WAY, IS NOW QUITE RECOVERED. . .

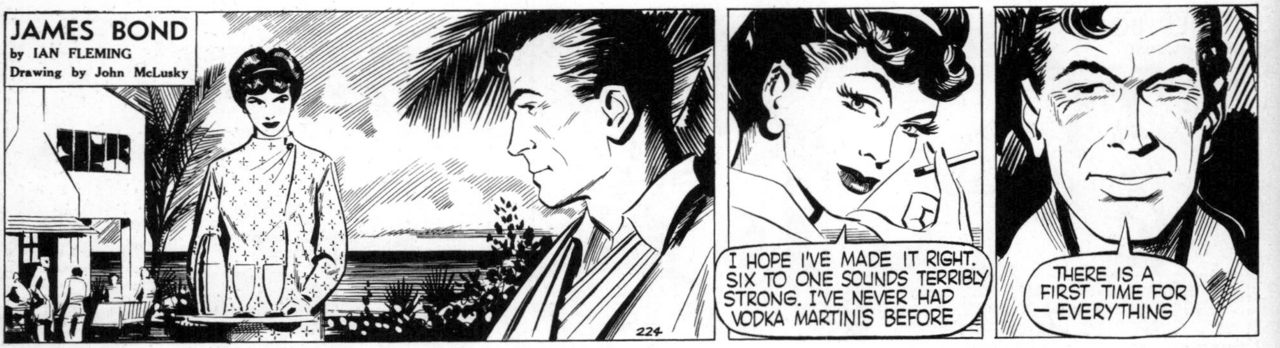
JAMES BOND
by IAN FLEMING
Drawing by John McLusky
224
I HOPE I'VE MADE IT RIGHT. SIX TO ONE SOUNDS TERRIBLY STRONG. I'VE NEVER HAD VODKA MARTINIS BEFORE
THERE IS A FIRST TIME FOR – EVERYTHING

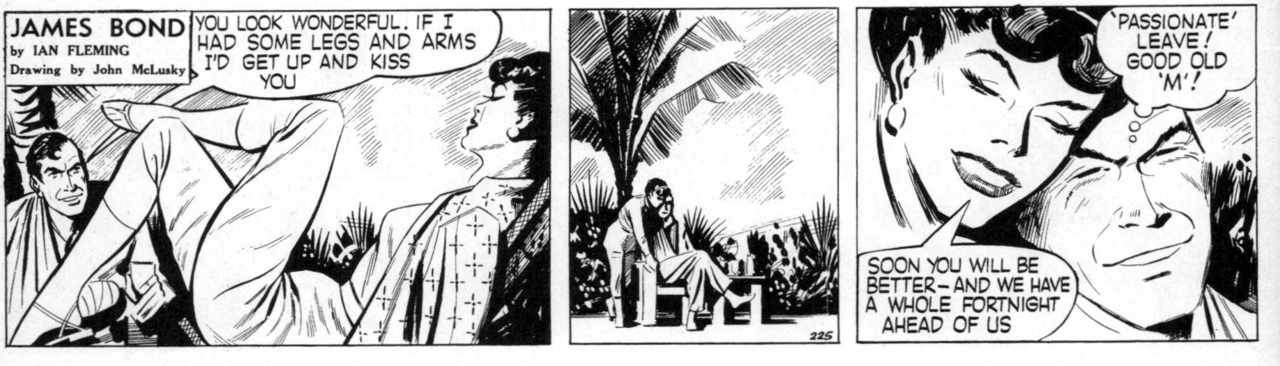
JAMES BOND
by IAN FLEMING
Drawing by John McLusky
YOU LOOK WONDERFUL. IF I HAD SOME LEGS AND ARMS I'D GET UP AND KISS YOU
225
'PASSIONATE' LEAVE! GOOD OLD 'M'!
SOON YOU WILL BE BETTER– AND WE HAVE A WHOLE FORTNIGHT AHEAD OF US

007

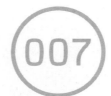

MOONRAKER

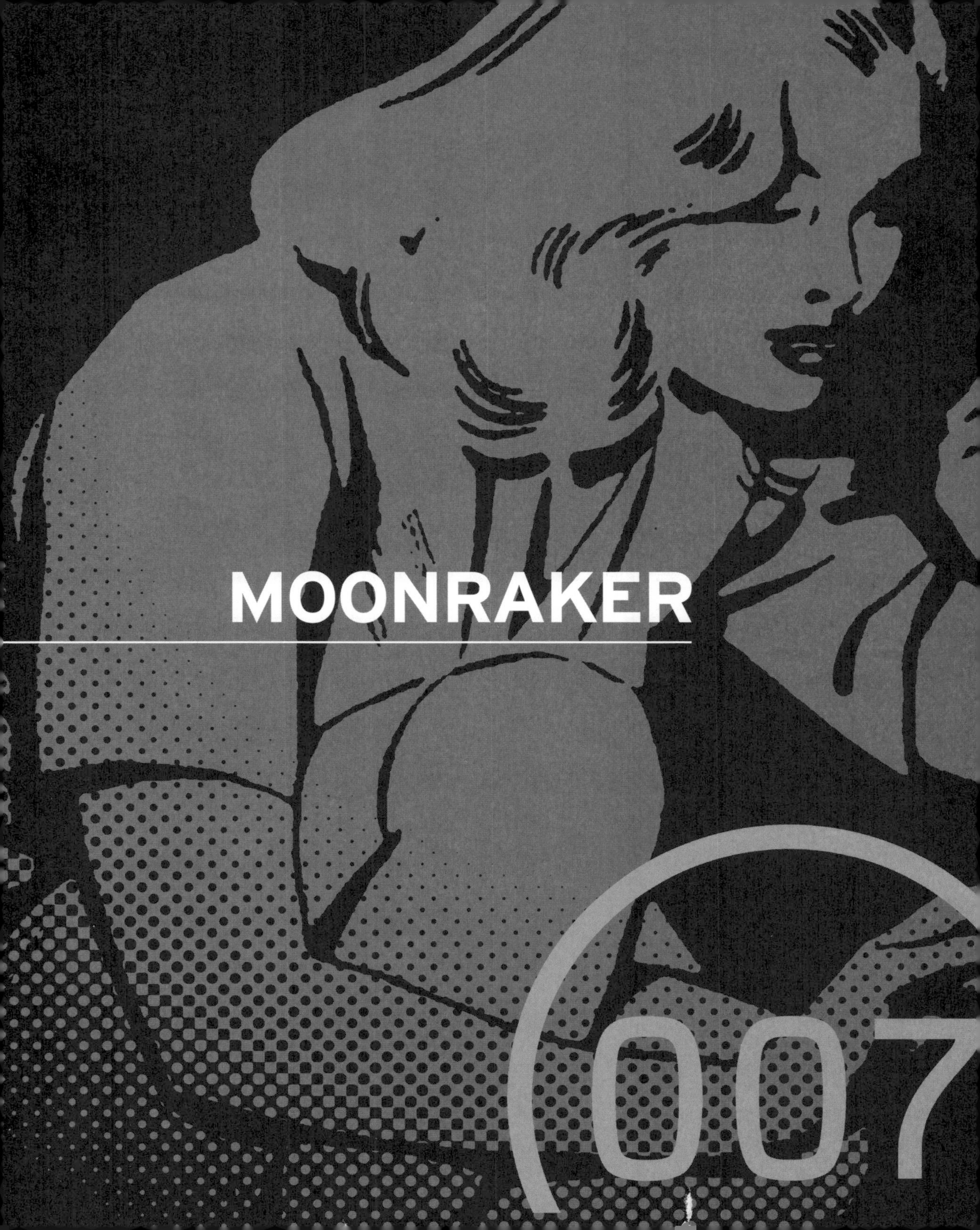
007

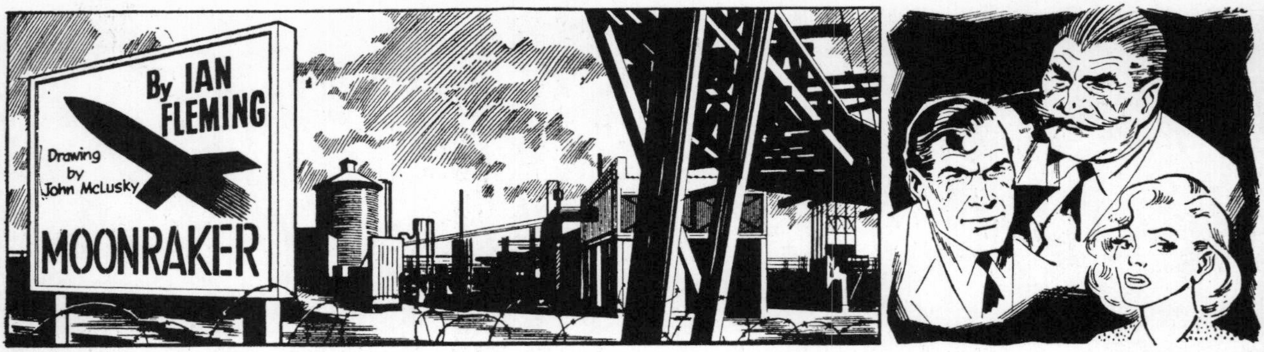
By IAN FLEMING
Drawing by John McLusky
MOONRAKER

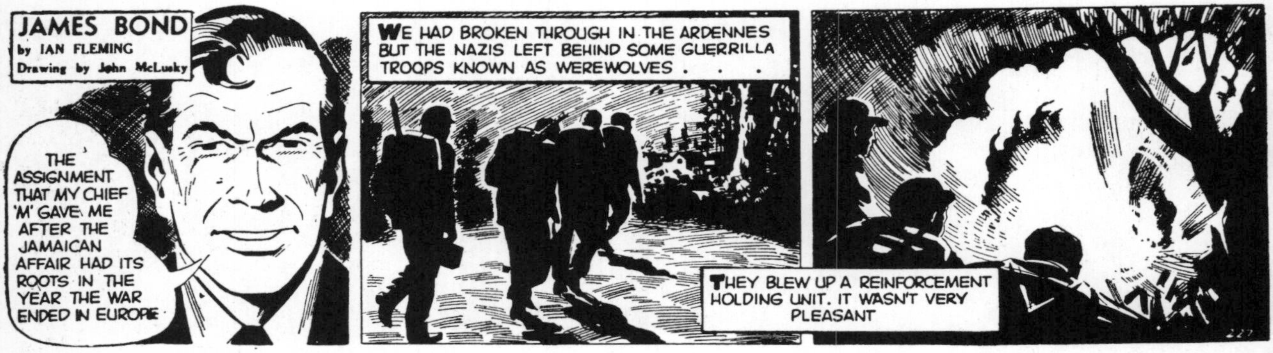
JAMES BOND
by IAN FLEMING
Drawing by John McLusky
THE ASSIGNMENT THAT MY CHIEF 'M' GAVE ME AFTER THE JAMAICAN AFFAIR HAD ITS ROOTS IN THE YEAR THE WAR ENDED IN EUROPE
WE HAD BROKEN THROUGH IN THE ARDENNES BUT THE NAZIS LEFT BEHIND SOME GUERRILLA TROOPS KNOWN AS WEREWOLVES . . .
THEY BLEW UP A REINFORCEMENT HOLDING UNIT. IT WASN'T VERY PLEASANT
227

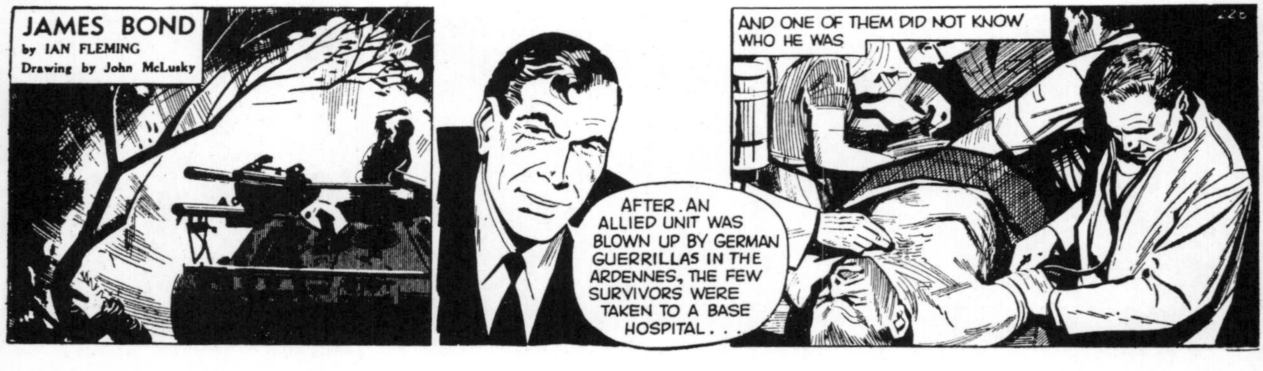
JAMES BOND
by IAN FLEMING
Drawing by John McLusky
AFTER AN ALLIED UNIT WAS BLOWN UP BY GERMAN GUERRILLAS IN THE ARDENNES, THE FEW SURVIVORS WERE TAKEN TO A BASE HOSPITAL . . .
AND ONE OF THEM DID NOT KNOW WHO HE WAS
228

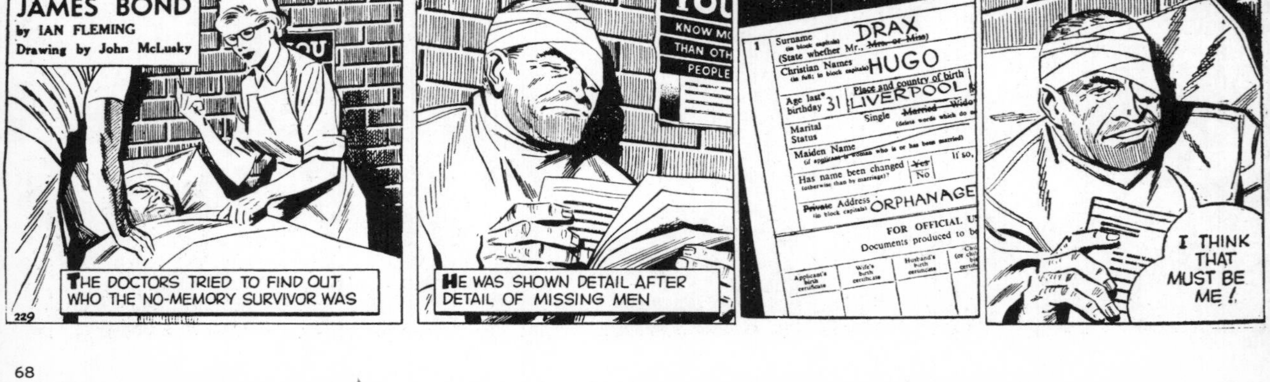
JAMES BOND
by IAN FLEMING
Drawing by John McLusky
THE DOCTORS TRIED TO FIND OUT WHO THE NO-MEMORY SURVIVOR WAS
229
YOU
KNOW MO
THAN OTH
PEOPLE
HE WAS SHOWN DETAIL AFTER DETAIL OF MISSING MEN
Surname
DRAX
(State whether Mr., Mrs. or Miss)
Christian Names
HUGO
Age last birthday 31
Place and country of birth
LIVERPOOL
Marital Status
Single
Married
Maiden Name
Has name been changed
Yes
No
Private Address
ORPHANAGE
FOR OFFICIAL U
Documents produced to be
I THINK THAT MUST BE ME!

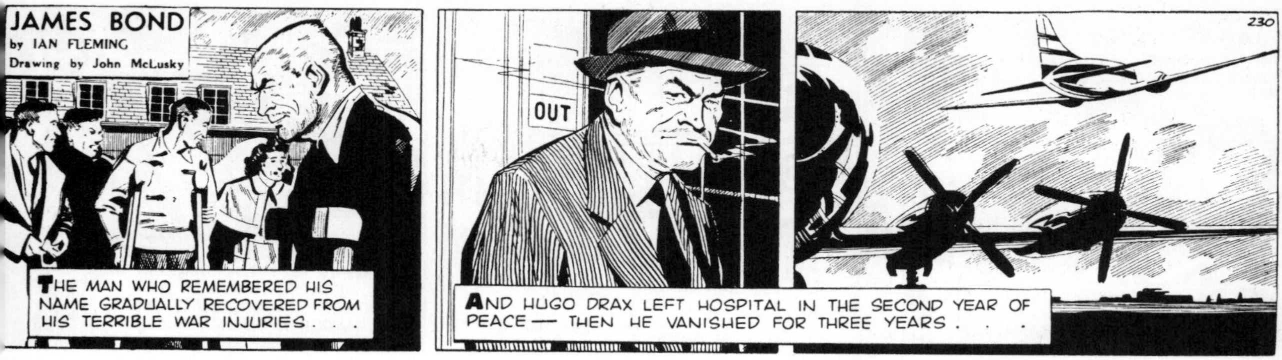
JAMES BOND
by IAN FLEMING
Drawing by John McLusky
230
THE MAN WHO REMEMBERED HIS NAME GRADUALLY RECOVERED FROM HIS TERRIBLE WAR INJURIES . . .
OUT
AND HUGO DRAX LEFT HOSPITAL IN THE SECOND YEAR OF PEACE — THEN HE VANISHED FOR THREE YEARS . . .

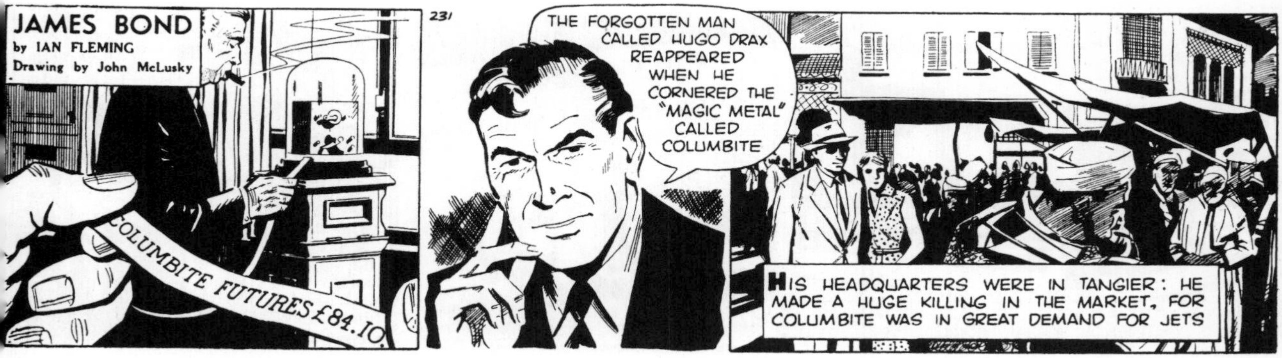
JAMES BOND
by IAN FLEMING
Drawing by John McLusky
231
COLUMBITE FUTURES £84.10
THE FORGOTTEN MAN CALLED HUGO DRAX REAPPEARED WHEN HE CORNERED THE "MAGIC METAL" CALLED COLUMBITE
HIS HEADQUARTERS WERE IN TANGIER: HE MADE A HUGE KILLING IN THE MARKET, FOR COLUMBITE WAS IN GREAT DEMAND FOR JETS

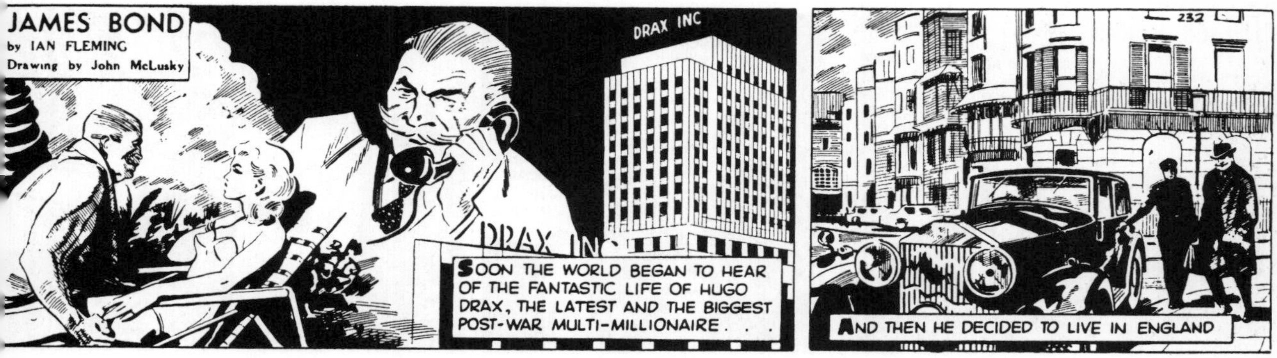
JAMES BOND
by IAN FLEMING
Drawing by John McLusky
DRAX INC
DRAX INC
SOON THE WORLD BEGAN TO HEAR OF THE FANTASTIC LIFE OF HUGO DRAX, THE LATEST AND THE BIGGEST POST-WAR MULTI-MILLIONAIRE . . .
232
AND THEN HE DECIDED TO LIVE IN ENGLAND

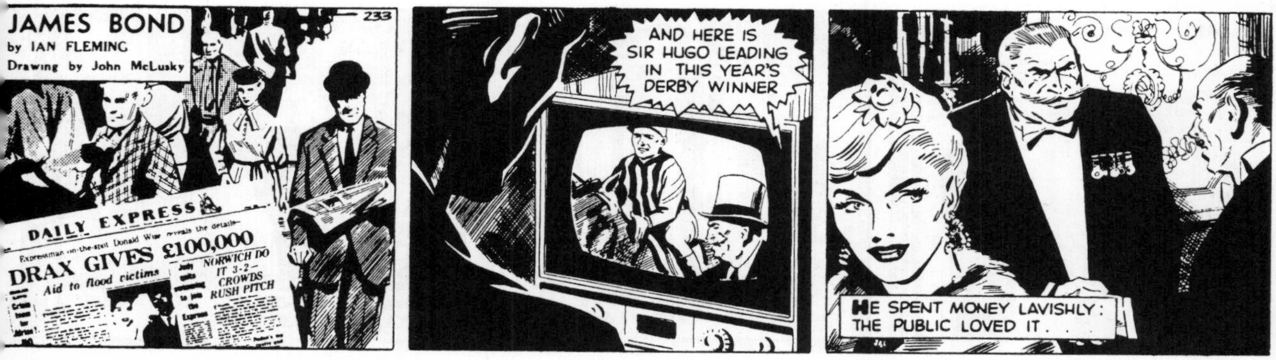
JAMES BOND
by IAN FLEMING
Drawing by John McLusky
233
DAILY EXPRESS
Expressman on-the-spot Donald Wise reveals the details
DRAX GIVES £100,000
Aid to flood victims
NORWICH DO IT 3-2— CROWDS RUSH PITCH
AND HERE IS SIR HUGO LEADING IN THIS YEAR'S DERBY WINNER
HE SPENT MONEY LAVISHLY: THE PUBLIC LOVED IT . .

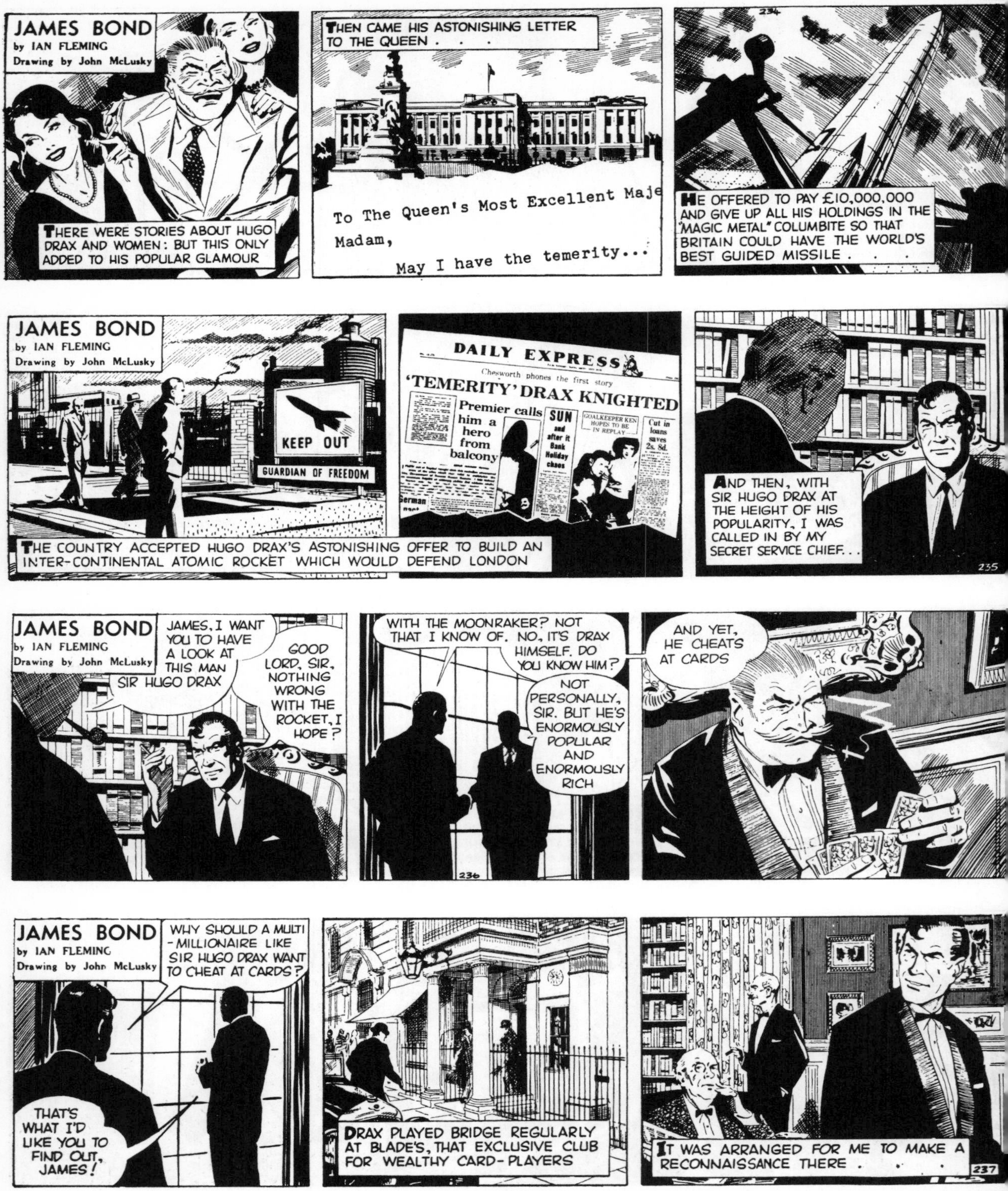
JAMES BOND
by IAN FLEMING
Drawing by John McLusky
THERE WERE STORIES ABOUT HUGO DRAX AND WOMEN: BUT THIS ONLY ADDED TO HIS POPULAR GLAMOUR
THEN CAME HIS ASTONISHING LETTER TO THE QUEEN . . .
To The Queen's Most Excellent Maje
Madam,
May I have the temerity...
234
HE OFFERED TO PAY £10,000,000 AND GIVE UP ALL HIS HOLDINGS IN THE "MAGIC METAL" COLUMBITE SO THAT BRITAIN COULD HAVE THE WORLD'S BEST GUIDED MISSILE . . .
JAMES BOND
by IAN FLEMING
Drawing by John McLusky
KEEP OUT
GUARDIAN OF FREEDOM
THE COUNTRY ACCEPTED HUGO DRAX'S ASTONISHING OFFER TO BUILD AN INTER-CONTINENTAL ATOMIC ROCKET WHICH WOULD DEFEND LONDON
DAILY EXPRESS
Chesworth phones the first story
'TEMERITY' DRAX KNIGHTED
Premier calls him a hero from balcony
SUN and after it Bank Holiday chaos
GOALKEEPER KEN HOPES TO BE IN REPLAY
Cut in loans saves 2s. 8d.
AND THEN, WITH SIR HUGO DRAX AT THE HEIGHT OF HIS POPULARITY, I WAS CALLED IN BY MY SECRET SERVICE CHIEF...
235
JAMES BOND
by IAN FLEMING
Drawing by John McLusky
JAMES, I WANT YOU TO HAVE A LOOK AT THIS MAN SIR HUGO DRAX
GOOD LORD, SIR, NOTHING WRONG WITH THE ROCKET, I HOPE?
WITH THE MOONRAKER? NOT THAT I KNOW OF. NO, IT'S DRAX HIMSELF. DO YOU KNOW HIM?
NOT PERSONALLY, SIR. BUT HE'S ENORMOUSLY POPULAR AND ENORMOUSLY RICH
236
AND YET, HE CHEATS AT CARDS
JAMES BOND
by IAN FLEMING
Drawing by John McLusky
WHY SHOULD A MULTI-MILLIONAIRE LIKE SIR HUGO DRAX WANT TO CHEAT AT CARDS?
THAT'S WHAT I'D LIKE YOU TO FIND OUT, JAMES!
DRAX PLAYED BRIDGE REGULARLY AT BLADE'S, THAT EXCLUSIVE CLUB FOR WEALTHY CARD-PLAYERS
IT WAS ARRANGED FOR ME TO MAKE A RECONNAISSANCE THERE . . .
237

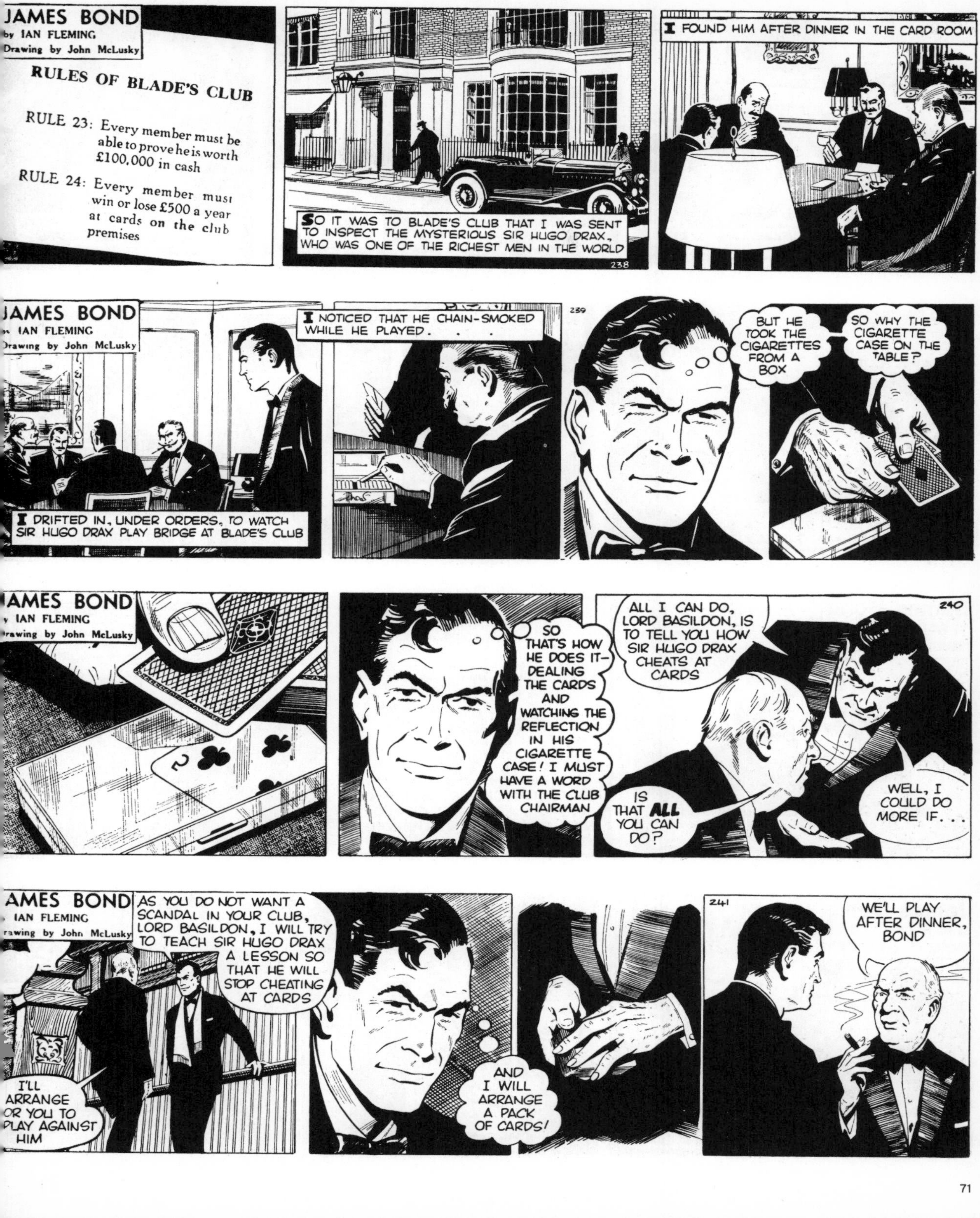
JAMES BOND
by IAN FLEMING
Drawing by John McLusky
RULES OF BLADE'S CLUB
RULE 23: Every member must be able to prove he is worth £100,000 in cash
RULE 24: Every member must win or lose £500 a year at cards on the club premises
SO IT WAS TO BLADE'S CLUB THAT I WAS SENT TO INSPECT THE MYSTERIOUS SIR HUGO DRAX, WHO WAS ONE OF THE RICHEST MEN IN THE WORLD
238
I FOUND HIM AFTER DINNER IN THE CARD ROOM
JAMES BOND
IAN FLEMING
Drawing by John McLusky
I DRIFTED IN, UNDER ORDERS, TO WATCH SIR HUGO DRAX PLAY BRIDGE AT BLADE'S CLUB
I NOTICED THAT HE CHAIN-SMOKED WHILE HE PLAYED . . .
239
BUT HE TOOK THE CIGARETTES FROM A BOX
SO WHY THE CIGARETTE CASE ON THE TABLE?
JAMES BOND
IAN FLEMING
Drawing by John McLusky
SO THAT'S HOW HE DOES IT-DEALING THE CARDS AND WATCHING THE REFLECTION IN HIS CIGARETTE CASE! I MUST HAVE A WORD WITH THE CLUB CHAIRMAN
240
ALL I CAN DO, LORD BASILDON, IS TO TELL YOU HOW SIR HUGO DRAX CHEATS AT CARDS
IS THAT ALL YOU CAN DO?
WELL, I COULD DO MORE IF. . .
JAMES BOND
IAN FLEMING
Drawing by John McLusky
AS YOU DO NOT WANT A SCANDAL IN YOUR CLUB, LORD BASILDON, I WILL TRY TO TEACH SIR HUGO DRAX A LESSON SO THAT HE WILL STOP CHEATING AT CARDS
I'LL ARRANGE OR YOU TO PLAY AGAINST HIM
AND I WILL ARRANGE A PACK OF CARDS!
241
WE'LL PLAY AFTER DINNER, BOND

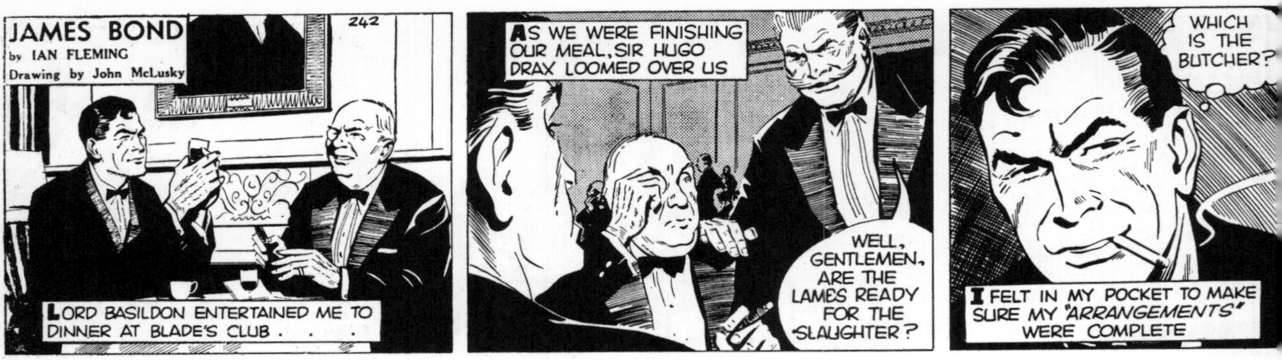
JAMES BOND
by IAN FLEMING
Drawing by John McLusky
242
LORD BASILDON ENTERTAINED ME TO DINNER AT BLADE'S CLUB . . .
AS WE WERE FINISHING OUR MEAL, SIR HUGO DRAX LOOMED OVER US
WELL, GENTLEMEN, ARE THE LAMES READY FOR THE SLAUGHTER?
WHICH IS THE BUTCHER?
I FELT IN MY POCKET TO MAKE SURE MY "ARRANGEMENTS" WERE COMPLETE

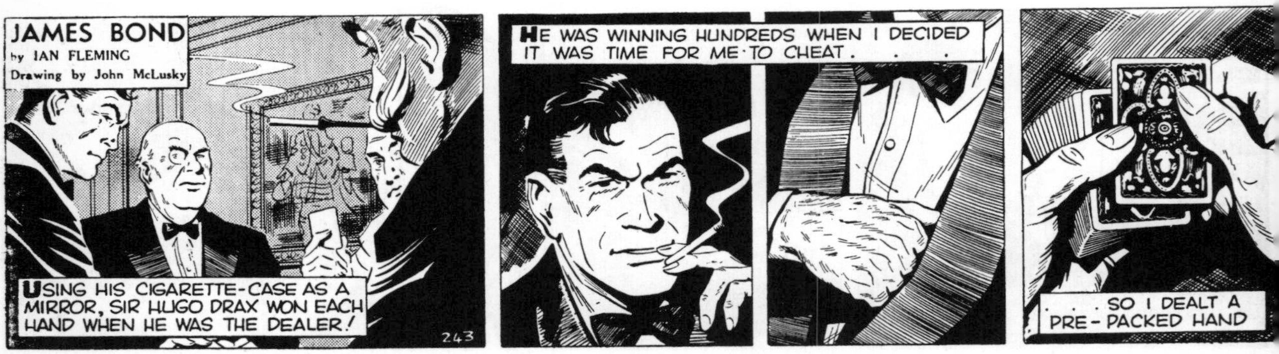
JAMES BOND
by IAN FLEMING
Drawing by John McLusky
USING HIS CIGARETTE-CASE AS A MIRROR, SIR HUGO DRAX WON EACH HAND WHEN HE WAS THE DEALER!
243
HE WAS WINNING HUNDREDS WHEN I DECIDED IT WAS TIME FOR ME TO CHEAT . . .
. . . SO I DEALT A PRE-PACKED HAND

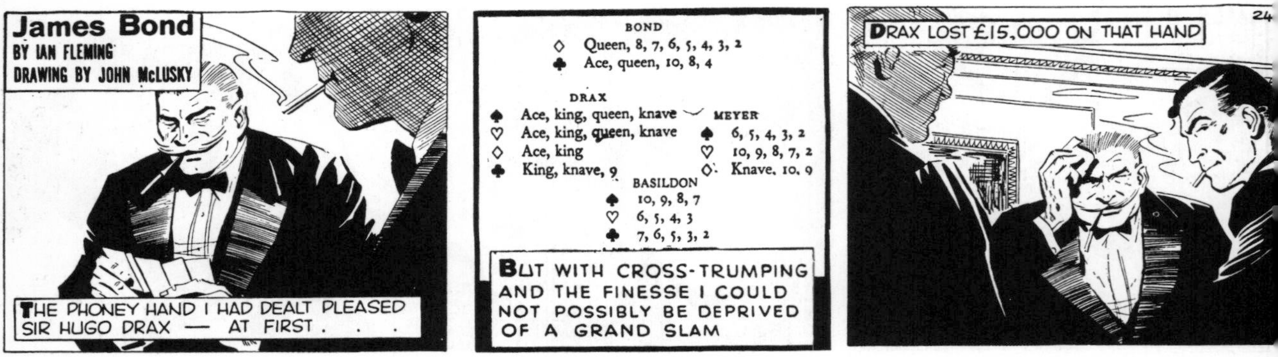
James Bond
BY IAN FLEMING
DRAWING BY JOHN McLUSKY
THE PHONEY HAND I HAD DEALT PLEASED SIR HUGO DRAX — AT FIRST . . .
BOND
♢ Queen, 8, 7, 6, 5, 4, 3, 2
♣ Ace, queen, 10, 8, 4
DRAX
♠ Ace, king, queen, knave
♡ Ace, king, queen, knave
♢ Ace, king
♣ King, knave, 9
MEYER
♠ 6, 5, 4, 3, 2
♡ 10, 9, 8, 7, 2
♢ Knave, 10, 9
BASILDON
♠ 10, 9, 8, 7
♡ 6, 5, 4, 3
♣ 7, 6, 5, 3, 2
BUT WITH CROSS-TRUMPING AND THE FINESSE I COULD NOT POSSIBLY BE DEPRIVED OF A GRAND SLAM
DRAX LOST £15,000 ON THAT HAND

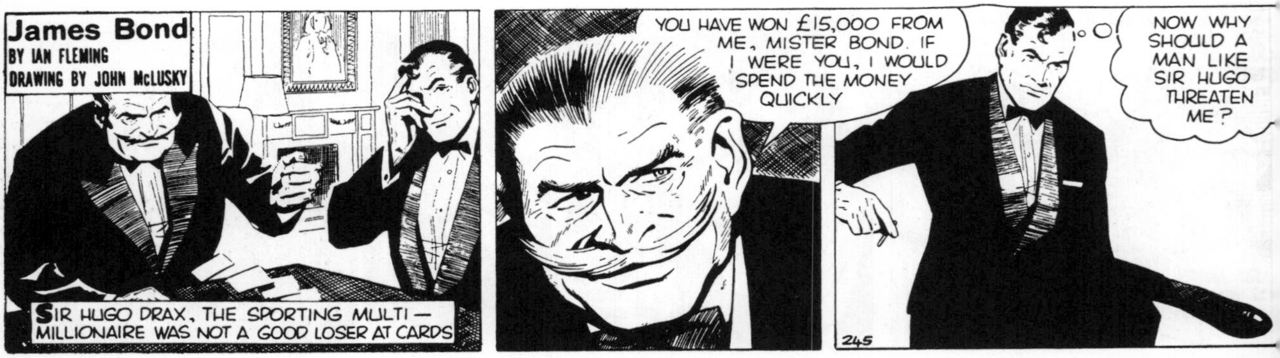
James Bond
BY IAN FLEMING
DRAWING BY JOHN McLUSKY
SIR HUGO DRAX, THE SPORTING MULTI—MILLIONAIRE WAS NOT A GOOD LOSER AT CARDS
YOU HAVE WON £15,000 FROM ME, MISTER BOND. IF I WERE YOU, I WOULD SPEND THE MONEY QUICKLY
NOW WHY SHOULD A MAN LIKE SIR HUGO THREATEN ME?
245

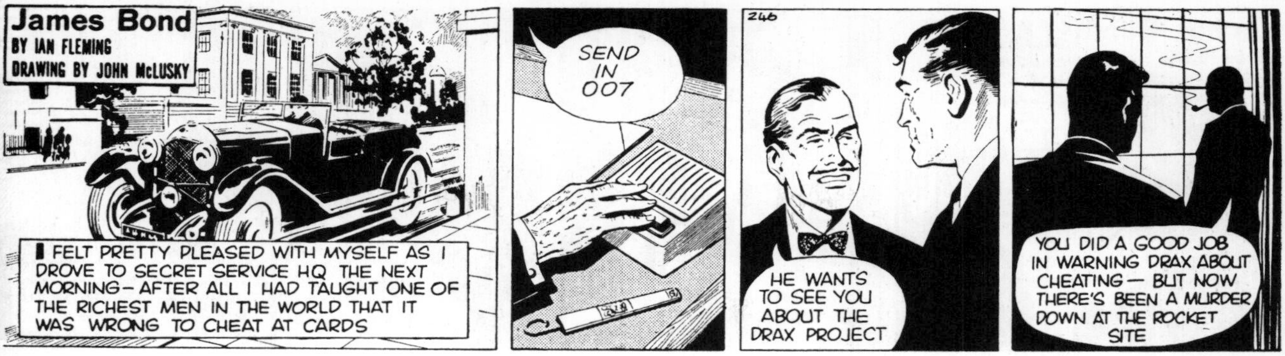
James Bond
BY IAN FLEMING
DRAWING BY JOHN McLUSKY
I FELT PRETTY PLEASED WITH MYSELF AS I DROVE TO SECRET SERVICE HQ THE NEXT MORNING — AFTER ALL I HAD TAUGHT ONE OF THE RICHEST MEN IN THE WORLD THAT IT WAS WRONG TO CHEAT AT CARDS
SEND IN 007
246
HE WANTS TO SEE YOU ABOUT THE DRAX PROJECT
YOU DID A GOOD JOB IN WARNING DRAX ABOUT CHEATING — BUT NOW THERE'S BEEN A MURDER DOWN AT THE ROCKET SITE

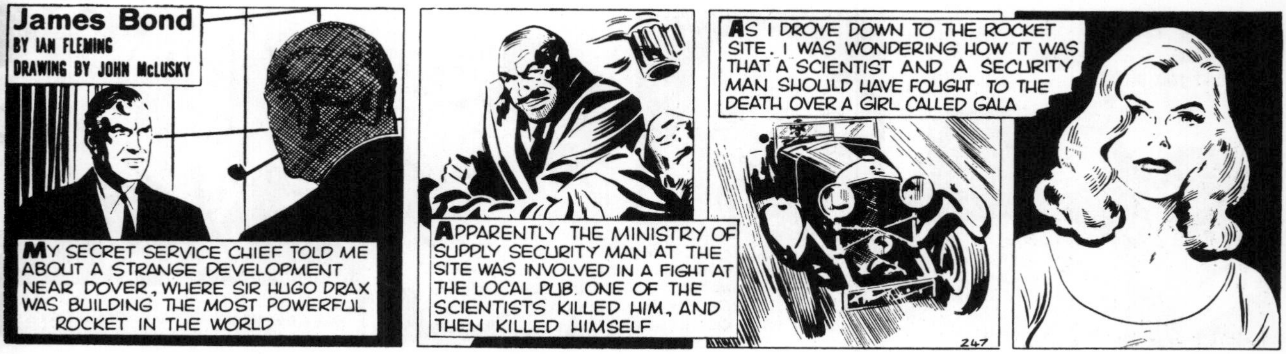
James Bond
BY IAN FLEMING
DRAWING BY JOHN McLUSKY
MY SECRET SERVICE CHIEF TOLD ME ABOUT A STRANGE DEVELOPMENT NEAR DOVER, WHERE SIR HUGO DRAX WAS BUILDING THE MOST POWERFUL ROCKET IN THE WORLD
APPARENTLY THE MINISTRY OF SUPPLY SECURITY MAN AT THE SITE WAS INVOLVED IN A FIGHT AT THE LOCAL PUB. ONE OF THE SCIENTISTS KILLED HIM, AND THEN KILLED HIMSELF
AS I DROVE DOWN TO THE ROCKET SITE, I WAS WONDERING HOW IT WAS THAT A SCIENTIST AND A SECURITY MAN SHOULD HAVE FOUGHT TO THE DEATH OVER A GIRL CALLED GALA
247

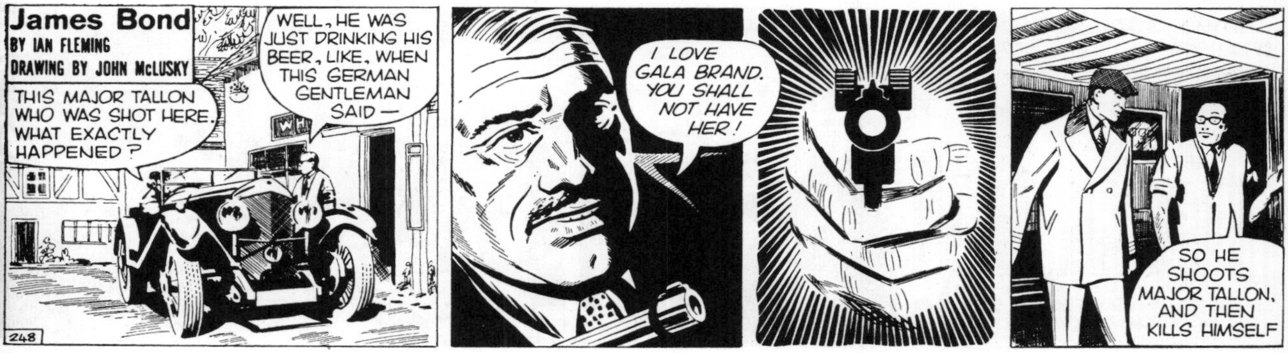
James Bond
BY IAN FLEMING
DRAWING BY JOHN McLUSKY
THIS MAJOR TALLON WHO WAS SHOT HERE. WHAT EXACTLY HAPPENED?
WELL, HE WAS JUST DRINKING HIS BEER, LIKE, WHEN THIS GERMAN GENTLEMAN SAID —
248
I LOVE GALA BRAND. YOU SHALL NOT HAVE HER!
SO HE SHOOTS MAJOR TALLON, AND THEN KILLS HIMSELF

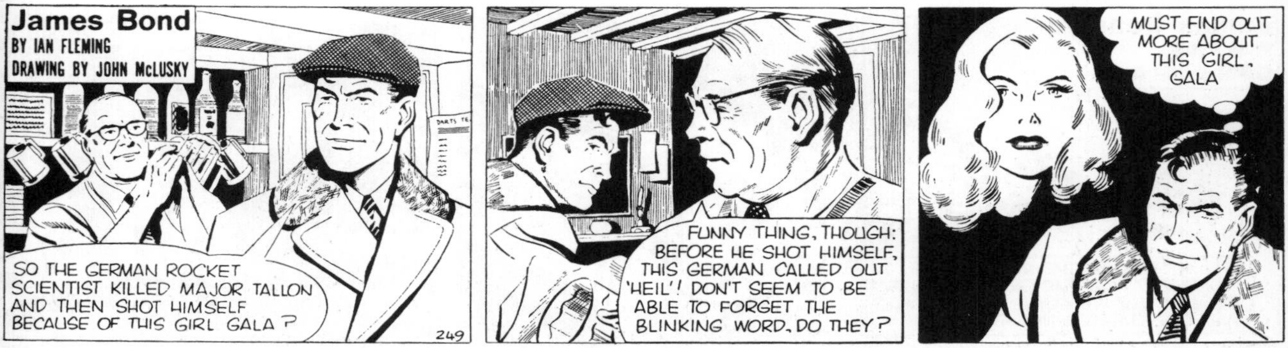
James Bond
BY IAN FLEMING
DRAWING BY JOHN McLUSKY
SO THE GERMAN ROCKET SCIENTIST KILLED MAJOR TALLON AND THEN SHOT HIMSELF BECAUSE OF THIS GIRL GALA?
249
FUNNY THING, THOUGH: BEFORE HE SHOT HIMSELF, THIS GERMAN CALLED OUT 'HEIL'! DON'T SEEM TO BE ABLE TO FORGET THE BLINKING WORD, DO THEY?
I MUST FIND OUT MORE ABOUT THIS GIRL, GALA

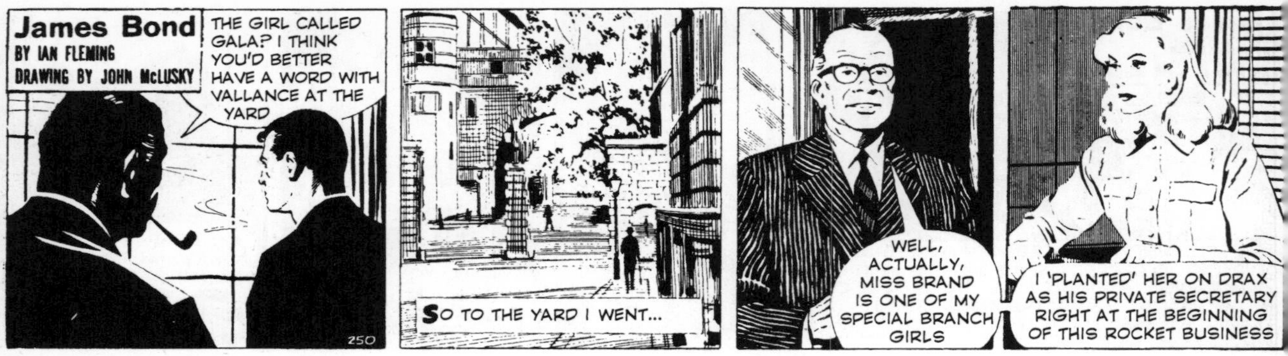
James Bond
BY IAN FLEMING
DRAWING BY JOHN McLUSKY
THE GIRL CALLED GALA? I THINK YOU'D BETTER HAVE A WORD WITH VALLANCE AT THE YARD
250
SO TO THE YARD I WENT...
WELL, ACTUALLY, MISS BRAND IS ONE OF MY SPECIAL BRANCH GIRLS
I 'PLANTED' HER ON DRAX AS HIS PRIVATE SECRETARY RIGHT AT THE BEGINNING OF THIS ROCKET BUSINESS

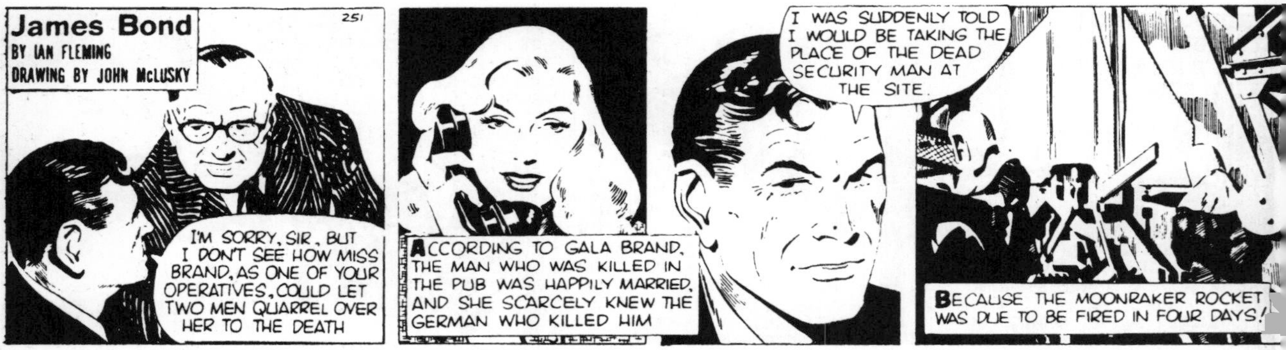
James Bond
BY IAN FLEMING
DRAWING BY JOHN McLUSKY
251
I'M SORRY, SIR, BUT I DON'T SEE HOW MISS BRAND, AS ONE OF YOUR OPERATIVES, COULD LET TWO MEN QUARREL OVER HER TO THE DEATH
ACCORDING TO GALA BRAND, THE MAN WHO WAS KILLED IN THE PUB WAS HAPPILY MARRIED, AND SHE SCARCELY KNEW THE GERMAN WHO KILLED HIM
I WAS SUDDENLY TOLD I WOULD BE TAKING THE PLACE OF THE DEAD SECURITY MAN AT THE SITE.
BECAUSE THE MOONRAKER ROCKET WAS DUE TO BE FIRED IN FOUR DAYS!

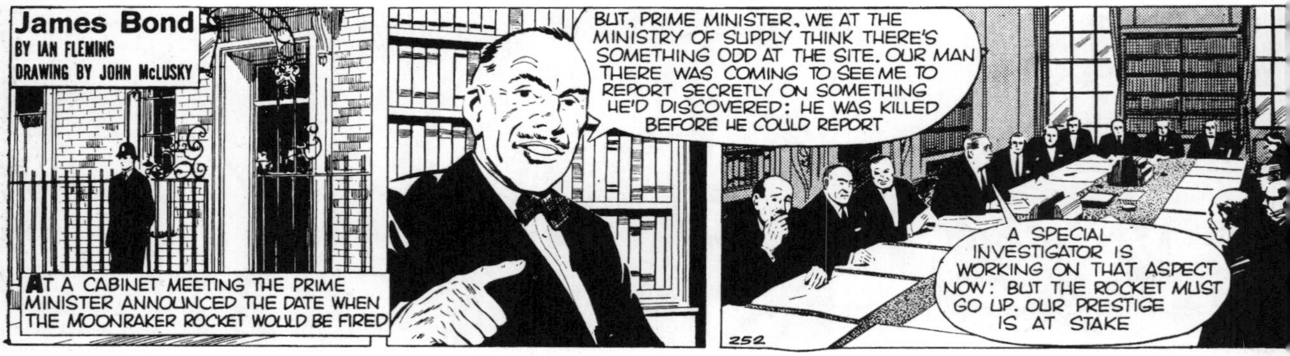
James Bond
BY IAN FLEMING
DRAWING BY JOHN McLUSKY
AT A CABINET MEETING THE PRIME MINISTER ANNOUNCED THE DATE WHEN THE MOONRAKER ROCKET WOULD BE FIRED
BUT, PRIME MINISTER, WE AT THE MINISTRY OF SUPPLY THINK THERE'S SOMETHING ODD AT THE SITE. OUR MAN THERE WAS COMING TO SEE ME TO REPORT SECRETLY ON SOMETHING HE'D DISCOVERED: HE WAS KILLED BEFORE HE COULD REPORT
A SPECIAL INVESTIGATOR IS WORKING ON THAT ASPECT NOW: BUT THE ROCKET MUST GO UP. OUR PRESTIGE IS AT STAKE
252

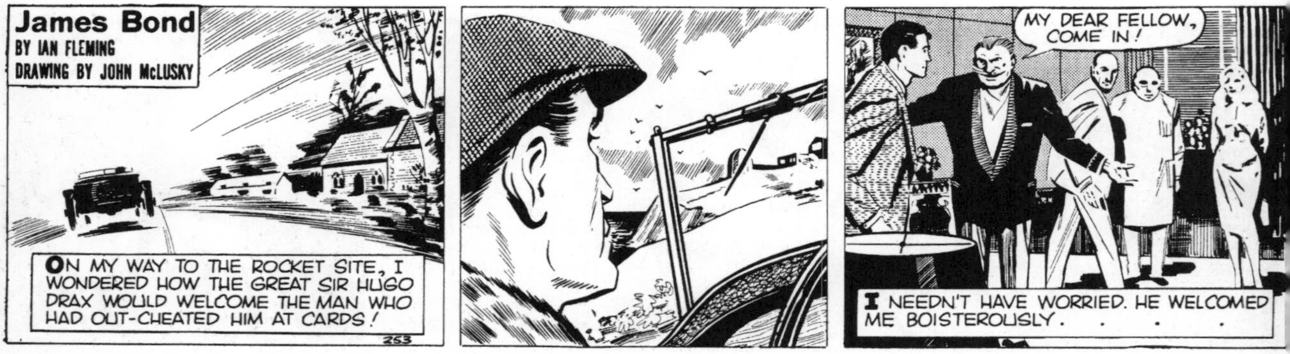
James Bond
BY IAN FLEMING
DRAWING BY JOHN McLUSKY
ON MY WAY TO THE ROCKET SITE, I WONDERED HOW THE GREAT SIR HUGO DRAX WOULD WELCOME THE MAN WHO HAD OUT-CHEATED HIM AT CARDS!
253
MY DEAR FELLOW, COME IN!
I NEEDN'T HAVE WORRIED. HE WELCOMED ME BOISTEROUSLY. . . .

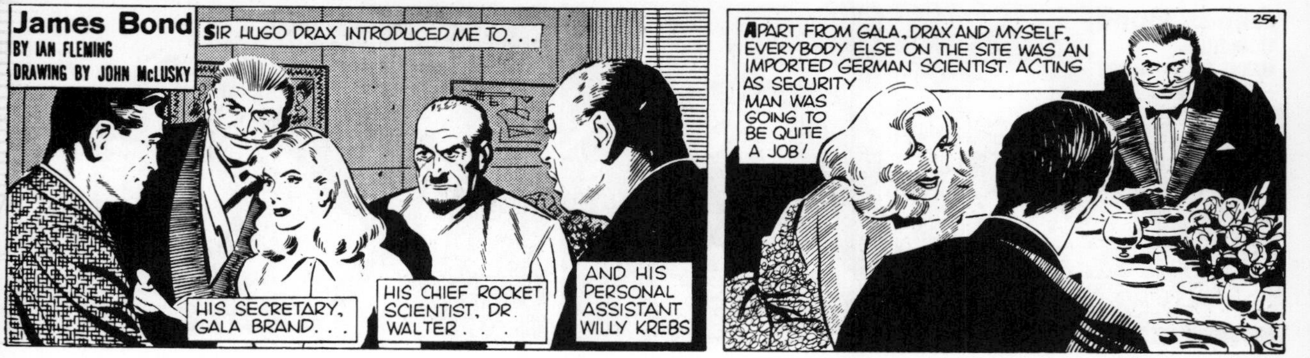
James Bond
BY IAN FLEMING
DRAWING BY JOHN McLUSKY
SIR HUGO DRAX INTRODUCED ME TO. . .
HIS SECRETARY, GALA BRAND. . .
HIS CHIEF ROCKET SCIENTIST, DR. WALTER . . .
AND HIS PERSONAL ASSISTANT WILLY KREBS
APART FROM GALA, DRAX AND MYSELF, EVERYBODY ELSE ON THE SITE WAS AN IMPORTED GERMAN SCIENTIST. ACTING AS SECURITY MAN WAS GOING TO BE QUITE A JOB!
254

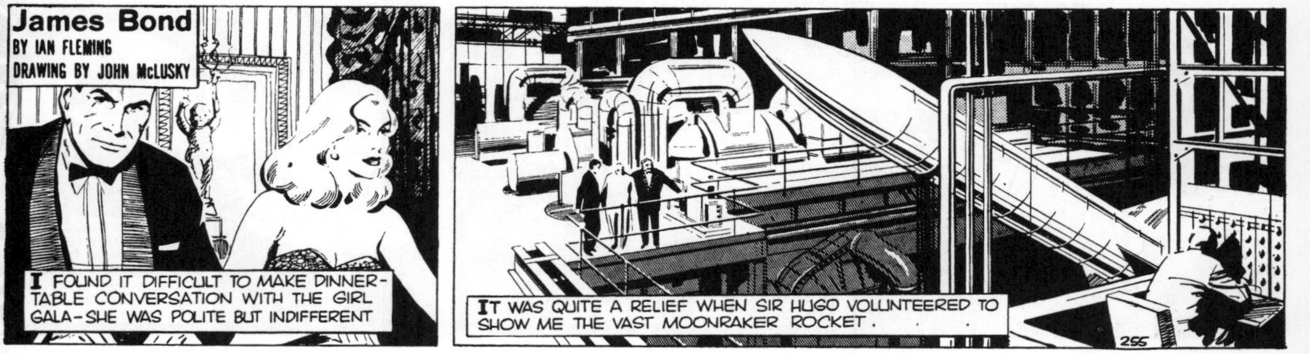
James Bond
BY IAN FLEMING
DRAWING BY JOHN McLUSKY
I FOUND IT DIFFICULT TO MAKE DINNER-TABLE CONVERSATION WITH THE GIRL GALA–SHE WAS POLITE BUT INDIFFERENT
IT WAS QUITE A RELIEF WHEN SIR HUGO VOLUNTEERED TO SHOW ME THE VAST MOONRAKER ROCKET . . .
255

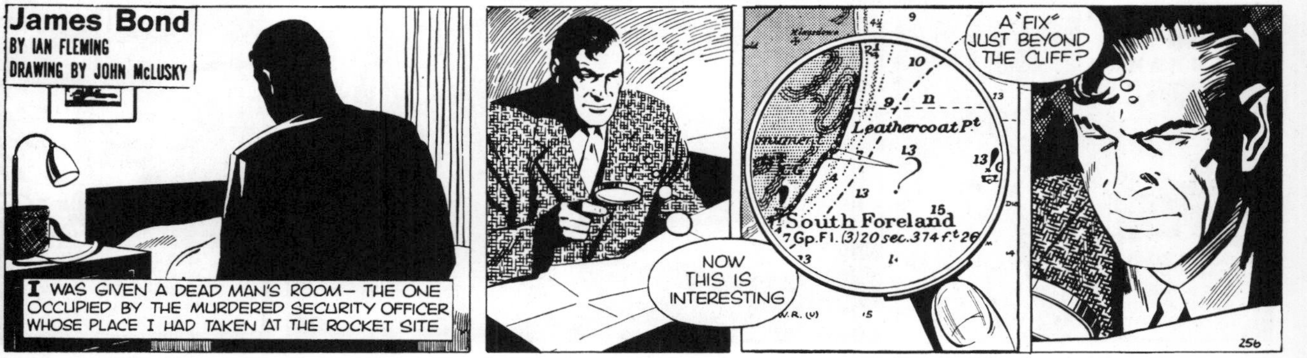
James Bond
BY IAN FLEMING
DRAWING BY JOHN McLUSKY
I WAS GIVEN A DEAD MAN'S ROOM– THE ONE OCCUPIED BY THE MURDERED SECURITY OFFICER WHOSE PLACE I HAD TAKEN AT THE ROCKET SITE
NOW THIS IS INTERESTING
Leathercoat Pt
South Foreland
A "FIX" JUST BEYOND THE CLIFF?
256

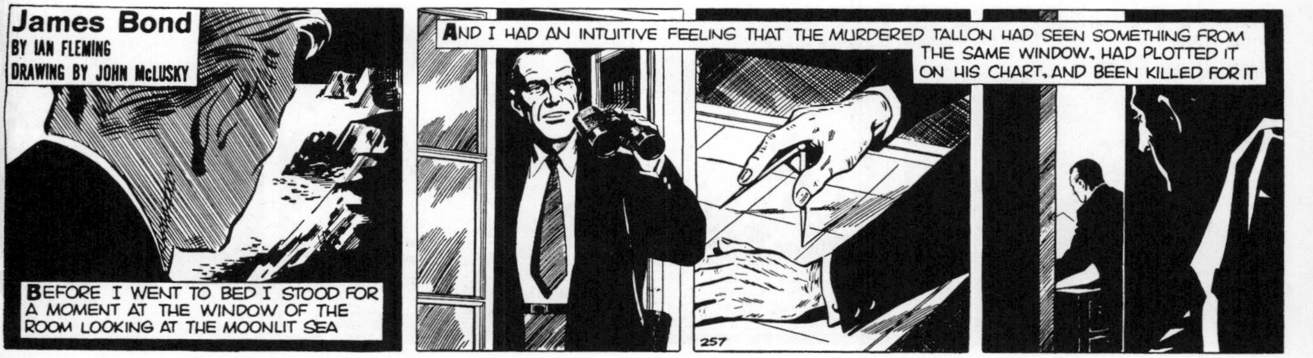
James Bond
BY IAN FLEMING
DRAWING BY JOHN McLUSKY
BEFORE I WENT TO BED I STOOD FOR A MOMENT AT THE WINDOW OF THE ROOM LOOKING AT THE MOONLIT SEA
AND I HAD AN INTUITIVE FEELING THAT THE MURDERED TALLON HAD SEEN SOMETHING FROM THE SAME WINDOW, HAD PLOTTED IT ON HIS CHART, AND BEEN KILLED FOR IT
257

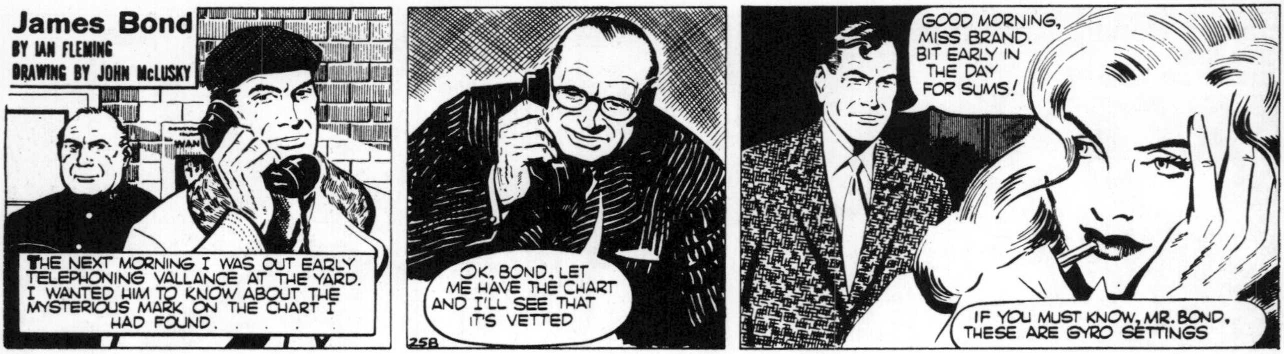
James Bond
BY IAN FLEMING
DRAWING BY JOHN McLUSKY
THE NEXT MORNING I WAS OUT EARLY TELEPHONING VALLANCE AT THE YARD. I WANTED HIM TO KNOW ABOUT THE MYSTERIOUS MARK ON THE CHART I HAD FOUND.
OK, BOND. LET ME HAVE THE CHART AND I'LL SEE THAT IT'S VETTED
258
GOOD MORNING, MISS BRAND. BIT EARLY IN THE DAY FOR SUMS!
IF YOU MUST KNOW, MR. BOND, THESE ARE GYRO SETTINGS

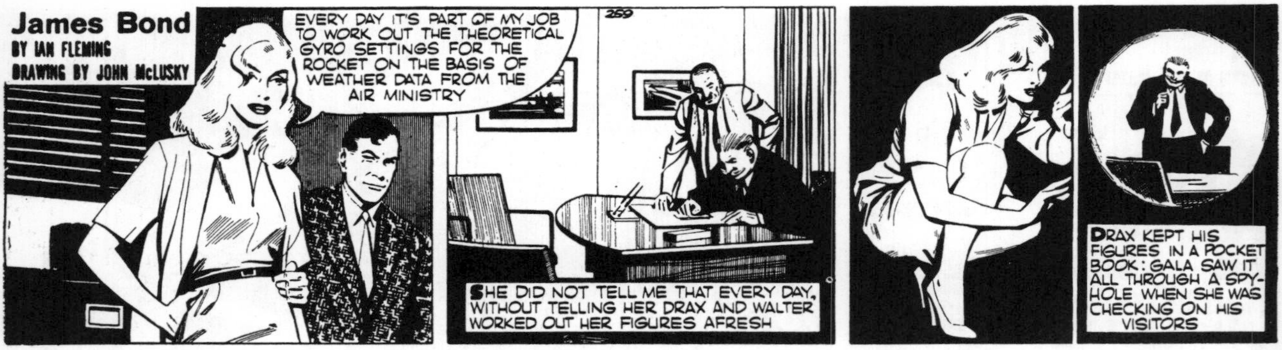
James Bond
BY IAN FLEMING
DRAWING BY JOHN McLUSKY
EVERY DAY IT'S PART OF MY JOB TO WORK OUT THE THEORETICAL GYRO SETTINGS FOR THE ROCKET ON THE BASIS OF WEATHER DATA FROM THE AIR MINISTRY
259
SHE DID NOT TELL ME THAT EVERY DAY, WITHOUT TELLING HER DRAX AND WALTER WORKED OUT HER FIGURES AFRESH
DRAX KEPT HIS FIGURES IN A POCKET BOOK: GALA SAW IT ALL THROUGH A SPY-HOLE WHEN SHE WAS CHECKING ON HIS VISITORS

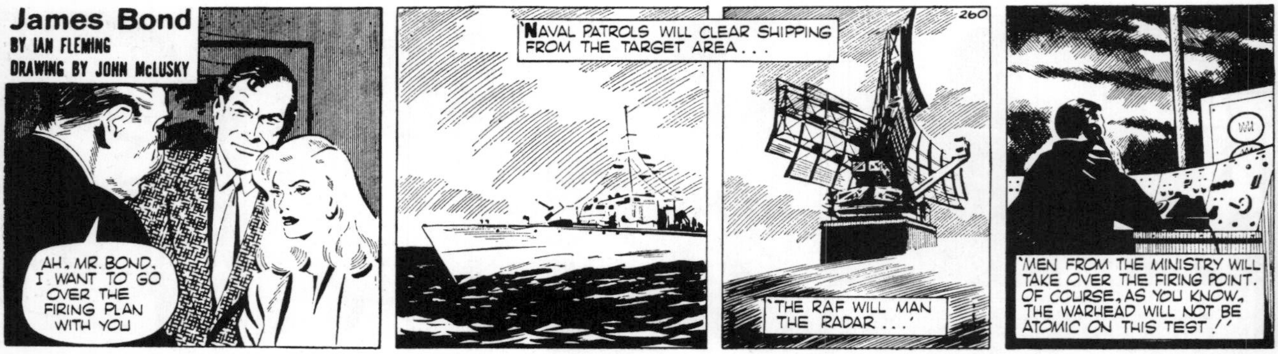
James Bond
BY IAN FLEMING
DRAWING BY JOHN McLUSKY
AH, MR. BOND. I WANT TO GO OVER THE FIRING PLAN WITH YOU
'NAVAL PATROLS WILL CLEAR SHIPPING FROM THE TARGET AREA . . .
260
'THE RAF WILL MAN THE RADAR . . .'
'MEN FROM THE MINISTRY WILL TAKE OVER THE FIRING POINT. OF COURSE, AS YOU KNOW, THE WARHEAD WILL NOT BE ATOMIC ON THIS TEST!'

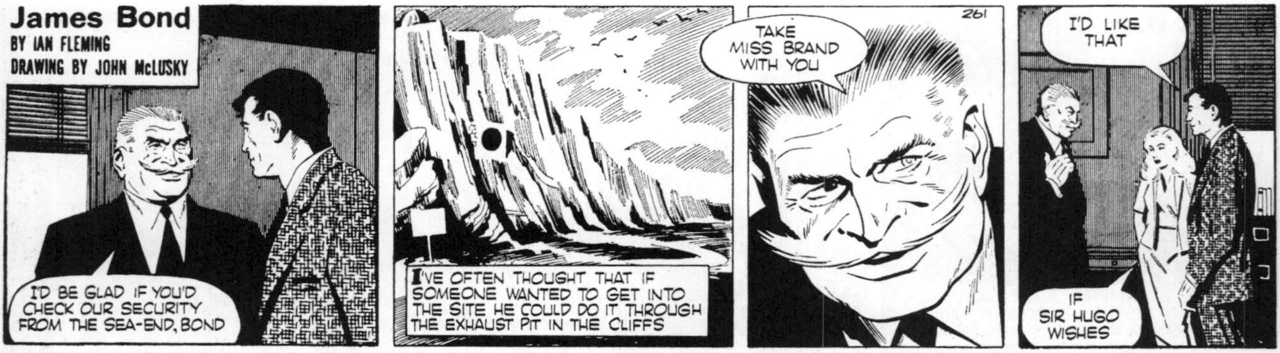
James Bond
BY IAN FLEMING
DRAWING BY JOHN McLUSKY
I'D BE GLAD IF YOU'D CHECK OUR SECURITY FROM THE SEA-END, BOND
I'VE OFTEN THOUGHT THAT IF SOMEONE WANTED TO GET INTO THE SITE HE COULD DO IT THROUGH THE EXHAUST PIT IN THE CLIFFS
261
TAKE MISS BRAND WITH YOU
I'D LIKE THAT
IF SIR HUGO WISHES

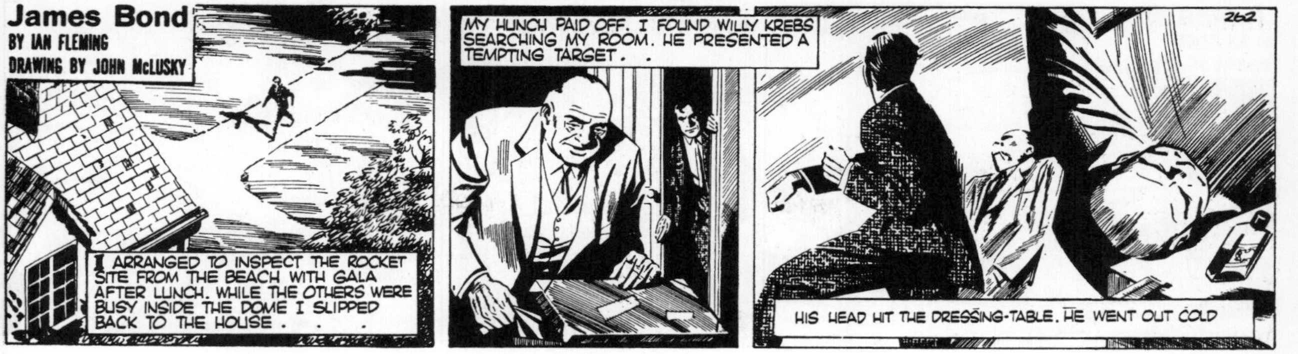
James Bond
BY IAN FLEMING
DRAWING BY JOHN McLUSKY
I ARRANGED TO INSPECT THE ROCKET SITE FROM THE BEACH WITH GALA AFTER LUNCH. WHILE THE OTHERS WERE BUSY INSIDE THE DOME I SLIPPED BACK TO THE HOUSE . . .
MY HUNCH PAID OFF. I FOUND WILLY KREBS SEARCHING MY ROOM. HE PRESENTED A TEMPTING TARGET . .
262
HIS HEAD HIT THE DRESSING-TABLE. HE WENT OUT COLD

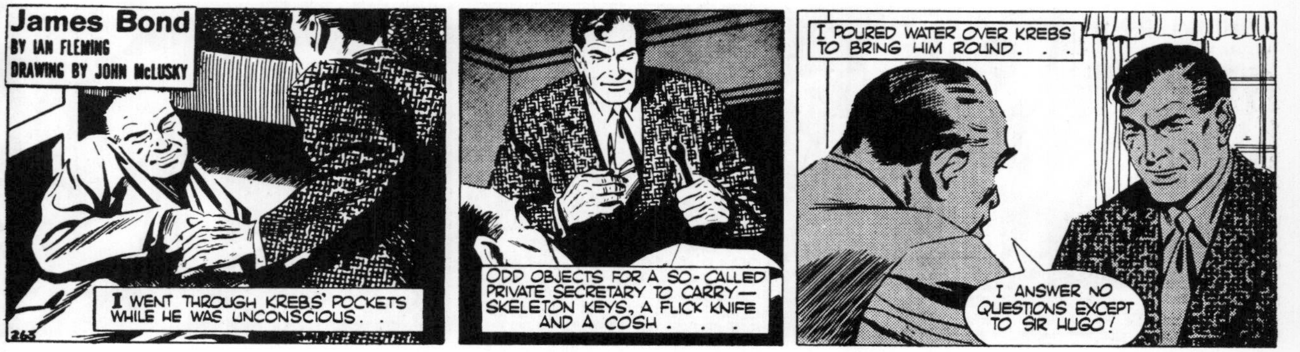
James Bond
BY IAN FLEMING
DRAWING BY JOHN McLUSKY
I WENT THROUGH KREBS' POCKETS WHILE HE WAS UNCONSCIOUS . .
263
ODD OBJECTS FOR A SO-CALLED PRIVATE SECRETARY TO CARRY— SKELETON KEYS, A FLICK KNIFE AND A COSH . . .
I POURED WATER OVER KREBS TO BRING HIM ROUND . . .
I ANSWER NO QUESTIONS EXCEPT TO SIR HUGO!

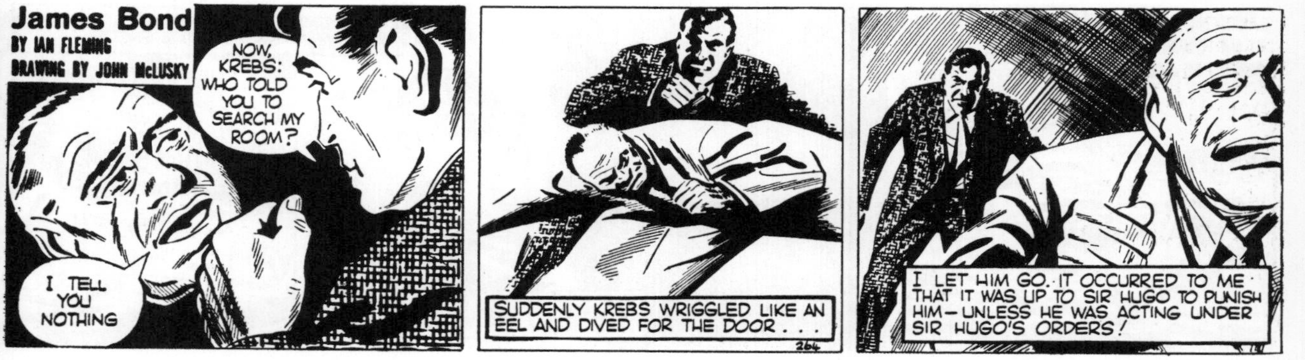
James Bond
BY IAN FLEMING
DRAWING BY JOHN McLUSKY
NOW, KREBS: WHO TOLD YOU TO SEARCH MY ROOM?
I TELL YOU NOTHING
SUDDENLY KREBS WRIGGLED LIKE AN EEL AND DIVED FOR THE DOOR . . .
264
I LET HIM GO. IT OCCURRED TO ME THAT IT WAS UP TO SIR HUGO TO PUNISH HIM—UNLESS HE WAS ACTING UNDER SIR HUGO'S ORDERS!

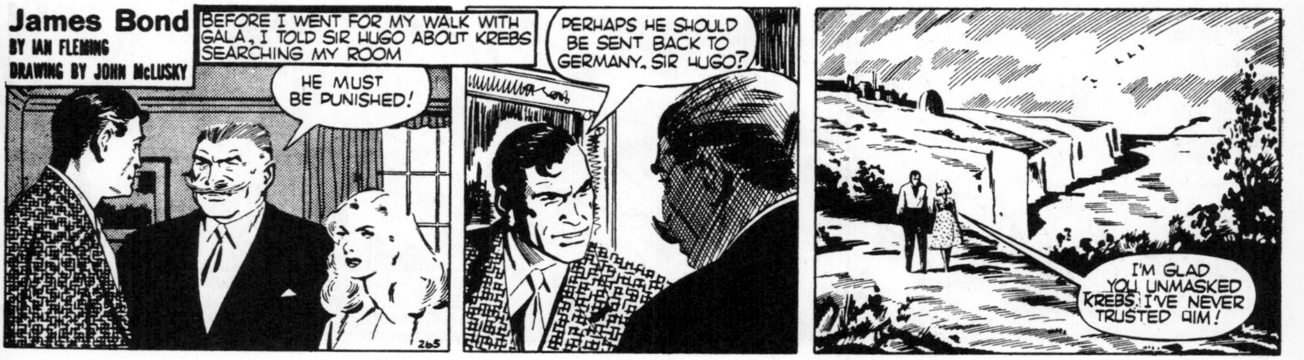
James Bond
BY IAN FLEMING
DRAWING BY JOHN McLUSKY
BEFORE I WENT FOR MY WALK WITH GALA, I TOLD SIR HUGO ABOUT KREBS SEARCHING MY ROOM
HE MUST BE PUNISHED!
PERHAPS HE SHOULD BE SENT BACK TO GERMANY, SIR HUGO?
265
I'M GLAD YOU UNMASKED KREBS. I'VE NEVER TRUSTED HIM!

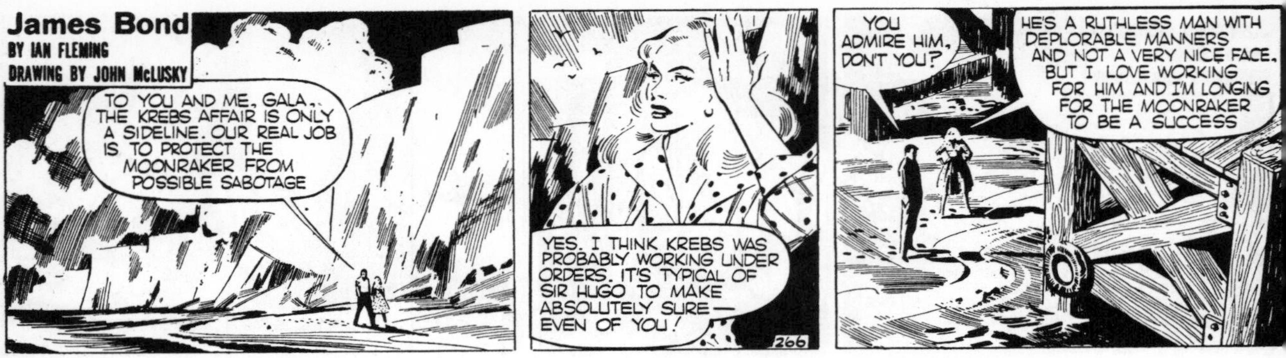
James Bond
BY IAN FLEMING
DRAWING BY JOHN McLUSKY
TO YOU AND ME, GALA, THE KREBS AFFAIR IS ONLY A SIDELINE. OUR REAL JOB IS TO PROTECT THE MOONRAKER FROM POSSIBLE SABOTAGE
YES. I THINK KREBS WAS PROBABLY WORKING UNDER ORDERS. IT'S TYPICAL OF SIR HUGO TO MAKE ABSOLUTELY SURE— EVEN OF YOU!
266
YOU ADMIRE HIM, DON'T YOU?
HE'S A RUTHLESS MAN WITH DEPLORABLE MANNERS AND NOT A VERY NICE FACE. BUT I LOVE WORKING FOR HIM AND I'M LONGING FOR THE MOONRAKER TO BE A SUCCESS

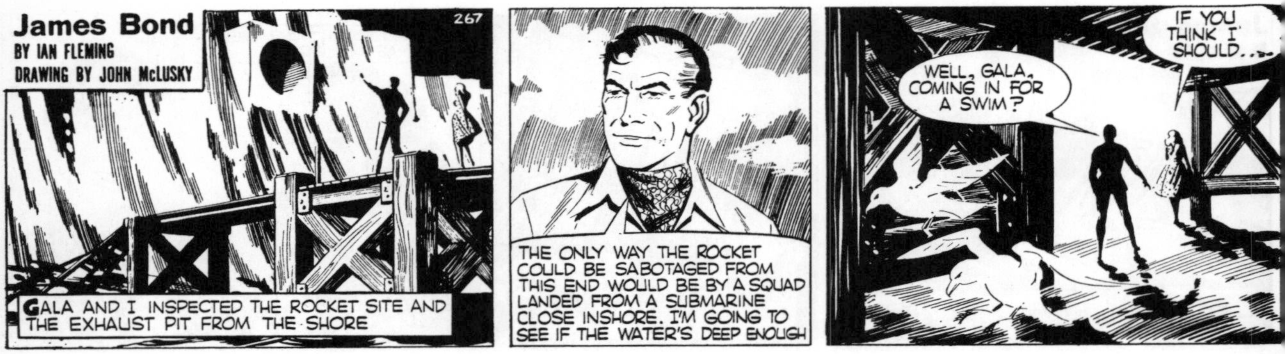
James Bond
BY IAN FLEMING
DRAWING BY JOHN McLUSKY
267
GALA AND I INSPECTED THE ROCKET SITE AND THE EXHAUST PIT FROM THE SHORE
THE ONLY WAY THE ROCKET COULD BE SABOTAGED FROM THIS END WOULD BE BY A SQUAD LANDED FROM A SUBMARINE CLOSE INSHORE. I'M GOING TO SEE IF THE WATER'S DEEP ENOUGH
WELL, GALA, COMING IN FOR A SWIM?
IF YOU THINK I SHOULD...

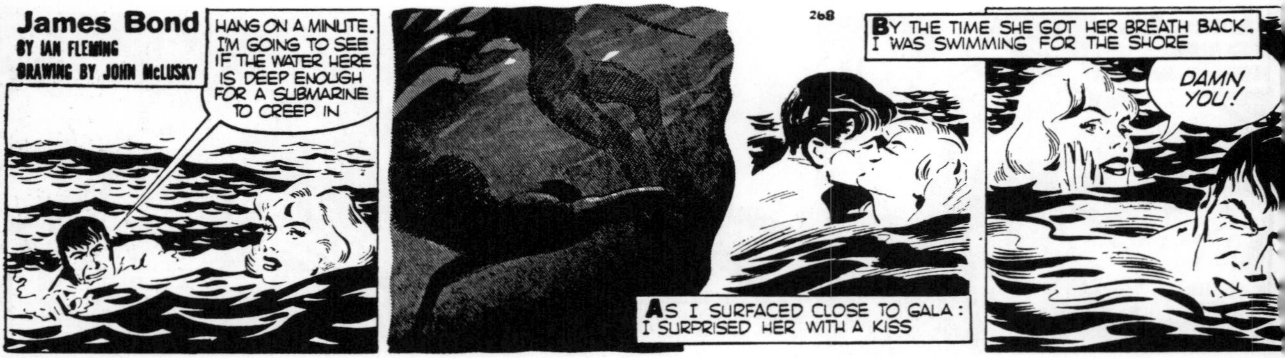
James Bond
BY IAN FLEMING
DRAWING BY JOHN McLUSKY
HANG ON A MINUTE. I'M GOING TO SEE IF THE WATER HERE IS DEEP ENOUGH FOR A SUBMARINE TO CREEP IN
268
AS I SURFACED CLOSE TO GALA: I SURPRISED HER WITH A KISS
BY THE TIME SHE GOT HER BREATH BACK. I WAS SWIMMING FOR THE SHORE
DAMN YOU!

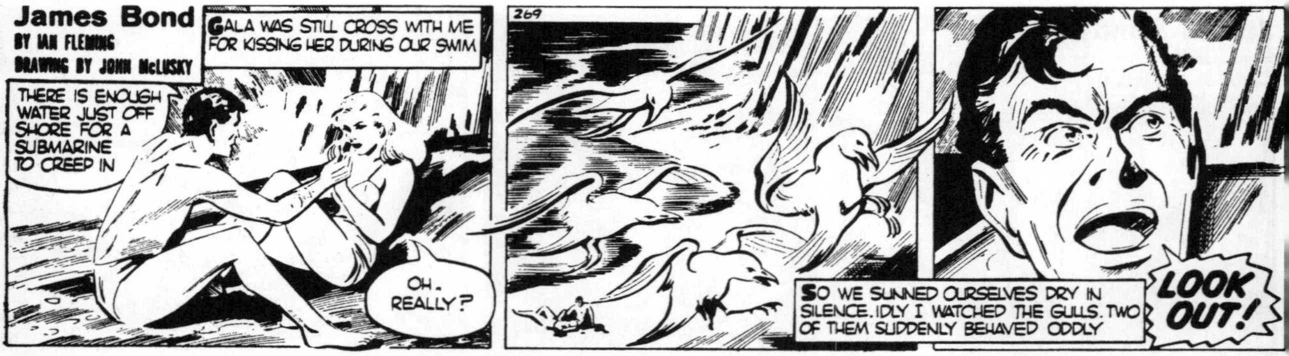
James Bond
BY IAN FLEMING
DRAWING BY JOHN McLUSKY
GALA WAS STILL CROSS WITH ME FOR KISSING HER DURING OUR SWIM
THERE IS ENOUGH WATER JUST OFF SHORE FOR A SUBMARINE TO CREEP IN
OH. REALLY?
269
SO WE SUNNED OURSELVES DRY IN SILENCE. IDLY I WATCHED THE GULLS. TWO OF THEM SUDDENLY BEHAVED ODDLY
LOOK OUT!

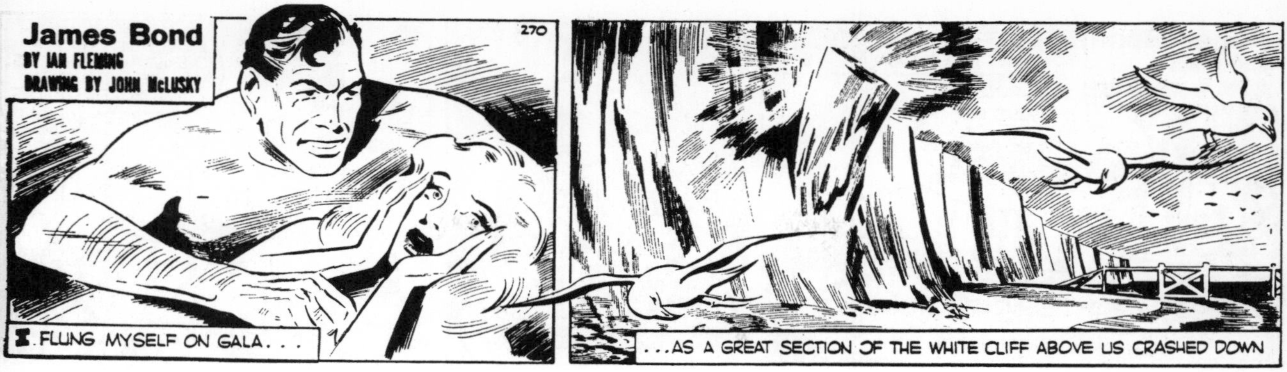
James Bond
BY IAN FLEMING
DRAWING BY JOHN McLUSKY
270
I. FLUNG MYSELF ON GALA . . .
. . . AS A GREAT SECTION OF THE WHITE CLIFF ABOVE US CRASHED DOWN

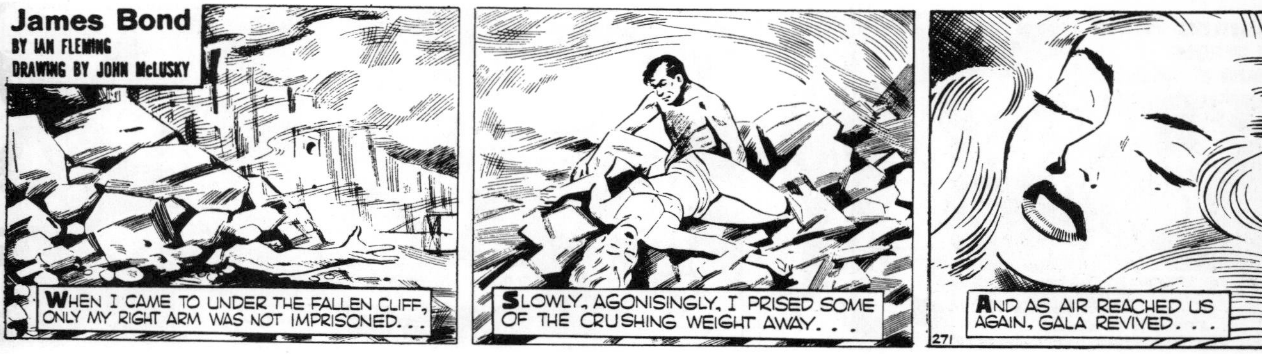
James Bond
BY IAN FLEMING
DRAWING BY JOHN McLUSKY
WHEN I CAME TO UNDER THE FALLEN CLIFF, ONLY MY RIGHT ARM WAS NOT IMPRISONED . . .
SLOWLY, AGONISINGLY, I PRISED SOME OF THE CRUSHING WEIGHT AWAY . . .
AND AS AIR REACHED US AGAIN, GALA REVIVED . . .
271

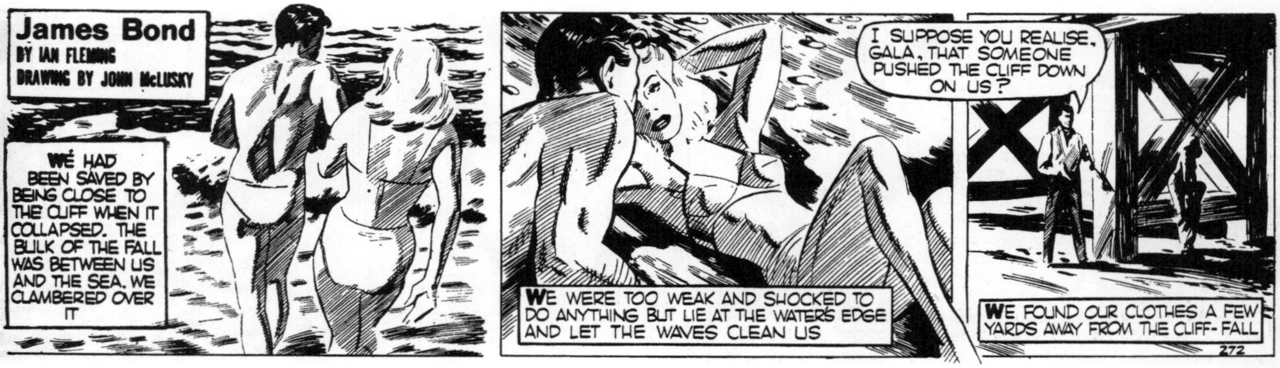
James Bond
BY IAN FLEMING
DRAWING BY JOHN McLUSKY
WE HAD BEEN SAVED BY BEING CLOSE TO THE CLIFF WHEN IT COLLAPSED. THE BULK OF THE FALL WAS BETWEEN US AND THE SEA. WE CLAMBERED OVER IT
WE WERE TOO WEAK AND SHOCKED TO DO ANYTHING BUT LIE AT THE WATER'S EDGE AND LET THE WAVES CLEAN US
I SUPPOSE YOU REALISE, GALA, THAT SOMEONE PUSHED THE CLIFF DOWN ON US?
WE FOUND OUR CLOTHES A FEW YARDS AWAY FROM THE CLIFF-FALL
272

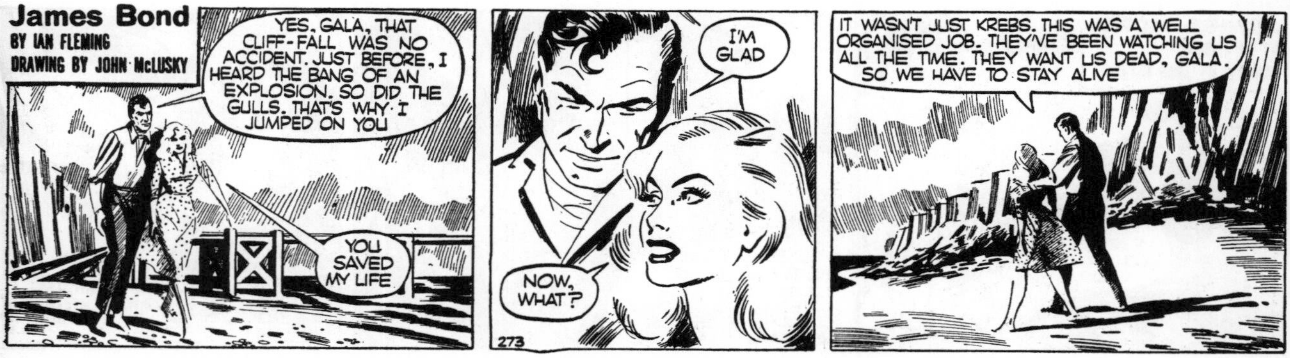
James Bond
BY IAN FLEMING
DRAWING BY JOHN McLUSKY
YES, GALA, THAT CLIFF-FALL WAS NO ACCIDENT. JUST BEFORE, I HEARD THE BANG OF AN EXPLOSION. SO DID THE GULLS. THAT'S WHY I JUMPED ON YOU
YOU SAVED MY LIFE
I'M GLAD
NOW, WHAT?
273
IT WASN'T JUST KREBS. THIS WAS A WELL ORGANISED JOB. THEY'VE BEEN WATCHING US ALL THE TIME. THEY WANT US DEAD, GALA. SO WE HAVE TO STAY ALIVE

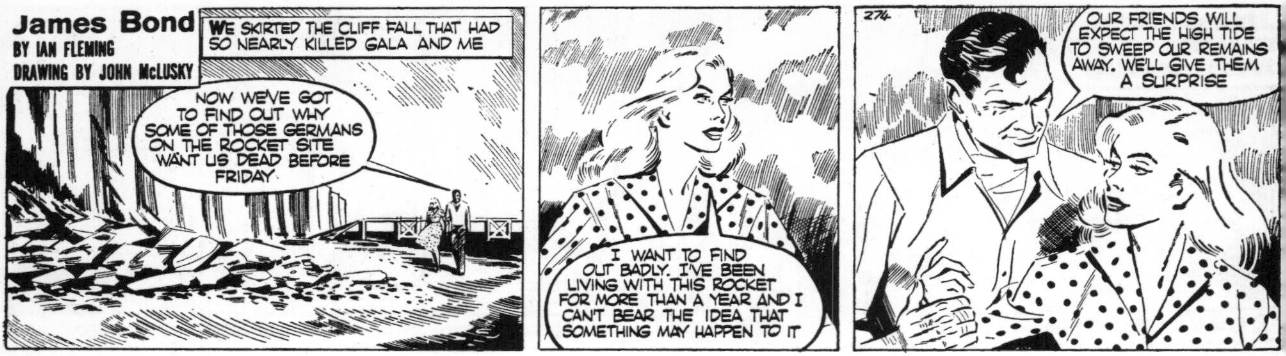
James Bond
BY IAN FLEMING
DRAWING BY JOHN McLUSKY
WE SKIRTED THE CLIFF FALL THAT HAD SO NEARLY KILLED GALA AND ME
NOW WE'VE GOT TO FIND OUT WHY SOME OF THOSE GERMANS ON THE ROCKET SITE WANT US DEAD BEFORE FRIDAY
I WANT TO FIND OUT BADLY. I'VE BEEN LIVING WITH THIS ROCKET FOR MORE THAN A YEAR AND I CAN'T BEAR THE IDEA THAT SOMETHING MAY HAPPEN TO IT
274
OUR FRIENDS WILL EXPECT THE HIGH TIDE TO SWEEP OUR REMAINS AWAY. WE'LL GIVE THEM A SURPRISE

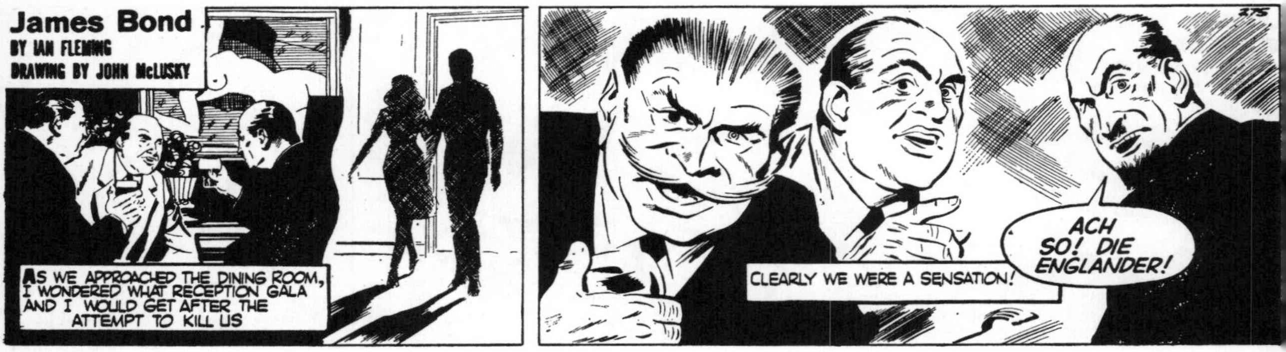
James Bond
BY IAN FLEMING
DRAWING BY JOHN McLUSKY
AS WE APPROACHED THE DINING ROOM, I WONDERED WHAT RECEPTION GALA AND I WOULD GET AFTER THE ATTEMPT TO KILL US
275
CLEARLY WE WERE A SENSATION!
ACH SO! DIE ENGLANDER!

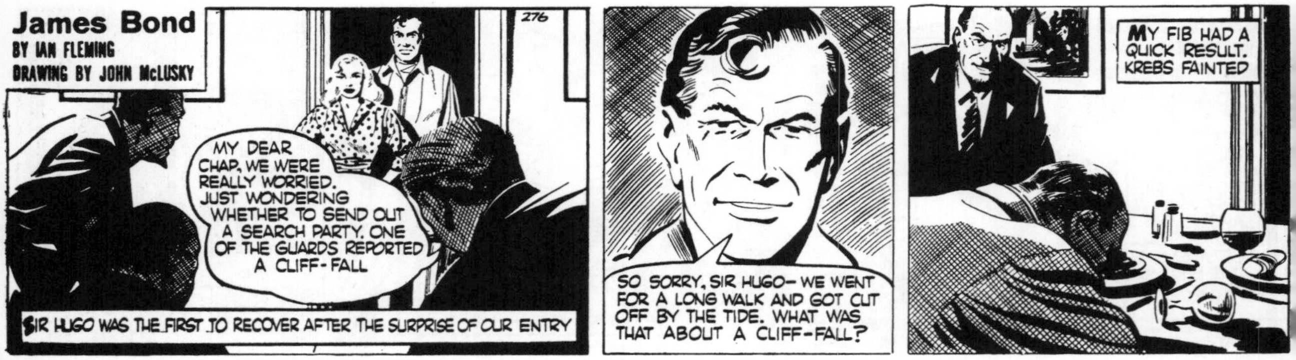
James Bond
BY IAN FLEMING
DRAWING BY JOHN McLUSKY
276
SIR HUGO WAS THE FIRST TO RECOVER AFTER THE SURPRISE OF OUR ENTRY
MY DEAR CHAP, WE WERE REALLY WORRIED. JUST WONDERING WHETHER TO SEND OUT A SEARCH PARTY. ONE OF THE GUARDS REPORTED A CLIFF-FALL
SO SORRY, SIR HUGO– WE WENT FOR A LONG WALK AND GOT CUT OFF BY THE TIDE. WHAT WAS THAT ABOUT A CLIFF-FALL?
MY FIB HAD A QUICK RESULT. KREBS FAINTED

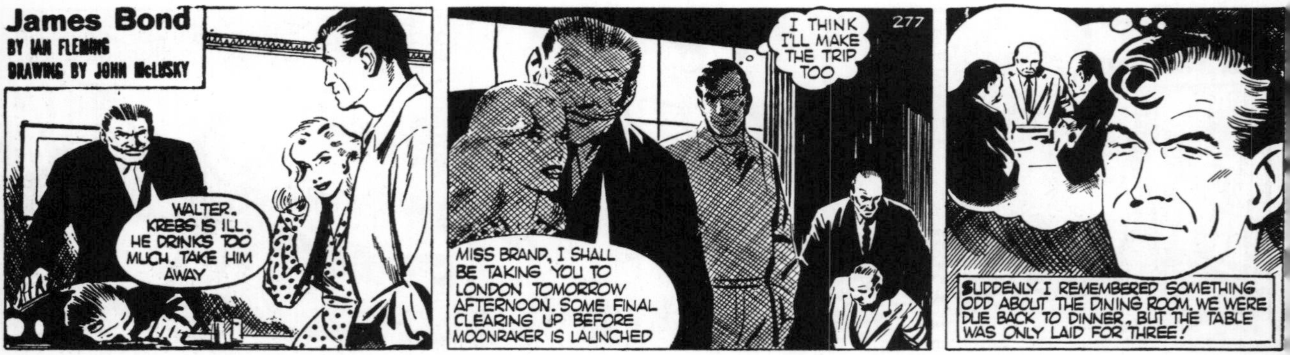
James Bond
BY IAN FLEMING
DRAWING BY JOHN McLUSKY
WALTER. KREBS IS ILL. HE DRINKS TOO MUCH. TAKE HIM AWAY
277
MISS BRAND, I SHALL BE TAKING YOU TO LONDON TOMORROW AFTERNOON. SOME FINAL CLEARING UP BEFORE MOONRAKER IS LAUNCHED
I THINK I'LL MAKE THE TRIP TOO
SUDDENLY I REMEMBERED SOMETHING ODD ABOUT THE DINING ROOM. WE WERE DUE BACK TO DINNER, BUT THE TABLE WAS ONLY LAID FOR THREE!

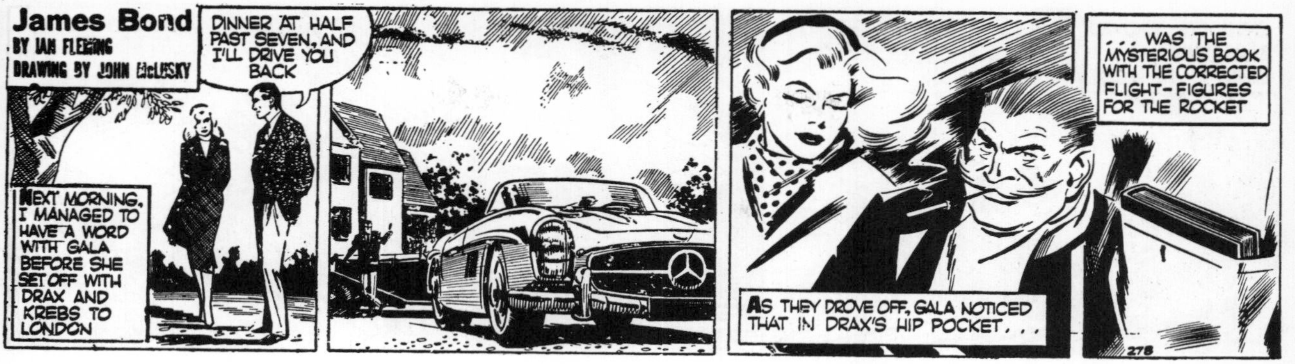
James Bond
BY IAN FLEMING
DRAWING BY JOHN McLUSKY
NEXT MORNING, I MANAGED TO HAVE A WORD WITH GALA BEFORE SHE SET OFF WITH DRAX AND KREBS TO LONDON
DINNER AT HALF PAST SEVEN, AND I'LL DRIVE YOU BACK
AS THEY DROVE OFF, GALA NOTICED THAT IN DRAX'S HIP POCKET . . .
. . . WAS THE MYSTERIOUS BOOK WITH THE CORRECTED FLIGHT-FIGURES FOR THE ROCKET
278

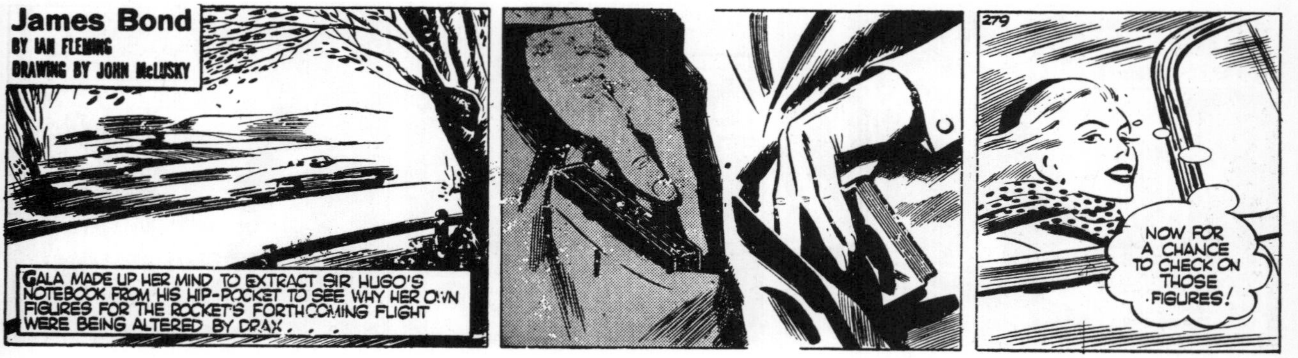
James Bond
BY IAN FLEMING
DRAWING BY JOHN McLUSKY
GALA MADE UP HER MIND TO EXTRACT SIR HUGO'S NOTEBOOK FROM HIS HIP-POCKET TO SEE WHY HER OWN FIGURES FOR THE ROCKET'S FORTHCOMING FLIGHT WERE BEING ALTERED BY DRAX . . .
279
NOW FOR A CHANCE TO CHECK ON THOSE FIGURES!

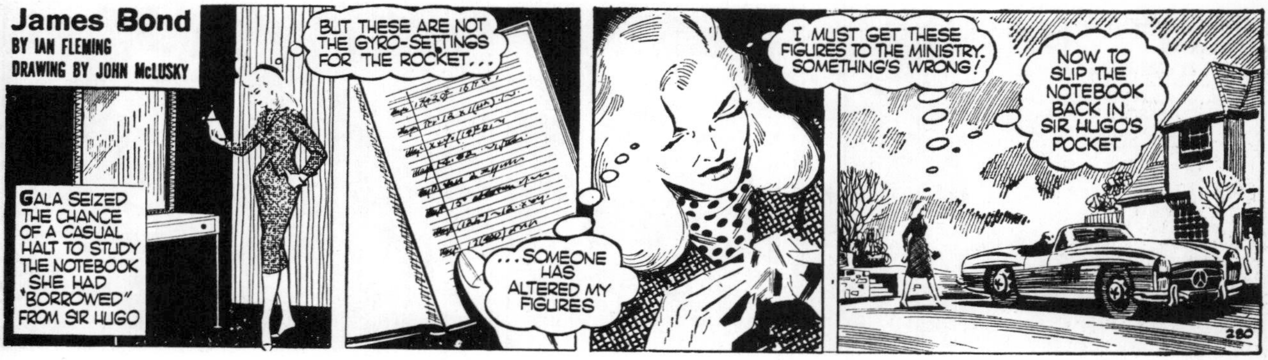
James Bond
BY IAN FLEMING
DRAWING BY JOHN McLUSKY
GALA SEIZED THE CHANCE OF A CASUAL HALT TO STUDY THE NOTEBOOK SHE HAD "BORROWED" FROM SIR HUGO
BUT THESE ARE NOT THE GYRO-SETTINGS FOR THE ROCKET . . .
. . . SOMEONE HAS ALTERED MY FIGURES
I MUST GET THESE FIGURES TO THE MINISTRY. SOMETHING'S WRONG!
NOW TO SLIP THE NOTEBOOK BACK IN SIR HUGO'S POCKET
280

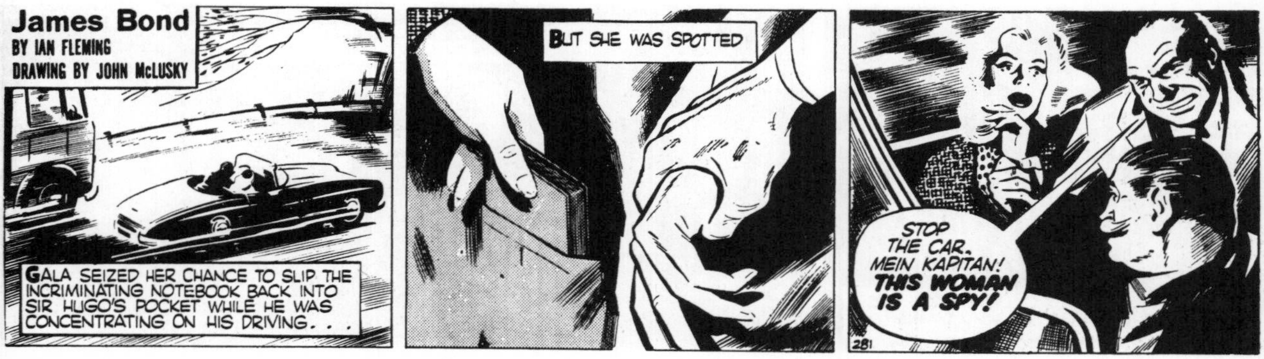
James Bond
BY IAN FLEMING
DRAWING BY JOHN McLUSKY
GALA SEIZED HER CHANCE TO SLIP THE INCRIMINATING NOTEBOOK BACK INTO SIR HUGO'S POCKET WHILE HE WAS CONCENTRATING ON HIS DRIVING . . .
BUT SHE WAS SPOTTED
STOP THE CAR, MEIN KAPITAN! THIS WOMAN IS A SPY!
281

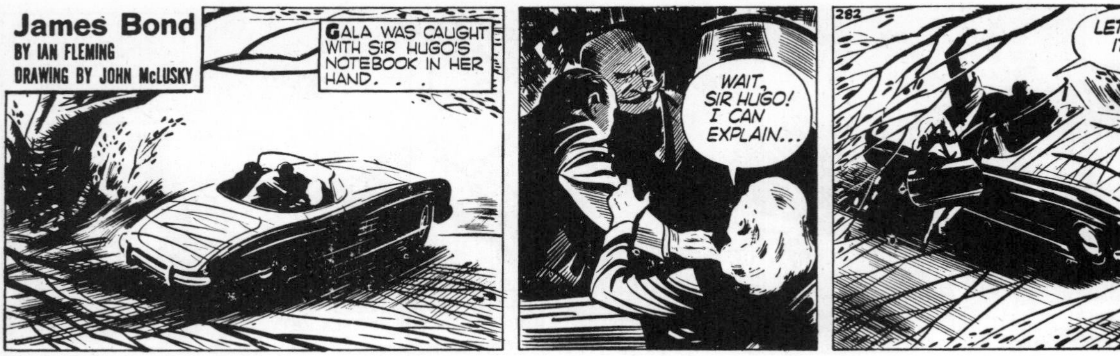
James Bond
BY IAN FLEMING
DRAWING BY JOHN McLUSKY
GALA WAS CAUGHT WITH SIR HUGO'S NOTEBOOK IN HER HAND . . .
282
WAIT, SIR HUGO! I CAN EXPLAIN...
LET HER HAVE IT, KREBS!

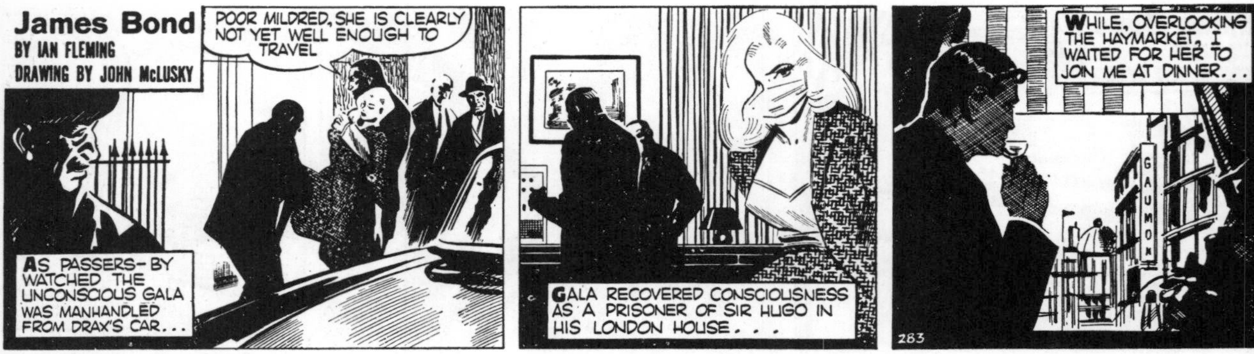
James Bond
BY IAN FLEMING
DRAWING BY JOHN McLUSKY
POOR MILDRED, SHE IS CLEARLY NOT YET WELL ENOUGH TO TRAVEL
AS PASSERS-BY WATCHED THE UNCONSCIOUS GALA WAS MANHANDLED FROM DRAX'S CAR...
GALA RECOVERED CONSCIOUSNESS AS A PRISONER OF SIR HUGO IN HIS LONDON HOUSE . . .
WHILE, OVERLOOKING THE HAYMARKET, I WAITED FOR HER TO JOIN ME AT DINNER...
GAUMON
283

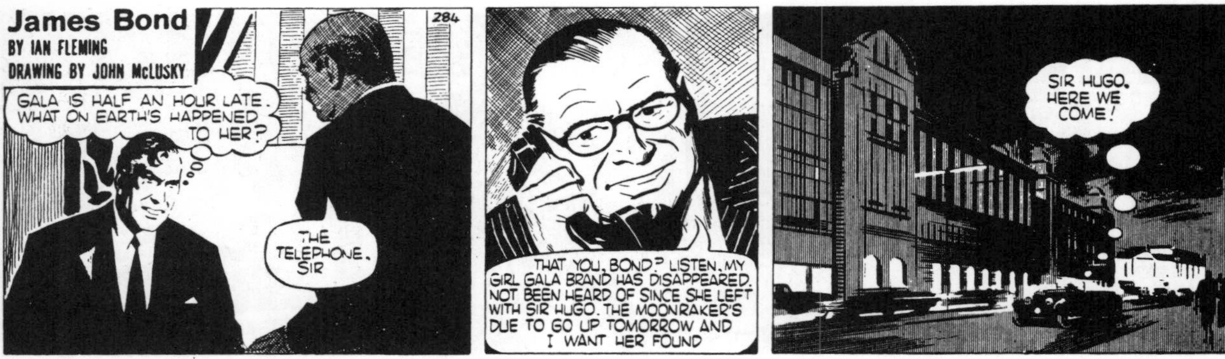
James Bond
BY IAN FLEMING
DRAWING BY JOHN McLUSKY
284
GALA IS HALF AN HOUR LATE. WHAT ON EARTH'S HAPPENED TO HER?
THE TELEPHONE, SIR
THAT YOU, BOND? LISTEN. MY GIRL GALA BRAND HAS DISAPPEARED. NOT BEEN HEARD OF SINCE SHE LEFT WITH SIR HUGO. THE MOONRAKER'S DUE TO GO UP TOMORROW AND I WANT HER FOUND
SIR HUGO. HERE WE COME!

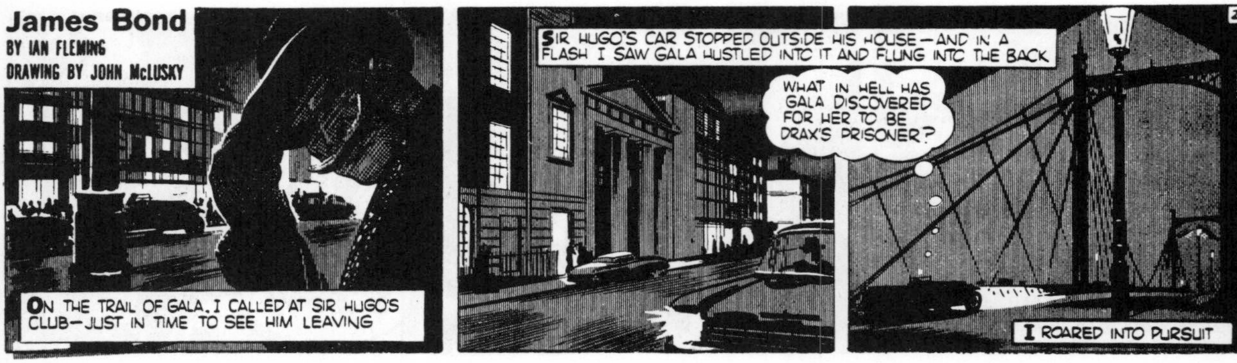
James Bond
BY IAN FLEMING
DRAWING BY JOHN McLUSKY
ON THE TRAIL OF GALA, I CALLED AT SIR HUGO'S CLUB—JUST IN TIME TO SEE HIM LEAVING
285
SIR HUGO'S CAR STOPPED OUTSIDE HIS HOUSE—AND IN A FLASH I SAW GALA HUSTLED INTO IT AND FLUNG INTO THE BACK
WHAT IN HELL HAS GALA DISCOVERED FOR HER TO BE DRAX'S PRISONER?
I ROARED INTO PURSUIT

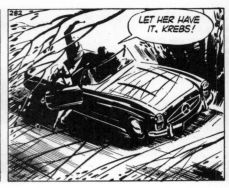

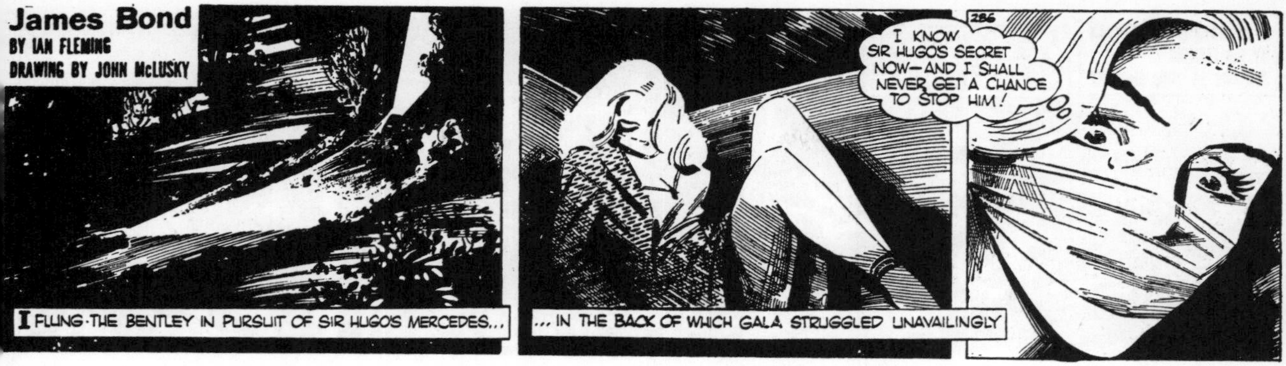
James Bond
BY IAN FLEMING
DRAWING BY JOHN McLUSKY
I FLUNG THE BENTLEY IN PURSUIT OF SIR HUGO'S MERCEDES...
286
... IN THE BACK OF WHICH GALA STRUGGLED UNAVAILINGLY
I KNOW SIR HUGO'S SECRET NOW—AND I SHALL NEVER GET A CHANCE TO STOP HIM!

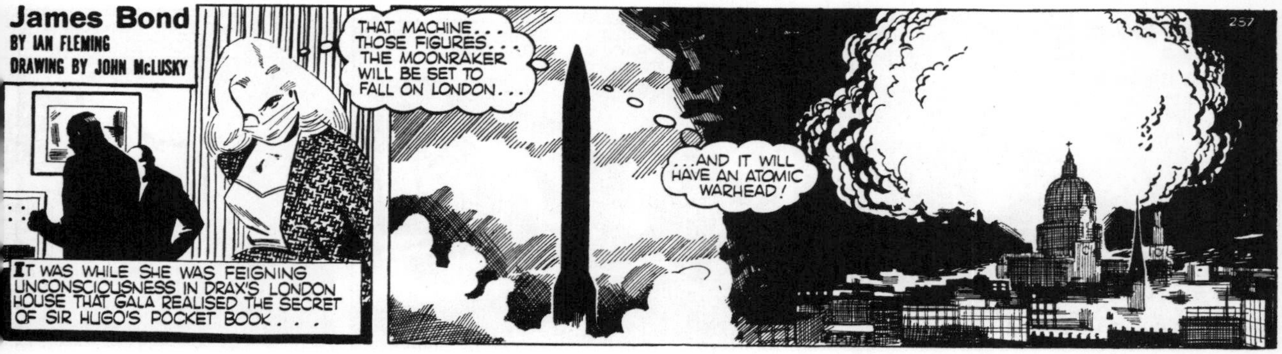
James Bond
BY IAN FLEMING
DRAWING BY JOHN McLUSKY
IT WAS WHILE SHE WAS FEIGNING UNCONSCIOUSNESS IN DRAX'S LONDON HOUSE THAT GALA REALISED THE SECRET OF SIR HUGO'S POCKET BOOK . . .
THAT MACHINE... THOSE FIGURES... THE MOONRAKER WILL BE SET TO FALL ON LONDON...
287
...AND IT WILL HAVE AN ATOMIC WARHEAD!

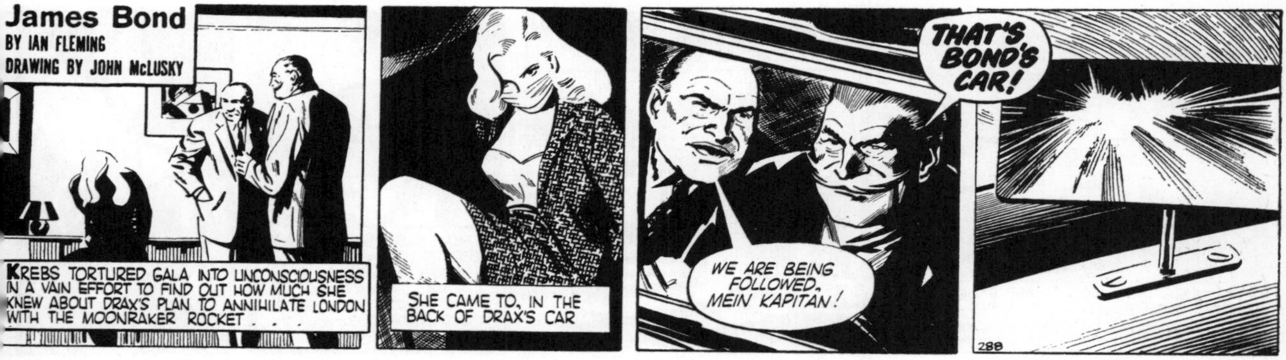
James Bond
BY IAN FLEMING
DRAWING BY JOHN McLUSKY
KREBS TORTURED GALA INTO UNCONSCIOUSNESS IN A VAIN EFFORT TO FIND OUT HOW MUCH SHE KNEW ABOUT DRAX'S PLAN TO ANNIHILATE LONDON WITH THE MOONRAKER ROCKET . . .
SHE CAME TO, IN THE BACK OF DRAX'S CAR
WE ARE BEING FOLLOWED, MEIN KAPITAN!
THAT'S BOND'S CAR!
288

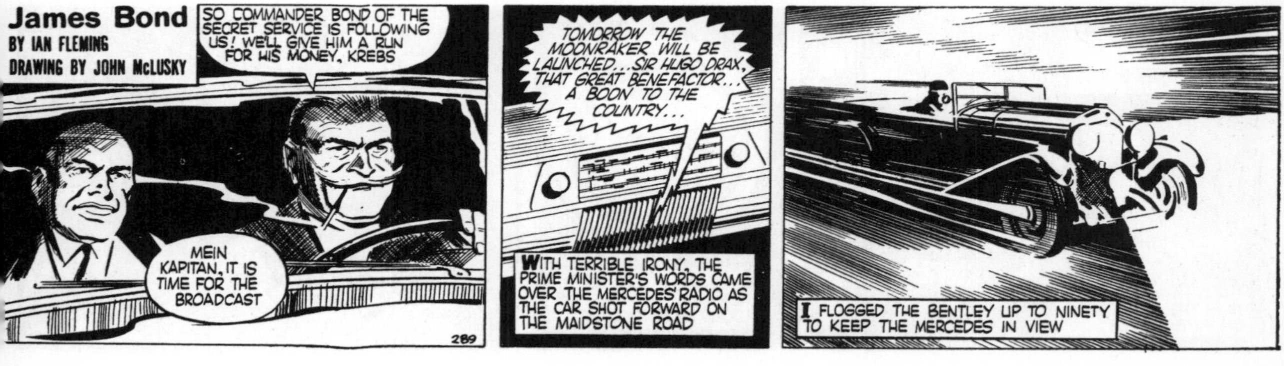
James Bond
BY IAN FLEMING
DRAWING BY JOHN McLUSKY
SO COMMANDER BOND OF THE SECRET SERVICE IS FOLLOWING US! WE'LL GIVE HIM A RUN FOR HIS MONEY, KREBS
MEIN KAPITAN, IT IS TIME FOR THE BROADCAST
289
TOMORROW THE MOONRAKER WILL BE LAUNCHED... SIR HUGO DRAX, THAT GREAT BENEFACTOR... A BOON TO THE COUNTRY...
WITH TERRIBLE IRONY, THE PRIME MINISTER'S WORDS CAME OVER THE MERCEDES' RADIO AS THE CAR SHOT FORWARD ON THE MAIDSTONE ROAD
I FLOGGED THE BENTLEY UP TO NINETY TO KEEP THE MERCEDES IN VIEW

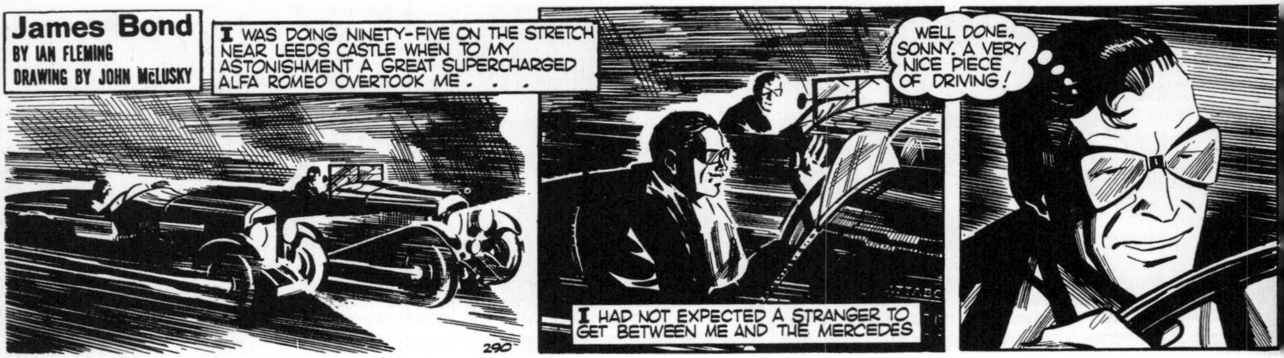
James Bond
BY IAN FLEMING
DRAWING BY JOHN McLUSKY
I WAS DOING NINETY-FIVE ON THE STRETCH NEAR LEEDS CASTLE WHEN TO MY ASTONISHMENT A GREAT SUPERCHARGED ALFA ROMEO OVERTOOK ME . . .
290
I HAD NOT EXPECTED A STRANGER TO GET BETWEEN ME AND THE MERCEDES
WELL DONE, SONNY. A VERY NICE PIECE OF DRIVING!

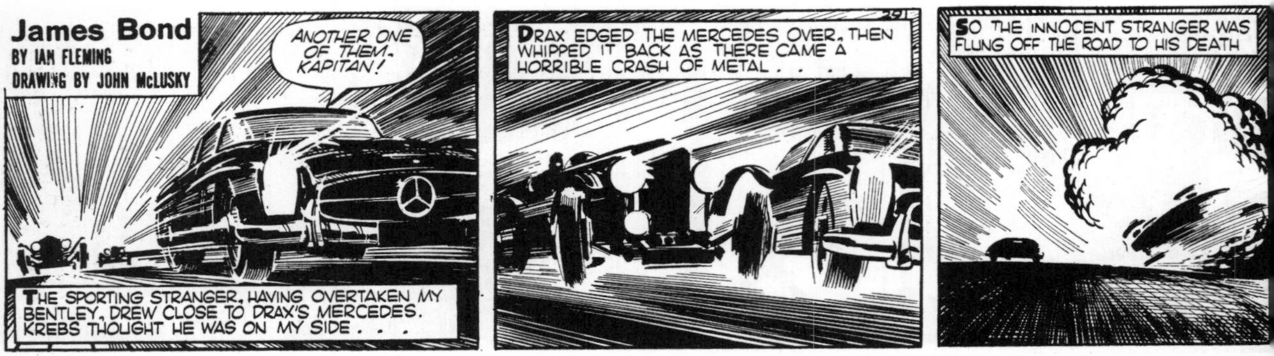
James Bond
BY IAN FLEMING
DRAWING BY JOHN McLUSKY
ANOTHER ONE OF THEM, KAPITAN!
THE SPORTING STRANGER, HAVING OVERTAKEN MY BENTLEY, DREW CLOSE TO DRAX'S MERCEDES. KREBS THOUGHT HE WAS ON MY SIDE . . .
291
DRAX EDGED THE MERCEDES OVER, THEN WHIPPED IT BACK AS THERE CAME A HORRIBLE CRASH OF METAL . . .
SO THE INNOCENT STRANGER WAS FLUNG OFF THE ROAD TO HIS DEATH

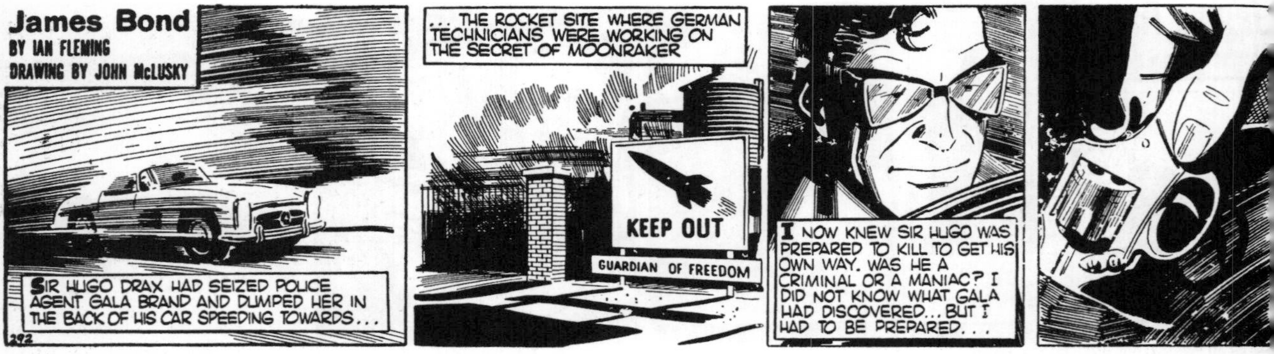
James Bond
BY IAN FLEMING
DRAWING BY JOHN McLUSKY
SIR HUGO DRAX HAD SEIZED POLICE AGENT GALA BRAND AND DUMPED HER IN THE BACK OF HIS CAR SPEEDING TOWARDS...
292
... THE ROCKET SITE WHERE GERMAN TECHNICIANS WERE WORKING ON THE SECRET OF MOONRAKER
KEEP OUT
GUARDIAN OF FREEDOM
I NOW KNEW SIR HUGO WAS PREPARED TO KILL TO GET HIS OWN WAY. WAS HE A CRIMINAL OR A MANIAC? I DID NOT KNOW WHAT GALA HAD DISCOVERED... BUT I HAD TO BE PREPARED...

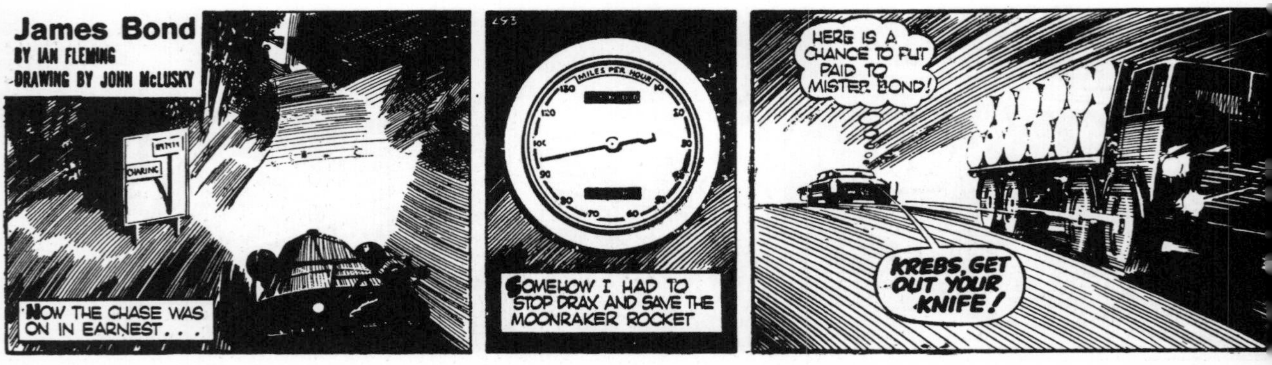
James Bond
BY IAN FLEMING
DRAWING BY JOHN McLUSKY
NOW THE CHASE WAS ON IN EARNEST . . .
293
MILES PER HOUR
SOMEHOW I HAD TO STOP DRAX AND SAVE THE MOONRAKER ROCKET
HERE IS A CHANCE TO PUT PAID TO MISTER BOND!
KREBS, GET OUT YOUR KNIFE!

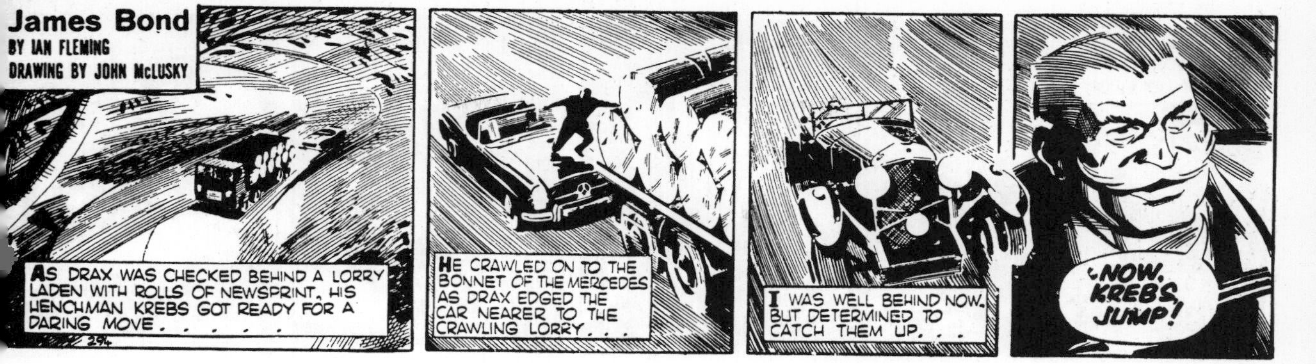
James Bond
BY IAN FLEMING
DRAWING BY JOHN McLUSKY
AS DRAX WAS CHECKED BEHIND A LORRY LADEN WITH ROLLS OF NEWSPRINT, HIS HENCHMAN KREBS GOT READY FOR A DARING MOVE . . . . .
HE CRAWLED ON TO THE BONNET OF THE MERCEDES AS DRAX EDGED THE CAR NEARER TO THE CRAWLING LORRY . . .
I WAS WELL BEHIND NOW. BUT DETERMINED TO CATCH THEM UP. . .
NOW, KREBS, JUMP!

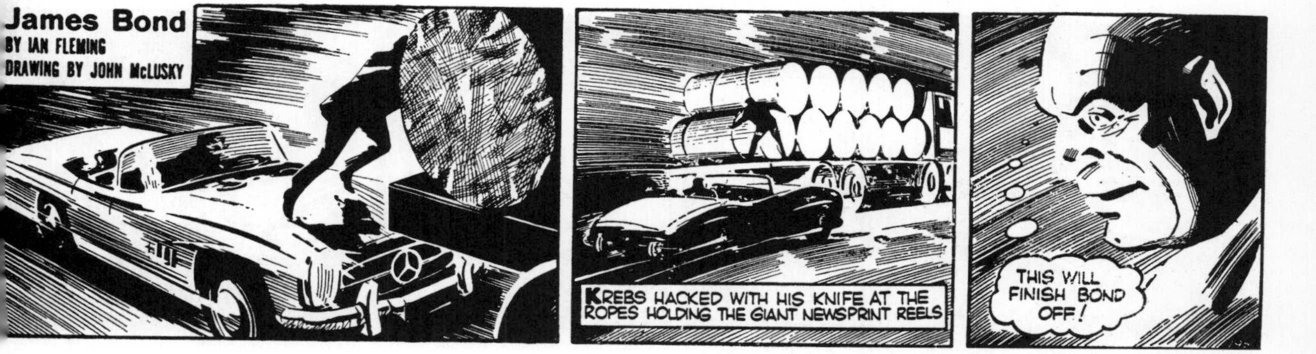
James Bond
BY IAN FLEMING
DRAWING BY JOHN McLUSKY
KREBS HACKED WITH HIS KNIFE AT THE ROPES HOLDING THE GIANT NEWSPRINT REELS
THIS WILL FINISH BOND OFF!

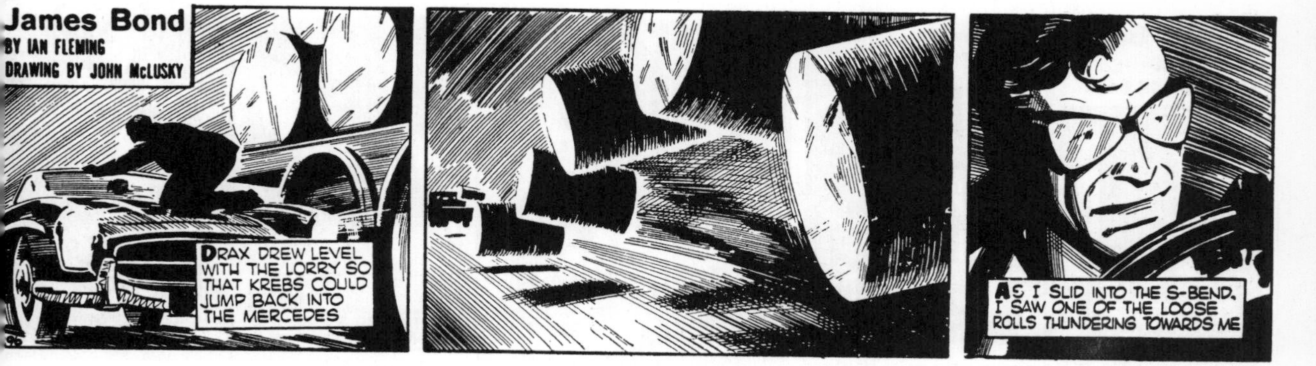
James Bond
BY IAN FLEMING
DRAWING BY JOHN McLUSKY
DRAX DREW LEVEL WITH THE LORRY SO THAT KREBS COULD JUMP BACK INTO THE MERCEDES
AS I SLID INTO THE S-BEND, I SAW ONE OF THE LOOSE ROLLS THUNDERING TOWARDS ME

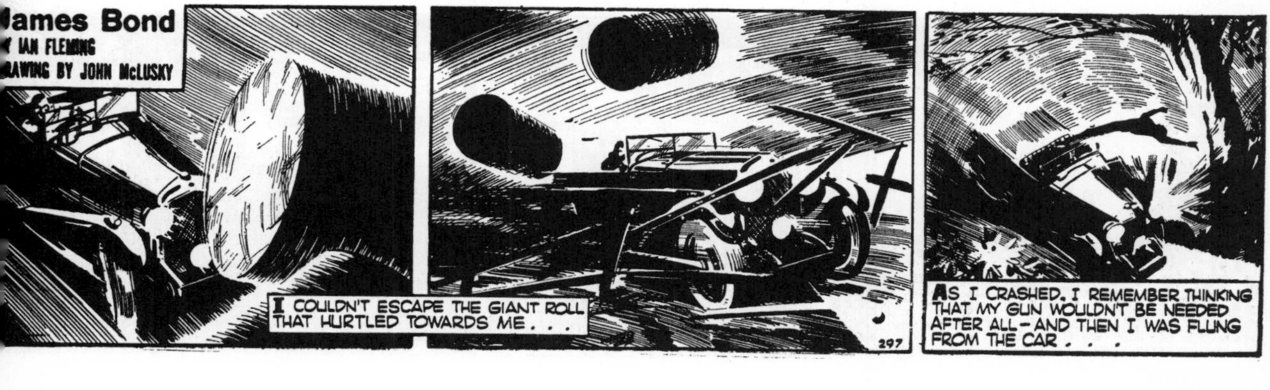
James Bond
IAN FLEMING
DRAWING BY JOHN McLUSKY
I COULDN'T ESCAPE THE GIANT ROLL THAT HURTLED TOWARDS ME . . .
297
AS I CRASHED, I REMEMBER THINKING THAT MY GUN WOULDN'T BE NEEDED AFTER ALL – AND THEN I WAS FLUNG FROM THE CAR . . .

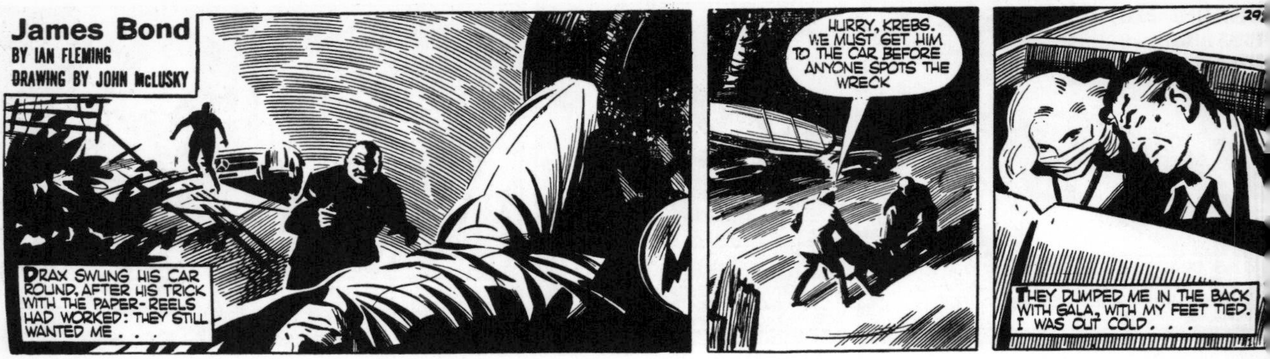
James Bond
BY IAN FLEMING
DRAWING BY JOHN McLUSKY
DRAX SWUNG HIS CAR ROUND, AFTER HIS TRICK WITH THE PAPER-REELS HAD WORKED: THEY STILL WANTED ME . . .
HURRY, KREBS. WE MUST GET HIM TO THE CAR BEFORE ANYONE SPOTS THE WRECK
THEY DUMPED ME IN THE BACK WITH GALA, WITH MY FEET TIED. I WAS OUT COLD . . .

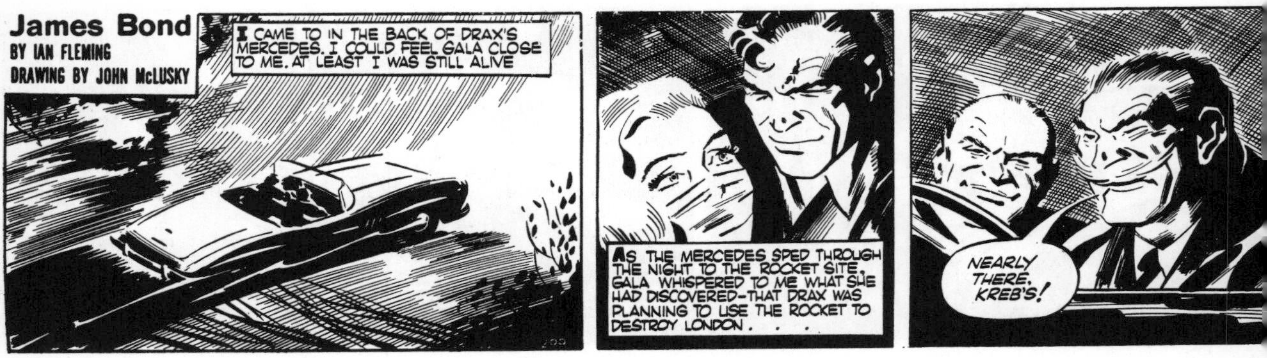
James Bond
BY IAN FLEMING
DRAWING BY JOHN McLUSKY
I CAME TO IN THE BACK OF DRAX'S MERCEDES. I COULD FEEL GALA CLOSE TO ME. AT LEAST I WAS STILL ALIVE
AS THE MERCEDES SPED THROUGH THE NIGHT TO THE ROCKET SITE, GALA WHISPERED TO ME WHAT SHE HAD DISCOVERED–THAT DRAX WAS PLANNING TO USE THE ROCKET TO DESTROY LONDON . . .
NEARLY THERE, KREB'S!

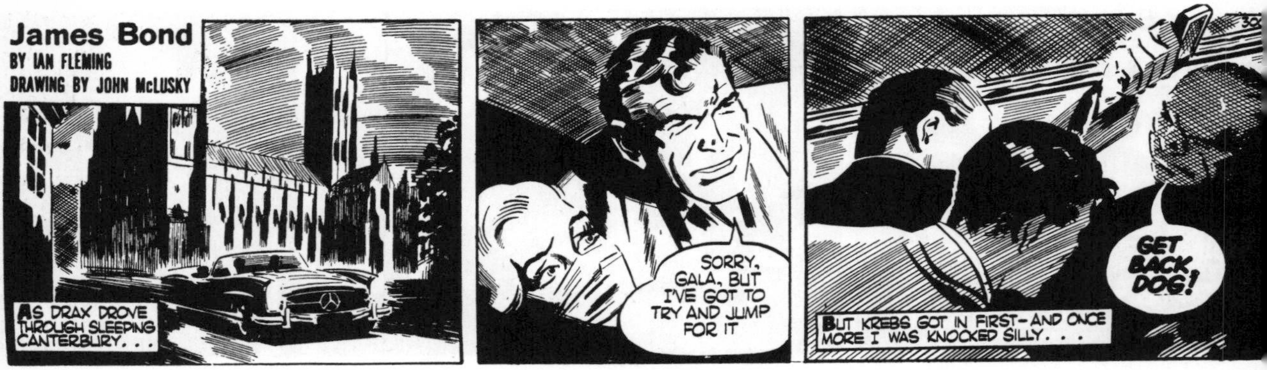
James Bond
BY IAN FLEMING
DRAWING BY JOHN McLUSKY
AS DRAX DROVE THROUGH SLEEPING CANTERBURY . . .
SORRY, GALA, BUT I'VE GOT TO TRY AND JUMP FOR IT
GET BACK DOG!
BUT KREBS GOT IN FIRST–AND ONCE MORE I WAS KNOCKED SILLY . . .

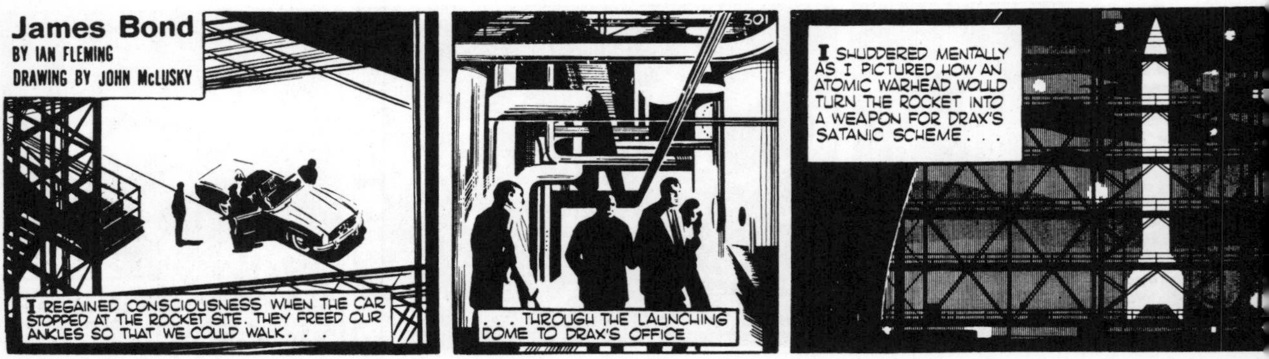
James Bond
BY IAN FLEMING
DRAWING BY JOHN McLUSKY
I REGAINED CONSCIOUSNESS WHEN THE CAR STOPPED AT THE ROCKET SITE. THEY FREED OUR ANKLES SO THAT WE COULD WALK . . .
301
. . . THROUGH THE LAUNCHING DOME TO DRAX'S OFFICE
I SHUDDERED MENTALLY AS I PICTURED HOW AN ATOMIC WARHEAD WOULD TURN THE ROCKET INTO A WEAPON FOR DRAX'S SATANIC SCHEME . . .

James Bond
BY IAN FLEMING
DRAWING BY JOHN McLUSKY

I WAS ONE OF THE BEST SHOTS IN THE BRANDENBURG DIVISION. SO DON'T MOVE, EITHER OF YOU

NOW DRAX LET HIS MASK DROP. NOW HE WAS ALL NAZI...

ONCE MORE GALA AND I WERE TRUSSED UP

AND KREBS WAS SENT TO FETCH A BLOW-LAMP

302

James Bond
BY IAN FLEMING
DRAWING BY JOHN McLUSKY

ALL RIGHT, BOND, DON'T FORGET, THERE'S NO FAIR PLAY HERE. KREBS WILL TAKE THE GIRL FIRST. HE IS AN EXPERT WITH THAT TORCH AS AN INSTRUMENT OF TORTURE

NOW, GALA BRAND, LET'S HAVE IT—WHO ARE YOU WORKING FOR?

GALA REMAINED SILENT

305

James Bond
BY IAN FLEMING
DRAWING BY JOHN McLUSKY

SINCE MISS BRAND WILL NOT TELL US FOR WHOM SHE IS WORKING, I REGRET THAT KREBS WILL HAVE TO USE A LITTLE PERSUASION

304

KREBS SENT A FLAME FLICKING TOWARDS GALA

STOP!

I COULD NOT LET KREBS DO IT. IN ANY CASE, THERE WERE CERTAIN THINGS IT WAS NOW POINTLESS TO HIDE

James Bond
BY IAN FLEMING
DRAWING BY JOHN McLUSKY

O.K., DRAX, HERE IT IS: MISS BRAND WORKS FOR SCOTLAND YARD. SO DO I

HOW INTERESTING... NOW, DOES ANYONE KNOW YOU ARE PRISONERS HERE?

305

IF I SAY 'YES', HE'LL SHOOT US BOTH: HE'S GOT NOTHING TO LOSE

NO—IF THEY DID, THEY'D BE HERE BY NOW

THAT'S TRUE. I CONGRATULATE YOU ON MAKING THE INTERVIEW SO HARMONIOUS. KREBS, YOU CAN PUT THAT BLOW-LAMP DOWN NOW

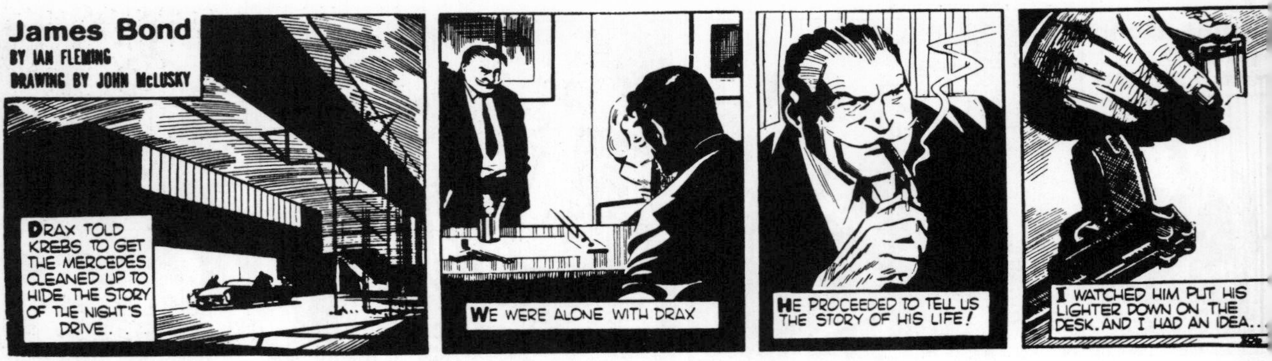
James Bond
BY IAN FLEMING
DRAWING BY JOHN McLUSKY
DRAX TOLD KREBS TO GET THE MERCEDES CLEANED UP TO HIDE THE STORY OF THE NIGHT'S DRIVE . .
WE WERE ALONE WITH DRAX
HE PROCEEDED TO TELL US THE STORY OF HIS LIFE!
I WATCHED HIM PUT HIS LIGHTER DOWN ON THE DESK, AND I HAD AN IDEA . . .

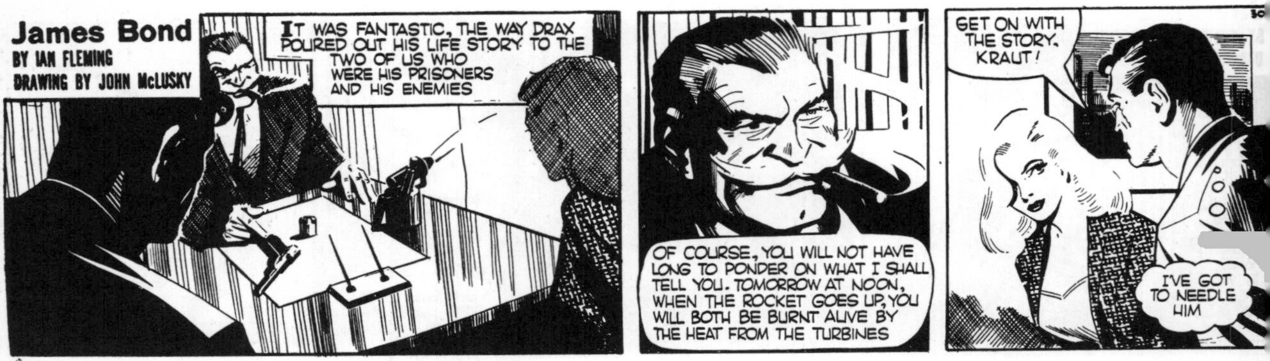
James Bond
BY IAN FLEMING
DRAWING BY JOHN McLUSKY
IT WAS FANTASTIC, THE WAY DRAX POURED OUT HIS LIFE STORY TO THE TWO OF US WHO WERE HIS PRISONERS AND HIS ENEMIES
OF COURSE, YOU WILL NOT HAVE LONG TO PONDER ON WHAT I SHALL TELL YOU. TOMORROW AT NOON, WHEN THE ROCKET GOES UP, YOU WILL BOTH BE BURNT ALIVE BY THE HEAT FROM THE TURBINES
GET ON WITH THE STORY, KRAUT!
I'VE GOT TO NEEDLE HIM

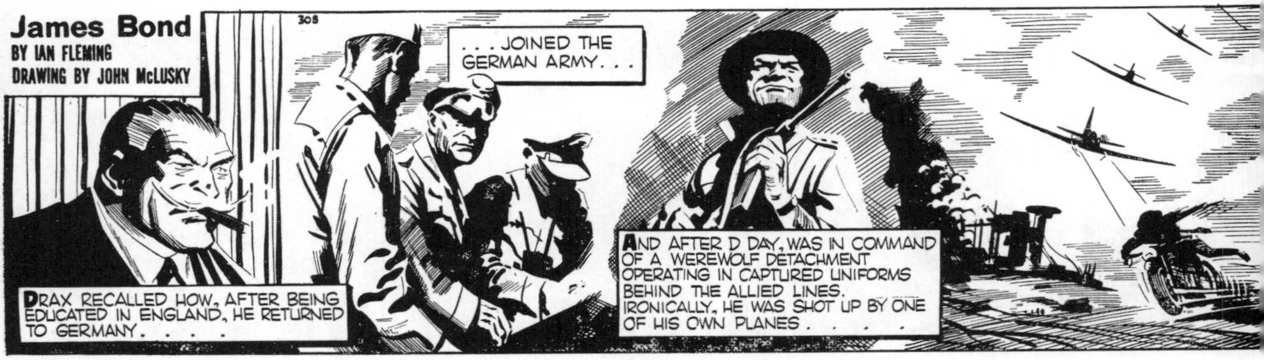
James Bond
BY IAN FLEMING
DRAWING BY JOHN McLUSKY
308
DRAX RECALLED HOW, AFTER BEING EDUCATED IN ENGLAND, HE RETURNED TO GERMANY . . . .
. . . JOINED THE GERMAN ARMY . . .
AND AFTER D DAY, WAS IN COMMAND OF A WEREWOLF DETACHMENT OPERATING IN CAPTURED UNIFORMS BEHIND THE ALLIED LINES. IRONICALLY, HE WAS SHOT UP BY ONE OF HIS OWN PLANES . . . .

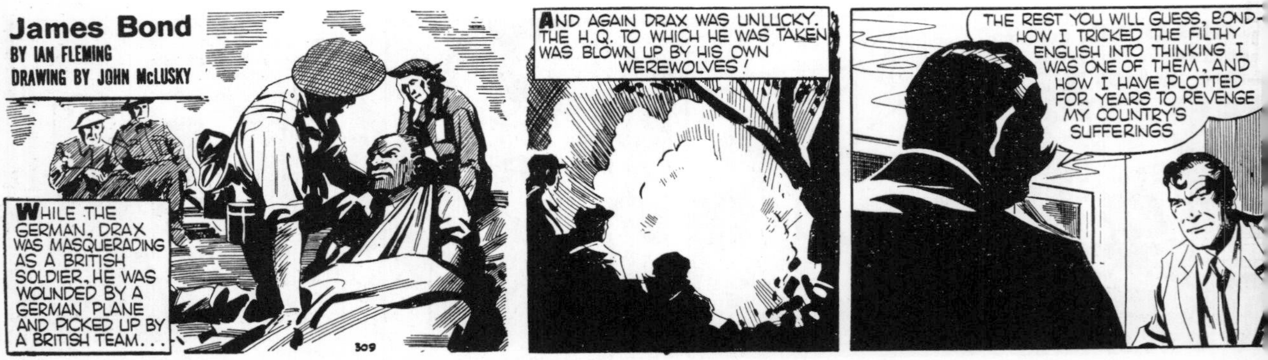
James Bond
BY IAN FLEMING
DRAWING BY JOHN McLUSKY
WHILE THE GERMAN, DRAX WAS MASQUERADING AS A BRITISH SOLDIER, HE WAS WOUNDED BY A GERMAN PLANE AND PICKED UP BY A BRITISH TEAM . . .
309
AND AGAIN DRAX WAS UNLUCKY. THE H.Q. TO WHICH HE WAS TAKEN WAS BLOWN UP BY HIS OWN WEREWOLVES!
THE REST YOU WILL GUESS, BOND- HOW I TRICKED THE FILTHY ENGLISH INTO THINKING I WAS ONE OF THEM, AND HOW I HAVE PLOTTED FOR YEARS TO REVENGE MY COUNTRY'S SUFFERINGS

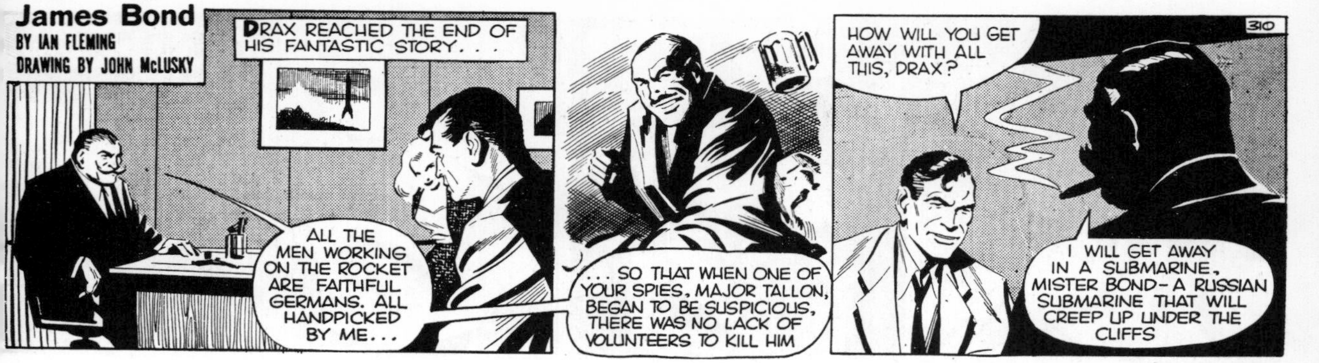
James Bond
BY IAN FLEMING
DRAWING BY JOHN McLUSKY
DRAX REACHED THE END OF HIS FANTASTIC STORY. . .
ALL THE MEN WORKING ON THE ROCKET ARE FAITHFUL GERMANS. ALL HANDPICKED BY ME. . .
. . . SO THAT WHEN ONE OF YOUR SPIES, MAJOR TALLON, BEGAN TO BE SUSPICIOUS, THERE WAS NO LACK OF VOLUNTEERS TO KILL HIM
310
HOW WILL YOU GET AWAY WITH ALL THIS, DRAX?
I WILL GET AWAY IN A SUBMARINE, MISTER BOND– A RUSSIAN SUBMARINE THAT WILL CREEP UP UNDER THE CLIFFS

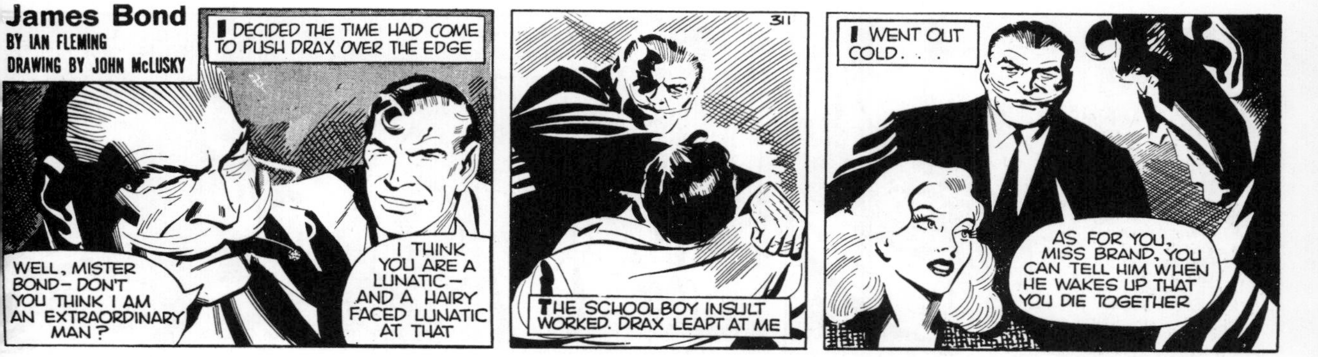
James Bond
BY IAN FLEMING
DRAWING BY JOHN McLUSKY
I DECIDED THE TIME HAD COME TO PUSH DRAX OVER THE EDGE
WELL, MISTER BOND– DON'T YOU THINK I AM AN EXTRAORDINARY MAN?
I THINK YOU ARE A LUNATIC– AND A HAIRY FACED LUNATIC AT THAT
311
THE SCHOOLBOY INSULT WORKED. DRAX LEAPT AT ME
I WENT OUT COLD. . .
AS FOR YOU, MISS BRAND, YOU CAN TELL HIM WHEN HE WAKES UP THAT YOU DIE TOGETHER

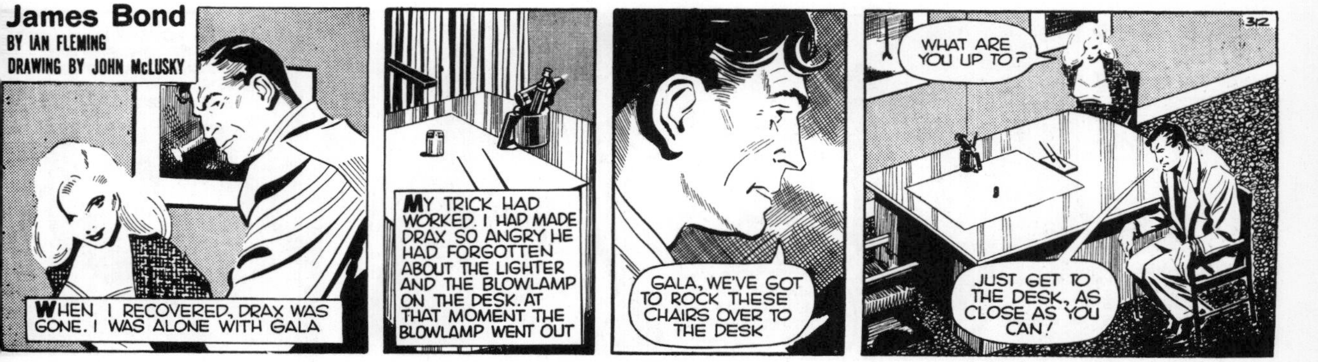
James Bond
BY IAN FLEMING
DRAWING BY JOHN McLUSKY
WHEN I RECOVERED, DRAX WAS GONE. I WAS ALONE WITH GALA
MY TRICK HAD WORKED. I HAD MADE DRAX SO ANGRY HE HAD FORGOTTEN ABOUT THE LIGHTER AND THE BLOWLAMP ON THE DESK. AT THAT MOMENT THE BLOWLAMP WENT OUT
GALA, WE'VE GOT TO ROCK THESE CHAIRS OVER TO THE DESK
312
WHAT ARE YOU UP TO?
JUST GET TO THE DESK, AS CLOSE AS YOU CAN!

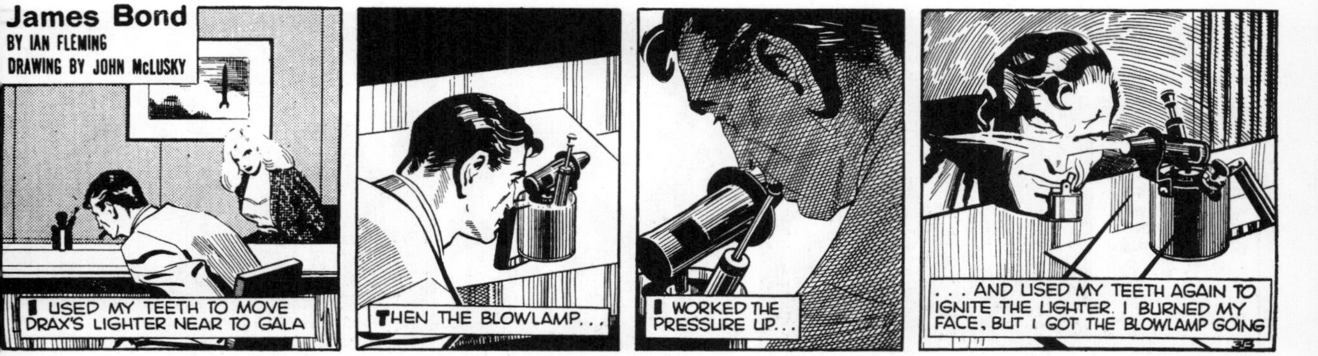
James Bond
BY IAN FLEMING
DRAWING BY JOHN McLUSKY
I USED MY TEETH TO MOVE DRAX'S LIGHTER NEAR TO GALA
THEN THE BLOWLAMP. . .
I WORKED THE PRESSURE UP. . .
. . . AND USED MY TEETH AGAIN TO IGNITE THE LIGHTER. I BURNED MY FACE, BUT I GOT THE BLOWLAMP GOING
313

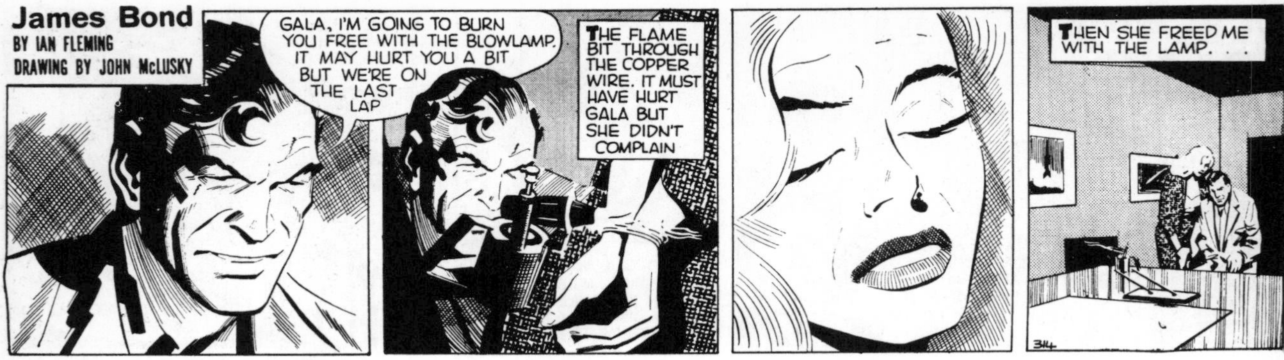
James Bond
BY IAN FLEMING
DRAWING BY JOHN McLUSKY
GALA, I'M GOING TO BURN YOU FREE WITH THE BLOWLAMP. IT MAY HURT YOU A BIT BUT WE'RE ON THE LAST LAP
THE FLAME BIT THROUGH THE COPPER WIRE. IT MUST HAVE HURT GALA BUT SHE DIDN'T COMPLAIN
THEN SHE FREED ME WITH THE LAMP. . .
314

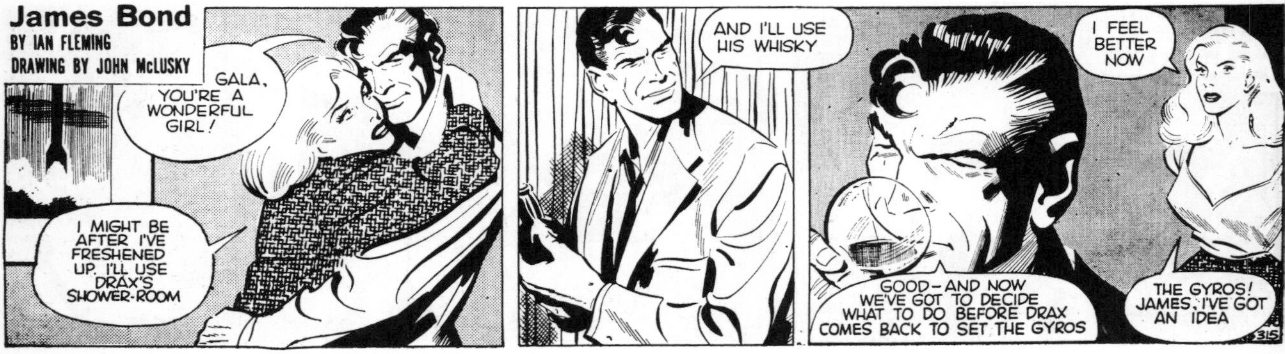
James Bond
BY IAN FLEMING
DRAWING BY JOHN McLUSKY
GALA, YOU'RE A WONDERFUL GIRL!
I MIGHT BE AFTER I'VE FRESHENED UP. I'LL USE DRAX'S SHOWER-ROOM
AND I'LL USE HIS WHISKY
I FEEL BETTER NOW
GOOD—AND NOW WE'VE GOT TO DECIDE WHAT TO DO BEFORE DRAX COMES BACK TO SET THE GYROS
THE GYROS! JAMES, I'VE GOT AN IDEA
315

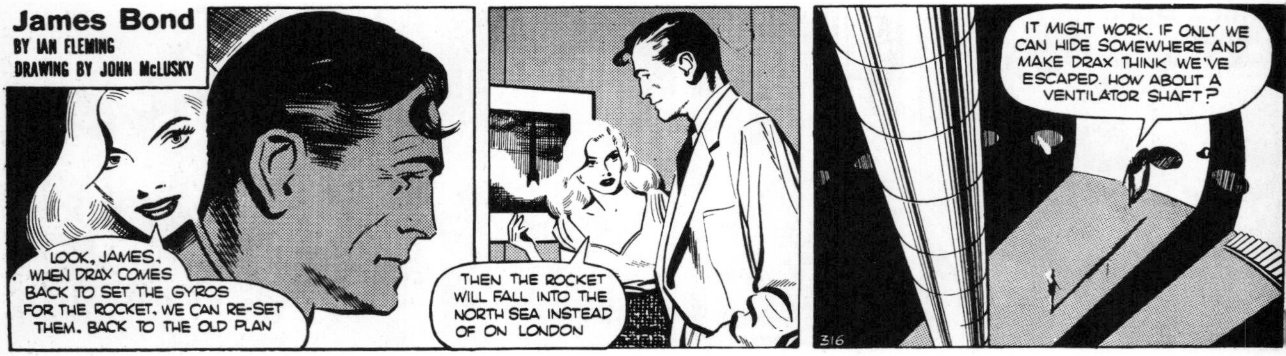
James Bond
BY IAN FLEMING
DRAWING BY JOHN McLUSKY
LOOK, JAMES. WHEN DRAX COMES BACK TO SET THE GYROS FOR THE ROCKET, WE CAN RE-SET THEM. BACK TO THE OLD PLAN
THEN THE ROCKET WILL FALL INTO THE NORTH SEA INSTEAD OF ON LONDON
IT MIGHT WORK. IF ONLY WE CAN HIDE SOMEWHERE AND MAKE DRAX THINK WE'VE ESCAPED. HOW ABOUT A VENTILATOR SHAFT?
316

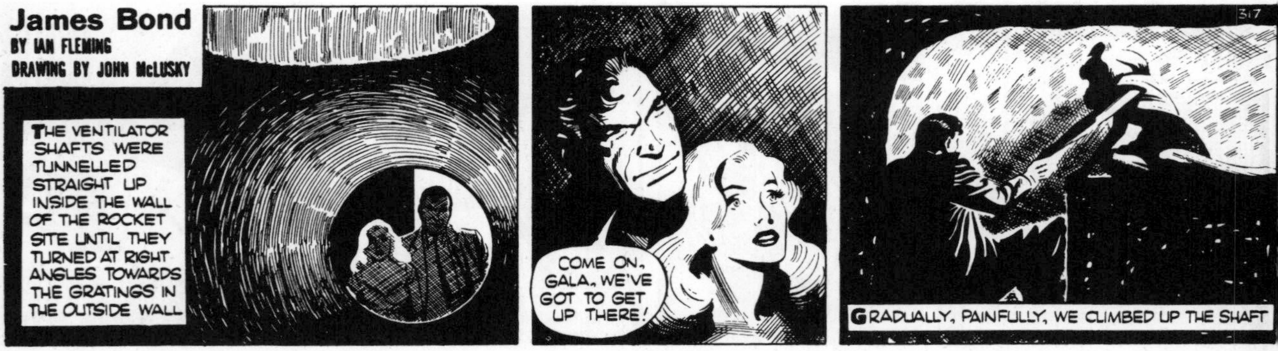
James Bond
BY IAN FLEMING
DRAWING BY JOHN McLUSKY
THE VENTILATOR SHAFTS WERE TUNNELLED STRAIGHT UP INSIDE THE WALL OF THE ROCKET SITE UNTIL THEY TURNED AT RIGHT ANGLES TOWARDS THE GRATINGS IN THE OUTSIDE WALL
COME ON, GALA. WE'VE GOT TO GET UP THERE!
317
GRADUALLY, PAINFULLY, WE CLIMBED UP THE SHAFT

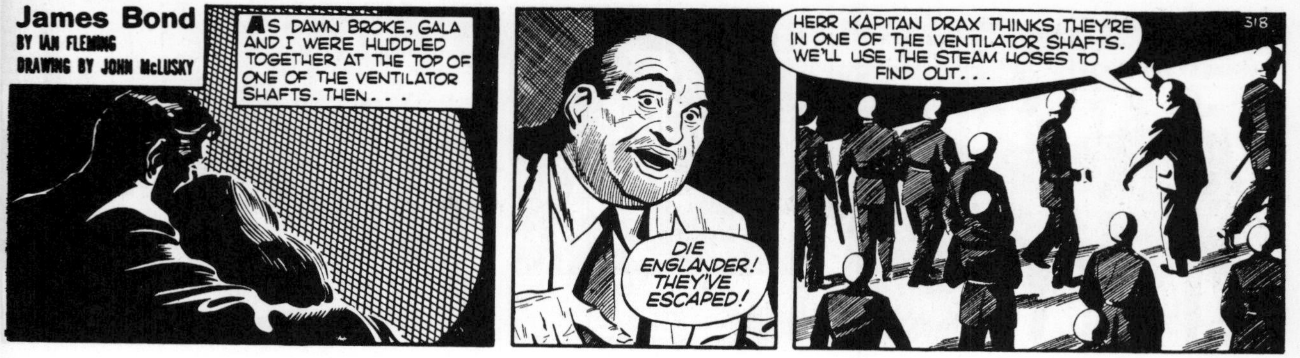
James Bond
BY IAN FLEMING
DRAWING BY JOHN McLUSKY
AS DAWN BROKE, GALA AND I WERE HUDDLED TOGETHER AT THE TOP OF ONE OF THE VENTILATOR SHAFTS. THEN . . .
DIE ENGLANDER! THEY'VE ESCAPED!
HERR KAPITAN DRAX THINKS THEY'RE IN ONE OF THE VENTILATOR SHAFTS. WE'LL USE THE STEAM HOSES TO FIND OUT . . .
318

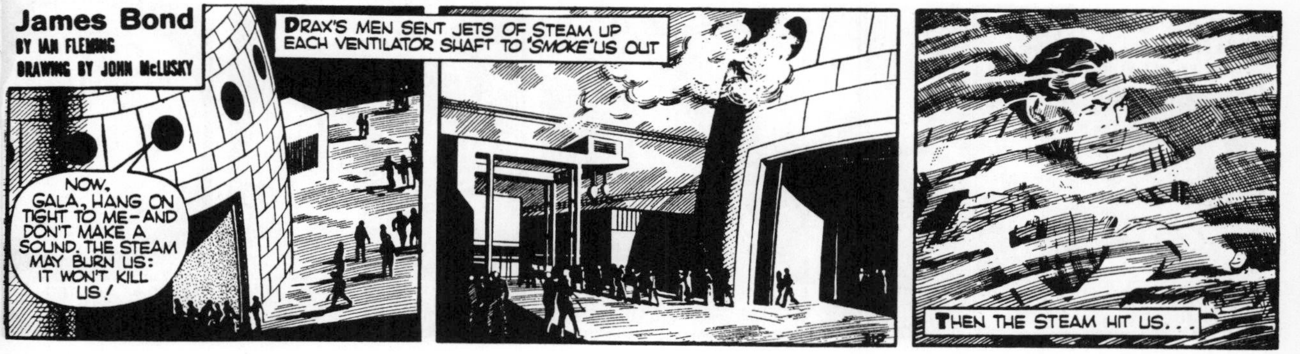
James Bond
BY IAN FLEMING
DRAWING BY JOHN McLUSKY
NOW, GALA, HANG ON TIGHT TO ME – AND DON'T MAKE A SOUND. THE STEAM MAY BURN US: IT WON'T KILL US!
DRAX'S MEN SENT JETS OF STEAM UP EACH VENTILATOR SHAFT TO 'SMOKE' US OUT
THEN THE STEAM HIT US . . .

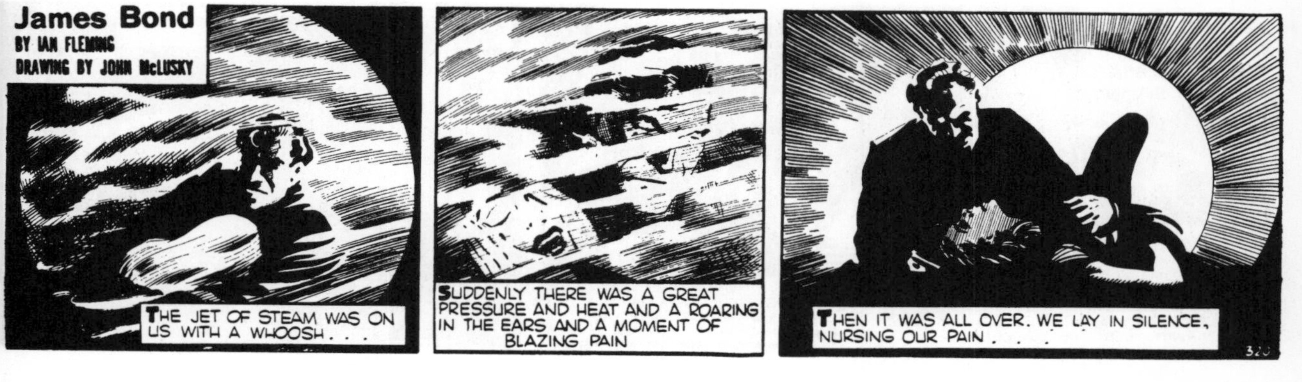
James Bond
BY IAN FLEMING
DRAWING BY JOHN McLUSKY
THE JET OF STEAM WAS ON US WITH A WHOOSH . . .
SUDDENLY THERE WAS A GREAT PRESSURE AND HEAT AND A ROARING IN THE EARS AND A MOMENT OF BLAZING PAIN
THEN IT WAS ALL OVER. WE LAY IN SILENCE, NURSING OUR PAIN . . .

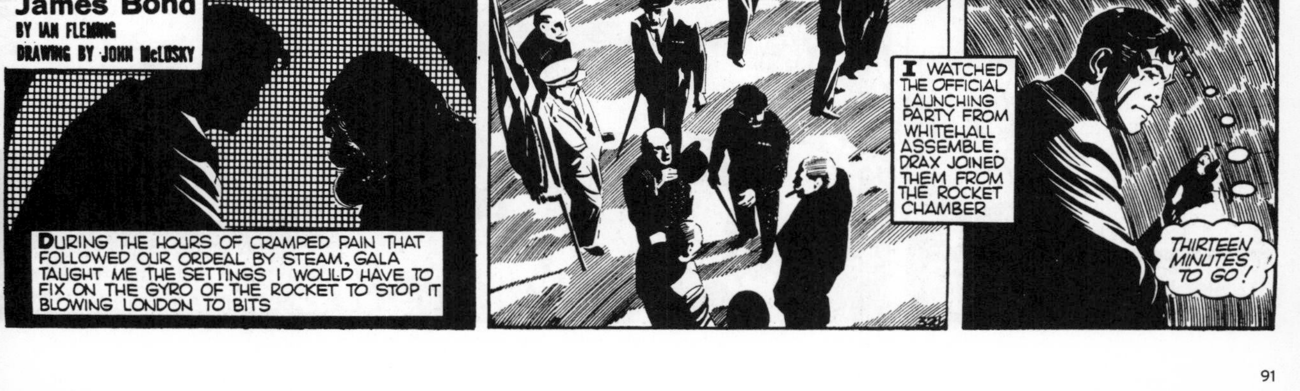
James Bond
BY IAN FLEMING
DRAWING BY JOHN McLUSKY
DURING THE HOURS OF CRAMPED PAIN THAT FOLLOWED OUR ORDEAL BY STEAM, GALA TAUGHT ME THE SETTINGS I WOULD HAVE TO FIX ON THE GYRO OF THE ROCKET TO STOP IT BLOWING LONDON TO BITS
I WATCHED THE OFFICIAL LAUNCHING PARTY FROM WHITEHALL ASSEMBLE. DRAX JOINED THEM FROM THE ROCKET CHAMBER
THIRTEEN MINUTES TO GO!

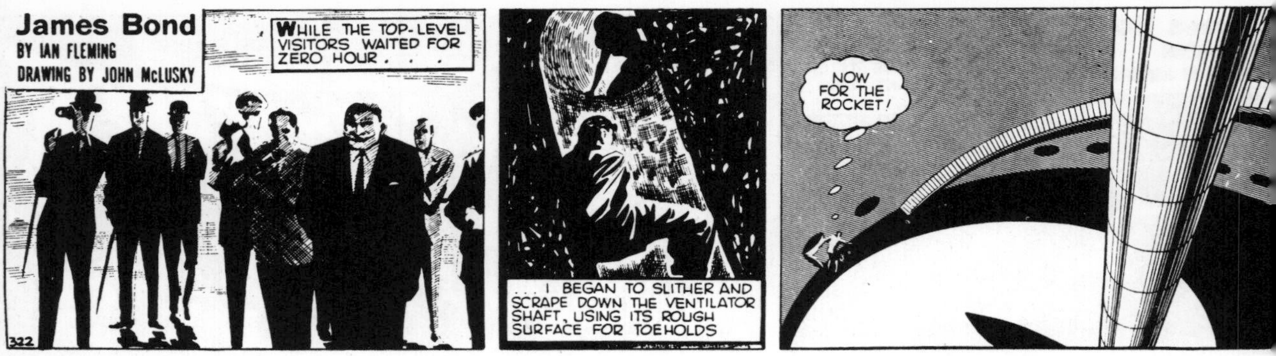
James Bond
BY IAN FLEMING
DRAWING BY JOHN McLUSKY
WHILE THE TOP-LEVEL VISITORS WAITED FOR ZERO HOUR . . .
322
. . . I BEGAN TO SLITHER AND SCRAPE DOWN THE VENTILATOR SHAFT, USING ITS ROUGH SURFACE FOR TOEHOLDS
NOW FOR THE ROCKET!

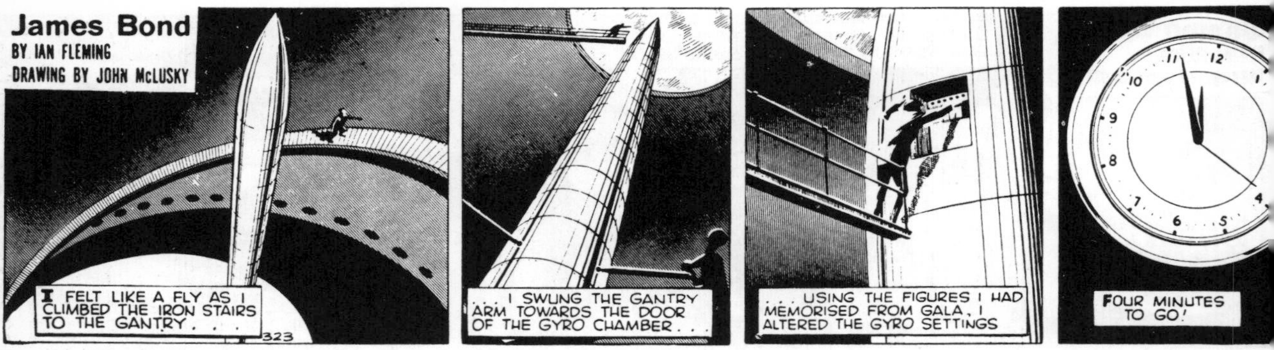
James Bond
BY IAN FLEMING
DRAWING BY JOHN McLUSKY
I FELT LIKE A FLY AS I CLIMBED THE IRON STAIRS TO THE GANTRY . . .
323
. . . I SWUNG THE GANTRY ARM TOWARDS THE DOOR OF THE GYRO CHAMBER . . .
. . . USING THE FIGURES I HAD MEMORISED FROM GALA, I ALTERED THE GYRO SETTINGS
FOUR MINUTES TO GO!

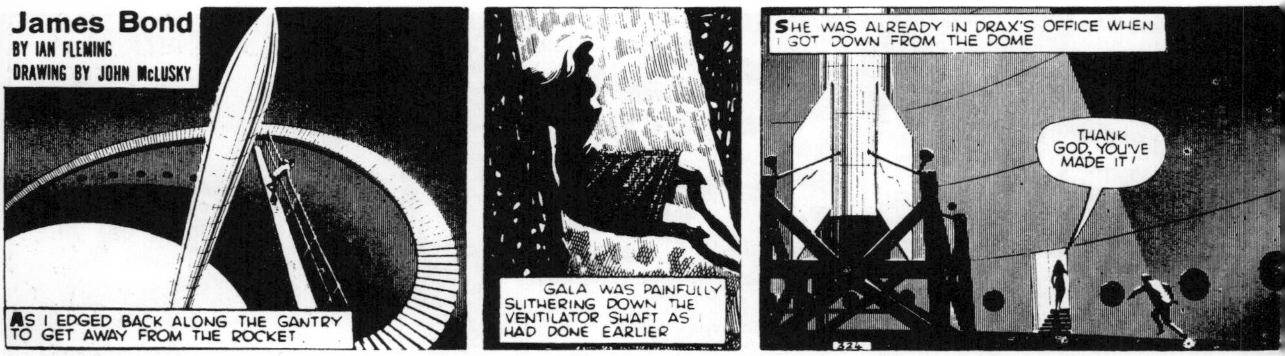
James Bond
BY IAN FLEMING
DRAWING BY JOHN McLUSKY
AS I EDGED BACK ALONG THE GANTRY TO GET AWAY FROM THE ROCKET . . .
GALA WAS PAINFULLY SLITHERING DOWN THE VENTILATOR SHAFT AS I HAD DONE EARLIER
SHE WAS ALREADY IN DRAX'S OFFICE WHEN I GOT DOWN FROM THE DOME
THANK GOD, YOU'VE MADE IT!
324

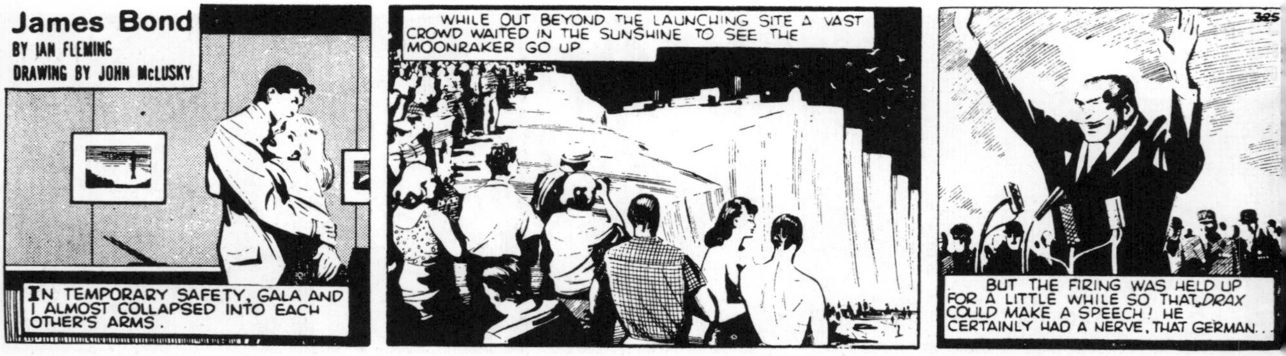
James Bond
BY IAN FLEMING
DRAWING BY JOHN McLUSKY
IN TEMPORARY SAFETY, GALA AND I ALMOST COLLAPSED INTO EACH OTHER'S ARMS .
WHILE OUT BEYOND THE LAUNCHING SITE A VAST CROWD WAITED IN THE SUNSHINE TO SEE THE MOONRAKER GO UP
325
BUT THE FIRING WAS HELD UP FOR A LITTLE WHILE SO THAT DRAX COULD MAKE A SPEECH! HE CERTAINLY HAD A NERVE, THAT GERMAN . . .

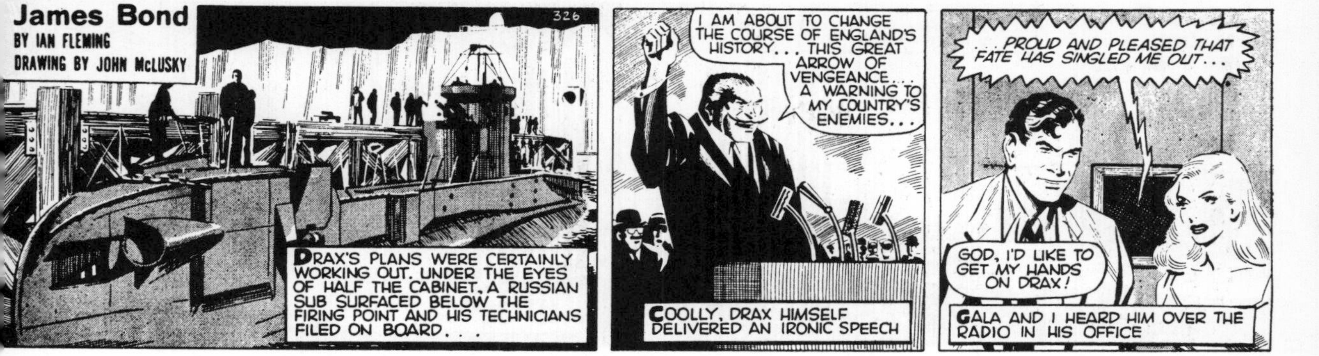
James Bond
BY IAN FLEMING
DRAWING BY JOHN McLUSKY
326
DRAX'S PLANS WERE CERTAINLY WORKING OUT. UNDER THE EYES OF HALF THE CABINET, A RUSSIAN SUB SURFACED BELOW THE FIRING POINT AND HIS TECHNICIANS FILED ON BOARD . . .
I AM ABOUT TO CHANGE THE COURSE OF ENGLAND'S HISTORY . . . THIS GREAT ARROW OF VENGEANCE . . . A WARNING TO MY COUNTRY'S ENEMIES . . .
COOLLY, DRAX HIMSELF DELIVERED AN IRONIC SPEECH
. . . PROUD AND PLEASED THAT FATE HAS SINGLED ME OUT . . .
GOD, I'D LIKE TO GET MY HANDS ON DRAX!
GALA AND I HEARD HIM OVER THE RADIO IN HIS OFFICE

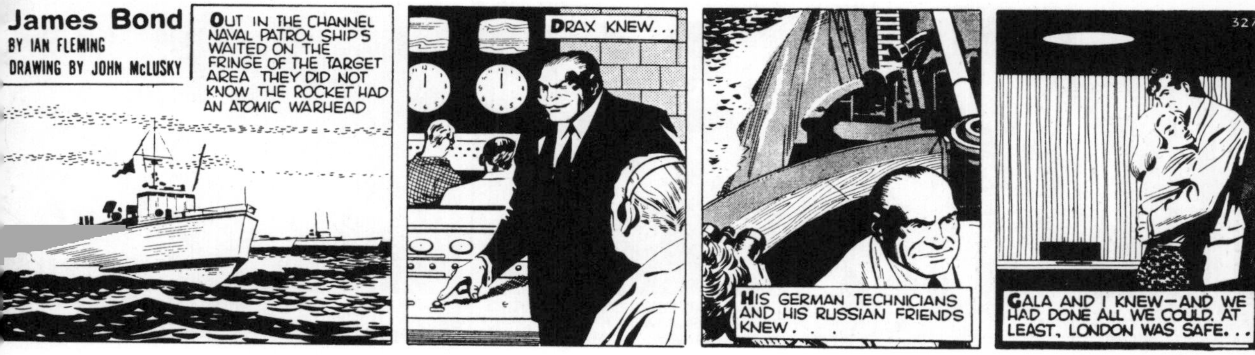
James Bond
BY IAN FLEMING
DRAWING BY JOHN McLUSKY
OUT IN THE CHANNEL NAVAL PATROL SHIPS WAITED ON THE FRINGE OF THE TARGET AREA. THEY DID NOT KNOW THE ROCKET HAD AN ATOMIC WARHEAD
DRAX KNEW . . .
HIS GERMAN TECHNICIANS AND HIS RUSSIAN FRIENDS KNEW . . .
327
GALA AND I KNEW—AND WE HAD DONE ALL WE COULD. AT LEAST, LONDON WAS SAFE . . .

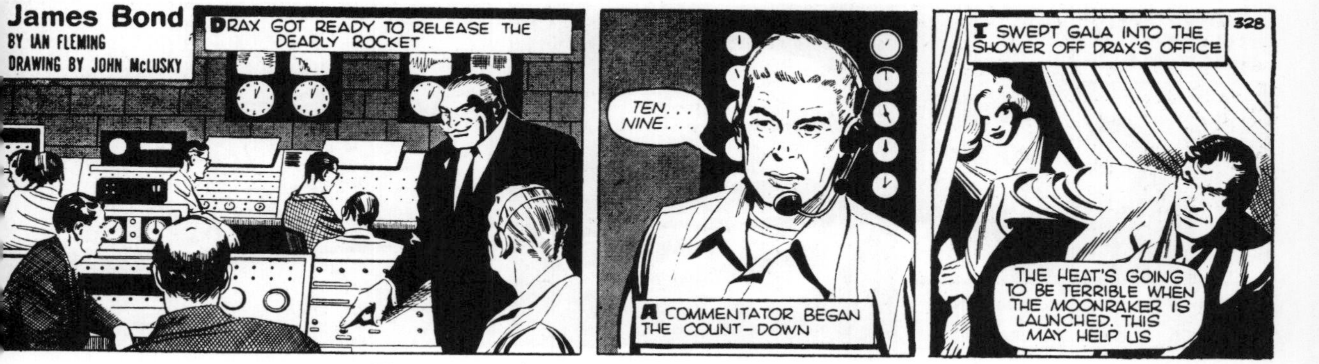
James Bond
BY IAN FLEMING
DRAWING BY JOHN McLUSKY
DRAX GOT READY TO RELEASE THE DEADLY ROCKET
TEN . . . NINE . . .
A COMMENTATOR BEGAN THE COUNT-DOWN
328
I SWEPT GALA INTO THE SHOWER OFF DRAX'S OFFICE
THE HEAT'S GOING TO BE TERRIBLE WHEN THE MOONRAKER IS LAUNCHED. THIS MAY HELP US

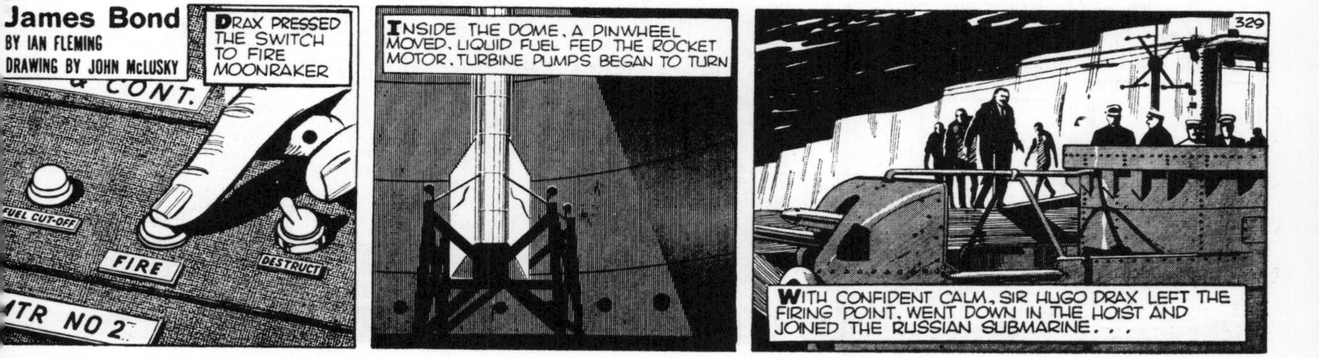
James Bond
BY IAN FLEMING
DRAWING BY JOHN McLUSKY
DRAX PRESSED THE SWITCH TO FIRE MOONRAKER
& CONT.
FUEL CUT-OFF
FIRE
DESTRUCT
MTR NO 2
INSIDE THE DOME, A PINWHEEL MOVED, LIQUID FUEL FED THE ROCKET MOTOR, TURBINE PUMPS BEGAN TO TURN
329
WITH CONFIDENT CALM, SIR HUGO DRAX LEFT THE FIRING POINT, WENT DOWN IN THE HOIST AND JOINED THE RUSSIAN SUBMARINE . . .

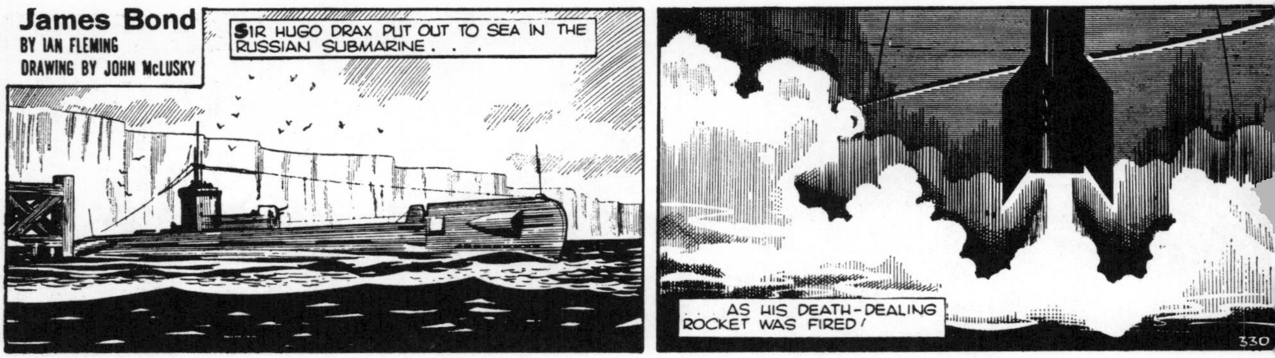
James Bond
BY IAN FLEMING
DRAWING BY JOHN McLUSKY
SIR HUGO DRAX PUT OUT TO SEA IN THE RUSSIAN SUBMARINE . . .
. . . AS HIS DEATH-DEALING ROCKET WAS FIRED!
330

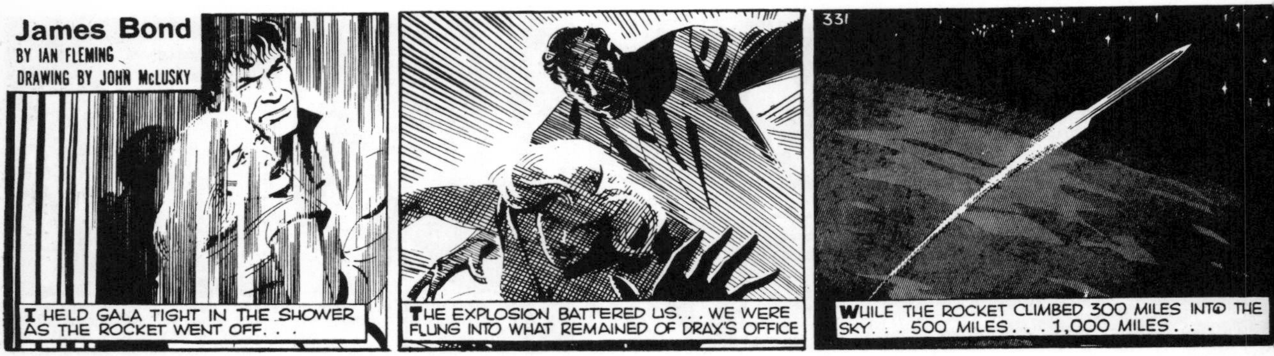
James Bond
BY IAN FLEMING
DRAWING BY JOHN McLUSKY
I HELD GALA TIGHT IN THE SHOWER AS THE ROCKET WENT OFF. . .
THE EXPLOSION BATTERED US. . . WE WERE FLUNG INTO WHAT REMAINED OF DRAX'S OFFICE
331
WHILE THE ROCKET CLIMBED 300 MILES INTO THE SKY. . . 500 MILES. . . 1,000 MILES. . .

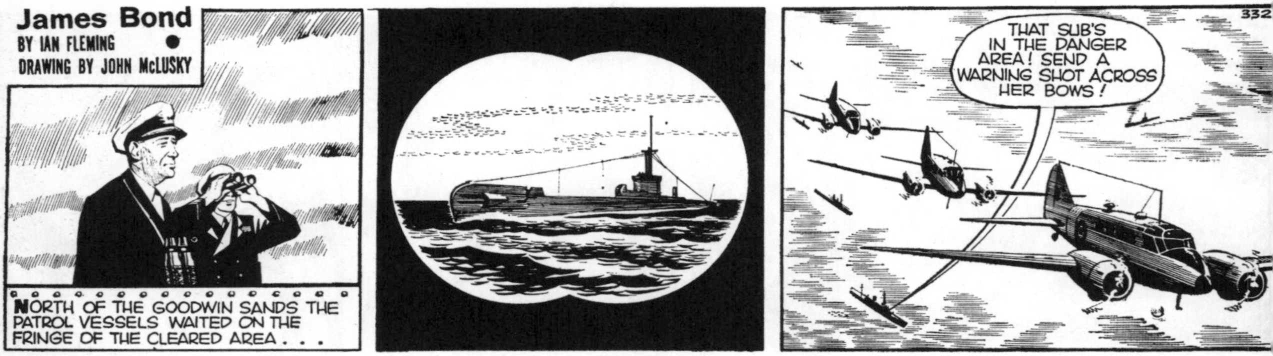
James Bond
BY IAN FLEMING
DRAWING BY JOHN McLUSKY
NORTH OF THE GOODWIN SANDS THE PATROL VESSELS WAITED ON THE FRINGE OF THE CLEARED AREA . . .
332
THAT SUB'S IN THE DANGER AREA! SEND A WARNING SHOT ACROSS HER BOWS!

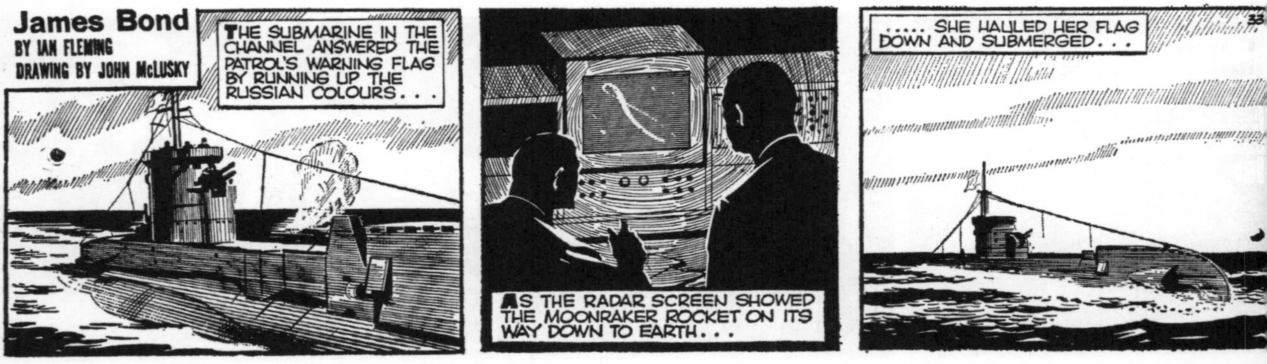
James Bond
BY IAN FLEMING
DRAWING BY JOHN McLUSKY
THE SUBMARINE IN THE CHANNEL ANSWERED THE PATROL'S WARNING FLAG BY RUNNING UP THE RUSSIAN COLOURS. . .
AS THE RADAR SCREEN SHOWED THE MOONRAKER ROCKET ON ITS WAY DOWN TO EARTH. . .
..... SHE HAULED HER FLAG DOWN AND SUBMERGED. . .

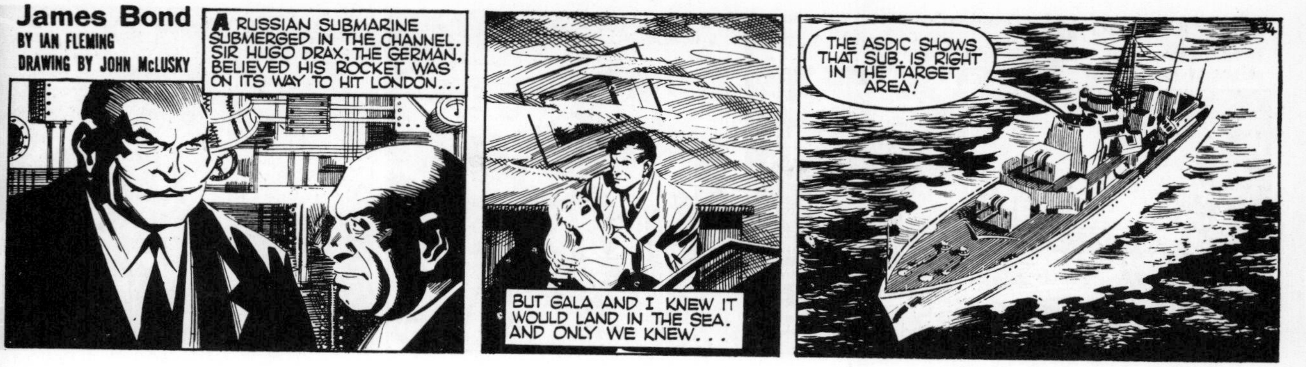
James Bond
BY IAN FLEMING
DRAWING BY JOHN McLUSKY
A RUSSIAN SUBMARINE SUBMERGED IN THE CHANNEL. SIR HUGO DRAX, THE GERMAN, BELIEVED HIS ROCKET WAS ON ITS WAY TO HIT LONDON...
BUT GALA AND I KNEW IT WOULD LAND IN THE SEA. AND ONLY WE KNEW...
334
THE ASDIC SHOWS THAT SUB. IS RIGHT IN THE TARGET AREA!

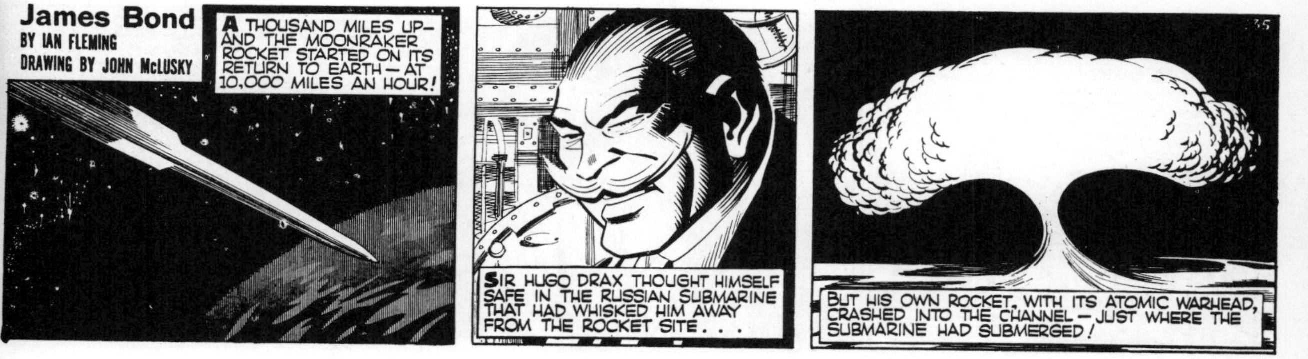
James Bond
BY IAN FLEMING
DRAWING BY JOHN McLUSKY
A THOUSAND MILES UP—AND THE MOONRAKER ROCKET STARTED ON ITS RETURN TO EARTH—AT 10,000 MILES AN HOUR!
SIR HUGO DRAX THOUGHT HIMSELF SAFE IN THE RUSSIAN SUBMARINE THAT HAD WHISKED HIM AWAY FROM THE ROCKET SITE...
335
BUT HIS OWN ROCKET, WITH ITS ATOMIC WARHEAD, CRASHED INTO THE CHANNEL—JUST WHERE THE SUBMARINE HAD SUBMERGED!

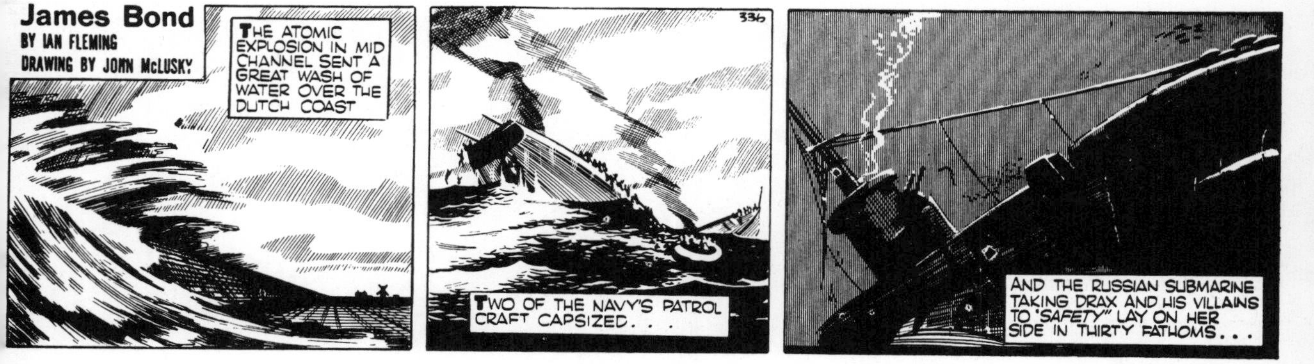
James Bond
BY IAN FLEMING
DRAWING BY JOHN McLUSKY
THE ATOMIC EXPLOSION IN MID CHANNEL SENT A GREAT WASH OF WATER OVER THE DUTCH COAST
336
TWO OF THE NAVY'S PATROL CRAFT CAPSIZED...
AND THE RUSSIAN SUBMARINE TAKING DRAX AND HIS VILLAINS TO "SAFETY" LAY ON HER SIDE IN THIRTY FATHOMS...

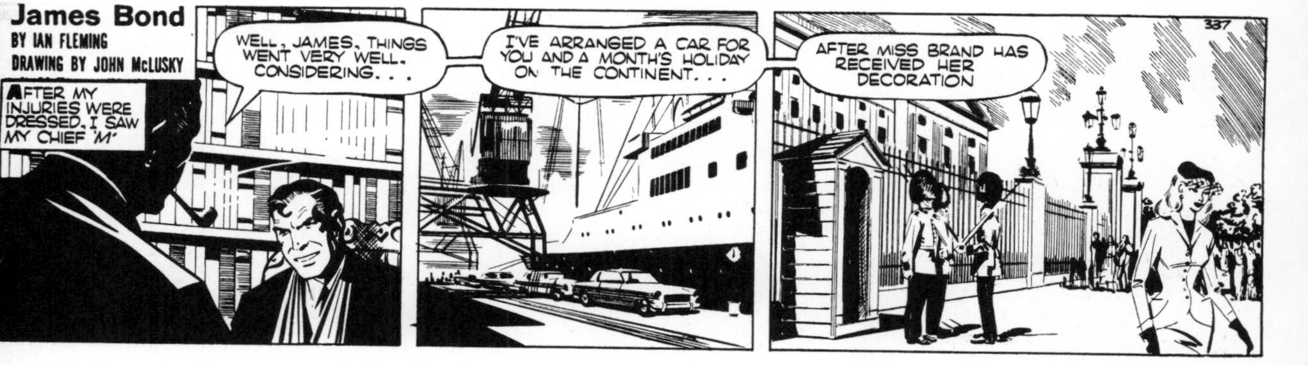
James Bond
BY IAN FLEMING
DRAWING BY JOHN McLUSKY
AFTER MY INJURIES WERE DRESSED, I SAW MY CHIEF 'M'
WELL, JAMES, THINGS WENT VERY WELL. CONSIDERING...
I'VE ARRANGED A CAR FOR YOU AND A MONTH'S HOLIDAY ON THE CONTINENT...
337
AFTER MISS BRAND HAS RECEIVED HER DECORATION

James Bond
BY IAN FLEMING
DRAWING BY JOHN McLUSKY
I HAD A RENDEZVOUS WITH GALA IN THE PARK . . .
THOSE SURGEONS DID A WONDERFUL JOB ON YOU, GALA
I WAS LUCKY, JAMES– THANKS TO YOU
AND CONGRATULATIONS ON THE GEORGE CROSS. YOU DESERVED IT
BUT WHY WAS THERE NO DECORATION FOR YOU, JAMES?
RULE OF THE SERVICE, GALA. STRICTLY ANON!
338

James Bond
BY IAN FLEMING
DRAWING BY JOHN McLUSKY
AND NOW, GALA, WE HAVE A MONTH'S HOLIDAY
HEAVENLY, JAMES. MY HONEYMOON!
339
JAMES, I'D LIKE YOU TO MEET MY FIANCE —DETECTIVE INSPECTOR VIVIAN!
SO I SAID GOODBYE TO GALA BRAND, AND SUDDENLY I FELT VERY LONELY. . .

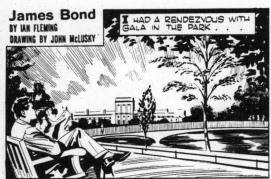

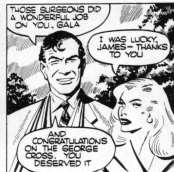

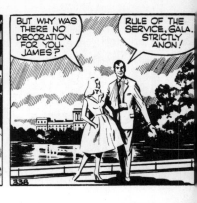

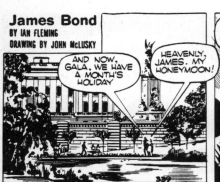

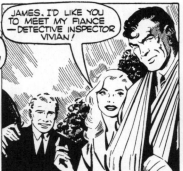

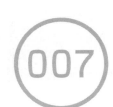

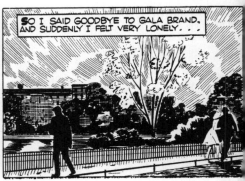

DIAMONDS ARE FOREVER

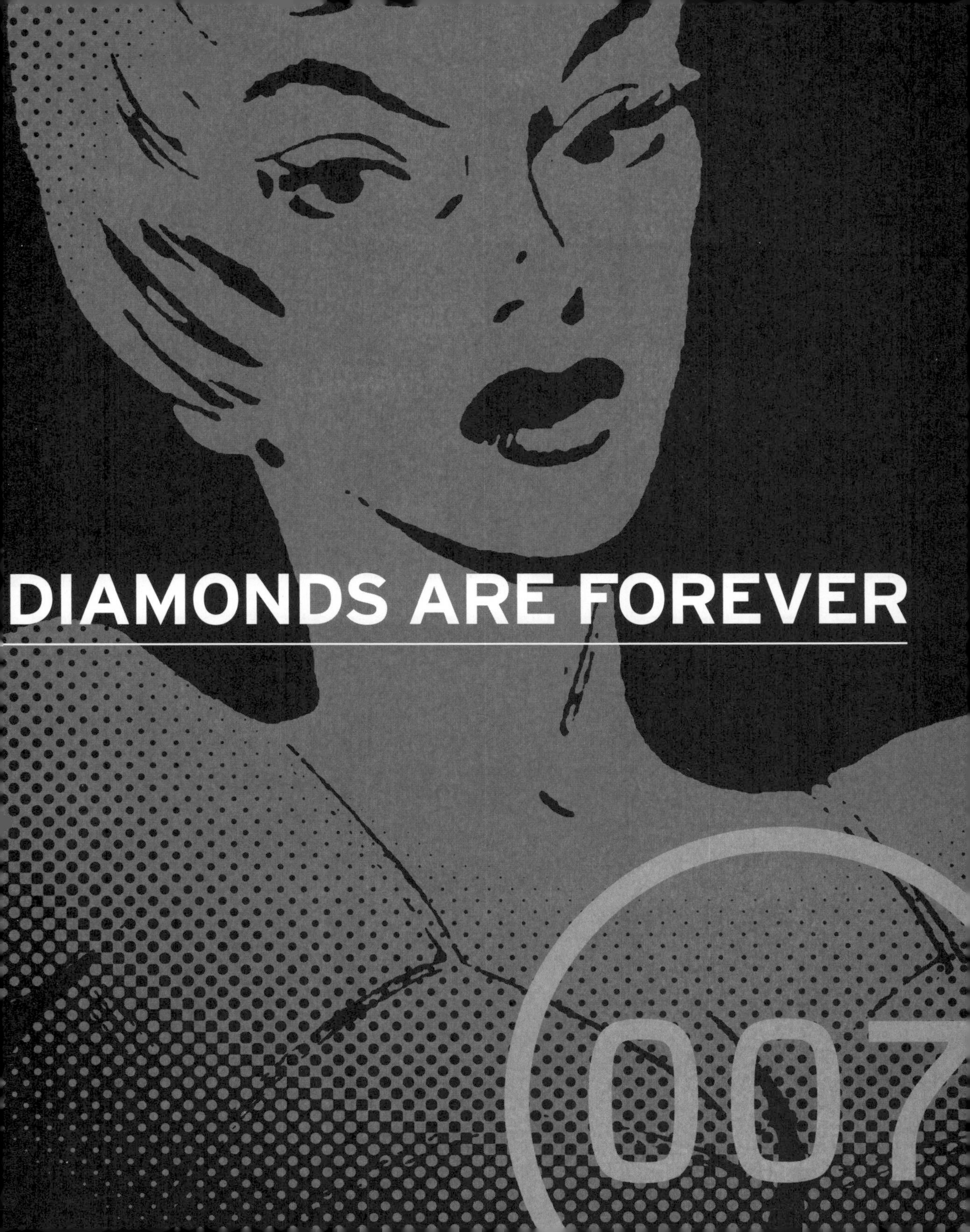

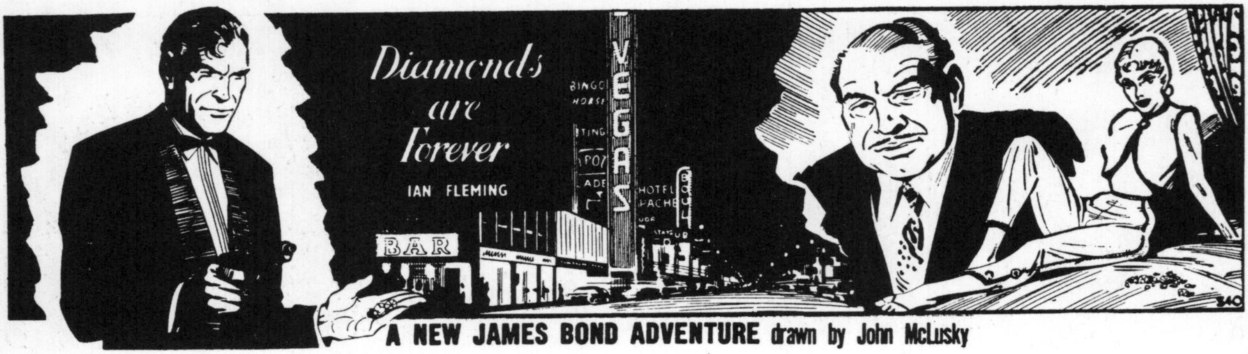
Diamonds are Forever
IAN FLEMING
BAR
VEGAS
HOTEL

A NEW JAMES BOND ADVENTURE drawn by John McLusky

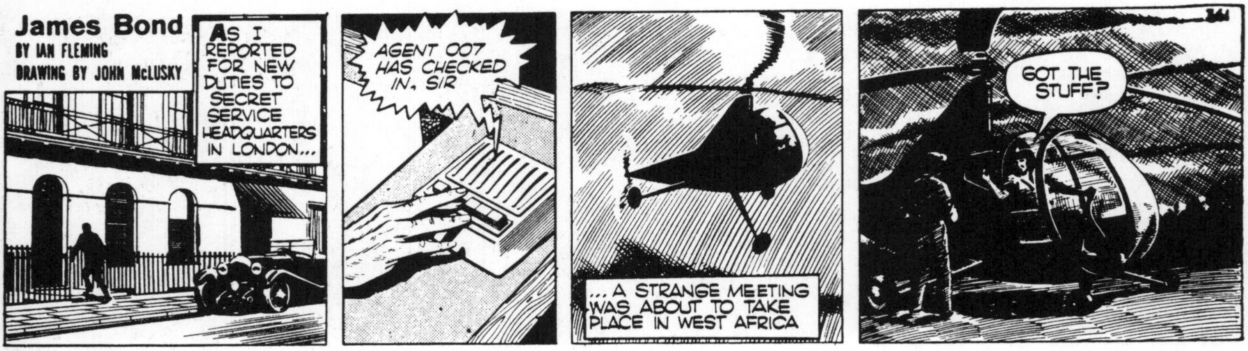
James Bond
BY IAN FLEMING
DRAWING BY JOHN McLUSKY
AS I REPORTED FOR NEW DUTIES TO SECRET SERVICE HEADQUARTERS IN LONDON...
AGENT 007 HAS CHECKED IN, SIR
... A STRANGE MEETING WAS ABOUT TO TAKE PLACE IN WEST AFRICA
GOT THE STUFF?

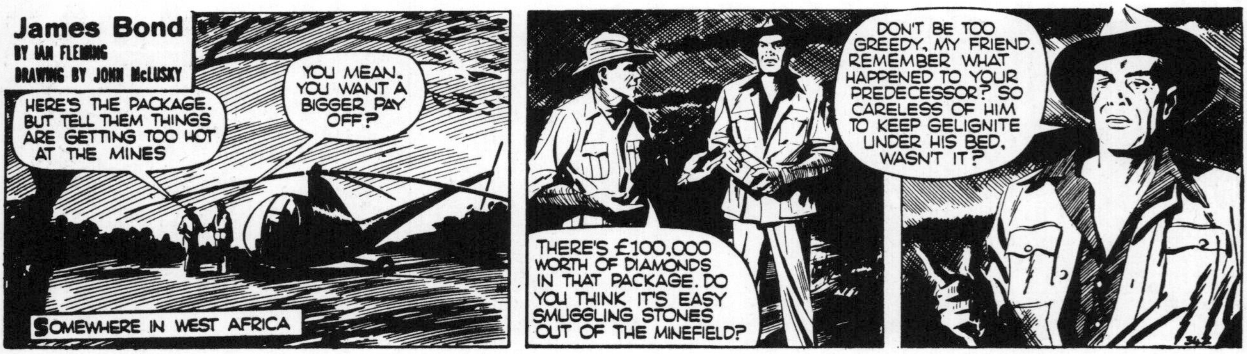
James Bond
BY IAN FLEMING
DRAWING BY JOHN McLUSKY
HERE'S THE PACKAGE. BUT TELL THEM THINGS ARE GETTING TOO HOT AT THE MINES
YOU MEAN, YOU WANT A BIGGER PAY OFF?
SOMEWHERE IN WEST AFRICA
THERE'S £100,000 WORTH OF DIAMONDS IN THAT PACKAGE. DO YOU THINK IT'S EASY SMUGGLING STONES OUT OF THE MINEFIELD?
DON'T BE TOO GREEDY, MY FRIEND. REMEMBER WHAT HAPPENED TO YOUR PREDECESSOR? SO CARELESS OF HIM TO KEEP GELIGNITE UNDER HIS BED, WASN'T IT?

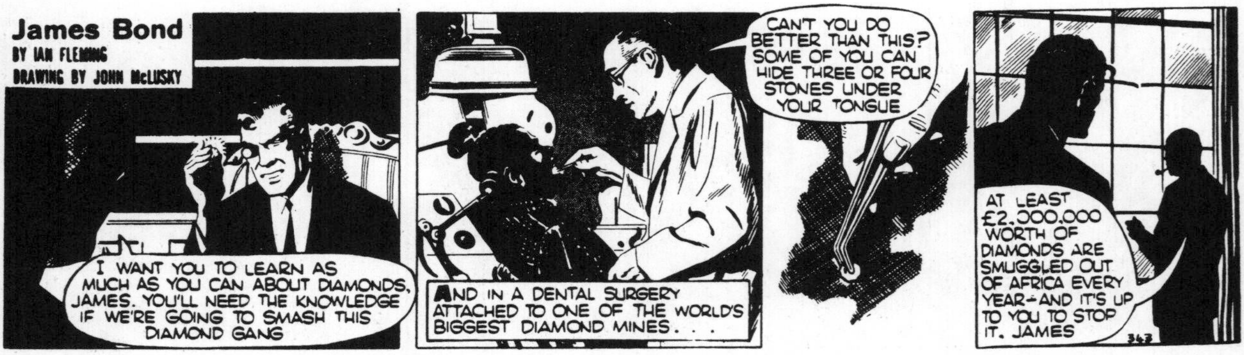
James Bond
BY IAN FLEMING
DRAWING BY JOHN McLUSKY
I WANT YOU TO LEARN AS MUCH AS YOU CAN ABOUT DIAMONDS, JAMES. YOU'LL NEED THE KNOWLEDGE IF WE'RE GOING TO SMASH THIS DIAMOND GANG
AND IN A DENTAL SURGERY ATTACHED TO ONE OF THE WORLD'S BIGGEST DIAMOND MINES . . .
CAN'T YOU DO BETTER THAN THIS? SOME OF YOU CAN HIDE THREE OR FOUR STONES UNDER YOUR TONGUE
AT LEAST £2,000,000 WORTH OF DIAMONDS ARE SMUGGLED OUT OF AFRICA EVERY YEAR—AND IT'S UP TO YOU TO STOP IT, JAMES

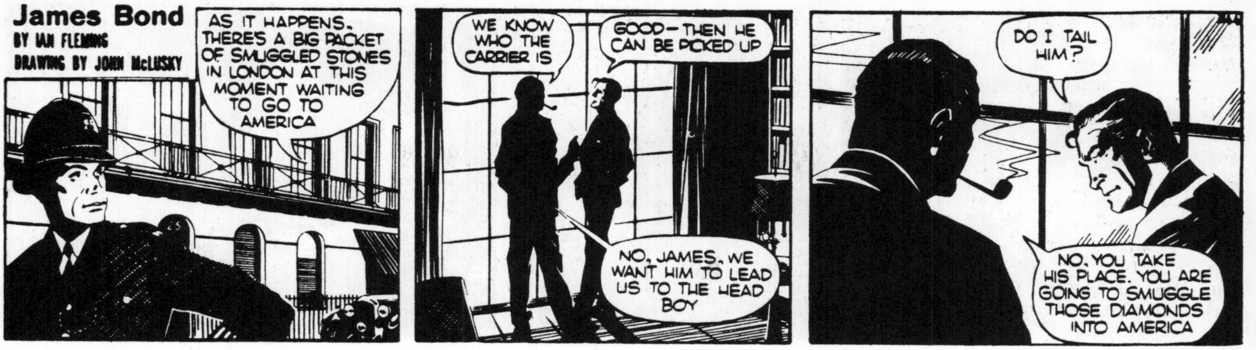
James Bond
BY IAN FLEMING
DRAWING BY JOHN McLUSKY
AS IT HAPPENS, THERE'S A BIG PACKET OF SMUGGLED STONES IN LONDON AT THIS MOMENT WAITING TO GO TO AMERICA
WE KNOW WHO THE CARRIER IS
GOOD—THEN HE CAN BE PICKED UP
NO, JAMES, WE WANT HIM TO LEAD US TO THE HEAD BOY
DO I TAIL HIM?
NO, YOU TAKE HIS PLACE. YOU ARE GOING TO SMUGGLE THOSE DIAMONDS INTO AMERICA

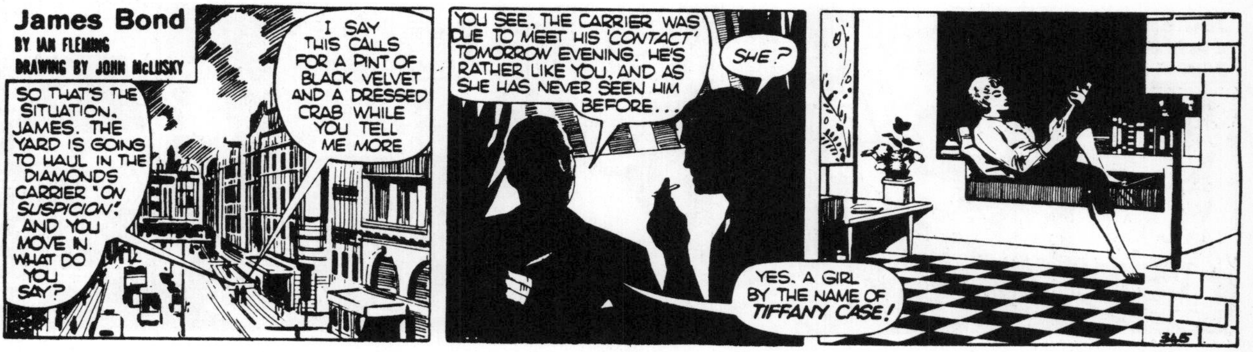
James Bond
BY IAN FLEMING
DRAWING BY JOHN McLUSKY
SO THAT'S THE SITUATION, JAMES. THE YARD IS GOING TO HAUL IN THE DIAMONDS CARRIER "ON *SUSPICION*" AND YOU MOVE IN. WHAT DO YOU SAY?
I SAY THIS CALLS FOR A PINT OF BLACK VELVET AND A DRESSED CRAB WHILE YOU TELL ME MORE
YOU SEE, THE CARRIER WAS DUE TO MEET HIS '*CONTACT*' TOMORROW EVENING. HE'S RATHER LIKE YOU, AND AS SHE HAS NEVER SEEN HIM BEFORE...
SHE?
YES. A GIRL BY THE NAME OF ***TIFFANY CASE!***
345

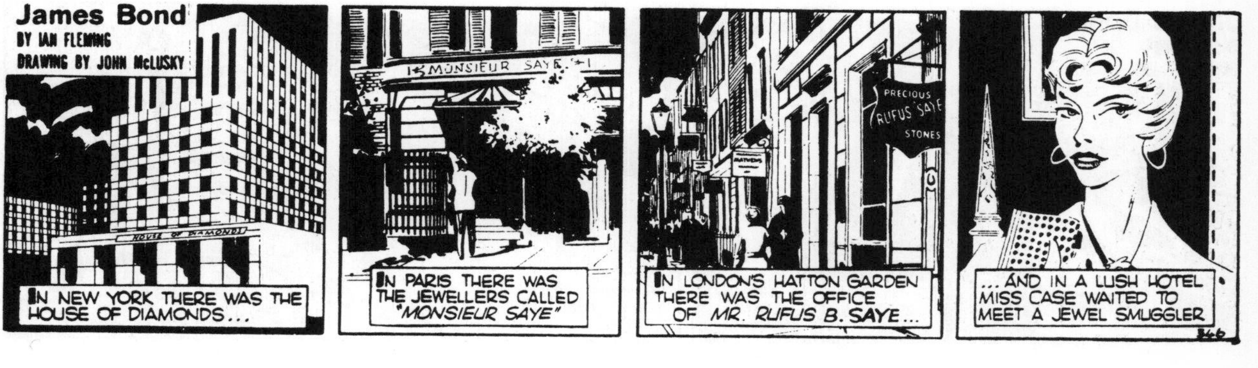
James Bond
BY IAN FLEMING
DRAWING BY JOHN McLUSKY
HOUSE OF DIAMONDS
IN NEW YORK THERE WAS THE HOUSE OF DIAMONDS...
MONSIEUR SAYE
IN PARIS THERE WAS THE JEWELLERS CALLED "*MONSIEUR SAYE*"
PRECIOUS
RUFUS SAYE
STONES
IN LONDON'S HATTON GARDEN THERE WAS THE OFFICE OF *MR. RUFUS B. SAYE*...
...AND IN A LUSH HOTEL MISS CASE WAITED TO MEET A JEWEL SMUGGLER
346

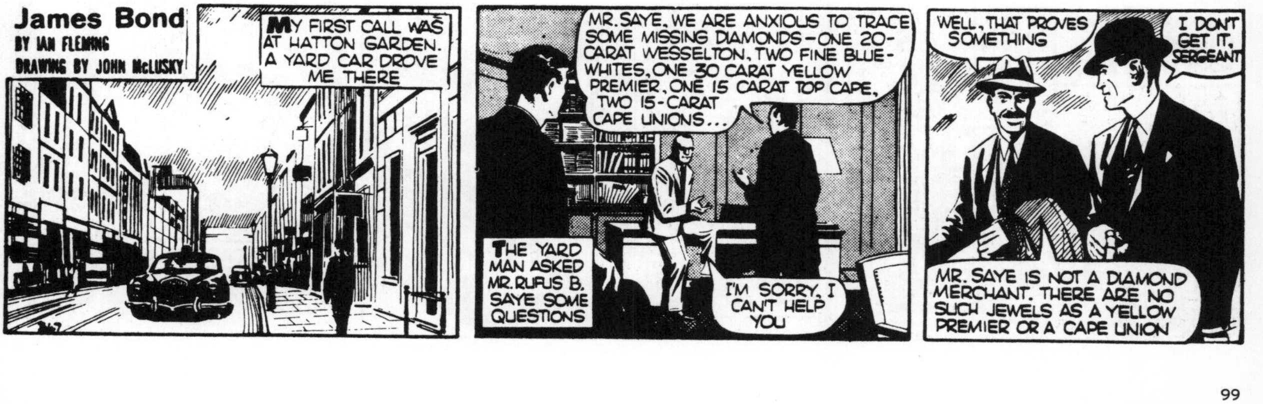
James Bond
BY IAN FLEMING
DRAWING BY JOHN McLUSKY
MY FIRST CALL WAS AT HATTON GARDEN. A YARD CAR DROVE ME THERE
MR. SAYE, WE ARE ANXIOUS TO TRACE SOME MISSING DIAMONDS—ONE 20-CARAT WESSELTON, TWO FINE BLUE-WHITES, ONE 30 CARAT YELLOW PREMIER, ONE 15 CARAT TOP CAPE, TWO 15-CARAT CAPE UNIONS...
THE YARD MAN ASKED MR. RUFUS B. SAYE SOME QUESTIONS
I'M SORRY, I CAN'T HELP YOU
WELL, THAT PROVES SOMETHING
I DON'T GET IT, SERGEANT
MR. SAYE IS NOT A DIAMOND MERCHANT. THERE ARE NO SUCH JEWELS AS A YELLOW PREMIER OR A CAPE UNION

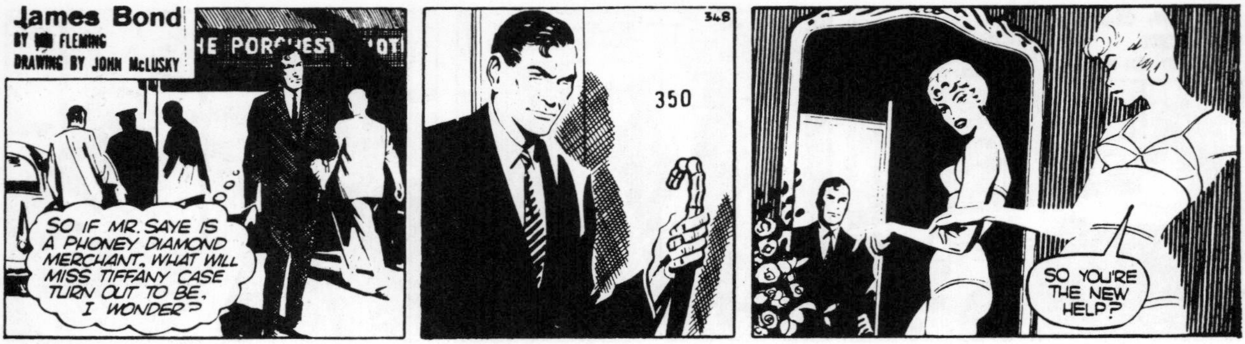

James Bond
BY FLEMING
DRAWING BY JOHN McLUSKY
SO IF MR. SAYE IS A PHONEY DIAMOND MERCHANT, WHAT WILL MISS TIFFANY CASE TURN OUT TO BE, I WONDER?
348
350
SO YOU'RE THE NEW HELP?

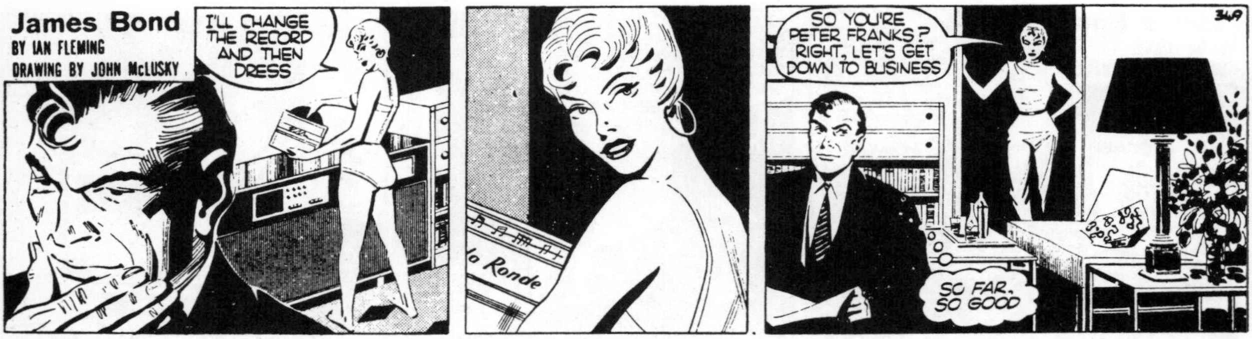

James Bond
BY IAN FLEMING
DRAWING BY JOHN McLUSKY
I'LL CHANGE THE RECORD AND THEN DRESS
349
SO YOU'RE PETER FRANKS? RIGHT, LET'S GET DOWN TO BUSINESS
SO FAR, SO GOOD

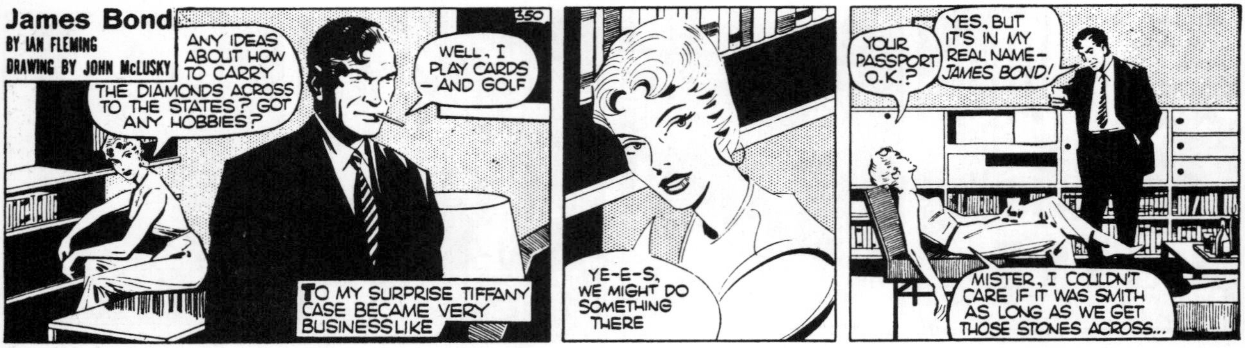

James Bond
BY IAN FLEMING
DRAWING BY JOHN McLUSKY
350
ANY IDEAS ABOUT HOW TO CARRY THE DIAMONDS ACROSS TO THE STATES? GOT ANY HOBBIES?
WELL, I PLAY CARDS —AND GOLF
TO MY SURPRISE TIFFANY CASE BECAME VERY BUSINESSLIKE
YE-E-S, WE MIGHT DO SOMETHING THERE
YOUR PASSPORT O.K.?
YES, BUT IT'S IN MY REAL NAME— JAMES BOND!
MISTER, I COULDN'T CARE IF IT WAS SMITH AS LONG AS WE GET THOSE STONES ACROSS...

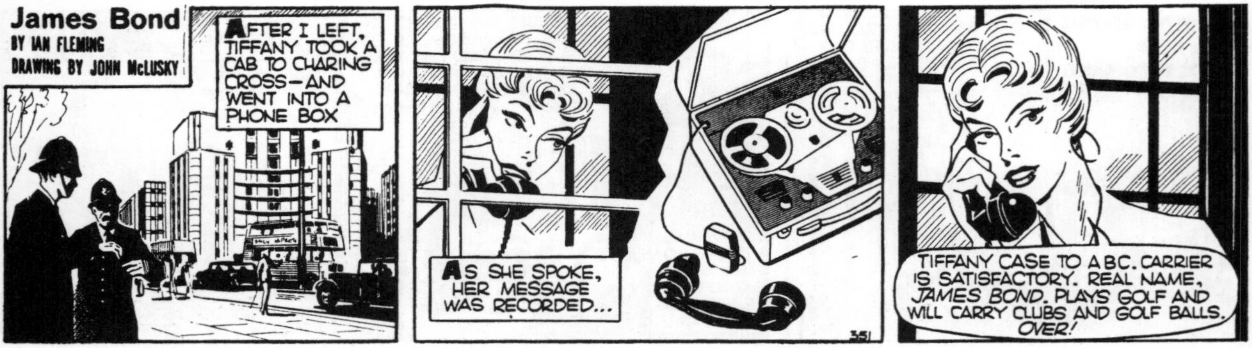

James Bond
BY IAN FLEMING
DRAWING BY JOHN McLUSKY
AFTER I LEFT, TIFFANY TOOK A CAB TO CHARING CROSS—AND WENT INTO A PHONE BOX
AS SHE SPOKE, HER MESSAGE WAS RECORDED...
351
TIFFANY CASE TO A.B.C. CARRIER IS SATISFACTORY. REAL NAME, JAMES BOND. PLAYS GOLF AND WILL CARRY CLUBS AND GOLF BALLS. OVER!

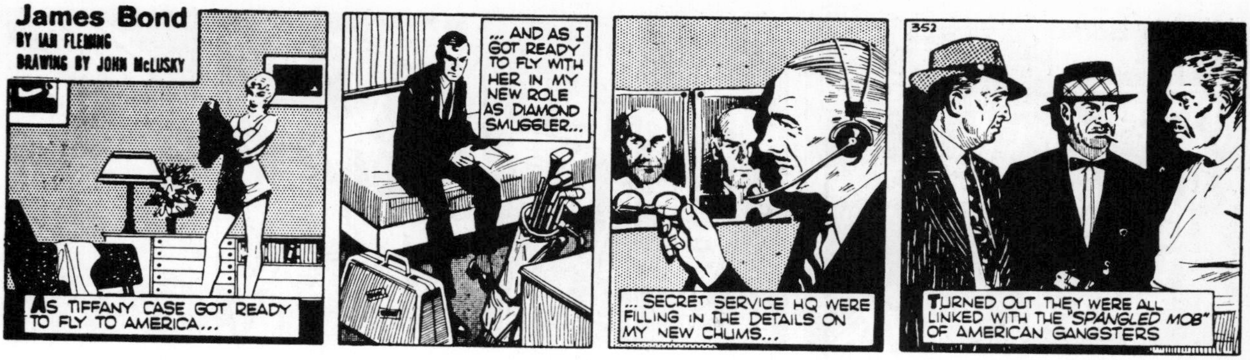
James Bond
BY IAN FLEMING
DRAWING BY JOHN McLUSKY
AS TIFFANY CASE GOT READY TO FLY TO AMERICA...
... AND AS I GOT READY TO FLY WITH HER IN MY NEW ROLE AS DIAMOND SMUGGLER...
... SECRET SERVICE HQ WERE FILLING IN THE DETAILS ON MY NEW CHUMS...
352
TURNED OUT THEY WERE ALL LINKED WITH THE "SPANGLED MOB" OF AMERICAN GANGSTERS

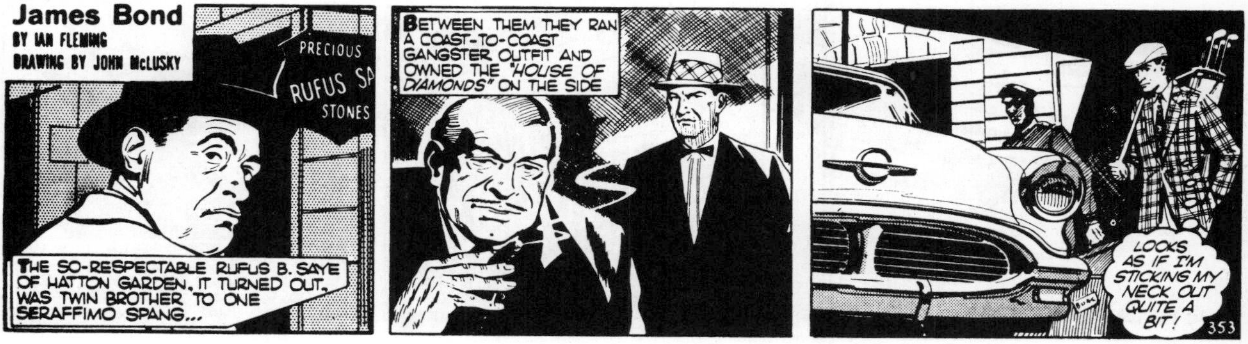
James Bond
BY IAN FLEMING
DRAWING BY JOHN McLUSKY
PRECIOUS
RUFUS SA
STONES
THE SO-RESPECTABLE RUFUS B. SAYE OF HATTON GARDEN, IT TURNED OUT, WAS TWIN BROTHER TO ONE SERAFFIMO SPANG...
BETWEEN THEM THEY RAN A COAST-TO-COAST GANGSTER OUTFIT AND OWNED THE "HOUSE OF DIAMONDS" ON THE SIDE
LOOKS AS IF I'M STICKING MY NECK OUT QUITE A BIT!
353

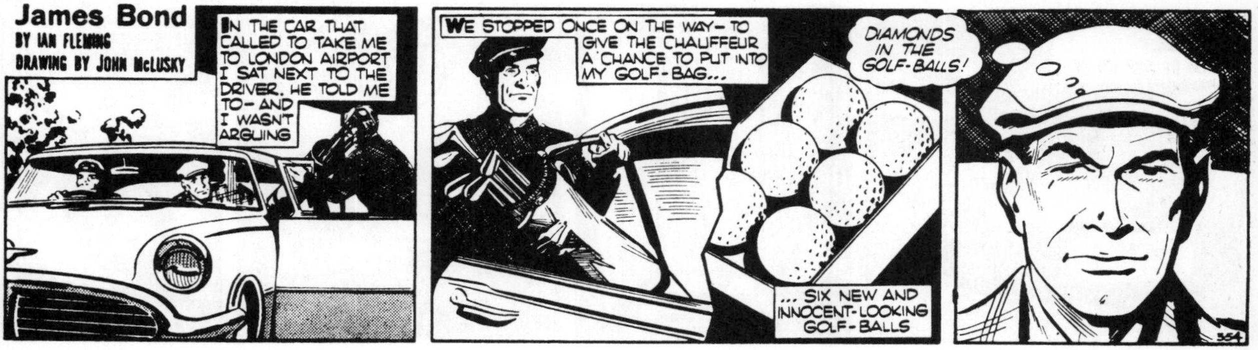
James Bond
BY IAN FLEMING
DRAWING BY JOHN McLUSKY
IN THE CAR THAT CALLED TO TAKE ME TO LONDON AIRPORT I SAT NEXT TO THE DRIVER. HE TOLD ME TO – AND I WASN'T ARGUING
WE STOPPED ONCE ON THE WAY – TO GIVE THE CHAUFFEUR A CHANCE TO PUT INTO MY GOLF-BAG...
... SIX NEW AND INNOCENT-LOOKING GOLF-BALLS
DIAMONDS IN THE GOLF-BALLS!
354

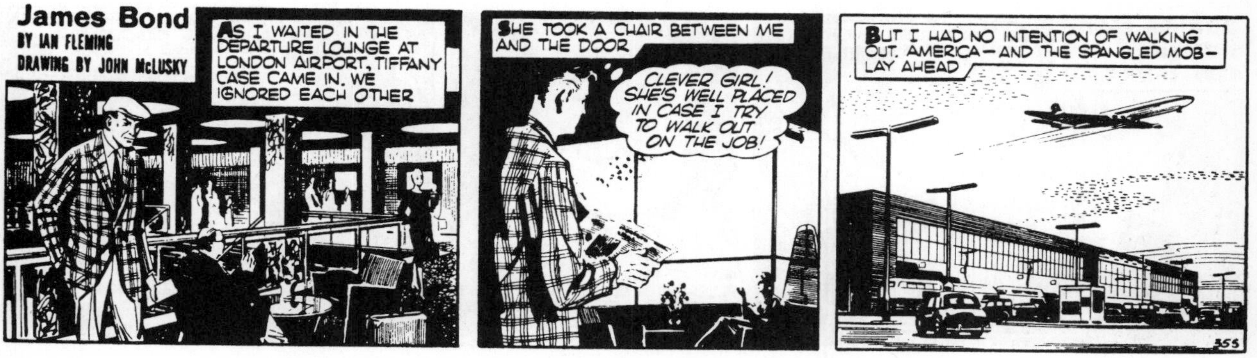
James Bond
BY IAN FLEMING
DRAWING BY JOHN McLUSKY
AS I WAITED IN THE DEPARTURE LOUNGE AT LONDON AIRPORT, TIFFANY CASE CAME IN. WE IGNORED EACH OTHER
SHE TOOK A CHAIR BETWEEN ME AND THE DOOR
CLEVER GIRL! SHE'S WELL PLACED IN CASE I TRY TO WALK OUT ON THE JOB!
BUT I HAD NO INTENTION OF WALKING OUT. AMERICA – AND THE SPANGLED MOB – LAY AHEAD
355

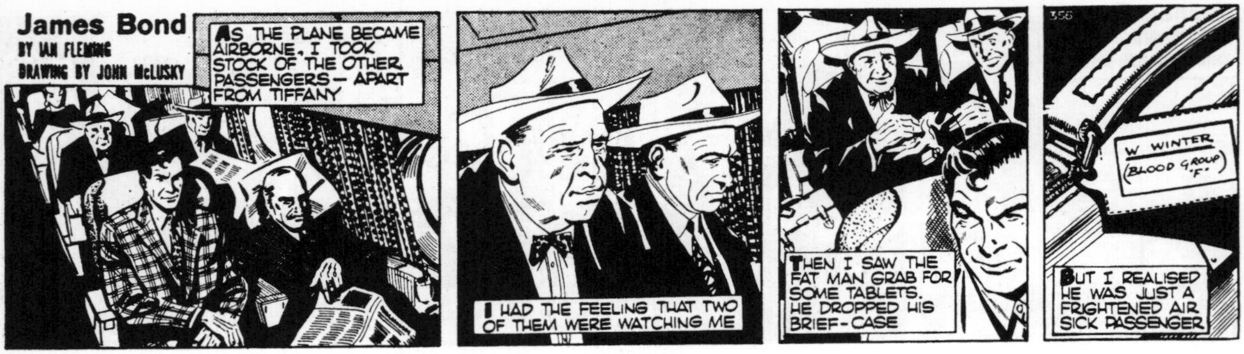
James Bond
BY IAN FLEMING
DRAWING BY JOHN McLUSKY
AS THE PLANE BECAME AIRBORNE, I TOOK STOCK OF THE OTHER PASSENGERS — APART FROM TIFFANY
I HAD THE FEELING THAT TWO OF THEM WERE WATCHING ME
THEN I SAW THE FAT MAN GRAB FOR SOME TABLETS. HE DROPPED HIS BRIEF-CASE
356
W WINTER
(BLOOD GROUP 'F')
BUT I REALISED HE WAS JUST A FRIGHTENED AIR SICK PASSENGER

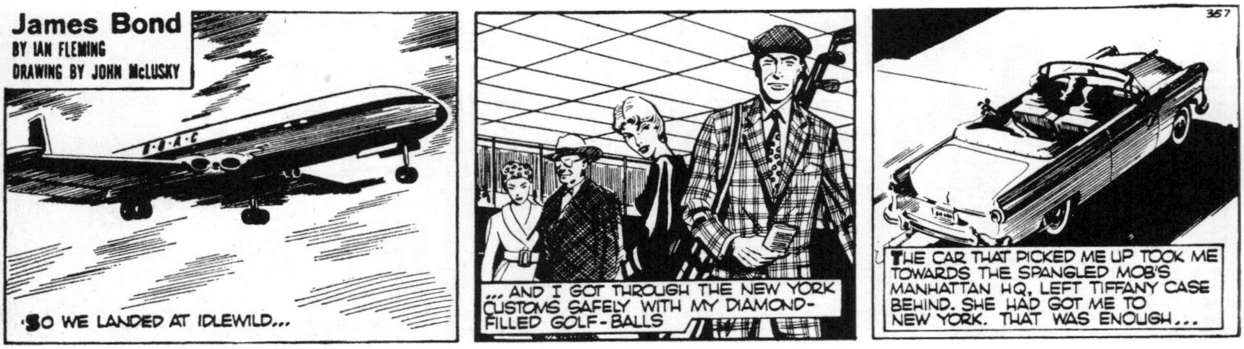
James Bond
BY IAN FLEMING
DRAWING BY JOHN McLUSKY
B.O.A.C
SO WE LANDED AT IDLEWILD...
... AND I GOT THROUGH THE NEW YORK CUSTOMS SAFELY WITH MY DIAMOND-FILLED GOLF-BALLS
357
THE CAR THAT PICKED ME UP TOOK ME TOWARDS THE SPANGLED MOB'S MANHATTAN HQ, LEFT TIFFANY CASE BEHIND. SHE HAD GOT ME TO NEW YORK. THAT WAS ENOUGH...

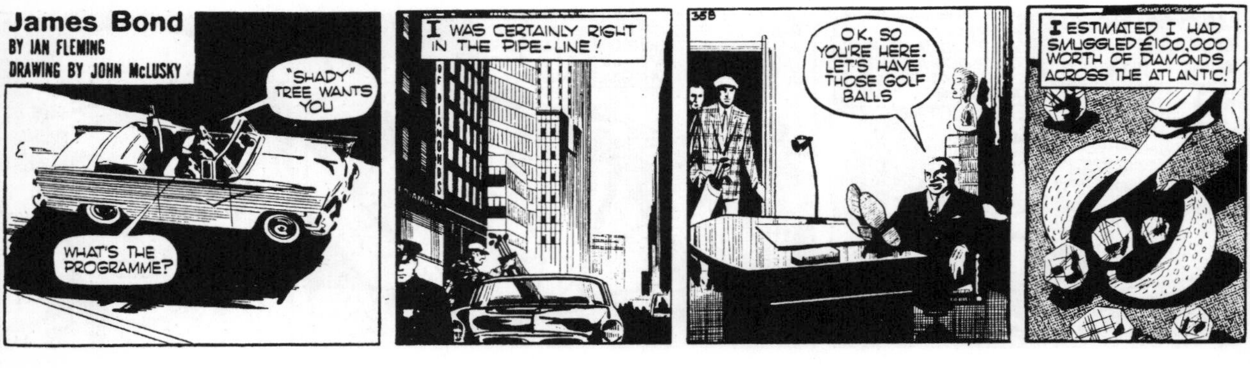
James Bond
BY IAN FLEMING
DRAWING BY JOHN McLUSKY
"SHADY" TREE WANTS YOU
WHAT'S THE PROGRAMME?
I WAS CERTAINLY RIGHT IN THE PIPE-LINE!
358
OK, SO YOU'RE HERE. LET'S HAVE THOSE GOLF BALLS
I ESTIMATED I HAD SMUGGLED £100,000 WORTH OF DIAMONDS ACROSS THE ATLANTIC!

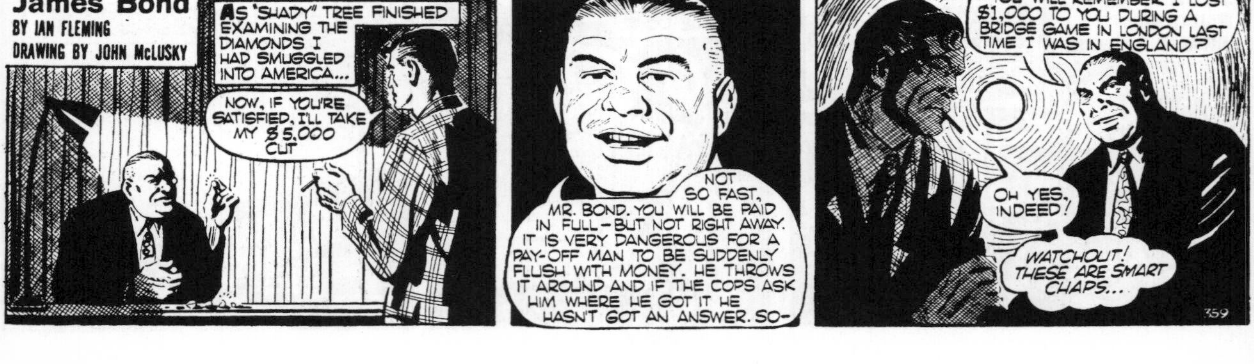
James Bond
BY IAN FLEMING
DRAWING BY JOHN McLUSKY
AS "SHADY" TREE FINISHED EXAMINING THE DIAMONDS I HAD SMUGGLED INTO AMERICA...
NOW, IF YOU'RE SATISFIED, I'LL TAKE MY $5,000 CUT
NOT SO FAST, MR. BOND. YOU WILL BE PAID IN FULL—BUT NOT RIGHT AWAY. IT IS VERY DANGEROUS FOR A PAY-OFF MAN TO BE SUDDENLY FLUSH WITH MONEY. HE THROWS IT AROUND AND IF THE COPS ASK HIM WHERE HE GOT IT HE HASN'T GOT AN ANSWER. SO-
-YOU WILL REMEMBER I LOST $1,000 TO YOU DURING A BRIDGE GAME IN LONDON LAST TIME I WAS IN ENGLAND?
OH YES, INDEED!
WATCHOUT! THESE ARE SMART CHAPS...
359

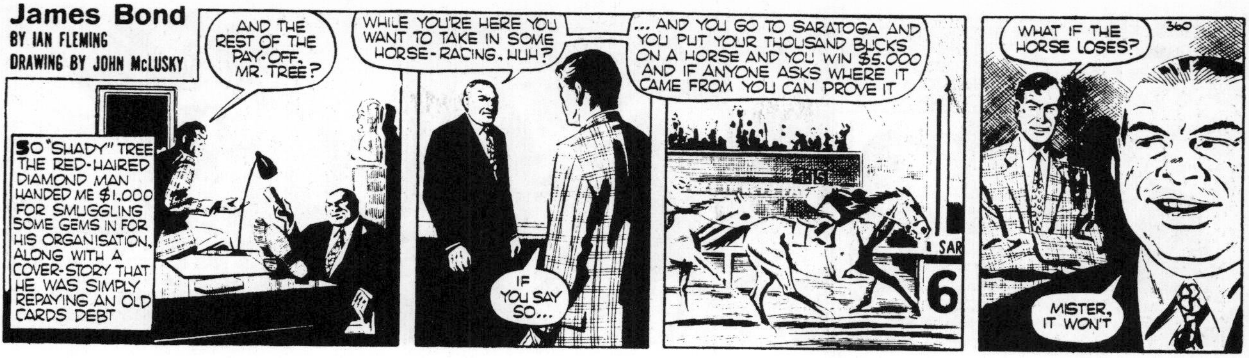
James Bond
BY IAN FLEMING
DRAWING BY JOHN McLUSKY
SO "SHADY" TREE THE RED-HAIRED DIAMOND MAN HANDED ME $1,000 FOR SMUGGLING SOME GEMS IN FOR HIS ORGANISATION, ALONG WITH A COVER-STORY THAT HE WAS SIMPLY REPAYING AN OLD CARDS DEBT
AND THE REST OF THE PAY-OFF, MR. TREE?
WHILE YOU'RE HERE YOU WANT TO TAKE IN SOME HORSE-RACING, HUH?
IF YOU SAY SO...
... AND YOU GO TO SARATOGA AND YOU PUT YOUR THOUSAND BUCKS ON A HORSE AND YOU WIN $5,000 AND IF ANYONE ASKS WHERE IT CAME FROM YOU CAN PROVE IT
SAR
6
360
WHAT IF THE HORSE LOSES?
MISTER, IT WON'T

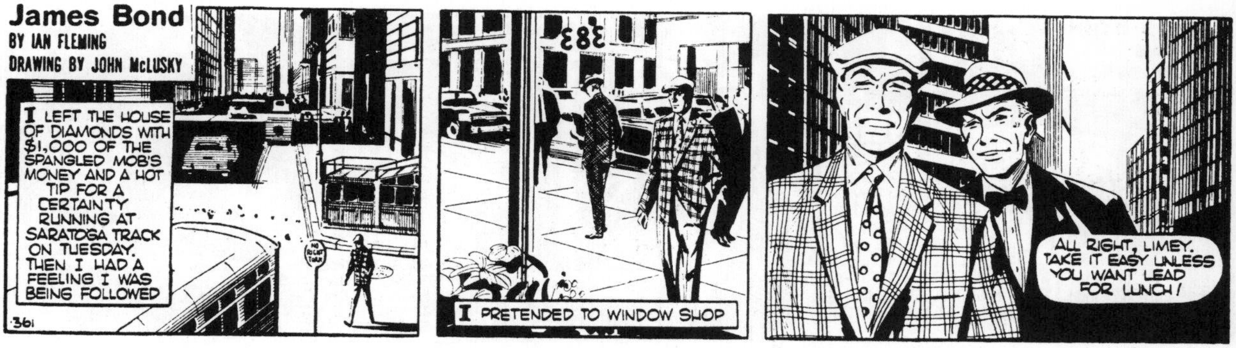
James Bond
BY IAN FLEMING
DRAWING BY JOHN McLUSKY
I LEFT THE HOUSE OF DIAMONDS WITH $1,000 OF THE SPANGLED MOB'S MONEY AND A HOT TIP FOR A CERTAINTY RUNNING AT SARATOGA TRACK ON TUESDAY. THEN I HAD A FEELING I WAS BEING FOLLOWED
361
383
I PRETENDED TO WINDOW SHOP
ALL RIGHT, LIMEY. TAKE IT EASY UNLESS YOU WANT LEAD FOR LUNCH!

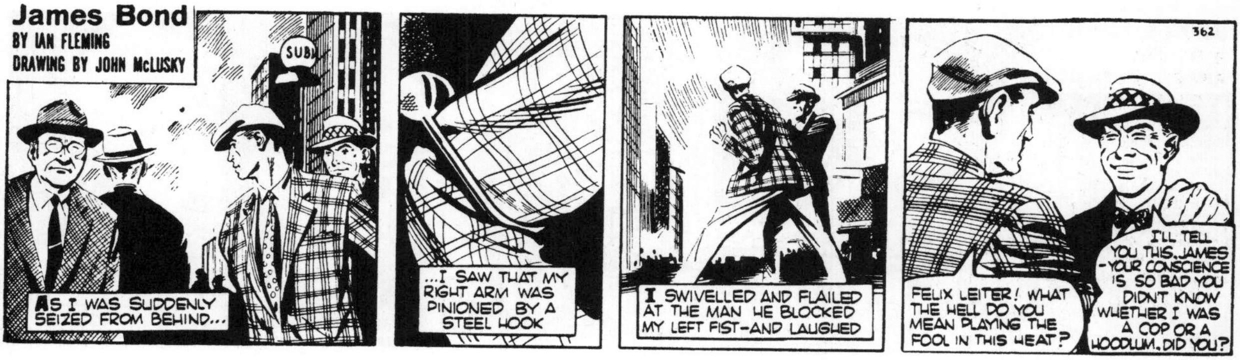
James Bond
BY IAN FLEMING
DRAWING BY JOHN McLUSKY
SUBW
AS I WAS SUDDENLY SEIZED FROM BEHIND...
...I SAW THAT MY RIGHT ARM WAS PINIONED BY A STEEL HOOK
I SWIVELLED AND FLAILED AT THE MAN HE BLOCKED MY LEFT FIST–AND LAUGHED
362
FELIX LEITER! WHAT THE HELL DO YOU MEAN PLAYING THE FOOL IN THIS HEAT?
I'LL TELL YOU THIS, JAMES –YOUR CONSCIENCE IS SO BAD YOU DIDN'T KNOW WHETHER I WAS A COP OR A HOODLUM, DID YOU?

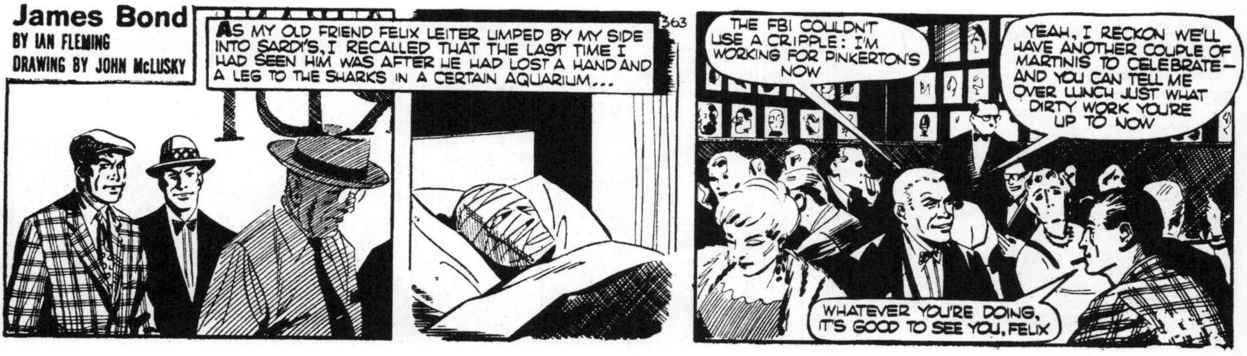
James Bond
BY IAN FLEMING
DRAWING BY JOHN McLUSKY
AS MY OLD FRIEND FELIX LEITER LIMPED BY MY SIDE INTO SARDI'S, I RECALLED THAT THE LAST TIME I HAD SEEN HIM WAS AFTER HE HAD LOST A HAND AND A LEG TO THE SHARKS IN A CERTAIN AQUARIUM...
363
THE FBI COULDN'T USE A CRIPPLE: I'M WORKING FOR PINKERTON'S NOW
YEAH, I RECKON WE'LL HAVE ANOTHER COUPLE OF MARTINIS TO CELEBRATE– AND YOU CAN TELL ME OVER LUNCH JUST WHAT DIRTY WORK YOU'RE UP TO NOW
WHATEVER YOU'RE DOING, IT'S GOOD TO SEE YOU, FELIX

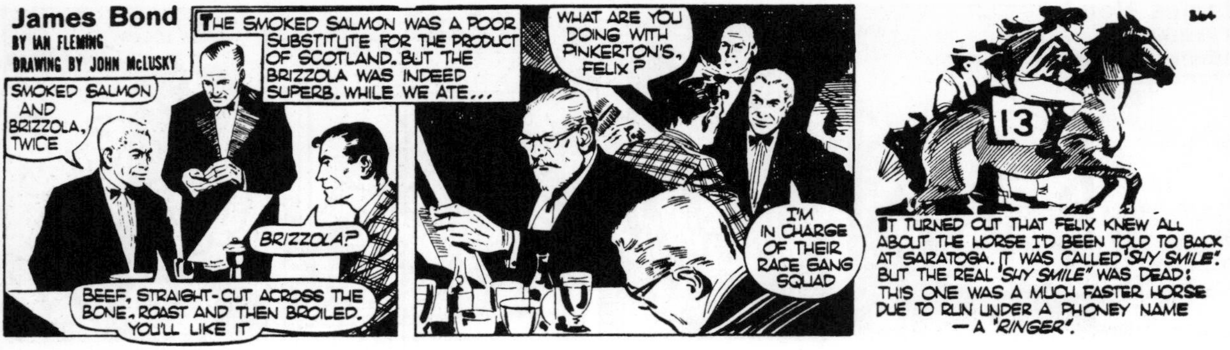
James Bond
BY IAN FLEMING
DRAWING BY JOHN McLUSKY
THE SMOKED SALMON WAS A POOR SUBSTITUTE FOR THE PRODUCT OF SCOTLAND. BUT THE BRIZZOLA WAS INDEED SUPERB. WHILE WE ATE...
SMOKED SALMON AND BRIZZOLA, TWICE
BRIZZOLA?
BEEF, STRAIGHT-CUT ACROSS THE BONE, ROAST AND THEN BROILED. YOU'LL LIKE IT
WHAT ARE YOU DOING WITH PINKERTON'S, FELIX?
I'M IN CHARGE OF THEIR RACE GANG SQUAD
364
13
IT TURNED OUT THAT FELIX KNEW ALL ABOUT THE HORSE I'D BEEN TOLD TO BACK AT SARATOGA. IT WAS CALLED 'SHY SMILE'. BUT THE REAL 'SHY SMILE' WAS DEAD: THIS ONE WAS A MUCH FASTER HORSE DUE TO RUN UNDER A PHONEY NAME — A 'RINGER'.

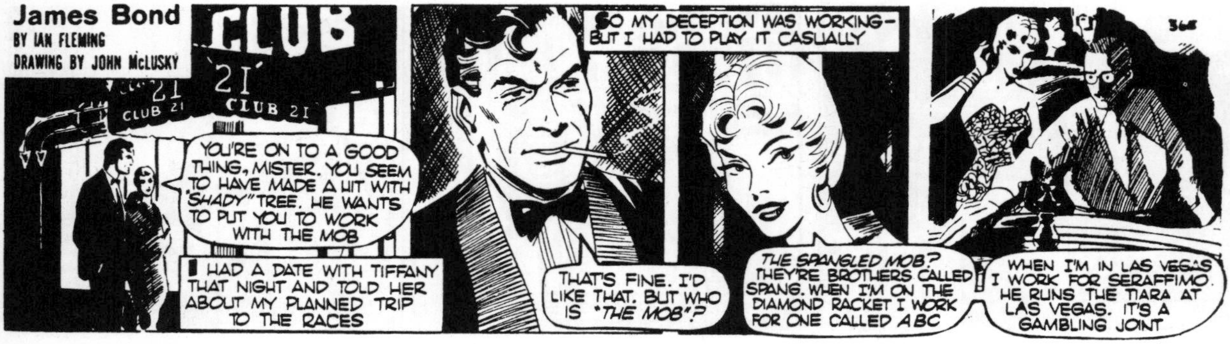
James Bond
BY IAN FLEMING
DRAWING BY JOHN McLUSKY
CLUB
21
CLUB 21
CLUB 21
YOU'RE ON TO A GOOD THING, MISTER. YOU SEEM TO HAVE MADE A HIT WITH 'SHADY' TREE. HE WANTS TO PUT YOU TO WORK WITH THE MOB
I HAD A DATE WITH TIFFANY THAT NIGHT AND TOLD HER ABOUT MY PLANNED TRIP TO THE RACES
SO MY DECEPTION WAS WORKING— BUT I HAD TO PLAY IT CASUALLY
THAT'S FINE. I'D LIKE THAT. BUT WHO IS "THE MOB"?
THE SPANGLED MOB? THEY'RE BROTHERS CALLED SPANG. WHEN I'M ON THE DIAMOND RACKET I WORK FOR ONE CALLED ABC
365
WHEN I'M IN LAS VEGAS I WORK FOR SERAFFIMO. HE RUNS THE TIARA AT LAS VEGAS. IT'S A GAMBLING JOINT

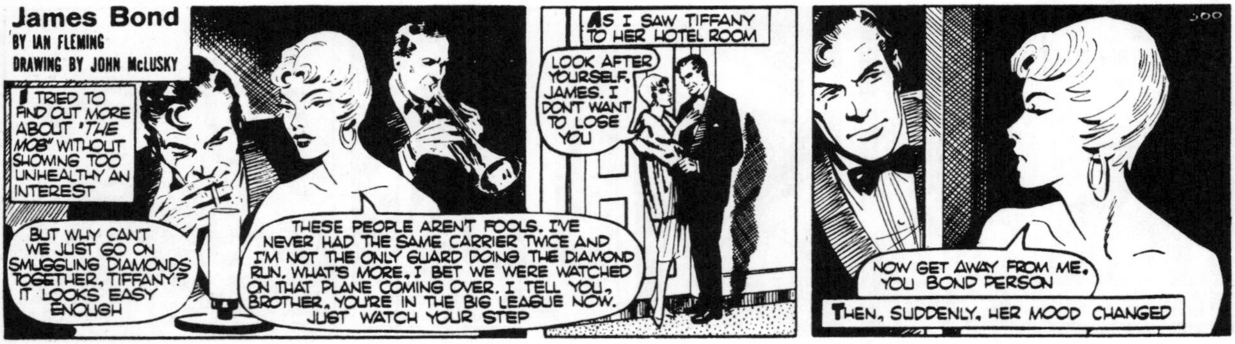
James Bond
BY IAN FLEMING
DRAWING BY JOHN McLUSKY
I TRIED TO FIND OUT MORE ABOUT 'THE MOB' WITHOUT SHOWING TOO UNHEALTHY AN INTEREST
BUT WHY CAN'T WE JUST GO ON SMUGGLING DIAMONDS TOGETHER, TIFFANY? IT LOOKS EASY ENOUGH
THESE PEOPLE AREN'T FOOLS. I'VE NEVER HAD THE SAME CARRIER TWICE AND I'M NOT THE ONLY GUARD DOING THE DIAMOND RUN. WHAT'S MORE, I BET WE WERE WATCHED ON THAT PLANE COMING OVER. I TELL YOU, BROTHER, YOU'RE IN THE BIG LEAGUE NOW. JUST WATCH YOUR STEP
AS I SAW TIFFANY TO HER HOTEL ROOM
LOOK AFTER YOURSELF, JAMES. I DON'T WANT TO LOSE YOU
NOW GET AWAY FROM ME, YOU BOND PERSON
THEN, SUDDENLY, HER MOOD CHANGED

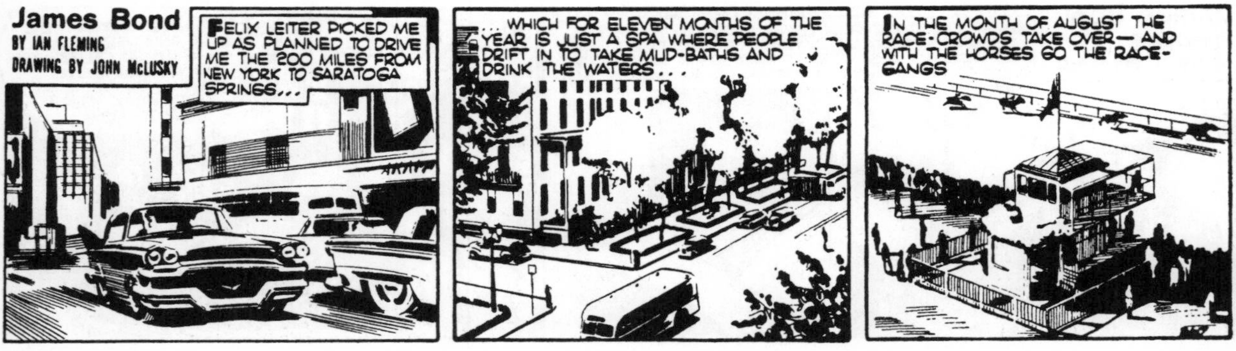
James Bond
BY IAN FLEMING
DRAWING BY JOHN McLUSKY
FELIX LEITER PICKED ME UP AS PLANNED TO DRIVE ME THE 200 MILES FROM NEW YORK TO SARATOGA SPRINGS...
... WHICH FOR ELEVEN MONTHS OF THE YEAR IS JUST A SPA WHERE PEOPLE DRIFT IN TO TAKE MUD-BATHS AND DRINK THE WATERS...
IN THE MONTH OF AUGUST THE RACE-CROWDS TAKE OVER— AND WITH THE HORSES GO THE RACE-GANGS

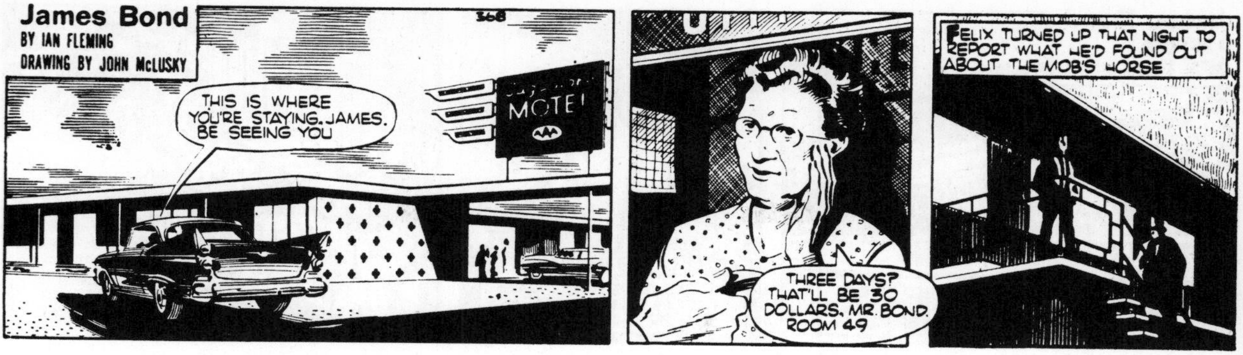
James Bond
BY IAN FLEMING
DRAWING BY JOHN McLUSKY
368
THIS IS WHERE YOU'RE STAYING, JAMES. BE SEEING YOU
MOTEL
THREE DAYS? THAT'LL BE 30 DOLLARS, MR. BOND. ROOM 49
FELIX TURNED UP THAT NIGHT TO REPORT WHAT HE'D FOUND OUT ABOUT THE MOB'S HORSE

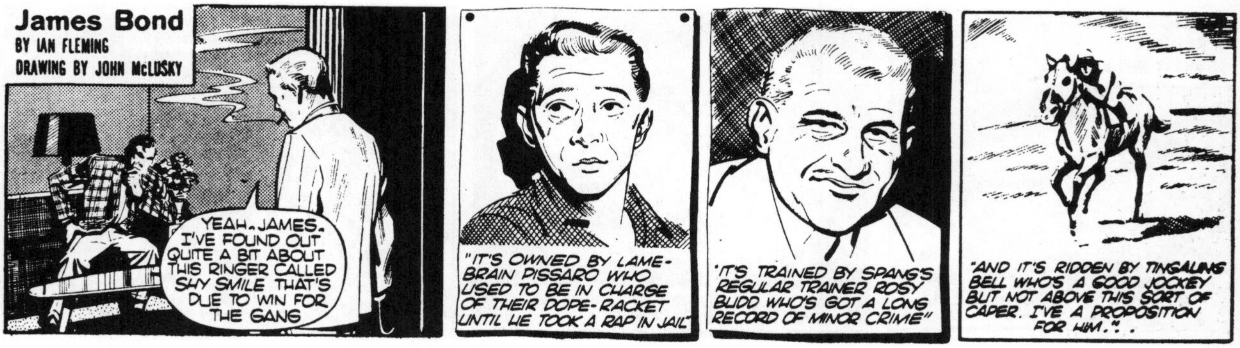
James Bond
BY IAN FLEMING
DRAWING BY JOHN McLUSKY
YEAH, JAMES. I'VE FOUND OUT QUITE A BIT ABOUT THIS RINGER CALLED *SHY SMILE* THAT'S DUE TO WIN FOR THE GANG
"IT'S OWNED BY LAME-BRAIN PISSARO WHO USED TO BE IN CHARGE OF THEIR DOPE-RACKET UNTIL HE TOOK A RAP IN JAIL"
"IT'S TRAINED BY SPANG'S REGULAR TRAINER ROSY BUDD WHO'S GOT A LONG RECORD OF MINOR CRIME"
"AND IT'S RIDDEN BY TINGALING BELL WHO'S A GOOD JOCKEY BUT NOT ABOVE THIS SORT OF CAPER. I'VE A PROPOSITION FOR HIM." . .

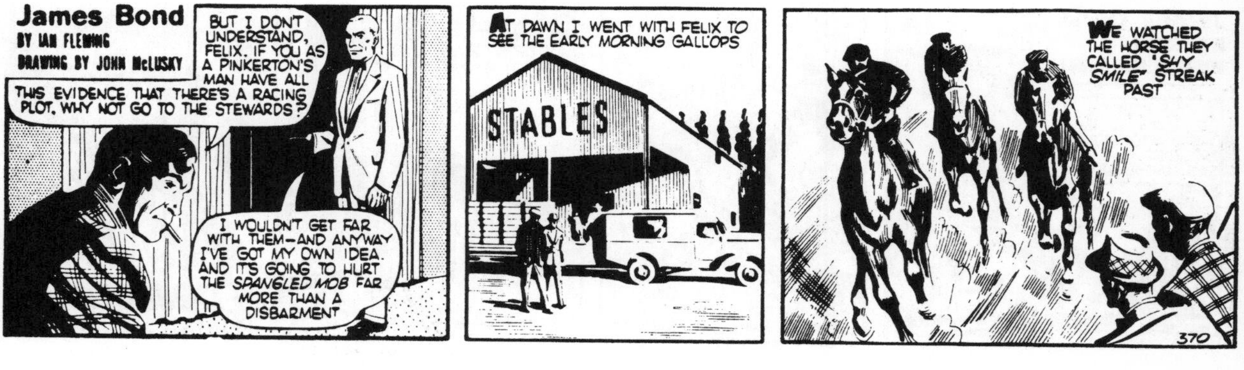
James Bond
BY IAN FLEMING
DRAWING BY JOHN McLUSKY
BUT I DON'T UNDERSTAND, FELIX. IF YOU AS A PINKERTON'S MAN HAVE ALL THIS EVIDENCE THAT THERE'S A RACING PLOT, WHY NOT GO TO THE STEWARDS?
I WOULDN'T GET FAR WITH THEM—AND ANYWAY I'VE GOT MY OWN IDEA. AND IT'S GOING TO HURT THE *SPANGLED MOB* FAR MORE THAN A DISBARMENT
AT DAWN I WENT WITH FELIX TO SEE THE EARLY MORNING GALLOPS
STABLES
WE WATCHED THE HORSE THEY CALLED "*SHY SMILE*" STREAK PAST
370

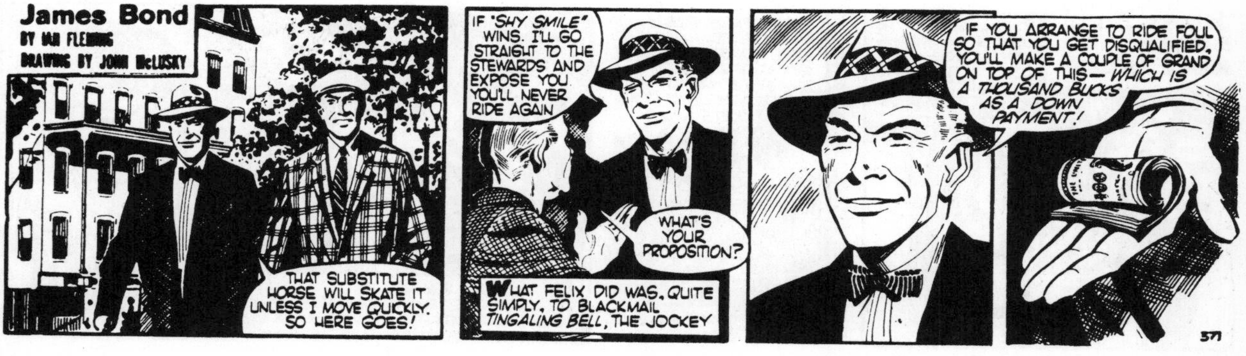
James Bond
BY IAN FLEMING
DRAWING BY JOHN McLUSKY
THAT SUBSTITUTE HORSE WILL SKATE IT UNLESS I MOVE QUICKLY. SO HERE GOES!
IF "*SHY SMILE*" WINS, I'LL GO STRAIGHT TO THE STEWARDS AND EXPOSE YOU. YOU'LL NEVER RIDE AGAIN
WHAT'S YOUR PROPOSITION?
WHAT FELIX DID WAS, QUITE SIMPLY, TO BLACKMAIL *TINGALING BELL*, THE JOCKEY
IF YOU ARRANGE TO RIDE FOUL SO THAT YOU GET DISQUALIFIED, YOU'LL MAKE A COUPLE OF GRAND ON TOP OF THIS—*WHICH IS A THOUSAND BUCKS AS A DOWN PAYMENT!*
371

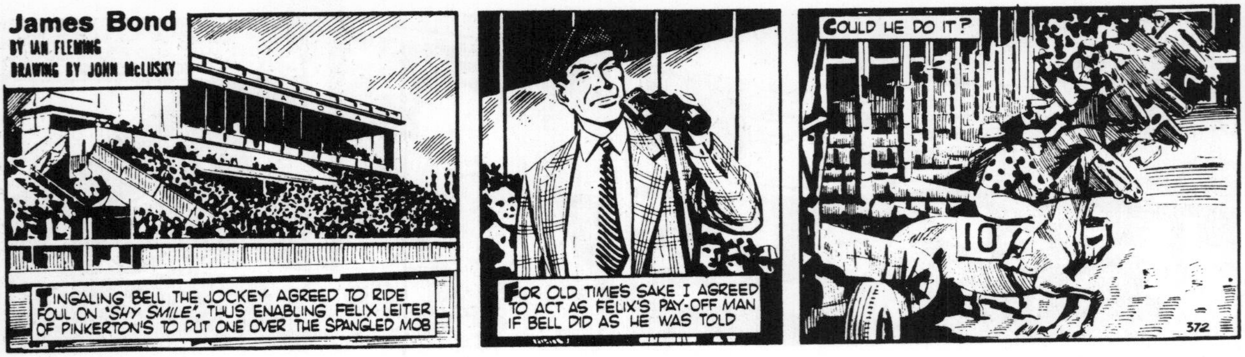
James Bond
BY IAN FLEMING
DRAWING BY JOHN McLUSKY
SARATOGA
TINGALING BELL THE JOCKEY AGREED TO RIDE FOUL ON 'SHY SMILE', THUS ENABLING FELIX LEITER OF PINKERTON'S TO PUT ONE OVER THE SPANGLED MOB
FOR OLD TIME'S SAKE I AGREED TO ACT AS FELIX'S PAY-OFF MAN IF BELL DID AS HE WAS TOLD
COULD HE DO IT?
10
372

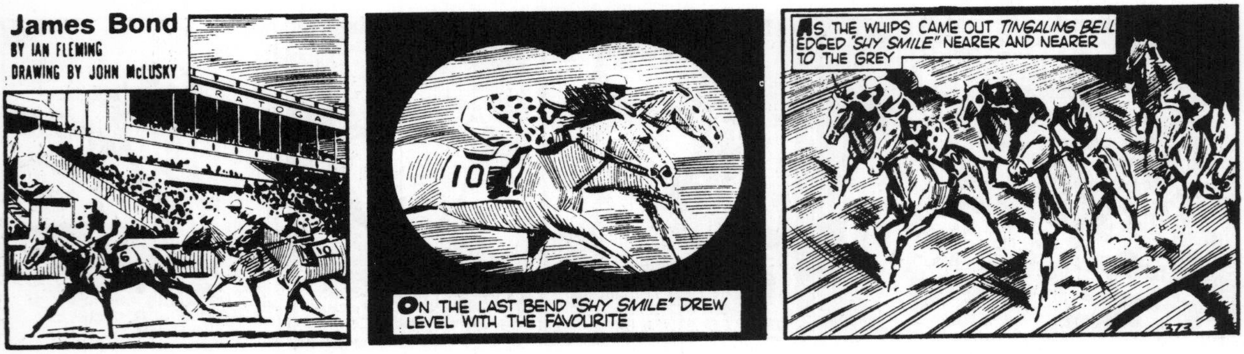
James Bond
BY IAN FLEMING
DRAWING BY JOHN McLUSKY
ARATOGA
6
10
10
ON THE LAST BEND "SHY SMILE" DREW LEVEL WITH THE FAVOURITE
AS THE WHIPS CAME OUT TINGALING BELL EDGED "SHY SMILE" NEARER AND NEARER TO THE GREY
373

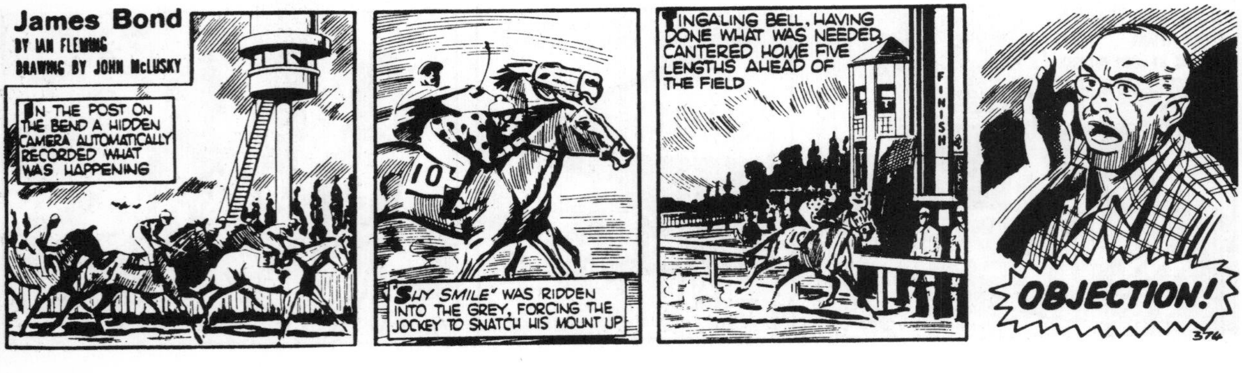
James Bond
BY IAN FLEMING
DRAWING BY JOHN McLUSKY
IN THE POST ON THE BEND A HIDDEN CAMERA AUTOMATICALLY RECORDED WHAT WAS HAPPENING
10
'SHY SMILE' WAS RIDDEN INTO THE GREY, FORCING THE JOCKEY TO SNATCH HIS MOUNT UP
TINGALING BELL, HAVING DONE WHAT WAS NEEDED, CANTERED HOME FIVE LENGTHS AHEAD OF THE FIELD
FINISH
OBJECTION!
374

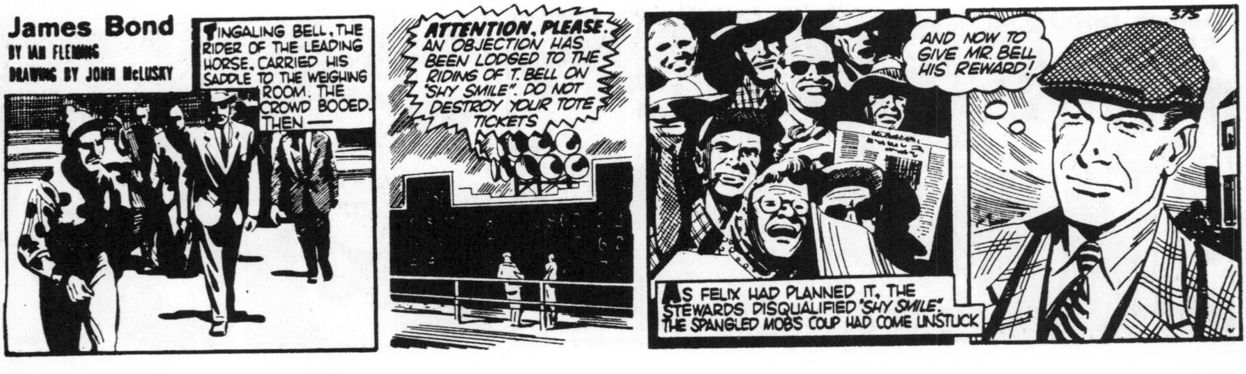
James Bond
BY IAN FLEMING
DRAWING BY JOHN McLUSKY
TINGALING BELL, THE RIDER OF THE LEADING HORSE, CARRIED HIS SADDLE TO THE WEIGHING ROOM. THE CROWD BOOED. THEN—
ATTENTION, PLEASE. AN OBJECTION HAS BEEN LODGED TO THE RIDINGS OF T. BELL ON "SHY SMILE". DO NOT DESTROY YOUR TOTE TICKETS
375
AND NOW TO GIVE MR. BELL HIS REWARD!
AS FELIX HAD PLANNED IT, THE STEWARDS DISQUALIFIED 'SHY SMILE'. THE SPANGLED MOB'S COUP HAD COME UNSTUCK

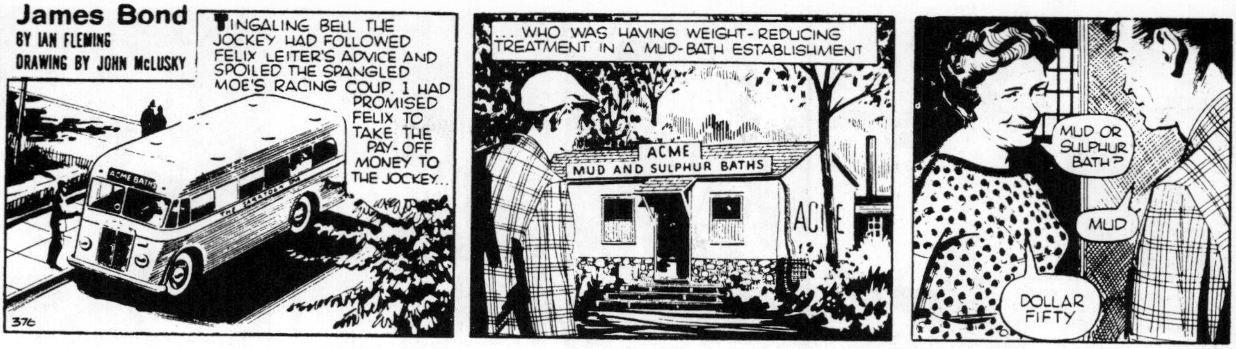
James Bond
BY IAN FLEMING
DRAWING BY JOHN McLUSKY
TINGALING BELL THE JOCKEY HAD FOLLOWED FELIX LEITER'S ADVICE AND SPOILED THE SPANGLED MOE'S RACING COUP. I HAD PROMISED FELIX TO TAKE THE PAY-OFF MONEY TO THE JOCKEY...
ACME BATHS
376
... WHO WAS HAVING WEIGHT-REDUCING TREATMENT IN A MUD-BATH ESTABLISHMENT
ACME
MUD AND SULPHUR BATHS
MUD OR SULPHUR BATH?
MUD
DOLLAR FIFTY

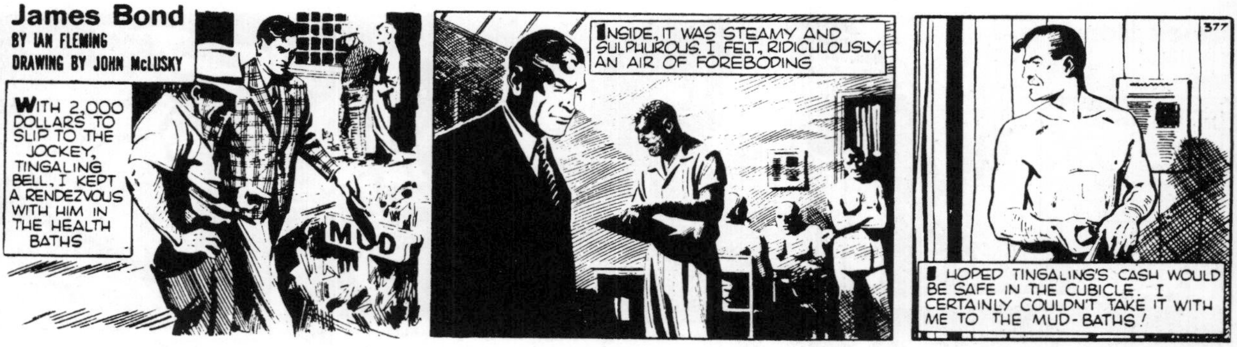
James Bond
BY IAN FLEMING
DRAWING BY JOHN McLUSKY
WITH 2,000 DOLLARS TO SLIP TO THE JOCKEY, TINGALING BELL, I KEPT A RENDEZVOUS WITH HIM IN THE HEALTH BATHS
MUD
INSIDE, IT WAS STEAMY AND SULPHUROUS. I FELT, RIDICULOUSLY, AN AIR OF FOREBODING
377
I HOPED TINGALING'S CASH WOULD BE SAFE IN THE CUBICLE. I CERTAINLY COULDN'T TAKE IT WITH ME TO THE MUD-BATHS!

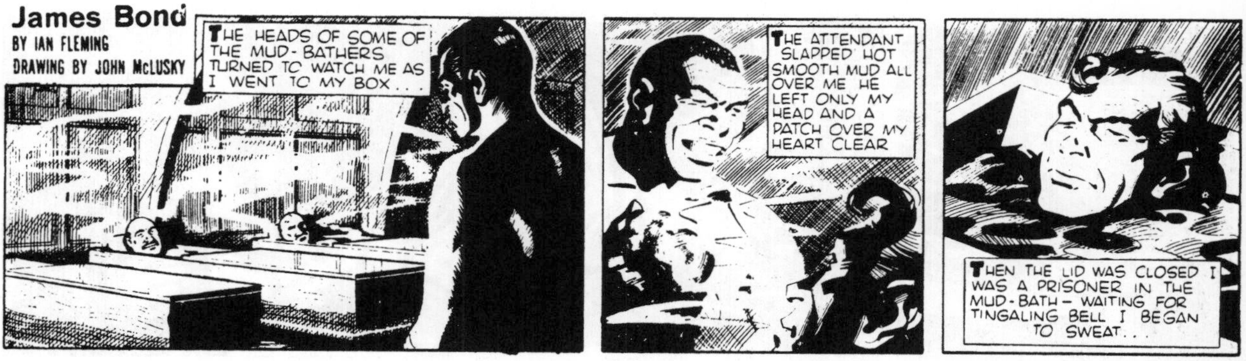
James Bond
BY IAN FLEMING
DRAWING BY JOHN McLUSKY
THE HEADS OF SOME OF THE MUD-BATHERS TURNED TO WATCH ME AS I WENT TO MY BOX...
THE ATTENDANT SLAPPED HOT SMOOTH MUD ALL OVER ME HE LEFT ONLY MY HEAD AND A PATCH OVER MY HEART CLEAR
THEN THE LID WAS CLOSED I WAS A PRISONER IN THE MUD-BATH – WAITING FOR TINGALING BELL I BEGAN TO SWEAT...

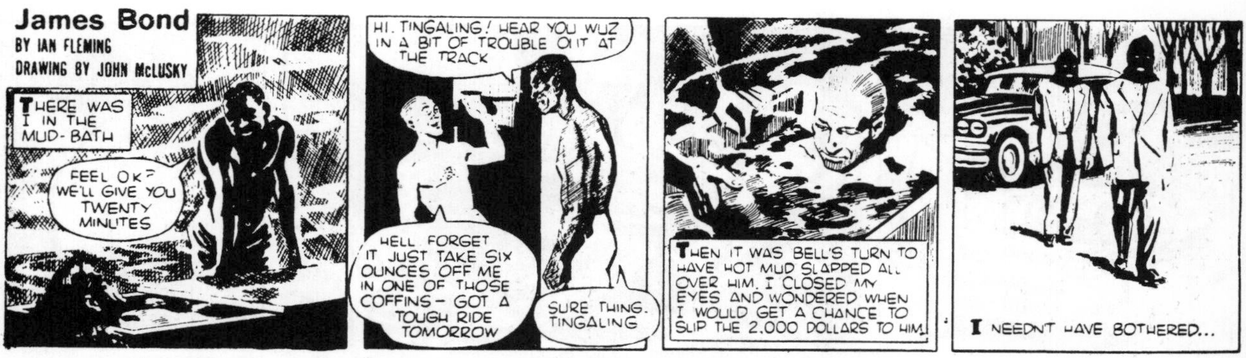
James Bond
BY IAN FLEMING
DRAWING BY JOHN McLUSKY
THERE WAS I IN THE MUD-BATH
FEEL OK? WE'LL GIVE YOU TWENTY MINUTES
HI. TINGALING! HEAR YOU WUZ IN A BIT OF TROUBLE OUT AT THE TRACK
HELL, FORGET IT JUST TAKE SIX OUNCES OFF ME IN ONE OF THOSE COFFINS – GOT A TOUGH RIDE TOMORROW
SURE THING. TINGALING
THEN IT WAS BELL'S TURN TO HAVE HOT MUD SLAPPED ALL OVER HIM. I CLOSED MY EYES AND WONDERED WHEN I WOULD GET A CHANCE TO SLIP THE 2,000 DOLLARS TO HIM.
I NEEDN'T HAVE BOTHERED...

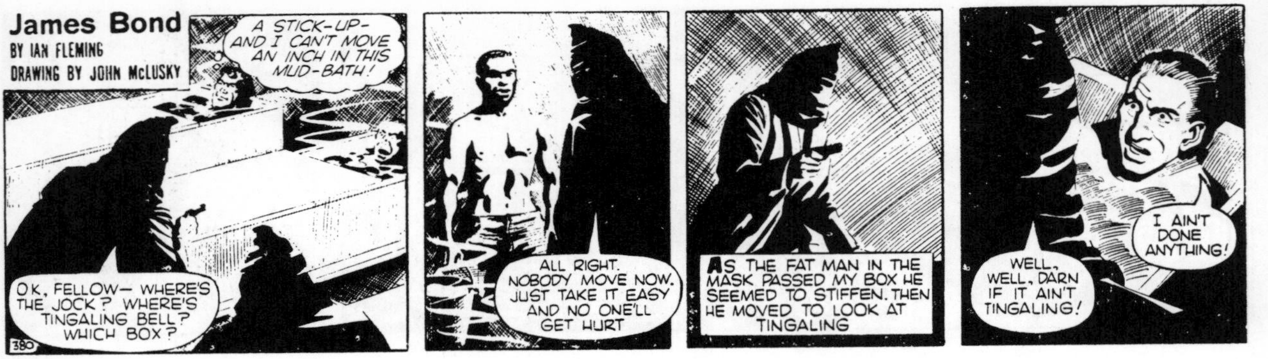
James Bond
BY IAN FLEMING
DRAWING BY JOHN McLUSKY
A STICK-UP– AND I CAN'T MOVE AN INCH IN THIS MUD-BATH!
O.K., FELLOW– WHERE'S THE JOCK? WHERE'S TINGALING BELL? WHICH BOX?
380
ALL RIGHT. NOBODY MOVE NOW. JUST TAKE IT EASY AND NO ONE'LL GET HURT
AS THE FAT MAN IN THE MASK PASSED MY BOX HE SEEMED TO STIFFEN. THEN HE MOVED TO LOOK AT TINGALING
WELL, WELL, DARN IF IT AIN'T TINGALING!
I AIN'T DONE ANYTHING!

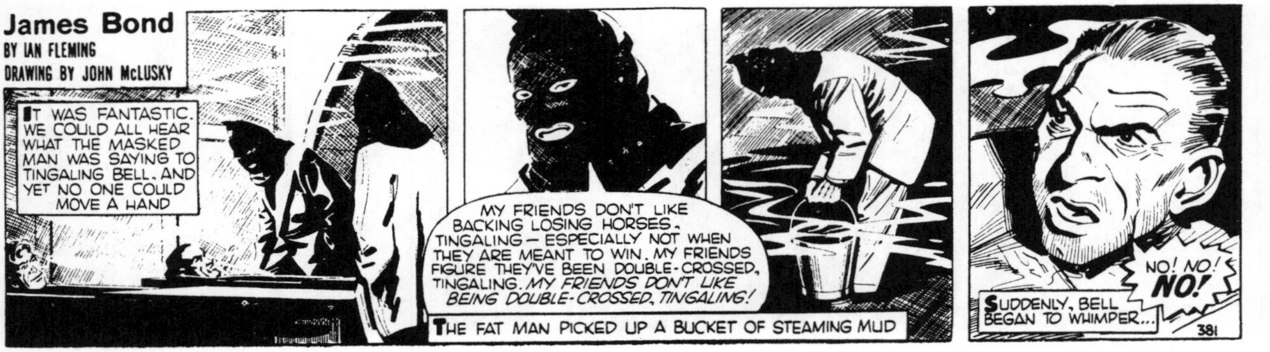
James Bond
BY IAN FLEMING
DRAWING BY JOHN McLUSKY
IT WAS FANTASTIC. WE COULD ALL HEAR WHAT THE MASKED MAN WAS SAYING TO TINGALING BELL. AND YET NO ONE COULD MOVE A HAND
MY FRIENDS DON'T LIKE BACKING LOSING HORSES, TINGALING – ESPECIALLY NOT WHEN THEY ARE MEANT TO WIN. MY FRIENDS FIGURE THEY'VE BEEN DOUBLE-CROSSED, TINGALING. MY FRIENDS DON'T LIKE BEING DOUBLE-CROSSED, TINGALING!
THE FAT MAN PICKED UP A BUCKET OF STEAMING MUD
NO! NO! NO!
SUDDENLY, BELL BEGAN TO WHIMPER...
381

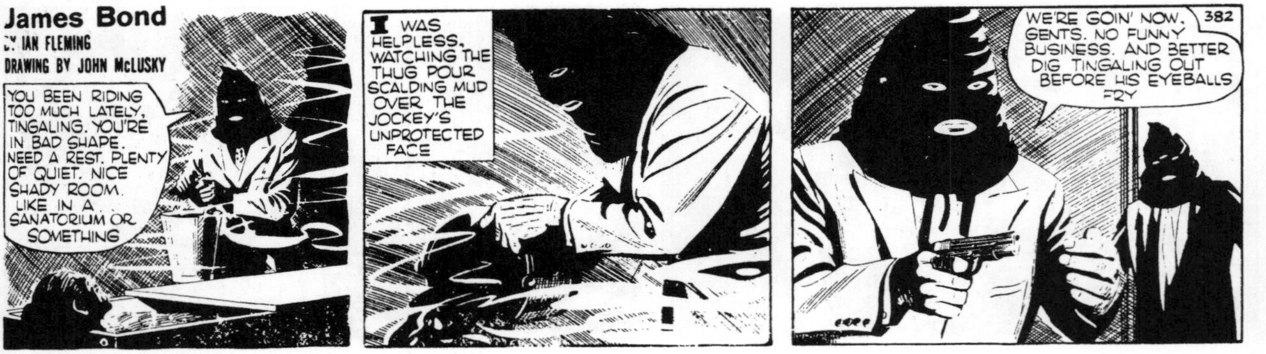
James Bond
BY IAN FLEMING
DRAWING BY JOHN McLUSKY
YOU BEEN RIDING TOO MUCH LATELY, TINGALING. YOU'RE IN BAD SHAPE. NEED A REST. PLENTY OF QUIET. NICE SHADY ROOM. LIKE IN A SANATORIUM OR SOMETHING
I WAS HELPLESS, WATCHING THE THUG POUR SCALDING MUD OVER THE JOCKEY'S UNPROTECTED FACE
WE'RE GOIN' NOW, GENTS. NO FUNNY BUSINESS. AND BETTER DIG TINGALING OUT BEFORE HIS EYEBALLS FRY
382

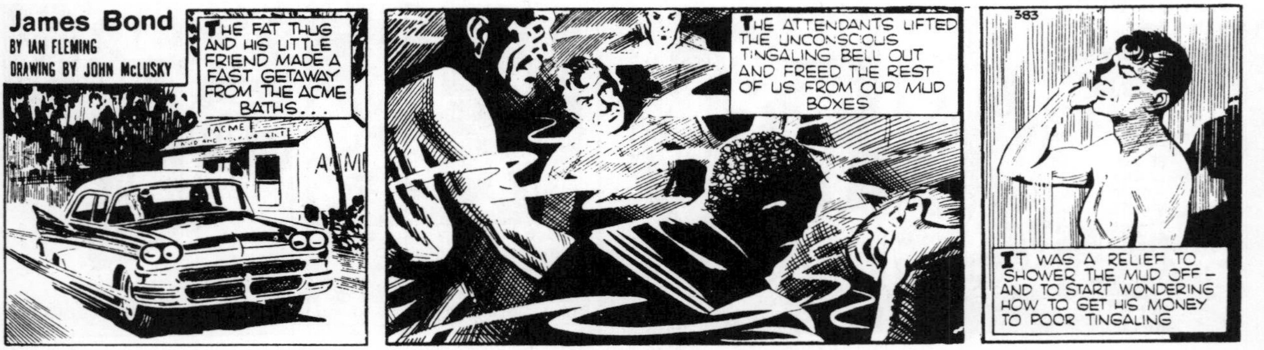
James Bond
BY IAN FLEMING
DRAWING BY JOHN McLUSKY
THE FAT THUG AND HIS LITTLE FRIEND MADE A FAST GETAWAY FROM THE ACME BATHS...
ACME
THE ATTENDANTS LIFTED THE UNCONSCIOUS TINGALING BELL OUT AND FREED THE REST OF US FROM OUR MUD BOXES
383
IT WAS A RELIEF TO SHOWER THE MUD OFF – AND TO START WONDERING HOW TO GET HIS MONEY TO POOR TINGALING

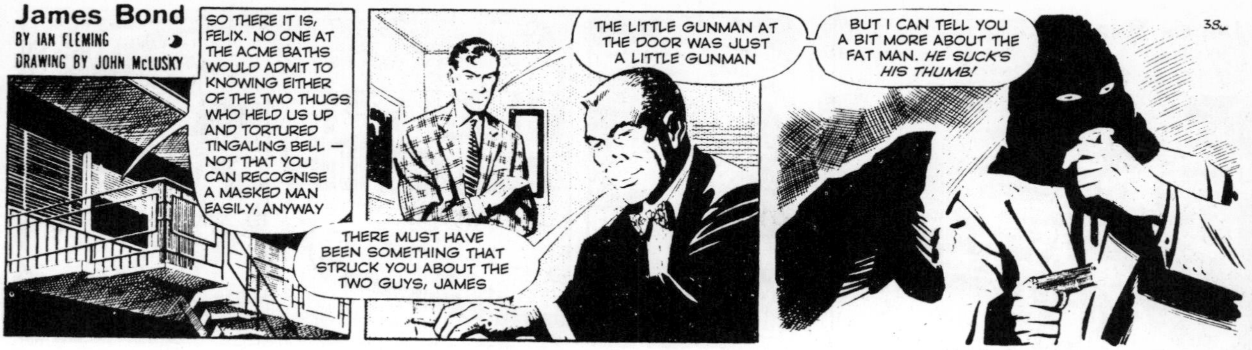
James Bond
BY IAN FLEMING
DRAWING BY JOHN McLUSKY
SO THERE IT IS, FELIX. NO ONE AT THE ACME BATHS WOULD ADMIT TO KNOWING EITHER OF THE TWO THUGS WHO HELD US UP AND TORTURED TINGALING BELL — NOT THAT YOU CAN RECOGNISE A MASKED MAN EASILY, ANYWAY
THERE MUST HAVE BEEN SOMETHING THAT STRUCK YOU ABOUT THE TWO GUYS, JAMES
THE LITTLE GUNMAN AT THE DOOR WAS JUST A LITTLE GUNMAN
BUT I CAN TELL YOU A BIT MORE ABOUT THE FAT MAN. *HE SUCK'S HIS THUMB!*
38

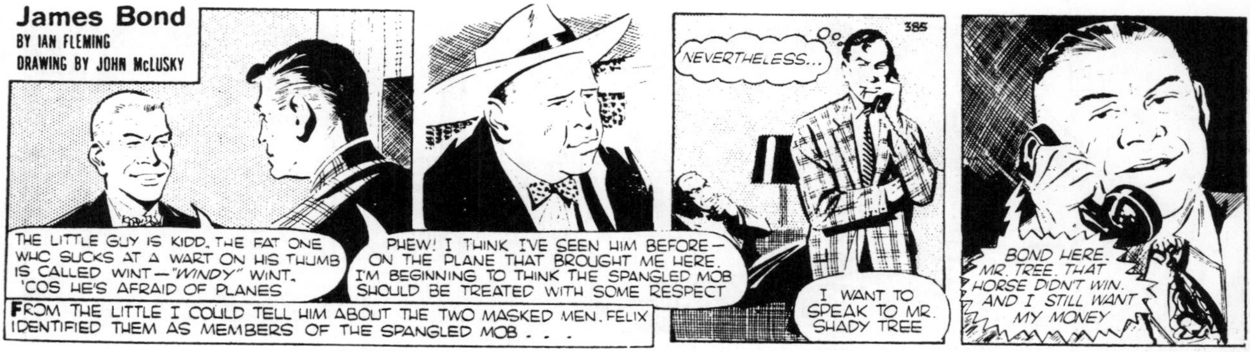
James Bond
BY IAN FLEMING
DRAWING BY JOHN McLUSKY
THE LITTLE GUY IS KIDD. THE FAT ONE WHO SUCKS AT A WART ON HIS THUMB IS CALLED WINT—"*WINDY*" WINT. 'COS HE'S AFRAID OF PLANES
PHEW! I THINK I'VE SEEN HIM BEFORE—ON THE PLANE THAT BROUGHT ME HERE. I'M BEGINNING TO THINK THE SPANGLED MOB SHOULD BE TREATED WITH SOME RESPECT
FROM THE LITTLE I COULD TELL HIM ABOUT THE TWO MASKED MEN, FELIX IDENTIFIED THEM AS MEMBERS OF THE SPANGLED MOB . . .
385
NEVERTHELESS...
I WANT TO SPEAK TO MR. SHADY TREE
BOND HERE. MR. TREE. THAT HORSE DIDN'T WIN. AND I STILL WANT MY MONEY

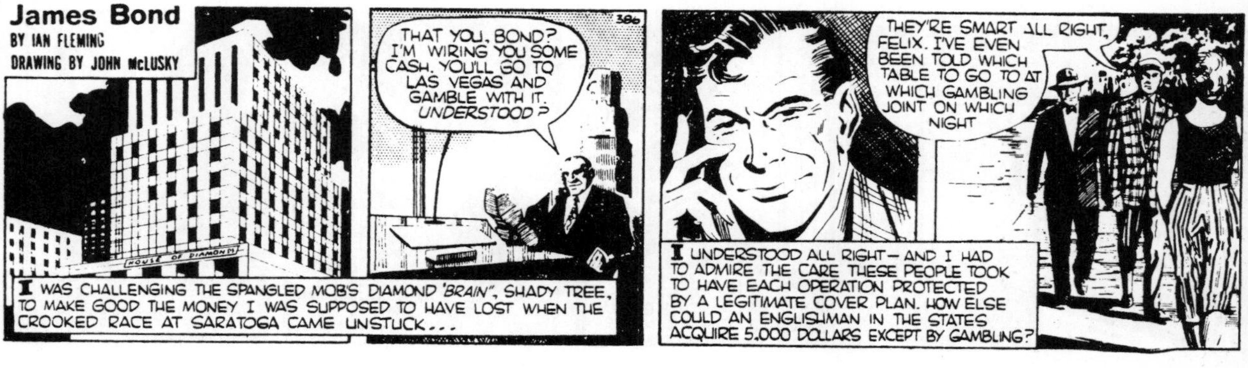
James Bond
BY IAN FLEMING
DRAWING BY JOHN McLUSKY
HOUSE OF DIAMONDS
386
THAT YOU, BOND? I'M WIRING YOU SOME CASH. YOU'LL GO TO LAS VEGAS AND GAMBLE WITH IT. *UNDERSTOOD?*
I WAS CHALLENGING THE SPANGLED MOB'S DIAMOND '*BRAIN*', SHADY TREE, TO MAKE GOOD THE MONEY I WAS SUPPOSED TO HAVE LOST WHEN THE CROOKED RACE AT SARATOGA CAME UNSTUCK . . .
THEY'RE SMART ALL RIGHT, FELIX. I'VE EVEN BEEN TOLD WHICH TABLE TO GO TO AT WHICH GAMBLING JOINT ON WHICH NIGHT
I UNDERSTOOD ALL RIGHT— AND I HAD TO ADMIRE THE CARE THESE PEOPLE TOOK TO HAVE EACH OPERATION PROTECTED BY A LEGITIMATE COVER PLAN. HOW ELSE COULD AN ENGLISHMAN IN THE STATES ACQUIRE 5,000 DOLLARS EXCEPT BY GAMBLING?

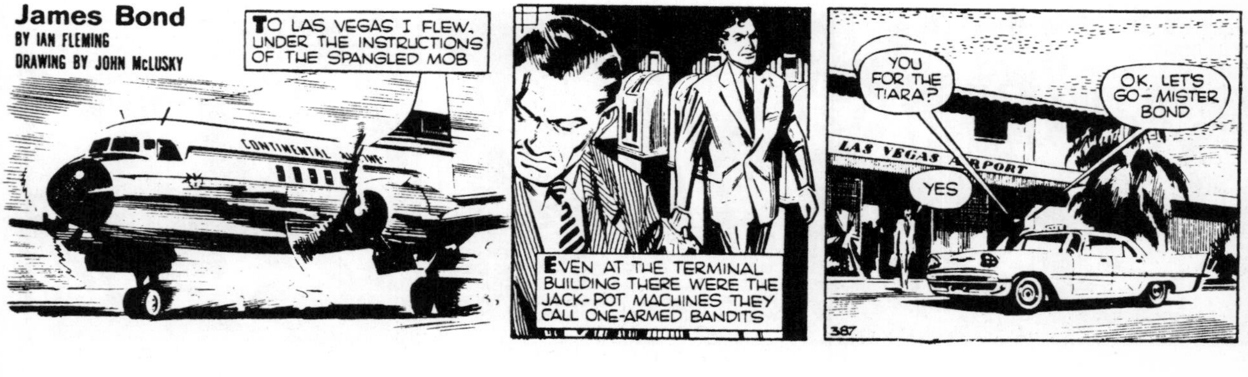
James Bond
BY IAN FLEMING
DRAWING BY JOHN McLUSKY
TO LAS VEGAS I FLEW, UNDER THE INSTRUCTIONS OF THE SPANGLED MOB
CONTINENTAL
EVEN AT THE TERMINAL BUILDING THERE WERE THE JACK-POT MACHINES THEY CALL ONE-ARMED BANDITS
LAS VEGAS AIRPORT
YOU FOR THE TIARA?
YES
OK. LET'S GO—MISTER BOND
387

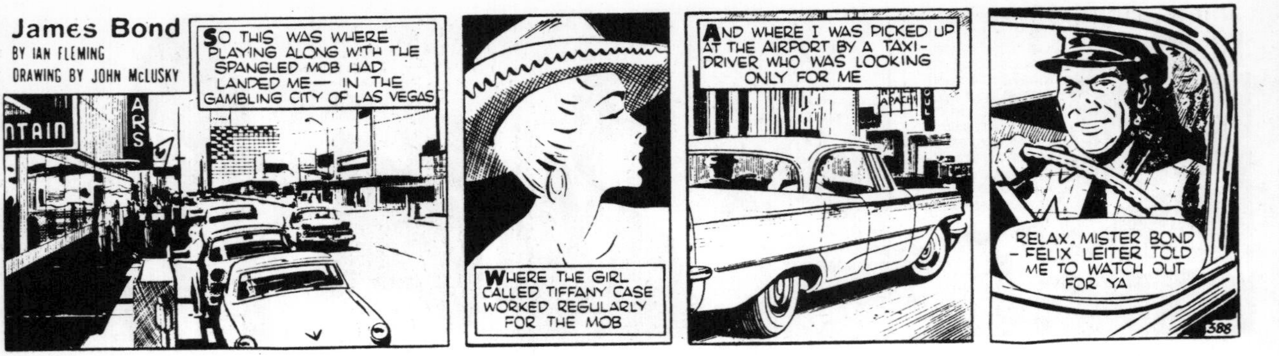
James Bond
BY IAN FLEMING
DRAWING BY JOHN McLUSKY
SO THIS WAS WHERE PLAYING ALONG WITH THE SPANGLED MOB HAD LANDED ME— IN THE GAMBLING CITY OF LAS VEGAS
WHERE THE GIRL CALLED TIFFANY CASE WORKED REGULARLY FOR THE MOB
AND WHERE I WAS PICKED UP AT THE AIRPORT BY A TAXI-DRIVER WHO WAS LOOKING ONLY FOR ME
RELAX. MISTER BOND - FELIX LEITER TOLD ME TO WATCH OUT FOR YA
388

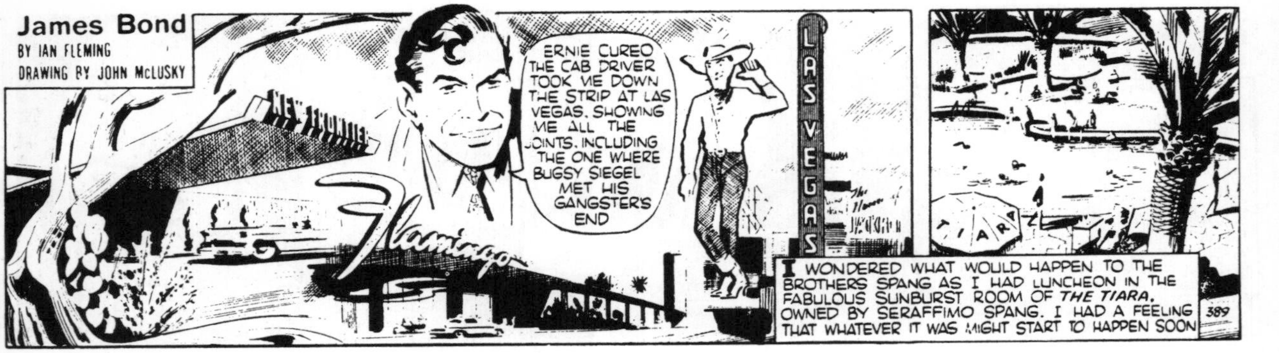
James Bond
BY IAN FLEMING
DRAWING BY JOHN McLUSKY
ERNIE CUREO THE CAB DRIVER TOOK ME DOWN THE STRIP AT LAS VEGAS. SHOWING ME ALL THE JOINTS. INCLUDING THE ONE WHERE BUGSY SIEGEL MET HIS GANGSTER'S END
LAS VEGAS
Flamingo
TIARA
I WONDERED WHAT WOULD HAPPEN TO THE BROTHERS SPANG AS I HAD LUNCHEON IN THE FABULOUS SUNBURST ROOM OF THE TIARA. OWNED BY SERAFFIMO SPANG. I HAD A FEELING THAT WHATEVER IT WAS MIGHT START TO HAPPEN SOON
389

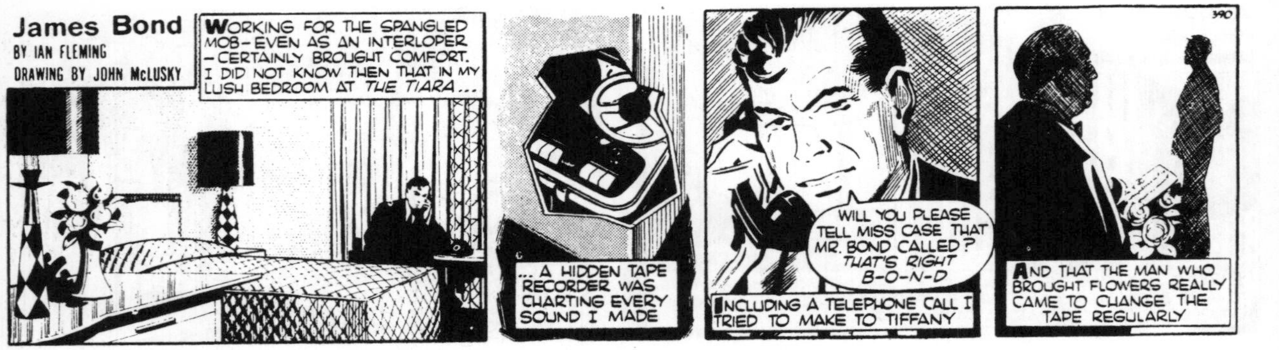
James Bond
BY IAN FLEMING
DRAWING BY JOHN McLUSKY
WORKING FOR THE SPANGLED MOB - EVEN AS AN INTERLOPER - CERTAINLY BROUGHT COMFORT. I DID NOT KNOW THEN THAT IN MY LUSH BEDROOM AT THE TIARA...
... A HIDDEN TAPE RECORDER WAS CHARTING EVERY SOUND I MADE
WILL YOU PLEASE TELL MISS CASE THAT MR. BOND CALLED? THAT'S RIGHT B-O-N-D
INCLUDING A TELEPHONE CALL I TRIED TO MAKE TO TIFFANY
390
AND THAT THE MAN WHO BROUGHT FLOWERS REALLY CAME TO CHANGE THE TAPE REGULARLY

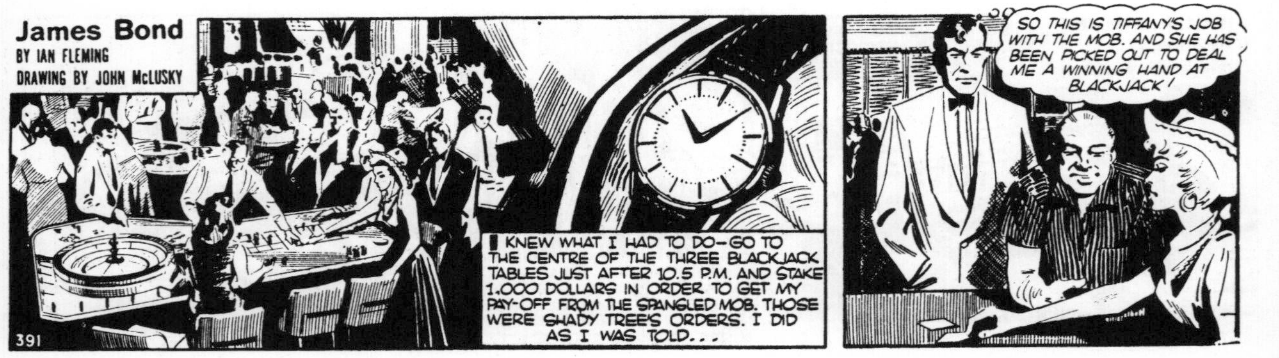
James Bond
BY IAN FLEMING
DRAWING BY JOHN McLUSKY
391
I KNEW WHAT I HAD TO DO - GO TO THE CENTRE OF THE THREE BLACKJACK TABLES JUST AFTER 10.5 P.M. AND STAKE 1,000 DOLLARS IN ORDER TO GET MY PAY-OFF FROM THE SPANGLED MOB. THOSE WERE SHADY TREE'S ORDERS. I DID AS I WAS TOLD...
SO THIS IS TIFFANY'S JOB WITH THE MOB. AND SHE HAS BEEN PICKED OUT TO DEAL ME A WINNING HAND AT BLACKJACK!

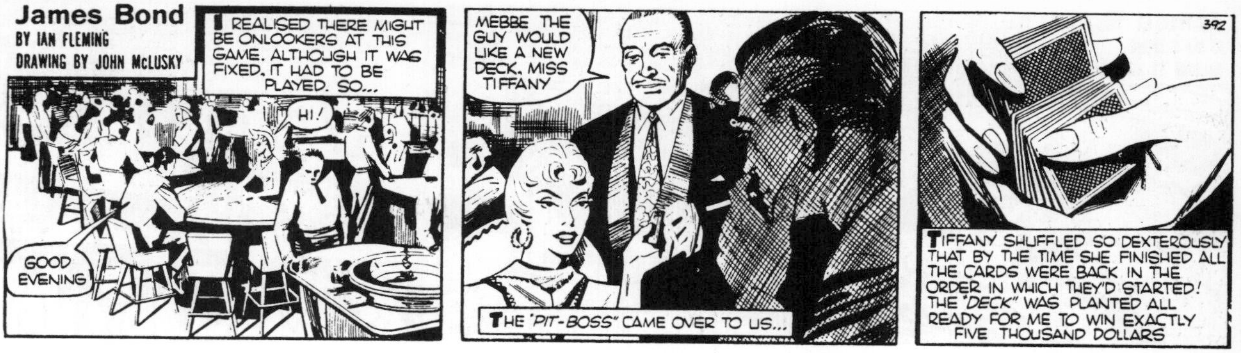
James Bond
BY IAN FLEMING
DRAWING BY JOHN McLUSKY
I REALISED THERE MIGHT BE ONLOOKERS AT THIS GAME. ALTHOUGH IT WAS FIXED, IT HAD TO BE PLAYED. SO...
HI!
GOOD EVENING
MEBBE THE GUY WOULD LIKE A NEW DECK, MISS TIFFANY
THE "PIT-BOSS" CAME OVER TO US...
392
TIFFANY SHUFFLED SO DEXTEROUSLY THAT BY THE TIME SHE FINISHED ALL THE CARDS WERE BACK IN THE ORDER IN WHICH THEY'D STARTED! THE "DECK" WAS PLANTED ALL READY FOR ME TO WIN EXACTLY FIVE THOUSAND DOLLARS

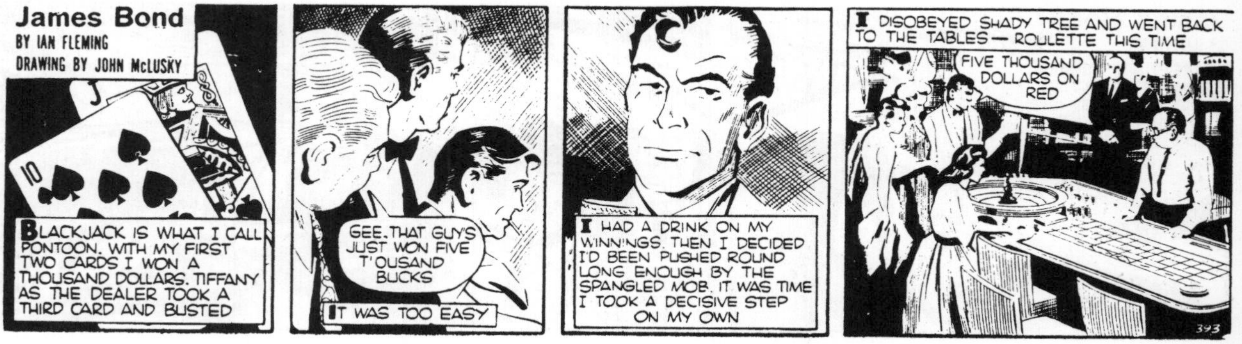
James Bond
BY IAN FLEMING
DRAWING BY JOHN McLUSKY
BLACKJACK IS WHAT I CALL PONTOON. WITH MY FIRST TWO CARDS I WON A THOUSAND DOLLARS. TIFFANY AS THE DEALER TOOK A THIRD CARD AND BUSTED
GEE, THAT GUY'S JUST WON FIVE T'OUSAND BUCKS
IT WAS TOO EASY
I HAD A DRINK ON MY WINNINGS. THEN I DECIDED I'D BEEN PUSHED ROUND LONG ENOUGH BY THE SPANGLED MOB. IT WAS TIME I TOOK A DECISIVE STEP ON MY OWN
I DISOBEYED SHADY TREE AND WENT BACK TO THE TABLES — ROULETTE THIS TIME
FIVE THOUSAND DOLLARS ON RED
393

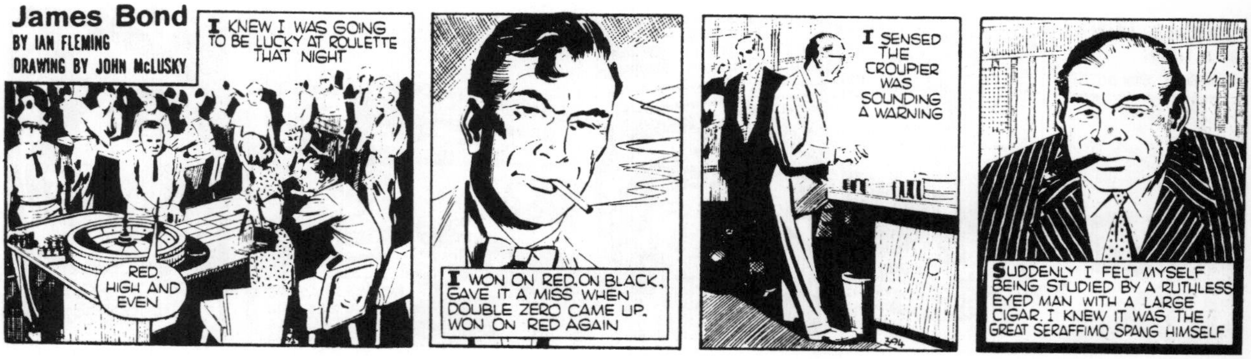
James Bond
BY IAN FLEMING
DRAWING BY JOHN McLUSKY
I KNEW I WAS GOING TO BE LUCKY AT ROULETTE THAT NIGHT
RED, HIGH AND EVEN
I WON ON RED, ON BLACK, GAVE IT A MISS WHEN DOUBLE ZERO CAME UP, WON ON RED AGAIN
I SENSED THE CROUPIER WAS SOUNDING A WARNING
394
SUDDENLY I FELT MYSELF BEING STUDIED BY A RUTHLESS EYED MAN WITH A LARGE CIGAR. I KNEW IT WAS THE GREAT SERAFFIMO SPANG HIMSELF

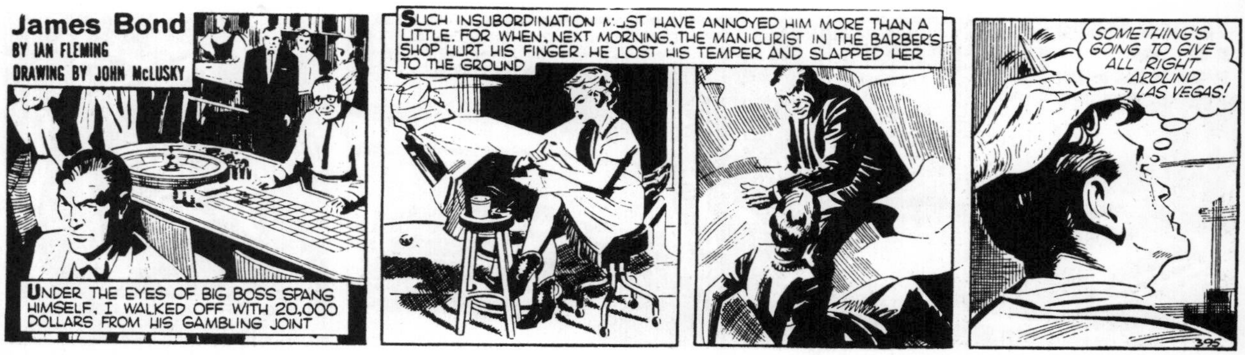
James Bond
BY IAN FLEMING
DRAWING BY JOHN McLUSKY
UNDER THE EYES OF BIG BOSS SPANG HIMSELF, I WALKED OFF WITH 20,000 DOLLARS FROM HIS GAMBLING JOINT
SUCH INSUBORDINATION MUST HAVE ANNOYED HIM MORE THAN A LITTLE. FOR WHEN, NEXT MORNING, THE MANICURIST IN THE BARBER'S SHOP HURT HIS FINGER, HE LOST HIS TEMPER AND SLAPPED HER TO THE GROUND
SOMETHING'S GOING TO GIVE ALL RIGHT AROUND LAS VEGAS!
395

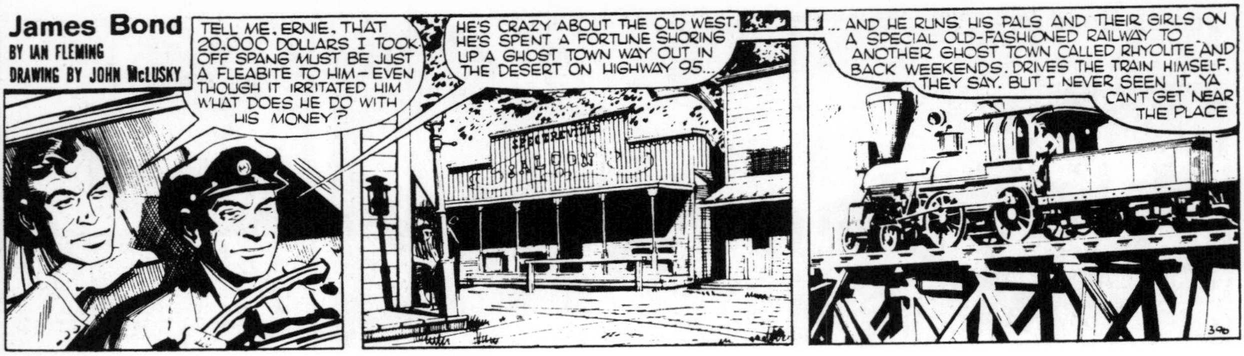
James Bond
BY IAN FLEMING
DRAWING BY JOHN McLUSKY
TELL ME, ERNIE, THAT 20,000 DOLLARS I TOOK OFF SPANG MUST BE JUST A FLEABITE TO HIM—EVEN THOUGH IT IRRITATED HIM WHAT DOES HE DO WITH HIS MONEY?
HE'S CRAZY ABOUT THE OLD WEST. HE'S SPENT A FORTUNE SHORING UP A GHOST TOWN WAY OUT IN THE DESERT ON HIGHWAY 95...
... AND HE RUNS HIS PALS AND THEIR GIRLS ON A SPECIAL OLD-FASHIONED RAILWAY TO ANOTHER GHOST TOWN CALLED RHYOLITE AND BACK WEEKENDS. DRIVES THE TRAIN HIMSELF, THEY SAY. BUT I NEVER SEEN IT. YA CAN'T GET NEAR THE PLACE
396

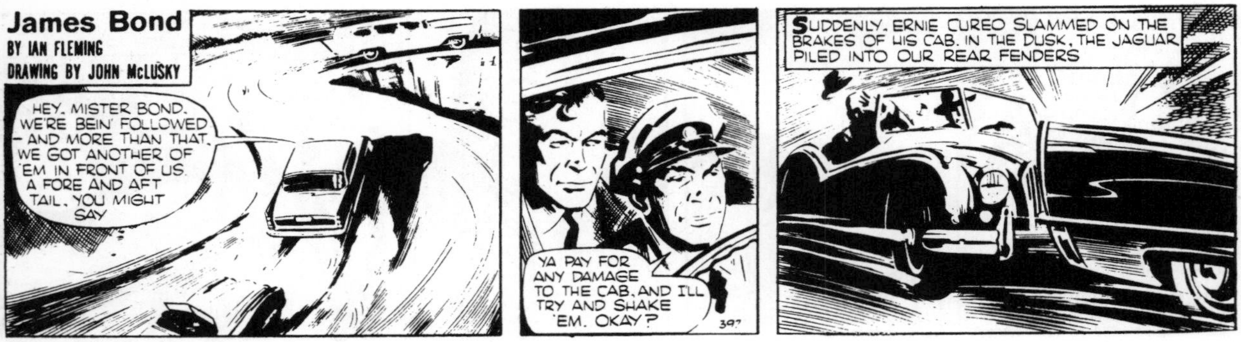
James Bond
BY IAN FLEMING
DRAWING BY JOHN McLUSKY
HEY, MISTER BOND. WE'RE BEIN' FOLLOWED —AND MORE THAN THAT. WE GOT ANOTHER OF 'EM IN FRONT OF US. A FORE AND AFT TAIL, YOU MIGHT SAY
YA PAY FOR ANY DAMAGE TO THE CAB, AND I'LL TRY AND SHAKE 'EM. OKAY?
397
SUDDENLY, ERNIE CUREO SLAMMED ON THE BRAKES OF HIS CAB. IN THE DUSK, THE JAGUAR PILED INTO OUR REAR FENDERS

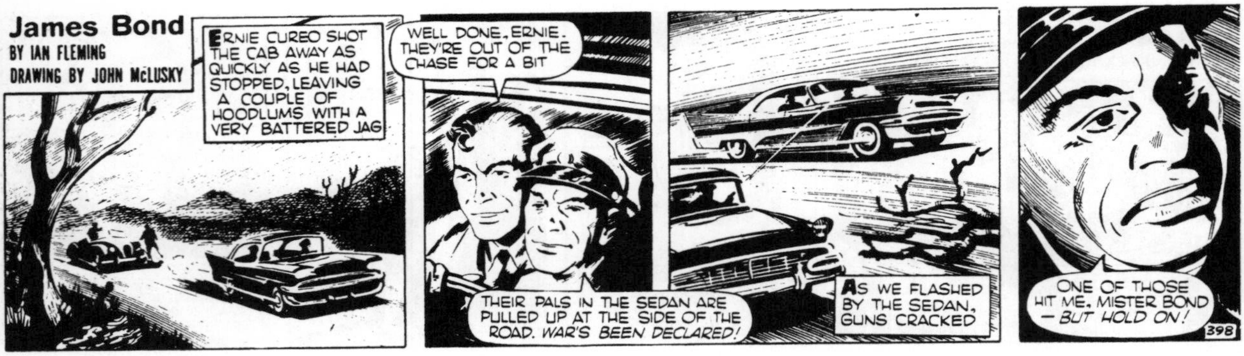
James Bond
BY IAN FLEMING
DRAWING BY JOHN McLUSKY
ERNIE CUREO SHOT THE CAB AWAY AS QUICKLY AS HE HAD STOPPED, LEAVING A COUPLE OF HOODLUMS WITH A VERY BATTERED JAG
WELL DONE, ERNIE. THEY'RE OUT OF THE CHASE FOR A BIT
THEIR PALS IN THE SEDAN ARE PULLED UP AT THE SIDE OF THE ROAD. *WAR'S BEEN DECLARED!*
AS WE FLASHED BY THE SEDAN, GUNS CRACKED
ONE OF THOSE HIT ME, MISTER BOND —*BUT HOLD ON!*
398

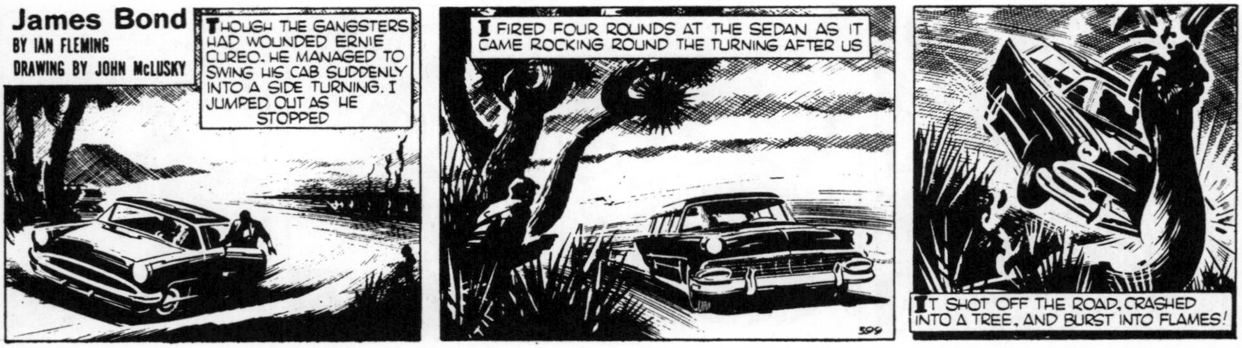
James Bond
BY IAN FLEMING
DRAWING BY JOHN McLUSKY
THOUGH THE GANGSTERS HAD WOUNDED ERNIE CUREO, HE MANAGED TO SWING HIS CAB SUDDENLY INTO A SIDE TURNING. I JUMPED OUT AS HE STOPPED
I FIRED FOUR ROUNDS AT THE SEDAN AS IT CAME ROCKING ROUND THE TURNING AFTER US
399
IT SHOT OFF THE ROAD, CRASHED INTO A TREE, AND BURST INTO FLAMES!

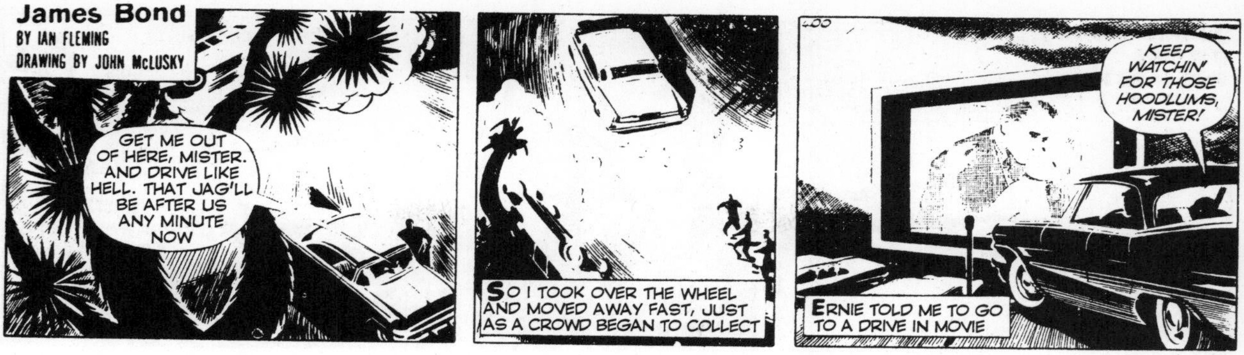
James Bond
BY IAN FLEMING
DRAWING BY JOHN McLUSKY
GET ME OUT OF HERE, MISTER. AND DRIVE LIKE HELL. THAT JAG'LL BE AFTER US ANY MINUTE NOW
SO I TOOK OVER THE WHEEL AND MOVED AWAY FAST, JUST AS A CROWD BEGAN TO COLLECT
400
KEEP WATCHIN' FOR THOSE HOODLUMS, MISTER!
ERNIE TOLD ME TO GO TO A DRIVE IN MOVIE

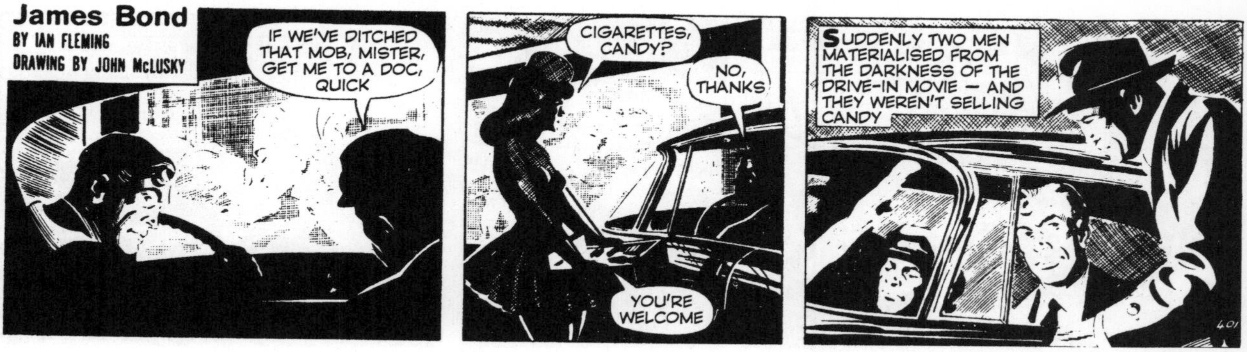
James Bond
BY IAN FLEMING
DRAWING BY JOHN McLUSKY
IF WE'VE DITCHED THAT MOB, MISTER, GET ME TO A DOC, QUICK
CIGARETTES, CANDY?
NO, THANKS
YOU'RE WELCOME
SUDDENLY TWO MEN MATERIALISED FROM THE DARKNESS OF THE DRIVE-IN MOVIE — AND THEY WEREN'T SELLING CANDY
401

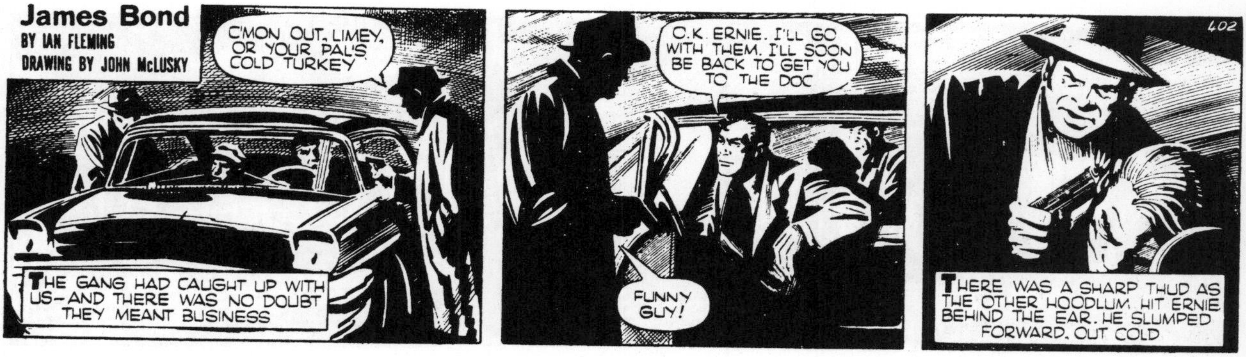
James Bond
BY IAN FLEMING
DRAWING BY JOHN McLUSKY
C'MON OUT, LIMEY, OR YOUR PAL'S COLD TURKEY
THE GANG HAD CAUGHT UP WITH US—AND THERE WAS NO DOUBT THEY MEANT BUSINESS
O.K. ERNIE. I'LL GO WITH THEM. I'LL SOON BE BACK TO GET YOU TO THE DOC
FUNNY GUY!
402
THERE WAS A SHARP THUD AS THE OTHER HOODLUM HIT ERNIE BEHIND THE EAR. HE SLUMPED FORWARD, OUT COLD

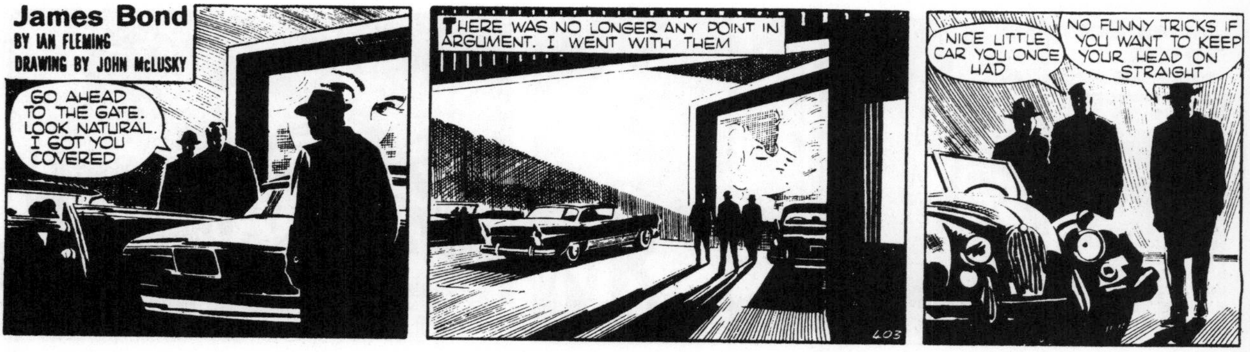
James Bond
BY IAN FLEMING
DRAWING BY JOHN McLUSKY
GO AHEAD TO THE GATE. LOOK NATURAL. I GOT YOU COVERED
THERE WAS NO LONGER ANY POINT IN ARGUMENT. I WENT WITH THEM
403
NICE LITTLE CAR YOU ONCE HAD
NO FUNNY TRICKS IF YOU WANT TO KEEP YOUR HEAD ON STRAIGHT

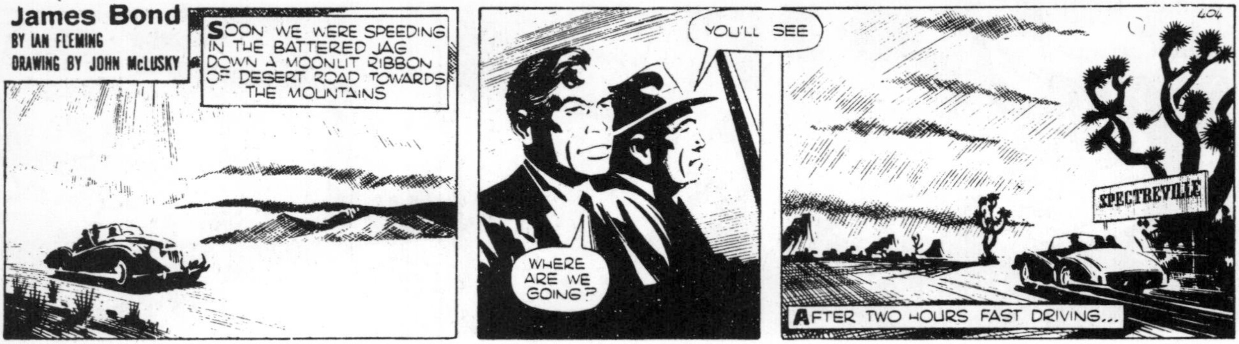
James Bond
BY IAN FLEMING
DRAWING BY JOHN McLUSKY
SOON WE WERE SPEEDING IN THE BATTERED JAG DOWN A MOONLIT RIBBON OF DESERT ROAD TOWARDS THE MOUNTAINS
YOU'LL SEE
WHERE ARE WE GOING?
404
SPECTREVILLE
AFTER TWO HOURS FAST DRIVING...

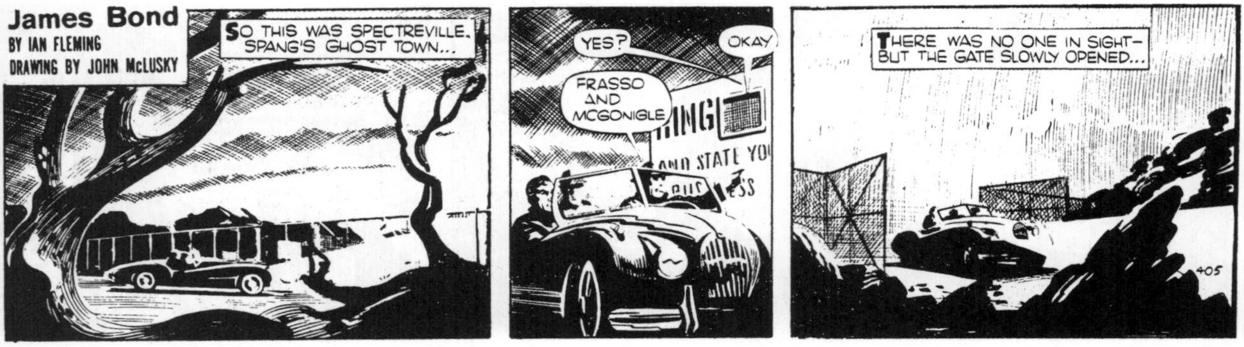
James Bond
BY IAN FLEMING
DRAWING BY JOHN McLUSKY
SO THIS WAS SPECTREVILLE. SPANG'S GHOST TOWN...
YES?
OKAY
FRASSO AND McGONIGLE
THERE WAS NO ONE IN SIGHT– BUT THE GATE SLOWLY OPENED...
405

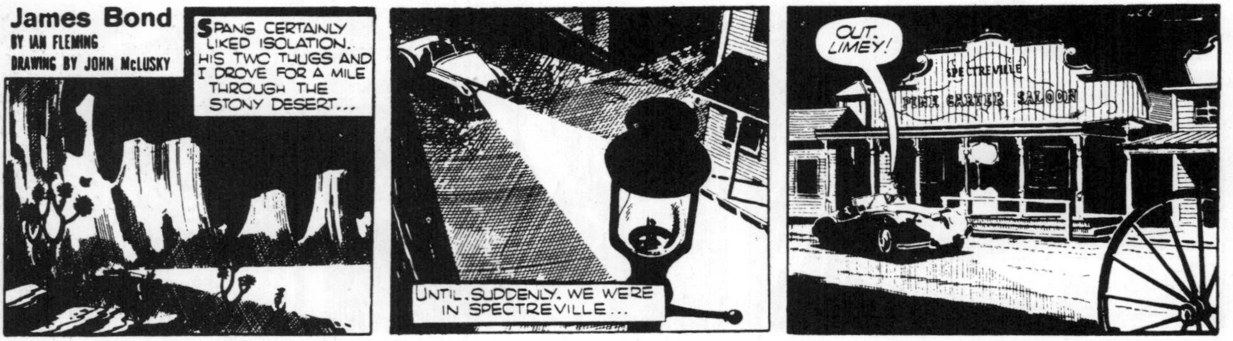
James Bond
BY IAN FLEMING
DRAWING BY JOHN McLUSKY
SPANG CERTAINLY LIKED ISOLATION. HIS TWO THUGS AND I DROVE FOR A MILE THROUGH THE STONY DESERT...
UNTIL, SUDDENLY, WE WERE IN SPECTREVILLE...
OUT, LIMEY!
SPECTREVILLE
PINK GARTER SALOON

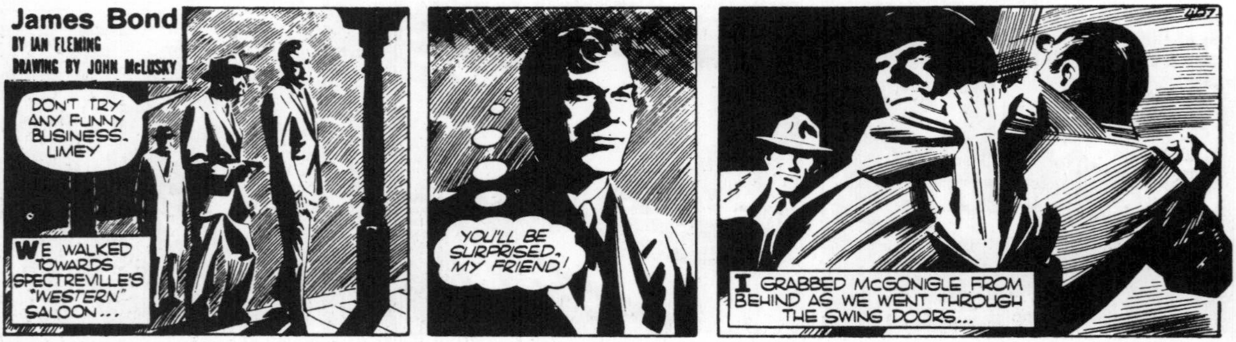
James Bond
BY IAN FLEMING
DRAWING BY JOHN McLUSKY
DON'T TRY ANY FUNNY BUSINESS, LIMEY
WE WALKED TOWARDS SPECTREVILLE'S "WESTERN" SALOON...
YOU'LL BE SURPRISED, MY FRIEND!
I GRABBED McGONIGLE FROM BEHIND AS WE WENT THROUGH THE SWING DOORS...

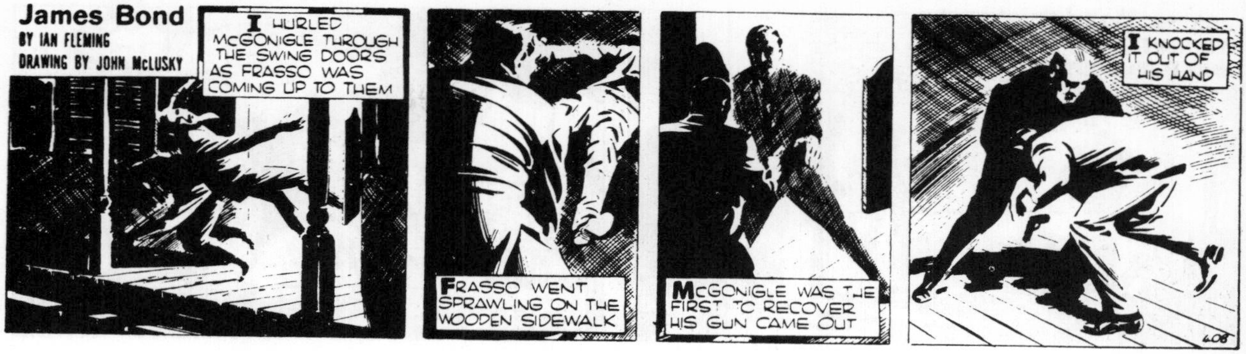
James Bond
BY IAN FLEMING
DRAWING BY JOHN McLUSKY
I HURLED McGONIGLE THROUGH THE SWING DOORS AS FRASSO WAS COMING UP TO THEM
FRASSO WENT SPRAWLING ON THE WOODEN SIDEWALK
McGONIGLE WAS THE FIRST TO RECOVER HIS GUN CAME OUT
I KNOCKED IT OUT OF HIS HAND
408

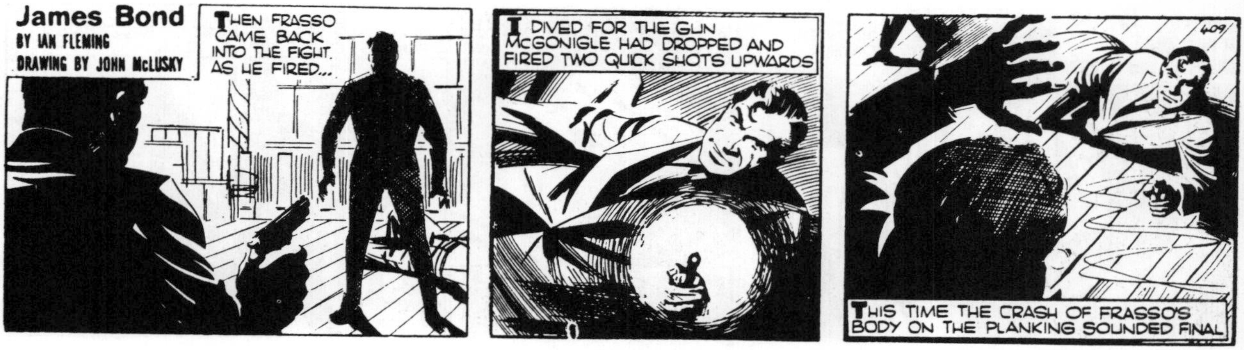
James Bond
BY IAN FLEMING
DRAWING BY JOHN McLUSKY
THEN FRASSO CAME BACK INTO THE FIGHT. AS HE FIRED...
I DIVED FOR THE GUN McGONIGLE HAD DROPPED AND FIRED TWO QUICK SHOTS UPWARDS
409
THIS TIME THE CRASH OF FRASSO'S BODY ON THE PLANKING SOUNDED FINAL

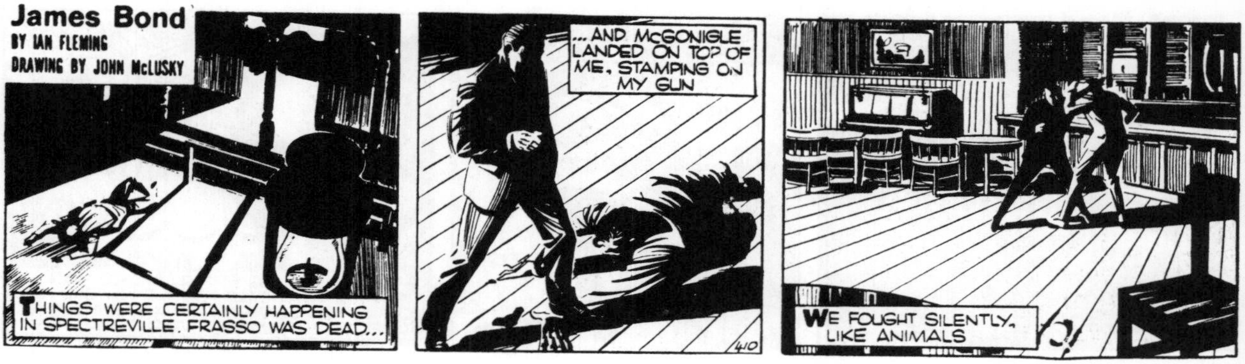
James Bond
BY IAN FLEMING
DRAWING BY JOHN McLUSKY
THINGS WERE CERTAINLY HAPPENING IN SPECTREVILLE. FRASSO WAS DEAD...
...AND McGONIGLE LANDED ON TOP OF ME, STAMPING ON MY GUN
410
WE FOUGHT SILENTLY, LIKE ANIMALS

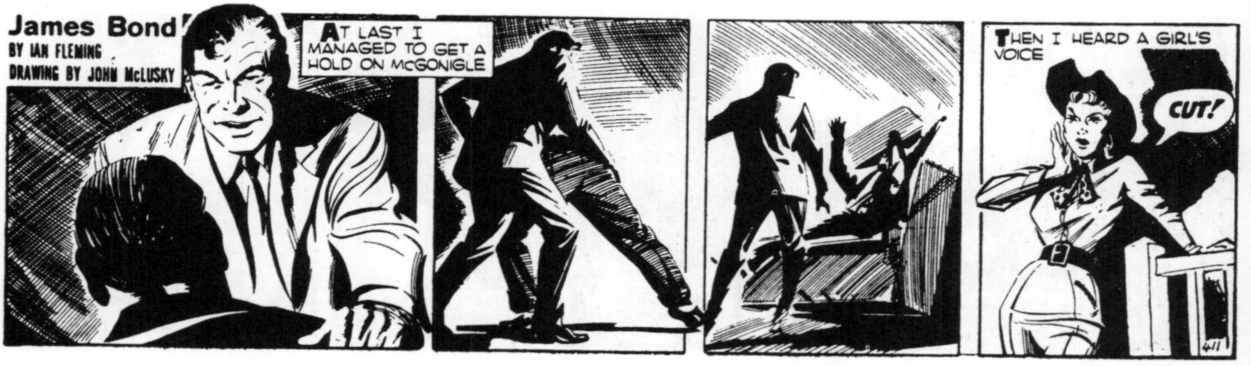
James Bond
BY IAN FLEMING
DRAWING BY JOHN McLUSKY
AT LAST I MANAGED TO GET A HOLD ON McGONIGLE
THEN I HEARD A GIRL'S VOICE
CUT!
411

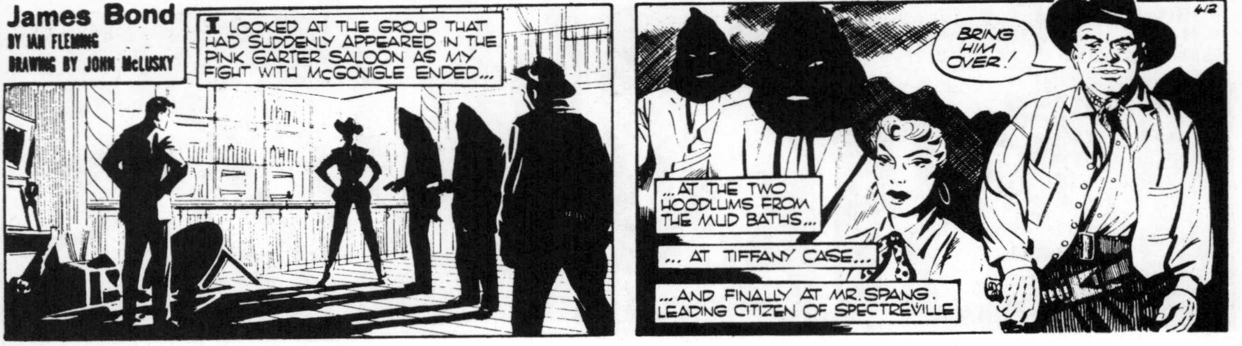
James Bond
BY IAN FLEMING
DRAWING BY JOHN McLUSKY
I LOOKED AT THE GROUP THAT HAD SUDDENLY APPEARED IN THE PINK GARTER SALOON AS MY FIGHT WITH McGONIGLE ENDED...
412
BRING HIM OVER!
...AT THE TWO HOODLUMS FROM THE MUD BATHS...
... AT TIFFANY CASE...
...AND FINALLY AT MR. SPANG. LEADING CITIZEN OF SPECTREVILLE

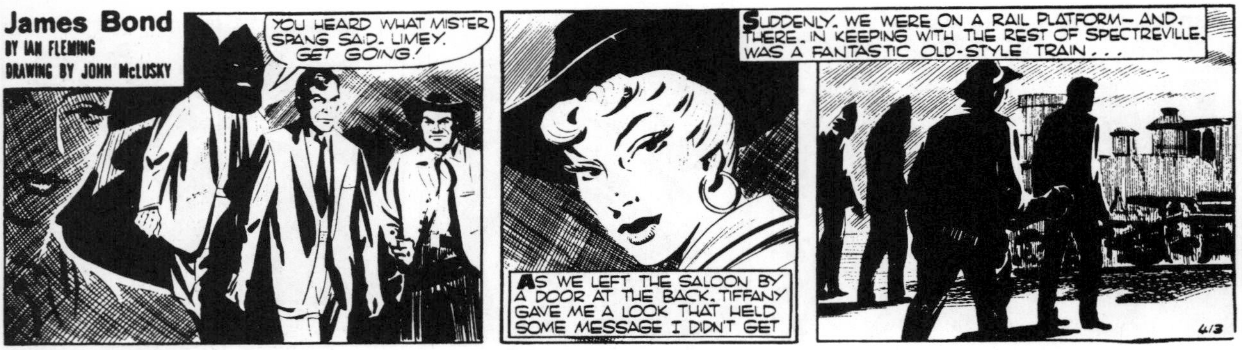
James Bond
BY IAN FLEMING
DRAWING BY JOHN McLUSKY
YOU HEARD WHAT MISTER SPANG SAID. LIMEY. GET GOING!
AS WE LEFT THE SALOON BY A DOOR AT THE BACK. TIFFANY GAVE ME A LOOK THAT HELD SOME MESSAGE I DIDN'T GET
SUDDENLY, WE WERE ON A RAIL PLATFORM—AND. THERE. IN KEEPING WITH THE REST OF SPECTREVILLE. WAS A FANTASTIC OLD-STYLE TRAIN . . .
413

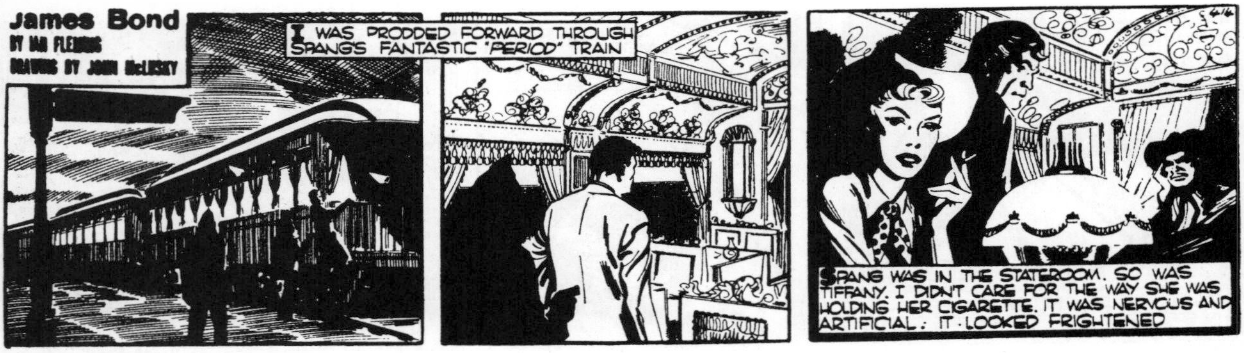
James Bond
BY IAN FLEMING
DRAWING BY JOHN McLUSKY
I WAS PRODDED FORWARD THROUGH SPANG'S FANTASTIC "PERIOD" TRAIN
414
SPANG WAS IN THE STATEROOM. SO WAS TIFFANY. I DIDN'T CARE FOR THE WAY SHE WAS HOLDING HER CIGARETTE. IT WAS NERVOUS AND ARTIFICIAL: IT LOOKED FRIGHTENED

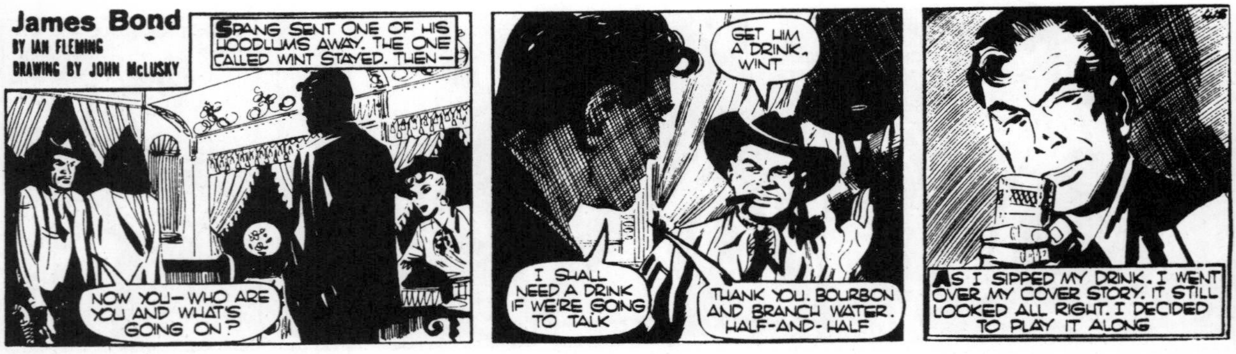
James Bond
BY IAN FLEMING
DRAWING BY JOHN McLUSKY
SPANG SENT ONE OF HIS HOODLUMS AWAY. THE ONE CALLED WINT STAYED. THEN—
NOW YOU—WHO ARE YOU AND WHAT'S GOING ON?
GET HIM A DRINK. WINT
I SHALL NEED A DRINK IF WE'RE GOING TO TALK
THANK YOU. BOURBON AND BRANCH WATER. HALF-AND-HALF
AS I SIPPED MY DRINK. I WENT OVER MY COVER STORY. IT STILL LOOKED ALL RIGHT. I DECIDED TO PLAY IT ALONG

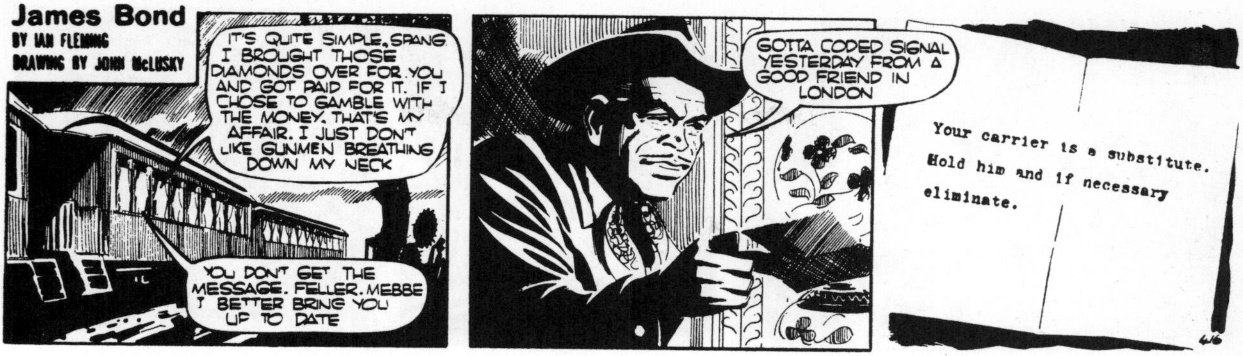
James Bond
BY IAN FLEMING
DRAWING BY JOHN McLUSKY
IT'S QUITE SIMPLE, SPANG. I BROUGHT THOSE DIAMONDS OVER FOR YOU AND GOT PAID FOR IT. IF I CHOSE TO GAMBLE WITH THE MONEY, THAT'S MY AFFAIR. I JUST DON'T LIKE GUNMEN BREATHING DOWN MY NECK
YOU DON'T GET THE MESSAGE, FELLER. MEBBE I BETTER BRING YOU UP TO DATE
GOTTA CODED SIGNAL YESTERDAY FROM A GOOD FRIEND IN LONDON
Your carrier is a substitute. Hold him and if necessary eliminate.
416

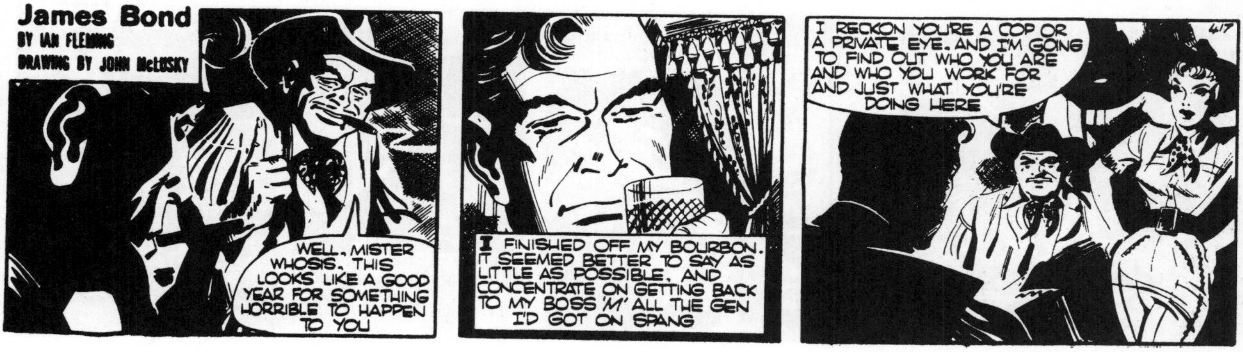
James Bond
BY IAN FLEMING
DRAWING BY JOHN McLUSKY
WELL, MISTER WHOSIS, THIS LOOKS LIKE A GOOD YEAR FOR SOMETHING HORRIBLE TO HAPPEN TO YOU
I FINISHED OFF MY BOURBON. IT SEEMED BETTER TO SAY AS LITTLE AS POSSIBLE, AND CONCENTRATE ON GETTING BACK TO MY BOSS 'M' ALL THE GEN I'D GOT ON SPANG
417
I RECKON YOU'RE A COP OR A PRIVATE EYE. AND I'M GOING TO FIND OUT WHO YOU ARE AND WHO YOU WORK FOR AND JUST WHAT YOU'RE DOING HERE

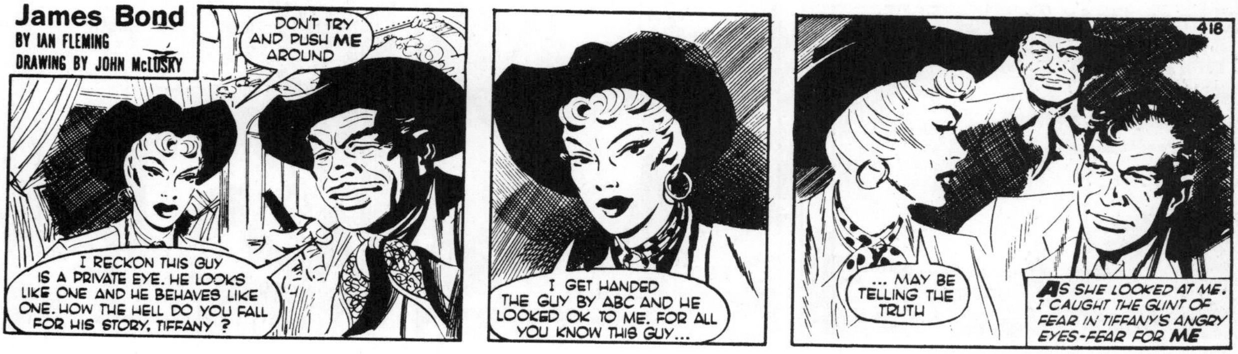
James Bond
BY IAN FLEMING
DRAWING BY JOHN McLUSKY
DON'T TRY AND PUSH ME AROUND
I RECKON THIS GUY IS A PRIVATE EYE. HE LOOKS LIKE ONE AND HE BEHAVES LIKE ONE. HOW THE HELL DO YOU FALL FOR HIS STORY, TIFFANY ?
I GET HANDED THE GUY BY ABC AND HE LOOKED OK TO ME. FOR ALL YOU KNOW THIS GUY...
418
... MAY BE TELLING THE TRUTH
AS SHE LOOKED AT ME, I CAUGHT THE GLINT OF FEAR IN TIFFANY'S ANGRY EYES-FEAR FOR ME

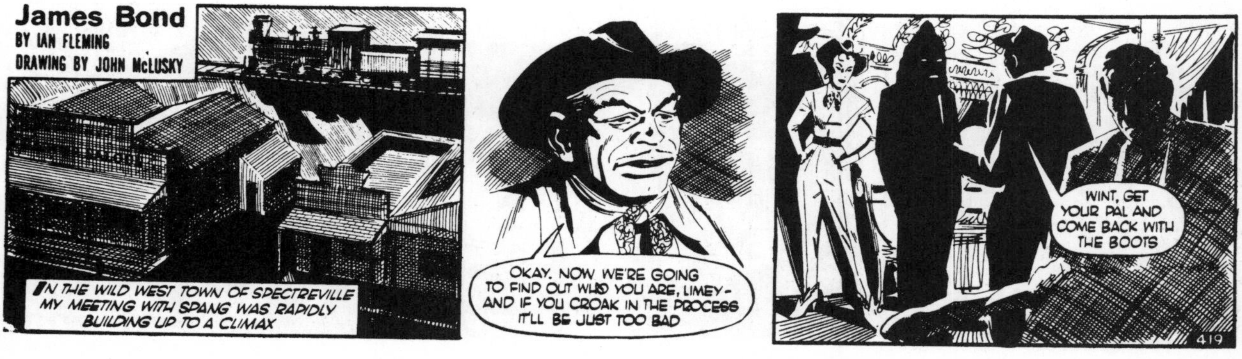
James Bond
BY IAN FLEMING
DRAWING BY JOHN McLUSKY
IN THE WILD WEST TOWN OF SPECTREVILLE MY MEETING WITH SPANG WAS RAPIDLY BUILDING UP TO A CLIMAX
OKAY. NOW WE'RE GOING TO FIND OUT WHO YOU ARE, LIMEY - AND IF YOU CROAK IN THE PROCESS IT'LL BE JUST TOO BAD
WINT, GET YOUR PAL AND COME BACK WITH THE BOOTS
419

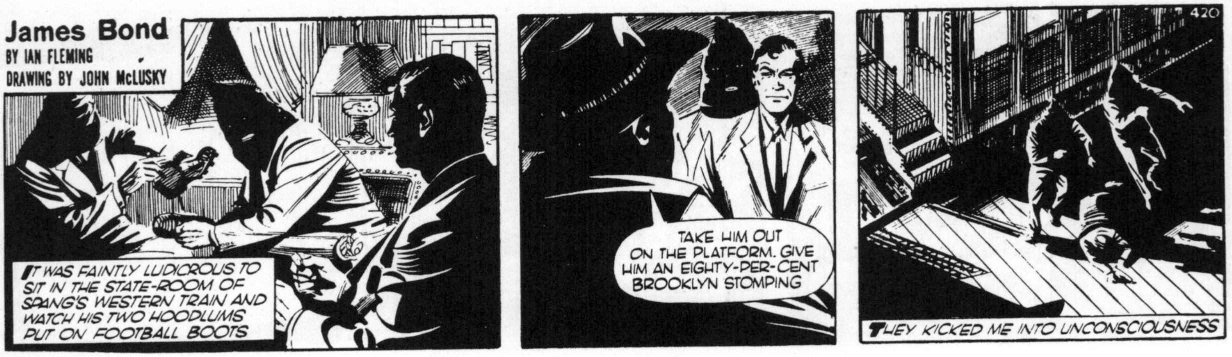
James Bond
BY IAN FLEMING
DRAWING BY JOHN McLUSKY
IT WAS FAINTLY LUDICROUS TO SIT IN THE STATE-ROOM OF SPANG'S WESTERN TRAIN AND WATCH HIS TWO HOODLUMS PUT ON FOOTBALL BOOTS
TAKE HIM OUT ON THE PLATFORM. GIVE HIM AN EIGHTY-PER-CENT BROOKLYN STOMPING
420
THEY KICKED ME INTO UNCONSCIOUSNESS

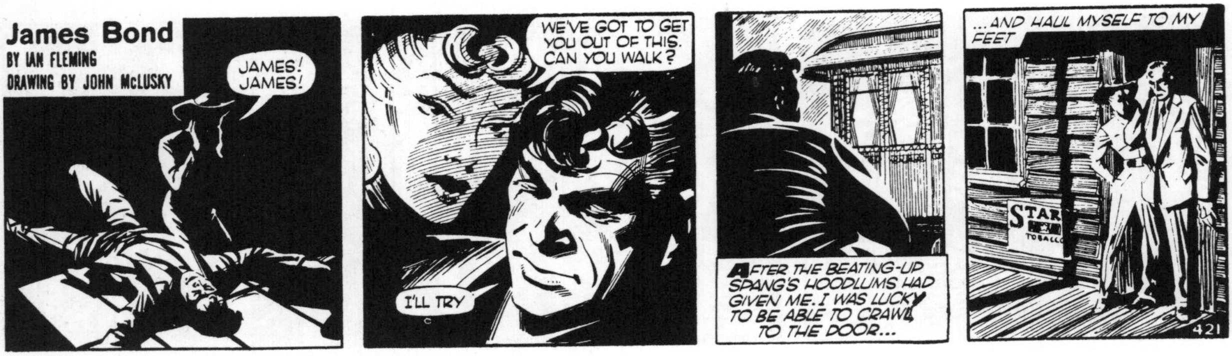
James Bond
BY IAN FLEMING
DRAWING BY JOHN McLUSKY
JAMES! JAMES!
WE'VE GOT TO GET YOU OUT OF THIS. CAN YOU WALK?
I'LL TRY
AFTER THE BEATING-UP SPANG'S HOODLUMS HAD GIVEN ME. I WAS LUCKY TO BE ABLE TO CRAWL TO THE DOOR...
...AND HAUL MYSELF TO MY FEET
421

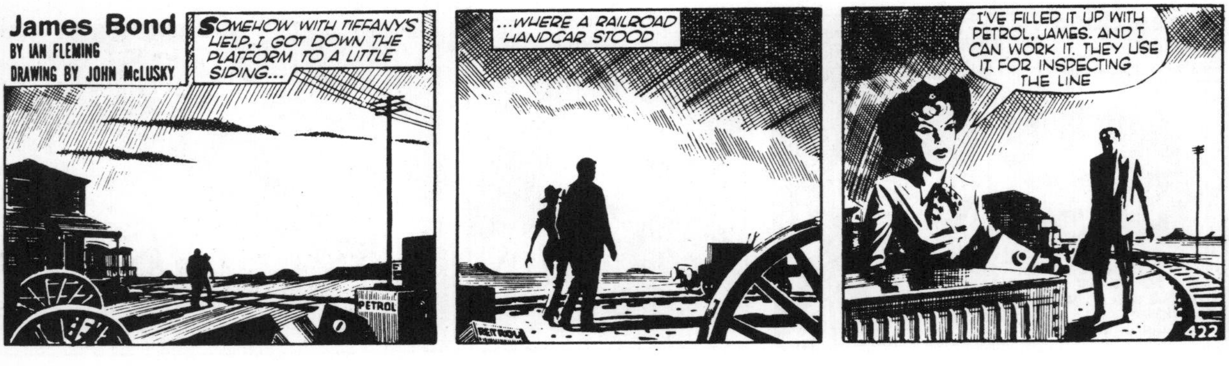
James Bond
BY IAN FLEMING
DRAWING BY JOHN McLUSKY
SOMEHOW WITH TIFFANY'S HELP, I GOT DOWN THE PLATFORM TO A LITTLE SIDING...
PETROL
...WHERE A RAILROAD HANDCAR STOOD
I'VE FILLED IT UP WITH PETROL, JAMES. AND I CAN WORK IT. THEY USE IT FOR INSPECTING THE LINE
422

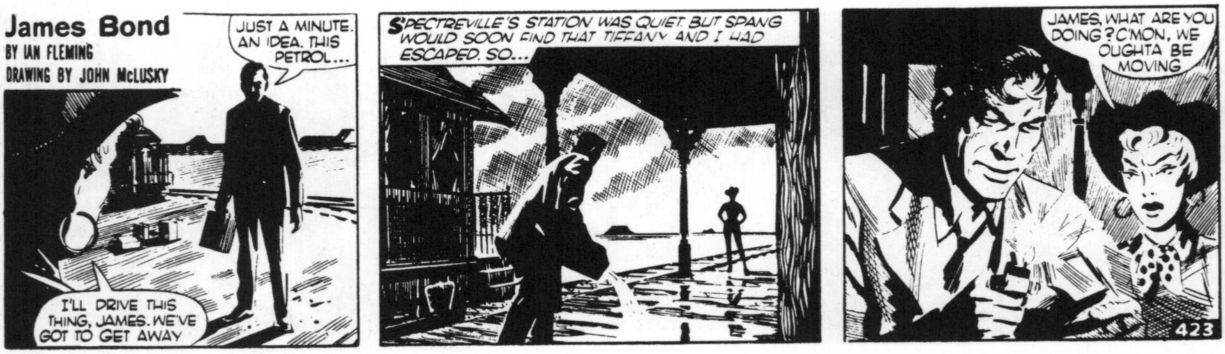
James Bond
BY IAN FLEMING
DRAWING BY JOHN McLUSKY
JUST A MINUTE. AN IDEA. THIS PETROL...
I'LL DRIVE THIS THING, JAMES. WE'VE GOT TO GET AWAY
SPECTREVILLE'S STATION WAS QUIET BUT SPANG WOULD SOON FIND THAT TIFFANY AND I HAD ESCAPED. SO...
JAMES, WHAT ARE YOU DOING? C'MON, WE OUGHTA BE MOVING
423

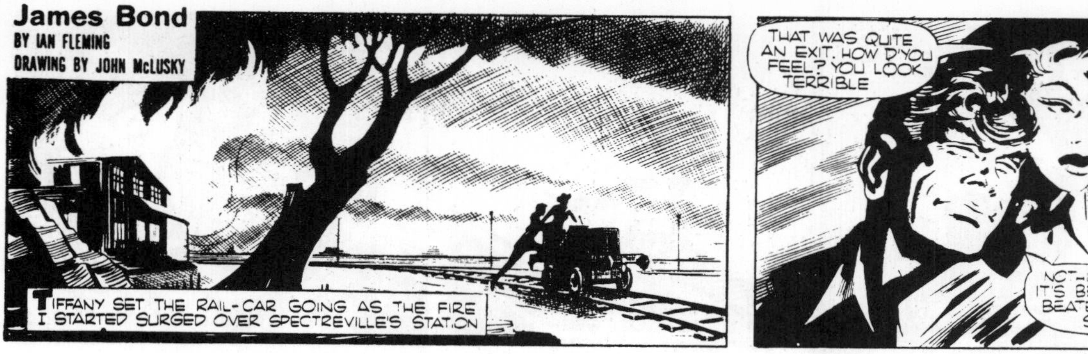
James Bond
BY IAN FLEMING
DRAWING BY JOHN McLUSKY
TIFFANY SET THE RAIL-CAR GOING AS THE FIRE I STARTED SURGED OVER SPECTREVILLE'S STATION
THAT WAS QUITE AN EXIT. HOW D'YOU FEEL? YOU LOOK TERRIBLE
NOTHING BROKEN. IT'S BETTER BEING BEATEN UP THAN SHOT!
424

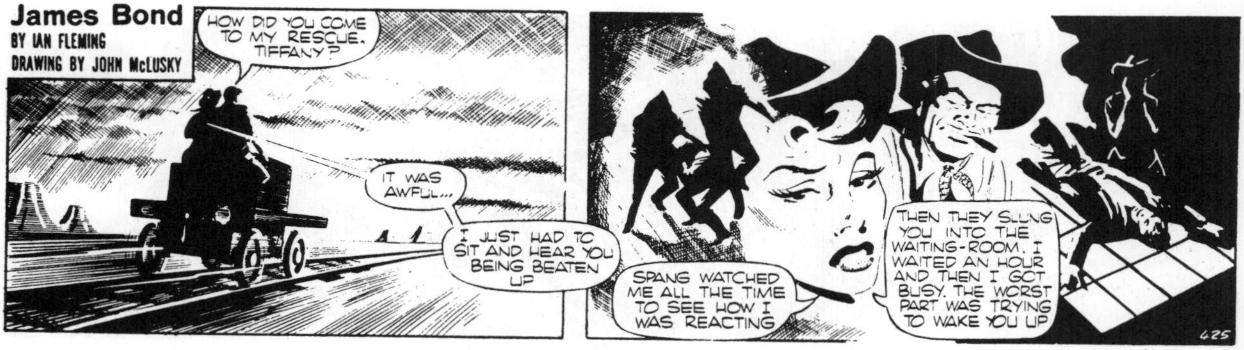
James Bond
BY IAN FLEMING
DRAWING BY JOHN McLUSKY
HOW DID YOU COME TO MY RESCUE, TIFFANY?
IT WAS AWFUL...
I JUST HAD TO SIT AND HEAR YOU BEING BEATEN UP
SPANG WATCHED ME ALL THE TIME TO SEE HOW I WAS REACTING
THEN THEY SLUNG YOU INTO THE WAITING-ROOM. I WAITED AN HOUR AND THEN I GOT BUSY. THE WORST PART WAS TRYING TO WAKE YOU UP
425

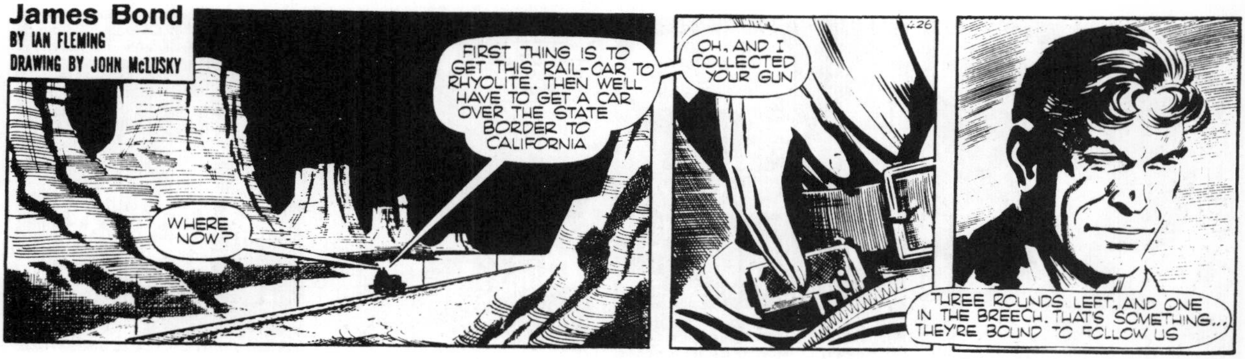
James Bond
BY IAN FLEMING
DRAWING BY JOHN McLUSKY
WHERE NOW?
FIRST THING IS TO GET THIS RAIL-CAR TO RHYOLITE. THEN WE'LL HAVE TO GET A CAR OVER THE STATE BORDER TO CALIFORNIA
426
OH, AND I COLLECTED YOUR GUN
THREE ROUNDS LEFT, AND ONE IN THE BREECH. THAT'S SOMETHING... THEY'RE BOUND TO FOLLOW US

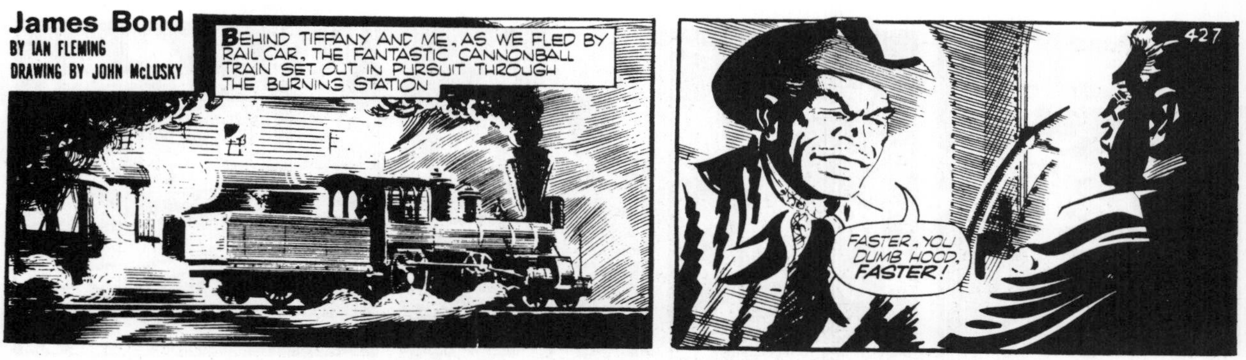
James Bond
BY IAN FLEMING
DRAWING BY JOHN McLUSKY
BEHIND TIFFANY AND ME, AS WE FLED BY RAIL CAR, THE FANTASTIC CANNONBALL TRAIN SET OUT IN PURSUIT THROUGH THE BURNING STATION
427
FASTER, YOU DUMB HOOD, FASTER!

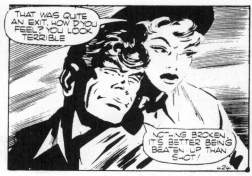

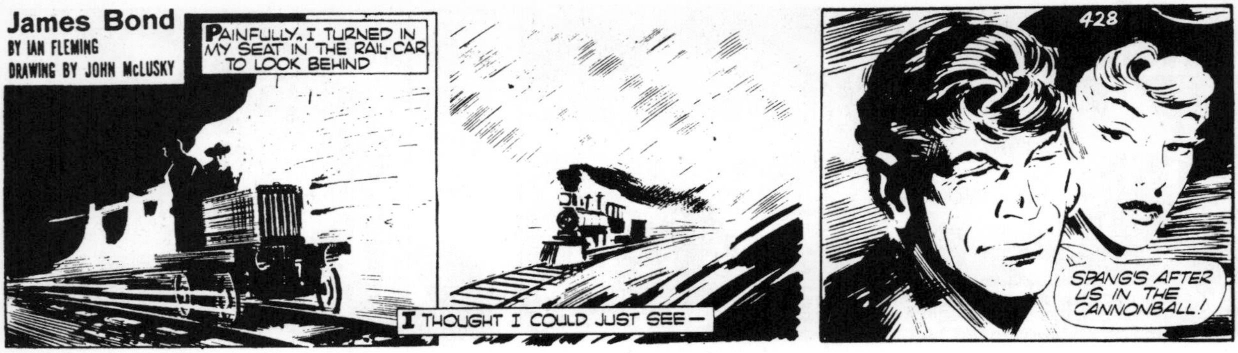
James Bond
BY IAN FLEMING
DRAWING BY JOHN McLUSKY
PAINFULLY, I TURNED IN MY SEAT IN THE RAIL-CAR TO LOOK BEHIND
I THOUGHT I COULD JUST SEE—
428
SPANG'S AFTER US IN THE CANNONBALL!

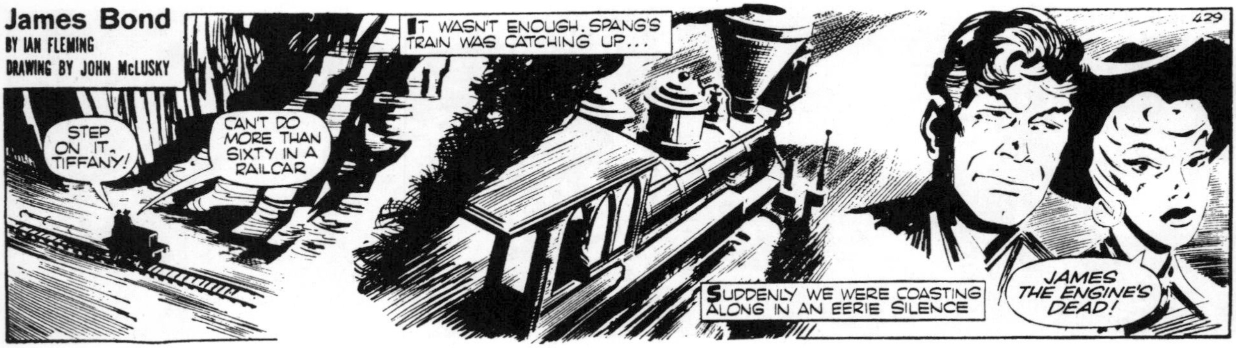
James Bond
BY IAN FLEMING
DRAWING BY JOHN McLUSKY
STEP ON IT, TIFFANY!
CAN'T DO MORE THAN SIXTY IN A RAILCAR
IT WASN'T ENOUGH. SPANG'S TRAIN WAS CATCHING UP...
429
SUDDENLY WE WERE COASTING ALONG IN AN EERIE SILENCE
JAMES THE ENGINE'S DEAD!

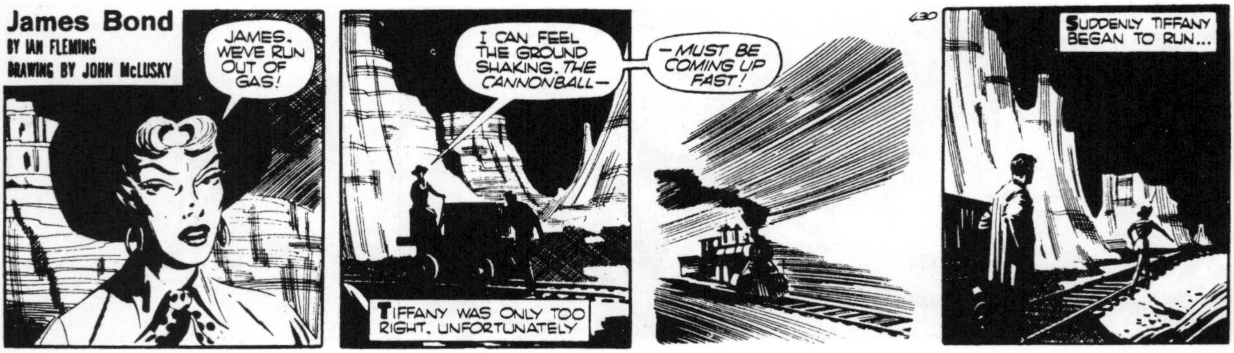
James Bond
BY IAN FLEMING
DRAWING BY JOHN McLUSKY
JAMES. WE'VE RUN OUT OF GAS!
I CAN FEEL THE GROUND SHAKING. THE CANNONBALL—
—MUST BE COMING UP FAST!
TIFFANY WAS ONLY TOO RIGHT, UNFORTUNATELY
430
SUDDENLY TIFFANY BEGAN TO RUN...

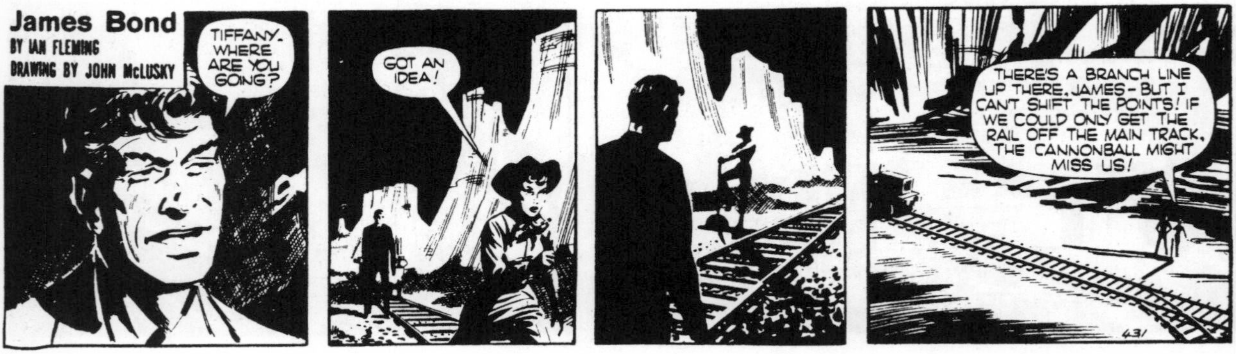
James Bond
BY IAN FLEMING
DRAWING BY JOHN McLUSKY
TIFFANY. WHERE ARE YOU GOING?
GOT AN IDEA!
THERE'S A BRANCH LINE UP THERE, JAMES– BUT I CANT SHIFT THE POINTS! IF WE COULD ONLY GET THE RAIL OFF THE MAIN TRACK, THE CANNONBALL MIGHT MISS US!
431

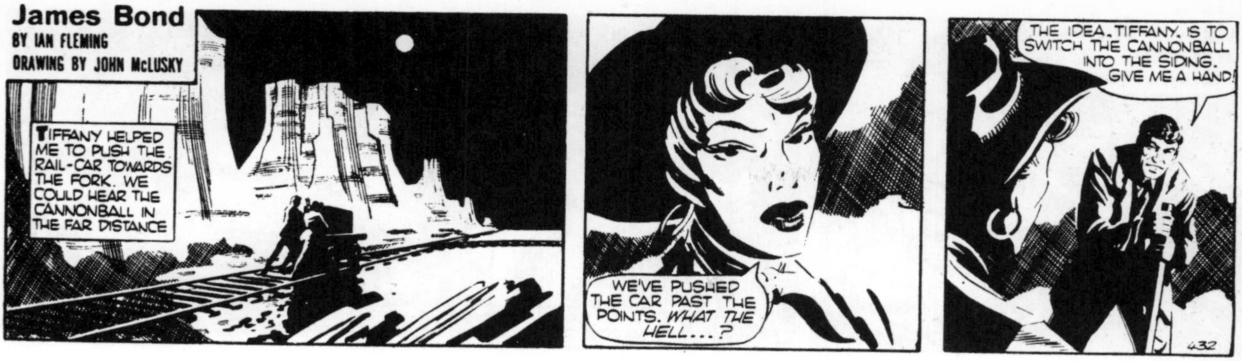
James Bond
BY IAN FLEMING
DRAWING BY JOHN McLUSKY
TIFFANY HELPED ME TO PUSH THE RAIL-CAR TOWARDS THE FORK. WE COULD HEAR THE CANNONBALL IN THE FAR DISTANCE
WE'VE PUSHED THE CAR PAST THE POINTS. WHAT THE HELL...?
THE IDEA, TIFFANY, IS TO SWITCH THE CANNONBALL INTO THE SIDING. GIVE ME A HAND!
432

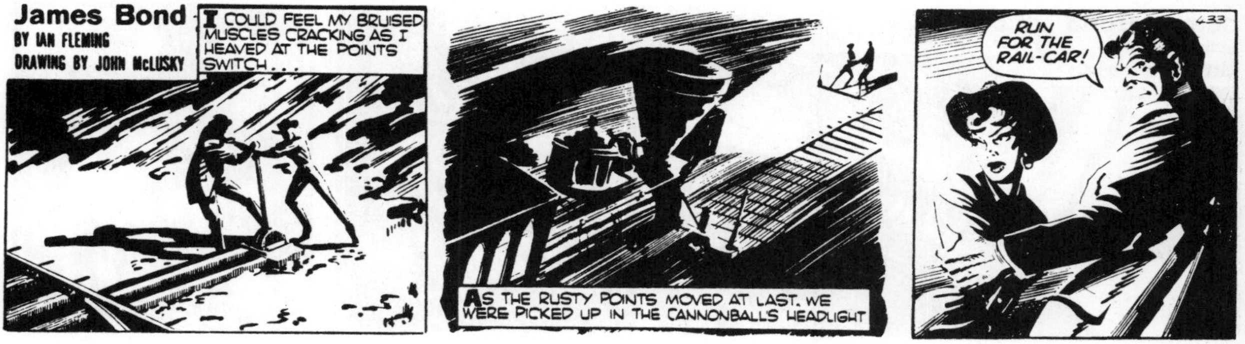
James Bond
BY IAN FLEMING
DRAWING BY JOHN McLUSKY
I COULD FEEL MY BRUISED MUSCLES CRACKING AS I HEAVED AT THE POINTS SWITCH...
AS THE RUSTY POINTS MOVED AT LAST, WE WERE PICKED UP IN THE CANNONBALL'S HEADLIGHT
433
RUN FOR THE RAIL-CAR!

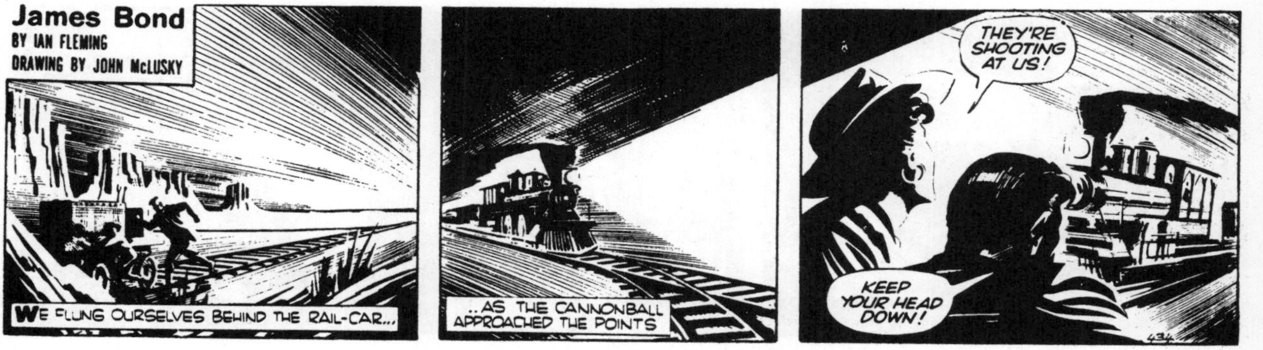
James Bond
BY IAN FLEMING
DRAWING BY JOHN McLUSKY
WE FLUNG OURSELVES BEHIND THE RAIL-CAR...
..AS THE CANNONBALL APPROACHED THE POINTS
THEY'RE SHOOTING AT US!
KEEP YOUR HEAD DOWN!
434

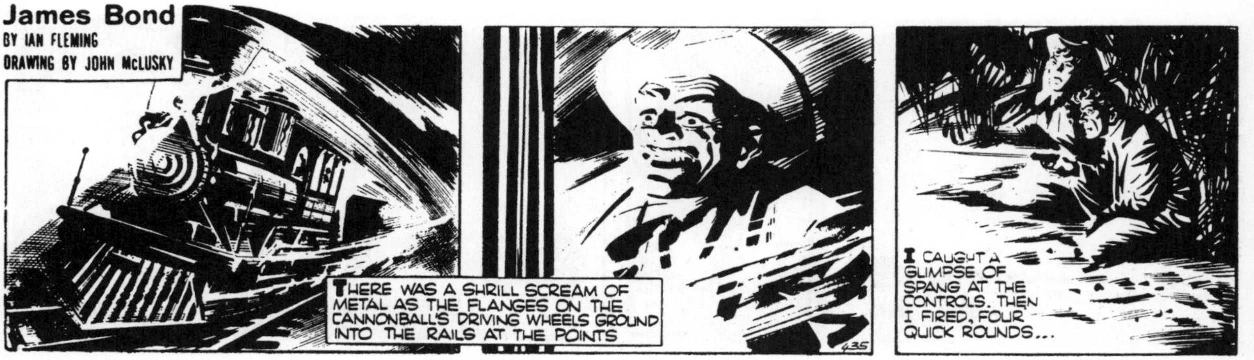
James Bond
BY IAN FLEMING
DRAWING BY JOHN McLUSKY
THERE WAS A SHRILL SCREAM OF METAL AS THE FLANGES ON THE CANNONBALL'S DRIVING WHEELS GROUND INTO THE RAILS AT THE POINTS
435
I CAUGHT A GLIMPSE OF SPANG AT THE CONTROLS. THEN I FIRED, FOUR QUICK ROUNDS...

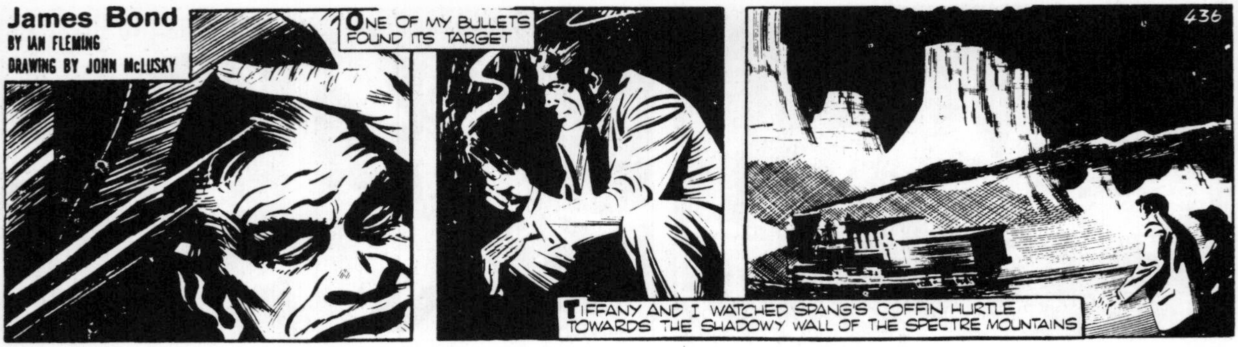
James Bond
BY IAN FLEMING
DRAWING BY JOHN McLUSKY
ONE OF MY BULLETS FOUND ITS TARGET
436
TIFFANY AND I WATCHED SPANG'S COFFIN HURTLE TOWARDS THE SHADOWY WALL OF THE SPECTRE MOUNTAINS

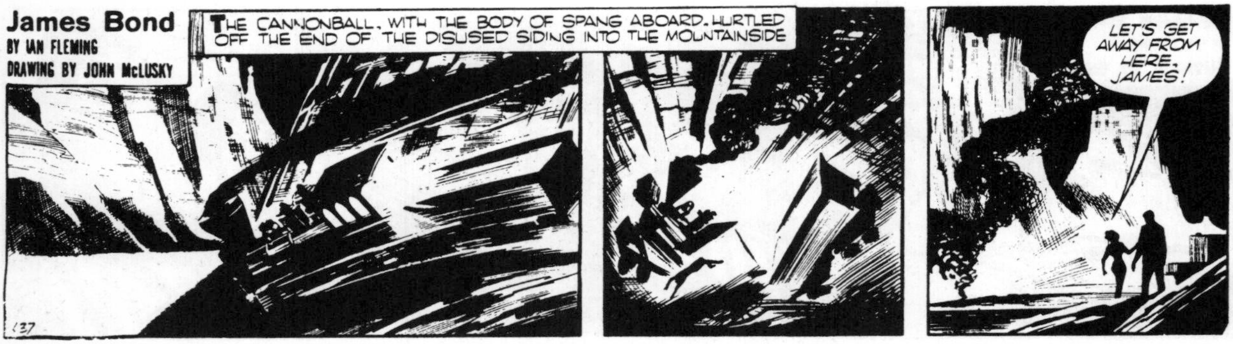
James Bond
BY IAN FLEMING
DRAWING BY JOHN McLUSKY
THE CANNONBALL, WITH THE BODY OF SPANG ABOARD, HURTLED OFF THE END OF THE DISUSED SIDING INTO THE MOUNTAINSIDE
LET'S GET AWAY FROM HERE, JAMES!

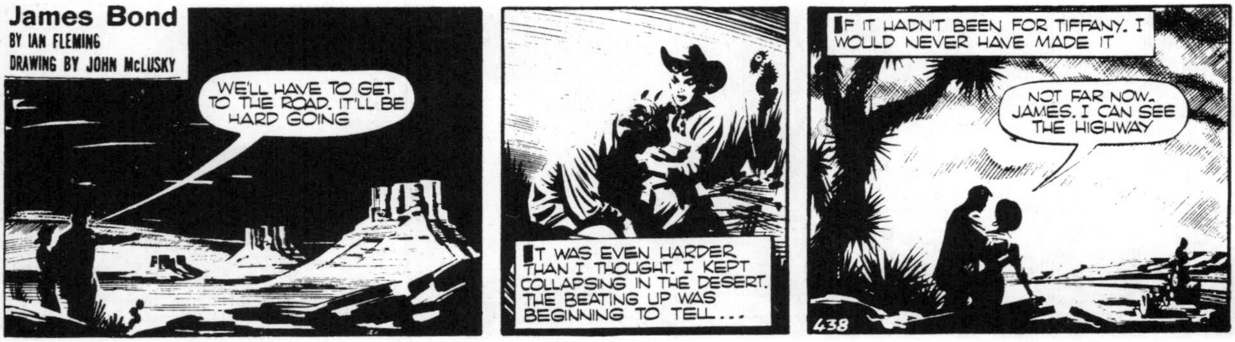
James Bond
BY IAN FLEMING
DRAWING BY JOHN McLUSKY
WE'LL HAVE TO GET TO THE ROAD. IT'LL BE HARD GOING
IT WAS EVEN HARDER THAN I THOUGHT. I KEPT COLLAPSING IN THE DESERT. THE BEATING UP WAS BEGINNING TO TELL...
IF IT HADN'T BEEN FOR TIFFANY, I WOULD NEVER HAVE MADE IT
NOT FAR NOW, JAMES. I CAN SEE THE HIGHWAY
438

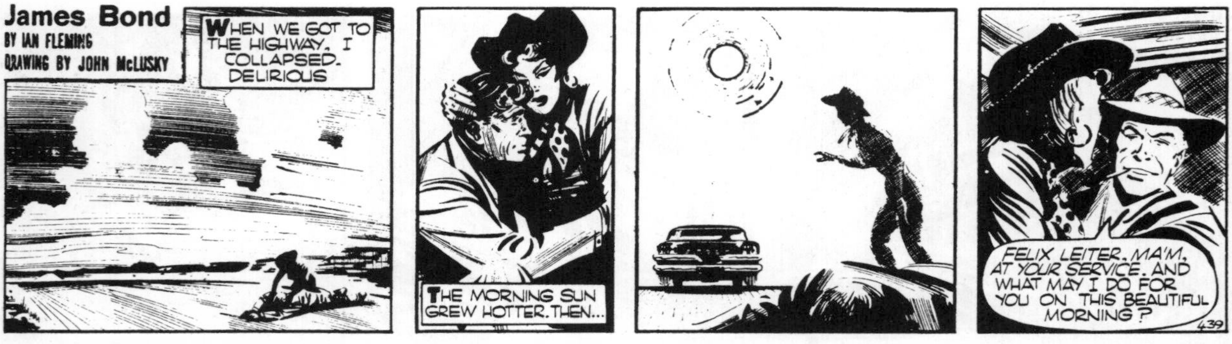
James Bond
BY IAN FLEMING
DRAWING BY JOHN McLUSKY
WHEN WE GOT TO THE HIGHWAY, I COLLAPSED. DELIRIOUS
THE MORNING SUN GREW HOTTER. THEN...
FELIX LEITER, MA'M, AT YOUR SERVICE. AND WHAT MAY I DO FOR YOU ON THIS BEAUTIFUL MORNING?
439

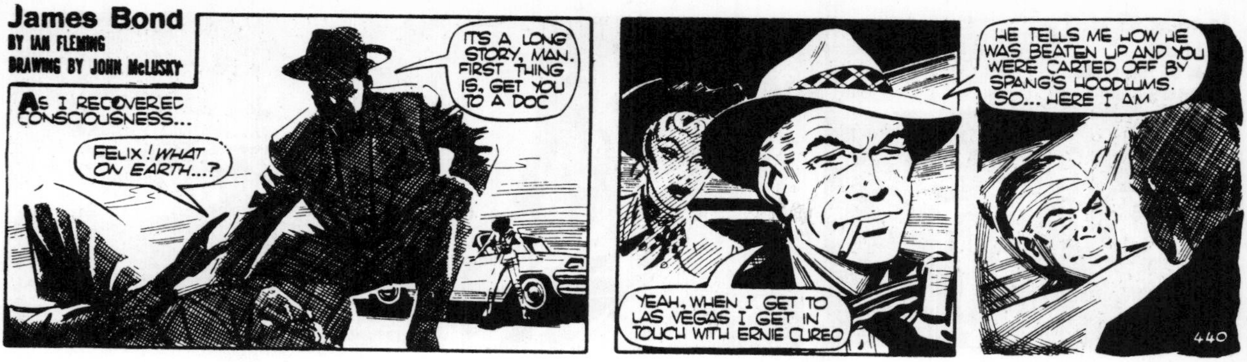
James Bond
BY IAN FLEMING
DRAWING BY JOHN McLUSKY
AS I RECOVERED CONSCIOUSNESS...
FELIX! WHAT ON EARTH...?
ITS A LONG STORY, MAN. FIRST THING IS, GET YOU TO A DOC
YEAH. WHEN I GET TO LAS VEGAS I GET IN TOUCH WITH ERNIE CUREO
HE TELLS ME HOW HE WAS BEATEN UP AND YOU WERE CARTED OFF BY SPANG'S HOODLUMS. SO... HERE I AM
440

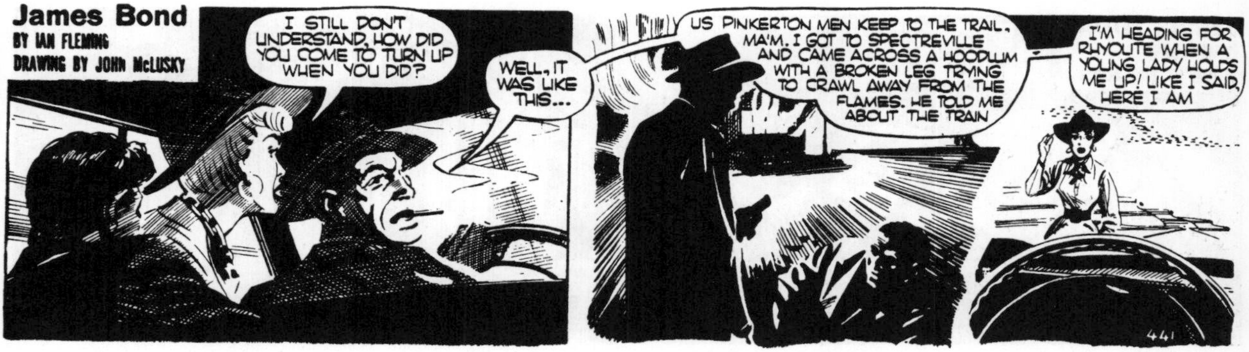
James Bond
BY IAN FLEMING
DRAWING BY JOHN McLUSKY
I STILL DON'T UNDERSTAND, HOW DID YOU COME TO TURN UP WHEN YOU DID?
WELL, IT WAS LIKE THIS...
US PINKERTON MEN KEEP TO THE TRAIL, MA'M. I GOT TO SPECTREVILLE AND CAME ACROSS A HOODLUM WITH A BROKEN LEG TRYING TO CRAWL AWAY FROM THE FLAMES. HE TOLD ME ABOUT THE TRAIN
I'M HEADING FOR RHYOLITE WHEN A YOUNG LADY HOLDS ME UP! LIKE I SAID, HERE I AM
441

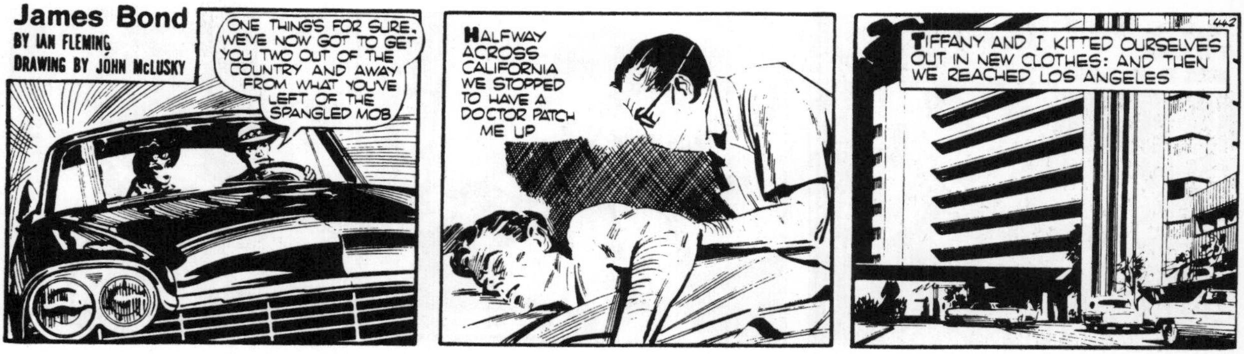
James Bond
BY IAN FLEMING
DRAWING BY JOHN McLUSKY
ONE THING'S FOR SURE. WEVE NOW GOT TO GET YOU TWO OUT OF THE COUNTRY AND AWAY FROM WHAT YOU'VE LEFT OF THE SPANGLED MOB
HALFWAY ACROSS CALIFORNIA WE STOPPED TO HAVE A DOCTOR PATCH ME UP
442
TIFFANY AND I KITTED OURSELVES OUT IN NEW CLOTHES: AND THEN WE REACHED LOS ANGELES

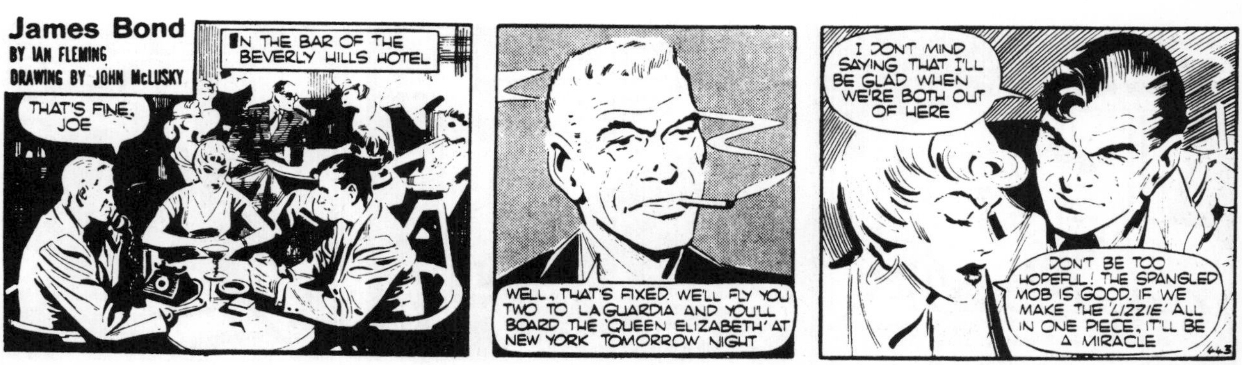
James Bond
BY IAN FLEMING
DRAWING BY JOHN McLUSKY
IN THE BAR OF THE BEVERLY HILLS HOTEL
THAT'S FINE, JOE
WELL, THAT'S FIXED. WE'LL FLY YOU TWO TO LA GUARDIA AND YOU'LL BOARD THE 'QUEEN ELIZABETH' AT NEW YORK TOMORROW NIGHT
I DONT MIND SAYING THAT I'LL BE GLAD WHEN WE'RE BOTH OUT OF HERE
DON'T BE TOO HOPEFUL! THE SPANGLED MOB IS GOOD. IF WE MAKE THE 'LIZZIE' ALL IN ONE PIECE, IT'LL BE A MIRACLE
443

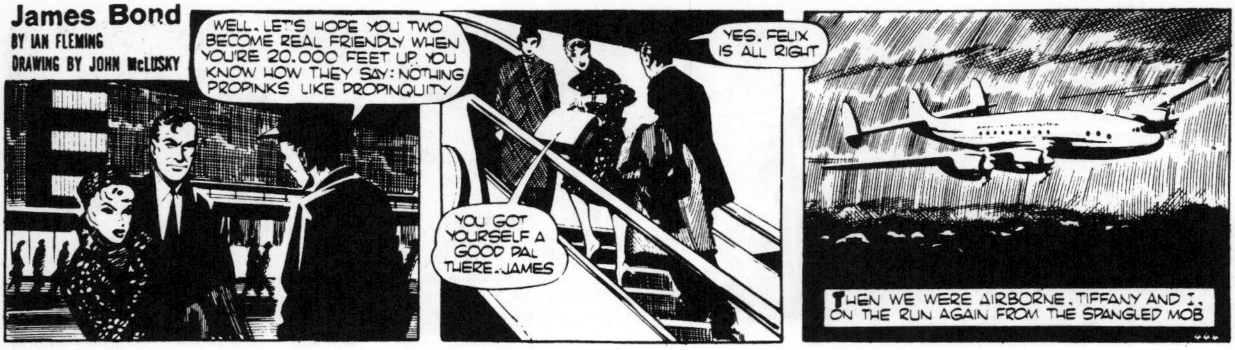
James Bond
BY IAN FLEMING
DRAWING BY JOHN McLUSKY
WELL, LET'S HOPE YOU TWO BECOME REAL FRIENDLY WHEN YOU'RE 20,000 FEET UP. YOU KNOW HOW THEY SAY: NOTHING PROPINKS LIKE PROPINQUITY
YOU GOT YOURSELF A GOOD PAL THERE, JAMES
YES, FELIX IS ALL RIGHT
THEN WE WERE AIRBORNE, TIFFANY AND I, ON THE RUN AGAIN FROM THE SPANGLED MOB
444

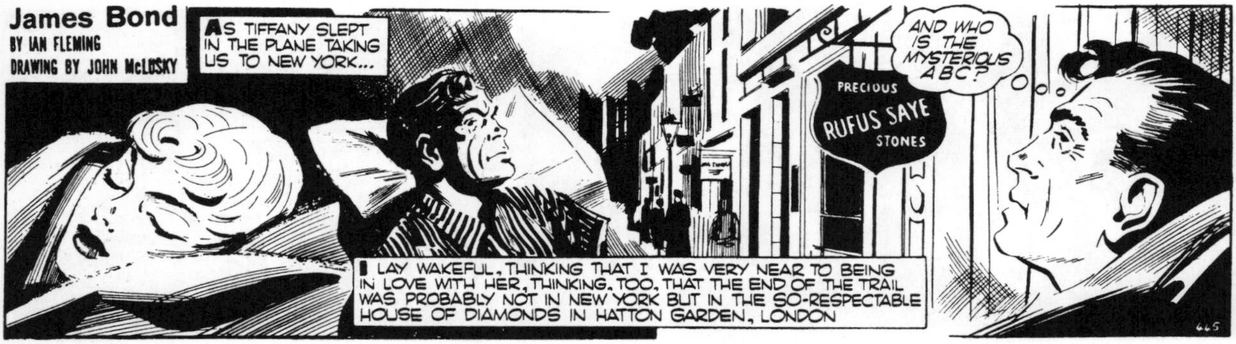
James Bond
BY IAN FLEMING
DRAWING BY JOHN McLUSKY
AS TIFFANY SLEPT IN THE PLANE TAKING US TO NEW YORK...
I LAY WAKEFUL, THINKING THAT I WAS VERY NEAR TO BEING IN LOVE WITH HER, THINKING, TOO, THAT THE END OF THE TRAIL WAS PROBABLY NOT IN NEW YORK BUT IN THE SO-RESPECTABLE HOUSE OF DIAMONDS IN HATTON GARDEN, LONDON
PRECIOUS
RUFUS SAYE
STONES
AND WHO IS THE MYSTERIOUS ABC?
445

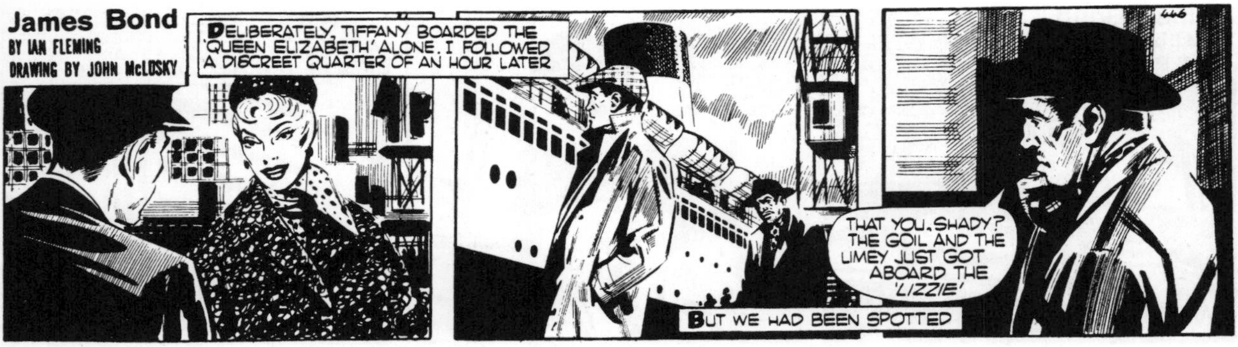
James Bond
BY IAN FLEMING
DRAWING BY JOHN McLUSKY
DELIBERATELY, TIFFANY BOARDED THE 'QUEEN ELIZABETH' ALONE. I FOLLOWED A DISCREET QUARTER OF AN HOUR LATER
BUT WE HAD BEEN SPOTTED
THAT YOU, SHADY? THE GOIL AND THE LIMEY JUST GOT ABOARD THE 'LIZZIE'
446

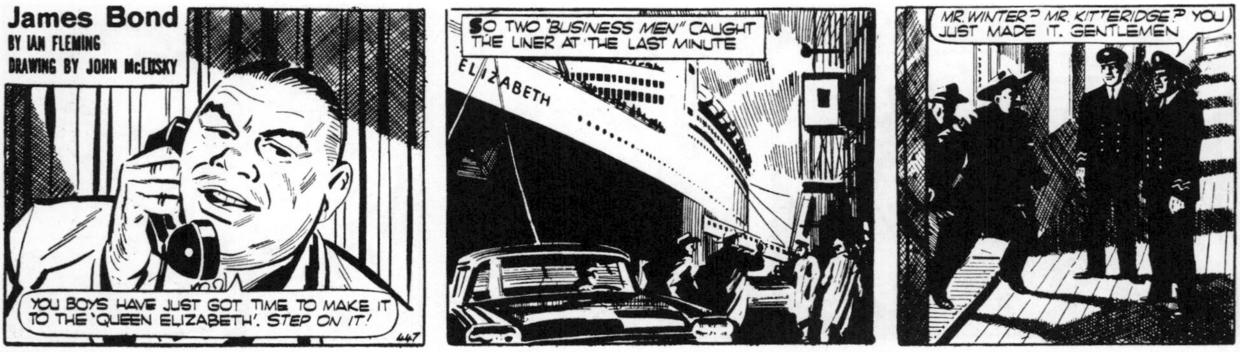
James Bond
BY IAN FLEMING
DRAWING BY JOHN McLUSKY
YOU BOYS HAVE JUST GOT TIME TO MAKE IT TO THE 'QUEEN ELIZABETH'. STEP ON IT!
447
SO TWO "BUSINESS MEN" CAUGHT THE LINER AT THE LAST MINUTE
ELIZABETH
MR. WINTER? MR. KITTERIDGE? YOU JUST MADE IT, GENTLEMEN

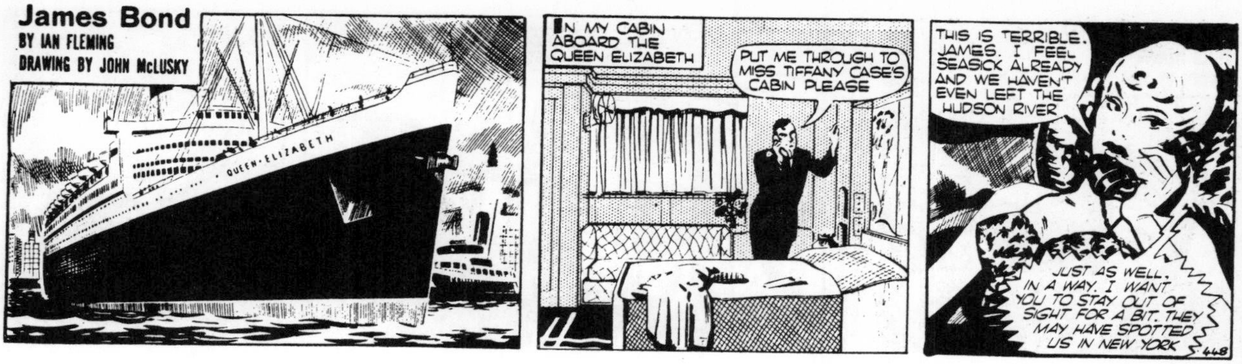
James Bond
BY IAN FLEMING
DRAWING BY JOHN McLUSKY
QUEEN ELIZABETH
IN MY CABIN ABOARD THE QUEEN ELIZABETH
PUT ME THROUGH TO MISS TIFFANY CASE'S CABIN PLEASE
THIS IS TERRIBLE, JAMES. I FEEL SEASICK ALREADY AND WE HAVEN'T EVEN LEFT THE HUDSON RIVER
JUST AS WELL, IN A WAY. I WANT YOU TO STAY OUT OF SIGHT FOR A BIT. THEY MAY HAVE SPOTTED US IN NEW YORK
448

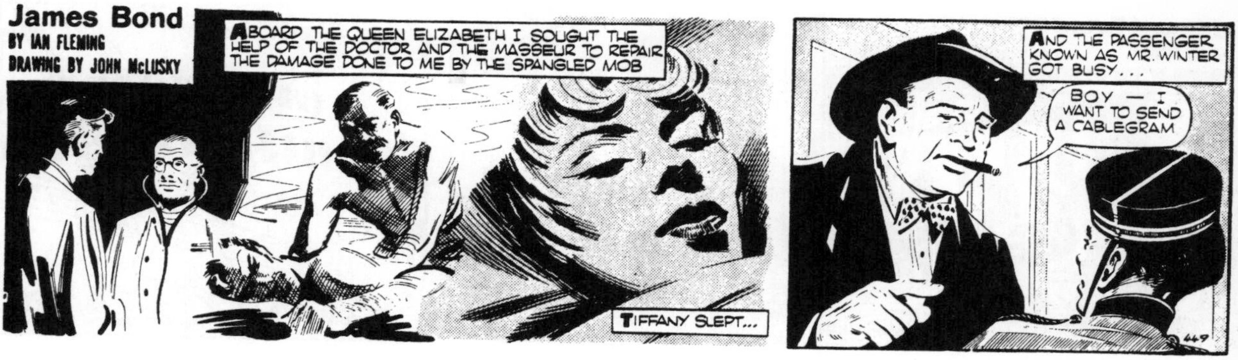
James Bond
BY IAN FLEMING
DRAWING BY JOHN McLUSKY
ABOARD THE QUEEN ELIZABETH I SOUGHT THE HELP OF THE DOCTOR AND THE MASSEUR TO REPAIR THE DAMAGE DONE TO ME BY THE SPANGLED MOB
TIFFANY SLEPT...
AND THE PASSENGER KNOWN AS MR. WINTER GOT BUSY...
BOY — I WANT TO SEND A CABLEGRAM
449

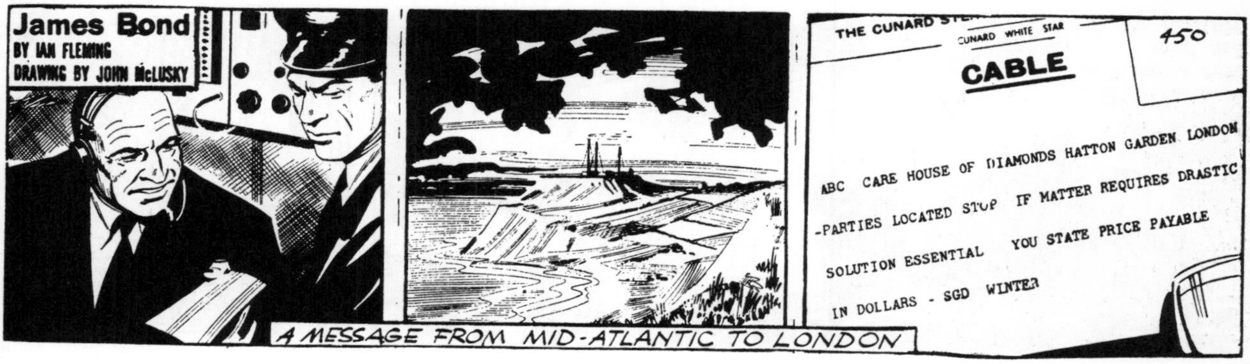
James Bond
BY IAN FLEMING
DRAWING BY JOHN McLUSKY
THE CUNARD
CUNARD WHITE STAR
450
CABLE
ABC CARE HOUSE OF DIAMONDS HATTON GARDEN LONDON
-PARTIES LOCATED STOP IF MATTER REQUIRES DRASTIC
SOLUTION ESSENTIAL YOU STATE PRICE PAYABLE
IN DOLLARS - SGD WINTER
A MESSAGE FROM MID-ATLANTIC TO LONDON

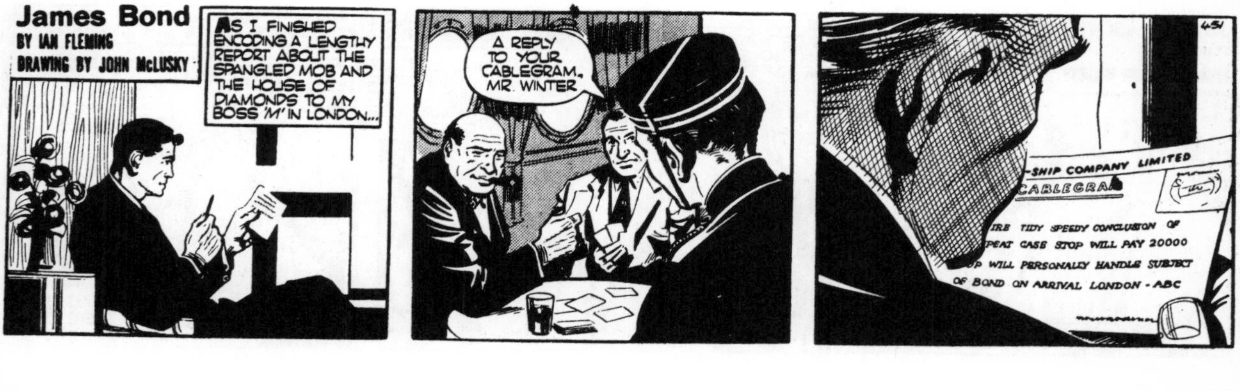
James Bond
BY IAN FLEMING
DRAWING BY JOHN McLUSKY
AS I FINISHED ENCODING A LENGTHY REPORT ABOUT THE SPANGLED MOB AND THE HOUSE OF DIAMONDS TO MY BOSS 'M' IN LONDON...
A REPLY TO YOUR CABLEGRAM, MR. WINTER
451
SHIP COMPANY LIMITED
CABLEGRA
IRE TIDY SPEEDY CONCLUSION OF
PEAT CASE STOP WILL PAY 20000
OP WILL PERSONALLY HANDLE SUBJECT
OF BOND ON ARRIVAL LONDON - ABC

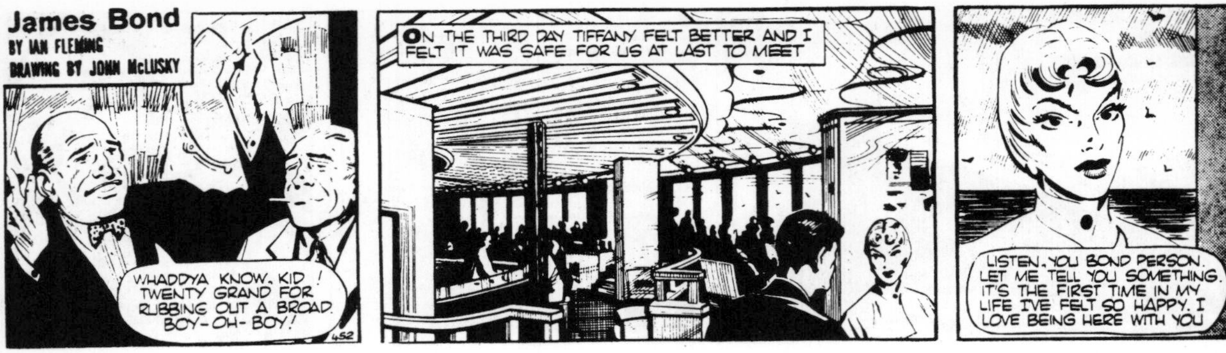
James Bond
BY IAN FLEMING
DRAWING BY JOHN McLUSKY
WHADDYA KNOW, KID! TWENTY GRAND FOR RUBBING OUT A BROAD. BOY-OH-BOY!
452
ON THE THIRD DAY TIFFANY FELT BETTER AND I FELT IT WAS SAFE FOR US AT LAST TO MEET
LISTEN, YOU BOND PERSON. LET ME TELL YOU SOMETHING. IT'S THE FIRST TIME IN MY LIFE I'VE FELT SO HAPPY. I LOVE BEING HERE WITH YOU

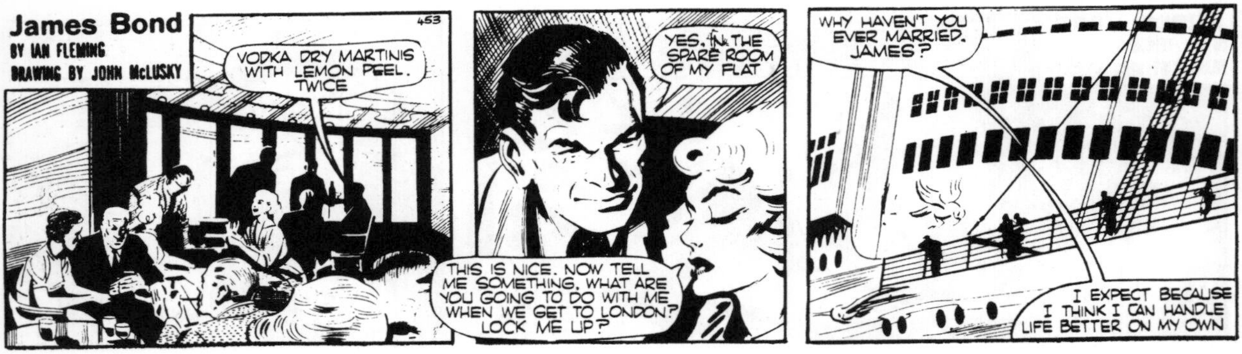
James Bond
BY IAN FLEMING
DRAWING BY JOHN McLUSKY
453
VODKA DRY MARTINIS WITH LEMON PEEL. TWICE
YES. IN THE SPARE ROOM OF MY FLAT
THIS IS NICE. NOW TELL ME SOMETHING. WHAT ARE YOU GOING TO DO WITH ME WHEN WE GET TO LONDON? LOCK ME UP?
WHY HAVEN'T YOU EVER MARRIED, JAMES?
I EXPECT BECAUSE I THINK I CAN HANDLE LIFE BETTER ON MY OWN

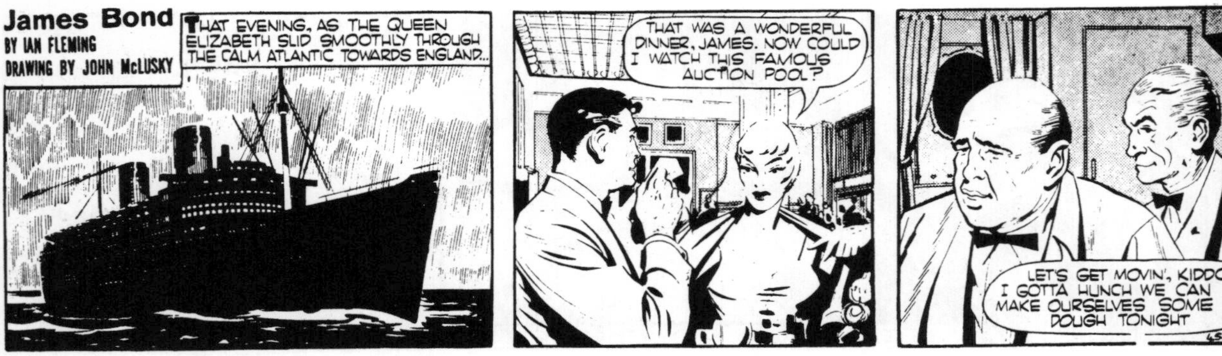
James Bond
BY IAN FLEMING
DRAWING BY JOHN McLUSKY
THAT EVENING, AS THE QUEEN ELIZABETH SLID SMOOTHLY THROUGH THE CALM ATLANTIC TOWARDS ENGLAND...
THAT WAS A WONDERFUL DINNER, JAMES. NOW COULD I WATCH THIS FAMOUS AUCTION POOL?
LET'S GET MOVIN', KIDDO. I GOTTA HUNCH WE CAN MAKE OURSELVES SOME DOUGH TONIGHT
454

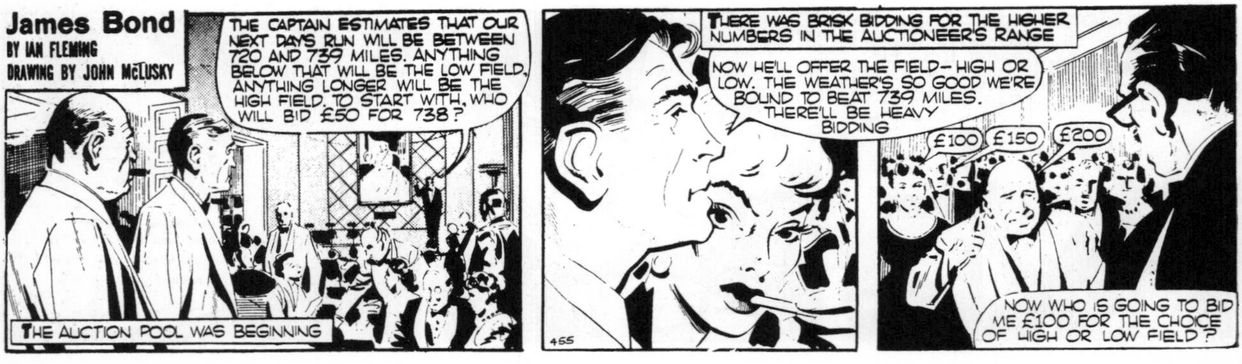
James Bond
BY IAN FLEMING
DRAWING BY JOHN McLUSKY
THE AUCTION POOL WAS BEGINNING
THE CAPTAIN ESTIMATES THAT OUR NEXT DAY'S RUN WILL BE BETWEEN 720 AND 739 MILES. ANYTHING BELOW THAT WILL BE THE LOW FIELD. ANYTHING LONGER WILL BE THE HIGH FIELD. TO START WITH, WHO WILL BID £50 FOR 738?
THERE WAS BRISK BIDDING FOR THE HIGHER NUMBERS IN THE AUCTIONEER'S RANGE
NOW HE'LL OFFER THE FIELD– HIGH OR LOW. THE WEATHER'S SO GOOD WE'RE BOUND TO BEAT 739 MILES. THERE'LL BE HEAVY BIDDING
£100
£150
£200
NOW WHO IS GOING TO BID ME £100 FOR THE CHOICE OF HIGH OR LOW FIELD?
455

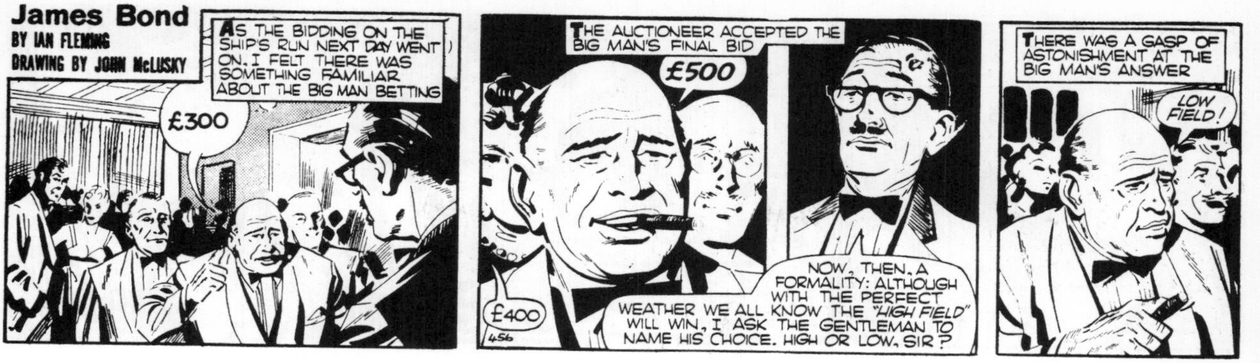
James Bond
BY IAN FLEMING
DRAWING BY JOHN McLUSKY
AS THE BIDDING ON THE SHIP'S RUN NEXT DAY WENT ON, I FELT THERE WAS SOMETHING FAMILIAR ABOUT THE BIG MAN BETTING
£300
THE AUCTIONEER ACCEPTED THE BIG MAN'S FINAL BID
£500
£400
456
NOW, THEN, A FORMALITY: ALTHOUGH WITH THE PERFECT WEATHER WE ALL KNOW THE "HIGH FIELD" WILL WIN, I ASK THE GENTLEMAN TO NAME HIS CHOICE. HIGH OR LOW, SIR?
THERE WAS A GASP OF ASTONISHMENT AT THE BIG MAN'S ANSWER
LOW FIELD!

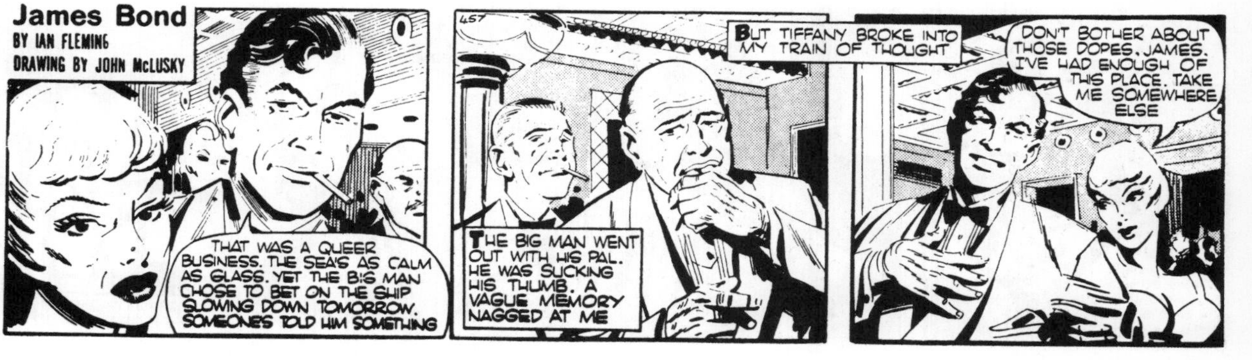
James Bond
BY IAN FLEMING
DRAWING BY JOHN McLUSKY
THAT WAS A QUEER BUSINESS. THE SEA'S AS CALM AS GLASS. YET THE BIG MAN CHOSE TO BET ON THE SHIP SLOWING DOWN TOMORROW. SOMEONE'S TOLD HIM SOMETHING
457
THE BIG MAN WENT OUT WITH HIS PAL. HE WAS SUCKING HIS THUMB. A VAGUE MEMORY NAGGED AT ME
BUT TIFFANY BROKE INTO MY TRAIN OF THOUGHT
DON'T BOTHER ABOUT THOSE DOPES, JAMES. I'VE HAD ENOUGH OF THIS PLACE. TAKE ME SOMEWHERE ELSE

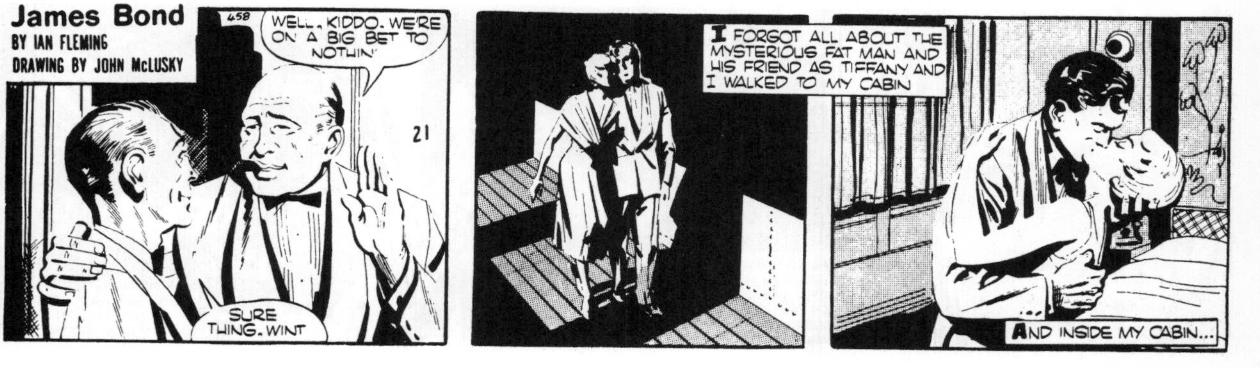
James Bond
BY IAN FLEMING
DRAWING BY JOHN McLUSKY
458
WELL, KIDDO, WE'RE ON A BIG BET TO NOTHIN'
21
SURE THING, WINT
I FORGOT ALL ABOUT THE MYSTERIOUS FAT MAN AND HIS FRIEND AS TIFFANY AND I WALKED TO MY CABIN
AND INSIDE MY CABIN...

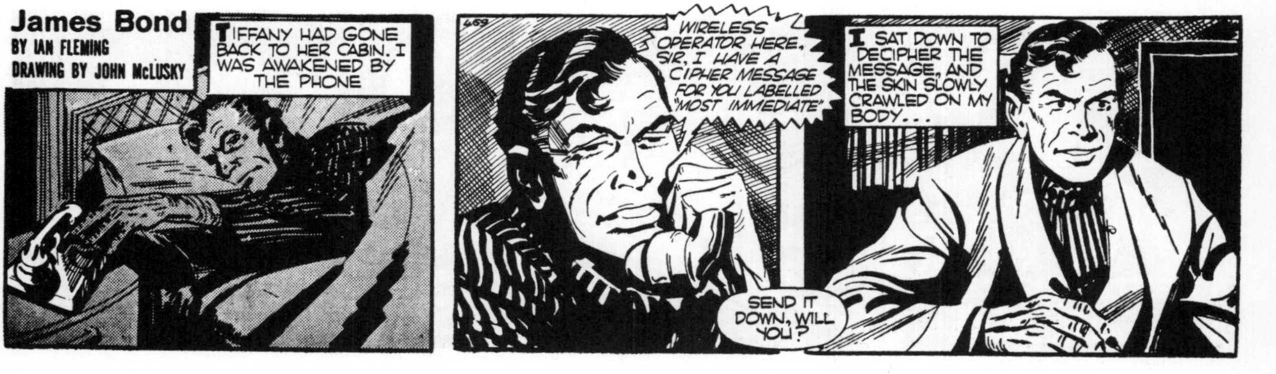
James Bond
BY IAN FLEMING
DRAWING BY JOHN McLUSKY
TIFFANY HAD GONE BACK TO HER CABIN. I WAS AWAKENED BY THE PHONE
459
WIRELESS OPERATOR HERE, SIR. I HAVE A CIPHER MESSAGE FOR YOU LABELLED "MOST IMMEDIATE"
SEND IT DOWN, WILL YOU?
I SAT DOWN TO DECIPHER THE MESSAGE, AND THE SKIN SLOWLY CRAWLED ON MY BODY...

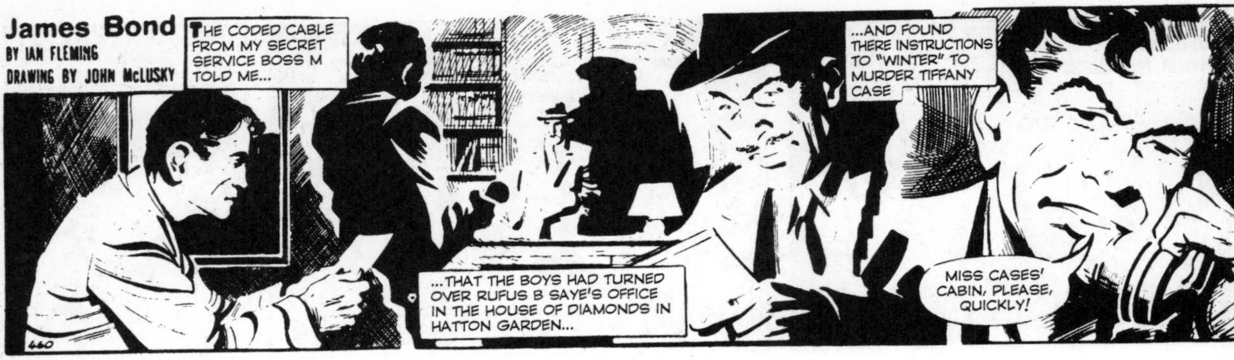
James Bond
BY IAN FLEMING
DRAWING BY JOHN McLUSKY
THE CODED CABLE FROM MY SECRET SERVICE BOSS M TOLD ME...
...THAT THE BOYS HAD TURNED OVER RUFUS B SAYE'S OFFICE IN THE HOUSE OF DIAMONDS IN HATTON GARDEN...
...AND FOUND THERE INSTRUCTIONS TO "WINTER" TO MURDER TIFFANY CASE
MISS CASES' CABIN, PLEASE, QUICKLY!

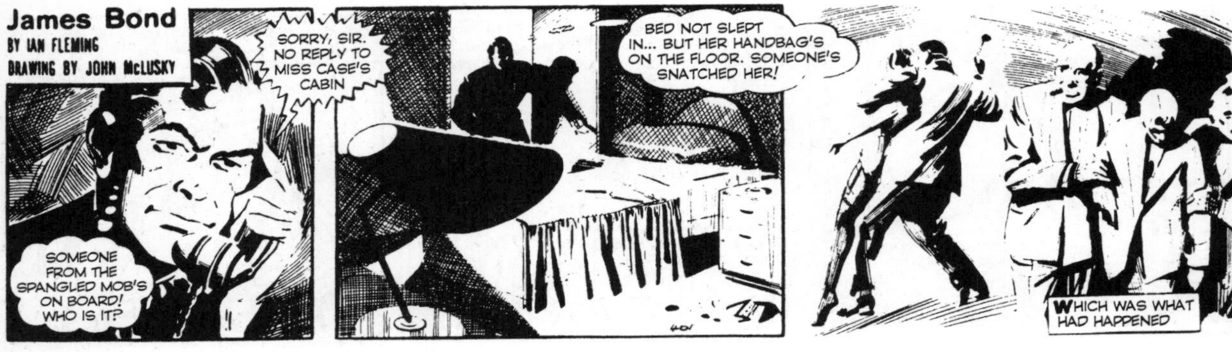
James Bond
BY IAN FLEMING
DRAWING BY JOHN McLUSKY
SORRY, SIR. NO REPLY TO MISS CASE'S CABIN
SOMEONE FROM THE SPANGLED MOB'S ON BOARD! WHO IS IT?
BED NOT SLEPT IN... BUT HER HANDBAG'S ON THE FLOOR. SOMEONE'S SNATCHED HER!
WHICH WAS WHAT HAD HAPPENED

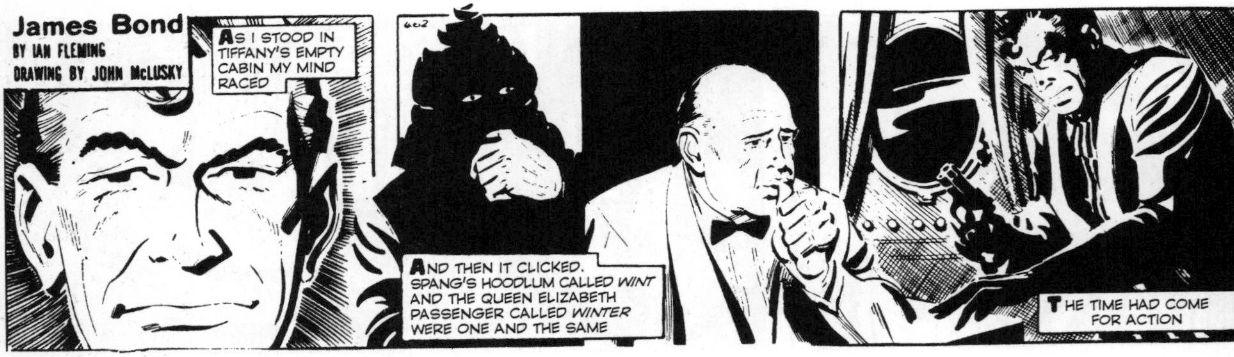
James Bond
BY IAN FLEMING
DRAWING BY JOHN McLUSKY
AS I STOOD IN TIFFANY'S EMPTY CABIN MY MIND RACED
AND THEN IT CLICKED. SPANG'S HOODLUM CALLED WINT AND THE QUEEN ELIZABETH PASSENGER CALLED WINTER WERE ONE AND THE SAME
THE TIME HAD COME FOR ACTION

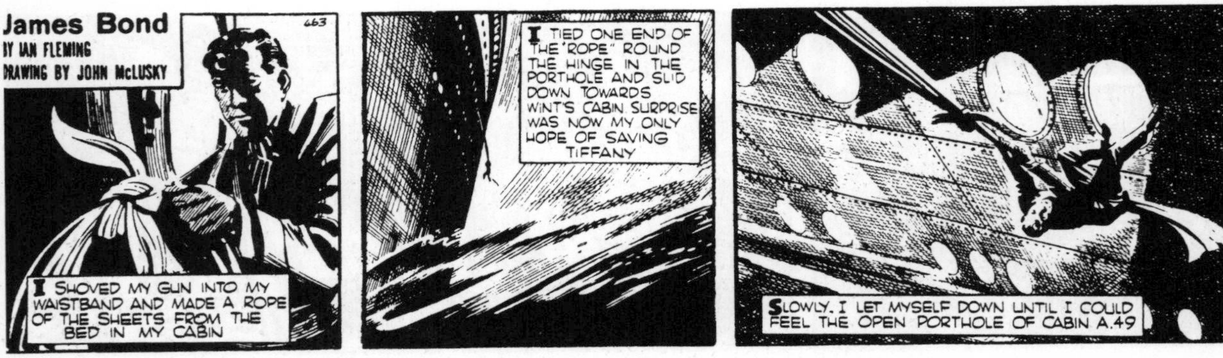
James Bond
BY IAN FLEMING
DRAWING BY JOHN McLUSKY
I SHOVED MY GUN INTO MY WAISTBAND AND MADE A ROPE OF THE SHEETS FROM THE BED IN MY CABIN
I TIED ONE END OF THE "ROPE" ROUND THE HINGE IN THE PORTHOLE AND SLID DOWN TOWARDS WINT'S CABIN. SURPRISE WAS NOW MY ONLY HOPE OF SAVING TIFFANY
SLOWLY, I LET MYSELF DOWN UNTIL I COULD FEEL THE OPEN PORTHOLE OF CABIN A.49

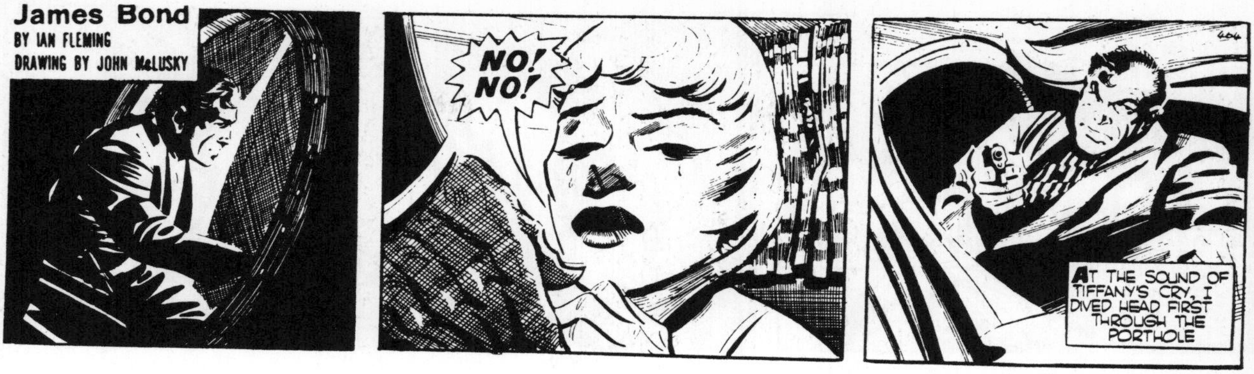

James Bond
BY IAN FLEMING
DRAWING BY JOHN McLUSKY
NO! NO!
AT THE SOUND OF TIFFANY'S CRY, I DIVED HEAD FIRST THROUGH THE PORTHOLE

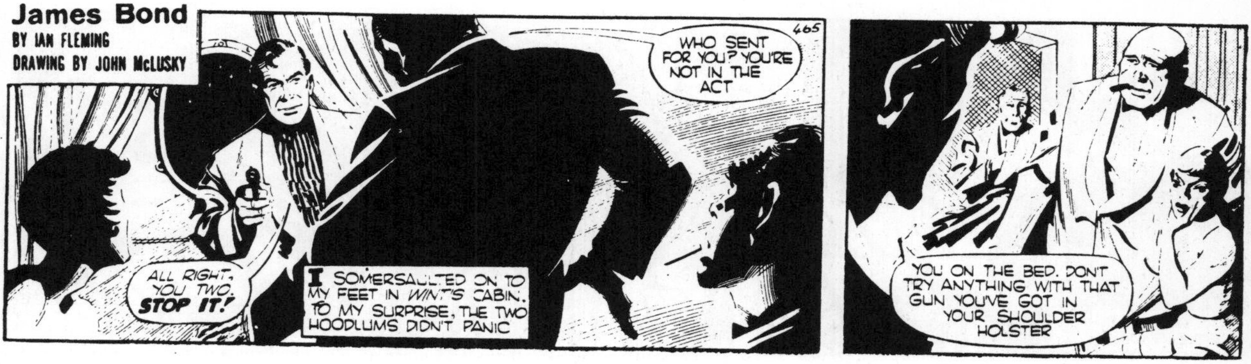

James Bond
BY IAN FLEMING
DRAWING BY JOHN McLUSKY
WHO SENT FOR YOU? YOU'RE NOT IN THE ACT
ALL RIGHT, YOU TWO. STOP IT!
I SOMERSAULTED ON TO MY FEET IN WINT'S CABIN. TO MY SURPRISE, THE TWO HOODLUMS DIDN'T PANIC
YOU ON THE BED. DON'T TRY ANYTHING WITH THAT GUN YOU'VE GOT IN YOUR SHOULDER HOLSTER

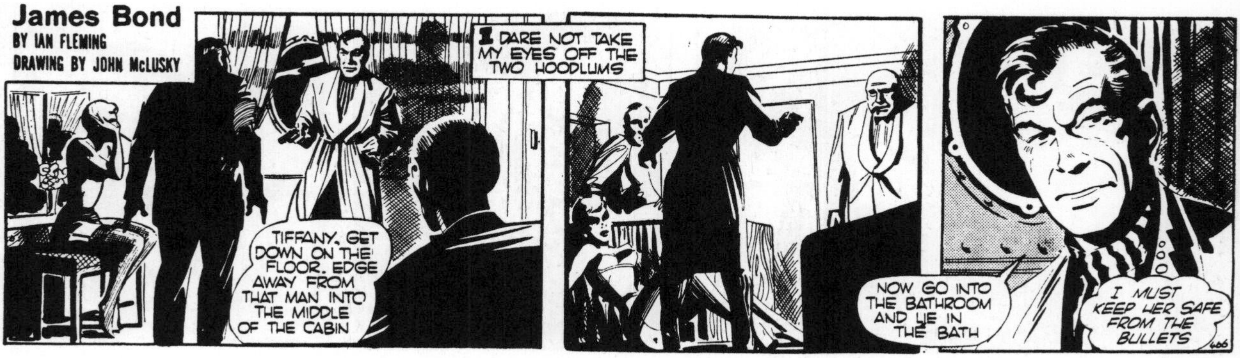

James Bond
BY IAN FLEMING
DRAWING BY JOHN McLUSKY
TIFFANY, GET DOWN ON THE FLOOR. EDGE AWAY FROM THAT MAN INTO THE MIDDLE OF THE CABIN
I DARE NOT TAKE MY EYES OFF THE TWO HOODLUMS
NOW GO INTO THE BATHROOM AND LIE IN THE BATH
I MUST KEEP HER SAFE FROM THE BULLETS

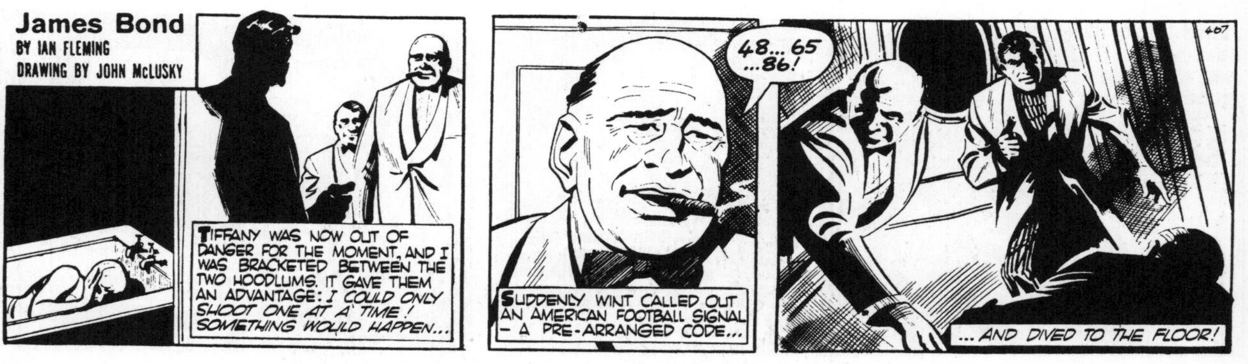

James Bond
BY IAN FLEMING
DRAWING BY JOHN McLUSKY
TIFFANY WAS NOW OUT OF DANGER FOR THE MOMENT, AND I WAS BRACKETED BETWEEN THE TWO HOODLUMS. IT GAVE THEM AN ADVANTAGE: I COULD ONLY SHOOT ONE AT A TIME! SOMETHING WOULD HAPPEN...
48... 65 ...86!
SUDDENLY WINT CALLED OUT AN AMERICAN FOOTBALL SIGNAL – A PRE-ARRANGED CODE...
... AND DIVED TO THE FLOOR!

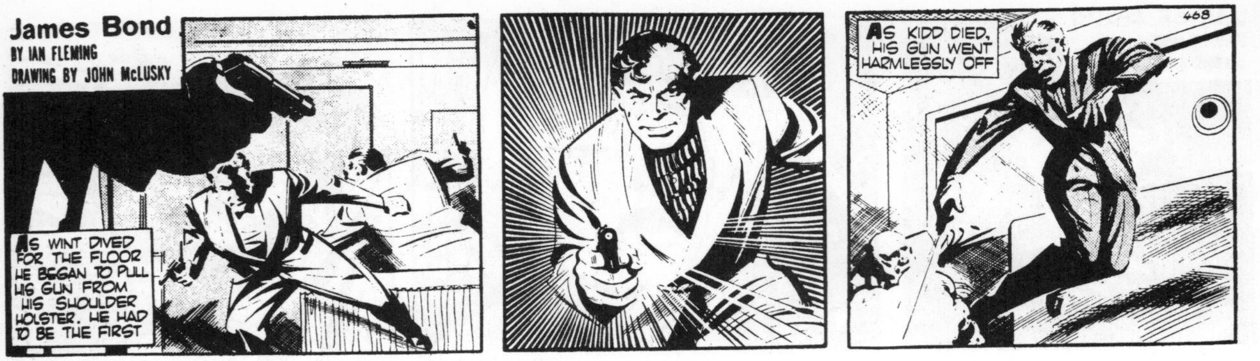
James Bond
BY IAN FLEMING
DRAWING BY JOHN McLUSKY
AS WINT DIVED FOR THE FLOOR HE BEGAN TO PULL HIS GUN FROM HIS SHOULDER HOLSTER. HE HAD TO BE THE FIRST
AS KIDD DIED, HIS GUN WENT HARMLESSLY OFF

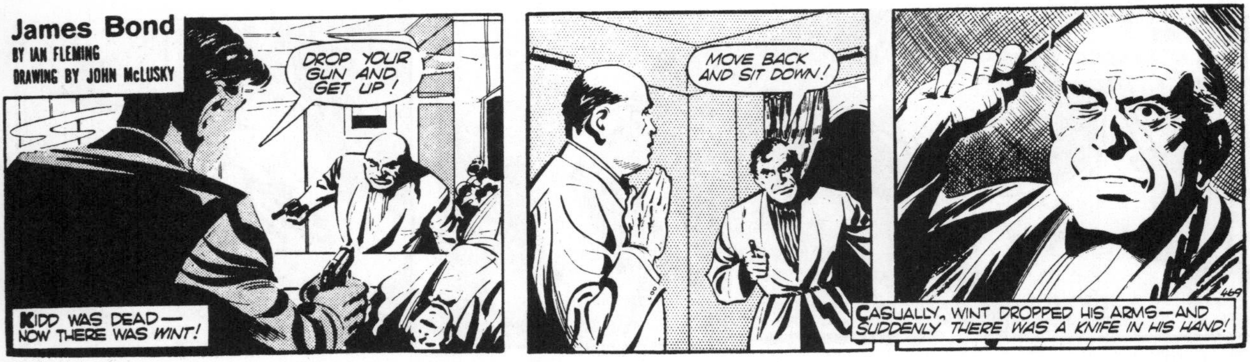
James Bond
BY IAN FLEMING
DRAWING BY JOHN McLUSKY
DROP YOUR GUN AND GET UP!
KIDD WAS DEAD— NOW THERE WAS WINT!
MOVE BACK AND SIT DOWN!
CASUALLY, WINT DROPPED HIS ARMS—AND SUDDENLY THERE WAS A KNIFE IN HIS HAND!

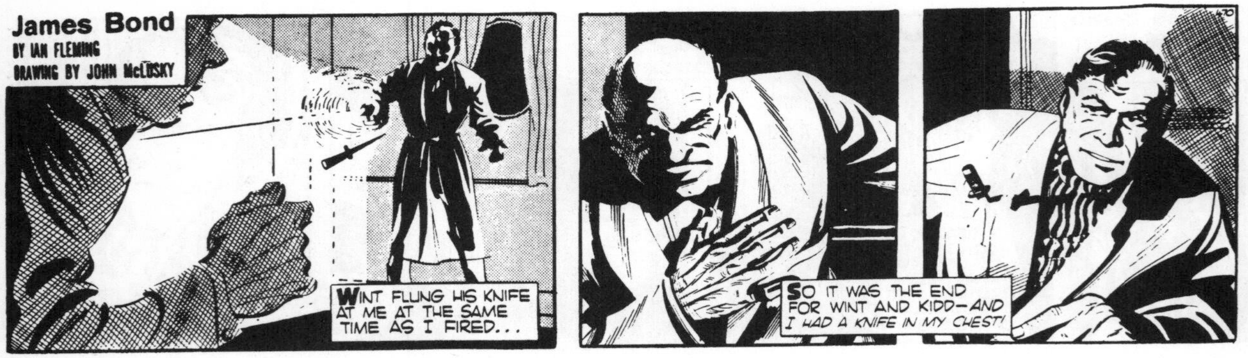
James Bond
BY IAN FLEMING
DRAWING BY JOHN McLUSKY
WINT FLUNG HIS KNIFE AT ME AT THE SAME TIME AS I FIRED...
SO IT WAS THE END FOR WINT AND KIDD—AND I HAD A KNIFE IN MY CHEST!

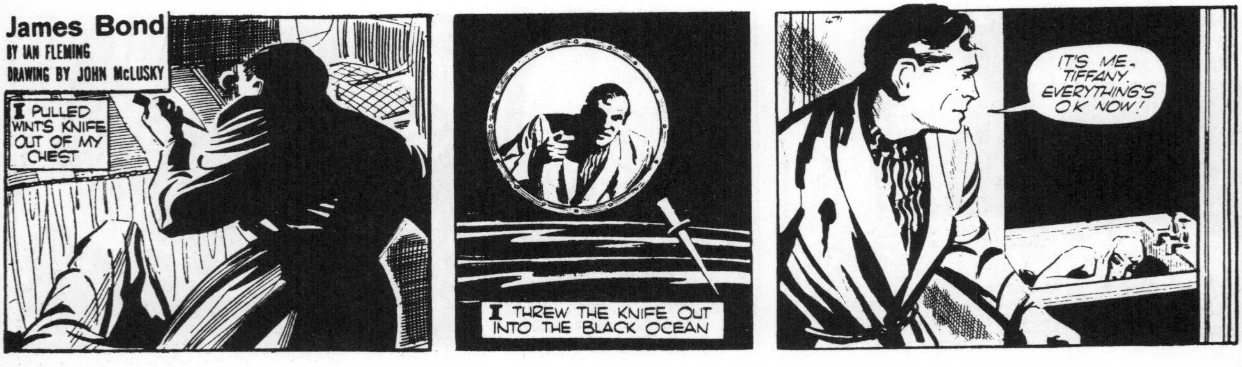
James Bond
BY IAN FLEMING
DRAWING BY JOHN McLUSKY
I PULLED WINT'S KNIFE OUT OF MY CHEST
I THREW THE KNIFE OUT INTO THE BLACK OCEAN
IT'S ME. TIFFANY. EVERYTHING'S OK NOW!

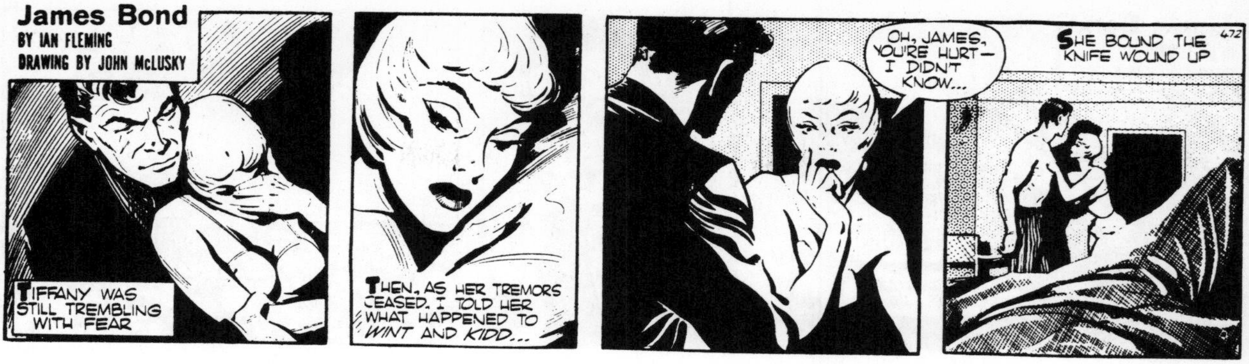
James Bond
BY IAN FLEMING
DRAWING BY JOHN McLUSKY
TIFFANY WAS STILL TREMBLING WITH FEAR
THEN, AS HER TREMORS CEASED, I TOLD HER WHAT HAPPENED TO WINT AND KIDD...
OH, JAMES, YOU'RE HURT— I DIDN'T KNOW...
472
SHE BOUND THE KNIFE WOUND UP

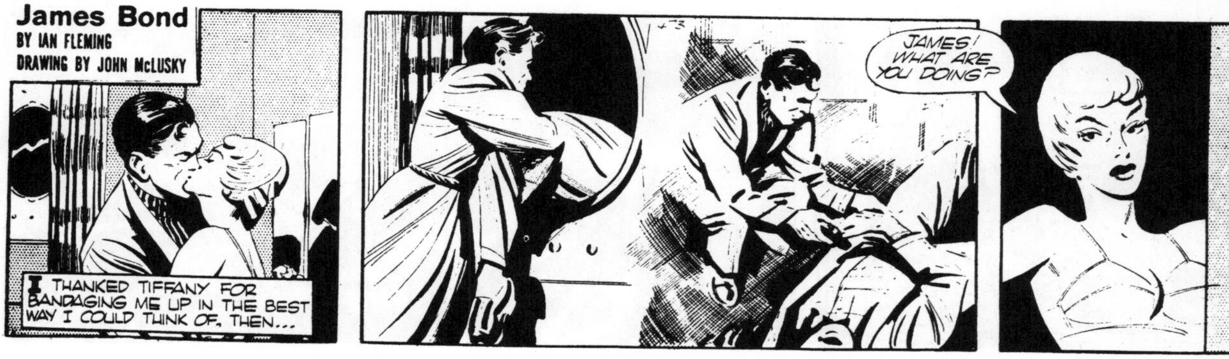
James Bond
BY IAN FLEMING
DRAWING BY JOHN McLUSKY
I THANKED TIFFANY FOR BANDAGING ME UP IN THE BEST WAY I COULD THINK OF. THEN...
473
JAMES! WHAT ARE YOU DOING?

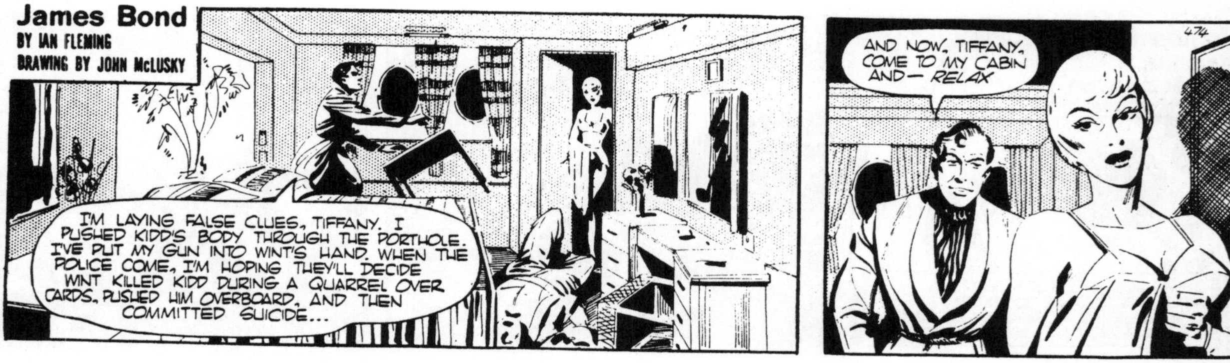
James Bond
BY IAN FLEMING
DRAWING BY JOHN McLUSKY
I'M LAYING FALSE CLUES, TIFFANY. I PUSHED KIDD'S BODY THROUGH THE PORTHOLE. I'VE PUT MY GUN INTO WINT'S HAND. WHEN THE POLICE COME, I'M HOPING THEY'LL DECIDE WINT KILLED KIDD DURING A QUARREL OVER CARDS, PUSHED HIM OVERBOARD, AND THEN COMMITTED SUICIDE...
474
AND NOW, TIFFANY, COME TO MY CABIN AND— RELAX

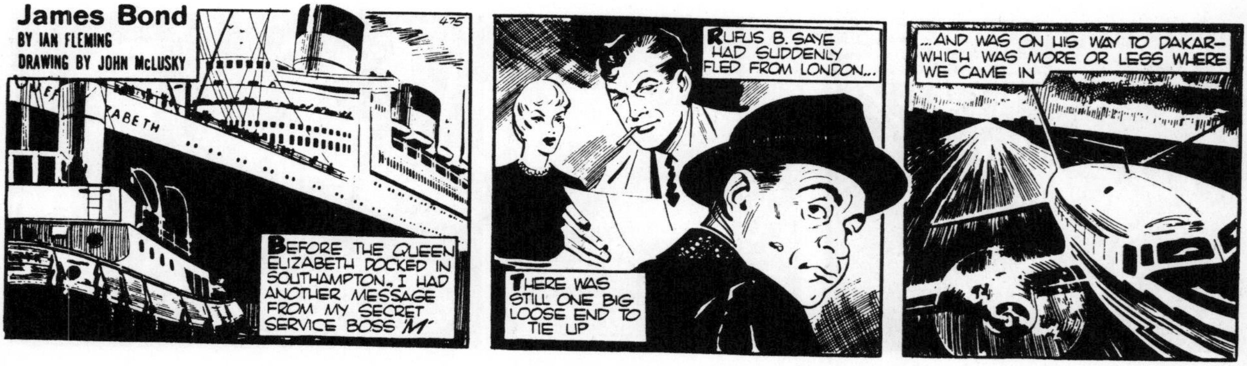
James Bond
BY IAN FLEMING
DRAWING BY JOHN McLUSKY
475
BEFORE THE QUEEN ELIZABETH DOCKED IN SOUTHAMPTON, I HAD ANOTHER MESSAGE FROM MY SECRET SERVICE BOSS 'M'
RUFUS B. SAYE HAD SUDDENLY FLED FROM LONDON...
THERE WAS STILL ONE BIG LOOSE END TO TIE UP
...AND WAS ON HIS WAY TO DAKAR— WHICH WAS MORE OR LESS WHERE WE CAME IN

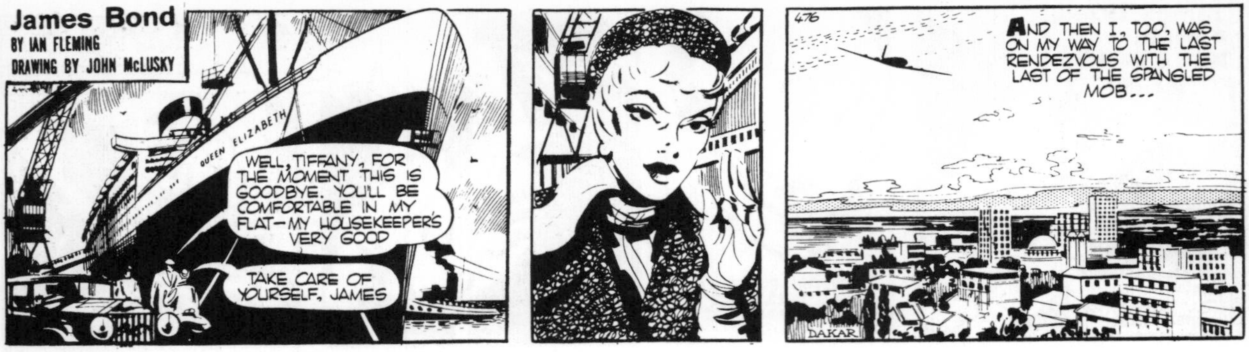
James Bond
BY IAN FLEMING
DRAWING BY JOHN McLUSKY
QUEEN ELIZABETH
WELL, TIFFANY, FOR THE MOMENT THIS IS GOODBYE. YOU'LL BE COMFORTABLE IN MY FLAT—MY HOUSEKEEPER'S VERY GOOD
TAKE CARE OF YOURSELF, JAMES
476
AND THEN I, TOO, WAS ON MY WAY TO THE LAST RENDEZVOUS WITH THE LAST OF THE SPANGLED MOB...
DAKAR

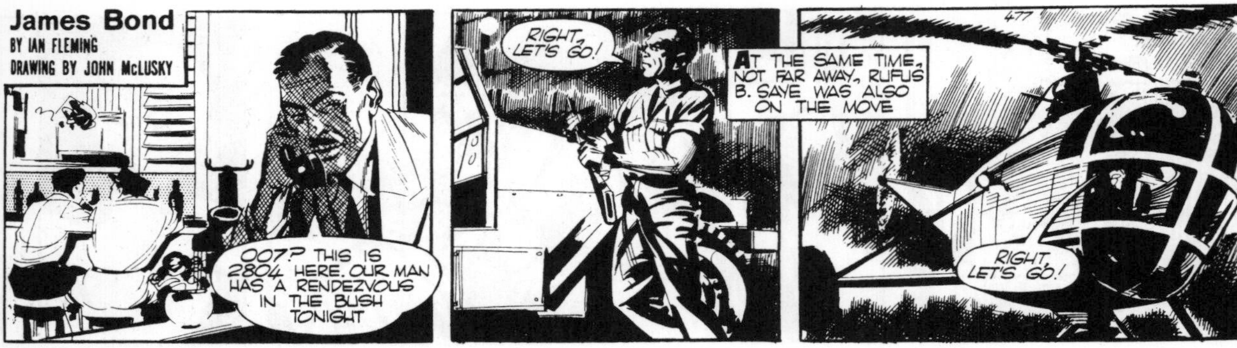
James Bond
BY IAN FLEMING
DRAWING BY JOHN McLUSKY
007? THIS IS 2804 HERE. OUR MAN HAS A RENDEZVOUS IN THE BUSH TONIGHT
RIGHT, LET'S GO!
AT THE SAME TIME, NOT FAR AWAY, RUFUS B. SAYE WAS ALSO ON THE MOVE
477
RIGHT, LET'S GO!

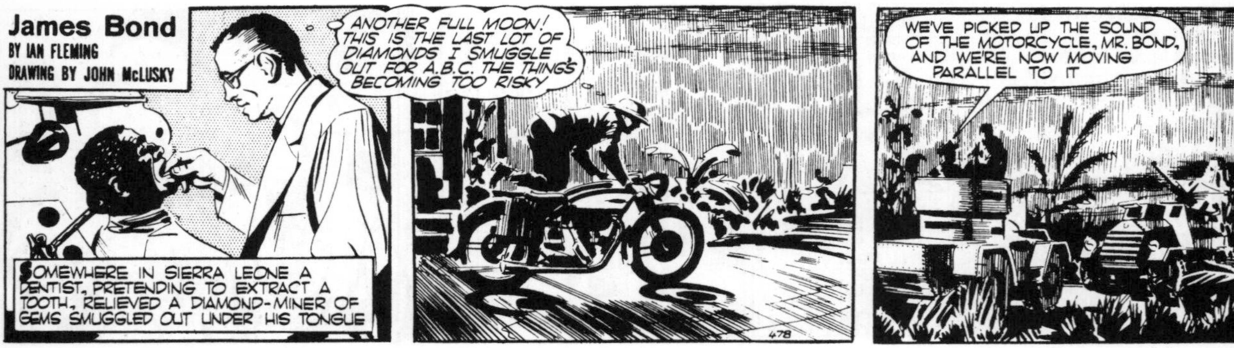
James Bond
BY IAN FLEMING
DRAWING BY JOHN McLUSKY
SOMEWHERE IN SIERRA LEONE A DENTIST, PRETENDING TO EXTRACT A TOOTH, RELIEVED A DIAMOND-MINER OF GEMS SMUGGLED OUT UNDER HIS TONGUE
ANOTHER FULL MOON! THIS IS THE LAST LOT OF DIAMONDS I SMUGGLE OUT FOR A.B.C. THE THING'S BECOMING TOO RISKY
478
WE'VE PICKED UP THE SOUND OF THE MOTORCYCLE, MR. BOND, AND WE'RE NOW MOVING PARALLEL TO IT

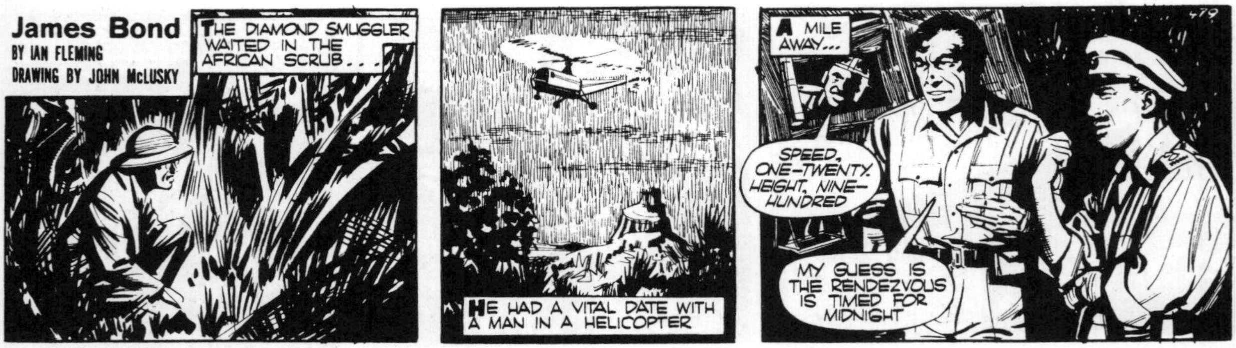
James Bond
BY IAN FLEMING
DRAWING BY JOHN McLUSKY
THE DIAMOND SMUGGLER WAITED IN THE AFRICAN SCRUB...
HE HAD A VITAL DATE WITH A MAN IN A HELICOPTER
479
A MILE AWAY...
SPEED, ONE-TWENTY. HEIGHT, NINE-HUNDRED
MY GUESS IS THE RENDEZVOUS IS TIMED FOR MIDNIGHT

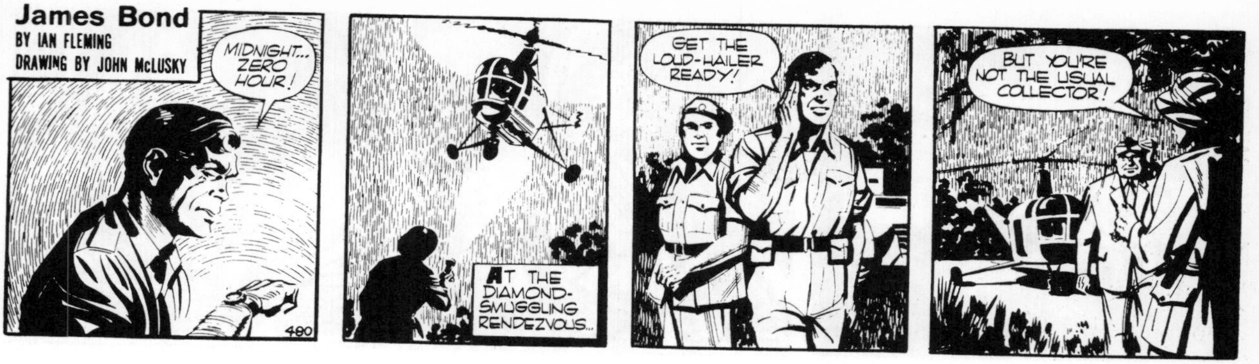
James Bond
BY IAN FLEMING
DRAWING BY JOHN McLUSKY
MIDNIGHT... ZERO HOUR!
480
AT THE DIAMOND-SMUGGLING RENDEZVOUS...
GET THE LOUD-HAILER READY!
BUT YOU'RE NOT THE USUAL COLLECTOR!

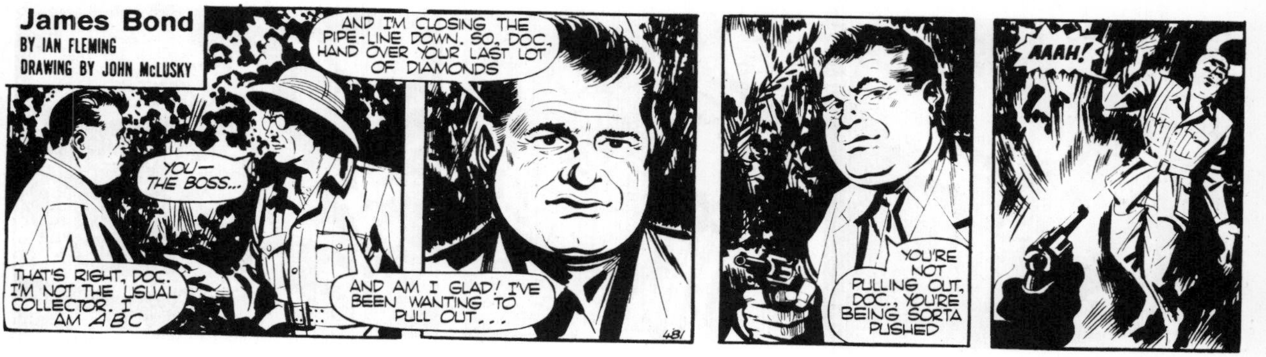
James Bond
BY IAN FLEMING
DRAWING BY JOHN McLUSKY
YOU—THE BOSS...
THAT'S RIGHT, DOC. I'M NOT THE USUAL COLLECTOR. I AM ABC
AND AM I GLAD! I'VE BEEN WANTING TO PULL OUT...
AND I'M CLOSING THE PIPE-LINE DOWN. SO, DOC, HAND OVER YOUR LAST LOT OF DIAMONDS
481
YOU'RE NOT PULLING OUT, DOC., YOU'RE BEING SORTA PUSHED
AAAH!

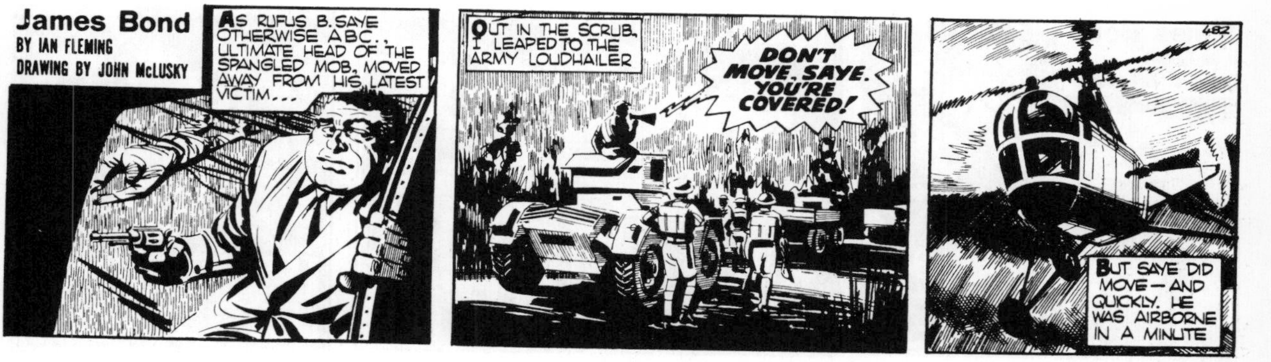
James Bond
BY IAN FLEMING
DRAWING BY JOHN McLUSKY
AS RUFUS B. SAYE OTHERWISE ABC., ULTIMATE HEAD OF THE SPANGLED MOB, MOVED AWAY FROM HIS LATEST VICTIM...
OUT IN THE SCRUB, I LEAPED TO THE ARMY LOUDHAILER
DON'T MOVE, SAYE. YOU'RE COVERED!
482
BUT SAYE DID MOVE—AND QUICKLY. HE WAS AIRBORNE IN A MINUTE

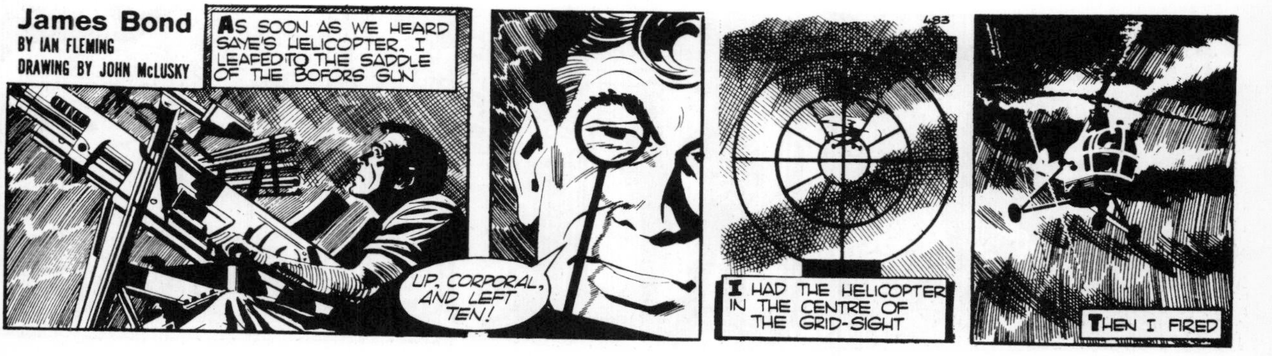
James Bond
BY IAN FLEMING
DRAWING BY JOHN McLUSKY
AS SOON AS WE HEARD SAYE'S HELICOPTER, I LEAPED TO THE SADDLE OF THE BOFORS GUN
UP, CORPORAL, AND LEFT TEN!
483
I HAD THE HELICOPTER IN THE CENTRE OF THE GRID-SIGHT
THEN I FIRED

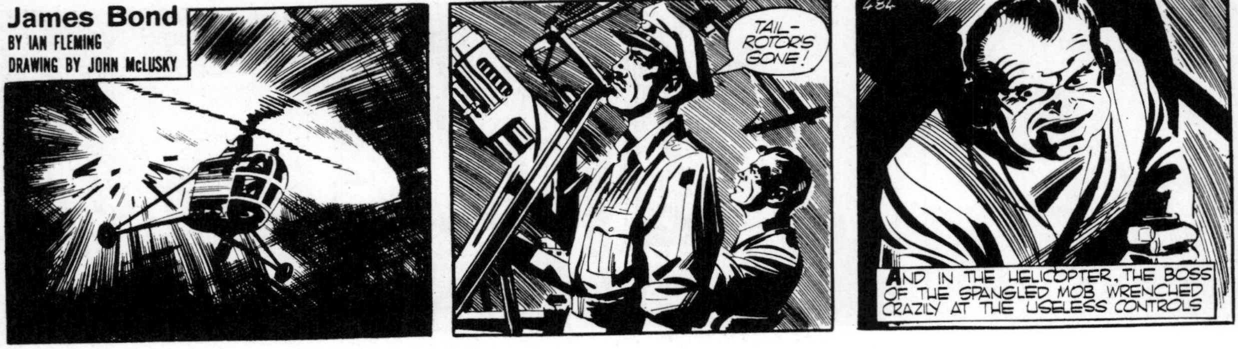
James Bond
BY IAN FLEMING
DRAWING BY JOHN McLUSKY
TAIL-ROTOR'S GONE!
484
AND IN THE HELICOPTER, THE BOSS OF THE SPANGLED MOB WRENCHED CRAZILY AT THE USELESS CONTROLS

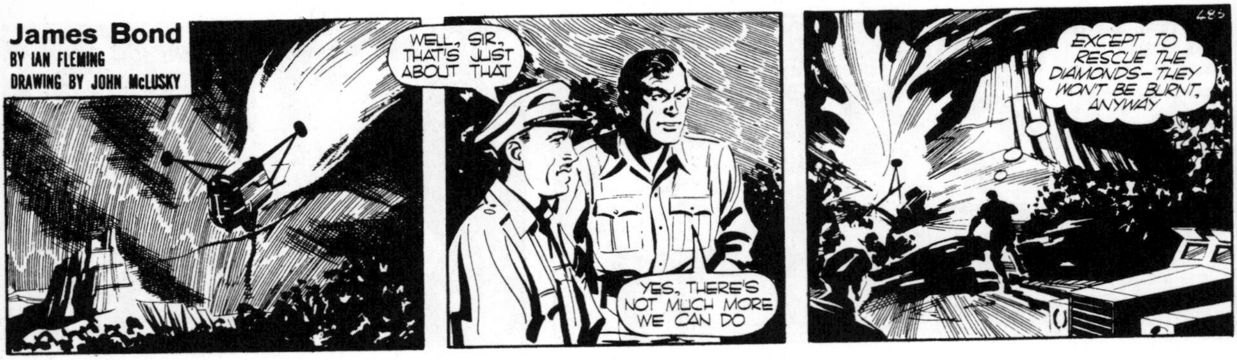
James Bond
BY IAN FLEMING
DRAWING BY JOHN McLUSKY
WELL, SIR, THAT'S JUST ABOUT THAT
YES, THERE'S NOT MUCH MORE WE CAN DO
485
EXCEPT TO RESCUE THE DIAMONDS—THEY WON'T BE BURNT, ANYWAY

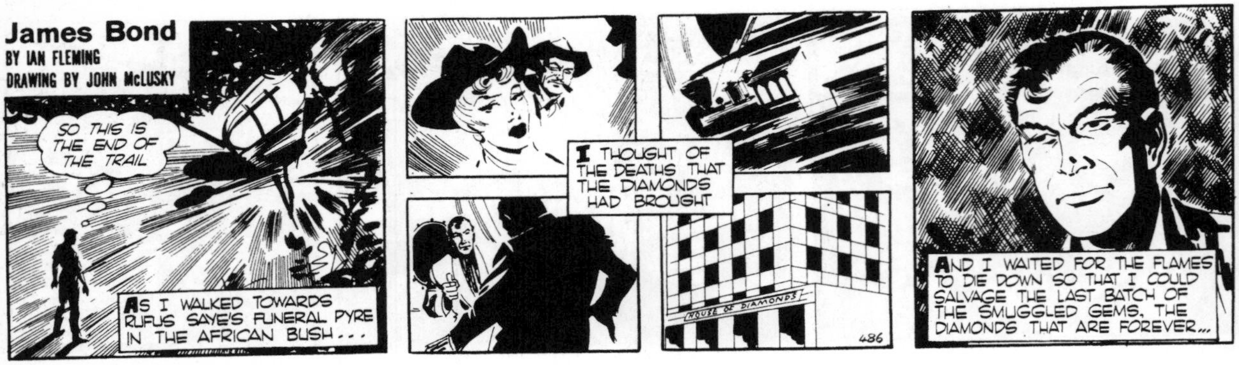
James Bond
BY IAN FLEMING
DRAWING BY JOHN McLUSKY
SO THIS IS THE END OF THE TRAIL
AS I WALKED TOWARDS RUFUS SAYE'S FUNERAL PYRE IN THE AFRICAN BUSH...
I THOUGHT OF THE DEATHS THAT THE DIAMONDS HAD BROUGHT
HOUSE OF DIAMONDS
486
AND I WAITED FOR THE FLAMES TO DIE DOWN SO THAT I COULD SALVAGE THE LAST BATCH OF THE SMUGGLED GEMS, THE DIAMONDS THAT ARE FOREVER...

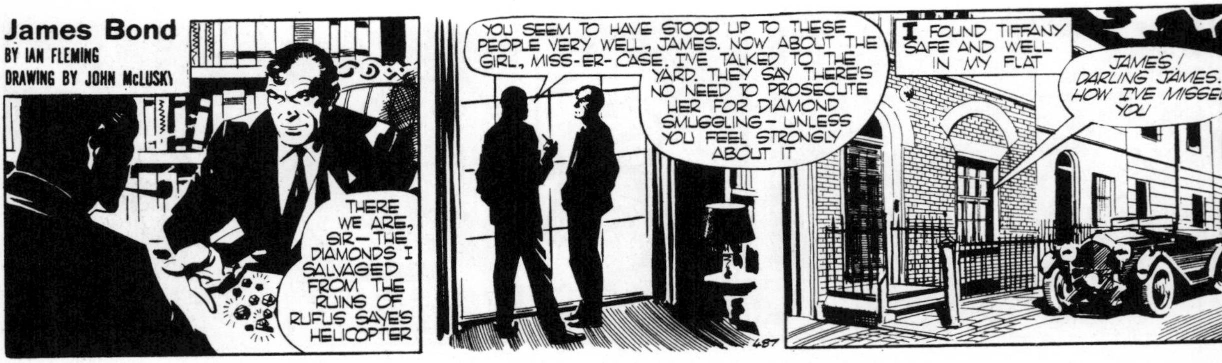
James Bond
BY IAN FLEMING
DRAWING BY JOHN McLUSKY
THERE WE ARE, SIR—THE DIAMONDS I SALVAGED FROM THE RUINS OF RUFUS SAYE'S HELICOPTER
YOU SEEM TO HAVE STOOD UP TO THESE PEOPLE VERY WELL, JAMES. NOW ABOUT THE GIRL, MISS-ER-CASE. I'VE TALKED TO THE YARD. THEY SAY THERE'S NO NEED TO PROSECUTE HER FOR DIAMOND SMUGGLING—UNLESS YOU FEEL STRONGLY ABOUT IT
487
I FOUND TIFFANY SAFE AND WELL IN MY FLAT
JAMES! DARLING JAMES. HOW I'VE MISSED YOU

FROM RUSSIA WITH LOVE

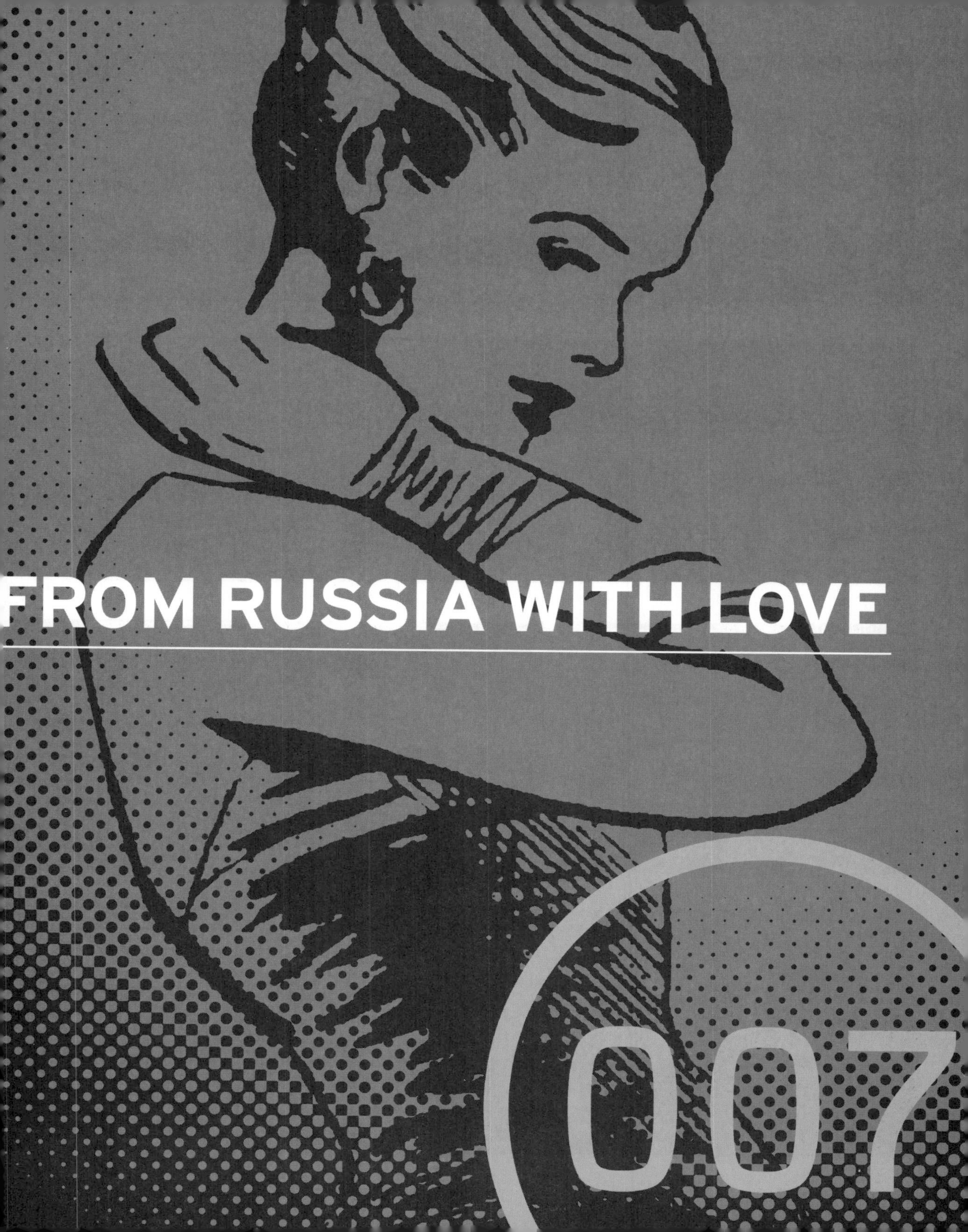
007

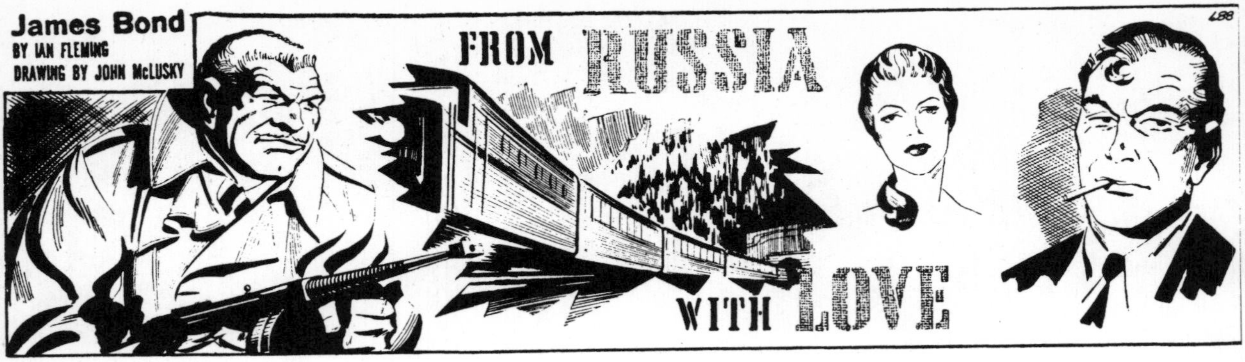

James Bond
BY IAN FLEMING
DRAWING BY JOHN McLUSKY
488
FROM RUSSIA WITH LOVE

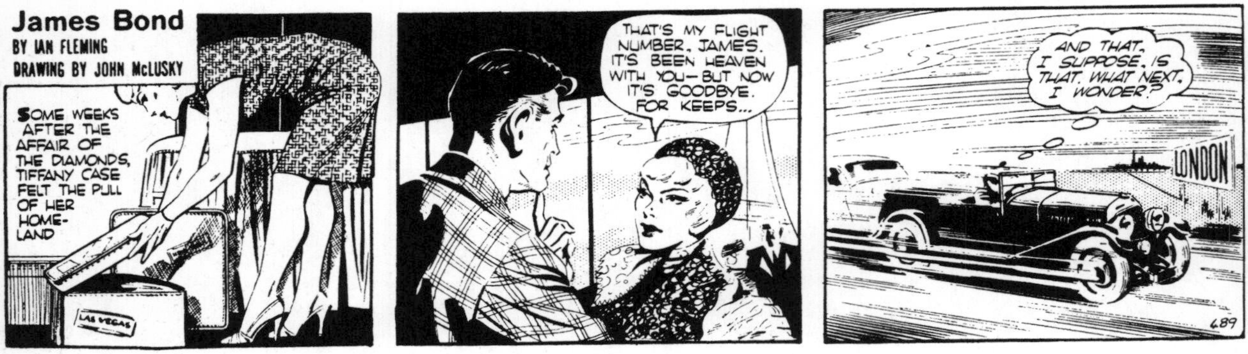

James Bond
BY IAN FLEMING
DRAWING BY JOHN McLUSKY
SOME WEEKS AFTER THE AFFAIR OF THE DIAMONDS, TIFFANY CASE FELT THE PULL OF HER HOME-LAND
LAS VEGAS
THAT'S MY FLIGHT NUMBER, JAMES. IT'S BEEN HEAVEN WITH YOU—BUT NOW IT'S GOODBYE. FOR KEEPS...
AND THAT, I SUPPOSE, IS THAT. WHAT NEXT, I WONDER?
LONDON
489

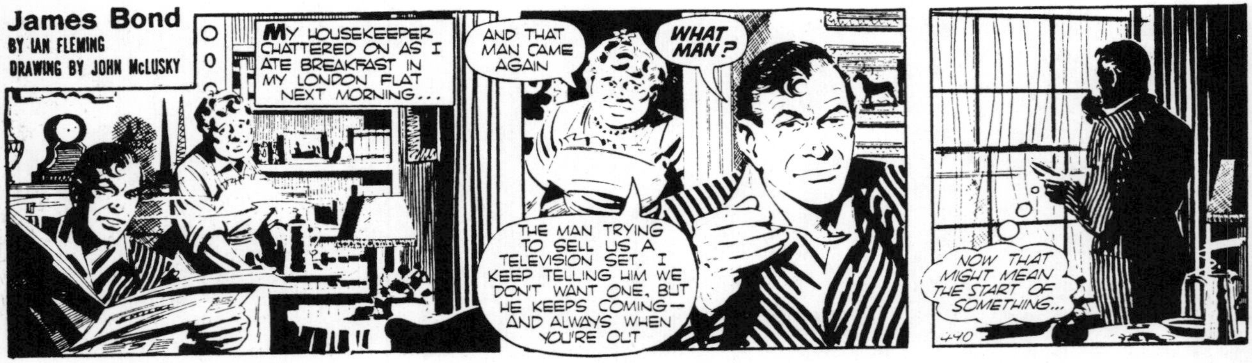

James Bond
BY IAN FLEMING
DRAWING BY JOHN McLUSKY
MY HOUSEKEEPER CHATTERED ON AS I ATE BREAKFAST IN MY LONDON FLAT NEXT MORNING...
AND THAT MAN CAME AGAIN
WHAT MAN?
THE MAN TRYING TO SELL US A TELEVISION SET. I KEEP TELLING HIM WE DON'T WANT ONE, BUT HE KEEPS COMING—AND ALWAYS WHEN YOU'RE OUT
NOW THAT MIGHT MEAN THE START OF SOMETHING...
490

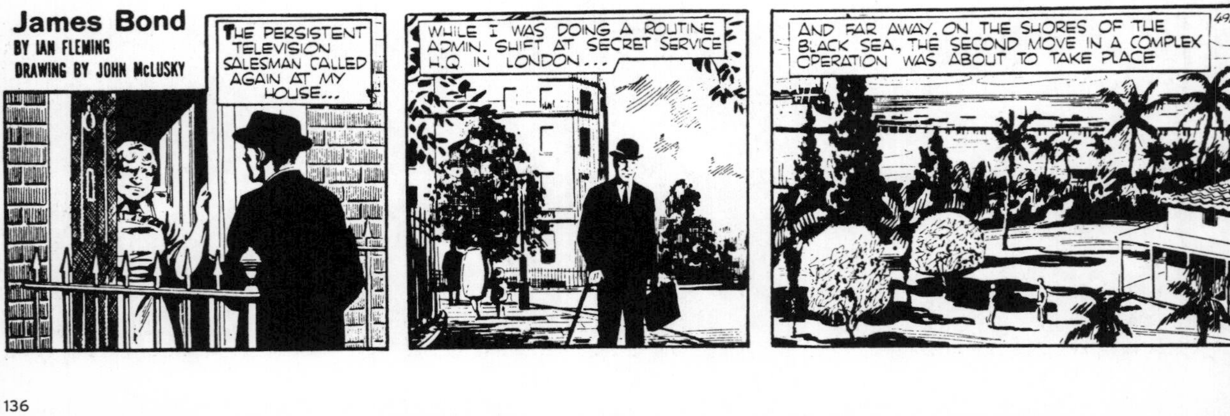

James Bond
BY IAN FLEMING
DRAWING BY JOHN McLUSKY
THE PERSISTENT TELEVISION SALESMAN CALLED AGAIN AT MY HOUSE...
WHILE I WAS DOING A ROUTINE ADMIN. SHIFT AT SECRET SERVICE H.Q IN LONDON...
491
AND FAR AWAY, ON THE SHORES OF THE BLACK SEA, THE SECOND MOVE IN A COMPLEX OPERATION WAS ABOUT TO TAKE PLACE

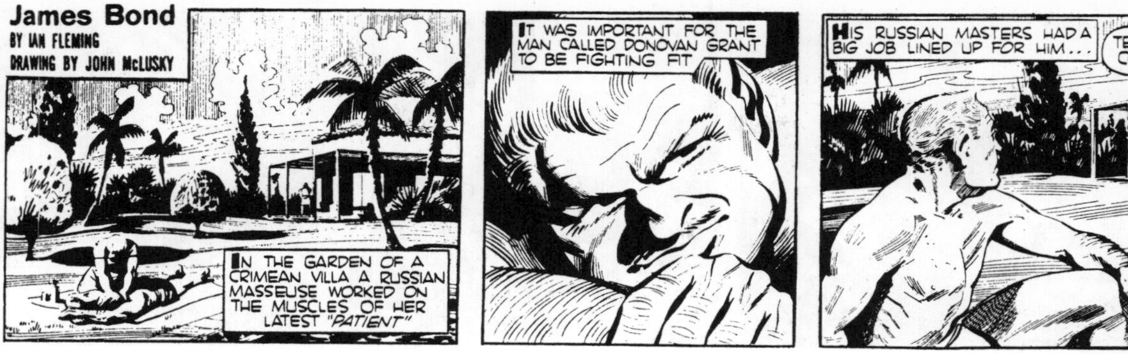
James Bond
BY IAN FLEMING
DRAWING BY JOHN McLUSKY
IN THE GARDEN OF A CRIMEAN VILLA A RUSSIAN MASSEUSE WORKED ON THE MUSCLES OF HER LATEST "PATIENT"
IT WAS IMPORTANT FOR THE MAN CALLED DONOVAN GRANT TO BE FIGHTING FIT
HIS RUSSIAN MASTERS HAD A BIG JOB LINED UP FOR HIM...
TELEPHONE, COMRADE!

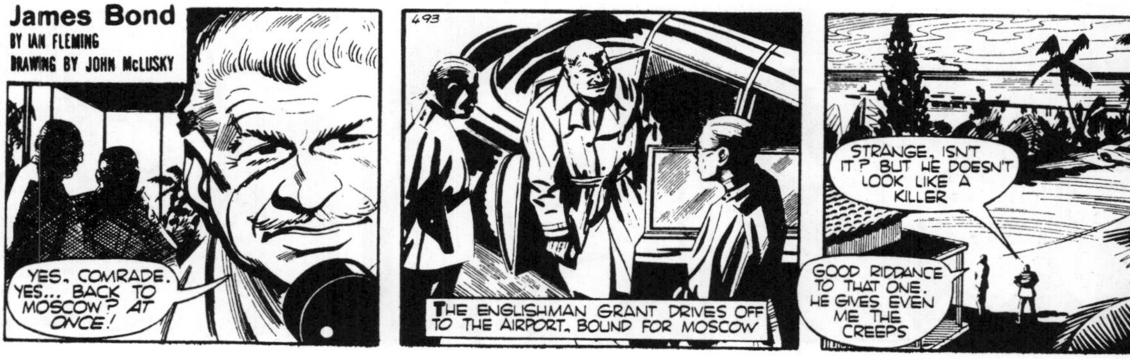
James Bond
BY IAN FLEMING
DRAWING BY JOHN McLUSKY
YES, COMRADE. YES... BACK TO MOSCOW? AT ONCE!
493
THE ENGLISHMAN GRANT DRIVES OFF TO THE AIRPORT, BOUND FOR MOSCOW
STRANGE, ISN'T IT? BUT HE DOESN'T LOOK LIKE A KILLER
GOOD RIDDANCE TO THAT ONE. HE GIVES EVEN ME THE CREEPS

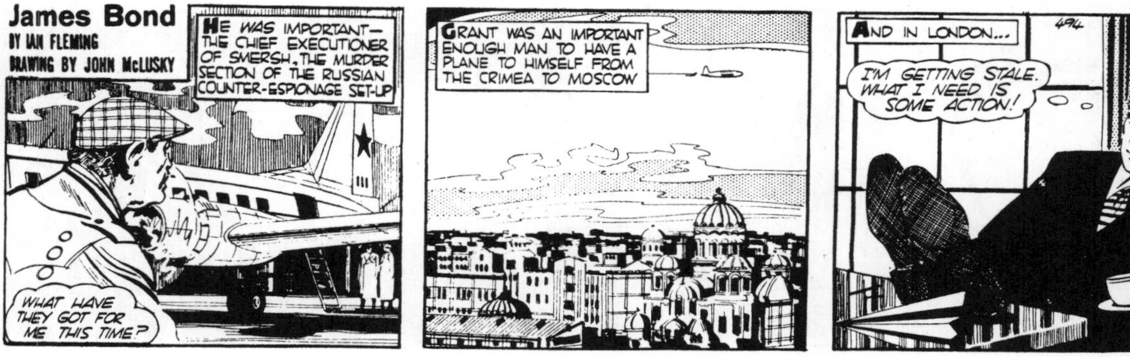
James Bond
BY IAN FLEMING
DRAWING BY JOHN McLUSKY
HE WAS IMPORTANT— THE CHIEF EXECUTIONER OF SMERSH, THE MURDER SECTION OF THE RUSSIAN COUNTER-ESPIONAGE SET-UP
WHAT HAVE THEY GOT FOR ME THIS TIME?
GRANT WAS AN IMPORTANT ENOUGH MAN TO HAVE A PLANE TO HIMSELF FROM THE CRIMEA TO MOSCOW
AND IN LONDON...
494
I'M GETTING STALE. WHAT I NEED IS SOME ACTION!

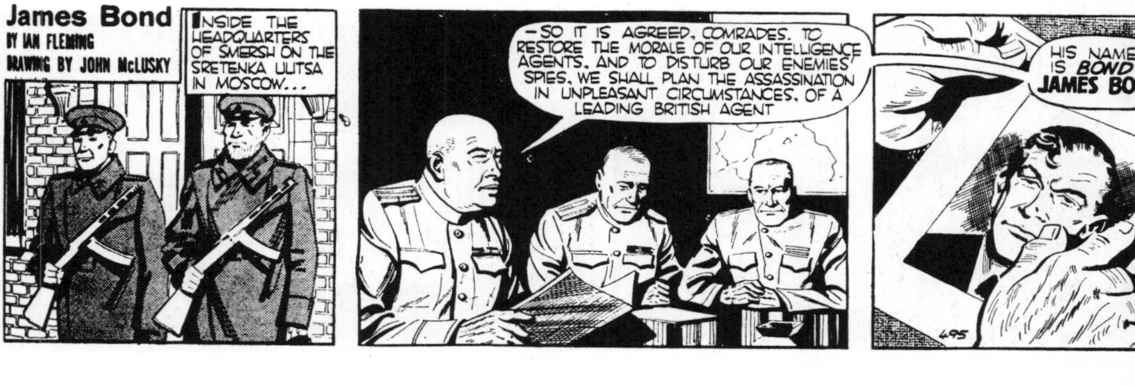
James Bond
BY IAN FLEMING
DRAWING BY JOHN McLUSKY
INSIDE THE HEADQUARTERS OF SMERSH ON THE SRETENKA ULITSA IN MOSCOW...
—SO IT IS AGREED, COMRADES, TO RESTORE THE MORALE OF OUR INTELLIGENCE AGENTS, AND TO DISTURB OUR ENEMIES' SPIES, WE SHALL PLAN THE ASSASSINATION IN UNPLEASANT CIRCUMSTANCES, OF A LEADING BRITISH AGENT
HIS NAME IS BOND— JAMES BOND!
495

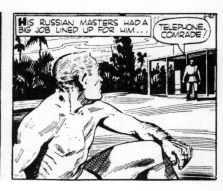

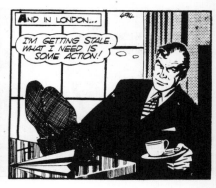

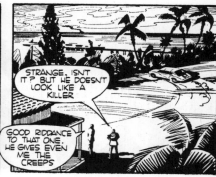

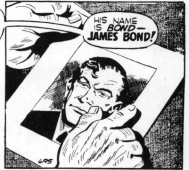

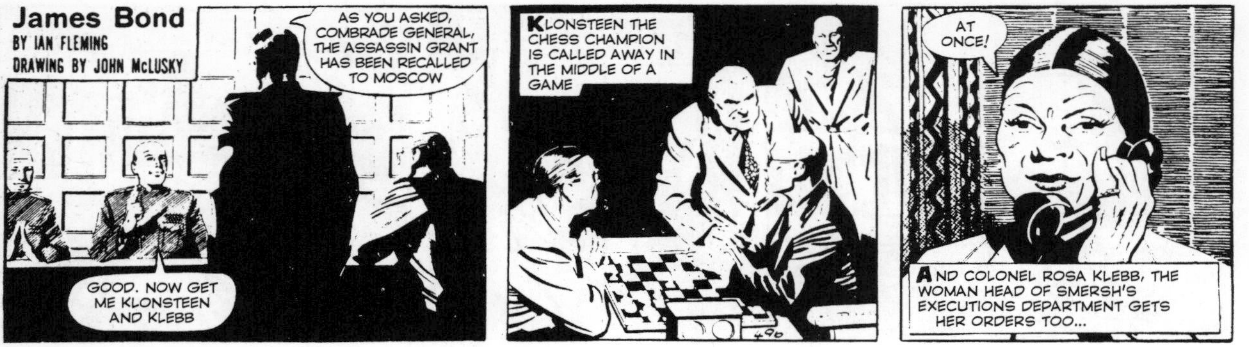
James Bond
BY IAN FLEMING
DRAWING BY JOHN McLUSKY
AS YOU ASKED, COMBRADE GENERAL, THE ASSASSIN GRANT HAS BEEN RECALLED TO MOSCOW
GOOD. NOW GET ME KLONSTEEN AND KLEBB
KLONSTEEN THE CHESS CHAMPION IS CALLED AWAY IN THE MIDDLE OF A GAME
AT ONCE!
AND COLONEL ROSA KLEBB, THE WOMAN HEAD OF SMERSH'S EXECUTIONS DEPARTMENT GETS HER ORDERS TOO...

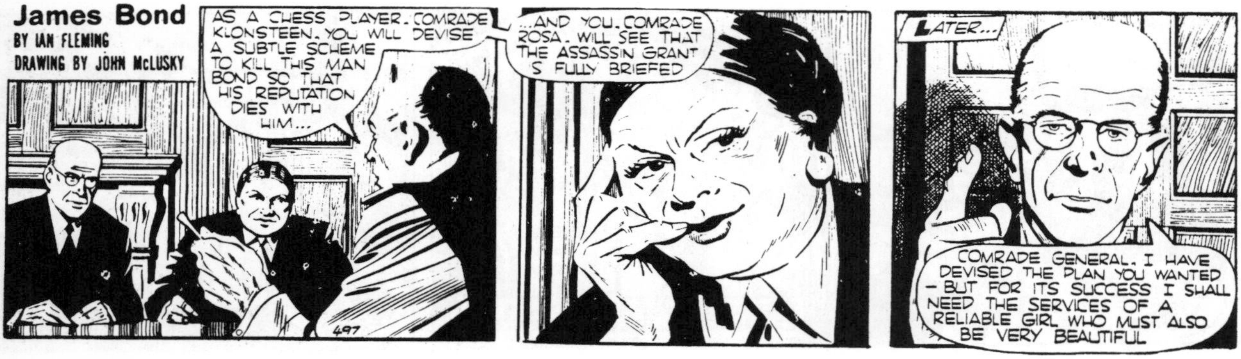
James Bond
BY IAN FLEMING
DRAWING BY JOHN McLUSKY
AS A CHESS PLAYER, COMRADE KLONSTEEN, YOU WILL DEVISE A SUBTLE SCHEME TO KILL THIS MAN BOND SO THAT HIS REPUTATION DIES WITH HIM...
...AND YOU, COMRADE ROSA, WILL SEE THAT THE ASSASSIN GRANT S FULLY BRIEFED
497
LATER...
COMRADE GENERAL, I HAVE DEVISED THE PLAN YOU WANTED - BUT FOR ITS SUCCESS I SHALL NEED THE SERVICES OF A RELIABLE GIRL WHO MUST ALSO BE VERY BEAUTIFUL

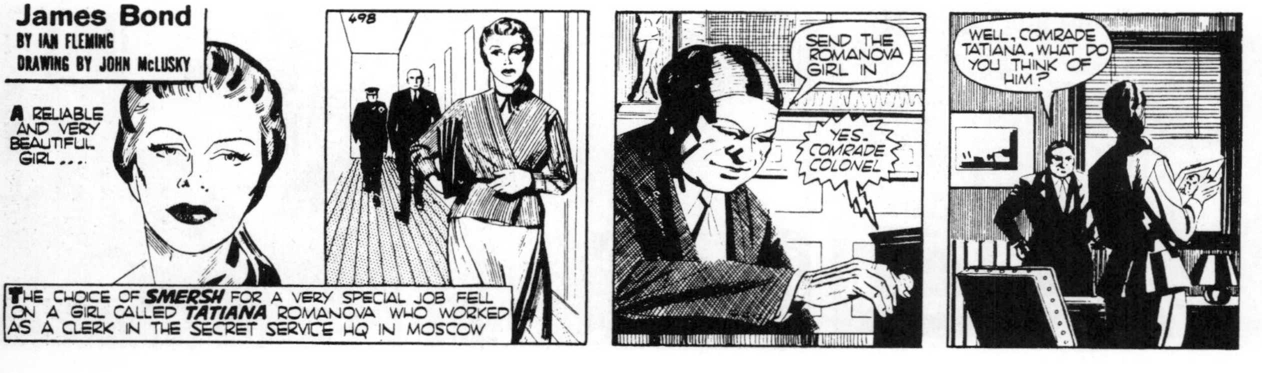
James Bond
BY IAN FLEMING
DRAWING BY JOHN McLUSKY
A RELIABLE AND VERY BEAUTIFUL GIRL...
498
THE CHOICE OF SMERSH FOR A VERY SPECIAL JOB FELL ON A GIRL CALLED TATIANA ROMANOVA WHO WORKED AS A CLERK IN THE SECRET SERVICE HQ IN MOSCOW
SEND THE ROMANOVA GIRL IN
YES, COMRADE COLONEL
WELL, COMRADE TATIANA, WHAT DO YOU THINK OF HIM?

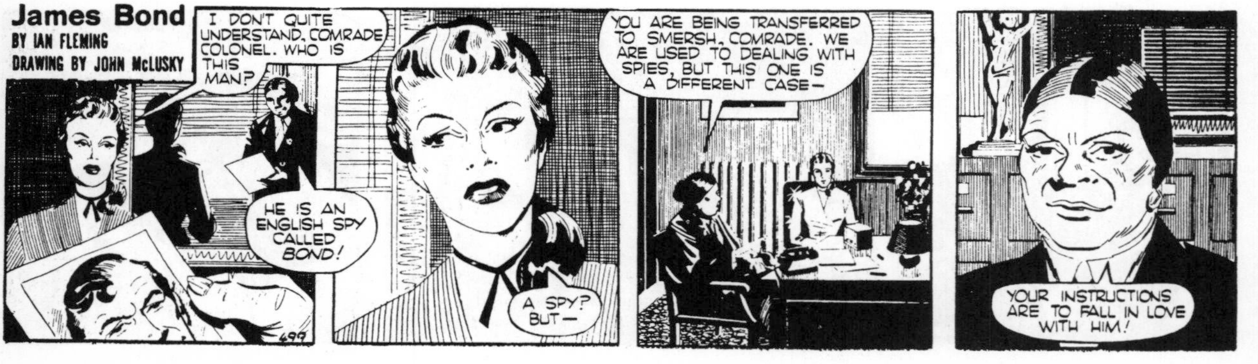
James Bond
BY IAN FLEMING
DRAWING BY JOHN McLUSKY
I DON'T QUITE UNDERSTAND, COMRADE COLONEL. WHO IS THIS MAN?
HE IS AN ENGLISH SPY CALLED BOND!
499
A SPY? BUT—
YOU ARE BEING TRANSFERRED TO SMERSH, COMRADE. WE ARE USED TO DEALING WITH SPIES, BUT THIS ONE IS A DIFFERENT CASE—
YOUR INSTRUCTIONS ARE TO FALL IN LOVE WITH HIM!

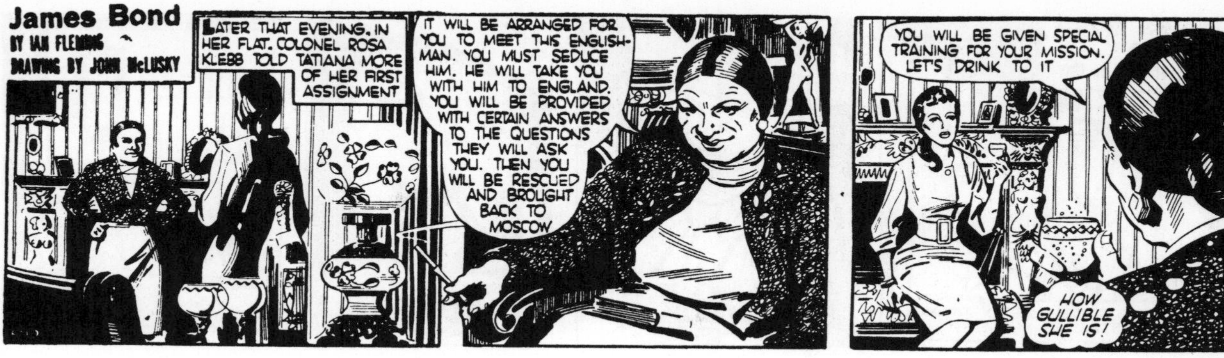
James Bond
BY IAN FLEMING
DRAWING BY JOHN McLUSKY
LATER THAT EVENING, IN HER FLAT, COLONEL ROSA KLEBB TOLD TATIANA MORE OF HER FIRST ASSIGNMENT
IT WILL BE ARRANGED FOR YOU TO MEET THIS ENGLISHMAN. YOU MUST SEDUCE HIM. HE WILL TAKE YOU WITH HIM TO ENGLAND. YOU WILL BE PROVIDED WITH CERTAIN ANSWERS TO THE QUESTIONS THEY WILL ASK YOU. THEN YOU WILL BE RESCUED AND BROUGHT BACK TO MOSCOW
YOU WILL BE GIVEN SPECIAL TRAINING FOR YOUR MISSION. LET'S DRINK TO IT
HOW GULLIBLE SHE IS!

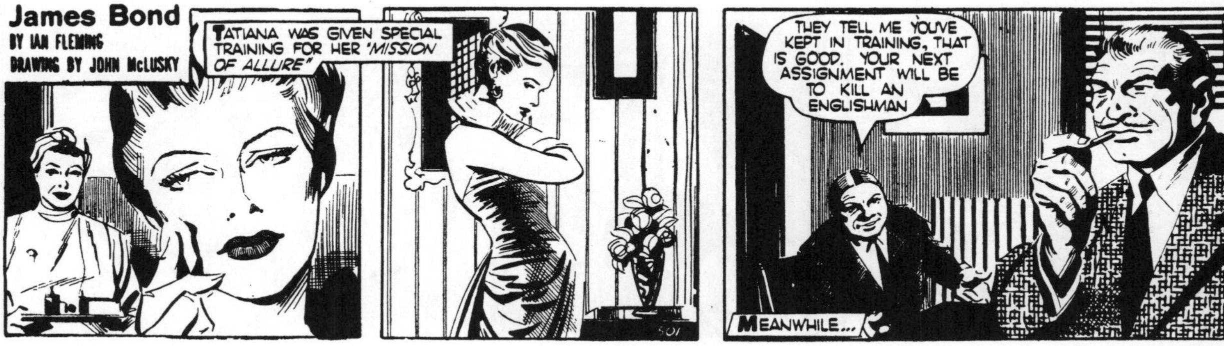
James Bond
BY IAN FLEMING
DRAWING BY JOHN McLUSKY
TATIANA WAS GIVEN SPECIAL TRAINING FOR HER "MISSION OF ALLURE"
501
MEANWHILE...
THEY TELL ME YOU'VE KEPT IN TRAINING, THAT IS GOOD. YOUR NEXT ASSIGNMENT WILL BE TO KILL AN ENGLISHMAN

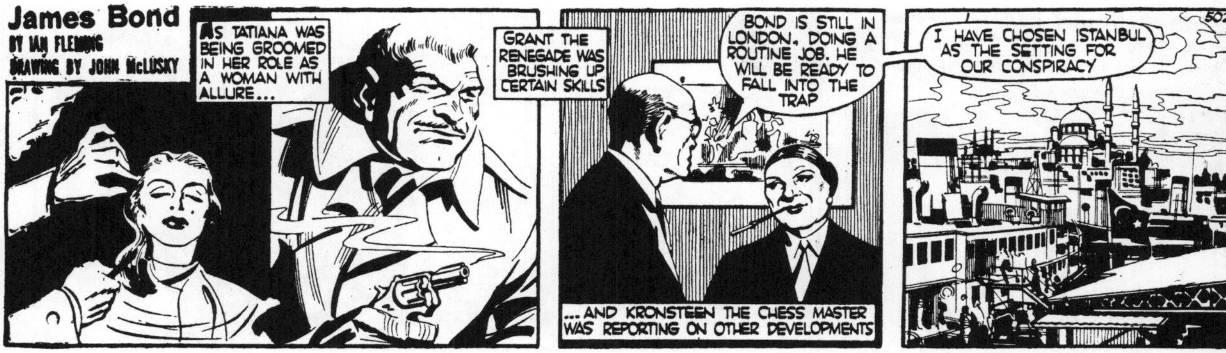
James Bond
BY IAN FLEMING
DRAWING BY JOHN McLUSKY
AS TATIANA WAS BEING GROOMED IN HER ROLE AS A WOMAN WITH ALLURE...
GRANT THE RENEGADE WAS BRUSHING UP CERTAIN SKILLS
...AND KRONSTEEN THE CHESS MASTER WAS REPORTING ON OTHER DEVELOPMENTS
BOND IS STILL IN LONDON, DOING A ROUTINE JOB. HE WILL BE READY TO FALL INTO THE TRAP
502
I HAVE CHOSEN ISTANBUL AS THE SETTING FOR OUR CONSPIRACY

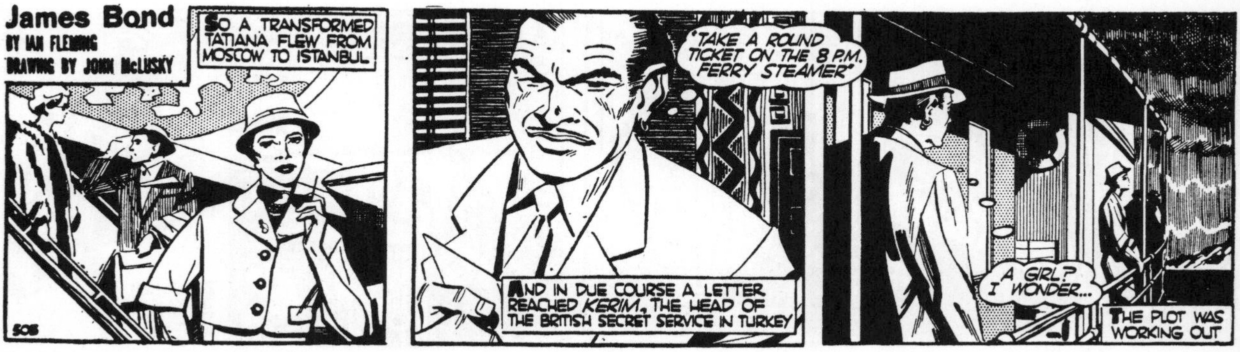
James Bond
BY IAN FLEMING
DRAWING BY JOHN McLUSKY
SO A TRANSFORMED TATIANA FLEW FROM MOSCOW TO ISTANBUL
503
AND IN DUE COURSE A LETTER REACHED KERIM, THE HEAD OF THE BRITISH SECRET SERVICE IN TURKEY
"TAKE A ROUND TICKET ON THE 8 P.M. FERRY STEAMER"
A GIRL? I WONDER...
THE PLOT WAS WORKING OUT

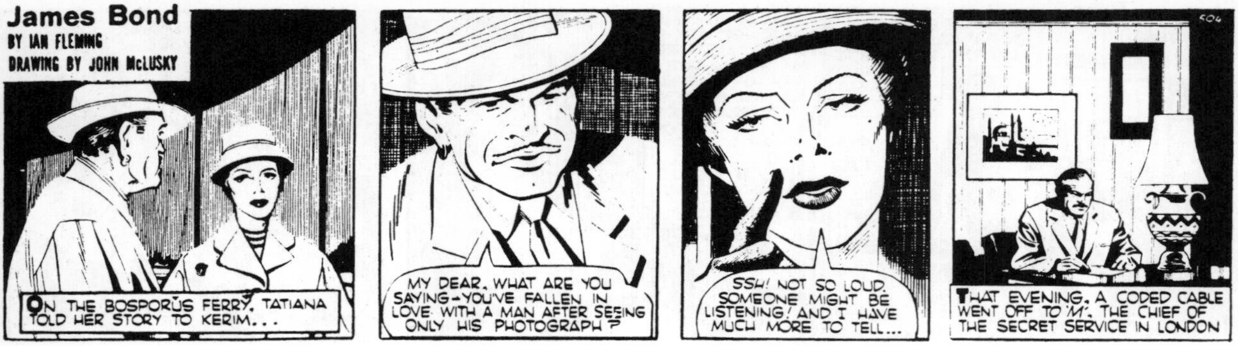
James Bond
BY IAN FLEMING
DRAWING BY JOHN McLUSKY
ON THE BOSPORUS FERRY, TATIANA TOLD HER STORY TO KERIM...
MY DEAR, WHAT ARE YOU SAYING–YOU'VE FALLEN IN LOVE WITH A MAN AFTER SEEING ONLY HIS PHOTOGRAPH?
SSH! NOT SO LOUD. SOMEONE MIGHT BE LISTENING! AND I HAVE MUCH MORE TO TELL...
504
THAT EVENING, A CODED CABLE WENT OFF TO 'M', THE CHIEF OF THE SECRET SERVICE IN LONDON

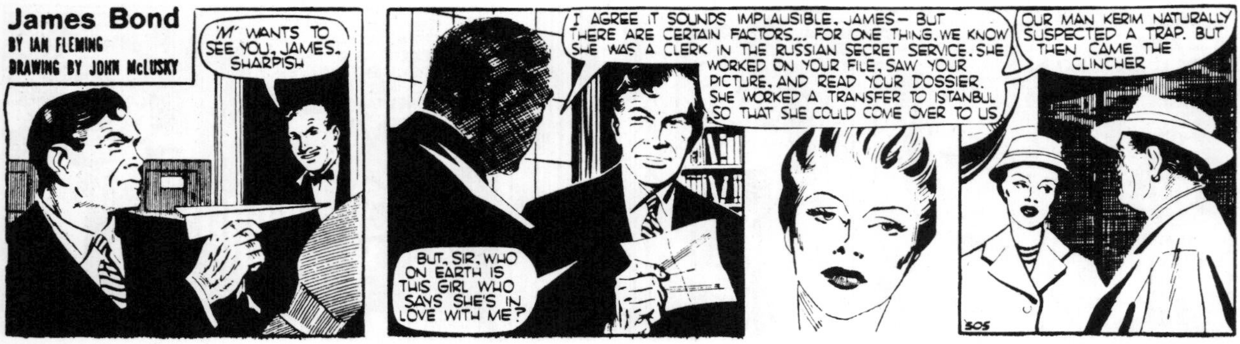
James Bond
BY IAN FLEMING
DRAWING BY JOHN McLUSKY
'M' WANTS TO SEE YOU, JAMES. SHARPISH
BUT, SIR, WHO ON EARTH IS THIS GIRL WHO SAYS SHE'S IN LOVE WITH ME?
I AGREE IT SOUNDS IMPLAUSIBLE, JAMES– BUT THERE ARE CERTAIN FACTORS... FOR ONE THING, WE KNOW SHE WAS A CLERK IN THE RUSSIAN SECRET SERVICE. SHE WORKED ON YOUR FILE, SAW YOUR PICTURE, AND READ YOUR DOSSIER. SHE WORKED A TRANSFER TO ISTANBUL SO THAT SHE COULD COME OVER TO US
OUR MAN KERIM NATURALLY SUSPECTED A TRAP. BUT THEN CAME THE CLINCHER
505

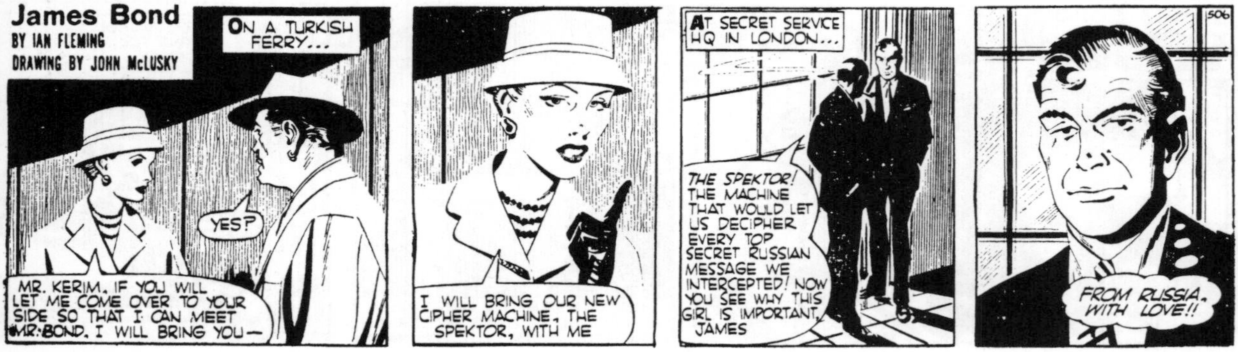
James Bond
BY IAN FLEMING
DRAWING BY JOHN McLUSKY
ON A TURKISH FERRY...
YES?
MR. KERIM, IF YOU WILL LET ME COME OVER TO YOUR SIDE SO THAT I CAN MEET MR. BOND, I WILL BRING YOU–
I WILL BRING OUR NEW CIPHER MACHINE, THE SPEKTOR, WITH ME
AT SECRET SERVICE HQ IN LONDON...
THE SPEKTOR! THE MACHINE THAT WOULD LET US DECIPHER EVERY TOP SECRET RUSSIAN MESSAGE WE INTERCEPTED! NOW YOU SEE WHY THIS GIRL IS IMPORTANT, JAMES
506
FROM RUSSIA, WITH LOVE!!

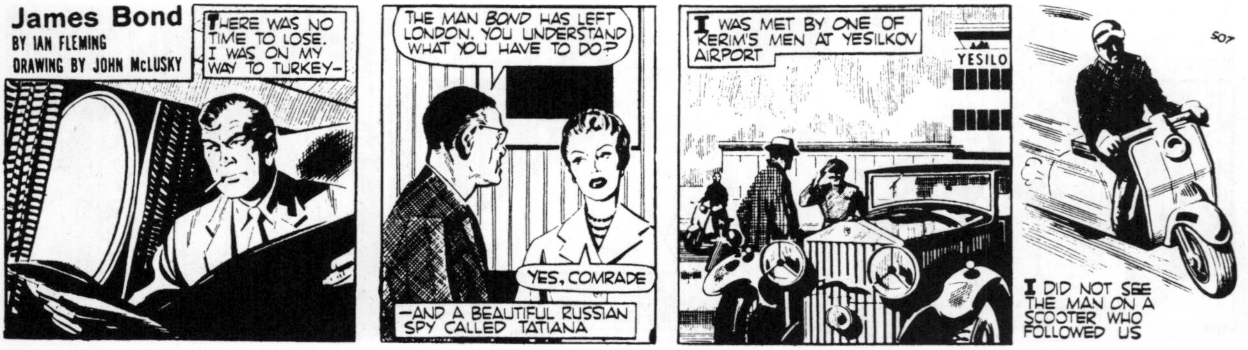
James Bond
BY IAN FLEMING
DRAWING BY JOHN McLUSKY
THERE WAS NO TIME TO LOSE. I WAS ON MY WAY TO TURKEY–
THE MAN BOND HAS LEFT LONDON. YOU UNDERSTAND WHAT YOU HAVE TO DO?
YES, COMRADE
–AND A BEAUTIFUL RUSSIAN SPY CALLED TATIANA
I WAS MET BY ONE OF KERIM'S MEN AT YESILKOV AIRPORT
YESILO
507
I DID NOT SEE THE MAN ON A SCOOTER WHO FOLLOWED US

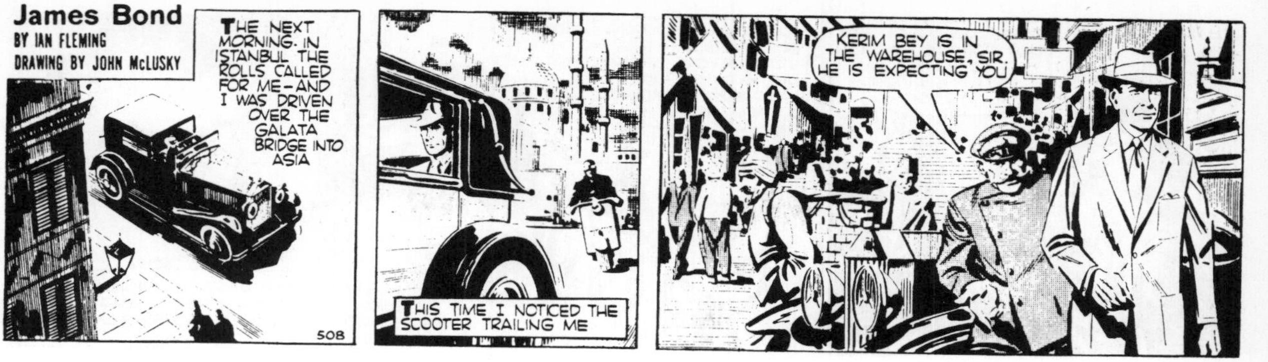
James Bond
BY IAN FLEMING
DRAWING BY JOHN McLUSKY
THE NEXT MORNING. IN ISTANBUL THE ROLLS CALLED FOR ME—AND I WAS DRIVEN OVER THE GALATA BRIDGE INTO ASIA
508
THIS TIME I NOTICED THE SCOOTER TRAILING ME
KERIM BEY IS IN THE WAREHOUSE, SIR. HE IS EXPECTING YOU

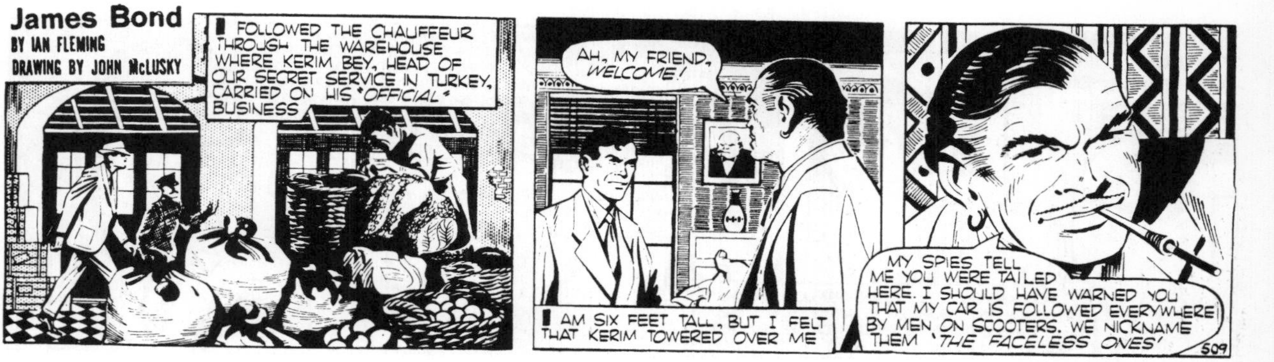
James Bond
BY IAN FLEMING
DRAWING BY JOHN McLUSKY
I FOLLOWED THE CHAUFFEUR THROUGH THE WAREHOUSE WHERE KERIM BEY, HEAD OF OUR SECRET SERVICE IN TURKEY, CARRIED ON HIS 'OFFICIAL' BUSINESS
AH, MY FRIEND, WELCOME!
I AM SIX FEET TALL, BUT I FELT THAT KERIM TOWERED OVER ME
MY SPIES TELL ME YOU WERE TAILED HERE. I SHOULD HAVE WARNED YOU THAT MY CAR IS FOLLOWED EVERYWHERE BY MEN ON SCOOTERS. WE NICKNAME THEM 'THE FACELESS ONES'
509

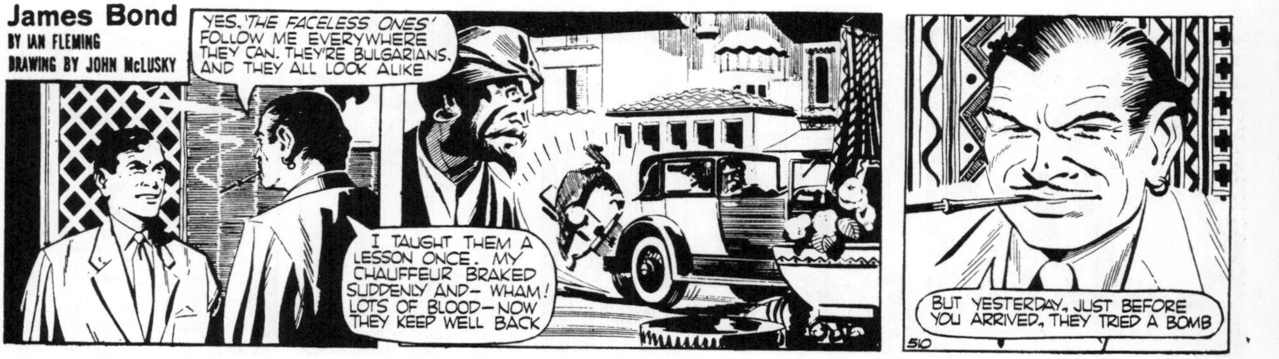
James Bond
BY IAN FLEMING
DRAWING BY JOHN McLUSKY
YES. 'THE FACELESS ONES' FOLLOW ME EVERYWHERE THEY CAN. THEY'RE BULGARIANS, AND THEY ALL LOOK ALIKE
I TAUGHT THEM A LESSON ONCE. MY CHAUFFEUR BRAKED SUDDENLY AND—WHAM! LOTS OF BLOOD—NOW THEY KEEP WELL BACK
510
BUT YESTERDAY, JUST BEFORE YOU ARRIVED, THEY TRIED A BOMB

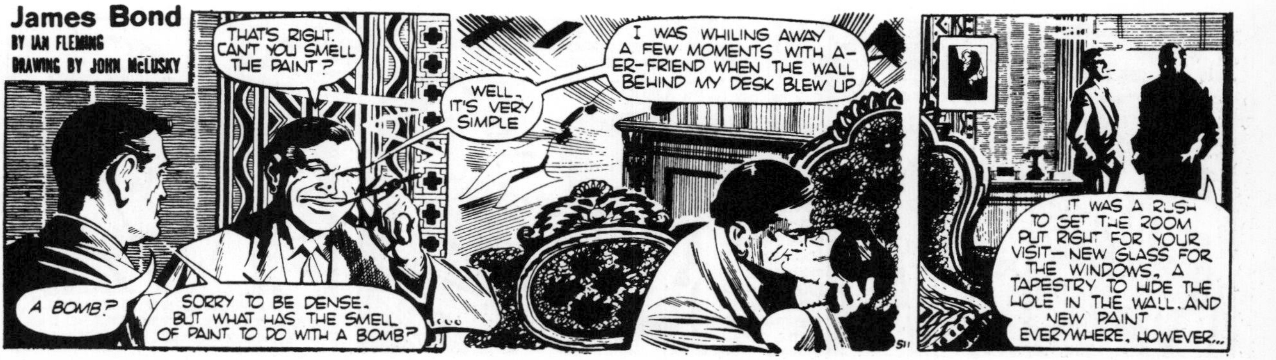
James Bond
BY IAN FLEMING
DRAWING BY JOHN McLUSKY
A BOMB?
THAT'S RIGHT. CAN'T YOU SMELL THE PAINT?
SORRY TO BE DENSE. BUT WHAT HAS THE SMELL OF PAINT TO DO WITH A BOMB?
WELL, IT'S VERY SIMPLE
I WAS WHILING AWAY A FEW MOMENTS WITH A-ER-FRIEND WHEN THE WALL BEHIND MY DESK BLEW UP
511
IT WAS A RUSH TO GET THE ROOM PUT RIGHT FOR YOUR VISIT—NEW GLASS FOR THE WINDOWS, A TAPESTRY TO HIDE THE HOLE IN THE WALL, AND NEW PAINT EVERYWHERE. HOWEVER...

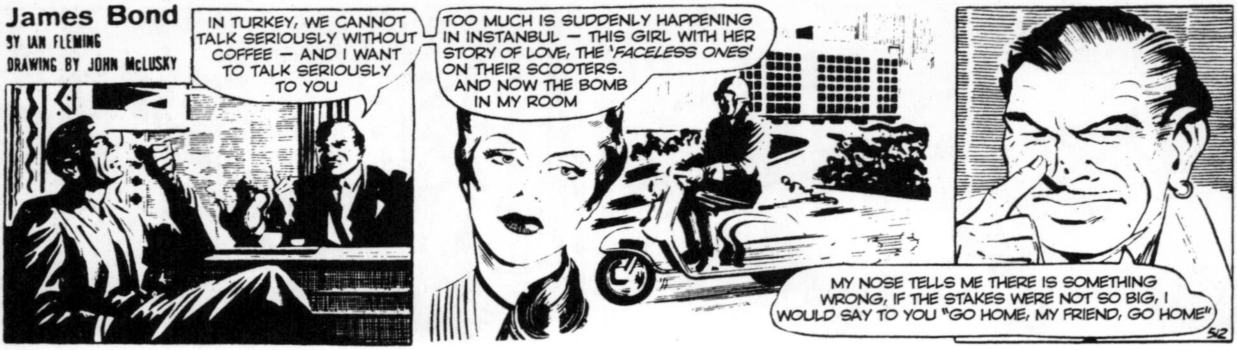
James Bond
BY IAN FLEMING
DRAWING BY JOHN McLUSKY
IN TURKEY, WE CANNOT TALK SERIOUSLY WITHOUT COFFEE — AND I WANT TO TALK SERIOUSLY TO YOU
TOO MUCH IS SUDDENLY HAPPENING IN INSTANBUL — THIS GIRL WITH HER STORY OF LOVE, THE '*FACELESS ONES*' ON THEIR SCOOTERS. AND NOW THE BOMB IN MY ROOM
MY NOSE TELLS ME THERE IS SOMETHING WRONG, IF THE STAKES WERE NOT SO BIG, I WOULD SAY TO YOU "GO HOME, MY FRIEND, GO HOME"
512

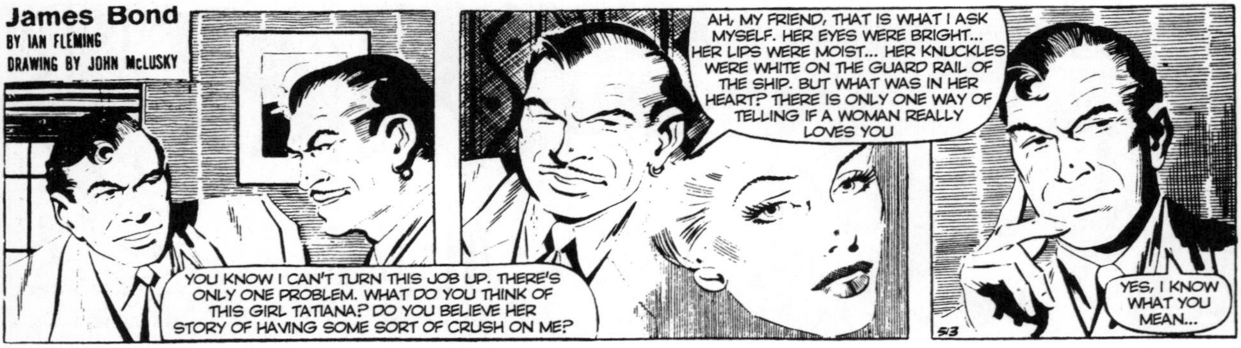
James Bond
BY IAN FLEMING
DRAWING BY JOHN McLUSKY
YOU KNOW I CAN'T TURN THIS JOB UP. THERE'S ONLY ONE PROBLEM. WHAT DO YOU THINK OF THIS GIRL TATIANA? DO YOU BELIEVE HER STORY OF HAVING SOME SORT OF CRUSH ON ME?
AH, MY FRIEND, THAT IS WHAT I ASK MYSELF. HER EYES WERE BRIGHT... HER LIPS WERE MOIST... HER KNUCKLES WERE WHITE ON THE GUARD RAIL OF THE SHIP. BUT WHAT WAS IN HER HEART? THERE IS ONLY ONE WAY OF TELLING IF A WOMAN REALLY LOVES YOU
513
YES, I KNOW WHAT YOU MEAN...

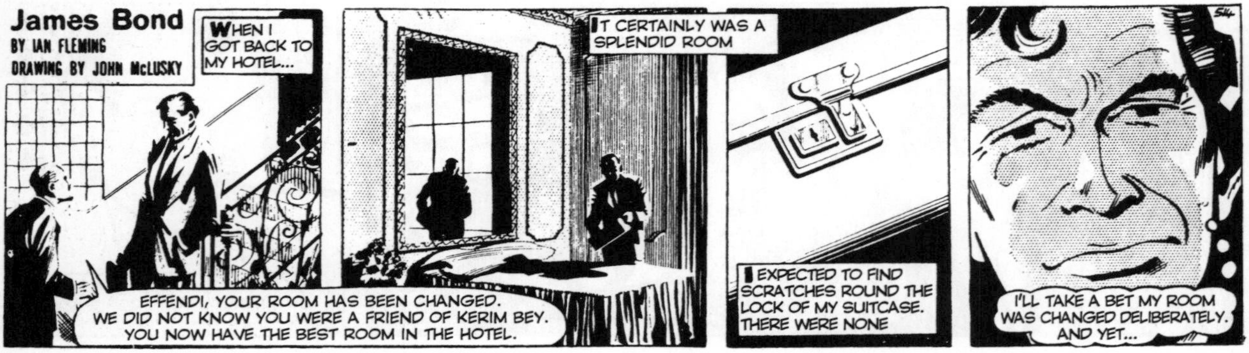
James Bond
BY IAN FLEMING
DRAWING BY JOHN McLUSKY
WHEN I GOT BACK TO MY HOTEL...
EFFENDI, YOUR ROOM HAS BEEN CHANGED. WE DID NOT KNOW YOU WERE A FRIEND OF KERIM BEY. YOU NOW HAVE THE BEST ROOM IN THE HOTEL.
IT CERTAINLY WAS A SPLENDID ROOM
I EXPECTED TO FIND SCRATCHES ROUND THE LOCK OF MY SUITCASE. THERE WERE NONE
514
I'LL TAKE A BET MY ROOM WAS CHANGED DELIBERATELY. AND YET...

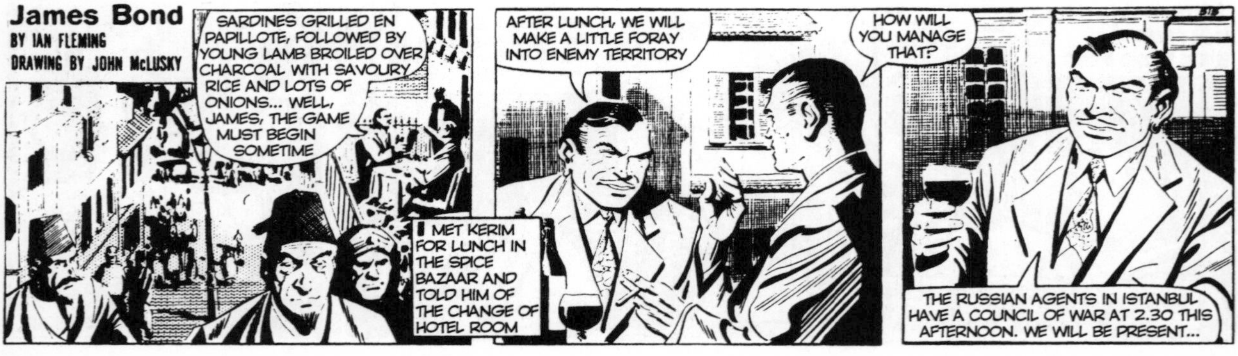
James Bond
BY IAN FLEMING
DRAWING BY JOHN McLUSKY
SARDINES GRILLED EN PAPILLOTE, FOLLOWED BY YOUNG LAMB BROILED OVER CHARCOAL WITH SAVOURY RICE AND LOTS OF ONIONS... WELL, JAMES, THE GAME MUST BEGIN SOMETIME
I MET KERIM FOR LUNCH IN THE SPICE BAZAAR AND TOLD HIM OF THE CHANGE OF HOTEL ROOM
AFTER LUNCH, WE WILL MAKE A LITTLE FORAY INTO ENEMY TERRITORY
HOW WILL YOU MANAGE THAT?
THE RUSSIAN AGENTS IN ISTANBUL HAVE A COUNCIL OF WAR AT 2.30 THIS AFTERNOON. WE WILL BE PRESENT...

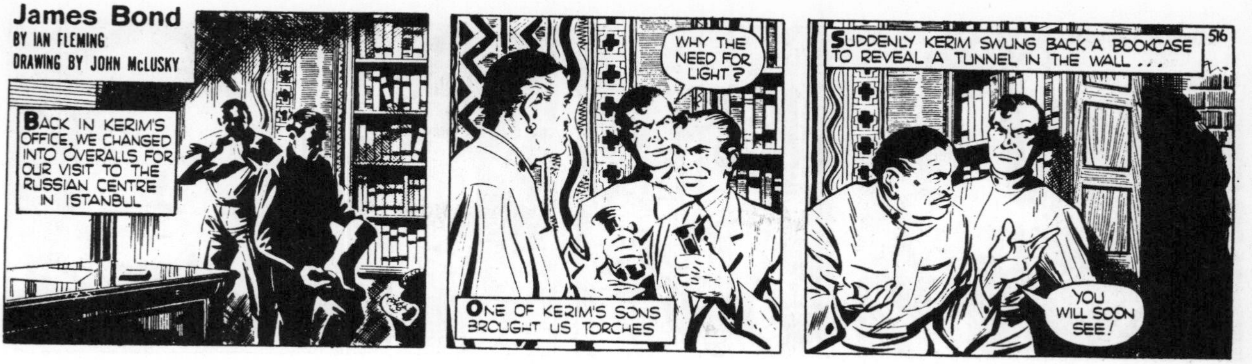
James Bond
BY IAN FLEMING
DRAWING BY JOHN McLUSKY
BACK IN KERIM'S OFFICE, WE CHANGED INTO OVERALLS FOR OUR VISIT TO THE RUSSIAN CENTRE IN ISTANBUL
WHY THE NEED FOR LIGHT?
ONE OF KERIM'S SONS BROUGHT US TORCHES
SUDDENLY KERIM SWUNG BACK A BOOKCASE TO REVEAL A TUNNEL IN THE WALL . . .
516
YOU WILL SOON SEE!

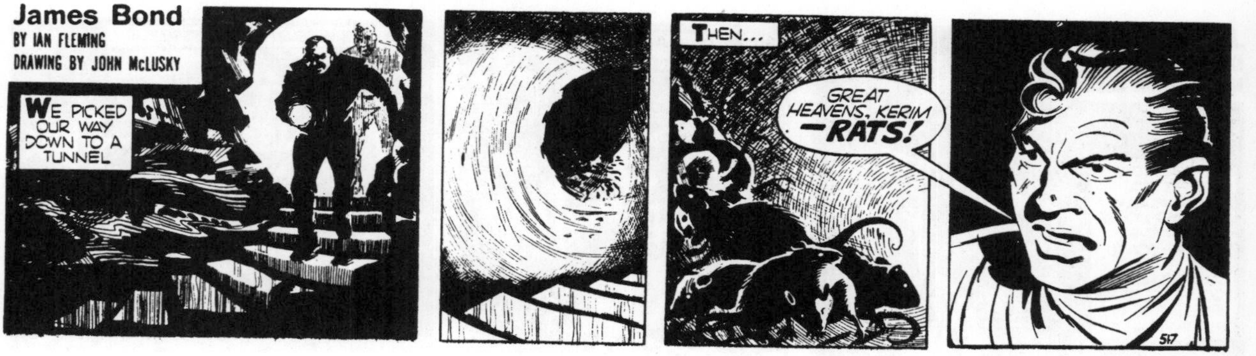
James Bond
BY IAN FLEMING
DRAWING BY JOHN McLUSKY
WE PICKED OUR WAY DOWN TO A TUNNEL
THEN...
GREAT HEAVENS, KERIM —RATS!
517

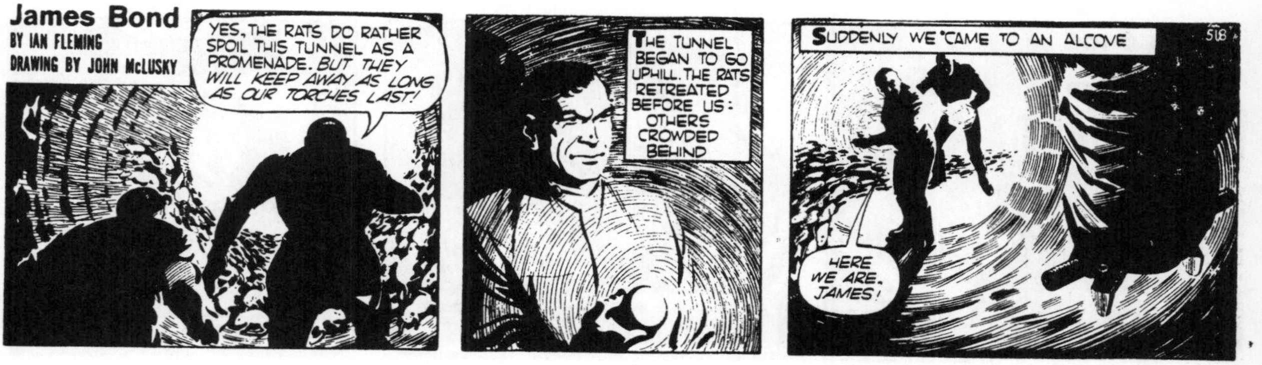
James Bond
BY IAN FLEMING
DRAWING BY JOHN McLUSKY
YES, THE RATS DO RATHER SPOIL THIS TUNNEL AS A PROMENADE. BUT THEY WILL KEEP AWAY AS LONG AS OUR TORCHES LAST!
THE TUNNEL BEGAN TO GO UPHILL. THE RATS RETREATED BEFORE US: OTHERS CROWDED BEHIND
SUDDENLY WE CAME TO AN ALCOVE
518
HERE WE ARE, JAMES!

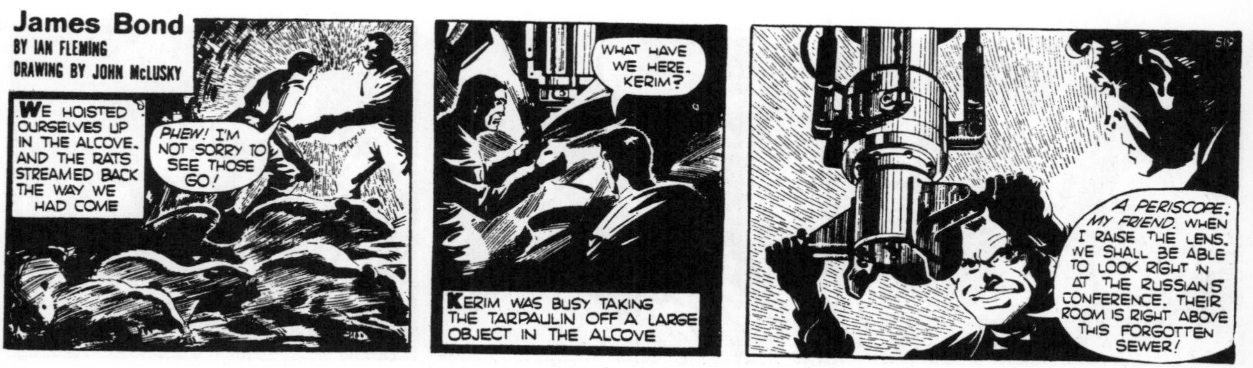
James Bond
BY IAN FLEMING
DRAWING BY JOHN McLUSKY
WE HOISTED OURSELVES UP IN THE ALCOVE, AND THE RATS STREAMED BACK THE WAY WE HAD COME
PHEW! I'M NOT SORRY TO SEE THOSE GO!
WHAT HAVE WE HERE, KERIM?
KERIM WAS BUSY TAKING THE TARPAULIN OFF A LARGE OBJECT IN THE ALCOVE
519
A PERISCOPE, MY FRIEND. WHEN I RAISE THE LENS, WE SHALL BE ABLE TO LOOK RIGHT IN AT THE RUSSIANS' CONFERENCE. THEIR ROOM IS RIGHT ABOVE THIS FORGOTTEN SEWER!

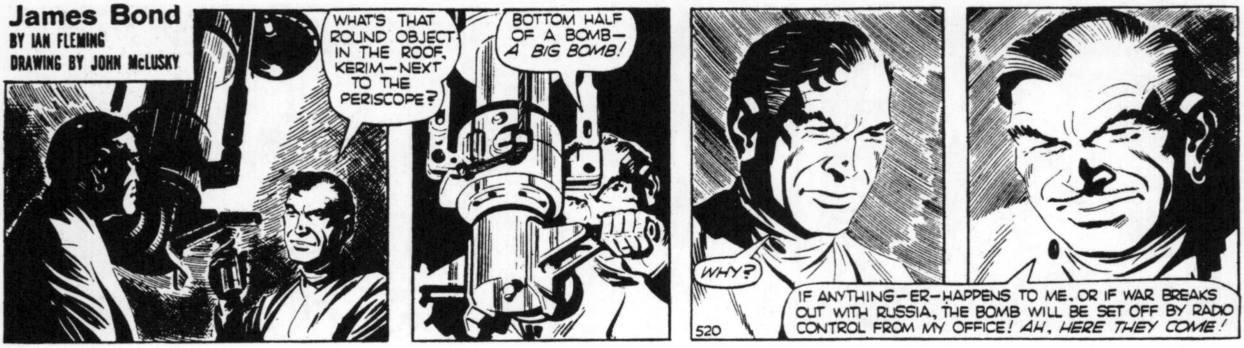
James Bond
BY IAN FLEMING
DRAWING BY JOHN McLUSKY
WHAT'S THAT ROUND OBJECT IN THE ROOF, KERIM—NEXT TO THE PERISCOPE?
BOTTOM HALF OF A BOMB—*A BIG BOMB!*
WHY?
IF ANYTHING—ER—HAPPENS TO ME, OR IF WAR BREAKS OUT WITH RUSSIA, THE BOMB WILL BE SET OFF BY RADIO CONTROL FROM MY OFFICE! *AH, HERE THEY COME!*
520

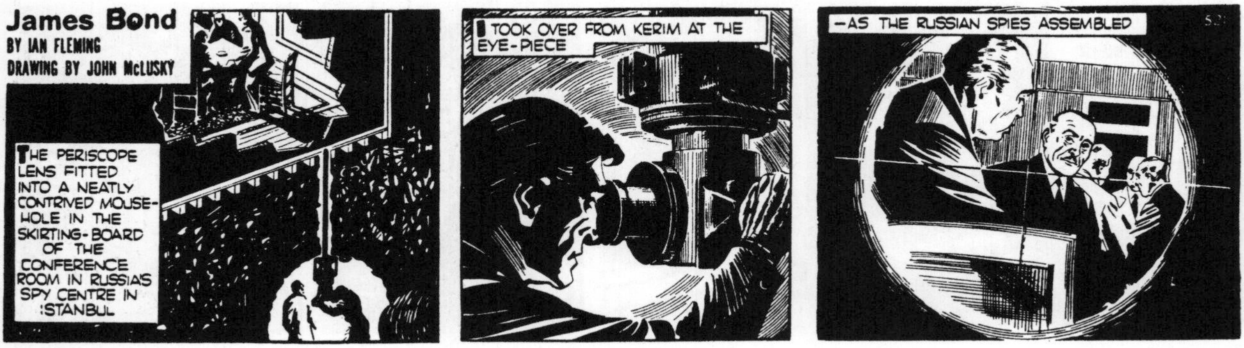
James Bond
BY IAN FLEMING
DRAWING BY JOHN McLUSKY
THE PERISCOPE LENS FITTED INTO A NEATLY CONTRIVED MOUSE-HOLE IN THE SKIRTING-BOARD OF THE CONFERENCE ROOM IN RUSSIA'S SPY CENTRE IN ISTANBUL
I TOOK OVER FROM KERIM AT THE EYE-PIECE
—AS THE RUSSIAN SPIES ASSEMBLED

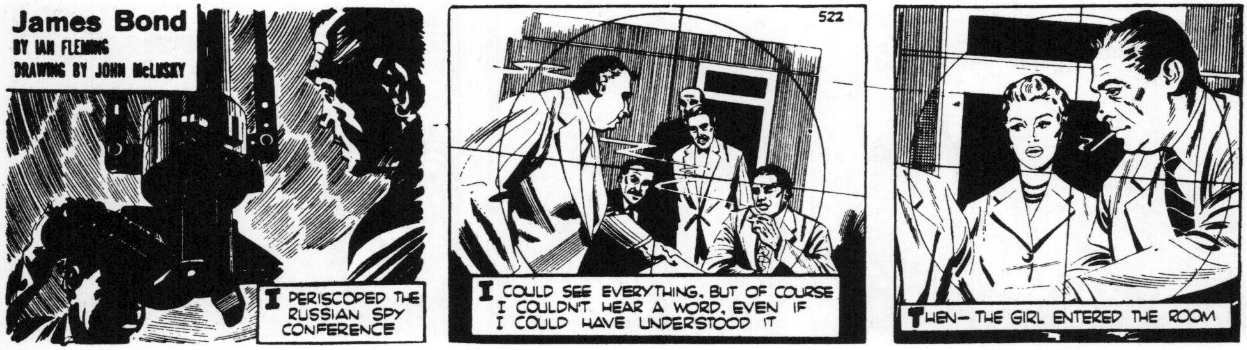
James Bond
BY IAN FLEMING
DRAWING BY JOHN McLUSKY
I PERISCOPED THE RUSSIAN SPY CONFERENCE
522
I COULD SEE EVERYTHING, BUT OF COURSE I COULDN'T HEAR A WORD, EVEN IF I COULD HAVE UNDERSTOOD IT
THEN—THE GIRL ENTERED THE ROOM

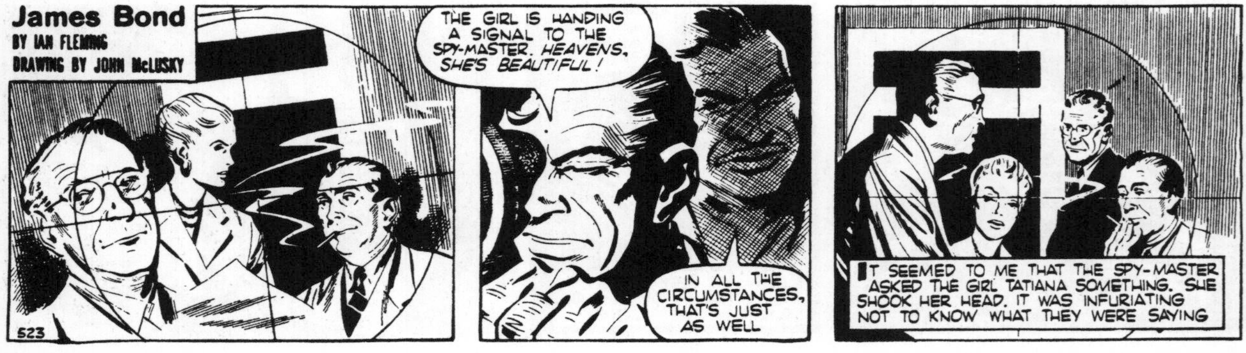
James Bond
BY IAN FLEMING
DRAWING BY JOHN McLUSKY
523
THE GIRL IS HANDING A SIGNAL TO THE SPY-MASTER. *HEAVENS, SHE'S BEAUTIFUL!*
IN ALL THE CIRCUMSTANCES, THAT'S JUST AS WELL
IT SEEMED TO ME THAT THE SPY-MASTER ASKED THE GIRL TATIANA SOMETHING. SHE SHOOK HER HEAD. IT WAS INFURIATING NOT TO KNOW WHAT THEY WERE SAYING

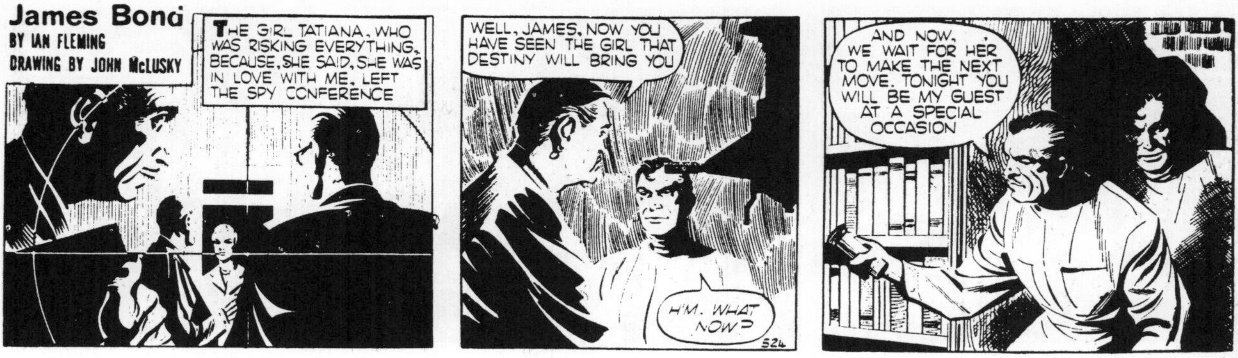
James Bond
BY IAN FLEMING
DRAWING BY JOHN McLUSKY
THE GIRL TATIANA, WHO WAS RISKING EVERYTHING, BECAUSE, SHE SAID, SHE WAS IN LOVE WITH ME, LEFT THE SPY CONFERENCE
WELL, JAMES, NOW YOU HAVE SEEN THE GIRL THAT DESTINY WILL BRING YOU
H'M. WHAT NOW?
524
AND NOW, WE WAIT FOR HER TO MAKE THE NEXT MOVE. TONIGHT YOU WILL BE MY GUEST AT A SPECIAL OCCASION

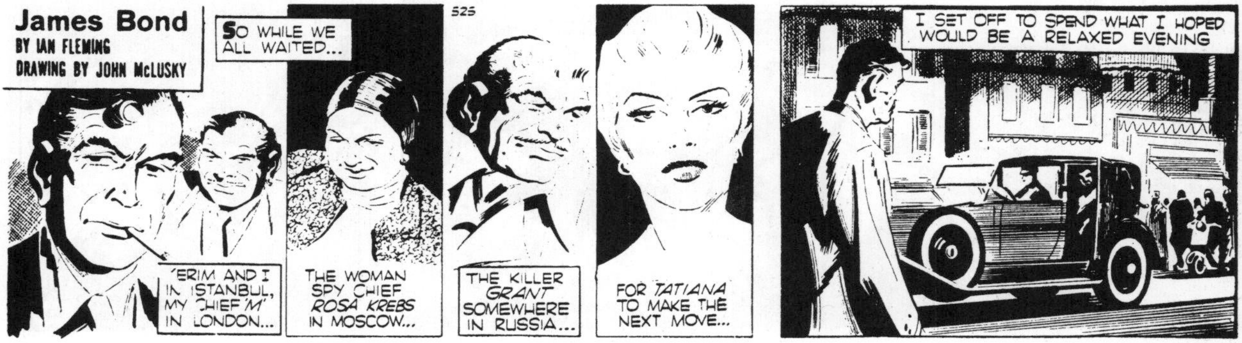
James Bond
BY IAN FLEMING
DRAWING BY JOHN McLUSKY
SO WHILE WE ALL WAITED...
525
KERIM AND I IN ISTANBUL, MY CHIEF 'M' IN LONDON...
THE WOMAN SPY CHIEF ROSA KREBS IN MOSCOW...
THE KILLER GRANT SOMEWHERE IN RUSSIA...
FOR TATIANA TO MAKE THE NEXT MOVE...
I SET OFF TO SPEND WHAT I HOPED WOULD BE A RELAXED EVENING

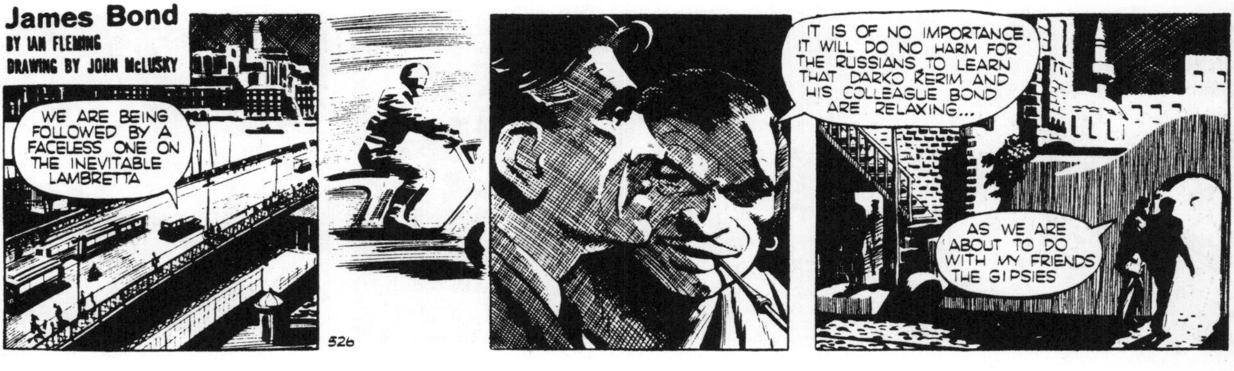
James Bond
BY IAN FLEMING
DRAWING BY JOHN McLUSKY
WE ARE BEING FOLLOWED BY A FACELESS ONE ON THE INEVITABLE LAMBRETTA
526
IT IS OF NO IMPORTANCE. IT WILL DO NO HARM FOR THE RUSSIANS TO LEARN THAT DARKO KERIM AND HIS COLLEAGUE BOND ARE RELAXING...
AS WE ARE ABOUT TO DO WITH MY FRIENDS THE GIPSIES

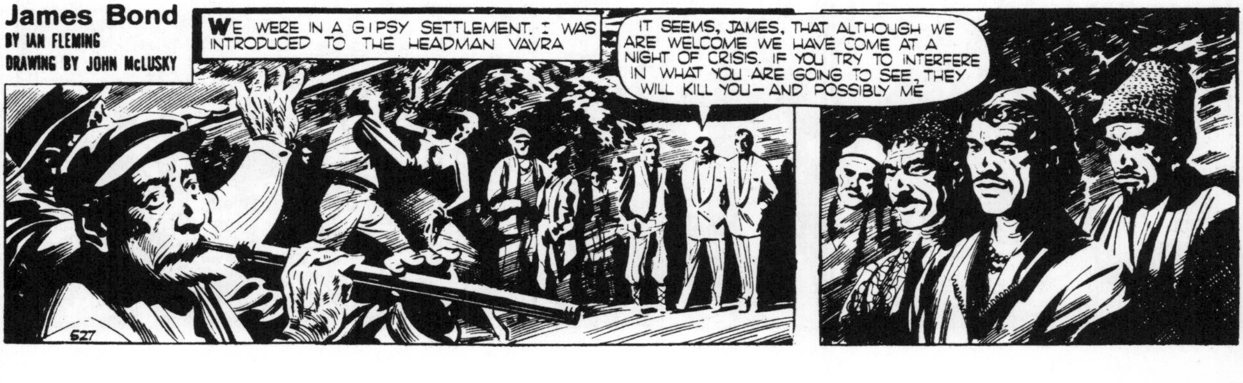
James Bond
BY IAN FLEMING
DRAWING BY JOHN McLUSKY
WE WERE IN A GIPSY SETTLEMENT. I WAS INTRODUCED TO THE HEADMAN VAVRA
IT SEEMS, JAMES, THAT ALTHOUGH WE ARE WELCOME WE HAVE COME AT A NIGHT OF CRISIS. IF YOU TRY TO INTERFERE IN WHAT YOU ARE GOING TO SEE, THEY WILL KILL YOU—AND POSSIBLY ME
527

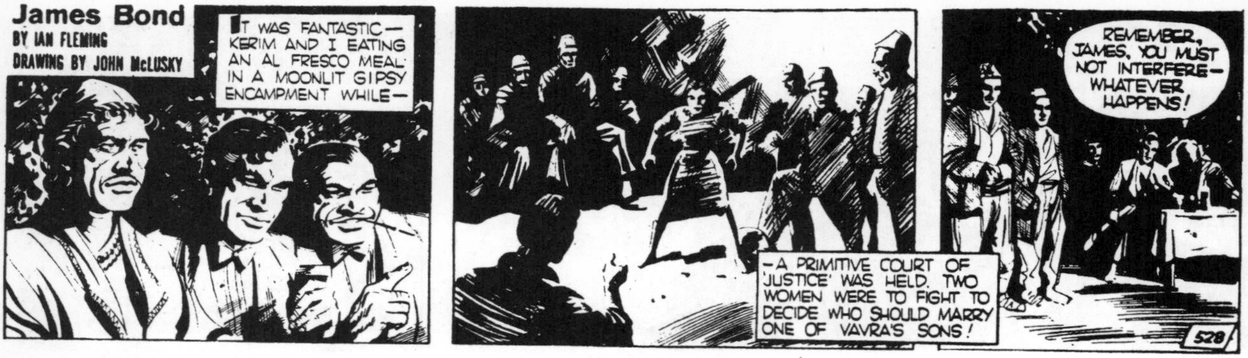
James Bond
BY IAN FLEMING
DRAWING BY JOHN McLUSKY
IT WAS FANTASTIC—KERIM AND I EATING AN AL FRESCO MEAL IN A MOONLIT GIPSY ENCAMPMENT WHILE—
—A PRIMITIVE COURT OF 'JUSTICE' WAS HELD. TWO WOMEN WERE TO FIGHT TO DECIDE WHO SHOULD MARRY ONE OF VAVRA'S SONS!
REMEMBER, JAMES, YOU MUST NOT INTERFERE—WHATEVER HAPPENS!
528

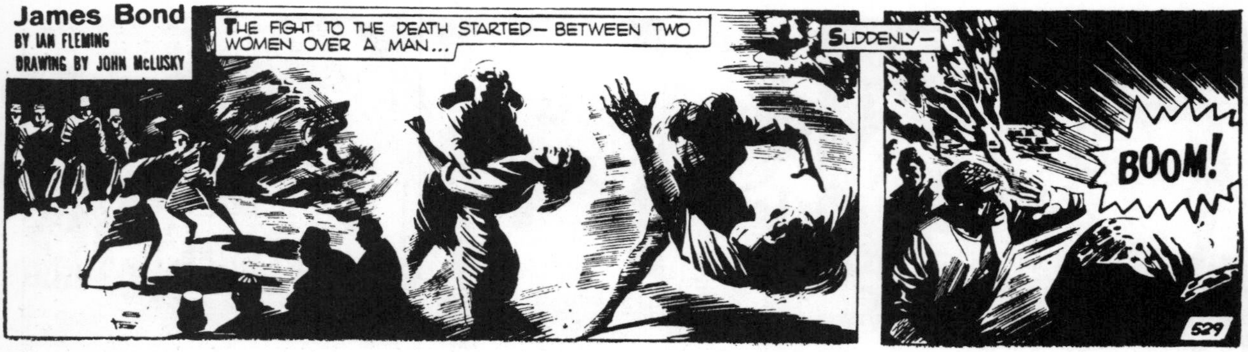
James Bond
BY IAN FLEMING
DRAWING BY JOHN McLUSKY
THE FIGHT TO THE DEATH STARTED— BETWEEN TWO WOMEN OVER A MAN...
SUDDENLY—
BOOM!
529

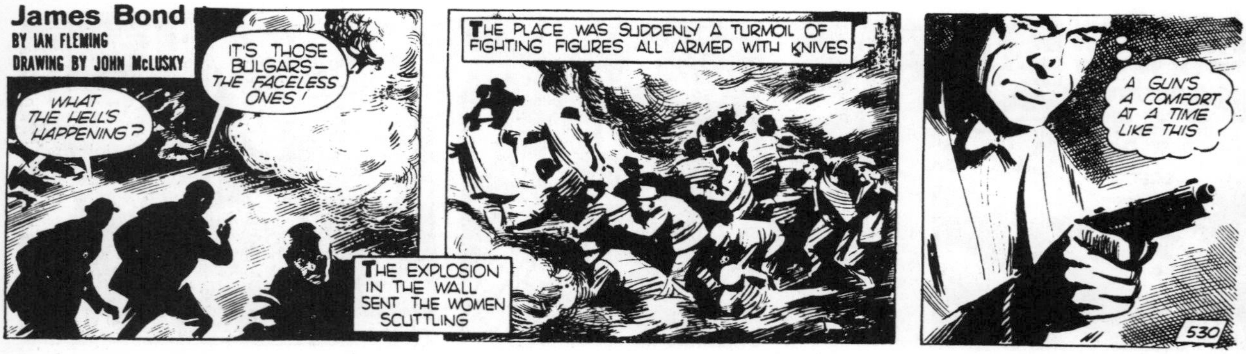
James Bond
BY IAN FLEMING
DRAWING BY JOHN McLUSKY
WHAT THE HELL'S HAPPENING?
IT'S THOSE BULGARS— THE FACELESS ONES!
THE EXPLOSION IN THE WALL SENT THE WOMEN SCUTTLING
THE PLACE WAS SUDDENLY A TURMOIL OF FIGHTING FIGURES ALL ARMED WITH KNIVES
A GUN'S A COMFORT AT A TIME LIKE THIS
530

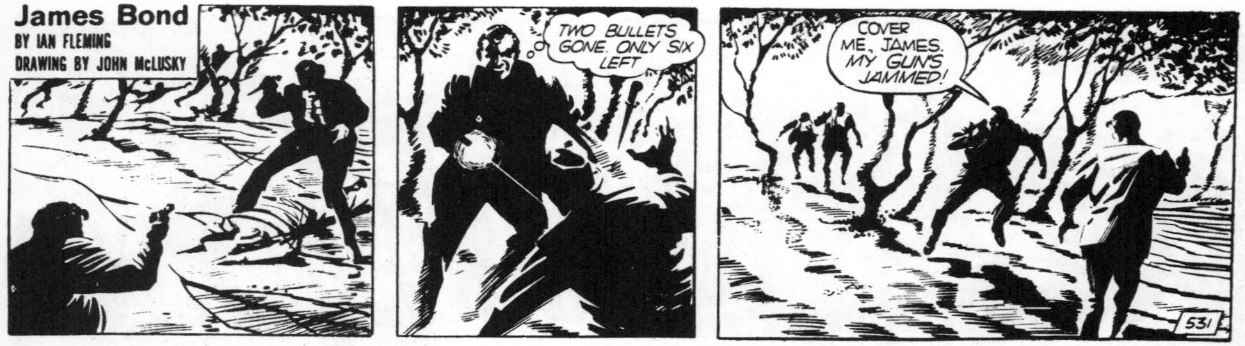
James Bond
BY IAN FLEMING
DRAWING BY JOHN McLUSKY
TWO BULLETS GONE. ONLY SIX LEFT
COVER ME, JAMES. MY GUN'S JAMMED!
531

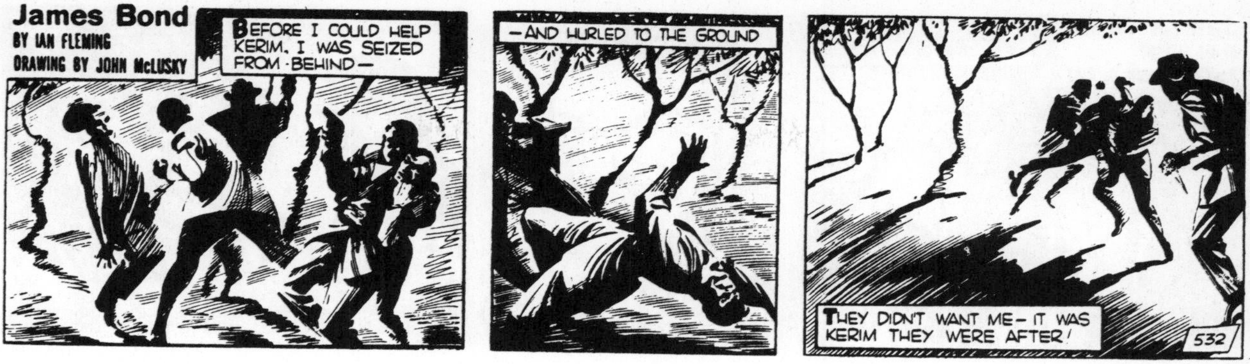
James Bond
BY IAN FLEMING
DRAWING BY JOHN McLUSKY
BEFORE I COULD HELP KERIM, I WAS SEIZED FROM BEHIND—
—AND HURLED TO THE GROUND
THEY DIDN'T WANT ME—IT WAS KERIM THEY WERE AFTER!
532

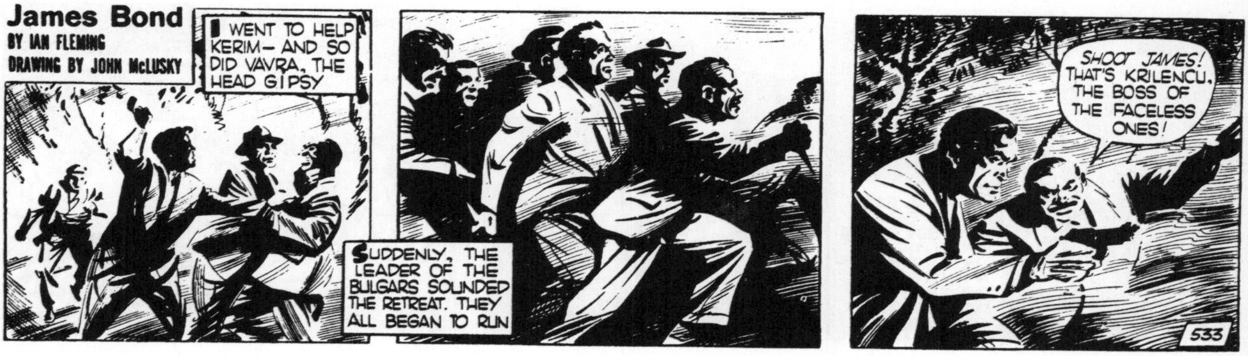
James Bond
BY IAN FLEMING
DRAWING BY JOHN McLUSKY
I WENT TO HELP KERIM—AND SO DID VAVRA, THE HEAD GIPSY
SUDDENLY, THE LEADER OF THE BULGARS SOUNDED THE RETREAT. THEY ALL BEGAN TO RUN
SHOOT JAMES! THAT'S KRILENCU, THE BOSS OF THE FACELESS ONES!
533

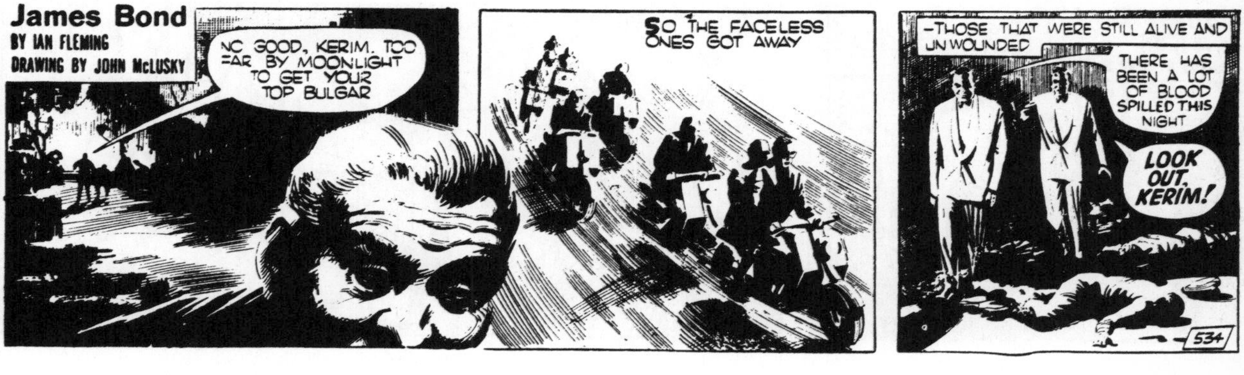
James Bond
BY IAN FLEMING
DRAWING BY JOHN McLUSKY
NO GOOD, KERIM. TOO FAR BY MOONLIGHT TO GET YOUR TOP BULGAR
SO THE FACELESS ONES GOT AWAY
—THOSE THAT WERE STILL ALIVE AND UNWOUNDED
THERE HAS BEEN A LOT OF BLOOD SPILLED THIS NIGHT
LOOK OUT, KERIM!
534

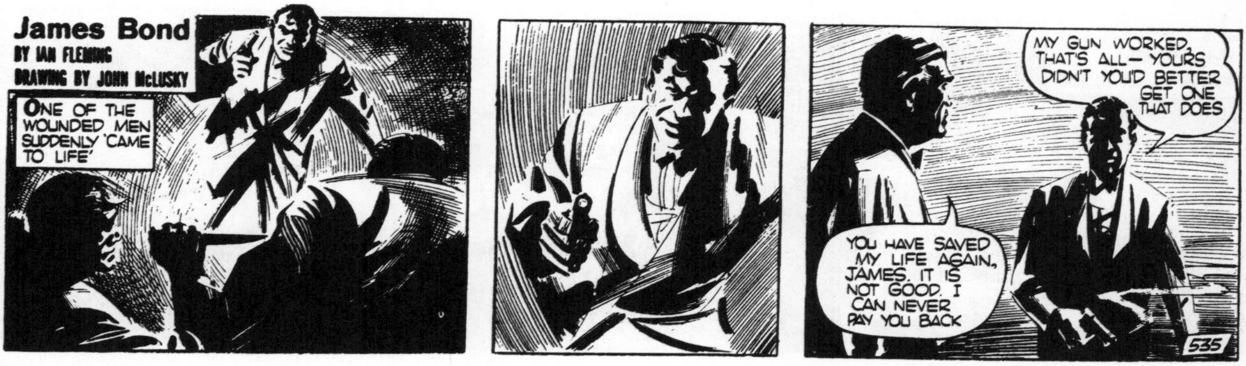
James Bond
BY IAN FLEMING
DRAWING BY JOHN McLUSKY
ONE OF THE WOUNDED MEN SUDDENLY 'CAME TO LIFE'
MY GUN WORKED, THAT'S ALL—YOURS DIDN'T. YOU'D BETTER GET ONE THAT DOES
YOU HAVE SAVED MY LIFE AGAIN, JAMES. IT IS NOT GOOD. I CAN NEVER PAY YOU BACK
535

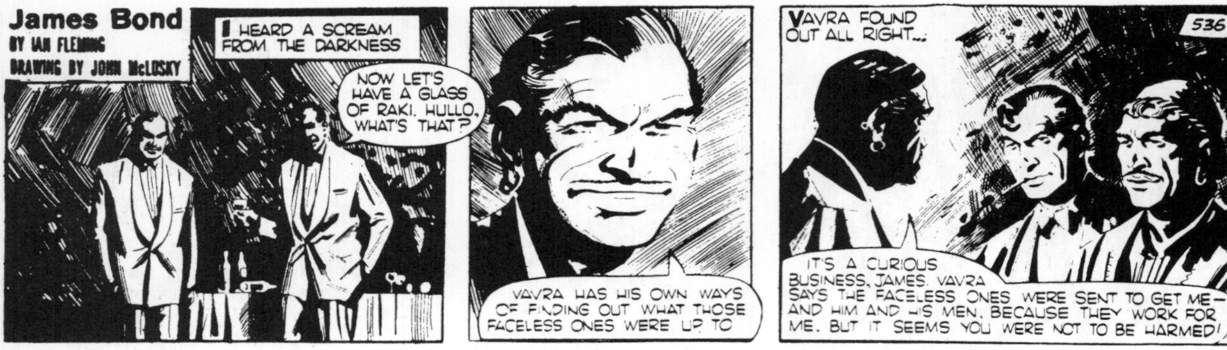
James Bond
BY IAN FLEMING
DRAWING BY JOHN McLUSKY
I HEARD A SCREAM FROM THE DARKNESS
NOW LET'S HAVE A GLASS OF RAKI. HULLO, WHAT'S THAT?
VAVRA HAS HIS OWN WAYS OF FINDING OUT WHAT THOSE FACELESS ONES WERE UP TO
VAVRA FOUND OUT ALL RIGHT...
536
IT'S A CURIOUS BUSINESS, JAMES. VAVRA SAYS THE FACELESS ONES WERE SENT TO GET ME— AND HIM AND HIS MEN, BECAUSE THEY WORK FOR ME. BUT IT SEEMS YOU WERE NOT TO BE HARMED!

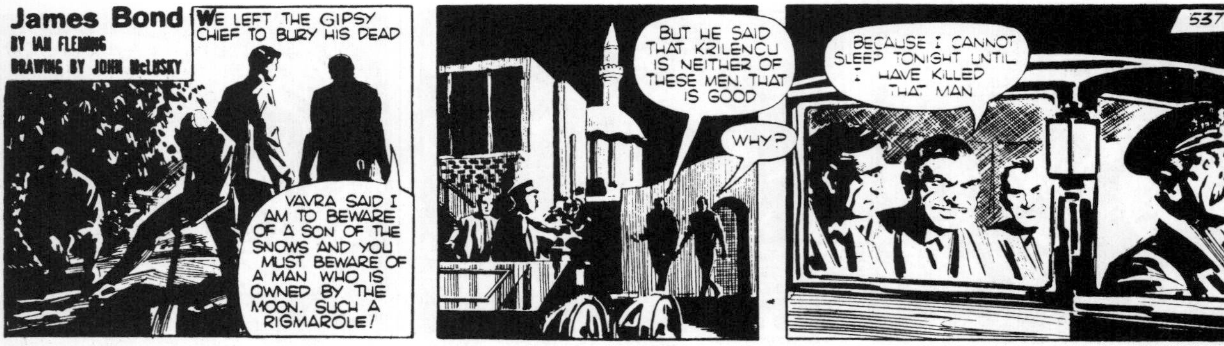
James Bond
BY IAN FLEMING
DRAWING BY JOHN McLUSKY
WE LEFT THE GIPSY CHIEF TO BURY HIS DEAD
VAVRA SAID I AM TO BEWARE OF A SON OF THE SNOWS AND YOU MUST BEWARE OF A MAN WHO IS OWNED BY THE MOON. SUCH A RIGMAROLE!
BUT HE SAID THAT KRILENCU IS NEITHER OF THESE MEN. THAT IS GOOD
WHY?
537
BECAUSE I CANNOT SLEEP TONIGHT UNTIL I HAVE KILLED THAT MAN

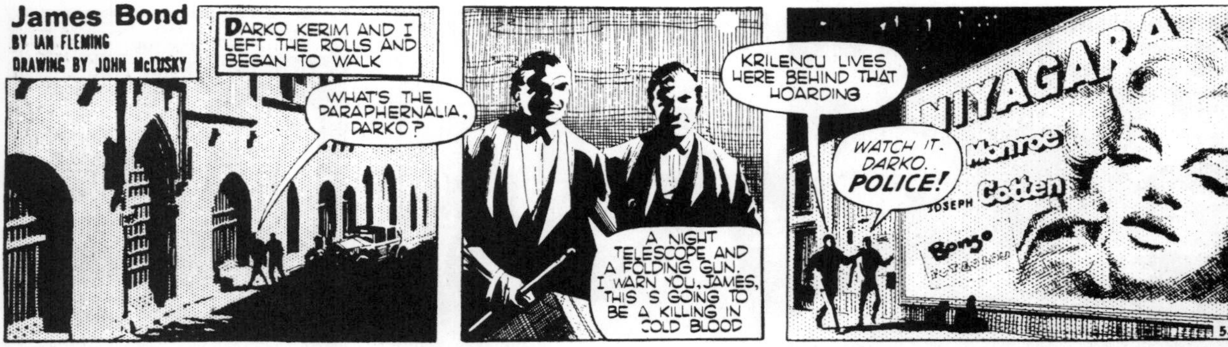
James Bond
BY IAN FLEMING
DRAWING BY JOHN McLUSKY
DARKO KERIM AND I LEFT THE ROLLS AND BEGAN TO WALK
WHAT'S THE PARAPHERNALIA, DARKO?
A NIGHT TELESCOPE AND A FOLDING GUN. I WARN YOU, JAMES, THIS 'S GOING TO BE A KILLING IN COLD BLOOD
KRILENCU LIVES HERE BEHIND THAT HOARDING
WATCH IT, DARKO. POLICE!
NIYAGARA
Monroe
JOSEPH Cotten
Bongo
538

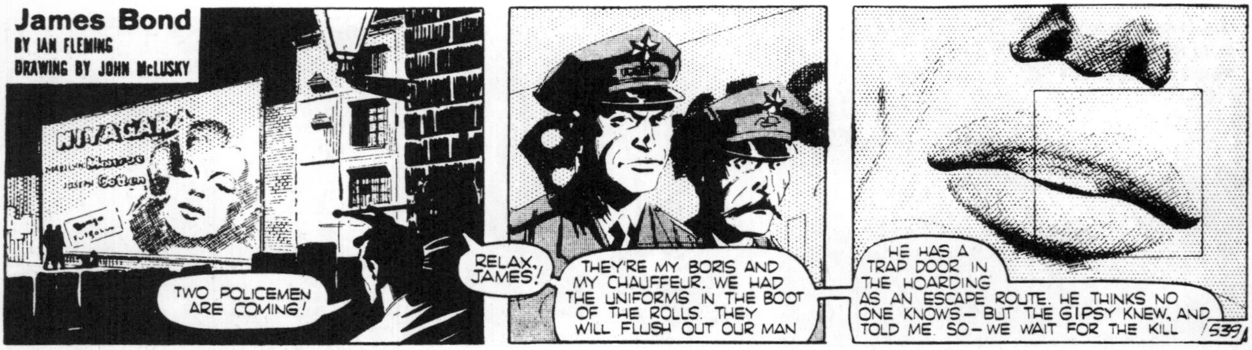
James Bond
BY IAN FLEMING
DRAWING BY JOHN McLUSKY
NIYAGARA
Monroe
JOSEPH Cotten
TWO POLICEMEN ARE COMING!
RELAX, JAMES!
THEY'RE MY BORIS AND MY CHAUFFEUR. WE HAD THE UNIFORMS IN THE BOOT OF THE ROLLS. THEY WILL FLUSH OUT OUR MAN
HE HAS A TRAP DOOR IN THE HOARDING AS AN ESCAPE ROUTE. HE THINKS NO ONE KNOWS— BUT THE GIPSY KNEW, AND TOLD ME. SO— WE WAIT FOR THE KILL
539

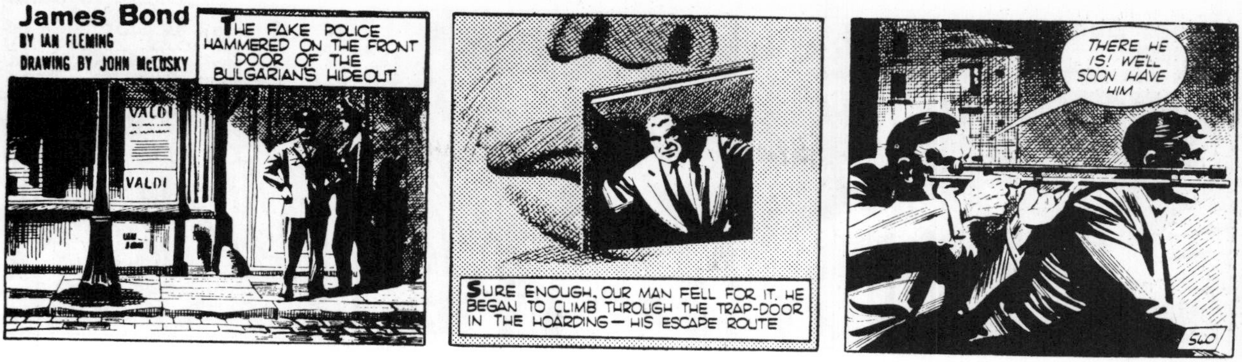
James Bond
BY IAN FLEMING
DRAWING BY JOHN McLUSKY
THE FAKE POLICE HAMMERED ON THE FRONT DOOR OF THE BULGARIAN'S HIDEOUT
VALDI
VALDI
SURE ENOUGH, OUR MAN FELL FOR IT. HE BEGAN TO CLIMB THROUGH THE TRAP-DOOR IN THE HOARDING—HIS ESCAPE ROUTE
THERE HE IS! WE'LL SOON HAVE HIM
540

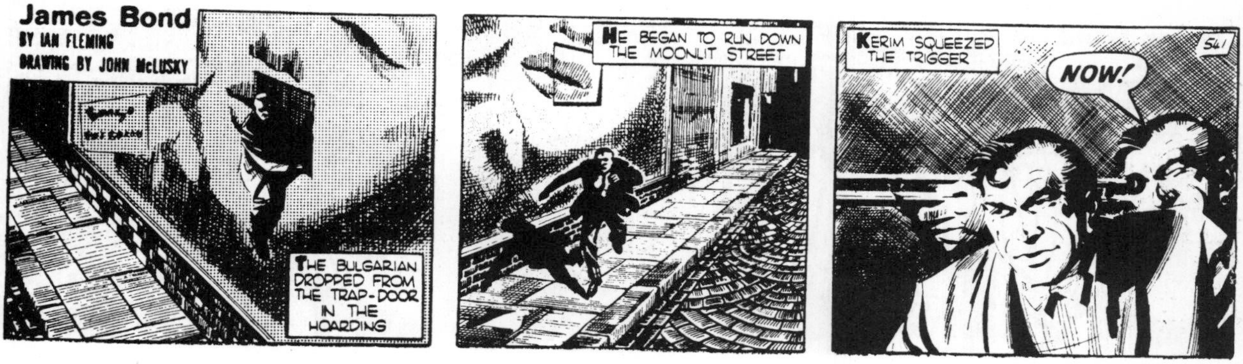
James Bond
BY IAN FLEMING
DRAWING BY JOHN McLUSKY
THE BULGARIAN DROPPED FROM THE TRAP-DOOR IN THE HOARDING
HE BEGAN TO RUN DOWN THE MOONLIT STREET
KERIM SQUEEZED THE TRIGGER
NOW!
541

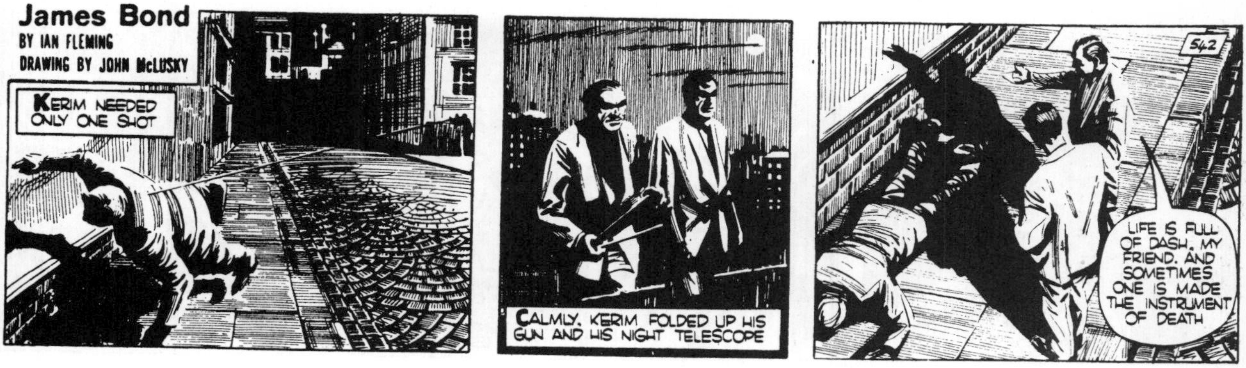
James Bond
BY IAN FLEMING
DRAWING BY JOHN McLUSKY
KERIM NEEDED ONLY ONE SHOT
CALMLY, KERIM FOLDED UP HIS GUN AND HIS NIGHT TELESCOPE
542
LIFE IS FULL OF DASH, MY FRIEND. AND SOMETIMES ONE IS MADE THE INSTRUMENT OF DEATH

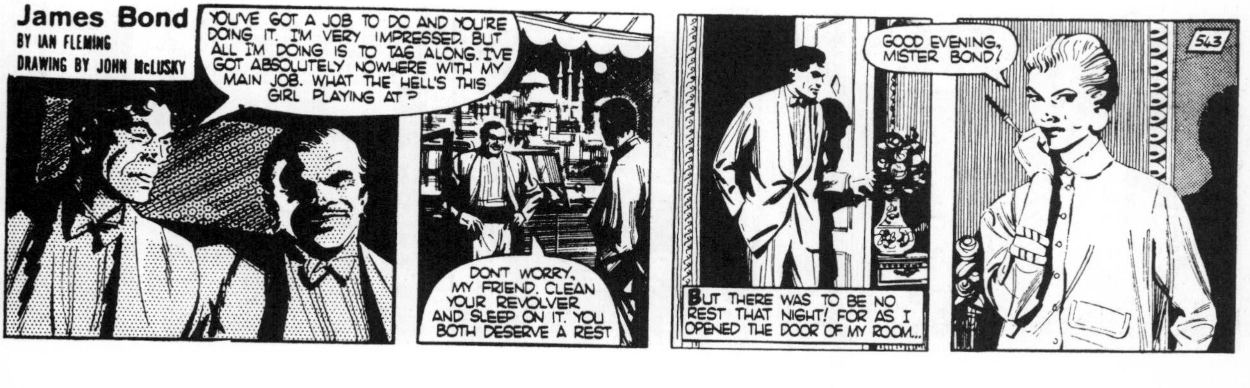
James Bond
BY IAN FLEMING
DRAWING BY JOHN McLUSKY
YOU'VE GOT A JOB TO DO AND YOU'RE DOING IT. I'M VERY IMPRESSED. BUT ALL I'M DOING IS TO TAG ALONG. I'VE GOT ABSOLUTELY NOWHERE WITH MY MAIN JOB. WHAT THE HELL'S THIS GIRL PLAYING AT?
DON'T WORRY, MY FRIEND. CLEAN YOUR REVOLVER AND SLEEP ON IT. YOU BOTH DESERVE A REST
BUT THERE WAS TO BE NO REST THAT NIGHT! FOR AS I OPENED THE DOOR OF MY ROOM...
543
GOOD EVENING, MISTER BOND!

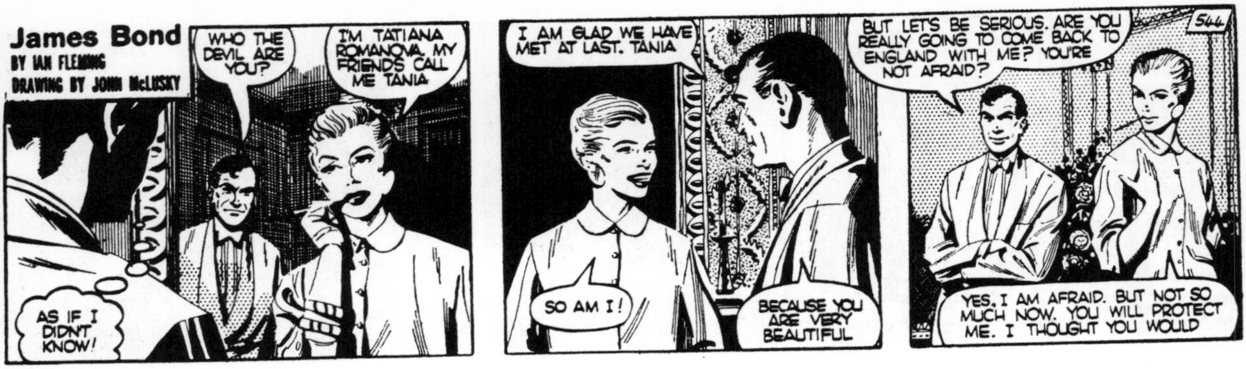
James Bond
BY IAN FLEMING
DRAWING BY JOHN McLUSKY
WHO THE DEVIL ARE YOU?
I'M TATIANA ROMANOVA. MY FRIENDS CALL ME TANIA
AS IF I DIDN'T KNOW!
I AM GLAD WE HAVE MET AT LAST, TANIA
SO AM I!
BECAUSE YOU ARE VERY BEAUTIFUL
544
BUT LET'S BE SERIOUS. ARE YOU REALLY GOING TO COME BACK TO ENGLAND WITH ME? YOU'RE NOT AFRAID?
YES, I AM AFRAID. BUT NOT SO MUCH NOW. YOU WILL PROTECT ME. I THOUGHT YOU WOULD

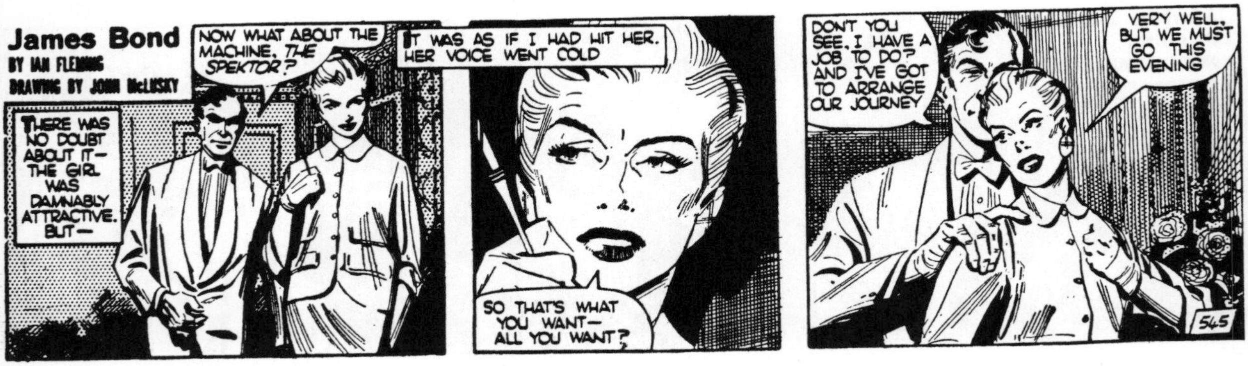
James Bond
BY IAN FLEMING
DRAWING BY JOHN McLUSKY
NOW WHAT ABOUT THE MACHINE, THE SPEKTOR?
THERE WAS NO DOUBT ABOUT IT— THE GIRL WAS DAMNABLY ATTRACTIVE. BUT—
IT WAS AS IF I HAD HIT HER. HER VOICE WENT COLD
SO THAT'S WHAT YOU WANT— ALL YOU WANT?
DON'T YOU SEE, I HAVE A JOB TO DO? AND I'VE GOT TO ARRANGE OUR JOURNEY
VERY WELL. BUT WE MUST GO THIS EVENING
545

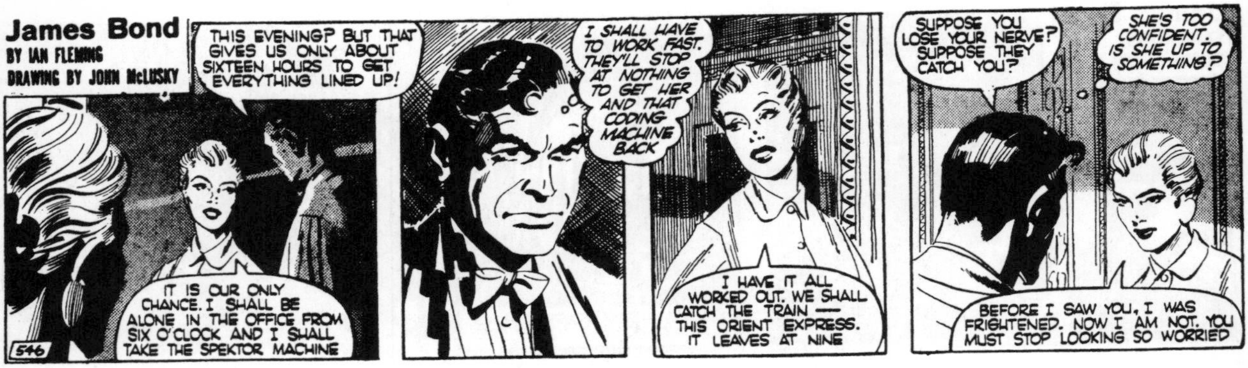
James Bond
BY IAN FLEMING
DRAWING BY JOHN McLUSKY
THIS EVENING? BUT THAT GIVES US ONLY ABOUT SIXTEEN HOURS TO GET EVERYTHING LINED UP!
IT IS OUR ONLY CHANCE. I SHALL BE ALONE IN THE OFFICE FROM SIX O'CLOCK AND I SHALL TAKE THE SPEKTOR MACHINE
546
I SHALL HAVE TO WORK FAST. THEY'LL STOP AT NOTHING TO GET HER AND THAT CODING MACHINE BACK
I HAVE IT ALL WORKED OUT. WE SHALL CATCH THE TRAIN — THIS ORIENT EXPRESS. IT LEAVES AT NINE
SUPPOSE YOU LOSE YOUR NERVE? SUPPOSE THEY CATCH YOU?
SHE'S TOO CONFIDENT. IS SHE UP TO SOMETHING?
BEFORE I SAW YOU, I WAS FRIGHTENED. NOW I AM NOT. YOU MUST STOP LOOKING SO WORRIED

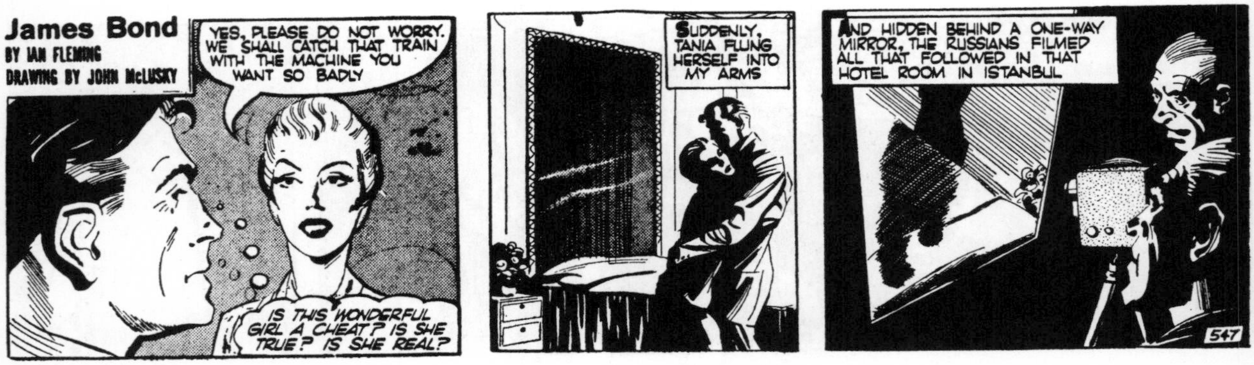
James Bond
BY IAN FLEMING
DRAWING BY JOHN McLUSKY
YES, PLEASE DO NOT WORRY. WE SHALL CATCH THAT TRAIN WITH THE MACHINE YOU WANT SO BADLY
IS THIS WONDERFUL GIRL A CHEAT? IS SHE TRUE? IS SHE REAL?
SUDDENLY, TANIA FLUNG HERSELF INTO MY ARMS
AND HIDDEN BEHIND A ONE-WAY MIRROR, THE RUSSIANS FILMED ALL THAT FOLLOWED IN THAT HOTEL ROOM IN ISTANBUL
547

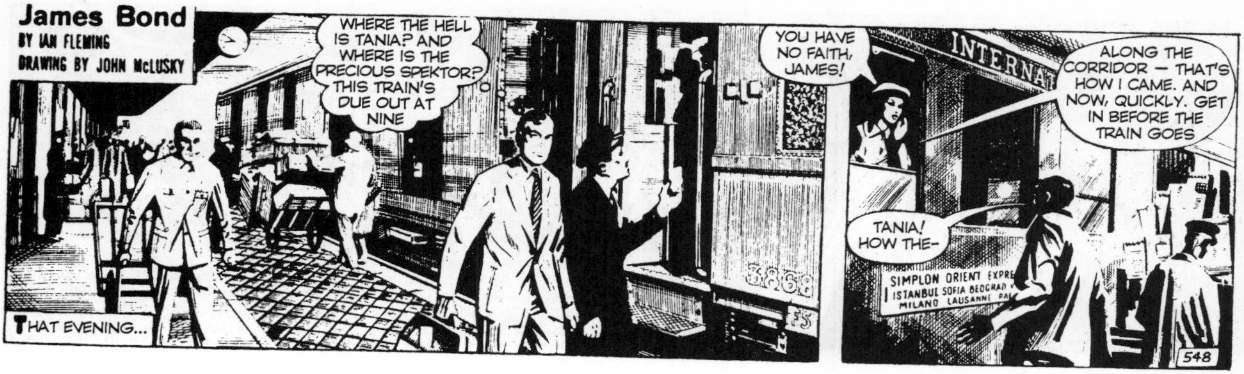
James Bond
BY IAN FLEMING
DRAWING BY JOHN McLUSKY
THAT EVENING...
WHERE THE HELL IS TANIA? AND WHERE IS THE PRECIOUS SPEKTOR? THIS TRAIN'S DUE OUT AT NINE
YOU HAVE NO FAITH, JAMES!
TANIA! HOW THE-
ALONG THE CORRIDOR — THAT'S HOW I CAME. AND NOW, QUICKLY. GET IN BEFORE THE TRAIN GOES
SIMPLON ORIENT EXPRE
ISTANBUL SOFIA BEOGRAD
MILANO LAUSANNE
548

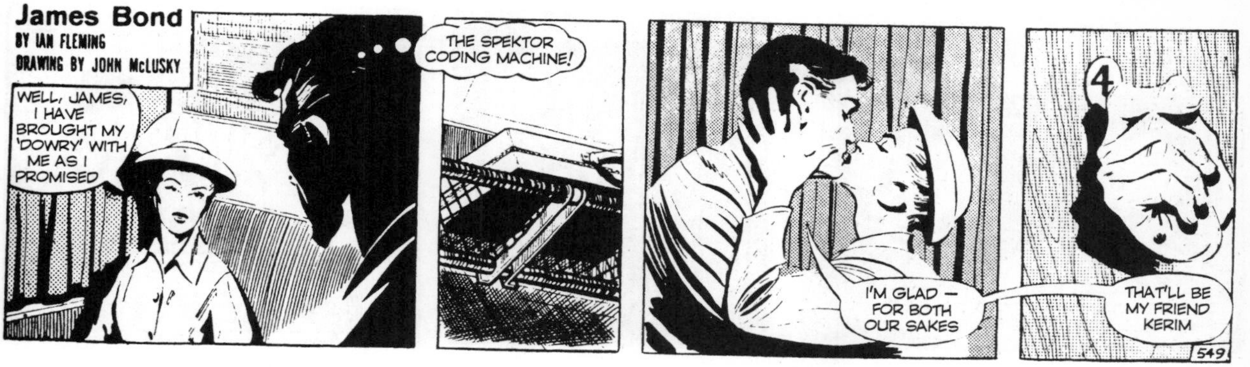
James Bond
BY IAN FLEMING
DRAWING BY JOHN McLUSKY
WELL, JAMES, I HAVE BROUGHT MY 'DOWRY' WITH ME AS I PROMISED
THE SPEKTOR CODING MACHINE!
I'M GLAD — FOR BOTH OUR SAKES
THAT'LL BE MY FRIEND KERIM
549

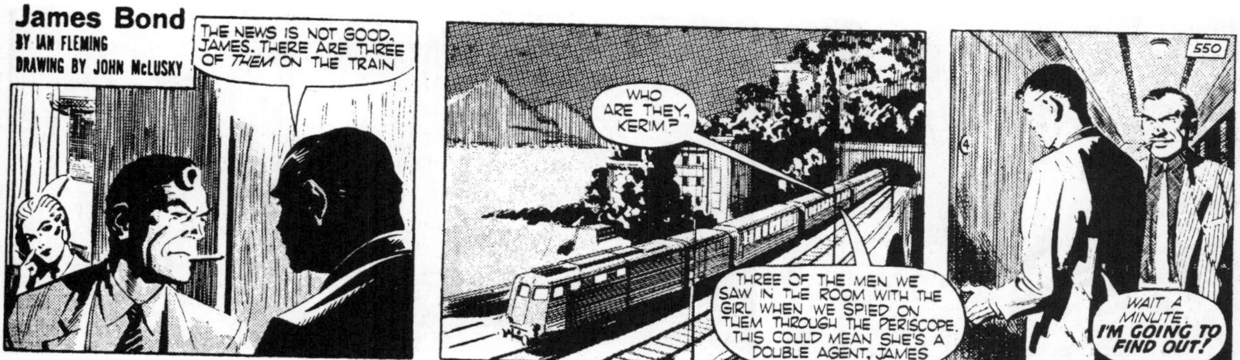
James Bond
BY IAN FLEMING
DRAWING BY JOHN McLUSKY
THE NEWS IS NOT GOOD, JAMES. THERE ARE THREE OF THEM ON THE TRAIN
WHO ARE THEY, KERIM?
THREE OF THE MEN WE SAW IN THE ROOM WITH THE GIRL WHEN WE SPIED ON THEM THROUGH THE PERISCOPE. THIS COULD MEAN SHE'S A DOUBLE AGENT, JAMES
WAIT A MINUTE. I'M GOING TO FIND OUT!
550

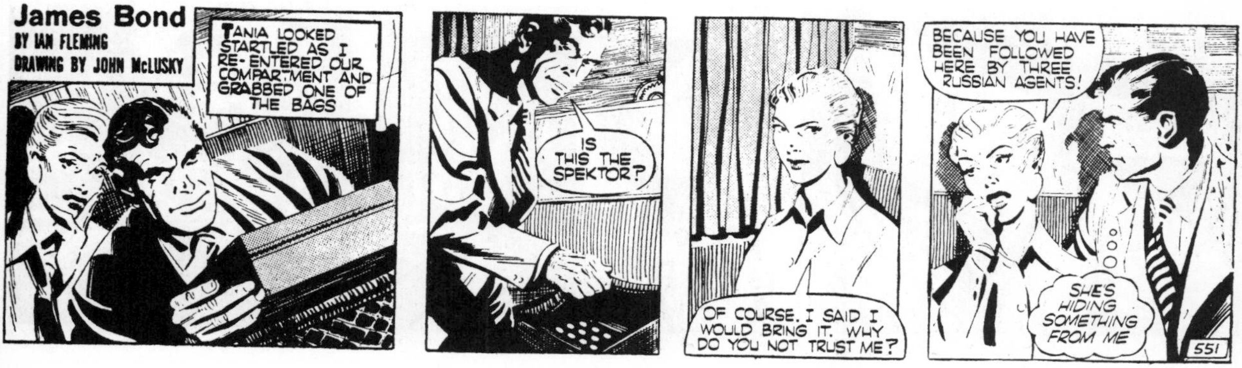
James Bond
BY IAN FLEMING
DRAWING BY JOHN McLUSKY
TANIA LOOKED STARTLED AS I RE-ENTERED OUR COMPARTMENT AND GRABBED ONE OF THE BAGS
IS THIS THE SPEKTOR?
OF COURSE. I SAID I WOULD BRING IT. WHY DO YOU NOT TRUST ME?
BECAUSE YOU HAVE BEEN FOLLOWED HERE BY THREE RUSSIAN AGENTS!
SHE'S HIDING SOMETHING FROM ME
551

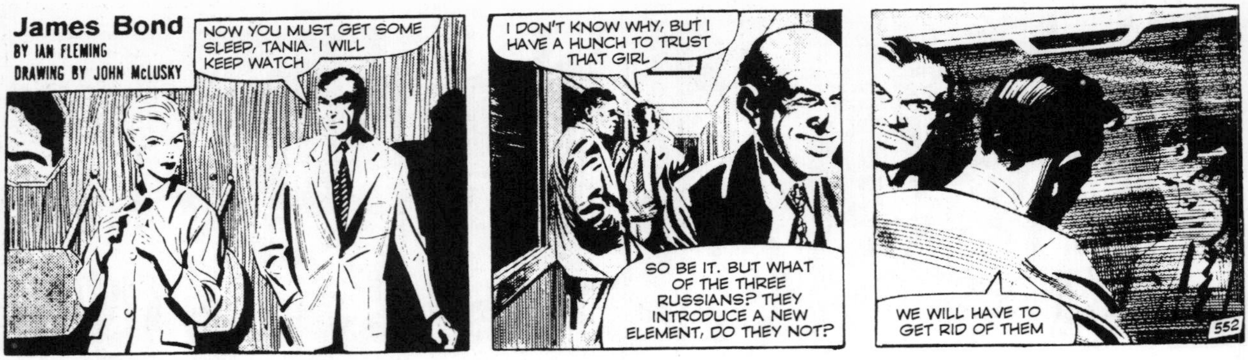
James Bond
BY IAN FLEMING
DRAWING BY JOHN McLUSKY
NOW YOU MUST GET SOME SLEEP, TANIA. I WILL KEEP WATCH
I DON'T KNOW WHY, BUT I HAVE A HUNCH TO TRUST THAT GIRL
SO BE IT. BUT WHAT OF THE THREE RUSSIANS? THEY INTRODUCE A NEW ELEMENT, DO THEY NOT?
WE WILL HAVE TO GET RID OF THEM
552

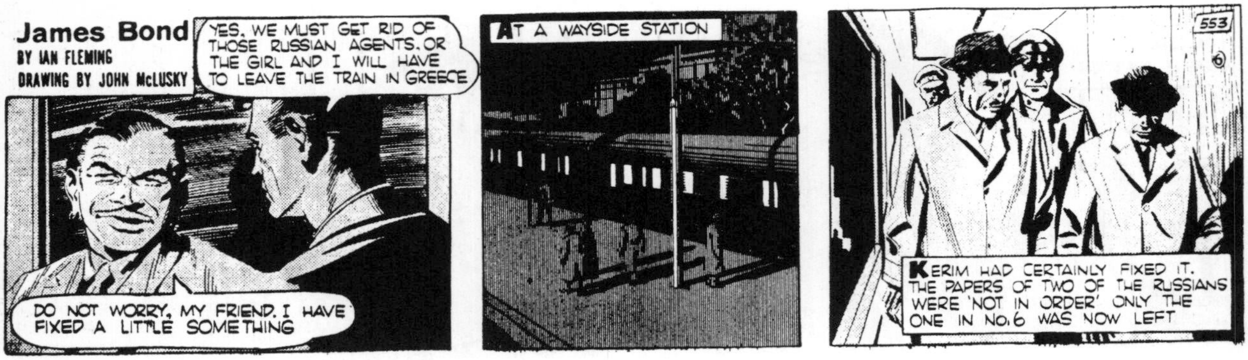
James Bond
BY IAN FLEMING
DRAWING BY JOHN McLUSKY
YES, WE MUST GET RID OF THOSE RUSSIAN AGENTS, OR THE GIRL AND I WILL HAVE TO LEAVE THE TRAIN IN GREECE
DO NOT WORRY, MY FRIEND. I HAVE FIXED A LITTLE SOMETHING
AT A WAYSIDE STATION
553
KERIM HAD CERTAINLY FIXED IT. THE PAPERS OF TWO OF THE RUSSIANS WERE 'NOT IN ORDER' ONLY THE ONE IN No. 6 WAS NOW LEFT

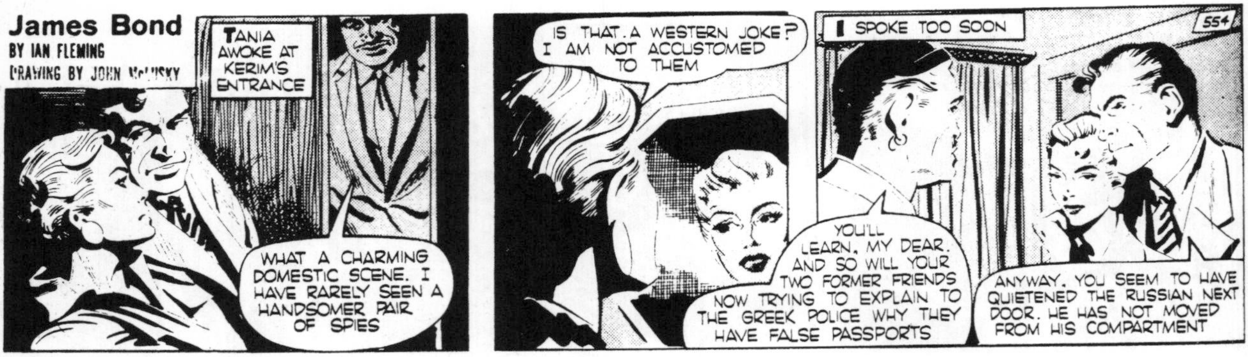
James Bond
BY IAN FLEMING
DRAWING BY JOHN McLUSKY
TANIA AWOKE AT KERIM'S ENTRANCE
WHAT A CHARMING DOMESTIC SCENE. I HAVE RARELY SEEN A HANDSOMER PAIR OF SPIES
IS THAT A WESTERN JOKE? I AM NOT ACCUSTOMED TO THEM
YOU'LL LEARN, MY DEAR. AND SO WILL YOUR TWO FORMER FRIENDS NOW TRYING TO EXPLAIN TO THE GREEK POLICE WHY THEY HAVE FALSE PASSPORTS
I SPOKE TOO SOON
554
ANYWAY, YOU SEEM TO HAVE QUIETENED THE RUSSIAN NEXT DOOR. HE HAS NOT MOVED FROM HIS COMPARTMENT

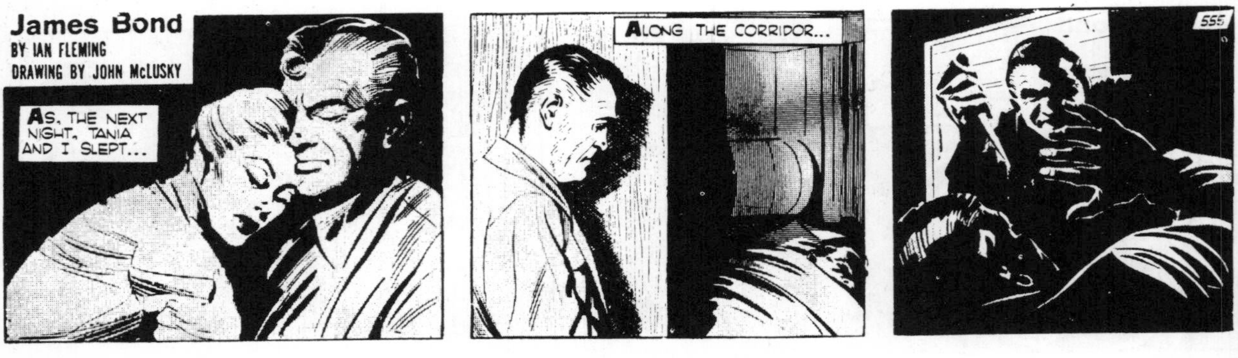
James Bond
BY IAN FLEMING
DRAWING BY JOHN McLUSKY
AS, THE NEXT NIGHT, TANIA AND I SLEPT...
ALONG THE CORRIDOR...
555

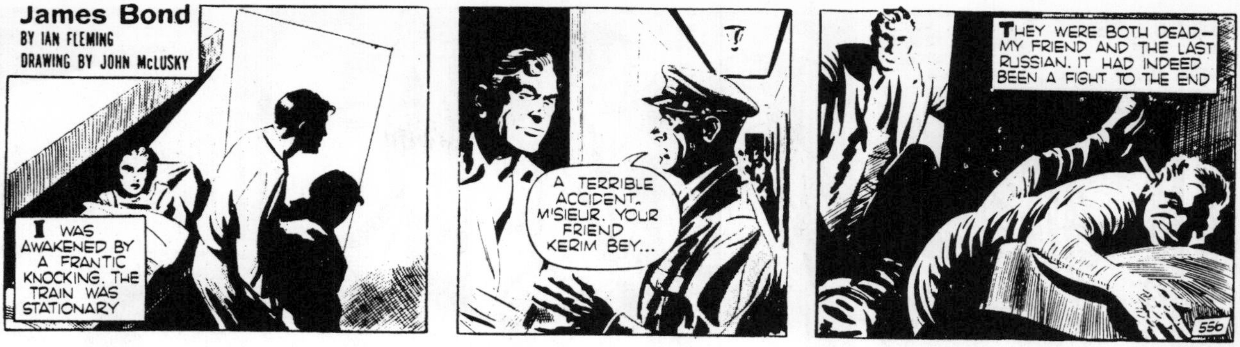
James Bond
BY IAN FLEMING
DRAWING BY JOHN McLUSKY
I WAS AWAKENED BY A FRANTIC KNOCKING. THE TRAIN WAS STATIONARY
A TERRIBLE ACCIDENT, M'SIEUR. YOUR FRIEND KERIM BEY...
THEY WERE BOTH DEAD—MY FRIEND AND THE LAST RUSSIAN. IT HAD INDEED BEEN A FIGHT TO THE END
556

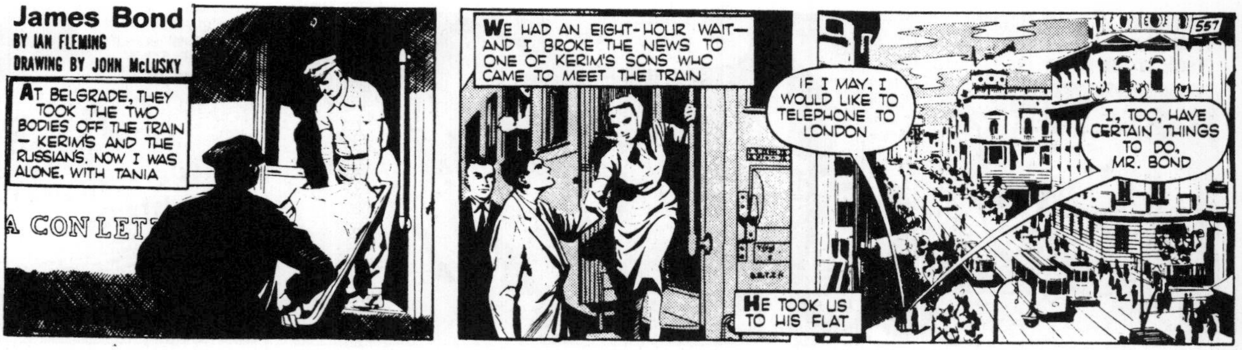
James Bond
BY IAN FLEMING
DRAWING BY JOHN McLUSKY
AT BELGRADE, THEY TOOK THE TWO BODIES OFF THE TRAIN – KERIM'S AND THE RUSSIAN'S. NOW I WAS ALONE, WITH TANIA
A CON LETT
WE HAD AN EIGHT-HOUR WAIT–AND I BROKE THE NEWS TO ONE OF KERIM'S SONS WHO CAME TO MEET THE TRAIN
HE TOOK US TO HIS FLAT
557
IF I MAY, I WOULD LIKE TO TELEPHONE TO LONDON
I, TOO, HAVE CERTAIN THINGS TO DO, MR. BOND

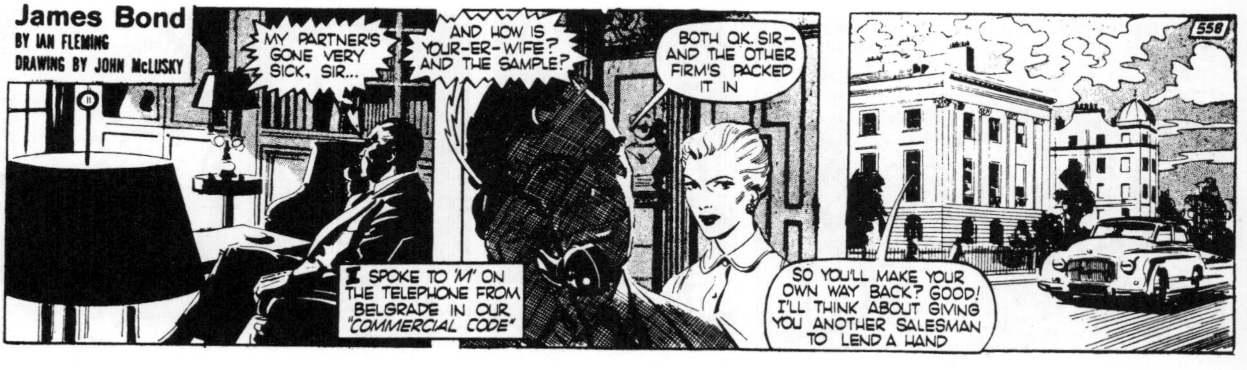
James Bond
BY IAN FLEMING
DRAWING BY JOHN McLUSKY
MY PARTNER'S GONE VERY SICK, SIR...
AND HOW IS YOUR-ER-WIFE? AND THE SAMPLE?
BOTH O.K. SIR–AND THE OTHER FIRM'S PACKED IT IN
I SPOKE TO 'M' ON THE TELEPHONE FROM BELGRADE IN OUR "COMMERCIAL CODE"
558
SO YOU'LL MAKE YOUR OWN WAY BACK? GOOD! I'LL THINK ABOUT GIVING YOU ANOTHER SALESMAN TO LEND A HAND

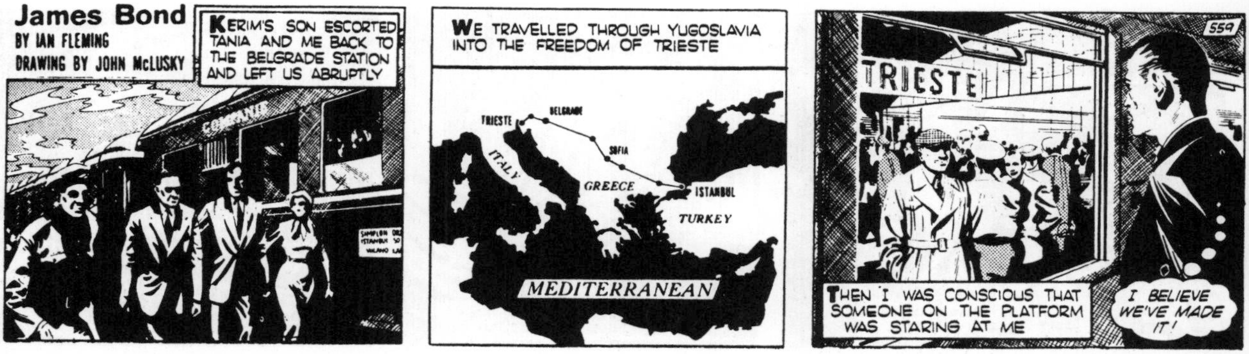
James Bond
BY IAN FLEMING
DRAWING BY JOHN McLUSKY
KERIM'S SON ESCORTED TANIA AND ME BACK TO THE BELGRADE STATION AND LEFT US ABRUPTLY
WE TRAVELLED THROUGH YUGOSLAVIA INTO THE FREEDOM OF TRIESTE
TRIESTE
BELGRADE
SOFIA
ITALY
GREECE
ISTANBUL
TURKEY
MEDITERRANEAN
559
TRIESTE
THEN I WAS CONSCIOUS THAT SOMEONE ON THE PLATFORM WAS STARING AT ME
I BELIEVE WE'VE MADE IT!

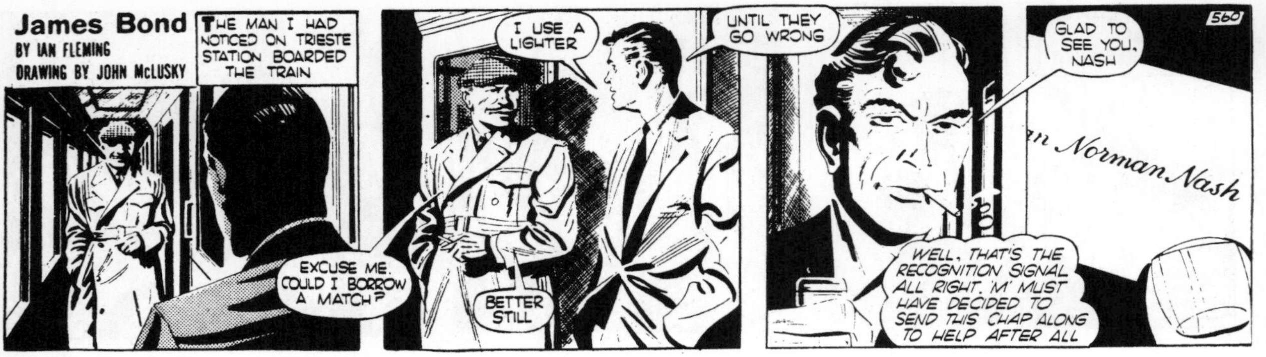
James Bond
BY IAN FLEMING
DRAWING BY JOHN McLUSKY
THE MAN I HAD NOTICED ON TRIESTE STATION BOARDED THE TRAIN
EXCUSE ME. COULD I BORROW A MATCH?
I USE A LIGHTER
UNTIL THEY GO WRONG
BETTER STILL
560
GLAD TO SEE YOU, NASH
n Norman Nash
WELL, THAT'S THE RECOGNITION SIGNAL ALL RIGHT. 'M' MUST HAVE DECIDED TO SEND THIS CHAP ALONG TO HELP AFTER ALL

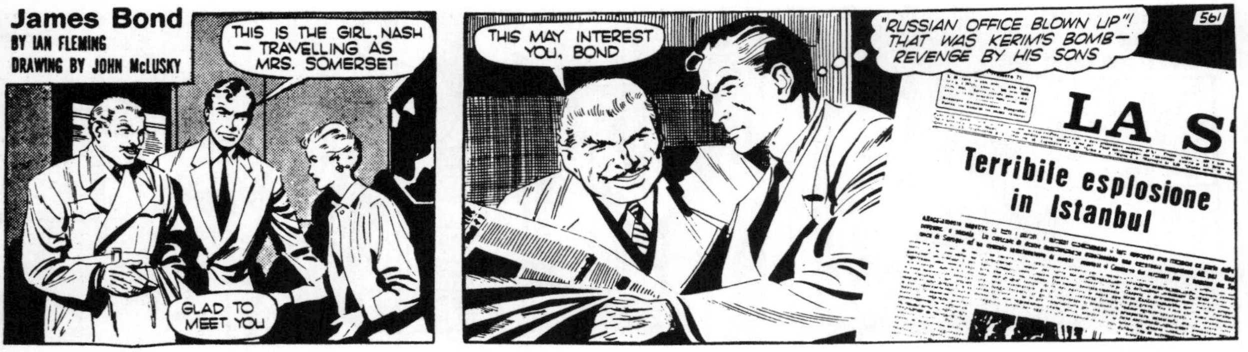
James Bond
BY IAN FLEMING
DRAWING BY JOHN McLUSKY
THIS IS THE GIRL, NASH — TRAVELLING AS MRS. SOMERSET
GLAD TO MEET YOU
THIS MAY INTEREST YOU, BOND
561
"RUSSIAN OFFICE BLOWN UP"! THAT WAS KERIM'S BOMB—REVENGE BY HIS SONS
LA S
Terribile esplosione in Istanbul

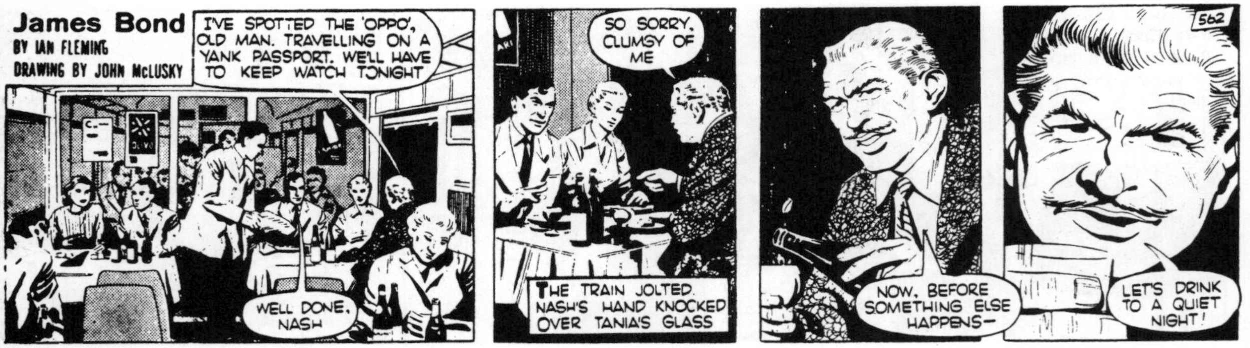
James Bond
BY IAN FLEMING
DRAWING BY JOHN McLUSKY
I'VE SPOTTED THE 'OPPO', OLD MAN. TRAVELLING ON A YANK PASSPORT. WE'LL HAVE TO KEEP WATCH TONIGHT
WELL DONE, NASH
SO SORRY, CLUMSY OF ME
THE TRAIN JOLTED. NASH'S HAND KNOCKED OVER TANIA'S GLASS
NOW, BEFORE SOMETHING ELSE HAPPENS—
562
LET'S DRINK TO A QUIET NIGHT!

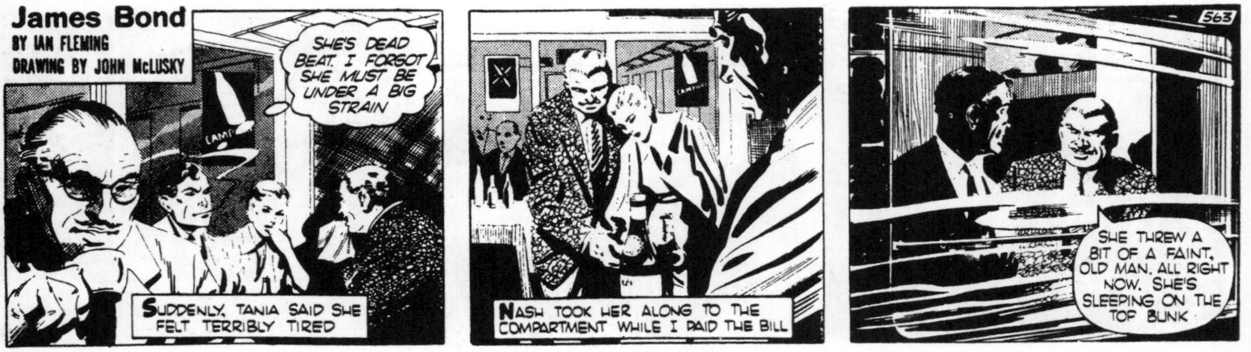
James Bond
BY IAN FLEMING
DRAWING BY JOHN McLUSKY
SHE'S DEAD BEAT. I FORGOT SHE MUST BE UNDER A BIG STRAIN
SUDDENLY, TANIA SAID SHE FELT TERRIBLY TIRED
NASH TOOK HER ALONG TO THE COMPARTMENT WHILE I PAID THE BILL
563
SHE THREW A BIT OF A FAINT, OLD MAN. ALL RIGHT NOW. SHE'S SLEEPING ON THE TOP BUNK

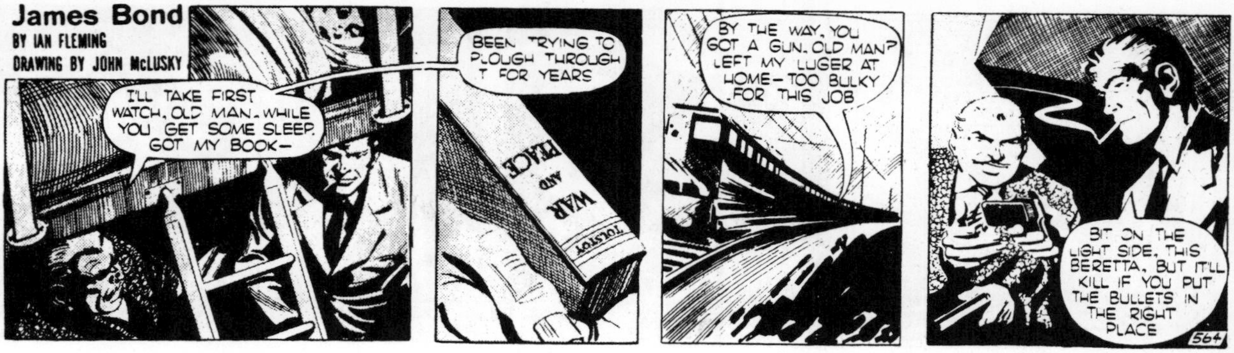
James Bond
BY IAN FLEMING
DRAWING BY JOHN McLUSKY
I'LL TAKE FIRST WATCH, OLD MAN - WHILE YOU GET SOME SLEEP. GOT MY BOOK-
BEEN TRYING TO PLOUGH THROUGH IT FOR YEARS
WAR AND PEACE
TOLSTOY
BY THE WAY, YOU GOT A GUN, OLD MAN? LEFT MY LUGER AT HOME - TOO BULKY FOR THIS JOB
BIT ON THE LIGHT SIDE, THIS BERETTA, BUT IT'LL KILL IF YOU PUT THE BULLETS IN THE RIGHT PLACE
564

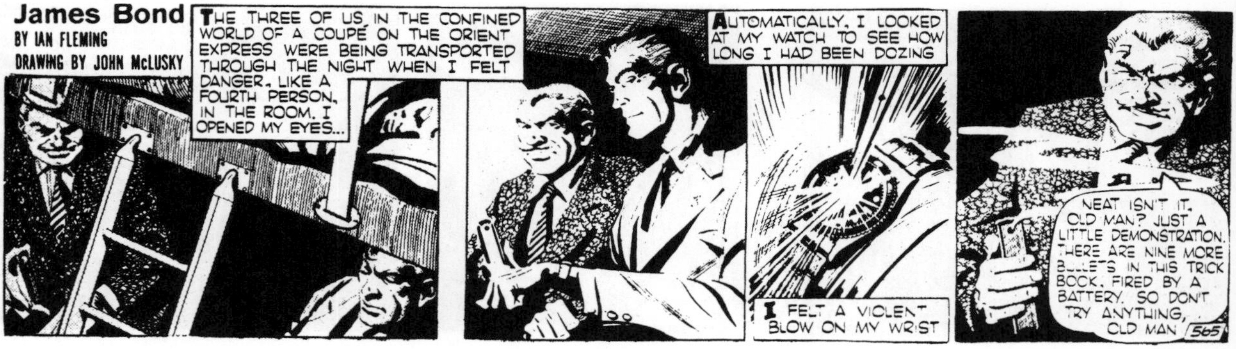
James Bond
BY IAN FLEMING
DRAWING BY JOHN McLUSKY
THE THREE OF US IN THE CONFINED WORLD OF A COUPÉ ON THE ORIENT EXPRESS WERE BEING TRANSPORTED THROUGH THE NIGHT WHEN I FELT DANGER. LIKE A FOURTH PERSON, IN THE ROOM. I OPENED MY EYES...
AUTOMATICALLY, I LOOKED AT MY WATCH TO SEE HOW LONG I HAD BEEN DOZING
I FELT A VIOLENT BLOW ON MY WRIST
NEAT ISN'T IT, OLD MAN? JUST A LITTLE DEMONSTRATION. THERE ARE NINE MORE BULLETS IN THIS TRICK BOOK, FIRED BY A BATTERY. SO DON'T TRY ANYTHING, OLD MAN
565

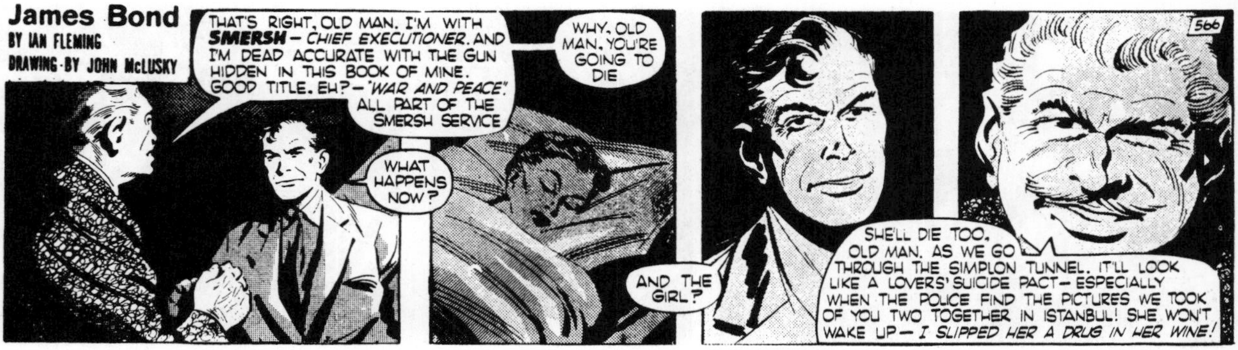
James Bond
BY IAN FLEMING
DRAWING BY JOHN McLUSKY
THAT'S RIGHT, OLD MAN. I'M WITH SMERSH - CHIEF EXECUTIONER. AND I'M DEAD ACCURATE WITH THE GUN HIDDEN IN THIS BOOK OF MINE. GOOD TITLE, EH? - "WAR AND PEACE". ALL PART OF THE SMERSH SERVICE
WHY, OLD MAN, YOU'RE GOING TO DIE
WHAT HAPPENS NOW?
566
AND THE GIRL?
SHE'LL DIE TOO, OLD MAN, AS WE GO THROUGH THE SIMPLON TUNNEL. IT'LL LOOK LIKE A LOVERS' SUICIDE PACT - ESPECIALLY WHEN THE POLICE FIND THE PICTURES WE TOOK OF YOU TWO TOGETHER IN ISTANBUL! SHE WON'T WAKE UP - I SLIPPED HER A DRUG IN HER WINE!

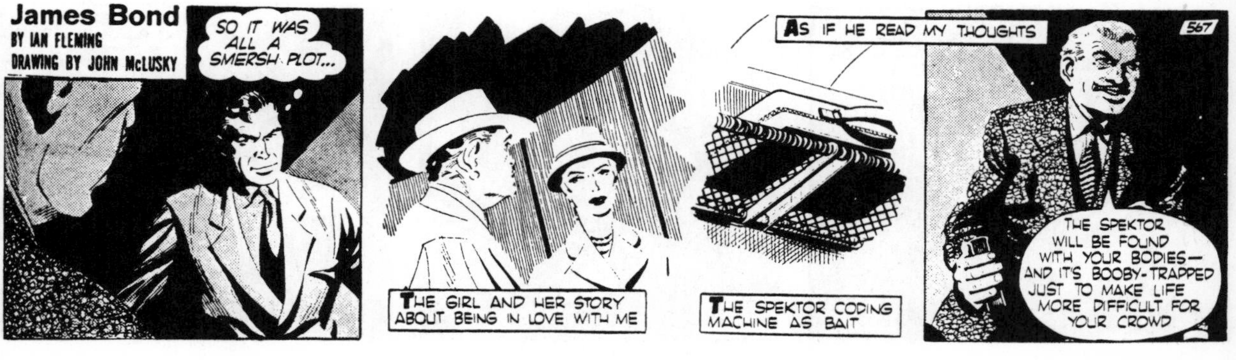
James Bond
BY IAN FLEMING
DRAWING BY JOHN McLUSKY
SO IT WAS ALL A SMERSH PLOT...
THE GIRL AND HER STORY ABOUT BEING IN LOVE WITH ME
THE SPEKTOR CODING MACHINE AS BAIT
AS IF HE READ MY THOUGHTS
567
THE SPEKTOR WILL BE FOUND WITH YOUR BODIES - AND IT'S BOOBY-TRAPPED JUST TO MAKE LIFE MORE DIFFICULT FOR YOUR CROWD

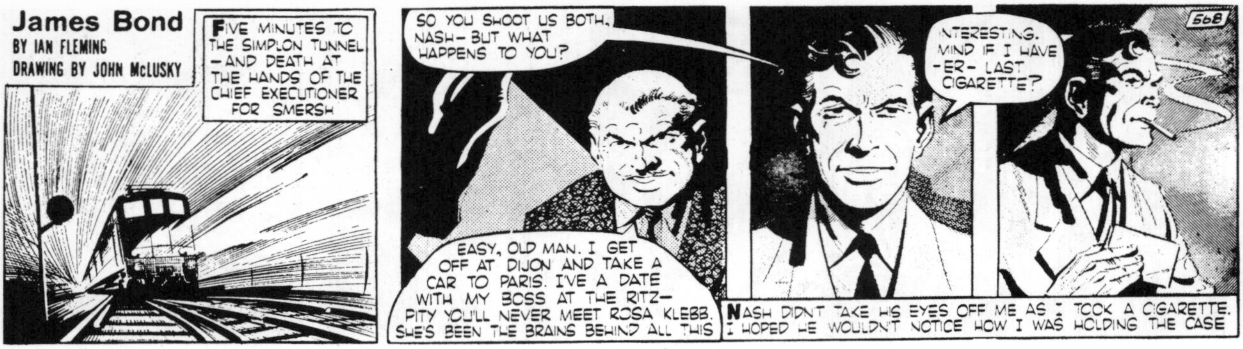
James Bond
BY IAN FLEMING
DRAWING BY JOHN McLUSKY
FIVE MINUTES TO THE SIMPLON TUNNEL —AND DEATH AT THE HANDS OF THE CHIEF EXECUTIONER FOR SMERSH
SO YOU SHOOT US BOTH, NASH— BUT WHAT HAPPENS TO YOU?
EASY, OLD MAN. I GET OFF AT DIJON AND TAKE A CAR TO PARIS. I'VE A DATE WITH MY BOSS AT THE RITZ— PITY YOU'LL NEVER MEET ROSA KLEBB. SHE'S BEEN THE BRAINS BEHIND ALL THIS
INTERESTING. MIND IF I HAVE —ER— LAST CIGARETTE?
568
NASH DIDN'T TAKE HIS EYES OFF ME AS I TOOK A CIGARETTE. I HOPED HE WOULDN'T NOTICE HOW I WAS HOLDING THE CASE

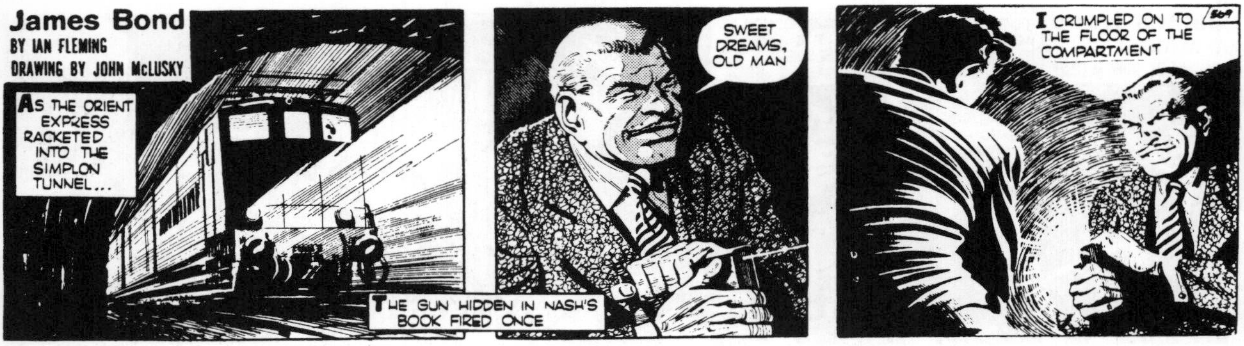
James Bond
BY IAN FLEMING
DRAWING BY JOHN McLUSKY
AS THE ORIENT EXPRESS RACKETED INTO THE SIMPLON TUNNEL...
SWEET DREAMS, OLD MAN
THE GUN HIDDEN IN NASH'S BOOK FIRED ONCE
I CRUMPLED ON TO THE FLOOR OF THE COMPARTMENT
569

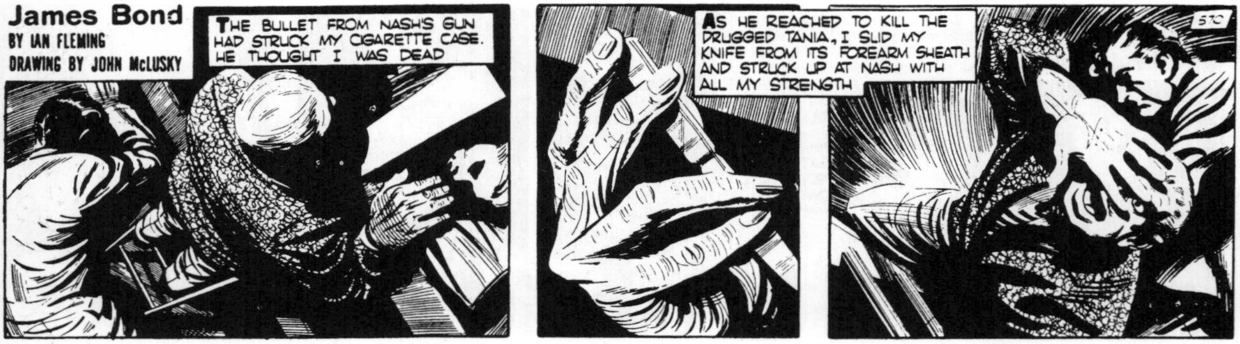
James Bond
BY IAN FLEMING
DRAWING BY JOHN McLUSKY
THE BULLET FROM NASH'S GUN HAD STRUCK MY CIGARETTE CASE. HE THOUGHT I WAS DEAD
AS HE REACHED TO KILL THE DRUGGED TANIA, I SLID MY KNIFE FROM ITS FOREARM SHEATH AND STRUCK UP AT NASH WITH ALL MY STRENGTH
570

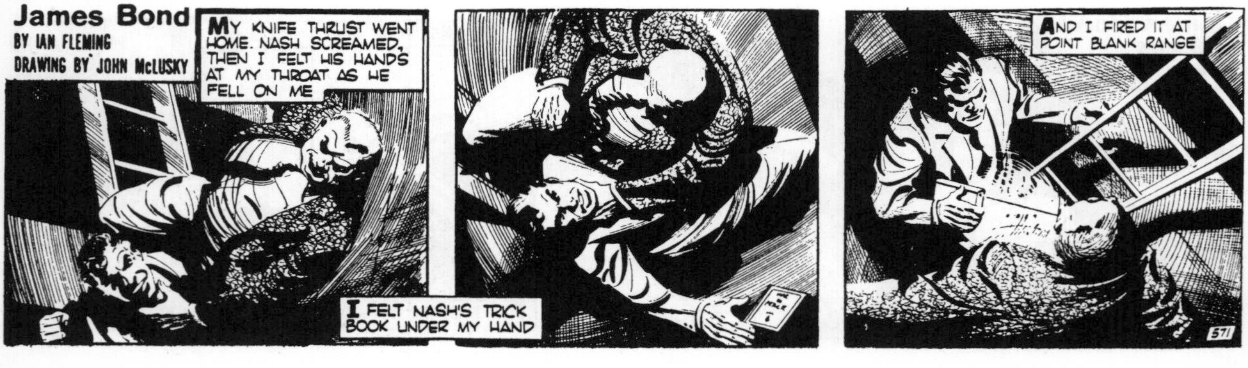
James Bond
BY IAN FLEMING
DRAWING BY JOHN McLUSKY
MY KNIFE THRUST WENT HOME. NASH SCREAMED, THEN I FELT HIS HANDS AT MY THROAT AS HE FELL ON ME
I FELT NASH'S TRICK BOOK UNDER MY HAND
AND I FIRED IT AT POINT BLANK RANGE
571

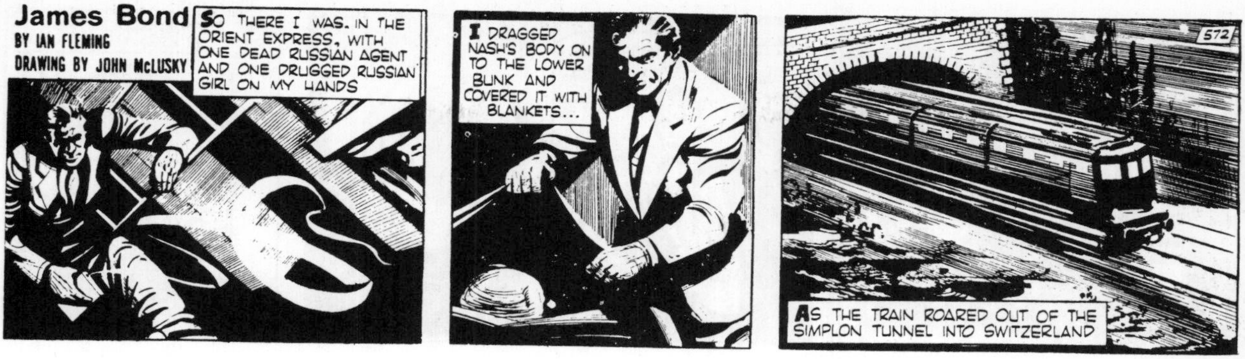
James Bond
BY IAN FLEMING
DRAWING BY JOHN McLUSKY
SO THERE I WAS, IN THE ORIENT EXPRESS, WITH ONE DEAD RUSSIAN AGENT AND ONE DRUGGED RUSSIAN GIRL ON MY HANDS
I DRAGGED NASH'S BODY ON TO THE LOWER BUNK AND COVERED IT WITH BLANKETS...
572
AS THE TRAIN ROARED OUT OF THE SIMPLON TUNNEL INTO SWITZERLAND

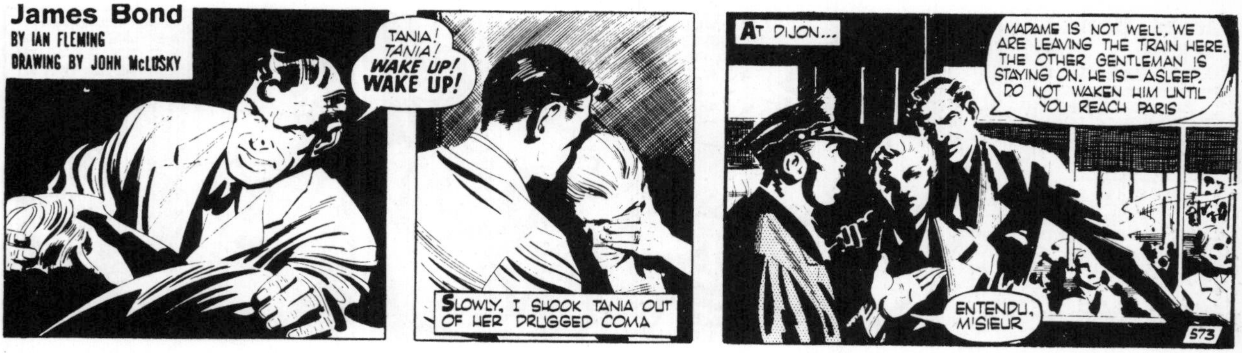
James Bond
BY IAN FLEMING
DRAWING BY JOHN McLUSKY
TANIA! TANIA! WAKE UP! WAKE UP!
SLOWLY, I SHOOK TANIA OUT OF HER DRUGGED COMA
AT DIJON...
MADAME IS NOT WELL. WE ARE LEAVING THE TRAIN HERE. THE OTHER GENTLEMAN IS STAYING ON. HE IS— ASLEEP. DO NOT WAKEN HIM UNTIL YOU REACH PARIS
ENTENDU, M'SIEUR
573

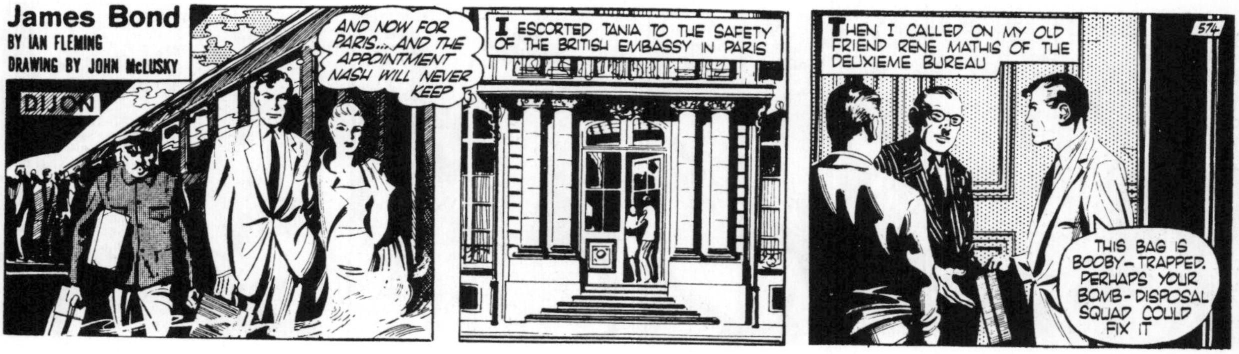
James Bond
BY IAN FLEMING
DRAWING BY JOHN McLUSKY
DIJON
AND NOW FOR PARIS... AND THE APPOINTMENT NASH WILL NEVER KEEP
I ESCORTED TANIA TO THE SAFETY OF THE BRITISH EMBASSY IN PARIS
574
THEN I CALLED ON MY OLD FRIEND RENE MATHIS OF THE DEUXIEME BUREAU
THIS BAG IS BOOBY-TRAPPED. PERHAPS YOUR BOMB-DISPOSAL SQUAD COULD FIX IT

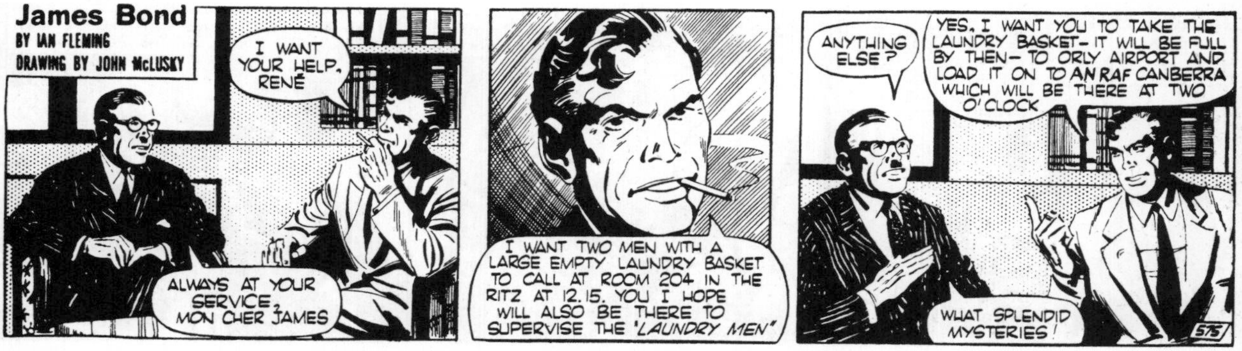
James Bond
BY IAN FLEMING
DRAWING BY JOHN McLUSKY
I WANT YOUR HELP, RENÉ
ALWAYS AT YOUR SERVICE, MON CHER JAMES
I WANT TWO MEN WITH A LARGE EMPTY LAUNDRY BASKET TO CALL AT ROOM 204 IN THE RITZ AT 12.15. YOU I HOPE WILL ALSO BE THERE TO SUPERVISE THE 'LAUNDRY MEN'
ANYTHING ELSE?
YES, I WANT YOU TO TAKE THE LAUNDRY BASKET— IT WILL BE FULL BY THEN— TO ORLY AIRPORT AND LOAD IT ON TO AN RAF CANBERRA WHICH WILL BE THERE AT TWO O'CLOCK
WHAT SPLENDID MYSTERIES!
575

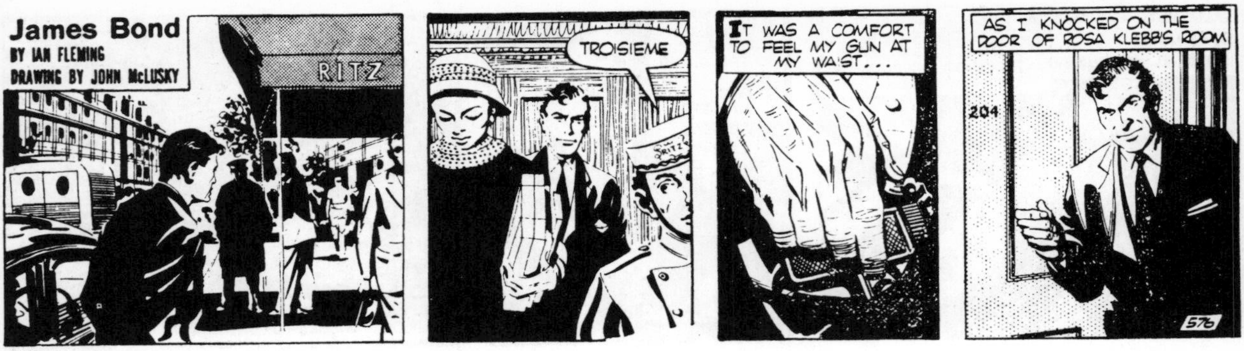
James Bond
BY IAN FLEMING
DRAWING BY JOHN McLUSKY
RITZ
TROISIEME
IT WAS A COMFORT TO FEEL MY GUN AT MY WAIST...
AS I KNOCKED ON THE DOOR OF ROSA KLEBB'S ROOM
204
576

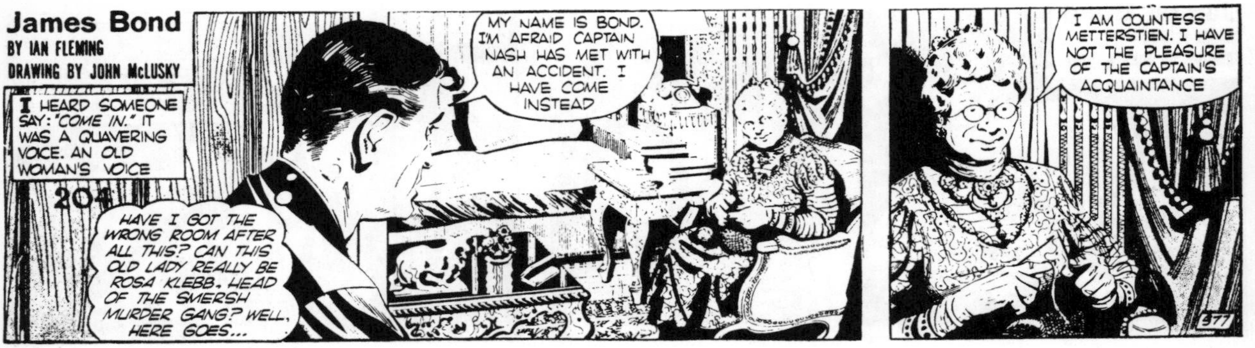
James Bond
BY IAN FLEMING
DRAWING BY JOHN McLUSKY
I HEARD SOMEONE SAY: "COME IN." IT WAS A QUAVERING VOICE. AN OLD WOMAN'S VOICE
204
HAVE I GOT THE WRONG ROOM AFTER ALL THIS? CAN THIS OLD LADY REALLY BE ROSA KLEBB. HEAD OF THE SMERSH MURDER GANG? WELL. HERE GOES...
MY NAME IS BOND. I'M AFRAID CAPTAIN NASH HAS MET WITH AN ACCIDENT. I HAVE COME INSTEAD
I AM COUNTESS METTERSTIEN. I HAVE NOT THE PLEASURE OF THE CAPTAIN'S ACQUAINTANCE
577

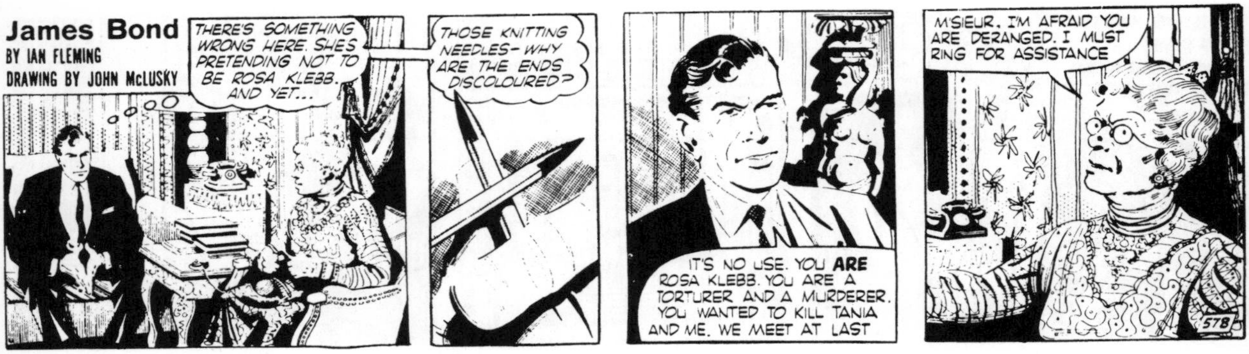
James Bond
BY IAN FLEMING
DRAWING BY JOHN McLUSKY
THERE'S SOMETHING WRONG HERE. SHES PRETENDING NOT TO BE ROSA KLEBB. AND YET...
THOSE KNITTING NEEDLES– WHY ARE THE ENDS DISCOLOURED?
IT'S NO USE. YOU ARE ROSA KLEBB. YOU ARE A TORTURER AND A MURDERER. YOU WANTED TO KILL TANIA AND ME. WE MEET AT LAST
M'SIEUR. I'M AFRAID YOU ARE DERANGED. I MUST RING FOR ASSISTANCE
578

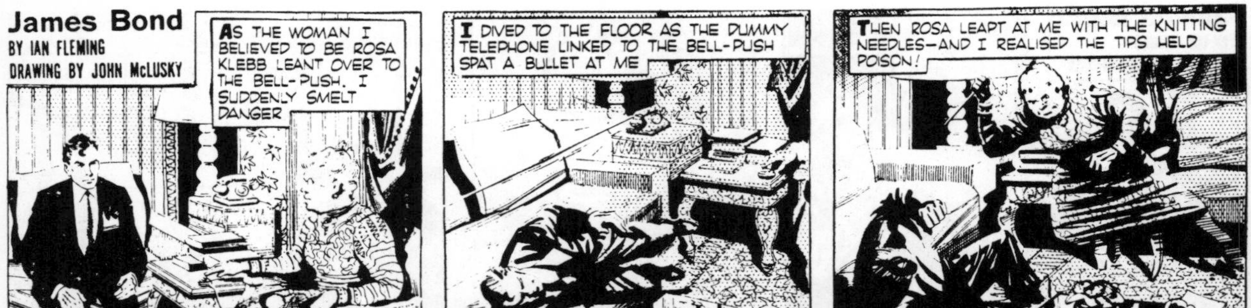
James Bond
BY IAN FLEMING
DRAWING BY JOHN McLUSKY
AS THE WOMAN I BELIEVED TO BE ROSA KLEBB LEANT OVER TO THE BELL-PUSH. I SUDDENLY SMELT DANGER
I DIVED TO THE FLOOR AS THE DUMMY TELEPHONE LINKED TO THE BELL-PUSH SPAT A BULLET AT ME
THEN ROSA LEAPT AT ME WITH THE KNITTING NEEDLES—AND I REALISED THE TIPS HELD POISON!
579

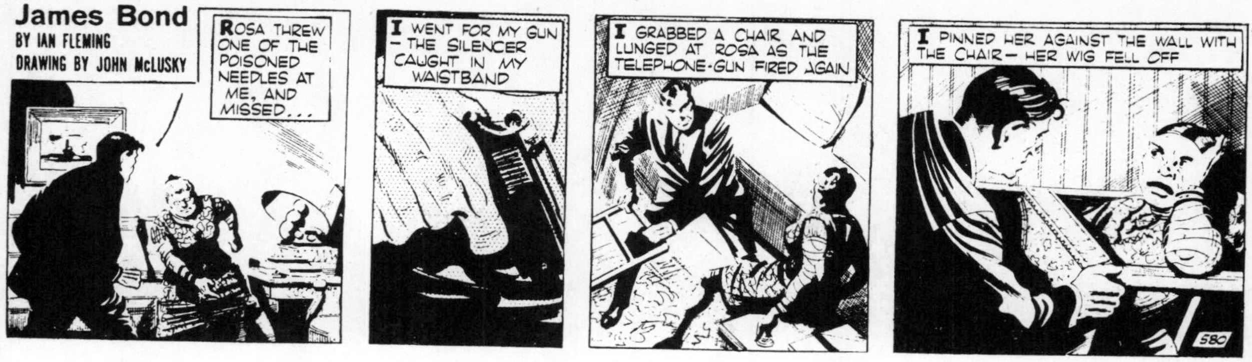
James Bond
BY IAN FLEMING
DRAWING BY JOHN McLUSKY
ROSA THREW ONE OF THE POISONED NEEDLES AT ME, AND MISSED...
I WENT FOR MY GUN – THE SILENCER CAUGHT IN MY WAISTBAND
I GRABBED A CHAIR AND LUNGED AT ROSA AS THE TELEPHONE-GUN FIRED AGAIN
I PINNED HER AGAINST THE WALL WITH THE CHAIR – HER WIG FELL OFF
580

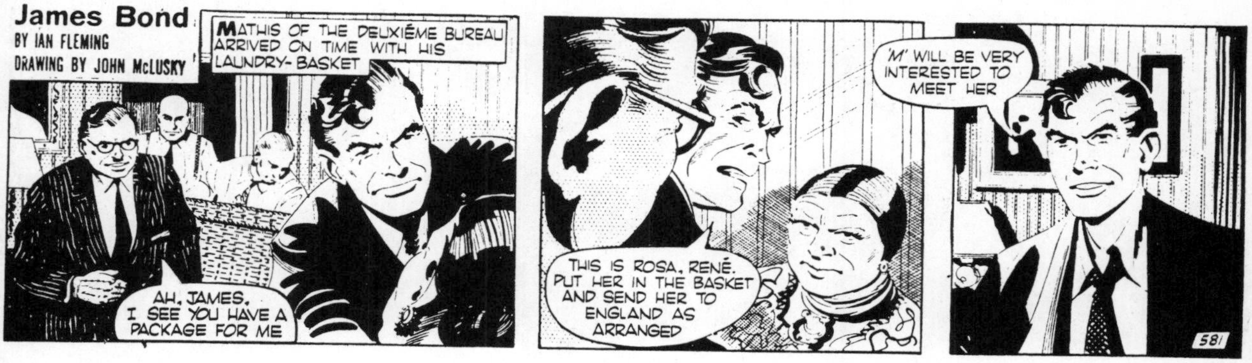
James Bond
BY IAN FLEMING
DRAWING BY JOHN McLUSKY
MATHIS OF THE DEUXIÉME BUREAU ARRIVED ON TIME WITH HIS LAUNDRY-BASKET
AH, JAMES. I SEE YOU HAVE A PACKAGE FOR ME
THIS IS ROSA, RENÉ. PUT HER IN THE BASKET AND SEND HER TO ENGLAND AS ARRANGED
'M' WILL BE VERY INTERESTED TO MEET HER
581

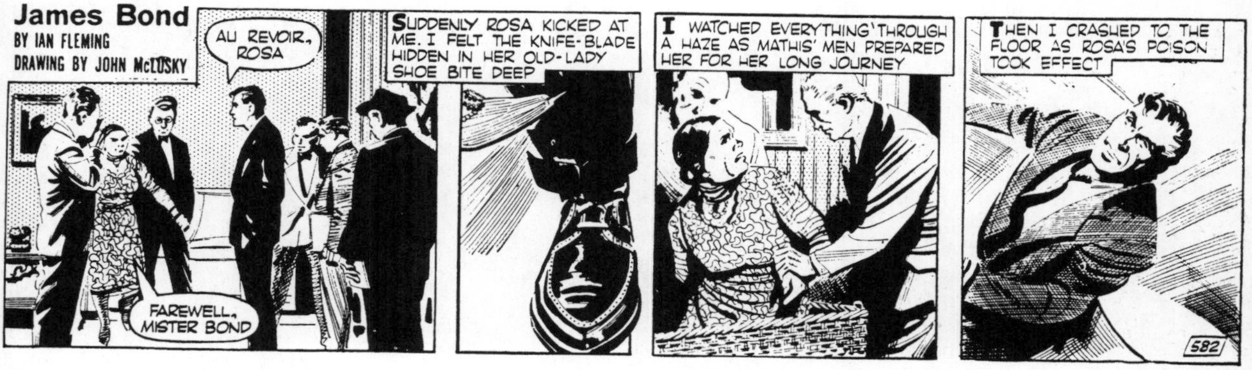
James Bond
BY IAN FLEMING
DRAWING BY JOHN McLUSKY
AU REVOIR, ROSA
FAREWELL, MISTER BOND
SUDDENLY ROSA KICKED AT ME. I FELT THE KNIFE-BLADE HIDDEN IN HER OLD-LADY SHOE BITE DEEP
I WATCHED EVERYTHING THROUGH A HAZE AS MATHIS' MEN PREPARED HER FOR HER LONG JOURNEY
THEN I CRASHED TO THE FLOOR AS ROSA'S POISON TOOK EFFECT
582

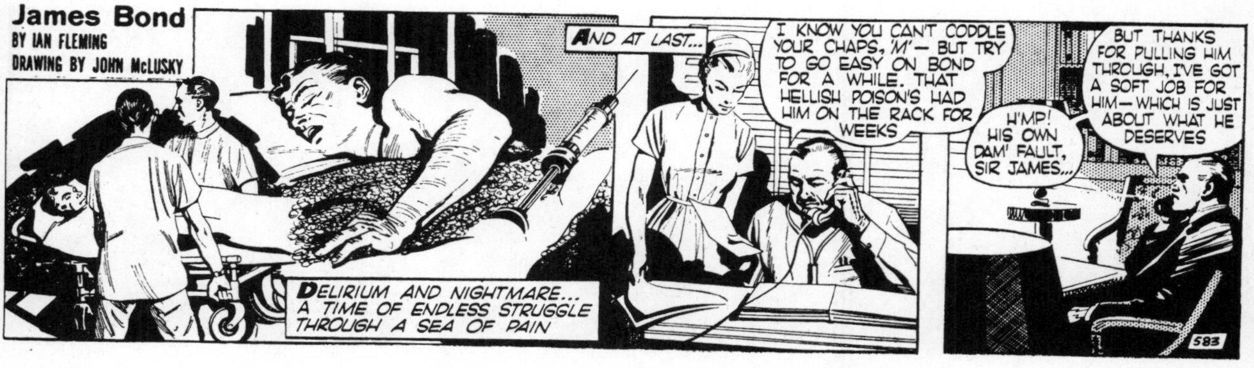
James Bond
BY IAN FLEMING
DRAWING BY JOHN McLUSKY
DELIRIUM AND NIGHTMARE... A TIME OF ENDLESS STRUGGLE THROUGH A SEA OF PAIN
AND AT LAST...
I KNOW YOU CAN'T CODDLE YOUR CHAPS, 'M' – BUT TRY TO GO EASY ON BOND FOR A WHILE. THAT HELLISH POISON'S HAD HIM ON THE RACK FOR WEEKS
H'MP! HIS OWN DAM' FAULT, SIR JAMES...
BUT THANKS FOR PULLING HIM THROUGH, I'VE GOT A SOFT JOB FOR HIM – WHICH IS JUST ABOUT WHAT HE DESERVES
583

DR NO

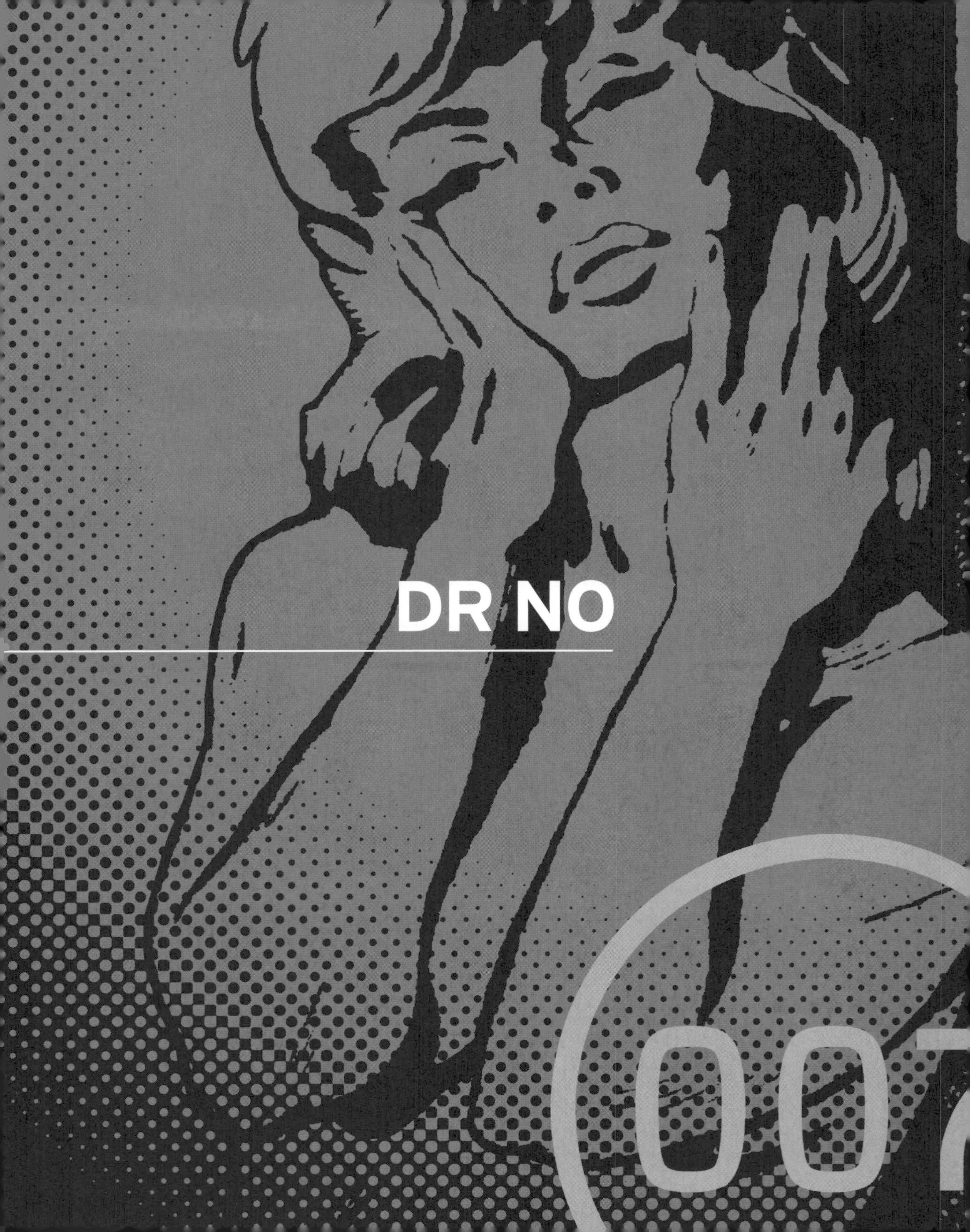

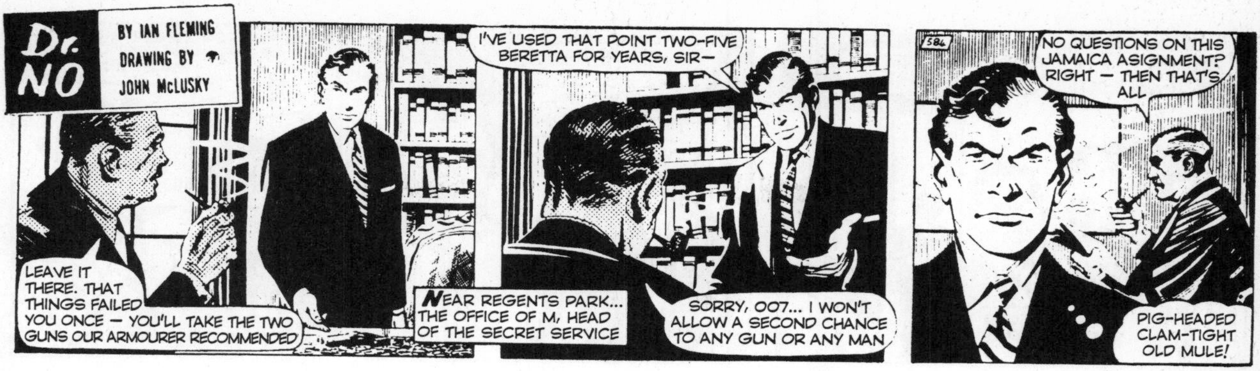
Dr. NO
BY IAN FLEMING
DRAWING BY JOHN McLUSKY
LEAVE IT THERE. THAT THINGS FAILED YOU ONCE — YOU'LL TAKE THE TWO GUNS OUR ARMOURER RECOMMENDED
NEAR REGENTS PARK... THE OFFICE OF M, HEAD OF THE SECRET SERVICE
I'VE USED THAT POINT TWO-FIVE BERETTA FOR YEARS, SIR—
SORRY, 007... I WON'T ALLOW A SECOND CHANCE TO ANY GUN OR ANY MAN
584
NO QUESTIONS ON THIS JAMAICA ASIGNMENT? RIGHT — THEN THAT'S ALL
PIG-HEADED CLAM-TIGHT OLD MULE!

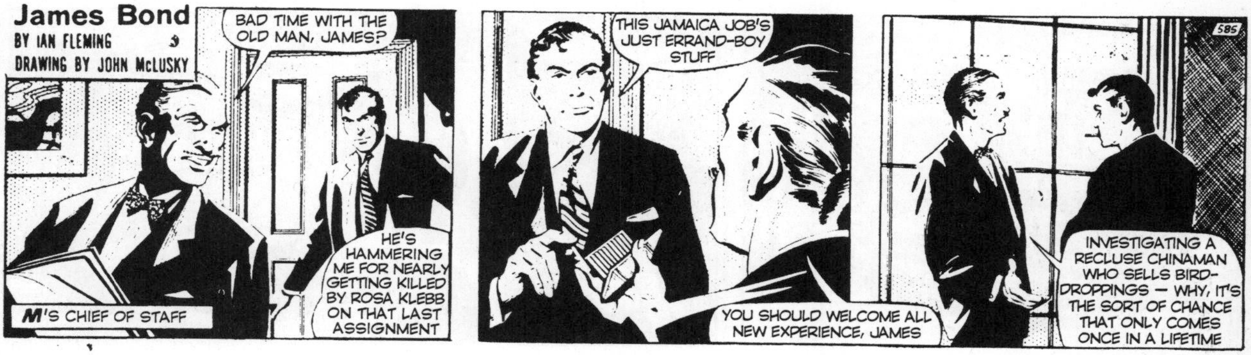
James Bond
BY IAN FLEMING
DRAWING BY JOHN McLUSKY
BAD TIME WITH THE OLD MAN, JAMES?
HE'S HAMMERING ME FOR NEARLY GETTING KILLED BY ROSA KLEBB ON THAT LAST ASSIGNMENT
M'S CHIEF OF STAFF
THIS JAMAICA JOB'S JUST ERRAND-BOY STUFF
YOU SHOULD WELCOME ALL NEW EXPERIENCE, JAMES
585
INVESTIGATING A RECLUSE CHINAMAN WHO SELLS BIRD-DROPPINGS — WHY, IT'S THE SORT OF CHANCE THAT ONLY COMES ONCE IN A LIFETIME

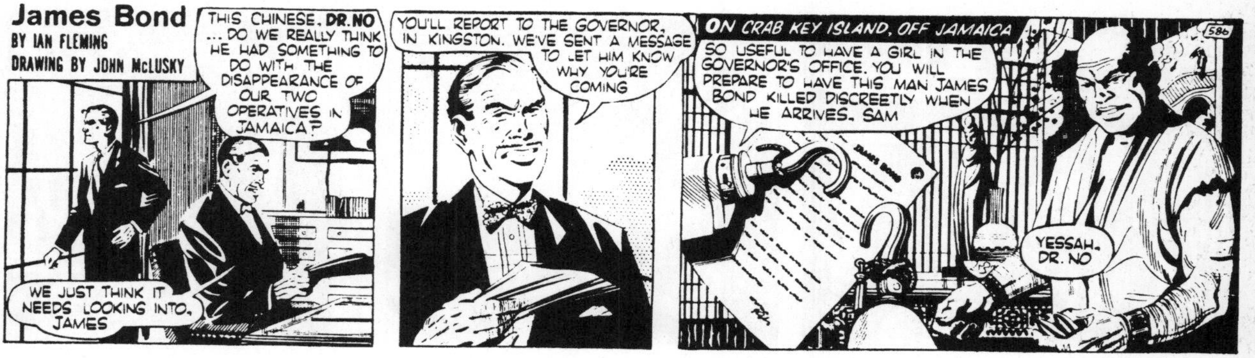
James Bond
BY IAN FLEMING
DRAWING BY JOHN McLUSKY
THIS CHINESE, DR. NO ... DO WE REALLY THINK HE HAD SOMETHING TO DO WITH THE DISAPPEARANCE OF OUR TWO OPERATIVES IN JAMAICA?
WE JUST THINK IT NEEDS LOOKING INTO, JAMES
YOU'LL REPORT TO THE GOVERNOR, IN KINGSTON. WE'VE SENT A MESSAGE TO LET HIM KNOW WHY YOU'RE COMING
ON CRAB KEY ISLAND, OFF JAMAICA
586
SO USEFUL TO HAVE A GIRL IN THE GOVERNOR'S OFFICE. YOU WILL PREPARE TO HAVE THIS MAN JAMES BOND KILLED DISCREETLY WHEN HE ARRIVES. SAM
YESSAH, DR. NO

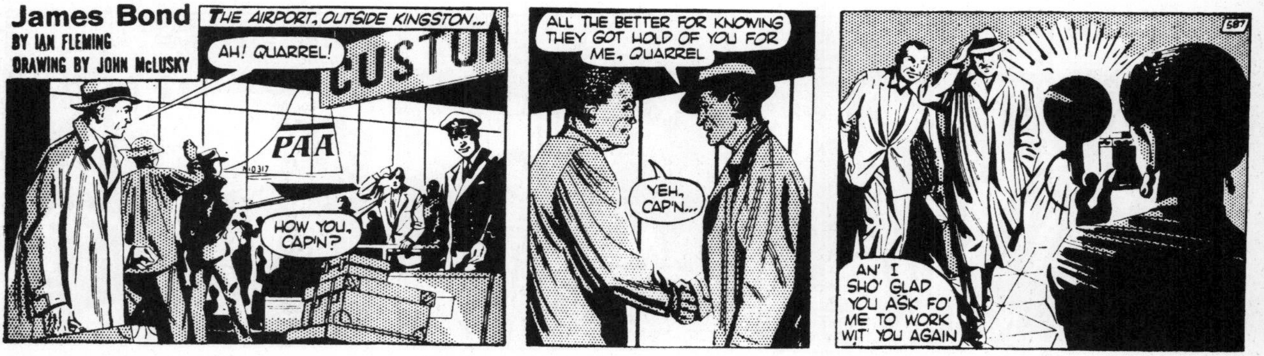
James Bond
BY IAN FLEMING
DRAWING BY JOHN McLUSKY
THE AIRPORT, OUTSIDE KINGSTON...
AH! QUARREL!
CUSTO
PAA
HOW YOU, CAP'N?
ALL THE BETTER FOR KNOWING THEY GOT HOLD OF YOU FOR ME, QUARREL
YEH, CAP'N...
587
AN' I SHO' GLAD YOU ASK FO' ME TO WORK WIT' YOU AGAIN

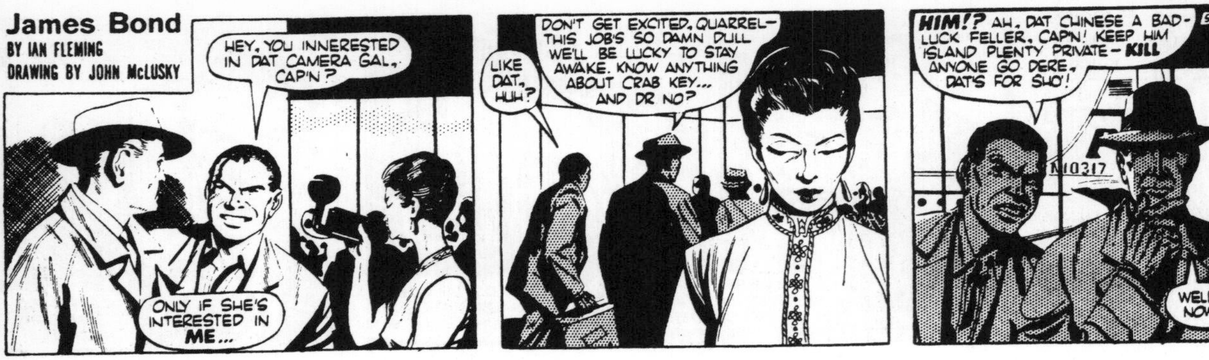
James Bond
BY IAN FLEMING
DRAWING BY JOHN McLUSKY
HEY, YOU INNERESTED IN DAT CAMERA GAL, CAP'N?
ONLY IF SHE'S INTERESTED IN ME...
LIKE DAT, HUH?
DON'T GET EXCITED, QUARREL— THIS JOB'S SO DAMN DULL WE'LL BE LUCKY TO STAY AWAKE. KNOW ANYTHING ABOUT CRAB KEY... AND DR NO?
588
HIM!? AH, DAT CHINESE A BAD-LUCK FELLER, CAP'N! KEEP HIM ISLAND PLENTY PRIVATE— KILL ANYONE GO DERE, DAT'S FOR SHO'!
WELL, NOW...!

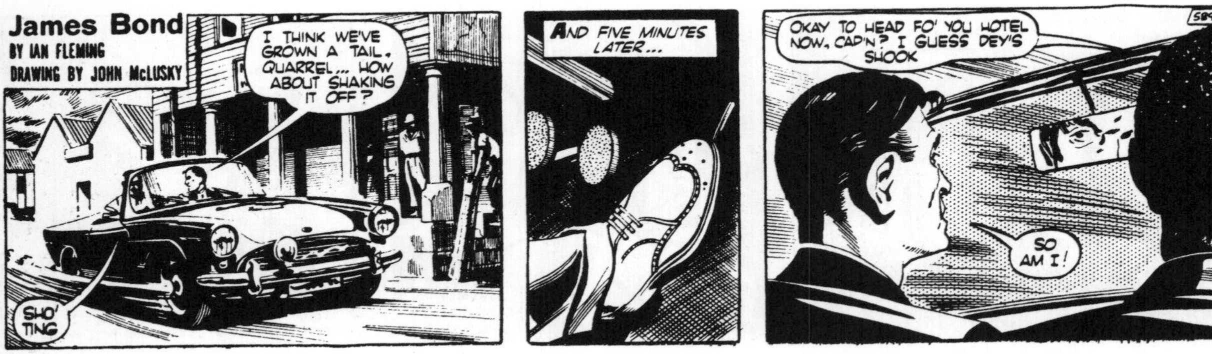
James Bond
BY IAN FLEMING
DRAWING BY JOHN McLUSKY
I THINK WE'VE GROWN A TAIL, QUARREL... HOW ABOUT SHAKING IT OFF?
SHO' TING
AND FIVE MINUTES LATER...
589
OKAY TO HEAD FO' YOU HOTEL NOW, CAP'N? I GUESS DEY'S SHOOK
SO AM I!

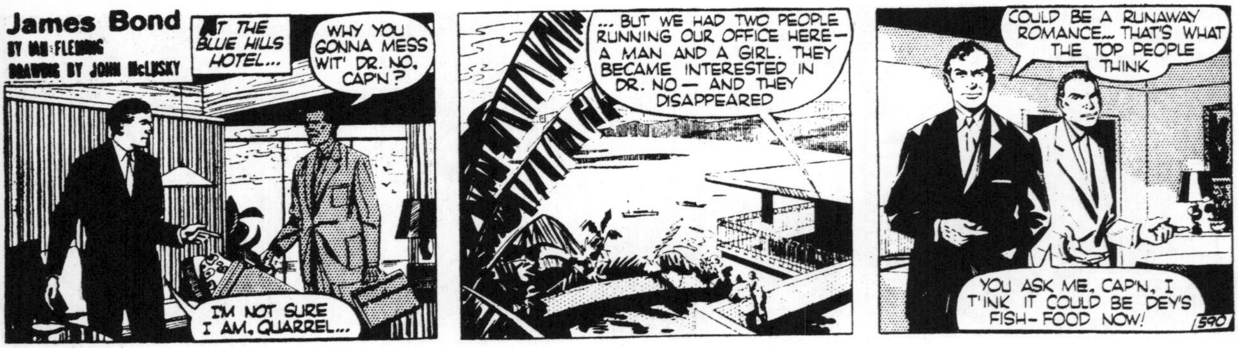
James Bond
BY IAN FLEMING
DRAWING BY JOHN McLUSKY
AT THE BLUE HILLS HOTEL...
WHY YOU GONNA MESS WIT' DR. NO, CAP'N?
I'M NOT SURE I AM, QUARREL...
... BUT WE HAD TWO PEOPLE RUNNING OUR OFFICE HERE— A MAN AND A GIRL. THEY BECAME INTERESTED IN DR. NO— AND THEY DISAPPEARED
COULD BE A RUNAWAY ROMANCE... THAT'S WHAT THE TOP PEOPLE THINK
YOU ASK ME, CAP'N, I T'INK IT COULD BE DEY'S FISH-FOOD NOW!
590

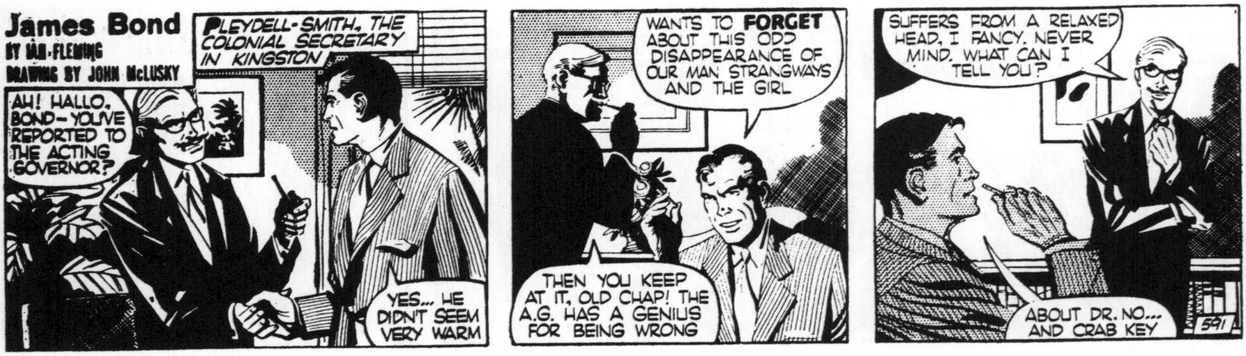
James Bond
BY IAN FLEMING
DRAWING BY JOHN McLUSKY
PLEYDELL-SMITH, THE COLONIAL SECRETARY IN KINGSTON
AH! HALLO, BOND— YOU'VE REPORTED TO THE ACTING GOVERNOR?
YES... HE DIDN'T SEEM VERY WARM
WANTS TO FORGET ABOUT THIS ODD DISAPPEARANCE OF OUR MAN STRANGWAYS AND THE GIRL
THEN YOU KEEP AT IT, OLD CHAP! THE A.G. HAS A GENIUS FOR BEING WRONG
SUFFERS FROM A RELAXED HEAD, I FANCY. NEVER MIND. WHAT CAN I TELL YOU?
ABOUT DR. NO... AND CRAB KEY
591

James Bond
BY IAN FLEMING
DRAWING BY JOHN McCLUSKY

CRAB KEY IS WHAT THEY CALL GUANERA — AN ISLAND WHERE UMPTEEN THOUSAND SEA-BIRDS, OF THE SPECIES GUANAY, DROP THEIR STUFF EVERY DAY

WHY?

EH? OH, YOU MEAN WHY ON THE ISLAND? CAN'T IMAGINE, OLD CHAP...

THROUGH NO FAULT OF MY OWN, I'M NOT A BIRD. BUT THEY'VE BEEN DOING JUST THAT SINCE ADAM — AND GUANO'S THE FINEST FERTILISER IN THE WORLD

592

James Bond
BY IAN FLEMING
DRAWING BY JOHN McCLUSKY

WE SOLD THE ISLAND TO THIS RUM CHINEE YEARS BACK. HE DIGS THE GUANO WITH HIS OWN LABOUR. SPENT A LOT ON INSTALLATIONS, BUT HE MUST BE MAKING A FORTUNE NOW

593

IS IT TRUE HE'S MADE A FORTRESS OF THE PLACE?

COULD BE... BUT SINCE HE *OWNS* IT, HE'S ENTITLED TO KEEP OFF TRESPASSERS

THERE ARE WEIRD RUMOURS, OF COURSE, BUT WE'VE HEARD NO ACTUAL COMPLAINTS ABOUT HIM

WE'VE HEARD NOTHING FROM STRANGWAYS, EITHER. IT'S A FACT OF LIFE THAT PEOPLE WHO DISAPPEAR *CAN'T* COMPLAIN

James Bond
BY IAN FLEMING
DRAWING BY JOHN McCLUSKY

QUARREL? I'VE MADE MY NUMBER WITH THE TOP BRASS. SEE YOU AT THE *JOY BOAT* THIS EVENING — SEVEN O'CLOCK

*A*ND ELSEWHERE...

BASKET OF FRUIT FROM KING'S HOUSE FOR YOU, MR. BOND, SAH

FRUIT...?

594

James Bond
BY IAN FLEMING
DRAWING BY JOHN McCLUSKY

RECEPTION? THIS BASKET OF FRUIT FROM KING'S HOUSE — HOW WAS IT DELIVERED?

BY MESSENGER, SIR — A COLOURED MAN SAID HE WAS FROM THE A.D.C'S OFFICE

THANK YOU...

595

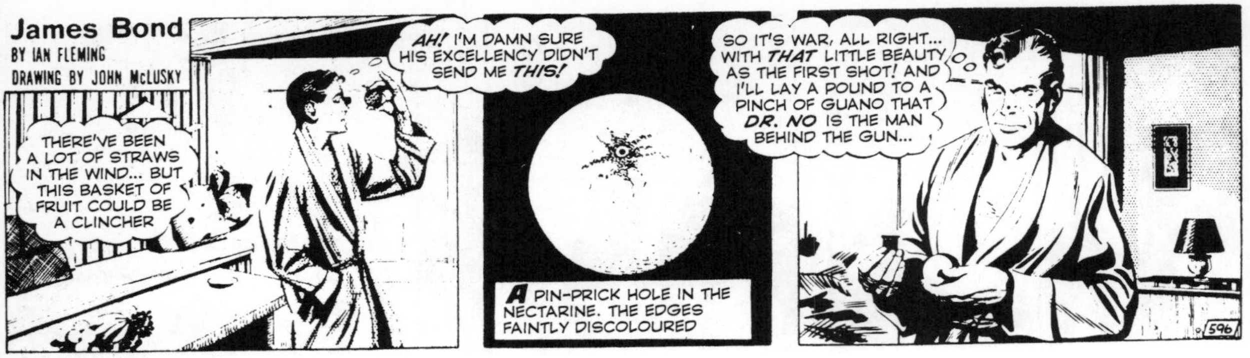
James Bond
BY IAN FLEMING
DRAWING BY JOHN McLUSKY
THERE'VE BEEN A LOT OF STRAWS IN THE WIND... BUT THIS BASKET OF FRUIT COULD BE A CLINCHER
AH! I'M DAMN SURE HIS EXCELLENCY DIDN'T SEND ME THIS!
A PIN-PRICK HOLE IN THE NECTARINE. THE EDGES FAINTLY DISCOLOURED
SO IT'S WAR, ALL RIGHT... WITH THAT LITTLE BEAUTY AS THE FIRST SHOT! AND I'LL LAY A POUND TO A PINCH OF GUANO THAT DR. NO IS THE MAN BEHIND THE GUN...
596

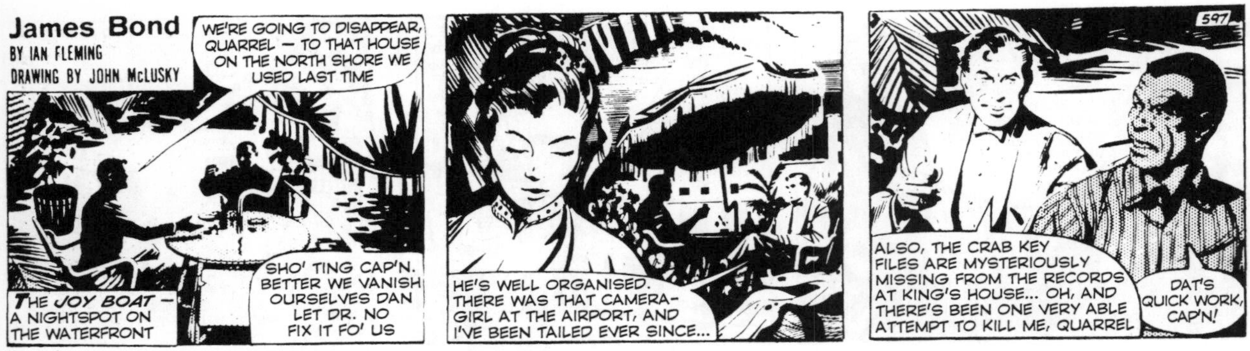
James Bond
BY IAN FLEMING
DRAWING BY JOHN McLUSKY
THE JOY BOAT — A NIGHTSPOT ON THE WATERFRONT
WE'RE GOING TO DISAPPEAR, QUARREL — TO THAT HOUSE ON THE NORTH SHORE WE USED LAST TIME
SHO' TING CAP'N. BETTER WE VANISH OURSELVES DAN LET DR. NO FIX IT FO' US
HE'S WELL ORGANISED. THERE WAS THAT CAMERA-GIRL AT THE AIRPORT, AND I'VE BEEN TAILED EVER SINCE...
597
ALSO, THE CRAB KEY FILES ARE MYSTERIOUSLY MISSING FROM THE RECORDS AT KING'S HOUSE... OH, AND THERE'S BEEN ONE VERY ABLE ATTEMPT TO KILL ME, QUARREL
DAT'S QUICK WORK, CAP'N!

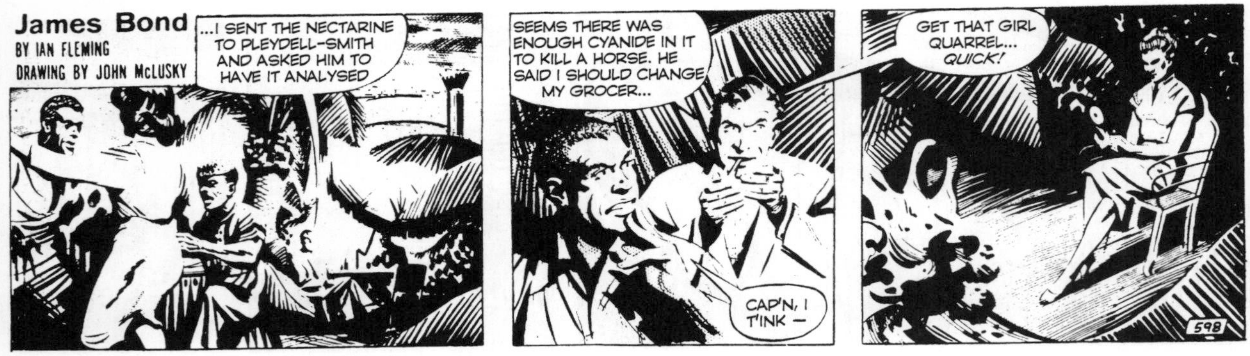
James Bond
BY IAN FLEMING
DRAWING BY JOHN McLUSKY
...I SENT THE NECTARINE TO PLEYDELL-SMITH AND ASKED HIM TO HAVE IT ANALYSED
SEEMS THERE WAS ENOUGH CYANIDE IN IT TO KILL A HORSE. HE SAID I SHOULD CHANGE MY GROCER...
CAP'N, I T'INK —
GET THAT GIRL QUARREL... QUICK!
598

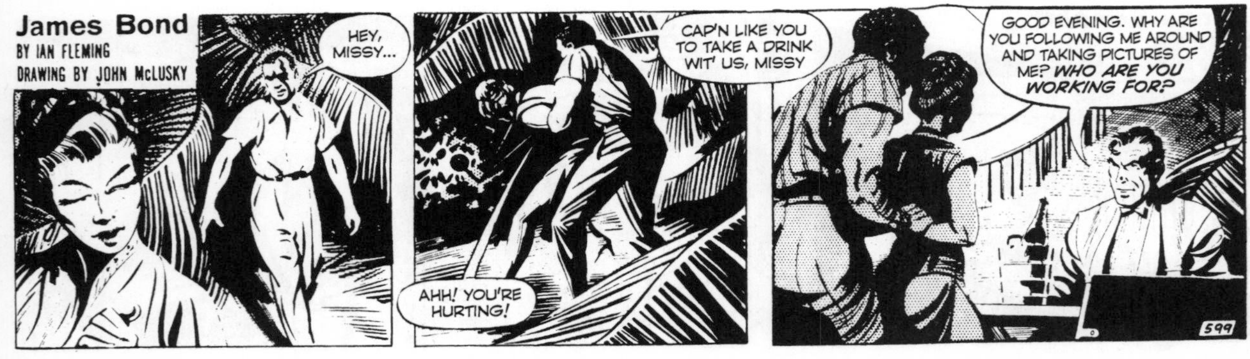
James Bond
BY IAN FLEMING
DRAWING BY JOHN McLUSKY
HEY, MISSY...
CAP'N LIKE YOU TO TAKE A DRINK WIT' US, MISSY
AHH! YOU'RE HURTING!
GOOD EVENING. WHY ARE YOU FOLLOWING ME AROUND AND TAKING PICTURES OF ME? WHO ARE YOU WORKING FOR?
599

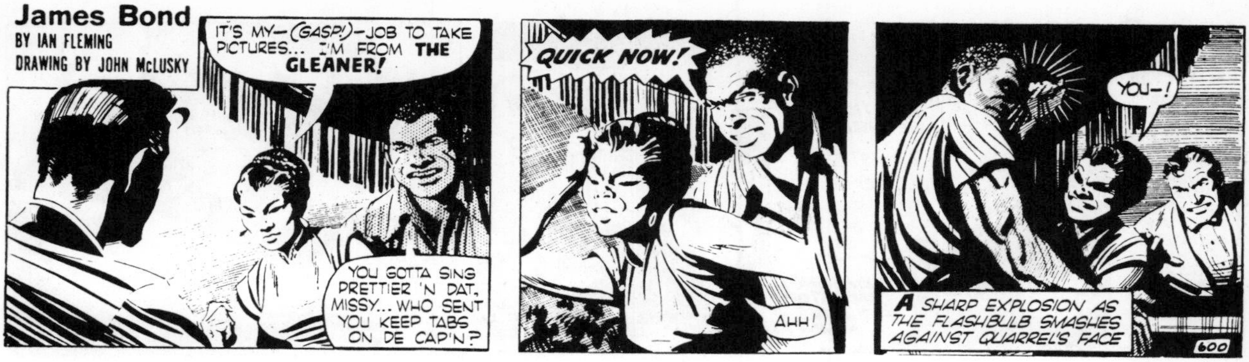
James Bond
BY IAN FLEMING
DRAWING BY JOHN McLUSKY
IT'S MY—(GASP!)—JOB TO TAKE PICTURES... I'M FROM THE GLEANER!
YOU GOTTA SING PRETTIER 'N DAT, MISSY... WHO SENT YOU KEEP TABS ON DE CAP'N?
QUICK NOW!
AHH!
YOU—!
A SHARP EXPLOSION AS THE FLASHBULB SMASHES AGAINST QUARREL'S FACE
600

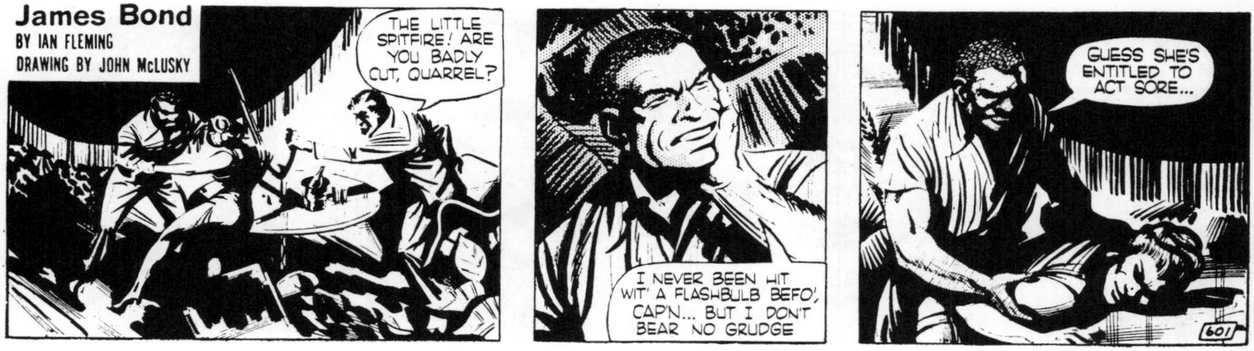
James Bond
BY IAN FLEMING
DRAWING BY JOHN McLUSKY
THE LITTLE SPITFIRE! ARE YOU BADLY CUT, QUARREL?
I NEVER BEEN HIT WIT' A FLASHBULB BEFO', CAP'N... BUT I DON'T BEAR NO GRUDGE
GUESS SHE'S ENTITLED TO ACT SORE...
601

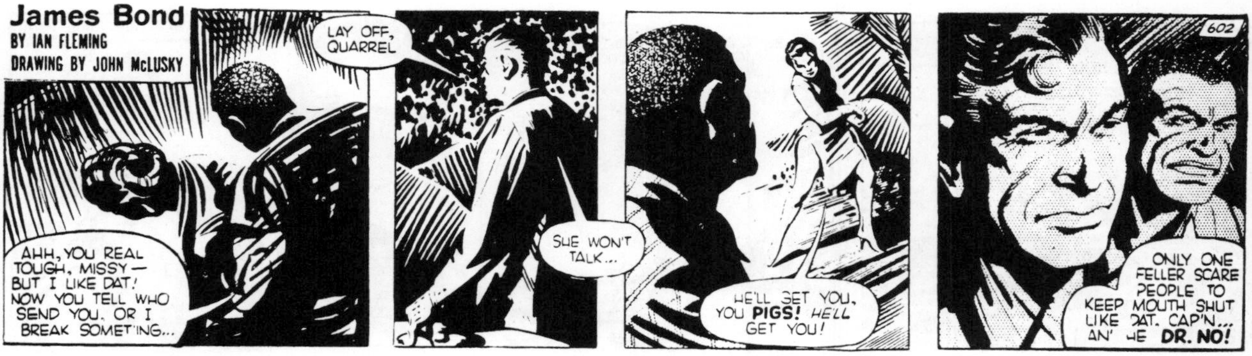
James Bond
BY IAN FLEMING
DRAWING BY JOHN McLUSKY
AHH, YOU REAL TOUGH, MISSY— BUT I LIKE DAT! NOW YOU TELL WHO SEND YOU. OR I BREAK SOMET'ING...
LAY OFF, QUARREL
SHE WON'T TALK...
HE'LL GET YOU, YOU PIGS! HE'LL GET YOU!
602
ONLY ONE FELLER SCARE PEOPLE TO KEEP MOUTH SHUT LIKE DAT, CAP'N... AN' HE DR. NO!

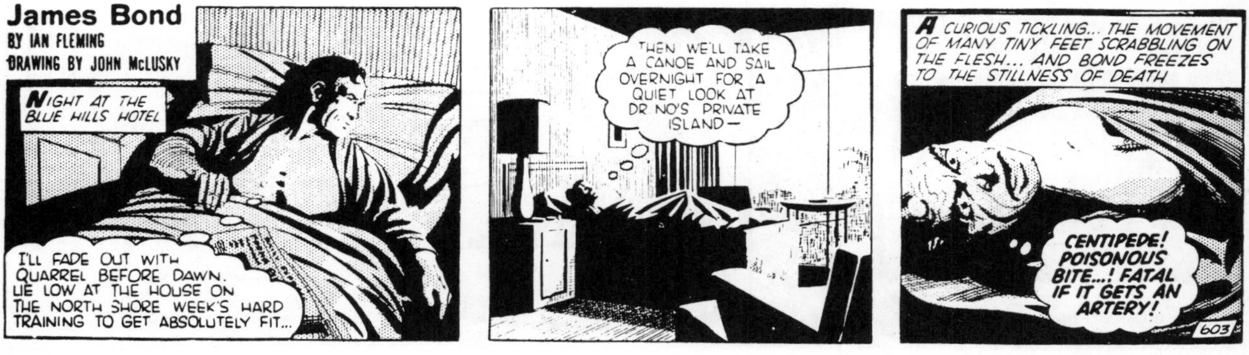
James Bond
BY IAN FLEMING
DRAWING BY JOHN McLUSKY
NIGHT AT THE BLUE HILLS HOTEL
I'LL FADE OUT WITH QUARREL BEFORE DAWN. LIE LOW AT THE HOUSE ON THE NORTH SHORE WEEK'S HARD TRAINING TO GET ABSOLUTELY FIT...
THEN WE'LL TAKE A CANOE AND SAIL OVERNIGHT FOR A QUIET LOOK AT DR NO'S PRIVATE ISLAND—
A CURIOUS TICKLING... THE MOVEMENT OF MANY TINY FEET SCRABBLING ON THE FLESH... AND BOND FREEZES TO THE STILLNESS OF DEATH
CENTIPEDE! POISONOUS BITE...! FATAL IF IT GETS AN ARTERY!
603

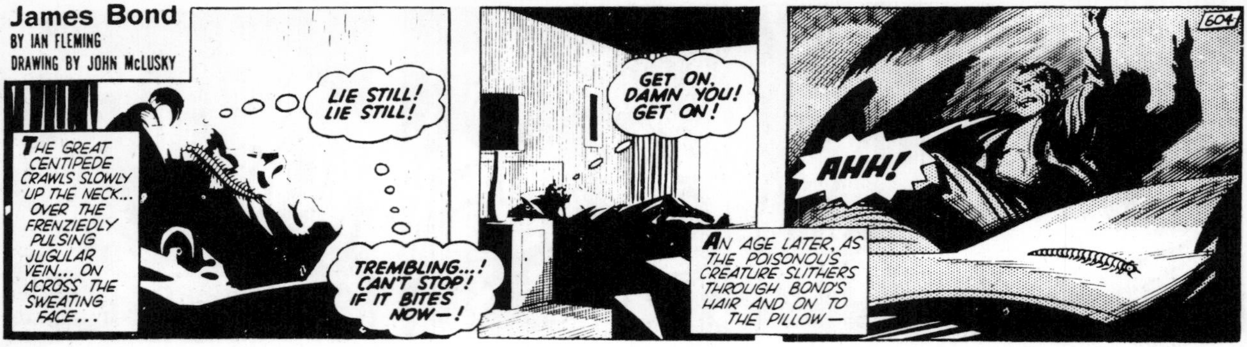
James Bond
BY IAN FLEMING
DRAWING BY JOHN McLUSKY
THE GREAT CENTIPEDE CRAWLS SLOWLY UP THE NECK... OVER THE FRENZIEDLY PULSING JUGULAR VEIN... ON ACROSS THE SWEATING FACE...
LIE STILL! LIE STILL!
TREMBLING...! CAN'T STOP! IF IT BITES NOW—!
GET ON, DAMN YOU! GET ON!
AN AGE LATER, AS THE POISONOUS CREATURE SLITHERS THROUGH BOND'S HAIR AND ON TO THE PILLOW—
604
AHH!

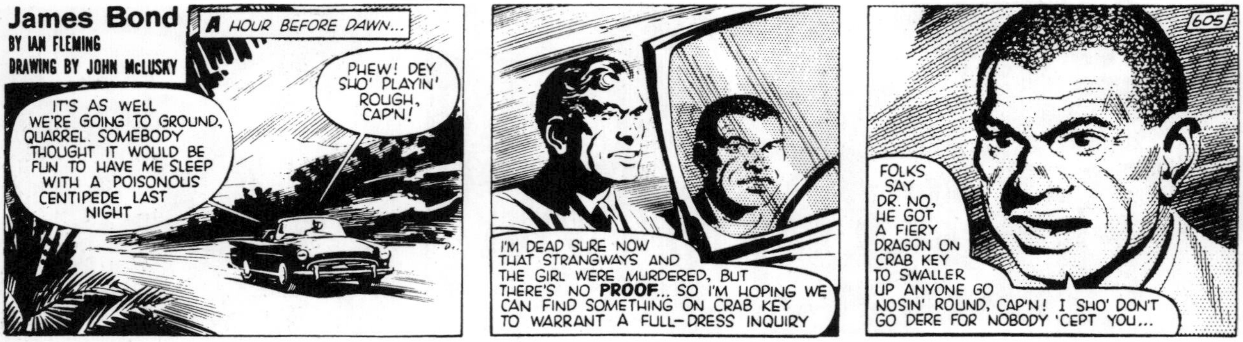
James Bond
BY IAN FLEMING
DRAWING BY JOHN McLUSKY
A HOUR BEFORE DAWN...
IT'S AS WELL WE'RE GOING TO GROUND, QUARREL. SOMEBODY THOUGHT IT WOULD BE FUN TO HAVE ME SLEEP WITH A POISONOUS CENTIPEDE LAST NIGHT
PHEW! DEY SHO' PLAYIN' ROUGH, CAP'N!
I'M DEAD SURE NOW THAT STRANGWAYS AND THE GIRL WERE MURDERED, BUT THERE'S NO **PROOF**.. SO I'M HOPING WE CAN FIND SOMETHING ON CRAB KEY TO WARRANT A FULL-DRESS INQUIRY
605
FOLKS SAY DR. NO, HE GOT A FIERY DRAGON ON CRAB KEY TO SWALLER UP ANYONE GO NOSIN' ROUND, CAP'N! I SHO' DON'T GO DERE FOR NOBODY 'CEPT YOU...

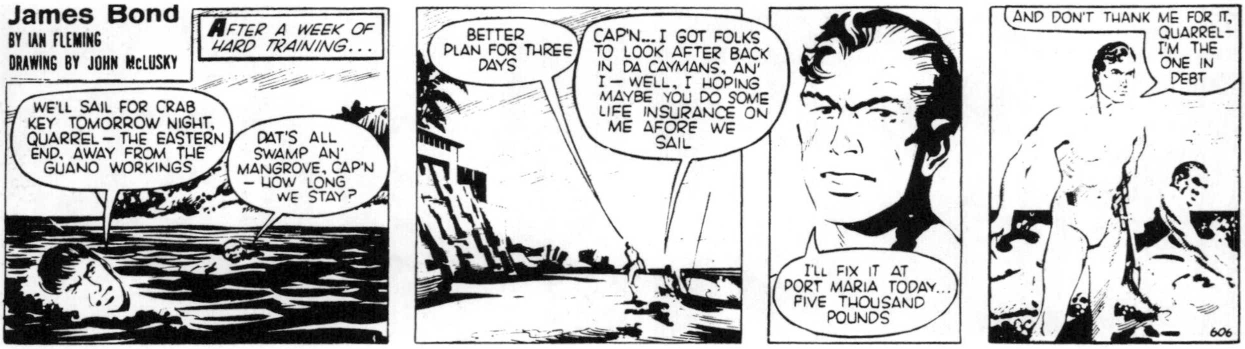
James Bond
BY IAN FLEMING
DRAWING BY JOHN McLUSKY
AFTER A WEEK OF HARD TRAINING...
WE'LL SAIL FOR CRAB KEY TOMORROW NIGHT, QUARREL—THE EASTERN END, AWAY FROM THE GUANO WORKINGS
DAT'S ALL SWAMP AN' MANGROVE, CAP'N — HOW LONG WE STAY?
BETTER PLAN FOR THREE DAYS
CAP'N... I GOT FOLKS TO LOOK AFTER BACK IN DA CAYMANS, AN' I — WELL, I HOPING MAYBE YOU DO SOME LIFE INSURANCE ON ME AFORE WE SAIL
I'LL FIX IT AT PORT MARIA TODAY... FIVE THOUSAND POUNDS
AND DON'T THANK ME FOR IT, QUARREL— I'M THE ONE IN DEBT
606

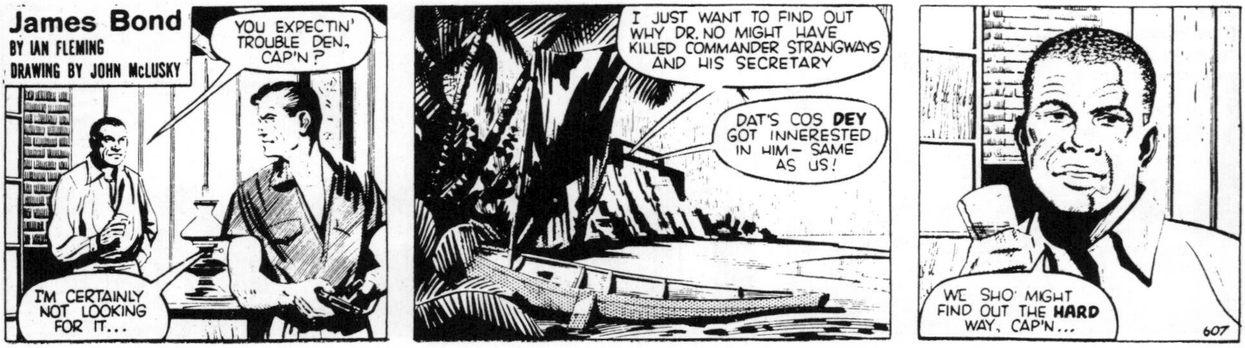
James Bond
BY IAN FLEMING
DRAWING BY JOHN McLUSKY
YOU EXPECTIN' TROUBLE DEN, CAP'N?
I'M CERTAINLY NOT LOOKING FOR IT...
I JUST WANT TO FIND OUT WHY DR. NO MIGHT HAVE KILLED COMMANDER STRANGWAYS AND HIS SECRETARY
DAT'S COS **DEY** GOT INNERESTED IN HIM— SAME AS US!
WE SHO' MIGHT FIND OUT THE **HARD** WAY, CAP'N...
607

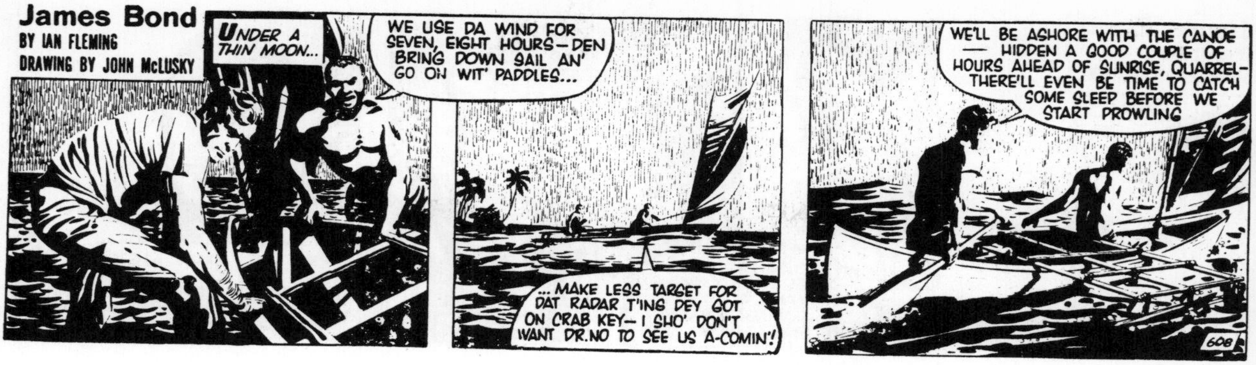
James Bond
BY IAN FLEMING
DRAWING BY JOHN McLUSKY
UNDER A THIN MOON...
WE USE DA WIND FOR SEVEN, EIGHT HOURS—DEN BRING DOWN SAIL AN' GO ON WIT' PADDLES...
...MAKE LESS TARGET FOR DAT RADAR T'ING DEY GOT ON CRAB KEY—I SHO' DON'T WANT DR.NO TO SEE US A-COMIN'!
WE'LL BE ASHORE WITH THE CANOE — HIDDEN A GOOD COUPLE OF HOURS AHEAD OF SUNRISE, QUARREL—THERE'LL EVEN BE TIME TO CATCH SOME SLEEP BEFORE WE START PROWLING
608

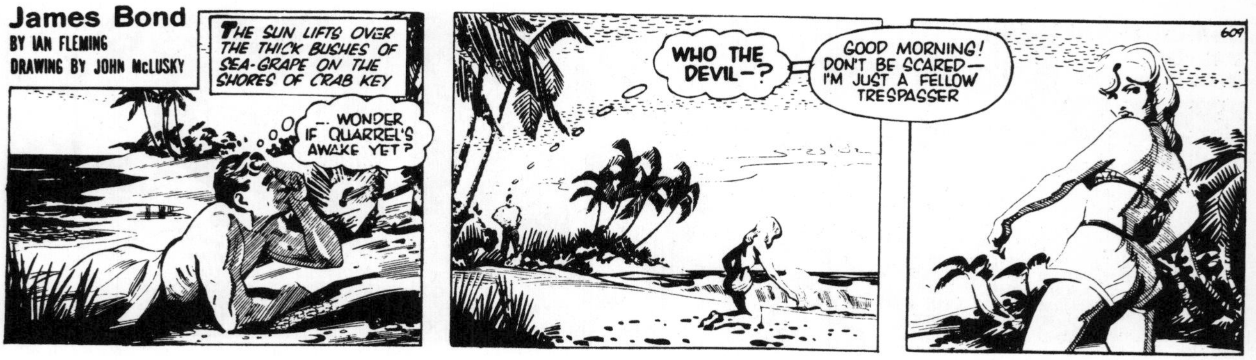
James Bond
BY IAN FLEMING
DRAWING BY JOHN McLUSKY
THE SUN LIFTS OVER THE THICK BUSHES OF SEA-GRAPE ON THE SHORES OF CRAB KEY
—. WONDER IF QUARREL'S AWAKE YET?
WHO THE DEVIL—?
GOOD MORNING! DON'T BE SCARED—I'M JUST A FELLOW TRESPASSER
609

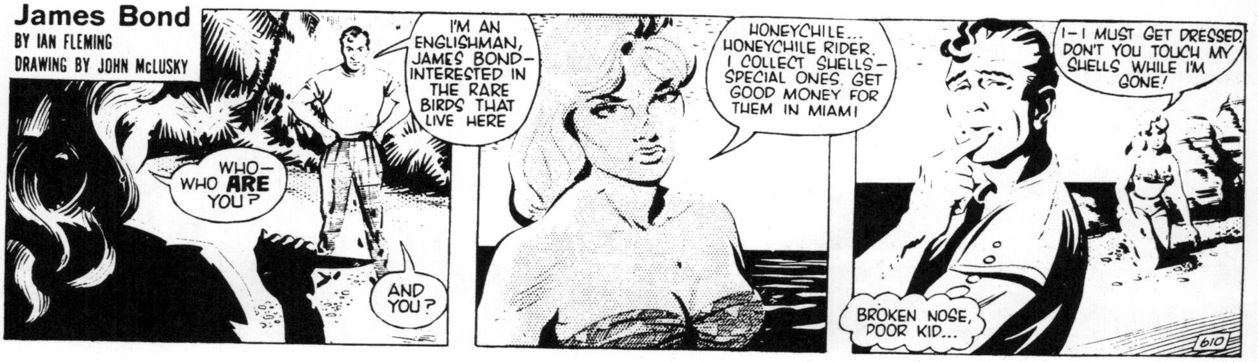
James Bond
BY IAN FLEMING
DRAWING BY JOHN McLUSKY
WHO—WHO ARE YOU?
I'M AN ENGLISHMAN, JAMES BOND—INTERESTED IN THE RARE BIRDS THAT LIVE HERE
AND YOU?
HONEYCHILE... HONEYCHILE RIDER. I COLLECT SHELLS—SPECIAL ONES. GET GOOD MONEY FOR THEM IN MIAMI
I—I MUST GET DRESSED. DON'T YOU TOUCH MY SHELLS WHILE I'M GONE!
BROKEN NOSE, POOR KID...
610

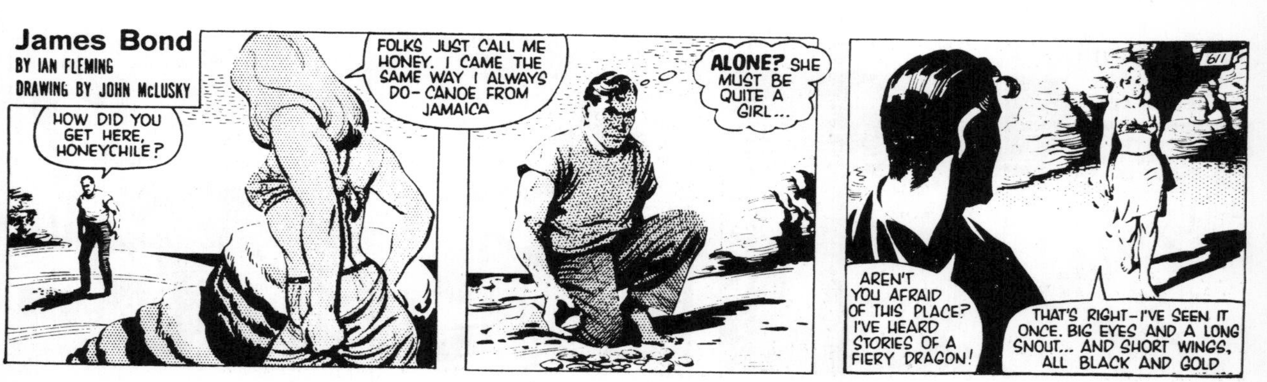
James Bond
BY IAN FLEMING
DRAWING BY JOHN McLUSKY
HOW DID YOU GET HERE, HONEYCHILE?
FOLKS JUST CALL ME HONEY. I CAME THE SAME WAY I ALWAYS DO—CANOE FROM JAMAICA
ALONE? SHE MUST BE QUITE A GIRL...
611
AREN'T YOU AFRAID OF THIS PLACE? I'VE HEARD STORIES OF A FIERY DRAGON!
THAT'S RIGHT—I'VE SEEN IT ONCE. BIG EYES AND A LONG SNOUT... AND SHORT WINGS, ALL BLACK AND GOLD

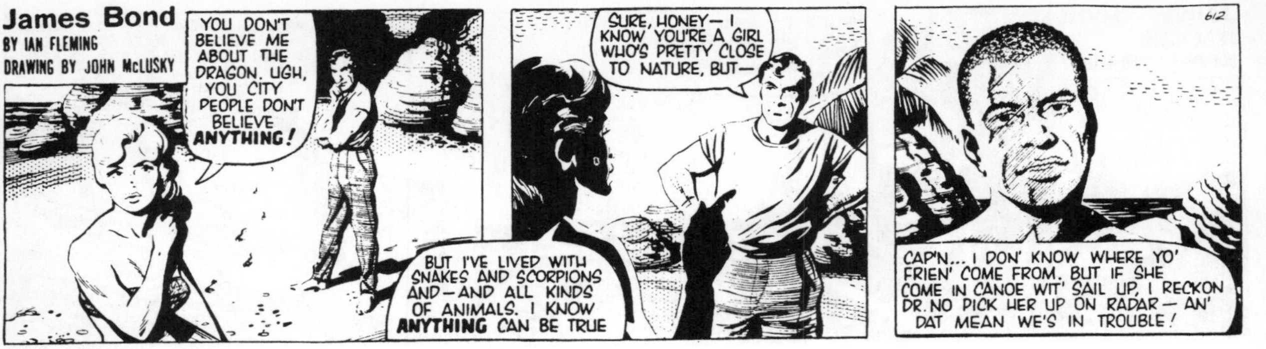
James Bond
BY IAN FLEMING
DRAWING BY JOHN McLUSKY
YOU DON'T BELIEVE ME ABOUT THE DRAGON. UGH, YOU CITY PEOPLE DON'T BELIEVE **ANYTHING**!
SURE, HONEY— I KNOW YOU'RE A GIRL WHO'S PRETTY CLOSE TO NATURE, BUT—
BUT I'VE LIVED WITH SNAKES AND SCORPIONS AND—AND ALL KINDS OF ANIMALS. I KNOW **ANYTHING** CAN BE TRUE
612
CAP'N... I DON' KNOW WHERE YO' FRIEN' COME FROM, BUT IF SHE COME IN CANOE WIT' SAIL UP, I RECKON DR. NO PICK HER UP ON RADAR— AN' DAT MEAN WE'S IN TROUBLE!

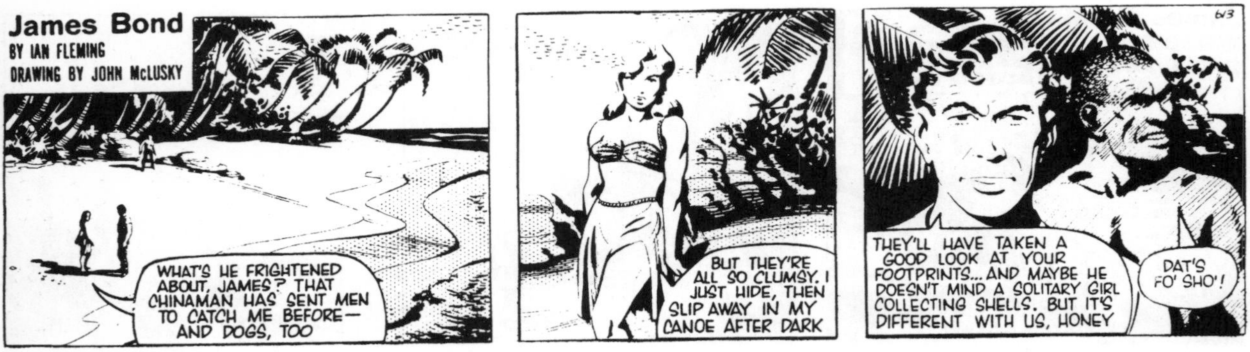
James Bond
BY IAN FLEMING
DRAWING BY JOHN McLUSKY
WHAT'S HE FRIGHTENED ABOUT, JAMES? THAT CHINAMAN HAS SENT MEN TO CATCH ME BEFORE— AND DOGS, TOO
BUT THEY'RE ALL SO CLUMSY. I JUST HIDE, THEN SLIP AWAY IN MY CANOE AFTER DARK
613
THEY'LL HAVE TAKEN A GOOD LOOK AT YOUR FOOTPRINTS... AND MAYBE HE DOESN'T MIND A SOLITARY GIRL COLLECTING SHELLS. BUT IT'S DIFFERENT WITH US, HONEY
DAT'S FO' SHO'!

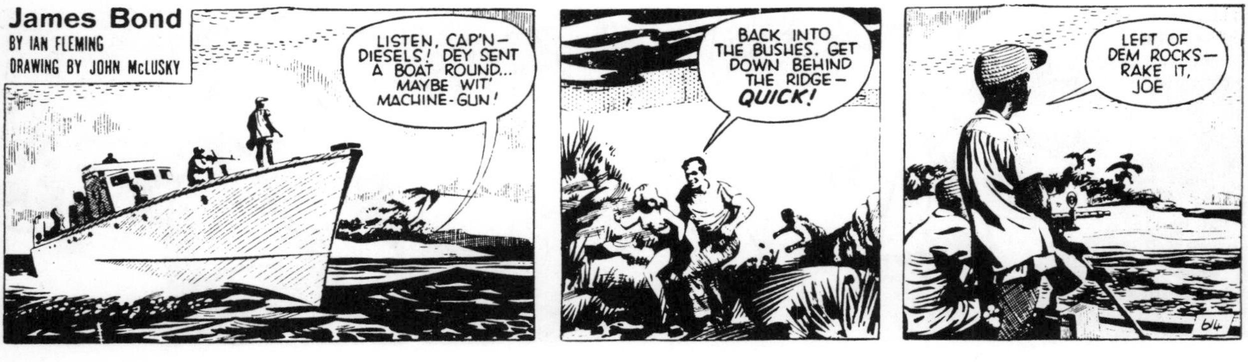
James Bond
BY IAN FLEMING
DRAWING BY JOHN McLUSKY
LISTEN, CAP'N— DIESELS! DEY SENT A BOAT ROUND... MAYBE WIT' MACHINE-GUN!
BACK INTO THE BUSHES. GET DOWN BEHIND THE RIDGE— **QUICK!**
LEFT OF DEM ROCKS— RAKE IT, JOE
614

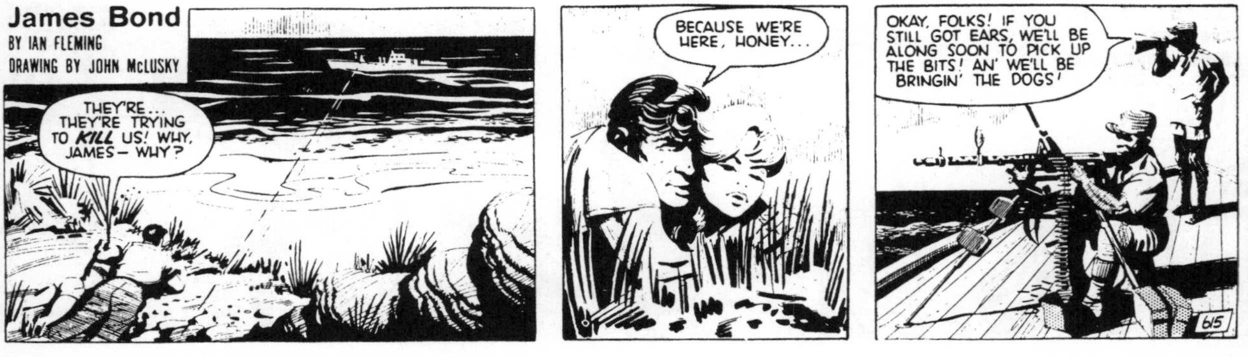
James Bond
BY IAN FLEMING
DRAWING BY JOHN McLUSKY
THEY'RE... THEY'RE TRYING TO **KILL** US! WHY, JAMES— WHY?
BECAUSE WE'RE HERE, HONEY...
OKAY, FOLKS! IF YOU STILL GOT EARS, WE'LL BE ALONG SOON TO PICK UP THE BITS! AN' WE'LL BE BRINGIN' THE DOGS!
615

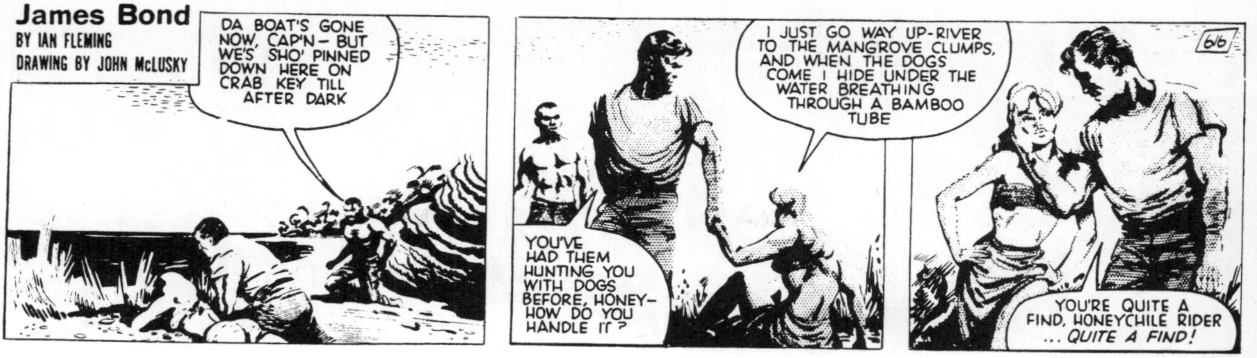
James Bond
BY IAN FLEMING
DRAWING BY JOHN McLUSKY
DA BOAT'S GONE NOW, CAP'N– BUT WE'S SHO' PINNED DOWN HERE ON CRAB KEY TILL AFTER DARK
YOU'VE HAD THEM HUNTING YOU WITH DOGS BEFORE, HONEY– HOW DO YOU HANDLE IT?
I JUST GO WAY UP-RIVER TO THE MANGROVE CLUMPS, AND WHEN THE DOGS COME I HIDE UNDER THE WATER BREATHING THROUGH A BAMBOO TUBE
616
YOU'RE QUITE A FIND, HONEYCHILE RIDER ... QUITE A FIND!

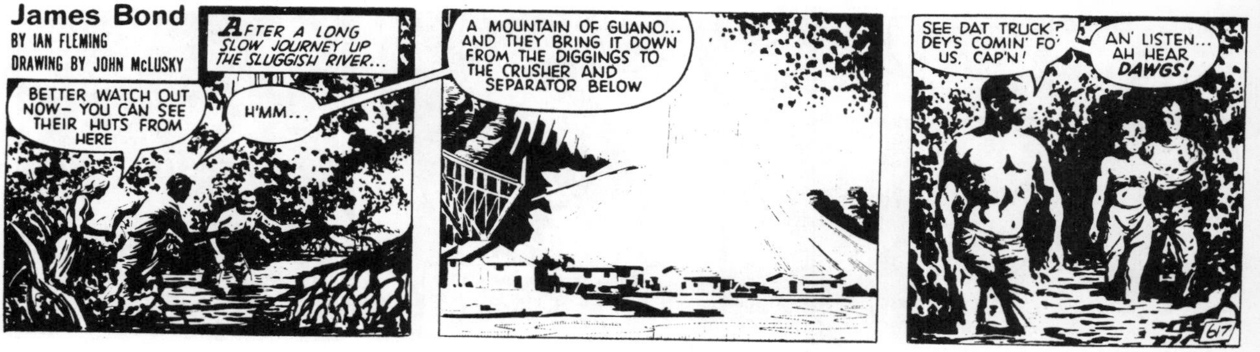
James Bond
BY IAN FLEMING
DRAWING BY JOHN McLUSKY
AFTER A LONG SLOW JOURNEY UP THE SLUGGISH RIVER...
BETTER WATCH OUT NOW– YOU CAN SEE THEIR HUTS FROM HERE
H'MM...
A MOUNTAIN OF GUANO... AND THEY BRING IT DOWN FROM THE DIGGINGS TO THE CRUSHER AND SEPARATOR BELOW
SEE DAT TRUCK? DEY'S COMIN' FO' US, CAP'N!
AN' LISTEN... AH HEAR DAWGS!
617

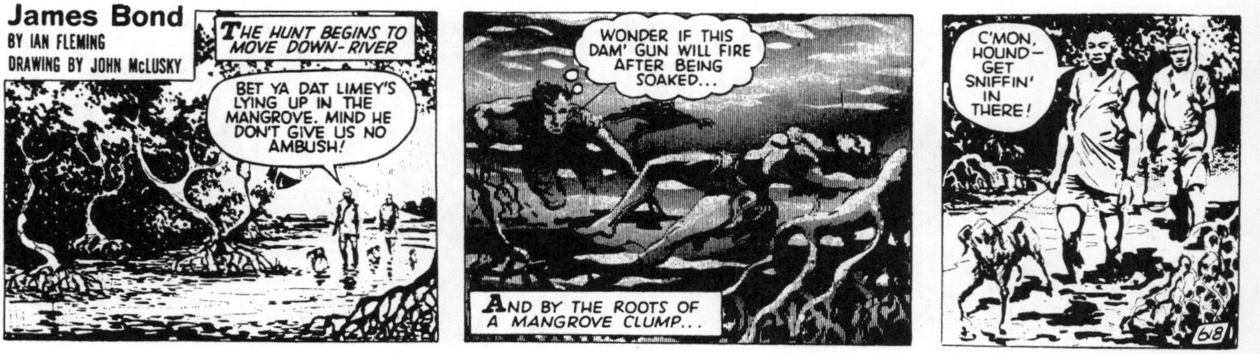
James Bond
BY IAN FLEMING
DRAWING BY JOHN McLUSKY
THE HUNT BEGINS TO MOVE DOWN-RIVER
BET YA DAT LIMEY'S LYING UP IN THE MANGROVE. MIND HE DON'T GIVE US NO AMBUSH!
WONDER IF THIS DAM' GUN WILL FIRE AFTER BEING SOAKED...
AND BY THE ROOTS OF A MANGROVE CLUMP...
C'MON, HOUND– GET SNIFFIN' IN THERE!
618

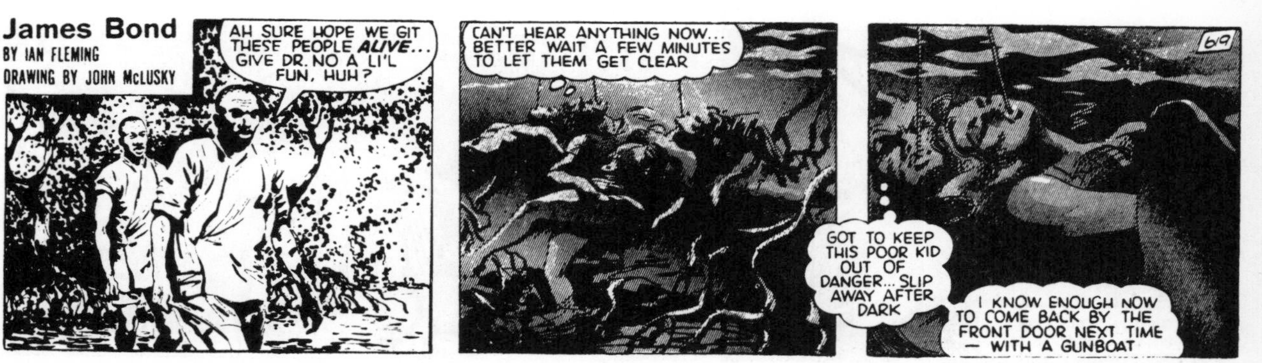
James Bond
BY IAN FLEMING
DRAWING BY JOHN McLUSKY
AH SURE HOPE WE GIT THESE PEOPLE ALIVE... GIVE DR. NO A LI'L FUN, HUH?
CAN'T HEAR ANYTHING NOW... BETTER WAIT A FEW MINUTES TO LET THEM GET CLEAR
619
GOT TO KEEP THIS POOR KID OUT OF DANGER... SLIP AWAY AFTER DARK
I KNOW ENOUGH NOW TO COME BACK BY THE FRONT DOOR NEXT TIME — WITH A GUNBOAT

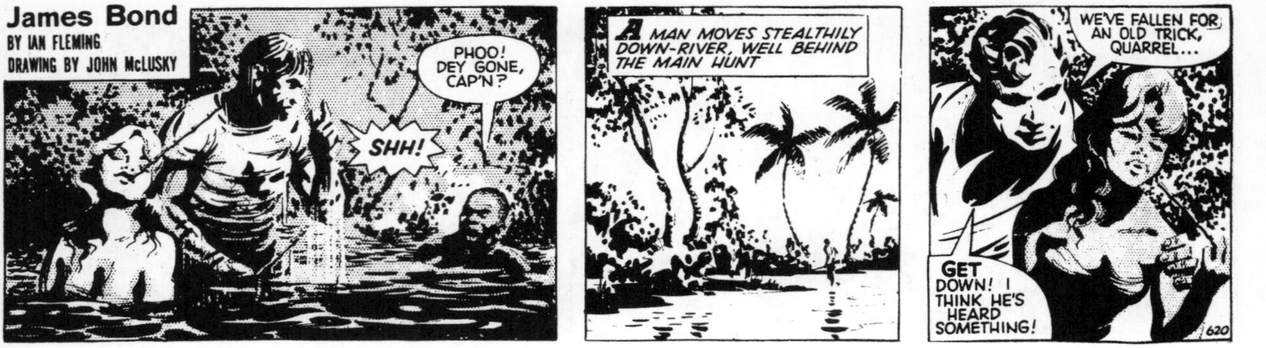
James Bond
BY IAN FLEMING
DRAWING BY JOHN McLUSKY
PHOO! DEY GONE, CAP'N?
SHH!
A MAN MOVES STEALTHILY DOWN-RIVER, WELL BEHIND THE MAIN HUNT
WE'VE FALLEN FOR AN OLD TRICK, QUARREL...
GET DOWN! I THINK HE'S HEARD SOMETHING!
620

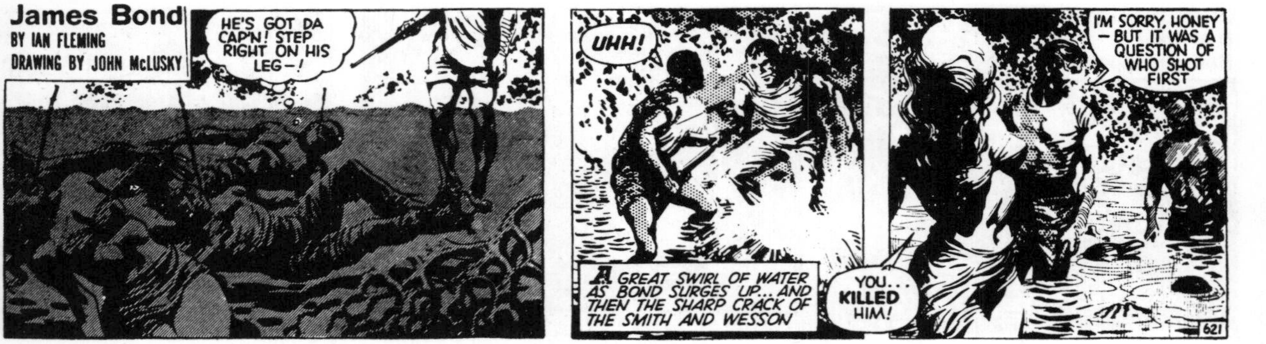
James Bond
BY IAN FLEMING
DRAWING BY JOHN McLUSKY
HE'S GOT DA CAP'N! STEP RIGHT ON HIS LEG—!
UHH!
A GREAT SWIRL OF WATER AS BOND SURGES UP... AND THEN THE SHARP CRACK OF THE SMITH AND WESSON
YOU... KILLED HIM!
I'M SORRY, HONEY — BUT IT WAS A QUESTION OF WHO SHOT FIRST
621

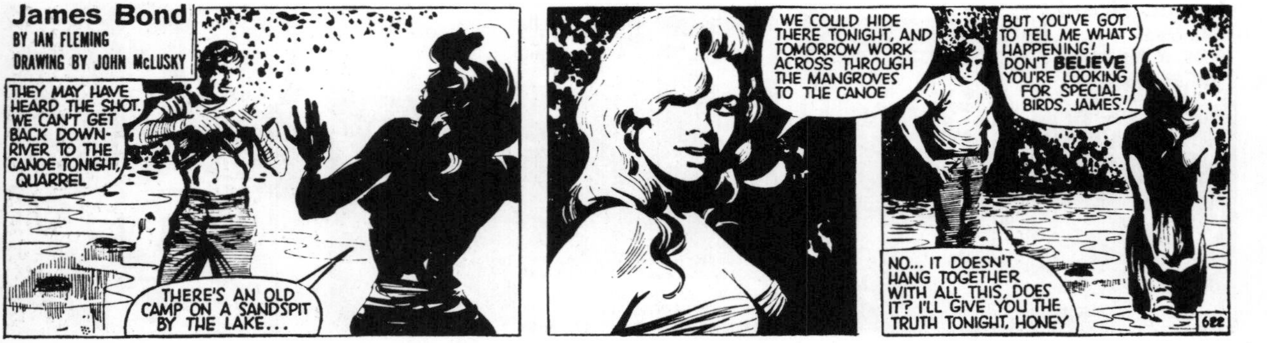
James Bond
BY IAN FLEMING
DRAWING BY JOHN McLUSKY
THEY MAY HAVE HEARD THE SHOT. WE CAN'T GET BACK DOWN-RIVER TO THE CANOE TONIGHT, QUARREL
THERE'S AN OLD CAMP ON A SANDSPIT BY THE LAKE...
WE COULD HIDE THERE TONIGHT, AND TOMORROW WORK ACROSS THROUGH THE MANGROVES TO THE CANOE
BUT YOU'VE GOT TO TELL ME WHAT'S HAPPENING! I DON'T BELIEVE YOU'RE LOOKING FOR SPECIAL BIRDS, JAMES!
NO... IT DOESN'T HANG TOGETHER WITH ALL THIS, DOES IT? I'LL GIVE YOU THE TRUTH TONIGHT, HONEY
622

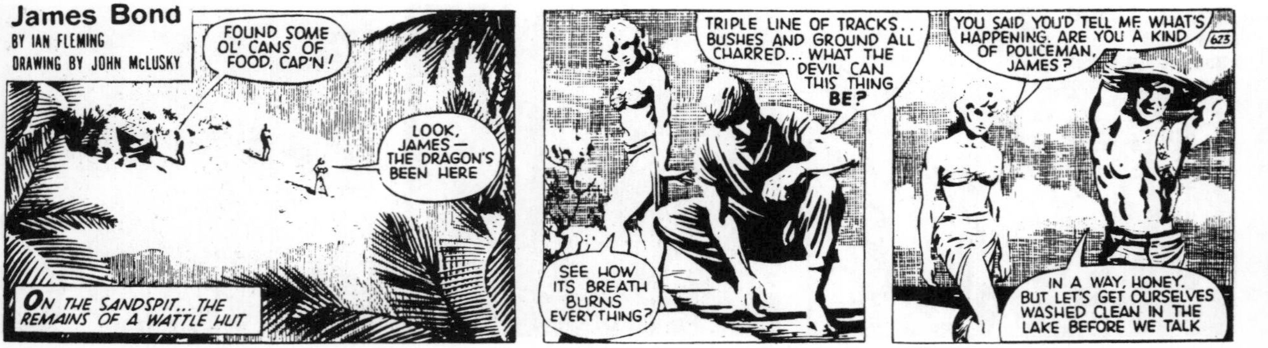
James Bond
BY IAN FLEMING
DRAWING BY JOHN McLUSKY
FOUND SOME OL' CANS OF FOOD, CAP'N!
LOOK, JAMES— THE DRAGON'S BEEN HERE
ON THE SANDSPIT... THE REMAINS OF A WATTLE HUT
TRIPLE LINE OF TRACKS... BUSHES AND GROUND ALL CHARRED... WHAT THE DEVIL CAN THIS THING BE?
SEE HOW ITS BREATH BURNS EVERYTHING?
YOU SAID YOU'D TELL ME WHAT'S HAPPENING. ARE YOU A KIND OF POLICEMAN, JAMES?
623
IN A WAY, HONEY. BUT LET'S GET OURSELVES WASHED CLEAN IN THE LAKE BEFORE WE TALK

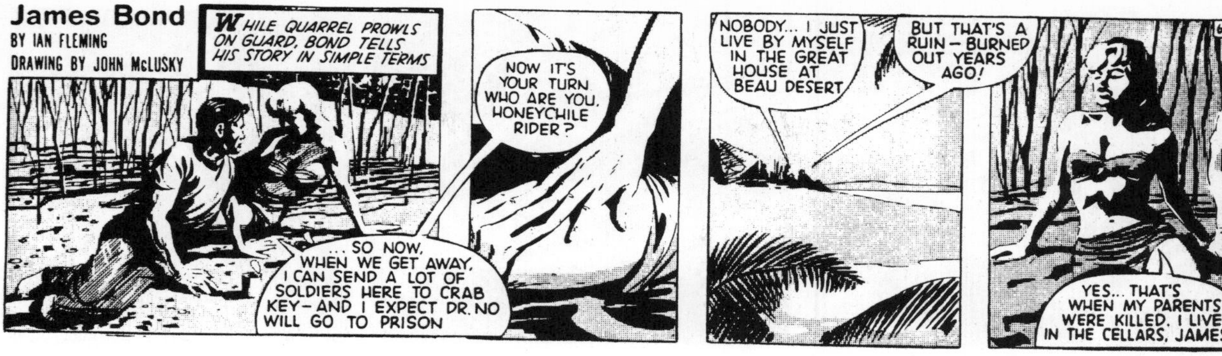
James Bond
BY IAN FLEMING
DRAWING BY JOHN McLUSKY
WHILE QUARREL PROWLS ON GUARD, BOND TELLS HIS STORY IN SIMPLE TERMS
... SO NOW, WHEN WE GET AWAY, I CAN SEND A LOT OF SOLDIERS HERE TO CRAB KEY—AND I EXPECT DR. NO WILL GO TO PRISON
NOW IT'S YOUR TURN. WHO ARE YOU, HONEYCHILE RIDER?
NOBODY... I JUST LIVE BY MYSELF IN THE GREAT HOUSE AT BEAU DESERT
BUT THAT'S A RUIN—BURNED OUT YEARS AGO!
624
YES... THAT'S WHEN MY PARENTS WERE KILLED. I LIVE IN THE CELLARS, JAMES

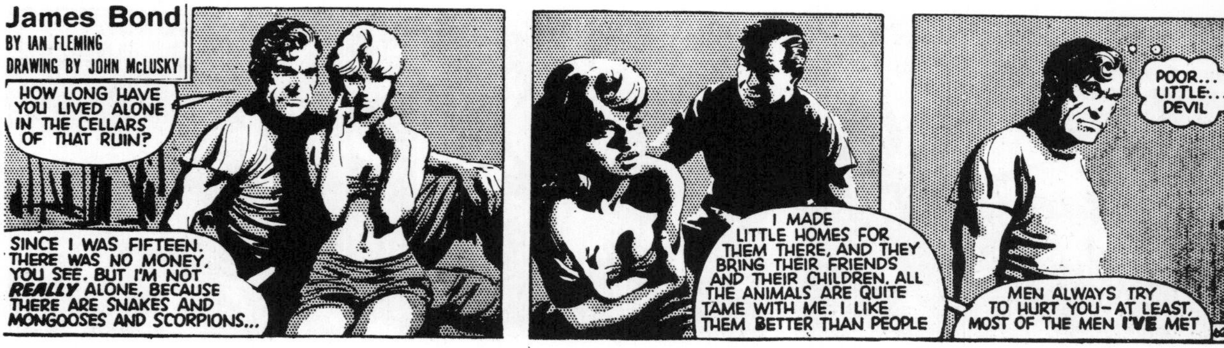
James Bond
BY IAN FLEMING
DRAWING BY JOHN McLUSKY
HOW LONG HAVE YOU LIVED ALONE IN THE CELLARS OF THAT RUIN?
SINCE I WAS FIFTEEN. THERE WAS NO MONEY, YOU SEE. BUT I'M NOT REALLY ALONE, BECAUSE THERE ARE SNAKES AND MONGOOSES AND SCORPIONS...
I MADE LITTLE HOMES FOR THEM THERE, AND THEY BRING THEIR FRIENDS AND THEIR CHILDREN. ALL THE ANIMALS ARE QUITE TAME WITH ME. I LIKE THEM BETTER THAN PEOPLE
POOR... LITTLE... DEVIL
MEN ALWAYS TRY TO HURT YOU—AT LEAST, MOST OF THE MEN I'VE MET
625

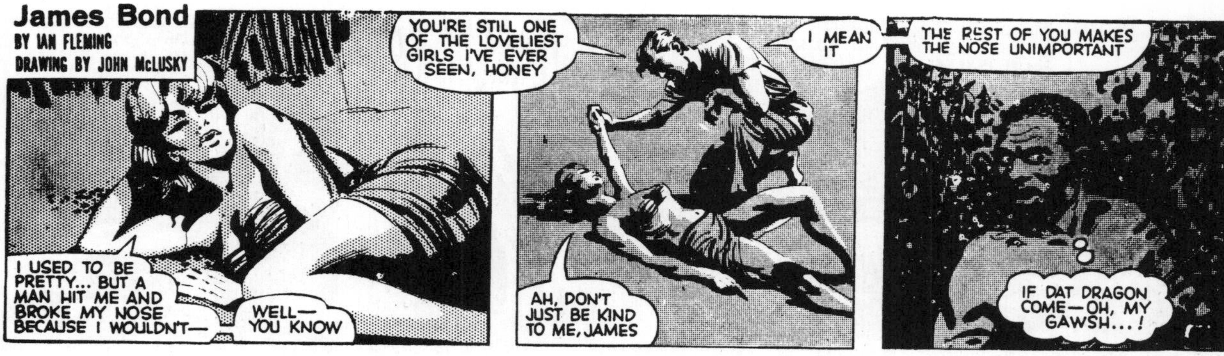
James Bond
BY IAN FLEMING
DRAWING BY JOHN McLUSKY
I USED TO BE PRETTY... BUT A MAN HIT ME AND BROKE MY NOSE BECAUSE I WOULDN'T—
WELL—YOU KNOW
YOU'RE STILL ONE OF THE LOVELIEST GIRLS I'VE EVER SEEN, HONEY
AH, DON'T JUST BE KIND TO ME, JAMES
I MEAN IT
THE REST OF YOU MAKES THE NOSE UNIMPORTANT
IF DAT DRAGON COME—OH, MY GAWSH...!

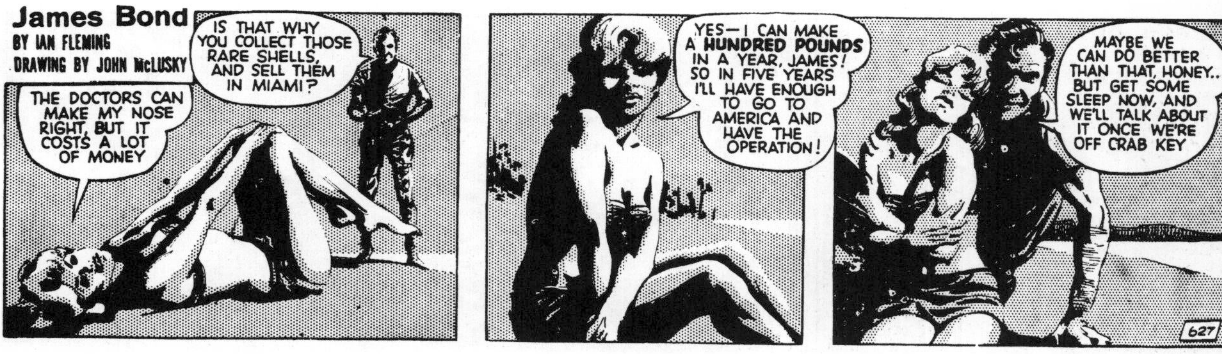
James Bond
BY IAN FLEMING
DRAWING BY JOHN McLUSKY
THE DOCTORS CAN MAKE MY NOSE RIGHT, BUT IT COSTS A LOT OF MONEY
IS THAT WHY YOU COLLECT THOSE RARE SHELLS, AND SELL THEM IN MIAMI?
YES—I CAN MAKE A HUNDRED POUNDS IN A YEAR, JAMES! SO IN FIVE YEARS I'LL HAVE ENOUGH TO GO TO AMERICA AND HAVE THE OPERATION!
MAYBE WE CAN DO BETTER THAN THAT, HONEY... BUT GET SOME SLEEP NOW, AND WE'LL TALK ABOUT IT ONCE WE'RE OFF CRAB KEY
627

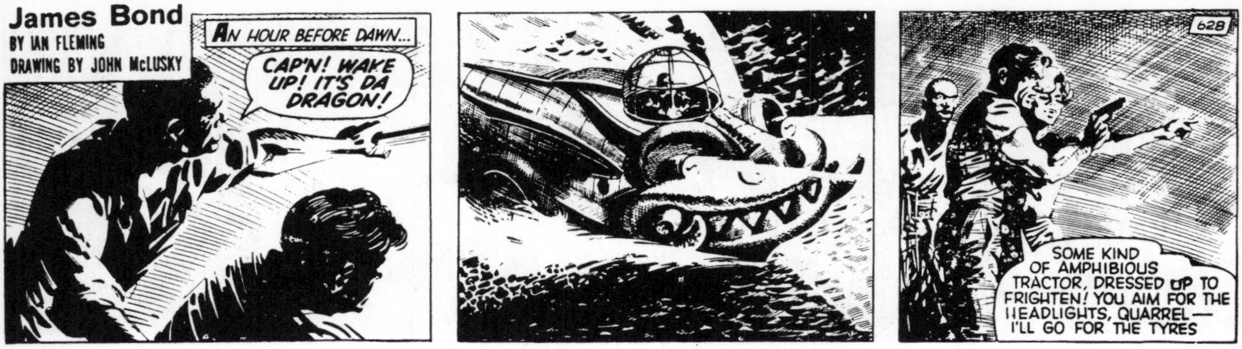
James Bond
BY IAN FLEMING
DRAWING BY JOHN McLUSKY
AN HOUR BEFORE DAWN...
CAP'N! WAKE UP! IT'S DA DRAGON!
628
SOME KIND OF AMPHIBIOUS TRACTOR, DRESSED UP TO FRIGHTEN! YOU AIM FOR THE HEADLIGHTS, QUARREL— I'LL GO FOR THE TYRES

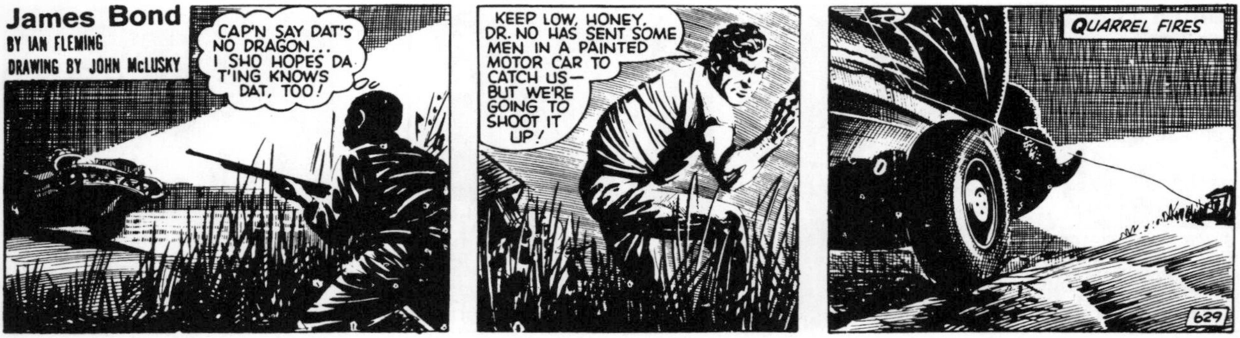
James Bond
BY IAN FLEMING
DRAWING BY JOHN McLUSKY
CAP'N SAY DAT'S NO DRAGON... I SHO HOPES DA T'ING KNOWS DAT, TOO!
KEEP LOW, HONEY. DR. NO HAS SENT SOME MEN IN A PAINTED MOTOR CAR TO CATCH US— BUT WE'RE GOING TO SHOOT IT UP!
QUARREL FIRES
629

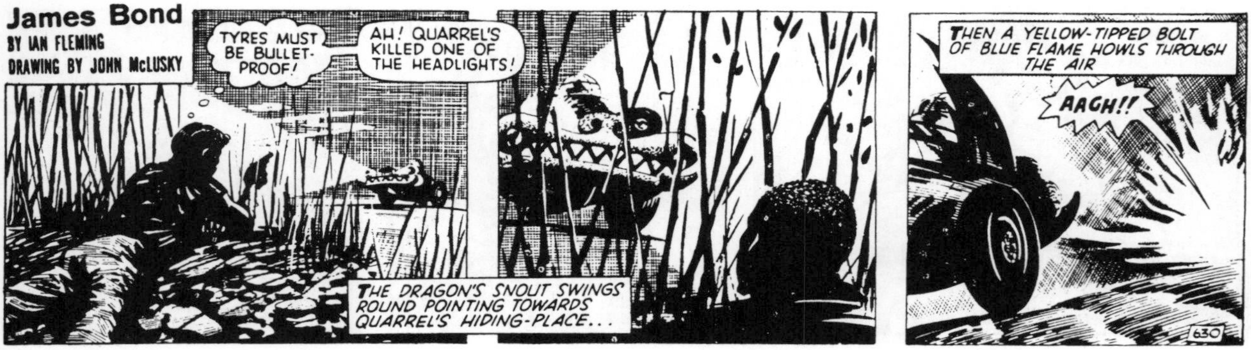
James Bond
BY IAN FLEMING
DRAWING BY JOHN McLUSKY
TYRES MUST BE BULLET-PROOF!
AH! QUARREL'S KILLED ONE OF THE HEADLIGHTS!
THE DRAGON'S SNOUT SWINGS ROUND POINTING TOWARDS QUARREL'S HIDING-PLACE...
THEN A YELLOW-TIPPED BOLT OF BLUE FLAME HOWLS THROUGH THE AIR
AAGH!!
630

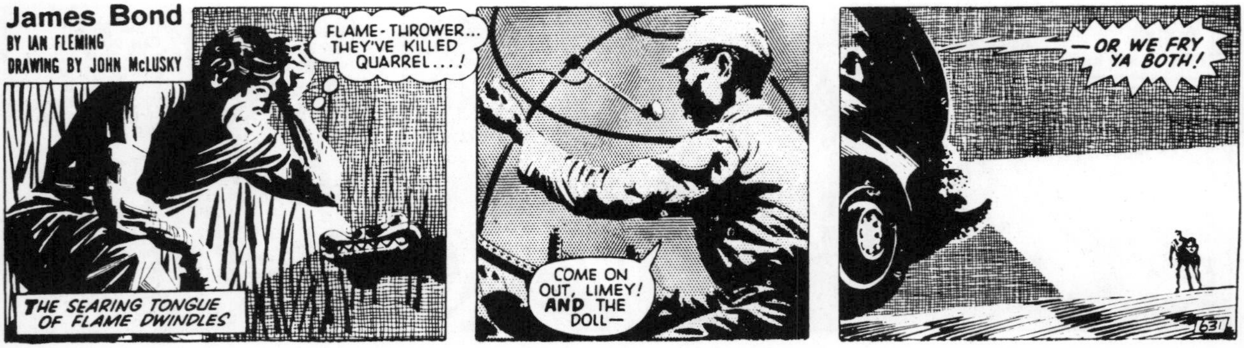
James Bond
BY IAN FLEMING
DRAWING BY JOHN McLUSKY
FLAME-THROWER... THEY'VE KILLED QUARREL...!
THE SEARING TONGUE OF FLAME DWINDLES
COME ON OUT, LIMEY! AND THE DOLL—
—OR WE FRY YA BOTH!
631

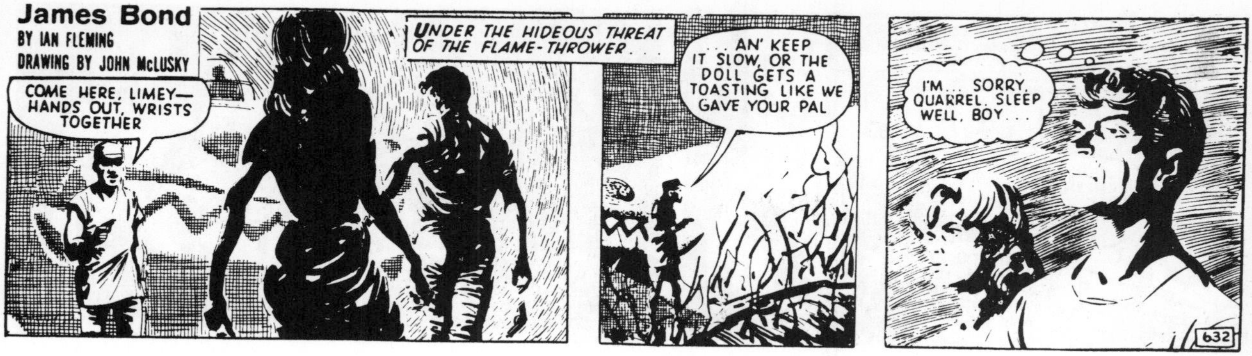
James Bond
BY IAN FLEMING
DRAWING BY JOHN McLUSKY
COME HERE, LIMEY— HANDS OUT, WRISTS TOGETHER
UNDER THE HIDEOUS THREAT OF THE FLAME-THROWER . . .
. . . AN' KEEP IT SLOW, OR THE DOLL GETS A TOASTING LIKE WE GAVE YOUR PAL
I'M . . . SORRY, QUARREL. SLEEP WELL, BOY . . .
632

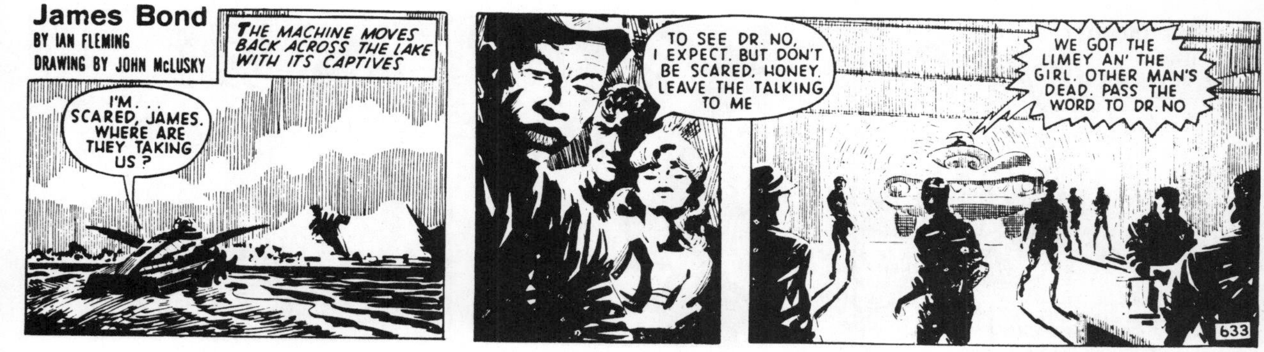
James Bond
BY IAN FLEMING
DRAWING BY JOHN McLUSKY
THE MACHINE MOVES BACK ACROSS THE LAKE WITH ITS CAPTIVES
I'M . . . SCARED, JAMES. WHERE ARE THEY TAKING US?
TO SEE DR. NO, I EXPECT. BUT DON'T BE SCARED, HONEY. LEAVE THE TALKING TO ME
WE GOT THE LIMEY AN' THE GIRL. OTHER MAN'S DEAD. PASS THE WORD TO DR. NO
633

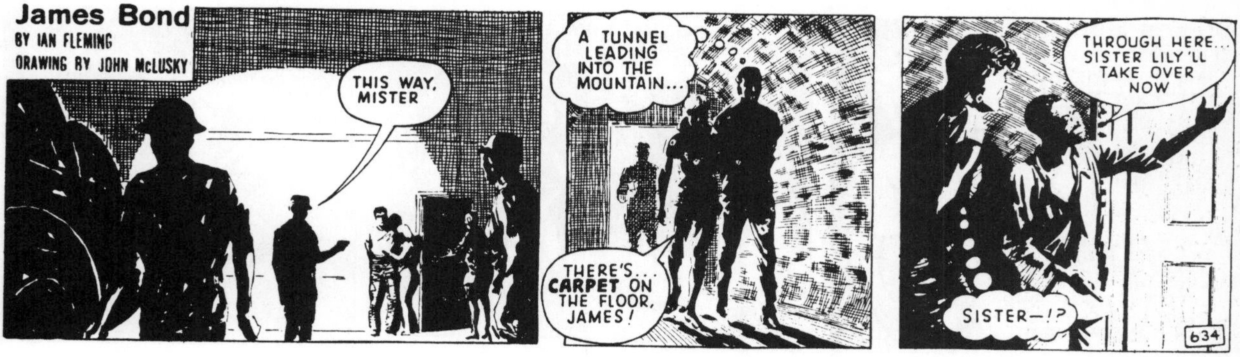
James Bond
BY IAN FLEMING
DRAWING BY JOHN McLUSKY
THIS WAY, MISTER
A TUNNEL LEADING INTO THE MOUNTAIN . . .
THERE'S . . . CARPET ON THE FLOOR, JAMES!
THROUGH HERE . . . SISTER LILY'LL TAKE OVER NOW
SISTER—!?
634

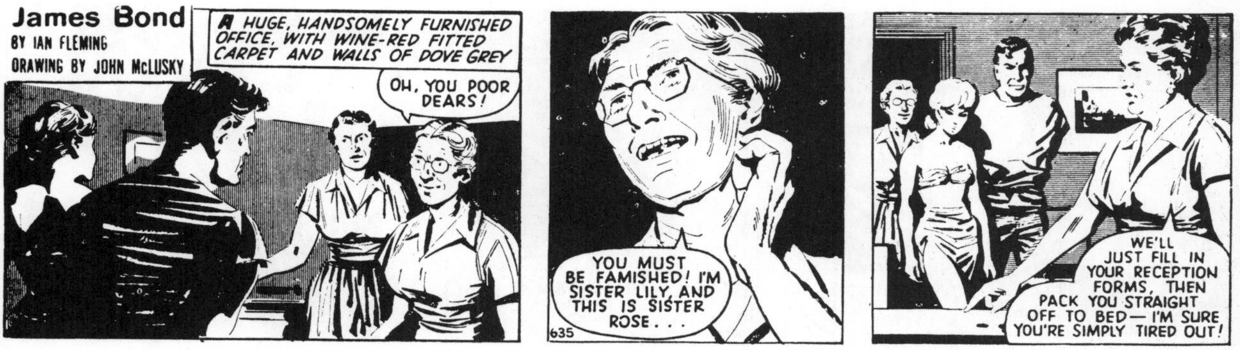
James Bond
BY IAN FLEMING
DRAWING BY JOHN McLUSKY
A HUGE, HANDSOMELY FURNISHED OFFICE, WITH WINE-RED FITTED CARPET AND WALLS OF DOVE GREY
OH, YOU POOR DEARS!
YOU MUST BE FAMISHED! I'M SISTER LILY, AND THIS IS SISTER ROSE . . .
635
WE'LL JUST FILL IN YOUR RECEPTION FORMS, THEN PACK YOU STRAIGHT OFF TO BED— I'M SURE YOU'RE SIMPLY TIRED OUT!

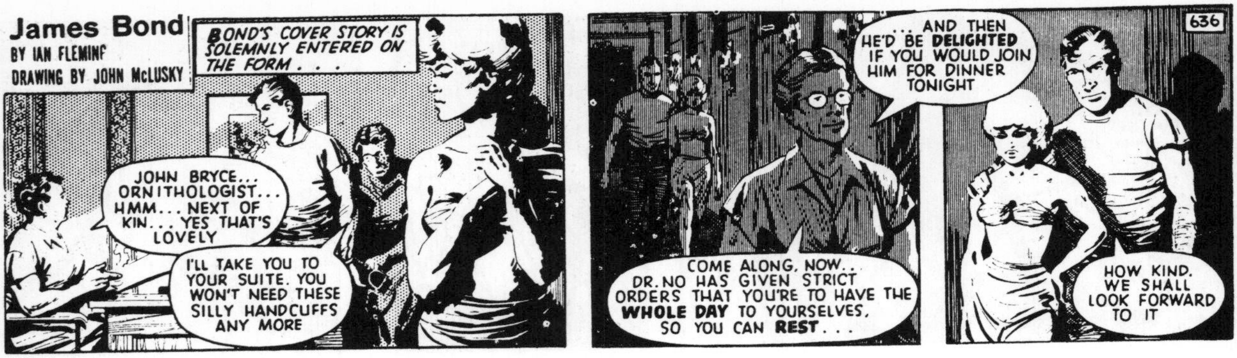
James Bond
BY IAN FLEMING
DRAWING BY JOHN McLUSKY
BOND'S COVER STORY IS SOLEMNLY ENTERED ON THE FORM . . .
JOHN BRYCE... ORNITHOLOGIST... HMM... NEXT OF KIN... YES THAT'S LOVELY
I'LL TAKE YOU TO YOUR SUITE. YOU WON'T NEED THESE SILLY HANDCUFFS ANY MORE
COME ALONG, NOW.. DR. NO HAS GIVEN STRICT ORDERS THAT YOU'RE TO HAVE THE WHOLE DAY TO YOURSELVES, SO YOU CAN REST . . .
636
... AND THEN HE'D BE DELIGHTED IF YOU WOULD JOIN HIM FOR DINNER TONIGHT
HOW KIND. WE SHALL LOOK FORWARD TO IT

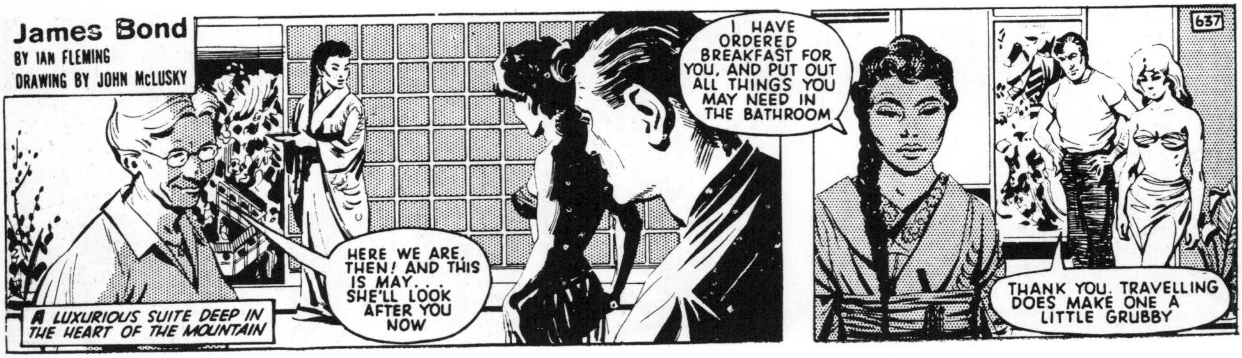
James Bond
BY IAN FLEMING
DRAWING BY JOHN McLUSKY
A LUXURIOUS SUITE DEEP IN THE HEART OF THE MOUNTAIN
HERE WE ARE, THEN! AND THIS IS MAY... SHE'LL LOOK AFTER YOU NOW
I HAVE ORDERED BREAKFAST FOR YOU, AND PUT OUT ALL THINGS YOU MAY NEED IN THE BATHROOM
637
THANK YOU. TRAVELLING DOES MAKE ONE A LITTLE GRUBBY

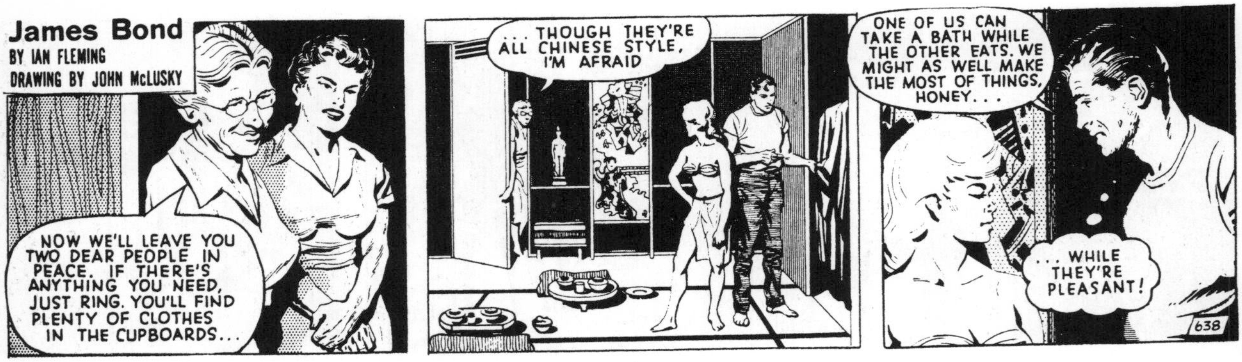
James Bond
BY IAN FLEMING
DRAWING BY JOHN McLUSKY
NOW WE'LL LEAVE YOU TWO DEAR PEOPLE IN PEACE. IF THERE'S ANYTHING YOU NEED, JUST RING. YOU'LL FIND PLENTY OF CLOTHES IN THE CUPBOARDS...
... THOUGH THEY'RE ALL CHINESE STYLE, I'M AFRAID
ONE OF US CAN TAKE A BATH WHILE THE OTHER EATS. WE MIGHT AS WELL MAKE THE MOST OF THINGS, HONEY...
... WHILE THEY'RE PLEASANT!
638

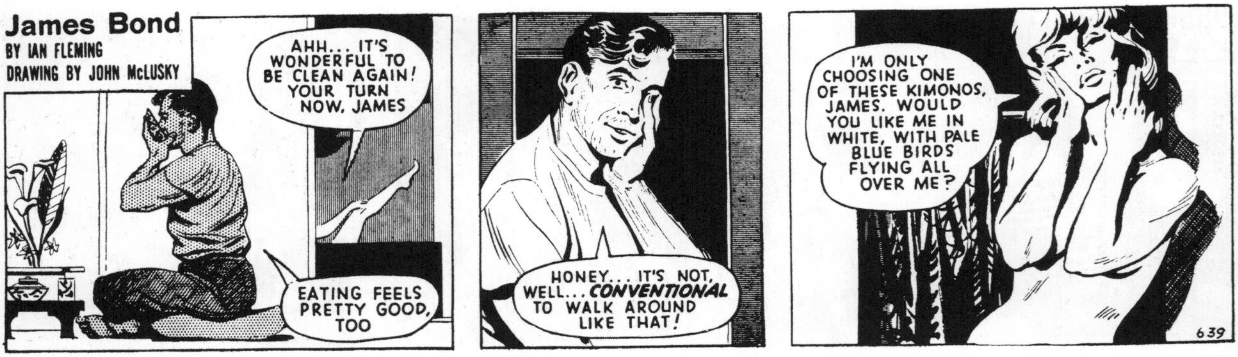
James Bond
BY IAN FLEMING
DRAWING BY JOHN McLUSKY
AHH... IT'S WONDERFUL TO BE CLEAN AGAIN! YOUR TURN NOW, JAMES
EATING FEELS PRETTY GOOD, TOO
HONEY... IT'S NOT, WELL... CONVENTIONAL TO WALK AROUND LIKE THAT!
I'M ONLY CHOOSING ONE OF THESE KIMONOS, JAMES. WOULD YOU LIKE ME IN WHITE, WITH PALE BLUE BIRDS FLYING ALL OVER ME?
639

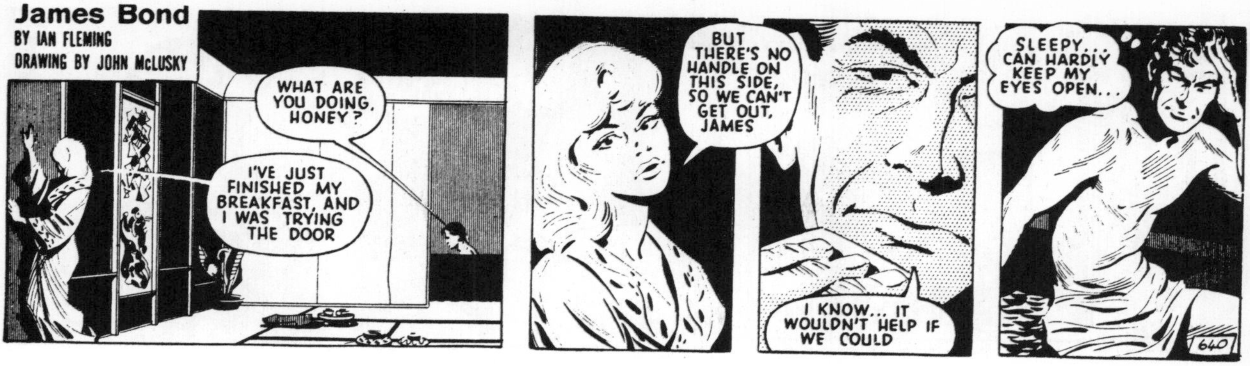
James Bond
BY IAN FLEMING
DRAWING BY JOHN McLUSKY
WHAT ARE YOU DOING, HONEY?
I'VE JUST FINISHED MY BREAKFAST, AND I WAS TRYING THE DOOR
BUT THERE'S NO HANDLE ON THIS SIDE, SO WE CAN'T GET OUT, JAMES
I KNOW... IT WOULDN'T HELP IF WE COULD
SLEEPY... CAN HARDLY KEEP MY EYES OPEN...
640

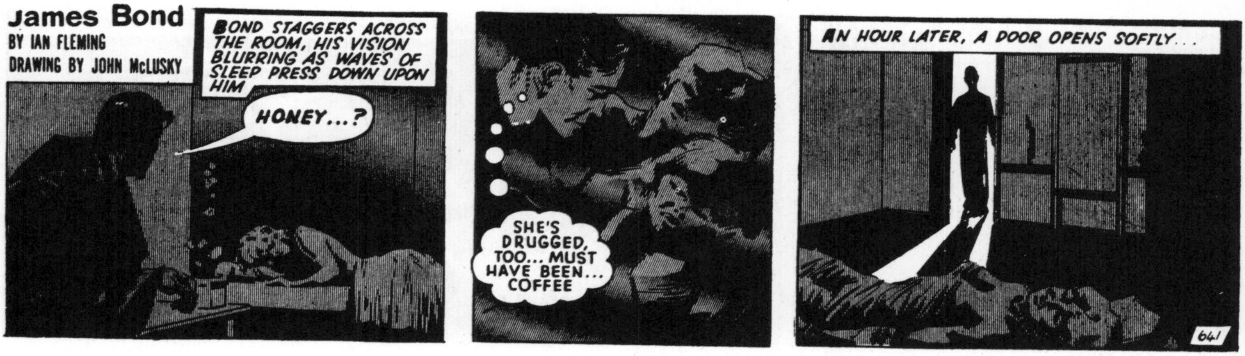
James Bond
BY IAN FLEMING
DRAWING BY JOHN McLUSKY
BOND STAGGERS ACROSS THE ROOM, HIS VISION BLURRING AS WAVES OF SLEEP PRESS DOWN UPON HIM
HONEY...?
SHE'S DRUGGED, TOO... MUST HAVE BEEN... COFFEE
AN HOUR LATER, A DOOR OPENS SOFTLY...
641

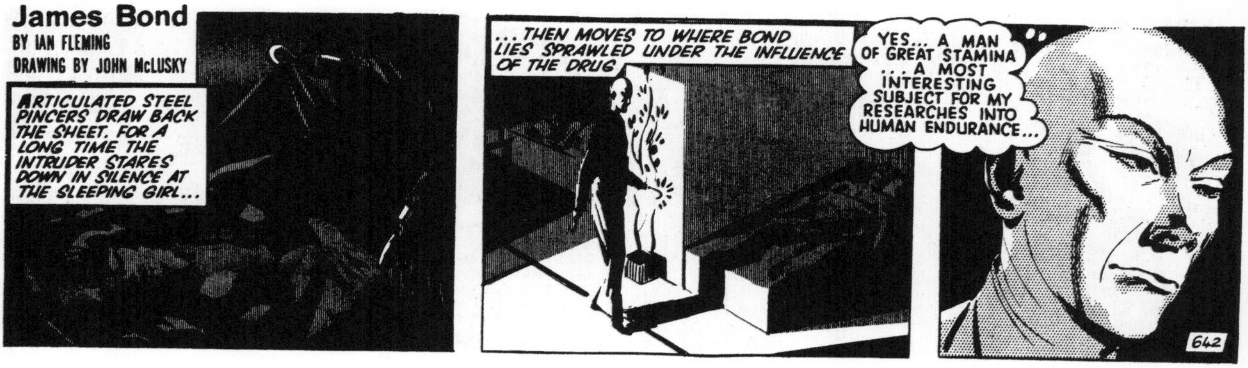
James Bond
BY IAN FLEMING
DRAWING BY JOHN McLUSKY
ARTICULATED STEEL PINCERS DRAW BACK THE SHEET. FOR A LONG TIME THE INTRUDER STARES DOWN IN SILENCE AT THE SLEEPING GIRL...
...THEN MOVES TO WHERE BOND LIES SPRAWLED UNDER THE INFLUENCE OF THE DRUG
YES... A MAN OF GREAT STAMINA ... A MOST INTERESTING SUBJECT FOR MY RESEARCHES INTO HUMAN ENDURANCE...
642

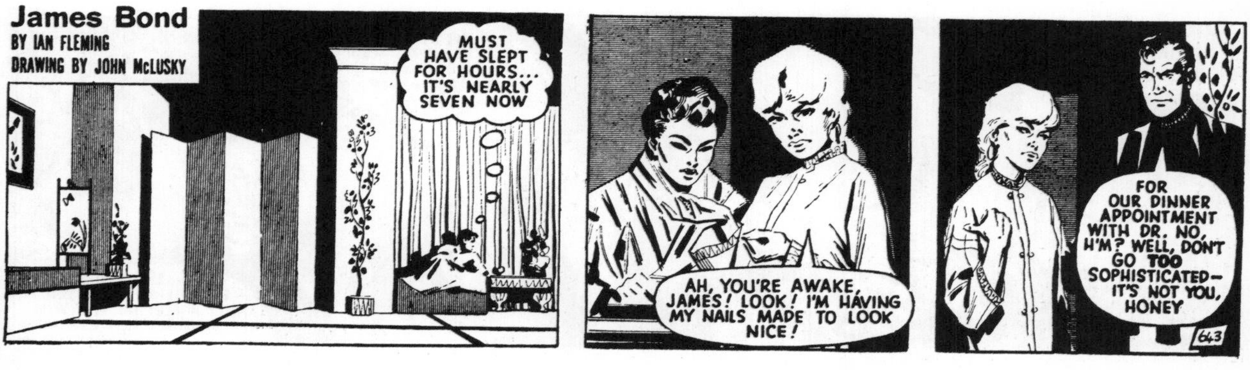
James Bond
BY IAN FLEMING
DRAWING BY JOHN McLUSKY
MUST HAVE SLEPT FOR HOURS... IT'S NEARLY SEVEN NOW
AH, YOU'RE AWAKE, JAMES! LOOK! I'M HAVING MY NAILS MADE TO LOOK NICE!
FOR OUR DINNER APPOINTMENT WITH DR. NO, H'M? WELL, DON'T GO TOO SOPHISTICATED— IT'S NOT YOU, HONEY
643

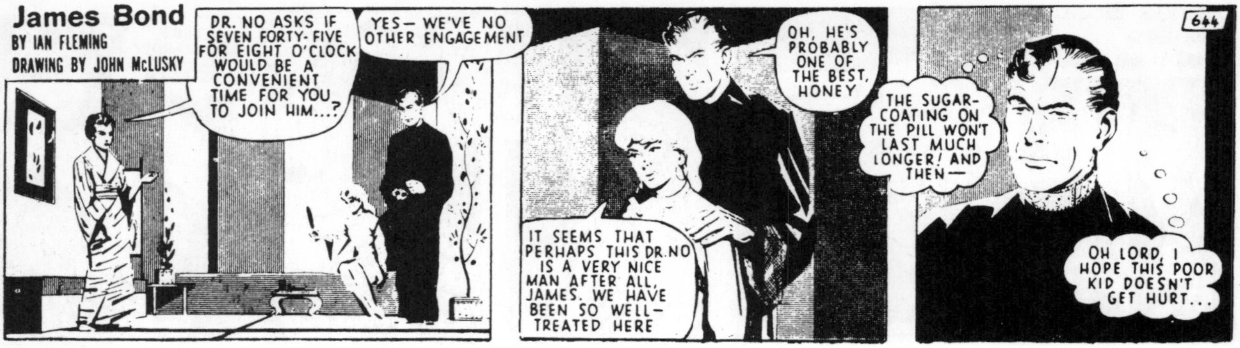
James Bond
BY IAN FLEMING
DRAWING BY JOHN McLUSKY
DR. NO ASKS IF SEVEN FORTY-FIVE FOR EIGHT O'CLOCK WOULD BE A CONVENIENT TIME FOR YOU TO JOIN HIM...?
YES— WE'VE NO OTHER ENGAGEMENT
IT SEEMS THAT PERHAPS THIS DR. NO IS A VERY NICE MAN AFTER ALL, JAMES. WE HAVE BEEN SO WELL-TREATED HERE
OH, HE'S PROBABLY ONE OF THE BEST, HONEY
644
THE SUGAR-COATING ON THE PILL WON'T LAST MUCH LONGER! AND THEN—
OH LORD, I HOPE THIS POOR KID DOESN'T GET HURT...

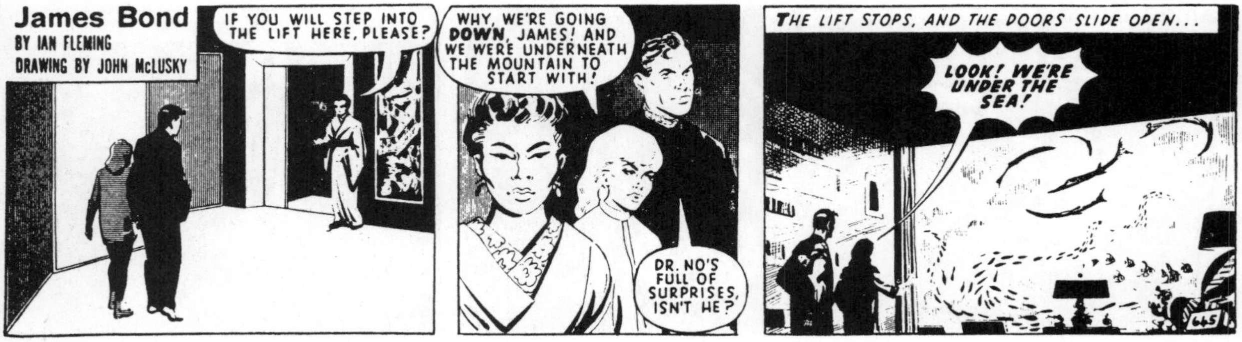
James Bond
BY IAN FLEMING
DRAWING BY JOHN McLUSKY
IF YOU WILL STEP INTO THE LIFT HERE, PLEASE?
WHY, WE'RE GOING DOWN, JAMES! AND WE WERE UNDERNEATH THE MOUNTAIN TO START WITH!
DR. NO'S FULL OF SURPRISES, ISN'T HE?
THE LIFT STOPS, AND THE DOORS SLIDE OPEN...
LOOK! WE'RE UNDER THE SEA!
645

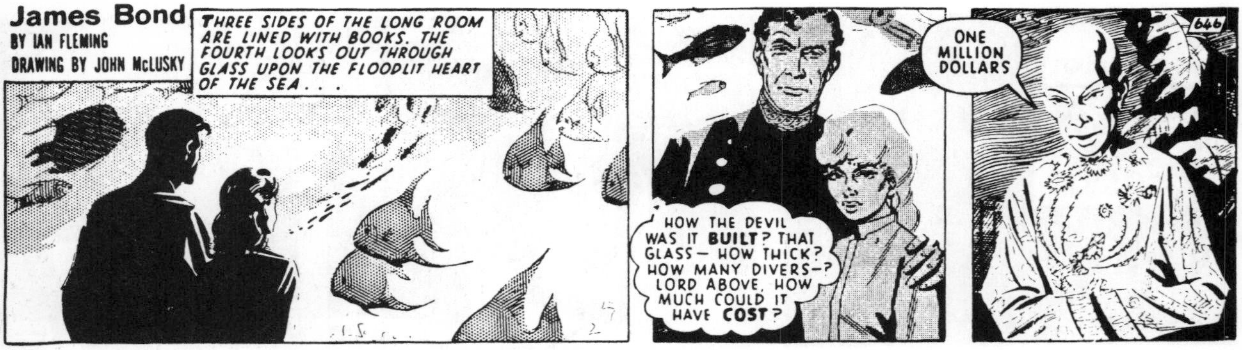
James Bond
BY IAN FLEMING
DRAWING BY JOHN McLUSKY
THREE SIDES OF THE LONG ROOM ARE LINED WITH BOOKS. THE FOURTH LOOKS OUT THROUGH GLASS UPON THE FLOODLIT HEART OF THE SEA . . .
HOW THE DEVIL WAS IT BUILT? THAT GLASS— HOW THICK? HOW MANY DIVERS—? LORD ABOVE, HOW MUCH COULD IT HAVE COST?
646
ONE MILLION DOLLARS

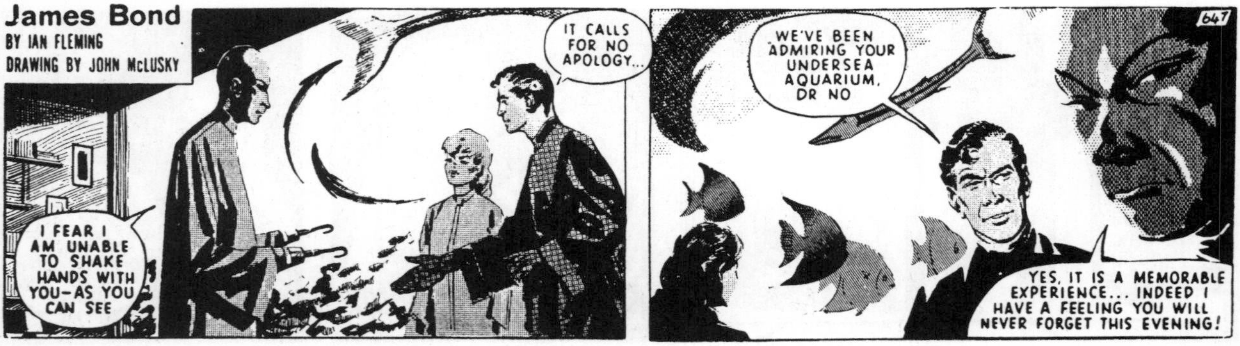
James Bond
BY IAN FLEMING
DRAWING BY JOHN McLUSKY
I FEAR I AM UNABLE TO SHAKE HANDS WITH YOU—AS YOU CAN SEE
IT CALLS FOR NO APOLOGY...
647
WE'VE BEEN ADMIRING YOUR UNDERSEA AQUARIUM, DR NO
YES, IT IS A MEMORABLE EXPERIENCE... INDEED I HAVE A FEELING YOU WILL NEVER FORGET THIS EVENING!

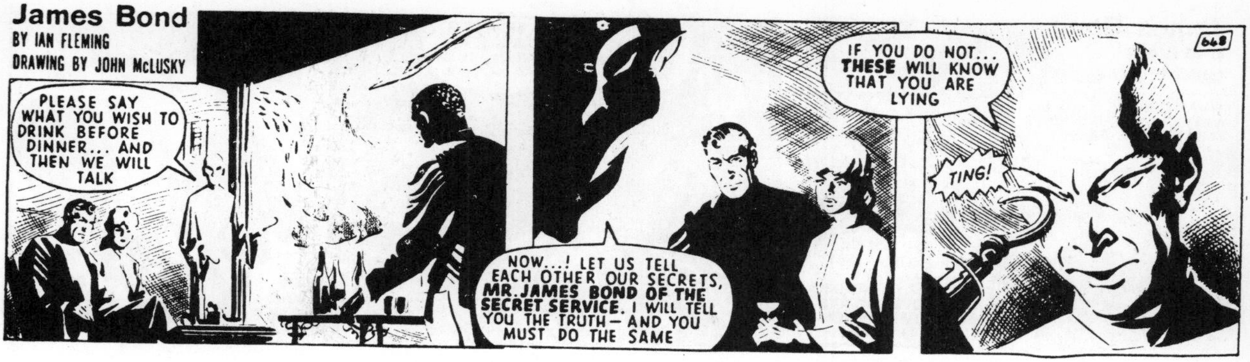
James Bond
BY IAN FLEMING
DRAWING BY JOHN McLUSKY
PLEASE SAY WHAT YOU WISH TO DRINK BEFORE DINNER... AND THEN WE WILL TALK
NOW...! LET US TELL EACH OTHER OUR SECRETS, MR. JAMES BOND OF THE SECRET SERVICE. I WILL TELL YOU THE TRUTH—AND YOU MUST DO THE SAME
648
IF YOU DO NOT... THESE WILL KNOW THAT YOU ARE LYING
TING!

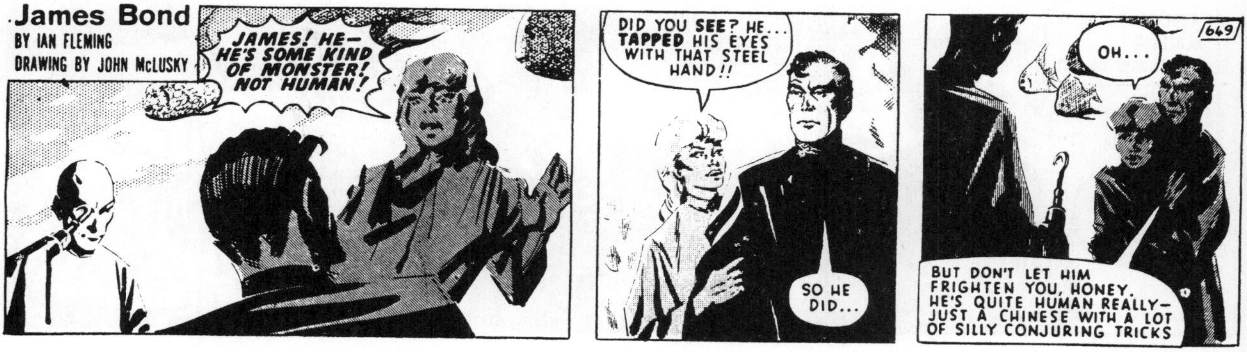
James Bond
BY IAN FLEMING
DRAWING BY JOHN McLUSKY
JAMES! HE—HE'S SOME KIND OF MONSTER! NOT HUMAN!
DID YOU SEE? HE... TAPPED HIS EYES WITH THAT STEEL HAND!!
SO HE DID...
649
OH...
BUT DON'T LET HIM FRIGHTEN YOU, HONEY. HE'S QUITE HUMAN REALLY—JUST A CHINESE WITH A LOT OF SILLY CONJURING TRICKS

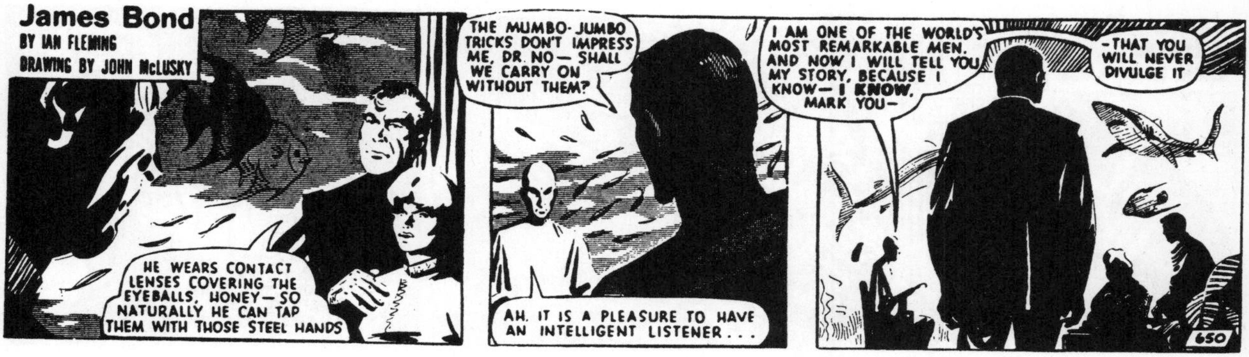
James Bond
BY IAN FLEMING
DRAWING BY JOHN McLUSKY
HE WEARS CONTACT LENSES COVERING THE EYEBALLS, HONEY—SO NATURALLY HE CAN TAP THEM WITH THOSE STEEL HANDS
THE MUMBO-JUMBO TRICKS DON'T IMPRESS ME, DR. NO—SHALL WE CARRY ON WITHOUT THEM?
AH. IT IS A PLEASURE TO HAVE AN INTELLIGENT LISTENER...
I AM ONE OF THE WORLD'S MOST REMARKABLE MEN. AND NOW I WILL TELL YOU MY STORY, BECAUSE I KNOW—I KNOW, MARK YOU—
—THAT YOU WILL NEVER DIVULGE IT
650

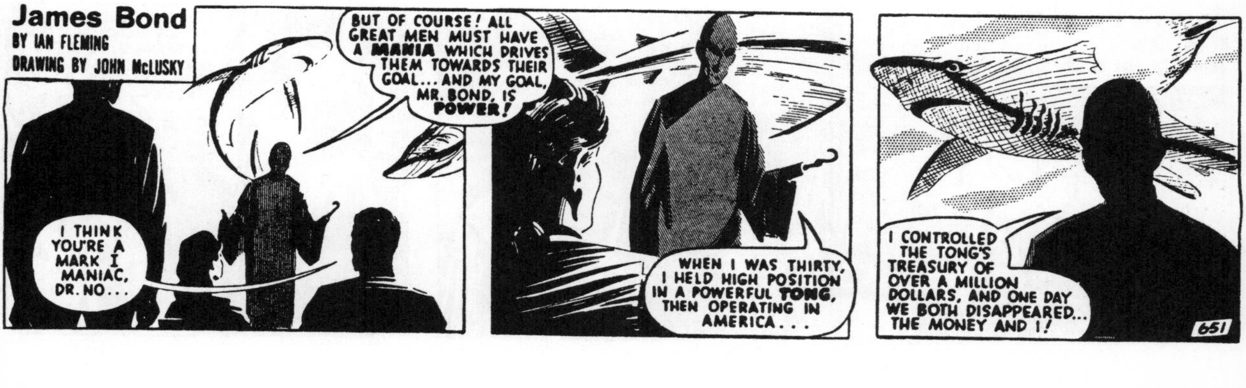
James Bond
BY IAN FLEMING
DRAWING BY JOHN McLUSKY
I THINK YOU'RE A MARK I MANIAC, DR. NO...
BUT OF COURSE! ALL GREAT MEN MUST HAVE A MANIA WHICH DRIVES THEM TOWARDS THEIR GOAL... AND MY GOAL, MR. BOND, IS POWER!
WHEN I WAS THIRTY, I HELD HIGH POSITION IN A POWERFUL TONG, THEN OPERATING IN AMERICA...
I CONTROLLED THE TONG'S TREASURY OF OVER A MILLION DOLLARS, AND ONE DAY WE BOTH DISAPPEARED... THE MONEY AND I!
651

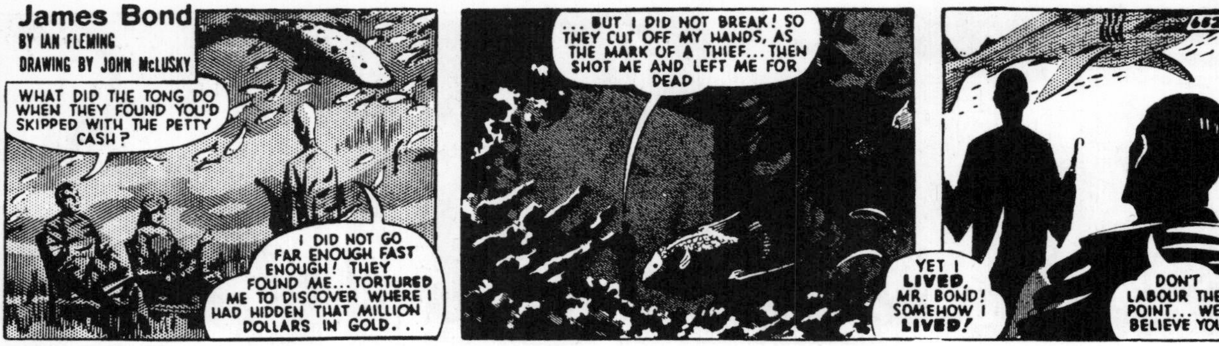
James Bond
BY IAN FLEMING
DRAWING BY JOHN McLUSKY
WHAT DID THE TONG DO WHEN THEY FOUND YOU'D SKIPPED WITH THE PETTY CASH?
I DID NOT GO FAR ENOUGH FAST ENOUGH! THEY FOUND ME... TORTURED ME TO DISCOVER WHERE I HAD HIDDEN THAT MILLION DOLLARS IN GOLD...
... BUT I DID NOT BREAK! SO THEY CUT OFF MY HANDS, AS THE MARK OF A THIEF... THEN SHOT ME AND LEFT ME FOR DEAD
652
YET I **LIVED,** MR. BOND! SOMEHOW I **LIVED!**
DON'T LABOUR THE POINT... WE BELIEVE YOU

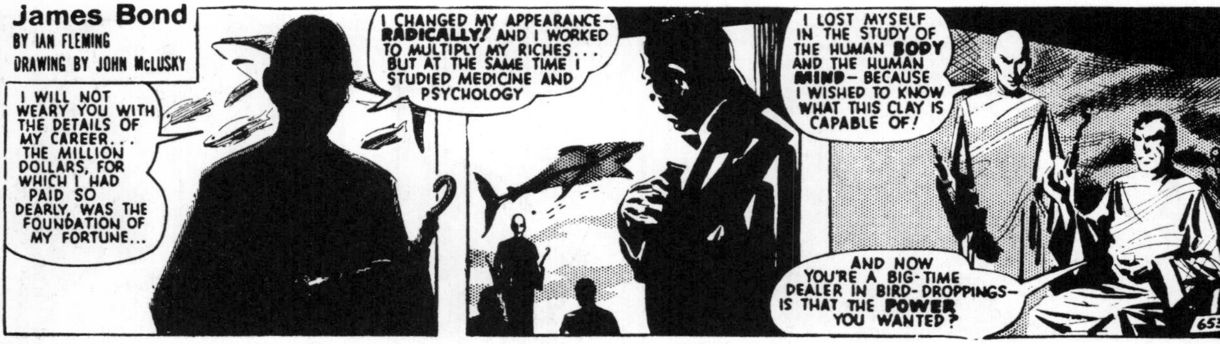
James Bond
BY IAN FLEMING
DRAWING BY JOHN McLUSKY
I WILL NOT WEARY YOU WITH THE DETAILS OF MY CAREER... THE MILLION DOLLARS, FOR WHICH I HAD PAID SO DEARLY, WAS THE FOUNDATION OF MY FORTUNE...
I CHANGED MY APPEARANCE— **RADICALLY!** AND I WORKED TO MULTIPLY MY RICHES... BUT AT THE SAME TIME I STUDIED MEDICINE AND PSYCHOLOGY
I LOST MYSELF IN THE STUDY OF THE HUMAN **BODY** AND THE HUMAN **MIND**— BECAUSE I WISHED TO KNOW WHAT THIS CLAY IS CAPABLE OF!
AND NOW YOU'RE A BIG-TIME DEALER IN BIRD-DROPPINGS— IS THAT THE **POWER** YOU WANTED?
653

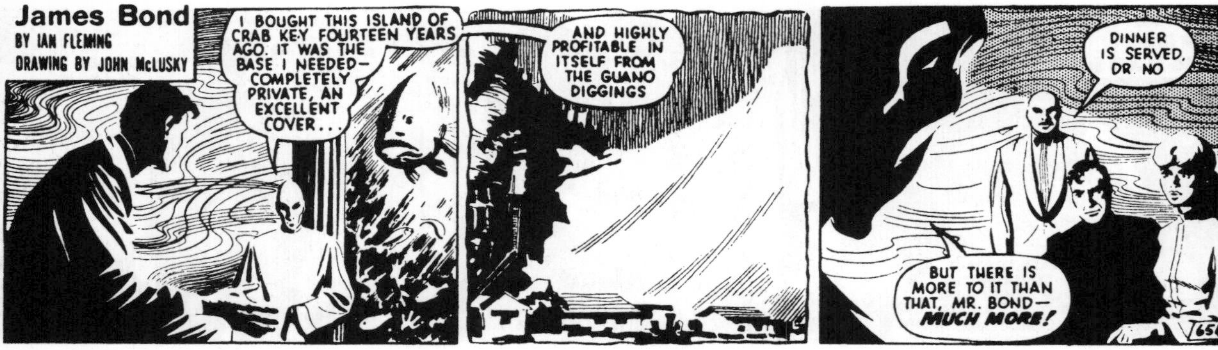
James Bond
BY IAN FLEMING
DRAWING BY JOHN McLUSKY
I BOUGHT THIS ISLAND OF CRAB KEY FOURTEEN YEARS AGO. IT WAS THE BASE I NEEDED— COMPLETELY PRIVATE, AN EXCELLENT COVER...
AND HIGHLY PROFITABLE IN ITSELF FROM THE GUANO DIGGINGS
DINNER IS SERVED, DR. NO
BUT THERE IS MORE TO IT THAN THAT, MR. BOND— **MUCH MORE!**
654

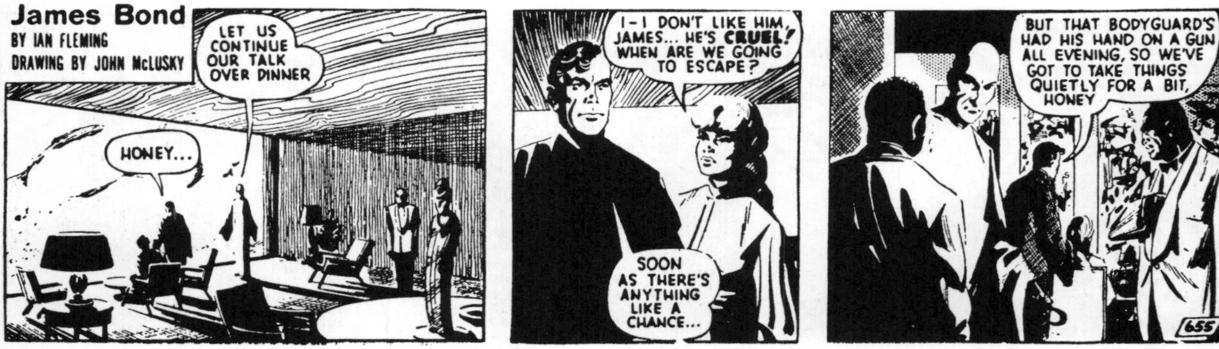
James Bond
BY IAN FLEMING
DRAWING BY JOHN McLUSKY
LET US CONTINUE OUR TALK OVER DINNER
HONEY...
I-I DON'T LIKE HIM, JAMES... HE'S **CRUEL!** WHEN ARE WE GOING TO ESCAPE?
SOON AS THERE'S ANYTHING LIKE A CHANCE...
BUT THAT BODYGUARD'S HAD HIS HAND ON A GUN ALL EVENING, SO WE'VE GOT TO TAKE THINGS QUIETLY FOR A BIT, HONEY
655

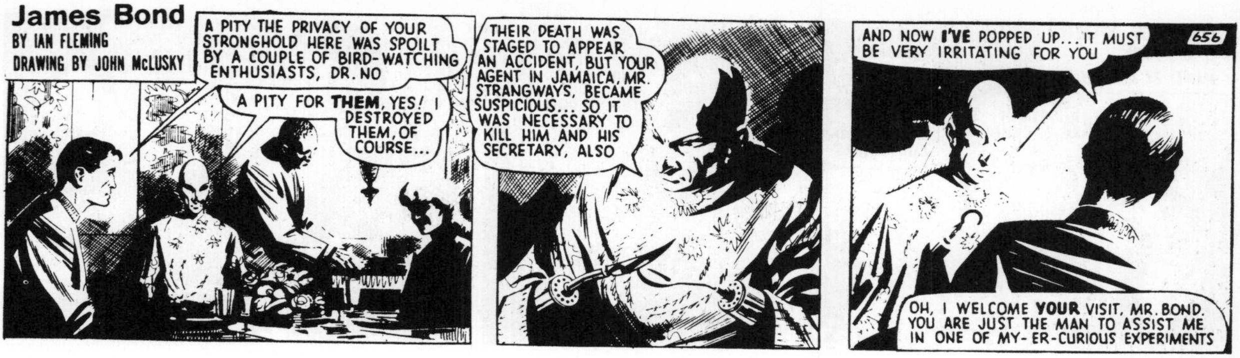
James Bond
BY IAN FLEMING
DRAWING BY JOHN McLUSKY
A PITY THE PRIVACY OF YOUR STRONGHOLD HERE WAS SPOILT BY A COUPLE OF BIRD-WATCHING ENTHUSIASTS, DR. NO
A PITY FOR **THEM**, YES! I DESTROYED THEM, OF COURSE...
THEIR DEATH WAS STAGED TO APPEAR AN ACCIDENT, BUT YOUR AGENT IN JAMAICA, MR. STRANGWAYS, BECAME SUSPICIOUS... SO IT WAS NECESSARY TO KILL HIM AND HIS SECRETARY, ALSO
656
AND NOW **I'VE** POPPED UP... IT MUST BE VERY IRRITATING FOR YOU
OH, I WELCOME **YOUR** VISIT, MR. BOND. YOU ARE JUST THE MAN TO ASSIST ME IN ONE OF MY-ER-CURIOUS EXPERIMENTS

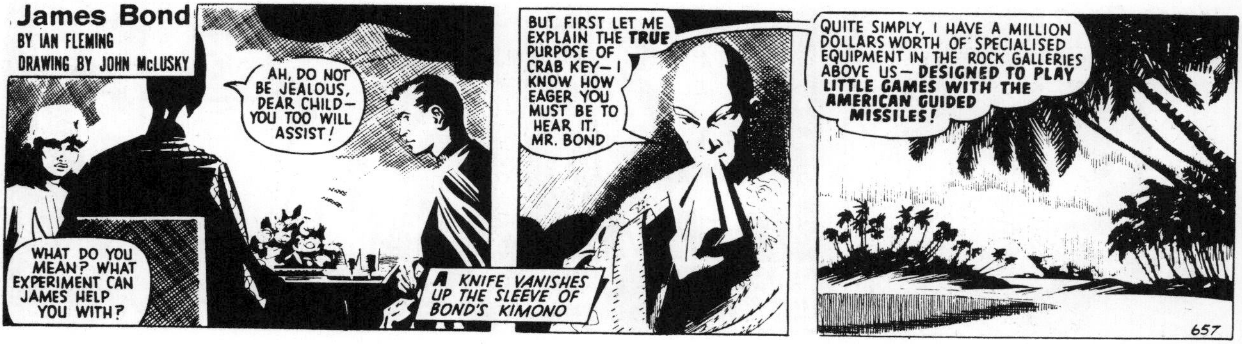
James Bond
BY IAN FLEMING
DRAWING BY JOHN McLUSKY
WHAT DO YOU MEAN? WHAT EXPERIMENT CAN JAMES HELP YOU WITH?
AH, DO NOT BE JEALOUS, DEAR CHILD— YOU TOO WILL ASSIST!
A KNIFE VANISHES UP THE SLEEVE OF BOND'S KIMONO
BUT FIRST LET ME EXPLAIN THE **TRUE** PURPOSE OF CRAB KEY— I KNOW HOW EAGER YOU MUST BE TO HEAR IT, MR. BOND
QUITE SIMPLY, I HAVE A MILLION DOLLARS WORTH OF SPECIALISED EQUIPMENT IN THE ROCK GALLERIES ABOVE US— **DESIGNED TO PLAY LITTLE GAMES WITH THE AMERICAN GUIDED MISSILES!**
657

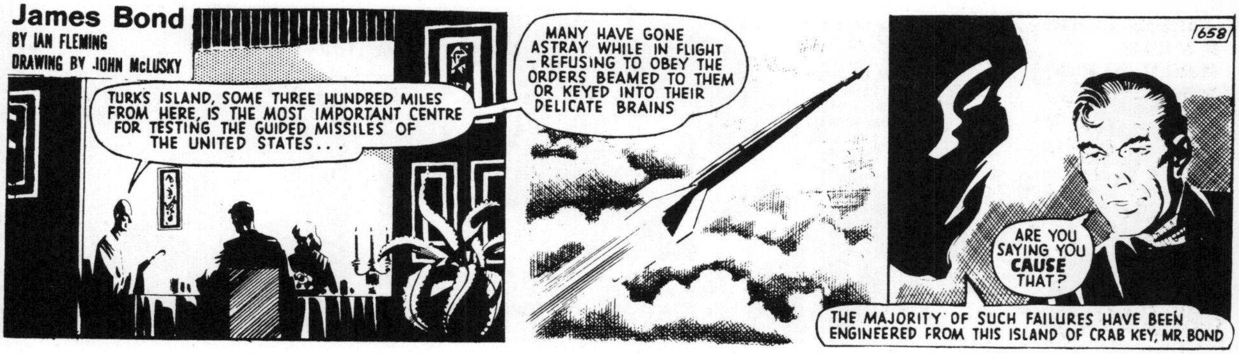
James Bond
BY IAN FLEMING
DRAWING BY JOHN McLUSKY
TURKS ISLAND, SOME THREE HUNDRED MILES FROM HERE, IS THE MOST IMPORTANT CENTRE FOR TESTING THE GUIDED MISSILES OF THE UNITED STATES...
MANY HAVE GONE ASTRAY WHILE IN FLIGHT —REFUSING TO OBEY THE ORDERS BEAMED TO THEM OR KEYED INTO THEIR DELICATE BRAINS
658
ARE YOU SAYING YOU **CAUSE** THAT?
THE MAJORITY OF SUCH FAILURES HAVE BEEN ENGINEERED FROM THIS ISLAND OF CRAB KEY, MR. BOND

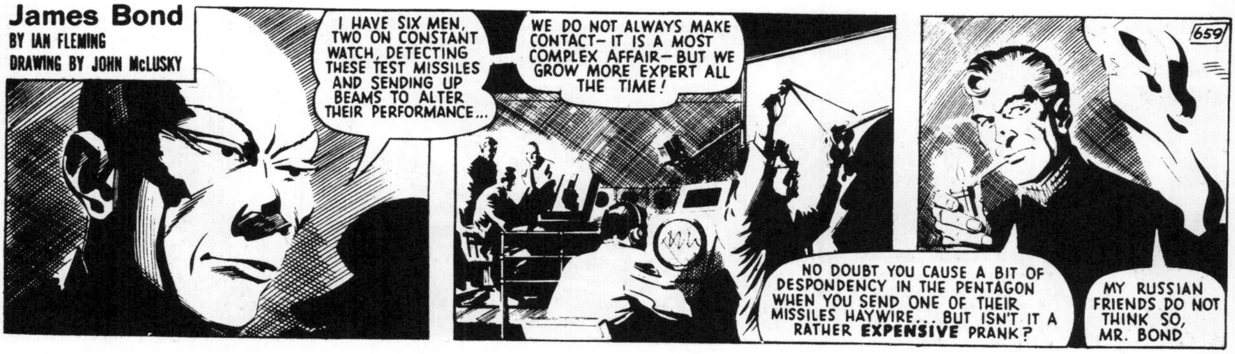
James Bond
BY IAN FLEMING
DRAWING BY JOHN McLUSKY
I HAVE SIX MEN, TWO ON CONSTANT WATCH, DETECTING THESE TEST MISSILES AND SENDING UP BEAMS TO ALTER THEIR PERFORMANCE...
WE DO NOT ALWAYS MAKE CONTACT— IT IS A MOST COMPLEX AFFAIR— BUT WE GROW MORE EXPERT ALL THE TIME!
NO DOUBT YOU CAUSE A BIT OF DESPONDENCY IN THE PENTAGON WHEN YOU SEND ONE OF THEIR MISSILES HAYWIRE... BUT ISN'T IT A RATHER **EXPENSIVE** PRANK?
659
MY RUSSIAN FRIENDS DO NOT THINK SO, MR. BOND

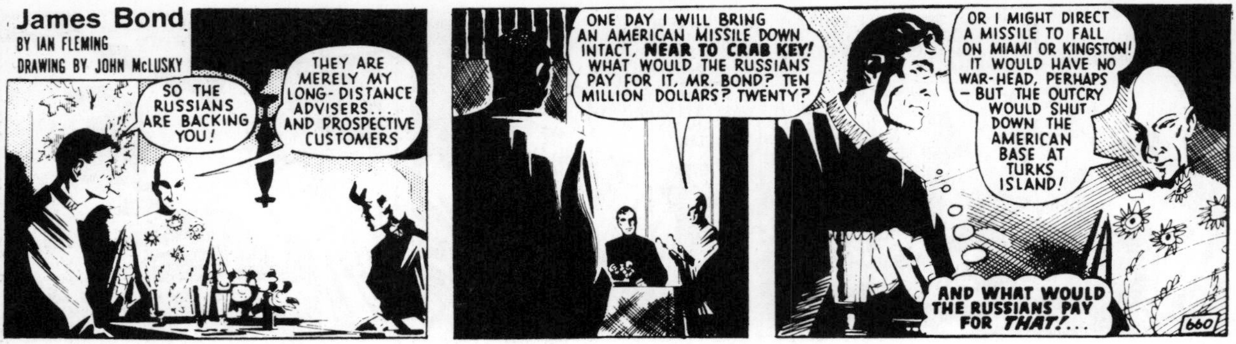
James Bond
BY IAN FLEMING
DRAWING BY JOHN McLUSKY
SO THE RUSSIANS ARE BACKING YOU!
THEY ARE MERELY MY LONG-DISTANCE ADVISERS... AND PROSPECTIVE CUSTOMERS
ONE DAY I WILL BRING AN AMERICAN MISSILE DOWN INTACT, NEAR TO CRAB KEY! WHAT WOULD THE RUSSIANS PAY FOR IT, MR. BOND? TEN MILLION DOLLARS? TWENTY?
OR I MIGHT DIRECT A MISSILE TO FALL ON MIAMI OR KINGSTON! IT WOULD HAVE NO WAR-HEAD, PERHAPS – BUT THE OUTCRY WOULD SHUT DOWN THE AMERICAN BASE AT TURKS ISLAND!
AND WHAT WOULD THE RUSSIANS PAY FOR THAT!...
660

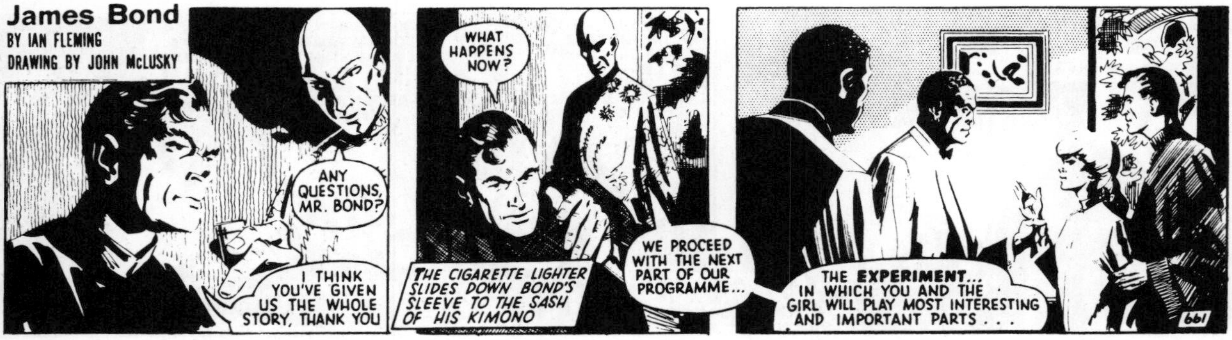
James Bond
BY IAN FLEMING
DRAWING BY JOHN McLUSKY
ANY QUESTIONS, MR. BOND?
I THINK YOU'VE GIVEN US THE WHOLE STORY, THANK YOU
WHAT HAPPENS NOW?
THE CIGARETTE LIGHTER SLIDES DOWN BOND'S SLEEVE TO THE SASH OF HIS KIMONO
WE PROCEED WITH THE NEXT PART OF OUR PROGRAMME...
THE EXPERIMENT... IN WHICH YOU AND THE GIRL WILL PLAY MOST INTERESTING AND IMPORTANT PARTS . . .
661

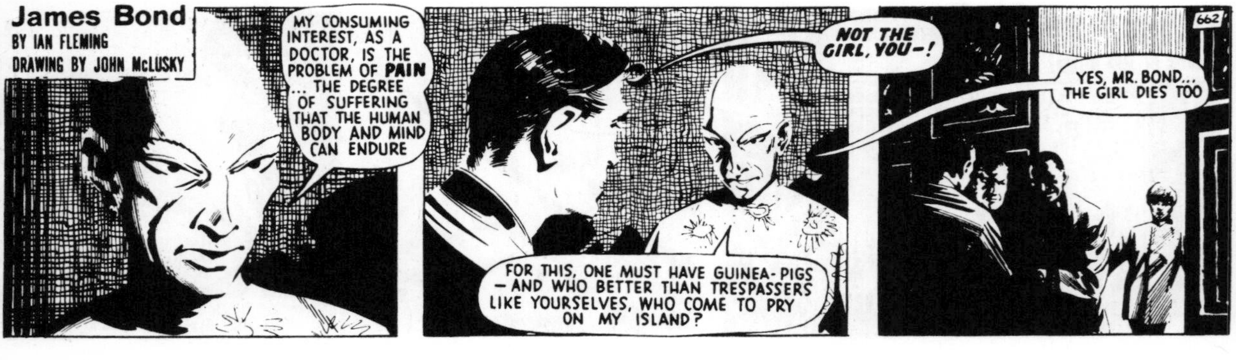
James Bond
BY IAN FLEMING
DRAWING BY JOHN McLUSKY
MY CONSUMING INTEREST, AS A DOCTOR, IS THE PROBLEM OF PAIN ... THE DEGREE OF SUFFERING THAT THE HUMAN BODY AND MIND CAN ENDURE
NOT THE GIRL, YOU–!
FOR THIS, ONE MUST HAVE GUINEA-PIGS – AND WHO BETTER THAN TRESPASSERS LIKE YOURSELVES, WHO COME TO PRY ON MY ISLAND?
662
YES, MR. BOND... THE GIRL DIES TOO

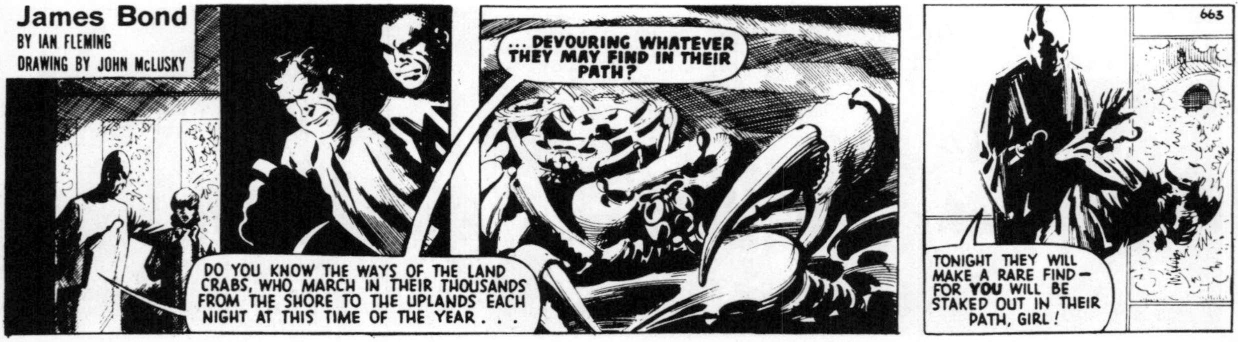
James Bond
BY IAN FLEMING
DRAWING BY JOHN McLUSKY
DO YOU KNOW THE WAYS OF THE LAND CRABS, WHO MARCH IN THEIR THOUSANDS FROM THE SHORE TO THE UPLANDS EACH NIGHT AT THIS TIME OF THE YEAR . . .
... DEVOURING WHATEVER THEY MAY FIND IN THEIR PATH?
663
TONIGHT THEY WILL MAKE A RARE FIND – FOR YOU WILL BE STAKED OUT IN THEIR PATH, GIRL!

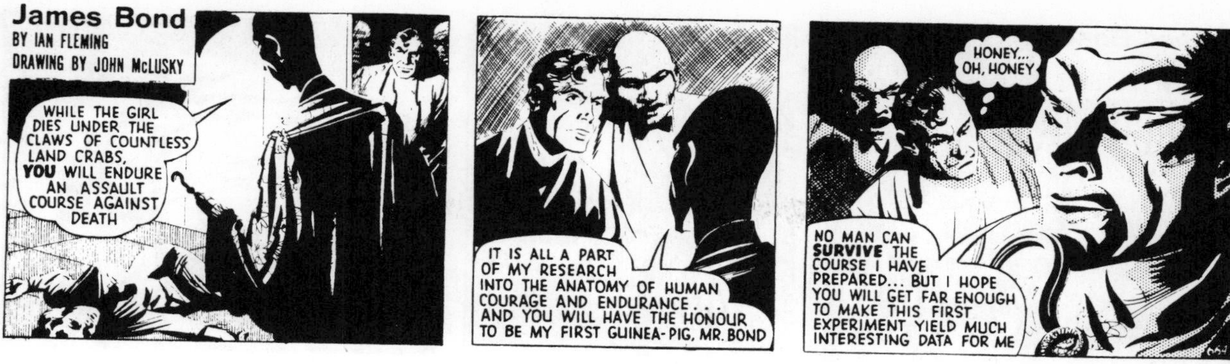
James Bond
BY IAN FLEMING
DRAWING BY JOHN McLUSKY
WHILE THE GIRL DIES UNDER THE CLAWS OF COUNTLESS LAND CRABS, **YOU** WILL ENDURE AN ASSAULT COURSE AGAINST DEATH
IT IS ALL A PART OF MY RESEARCH INTO THE ANATOMY OF HUMAN COURAGE AND ENDURANCE... AND YOU WILL HAVE THE HONOUR TO BE MY FIRST GUINEA-PIG, MR. BOND
HONEY... OH, HONEY
NO MAN CAN **SURVIVE** THE COURSE I HAVE PREPARED... BUT I HOPE YOU WILL GET FAR ENOUGH TO MAKE THIS FIRST EXPERIMENT YIELD MUCH INTERESTING DATA FOR ME
664

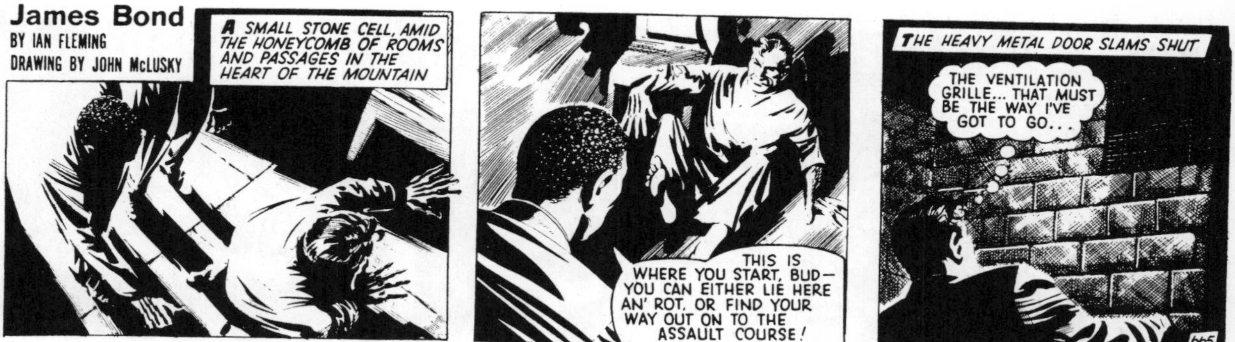
James Bond
BY IAN FLEMING
DRAWING BY JOHN McLUSKY
A SMALL STONE CELL, AMID THE HONEYCOMB OF ROOMS AND PASSAGES IN THE HEART OF THE MOUNTAIN
THIS IS WHERE YOU START, BUD— YOU CAN EITHER LIE HERE AN' ROT, OR FIND YOUR WAY OUT ON TO THE ASSAULT COURSE!
THE HEAVY METAL DOOR SLAMS SHUT
THE VENTILATION GRILLE... THAT MUST BE THE WAY I'VE GOT TO GO...
665

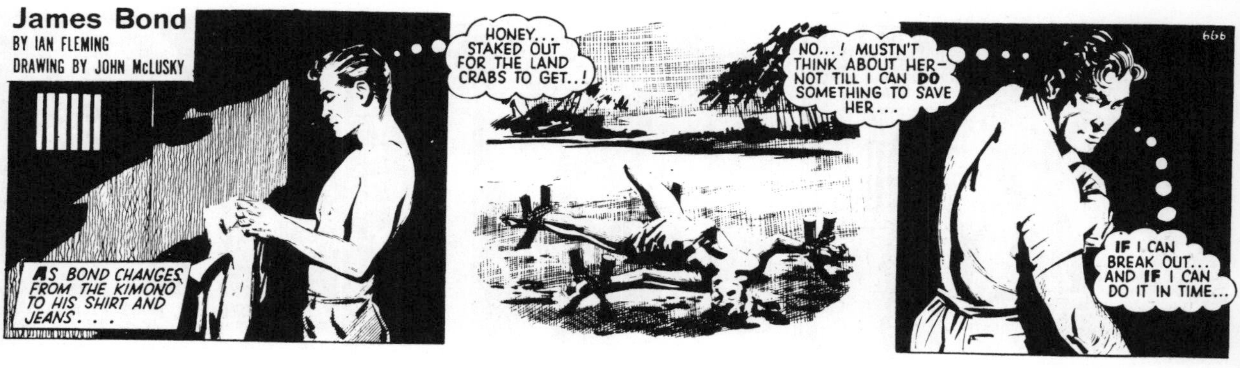
James Bond
BY IAN FLEMING
DRAWING BY JOHN McLUSKY
AS BOND CHANGES FROM THE KIMONO TO HIS SHIRT AND JEANS...
HONEY... STAKED OUT FOR THE LAND CRABS TO GET..!
NO...! MUSTN'T THINK ABOUT HER— NOT TILL I CAN **DO** SOMETHING TO SAVE HER...
666
IF I CAN BREAK OUT... AND **IF** I CAN DO IT IN TIME...

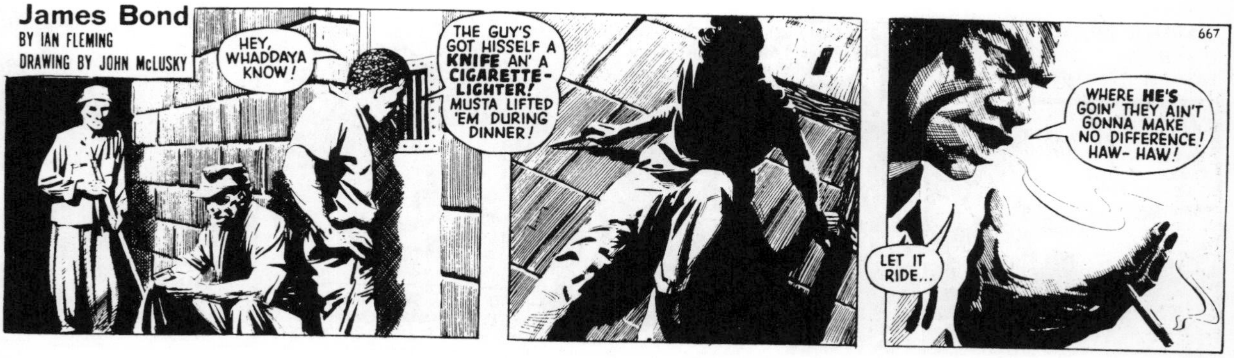
James Bond
BY IAN FLEMING
DRAWING BY JOHN McLUSKY
HEY, WHADDAYA KNOW!
THE GUY'S GOT HISSELF A **KNIFE** AN' A **CIGARETTE-LIGHTER!** MUSTA LIFTED 'EM DURING DINNER!
667
WHERE **HE'S** GOIN' THEY AIN'T GONNA MAKE NO DIFFERENCE! HAW-HAW!
LET IT RIDE...

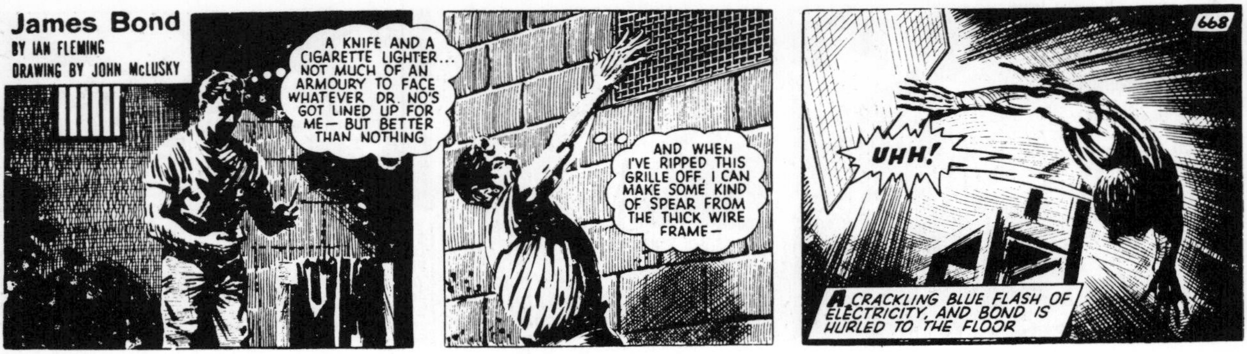
James Bond
BY IAN FLEMING
DRAWING BY JOHN McLUSKY
A KNIFE AND A CIGARETTE LIGHTER... NOT MUCH OF AN ARMOURY TO FACE WHATEVER DR. NO'S GOT LINED UP FOR ME— BUT BETTER THAN NOTHING
AND WHEN I'VE RIPPED THIS GRILLE OFF, I CAN MAKE SOME KIND OF SPEAR FROM THE THICK WIRE FRAME—
668
UHH!
A CRACKLING BLUE FLASH OF ELECTRICITY, AND BOND IS HURLED TO THE FLOOR

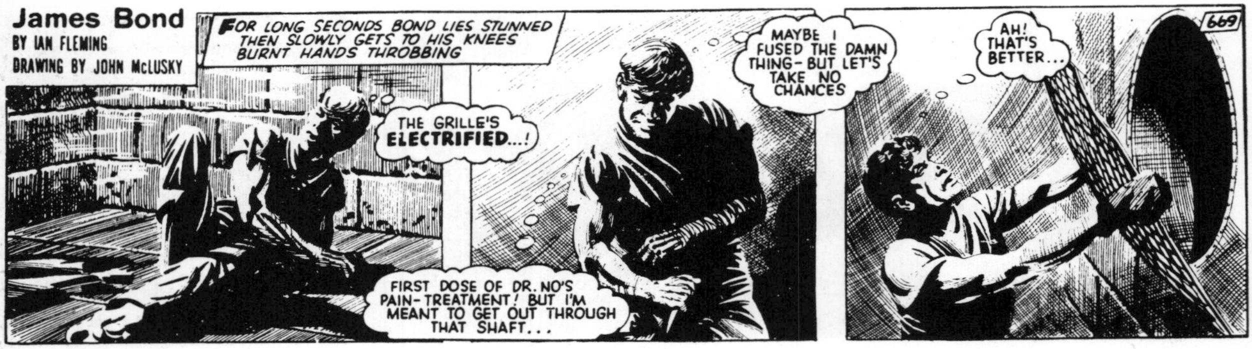
James Bond
BY IAN FLEMING
DRAWING BY JOHN McLUSKY
FOR LONG SECONDS BOND LIES STUNNED THEN SLOWLY GETS TO HIS KNEES BURNT HANDS THROBBING
THE GRILLE'S ELECTRIFIED...!
FIRST DOSE OF DR. NO'S PAIN-TREATMENT! BUT I'M MEANT TO GET OUT THROUGH THAT SHAFT...
MAYBE I FUSED THE DAMN THING- BUT LET'S TAKE NO CHANCES
669
AH! THAT'S BETTER...

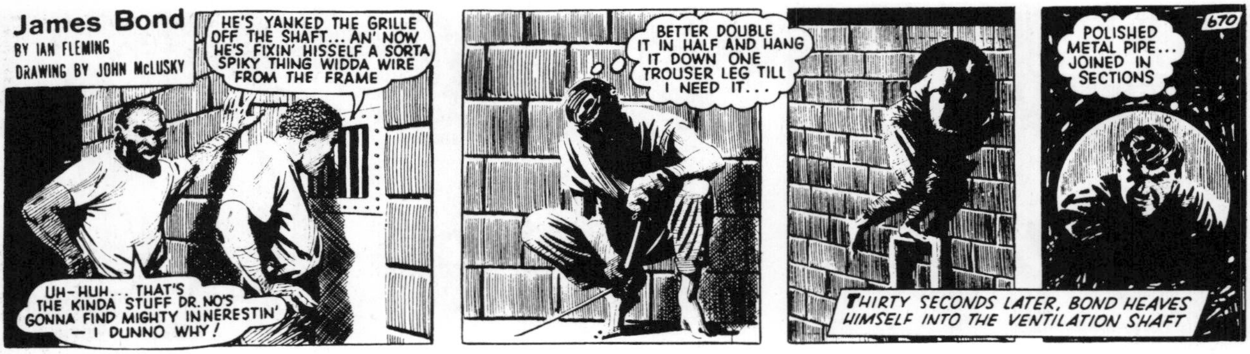
James Bond
BY IAN FLEMING
DRAWING BY JOHN McLUSKY
HE'S YANKED THE GRILLE OFF THE SHAFT... AN' NOW HE'S FIXIN' HISSELF A SORTA SPIKY THING WIDDA WIRE FROM THE FRAME
UH-HUH... THAT'S THE KINDA STUFF DR. NO'S GONNA FIND MIGHTY INNERESTIN' — I DUNNO WHY!
BETTER DOUBLE IT IN HALF AND HANG IT DOWN ONE TROUSER LEG TILL I NEED IT...
670
POLISHED METAL PIPE... JOINED IN SECTIONS
THIRTY SECONDS LATER, BOND HEAVES HIMSELF INTO THE VENTILATION SHAFT

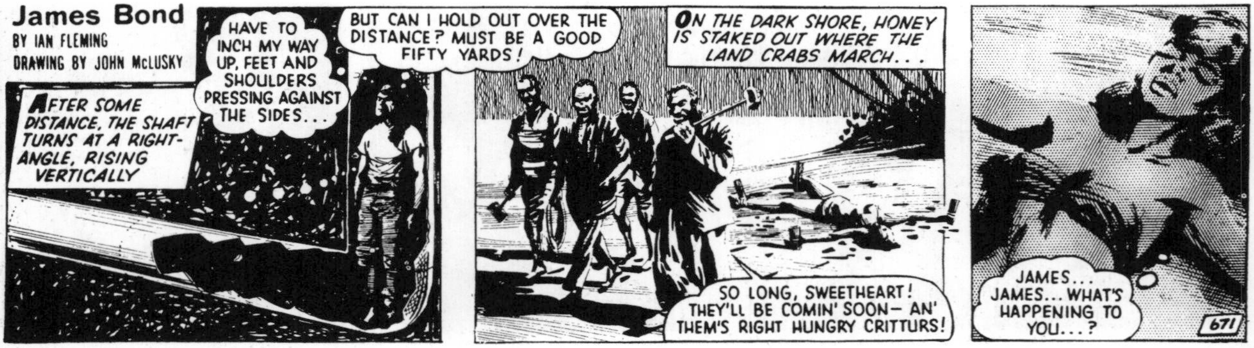
James Bond
BY IAN FLEMING
DRAWING BY JOHN McLUSKY
AFTER SOME DISTANCE, THE SHAFT TURNS AT A RIGHT-ANGLE, RISING VERTICALLY
HAVE TO INCH MY WAY UP, FEET AND SHOULDERS PRESSING AGAINST THE SIDES...
BUT CAN I HOLD OUT OVER THE DISTANCE? MUST BE A GOOD FIFTY YARDS!
ON THE DARK SHORE, HONEY IS STAKED OUT WHERE THE LAND CRABS MARCH...
SO LONG, SWEETHEART! THEY'LL BE COMIN' SOON— AN' THEM'S RIGHT HUNGRY CRITTURS!
JAMES... JAMES... WHAT'S HAPPENING TO YOU...?
671

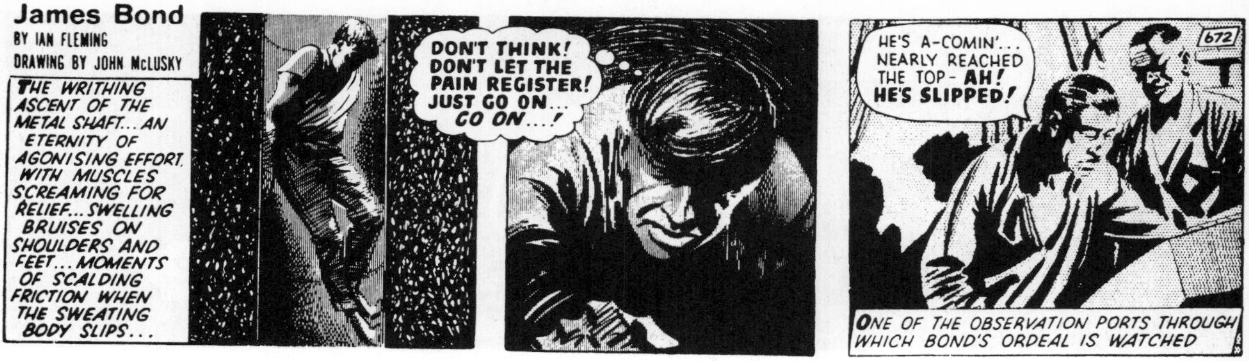
James Bond
BY IAN FLEMING
DRAWING BY JOHN McLUSKY
THE WRITHING ASCENT OF THE METAL SHAFT... AN ETERNITY OF AGONISING EFFORT, WITH MUSCLES SCREAMING FOR RELIEF... SWELLING BRUISES ON SHOULDERS AND FEET... MOMENTS OF SCALDING FRICTION WHEN THE SWEATING BODY SLIPS...
DON'T THINK! DON'T LET THE PAIN REGISTER! JUST GO ON... GO ON...!
672
HE'S A-COMIN'... NEARLY REACHED THE TOP- AH! HE'S SLIPPED!
ONE OF THE OBSERVATION PORTS THROUGH WHICH BOND'S ORDEAL IS WATCHED

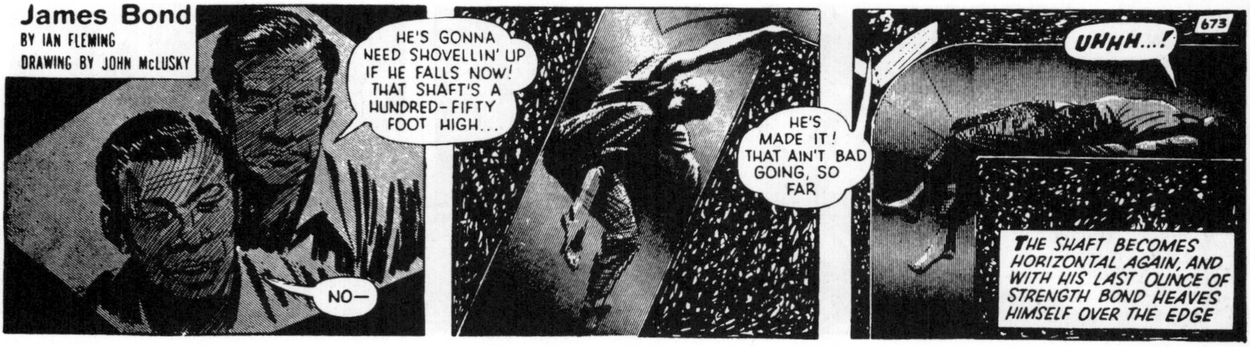
James Bond
BY IAN FLEMING
DRAWING BY JOHN McLUSKY
HE'S GONNA NEED SHOVELLIN' UP IF HE FALLS NOW! THAT SHAFT'S A HUNDRED-FIFTY FOOT HIGH...
NO—
HE'S MADE IT! THAT AIN'T BAD GOING, SO FAR
673
UHHH...!
THE SHAFT BECOMES HORIZONTAL AGAIN, AND WITH HIS LAST OUNCE OF STRENGTH BOND HEAVES HIMSELF OVER THE EDGE

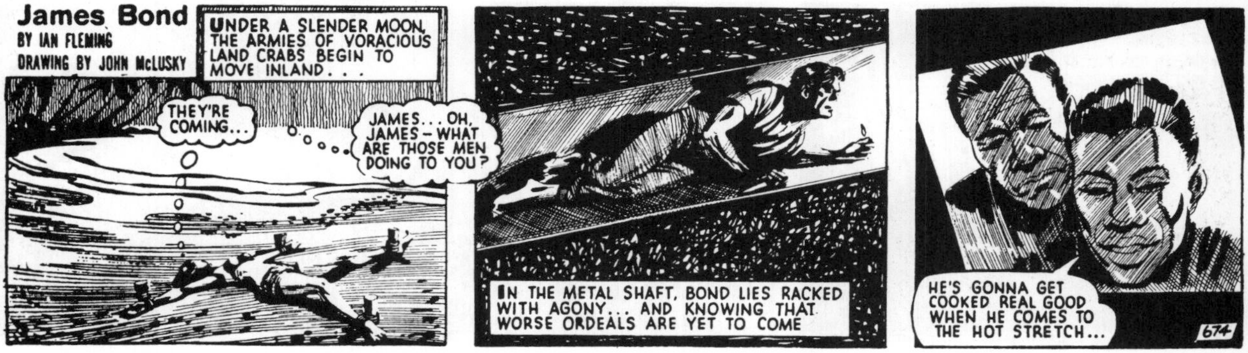
James Bond
BY IAN FLEMING
DRAWING BY JOHN McLUSKY
UNDER A SLENDER MOON, THE ARMIES OF VORACIOUS LAND CRABS BEGIN TO MOVE INLAND...
THEY'RE COMING...
JAMES... OH, JAMES – WHAT ARE THOSE MEN DOING TO YOU?
IN THE METAL SHAFT, BOND LIES RACKED WITH AGONY... AND KNOWING THAT WORSE ORDEALS ARE YET TO COME
HE'S GONNA GET COOKED REAL GOOD WHEN HE COMES TO THE HOT STRETCH...
674

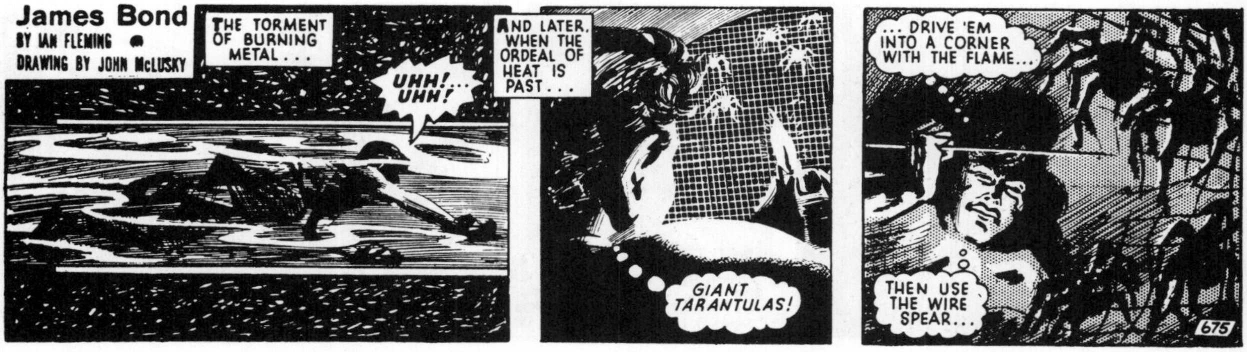
James Bond
BY IAN FLEMING
DRAWING BY JOHN McLUSKY
THE TORMENT OF BURNING METAL...
UHH!... UHH!
AND LATER, WHEN THE ORDEAL OF HEAT IS PAST...
GIANT TARANTULAS!
... DRIVE 'EM INTO A CORNER WITH THE FLAME...
THEN USE THE WIRE SPEAR...
675

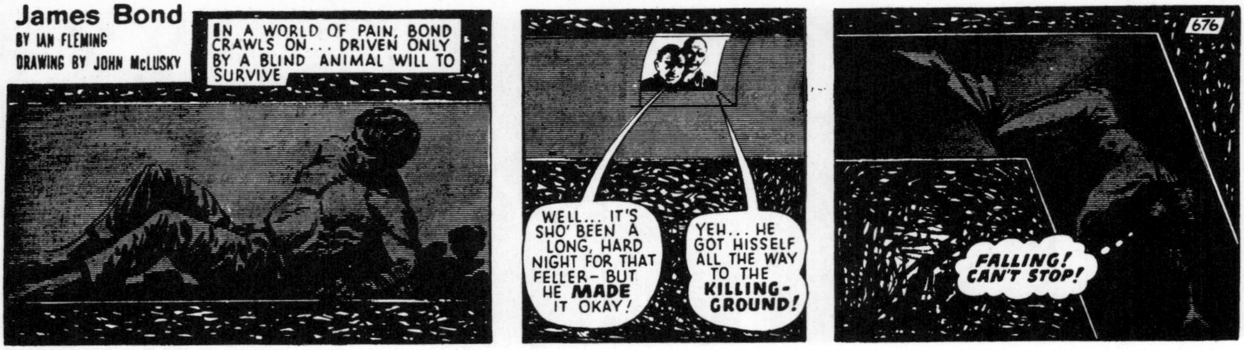
James Bond
BY IAN FLEMING
DRAWING BY JOHN McLUSKY
IN A WORLD OF PAIN, BOND CRAWLS ON... DRIVEN ONLY BY A BLIND ANIMAL WILL TO SURVIVE
WELL... IT'S SHO' BEEN A LONG, HARD NIGHT FOR THAT FELLER– BUT HE MADE IT OKAY!
YEH... HE GOT HISSELF ALL THE WAY TO THE KILLING-GROUND!
676
FALLING! CAN'T STOP!

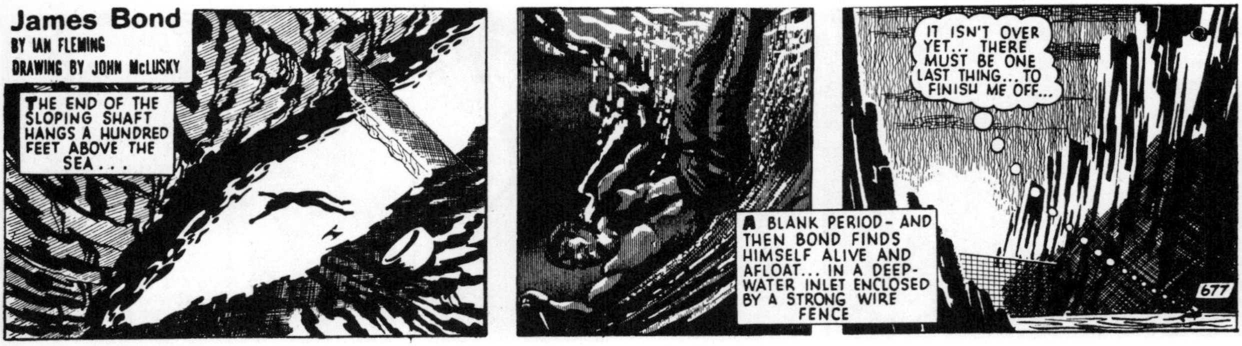
James Bond
BY IAN FLEMING
DRAWING BY JOHN McLUSKY
THE END OF THE SLOPING SHAFT HANGS A HUNDRED FEET ABOVE THE SEA...
A BLANK PERIOD– AND THEN BOND FINDS HIMSELF ALIVE AND AFLOAT... IN A DEEP-WATER INLET ENCLOSED BY A STRONG WIRE FENCE
IT ISN'T OVER YET... THERE MUST BE ONE LAST THING... TO FINISH ME OFF...
677

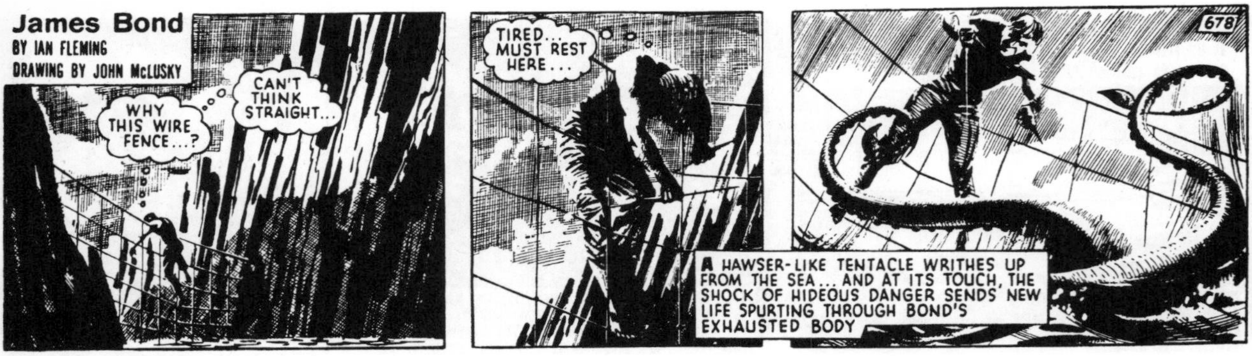
James Bond
BY IAN FLEMING
DRAWING BY JOHN McLUSKY
WHY THIS WIRE FENCE...?
CAN'T THINK STRAIGHT...
TIRED... MUST REST HERE...
678
A HAWSER-LIKE TENTACLE WRITHES UP FROM THE SEA... AND AT ITS TOUCH, THE SHOCK OF HIDEOUS DANGER SENDS NEW LIFE SPURTING THROUGH BOND'S EXHAUSTED BODY

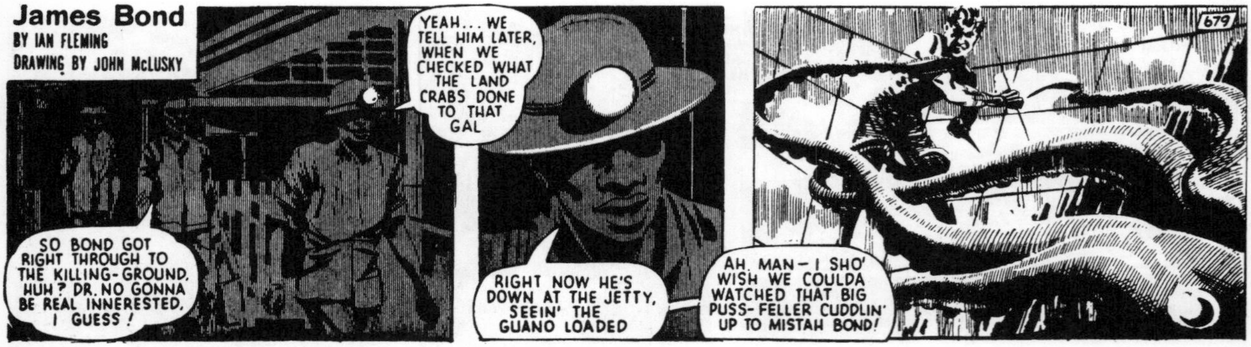
James Bond
BY IAN FLEMING
DRAWING BY JOHN McLUSKY
SO BOND GOT RIGHT THROUGH TO THE KILLING-GROUND, HUH? DR. NO GONNA BE REAL INNERESTED, I GUESS!
YEAH... WE TELL HIM LATER, WHEN WE CHECKED WHAT THE LAND CRABS DONE TO THAT GAL
RIGHT NOW HE'S DOWN AT THE JETTY, SEEIN' THE GUANO LOADED
AH, MAN– I SHO' WISH WE COULDA WATCHED THAT BIG PUSS-FELLER CUDDLIN' UP TO MISTAH BOND!
679

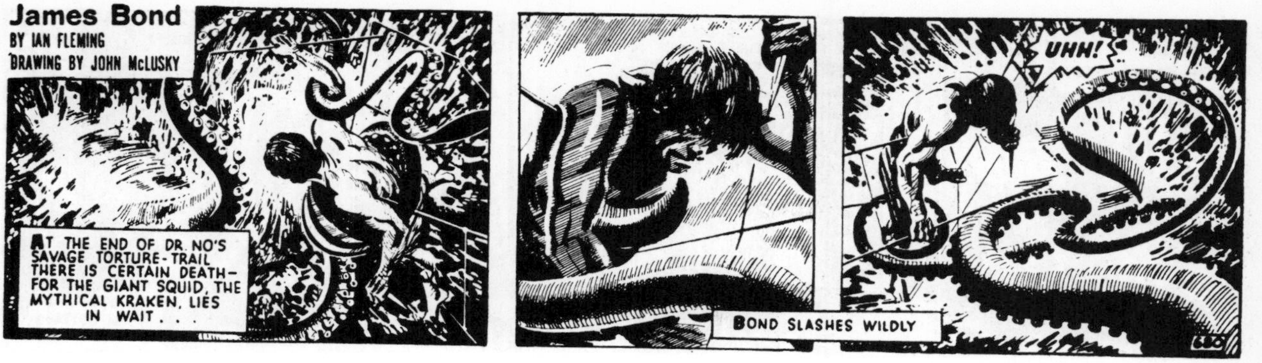
James Bond
BY IAN FLEMING
DRAWING BY JOHN McLUSKY
AT THE END OF DR. NO'S SAVAGE TORTURE-TRAIL THERE IS CERTAIN DEATH— FOR THE GIANT SQUID, THE MYTHICAL KRAKEN, LIES IN WAIT . . .
BOND SLASHES WILDLY
UHH!
680

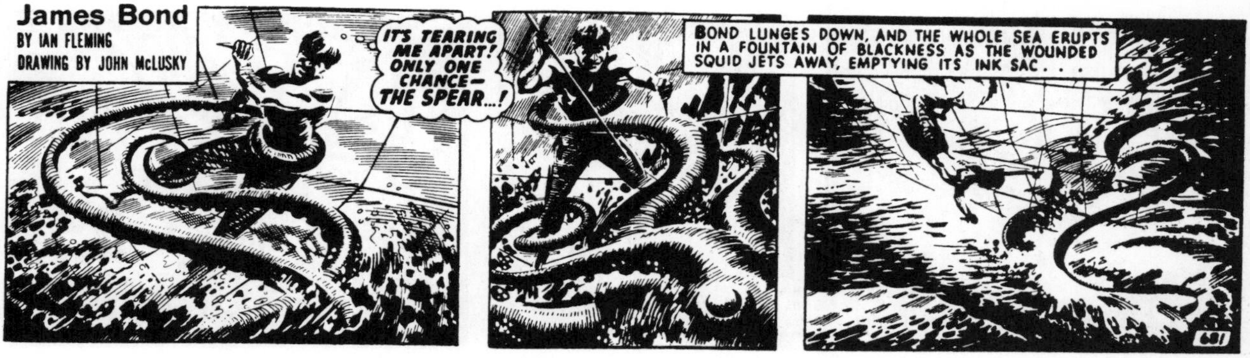
James Bond
BY IAN FLEMING
DRAWING BY JOHN McLUSKY
IT'S TEARING ME APART! ONLY ONE CHANCE— THE SPEAR...!
BOND LUNGES DOWN, AND THE WHOLE SEA ERUPTS IN A FOUNTAIN OF BLACKNESS AS THE WOUNDED SQUID JETS AWAY, EMPTYING ITS INK SAC . . .
681

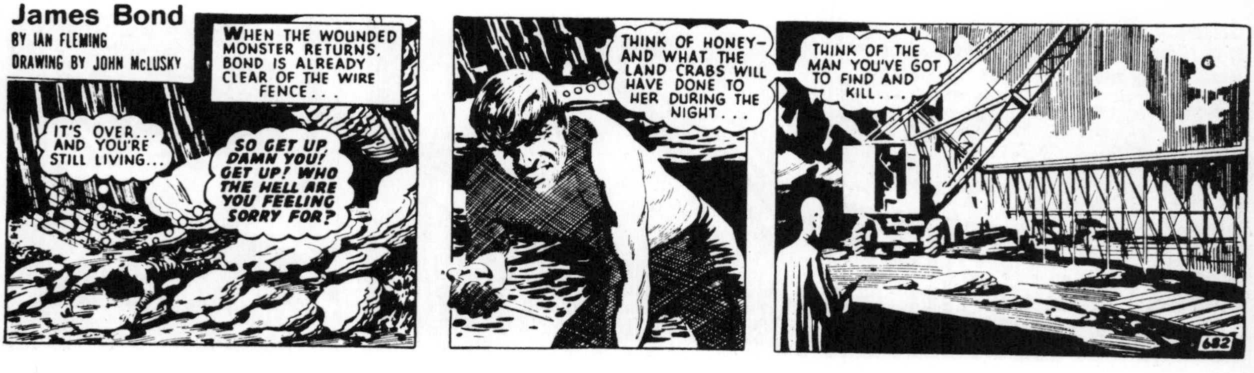
James Bond
BY IAN FLEMING
DRAWING BY JOHN McLUSKY
WHEN THE WOUNDED MONSTER RETURNS, BOND IS ALREADY CLEAR OF THE WIRE FENCE . . .
IT'S OVER... AND YOU'RE STILL LIVING...
SO GET UP, DAMN YOU! GET UP! WHO THE HELL ARE YOU FEELING SORRY FOR?
THINK OF HONEY— AND WHAT THE LAND CRABS WILL HAVE DONE TO HER DURING THE NIGHT . . .
THINK OF THE MAN YOU'VE GOT TO FIND AND KILL . . .
682

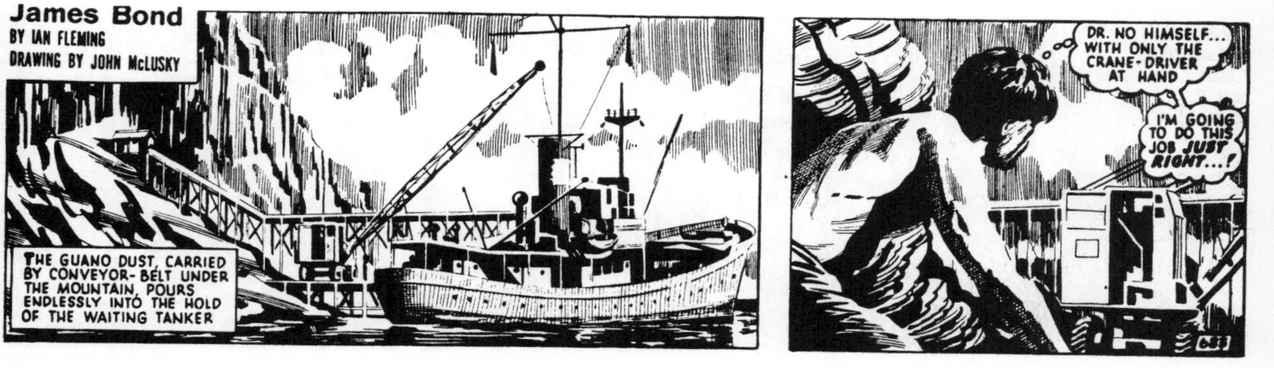
James Bond
BY IAN FLEMING
DRAWING BY JOHN McLUSKY
THE GUANO DUST, CARRIED BY CONVEYOR-BELT UNDER THE MOUNTAIN, POURS ENDLESSLY INTO THE HOLD OF THE WAITING TANKER
DR. NO HIMSELF... WITH ONLY THE CRANE-DRIVER AT HAND
I'M GOING TO DO THIS JOB JUST RIGHT...!
683

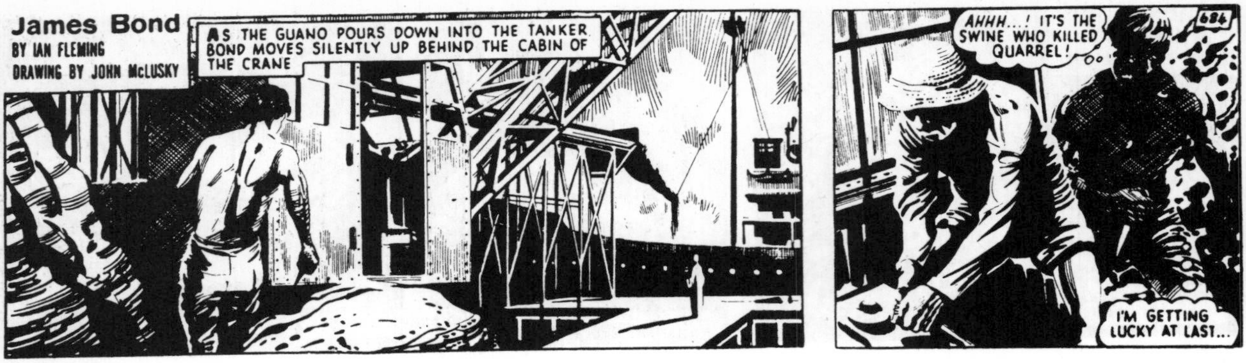
James Bond
BY IAN FLEMING
DRAWING BY JOHN McLUSKY
AS THE GUANO POURS DOWN INTO THE TANKER BOND MOVES SILENTLY UP BEHIND THE CABIN OF THE CRANE
684
AHHH...! IT'S THE SWINE WHO KILLED QUARREL!
I'M GETTING LUCKY AT LAST...

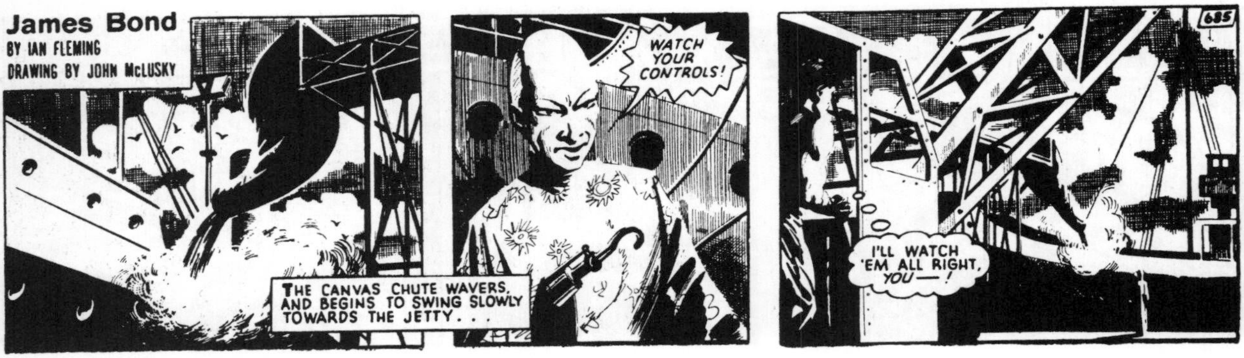
James Bond
BY IAN FLEMING
DRAWING BY JOHN McLUSKY
THE CANVAS CHUTE WAVERS, AND BEGINS TO SWING SLOWLY TOWARDS THE JETTY...
WATCH YOUR CONTROLS!
685
I'LL WATCH 'EM ALL RIGHT, YOU—!

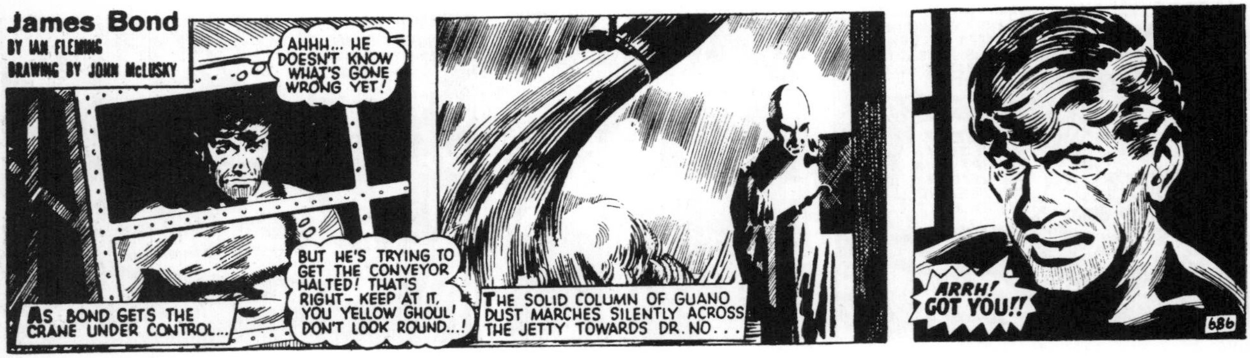
James Bond
BY IAN FLEMING
DRAWING BY JOHN McLUSKY
AHHH... HE DOESN'T KNOW WHAT'S GONE WRONG YET!
AS BOND GETS THE CRANE UNDER CONTROL...
BUT HE'S TRYING TO GET THE CONVEYOR HALTED! THAT'S RIGHT– KEEP AT IT, YOU YELLOW GHOUL! DON'T LOOK ROUND...!
THE SOLID COLUMN OF GUANO DUST MARCHES SILENTLY ACROSS THE JETTY TOWARDS DR. NO...
ARRH! GOT YOU!!
686

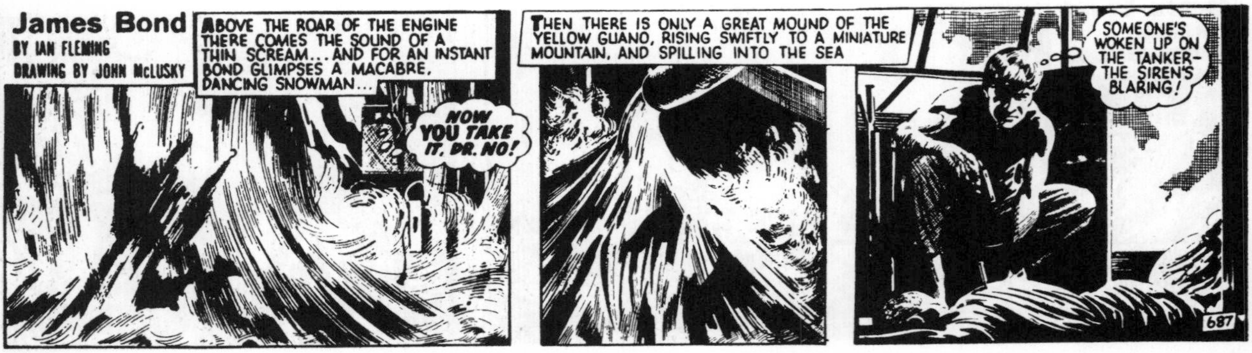
James Bond
BY IAN FLEMING
DRAWING BY JOHN McLUSKY
ABOVE THE ROAR OF THE ENGINE THERE COMES THE SOUND OF A THIN SCREAM... AND FOR AN INSTANT BOND GLIMPSES A MACABRE, DANCING SNOWMAN...
NOW YOU TAKE IT, DR. NO!
THEN THERE IS ONLY A GREAT MOUND OF THE YELLOW GUANO, RISING SWIFTLY TO A MINIATURE MOUNTAIN, AND SPILLING INTO THE SEA
SOMEONE'S WOKEN UP ON THE TANKER– THE SIREN'S BLARING!
687

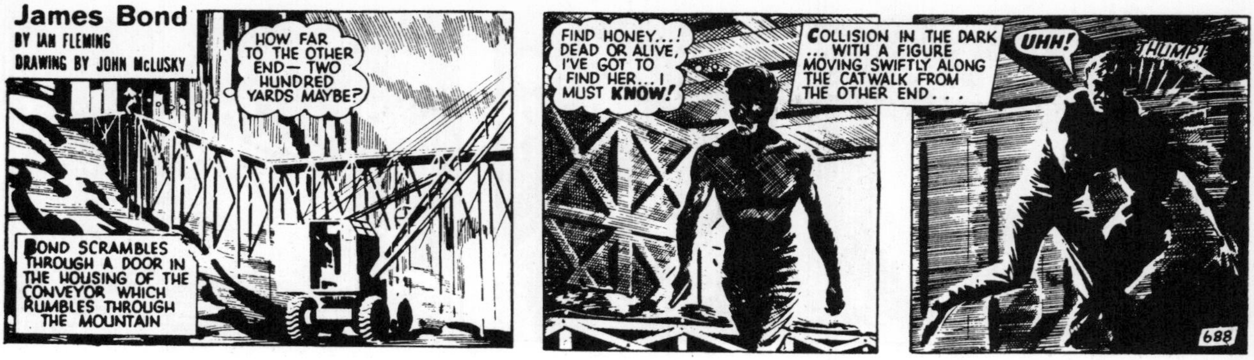
James Bond
BY IAN FLEMING
DRAWING BY JOHN McLUSKY
HOW FAR TO THE OTHER END— TWO HUNDRED YARDS MAYBE?
BOND SCRAMBLES THROUGH A DOOR IN THE HOUSING OF THE CONVEYOR WHICH RUMBLES THROUGH THE MOUNTAIN
FIND HONEY...! DEAD OR ALIVE, I'VE GOT TO FIND HER... I MUST KNOW!
COLLISION IN THE DARK ... WITH A FIGURE MOVING SWIFTLY ALONG THE CATWALK FROM THE OTHER END . . .
UHH!
THUMP!
688

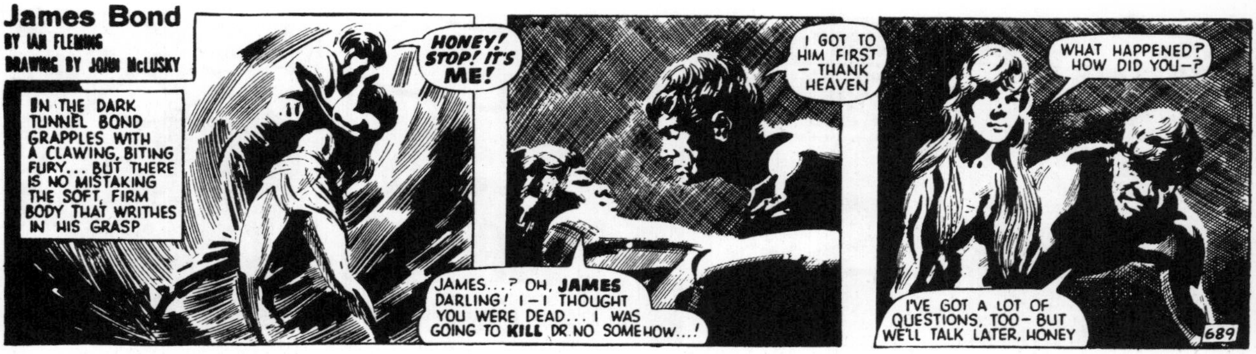
James Bond
BY IAN FLEMING
DRAWING BY JOHN McLUSKY
IN THE DARK TUNNEL BOND GRAPPLES WITH A CLAWING, BITING FURY... BUT THERE IS NO MISTAKING THE SOFT, FIRM BODY THAT WRITHES IN HIS GRASP
HONEY! STOP! IT'S ME!
I GOT TO HIM FIRST — THANK HEAVEN
JAMES...? OH, JAMES DARLING! I—I THOUGHT YOU WERE DEAD... I WAS GOING TO KILL DR NO SOMEHOW...!
WHAT HAPPENED? HOW DID YOU—?
I'VE GOT A LOT OF QUESTIONS, TOO— BUT WE'LL TALK LATER, HONEY
689

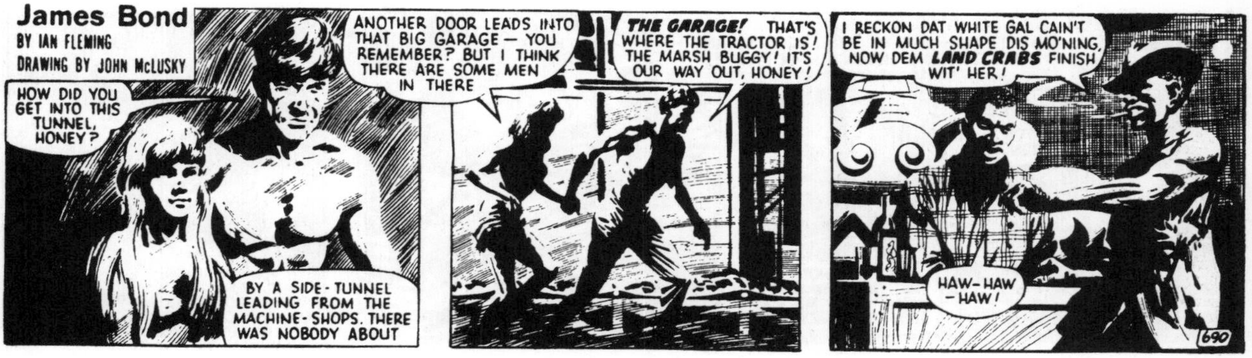
James Bond
BY IAN FLEMING
DRAWING BY JOHN McLUSKY
HOW DID YOU GET INTO THIS TUNNEL, HONEY?
BY A SIDE-TUNNEL LEADING FROM THE MACHINE-SHOPS. THERE WAS NOBODY ABOUT
ANOTHER DOOR LEADS INTO THAT BIG GARAGE — YOU REMEMBER? BUT I THINK THERE ARE SOME MEN IN THERE
THE GARAGE! THAT'S WHERE THE TRACTOR IS! THE MARSH BUGGY! IT'S OUR WAY OUT, HONEY!
I RECKON DAT WHITE GAL CAIN'T BE IN MUCH SHAPE DIS MO'NING, NOW DEM LAND CRABS FINISH WIT' HER!
HAW-HAW -HAW!
690

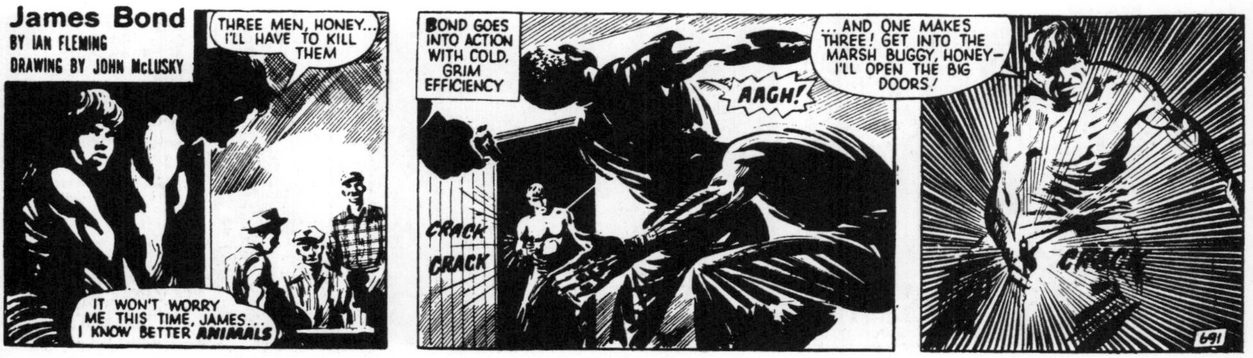
James Bond
BY IAN FLEMING
DRAWING BY JOHN McLUSKY
THREE MEN, HONEY... I'LL HAVE TO KILL THEM
IT WON'T WORRY ME THIS TIME, JAMES... I KNOW BETTER ANIMALS
BOND GOES INTO ACTION WITH COLD, GRIM EFFICIENCY
AAGH!
CRACK
CRACK
... AND ONE MAKES THREE! GET INTO THE MARSH BUGGY, HONEY— I'LL OPEN THE BIG DOORS!
CRACK
691

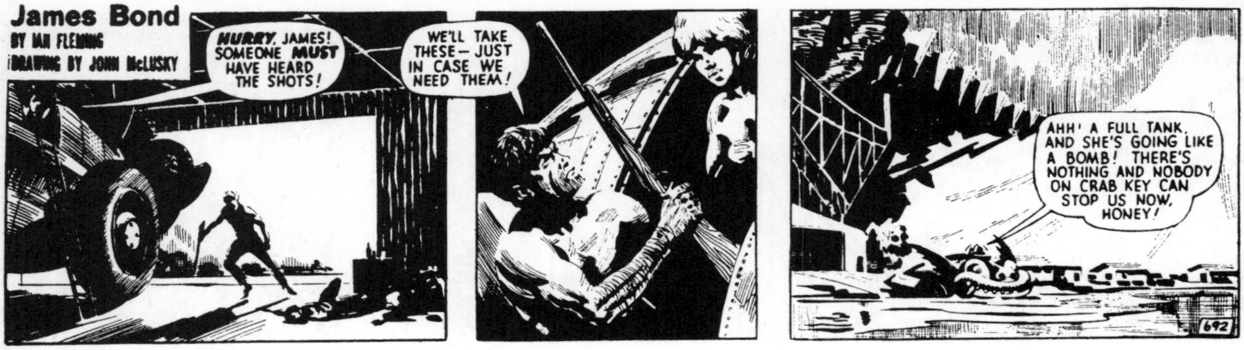
James Bond
BY IAN FLEMING
DRAWING BY JOHN McLUSKY
HURRY, JAMES! SOMEONE MUST HAVE HEARD THE SHOTS!
WE'LL TAKE THESE — JUST IN CASE WE NEED THEM!
AHH! A FULL TANK, AND SHE'S GOING LIKE A BOMB! THERE'S NOTHING AND NOBODY ON CRAB KEY CAN STOP US NOW, HONEY!
692

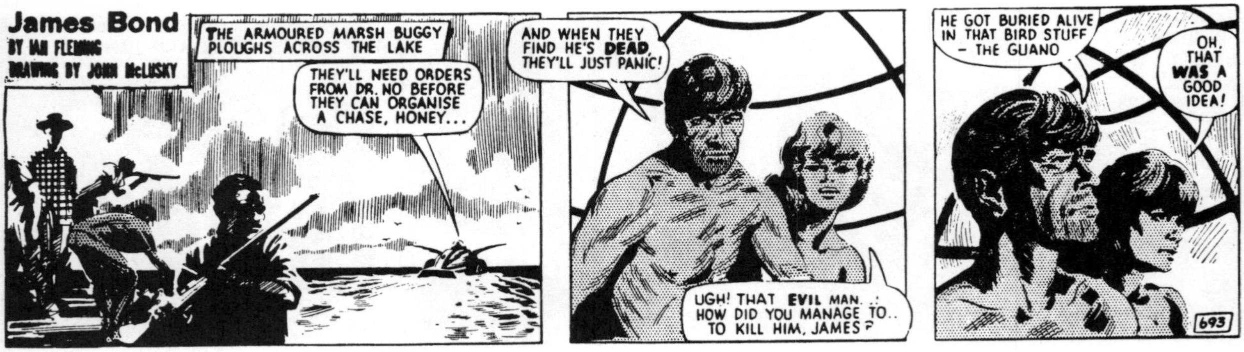
James Bond
BY IAN FLEMING
DRAWING BY JOHN McLUSKY
THE ARMOURED MARSH BUGGY PLOUGHS ACROSS THE LAKE
THEY'LL NEED ORDERS FROM DR. NO BEFORE THEY CAN ORGANISE A CHASE, HONEY...
AND WHEN THEY FIND HE'S DEAD, THEY'LL JUST PANIC!
UGH! THAT EVIL MAN.. HOW DID YOU MANAGE TO.. TO KILL HIM, JAMES?
HE GOT BURIED ALIVE IN THAT BIRD STUFF – THE GUANO
OH. THAT WAS A GOOD IDEA!
693

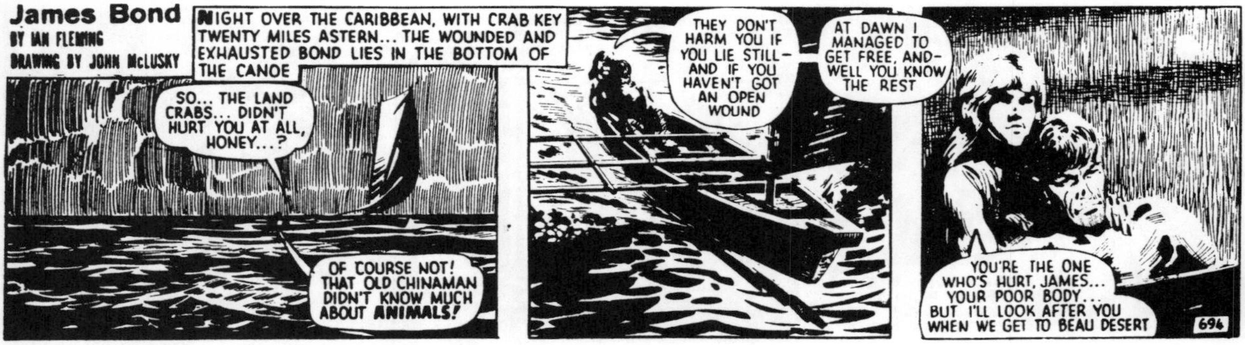
James Bond
BY IAN FLEMING
DRAWING BY JOHN McLUSKY
NIGHT OVER THE CARIBBEAN, WITH CRAB KEY TWENTY MILES ASTERN... THE WOUNDED AND EXHAUSTED BOND LIES IN THE BOTTOM OF THE CANOE
SO... THE LAND CRABS... DIDN'T HURT YOU AT ALL, HONEY...?
OF COURSE NOT! THAT OLD CHINAMAN DIDN'T KNOW MUCH ABOUT ANIMALS!
THEY DON'T HARM YOU IF YOU LIE STILL – AND IF YOU HAVEN'T GOT AN OPEN WOUND
AT DAWN I MANAGED TO GET FREE, AND – WELL YOU KNOW THE REST
YOU'RE THE ONE WHO'S HURT, JAMES... YOUR POOR BODY... BUT I'LL LOOK AFTER YOU WHEN WE GET TO BEAU DESERT
694

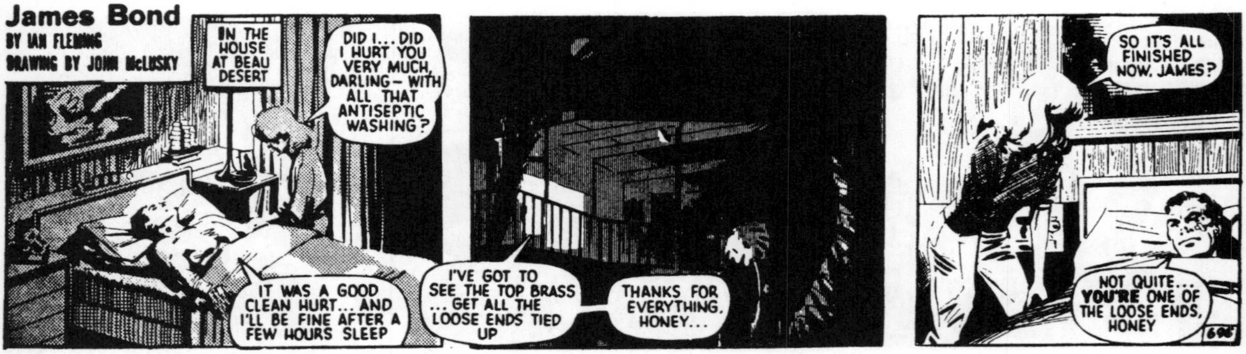
James Bond
BY IAN FLEMING
DRAWING BY JOHN McLUSKY
IN THE HOUSE AT BEAU DESERT
DID I... DID I HURT YOU VERY MUCH, DARLING – WITH ALL THAT ANTISEPTIC WASHING?
IT WAS A GOOD CLEAN HURT... AND I'LL BE FINE AFTER A FEW HOURS SLEEP
I'VE GOT TO SEE THE TOP BRASS ... GET ALL THE LOOSE ENDS TIED UP
THANKS FOR EVERYTHING, HONEY...
SO IT'S ALL FINISHED NOW, JAMES?
NOT QUITE... YOU'RE ONE OF THE LOOSE ENDS, HONEY

James Bond
BY IAN FLEMING
DRAWING BY JOHN McLUSKY

PLEYDELL-SMITH, COLONIAL SECRETARY IN KINGSTON

ALL FIXED, OLD MAN - THE A.G.'S SENT OFF A GUNBOAT AND A LOAD OF MILITARY TO CRAB KEY. WE'LL HANDLE ALL THE MOPPING-UP DETAILS

GOOD

YES - WE'LL BE BACK IN A FEW WEEKS. I'VE CABLED MY CHIEF FOR LEAVE

696

SO YOU'RE TAKING THIS GIRL HONEY TO NEW YORK, TO HAVE HER BROKEN NOSE PUT RIGHT?

YOU'LL GET IT - ON MEDICAL GROUNDS ALONE, OLD MAN! I'VE PUT IN QUITE A STARTLING LITTLE REPORT ON YOU MYSELF, YOU KNOW...

James Bond
BY IAN FLEMING
DRAWING BY JOHN McLUSKY

BOND'S HOUSE AT BEAU DESERT...

AND WHEN YOU COME BACK THERE'LL BE A JOB FOR YOU HERE WITH THE JAMAICA INSTITUTE-TO DO WITH NATURAL HISTORY. I THINK YOU CAN TELL THEM A THING OR TWO!

OH, JAMES ...IT'S LIKE A WONDERFUL DREAM

AND YOU'LL BE WITH ME **ALL THE TIME** IN NEW YORK - WHILE THE DOCTORS FIX MY NOSE SO I'M PRETTY AGAIN!

YOU'RE PRETTY NOW, HONEY. IN FACT YOU'RE BEAUTIFUL, THE MOST BEAUTIFUL GIRL I'VE EVER...

697

...KISSED

End of story

007

GOLDFINGER

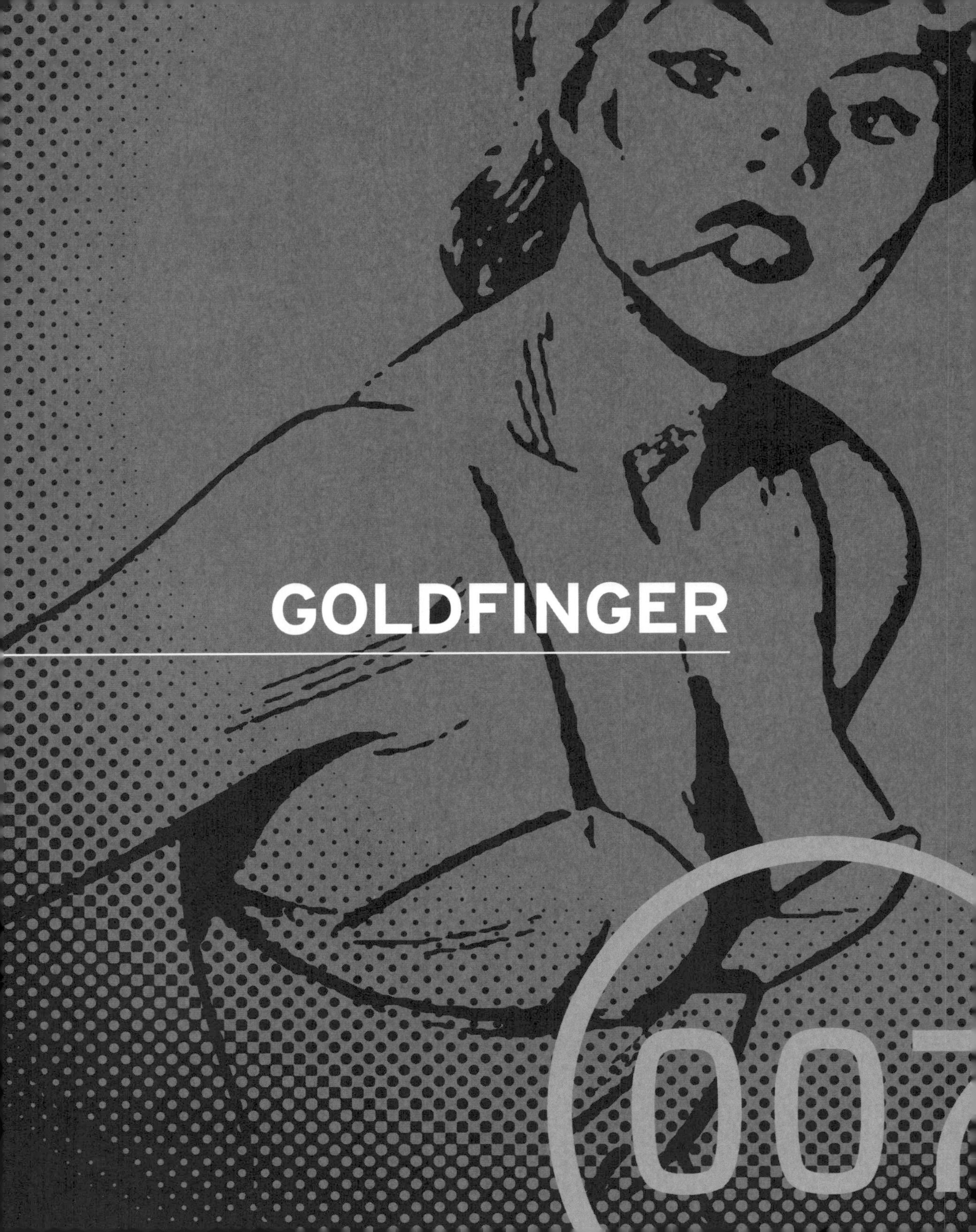
007

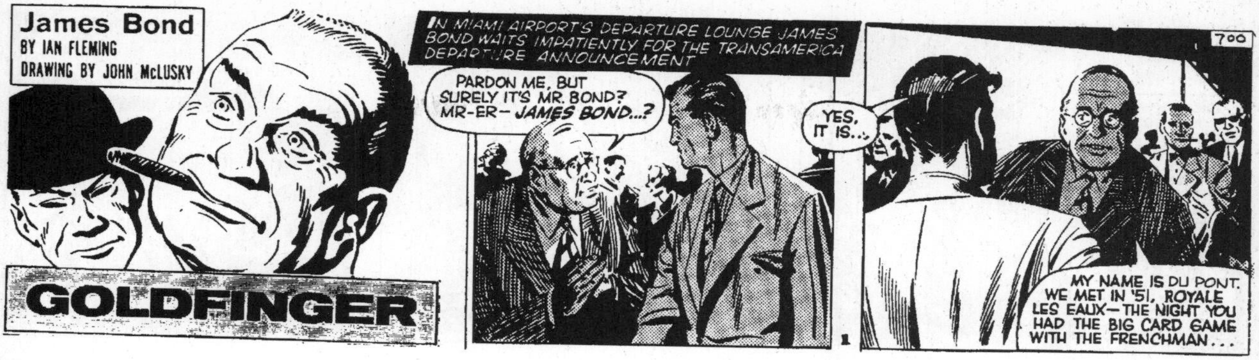
James Bond
BY IAN FLEMING
DRAWING BY JOHN McLUSKY
GOLDFINGER
IN MIAMI AIRPORT'S DEPARTURE LOUNGE JAMES BOND WAITS IMPATIENTLY FOR THE TRANSAMERICA DEPARTURE ANNOUNCEMENT
PARDON ME, BUT SURELY IT'S MR. BOND? MR-ER- JAMES BOND...?
700
YES, IT IS...
MY NAME IS DU PONT. WE MET IN '51, ROYALE LES EAUX—THE NIGHT YOU HAD THE BIG CARD GAME WITH THE FRENCHMAN...

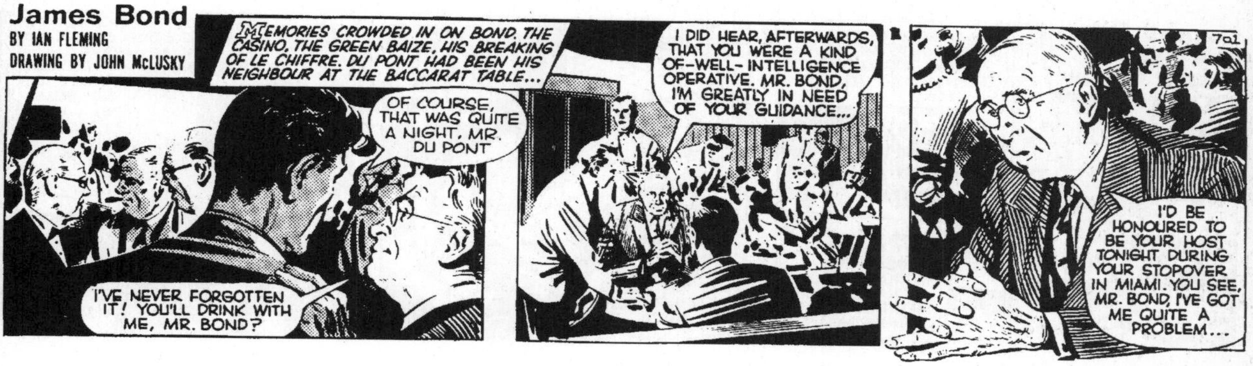
James Bond
BY IAN FLEMING
DRAWING BY JOHN McLUSKY
MEMORIES CROWDED IN ON BOND. THE CASINO, THE GREEN BAIZE, HIS BREAKING OF LE CHIFFRE. DU PONT HAD BEEN HIS NEIGHBOUR AT THE BACCARAT TABLE...
OF COURSE, THAT WAS QUITE A NIGHT, MR. DU PONT
I'VE NEVER FORGOTTEN IT! YOU'LL DRINK WITH ME, MR. BOND?
I DID HEAR, AFTERWARDS, THAT YOU WERE A KIND OF-WELL- INTELLIGENCE OPERATIVE. MR. BOND, I'M GREATLY IN NEED OF YOUR GUIDANCE...
701
I'D BE HONOURED TO BE YOUR HOST TONIGHT DURING YOUR STOPOVER IN MIAMI. YOU SEE, MR. BOND, I'VE GOT ME QUITE A PROBLEM...

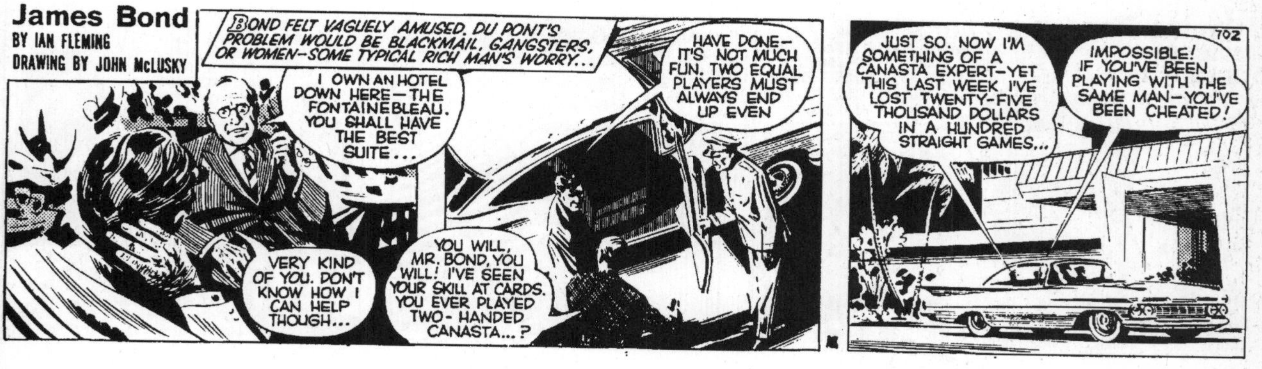
James Bond
BY IAN FLEMING
DRAWING BY JOHN McLUSKY
BOND FELT VAGUELY AMUSED. DU PONT'S PROBLEM WOULD BE BLACKMAIL, GANGSTERS, OR WOMEN—SOME TYPICAL RICH MAN'S WORRY...
I OWN AN HOTEL DOWN HERE—THE FONTAINEBLEAU. YOU SHALL HAVE THE BEST SUITE...
VERY KIND OF YOU. DON'T KNOW HOW I CAN HELP THOUGH...
YOU WILL, MR. BOND, YOU WILL! I'VE SEEN YOUR SKILL AT CARDS. YOU EVER PLAYED TWO- HANDED CANASTA...?
HAVE DONE— IT'S NOT MUCH FUN. TWO EQUAL PLAYERS MUST ALWAYS END UP EVEN
702
JUST SO. NOW I'M SOMETHING OF A CANASTA EXPERT-YET THIS LAST WEEK I'VE LOST TWENTY-FIVE THOUSAND DOLLARS IN A HUNDRED STRAIGHT GAMES...
IMPOSSIBLE! IF YOU'VE BEEN PLAYING WITH THE SAME MAN—YOU'VE BEEN CHEATED!

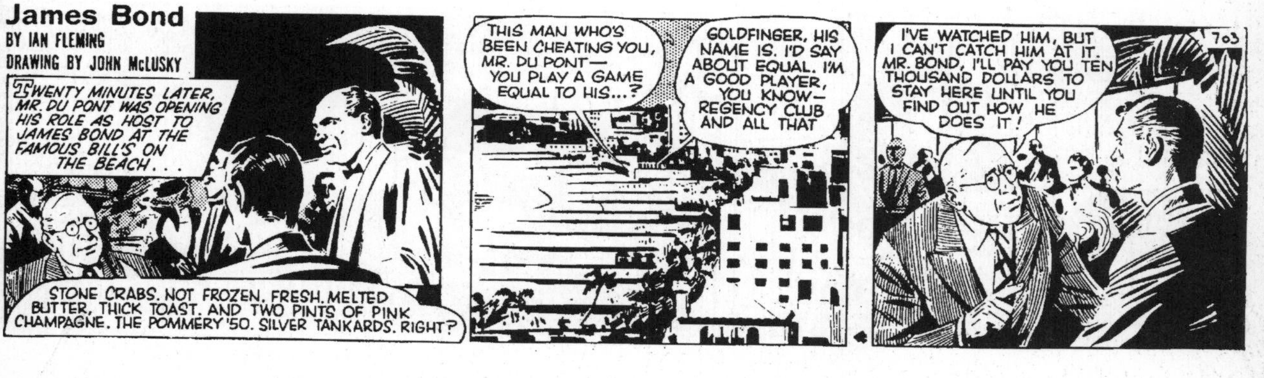
James Bond
BY IAN FLEMING
DRAWING BY JOHN McLUSKY
TWENTY MINUTES LATER, MR. DU PONT WAS OPENING HIS ROLE AS HOST TO JAMES BOND AT THE FAMOUS BILL'S ON THE BEACH...
STONE CRABS. NOT FROZEN. FRESH. MELTED BUTTER. THICK TOAST. AND TWO PINTS OF PINK CHAMPAGNE. THE POMMERY '50. SILVER TANKARDS. RIGHT?
THIS MAN WHO'S BEEN CHEATING YOU, MR. DU PONT— YOU PLAY A GAME EQUAL TO HIS...?
GOLDFINGER, HIS NAME IS. I'D SAY ABOUT EQUAL. I'M A GOOD PLAYER, YOU KNOW— REGENCY CLUB AND ALL THAT
703
I'VE WATCHED HIM, BUT I CAN'T CATCH HIM AT IT. MR. BOND, I'LL PAY YOU TEN THOUSAND DOLLARS TO STAY HERE UNTIL YOU FIND OUT HOW HE DOES IT!

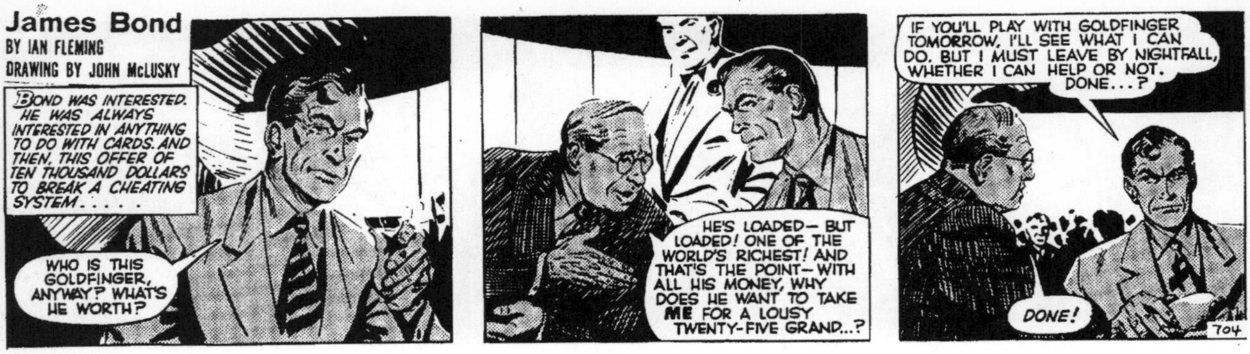
James Bond
BY IAN FLEMING
DRAWING BY JOHN McLUSKY
BOND WAS INTERESTED. HE WAS ALWAYS INTERESTED IN ANYTHING TO DO WITH CARDS. AND THEN, THIS OFFER OF TEN THOUSAND DOLLARS TO BREAK A CHEATING SYSTEM.....
WHO IS THIS GOLDFINGER, ANYWAY? WHAT'S HE WORTH?
HE'S LOADED— BUT LOADED! ONE OF THE WORLD'S RICHEST! AND THAT'S THE POINT— WITH ALL HIS MONEY, WHY DOES HE WANT TO TAKE ME FOR A LOUSY TWENTY-FIVE GRAND...?
IF YOU'LL PLAY WITH GOLDFINGER TOMORROW, I'LL SEE WHAT I CAN DO. BUT I MUST LEAVE BY NIGHTFALL, WHETHER I CAN HELP OR NOT. DONE...?
DONE!
704

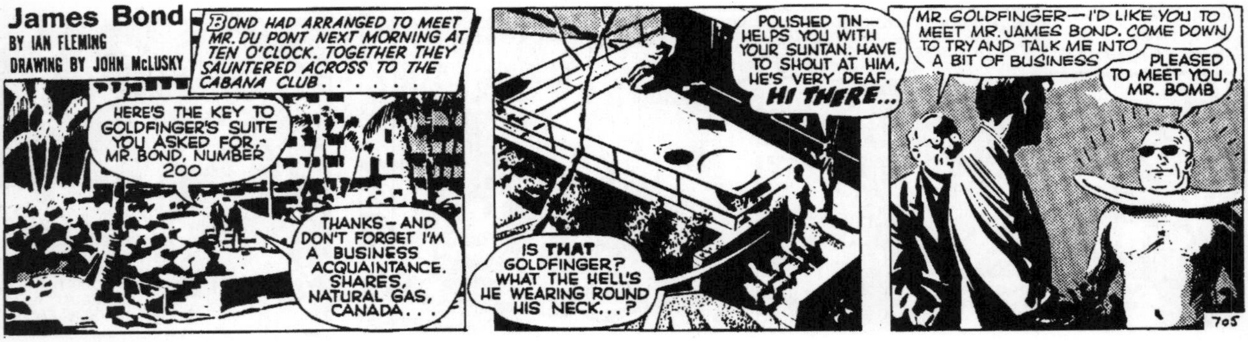
James Bond
BY IAN FLEMING
DRAWING BY JOHN McLUSKY
BOND HAD ARRANGED TO MEET MR. DU PONT NEXT MORNING AT TEN O'CLOCK. TOGETHER THEY SAUNTERED ACROSS TO THE CABANA CLUB.......
HERE'S THE KEY TO GOLDFINGER'S SUITE YOU ASKED FOR, MR. BOND, NUMBER 200
THANKS— AND DON'T FORGET I'M A BUSINESS ACQUAINTANCE. SHARES, NATURAL GAS, CANADA...
POLISHED TIN— HELPS YOU WITH YOUR SUNTAN. HAVE TO SHOUT AT HIM, HE'S VERY DEAF. HI THERE...
IS THAT GOLDFINGER? WHAT THE HELL'S HE WEARING ROUND HIS NECK...?
MR. GOLDFINGER— I'D LIKE YOU TO MEET MR. JAMES BOND. COME DOWN TO TRY AND TALK ME INTO A BIT OF BUSINESS
PLEASED TO MEET YOU, MR. BOMB
705

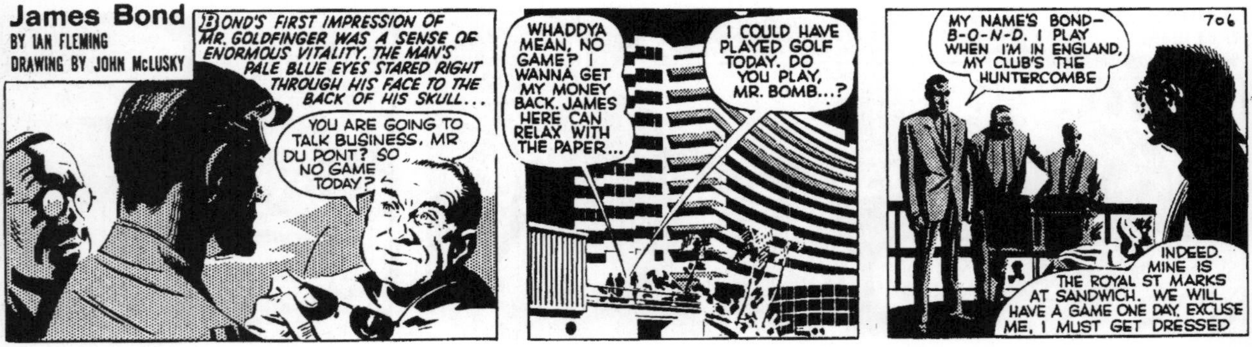
James Bond
BY IAN FLEMING
DRAWING BY JOHN McLUSKY
BOND'S FIRST IMPRESSION OF MR. GOLDFINGER WAS A SENSE OF ENORMOUS VITALITY. THE MAN'S PALE BLUE EYES STARED RIGHT THROUGH HIS FACE TO THE BACK OF HIS SKULL...
YOU ARE GOING TO TALK BUSINESS, MR DU PONT? SO NO GAME TODAY?
WHADDYA MEAN, NO GAME? I WANNA GET MY MONEY BACK. JAMES HERE CAN RELAX WITH THE PAPER...
I COULD HAVE PLAYED GOLF TODAY. DO YOU PLAY, MR. BOMB...?
706
MY NAME'S BOND— B-O-N-D. I PLAY WHEN I'M IN ENGLAND, MY CLUB'S THE HUNTERCOMBE
INDEED. MINE IS THE ROYAL ST MARKS AT SANDWICH. WE WILL HAVE A GAME ONE DAY. EXCUSE ME, I MUST GET DRESSED

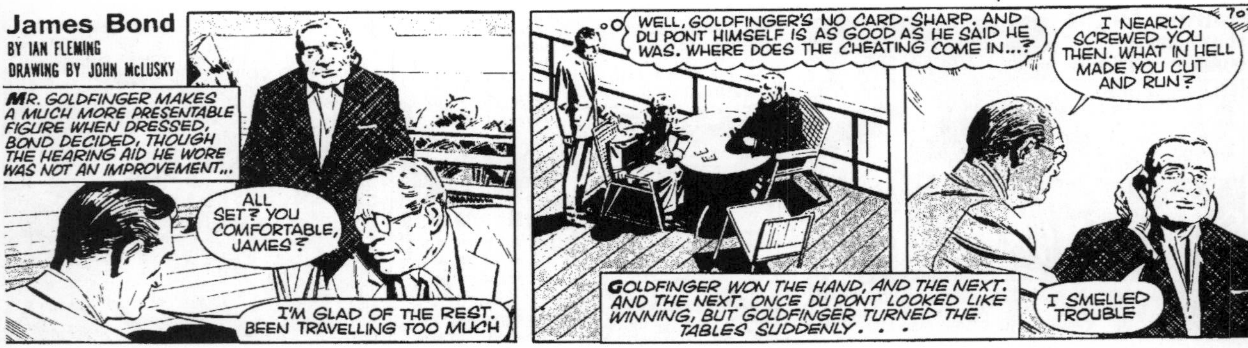
James Bond
BY IAN FLEMING
DRAWING BY JOHN McLUSKY
MR. GOLDFINGER MAKES A MUCH MORE PRESENTABLE FIGURE WHEN DRESSED, BOND DECIDED, THOUGH THE HEARING AID HE WORE WAS NOT AN IMPROVEMENT...
ALL SET? YOU COMFORTABLE, JAMES?
I'M GLAD OF THE REST. BEEN TRAVELLING TOO MUCH
WELL, GOLDFINGER'S NO CARD-SHARP. AND DU PONT HIMSELF IS AS GOOD AS HE SAID HE WAS. WHERE DOES THE CHEATING COME IN...?
GOLDFINGER WON THE HAND, AND THE NEXT. AND THE NEXT. ONCE DU PONT LOOKED LIKE WINNING, BUT GOLDFINGER TURNED THE TABLES SUDDENLY...
707
I NEARLY SCREWED YOU THEN. WHAT IN HELL MADE YOU CUT AND RUN?
I SMELLED TROUBLE

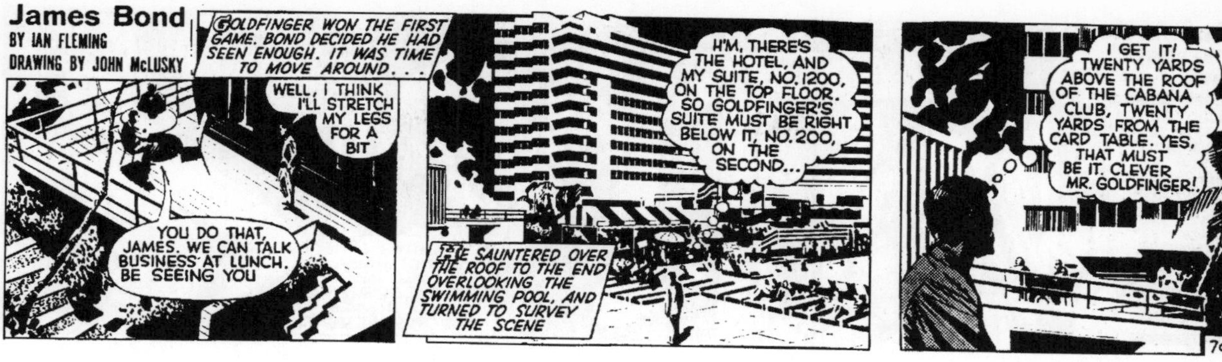
James Bond
BY IAN FLEMING
DRAWING BY JOHN McLUSKY
GOLDFINGER WON THE FIRST GAME. BOND DECIDED HE HAD SEEN ENOUGH. IT WAS TIME TO MOVE AROUND . . .
WELL, I THINK I'LL STRETCH MY LEGS FOR A BIT
YOU DO THAT, JAMES. WE CAN TALK BUSINESS AT LUNCH. BE SEEING YOU
H'M, THERE'S THE HOTEL, AND MY SUITE, NO. 1200, ON THE TOP FLOOR. SO GOLDFINGER'S SUITE MUST BE RIGHT BELOW IT, NO. 200, ON THE SECOND...
HE SAUNTERED OVER THE ROOF TO THE END OVERLOOKING THE SWIMMING POOL, AND TURNED TO SURVEY THE SCENE
I GET IT! TWENTY YARDS ABOVE THE ROOF OF THE CABANA CLUB, TWENTY YARDS FROM THE CARD TABLE. YES, THAT MUST BE IT. CLEVER MR. GOLDFINGER!
708

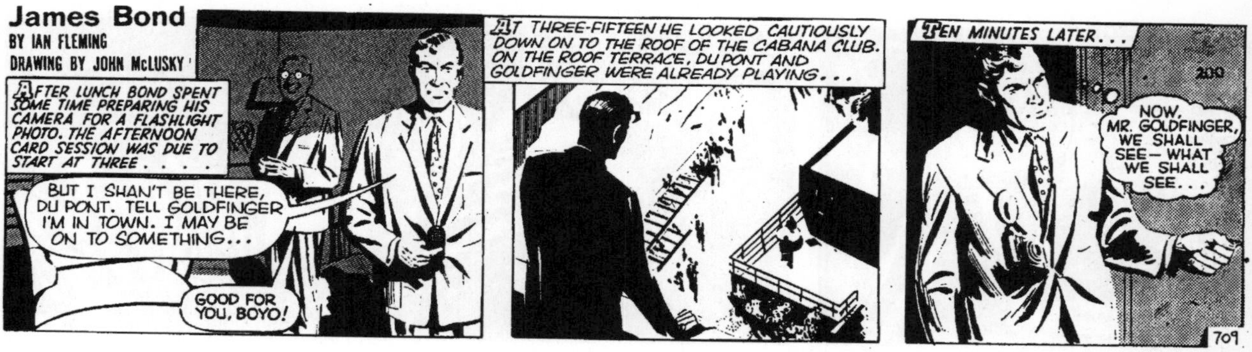
James Bond
BY IAN FLEMING
DRAWING BY JOHN McLUSKY
AFTER LUNCH BOND SPENT SOME TIME PREPARING HIS CAMERA FOR A FLASHLIGHT PHOTO. THE AFTERNOON CARD SESSION WAS DUE TO START AT THREE . . . .
BUT I SHAN'T BE THERE, DU PONT. TELL GOLDFINGER I'M IN TOWN. I MAY BE ON TO SOMETHING...
GOOD FOR YOU, BOYO!
AT THREE-FIFTEEN HE LOOKED CAUTIOUSLY DOWN ON TO THE ROOF OF THE CABANA CLUB. ON THE ROOF TERRACE, DU PONT AND GOLDFINGER WERE ALREADY PLAYING . . .
TEN MINUTES LATER . . .
200
NOW, MR. GOLDFINGER, WE SHALL SEE– WHAT WE SHALL SEE . . .
709

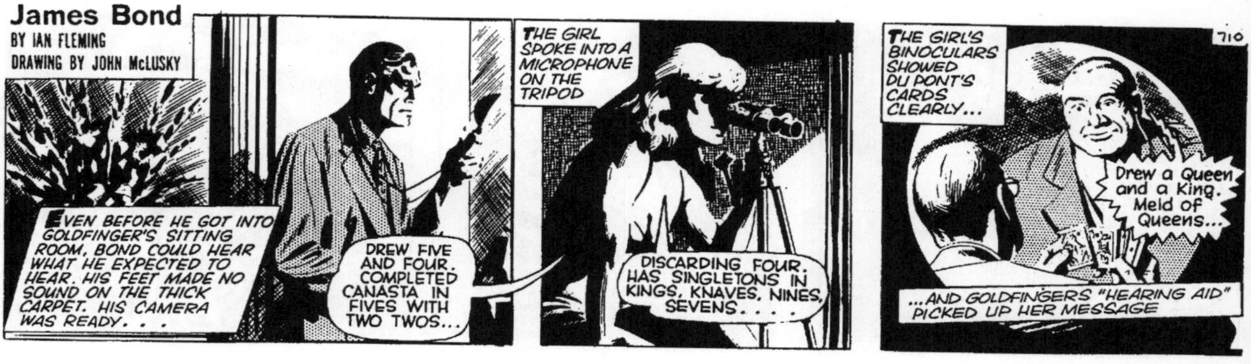
James Bond
BY IAN FLEMING
DRAWING BY JOHN McLUSKY
EVEN BEFORE HE GOT INTO GOLDFINGER'S SITTING ROOM, BOND COULD HEAR WHAT HE EXPECTED TO HEAR. HIS FEET MADE NO SOUND ON THE THICK CARPET. HIS CAMERA WAS READY . . .
DREW FIVE AND FOUR. COMPLETED CANASTA IN FIVES WITH TWO TWOS...
THE GIRL SPOKE INTO A MICROPHONE ON THE TRIPOD
DISCARDING FOUR. HAS SINGLETONS IN KINGS, KNAVES, NINES, SEVENS . . . .
710
THE GIRL'S BINOCULARS SHOWED DU PONT'S CARDS CLEARLY...
Drew a Queen and a King. Meld of Queens...
...AND GOLDFINGER'S "HEARING AID" PICKED UP HER MESSAGE

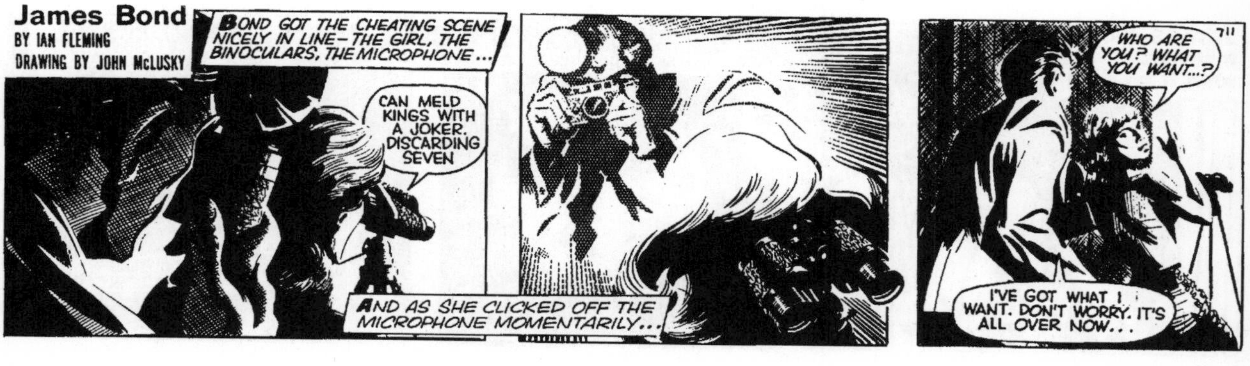
James Bond
BY IAN FLEMING
DRAWING BY JOHN McLUSKY
BOND GOT THE CHEATING SCENE NICELY IN LINE– THE GIRL, THE BINOCULARS, THE MICROPHONE . . .
CAN MELD KINGS WITH A JOKER. DISCARDING SEVEN
AND AS SHE CLICKED OFF THE MICROPHONE MOMENTARILY...
711
WHO ARE YOU? WHAT YOU WANT...?
I'VE GOT WHAT I WANT. DON'T WORRY. IT'S ALL OVER NOW...

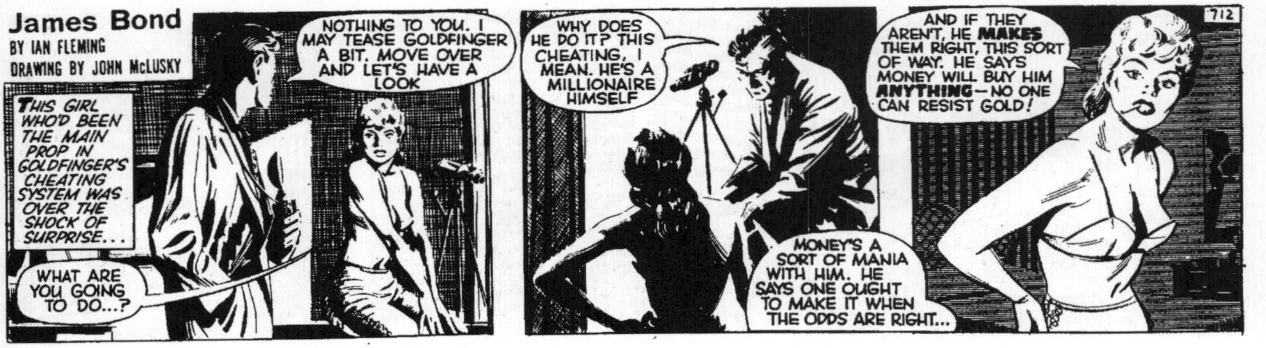
James Bond
BY IAN FLEMING
DRAWING BY JOHN McLUSKY
THIS GIRL WHO'D BEEN THE MAIN PROP IN GOLDFINGER'S CHEATING SYSTEM WAS OVER THE SHOCK OF SURPRISE...
WHAT ARE YOU GOING TO DO...?
NOTHING TO YOU. I MAY TEASE GOLDFINGER A BIT. MOVE OVER AND LET'S HAVE A LOOK
WHY DOES HE DO IT? THIS CHEATING, I MEAN. HE'S A MILLIONAIRE HIMSELF
MONEY'S A SORT OF MANIA WITH HIM. HE SAYS ONE OUGHT TO MAKE IT WHEN THE ODDS ARE RIGHT...
AND IF THEY AREN'T, HE MAKES THEM RIGHT, THIS SORT OF WAY. HE SAYS MONEY WILL BUY HIM ANYTHING—NO ONE CAN RESIST GOLD!
712

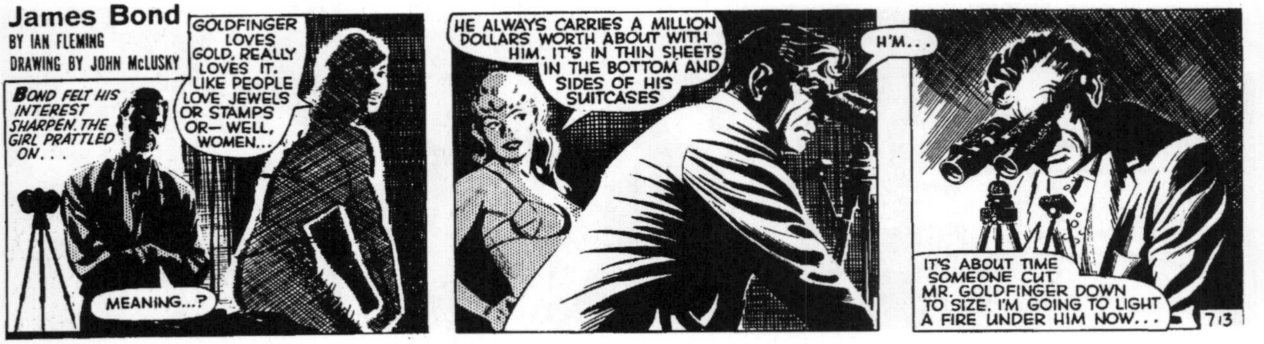
James Bond
BY IAN FLEMING
DRAWING BY JOHN McLUSKY
BOND FELT HIS INTEREST SHARPEN. THE GIRL PRATTLED ON...
GOLDFINGER LOVES GOLD, REALLY LOVES IT. LIKE PEOPLE LOVE JEWELS OR STAMPS OR— WELL, WOMEN...
MEANING...?
HE ALWAYS CARRIES A MILLION DOLLARS WORTH ABOUT WITH HIM. IT'S IN THIN SHEETS IN THE BOTTOM AND SIDES OF HIS SUITCASES
H'M...
IT'S ABOUT TIME SOMEONE CUT MR. GOLDFINGER DOWN TO SIZE. I'M GOING TO LIGHT A FIRE UNDER HIM NOW...
713

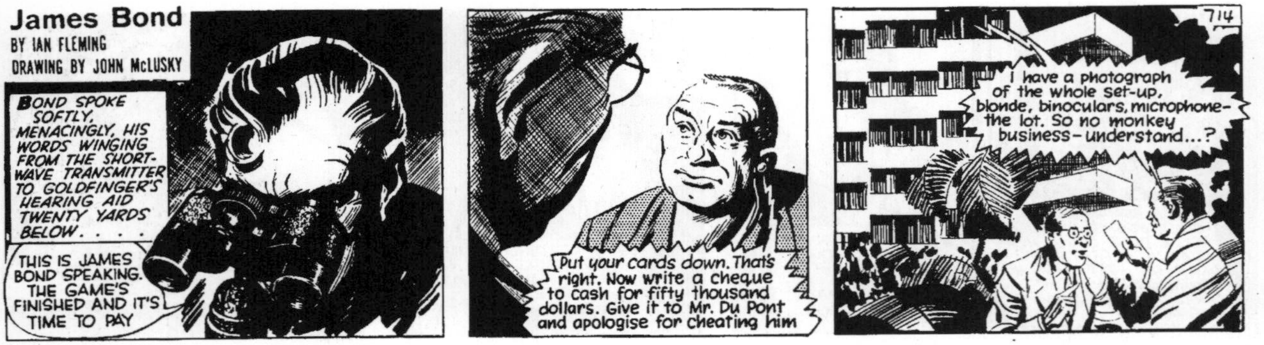
James Bond
BY IAN FLEMING
DRAWING BY JOHN McLUSKY
BOND SPOKE SOFTLY, MENACINGLY, HIS WORDS WINGING FROM THE SHORT-WAVE TRANSMITTER TO GOLDFINGER'S HEARING AID TWENTY YARDS BELOW....
THIS IS JAMES BOND SPEAKING. THE GAME'S FINISHED AND IT'S TIME TO PAY
Put your cards down. That's right. Now write a cheque to cash for fifty thousand dollars. Give it to Mr. Du Pont and apologise for cheating him
714
I have a photograph of the whole set-up, blonde, binoculars, microphone—the lot. So no monkey business—understand...?

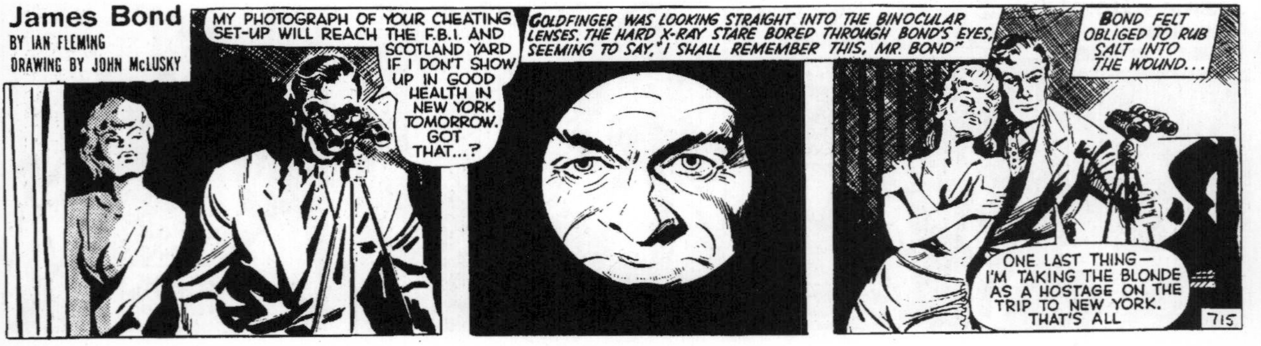
James Bond
BY IAN FLEMING
DRAWING BY JOHN McLUSKY
MY PHOTOGRAPH OF YOUR CHEATING SET-UP WILL REACH THE F.B.I. AND SCOTLAND YARD IF I DON'T SHOW UP IN GOOD HEALTH IN NEW YORK TOMORROW. GOT THAT...?
GOLDFINGER WAS LOOKING STRAIGHT INTO THE BINOCULAR LENSES. THE HARD X-RAY STARE BORED THROUGH BOND'S EYES, SEEMING TO SAY, "I SHALL REMEMBER THIS, MR. BOND"
BOND FELT OBLIGED TO RUB SALT INTO THE WOUND...
ONE LAST THING— I'M TAKING THE BLONDE AS A HOSTAGE ON THE TRIP TO NEW YORK. THAT'S ALL
715

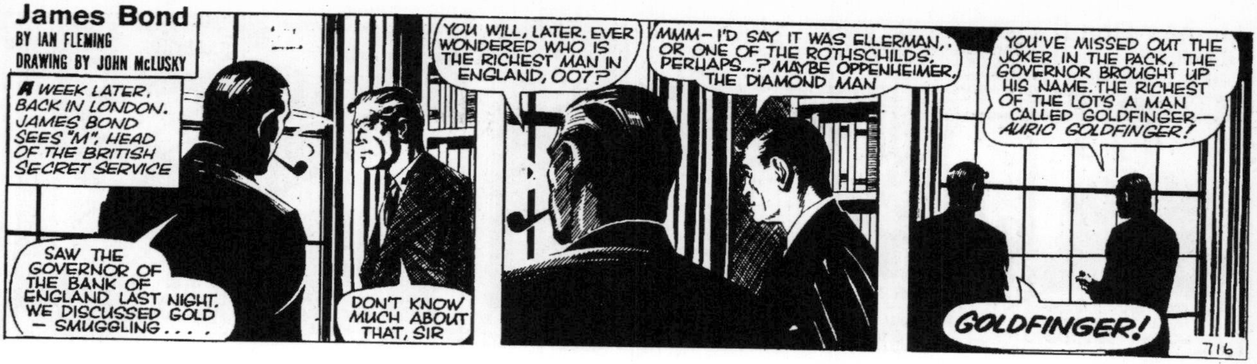
James Bond
BY IAN FLEMING
DRAWING BY JOHN McLUSKY
A WEEK LATER. BACK IN LONDON. JAMES BOND SEES "M", HEAD OF THE BRITISH SECRET SERVICE
SAW THE GOVERNOR OF THE BANK OF ENGLAND LAST NIGHT. WE DISCUSSED GOLD — SMUGGLING . . . .
DON'T KNOW MUCH ABOUT THAT, SIR
YOU WILL, LATER. EVER WONDERED WHO IS THE RICHEST MAN IN ENGLAND, 007?
MMM— I'D SAY IT WAS ELLERMAN, OR ONE OF THE ROTHSCHILDS, PERHAPS....? MAYBE OPPENHEIMER, THE DIAMOND MAN
YOU'VE MISSED OUT THE JOKER IN THE PACK, THE GOVERNOR BROUGHT UP HIS NAME. THE RICHEST OF THE LOT'S A MAN CALLED GOLDFINGER— AURIC GOLDFINGER!
GOLDFINGER!
716

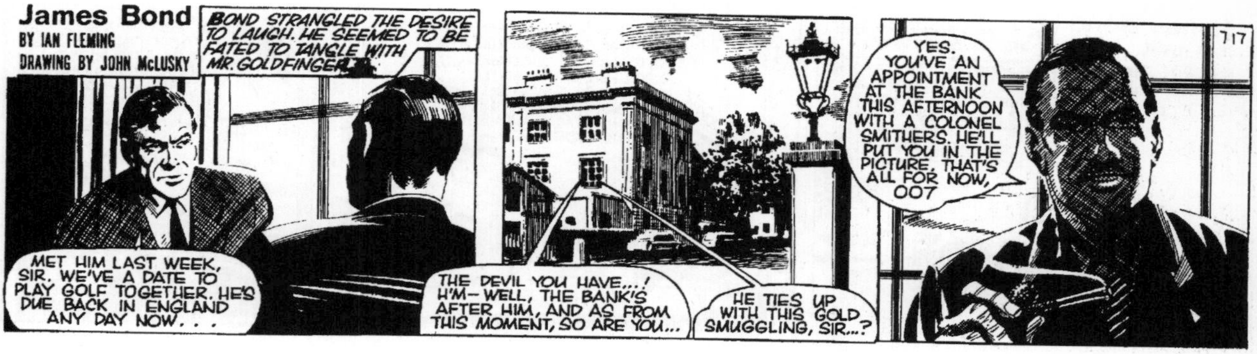
James Bond
BY IAN FLEMING
DRAWING BY JOHN McLUSKY
BOND STRANGLED THE DESIRE TO LAUGH. HE SEEMED TO BE FATED TO TANGLE WITH MR. GOLDFINGER
MET HIM LAST WEEK, SIR. WE'VE A DATE TO PLAY GOLF TOGETHER. HE'S DUE BACK IN ENGLAND ANY DAY NOW . . .
THE DEVIL YOU HAVE...! H'M— WELL, THE BANK'S AFTER HIM, AND AS FROM THIS MOMENT, SO ARE YOU...
HE TIES UP WITH THIS GOLD SMUGGLING, SIR...?
717
YES. YOU'VE AN APPOINTMENT AT THE BANK THIS AFTERNOON WITH A COLONEL SMITHERS. HE'LL PUT YOU IN THE PICTURE, THAT'S ALL FOR NOW, 007

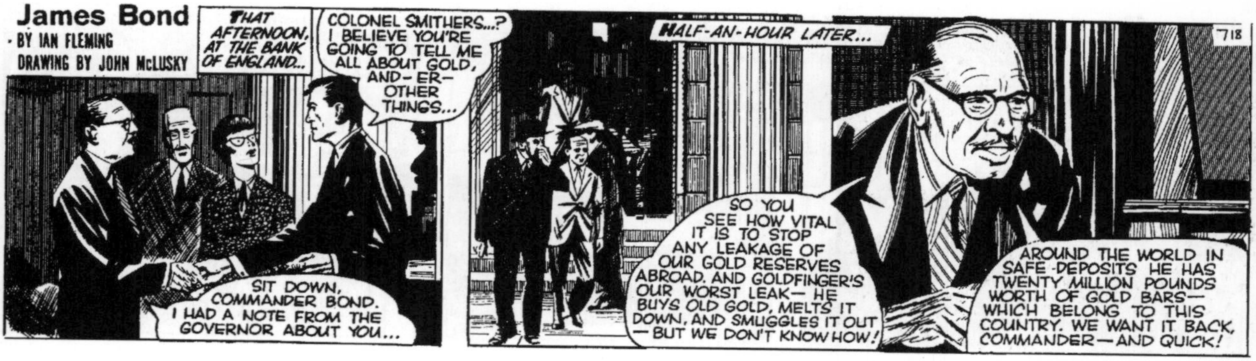
James Bond
BY IAN FLEMING
DRAWING BY JOHN McLUSKY
THAT AFTERNOON, AT THE BANK OF ENGLAND...
COLONEL SMITHERS...? I BELIEVE YOU'RE GOING TO TELL ME ALL ABOUT GOLD, AND— ER— OTHER THINGS...
SIT DOWN, COMMANDER BOND. I HAD A NOTE FROM THE GOVERNOR ABOUT YOU...
HALF-AN-HOUR LATER...
718
SO YOU SEE HOW VITAL IT IS TO STOP ANY LEAKAGE OF OUR GOLD RESERVES ABROAD. AND GOLDFINGER'S OUR WORST LEAK— HE BUYS OLD GOLD, MELTS IT DOWN, AND SMUGGLES IT OUT — BUT WE DON'T KNOW HOW!
AROUND THE WORLD IN SAFE-DEPOSITS HE HAS TWENTY MILLION POUNDS WORTH OF GOLD BARS— WHICH BELONG TO THIS COUNTRY. WE WANT IT BACK, COMMANDER — AND QUICK!

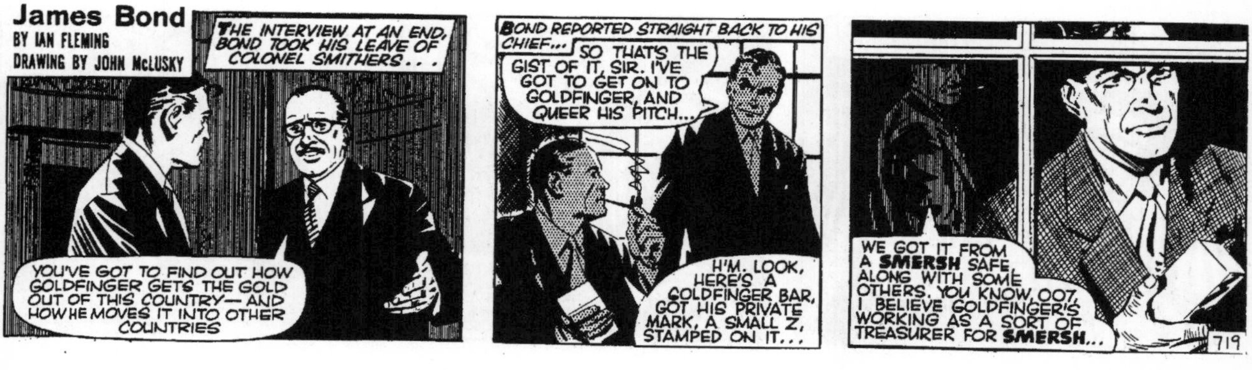
James Bond
BY IAN FLEMING
DRAWING BY JOHN McLUSKY
THE INTERVIEW AT AN END, BOND TOOK HIS LEAVE OF COLONEL SMITHERS . . .
YOU'VE GOT TO FIND OUT HOW GOLDFINGER GETS THE GOLD OUT OF THIS COUNTRY— AND HOW HE MOVES IT INTO OTHER COUNTRIES
BOND REPORTED STRAIGHT BACK TO HIS CHIEF...
SO THAT'S THE GIST OF IT, SIR. I'VE GOT TO GET ON TO GOLDFINGER, AND QUEER HIS PITCH...
H'M. LOOK, HERE'S A GOLDFINGER BAR, GOT HIS PRIVATE MARK, A SMALL Z, STAMPED ON IT...
WE GOT IT FROM A SMERSH SAFE ALONG WITH SOME OTHERS. YOU KNOW, 007, I BELIEVE GOLDFINGER'S WORKING AS A SORT OF TREASURER FOR SMERSH...
719

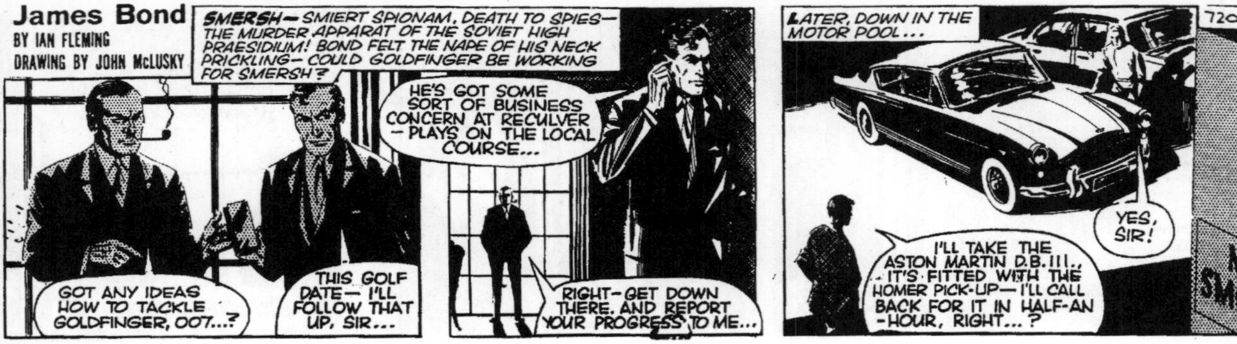

James Bond
BY IAN FLEMING
DRAWING BY JOHN McLUSKY
SMERSH— SMIERT SPIONAM, DEATH TO SPIES— THE MURDER APPARAT OF THE SOVIET HIGH PRAESIDIUM! BOND FELT THE NAPE OF HIS NECK PRICKLING— COULD GOLDFINGER BE WORKING FOR SMERSH?
GOT ANY IDEAS HOW TO TACKLE GOLDFINGER, 007...?
THIS GOLF DATE— I'LL FOLLOW THAT UP, SIR...
HE'S GOT SOME SORT OF BUSINESS CONCERN AT RECULVER —PLAYS ON THE LOCAL COURSE...
RIGHT—GET DOWN THERE. AND REPORT YOUR PROGRESS TO ME...
LATER, DOWN IN THE MOTOR POOL...
720
YES, SIR!
I'LL TAKE THE ASTON MARTIN D.B.III., IT'S FITTED WITH THE HOMER PICK-UP—I'LL CALL BACK FOR IT IN HALF-AN-HOUR, RIGHT...?

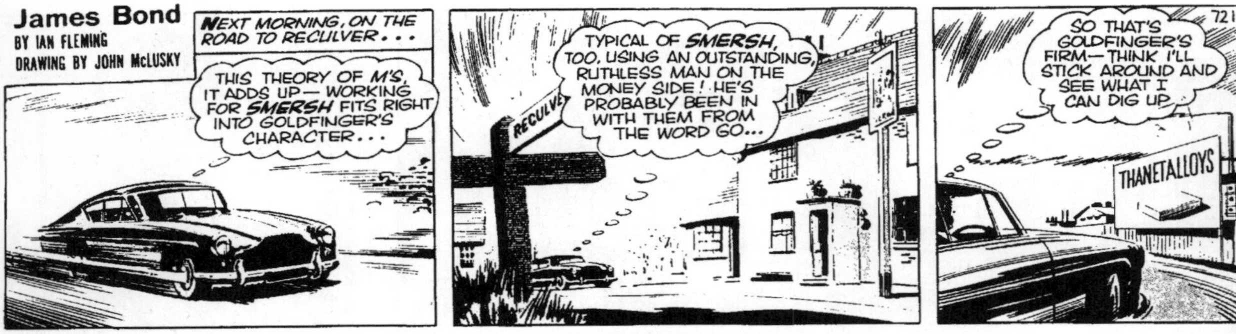

James Bond
BY IAN FLEMING
DRAWING BY JOHN McLUSKY
NEXT MORNING, ON THE ROAD TO RECULVER...
THIS THEORY OF M'S, IT ADDS UP— WORKING FOR SMERSH FITS RIGHT INTO GOLDFINGER'S CHARACTER...
TYPICAL OF SMERSH, TOO, USING AN OUTSTANDING, RUTHLESS MAN ON THE MONEY SIDE! HE'S PROBABLY BEEN IN WITH THEM FROM THE WORD GO...
RECULVE
721
SO THAT'S GOLDFINGER'S FIRM— THINK I'LL STICK AROUND AND SEE WHAT I CAN DIG UP...
THANETALLOYS

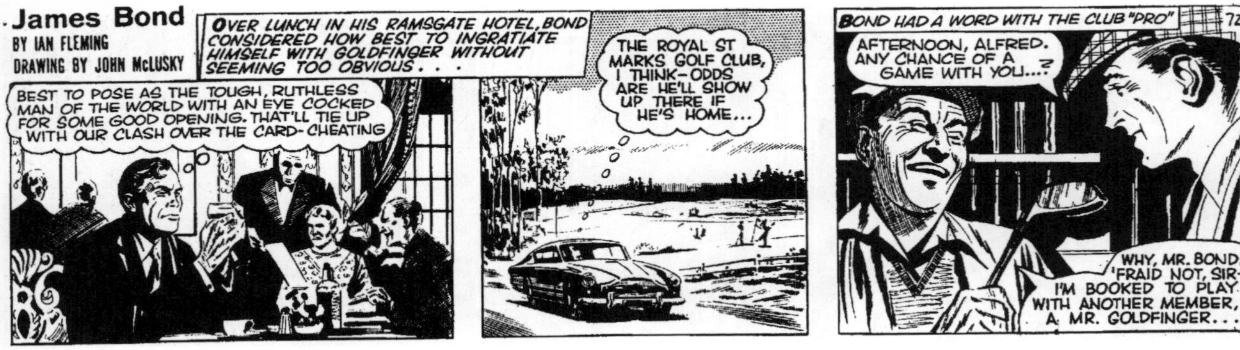

James Bond
BY IAN FLEMING
DRAWING BY JOHN McLUSKY
OVER LUNCH IN HIS RAMSGATE HOTEL, BOND CONSIDERED HOW BEST TO INGRATIATE HIMSELF WITH GOLDFINGER WITHOUT SEEMING TOO OBVIOUS...
BEST TO POSE AS THE TOUGH, RUTHLESS MAN OF THE WORLD WITH AN EYE COCKED FOR SOME GOOD OPENING. THAT'LL TIE UP WITH OUR CLASH OVER THE CARD-CHEATING
THE ROYAL ST MARKS GOLF CLUB, I THINK—ODDS ARE HE'LL SHOW UP THERE IF HE'S HOME...
BOND HAD A WORD WITH THE CLUB "PRO"
722
AFTERNOON, ALFRED. ANY CHANCE OF A GAME WITH YOU...?
WHY, MR. BOND! 'FRAID NOT, SIR— I'M BOOKED TO PLAY WITH ANOTHER MEMBER, A MR. GOLDFINGER...

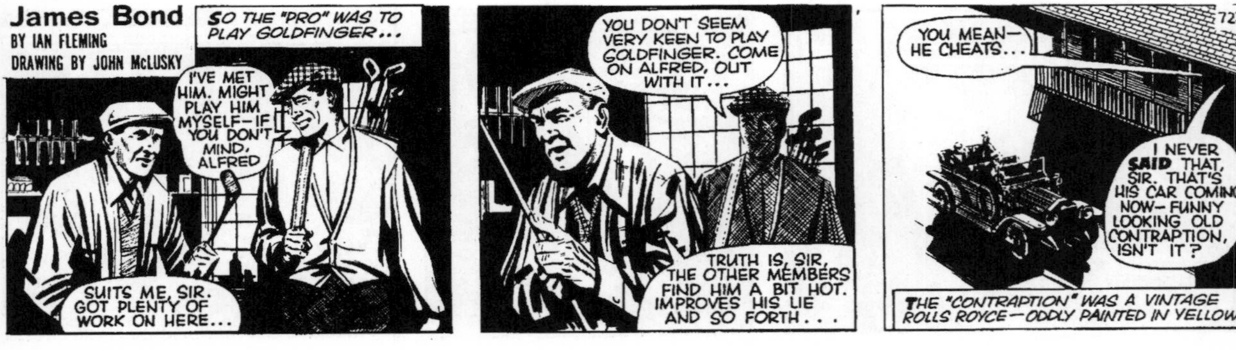

James Bond
BY IAN FLEMING
DRAWING BY JOHN McLUSKY
SO THE "PRO" WAS TO PLAY GOLDFINGER...
I'VE MET HIM. MIGHT PLAY HIM MYSELF—IF YOU DON'T MIND, ALFRED
SUITS ME, SIR. GOT PLENTY OF WORK ON HERE...
YOU DON'T SEEM VERY KEEN TO PLAY GOLDFINGER. COME ON ALFRED, OUT WITH IT...
TRUTH IS, SIR, THE OTHER MEMBERS FIND HIM A BIT HOT. IMPROVES HIS LIE AND SO FORTH...
723
YOU MEAN— HE CHEATS...?
I NEVER SAID THAT, SIR. THAT'S HIS CAR COMING NOW— FUNNY LOOKING OLD CONTRAPTION, ISN'T IT?
THE "CONTRAPTION" WAS A VINTAGE ROLLS ROYCE—ODDLY PAINTED IN YELLOW

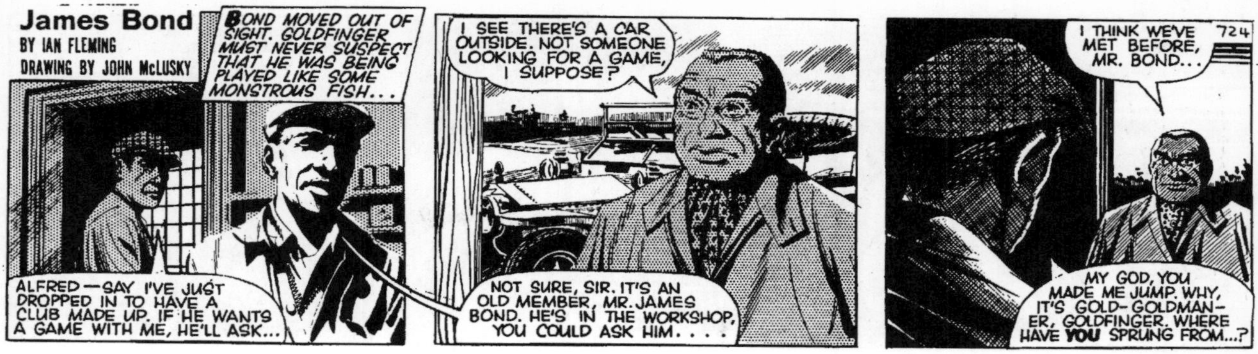
James Bond
BY IAN FLEMING
DRAWING BY JOHN McLUSKY
BOND MOVED OUT OF SIGHT. GOLDFINGER MUST NEVER SUSPECT THAT HE WAS BEING PLAYED LIKE SOME MONSTROUS FISH...
ALFRED—SAY I'VE JUST DROPPED IN TO HAVE A CLUB MADE UP. IF HE WANTS A GAME WITH ME, HE'LL ASK...
I SEE THERE'S A CAR OUTSIDE. NOT SOMEONE LOOKING FOR A GAME, I SUPPOSE?
NOT SURE, SIR. IT'S AN OLD MEMBER, MR. JAMES BOND. HE'S IN THE WORKSHOP, YOU COULD ASK HIM. . . .
724
I THINK WE'VE MET BEFORE, MR. BOND...
MY GOD, YOU MADE ME JUMP. WHY, IT'S GOLD-GOLDMAN-ER, GOLDFINGER. WHERE HAVE **YOU** SPRUNG FROM...?

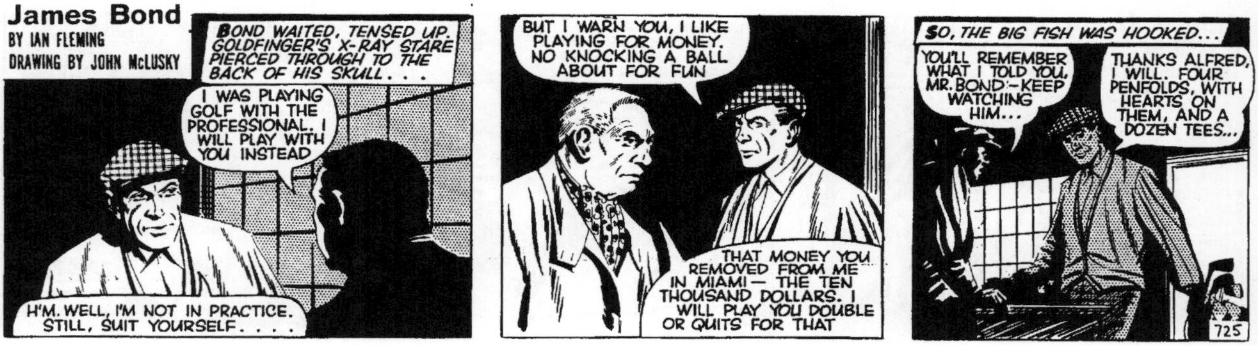
James Bond
BY IAN FLEMING
DRAWING BY JOHN McLUSKY
BOND WAITED, TENSED UP. GOLDFINGER'S X-RAY STARE PIERCED THROUGH TO THE BACK OF HIS SKULL . . .
I WAS PLAYING GOLF WITH THE PROFESSIONAL. I WILL PLAY WITH YOU INSTEAD
H'M. WELL, I'M NOT IN PRACTICE. STILL, SUIT YOURSELF. . . .
BUT I WARN YOU, I LIKE PLAYING FOR MONEY. NO KNOCKING A BALL ABOUT FOR FUN
THAT MONEY YOU REMOVED FROM ME IN MIAMI— THE TEN THOUSAND DOLLARS. I WILL PLAY YOU DOUBLE OR QUITS FOR THAT
SO, THE BIG FISH WAS HOOKED...
YOU'LL REMEMBER WHAT I TOLD YOU, MR. BOND—KEEP WATCHING HIM...
THANKS ALFRED, I WILL. FOUR PENFOLDS, WITH HEARTS ON THEM, AND A DOZEN TEES...
725

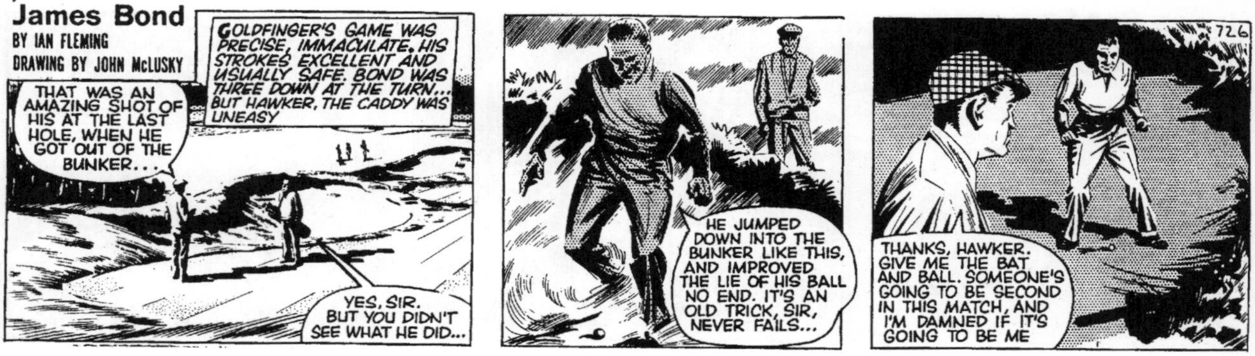
James Bond
BY IAN FLEMING
DRAWING BY JOHN McLUSKY
GOLDFINGER'S GAME WAS PRECISE, IMMACULATE. HIS STROKES EXCELLENT AND USUALLY SAFE. BOND WAS THREE DOWN AT THE TURN... BUT HAWKER, THE CADDY WAS UNEASY
THAT WAS AN AMAZING SHOT OF HIS AT THE LAST HOLE, WHEN HE GOT OUT OF THE BUNKER...
YES, SIR. BUT YOU DIDN'T SEE WHAT HE DID...
HE JUMPED DOWN INTO THE BUNKER LIKE THIS, AND IMPROVED THE LIE OF HIS BALL NO END. IT'S AN OLD TRICK, SIR, NEVER FAILS...
726
THANKS, HAWKER. GIVE ME THE BAT AND BALL. SOMEONE'S GOING TO BE SECOND IN THIS MATCH, AND I'M DAMNED IF IT'S GOING TO BE ME

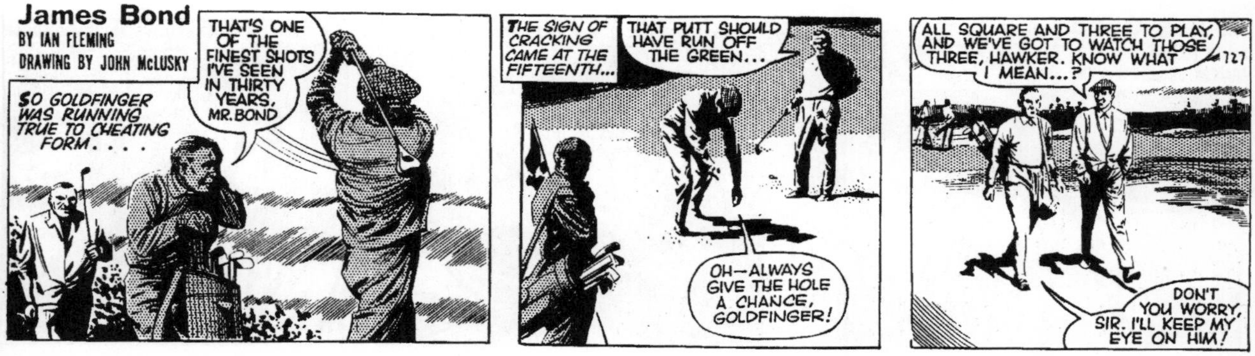
James Bond
BY IAN FLEMING
DRAWING BY JOHN McLUSKY
SO GOLDFINGER WAS RUNNING TRUE TO CHEATING FORM . . . .
THAT'S ONE OF THE FINEST SHOTS I'VE SEEN IN THIRTY YEARS, MR. BOND
THE SIGN OF CRACKING CAME AT THE FIFTEENTH...
THAT PUTT SHOULD HAVE RUN OFF THE GREEN...
OH—ALWAYS GIVE THE HOLE A CHANCE, GOLDFINGER!
ALL SQUARE AND THREE TO PLAY, AND WE'VE GOT TO WATCH THOSE THREE, HAWKER. KNOW WHAT I MEAN...?
727
DON'T YOU WORRY, SIR. I'LL KEEP MY EYE ON HIM!

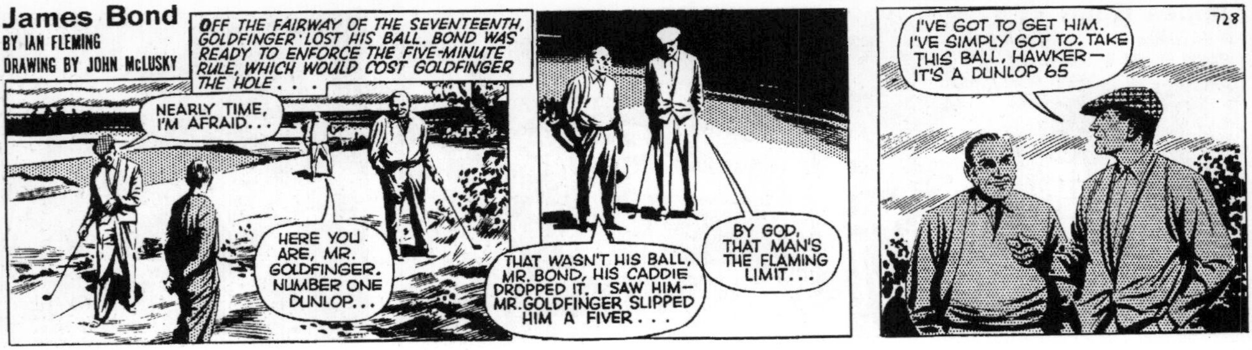
James Bond
BY IAN FLEMING
DRAWING BY JOHN McLUSKY
OFF THE FAIRWAY OF THE SEVENTEENTH, GOLDFINGER LOST HIS BALL. BOND WAS READY TO ENFORCE THE FIVE-MINUTE RULE, WHICH WOULD COST GOLDFINGER THE HOLE . . .
NEARLY TIME, I'M AFRAID...
HERE YOU ARE, MR. GOLDFINGER. NUMBER ONE DUNLOP...
THAT WASN'T HIS BALL, MR. BOND, HIS CADDIE DROPPED IT. I SAW HIM–MR. GOLDFINGER SLIPPED HIM A FIVER . . .
BY GOD, THAT MAN'S THE FLAMING LIMIT...
728
I'VE GOT TO GET HIM. I'VE SIMPLY GOT TO. TAKE THIS BALL, HAWKER– IT'S A DUNLOP 65

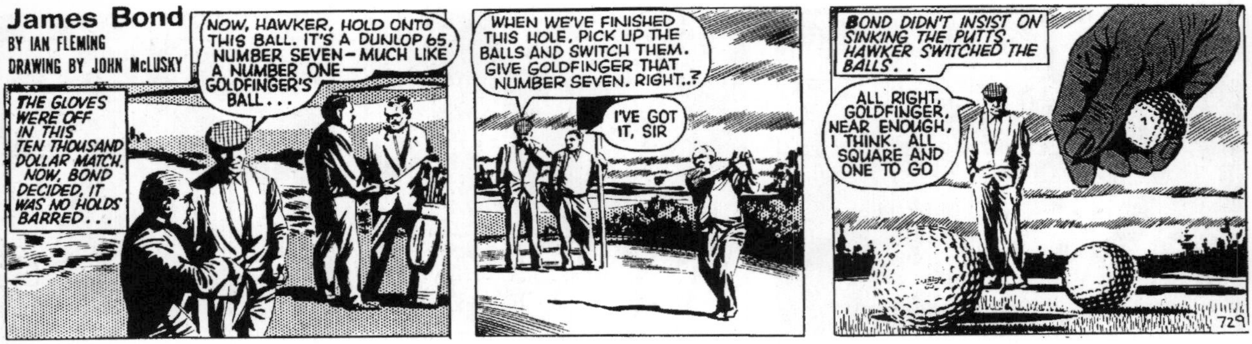
James Bond
BY IAN FLEMING
DRAWING BY JOHN McLUSKY
THE GLOVES WERE OFF IN THIS TEN THOUSAND DOLLAR MATCH. NOW, BOND DECIDED, IT WAS NO HOLDS BARRED...
NOW, HAWKER, HOLD ONTO THIS BALL. IT'S A DUNLOP 65, NUMBER SEVEN – MUCH LIKE A NUMBER ONE– GOLDFINGER'S BALL...
WHEN WE'VE FINISHED THIS HOLE, PICK UP THE BALLS AND SWITCH THEM. GIVE GOLDFINGER THAT NUMBER SEVEN. RIGHT..?
I'VE GOT IT, SIR
BOND DIDN'T INSIST ON SINKING THE PUTTS. HAWKER SWITCHED THE BALLS . . .
ALL RIGHT, GOLDFINGER, NEAR ENOUGH, I THINK. ALL SQUARE AND ONE TO GO
729

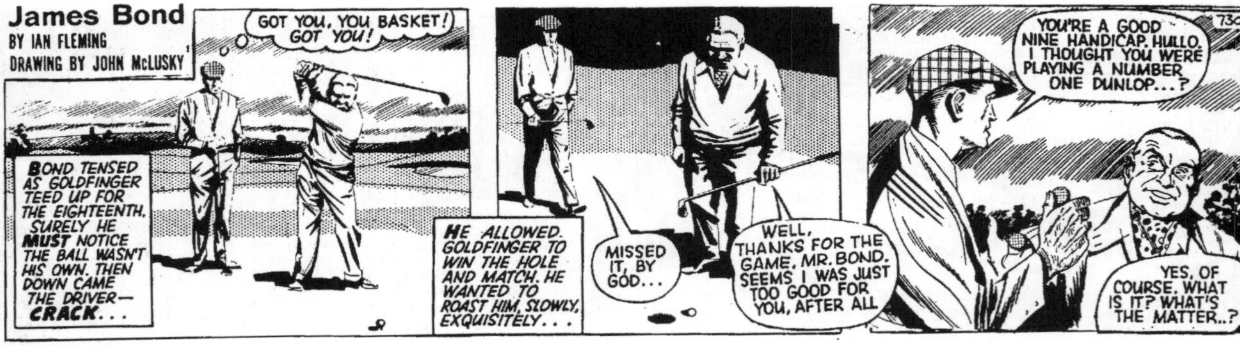
James Bond
BY IAN FLEMING
DRAWING BY JOHN McLUSKY
GOT YOU, YOU BASKET! GOT YOU!
BOND TENSED AS GOLDFINGER TEED UP FOR THE EIGHTEENTH. SURELY HE MUST NOTICE THE BALL WASN'T HIS OWN. THEN DOWN CAME THE DRIVER– CRACK...
HE ALLOWED. GOLDFINGER TO WIN THE HOLE AND MATCH. HE WANTED TO ROAST HIM, SLOWLY, EXQUISITELY . . .
MISSED IT, BY GOD...
WELL, THANKS FOR THE GAME, MR. BOND. SEEMS I WAS JUST TOO GOOD FOR YOU, AFTER ALL
730
YOU'RE A GOOD NINE HANDICAP. HULLO, I THOUGHT YOU WERE PLAYING A NUMBER ONE DUNLOP...?
YES, OF COURSE. WHAT IS IT? WHAT'S THE MATTER..?

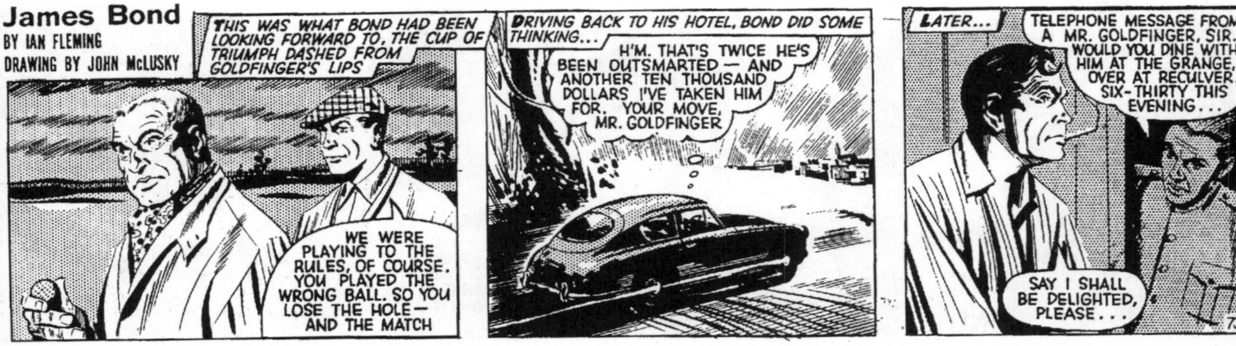
James Bond
BY IAN FLEMING
DRAWING BY JOHN McLUSKY
THIS WAS WHAT BOND HAD BEEN LOOKING FORWARD TO, THE CUP OF TRIUMPH DASHED FROM GOLDFINGER'S LIPS
WE WERE PLAYING TO THE RULES, OF COURSE. YOU PLAYED THE WRONG BALL. SO YOU LOSE THE HOLE– AND THE MATCH
DRIVING BACK TO HIS HOTEL, BOND DID SOME THINKING...
H'M. THAT'S TWICE HE'S BEEN OUTSMARTED – AND ANOTHER TEN THOUSAND DOLLARS I'VE TAKEN HIM FOR. YOUR MOVE, MR. GOLDFINGER
LATER...
TELEPHONE MESSAGE FROM A MR. GOLDFINGER, SIR. WOULD YOU DINE WITH HIM AT THE GRANGE, OVER AT RECULVER. SIX-THIRTY THIS EVENING...
SAY I SHALL BE DELIGHTED, PLEASE...
731

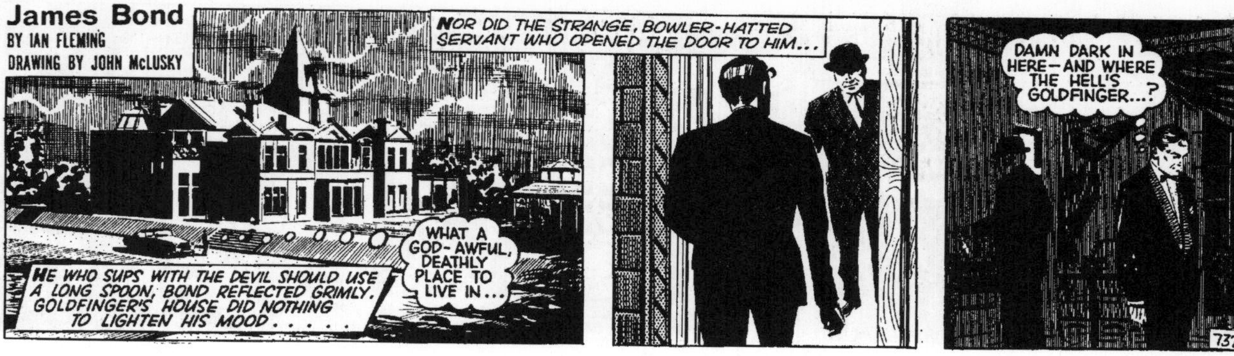
James Bond
BY IAN FLEMING
DRAWING BY JOHN McLUSKY
HE WHO SUPS WITH THE DEVIL SHOULD USE A LONG SPOON, BOND REFLECTED GRIMLY. GOLDFINGER'S HOUSE DID NOTHING TO LIGHTEN HIS MOOD . . . . .
WHAT A GOD-AWFUL, DEATHLY PLACE TO LIVE IN...
NOR DID THE STRANGE, BOWLER-HATTED SERVANT WHO OPENED THE DOOR TO HIM...
DAMN DARK IN HERE—AND WHERE THE HELL'S GOLDFINGER...?
732

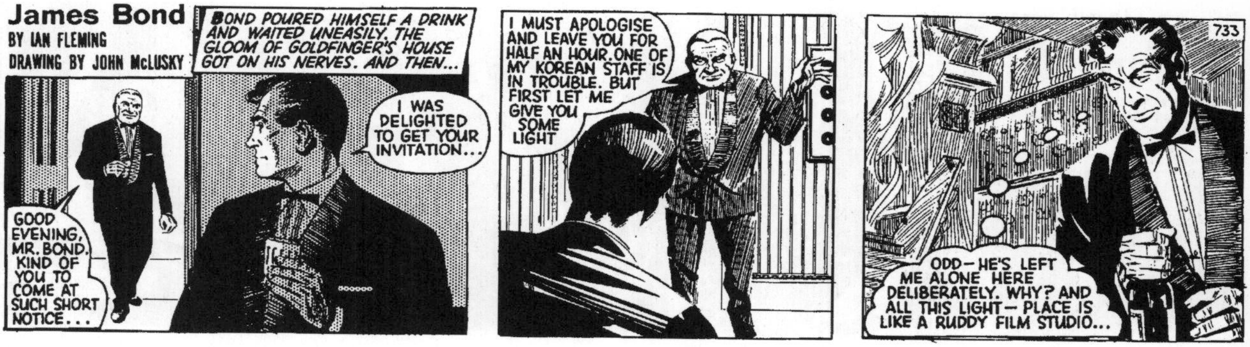
James Bond
BY IAN FLEMING
DRAWING BY JOHN McLUSKY
BOND POURED HIMSELF A DRINK AND WAITED UNEASILY. THE GLOOM OF GOLDFINGER'S HOUSE GOT ON HIS NERVES. AND THEN...
GOOD EVENING, MR. BOND. KIND OF YOU TO COME AT SUCH SHORT NOTICE...
I WAS DELIGHTED TO GET YOUR INVITATION...
I MUST APOLOGISE AND LEAVE YOU FOR HALF AN HOUR. ONE OF MY KOREAN STAFF IS IN TROUBLE. BUT FIRST LET ME GIVE YOU SOME LIGHT
733
ODD—HE'S LEFT ME ALONE HERE DELIBERATELY. WHY? AND ALL THIS LIGHT—PLACE IS LIKE A RUDDY FILM STUDIO...

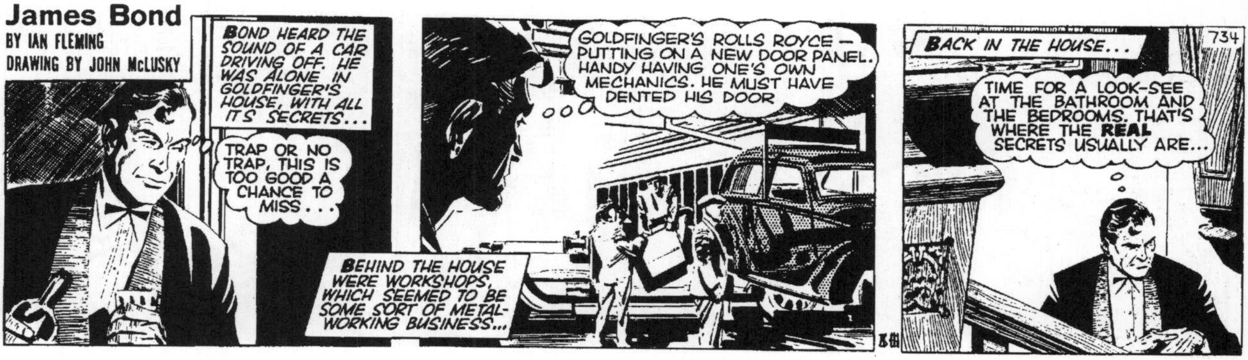
James Bond
BY IAN FLEMING
DRAWING BY JOHN McLUSKY
BOND HEARD THE SOUND OF A CAR DRIVING OFF. HE WAS ALONE IN GOLDFINGER'S HOUSE, WITH ALL IT'S SECRETS...
TRAP OR NO TRAP, THIS IS TOO GOOD A CHANCE TO MISS . . .
GOLDFINGER'S ROLLS ROYCE—PUTTING ON A NEW DOOR PANEL. HANDY HAVING ONE'S OWN MECHANICS. HE MUST HAVE DENTED HIS DOOR
BEHIND THE HOUSE WERE WORKSHOPS, WHICH SEEMED TO BE SOME SORT OF METAL-WORKING BUSINESS...
BACK IN THE HOUSE...
734
TIME FOR A LOOK-SEE AT THE BATHROOM AND THE BEDROOMS. THAT'S WHERE THE REAL SECRETS USUALLY ARE...

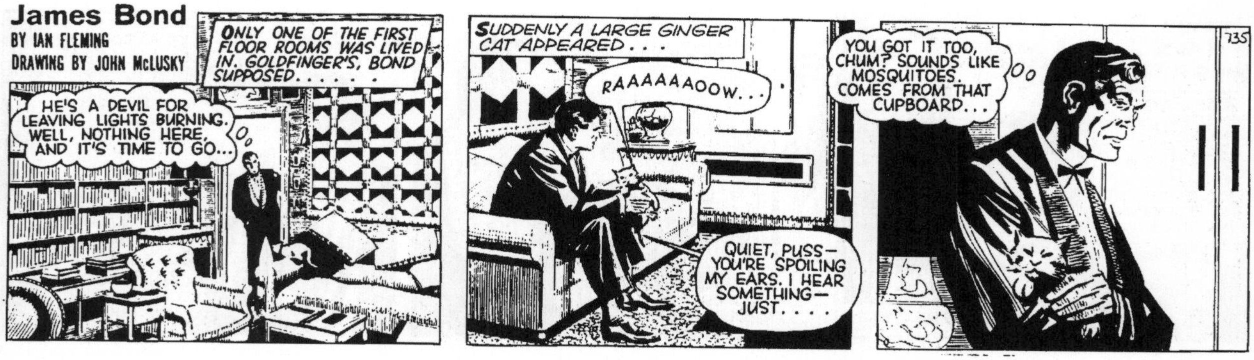
James Bond
BY IAN FLEMING
DRAWING BY JOHN McLUSKY
ONLY ONE OF THE FIRST FLOOR ROOMS WAS LIVED IN. GOLDFINGER'S, BOND SUPPOSED . . . . . .
HE'S A DEVIL FOR LEAVING LIGHTS BURNING. WELL, NOTHING HERE, AND IT'S TIME TO GO...
SUDDENLY A LARGE GINGER CAT APPEARED . . .
RAAAAAAOOW...
QUIET, PUSS—YOU'RE SPOILING MY EARS. I HEAR SOMETHING—JUST. . .
YOU GOT IT TOO, CHUM? SOUNDS LIKE MOSQUITOES. COMES FROM THAT CUPBOARD...
735

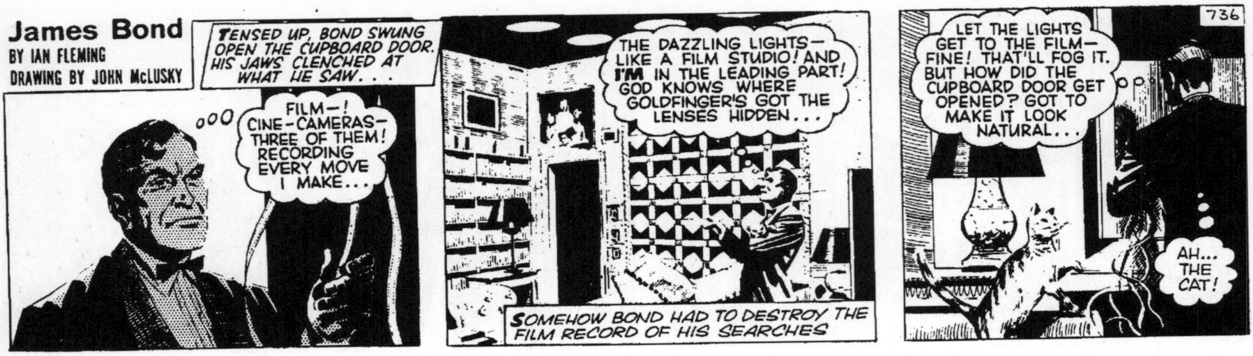
James Bond
BY IAN FLEMING
DRAWING BY JOHN McLUSKY
TENSED UP, BOND SWUNG OPEN THE CUPBOARD DOOR. HIS JAWS CLENCHED AT WHAT HE SAW . . .
FILM—! CINE-CAMERAS—THREE OF THEM! RECORDING EVERY MOVE I MAKE...
THE DAZZLING LIGHTS—LIKE A FILM STUDIO! AND I'M IN THE LEADING PART! GOD KNOWS WHERE GOLDFINGER'S GOT THE LENSES HIDDEN...
SOMEHOW BOND HAD TO DESTROY THE FILM RECORD OF HIS SEARCHES
736
LET THE LIGHTS GET TO THE FILM—FINE! THAT'LL FOG IT. BUT HOW DID THE CUPBOARD DOOR GET OPENED? GOT TO MAKE IT LOOK NATURAL...
AH... THE CAT!

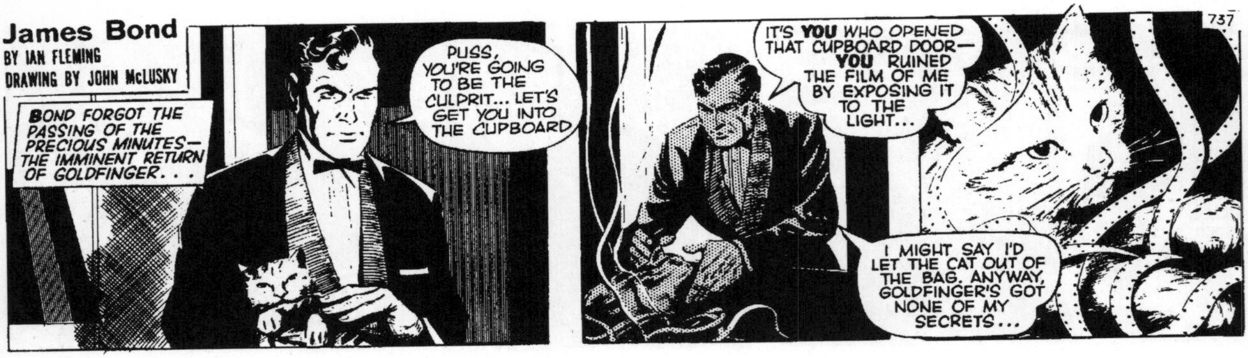
James Bond
BY IAN FLEMING
DRAWING BY JOHN McLUSKY
BOND FORGOT THE PASSING OF THE PRECIOUS MINUTES—THE IMMINENT RETURN OF GOLDFINGER . . .
PUSS, YOU'RE GOING TO BE THE CULPRIT... LET'S GET YOU INTO THE CUPBOARD
737
IT'S YOU WHO OPENED THAT CUPBOARD DOOR—YOU RUINED THE FILM OF ME BY EXPOSING IT TO THE LIGHT...
I MIGHT SAY I'D LET THE CAT OUT OF THE BAG. ANYWAY, GOLDFINGER'S GOT NONE OF MY SECRETS...

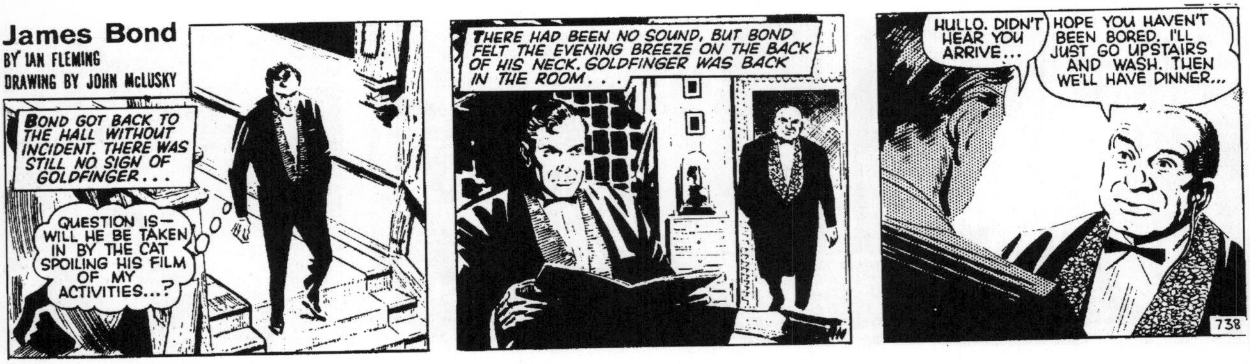
James Bond
BY IAN FLEMING
DRAWING BY JOHN McLUSKY
BOND GOT BACK TO THE HALL WITHOUT INCIDENT. THERE WAS STILL NO SIGN OF GOLDFINGER...
QUESTION IS—WILL HE BE TAKEN IN BY THE CAT SPOILING HIS FILM OF MY ACTIVITIES...?
THERE HAD BEEN NO SOUND, BUT BOND FELT THE EVENING BREEZE ON THE BACK OF HIS NECK. GOLDFINGER WAS BACK IN THE ROOM . . .
HULLO. DIDN'T HEAR YOU ARRIVE...
HOPE YOU HAVEN'T BEEN BORED. I'LL JUST GO UPSTAIRS AND WASH. THEN WE'LL HAVE DINNER...
738

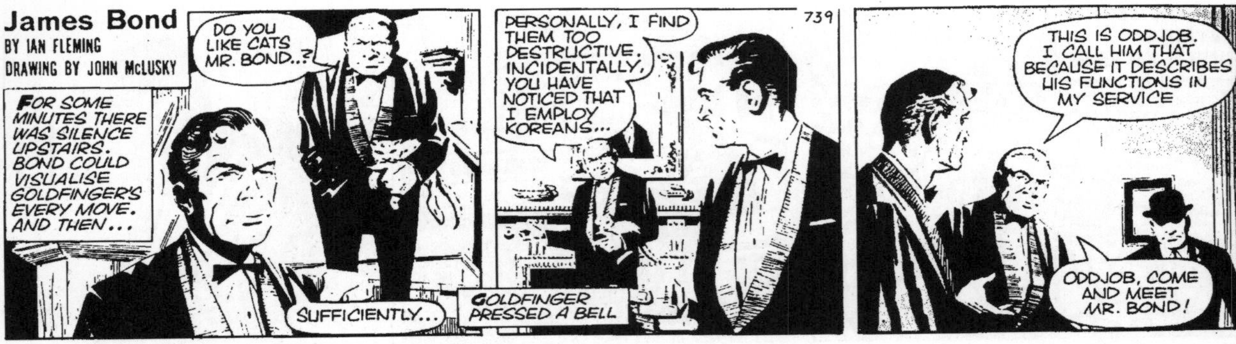
James Bond
BY IAN FLEMING
DRAWING BY JOHN McLUSKY
FOR SOME MINUTES THERE WAS SILENCE UPSTAIRS. BOND COULD VISUALISE GOLDFINGER'S EVERY MOVE. AND THEN...
DO YOU LIKE CATS MR. BOND..?
SUFFICIENTLY...
739
PERSONALLY, I FIND THEM TOO DESTRUCTIVE. INCIDENTALLY, YOU HAVE NOTICED THAT I EMPLOY KOREANS...
GOLDFINGER PRESSED A BELL
THIS IS ODDJOB. I CALL HIM THAT BECAUSE IT DESCRIBES HIS FUNCTIONS IN MY SERVICE
ODDJOB, COME AND MEET MR. BOND!

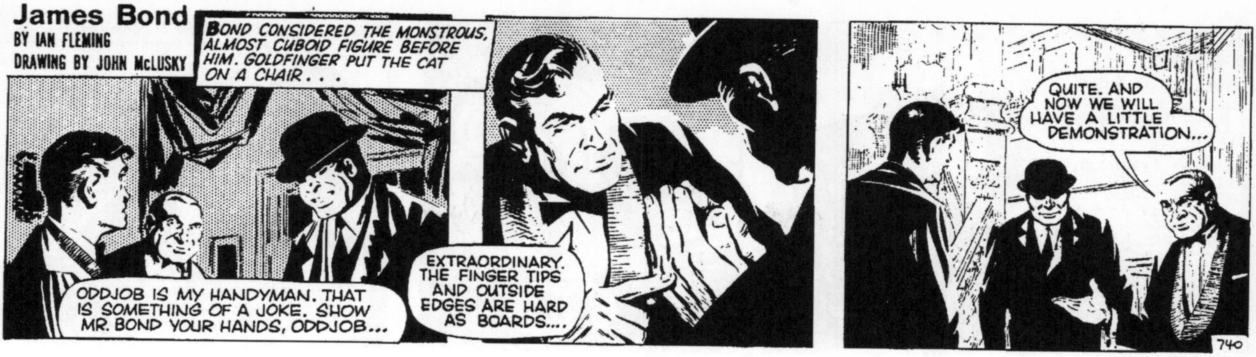
James Bond
BY IAN FLEMING
DRAWING BY JOHN McLUSKY
ODDJOB IS MY HANDYMAN. THAT IS SOMETHING OF A JOKE. SHOW MR. BOND YOUR HANDS, ODDJOB...
BOND CONSIDERED THE MONSTROUS, ALMOST CUBOID FIGURE BEFORE HIM. GOLDFINGER PUT THE CAT ON A CHAIR . . .
EXTRAORDINARY. THE FINGER TIPS AND OUTSIDE EDGES ARE HARD AS BOARDS....
QUITE. AND NOW WE WILL HAVE A LITTLE DEMONSTRATION...
740

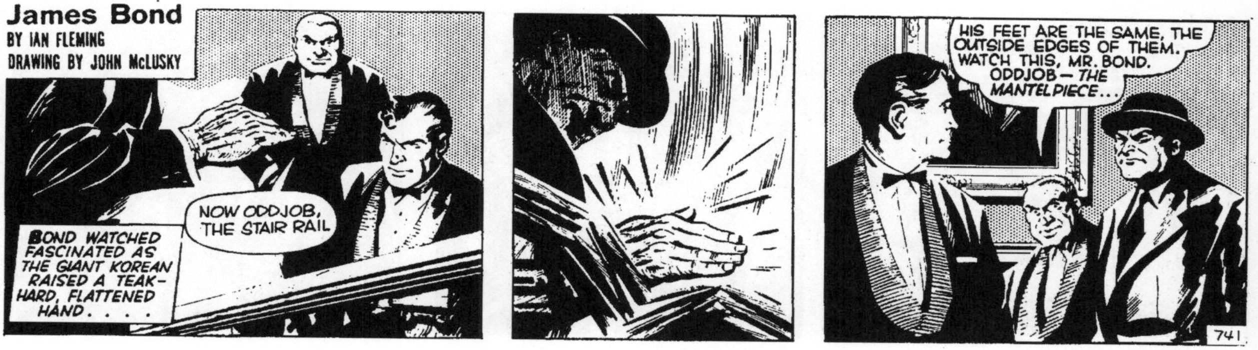
James Bond
BY IAN FLEMING
DRAWING BY JOHN McLUSKY
BOND WATCHED FASCINATED AS THE GIANT KOREAN RAISED A TEAK-HARD, FLATTENED HAND . . . .
NOW ODDJOB, THE STAIR RAIL
HIS FEET ARE THE SAME, THE OUTSIDE EDGES OF THEM. WATCH THIS, MR. BOND. ODDJOB — THE MANTELPIECE...
741

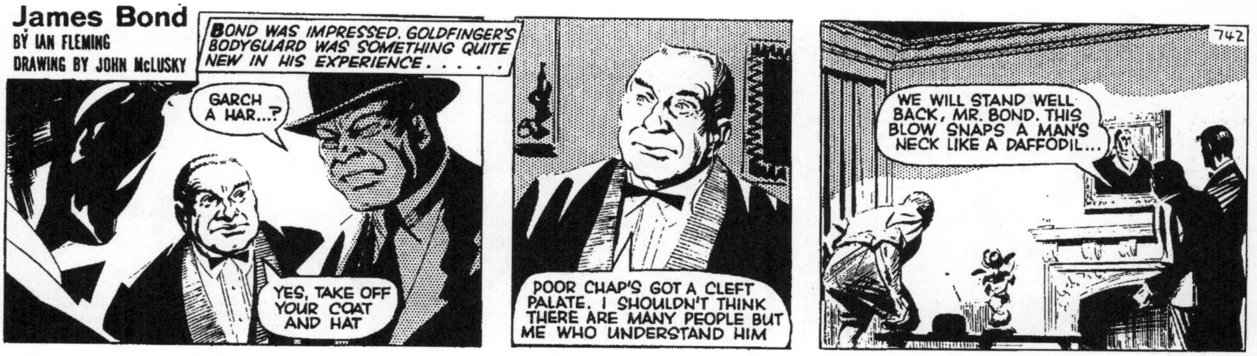
James Bond
BY IAN FLEMING
DRAWING BY JOHN McLUSKY
BOND WAS IMPRESSED. GOLDFINGER'S BODYGUARD WAS SOMETHING QUITE NEW IN HIS EXPERIENCE . . . .
GARCH A HAR...?
YES, TAKE OFF YOUR COAT AND HAT
POOR CHAP'S GOT A CLEFT PALATE. I SHOULDN'T THINK THERE ARE MANY PEOPLE BUT ME WHO UNDERSTAND HIM
742
WE WILL STAND WELL BACK, MR. BOND. THIS BLOW SNAPS A MAN'S NECK LIKE A DAFFODIL...

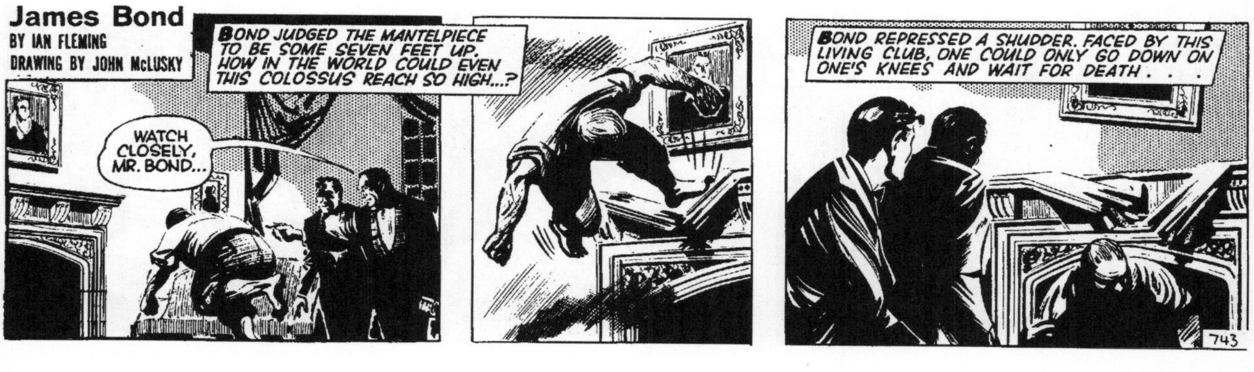
James Bond
BY IAN FLEMING
DRAWING BY JOHN McLUSKY
WATCH CLOSELY, MR. BOND...
BOND JUDGED THE MANTELPIECE TO BE SOME SEVEN FEET UP. HOW IN THE WORLD COULD EVEN THIS COLOSSUS REACH SO HIGH...?
BOND REPRESSED A SHUDDER. FACED BY THIS LIVING CLUB, ONE COULD ONLY GO DOWN ON ONE'S KNEES AND WAIT FOR DEATH . . .
743

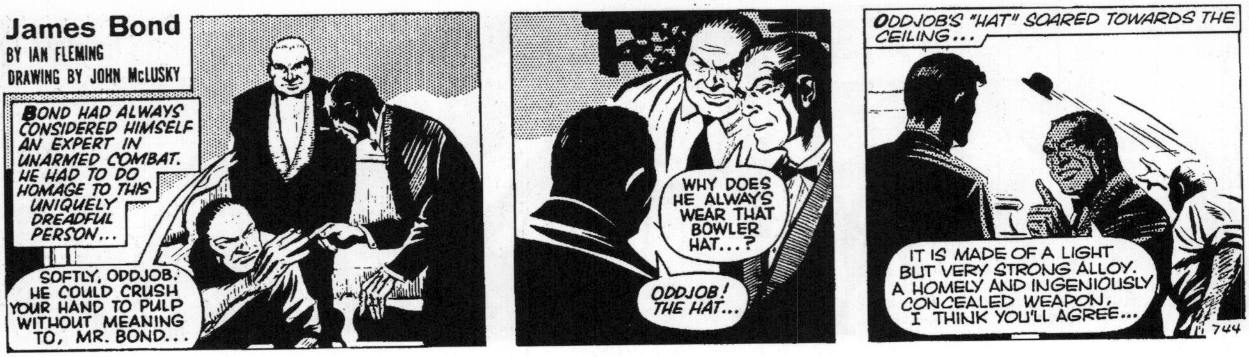
James Bond
BY IAN FLEMING
DRAWING BY JOHN McLUSKY
BOND HAD ALWAYS CONSIDERED HIMSELF AN EXPERT IN UNARMED COMBAT. HE HAD TO DO HOMAGE TO THIS UNIQUELY DREADFUL PERSON...
SOFTLY, ODDJOB: HE COULD CRUSH YOUR HAND TO PULP WITHOUT MEANING TO, MR. BOND...
WHY DOES HE ALWAYS WEAR THAT BOWLER HAT...?
ODDJOB! THE HAT...
ODDJOB'S "HAT" SOARED TOWARDS THE CEILING...
IT IS MADE OF A LIGHT BUT VERY STRONG ALLOY. A HOMELY AND INGENIOUSLY CONCEALED WEAPON, I THINK YOU'LL AGREE...
744

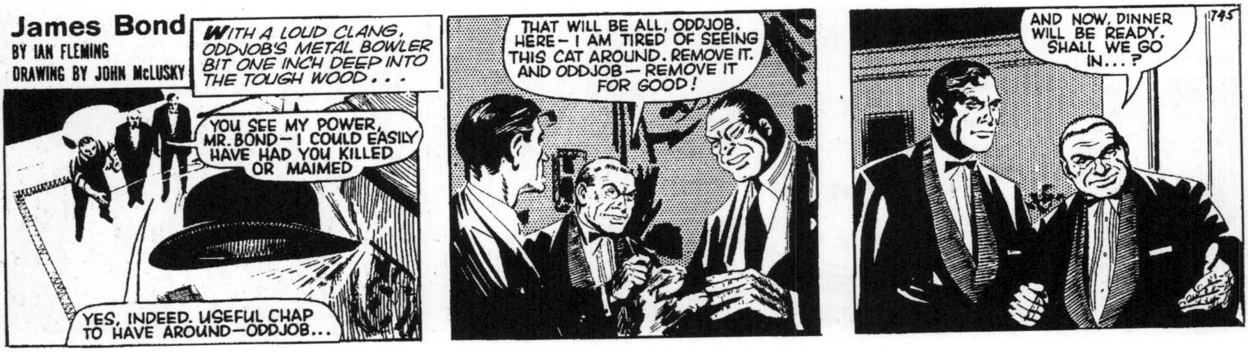
James Bond
BY IAN FLEMING
DRAWING BY JOHN McLUSKY
WITH A LOUD CLANG, ODDJOB'S METAL BOWLER BIT ONE INCH DEEP INTO THE TOUGH WOOD . . .
YOU SEE MY POWER, MR. BOND—I COULD EASILY HAVE HAD YOU KILLED OR MAIMED
YES, INDEED. USEFUL CHAP TO HAVE AROUND—ODDJOB...
THAT WILL BE ALL, ODDJOB. HERE—I AM TIRED OF SEEING THIS CAT AROUND. REMOVE IT. AND ODDJOB—REMOVE IT FOR GOOD!
AND NOW, DINNER WILL BE READY. SHALL WE GO IN...?
745

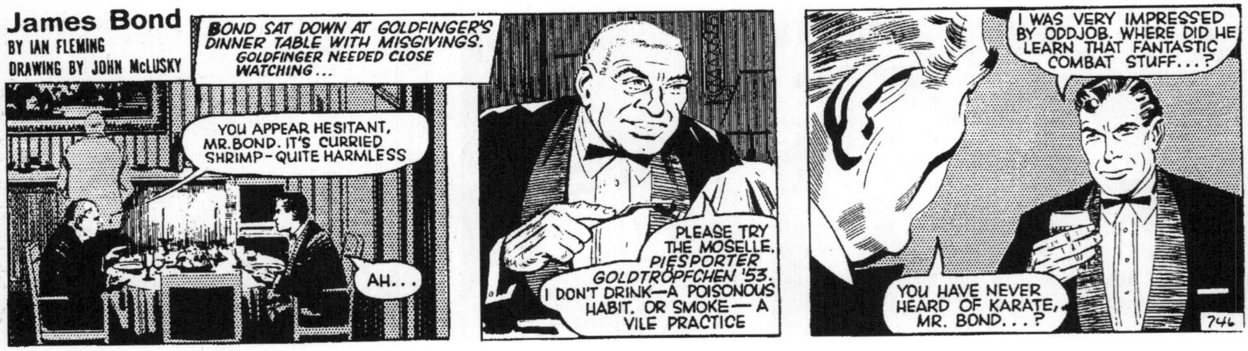
James Bond
BY IAN FLEMING
DRAWING BY JOHN McLUSKY
BOND SAT DOWN AT GOLDFINGER'S DINNER TABLE WITH MISGIVINGS. GOLDFINGER NEEDED CLOSE WATCHING...
YOU APPEAR HESITANT, MR. BOND. IT'S CURRIED SHRIMP-QUITE HARMLESS
AH...
PLEASE TRY THE MOSELLE, PIESPORTER GOLDTROPFCHEN '53. I DON'T DRINK—A POISONOUS HABIT. OR SMOKE— A VILE PRACTICE
I WAS VERY IMPRESSED BY ODDJOB. WHERE DID HE LEARN THAT FANTASTIC COMBAT STUFF...?
YOU HAVE NEVER HEARD OF KARATE, MR. BOND...?
746

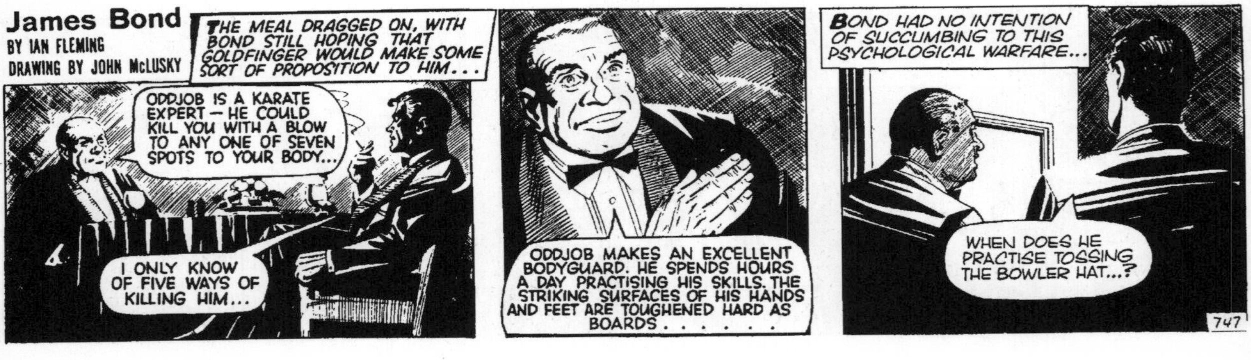
James Bond
BY IAN FLEMING
DRAWING BY JOHN McLUSKY
THE MEAL DRAGGED ON, WITH BOND STILL HOPING THAT GOLDFINGER WOULD MAKE SOME SORT OF PROPOSITION TO HIM...
ODDJOB IS A KARATE EXPERT—HE COULD KILL YOU WITH A BLOW TO ANY ONE OF SEVEN SPOTS TO YOUR BODY...
I ONLY KNOW OF FIVE WAYS OF KILLING HIM...
ODDJOB MAKES AN EXCELLENT BODYGUARD. HE SPENDS HOURS A DAY PRACTISING HIS SKILLS. THE STRIKING SURFACES OF HIS HANDS AND FEET ARE TOUGHENED HARD AS BOARDS . . . . . .
BOND HAD NO INTENTION OF SUCCUMBING TO THIS PSYCHOLOGICAL WARFARE...
WHEN DOES HE PRACTISE TOSSING THE BOWLER HAT...?
747

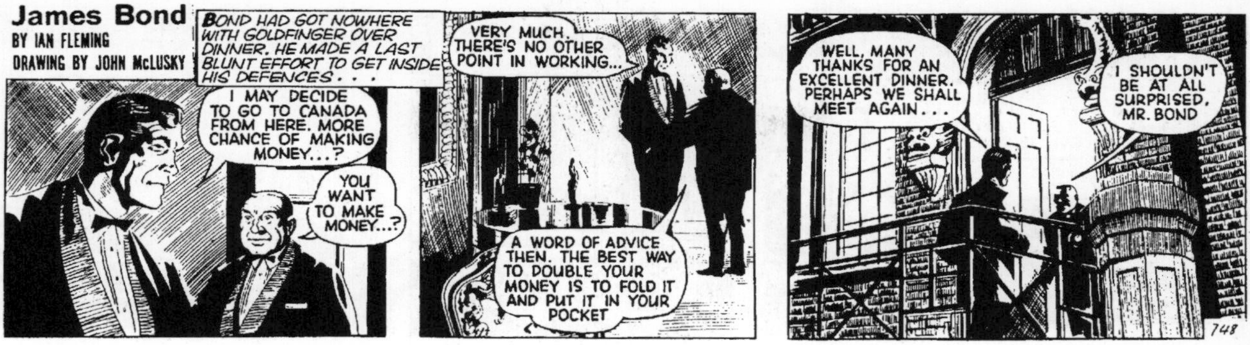
James Bond
BY IAN FLEMING
DRAWING BY JOHN McLUSKY
BOND HAD GOT NOWHERE WITH GOLDFINGER OVER DINNER. HE MADE A LAST BLUNT EFFORT TO GET INSIDE HIS DEFENCES . . .
I MAY DECIDE TO GO TO CANADA FROM HERE. MORE CHANCE OF MAKING MONEY...?
YOU WANT TO MAKE MONEY...?
VERY MUCH. THERE'S NO OTHER POINT IN WORKING...
A WORD OF ADVICE THEN. THE BEST WAY TO DOUBLE YOUR MONEY IS TO FOLD IT AND PUT IT IN YOUR POCKET
WELL, MANY THANKS FOR AN EXCELLENT DINNER. PERHAPS WE SHALL MEET AGAIN . . .
I SHOULDN'T BE AT ALL SURPRISED, MR. BOND
748

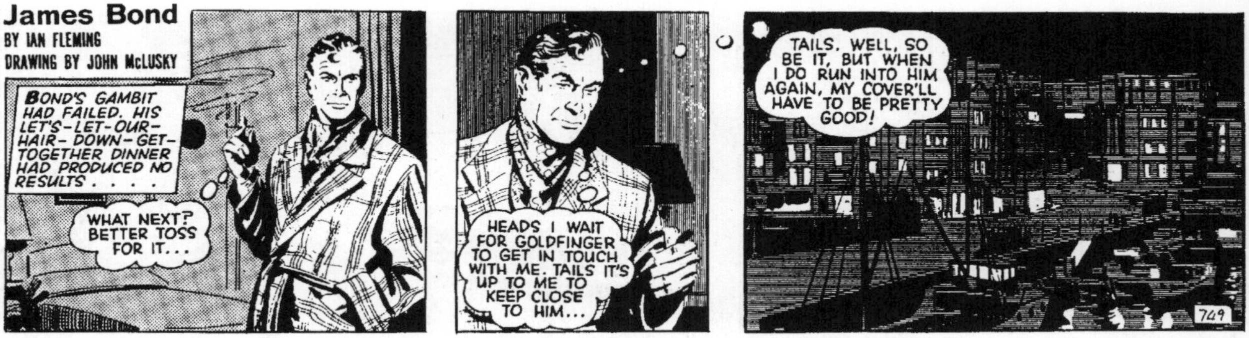
James Bond
BY IAN FLEMING
DRAWING BY JOHN McLUSKY
BOND'S GAMBIT HAD FAILED. HIS LET'S-LET-OUR-HAIR-DOWN-GET-TOGETHER DINNER HAD PRODUCED NO RESULTS . . . .
WHAT NEXT? BETTER TOSS FOR IT...
HEADS I WAIT FOR GOLDFINGER TO GET IN TOUCH WITH ME. TAILS IT'S UP TO ME TO KEEP CLOSE TO HIM...
TAILS. WELL, SO BE IT, BUT WHEN I DO RUN INTO HIM AGAIN, MY COVER'LL HAVE TO BE PRETTY GOOD!
749

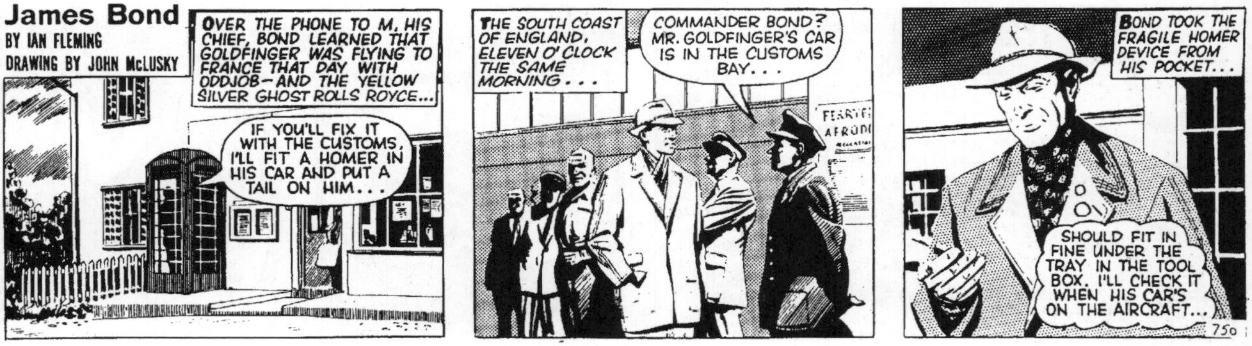
James Bond
BY IAN FLEMING
DRAWING BY JOHN McLUSKY
OVER THE PHONE TO M, HIS CHIEF, BOND LEARNED THAT GOLDFINGER WAS FLYING TO FRANCE THAT DAY WITH ODDJOB—AND THE YELLOW SILVER GHOST ROLLS ROYCE...
IF YOU'LL FIX IT WITH THE CUSTOMS, I'LL FIT A HOMER IN HIS CAR AND PUT A TAIL ON HIM...
THE SOUTH COAST OF ENGLAND, ELEVEN O' CLOCK THE SAME MORNING . . .
COMMANDER BOND? MR. GOLDFINGER'S CAR IS IN THE CUSTOMS BAY. . .
BOND TOOK THE FRAGILE HOMER DEVICE FROM HIS POCKET...
SHOULD FIT IN FINE UNDER THE TRAY IN THE TOOL BOX. I'LL CHECK IT WHEN HIS CAR'S ON THE AIRCRAFT...
750

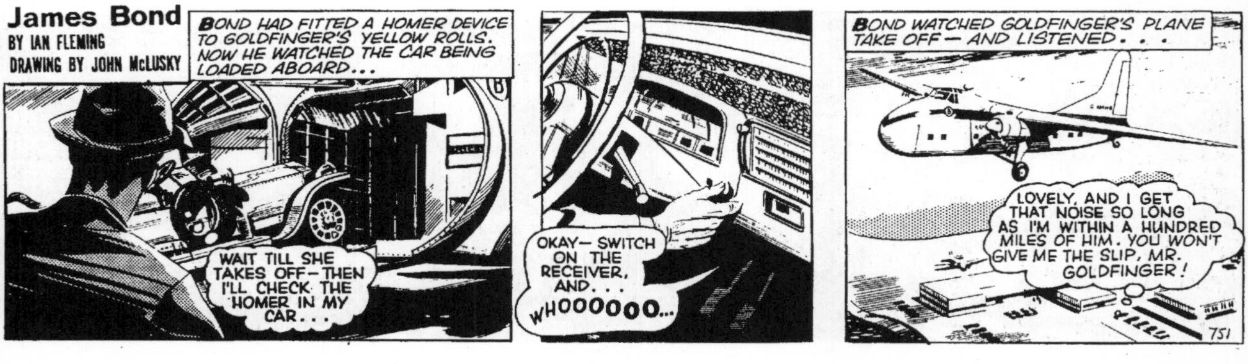
James Bond
BY IAN FLEMING
DRAWING BY JOHN McLUSKY
BOND HAD FITTED A HOMER DEVICE TO GOLDFINGER'S YELLOW ROLLS. NOW HE WATCHED THE CAR BEING LOADED ABOARD...
WAIT TILL SHE TAKES OFF—THEN I'LL CHECK THE HOMER IN MY CAR...
OKAY—SWITCH ON THE RECEIVER, AND. . .
WHOOOOOO...
BOND WATCHED GOLDFINGER'S PLANE TAKE OFF — AND LISTENED . . .
LOVELY, AND I GET THAT NOISE SO LONG AS I'M WITHIN A HUNDRED MILES OF HIM. YOU WON'T GIVE ME THE SLIP, MR. GOLDFINGER!
751

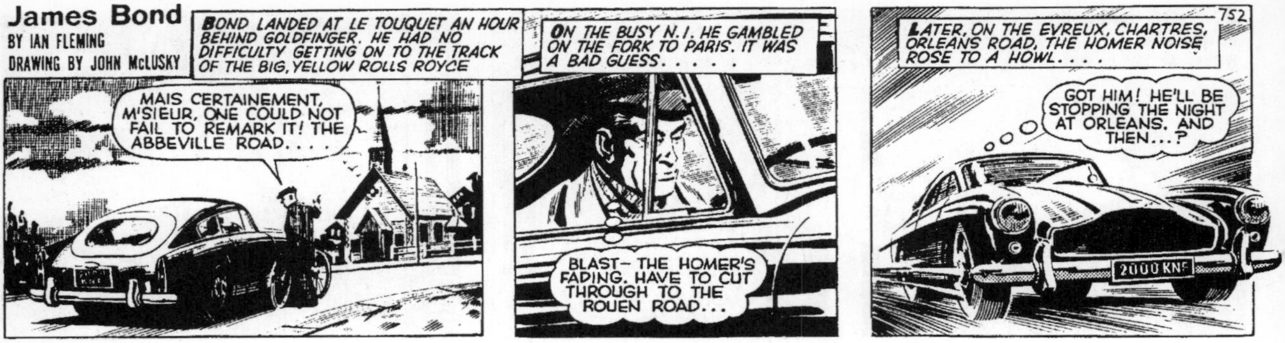
James Bond
BY IAN FLEMING
DRAWING BY JOHN McLUSKY
BOND LANDED AT LE TOUQUET AN HOUR BEHIND GOLDFINGER. HE HAD NO DIFFICULTY GETTING ON TO THE TRACK OF THE BIG, YELLOW ROLLS ROYCE
MAIS CERTAINEMENT, M'SIEUR, ONE COULD NOT FAIL TO REMARK IT! THE ABBEVILLE ROAD. . . .
ON THE BUSY N.I. HE GAMBLED ON THE FORK TO PARIS. IT WAS A BAD GUESS . . . . .
BLAST– THE HOMER'S FADING. HAVE TO CUT THROUGH TO THE ROUEN ROAD. . .
752
LATER, ON THE EVREUX, CHARTRES, ORLEANS ROAD, THE HOMER NOISE ROSE TO A HOWL. . . .
GOT HIM! HE'LL BE STOPPING THE NIGHT AT ORLEANS. AND THEN. . .?
2000 KNE

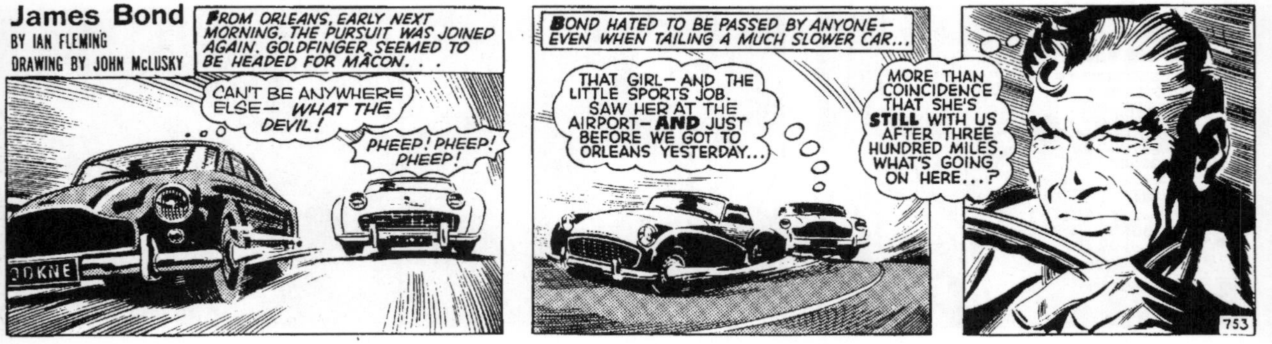
James Bond
BY IAN FLEMING
DRAWING BY JOHN McLUSKY
FROM ORLEANS, EARLY NEXT MORNING, THE PURSUIT WAS JOINED AGAIN. GOLDFINGER SEEMED TO BE HEADED FOR MÂCON . . .
CAN'T BE ANYWHERE ELSE– WHAT THE DEVIL!
PHEEP! PHEEP! PHEEP!
BOND HATED TO BE PASSED BY ANYONE– EVEN WHEN TAILING A MUCH SLOWER CAR. . .
THAT GIRL– AND THE LITTLE SPORTS JOB. SAW HER AT THE AIRPORT– AND JUST BEFORE WE GOT TO ORLEANS YESTERDAY. . .
MORE THAN COINCIDENCE THAT SHE'S STILL WITH US AFTER THREE HUNDRED MILES. WHAT'S GOING ON HERE. . .?
753

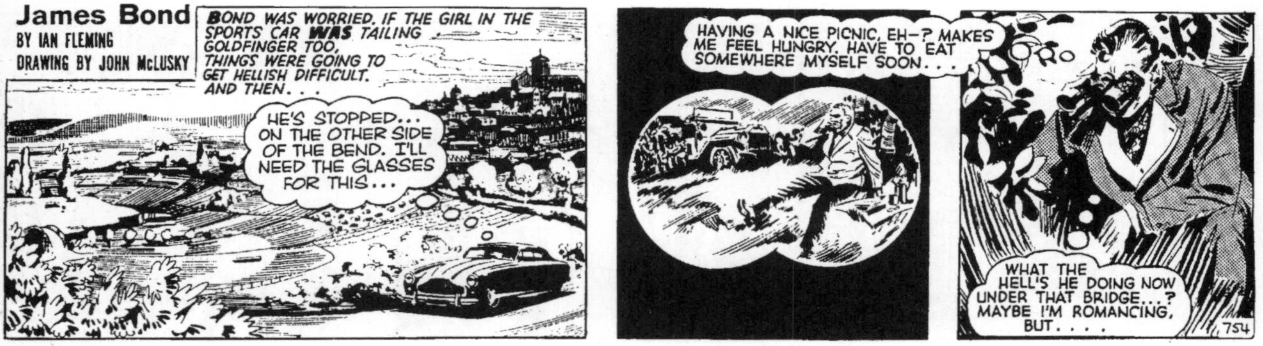
James Bond
BY IAN FLEMING
DRAWING BY JOHN McLUSKY
BOND WAS WORRIED. IF THE GIRL IN THE SPORTS CAR WAS TAILING GOLDFINGER TOO, THINGS WERE GOING TO GET HELLISH DIFFICULT. AND THEN. . .
HE'S STOPPED. . . ON THE OTHER SIDE OF THE BEND. I'LL NEED THE GLASSES FOR THIS. . .
HAVING A NICE PICNIC, EH–? MAKES ME FEEL HUNGRY. HAVE TO EAT SOMEWHERE MYSELF SOON. . .
WHAT THE HELL'S HE DOING NOW UNDER THAT BRIDGE. . .? MAYBE I'M ROMANCING, BUT. . . .
754

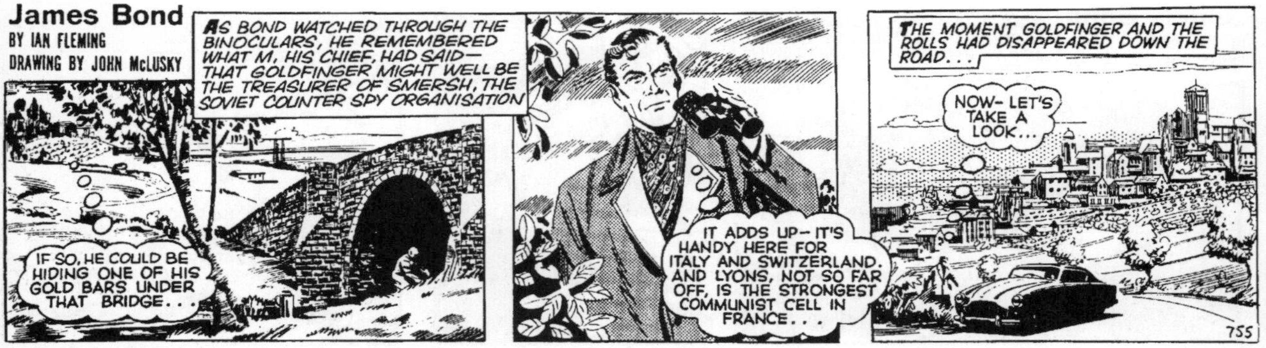
James Bond
BY IAN FLEMING
DRAWING BY JOHN McLUSKY
AS BOND WATCHED THROUGH THE BINOCULARS, HE REMEMBERED WHAT M, HIS CHIEF, HAD SAID– THAT GOLDFINGER MIGHT WELL BE THE TREASURER OF SMERSH, THE SOVIET COUNTER SPY ORGANISATION
IF SO, HE COULD BE HIDING ONE OF HIS GOLD BARS UNDER THAT BRIDGE. . .
IT ADDS UP– IT'S HANDY HERE FOR ITALY AND SWITZERLAND. AND LYONS, NOT SO FAR OFF, IS THE STRONGEST COMMUNIST CELL IN FRANCE. . .
THE MOMENT GOLDFINGER AND THE ROLLS HAD DISAPPEARED DOWN THE ROAD. . .
NOW– LET'S TAKE A LOOK. . .
755

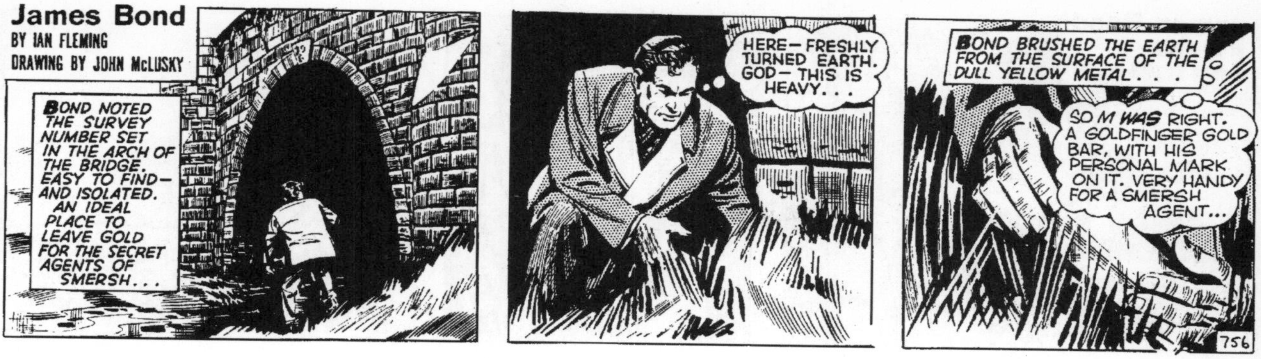
James Bond
BY IAN FLEMING
DRAWING BY JOHN McLUSKY
BOND NOTED THE SURVEY NUMBER SET IN THE ARCH OF THE BRIDGE. EASY TO FIND– AND ISOLATED. AN IDEAL PLACE TO LEAVE GOLD FOR THE SECRET AGENTS OF SMERSH . . .
HERE– FRESHLY TURNED EARTH. GOD– THIS IS HEAVY . . .
BOND BRUSHED THE EARTH FROM THE SURFACE OF THE DULL YELLOW METAL . . .
SO M WAS RIGHT. A GOLDFINGER GOLD BAR, WITH HIS PERSONAL MARK ON IT. VERY HANDY FOR A SMERSH AGENT...
756

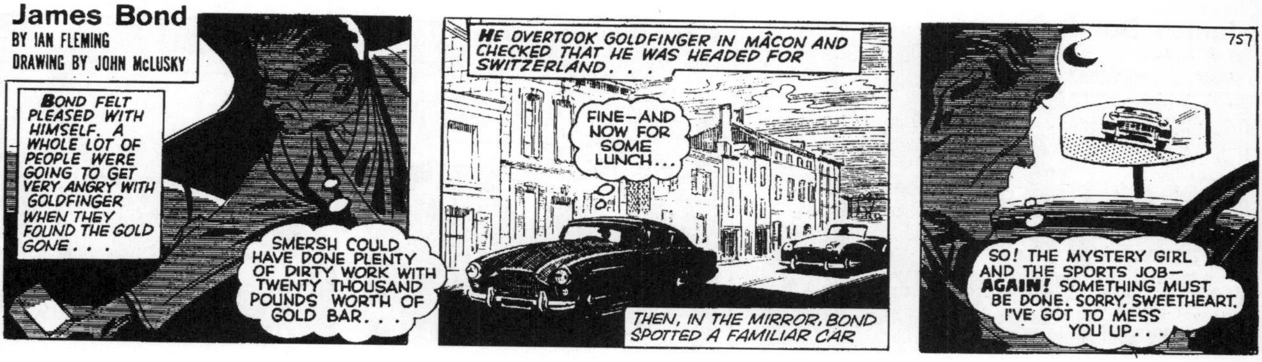
James Bond
BY IAN FLEMING
DRAWING BY JOHN McLUSKY
BOND FELT PLEASED WITH HIMSELF. A WHOLE LOT OF PEOPLE WERE GOING TO GET VERY ANGRY WITH GOLDFINGER WHEN THEY FOUND THE GOLD GONE . . .
SMERSH COULD HAVE DONE PLENTY OF DIRTY WORK WITH TWENTY THOUSAND POUNDS WORTH OF GOLD BAR . . .
HE OVERTOOK GOLDFINGER IN MÂCON AND CHECKED THAT HE WAS HEADED FOR SWITZERLAND . . .
FINE– AND NOW FOR SOME LUNCH...
THEN, IN THE MIRROR, BOND SPOTTED A FAMILIAR CAR
757
SO! THE MYSTERY GIRL AND THE SPORTS JOB– AGAIN! SOMETHING MUST BE DONE. SORRY, SWEETHEART. I'VE GOT TO MESS YOU UP . . .

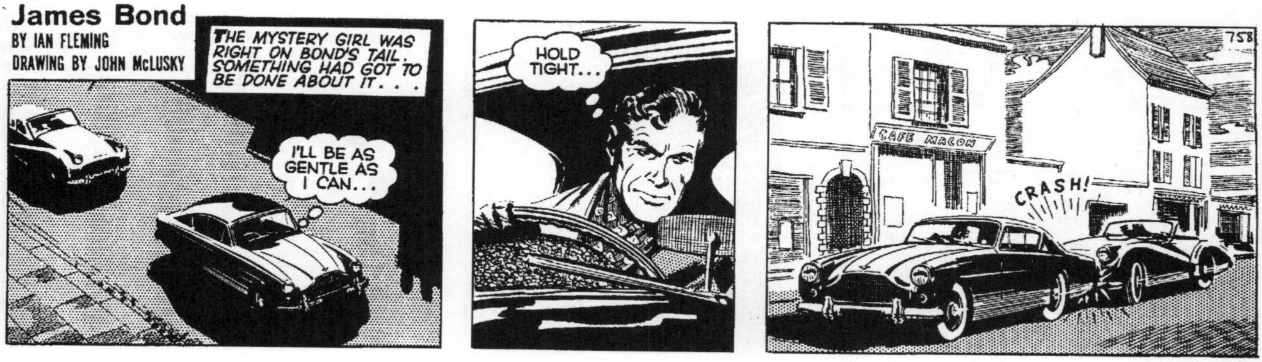
James Bond
BY IAN FLEMING
DRAWING BY JOHN McLUSKY
THE MYSTERY GIRL WAS RIGHT ON BOND'S TAIL. SOMETHING HAD GOT TO BE DONE ABOUT IT . . .
I'LL BE AS GENTLE AS I CAN...
HOLD TIGHT...
758
CAFE MACON
CRASH!

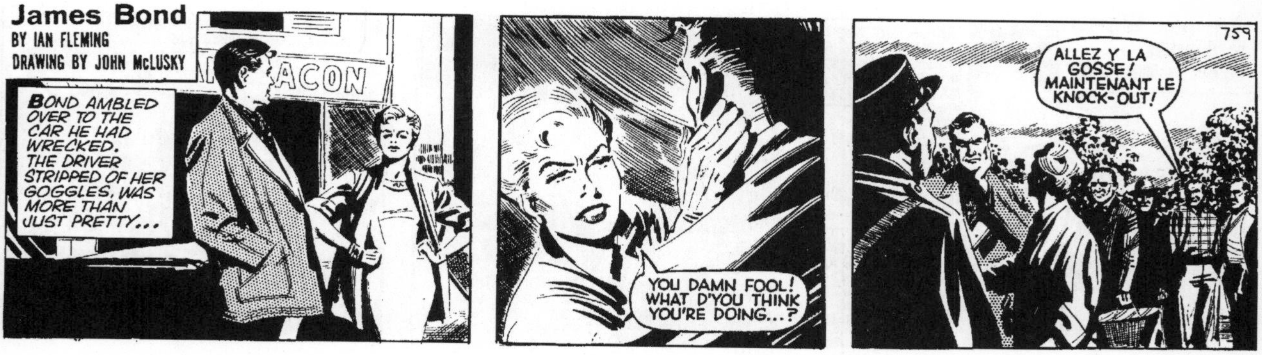
James Bond
BY IAN FLEMING
DRAWING BY JOHN McLUSKY
BOND AMBLED OVER TO THE CAR HE HAD WRECKED. THE DRIVER STRIPPED OF HER GOGGLES, WAS MORE THAN JUST PRETTY...
ACON
YOU DAMN FOOL! WHAT D'YOU THINK YOU'RE DOING...?
759
ALLEZ Y LA GOSSE! MAINTENANT LE KNOCK-OUT!

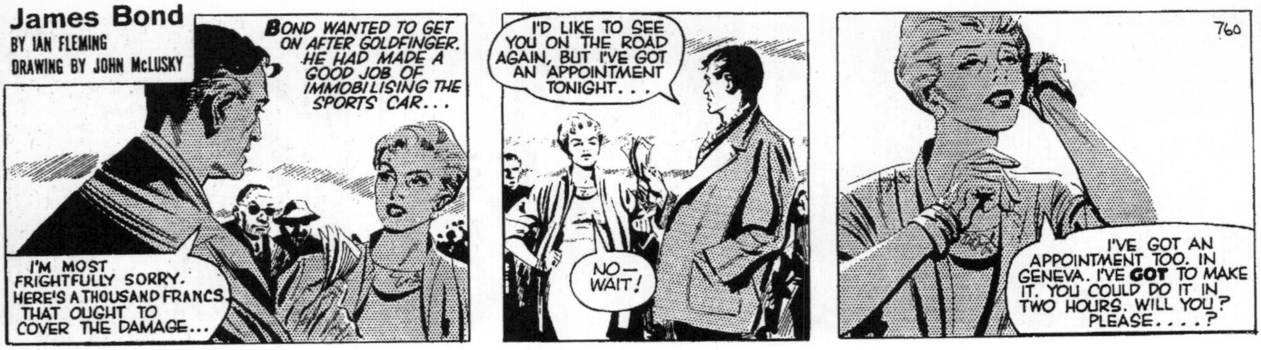
James Bond
BY IAN FLEMING
DRAWING BY JOHN McLUSKY
BOND WANTED TO GET ON AFTER GOLDFINGER. HE HAD MADE A GOOD JOB OF IMMOBILISING THE SPORTS CAR...
I'M MOST FRIGHTFULLY SORRY. HERE'S A THOUSAND FRANCS. THAT OUGHT TO COVER THE DAMAGE...
I'D LIKE TO SEE YOU ON THE ROAD AGAIN, BUT I'VE GOT AN APPOINTMENT TONIGHT...
NO— WAIT!
760
I'VE GOT AN APPOINTMENT TOO. IN GENEVA. I'VE GOT TO MAKE IT. YOU COULD DO IT IN TWO HOURS. WILL YOU? PLEASE....?

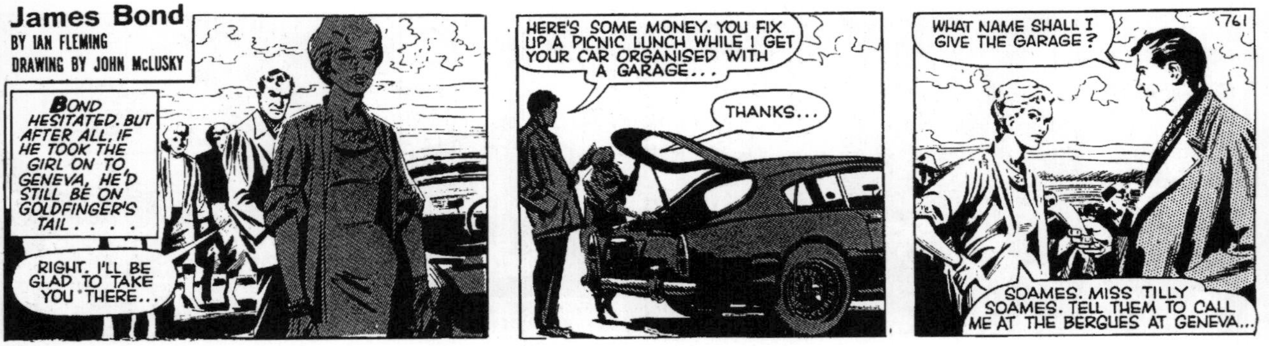
James Bond
BY IAN FLEMING
DRAWING BY JOHN McLUSKY
BOND HESITATED. BUT AFTER ALL, IF HE TOOK THE GIRL ON TO GENEVA, HE'D STILL BE ON GOLDFINGER'S TAIL....
RIGHT. I'LL BE GLAD TO TAKE YOU THERE...
HERE'S SOME MONEY. YOU FIX UP A PICNIC LUNCH WHILE I GET YOUR CAR ORGANISED WITH A GARAGE...
THANKS...
761
WHAT NAME SHALL I GIVE THE GARAGE?
SOAMES. MISS TILLY SOAMES. TELL THEM TO CALL ME AT THE BERGUES AT GENEVA...

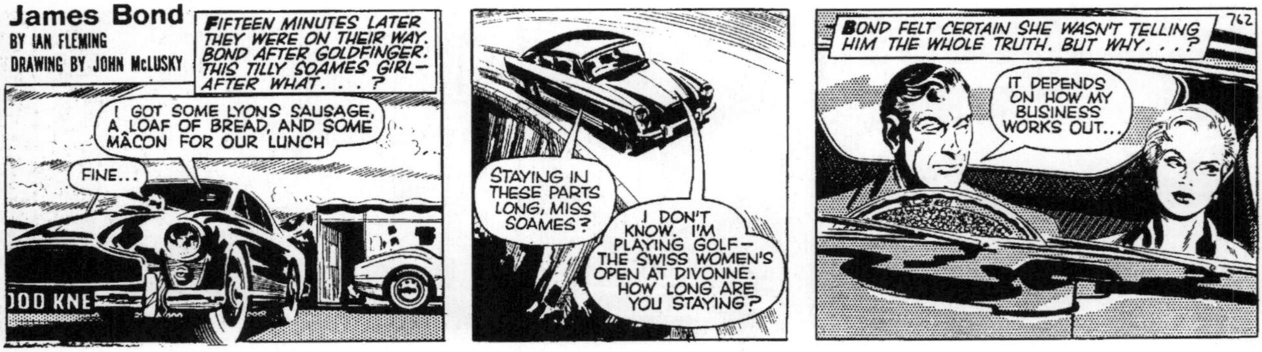
James Bond
BY IAN FLEMING
DRAWING BY JOHN McLUSKY
FIFTEEN MINUTES LATER THEY WERE ON THEIR WAY. BOND AFTER GOLDFINGER. THIS TILLY SOAMES GIRL— AFTER WHAT...?
I GOT SOME LYONS SAUSAGE, A LOAF OF BREAD, AND SOME MÂCON FOR OUR LUNCH
FINE...
STAYING IN THESE PARTS LONG, MISS SOAMES?
I DON'T KNOW. I'M PLAYING GOLF— THE SWISS WOMEN'S OPEN AT DIVONNE. HOW LONG ARE YOU STAYING?
762
BOND FELT CERTAIN SHE WASN'T TELLING HIM THE WHOLE TRUTH. BUT WHY...?
IT DEPENDS ON HOW MY BUSINESS WORKS OUT...

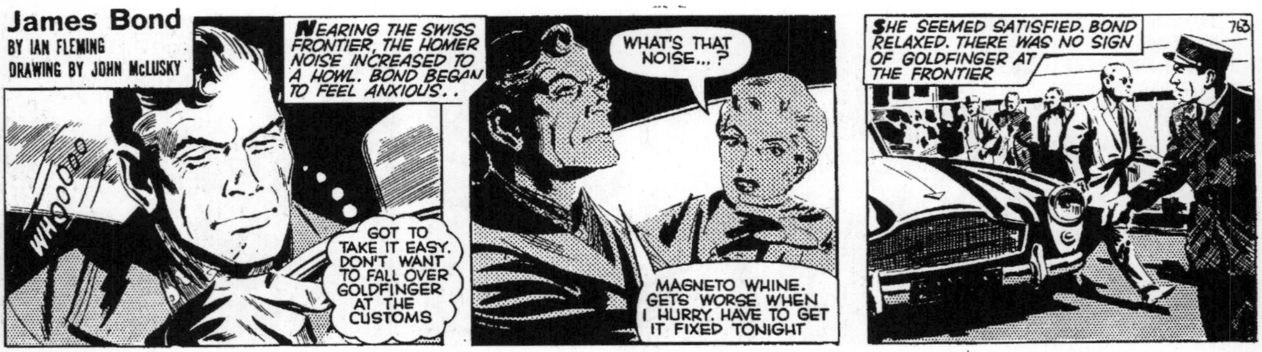
James Bond
BY IAN FLEMING
DRAWING BY JOHN McLUSKY
NEARING THE SWISS FRONTIER, THE HOMER NOISE INCREASED TO A HOWL. BOND BEGAN TO FEEL ANXIOUS..
WHOOOOO
GOT TO TAKE IT EASY. DON'T WANT TO FALL OVER GOLDFINGER AT THE CUSTOMS
WHAT'S THAT NOISE...?
MAGNETO WHINE. GETS WORSE WHEN I HURRY. HAVE TO GET IT FIXED TONIGHT
763
SHE SEEMED SATISFIED. BOND RELAXED. THERE WAS NO SIGN OF GOLDFINGER AT THE FRONTIER

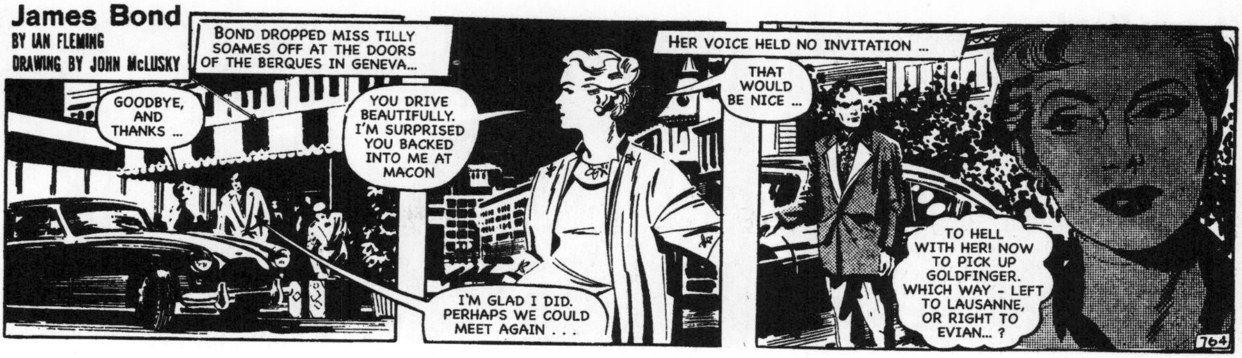
James Bond
BY IAN FLEMING
DRAWING BY JOHN McLUSKY
BOND DROPPED MISS TILLY SOAMES OFF AT THE DOORS OF THE BERQUES IN GENEVA...
GOODBYE, AND THANKS ...
YOU DRIVE BEAUTIFULLY. I'M SURPRISED YOU BACKED INTO ME AT MACON
I'M GLAD I DID. PERHAPS WE COULD MEET AGAIN . . .
HER VOICE HELD NO INVITATION ...
THAT WOULD BE NICE ...
TO HELL WITH HER! NOW TO PICK UP GOLDFINGER. WHICH WAY - LEFT TO LAUSANNE, OR RIGHT TO EVIAN... ?
764

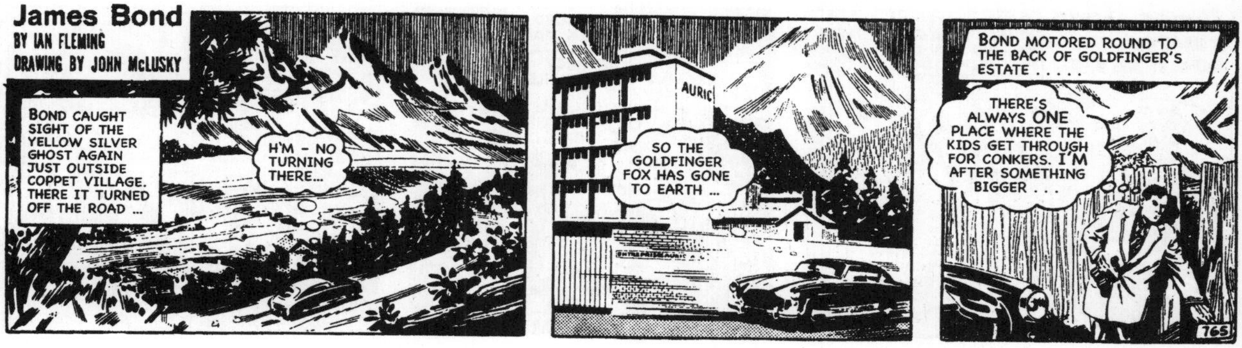
James Bond
BY IAN FLEMING
DRAWING BY JOHN McLUSKY
BOND CAUGHT SIGHT OF THE YELLOW SILVER GHOST AGAIN JUST OUTSIDE COPPET VILLAGE. THERE IT TURNED OFF THE ROAD ...
H'M - NO TURNING THERE...
AURIC
SO THE GOLDFINGER FOX HAS GONE TO EARTH ...
BOND MOTORED ROUND TO THE BACK OF GOLDFINGER'S ESTATE . . . . .
THERE'S ALWAYS ONE PLACE WHERE THE KIDS GET THROUGH FOR CONKERS. I'M AFTER SOMETHING BIGGER . . .
765

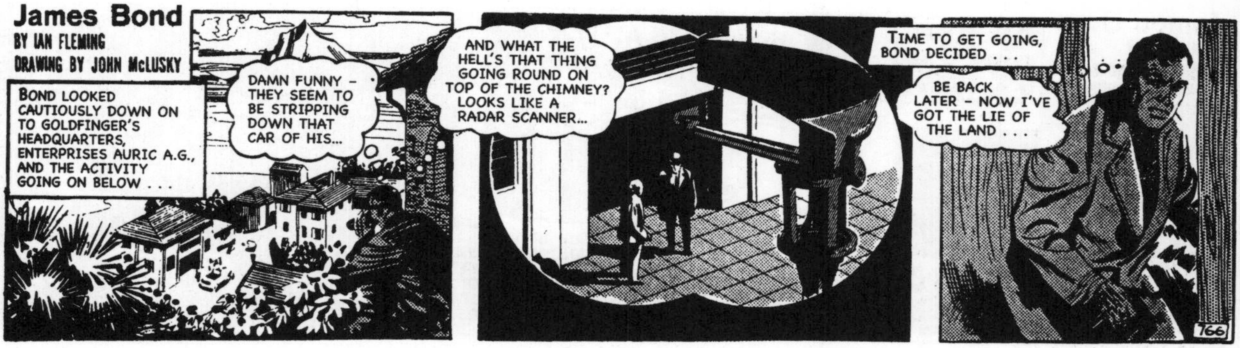
James Bond
BY IAN FLEMING
DRAWING BY JOHN McLUSKY
BOND LOOKED CAUTIOUSLY DOWN ON TO GOLDFINGER'S HEADQUARTERS, ENTERPRISES AURIC A.G., AND THE ACTIVITY GOING ON BELOW . . .
DAMN FUNNY - THEY SEEM TO BE STRIPPING DOWN THAT CAR OF HIS...
AND WHAT THE HELL'S THAT THING GOING ROUND ON TOP OF THE CHIMNEY? LOOKS LIKE A RADAR SCANNER...
TIME TO GET GOING, BOND DECIDED . . .
BE BACK LATER - NOW I'VE GOT THE LIE OF THE LAND . . .
766

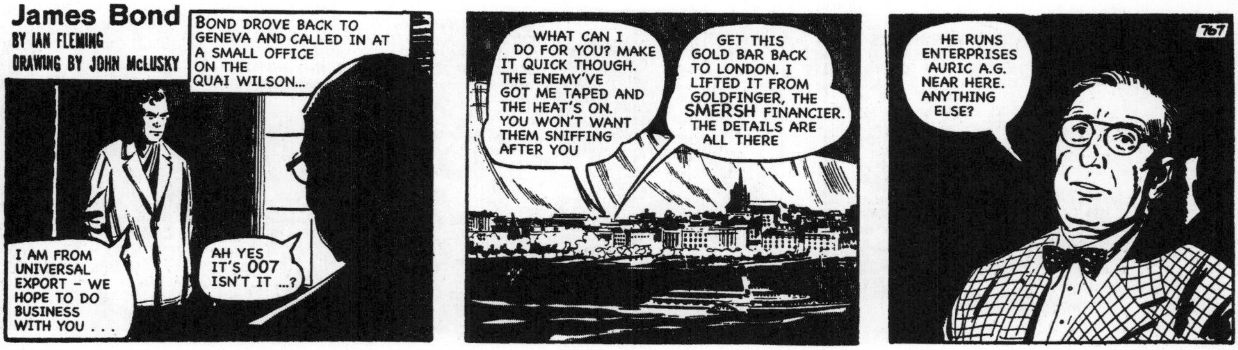
James Bond
BY IAN FLEMING
DRAWING BY JOHN McLUSKY
BOND DROVE BACK TO GENEVA AND CALLED IN AT A SMALL OFFICE ON THE QUAI WILSON...
I AM FROM UNIVERSAL EXPORT - WE HOPE TO DO BUSINESS WITH YOU . . .
AH YES IT'S 007 ISN'T IT ...?
WHAT CAN I DO FOR YOU? MAKE IT QUICK THOUGH. THE ENEMY'VE GOT ME TAPED AND THE HEAT'S ON. YOU WON'T WANT THEM SNIFFING AFTER YOU
GET THIS GOLD BAR BACK TO LONDON. I LIFTED IT FROM GOLDFINGER, THE SMERSH FINANCIER. THE DETAILS ARE ALL THERE
767
HE RUNS ENTERPRISES AURIC A.G. NEAR HERE. ANYTHING ELSE?

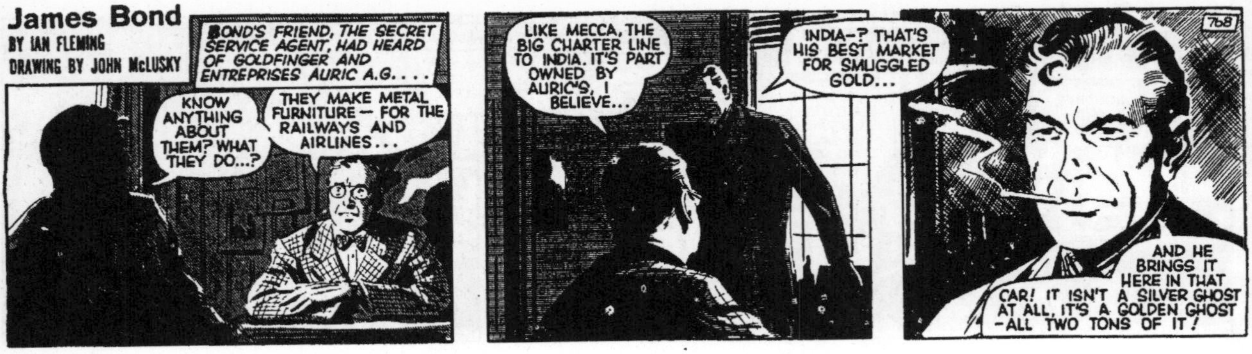
James Bond
BY IAN FLEMING
DRAWING BY JOHN McLUSKY
BOND'S FRIEND, THE SECRET SERVICE AGENT, HAD HEARD OF GOLDFINGER AND ENTREPRISES AURIC A.G. . . .
KNOW ANYTHING ABOUT THEM? WHAT THEY DO...?
THEY MAKE METAL FURNITURE — FOR THE RAILWAYS AND AIRLINES...
LIKE MECCA, THE BIG CHARTER LINE TO INDIA. IT'S PART OWNED BY AURIC'S, I BELIEVE...
INDIA-? THAT'S HIS BEST MARKET FOR SMUGGLED GOLD...
768
AND HE BRINGS IT HERE IN THAT CAR! IT ISN'T A SILVER GHOST AT ALL, IT'S A GOLDEN GHOST -ALL TWO TONS OF IT!

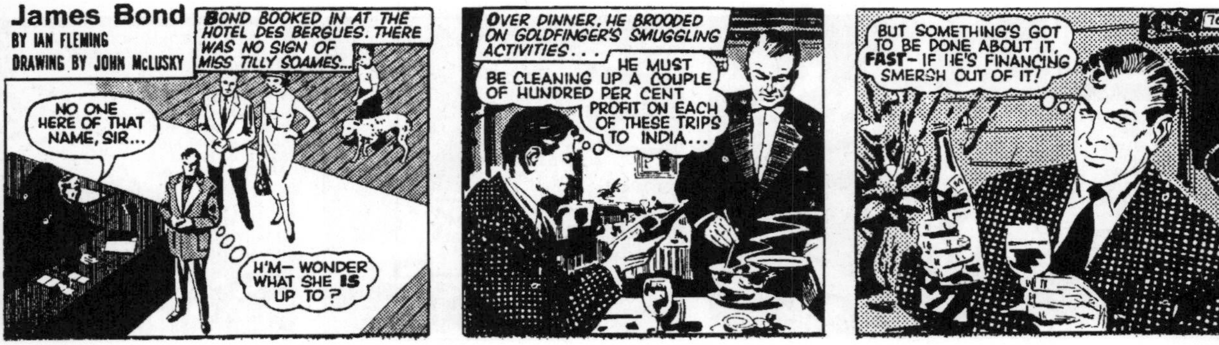
James Bond
BY IAN FLEMING
DRAWING BY JOHN McLUSKY
BOND BOOKED IN AT THE HOTEL DES BERGUES. THERE WAS NO SIGN OF MISS TILLY SOAMES...
NO ONE HERE OF THAT NAME, SIR...
H'M- WONDER WHAT SHE IS UP TO?
OVER DINNER, HE BROODED ON GOLDFINGER'S SMUGGLING ACTIVITIES...
HE MUST BE CLEANING UP A COUPLE OF HUNDRED PER CENT PROFIT ON EACH OF THESE TRIPS TO INDIA...
769
BUT SOMETHING'S GOT TO BE DONE ABOUT IT, FAST- IF HE'S FINANCING SMERSH OUT OF IT!

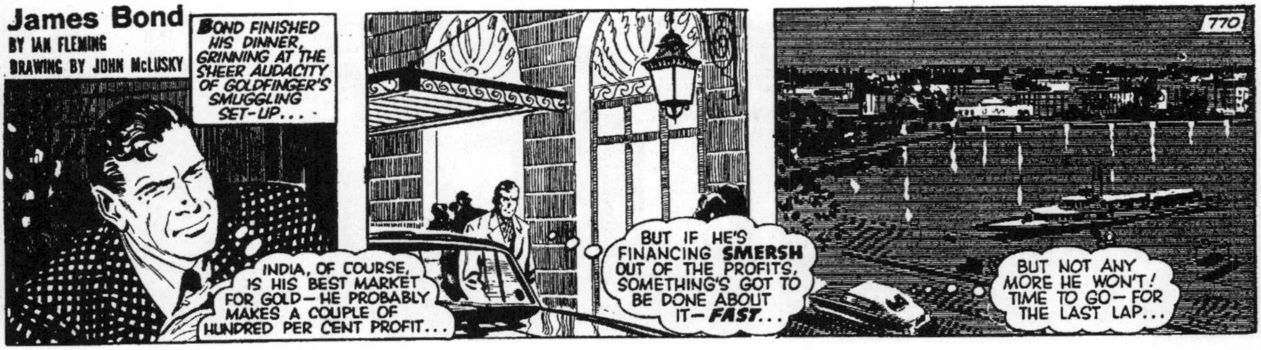
James Bond
BY IAN FLEMING
DRAWING BY JOHN McLUSKY
BOND FINISHED HIS DINNER, GRINNING AT THE SHEER AUDACITY OF GOLDFINGER'S SMUGGLING SET-UP...
INDIA, OF COURSE, IS HIS BEST MARKET FOR GOLD- HE PROBABLY MAKES A COUPLE OF HUNDRED PER CENT PROFIT...
BUT IF HE'S FINANCING SMERSH OUT OF THE PROFITS, SOMETHING'S GOT TO BE DONE ABOUT IT- FAST...
770
BUT NOT ANY MORE HE WON'T! TIME TO GO- FOR THE LAST LAP...

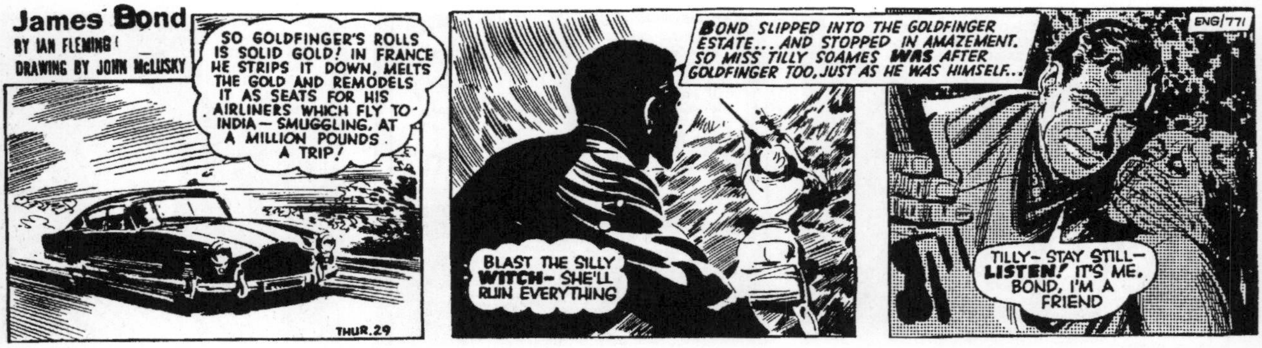
James Bond
BY IAN FLEMING
DRAWING BY JOHN McLUSKY
SO GOLDFINGER'S ROLLS IS SOLID GOLD! IN FRANCE HE STRIPS IT DOWN, MELTS THE GOLD AND REMODELS IT AS SEATS FOR HIS AIRLINERS WHICH FLY TO INDIA- SMUGGLING, AT A MILLION POUNDS A TRIP!
THUR.29
BOND SLIPPED INTO THE GOLDFINGER ESTATE... AND STOPPED IN AMAZEMENT. SO MISS TILLY SOAMES WAS AFTER GOLDFINGER TOO, JUST AS HE WAS HIMSELF...
BLAST THE SILLY WITCH- SHE'LL RUIN EVERYTHING
ENG/771
TILLY- STAY STILL- LISTEN! IT'S ME, BOND, I'M A FRIEND

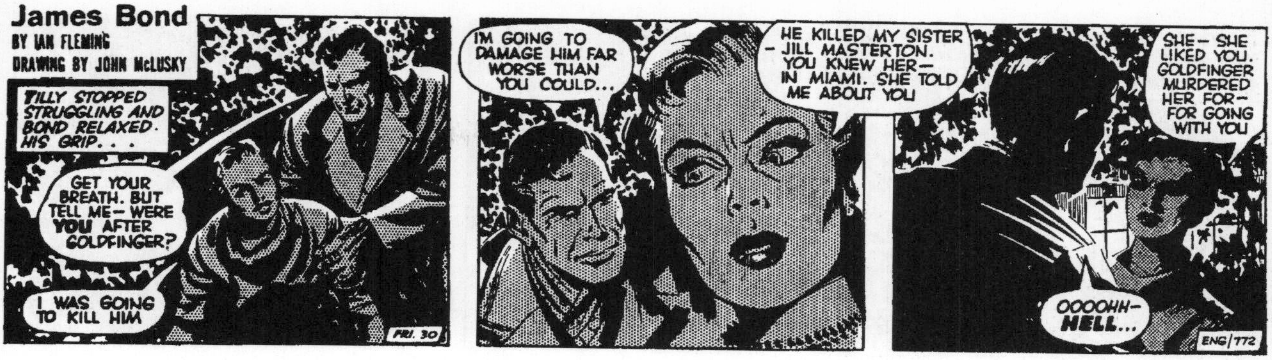
James Bond
BY IAN FLEMING
DRAWING BY JOHN McLUSKY
TILLY STOPPED STRUGGLING AND BOND RELAXED HIS GRIP. . .
GET YOUR BREATH. BUT TELL ME– WERE YOU AFTER GOLDFINGER?
I WAS GOING TO KILL HIM
FRI. 30
I'M GOING TO DAMAGE HIM FAR WORSE THAN YOU COULD...
HE KILLED MY SISTER – JILL MASTERTON. YOU KNEW HER– IN MIAMI. SHE TOLD ME ABOUT YOU
SHE– SHE LIKED YOU. GOLDFINGER MURDERED HER FOR– FOR GOING WITH YOU
OOOOHH– HELL...
ENG/772

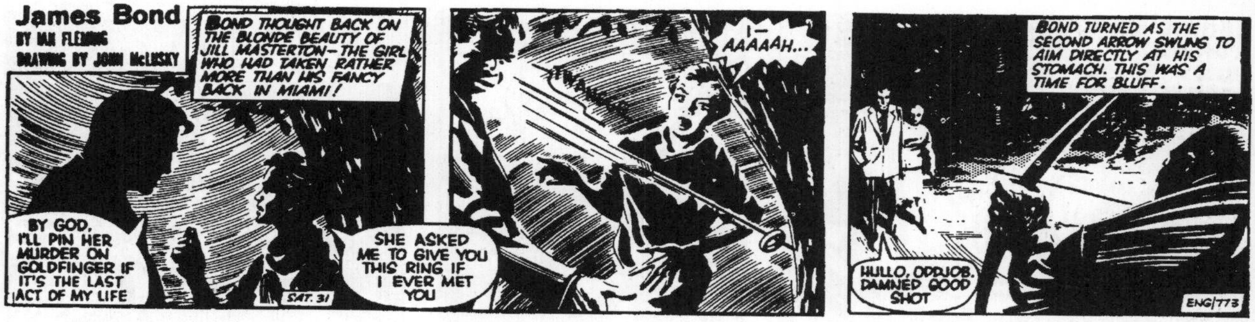
James Bond
BY IAN FLEMING
DRAWING BY JOHN McLUSKY
BOND THOUGHT BACK ON THE BLONDE BEAUTY OF JILL MASTERTON– THE GIRL WHO HAD TAKEN RATHER MORE THAN HIS FANCY BACK IN MIAMI!
BY GOD, I'LL PIN HER MURDER ON GOLDFINGER IF IT'S THE LAST ACT OF MY LIFE
SAT. 31
SHE ASKED ME TO GIVE YOU THIS RING IF I EVER MET YOU
I– AAAAAH...
BOND TURNED AS THE SECOND ARROW SWUNG TO AIM DIRECTLY AT HIS STOMACH. THIS WAS A TIME FOR BLUFF. . .
HULLO, ODDJOB. DAMNED GOOD SHOT
ENG/773

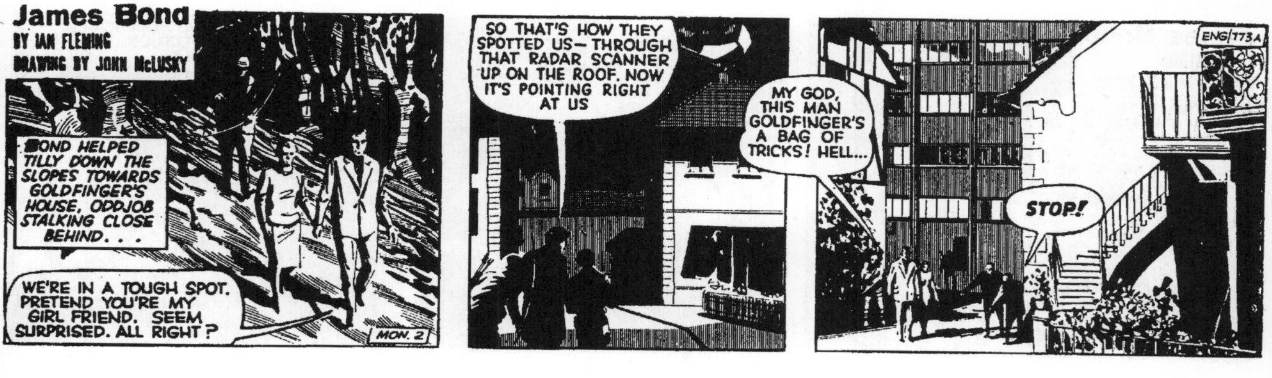
James Bond
BY IAN FLEMING
DRAWING BY JOHN McLUSKY
BOND HELPED TILLY DOWN THE SLOPES TOWARDS GOLDFINGER'S HOUSE, ODDJOB STALKING CLOSE BEHIND. . .
WE'RE IN A TOUGH SPOT. PRETEND YOU'RE MY GIRL FRIEND. SEEM SURPRISED. ALL RIGHT?
MON. 2
SO THAT'S HOW THEY SPOTTED US– THROUGH THAT RADAR SCANNER UP ON THE ROOF. NOW IT'S POINTING RIGHT AT US
MY GOD, THIS MAN GOLDFINGER'S A BAG OF TRICKS! HELL...
ENG/773A
STOP!

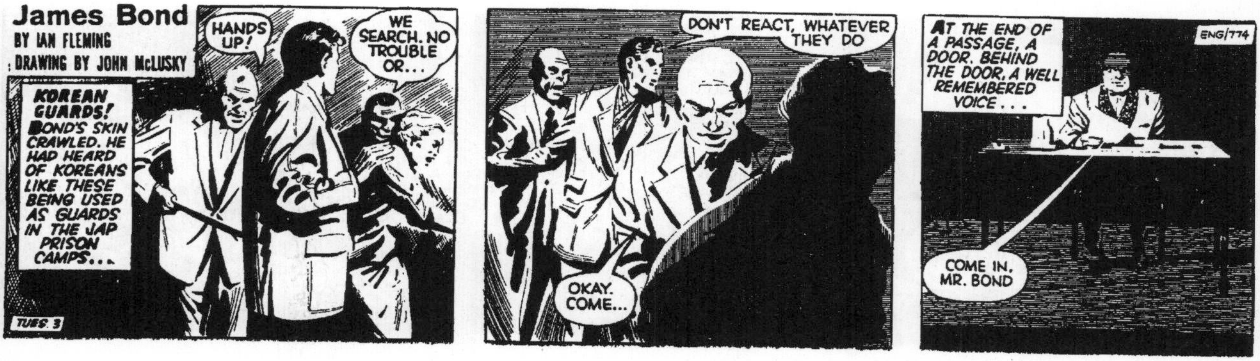
James Bond
BY IAN FLEMING
DRAWING BY JOHN McLUSKY
HANDS UP!
WE SEARCH. NO TROUBLE OR...
KOREAN GUARDS! BOND'S SKIN CRAWLED. HE HAD HEARD OF KOREANS LIKE THESE BEING USED AS GUARDS IN THE JAP PRISON CAMPS...
TUES. 3
DON'T REACT, WHATEVER THEY DO
OKAY. COME...
AT THE END OF A PASSAGE, A DOOR. BEHIND THE DOOR, A WELL REMEMBERED VOICE . . .
ENG/774
COME IN, MR. BOND

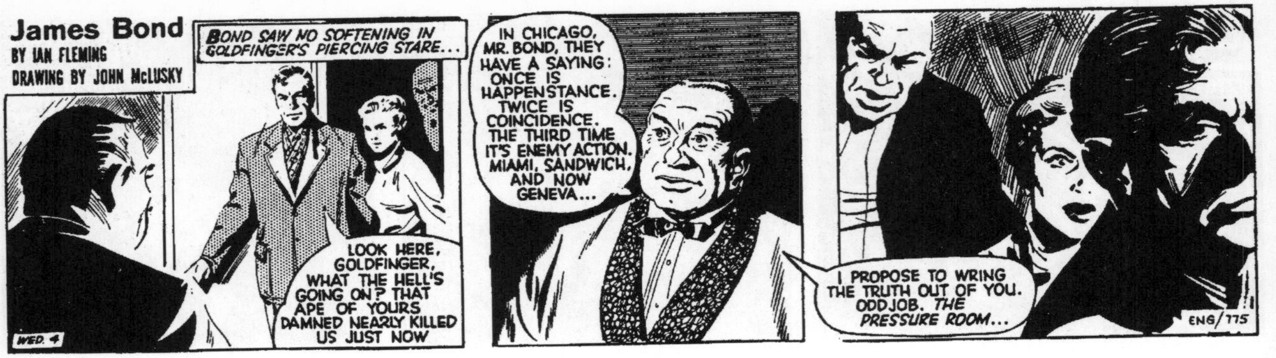
James Bond
BY IAN FLEMING
DRAWING BY JOHN McLUSKY
BOND SAW NO SOFTENING IN GOLDFINGER'S PIERCING STARE...
LOOK HERE, GOLDFINGER, WHAT THE HELL'S GOING ON? THAT APE OF YOURS DAMNED NEARLY KILLED US JUST NOW
WED. 4
IN CHICAGO, MR. BOND, THEY HAVE A SAYING: ONCE IS HAPPENSTANCE. TWICE IS COINCIDENCE. THE THIRD TIME IT'S ENEMY ACTION. MIAMI, SANDWICH, AND NOW GENEVA...
I PROPOSE TO WRING THE TRUTH OUT OF YOU. ODDJOB. THE PRESSURE ROOM...
ENG/775

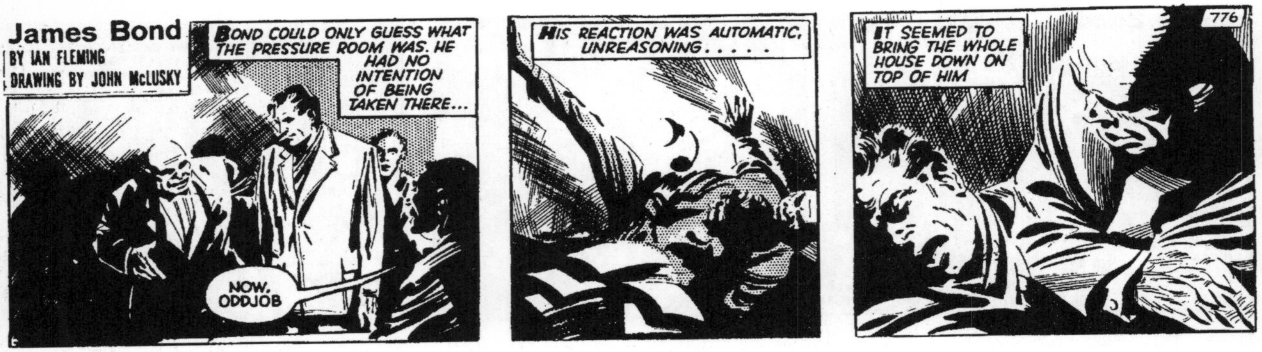
James Bond
BY IAN FLEMING
DRAWING BY JOHN McLUSKY
BOND COULD ONLY GUESS WHAT THE PRESSURE ROOM WAS. HE HAD NO INTENTION OF BEING TAKEN THERE...
NOW, ODDJOB
HIS REACTION WAS AUTOMATIC, UNREASONING.....
776
IT SEEMED TO BRING THE WHOLE HOUSE DOWN ON TOP OF HIM

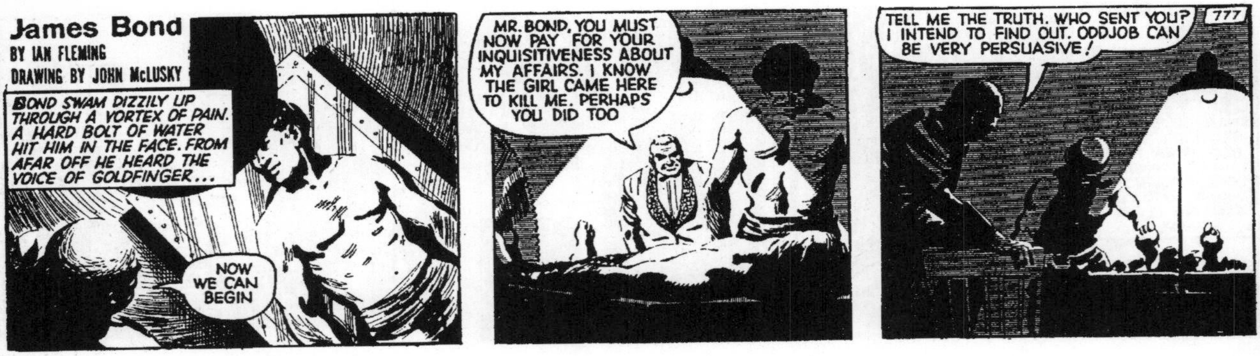
James Bond
BY IAN FLEMING
DRAWING BY JOHN McLUSKY
BOND SWAM DIZZILY UP THROUGH A VORTEX OF PAIN. A HARD BOLT OF WATER HIT HIM IN THE FACE. FROM AFAR OFF HE HEARD THE VOICE OF GOLDFINGER...
NOW WE CAN BEGIN
MR. BOND, YOU MUST NOW PAY FOR YOUR INQUISITIVENESS ABOUT MY AFFAIRS. I KNOW THE GIRL CAME HERE TO KILL ME. PERHAPS YOU DID TOO
TELL ME THE TRUTH. WHO SENT YOU? I INTEND TO FIND OUT. ODDJOB CAN BE VERY PERSUASIVE!
777

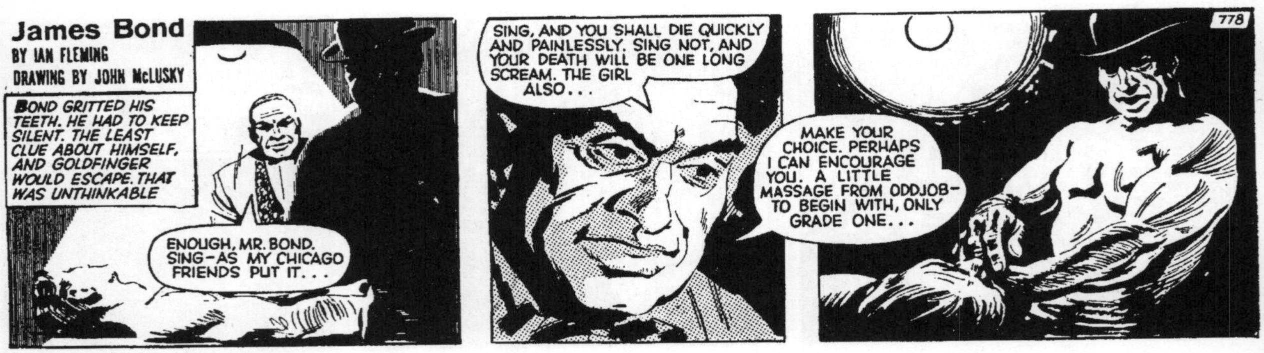
James Bond
BY IAN FLEMING
DRAWING BY JOHN McLUSKY
BOND GRITTED HIS TEETH. HE HAD TO KEEP SILENT. THE LEAST CLUE ABOUT HIMSELF, AND GOLDFINGER WOULD ESCAPE. THAT WAS UNTHINKABLE
ENOUGH, MR. BOND. SING–AS MY CHICAGO FRIENDS PUT IT...
SING, AND YOU SHALL DIE QUICKLY AND PAINLESSLY. SING NOT, AND YOUR DEATH WILL BE ONE LONG SCREAM. THE GIRL ALSO...
778
MAKE YOUR CHOICE. PERHAPS I CAN ENCOURAGE YOU. A LITTLE MASSAGE FROM ODDJOB– TO BEGIN WITH, ONLY GRADE ONE...

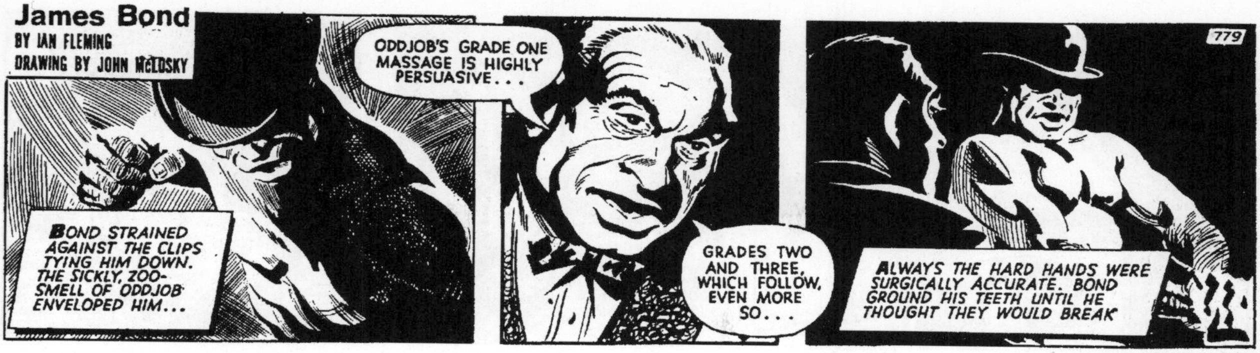
James Bond
BY IAN FLEMING
DRAWING BY JOHN McLUSKY
779
BOND STRAINED AGAINST THE CLIPS TYING HIM DOWN. THE SICKLY, ZOO-SMELL OF ODDJOB ENVELOPED HIM...
ODDJOB'S GRADE ONE MASSAGE IS HIGHLY PERSUASIVE...
GRADES TWO AND THREE, WHICH FOLLOW, EVEN MORE SO...
ALWAYS THE HARD HANDS WERE SURGICALLY ACCURATE. BOND GROUND HIS TEETH UNTIL HE THOUGHT THEY WOULD BREAK

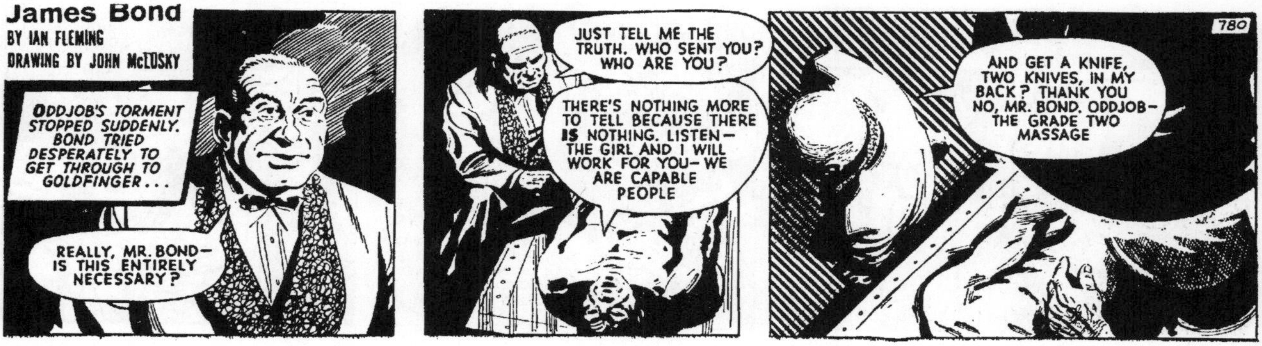
James Bond
BY IAN FLEMING
DRAWING BY JOHN McLUSKY
780
ODDJOB'S TORMENT STOPPED SUDDENLY. BOND TRIED DESPERATELY TO GET THROUGH TO GOLDFINGER...
REALLY, MR. BOND—IS THIS ENTIRELY NECESSARY?
JUST TELL ME THE TRUTH. WHO SENT YOU? WHO ARE YOU?
THERE'S NOTHING MORE TO TELL BECAUSE THERE IS NOTHING. LISTEN—THE GIRL AND I WILL WORK FOR YOU—WE ARE CAPABLE PEOPLE
AND GET A KNIFE, TWO KNIVES, IN MY BACK? THANK YOU NO, MR. BOND. ODDJOB—THE GRADE TWO MASSAGE

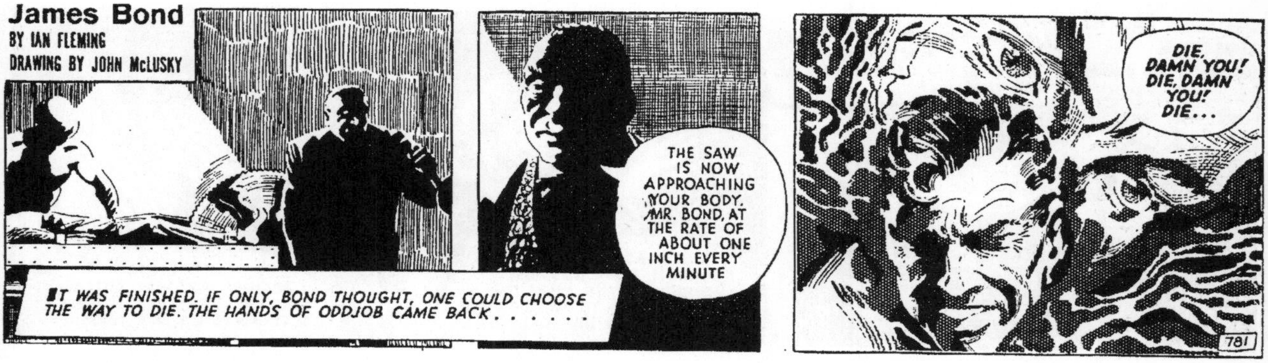
James Bond
BY IAN FLEMING
DRAWING BY JOHN McLUSKY
IT WAS FINISHED. IF ONLY, BOND THOUGHT, ONE COULD CHOOSE THE WAY TO DIE. THE HANDS OF ODDJOB CAME BACK......
THE SAW IS NOW APPROACHING YOUR BODY, MR. BOND, AT THE RATE OF ABOUT ONE INCH EVERY MINUTE
DIE, DAMN YOU! DIE, DAMN YOU! DIE...
781

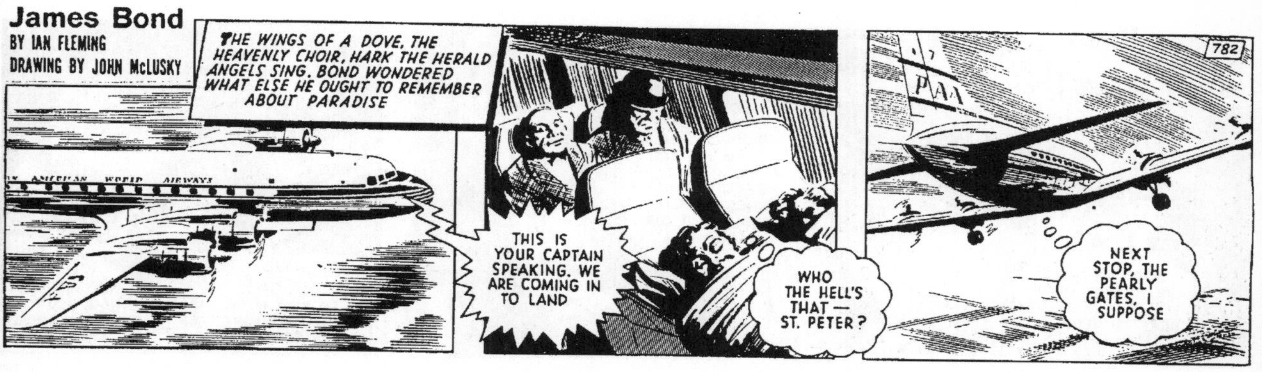
James Bond
BY IAN FLEMING
DRAWING BY JOHN McLUSKY
THE WINGS OF A DOVE, THE HEAVENLY CHOIR, HARK THE HERALD ANGELS SING. BOND WONDERED WHAT ELSE HE OUGHT TO REMEMBER ABOUT PARADISE
THIS IS YOUR CAPTAIN SPEAKING. WE ARE COMING IN TO LAND
WHO THE HELL'S THAT—ST. PETER?
782
NEXT STOP, THE PEARLY GATES, I SUPPOSE

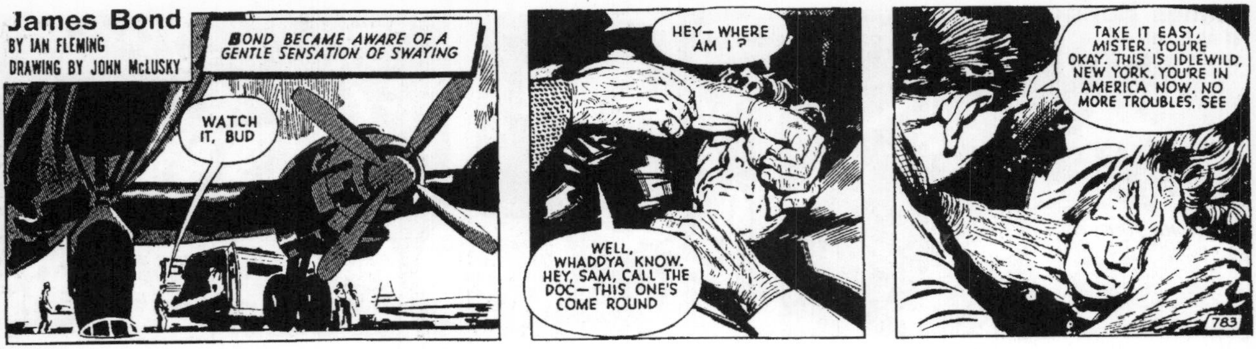
James Bond
BY IAN FLEMING
DRAWING BY JOHN McLUSKY
BOND BECAME AWARE OF A GENTLE SENSATION OF SWAYING
WATCH IT, BUD
HEY—WHERE AM I?
WELL, WHADDYA KNOW. HEY, SAM, CALL THE DOC—THIS ONE'S COME ROUND
TAKE IT EASY, MISTER. YOU'RE OKAY. THIS IS IDLEWILD, NEW YORK. YOU'RE IN AMERICA NOW. NO MORE TROUBLES, SEE
783

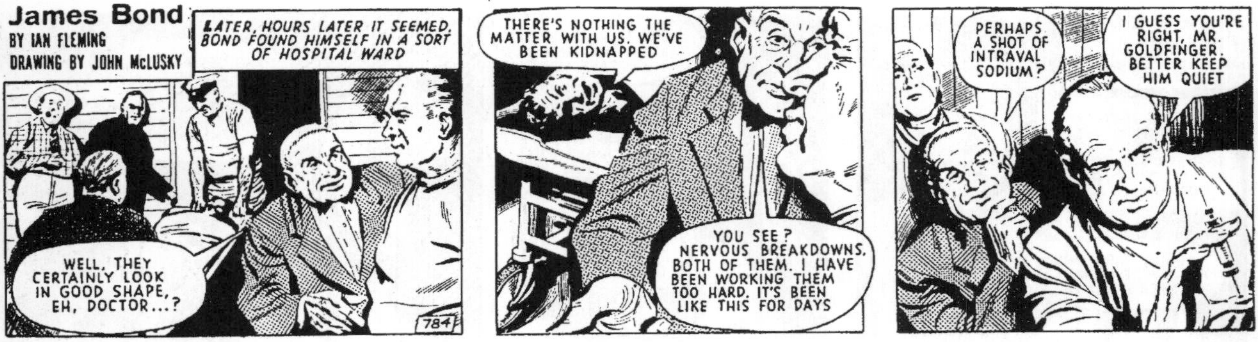
James Bond
BY IAN FLEMING
DRAWING BY JOHN McLUSKY
LATER, HOURS LATER IT SEEMED, BOND FOUND HIMSELF IN A SORT OF HOSPITAL WARD
WELL, THEY CERTAINLY LOOK IN GOOD SHAPE, EH, DOCTOR...?
784
THERE'S NOTHING THE MATTER WITH US. WE'VE BEEN KIDNAPPED
YOU SEE? NERVOUS BREAKDOWNS, BOTH OF THEM. I HAVE BEEN WORKING THEM TOO HARD. IT'S BEEN LIKE THIS FOR DAYS
PERHAPS A SHOT OF INTRAVAL SODIUM?
I GUESS YOU'RE RIGHT, MR. GOLDFINGER. BETTER KEEP HIM QUIET

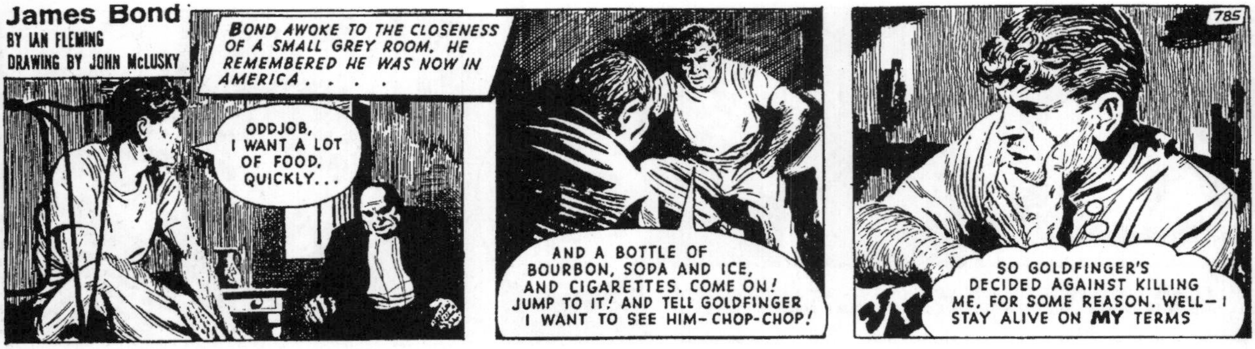
James Bond
BY IAN FLEMING
DRAWING BY JOHN McLUSKY
BOND AWOKE TO THE CLOSENESS OF A SMALL GREY ROOM. HE REMEMBERED HE WAS NOW IN AMERICA . . . .
ODDJOB, I WANT A LOT OF FOOD, QUICKLY...
AND A BOTTLE OF BOURBON, SODA AND ICE, AND CIGARETTES. COME ON! JUMP TO IT! AND TELL GOLDFINGER I WANT TO SEE HIM-CHOP-CHOP!
785
SO GOLDFINGER'S DECIDED AGAINST KILLING ME, FOR SOME REASON. WELL—I STAY ALIVE ON MY TERMS

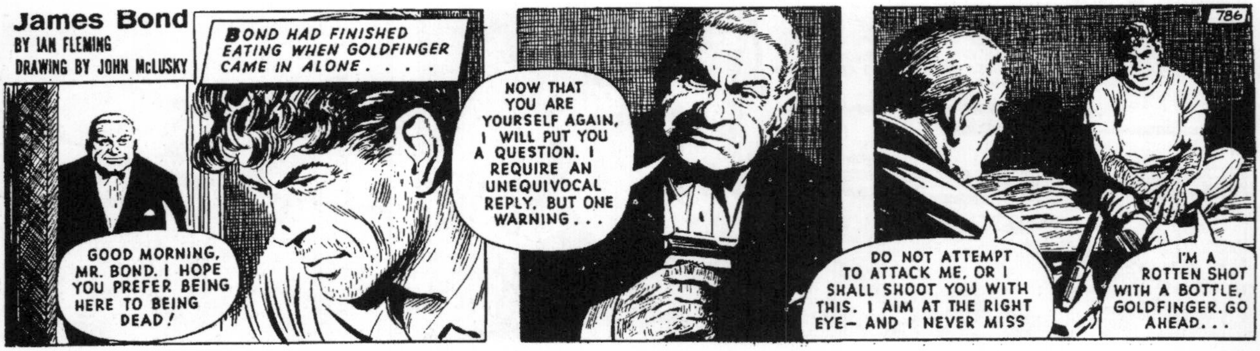
James Bond
BY IAN FLEMING
DRAWING BY JOHN McLUSKY
BOND HAD FINISHED EATING WHEN GOLDFINGER CAME IN ALONE . . . .
GOOD MORNING, MR. BOND. I HOPE YOU PREFER BEING HERE TO BEING DEAD!
NOW THAT YOU ARE YOURSELF AGAIN, I WILL PUT YOU A QUESTION. I REQUIRE AN UNEQUIVOCAL REPLY. BUT ONE WARNING...
786
DO NOT ATTEMPT TO ATTACK ME, OR I SHALL SHOOT YOU WITH THIS. I AIM AT THE RIGHT EYE—AND I NEVER MISS
I'M A ROTTEN SHOT WITH A BOTTLE, GOLDFINGER. GO AHEAD...

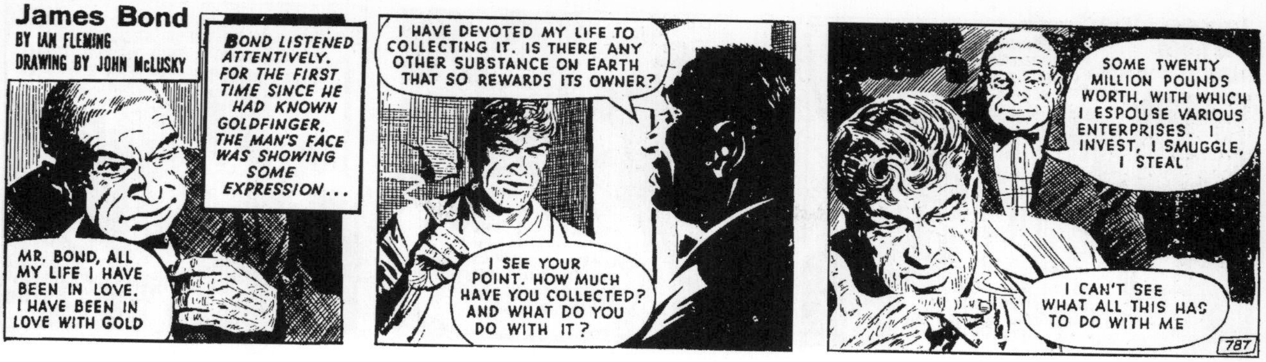
James Bond
BY IAN FLEMING
DRAWING BY JOHN McLUSKY
BOND LISTENED ATTENTIVELY. FOR THE FIRST TIME SINCE HE HAD KNOWN GOLDFINGER, THE MAN'S FACE WAS SHOWING SOME EXPRESSION...
MR. BOND, ALL MY LIFE I HAVE BEEN IN LOVE. I HAVE BEEN IN LOVE WITH GOLD
I HAVE DEVOTED MY LIFE TO COLLECTING IT. IS THERE ANY OTHER SUBSTANCE ON EARTH THAT SO REWARDS ITS OWNER?
I SEE YOUR POINT. HOW MUCH HAVE YOU COLLECTED? AND WHAT DO YOU DO WITH IT?
SOME TWENTY MILLION POUNDS WORTH, WITH WHICH I ESPOUSE VARIOUS ENTERPRISES. I INVEST, I SMUGGLE, I STEAL
I CAN'T SEE WHAT ALL THIS HAS TO DO WITH ME
787

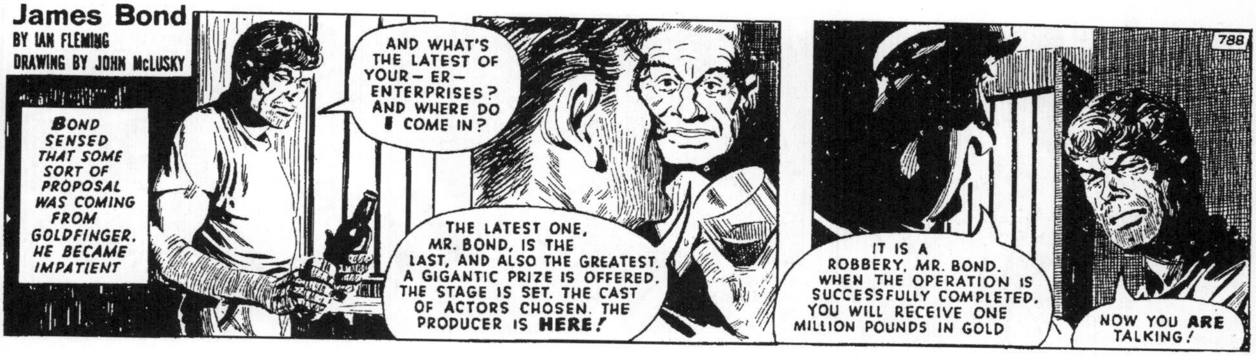
James Bond
BY IAN FLEMING
DRAWING BY JOHN McLUSKY
BOND SENSED THAT SOME SORT OF PROPOSAL WAS COMING FROM GOLDFINGER. HE BECAME IMPATIENT
AND WHAT'S THE LATEST OF YOUR—ER—ENTERPRISES? AND WHERE DO I COME IN?
THE LATEST ONE, MR. BOND, IS THE LAST, AND ALSO THE GREATEST. A GIGANTIC PRIZE IS OFFERED. THE STAGE IS SET. THE CAST OF ACTORS CHOSEN. THE PRODUCER IS HERE!
788
IT IS A ROBBERY, MR. BOND. WHEN THE OPERATION IS SUCCESSFULLY COMPLETED, YOU WILL RECEIVE ONE MILLION POUNDS IN GOLD
NOW YOU ARE TALKING!

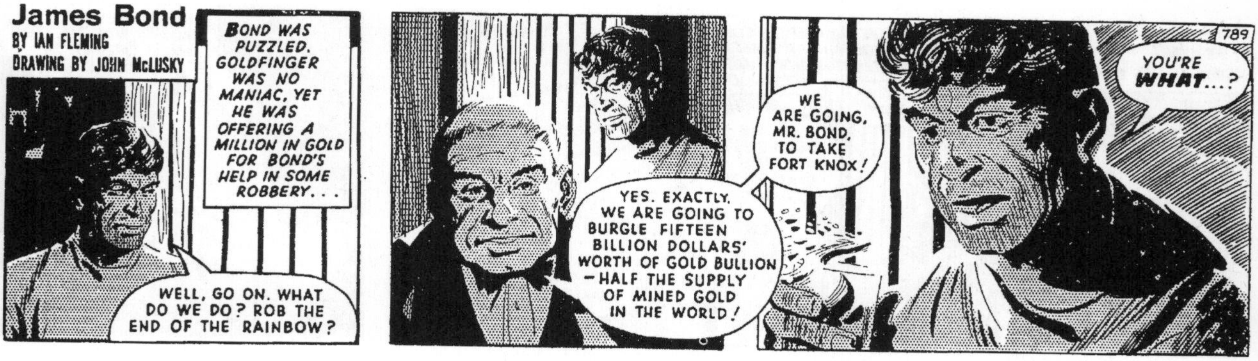
James Bond
BY IAN FLEMING
DRAWING BY JOHN McLUSKY
BOND WAS PUZZLED. GOLDFINGER WAS NO MANIAC, YET HE WAS OFFERING A MILLION IN GOLD FOR BOND'S HELP IN SOME ROBBERY...
WELL, GO ON. WHAT DO WE DO? ROB THE END OF THE RAINBOW?
WE ARE GOING, MR. BOND, TO TAKE FORT KNOX!
YES. EXACTLY. WE ARE GOING TO BURGLE FIFTEEN BILLION DOLLARS' WORTH OF GOLD BULLION —HALF THE SUPPLY OF MINED GOLD IN THE WORLD!
789
YOU'RE WHAT...?

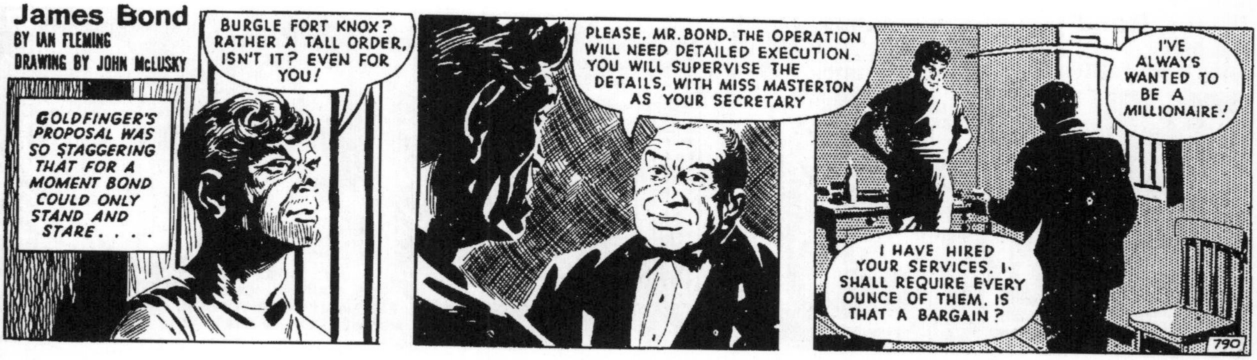
James Bond
BY IAN FLEMING
DRAWING BY JOHN McLUSKY
BURGLE FORT KNOX? RATHER A TALL ORDER, ISN'T IT? EVEN FOR YOU!
GOLDFINGER'S PROPOSAL WAS SO STAGGERING THAT FOR A MOMENT BOND COULD ONLY STAND AND STARE....
PLEASE, MR. BOND. THE OPERATION WILL NEED DETAILED EXECUTION. YOU WILL SUPERVISE THE DETAILS, WITH MISS MASTERTON AS YOUR SECRETARY
I'VE ALWAYS WANTED TO BE A MILLIONAIRE!
I HAVE HIRED YOUR SERVICES. I SHALL REQUIRE EVERY OUNCE OF THEM. IS THAT A BARGAIN?
790

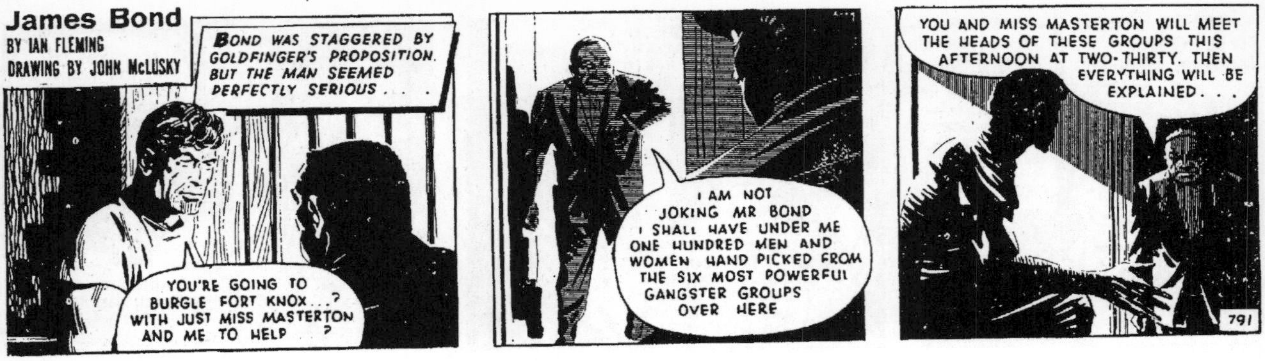
James Bond
BY IAN FLEMING
DRAWING BY JOHN McLUSKY
BOND WAS STAGGERED BY GOLDFINGER'S PROPOSITION. BUT THE MAN SEEMED PERFECTLY SERIOUS . . .
YOU'RE GOING TO BURGLE FORT KNOX...? WITH JUST MISS MASTERTON AND ME TO HELP . . ?
I AM NOT JOKING MR BOND I SHALL HAVE UNDER ME ONE HUNDRED MEN AND WOMEN HAND PICKED FROM THE SIX MOST POWERFUL GANGSTER GROUPS OVER HERE
YOU AND MISS MASTERTON WILL MEET THE HEADS OF THESE GROUPS THIS AFTERNOON AT TWO-THIRTY. THEN EVERYTHING WILL BE EXPLAINED . . .
791

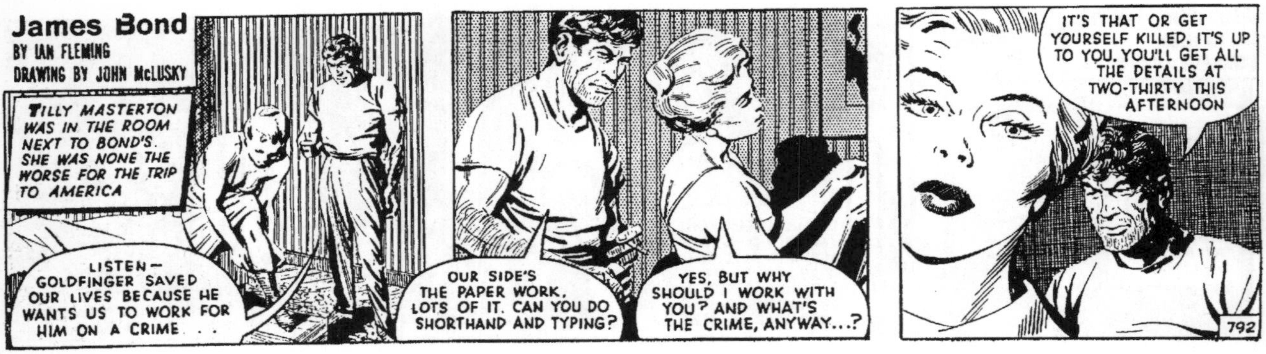
James Bond
BY IAN FLEMING
DRAWING BY JOHN McLUSKY
TILLY MASTERTON WAS IN THE ROOM NEXT TO BOND'S. SHE WAS NONE THE WORSE FOR THE TRIP TO AMERICA
LISTEN— GOLDFINGER SAVED OUR LIVES BECAUSE HE WANTS US TO WORK FOR HIM ON A CRIME . . .
OUR SIDE'S THE PAPER WORK, LOTS OF IT. CAN YOU DO SHORTHAND AND TYPING?
YES, BUT WHY SHOULD I WORK WITH YOU? AND WHAT'S THE CRIME, ANYWAY...?
IT'S THAT OR GET YOURSELF KILLED. IT'S UP TO YOU. YOU'LL GET ALL THE DETAILS AT TWO-THIRTY THIS AFTERNOON
792

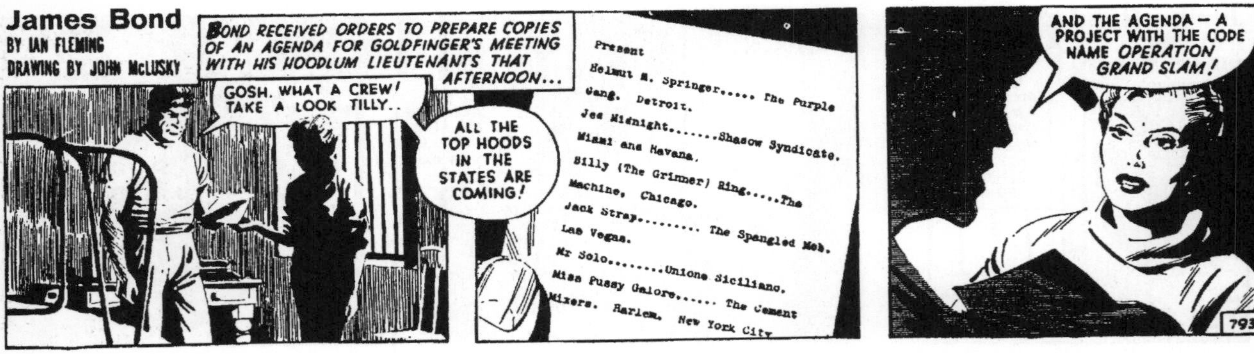
James Bond
BY IAN FLEMING
DRAWING BY JOHN McLUSKY
BOND RECEIVED ORDERS TO PREPARE COPIES OF AN AGENDA FOR GOLDFINGER'S MEETING WITH HIS HOODLUM LIEUTENANTS THAT AFTERNOON...
GOSH. WHAT A CREW! TAKE A LOOK TILLY..
ALL THE TOP HOODS IN THE STATES ARE COMING!
Present
Helmut M. Springer..... The Purple Gang. Detroit.
Jed Midnight.......Shadow Syndicate. Miami and Havana.
Billy (The Grinner) Ring.....The Machine, Chicago.
Jack Strap........ The Spangled Mob. Las Vegas.
Mr Solo.......Unione Siciliano.
Miss Pussy Galore...... The Cement Mixers. Harlem. New York City
AND THE AGENDA—A PROJECT WITH THE CODE NAME OPERATION GRAND SLAM!
793

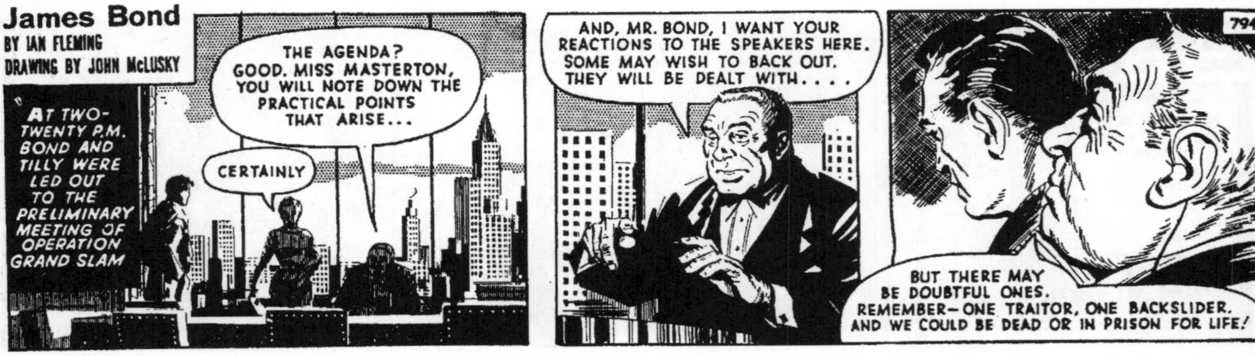
James Bond
BY IAN FLEMING
DRAWING BY JOHN McLUSKY
AT TWO-TWENTY P.M. BOND AND TILLY WERE LED OUT TO THE PRELIMINARY MEETING OF OPERATION GRAND SLAM
THE AGENDA? GOOD. MISS MASTERTON, YOU WILL NOTE DOWN THE PRACTICAL POINTS THAT ARISE...
CERTAINLY
AND, MR. BOND, I WANT YOUR REACTIONS TO THE SPEAKERS HERE. SOME MAY WISH TO BACK OUT. THEY WILL BE DEALT WITH....
794
BUT THERE MAY BE DOUBTFUL ONES. REMEMBER—ONE TRAITOR, ONE BACKSLIDER, AND WE COULD BE DEAD OR IN PRISON FOR LIFE!

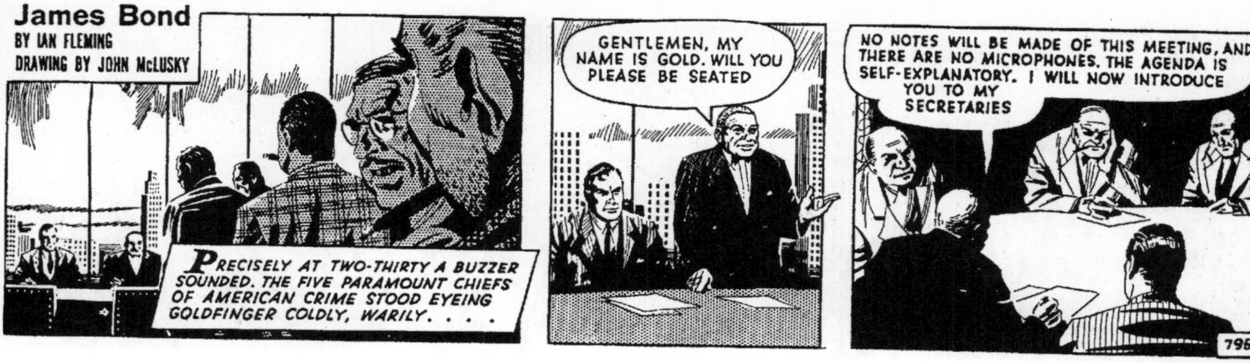
James Bond
BY IAN FLEMING
DRAWING BY JOHN McLUSKY
PRECISELY AT TWO-THIRTY A BUZZER SOUNDED. THE FIVE PARAMOUNT CHIEFS OF AMERICAN CRIME STOOD EYEING GOLDFINGER COLDLY, WARILY. . . .
GENTLEMEN, MY NAME IS GOLD. WILL YOU PLEASE BE SEATED
NO NOTES WILL BE MADE OF THIS MEETING, AND THERE ARE NO MICROPHONES. THE AGENDA IS SELF-EXPLANATORY. I WILL NOW INTRODUCE YOU TO MY SECRETARIES
795

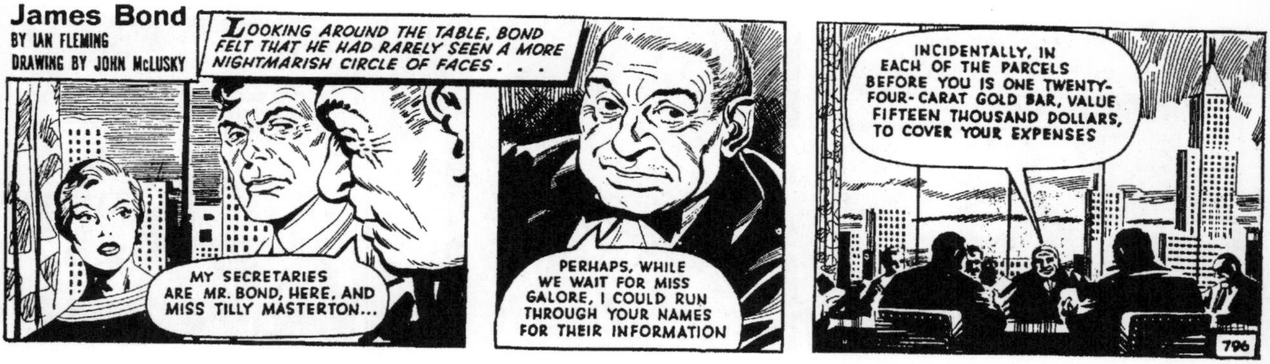
James Bond
BY IAN FLEMING
DRAWING BY JOHN McLUSKY
LOOKING AROUND THE TABLE, BOND FELT THAT HE HAD RARELY SEEN A MORE NIGHTMARISH CIRCLE OF FACES . . .
MY SECRETARIES ARE MR. BOND, HERE, AND MISS TILLY MASTERTON...
PERHAPS, WHILE WE WAIT FOR MISS GALORE, I COULD RUN THROUGH YOUR NAMES FOR THEIR INFORMATION
INCIDENTALLY, IN EACH OF THE PARCELS BEFORE YOU IS ONE TWENTY-FOUR-CARAT GOLD BAR, VALUE FIFTEEN THOUSAND DOLLARS, TO COVER YOUR EXPENSES
796

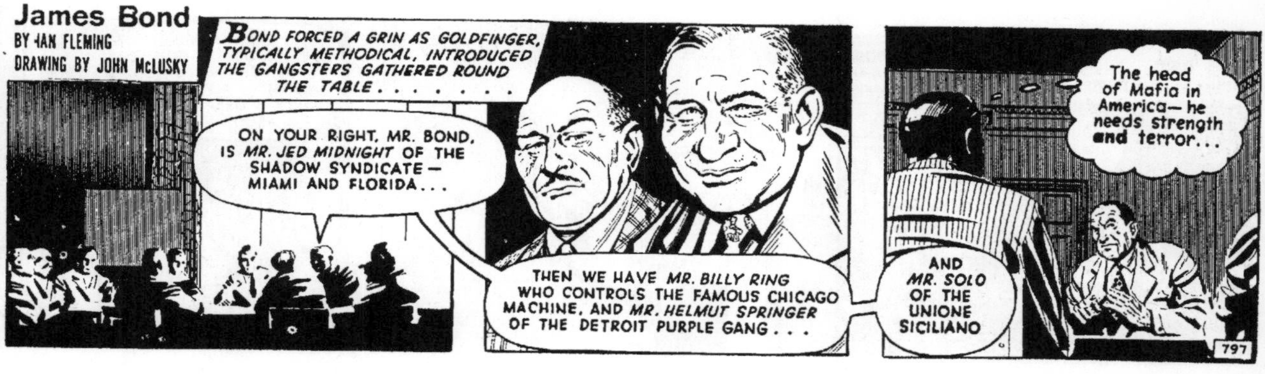
James Bond
BY IAN FLEMING
DRAWING BY JOHN McLUSKY
BOND FORCED A GRIN AS GOLDFINGER, TYPICALLY METHODICAL, INTRODUCED THE GANGSTERS GATHERED ROUND THE TABLE . . . .
ON YOUR RIGHT, MR. BOND, IS MR. JED MIDNIGHT OF THE SHADOW SYNDICATE— MIAMI AND FLORIDA . . .
THEN WE HAVE MR. BILLY RING WHO CONTROLS THE FAMOUS CHICAGO MACHINE, AND MR. HELMUT SPRINGER OF THE DETROIT PURPLE GANG . . .
The head of Mafia in America— he needs strength and terror...
AND MR. SOLO OF THE UNIONE SICILIANO
797

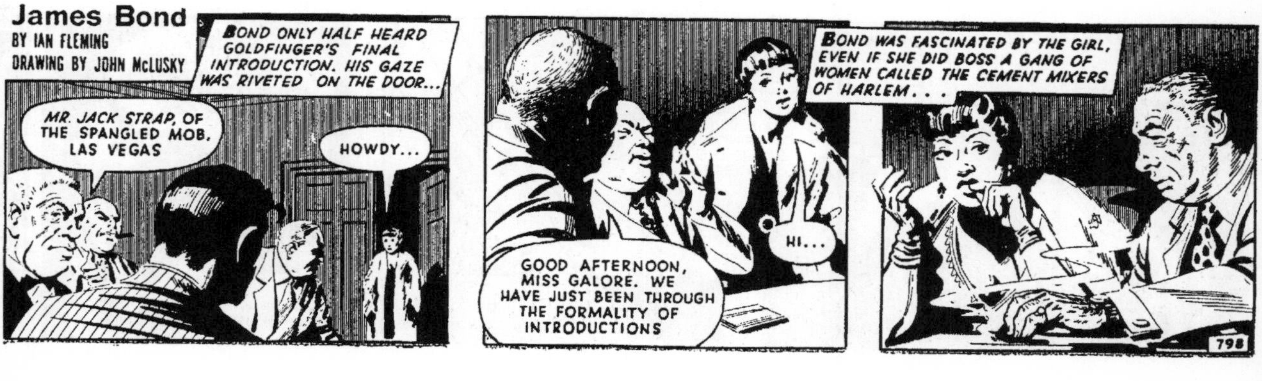
James Bond
BY IAN FLEMING
DRAWING BY JOHN McLUSKY
BOND ONLY HALF HEARD GOLDFINGER'S FINAL INTRODUCTION. HIS GAZE WAS RIVETED ON THE DOOR...
MR. JACK STRAP, OF THE SPANGLED MOB, LAS VEGAS
HOWDY...
HI...
GOOD AFTERNOON, MISS GALORE. WE HAVE JUST BEEN THROUGH THE FORMALITY OF INTRODUCTIONS
BOND WAS FASCINATED BY THE GIRL, EVEN IF SHE DID BOSS A GANG OF WOMEN CALLED THE CEMENT MIXERS OF HARLEM . . .
798

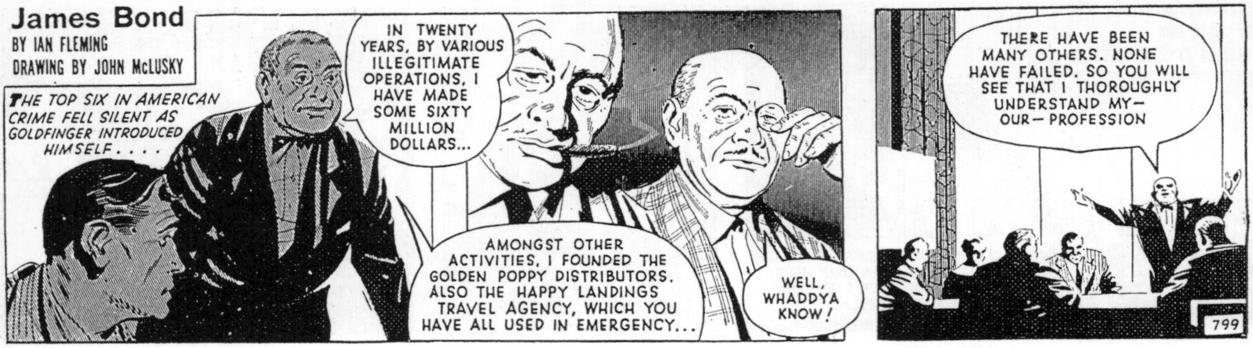
James Bond
BY IAN FLEMING
DRAWING BY JOHN McLUSKY
THE TOP SIX IN AMERICAN CRIME FELL SILENT AS GOLDFINGER INTRODUCED HIMSELF . . . .
IN TWENTY YEARS, BY VARIOUS ILLEGITIMATE OPERATIONS, I HAVE MADE SOME SIXTY MILLION DOLLARS...
AMONGST OTHER ACTIVITIES, I FOUNDED THE GOLDEN POPPY DISTRIBUTORS. ALSO THE HAPPY LANDINGS TRAVEL AGENCY, WHICH YOU HAVE ALL USED IN EMERGENCY...
WELL, WHADDYA KNOW!
THERE HAVE BEEN MANY OTHERS. NONE HAVE FAILED. SO YOU WILL SEE THAT I THOROUGHLY UNDERSTAND MY— OUR— PROFESSION
799

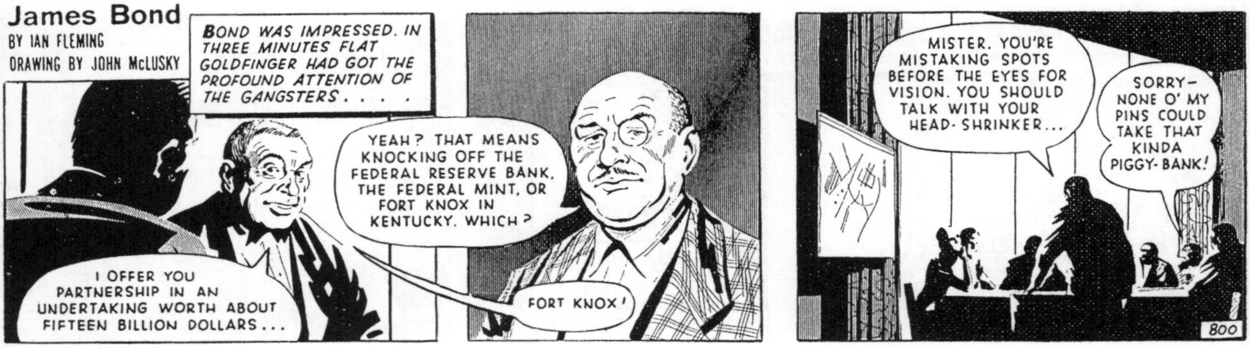
James Bond
BY IAN FLEMING
DRAWING BY JOHN McLUSKY
BOND WAS IMPRESSED. IN THREE MINUTES FLAT GOLDFINGER HAD GOT THE PROFOUND ATTENTION OF THE GANGSTERS . . . .
I OFFER YOU PARTNERSHIP IN AN UNDERTAKING WORTH ABOUT FIFTEEN BILLION DOLLARS...
YEAH? THAT MEANS KNOCKING OFF THE FEDERAL RESERVE BANK, THE FEDERAL MINT, OR FORT KNOX IN KENTUCKY. WHICH?
FORT KNOX!
MISTER, YOU'RE MISTAKING SPOTS BEFORE THE EYES FOR VISION. YOU SHOULD TALK WITH YOUR HEAD-SHRINKER...
SORRY— NONE O' MY PINS COULD TAKE THAT KINDA PIGGY-BANK!
800

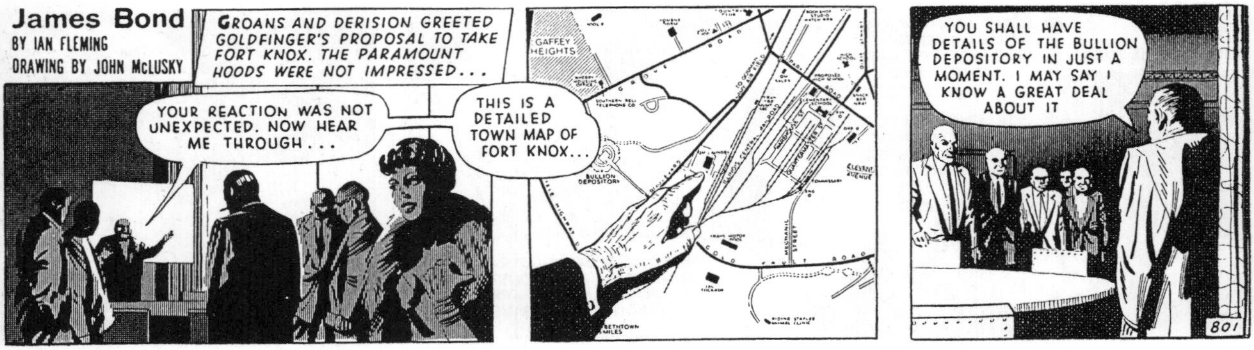
James Bond
BY IAN FLEMING
DRAWING BY JOHN McLUSKY
GROANS AND DERISION GREETED GOLDFINGER'S PROPOSAL TO TAKE FORT KNOX. THE PARAMOUNT HOODS WERE NOT IMPRESSED...
YOUR REACTION WAS NOT UNEXPECTED. NOW HEAR ME THROUGH...
THIS IS A DETAILED TOWN MAP OF FORT KNOX...
GAFFEY HEIGHTS
BULLION DEPOSITORY
YOU SHALL HAVE DETAILS OF THE BULLION DEPOSITORY IN JUST A MOMENT. I MAY SAY I KNOW A GREAT DEAL ABOUT IT
801

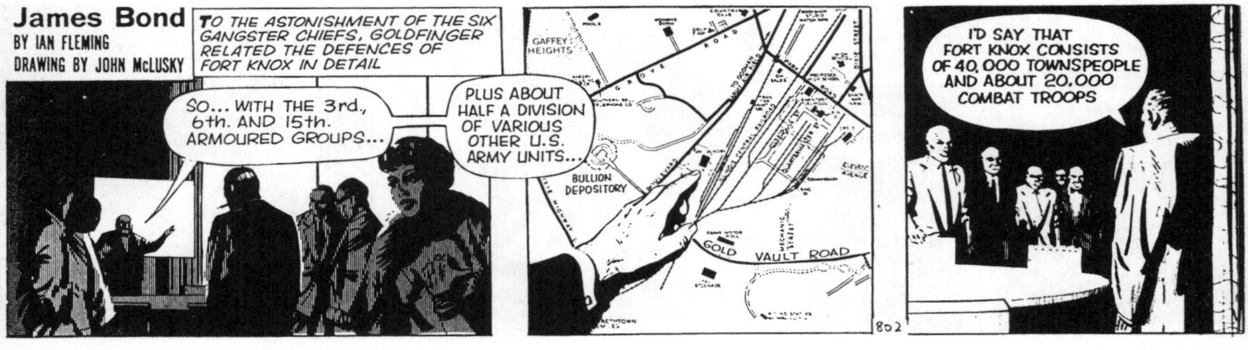
James Bond
BY IAN FLEMING
DRAWING BY JOHN McLUSKY
TO THE ASTONISHMENT OF THE SIX GANGSTER CHIEFS, GOLDFINGER RELATED THE DEFENCES OF FORT KNOX IN DETAIL
SO... WITH THE 3rd., 6th. AND 15th. ARMOURED GROUPS...
PLUS ABOUT HALF A DIVISION OF VARIOUS OTHER U.S. ARMY UNITS...
GAFFEY HEIGHTS
BULLION DEPOSITORY
MECHANIC STREET
GOLD VAULT ROAD
802
I'D SAY THAT FORT KNOX CONSISTS OF 40,000 TOWNSPEOPLE AND ABOUT 20,000 COMBAT TROOPS

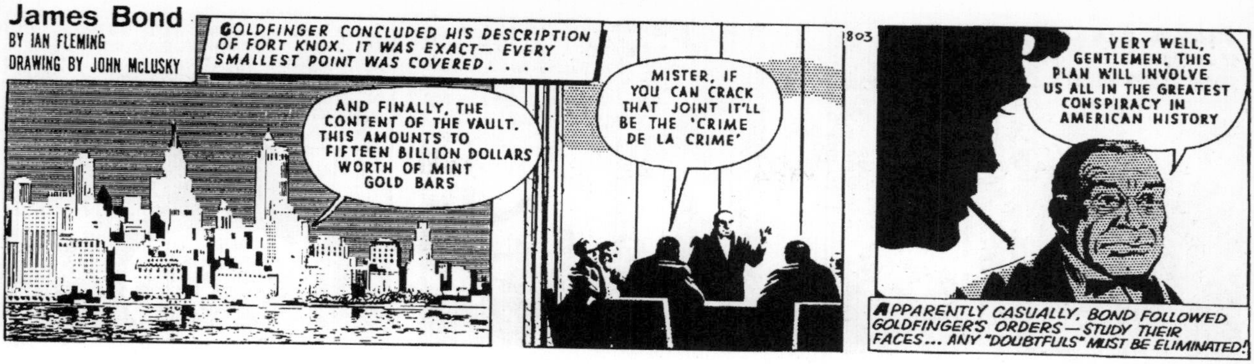
James Bond
BY IAN FLEMING
DRAWING BY JOHN McLUSKY
GOLDFINGER CONCLUDED HIS DESCRIPTION OF FORT KNOX. IT WAS EXACT— EVERY SMALLEST POINT WAS COVERED . . . .
AND FINALLY, THE CONTENT OF THE VAULT. THIS AMOUNTS TO FIFTEEN BILLION DOLLARS WORTH OF MINT GOLD BARS
MISTER, IF YOU CAN CRACK THAT JOINT IT'LL BE THE 'CRIME DE LA CRIME'
803
VERY WELL, GENTLEMEN, THIS PLAN WILL INVOLVE US ALL IN THE GREATEST CONSPIRACY IN AMERICAN HISTORY
APPARENTLY CASUALLY, BOND FOLLOWED GOLDFINGER'S ORDERS — STUDY THEIR FACES... ANY "DOUBTFULS" MUST BE ELIMINATED!

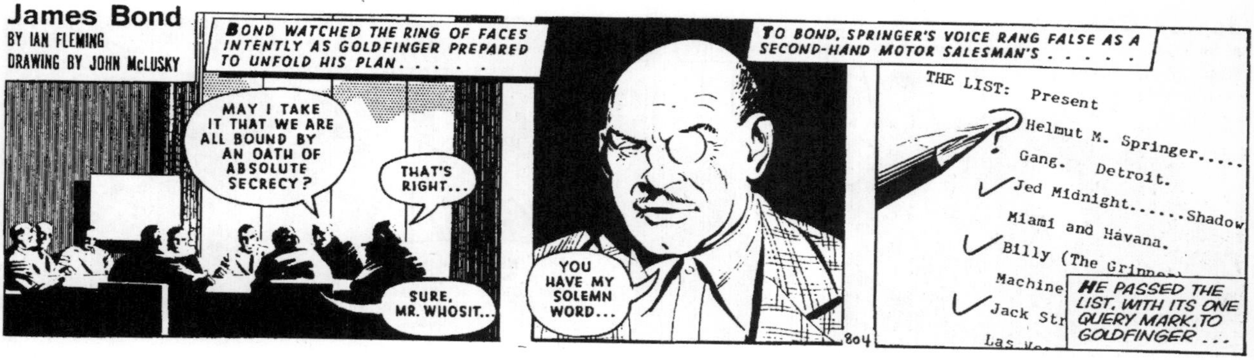
James Bond
BY IAN FLEMING
DRAWING BY JOHN McLUSKY
BOND WATCHED THE RING OF FACES INTENTLY AS GOLDFINGER PREPARED TO UNFOLD HIS PLAN . . . . .
MAY I TAKE IT THAT WE ARE ALL BOUND BY AN OATH OF ABSOLUTE SECRECY?
THAT'S RIGHT...
SURE, MR. WHOSIT...
YOU HAVE MY SOLEMN WORD...
804
TO BOND, SPRINGER'S VOICE RANG FALSE AS A SECOND-HAND MOTOR SALESMAN'S . . . . .
THE LIST: Present
Helmut M. Springer.....
Gang. Detroit.
Jed Midnight......Shadow
Miami and Havana.
Billy (The Grinn
Machine
Jack Str
HE PASSED THE LIST, WITH ITS ONE QUERY MARK, TO GOLDFINGER . . .

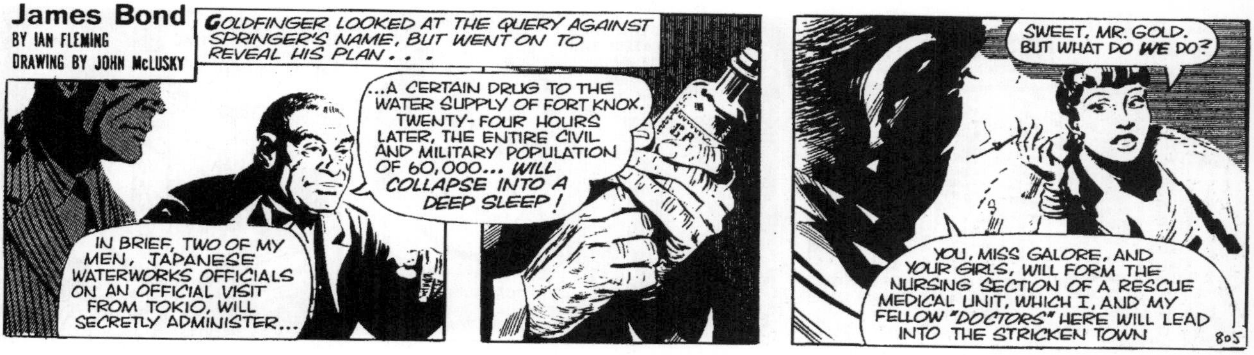
James Bond
BY IAN FLEMING
DRAWING BY JOHN McLUSKY
GOLDFINGER LOOKED AT THE QUERY AGAINST SPRINGER'S NAME, BUT WENT ON TO REVEAL HIS PLAN . . .
IN BRIEF, TWO OF MY MEN, JAPANESE WATERWORKS OFFICIALS ON AN OFFICIAL VISIT FROM TOKIO, WILL SECRETLY ADMINISTER...
...A CERTAIN DRUG TO THE WATER SUPPLY OF FORT KNOX. TWENTY-FOUR HOURS LATER, THE ENTIRE CIVIL AND MILITARY POPULATION OF 60,000... WILL COLLAPSE INTO A DEEP SLEEP!
SWEET, MR. GOLD. BUT WHAT DO WE DO?
YOU, MISS GALORE, AND YOUR GIRLS, WILL FORM THE NURSING SECTION OF A RESCUE MEDICAL UNIT, WHICH I, AND MY FELLOW "DOCTORS" HERE WILL LEAD INTO THE STRICKEN TOWN
805

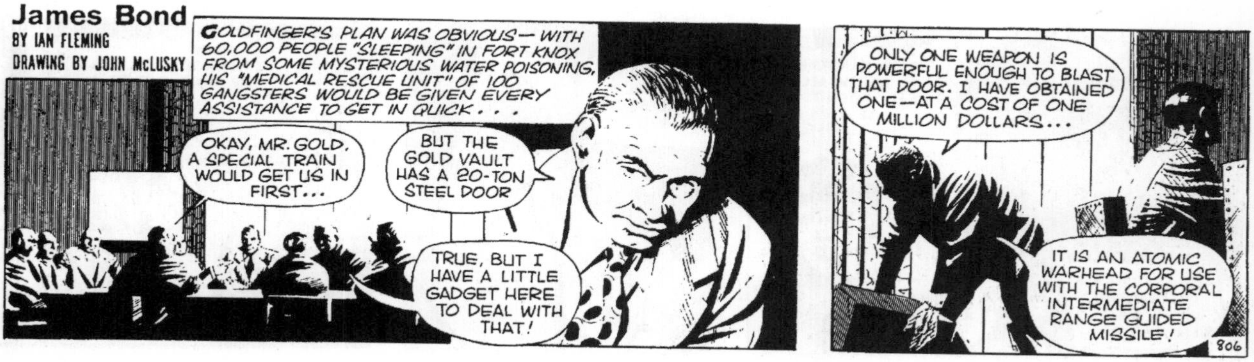
James Bond
BY IAN FLEMING
DRAWING BY JOHN McLUSKY
GOLDFINGER'S PLAN WAS OBVIOUS — WITH 60,000 PEOPLE "SLEEPING" IN FORT KNOX FROM SOME MYSTERIOUS WATER POISONING, HIS "MEDICAL RESCUE UNIT" OF 100 GANGSTERS WOULD BE GIVEN EVERY ASSISTANCE TO GET IN QUICK . . .
OKAY, MR. GOLD, A SPECIAL TRAIN WOULD GET US IN FIRST...
BUT THE GOLD VAULT HAS A 20-TON STEEL DOOR
TRUE, BUT I HAVE A LITTLE GADGET HERE TO DEAL WITH THAT!
ONLY ONE WEAPON IS POWERFUL ENOUGH TO BLAST THAT DOOR. I HAVE OBTAINED ONE — AT A COST OF ONE MILLION DOLLARS...
IT IS AN ATOMIC WARHEAD FOR USE WITH THE CORPORAL INTERMEDIATE RANGE GUIDED MISSILE!
806

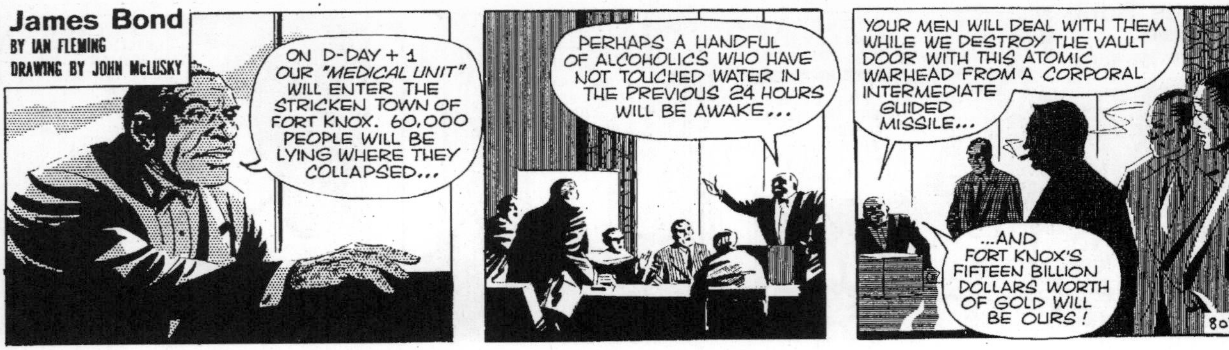
James Bond
BY IAN FLEMING
DRAWING BY JOHN McLUSKY
ON D-DAY + 1 OUR "MEDICAL UNIT" WILL ENTER THE STRICKEN TOWN OF FORT KNOX. 60,000 PEOPLE WILL BE LYING WHERE THEY COLLAPSED...
PERHAPS A HANDFUL OF ALCOHOLICS WHO HAVE NOT TOUCHED WATER IN THE PREVIOUS 24 HOURS WILL BE AWAKE...
YOUR MEN WILL DEAL WITH THEM WHILE WE DESTROY THE VAULT DOOR WITH THIS ATOMIC WARHEAD FROM A CORPORAL INTERMEDIATE GUIDED MISSILE...
...AND FORT KNOX'S FIFTEEN BILLION DOLLARS WORTH OF GOLD WILL BE OURS!
807

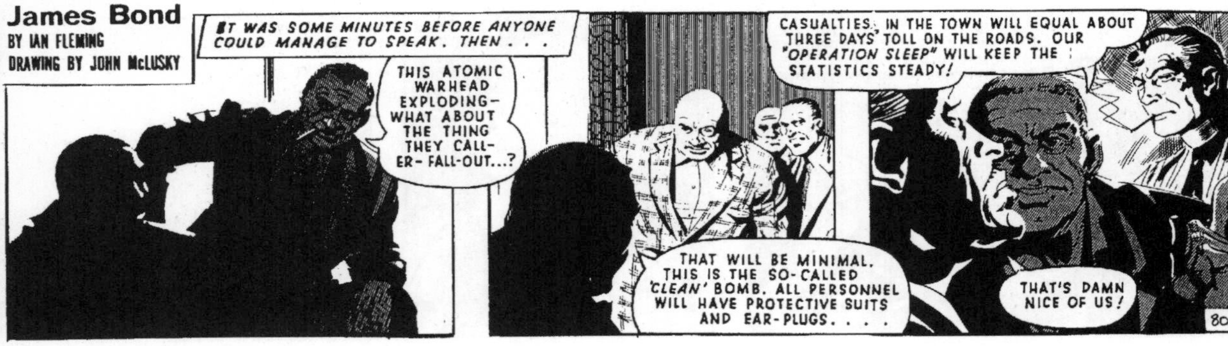
James Bond
BY IAN FLEMING
DRAWING BY JOHN McLUSKY
IT WAS SOME MINUTES BEFORE ANYONE COULD MANAGE TO SPEAK. THEN . . .
THIS ATOMIC WARHEAD EXPLODING- WHAT ABOUT THE THING THEY CALL- ER- FALL-OUT...?
THAT WILL BE MINIMAL. THIS IS THE SO-CALLED 'CLEAN' BOMB. ALL PERSONNEL WILL HAVE PROTECTIVE SUITS AND EAR-PLUGS. . . .
CASUALTIES IN THE TOWN WILL EQUAL ABOUT THREE DAYS' TOLL ON THE ROADS. OUR "OPERATION SLEEP" WILL KEEP THE STATISTICS STEADY!
THAT'S DAMN NICE OF US!
808

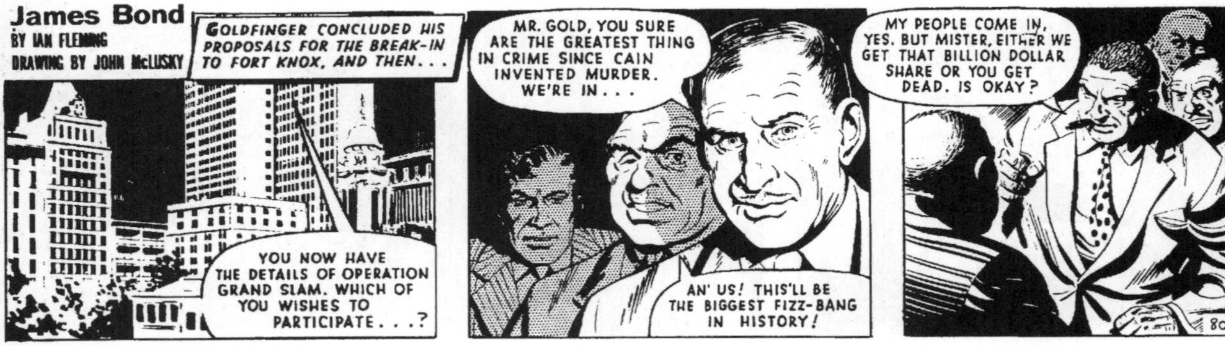
James Bond
BY IAN FLEMING
DRAWING BY JOHN McLUSKY
GOLDFINGER CONCLUDED HIS PROPOSALS FOR THE BREAK-IN TO FORT KNOX, AND THEN . . .
YOU NOW HAVE THE DETAILS OF OPERATION GRAND SLAM. WHICH OF YOU WISHES TO PARTICIPATE . . .?
MR. GOLD, YOU SURE ARE THE GREATEST THING IN CRIME SINCE CAIN INVENTED MURDER. WE'RE IN . . .
AN' US! THIS'LL BE THE BIGGEST FIZZ-BANG IN HISTORY!
MY PEOPLE COME IN, YES. BUT MISTER, EITHER WE GET THAT BILLION DOLLAR SHARE OR YOU GET DEAD. IS OKAY?
809

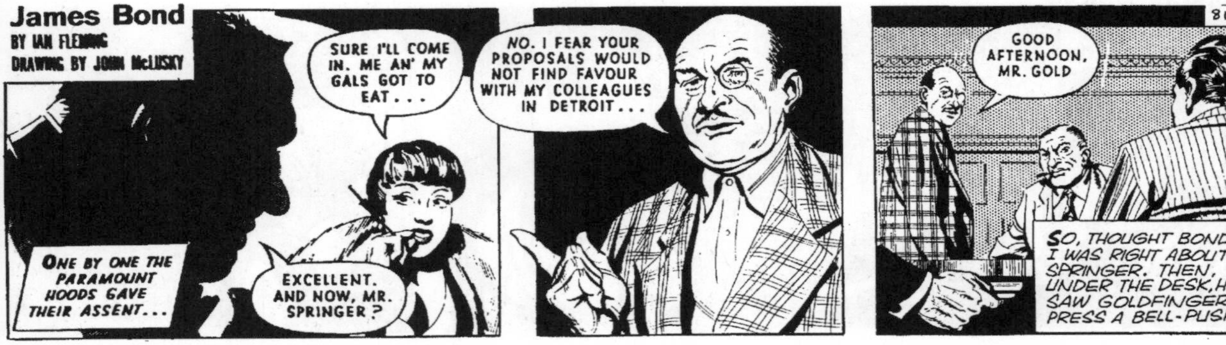
James Bond
BY IAN FLEMING
DRAWING BY JOHN McLUSKY
ONE BY ONE THE PARAMOUNT HOODS GAVE THEIR ASSENT...
SURE I'LL COME IN. ME AN' MY GALS GOT TO EAT . . .
EXCELLENT. AND NOW, MR. SPRINGER?
NO. I FEAR YOUR PROPOSALS WOULD NOT FIND FAVOUR WITH MY COLLEAGUES IN DETROIT . . .
810
GOOD AFTERNOON, MR. GOLD
SO, THOUGHT BOND, I WAS RIGHT ABOUT SPRINGER. THEN, UNDER THE DESK, HE SAW GOLDFINGER PRESS A BELL-PUSH

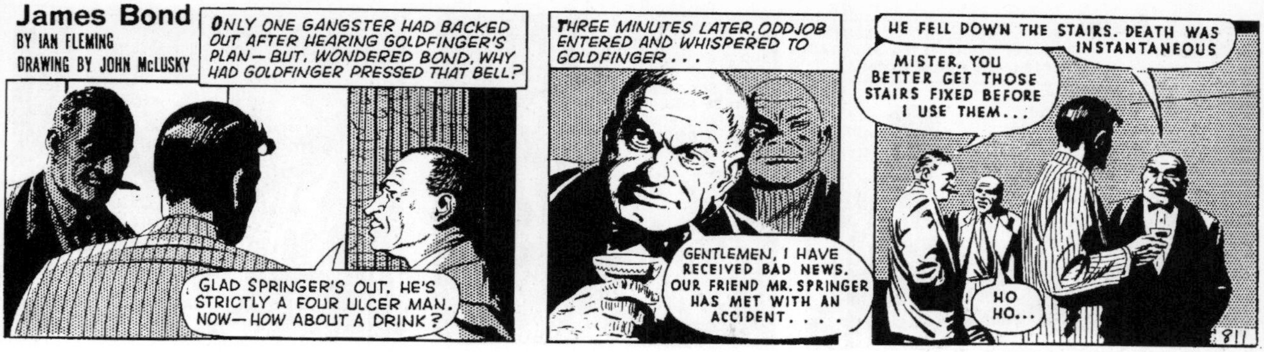
James Bond
BY IAN FLEMING
DRAWING BY JOHN McLUSKY
ONLY ONE GANGSTER HAD BACKED OUT AFTER HEARING GOLDFINGER'S PLAN— BUT, WONDERED BOND, WHY HAD GOLDFINGER PRESSED THAT BELL?
GLAD SPRINGER'S OUT. HE'S STRICTLY A FOUR ULCER MAN. NOW—HOW ABOUT A DRINK?
THREE MINUTES LATER, ODDJOB ENTERED AND WHISPERED TO GOLDFINGER . . .
GENTLEMEN, I HAVE RECEIVED BAD NEWS. OUR FRIEND MR. SPRINGER HAS MET WITH AN ACCIDENT . . . .
HE FELL DOWN THE STAIRS. DEATH WAS INSTANTANEOUS
MISTER, YOU BETTER GET THOSE STAIRS FIXED BEFORE I USE THEM . . .
HO HO...
811

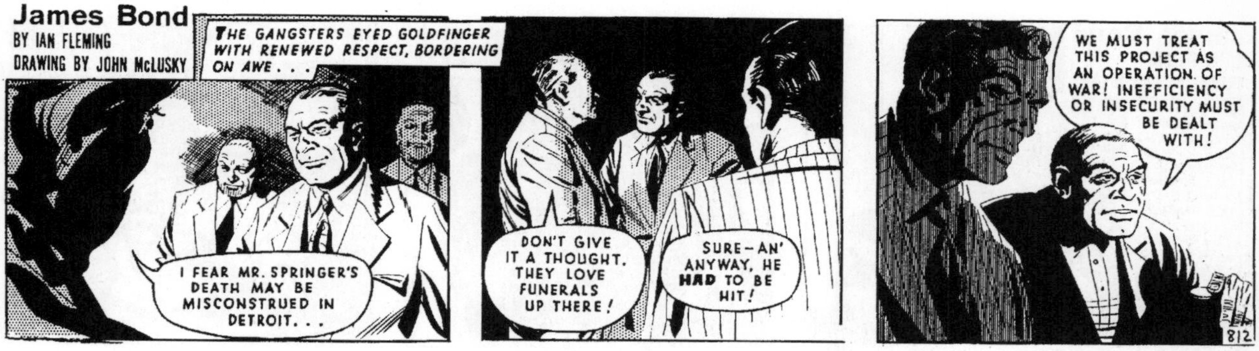
James Bond
BY IAN FLEMING
DRAWING BY JOHN McLUSKY
THE GANGSTERS EYED GOLDFINGER WITH RENEWED RESPECT, BORDERING ON AWE . . .
I FEAR MR. SPRINGER'S DEATH MAY BE MISCONSTRUED IN DETROIT. . .
DON'T GIVE IT A THOUGHT. THEY LOVE FUNERALS UP THERE!
SURE—AN' ANYWAY, HE HAD TO BE HIT!
WE MUST TREAT THIS PROJECT AS AN OPERATION OF WAR! INEFFICIENCY OR INSECURITY MUST BE DEALT WITH!
812

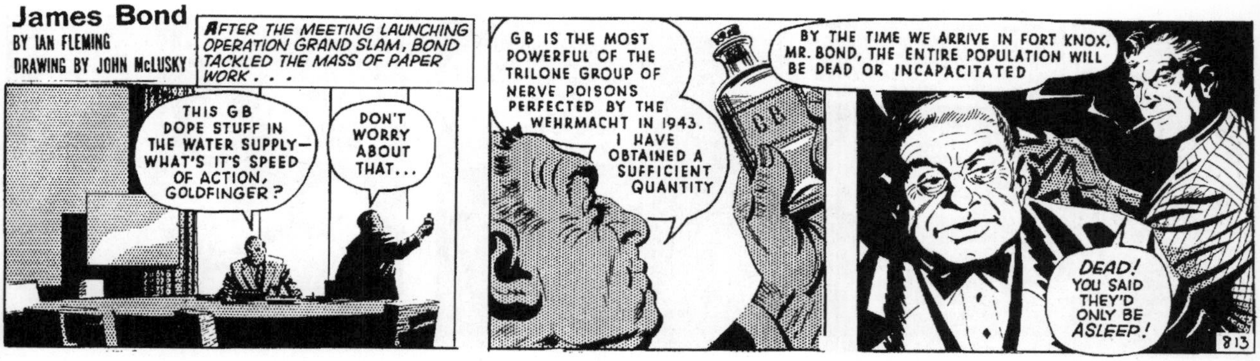
James Bond
BY IAN FLEMING
DRAWING BY JOHN McLUSKY
AFTER THE MEETING LAUNCHING OPERATION GRAND SLAM, BOND TACKLED THE MASS OF PAPER WORK . . .
THIS GB DOPE STUFF IN THE WATER SUPPLY— WHAT'S IT'S SPEED OF ACTION, GOLDFINGER?
DON'T WORRY ABOUT THAT...
GB IS THE MOST POWERFUL OF THE TRILONE GROUP OF NERVE POISONS PERFECTED BY THE WEHRMACHT IN 1943. I HAVE OBTAINED A SUFFICIENT QUANTITY
GB
BY THE TIME WE ARRIVE IN FORT KNOX, MR. BOND, THE ENTIRE POPULATION WILL BE DEAD OR INCAPACITATED
DEAD! YOU SAID THEY'D ONLY BE ASLEEP!
813

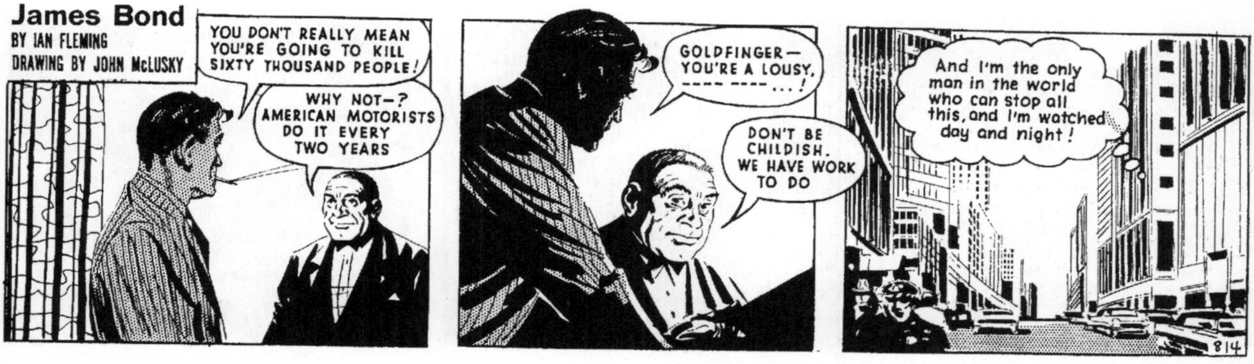
James Bond
BY IAN FLEMING
DRAWING BY JOHN McLUSKY
YOU DON'T REALLY MEAN YOU'RE GOING TO KILL SIXTY THOUSAND PEOPLE!
WHY NOT—? AMERICAN MOTORISTS DO IT EVERY TWO YEARS
GOLDFINGER— YOU'RE A LOUSY, ---- ---- ...!
DON'T BE CHILDISH. WE HAVE WORK TO DO
And I'm the only man in the world who can stop all this, and I'm watched day and night!
814

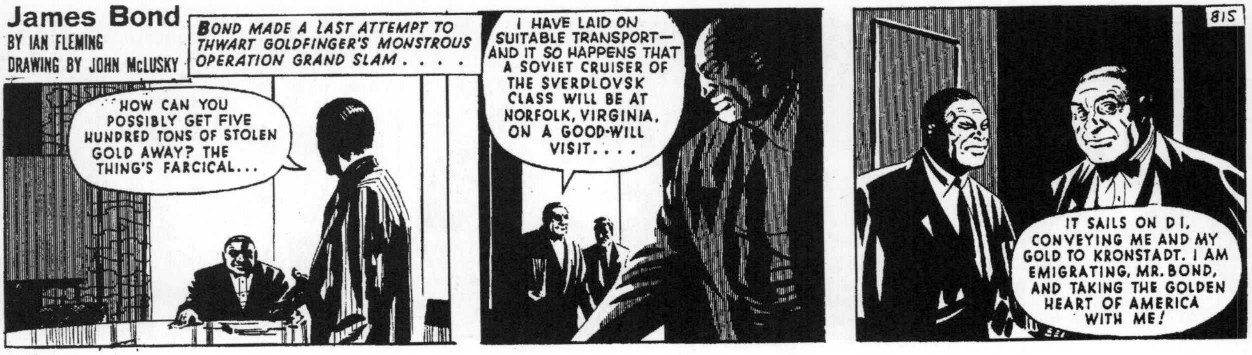

James Bond
BY IAN FLEMING
DRAWING BY JOHN McLUSKY
BOND MADE A LAST ATTEMPT TO THWART GOLDFINGER'S MONSTROUS OPERATION GRAND SLAM . . . .
HOW CAN YOU POSSIBLY GET FIVE HUNDRED TONS OF STOLEN GOLD AWAY? THE THING'S FARCICAL...
I HAVE LAID ON SUITABLE TRANSPORT— AND IT SO HAPPENS THAT A SOVIET CRUISER OF THE SVERDLOVSK CLASS WILL BE AT NORFOLK, VIRGINIA, ON A GOOD-WILL VISIT. . . .
815
IT SAILS ON D I, CONVEYING ME AND MY GOLD TO KRONSTADT. I AM EMIGRATING, MR. BOND, AND TAKING THE GOLDEN HEART OF AMERICA WITH ME!

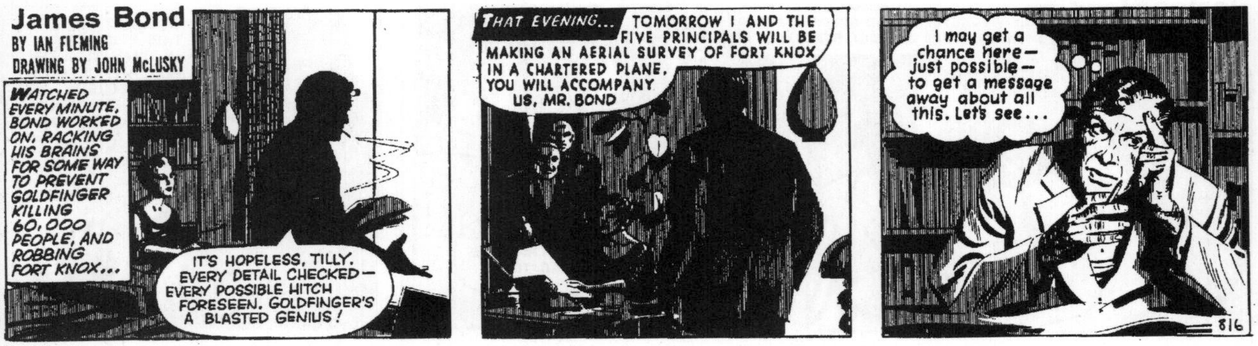

James Bond
BY IAN FLEMING
DRAWING BY JOHN McLUSKY
WATCHED EVERY MINUTE, BOND WORKED ON, RACKING HIS BRAINS FOR SOME WAY TO PREVENT GOLDFINGER KILLING 60,000 PEOPLE, AND ROBBING FORT KNOX...
IT'S HOPELESS, TILLY. EVERY DETAIL CHECKED— EVERY POSSIBLE HITCH FORESEEN. GOLDFINGER'S A BLASTED GENIUS!
THAT EVENING...
TOMORROW I AND THE FIVE PRINCIPALS WILL BE MAKING AN AERIAL SURVEY OF FORT KNOX IN A CHARTERED PLANE. YOU WILL ACCOMPANY US, MR. BOND
I may get a chance here— just possible— to get a message away about all this. Let's see...
816

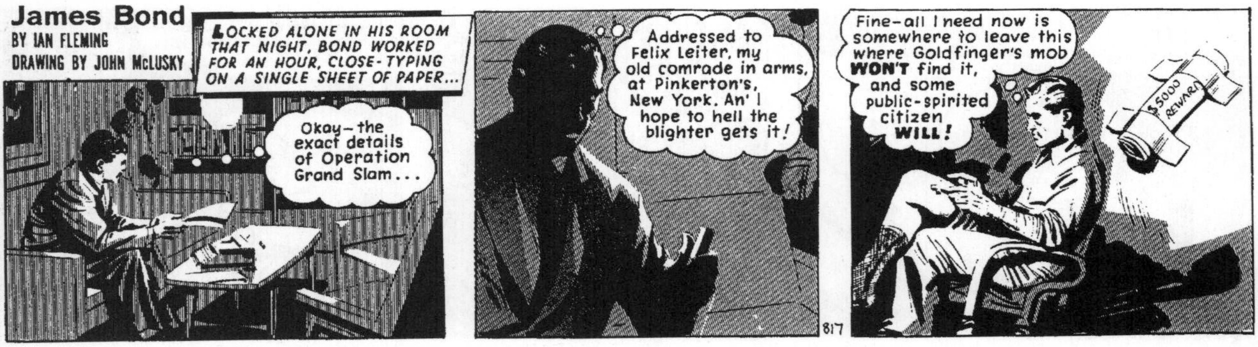

James Bond
BY IAN FLEMING
DRAWING BY JOHN McLUSKY
LOCKED ALONE IN HIS ROOM THAT NIGHT, BOND WORKED FOR AN HOUR, CLOSE-TYPING ON A SINGLE SHEET OF PAPER...
Okay—the exact details of Operation Grand Slam...
Addressed to Felix Leiter, my old comrade in arms, at Pinkerton's, New York. An' I hope to hell the blighter gets it!
817
Fine—all I need now is somewhere to leave this where Goldfinger's mob WON'T find it, and some public-spirited citizen WILL!
$5000 REWARD

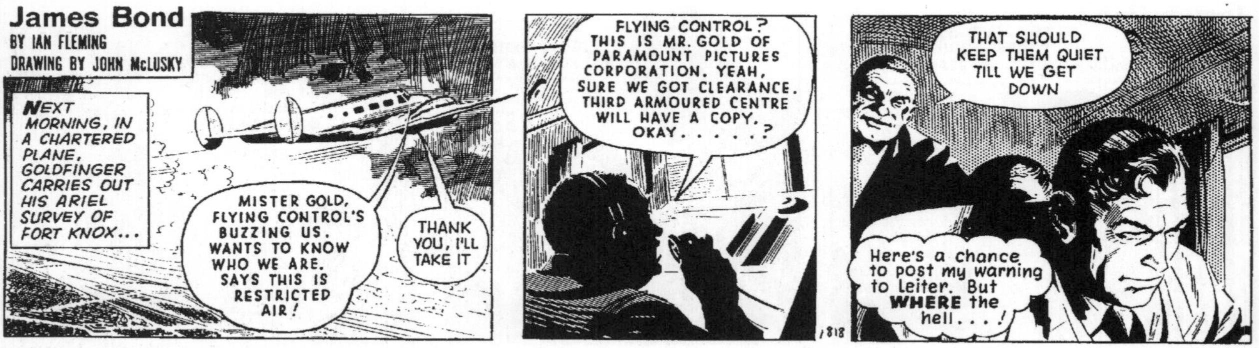

James Bond
BY IAN FLEMING
DRAWING BY JOHN McLUSKY
NEXT MORNING, IN A CHARTERED PLANE, GOLDFINGER CARRIES OUT HIS ARIEL SURVEY OF FORT KNOX...
MISTER GOLD, FLYING CONTROL'S BUZZING US. WANTS TO KNOW WHO WE ARE. SAYS THIS IS RESTRICTED AIR!
THANK YOU, I'LL TAKE IT
FLYING CONTROL? THIS IS MR. GOLD OF PARAMOUNT PICTURES CORPORATION. YEAH, SURE WE GOT CLEARANCE. THIRD ARMOURED CENTRE WILL HAVE A COPY. OKAY. . . . .?
818
THAT SHOULD KEEP THEM QUIET TILL WE GET DOWN
Here's a chance to post my warning to Leiter. But WHERE the hell. . . !

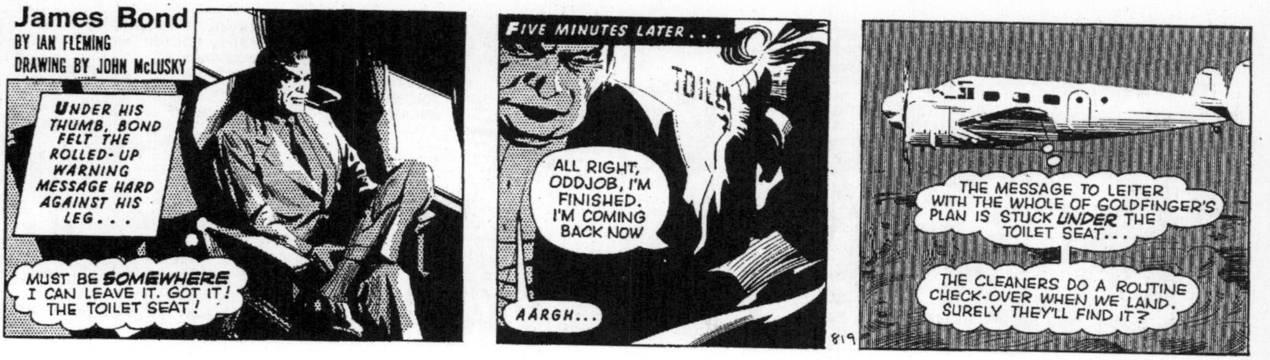
James Bond
BY IAN FLEMING
DRAWING BY JOHN McLUSKY
UNDER HIS THUMB, BOND FELT THE ROLLED-UP WARNING MESSAGE HARD AGAINST HIS LEG . . .
MUST BE SOMEWHERE I CAN LEAVE IT. GOT IT! THE TOILET SEAT!
FIVE MINUTES LATER . . .
TOILE
ALL RIGHT, ODDJOB, I'M FINISHED. I'M COMING BACK NOW
AARGH . . .
819
THE MESSAGE TO LEITER WITH THE WHOLE OF GOLDFINGER'S PLAN IS STUCK UNDER THE TOILET SEAT . . .
THE CLEANERS DO A ROUTINE CHECK-OVER WHEN WE LAND. SURELY THEY'LL FIND IT?

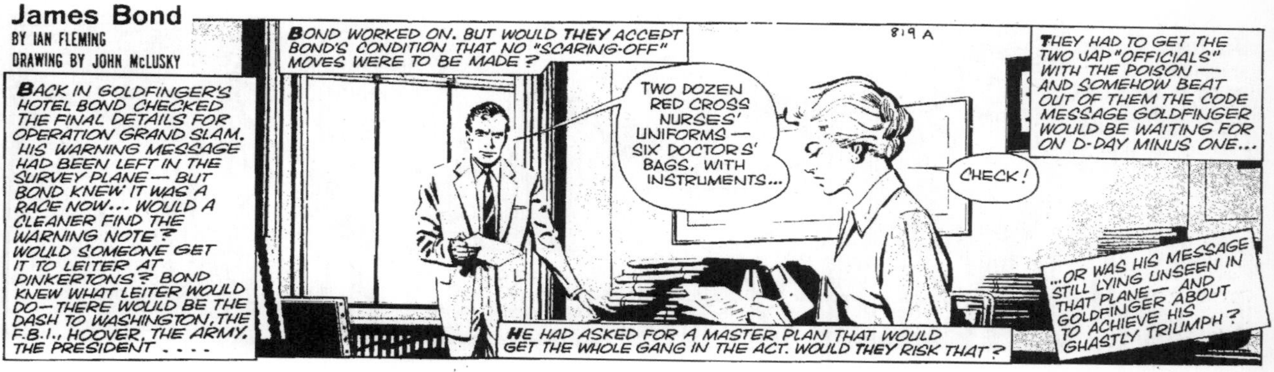
James Bond
BY IAN FLEMING
DRAWING BY JOHN McLUSKY
BACK IN GOLDFINGER'S HOTEL BOND CHECKED THE FINAL DETAILS FOR OPERATION GRAND SLAM. HIS WARNING MESSAGE HAD BEEN LEFT IN THE SURVEY PLANE — BUT BOND KNEW IT WAS A RACE NOW . . . WOULD A CLEANER FIND THE WARNING NOTE? WOULD SOMEONE GET IT TO LEITER AT PINKERTONS? BOND KNEW WHAT LEITER WOULD DO — THERE WOULD BE THE DASH TO WASHINGTON, THE F.B.I., HOOVER, THE ARMY, THE PRESIDENT . . . .
BOND WORKED ON. BUT WOULD THEY ACCEPT BOND'S CONDITION THAT NO "SCARING-OFF" MOVES WERE TO BE MADE?
819 A
TWO DOZEN RED CROSS NURSES' UNIFORMS — SIX DOCTORS' BAGS, WITH INSTRUMENTS . . .
CHECK!
HE HAD ASKED FOR A MASTER PLAN THAT WOULD GET THE WHOLE GANG IN THE ACT. WOULD THEY RISK THAT?
THEY HAD TO GET THE TWO JAP "OFFICIALS" WITH THE POISON — AND SOMEHOW BEAT OUT OF THEM THE CODE MESSAGE GOLDFINGER WOULD BE WAITING FOR ON D-DAY MINUS ONE . . .
. . . OR WAS HIS MESSAGE STILL LYING UNSEEN IN THAT PLANE — AND GOLDFINGER ABOUT TO ACHIEVE HIS GHASTLY TRIUMPH?

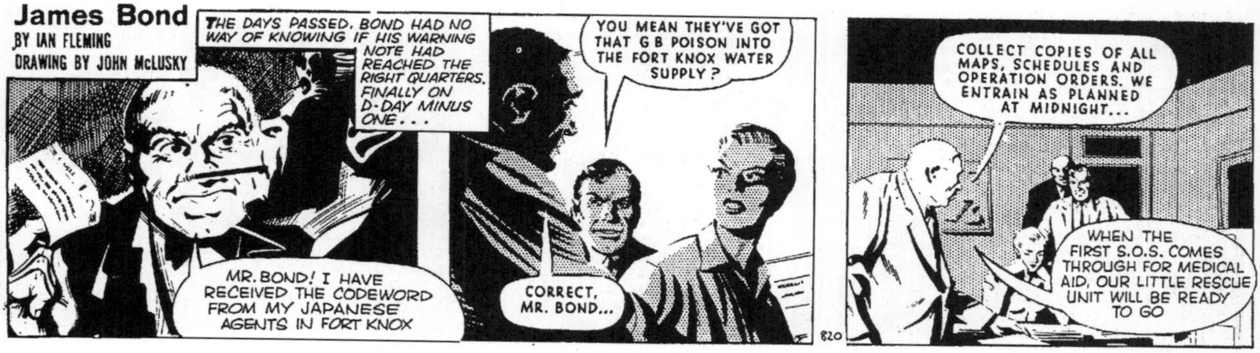
James Bond
BY IAN FLEMING
DRAWING BY JOHN McLUSKY
THE DAYS PASSED. BOND HAD NO WAY OF KNOWING IF HIS WARNING NOTE HAD REACHED THE RIGHT QUARTERS. FINALLY ON D-DAY MINUS ONE . . .
MR. BOND! I HAVE RECEIVED THE CODEWORD FROM MY JAPANESE AGENTS IN FORT KNOX
YOU MEAN THEY'VE GOT THAT G B POISON INTO THE FORT KNOX WATER SUPPLY?
CORRECT, MR. BOND . . .
820
COLLECT COPIES OF ALL MAPS, SCHEDULES AND OPERATION ORDERS. WE ENTRAIN AS PLANNED AT MIDNIGHT . . .
WHEN THE FIRST S.O.S. COMES THROUGH FOR MEDICAL AID, OUR LITTLE RESCUE UNIT WILL BE READY TO GO

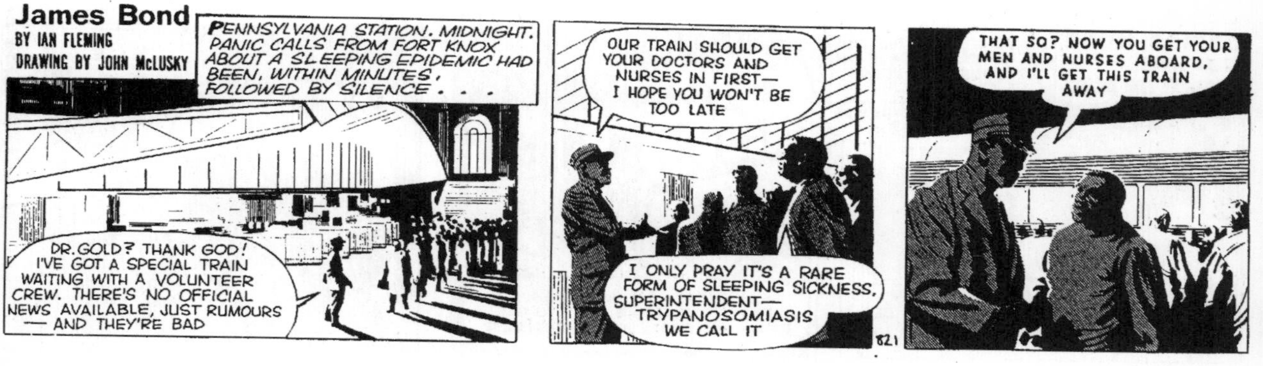
James Bond
BY IAN FLEMING
DRAWING BY JOHN McLUSKY
PENNSYLVANIA STATION. MIDNIGHT. PANIC CALLS FROM FORT KNOX ABOUT A SLEEPING EPIDEMIC HAD BEEN, WITHIN MINUTES, FOLLOWED BY SILENCE . . .
DR. GOLD? THANK GOD! I'VE GOT A SPECIAL TRAIN WAITING WITH A VOLUNTEER CREW. THERE'S NO OFFICIAL NEWS AVAILABLE, JUST RUMOURS — AND THEY'RE BAD
OUR TRAIN SHOULD GET YOUR DOCTORS AND NURSES IN FIRST — I HOPE YOU WON'T BE TOO LATE
I ONLY PRAY IT'S A RARE FORM OF SLEEPING SICKNESS, SUPERINTENDENT — TRYPANOSOMIASIS WE CALL IT
821
THAT SO? NOW YOU GET YOUR MEN AND NURSES ABOARD, AND I'LL GET THIS TRAIN AWAY

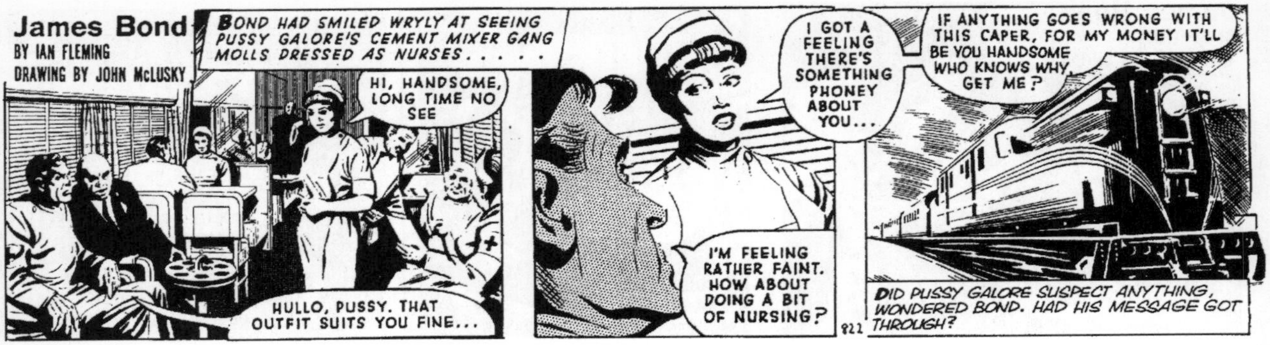
James Bond
BY IAN FLEMING
DRAWING BY JOHN McLUSKY
BOND HAD SMILED WRYLY AT SEEING PUSSY GALORE'S CEMENT MIXER GANG MOLLS DRESSED AS NURSES . . . . .
HI, HANDSOME, LONG TIME NO SEE
HULLO, PUSSY. THAT OUTFIT SUITS YOU FINE...
I GOT A FEELING THERE'S SOMETHING PHONEY ABOUT YOU...
I'M FEELING RATHER FAINT. HOW ABOUT DOING A BIT OF NURSING?
IF ANYTHING GOES WRONG WITH THIS CAPER, FOR MY MONEY IT'LL BE YOU HANDSOME WHO KNOWS WHY, GET ME?
DID PUSSY GALORE SUSPECT ANYTHING, WONDERED BOND. HAD HIS MESSAGE GOT THROUGH?
822

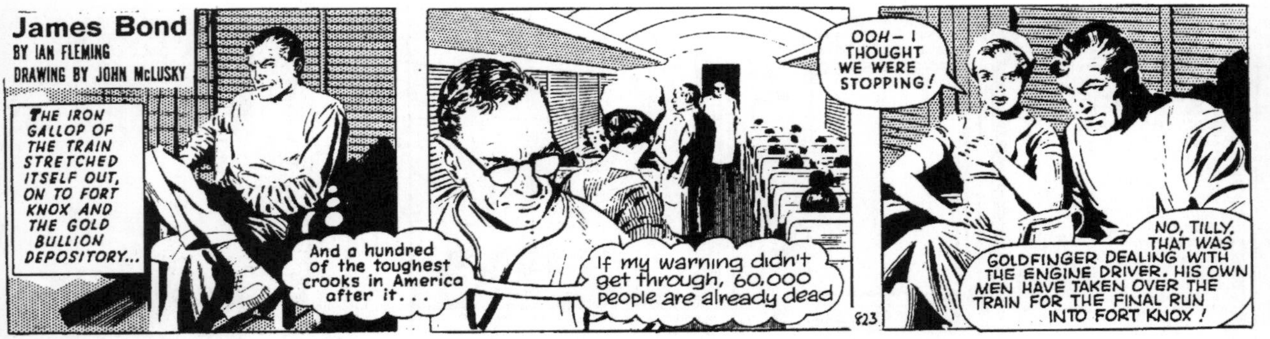
James Bond
BY IAN FLEMING
DRAWING BY JOHN McLUSKY
THE IRON GALLOP OF THE TRAIN STRETCHED ITSELF OUT, ON TO FORT KNOX AND THE GOLD BULLION DEPOSITORY...
And a hundred of the toughest crooks in America after it . . .
If my warning didn't get through, 60,000 people are already dead
OOH – I THOUGHT WE WERE STOPPING!
NO, TILLY. THAT WAS GOLDFINGER DEALING WITH THE ENGINE DRIVER. HIS OWN MEN HAVE TAKEN OVER THE TRAIN FOR THE FINAL RUN INTO FORT KNOX!
823

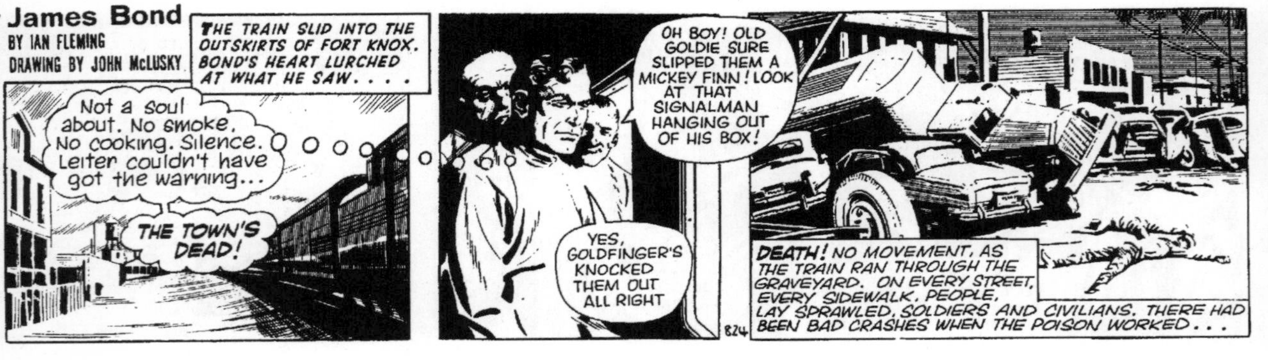
James Bond
BY IAN FLEMING
DRAWING BY JOHN McLUSKY
THE TRAIN SLID INTO THE OUTSKIRTS OF FORT KNOX. BOND'S HEART LURCHED AT WHAT HE SAW . . . .
Not a soul about. No smoke. No cooking. Silence. Leiter couldn't have got the warning...
THE TOWN'S DEAD!
OH BOY! OLD GOLDIE SURE SLIPPED THEM A MICKEY FINN! LOOK AT THAT SIGNALMAN HANGING OUT OF HIS BOX!
YES, GOLDFINGER'S KNOCKED THEM OUT ALL RIGHT
DEATH! NO MOVEMENT, AS THE TRAIN RAN THROUGH THE GRAVEYARD. ON EVERY STREET, EVERY SIDEWALK, PEOPLE, LAY SPRAWLED, SOLDIERS AND CIVILIANS. THERE HAD BEEN BAD CRASHES WHEN THE POISON WORKED . . .
824

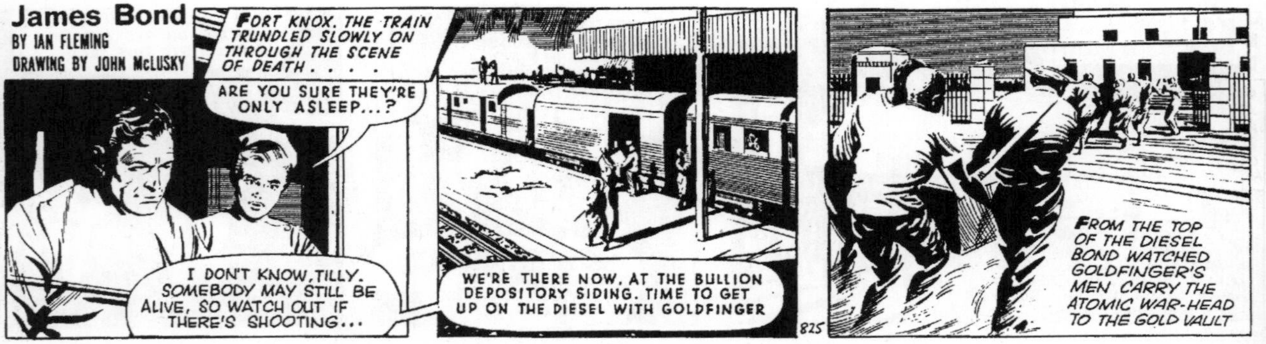
James Bond
BY IAN FLEMING
DRAWING BY JOHN McLUSKY
FORT KNOX. THE TRAIN TRUNDLED SLOWLY ON THROUGH THE SCENE OF DEATH . . . .
ARE YOU SURE THEY'RE ONLY ASLEEP...?
I DON'T KNOW, TILLY. SOMEBODY MAY STILL BE ALIVE, SO WATCH OUT IF THERE'S SHOOTING...
WE'RE THERE NOW, AT THE BULLION DEPOSITORY SIDING. TIME TO GET UP ON THE DIESEL WITH GOLDFINGER
FROM THE TOP OF THE DIESEL BOND WATCHED GOLDFINGER'S MEN CARRY THE ATOMIC WAR-HEAD TO THE GOLD VAULT
825

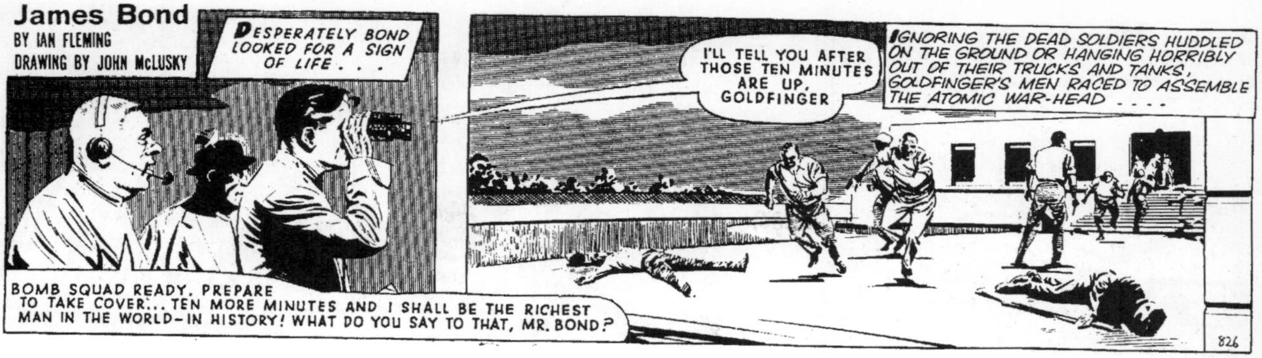
James Bond
BY IAN FLEMING
DRAWING BY JOHN McLUSKY
DESPERATELY BOND LOOKED FOR A SIGN OF LIFE . . .
I'LL TELL YOU AFTER THOSE TEN MINUTES ARE UP, GOLDFINGER
BOMB SQUAD READY. PREPARE TO TAKE COVER... TEN MORE MINUTES AND I SHALL BE THE RICHEST MAN IN THE WORLD–IN HISTORY! WHAT DO YOU SAY TO THAT, MR. BOND?
IGNORING THE DEAD SOLDIERS HUDDLED ON THE GROUND OR HANGING HORRIBLY OUT OF THEIR TRUCKS AND TANKS, GOLDFINGER'S MEN RACED TO ASSEMBLE THE ATOMIC WAR-HEAD . . .
826

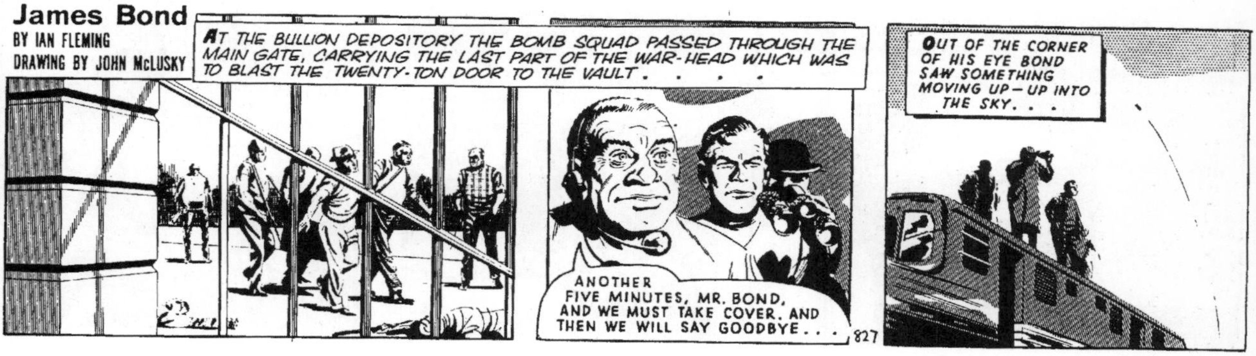
James Bond
BY IAN FLEMING
DRAWING BY JOHN McLUSKY
AT THE BULLION DEPOSITORY THE BOMB SQUAD PASSED THROUGH THE MAIN GATE, CARRYING THE LAST PART OF THE WAR-HEAD WHICH WAS TO BLAST THE TWENTY-TON DOOR TO THE VAULT . . . .
ANOTHER FIVE MINUTES, MR. BOND, AND WE MUST TAKE COVER. AND THEN WE WILL SAY GOODBYE . . .
827
OUT OF THE CORNER OF HIS EYE BOND SAW SOMETHING MOVING UP—UP INTO THE SKY. . .

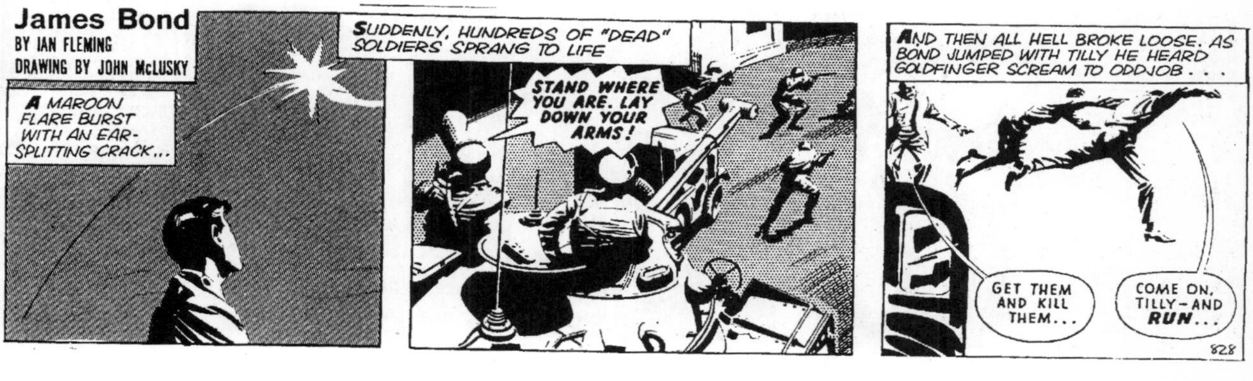
James Bond
BY IAN FLEMING
DRAWING BY JOHN McLUSKY
A MAROON FLARE BURST WITH AN EAR-SPLITTING CRACK...
SUDDENLY, HUNDREDS OF "DEAD" SOLDIERS SPRANG TO LIFE
STAND WHERE YOU ARE. LAY DOWN YOUR ARMS!
AND THEN ALL HELL BROKE LOOSE. AS BOND JUMPED WITH TILLY HE HEARD GOLDFINGER SCREAM TO ODDJOB . . .
GET THEM AND KILL THEM...
COME ON, TILLY–AND RUN...
828

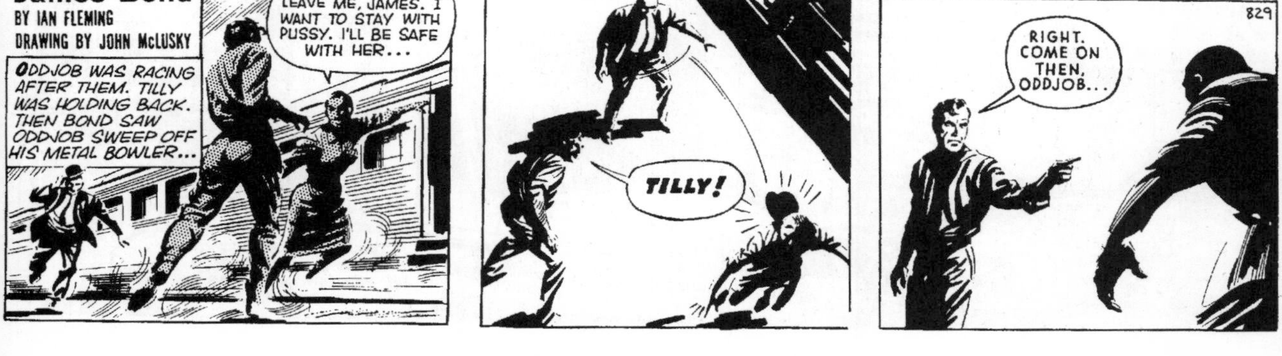
James Bond
BY IAN FLEMING
DRAWING BY JOHN McLUSKY
ODDJOB WAS RACING AFTER THEM. TILLY WAS HOLDING BACK. THEN BOND SAW ODDNOB SWEEP OFF HIS METAL BOWLER...
LEAVE ME, JAMES. I WANT TO STAY WITH PUSSY. I'LL BE SAFE WITH HER...
TILLY!
829
RIGHT. COME ON THEN, ODDJOB...

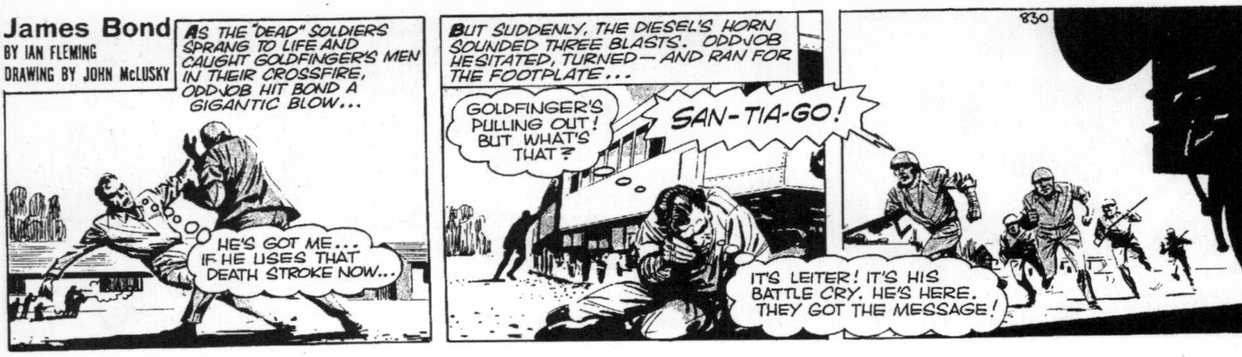
James Bond
BY IAN FLEMING
DRAWING BY JOHN McLUSKY
AS THE "DEAD" SOLDIERS SPRANG TO LIFE AND CAUGHT GOLDFINGER'S MEN IN THEIR CROSSFIRE, ODDJOB HIT BOND A GIGANTIC BLOW...
HE'S GOT ME... IF HE USES THAT DEATH STROKE NOW...
BUT SUDDENLY, THE DIESEL'S HORN SOUNDED THREE BLASTS. ODDJOB HESITATED, TURNED— AND RAN FOR THE FOOTPLATE...
GOLDFINGER'S PULLING OUT! BUT WHAT'S THAT?
SAN-TIA-GO!
830
IT'S LEITER! IT'S HIS BATTLE CRY. HE'S HERE. THEY GOT THE MESSAGE!

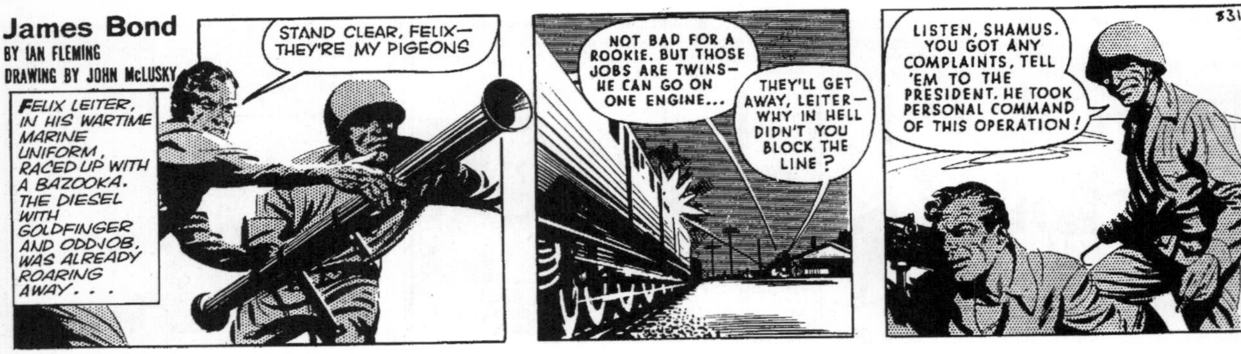
James Bond
BY IAN FLEMING
DRAWING BY JOHN McLUSKY
STAND CLEAR, FELIX— THEY'RE MY PIGEONS
FELIX LEITER, IN HIS WARTIME MARINE UNIFORM, RACED UP WITH A BAZOOKA. THE DIESEL WITH GOLDFINGER AND ODDJOB, WAS ALREADY ROARING AWAY...
NOT BAD FOR A ROOKIE. BUT THOSE JOBS ARE TWINS— HE CAN GO ON ONE ENGINE...
THEY'LL GET AWAY, LEITER— WHY IN HELL DIDN'T YOU BLOCK THE LINE?
831
LISTEN, SHAMUS. YOU GOT ANY COMPLAINTS, TELL 'EM TO THE PRESIDENT. HE TOOK PERSONAL COMMAND OF THIS OPERATION!

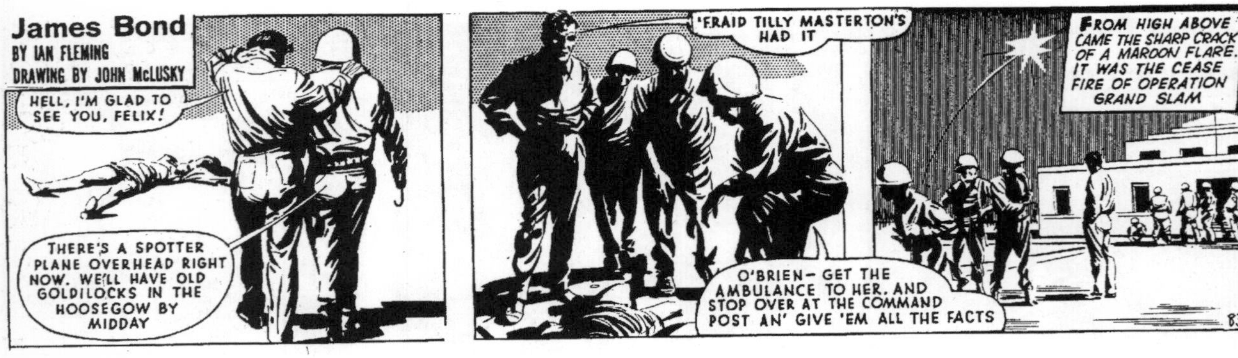
James Bond
BY IAN FLEMING
DRAWING BY JOHN McLUSKY
HELL, I'M GLAD TO SEE YOU, FELIX!
THERE'S A SPOTTER PLANE OVERHEAD RIGHT NOW. WE'LL HAVE OLD GOLDILOCKS IN THE HOOSEGOW BY MIDDAY
'FRAID TILLY MASTERTON'S HAD IT
O'BRIEN— GET THE AMBULANCE TO HER, AND STOP OVER AT THE COMMAND POST AN' GIVE 'EM ALL THE FACTS
FROM HIGH ABOVE CAME THE SHARP CRACK OF A MAROON FLARE. IT WAS THE CEASE FIRE OF OPERATION GRAND SLAM
832

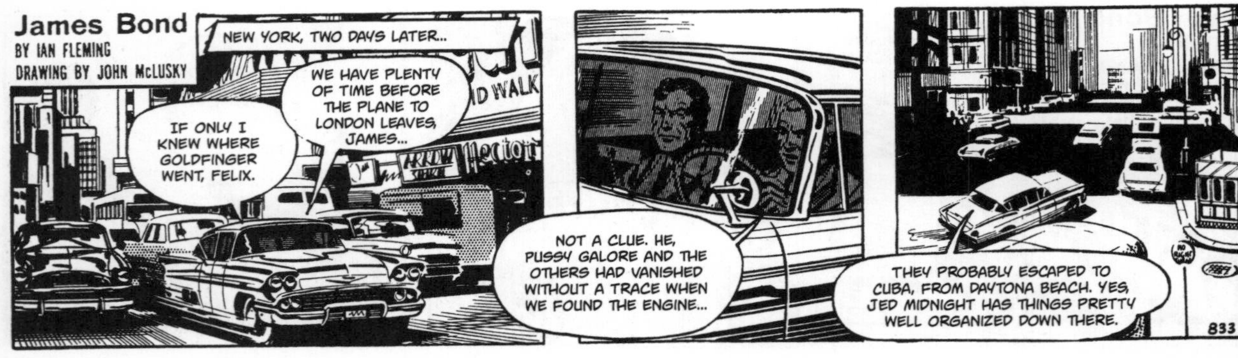
James Bond
BY IAN FLEMING
DRAWING BY JOHN McLUSKY
NEW YORK, TWO DAYS LATER...
IF ONLY I KNEW WHERE GOLDFINGER WENT, FELIX.
WE HAVE PLENTY OF TIME BEFORE THE PLANE TO LONDON LEAVES, JAMES...
NOT A CLUE. HE, PUSSY GALORE AND THE OTHERS HAD VANISHED WITHOUT A TRACE WHEN WE FOUND THE ENGINE...
THEY PROBABLY ESCAPED TO CUBA, FROM DAYTONA BEACH. YES, JED MIDNIGHT HAS THINGS PRETTY WELL ORGANIZED DOWN THERE.
833

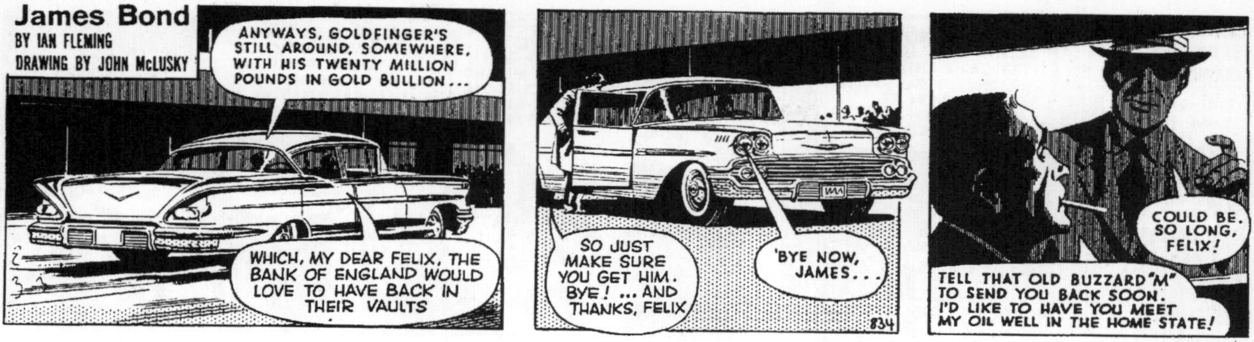
James Bond
BY IAN FLEMING
DRAWING BY JOHN McLUSKY
ANYWAYS, GOLDFINGER'S STILL AROUND, SOMEWHERE, WITH HIS TWENTY MILLION POUNDS IN GOLD BULLION...
WHICH, MY DEAR FELIX, THE BANK OF ENGLAND WOULD LOVE TO HAVE BACK IN THEIR VAULTS
SO JUST MAKE SURE YOU GET HIM. BYE! ... AND THANKS, FELIX
'BYE NOW, JAMES...
834
COULD BE. SO LONG, FELIX!
TELL THAT OLD BUZZARD "M" TO SEND YOU BACK SOON. I'D LIKE TO HAVE YOU MEET MY OIL WELL IN THE HOME STATE!

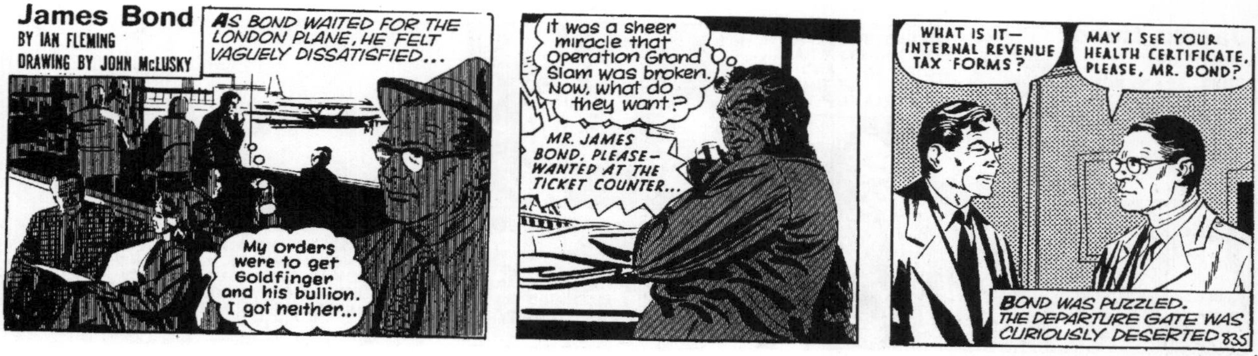
James Bond
BY IAN FLEMING
DRAWING BY JOHN McLUSKY
AS BOND WAITED FOR THE LONDON PLANE, HE FELT VAGUELY DISSATISFIED...
My orders were to get Goldfinger and his bullion. I got neither...
It was a sheer miracle that Operation Grand Slam was broken. Now, what do they want?
MR. JAMES BOND. PLEASE—WANTED AT THE TICKET COUNTER...
WHAT IS IT—INTERNAL REVENUE TAX FORMS?
MAY I SEE YOUR HEALTH CERTIFICATE, PLEASE, MR. BOND?
BOND WAS PUZZLED. THE DEPARTURE GATE WAS CURIOUSLY DESERTED
835

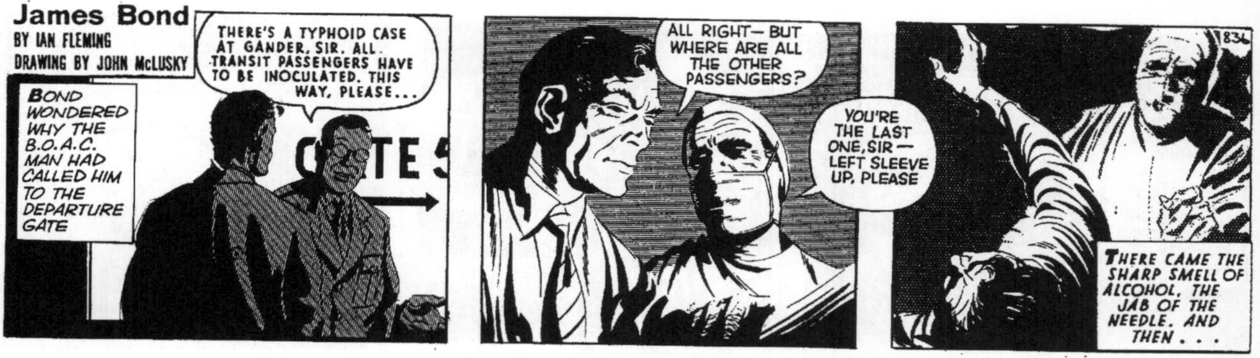
James Bond
BY IAN FLEMING
DRAWING BY JOHN McLUSKY
THERE'S A TYPHOID CASE AT GANDER, SIR. ALL TRANSIT PASSENGERS HAVE TO BE INOCULATED. THIS WAY, PLEASE...
BOND WONDERED WHY THE B.O.A.C. MAN HAD CALLED HIM TO THE DEPARTURE GATE
ALL RIGHT—BUT WHERE ARE ALL THE OTHER PASSENGERS?
YOU'RE THE LAST ONE, SIR—LEFT SLEEVE UP, PLEASE
836
THERE CAME THE SHARP SMELL OF ALCOHOL, THE JAB OF THE NEEDLE, AND THEN . . .

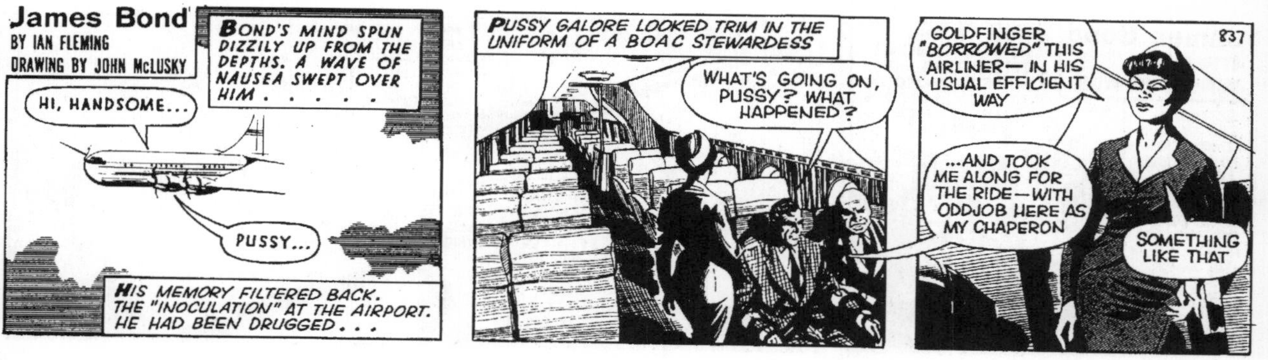
James Bond
BY IAN FLEMING
DRAWING BY JOHN McLUSKY
BOND'S MIND SPUN DIZZILY UP FROM THE DEPTHS. A WAVE OF NAUSEA SWEPT OVER HIM . . . . .
HI, HANDSOME...
PUSSY...
HIS MEMORY FILTERED BACK. THE "INOCULATION" AT THE AIRPORT. HE HAD BEEN DRUGGED . . .
PUSSY GALORE LOOKED TRIM IN THE UNIFORM OF A BOAC STEWARDESS
WHAT'S GOING ON, PUSSY? WHAT HAPPENED?
GOLDFINGER "BORROWED" THIS AIRLINER—IN HIS USUAL EFFICIENT WAY
...AND TOOK ME ALONG FOR THE RIDE—WITH ODDJOB HERE AS MY CHAPERON
SOMETHING LIKE THAT
837

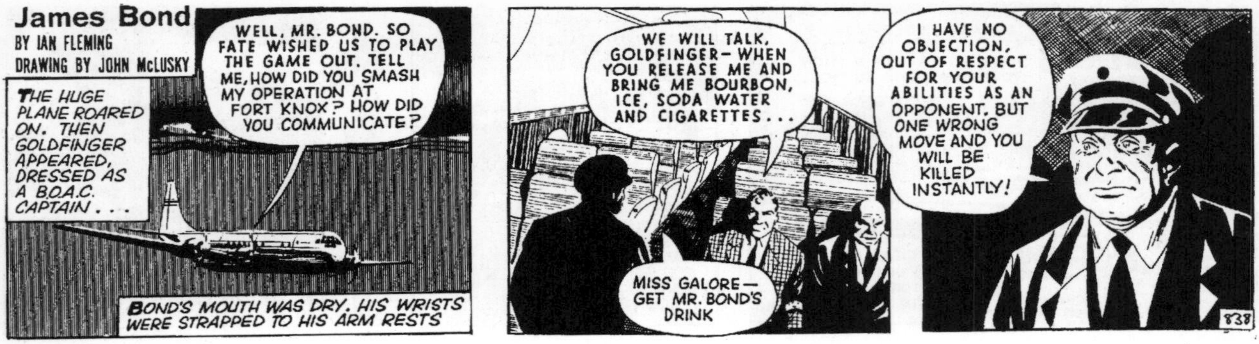
James Bond
BY IAN FLEMING
DRAWING BY JOHN McLUSKY
THE HUGE PLANE ROARED ON. THEN GOLDFINGER APPEARED, DRESSED AS A B.O.A.C. CAPTAIN . . .
WELL, MR. BOND. SO FATE WISHED US TO PLAY THE GAME OUT. TELL ME, HOW DID YOU SMASH MY OPERATION AT FORT KNOX? HOW DID YOU COMMUNICATE?
BOND'S MOUTH WAS DRY. HIS WRISTS WERE STRAPPED TO HIS ARM RESTS
WE WILL TALK, GOLDFINGER— WHEN YOU RELEASE ME AND BRING ME BOURBON, ICE, SODA WATER AND CIGARETTES . . .
MISS GALORE— GET MR. BOND'S DRINK
I HAVE NO OBJECTION, OUT OF RESPECT FOR YOUR ABILITIES AS AN OPPONENT. BUT ONE WRONG MOVE AND YOU WILL BE KILLED INSTANTLY!
838

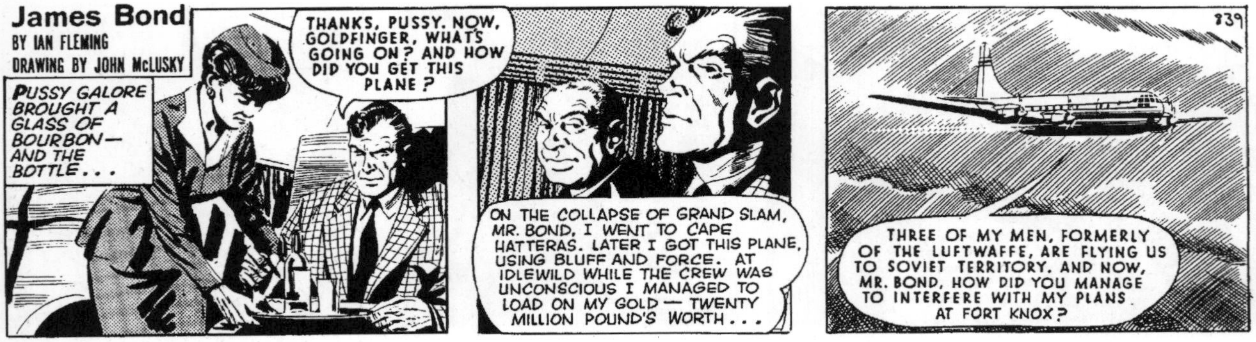
James Bond
BY IAN FLEMING
DRAWING BY JOHN McLUSKY
PUSSY GALORE BROUGHT A GLASS OF BOURBON— AND THE BOTTLE . . .
THANKS, PUSSY. NOW, GOLDFINGER, WHAT'S GOING ON? AND HOW DID YOU GET THIS PLANE?
ON THE COLLAPSE OF GRAND SLAM, MR. BOND, I WENT TO CAPE HATTERAS. LATER I GOT THIS PLANE, USING BLUFF AND FORCE. AT IDLEWILD WHILE THE CREW WAS UNCONSCIOUS I MANAGED TO LOAD ON MY GOLD — TWENTY MILLION POUND'S WORTH . . .
839
THREE OF MY MEN, FORMERLY OF THE LUFTWAFFE, ARE FLYING US TO SOVIET TERRITORY. AND NOW, MR. BOND, HOW DID YOU MANAGE TO INTERFERE WITH MY PLANS AT FORT KNOX?

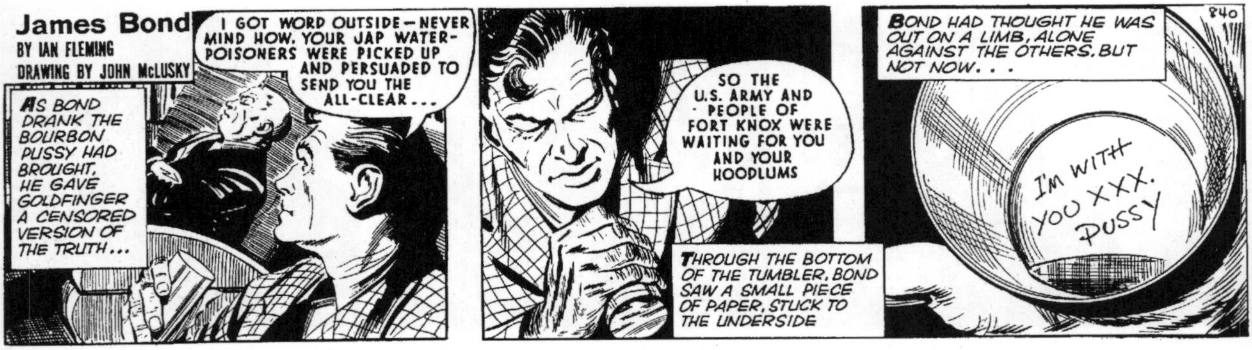
James Bond
BY IAN FLEMING
DRAWING BY JOHN McLUSKY
AS BOND DRANK THE BOURBON PUSSY HAD BROUGHT, HE GAVE GOLDFINGER A CENSORED VERSION OF THE TRUTH...
I GOT WORD OUTSIDE—NEVER MIND HOW. YOUR JAP WATER-POISONERS WERE PICKED UP AND PERSUADED TO SEND YOU THE ALL-CLEAR...
SO THE U.S. ARMY AND PEOPLE OF FORT KNOX WERE WAITING FOR YOU AND YOUR HOODLUMS
THROUGH THE BOTTOM OF THE TUMBLER, BOND SAW A SMALL PIECE OF PAPER, STUCK TO THE UNDERSIDE
840
BOND HAD THOUGHT HE WAS OUT ON A LIMB, ALONE AGAINST THE OTHERS. BUT NOT NOW. . .
I'M WITH YOU XXX. PUSSY

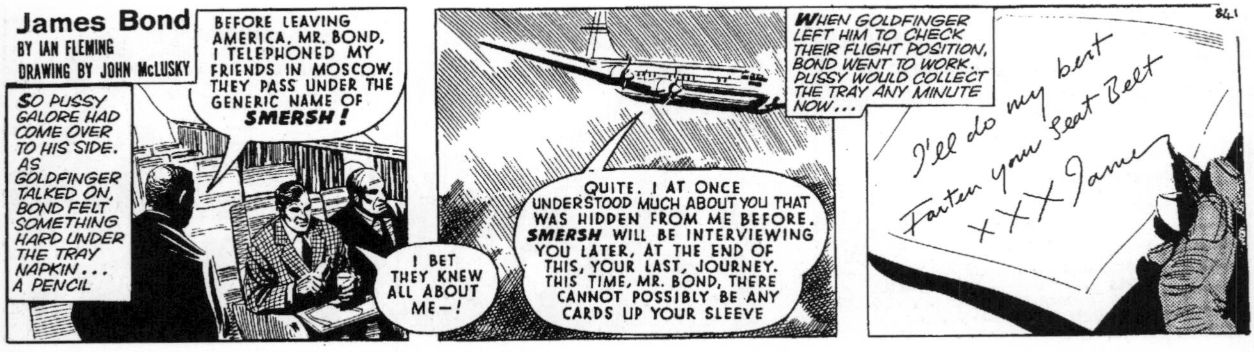
James Bond
BY IAN FLEMING
DRAWING BY JOHN McLUSKY
SO PUSSY GALORE HAD COME OVER TO HIS SIDE. AS GOLDFINGER TALKED ON, BOND FELT SOMETHING HARD UNDER THE TRAY NAPKIN . . . A PENCIL
BEFORE LEAVING AMERICA, MR. BOND, I TELEPHONED MY FRIENDS IN MOSCOW. THEY PASS UNDER THE GENERIC NAME OF SMERSH!
I BET THEY KNEW ALL ABOUT ME—!
QUITE. I AT ONCE UNDERSTOOD MUCH ABOUT YOU THAT WAS HIDDEN FROM ME BEFORE. SMERSH WILL BE INTERVIEWING YOU LATER, AT THE END OF THIS, YOUR LAST, JOURNEY. THIS TIME, MR. BOND, THERE CANNOT POSSIBLY BE ANY CARDS UP YOUR SLEEVE
841
WHEN GOLDFINGER LEFT HIM TO CHECK THEIR FLIGHT POSITION, BOND WENT TO WORK. PUSSY WOULD COLLECT THE TRAY ANY MINUTE NOW...
I'll do my best
Fasten your Seat Belt
XXX James

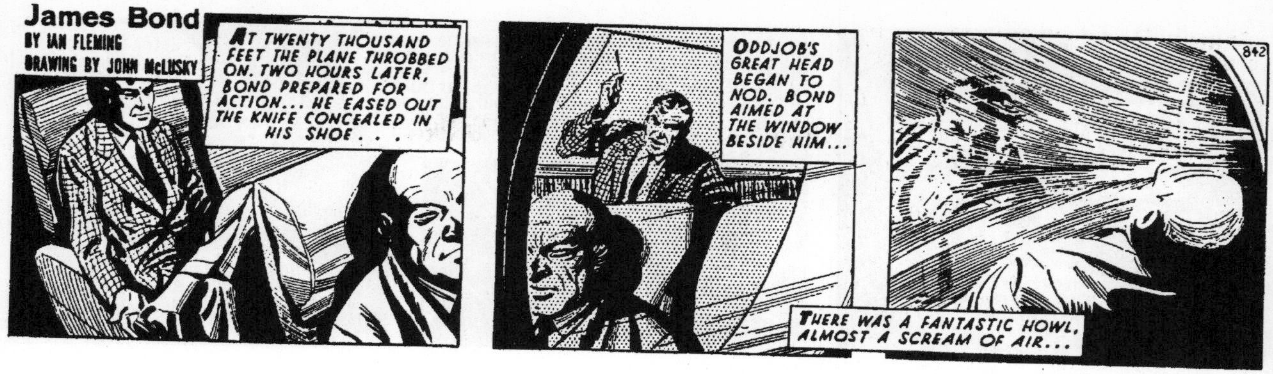

James Bond
BY IAN FLEMING
DRAWING BY JOHN McLUSKY
AT TWENTY THOUSAND FEET THE PLANE THROBBED ON. TWO HOURS LATER, BOND PREPARED FOR ACTION... HE EASED OUT THE KNIFE CONCEALED IN HIS SHOE . . .
ODDJOB'S GREAT HEAD BEGAN TO NOD. BOND AIMED AT THE WINDOW BESIDE HIM...
842
THERE WAS A FANTASTIC HOWL, ALMOST A SCREAM OF AIR...

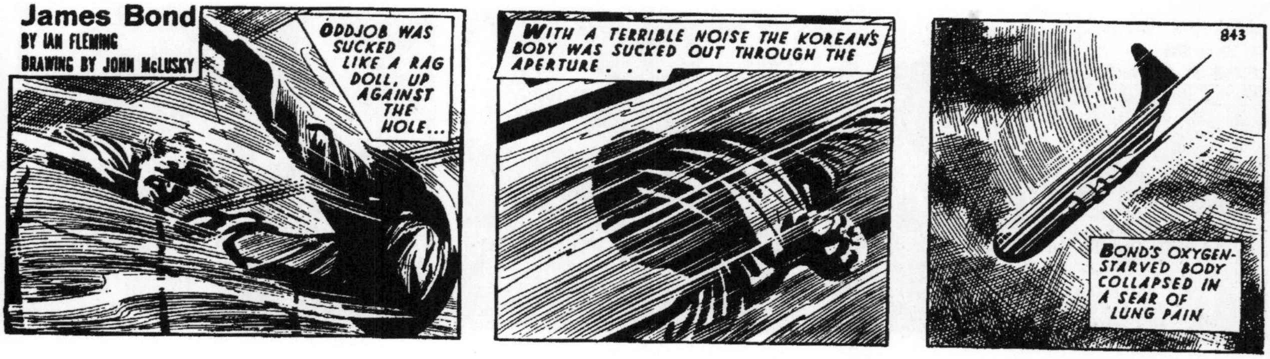

James Bond
BY IAN FLEMING
DRAWING BY JOHN McLUSKY
ODDJOB WAS SUCKED LIKE A RAG DOLL, UP AGAINST THE HOLE...
WITH A TERRIBLE NOISE THE KOREAN'S BODY WAS SUCKED OUT THROUGH THE APERTURE . . .
843
BOND'S OXYGEN-STARVED BODY COLLAPSED IN A SEAR OF LUNG PAIN

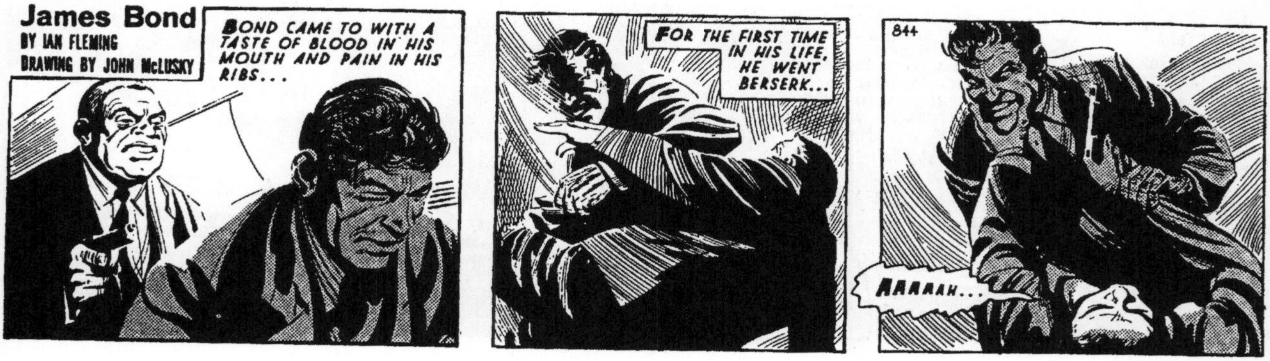

James Bond
BY IAN FLEMING
DRAWING BY JOHN McLUSKY
BOND CAME TO WITH A TASTE OF BLOOD IN HIS MOUTH AND PAIN IN HIS RIBS...
FOR THE FIRST TIME IN HIS LIFE, HE WENT BERSERK...
844
AAAAAH...

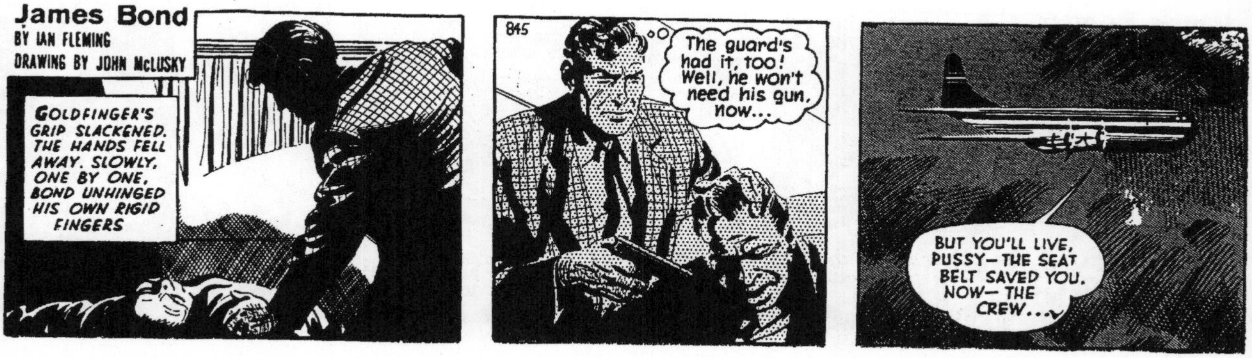

James Bond
BY IAN FLEMING
DRAWING BY JOHN McLUSKY
GOLDFINGER'S GRIP SLACKENED. THE HANDS FELL AWAY. SLOWLY, ONE BY ONE, BOND UNHINGED HIS OWN RIGID FINGERS
845
The guard's had it, too! Well, he won't need his gun, now...
BUT YOU'LL LIVE, PUSSY—THE SEAT BELT SAVED YOU. NOW—THE CREW...

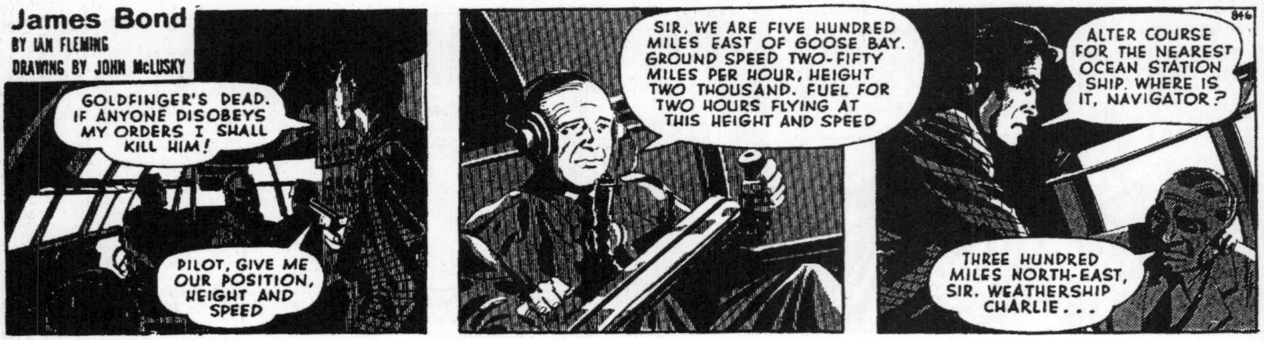
James Bond
BY IAN FLEMING
DRAWING BY JOHN McLUSKY
GOLDFINGER'S DEAD. IF ANYONE DISOBEYS MY ORDERS I SHALL KILL HIM!
PILOT, GIVE ME OUR POSITION, HEIGHT AND SPEED
SIR, WE ARE FIVE HUNDRED MILES EAST OF GOOSE BAY. GROUND SPEED TWO-FIFTY MILES PER HOUR, HEIGHT TWO THOUSAND. FUEL FOR TWO HOURS FLYING AT THIS HEIGHT AND SPEED
846
ALTER COURSE FOR THE NEAREST OCEAN STATION SHIP. WHERE IS IT, NAVIGATOR?
THREE HUNDRED MILES NORTH-EAST, SIR. WEATHERSHIP CHARLIE . . .

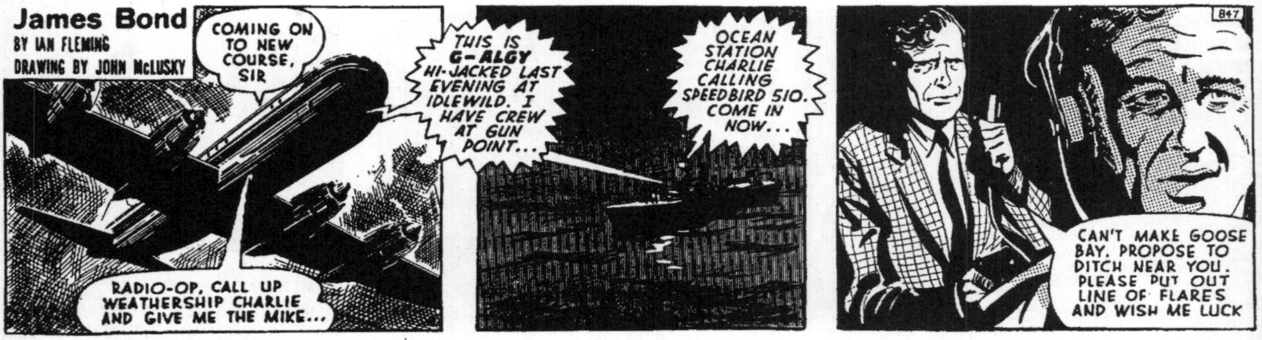
James Bond
BY IAN FLEMING
DRAWING BY JOHN McLUSKY
COMING ON TO NEW COURSE, SIR
RADIO-OP, CALL UP WEATHERSHIP CHARLIE AND GIVE ME THE MIKE...
THIS IS G-ALGY HI-JACKED LAST EVENING AT IDLEWILD. I HAVE CREW AT GUN POINT...
OCEAN STATION CHARLIE CALLING SPEEDBIRD 510. COME IN NOW...
847
CAN'T MAKE GOOSE BAY. PROPOSE TO DITCH NEAR YOU. PLEASE PUT OUT LINE OF FLARES AND WISH ME LUCK

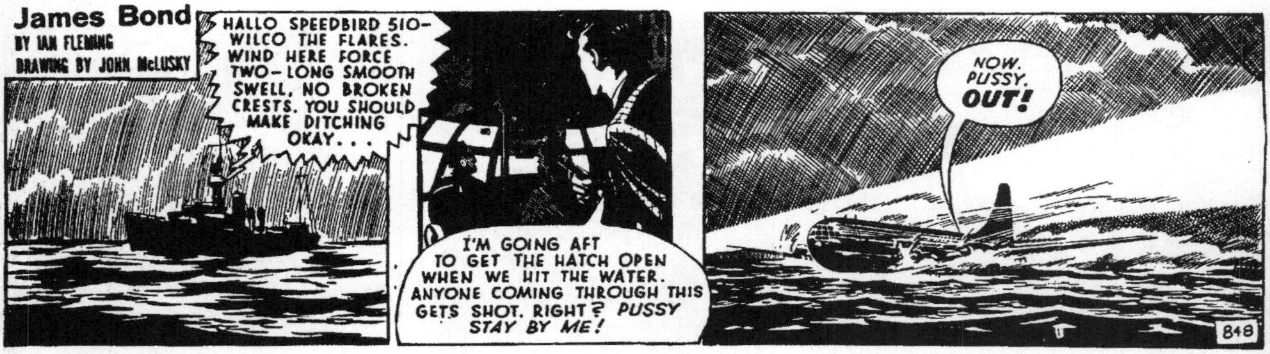
James Bond
BY IAN FLEMING
DRAWING BY JOHN McLUSKY
HALLO SPEEDBIRD 510-WILCO THE FLARES. WIND HERE FORCE TWO-LONG SMOOTH SWELL, NO BROKEN CRESTS. YOU SHOULD MAKE DITCHING OKAY . . .
I'M GOING AFT TO GET THE HATCH OPEN WHEN WE HIT THE WATER. ANYONE COMING THROUGH THIS GETS SHOT. RIGHT? PUSSY STAY BY ME!
NOW. PUSSY. OUT!
848

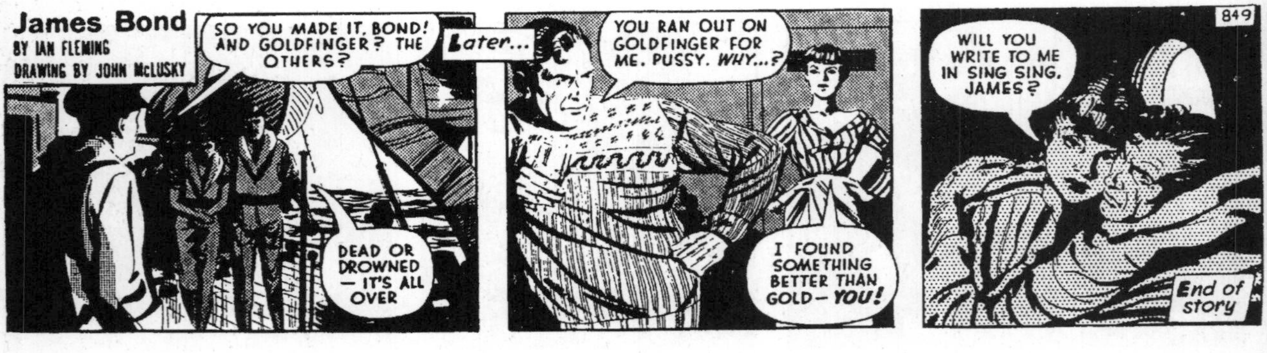
James Bond
BY IAN FLEMING
DRAWING BY JOHN McLUSKY
SO YOU MADE IT, BOND! AND GOLDFINGER? THE OTHERS?
DEAD OR DROWNED —IT'S ALL OVER
Later...
YOU RAN OUT ON GOLDFINGER FOR ME. PUSSY. WHY...?
I FOUND SOMETHING BETTER THAN GOLD—YOU!
849
WILL YOU WRITE TO ME IN SING SING, JAMES?
End of story

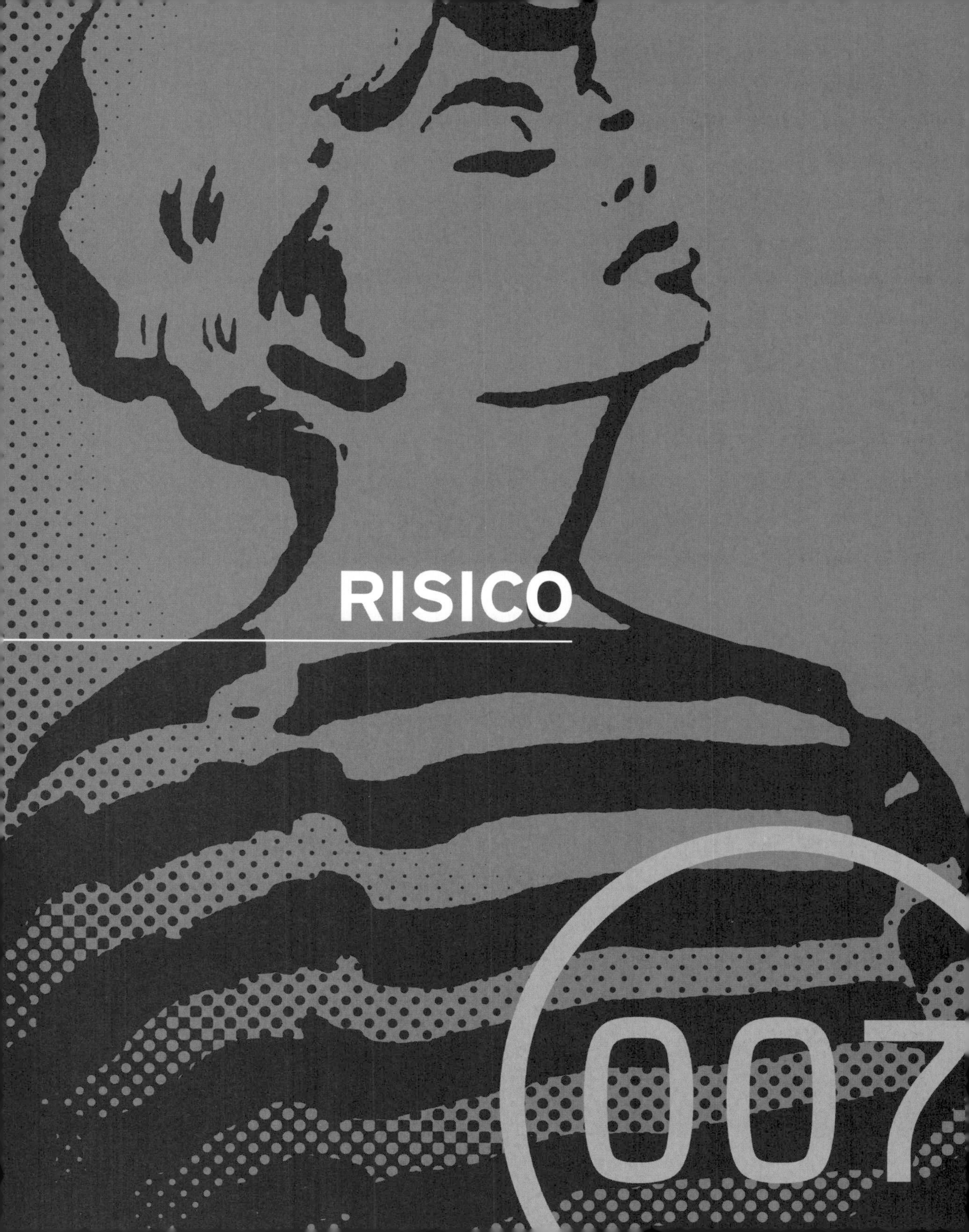

RISICO

007

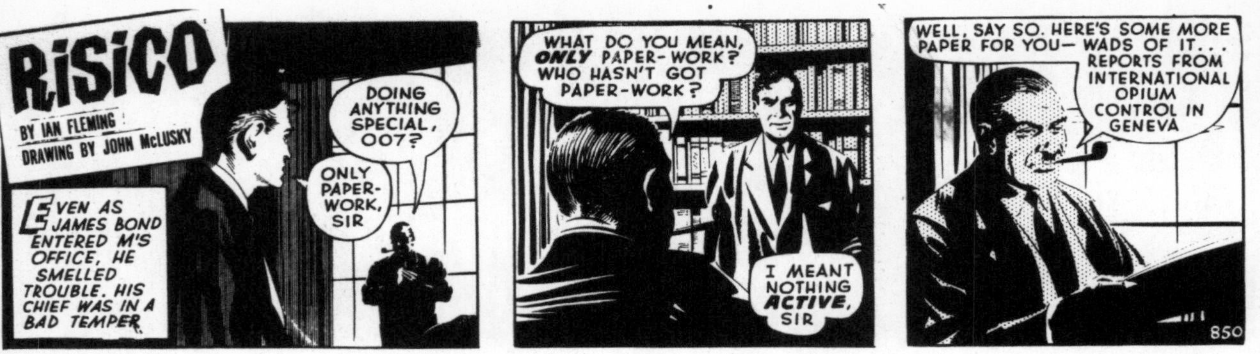
RISICO
BY IAN FLEMING
DRAWING BY JOHN McLUSKY
EVEN AS JAMES BOND ENTERED M'S OFFICE, HE SMELLED TROUBLE. HIS CHIEF WAS IN A BAD TEMPER
DOING ANYTHING SPECIAL, 007?
ONLY PAPER-WORK, SIR
WHAT DO YOU MEAN, ONLY PAPER-WORK? WHO HASN'T GOT PAPER-WORK?
I MEANT NOTHING ACTIVE, SIR
WELL, SAY SO. HERE'S SOME MORE PAPER FOR YOU— WADS OF IT... REPORTS FROM INTERNATIONAL OPIUM CONTROL IN GENEVA
850

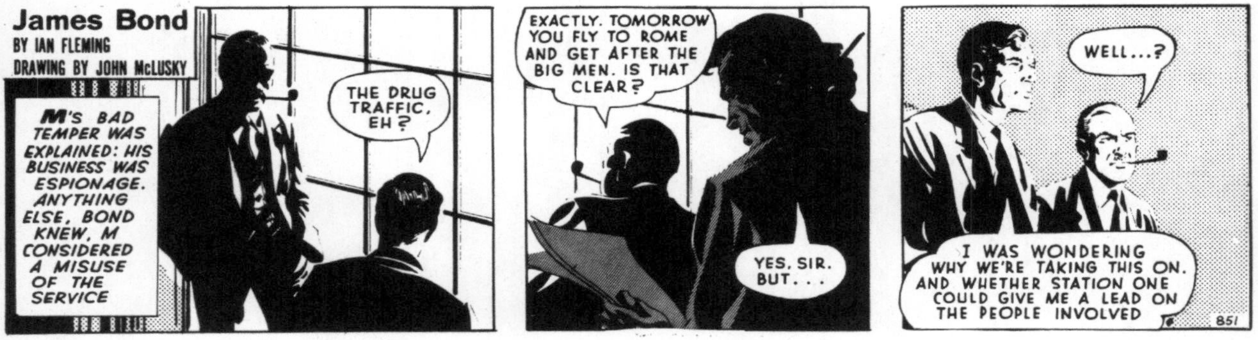
James Bond
BY IAN FLEMING
DRAWING BY JOHN McLUSKY
M'S BAD TEMPER WAS EXPLAINED: HIS BUSINESS WAS ESPIONAGE. ANYTHING ELSE, BOND KNEW, M CONSIDERED A MISUSE OF THE SERVICE
THE DRUG TRAFFIC, EH?
EXACTLY. TOMORROW YOU FLY TO ROME AND GET AFTER THE BIG MEN. IS THAT CLEAR?
YES, SIR. BUT...
WELL...?
I WAS WONDERING WHY WE'RE TAKING THIS ON. AND WHETHER STATION ONE COULD GIVE ME A LEAD ON THE PEOPLE INVOLVED
851

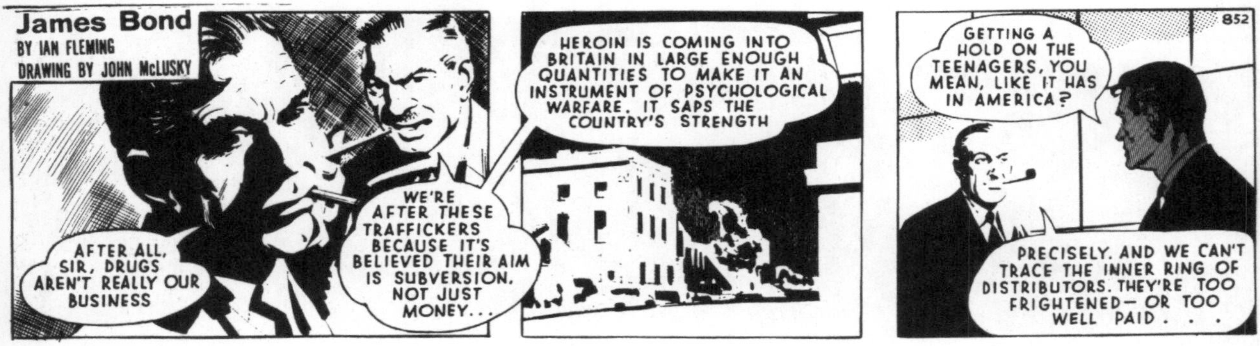
James Bond
BY IAN FLEMING
DRAWING BY JOHN McLUSKY
AFTER ALL, SIR, DRUGS AREN'T REALLY OUR BUSINESS
WE'RE AFTER THESE TRAFFICKERS BECAUSE IT'S BELIEVED THEIR AIM IS SUBVERSION. NOT JUST MONEY...
HEROIN IS COMING INTO BRITAIN IN LARGE ENOUGH QUANTITIES TO MAKE IT AN INSTRUMENT OF PSYCHOLOGICAL WARFARE. IT SAPS THE COUNTRY'S STRENGTH
852
GETTING A HOLD ON THE TEENAGERS, YOU MEAN, LIKE IT HAS IN AMERICA?
PRECISELY. AND WE CAN'T TRACE THE INNER RING OF DISTRIBUTORS. THEY'RE TOO FRIGHTENED— OR TOO WELL PAID . . .

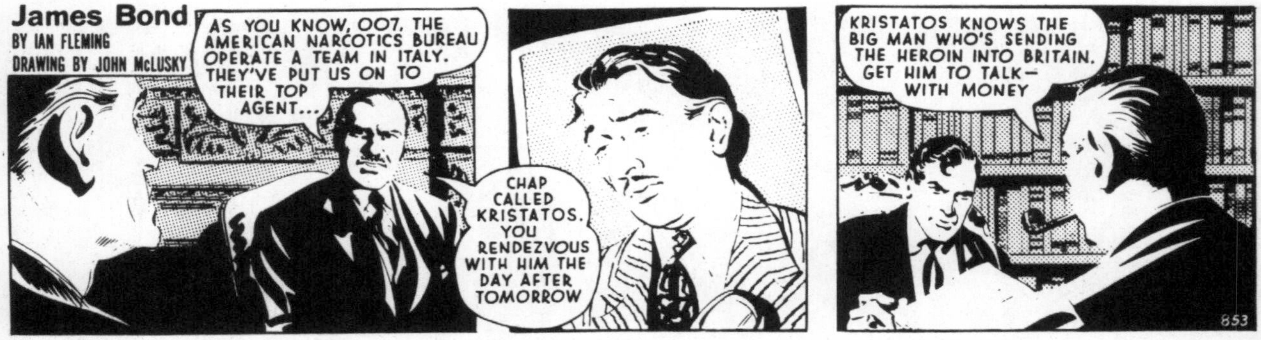
James Bond
BY IAN FLEMING
DRAWING BY JOHN McLUSKY
AS YOU KNOW, 007, THE AMERICAN NARCOTICS BUREAU OPERATE A TEAM IN ITALY. THEY'VE PUT US ON TO THEIR TOP AGENT...
CHAP CALLED KRISTATOS. YOU RENDEZVOUS WITH HIM THE DAY AFTER TOMORROW
KRISTATOS KNOWS THE BIG MAN WHO'S SENDING THE HEROIN INTO BRITAIN. GET HIM TO TALK— WITH MONEY
853

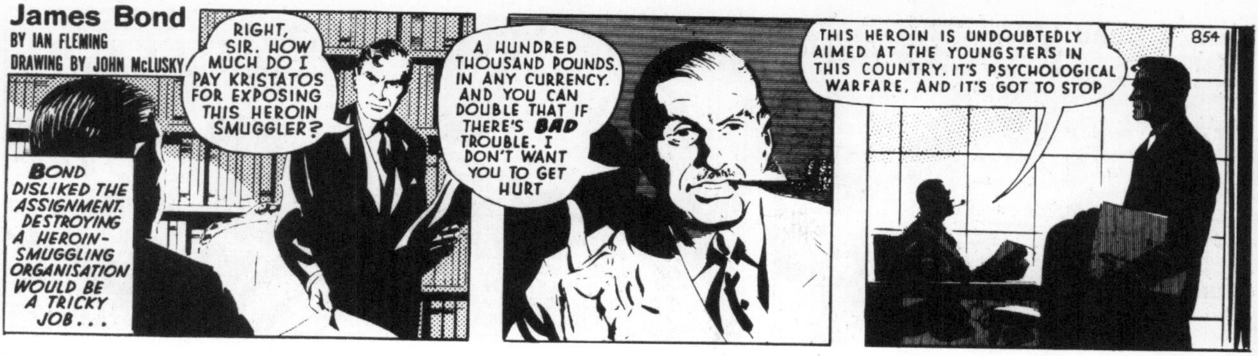
James Bond
BY IAN FLEMING
DRAWING BY JOHN McLUSKY
BOND DISLIKED THE ASSIGNMENT. DESTROYING A HEROIN-SMUGGLING ORGANISATION WOULD BE A TRICKY JOB . . .
RIGHT, SIR. HOW MUCH DO I PAY KRISTATOS FOR EXPOSING THIS HEROIN SMUGGLER?
A HUNDRED THOUSAND POUNDS. IN ANY CURRENCY. AND YOU CAN DOUBLE THAT IF THERE'S BAD TROUBLE. I DON'T WANT YOU TO GET HURT
854
THIS HEROIN IS UNDOUBTEDLY AIMED AT THE YOUNGSTERS IN THIS COUNTRY. IT'S PSYCHOLOGICAL WARFARE, AND IT'S GOT TO STOP

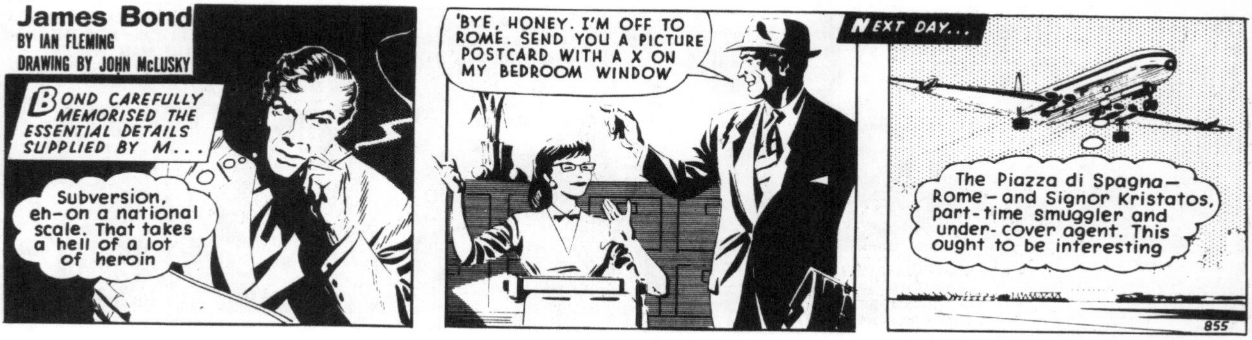
James Bond
BY IAN FLEMING
DRAWING BY JOHN McLUSKY
BOND CAREFULLY MEMORISED THE ESSENTIAL DETAILS SUPPLIED BY M . . .
Subversion, eh–on a national scale. That takes a hell of a lot of heroin
'BYE, HONEY. I'M OFF TO ROME. SEND YOU A PICTURE POSTCARD WITH A X ON MY BEDROOM WINDOW
NEXT DAY...
The Piazza di Spagna–Rome–and Signor Kristatos, part-time smuggler and under-cover agent. This ought to be interesting
855

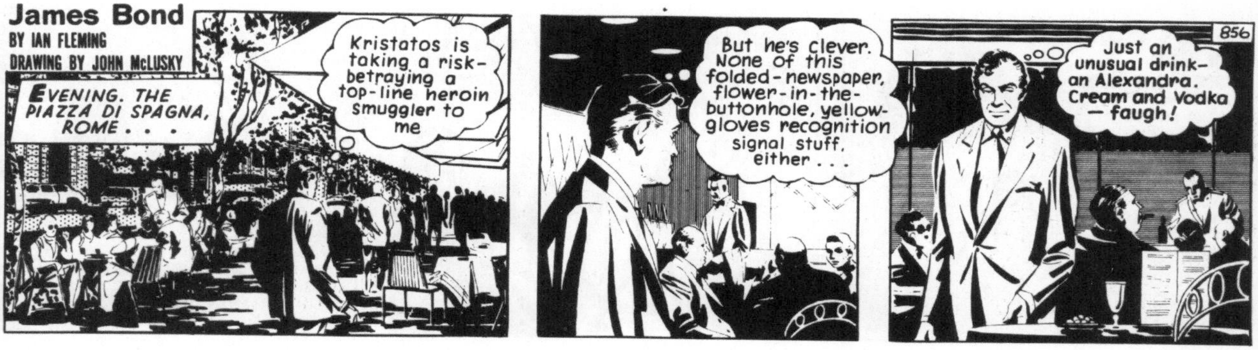
James Bond
BY IAN FLEMING
DRAWING BY JOHN McLUSKY
EVENING. THE PIAZZA DI SPAGNA, ROME . . .
Kristatos is taking a risk–betraying a top-line heroin smuggler to me
But he's clever. None of this folded-newspaper, flower-in-the-buttonhole, yellow-gloves recognition signal stuff, either . . .
856
Just an unusual drink–an Alexandra. Cream and Vodka –faugh!

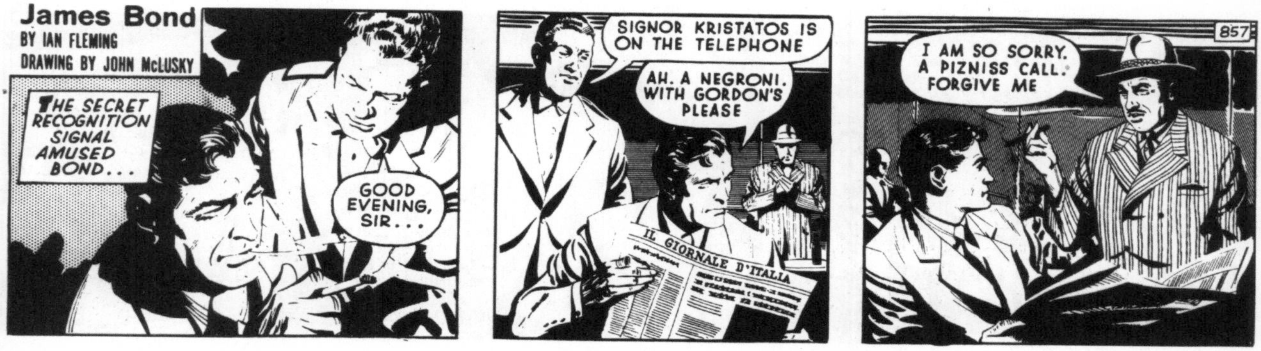
James Bond
BY IAN FLEMING
DRAWING BY JOHN McLUSKY
THE SECRET RECOGNITION SIGNAL AMUSED BOND . . .
GOOD EVENING, SIR . . .
SIGNOR KRISTATOS IS ON THE TELEPHONE
AH. A NEGRONI. WITH GORDON'S PLEASE
IL GIORNALE D'ITALIA
857
I AM SO SORRY. A PIZNISS CALL. FORGIVE ME

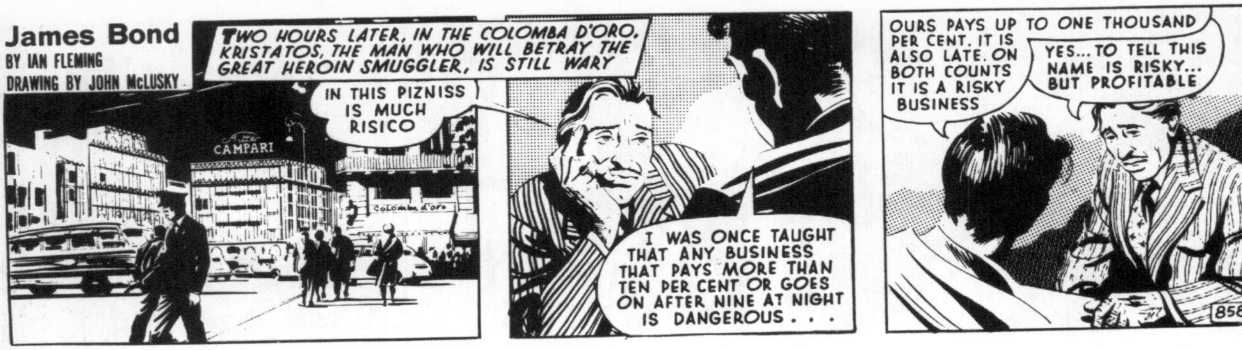
James Bond
BY IAN FLEMING
DRAWING BY JOHN McLUSKY
TWO HOURS LATER, IN THE COLOMBA D'ORO, KRISTATOS, THE MAN WHO WILL BETRAY THE GREAT HEROIN SMUGGLER, IS STILL WARY
IN THIS PIZNISS IS MUCH RISICO
CAMPARI
I WAS ONCE TAUGHT THAT ANY BUSINESS THAT PAYS MORE THAN TEN PER CENT OR GOES ON AFTER NINE AT NIGHT IS DANGEROUS . . .
OURS PAYS UP TO ONE THOUSAND PER CENT. IT IS ALSO LATE. ON BOTH COUNTS IT IS A RISKY BUSINESS
YES... TO TELL THIS NAME IS RISKY... BUT PROFITABLE
858

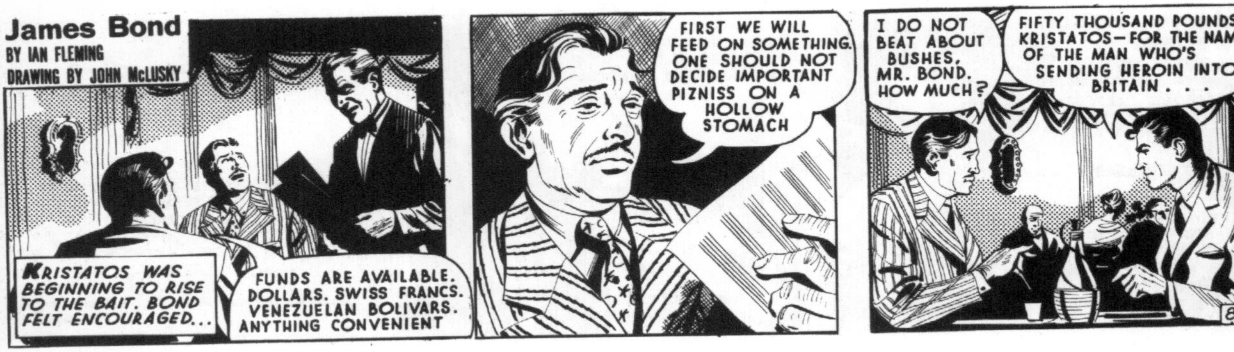
James Bond
BY IAN FLEMING
DRAWING BY JOHN McLUSKY
KRISTATOS WAS BEGINNING TO RISE TO THE BAIT. BOND FELT ENCOURAGED...
FUNDS ARE AVAILABLE. DOLLARS. SWISS FRANCS. VENEZUELAN BOLIVARS. ANYTHING CONVENIENT
FIRST WE WILL FEED ON SOMETHING. ONE SHOULD NOT DECIDE IMPORTANT PIZNISS ON A HOLLOW STOMACH
I DO NOT BEAT ABOUT BUSHES, MR. BOND. HOW MUCH?
FIFTY THOUSAND POUNDS, KRISTATOS—FOR THE NAME OF THE MAN WHO'S SENDING HEROIN INTO BRITAIN . . .
859

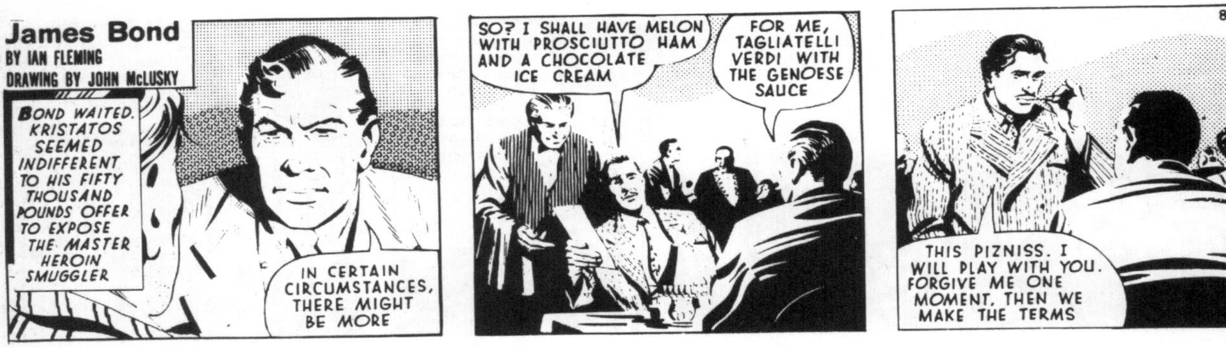
James Bond
BY IAN FLEMING
DRAWING BY JOHN McLUSKY
BOND WAITED. KRISTATOS SEEMED INDIFFERENT TO HIS FIFTY THOUSAND POUNDS OFFER TO EXPOSE THE MASTER HEROIN SMUGGLER
IN CERTAIN CIRCUMSTANCES, THERE MIGHT BE MORE
SO? I SHALL HAVE MELON WITH PROSCIUTTO HAM AND A CHOCOLATE ICE CREAM
FOR ME, TAGLIATELLI VERDI WITH THE GENOESE SAUCE
860
THIS PIZNISS. I WILL PLAY WITH YOU. FORGIVE ME ONE MOMENT, THEN WE MAKE THE TERMS

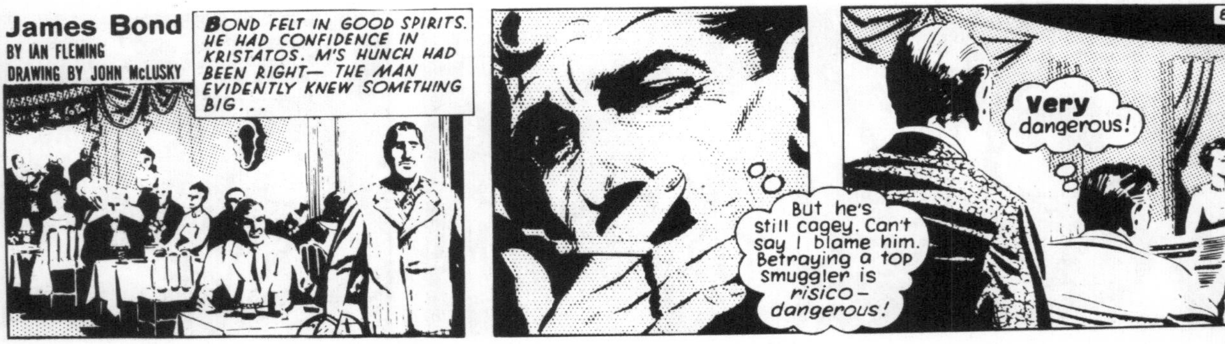
James Bond
BY IAN FLEMING
DRAWING BY JOHN McLUSKY
BOND FELT IN GOOD SPIRITS. HE HAD CONFIDENCE IN KRISTATOS. M'S HUNCH HAD BEEN RIGHT— THE MAN EVIDENTLY KNEW SOMETHING BIG...
But he's still cagey. Can't say I blame him. Betraying a top smuggler is risico—dangerous!
861
Very dangerous!

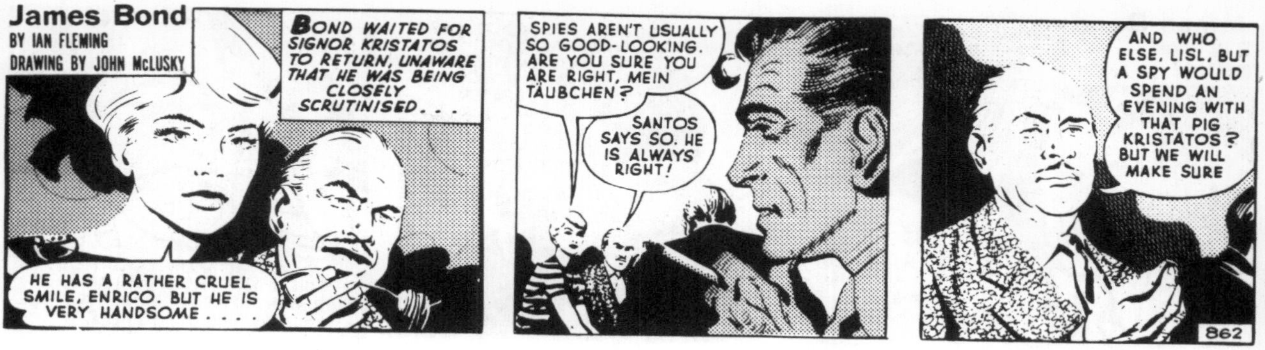
James Bond
BY IAN FLEMING
DRAWING BY JOHN McLUSKY
BOND WAITED FOR SIGNOR KRISTATOS TO RETURN, UNAWARE THAT HE WAS BEING CLOSELY SCRUTINISED . . .
HE HAS A RATHER CRUEL SMILE, ENRICO. BUT HE IS VERY HANDSOME . . .
SPIES AREN'T USUALLY SO GOOD-LOOKING. ARE YOU SURE YOU ARE RIGHT, MEIN TÄUBCHEN?
SANTOS SAYS SO. HE IS ALWAYS RIGHT!
AND WHO ELSE, LISL, BUT A SPY WOULD SPEND AN EVENING WITH THAT PIG KRISTATOS? BUT WE WILL MAKE SURE
862

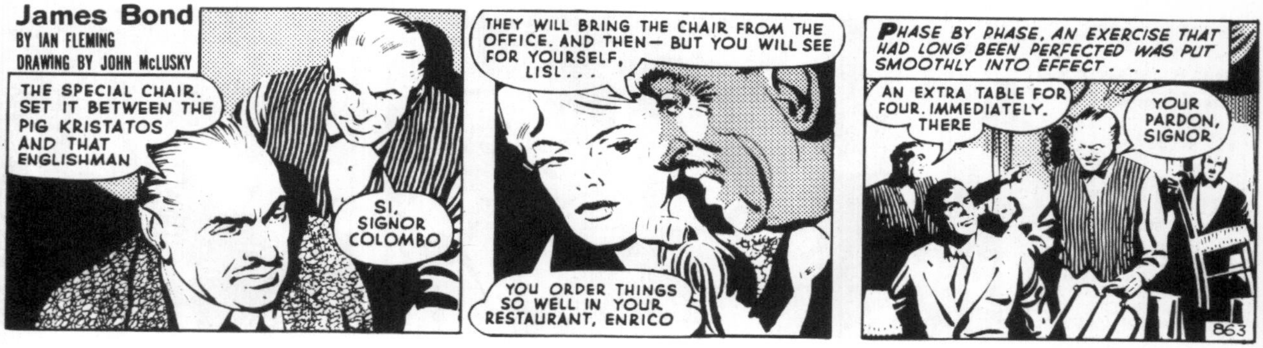
James Bond
BY IAN FLEMING
DRAWING BY JOHN McLUSKY
THE SPECIAL CHAIR. SET IT BETWEEN THE PIG KRISTATOS AND THAT ENGLISHMAN
SI, SIGNOR COLOMBO
THEY WILL BRING THE CHAIR FROM THE OFFICE. AND THEN— BUT YOU WILL SEE FOR YOURSELF, LISL . . .
YOU ORDER THINGS SO WELL IN YOUR RESTAURANT, ENRICO
PHASE BY PHASE, AN EXERCISE THAT HAD LONG BEEN PERFECTED WAS PUT SMOOTHLY INTO EFFECT . . .
AN EXTRA TABLE FOR FOUR. IMMEDIATELY. THERE
YOUR PARDON, SIGNOR
863

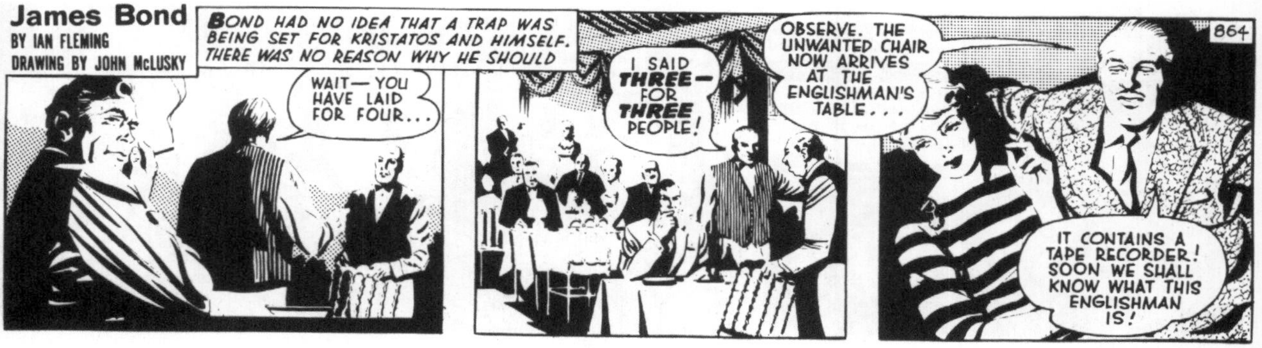
James Bond
BY IAN FLEMING
DRAWING BY JOHN McLUSKY
BOND HAD NO IDEA THAT A TRAP WAS BEING SET FOR KRISTATOS AND HIMSELF. THERE WAS NO REASON WHY HE SHOULD
WAIT— YOU HAVE LAID FOR FOUR...
I SAID THREE— FOR THREE PEOPLE!
OBSERVE. THE UNWANTED CHAIR NOW ARRIVES AT THE ENGLISHMAN'S TABLE . . .
IT CONTAINS A TAPE RECORDER! SOON WE SHALL KNOW WHAT THIS ENGLISHMAN IS!
864

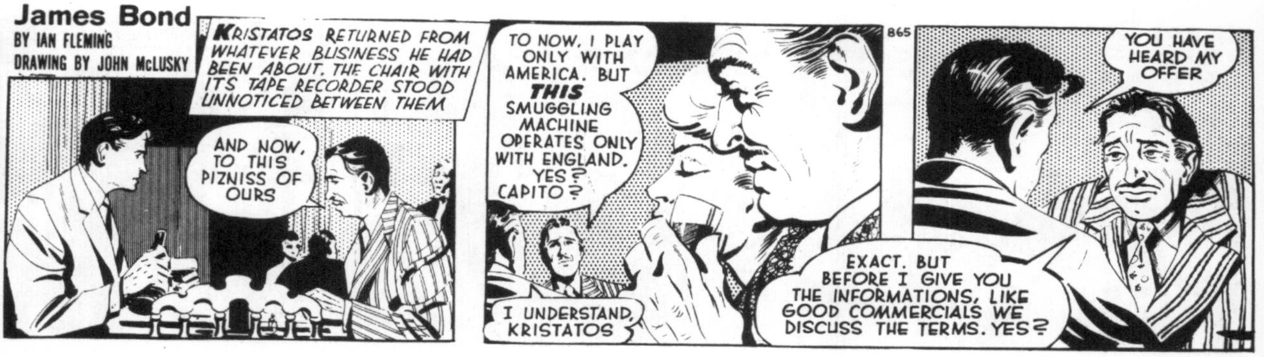
James Bond
BY IAN FLEMING
DRAWING BY JOHN McLUSKY
KRISTATOS RETURNED FROM WHATEVER BUSINESS HE HAD BEEN ABOUT. THE CHAIR WITH ITS TAPE RECORDER STOOD UNNOTICED BETWEEN THEM
AND NOW, TO THIS PIZNISS OF OURS
TO NOW, I PLAY ONLY WITH AMERICA. BUT THIS SMUGGLING MACHINE OPERATES ONLY WITH ENGLAND. YES? CAPITO?
I UNDERSTAND, KRISTATOS
865
YOU HAVE HEARD MY OFFER
EXACT. BUT BEFORE I GIVE YOU THE INFORMATIONS, LIKE GOOD COMMERCIALS WE DISCUSS THE TERMS. YES?

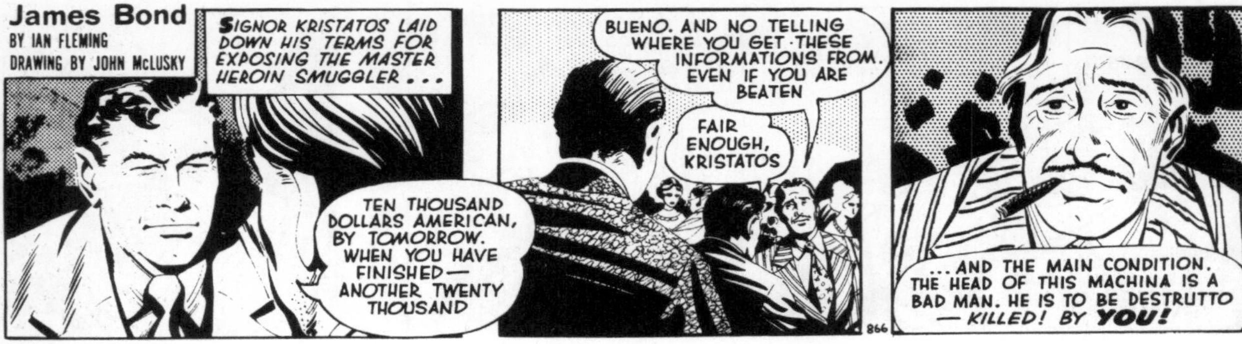
James Bond
BY IAN FLEMING
DRAWING BY JOHN McLUSKY
SIGNOR KRISTATOS LAID DOWN HIS TERMS FOR EXPOSING THE MASTER HEROIN SMUGGLER . . .
TEN THOUSAND DOLLARS AMERICAN, BY TOMORROW. WHEN YOU HAVE FINISHED— ANOTHER TWENTY THOUSAND
BUENO. AND NO TELLING WHERE YOU GET THESE INFORMATIONS FROM. EVEN IF YOU ARE BEATEN
FAIR ENOUGH, KRISTATOS
866
...AND THE MAIN CONDITION. THE HEAD OF THIS MACHINA IS A BAD MAN. HE IS TO BE DESTRUTTO — KILLED! BY YOU!

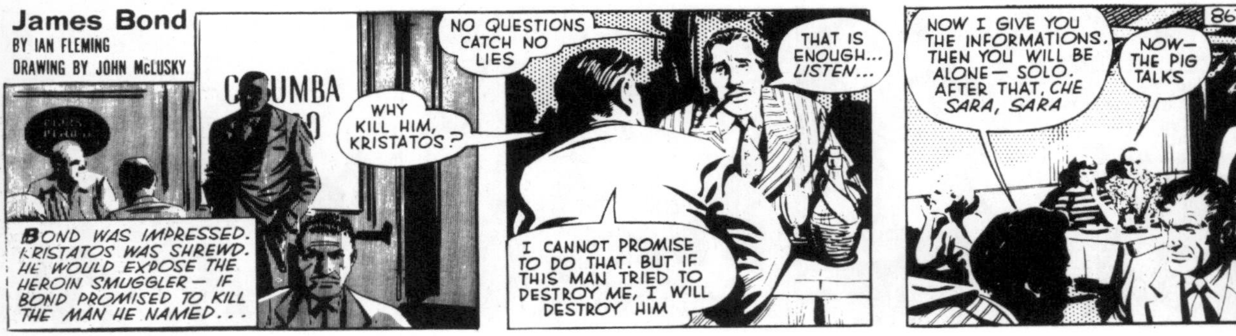
James Bond
BY IAN FLEMING
DRAWING BY JOHN McLUSKY
WHY KILL HIM, KRISTATOS?
BOND WAS IMPRESSED. KRISTATOS WAS SHREWD. HE WOULD EXPOSE THE HEROIN SMUGGLER— IF BOND PROMISED TO KILL THE MAN HE NAMED . . .
NO QUESTIONS CATCH NO LIES
THAT IS ENOUGH... LISTEN...
I CANNOT PROMISE TO DO THAT. BUT IF THIS MAN TRIED TO DESTROY ME, I WILL DESTROY HIM
867
NOW I GIVE YOU THE INFORMATIONS. THEN YOU WILL BE ALONE— SOLO. AFTER THAT, CHE SARA, SARA
NOW— THE PIG TALKS

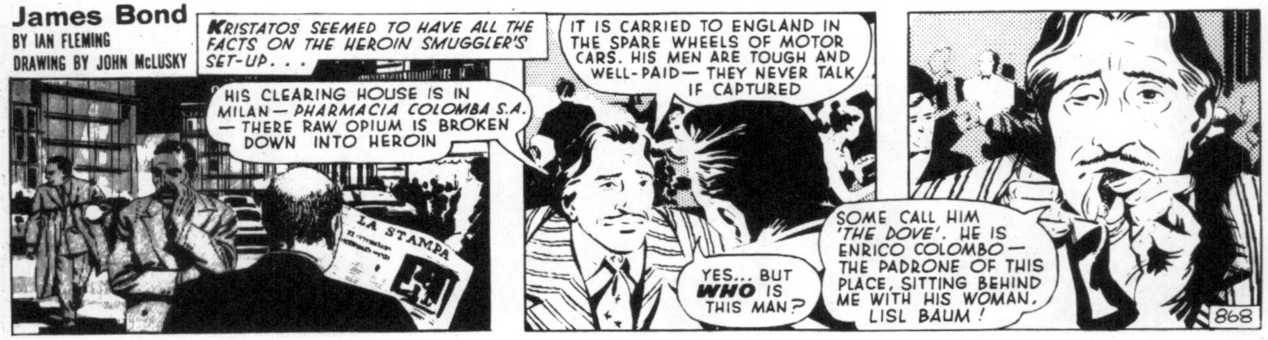
James Bond
BY IAN FLEMING
DRAWING BY JOHN McLUSKY
KRISTATOS SEEMED TO HAVE ALL THE FACTS ON THE HEROIN SMUGGLER'S SET-UP . . .
HIS CLEARING HOUSE IS IN MILAN— PHARMACIA COLOMBA S.A. — THERE RAW OPIUM IS BROKEN DOWN INTO HEROIN
LA STAMPA
IT IS CARRIED TO ENGLAND IN THE SPARE WHEELS OF MOTOR CARS. HIS MEN ARE TOUGH AND WELL-PAID— THEY NEVER TALK IF CAPTURED
YES... BUT WHO IS THIS MAN?
SOME CALL HIM 'THE DOVE'. HE IS ENRICO COLOMBO— THE PADRONE OF THIS PLACE, SITTING BEHIND ME WITH HIS WOMAN, LISL BAUM!
868

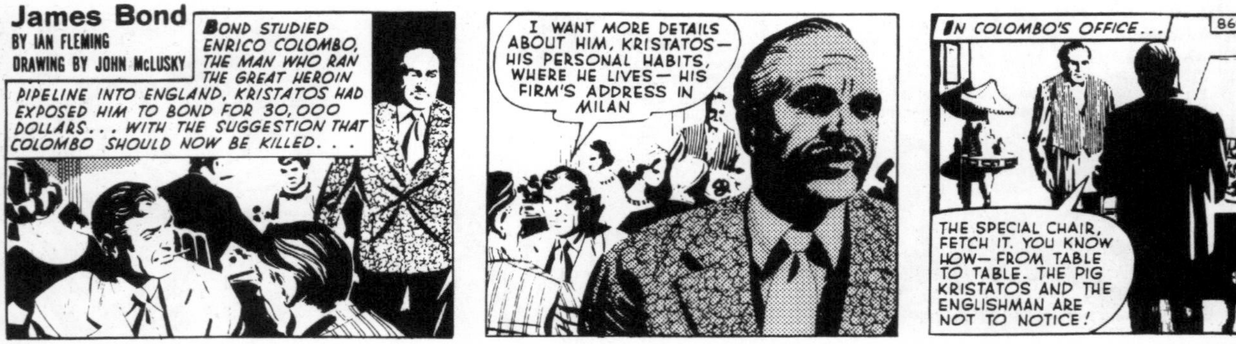
James Bond
BY IAN FLEMING
DRAWING BY JOHN McLUSKY
BOND STUDIED ENRICO COLOMBO, THE MAN WHO RAN THE GREAT HEROIN PIPELINE INTO ENGLAND, KRISTATOS HAD EXPOSED HIM TO BOND FOR 30,000 DOLLARS . . . WITH THE SUGGESTION THAT COLOMBO SHOULD NOW BE KILLED . . .
I WANT MORE DETAILS ABOUT HIM, KRISTATOS— HIS PERSONAL HABITS, WHERE HE LIVES— HIS FIRM'S ADDRESS IN MILAN
IN COLOMBO'S OFFICE . . .
869
THE SPECIAL CHAIR, FETCH IT. YOU KNOW HOW— FROM TABLE TO TABLE. THE PIG KRISTATOS AND THE ENGLISHMAN ARE NOT TO NOTICE!

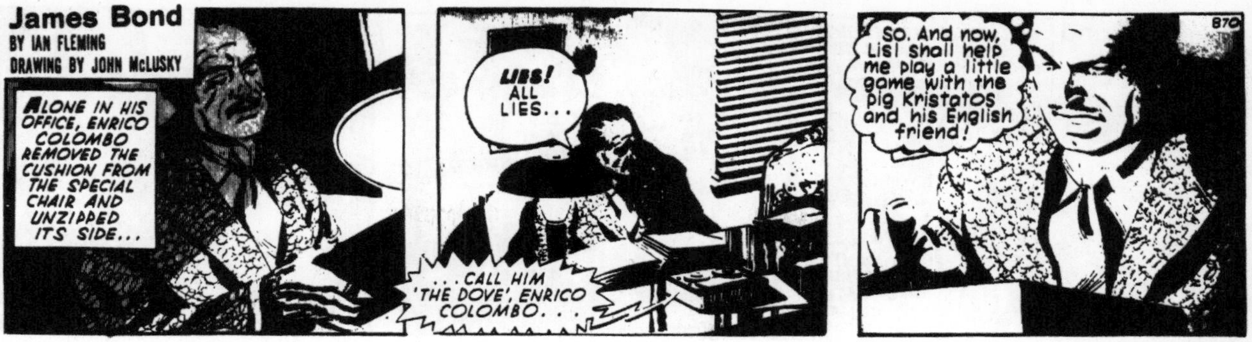
James Bond
BY IAN FLEMING
DRAWING BY JOHN McLUSKY
ALONE IN HIS OFFICE, ENRICO COLOMBO REMOVED THE CUSHION FROM THE SPECIAL CHAIR AND UNZIPPED ITS SIDE...
LIES! ALL LIES...
...CALL HIM 'THE DOVE', ENRICO COLOMBO...
870
So. And now, Lisl shall help me play a little game with the pig Kristatos and his English friend!

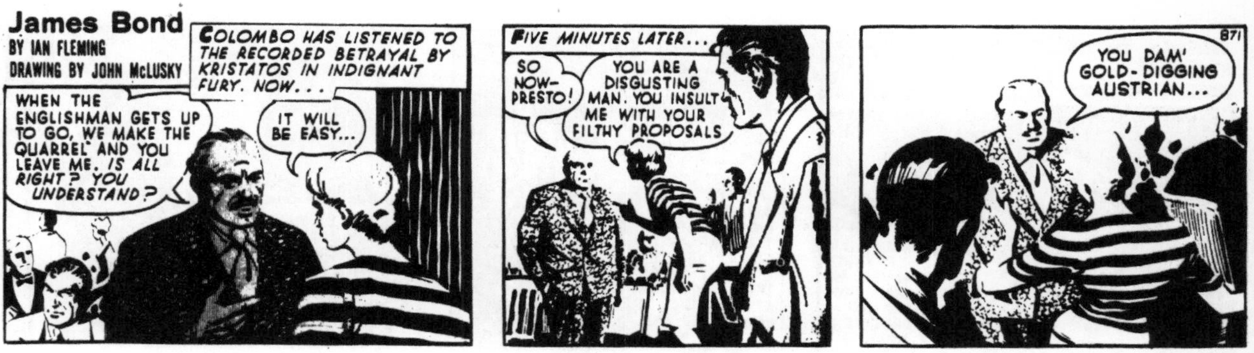
James Bond
BY IAN FLEMING
DRAWING BY JOHN McLUSKY
COLOMBO HAS LISTENED TO THE RECORDED BETRAYAL BY KRISTATOS IN INDIGNANT FURY. NOW...
WHEN THE ENGLISHMAN GETS UP TO GO, WE MAKE THE QUARREL AND YOU LEAVE ME. IS ALL RIGHT? YOU UNDERSTAND?
IT WILL BE EASY...
FIVE MINUTES LATER...
SO NOW-PRESTO!
YOU ARE A DISGUSTING MAN. YOU INSULT ME WITH YOUR FILTHY PROPOSALS
871
YOU DAM' GOLD-DIGGING AUSTRIAN...

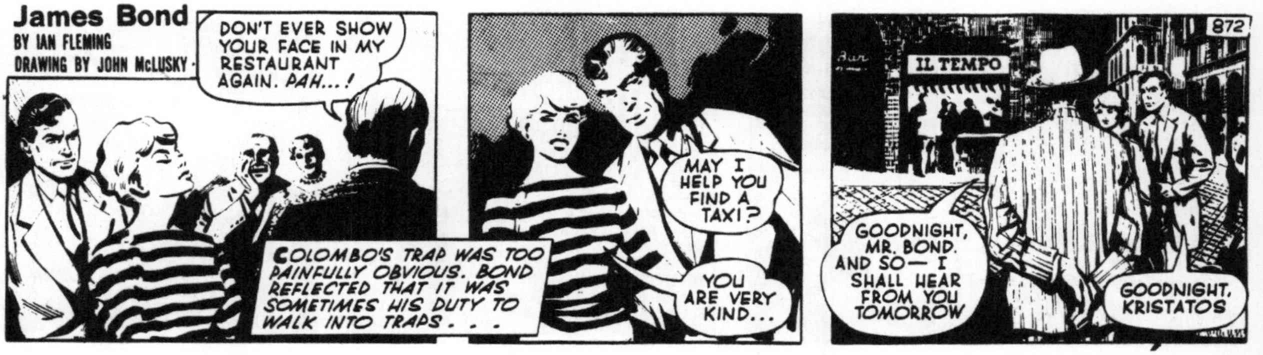
James Bond
BY IAN FLEMING
DRAWING BY JOHN McLUSKY
DON'T EVER SHOW YOUR FACE IN MY RESTAURANT AGAIN. PAH...!
COLOMBO'S TRAP WAS TOO PAINFULLY OBVIOUS. BOND REFLECTED THAT IT WAS SOMETIMES HIS DUTY TO WALK INTO TRAPS...
MAY I HELP YOU FIND A TAXI?
YOU ARE VERY KIND...
872
IL TEMPO
GOODNIGHT, MR. BOND. AND SO— I SHALL HEAR FROM YOU TOMORROW
GOODNIGHT, KRISTATOS

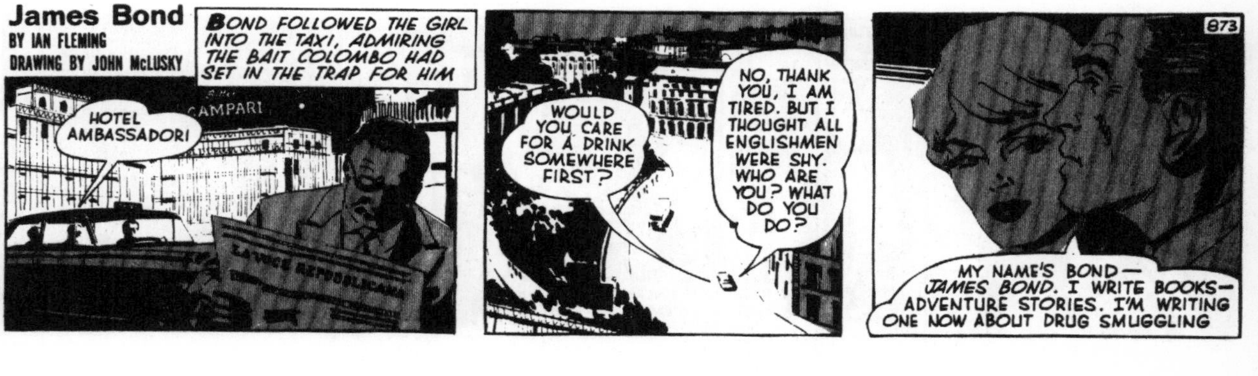
James Bond
BY IAN FLEMING
DRAWING BY JOHN McLUSKY
BOND FOLLOWED THE GIRL INTO THE TAXI, ADMIRING THE BAIT COLOMBO HAD SET IN THE TRAP FOR HIM
CAMPARI
HOTEL AMBASSADORI
WOULD YOU CARE FOR A DRINK SOMEWHERE FIRST?
NO, THANK YOU, I AM TIRED. BUT I THOUGHT ALL ENGLISHMEN WERE SHY. WHO ARE YOU? WHAT DO YOU DO?
873
MY NAME'S BOND— JAMES BOND. I WRITE BOOKS— ADVENTURE STORIES. I'M WRITING ONE NOW ABOUT DRUG SMUGGLING

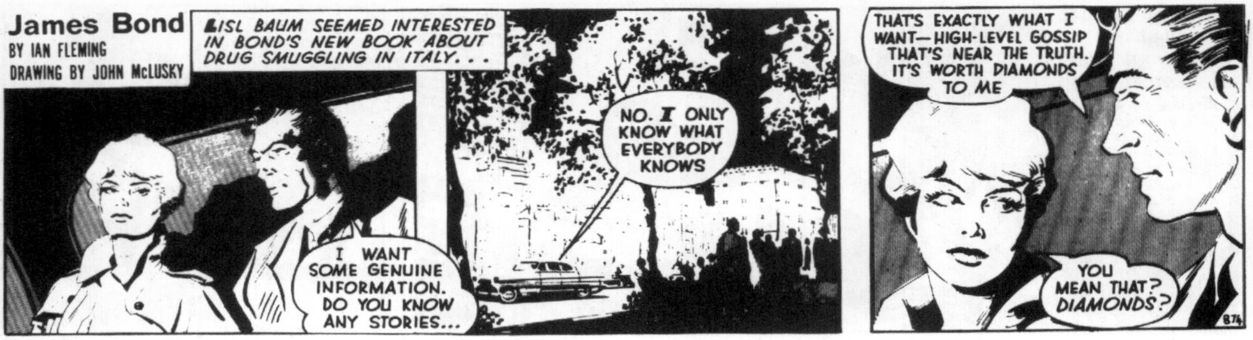
James Bond
BY IAN FLEMING
DRAWING BY JOHN McLUSKY
LISL BAUM SEEMED INTERESTED IN BOND'S NEW BOOK ABOUT DRUG SMUGGLING IN ITALY...
I WANT SOME GENUINE INFORMATION. DO YOU KNOW ANY STORIES...
NO. I ONLY KNOW WHAT EVERYBODY KNOWS
THAT'S EXACTLY WHAT I WANT—HIGH-LEVEL GOSSIP THAT'S NEAR THE TRUTH. IT'S WORTH DIAMONDS TO ME
YOU MEAN THAT? DIAMONDS?
874

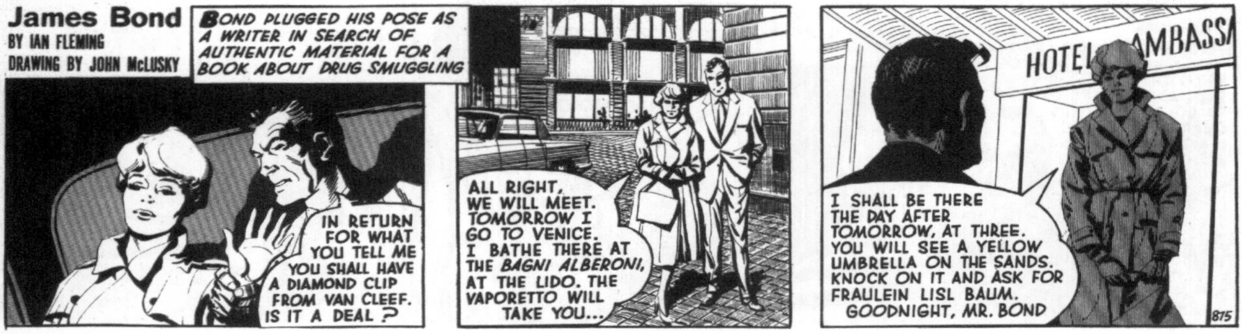
James Bond
BY IAN FLEMING
DRAWING BY JOHN McLUSKY
BOND PLUGGED HIS POSE AS A WRITER IN SEARCH OF AUTHENTIC MATERIAL FOR A BOOK ABOUT DRUG SMUGGLING
IN RETURN FOR WHAT YOU TELL ME YOU SHALL HAVE A DIAMOND CLIP FROM VAN CLEEF. IS IT A DEAL?
ALL RIGHT, WE WILL MEET. TOMORROW I GO TO VENICE. I BATHE THERE AT THE BAGNI ALBERONI, AT THE LIDO. THE VAPORETTO WILL TAKE YOU...
HOTEL AMBASS
I SHALL BE THERE THE DAY AFTER TOMORROW, AT THREE. YOU WILL SEE A YELLOW UMBRELLA ON THE SANDS. KNOCK ON IT AND ASK FOR FRAULEIN LISL BAUM. GOODNIGHT, MR. BOND
875

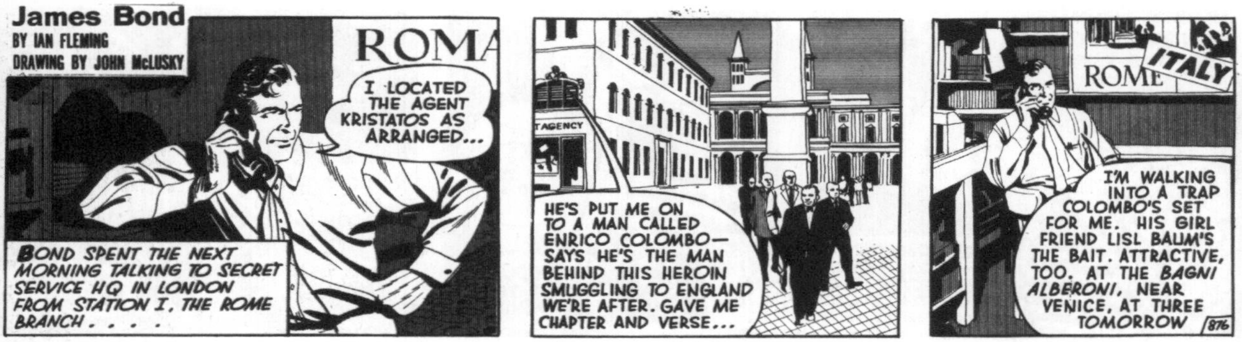
James Bond
BY IAN FLEMING
DRAWING BY JOHN McLUSKY
ROMA
I LOCATED THE AGENT KRISTATOS AS ARRANGED...
BOND SPENT THE NEXT MORNING TALKING TO SECRET SERVICE HQ IN LONDON FROM STATION I, THE ROME BRANCH...
AGENCY
HE'S PUT ME ON TO A MAN CALLED ENRICO COLOMBO—SAYS HE'S THE MAN BEHIND THIS HEROIN SMUGGLING TO ENGLAND WE'RE AFTER. GAVE ME CHAPTER AND VERSE...
ROME
ITALY
I'M WALKING INTO A TRAP COLOMBO'S SET FOR ME. HIS GIRL FRIEND LISL BAUM'S THE BAIT. ATTRACTIVE, TOO. AT THE BAGNI ALBERONI, NEAR VENICE, AT THREE TOMORROW
876

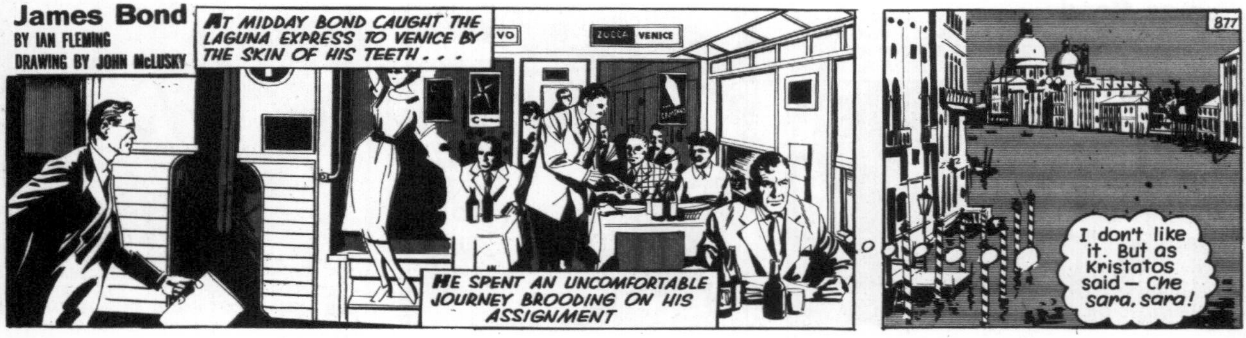
James Bond
BY IAN FLEMING
DRAWING BY JOHN McLUSKY
AT MIDDAY BOND CAUGHT THE LAGUNA EXPRESS TO VENICE BY THE SKIN OF HIS TEETH...
VENICE
HE SPENT AN UNCOMFORTABLE JOURNEY BROODING ON HIS ASSIGNMENT
877
I don't like it. But as Kristatos said — Che sara, sara!

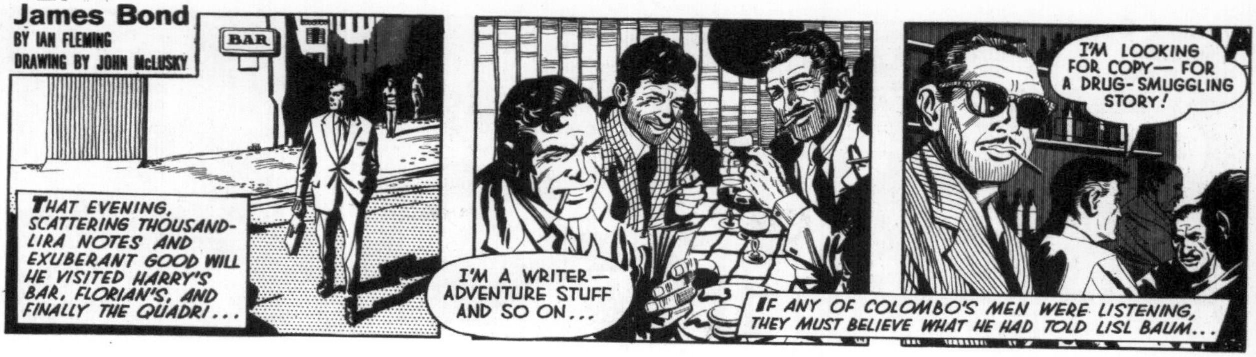

James Bond
BY IAN FLEMING
DRAWING BY JOHN McLUSKY
BAR
THAT EVENING, SCATTERING THOUSAND-LIRA NOTES AND EXUBERANT GOOD WILL HE VISITED HARRY'S BAR, FLORIAN'S, AND FINALLY THE QUADRI...
I'M A WRITER— ADVENTURE STUFF AND SO ON...
I'M LOOKING FOR COPY— FOR A DRUG-SMUGGLING STORY!
IF ANY OF COLOMBO'S MEN WERE LISTENING, THEY MUST BELIEVE WHAT HE HAD TOLD LISL BAUM...

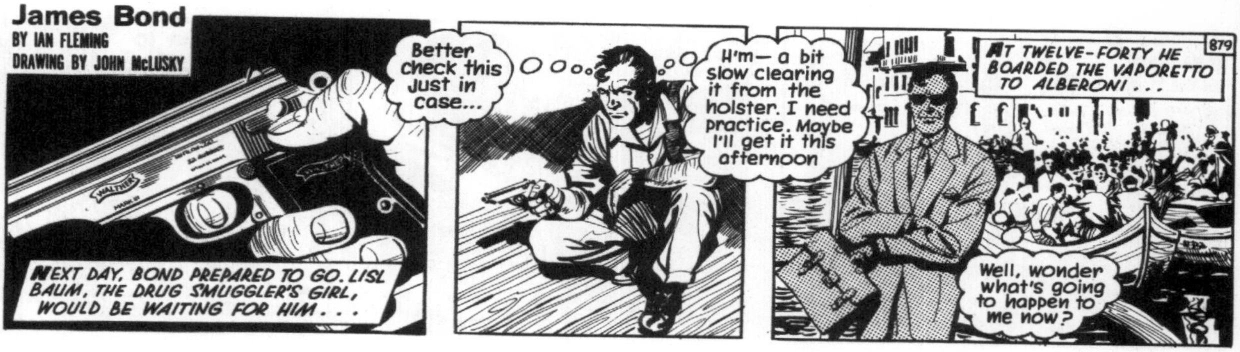

James Bond
BY IAN FLEMING
DRAWING BY JOHN McLUSKY
Better check this just in case...
NEXT DAY, BOND PREPARED TO GO. LISL BAUM, THE DRUG SMUGGLER'S GIRL, WOULD BE WAITING FOR HIM...
H'm— a bit slow clearing it from the holster. I need practice. Maybe I'll get it this afternoon
879
AT TWELVE-FORTY HE BOARDED THE VAPORETTO TO ALBERONI...
Well, wonder what's going to happen to me now?

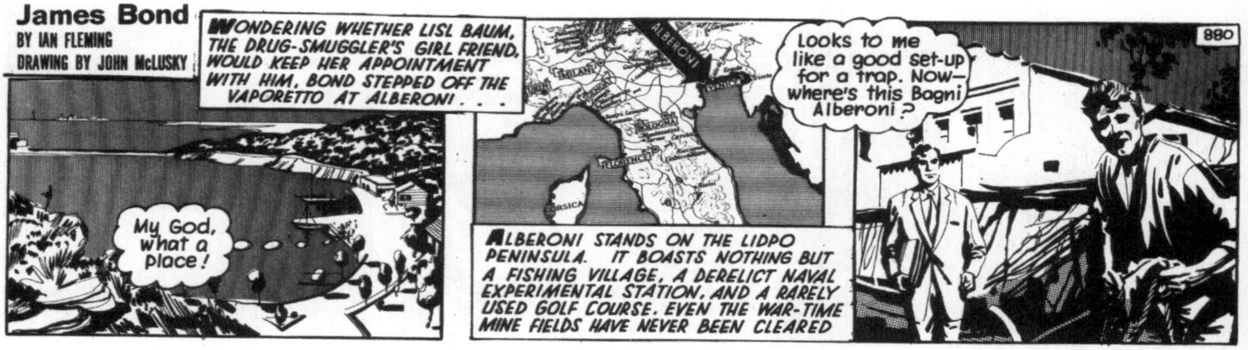

James Bond
BY IAN FLEMING
DRAWING BY JOHN McLUSKY
WONDERING WHETHER LISL BAUM, THE DRUG-SMUGGLER'S GIRL FRIEND, WOULD KEEP HER APPOINTMENT WITH HIM, BOND STEPPED OFF THE VAPORETTO AT ALBERONI...
My God, what a place!
ALBERONI
MILAN
BOLOGNA
FLORENCE
CORSICA
ALBERONI STANDS ON THE LIDPO PENINSULA. IT BOASTS NOTHING BUT A FISHING VILLAGE, A DERELICT NAVAL EXPERIMENTAL STATION, AND A RARELY USED GOLF COURSE. EVEN THE WAR-TIME MINE FIELDS HAVE NEVER BEEN CLEARED
880
Looks to me like a good set-up for a trap. Now— where's this Bagni Alberoni?

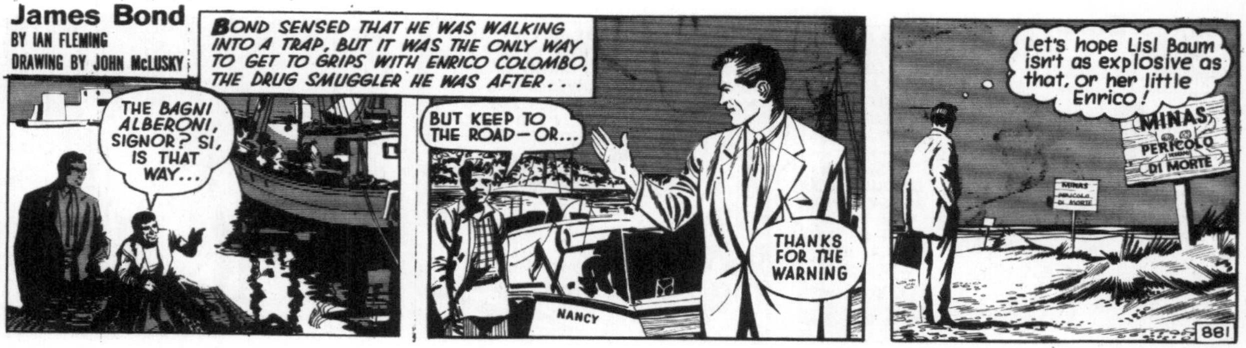

James Bond
BY IAN FLEMING
DRAWING BY JOHN McLUSKY
BOND SENSED THAT HE WAS WALKING INTO A TRAP, BUT IT WAS THE ONLY WAY TO GET TO GRIPS WITH ENRICO COLOMBO, THE DRUG SMUGGLER HE WAS AFTER...
THE BAGNI ALBERONI, SIGNOR? SI, IS THAT WAY...
BUT KEEP TO THE ROAD—OR...
THANKS FOR THE WARNING
NANCY
Let's hope Lisl Baum isn't as explosive as that, or her little Enrico!
MINAS
PERICOLO
DI MORTE
881

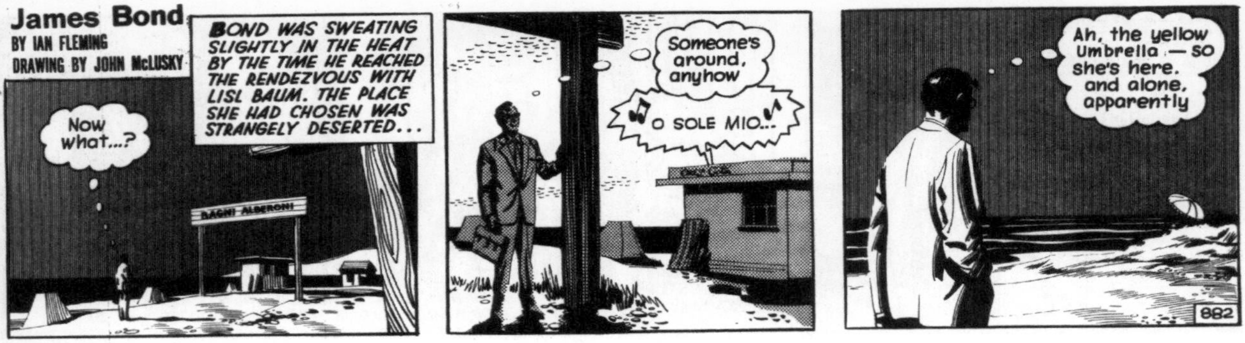
James Bond
BY IAN FLEMING
DRAWING BY JOHN McLUSKY
BOND WAS SWEATING SLIGHTLY IN THE HEAT BY THE TIME HE REACHED THE RENDEZVOUS WITH LISL BAUM. THE PLACE SHE HAD CHOSEN WAS STRANGELY DESERTED...
Now what...?
BAGNI ALBERONI
Someone's around, anyhow
O SOLE MIO...
Ah, the yellow umbrella — so she's here. and alone, apparently
882

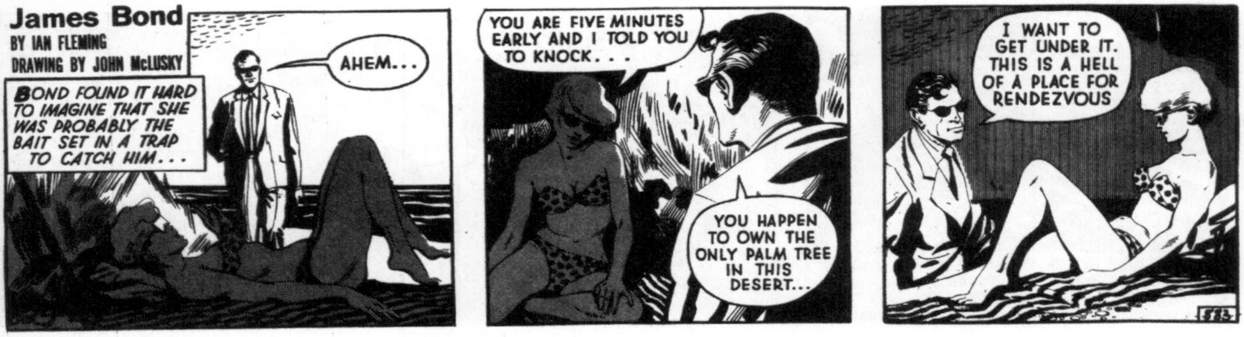
James Bond
BY IAN FLEMING
DRAWING BY JOHN McLUSKY
BOND FOUND IT HARD TO IMAGINE THAT SHE WAS PROBABLY THE BAIT SET IN A TRAP TO CATCH HIM...
AHEM...
YOU ARE FIVE MINUTES EARLY AND I TOLD YOU TO KNOCK...
YOU HAPPEN TO OWN THE ONLY PALM TREE IN THIS DESERT...
I WANT TO GET UNDER IT. THIS IS A HELL OF A PLACE FOR RENDEZVOUS

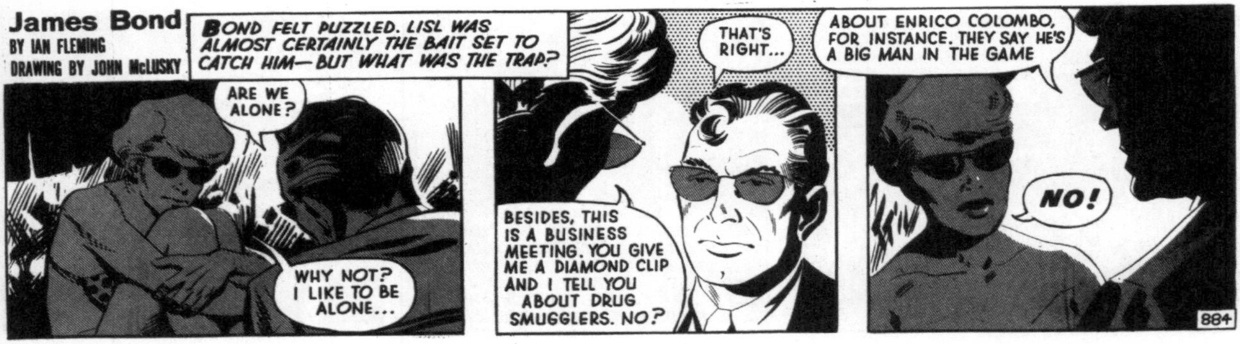
James Bond
BY IAN FLEMING
DRAWING BY JOHN McLUSKY
BOND FELT PUZZLED. LISL WAS ALMOST CERTAINLY THE BAIT SET TO CATCH HIM— BUT WHAT WAS THE TRAP?
ARE WE ALONE?
WHY NOT? I LIKE TO BE ALONE...
THAT'S RIGHT...
BESIDES, THIS IS A BUSINESS MEETING. YOU GIVE ME A DIAMOND CLIP AND I TELL YOU ABOUT DRUG SMUGGLERS. NO?
ABOUT ENRICO COLOMBO, FOR INSTANCE. THEY SAY HE'S A BIG MAN IN THE GAME
NO!
884

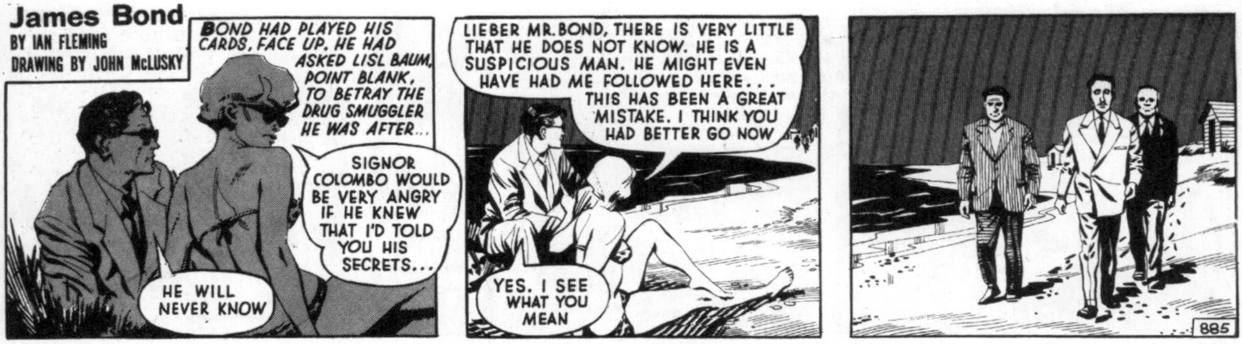
James Bond
BY IAN FLEMING
DRAWING BY JOHN McLUSKY
BOND HAD PLAYED HIS CARDS, FACE UP. HE HAD ASKED LISL BAUM, POINT BLANK, TO BETRAY THE DRUG SMUGGLER HE WAS AFTER...
SIGNOR COLOMBO WOULD BE VERY ANGRY IF HE KNEW THAT I'D TOLD YOU HIS SECRETS...
HE WILL NEVER KNOW
LIEBER MR. BOND, THERE IS VERY LITTLE THAT HE DOES NOT KNOW. HE IS A SUSPICIOUS MAN. HE MIGHT EVEN HAVE HAD ME FOLLOWED HERE... THIS HAS BEEN A GREAT MISTAKE. I THINK YOU HAD BETTER GO NOW
YES. I SEE WHAT YOU MEAN
885

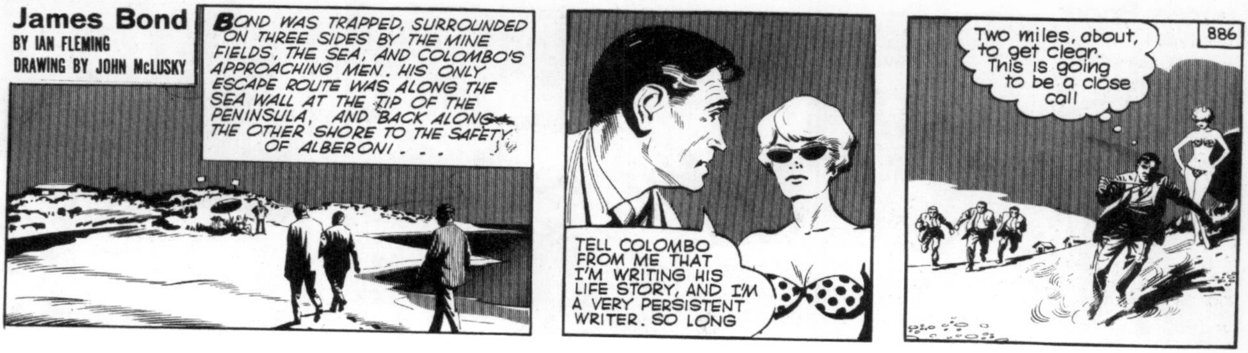
James Bond
BY IAN FLEMING
DRAWING BY JOHN McLUSKY
BOND WAS TRAPPED, SURROUNDED ON THREE SIDES BY THE MINE FIELDS, THE SEA, AND COLOMBO'S APPROACHING MEN. HIS ONLY ESCAPE ROUTE WAS ALONG THE SEA WALL AT THE TIP OF THE PENINSULA, AND BACK ALONG THE OTHER SHORE TO THE SAFETY OF ALBERONI . . .
TELL COLOMBO FROM ME THAT I'M WRITING HIS LIFE STORY, AND I'M A VERY PERSISTENT WRITER. SO LONG
886
Two miles, about, to get clear. This is going to be a close call

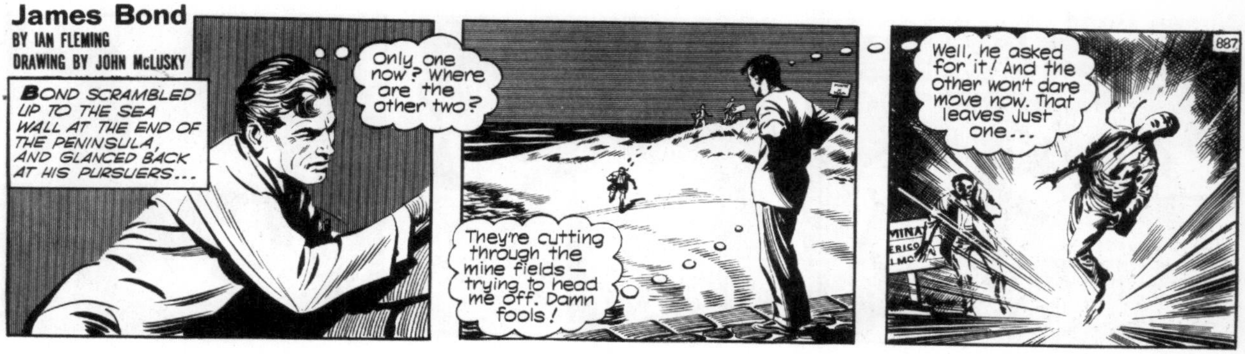
James Bond
BY IAN FLEMING
DRAWING BY JOHN McLUSKY
BOND SCRAMBLED UP TO THE SEA WALL AT THE END OF THE PENINSULA, AND GLANCED BACK AT HIS PURSUERS...
Only one now? Where are the other two?
They're cutting through the mine fields — trying to head me off. Damn fools!
887
Well, he asked for it! And the other won't dare move now. That leaves just one...

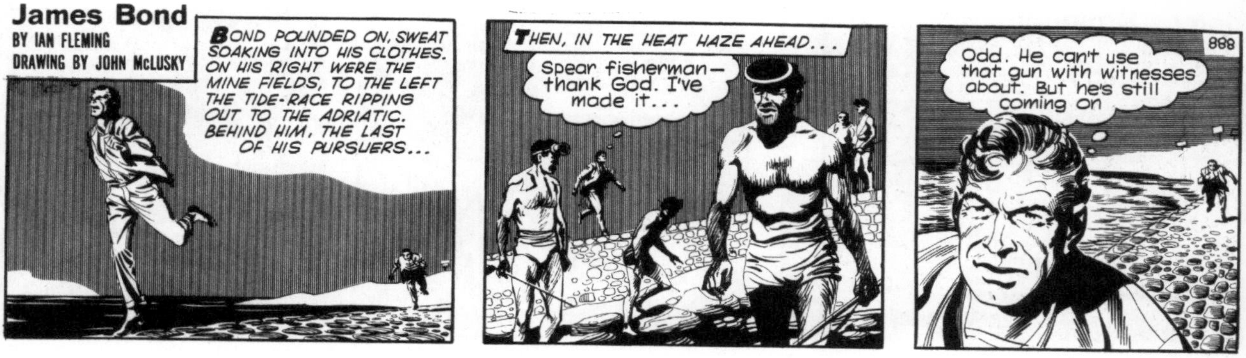
James Bond
BY IAN FLEMING
DRAWING BY JOHN McLUSKY
BOND POUNDED ON, SWEAT SOAKING INTO HIS CLOTHES. ON HIS RIGHT WERE THE MINE FIELDS, TO THE LEFT THE TIDE-RACE RIPPING OUT TO THE ADRIATIC. BEHIND HIM, THE LAST OF HIS PURSUERS...
THEN, IN THE HEAT HAZE AHEAD...
Spear fisherman — thank God. I've made it...
888
Odd. He can't use that gun with witnesses about. But he's still coming on

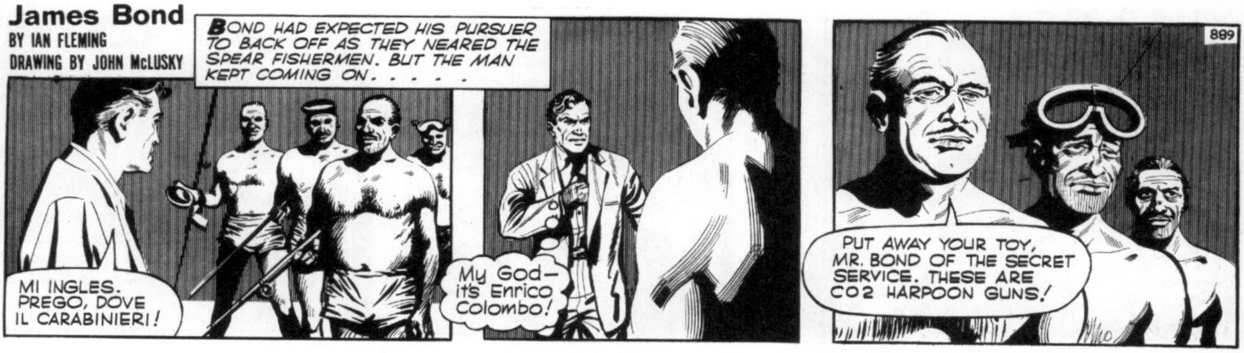
James Bond
BY IAN FLEMING
DRAWING BY JOHN McLUSKY
BOND HAD EXPECTED HIS PURSUER TO BACK OFF AS THEY NEARED THE SPEAR FISHERMEN. BUT THE MAN KEPT COMING ON. . . . .
MI INGLES. PREGO, DOVE IL CARABINIERI!
My God — it's Enrico Colombo!
889
PUT AWAY YOUR TOY, MR. BOND OF THE SECRET SERVICE. THESE ARE CO2 HARPOON GUNS!

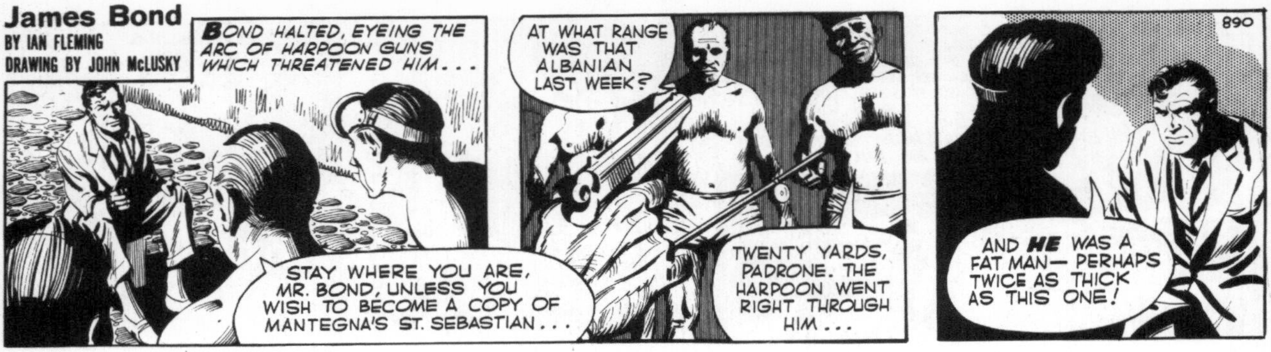
James Bond
BY IAN FLEMING
DRAWING BY JOHN McLUSKY
BOND HALTED, EYEING THE ARC OF HARPOON GUNS WHICH THREATENED HIM . . .
STAY WHERE YOU ARE, MR. BOND, UNLESS YOU WISH TO BECOME A COPY OF MANTEGNA'S ST. SEBASTIAN . . .
AT WHAT RANGE WAS THAT ALBANIAN LAST WEEK?
TWENTY YARDS, PADRONE. THE HARPOON WENT RIGHT THROUGH HIM . . .
890
AND HE WAS A FAT MAN— PERHAPS TWICE AS THICK AS THIS ONE!

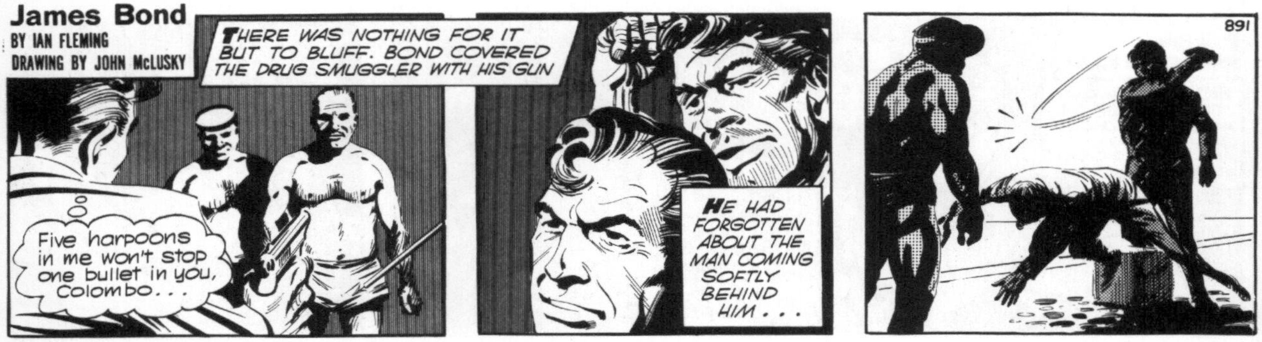
James Bond
BY IAN FLEMING
DRAWING BY JOHN McLUSKY
THERE WAS NOTHING FOR IT BUT TO BLUFF. BOND COVERED THE DRUG SMUGGLER WITH HIS GUN
Five harpoons in me won't stop one bullet in you, Colombo . . .
HE HAD FORGOTTEN ABOUT THE MAN COMING SOFTLY BEHIND HIM . . .
891

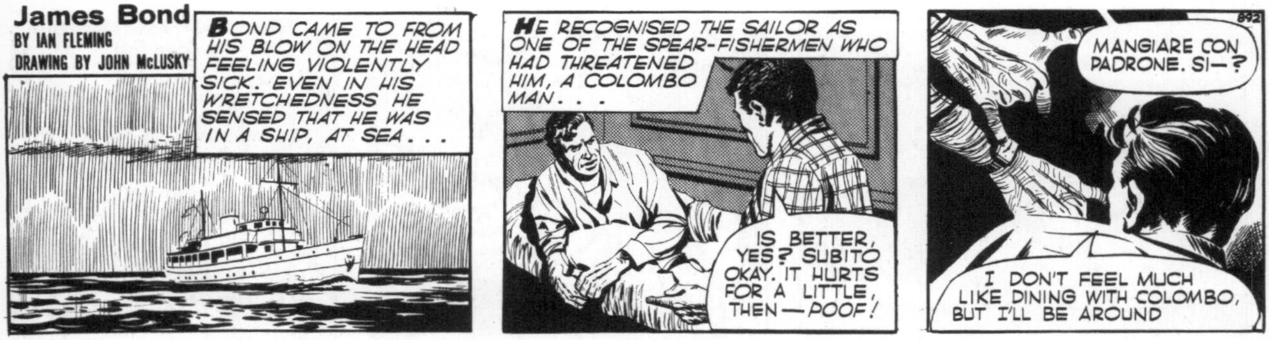
James Bond
BY IAN FLEMING
DRAWING BY JOHN McLUSKY
BOND CAME TO FROM HIS BLOW ON THE HEAD FEELING VIOLENTLY SICK. EVEN IN HIS WRETCHEDNESS HE SENSED THAT HE WAS IN A SHIP, AT SEA . . .
HE RECOGNISED THE SAILOR AS ONE OF THE SPEAR-FISHERMEN WHO HAD THREATENED HIM, A COLOMBO MAN . . .
IS BETTER, YES? SUBITO OKAY. IT HURTS FOR A LITTLE, THEN—POOF!
892
MANGIARE CON PADRONE. SI—?
I DON'T FEEL MUCH LIKE DINING WITH COLOMBO, BUT I'LL BE AROUND

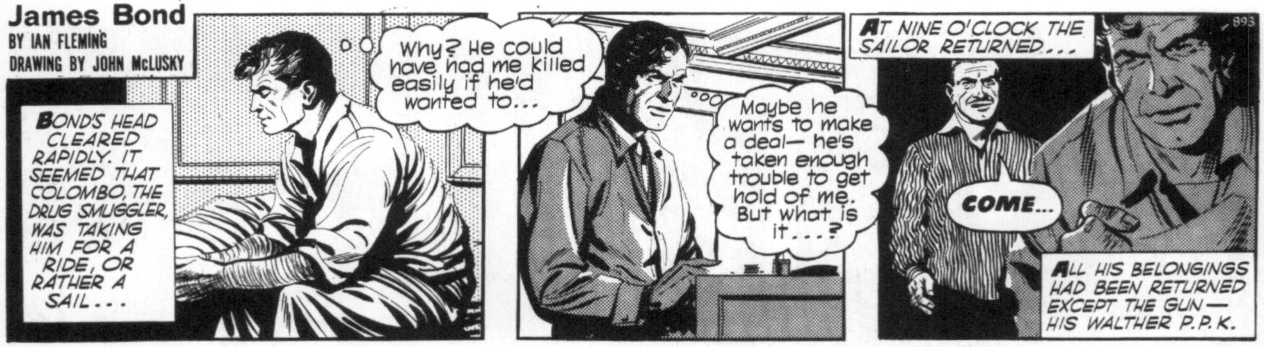
James Bond
BY IAN FLEMING
DRAWING BY JOHN McLUSKY
BOND'S HEAD CLEARED RAPIDLY. IT SEEMED THAT COLOMBO, THE DRUG SMUGGLER, WAS TAKING HIM FOR A RIDE, OR RATHER A SAIL . . .
Why? He could have had me killed easily if he'd wanted to...
Maybe he wants to make a deal— he's taken enough trouble to get hold of me. But what is it . . . ?
AT NINE O'CLOCK THE SAILOR RETURNED . . .
893
COME...
ALL HIS BELONGINGS HAD BEEN RETURNED EXCEPT THE GUN— HIS WALTHER P.P.K.

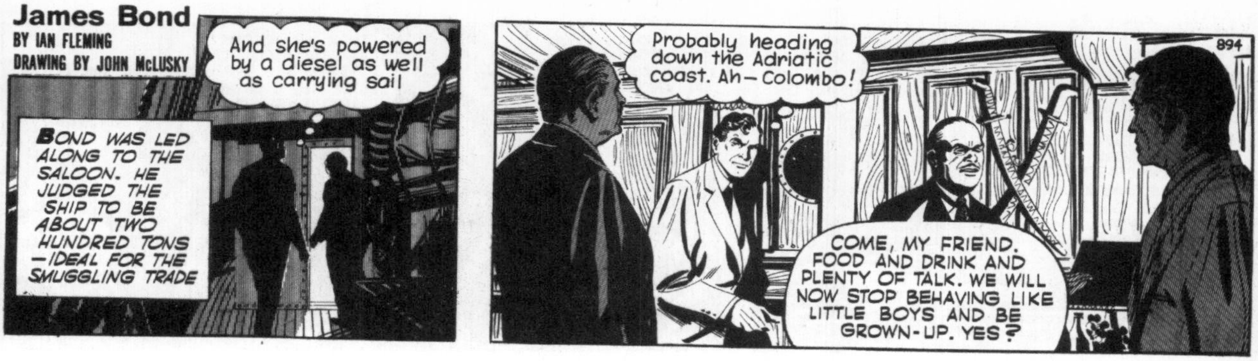
James Bond
BY IAN FLEMING
DRAWING BY JOHN McLUSKY
And she's powered by a diesel as well as carrying sail
BOND WAS LED ALONG TO THE SALOON. HE JUDGED THE SHIP TO BE ABOUT TWO HUNDRED TONS —IDEAL FOR THE SMUGGLING TRADE
Probably heading down the Adriatic coast. Ah—Colombo!
894
COME, MY FRIEND. FOOD AND DRINK AND PLENTY OF TALK. WE WILL NOW STOP BEHAVING LIKE LITTLE BOYS AND BE GROWN-UP. YES?

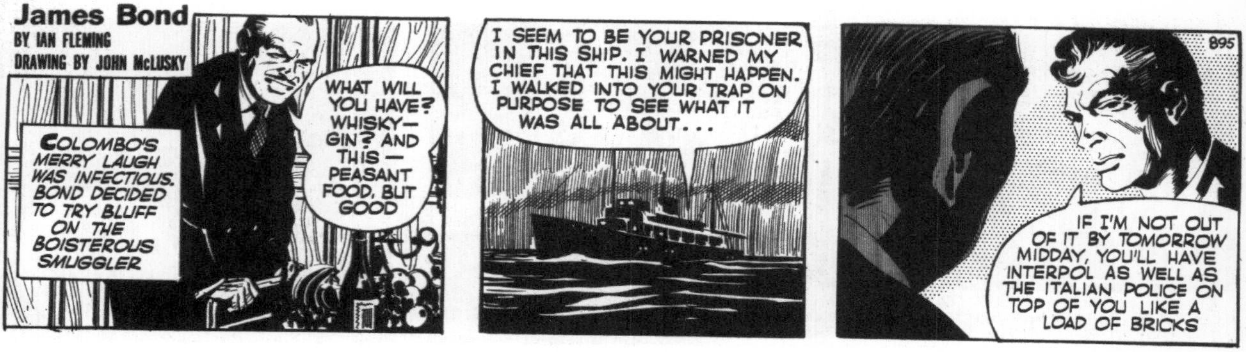
James Bond
BY IAN FLEMING
DRAWING BY JOHN McLUSKY
COLOMBO'S MERRY LAUGH WAS INFECTIOUS. BOND DECIDED TO TRY BLUFF ON THE BOISTEROUS SMUGGLER
WHAT WILL YOU HAVE? WHISKY—GIN? AND THIS—PEASANT FOOD, BUT GOOD
I SEEM TO BE YOUR PRISONER IN THIS SHIP. I WARNED MY CHIEF THAT THIS MIGHT HAPPEN. I WALKED INTO YOUR TRAP ON PURPOSE TO SEE WHAT IT WAS ALL ABOUT...
895
IF I'M NOT OUT OF IT BY TOMORROW MIDDAY, YOU'LL HAVE INTERPOL AS WELL AS THE ITALIAN POLICE ON TOP OF YOU LIKE A LOAD OF BRICKS

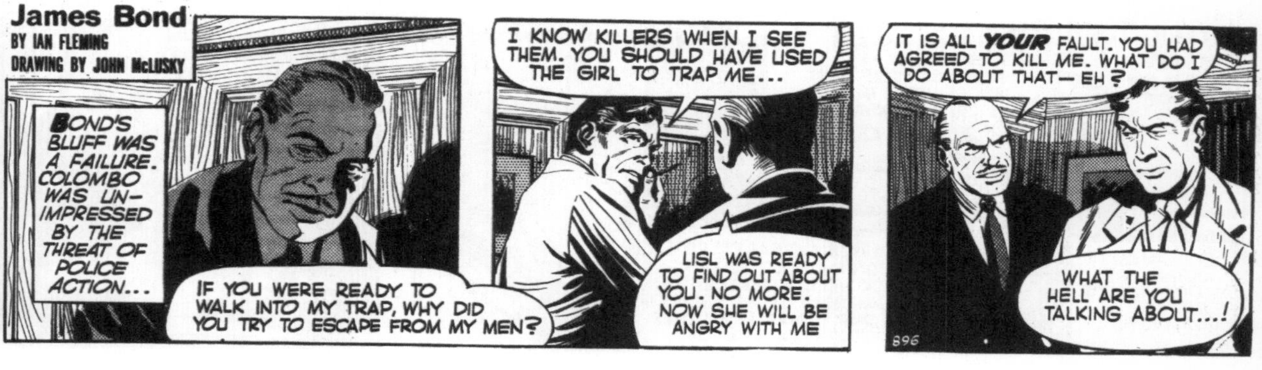
James Bond
BY IAN FLEMING
DRAWING BY JOHN McLUSKY
BOND'S BLUFF WAS A FAILURE. COLOMBO WAS UN-IMPRESSED BY THE THREAT OF POLICE ACTION...
IF YOU WERE READY TO WALK INTO MY TRAP, WHY DID YOU TRY TO ESCAPE FROM MY MEN?
I KNOW KILLERS WHEN I SEE THEM. YOU SHOULD HAVE USED THE GIRL TO TRAP ME...
LISL WAS READY TO FIND OUT ABOUT YOU. NO MORE. NOW SHE WILL BE ANGRY WITH ME
IT IS ALL YOUR FAULT. YOU HAD AGREED TO KILL ME. WHAT DO I DO ABOUT THAT—EH?
WHAT THE HELL ARE YOU TALKING ABOUT...!
896

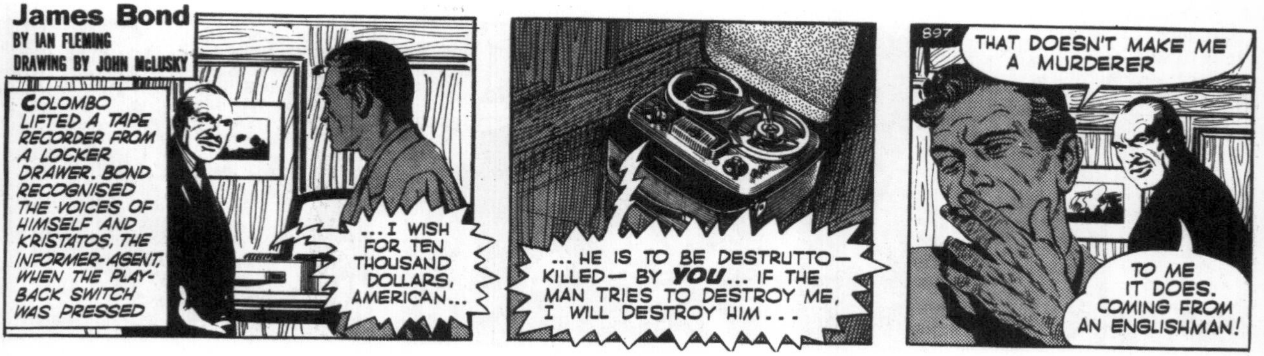
James Bond
BY IAN FLEMING
DRAWING BY JOHN McLUSKY
COLOMBO LIFTED A TAPE RECORDER FROM A LOCKER DRAWER. BOND RECOGNISED THE VOICES OF HIMSELF AND KRISTATOS, THE INFORMER-AGENT, WHEN THE PLAY-BACK SWITCH WAS PRESSED
...I WISH FOR TEN THOUSAND DOLLARS, AMERICAN...
... HE IS TO BE DESTRUTTO—KILLED—BY YOU... IF THE MAN TRIES TO DESTROY ME, I WILL DESTROY HIM...
897
THAT DOESN'T MAKE ME A MURDERER
TO ME IT DOES. COMING FROM AN ENGLISHMAN!

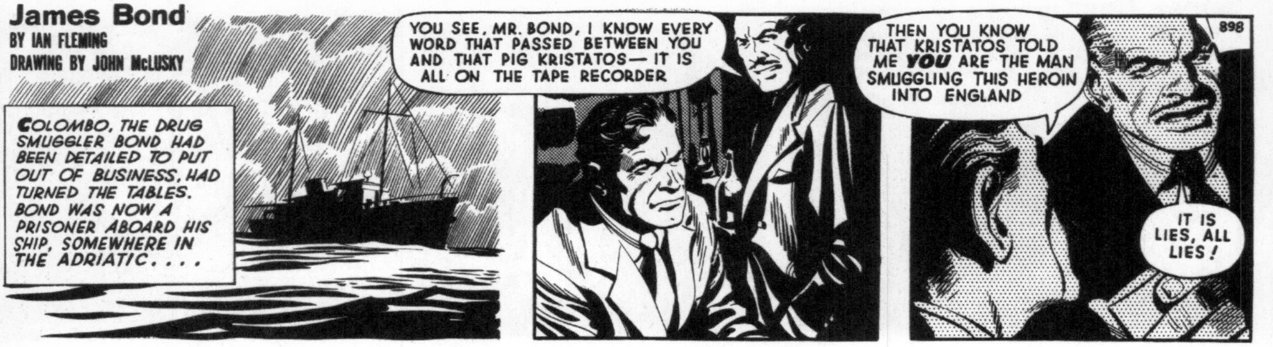
James Bond
BY IAN FLEMING
DRAWING BY JOHN McLUSKY
COLOMBO, THE DRUG SMUGGLER BOND HAD BEEN DETAILED TO PUT OUT OF BUSINESS, HAD TURNED THE TABLES. BOND WAS NOW A PRISONER ABOARD HIS SHIP, SOMEWHERE IN THE ADRIATIC. . . .
YOU SEE, MR. BOND, I KNOW EVERY WORD THAT PASSED BETWEEN YOU AND THAT PIG KRISTATOS— IT IS ALL ON THE TAPE RECORDER
898
THEN YOU KNOW THAT KRISTATOS TOLD ME YOU ARE THE MAN SMUGGLING THIS HEROIN INTO ENGLAND
IT IS LIES, ALL LIES!

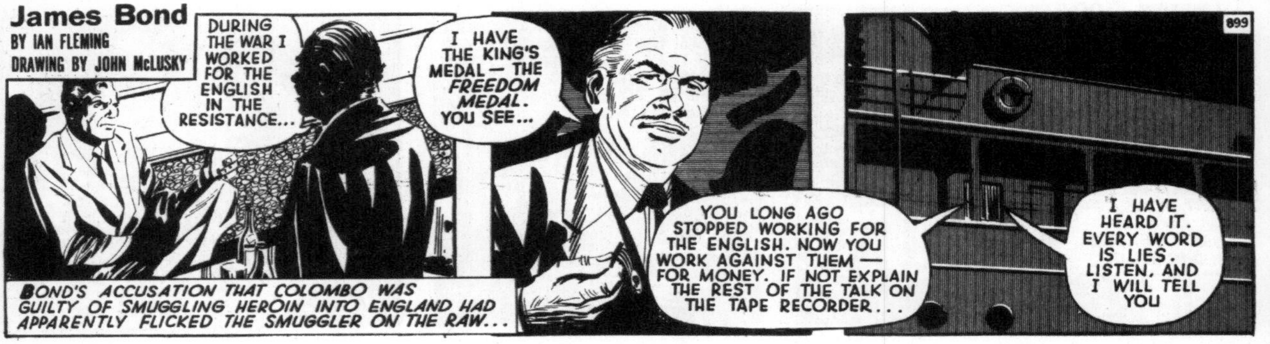
James Bond
BY IAN FLEMING
DRAWING BY JOHN McLUSKY
DURING THE WAR I WORKED FOR THE ENGLISH IN THE RESISTANCE...
BOND'S ACCUSATION THAT COLOMBO WAS GUILTY OF SMUGGLING HEROIN INTO ENGLAND HAD APPARENTLY FLICKED THE SMUGGLER ON THE RAW...
I HAVE THE KING'S MEDAL— THE FREEDOM MEDAL. YOU SEE...
899
YOU LONG AGO STOPPED WORKING FOR THE ENGLISH. NOW YOU WORK AGAINST THEM — FOR MONEY. IF NOT EXPLAIN THE REST OF THE TALK ON THE TAPE RECORDER . . .
I HAVE HEARD IT. EVERY WORD IS LIES. LISTEN, AND I WILL TELL YOU

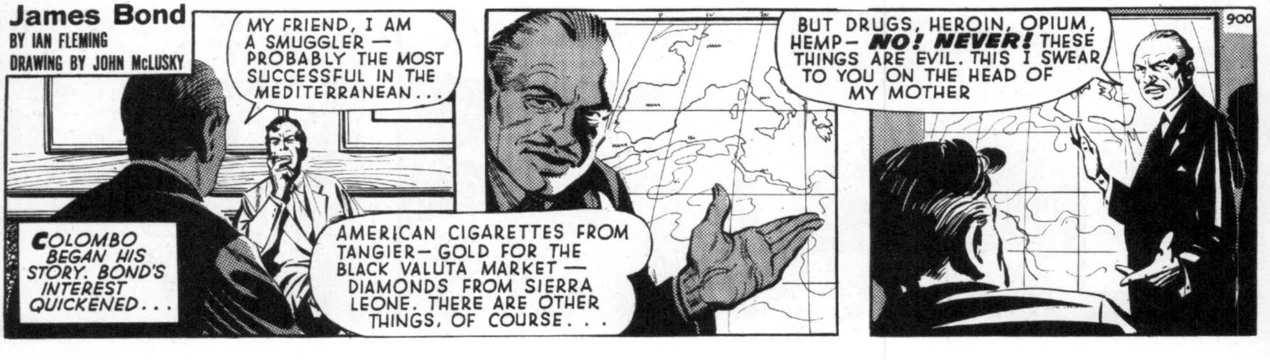
James Bond
BY IAN FLEMING
DRAWING BY JOHN McLUSKY
MY FRIEND, I AM A SMUGGLER — PROBABLY THE MOST SUCCESSFUL IN THE MEDITERRANEAN . . .
COLOMBO BEGAN HIS STORY. BOND'S INTEREST QUICKENED . . .
AMERICAN CIGARETTES FROM TANGIER— GOLD FOR THE BLACK VALUTA MARKET — DIAMONDS FROM SIERRA LEONE. THERE ARE OTHER THINGS, OF COURSE . . .
900
BUT DRUGS, HEROIN, OPIUM, HEMP— NO! NEVER! THESE THINGS ARE EVIL. THIS I SWEAR TO YOU ON THE HEAD OF MY MOTHER

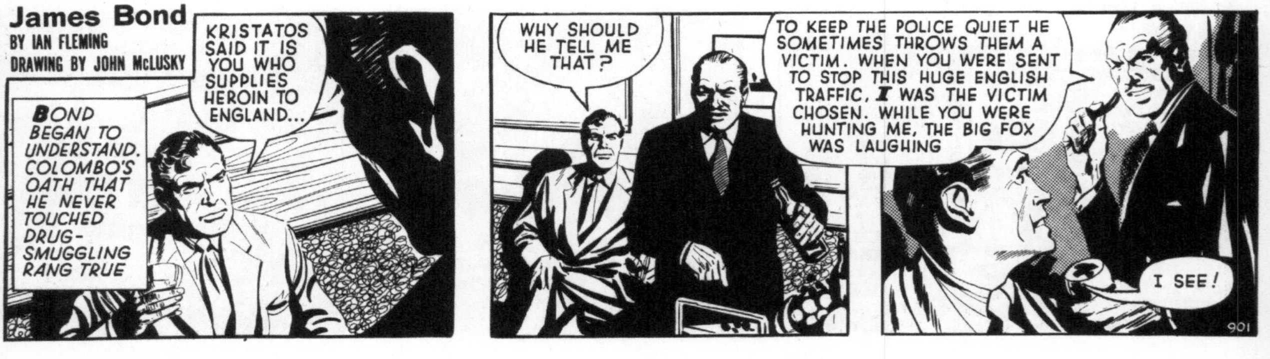
James Bond
BY IAN FLEMING
DRAWING BY JOHN McLUSKY
BOND BEGAN TO UNDERSTAND. COLOMBO'S OATH THAT HE NEVER TOUCHED DRUG-SMUGGLING RANG TRUE
KRISTATOS SAID IT IS YOU WHO SUPPLIES HEROIN TO ENGLAND...
WHY SHOULD HE TELL ME THAT?
TO KEEP THE POLICE QUIET HE SOMETIMES THROWS THEM A VICTIM. WHEN YOU WERE SENT TO STOP THIS HUGE ENGLISH TRAFFIC, I WAS THE VICTIM CHOSEN. WHILE YOU WERE HUNTING ME, THE BIG FOX WAS LAUGHING
I SEE!
901

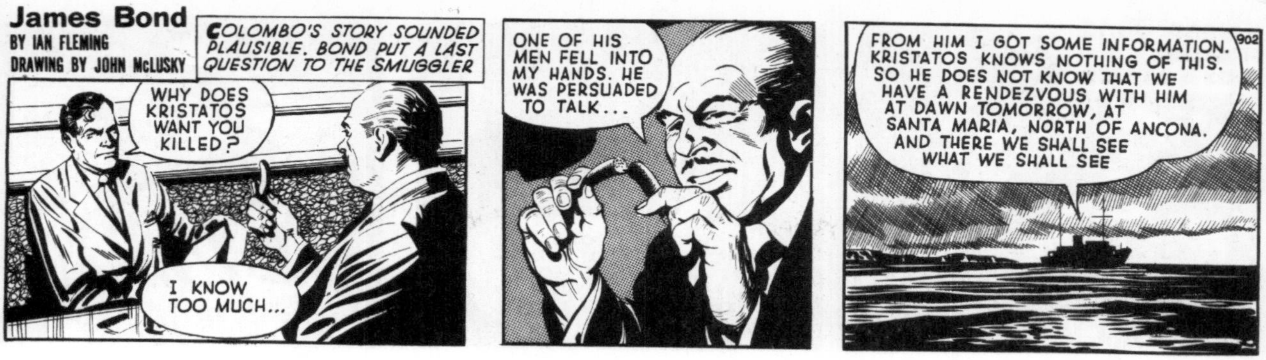
James Bond
BY IAN FLEMING
DRAWING BY JOHN McLUSKY
COLOMBO'S STORY SOUNDED PLAUSIBLE. BOND PUT A LAST QUESTION TO THE SMUGGLER
WHY DOES KRISTATOS WANT YOU KILLED?
I KNOW TOO MUCH...
ONE OF HIS MEN FELL INTO MY HANDS. HE WAS PERSUADED TO TALK...
FROM HIM I GOT SOME INFORMATION. KRISTATOS KNOWS NOTHING OF THIS. SO HE DOES NOT KNOW THAT WE HAVE A RENDEZVOUS WITH HIM AT DAWN TOMORROW, AT SANTA MARIA, NORTH OF ANCONA. AND THERE WE SHALL SEE WHAT WE SHALL SEE
902

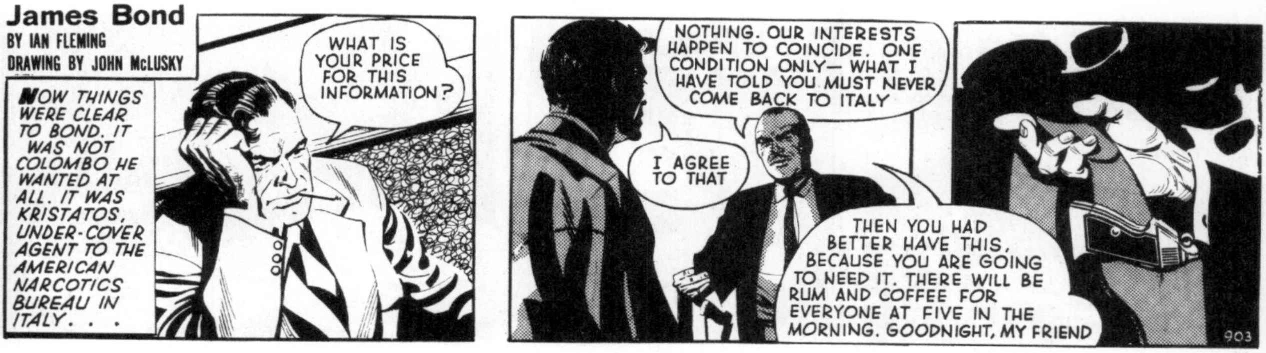
James Bond
BY IAN FLEMING
DRAWING BY JOHN McLUSKY
NOW THINGS WERE CLEAR TO BOND. IT WAS NOT COLOMBO HE WANTED AT ALL. IT WAS KRISTATOS, UNDER-COVER AGENT TO THE AMERICAN NARCOTICS BUREAU IN ITALY . . .
WHAT IS YOUR PRICE FOR THIS INFORMATION?
NOTHING. OUR INTERESTS HAPPEN TO COINCIDE. ONE CONDITION ONLY— WHAT I HAVE TOLD YOU MUST NEVER COME BACK TO ITALY
I AGREE TO THAT
THEN YOU HAD BETTER HAVE THIS, BECAUSE YOU ARE GOING TO NEED IT. THERE WILL BE RUM AND COFFEE FOR EVERYONE AT FIVE IN THE MORNING. GOODNIGHT, MY FRIEND
903

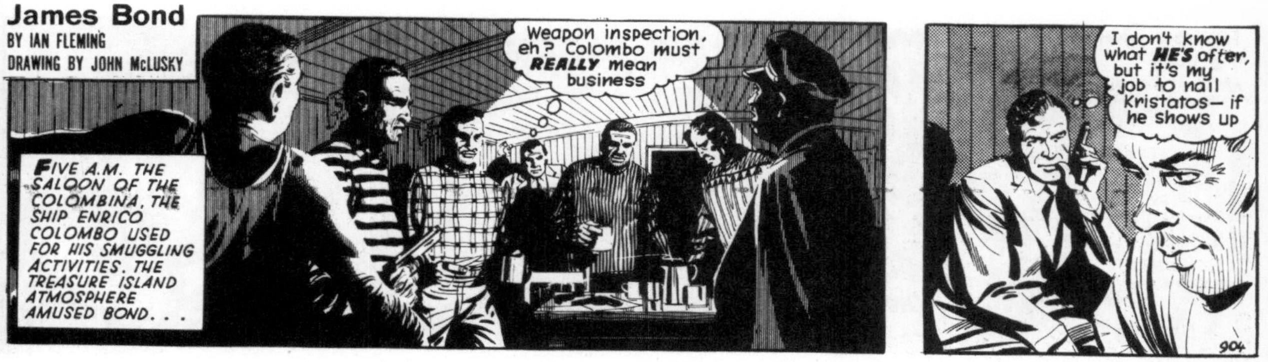
James Bond
BY IAN FLEMING
DRAWING BY JOHN McLUSKY
FIVE A.M. THE SALOON OF THE COLOMBINA, THE SHIP ENRICO COLOMBO USED FOR HIS SMUGGLING ACTIVITIES. THE TREASURE ISLAND ATMOSPHERE AMUSED BOND . . .
Weapon inspection, eh? Colombo must REALLY mean business
I don't know what HE'S after, but it's my job to nail Kristatos— if he shows up
904

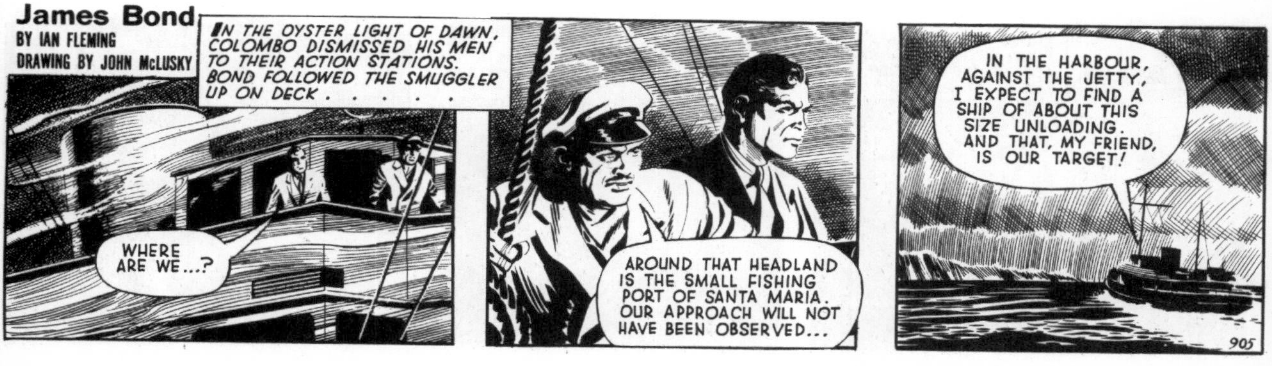
James Bond
BY IAN FLEMING
DRAWING BY JOHN McLUSKY
IN THE OYSTER LIGHT OF DAWN, COLOMBO DISMISSED HIS MEN TO THEIR ACTION STATIONS. BOND FOLLOWED THE SMUGGLER UP ON DECK . . . . .
WHERE ARE WE...?
AROUND THAT HEADLAND IS THE SMALL FISHING PORT OF SANTA MARIA. OUR APPROACH WILL NOT HAVE BEEN OBSERVED...
IN THE HARBOUR, AGAINST THE JETTY, I EXPECT TO FIND A SHIP OF ABOUT THIS SIZE UNLOADING. AND THAT, MY FRIEND, IS OUR TARGET!
905

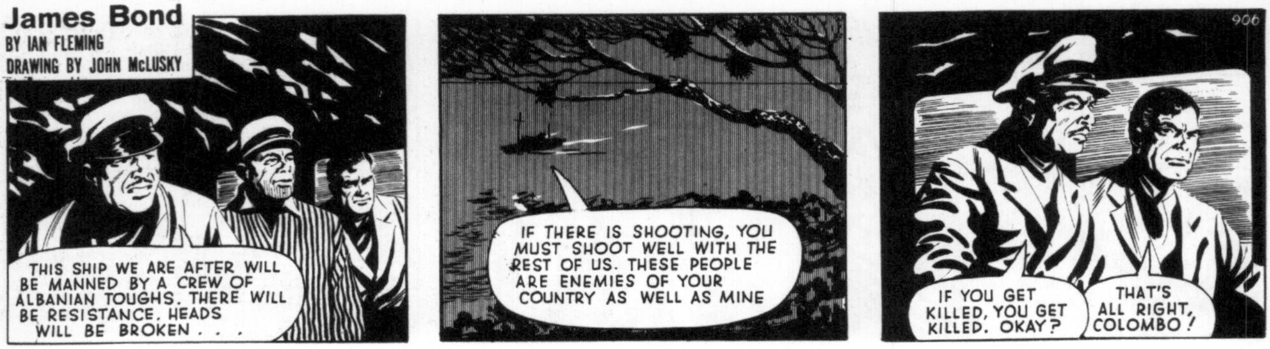
James Bond
BY IAN FLEMING
DRAWING BY JOHN McLUSKY
THIS SHIP WE ARE AFTER WILL BE MANNED BY A CREW OF ALBANIAN TOUGHS. THERE WILL BE RESISTANCE. HEADS WILL BE BROKEN . . .
IF THERE IS SHOOTING, YOU MUST SHOOT WELL WITH THE REST OF US. THESE PEOPLE ARE ENEMIES OF YOUR COUNTRY AS WELL AS MINE
906
IF YOU GET KILLED, YOU GET KILLED. OKAY?
THAT'S ALL RIGHT, COLOMBO!

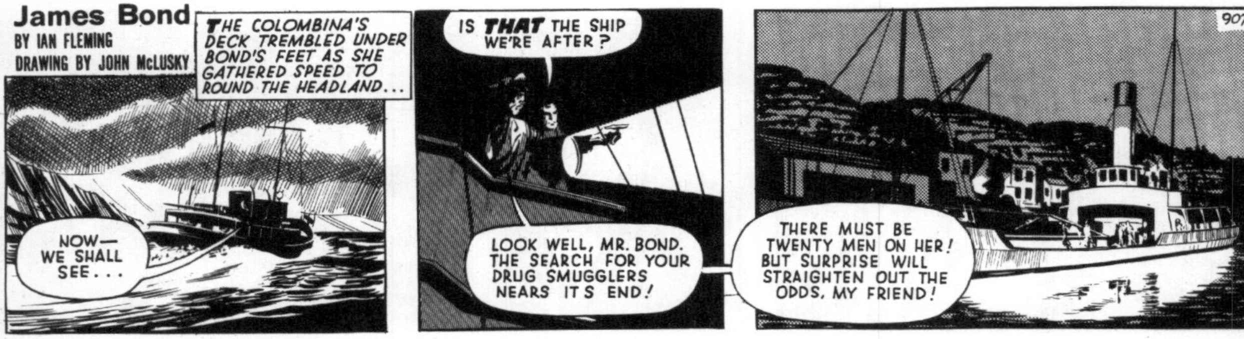
James Bond
BY IAN FLEMING
DRAWING BY JOHN McLUSKY
THE COLOMBINA'S DECK TREMBLED UNDER BOND'S FEET AS SHE GATHERED SPEED TO ROUND THE HEADLAND...
NOW— WE SHALL SEE...
IS THAT THE SHIP WE'RE AFTER?
LOOK WELL, MR. BOND. THE SEARCH FOR YOUR DRUG SMUGGLERS NEARS ITS END!
907
THERE MUST BE TWENTY MEN ON HER! BUT SURPRISE WILL STRAIGHTEN OUT THE ODDS, MY FRIEND!

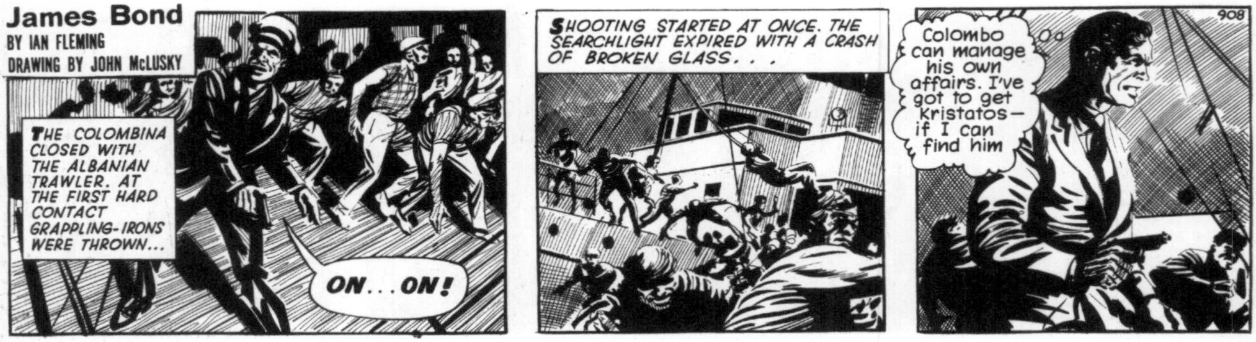
James Bond
BY IAN FLEMING
DRAWING BY JOHN McLUSKY
THE COLOMBINA CLOSED WITH THE ALBANIAN TRAWLER. AT THE FIRST HARD CONTACT GRAPPLING-IRONS WERE THROWN...
ON...ON!
SHOOTING STARTED AT ONCE. THE SEARCHLIGHT EXPIRED WITH A CRASH OF BROKEN GLASS. . .
908
Colombo can manage his own affairs. I've got to get Kristatos— if I can find him

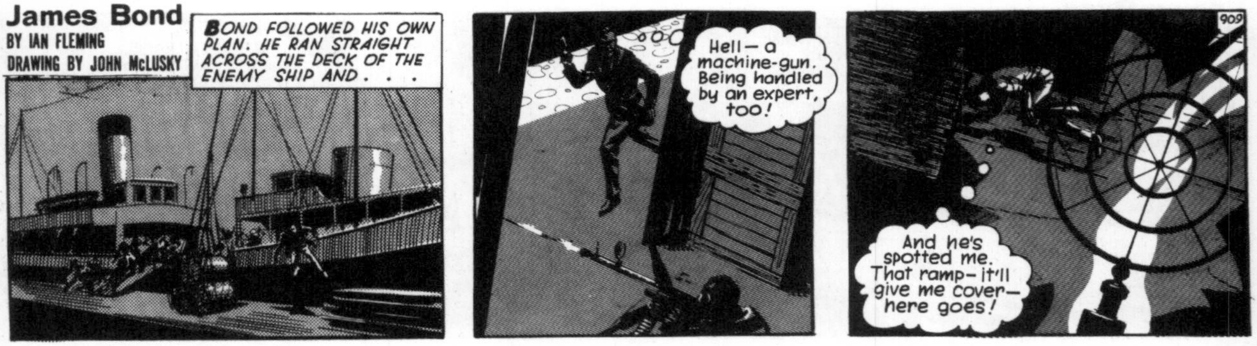
James Bond
BY IAN FLEMING
DRAWING BY JOHN McLUSKY
BOND FOLLOWED HIS OWN PLAN. HE RAN STRAIGHT ACROSS THE DECK OF THE ENEMY SHIP AND . . .
Hell—a machine-gun. Being handled by an expert, too!
909
And he's spotted me. That ramp—it'll give me cover— here goes!

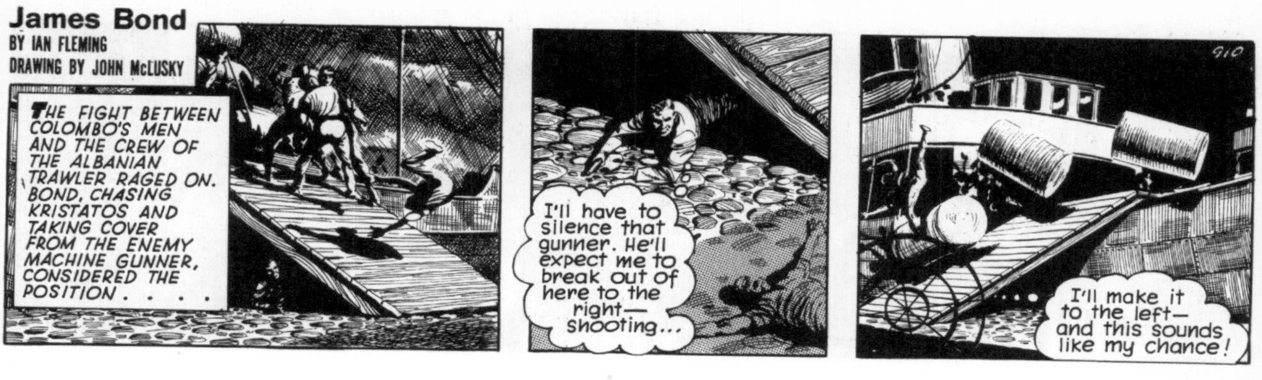
James Bond
BY IAN FLEMING
DRAWING BY JOHN McLUSKY
THE FIGHT BETWEEN COLOMBO'S MEN AND THE CREW OF THE ALBANIAN TRAWLER RAGED ON. BOND, CHASING KRISTATOS AND TAKING COVER FROM THE ENEMY MACHINE GUNNER, CONSIDERED THE POSITION . . . .
I'll have to silence that gunner. He'll expect me to break out of here to the right— shooting...
910
I'll make it to the left— and this sounds like my chance!

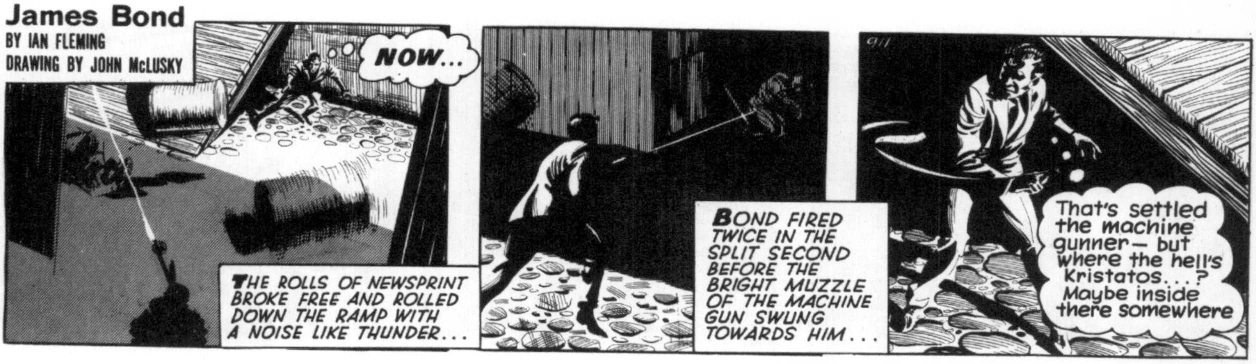
James Bond
BY IAN FLEMING
DRAWING BY JOHN McLUSKY
NOW...
THE ROLLS OF NEWSPRINT BROKE FREE AND ROLLED DOWN THE RAMP WITH A NOISE LIKE THUNDER...
BOND FIRED TWICE IN THE SPLIT SECOND BEFORE THE BRIGHT MUZZLE OF THE MACHINE GUN SWUNG TOWARDS HIM...
911
That's settled the machine gunner— but where the hell's Kristatos...? Maybe inside there somewhere

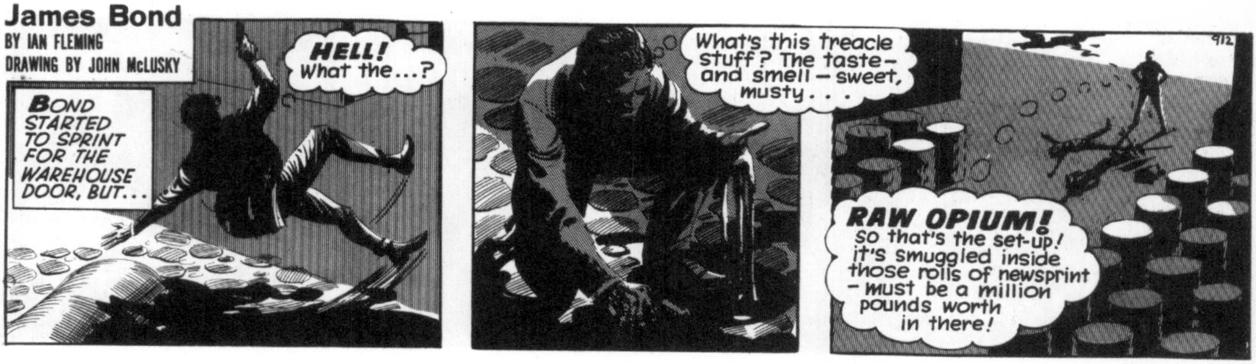
James Bond
BY IAN FLEMING
DRAWING BY JOHN McLUSKY
BOND STARTED TO SPRINT FOR THE WAREHOUSE DOOR, BUT...
HELL! What the...?
What's this treacle stuff? The taste— and smell — sweet, musty . . .
912
RAW OPIUM! so that's the set-up! it's smuggled inside those rolls of newsprint — must be a million pounds worth in there!

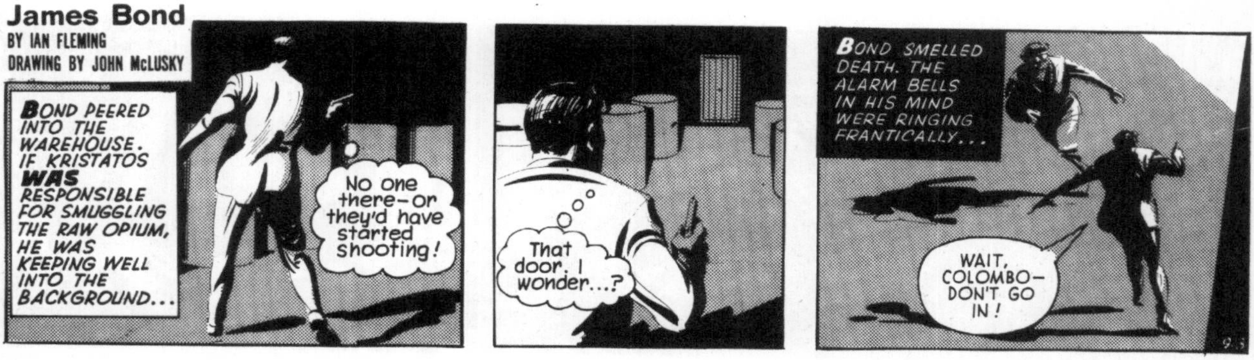
James Bond
BY IAN FLEMING
DRAWING BY JOHN McLUSKY
BOND PEERED INTO THE WAREHOUSE. IF KRISTATOS WAS RESPONSIBLE FOR SMUGGLING THE RAW OPIUM, HE WAS KEEPING WELL INTO THE BACKGROUND...
No one there—or they'd have started shooting!
That door. I wonder...?
BOND SMELLED DEATH. THE ALARM BELLS IN HIS MIND WERE RINGING FRANTICALLY...
WAIT, COLOMBO— DON'T GO IN!

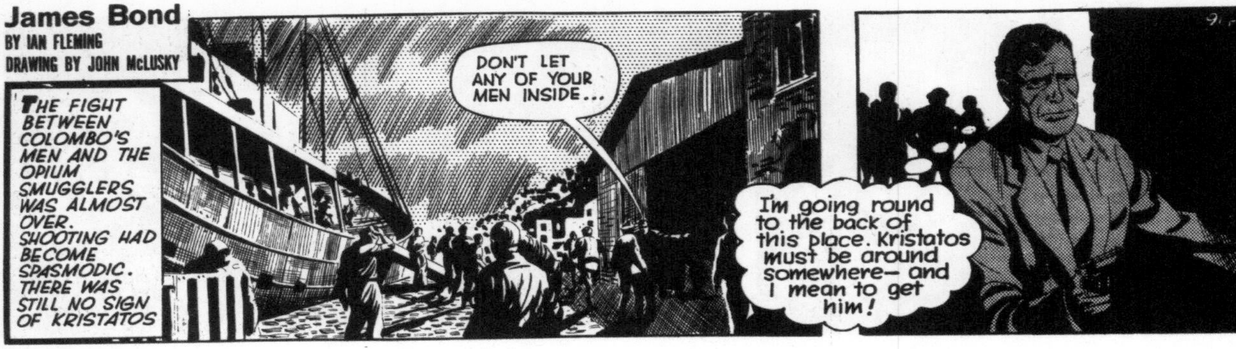
James Bond
BY IAN FLEMING
DRAWING BY JOHN McLUSKY
THE FIGHT BETWEEN COLOMBO'S MEN AND THE OPIUM SMUGGLERS WAS ALMOST OVER. SHOOTING HAD BECOME SPASMODIC. THERE WAS STILL NO SIGN OF KRISTATOS
DON'T LET ANY OF YOUR MEN INSIDE...
I'm going round to the back of this place. Kristatos must be around somewhere— and I mean to get him!

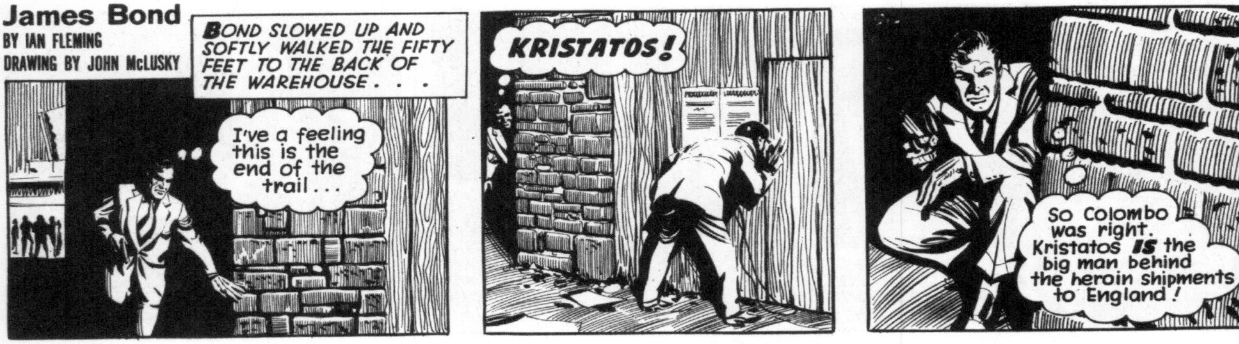
James Bond
BY IAN FLEMING
DRAWING BY JOHN McLUSKY
BOND SLOWED UP AND SOFTLY WALKED THE FIFTY FEET TO THE BACK OF THE WAREHOUSE . . .
I've a feeling this is the end of the trail...
KRISTATOS!
So Colombo was right. Kristatos IS the big man behind the heroin shipments to England!

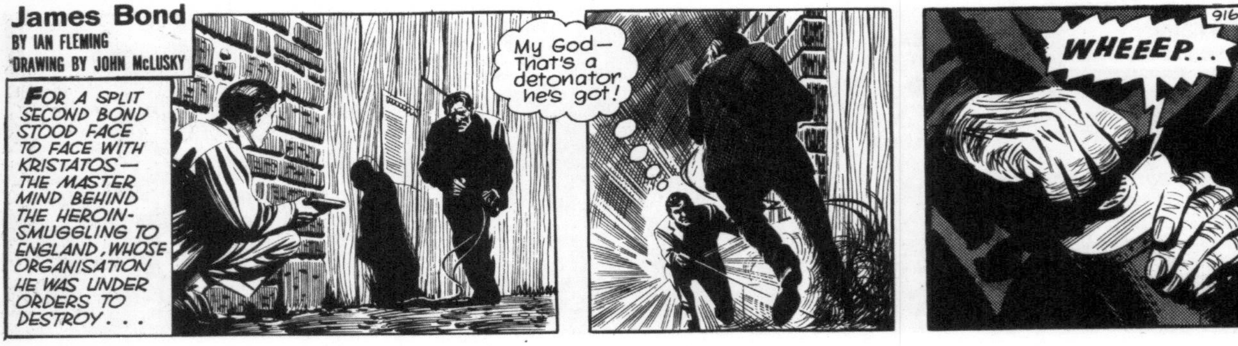
James Bond
BY IAN FLEMING
DRAWING BY JOHN McLUSKY
FOR A SPLIT SECOND BOND STOOD FACE TO FACE WITH KRISTATOS— THE MASTER MIND BEHIND THE HEROIN-SMUGGLING TO ENGLAND, WHOSE ORGANISATION HE WAS UNDER ORDERS TO DESTROY . . .
My God— That's a detonator he's got!
916
WHEEEP...

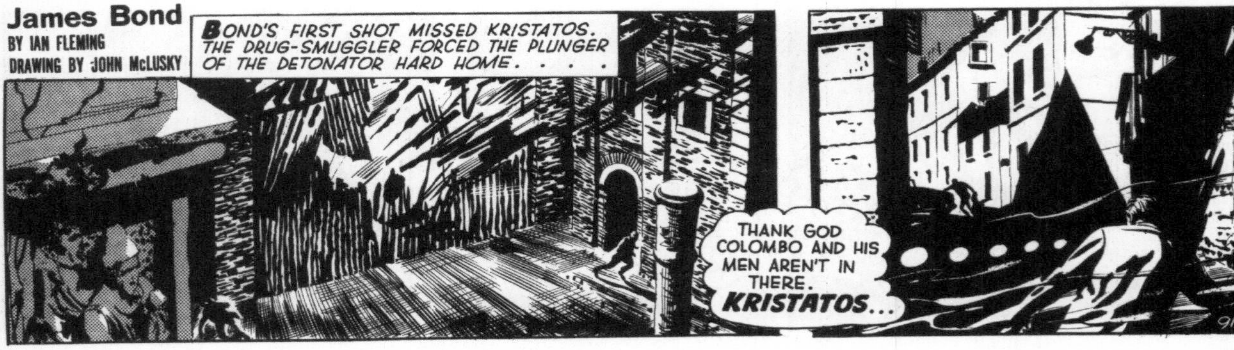
James Bond
BY IAN FLEMING
DRAWING BY JOHN McLUSKY
BOND'S FIRST SHOT MISSED KRISTATOS. THE DRUG-SMUGGLER FORCED THE PLUNGER OF THE DETONATOR HARD HOME . . . .
THANK GOD COLOMBO AND HIS MEN AREN'T IN THERE. KRISTATOS...
917

James Bond
BY IAN FLEMING
DRAWING BY JOHN McLUSKY

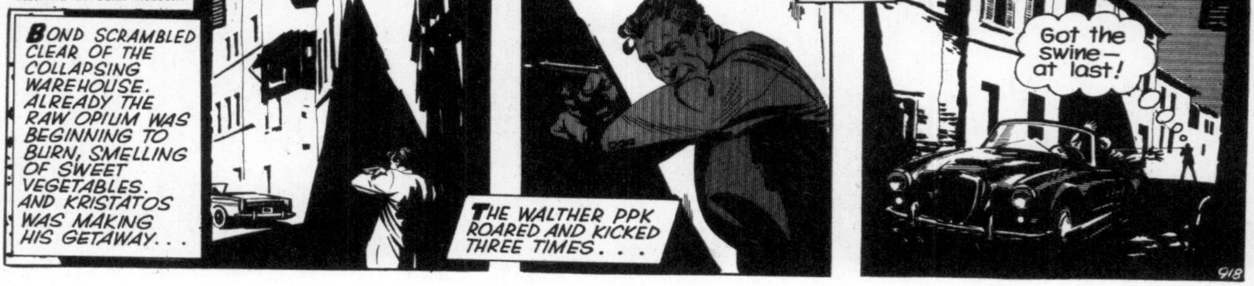
BOND SCRAMBLED CLEAR OF THE COLLAPSING WAREHOUSE. ALREADY THE RAW OPIUM WAS BEGINNING TO BURN, SMELLING OF SWEET VEGETABLES. AND KRISTATOS WAS MAKING HIS GETAWAY...
THE WALTHER PPK ROARED AND KICKED THREE TIMES...
AND...
Got the swine– at last!
918

James Bond
BY IAN FLEMING
DRAWING BY JOHN McLUSKY

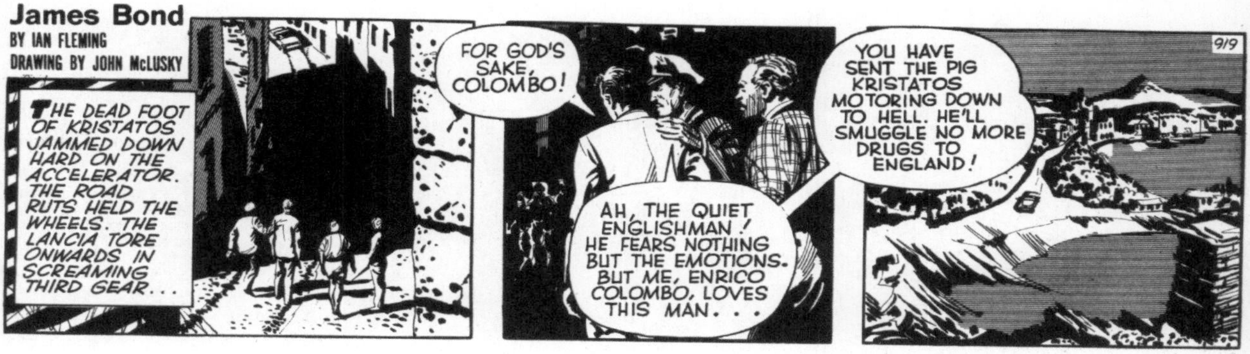
THE DEAD FOOT OF KRISTATOS JAMMED DOWN HARD ON THE ACCELERATOR. THE ROAD RUTS HELD THE WHEELS. THE LANCIA TORE ONWARDS IN SCREAMING THIRD GEAR...
FOR GOD'S SAKE, COLOMBO!
AH, THE QUIET ENGLISHMAN! HE FEARS NOTHING BUT THE EMOTIONS. BUT ME, ENRICO COLOMBO, LOVES THIS MAN...
YOU HAVE SENT THE PIG KRISTATOS MOTORING DOWN TO HELL. HE'LL SMUGGLE NO MORE DRUGS TO ENGLAND!
919

James Bond
BY IAN FLEMING
DRAWING BY JOHN McLUSKY

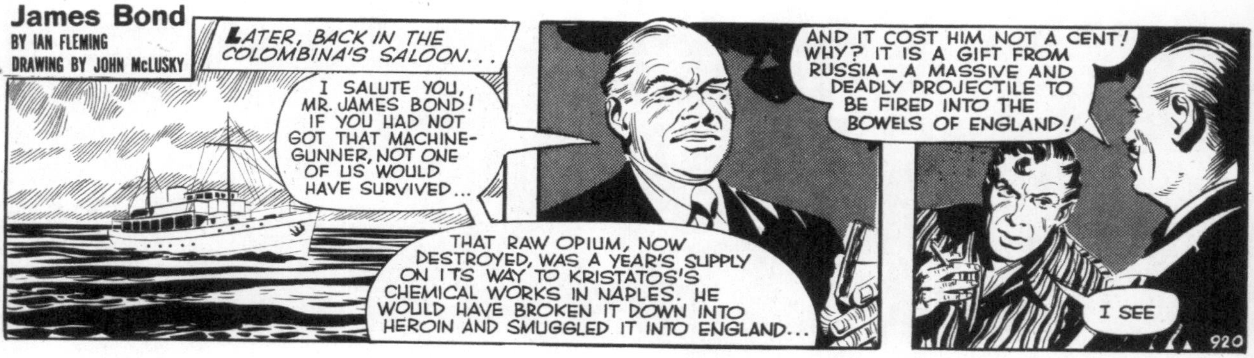
LATER, BACK IN THE COLOMBINA'S SALOON...
I SALUTE YOU, MR. JAMES BOND! IF YOU HAD NOT GOT THAT MACHINE-GUNNER, NOT ONE OF US WOULD HAVE SURVIVED...
THAT RAW OPIUM, NOW DESTROYED, WAS A YEAR'S SUPPLY ON ITS WAY TO KRISTATOS'S CHEMICAL WORKS IN NAPLES. HE WOULD HAVE BROKEN IT DOWN INTO HEROIN AND SMUGGLED IT INTO ENGLAND...
AND IT COST HIM NOT A CENT! WHY? IT IS A GIFT FROM RUSSIA– A MASSIVE AND DEADLY PROJECTILE TO BE FIRED INTO THE BOWELS OF ENGLAND!
I SEE
920

James Bond
BY IAN FLEMING
DRAWING BY JOHN McLUSKY

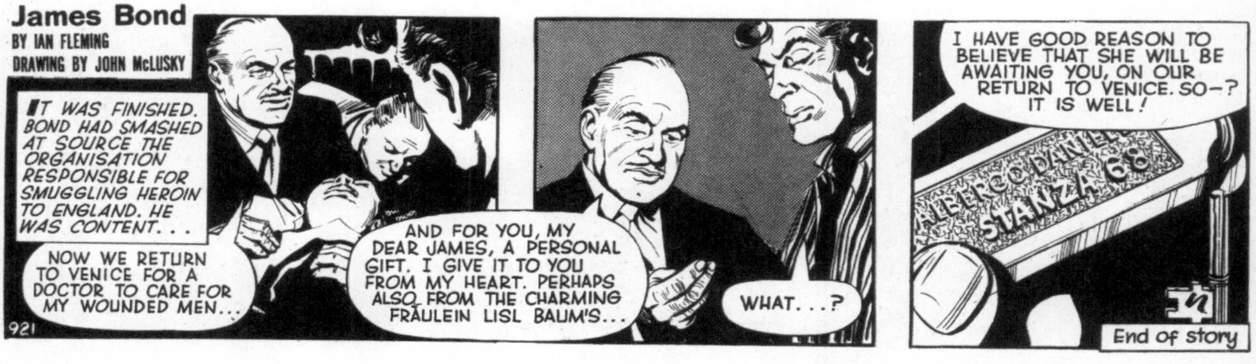
IT WAS FINISHED. BOND HAD SMASHED AT SOURCE THE ORGANISATION RESPONSIBLE FOR SMUGGLING HEROIN TO ENGLAND. HE WAS CONTENT...
NOW WE RETURN TO VENICE FOR A DOCTOR TO CARE FOR MY WOUNDED MEN...
921
AND FOR YOU, MY DEAR JAMES, A PERSONAL GIFT. I GIVE IT TO YOU FROM MY HEART. PERHAPS ALSO FROM THE CHARMING FRÄULEIN LISL BAUM'S...
WHAT...?
I HAVE GOOD REASON TO BELIEVE THAT SHE WILL BE AWAITING YOU, ON OUR RETURN TO VENICE. SO–? IT IS WELL!
STANZA 68
End of story

FROM A VIEW TO A KILL

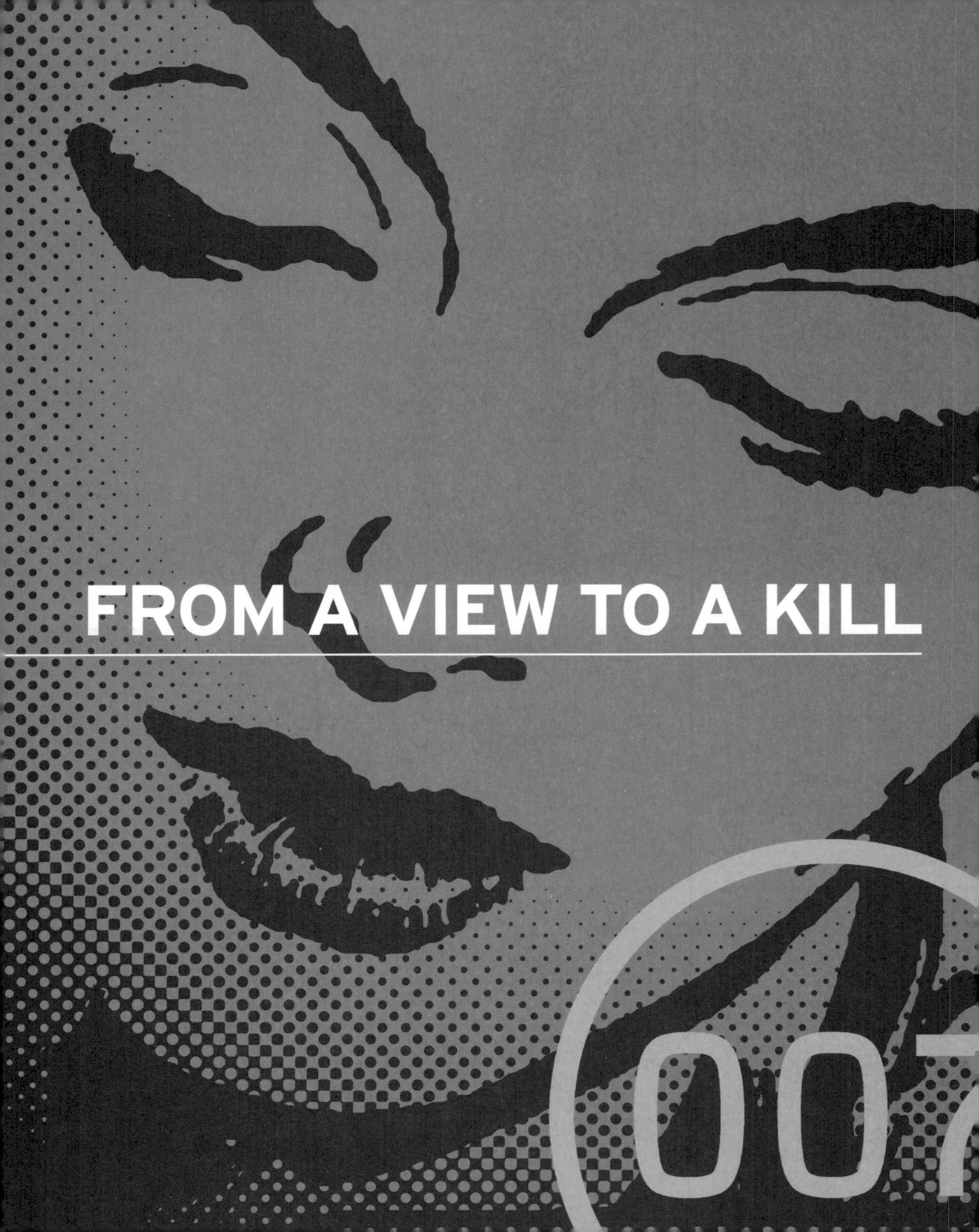

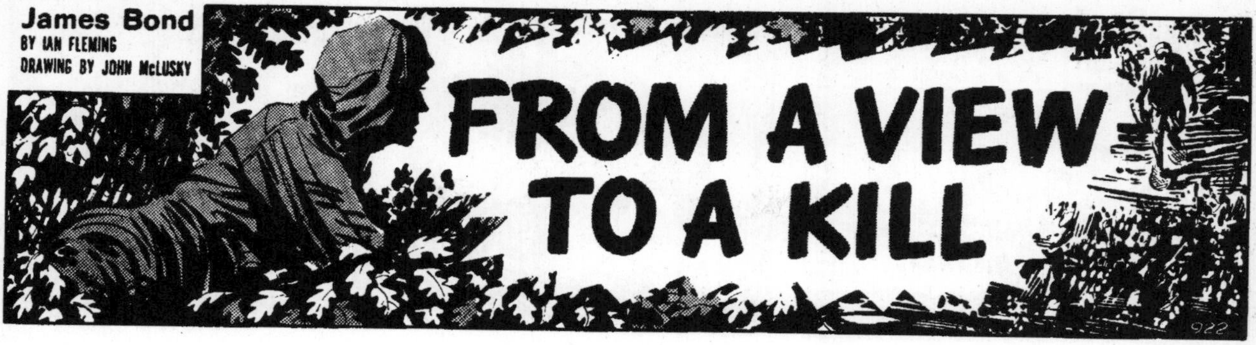
James Bond
BY IAN FLEMING
DRAWING BY JOHN McLUSKY
FROM A VIEW TO A KILL
922

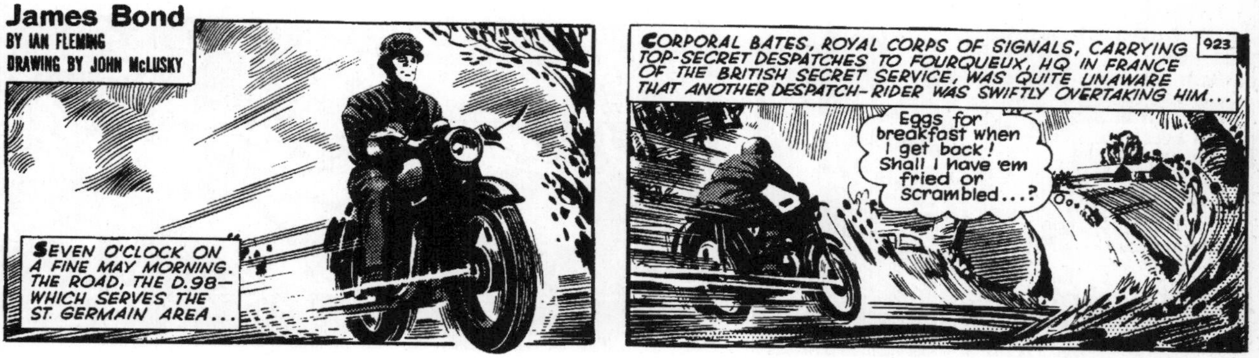
James Bond
BY IAN FLEMING
DRAWING BY JOHN McLUSKY
SEVEN O'CLOCK ON A FINE MAY MORNING. THE ROAD, THE D.98— WHICH SERVES THE ST. GERMAIN AREA...
923
CORPORAL BATES, ROYAL CORPS OF SIGNALS, CARRYING TOP-SECRET DESPATCHES TO FOURQUEUX, HQ IN FRANCE OF THE BRITISH SECRET SERVICE, WAS QUITE UNAWARE THAT ANOTHER DESPATCH-RIDER WAS SWIFTLY OVERTAKING HIM...
Eggs for breakfast when I get back! Shall I have 'em fried or scrambled...?

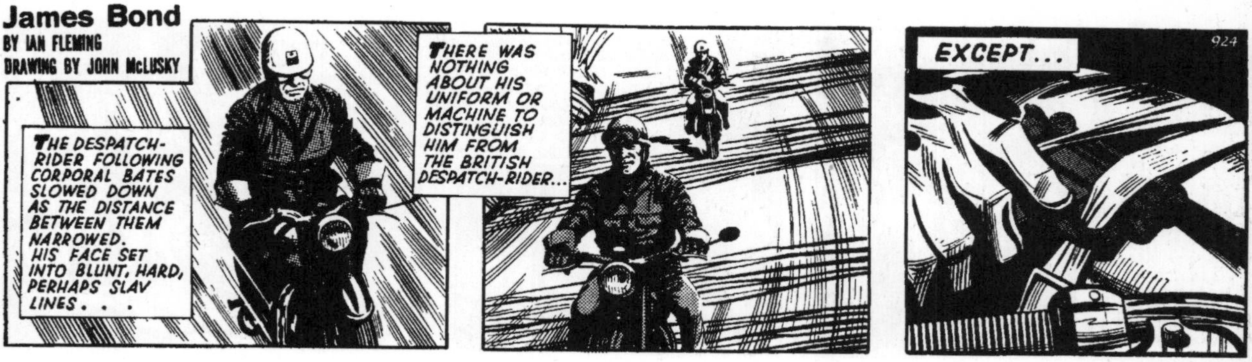
James Bond
BY IAN FLEMING
DRAWING BY JOHN McLUSKY
THE DESPATCH-RIDER FOLLOWING CORPORAL BATES SLOWED DOWN AS THE DISTANCE BETWEEN THEM NARROWED. HIS FACE SET INTO BLUNT, HARD, PERHAPS SLAV LINES . . .
THERE WAS NOTHING ABOUT HIS UNIFORM OR MACHINE TO DISTINGUISH HIM FROM THE BRITISH DESPATCH-RIDER...
924
EXCEPT...

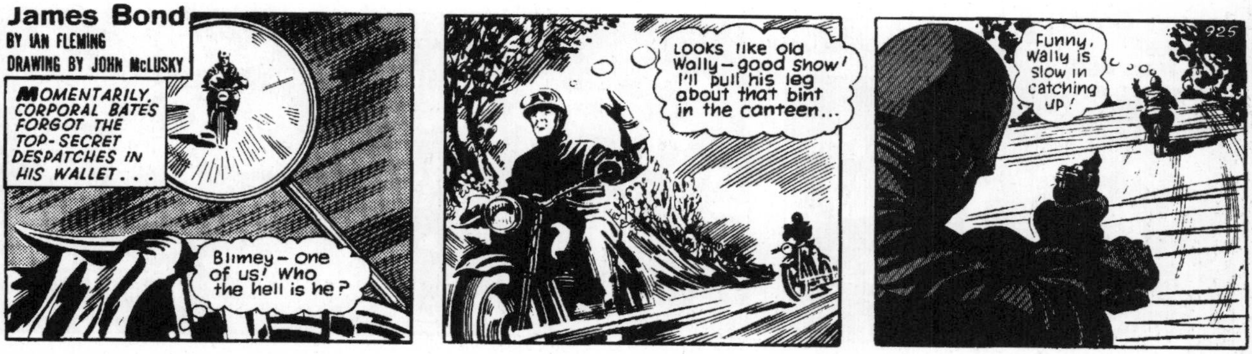
James Bond
BY IAN FLEMING
DRAWING BY JOHN McLUSKY
MOMENTARILY, CORPORAL BATES FORGOT THE TOP-SECRET DESPATCHES IN HIS WALLET...
Blimey — One of us! Who the hell is he?
Looks like old Wally — good show! I'll pull his leg about that bint in the canteen...
925
Funny, Wally is slow in catching up!

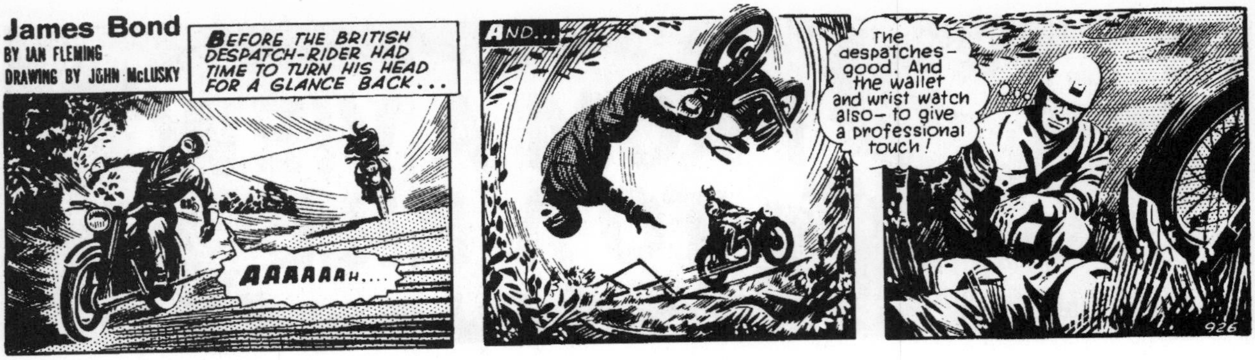
James Bond
BY IAN FLEMING
DRAWING BY JOHN McLUSKY
BEFORE THE BRITISH DESPATCH-RIDER HAD TIME TO TURN HIS HEAD FOR A GLANCE BACK...
AAAAAAH....
AND...
The despatches- good. And the wallet and wrist watch also- to give a professional touch!
926

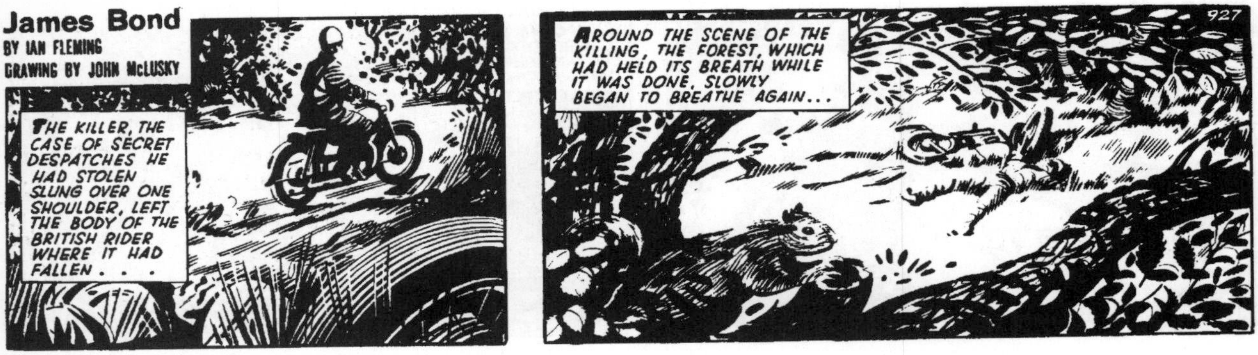
James Bond
BY IAN FLEMING
DRAWING BY JOHN McLUSKY
THE KILLER, THE CASE OF SECRET DESPATCHES HE HAD STOLEN SLUNG OVER ONE SHOULDER, LEFT THE BODY OF THE BRITISH RIDER WHERE IT HAD FALLEN . . .
AROUND THE SCENE OF THE KILLING, THE FOREST, WHICH HAD HELD ITS BREATH WHILE IT WAS DONE, SLOWLY BEGAN TO BREATHE AGAIN...
927

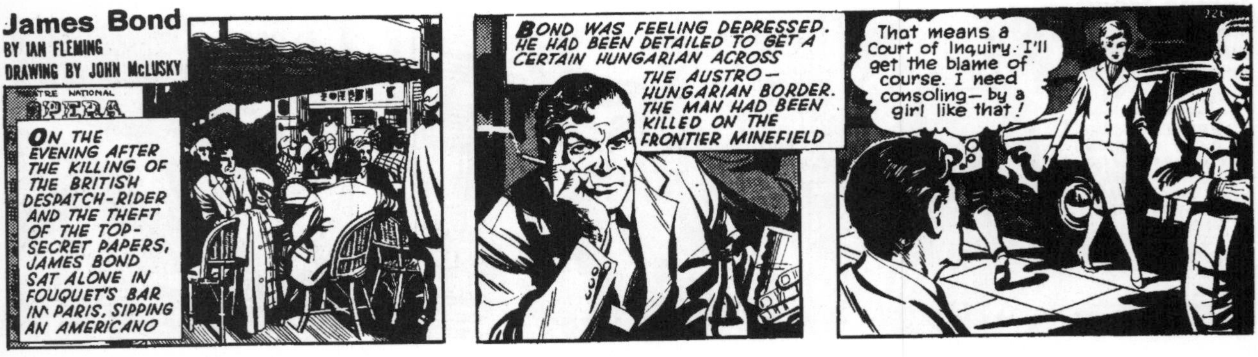
James Bond
BY IAN FLEMING
DRAWING BY JOHN McLUSKY
OPERA
ON THE EVENING AFTER THE KILLING OF THE BRITISH DESPATCH-RIDER AND THE THEFT OF THE TOP-SECRET PAPERS, JAMES BOND SAT ALONE IN FOUQUET'S BAR IN PARIS, SIPPING AN AMERICANO
BOND WAS FEELING DEPRESSED. HE HAD BEEN DETAILED TO GET A CERTAIN HUNGARIAN ACROSS THE AUSTRO-HUNGARIAN BORDER. THE MAN HAD BEEN KILLED ON THE FRONTIER MINEFIELD
That means a Court of Inquiry. I'll get the blame of course. I need consoling- by a girl like that!

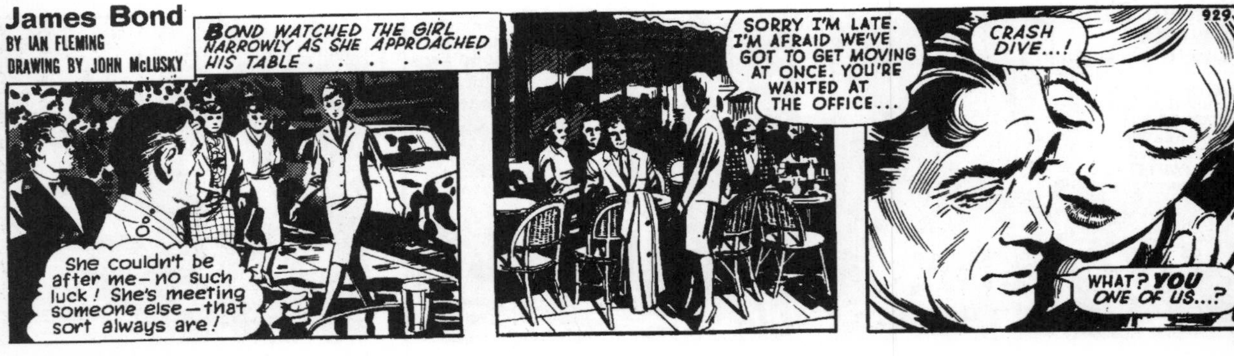
James Bond
BY IAN FLEMING
DRAWING BY JOHN McLUSKY
BOND WATCHED THE GIRL NARROWLY AS SHE APPROACHED HIS TABLE . . . . .
She couldn't be after me- no such luck! She's meeting someone else- that sort always are!
SORRY I'M LATE. I'M AFRAID WE'VE GOT TO GET MOVING AT ONCE. YOU'RE WANTED AT THE OFFICE...
929
CRASH DIVE...!
WHAT? YOU ONE OF US...?

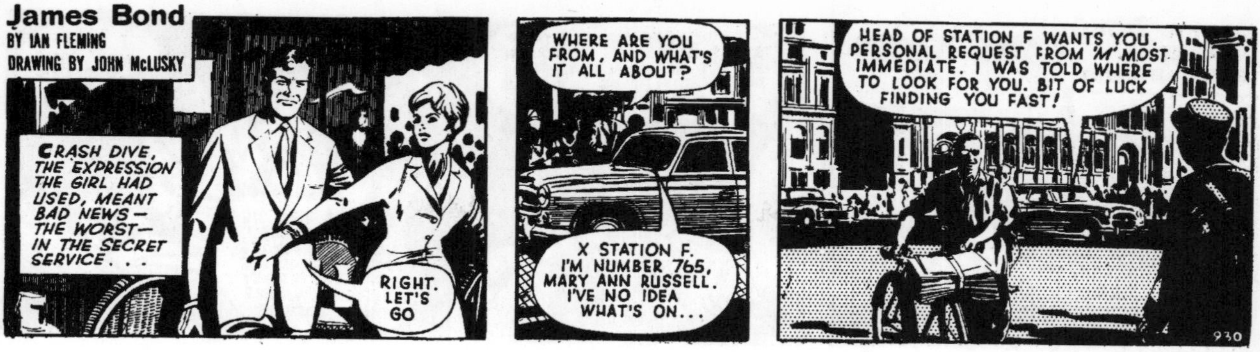
James Bond
BY IAN FLEMING
DRAWING BY JOHN McLUSKY
CRASH DIVE, THE EXPRESSION THE GIRL HAD USED, MEANT BAD NEWS — THE WORST — IN THE SECRET SERVICE . . .
RIGHT. LET'S GO
WHERE ARE YOU FROM, AND WHAT'S IT ALL ABOUT?
X STATION F. I'M NUMBER 765, MARY ANN RUSSELL. I'VE NO IDEA WHAT'S ON...
HEAD OF STATION F WANTS YOU. PERSONAL REQUEST FROM 'M' MOST IMMEDIATE. I WAS TOLD WHERE TO LOOK FOR YOU. BIT OF LUCK FINDING YOU FAST!
930

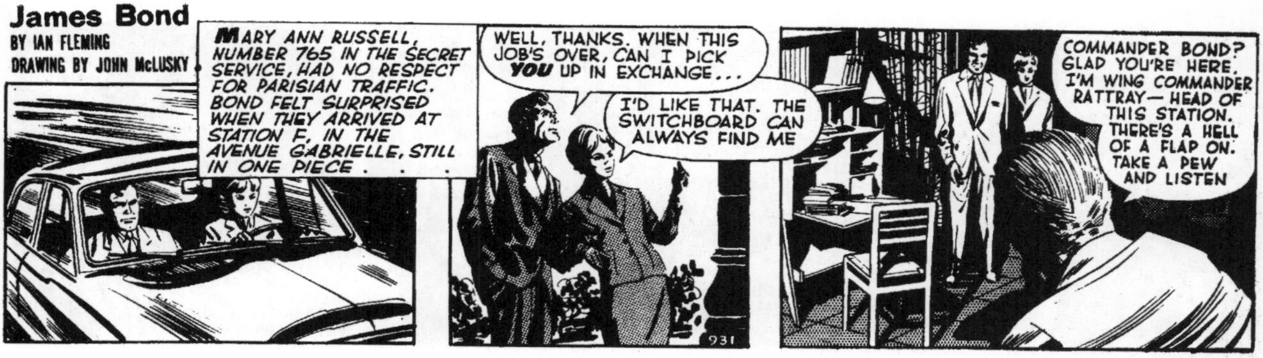
James Bond
BY IAN FLEMING
DRAWING BY JOHN McLUSKY
MARY ANN RUSSELL, NUMBER 765 IN THE SECRET SERVICE, HAD NO RESPECT FOR PARISIAN TRAFFIC. BOND FELT SURPRISED WHEN THEY ARRIVED AT STATION F, IN THE AVENUE GABRIELLE, STILL IN ONE PIECE . . .
WELL, THANKS. WHEN THIS JOB'S OVER, CAN I PICK YOU UP IN EXCHANGE...
I'D LIKE THAT. THE SWITCHBOARD CAN ALWAYS FIND ME
COMMANDER BOND? GLAD YOU'RE HERE. I'M WING COMMANDER RATTRAY— HEAD OF THIS STATION. THERE'S A HELL OF A FLAP ON. TAKE A PEW AND LISTEN
931

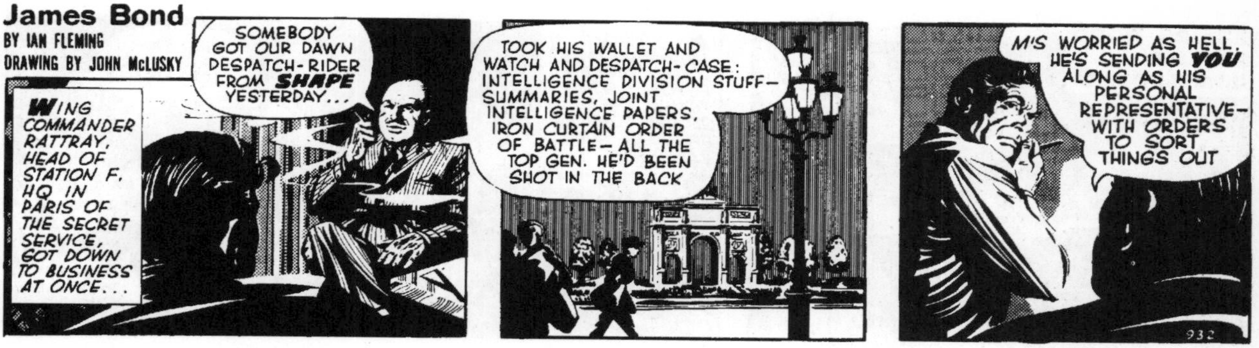
James Bond
BY IAN FLEMING
DRAWING BY JOHN McLUSKY
WING COMMANDER RATTRAY, HEAD OF STATION F, HQ IN PARIS OF THE SECRET SERVICE, GOT DOWN TO BUSINESS AT ONCE...
SOMEBODY GOT OUR DAWN DESPATCH-RIDER FROM SHAPE YESTERDAY...
TOOK HIS WALLET AND WATCH AND DESPATCH-CASE: INTELLIGENCE DIVISION STUFF— SUMMARIES, JOINT INTELLIGENCE PAPERS, IRON CURTAIN ORDER OF BATTLE— ALL THE TOP GEN. HE'D BEEN SHOT IN THE BACK
M'S WORRIED AS HELL. HE'S SENDING YOU ALONG AS HIS PERSONAL REPRESENTATIVE— WITH ORDERS TO SORT THINGS OUT
932

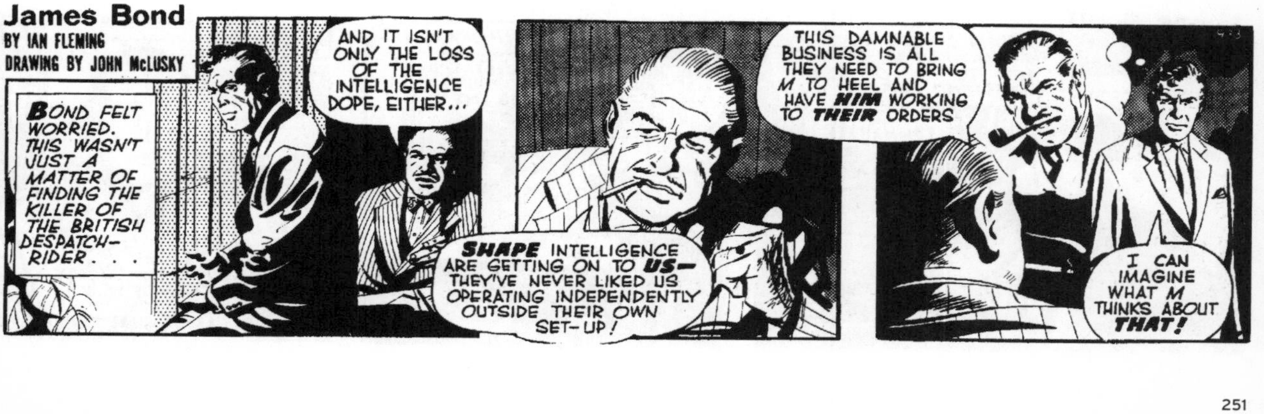
James Bond
BY IAN FLEMING
DRAWING BY JOHN McLUSKY
BOND FELT WORRIED. THIS WASN'T JUST A MATTER OF FINDING THE KILLER OF THE BRITISH DESPATCH-RIDER . . .
AND IT ISN'T ONLY THE LOSS OF THE INTELLIGENCE DOPE, EITHER...
SHAPE INTELLIGENCE ARE GETTING ON TO US— THEY'VE NEVER LIKED US OPERATING INDEPENDENTLY OUTSIDE THEIR OWN SET-UP!
THIS DAMNABLE BUSINESS IS ALL THEY NEED TO BRING M TO HEEL AND HAVE HIM WORKING TO THEIR ORDERS
I CAN IMAGINE WHAT M THINKS ABOUT THAT!

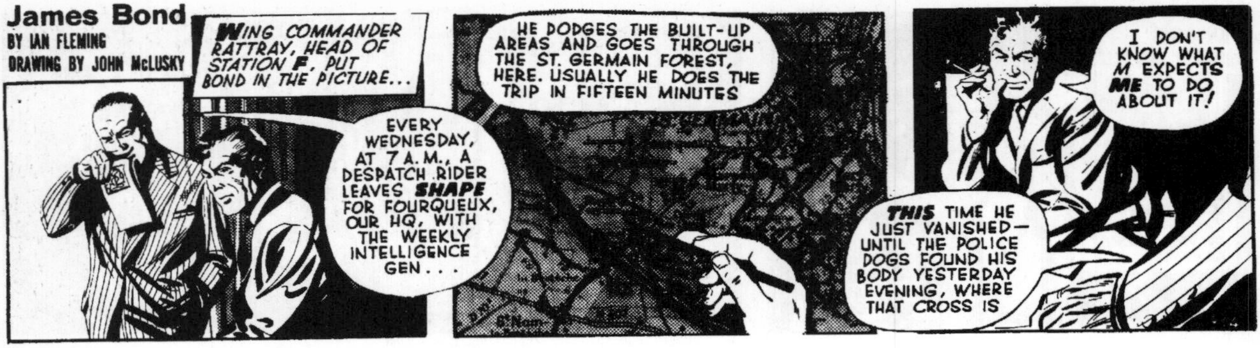
James Bond
BY IAN FLEMING
DRAWING BY JOHN McLUSKY
WING COMMANDER RATTRAY, HEAD OF STATION F, PUT BOND IN THE PICTURE...
EVERY WEDNESDAY, AT 7 A.M., A DESPATCH RIDER LEAVES SHAPE FOR FOURQUEUX, OUR HQ, WITH THE WEEKLY INTELLIGENCE GEN...
HE DODGES THE BUILT-UP AREAS AND GOES THROUGH THE ST. GERMAIN FOREST, HERE. USUALLY HE DOES THE TRIP IN FIFTEEN MINUTES
THIS TIME HE JUST VANISHED— UNTIL THE POLICE DOGS FOUND HIS BODY YESTERDAY EVENING, WHERE THAT CROSS IS
I DON'T KNOW WHAT M EXPECTS ME TO DO ABOUT IT!

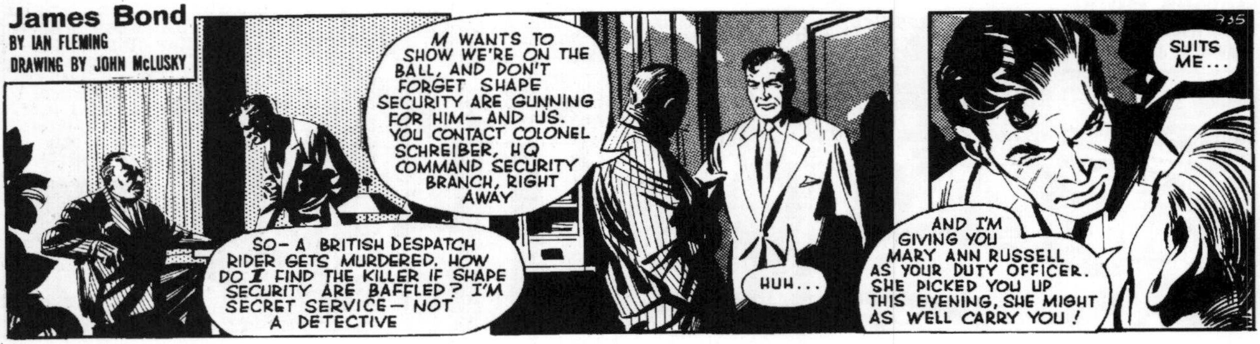
James Bond
BY IAN FLEMING
DRAWING BY JOHN McLUSKY
SO— A BRITISH DESPATCH RIDER GETS MURDERED. HOW DO I FIND THE KILLER IF SHAPE SECURITY ARE BAFFLED? I'M SECRET SERVICE— NOT A DETECTIVE
M WANTS TO SHOW WE'RE ON THE BALL, AND DON'T FORGET SHAPE SECURITY ARE GUNNING FOR HIM— AND US. YOU CONTACT COLONEL SCHREIBER, HQ COMMAND SECURITY BRANCH, RIGHT AWAY
HUH...
AND I'M GIVING YOU MARY ANN RUSSELL AS YOUR DUTY OFFICER. SHE PICKED YOU UP THIS EVENING, SHE MIGHT AS WELL CARRY YOU!
SUITS ME...

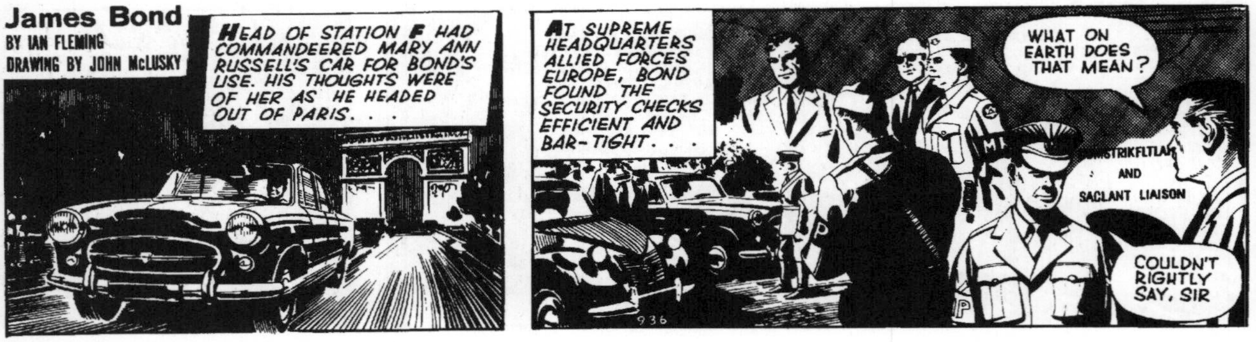
James Bond
BY IAN FLEMING
DRAWING BY JOHN McLUSKY
HEAD OF STATION F HAD COMMANDEERED MARY ANN RUSSELL'S CAR FOR BOND'S USE. HIS THOUGHTS WERE OF HER AS HE HEADED OUT OF PARIS...
AT SUPREME HEADQUARTERS ALLIED FORCES EUROPE, BOND FOUND THE SECURITY CHECKS EFFICIENT AND BAR-TIGHT...
WHAT ON EARTH DOES THAT MEAN?
AND
SACLANT LIAISON
COULDN'T RIGHTLY SAY, SIR

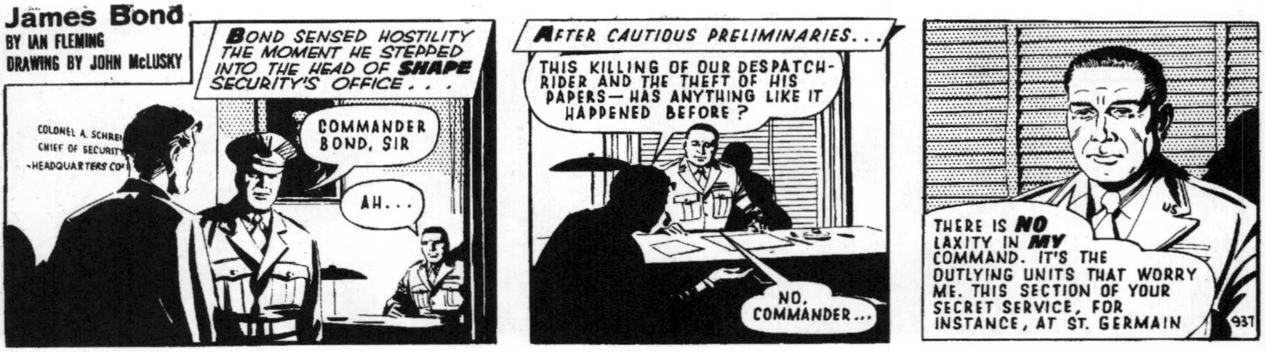
James Bond
BY IAN FLEMING
DRAWING BY JOHN McLUSKY
BOND SENSED HOSTILITY THE MOMENT HE STEPPED INTO THE HEAD OF SHAPE SECURITY'S OFFICE...
COMMANDER BOND, SIR
AH...
AFTER CAUTIOUS PRELIMINARIES...
THIS KILLING OF OUR DESPATCH-RIDER AND THE THEFT OF HIS PAPERS— HAS ANYTHING LIKE IT HAPPENED BEFORE?
NO, COMMANDER...
THERE IS NO LAXITY IN MY COMMAND. IT'S THE OUTLYING UNITS THAT WORRY ME. THIS SECTION OF YOUR SECRET SERVICE, FOR INSTANCE, AT ST. GERMAIN

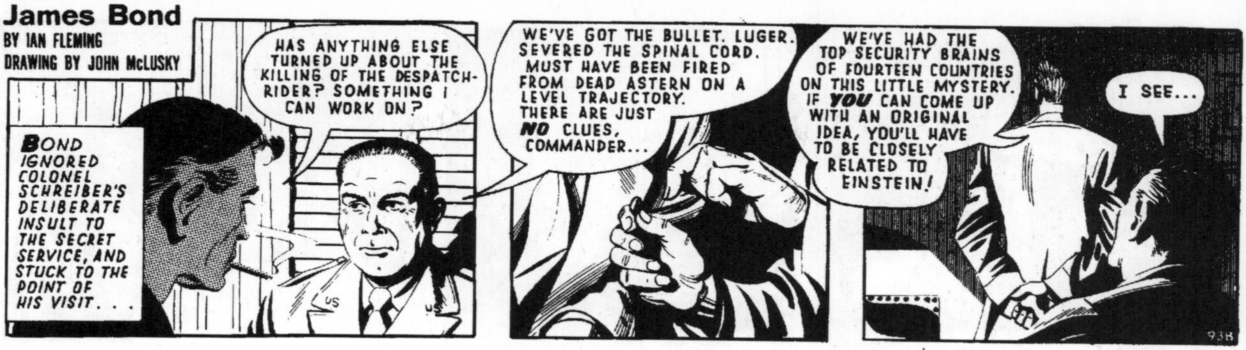
James Bond
BY IAN FLEMING
DRAWING BY JOHN McLUSKY
BOND IGNORED COLONEL SCHREIBER'S DELIBERATE INSULT TO THE SECRET SERVICE, AND STUCK TO THE POINT OF HIS VISIT . . .
HAS ANYTHING ELSE TURNED UP ABOUT THE KILLING OF THE DESPATCH-RIDER? SOMETHING I CAN WORK ON?
US
WE'VE GOT THE BULLET. LUGER. SEVERED THE SPINAL CORD. MUST HAVE BEEN FIRED FROM DEAD ASTERN ON A LEVEL TRAJECTORY. THERE ARE JUST NO CLUES, COMMANDER...
WE'VE HAD THE TOP SECURITY BRAINS OF FOURTEEN COUNTRIES ON THIS LITTLE MYSTERY. IF YOU CAN COME UP WITH AN ORIGINAL IDEA, YOU'LL HAVE TO BE CLOSELY RELATED TO EINSTEIN!
I SEE...
938

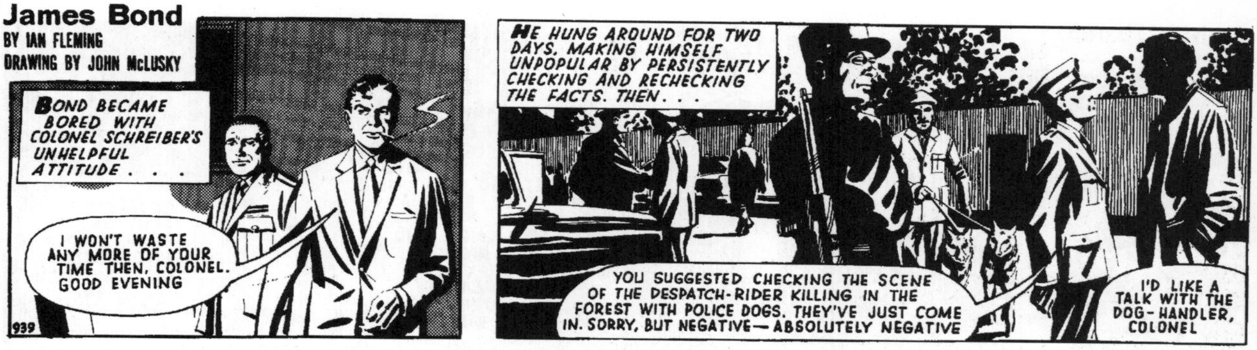
James Bond
BY IAN FLEMING
DRAWING BY JOHN McLUSKY
BOND BECAME BORED WITH COLONEL SCHREIBER'S UNHELPFUL ATTITUDE . . .
I WON'T WASTE ANY MORE OF YOUR TIME THEN, COLONEL. GOOD EVENING
939
HE HUNG AROUND FOR TWO DAYS, MAKING HIMSELF UNPOPULAR BY PERSISTENTLY CHECKING AND RECHECKING THE FACTS. THEN. . .
YOU SUGGESTED CHECKING THE SCENE OF THE DESPATCH-RIDER KILLING IN THE FOREST WITH POLICE DOGS. THEY'VE JUST COME IN. SORRY, BUT NEGATIVE— ABSOLUTELY NEGATIVE
I'D LIKE A TALK WITH THE DOG-HANDLER, COLONEL

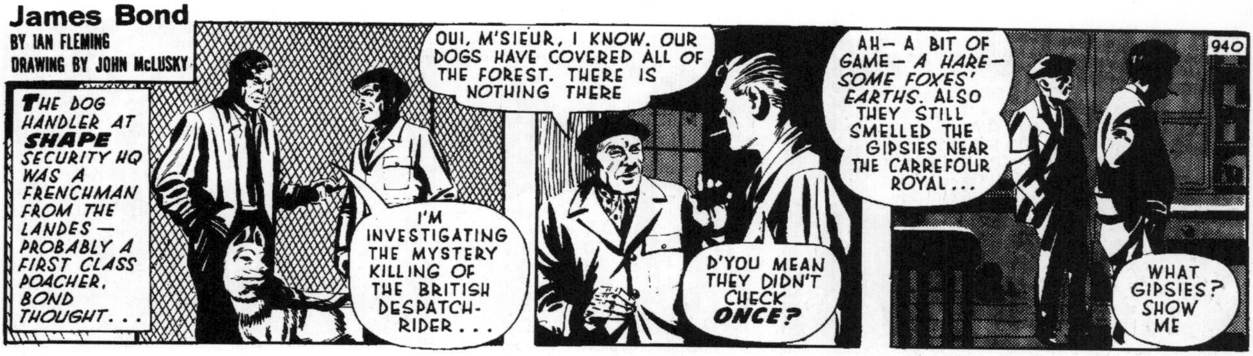
James Bond
BY IAN FLEMING
DRAWING BY JOHN McLUSKY
THE DOG HANDLER AT SHAPE SECURITY HQ WAS A FRENCHMAN FROM THE LANDES — PROBABLY A FIRST CLASS POACHER, BOND THOUGHT. . .
I'M INVESTIGATING THE MYSTERY KILLING OF THE BRITISH DESPATCH-RIDER . . .
OUI, M'SIEUR, I KNOW. OUR DOGS HAVE COVERED ALL OF THE FOREST. THERE IS NOTHING THERE
D'YOU MEAN THEY DIDN'T CHECK ONCE?
940
AH— A BIT OF GAME— A HARE— SOME FOXES' EARTHS. ALSO THEY STILL SMELLED THE GIPSIES NEAR THE CARREFOUR ROYAL...
WHAT GIPSIES? SHOW ME

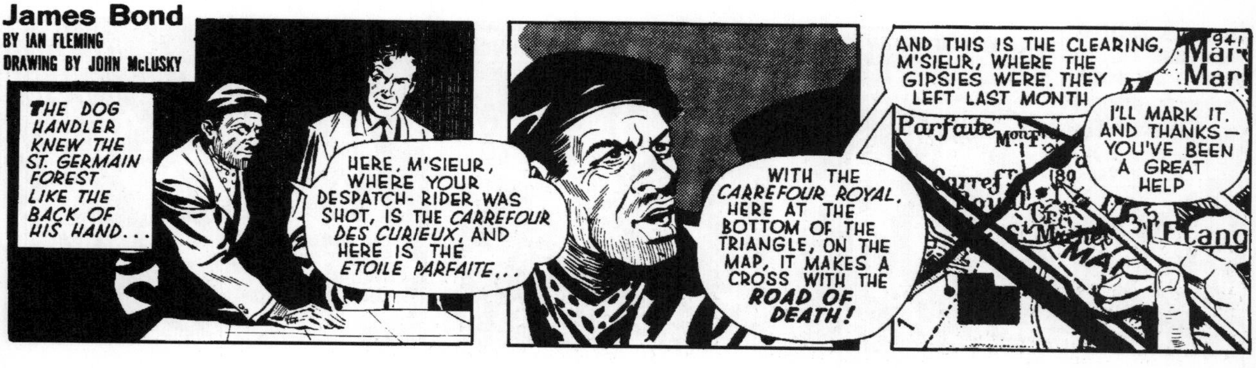
James Bond
BY IAN FLEMING
DRAWING BY JOHN McLUSKY
THE DOG HANDLER KNEW THE ST. GERMAIN FOREST LIKE THE BACK OF HIS HAND...
HERE, M'SIEUR, WHERE YOUR DESPATCH-RIDER WAS SHOT, IS THE CARREFOUR DES CURIEUX, AND HERE IS THE ETOILE PARFAITE...
WITH THE CARREFOUR ROYAL, HERE AT THE BOTTOM OF THE TRIANGLE, ON THE MAP, IT MAKES A CROSS WITH THE ROAD OF DEATH!
941
AND THIS IS THE CLEARING, M'SIEUR, WHERE THE GIPSIES WERE. THEY LEFT LAST MONTH
I'LL MARK IT. AND THANKS— YOU'VE BEEN A GREAT HELP
Parfaite
l'Etang

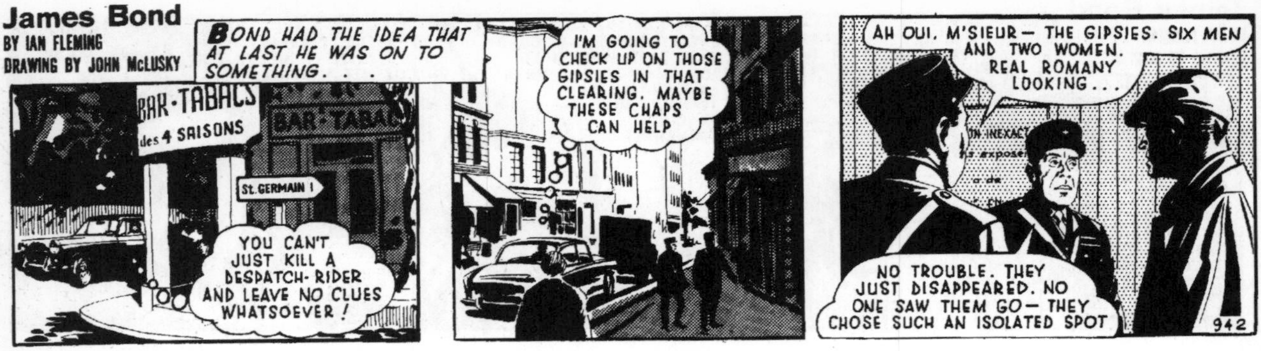
James Bond
BY IAN FLEMING
DRAWING BY JOHN McLUSKY
BOND HAD THE IDEA THAT AT LAST HE WAS ON TO SOMETHING. . .
BAR-TABACS des 4 SAISONS
BAR-TABAC
St. GERMAIN !
YOU CAN'T JUST KILL A DESPATCH-RIDER AND LEAVE NO CLUES WHATSOEVER !
I'M GOING TO CHECK UP ON THOSE GIPSIES IN THAT CLEARING. MAYBE THESE CHAPS CAN HELP
AH OUI, M'SIEUR — THE GIPSIES. SIX MEN AND TWO WOMEN. REAL ROMANY LOOKING...
NO TROUBLE. THEY JUST DISAPPEARED. NO ONE SAW THEM GO — THEY CHOSE SUCH AN ISOLATED SPOT
942

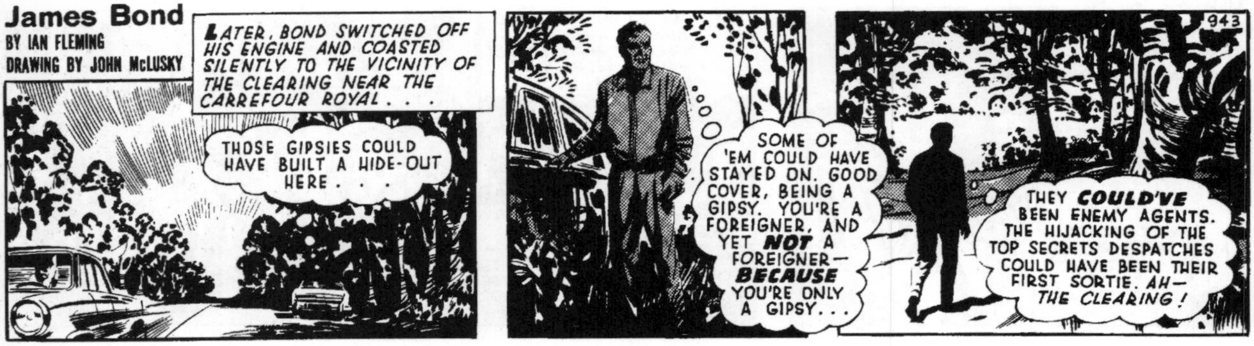
James Bond
BY IAN FLEMING
DRAWING BY JOHN McLUSKY
LATER, BOND SWITCHED OFF HIS ENGINE AND COASTED SILENTLY TO THE VICINITY OF THE CLEARING NEAR THE CARREFOUR ROYAL . . .
THOSE GIPSIES COULD HAVE BUILT A HIDE-OUT HERE . . .
SOME OF 'EM COULD HAVE STAYED ON. GOOD COVER, BEING A GIPSY. YOU'RE A FOREIGNER, AND YET NOT A FOREIGNER — BECAUSE YOU'RE ONLY A GIPSY...
943
THEY COULD'VE BEEN ENEMY AGENTS. THE HIJACKING OF THE TOP SECRETS DESPATCHES COULD HAVE BEEN THEIR FIRST SORTIE. AH — THE CLEARING !

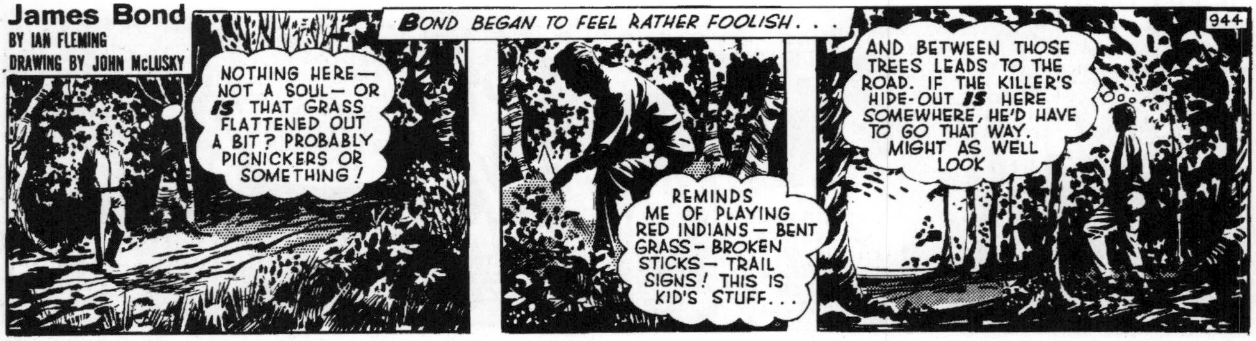
James Bond
BY IAN FLEMING
DRAWING BY JOHN McLUSKY
BOND BEGAN TO FEEL RATHER FOOLISH. . .
NOTHING HERE — NOT A SOUL — OR IS THAT GRASS FLATTENED OUT A BIT? PROBABLY PICNICKERS OR SOMETHING !
REMINDS ME OF PLAYING RED INDIANS — BENT GRASS — BROKEN STICKS — TRAIL SIGNS ! THIS IS KID'S STUFF...
944
AND BETWEEN THOSE TREES LEADS TO THE ROAD. IF THE KILLER'S HIDE-OUT IS HERE SOMEWHERE, HE'D HAVE TO GO THAT WAY. MIGHT AS WELL LOOK

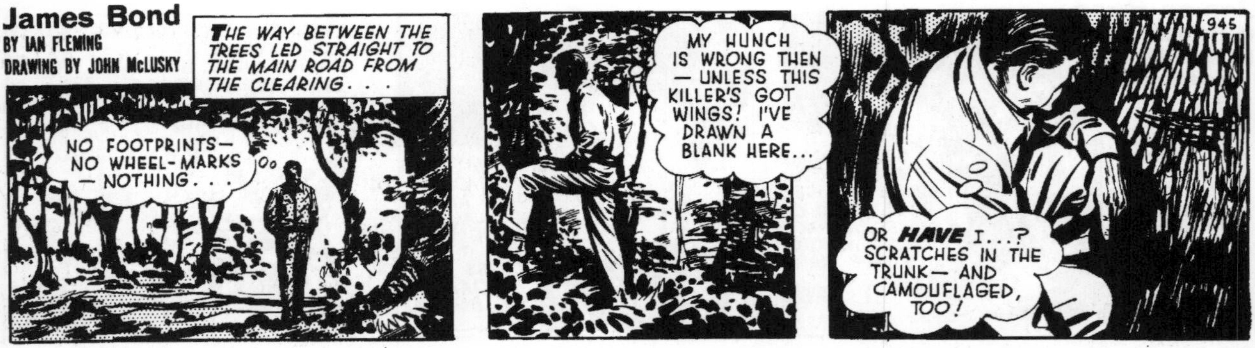
James Bond
BY IAN FLEMING
DRAWING BY JOHN McLUSKY
THE WAY BETWEEN THE TREES LED STRAIGHT TO THE MAIN ROAD FROM THE CLEARING. . .
NO FOOTPRINTS — NO WHEEL-MARKS — NOTHING. . .
MY HUNCH IS WRONG THEN — UNLESS THIS KILLER'S GOT WINGS! I'VE DRAWN A BLANK HERE...
945
OR HAVE I...? SCRATCHES IN THE TRUNK — AND CAMOUFLAGED, TOO !

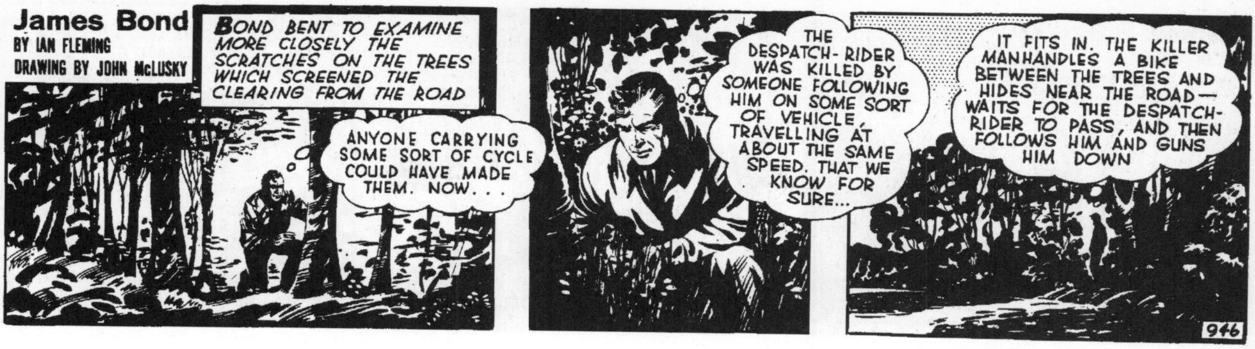

James Bond
BY IAN FLEMING
DRAWING BY JOHN McLUSKY
BOND BENT TO EXAMINE MORE CLOSELY THE SCRATCHES ON THE TREES WHICH SCREENED THE CLEARING FROM THE ROAD
ANYONE CARRYING SOME SORT OF CYCLE COULD HAVE MADE THEM. NOW . . .
THE DESPATCH-RIDER WAS KILLED BY SOMEONE FOLLOWING HIM ON SOME SORT OF VEHICLE, TRAVELLING AT ABOUT THE SAME SPEED. THAT WE KNOW FOR SURE...
IT FITS IN. THE KILLER MANHANDLES A BIKE BETWEEN THE TREES AND HIDES NEAR THE ROAD— WAITS FOR THE DESPATCH-RIDER TO PASS, AND THEN FOLLOWS HIM AND GUNS HIM DOWN
946

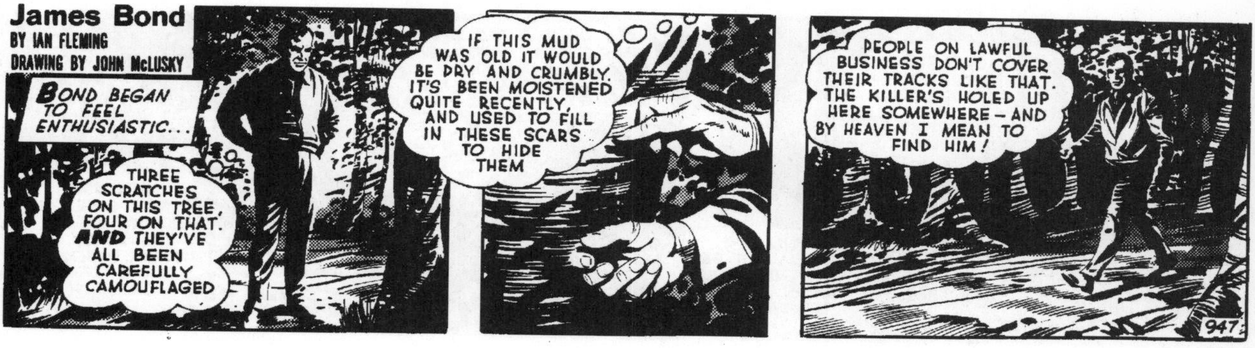

James Bond
BY IAN FLEMING
DRAWING BY JOHN McLUSKY
BOND BEGAN TO FEEL ENTHUSIASTIC...
THREE SCRATCHES ON THIS TREE, FOUR ON THAT. AND THEY'VE ALL BEEN CAREFULLY CAMOUFLAGED
IF THIS MUD WAS OLD IT WOULD BE DRY AND CRUMBLY. IT'S BEEN MOISTENED QUITE RECENTLY, AND USED TO FILL IN THESE SCARS TO HIDE THEM
PEOPLE ON LAWFUL BUSINESS DON'T COVER THEIR TRACKS LIKE THAT. THE KILLER'S HOLED UP HERE SOMEWHERE—AND BY HEAVEN I MEAN TO FIND HIM!
947

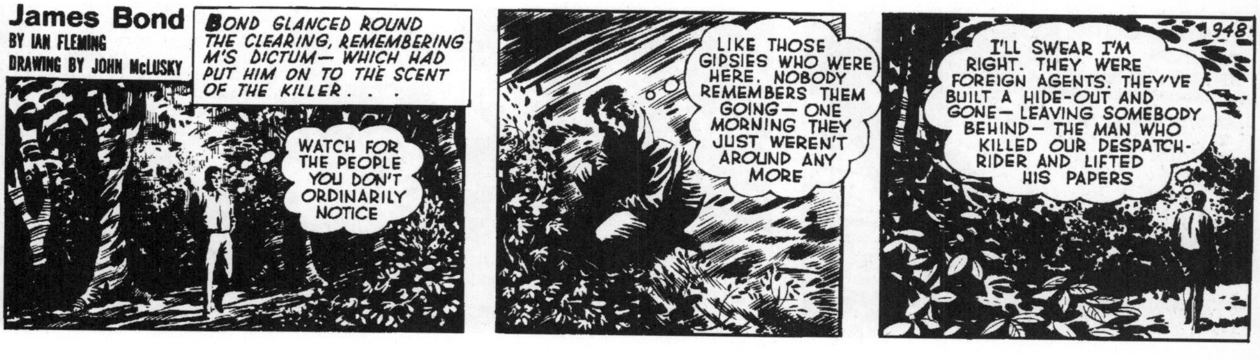

James Bond
BY IAN FLEMING
DRAWING BY JOHN McLUSKY
BOND GLANCED ROUND THE CLEARING, REMEMBERING M'S DICTUM— WHICH HAD PUT HIM ON TO THE SCENT OF THE KILLER . . .
WATCH FOR THE PEOPLE YOU DON'T ORDINARILY NOTICE
LIKE THOSE GIPSIES WHO WERE HERE. NOBODY REMEMBERS THEM GOING— ONE MORNING THEY JUST WEREN'T AROUND ANY MORE
948
I'LL SWEAR I'M RIGHT. THEY WERE FOREIGN AGENTS. THEY'VE BUILT A HIDE-OUT AND GONE— LEAVING SOMEBODY BEHIND— THE MAN WHO KILLED OUR DESPATCH-RIDER AND LIFTED HIS PAPERS

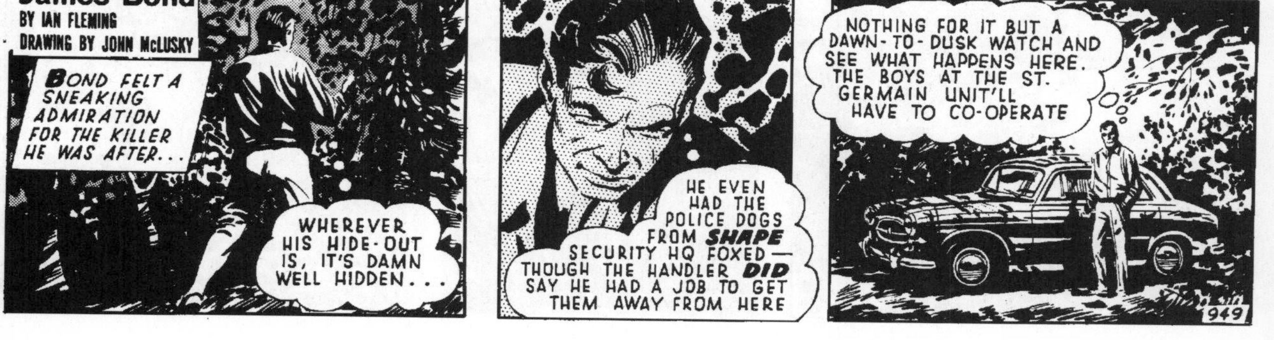

James Bond
BY IAN FLEMING
DRAWING BY JOHN McLUSKY
BOND FELT A SNEAKING ADMIRATION FOR THE KILLER HE WAS AFTER...
WHEREVER HIS HIDE-OUT IS, IT'S DAMN WELL HIDDEN . . .
HE EVEN HAD THE POLICE DOGS FROM SHAPE SECURITY HQ FOXED— THOUGH THE HANDLER DID SAY HE HAD A JOB TO GET THEM AWAY FROM HERE
NOTHING FOR IT BUT A DAWN-TO-DUSK WATCH AND SEE WHAT HAPPENS HERE. THE BOYS AT THE ST. GERMAIN UNIT'LL HAVE TO CO-OPERATE
949

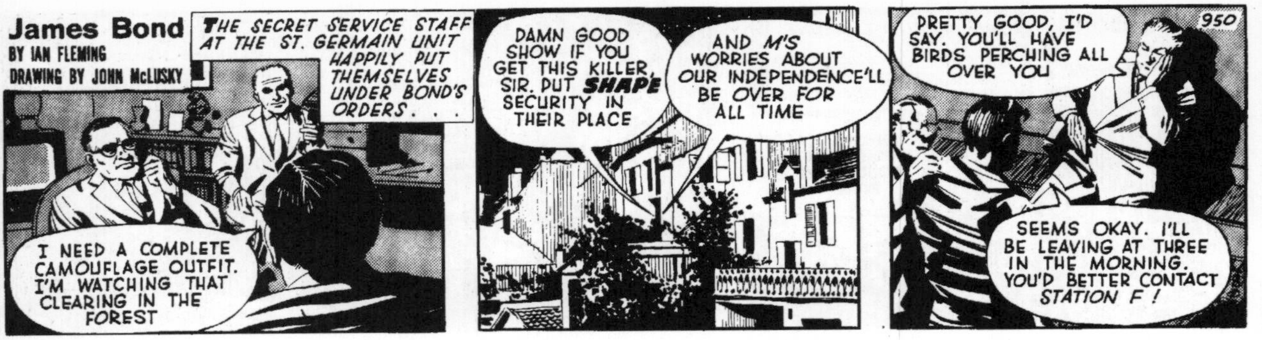
James Bond
BY IAN FLEMING
DRAWING BY JOHN McLUSKY
THE SECRET SERVICE STAFF AT THE ST. GERMAIN UNIT HAPPILY PUT THEMSELVES UNDER BOND'S ORDERS . . .
I NEED A COMPLETE CAMOUFLAGE OUTFIT. I'M WATCHING THAT CLEARING IN THE FOREST
DAMN GOOD SHOW IF YOU GET THIS KILLER, SIR. PUT SHAPE SECURITY IN THEIR PLACE
AND M'S WORRIES ABOUT OUR INDEPENDENCE'LL BE OVER FOR ALL TIME
950
PRETTY GOOD, I'D SAY. YOU'LL HAVE BIRDS PERCHING ALL OVER YOU
SEEMS OKAY. I'LL BE LEAVING AT THREE IN THE MORNING. YOU'D BETTER CONTACT STATION F !

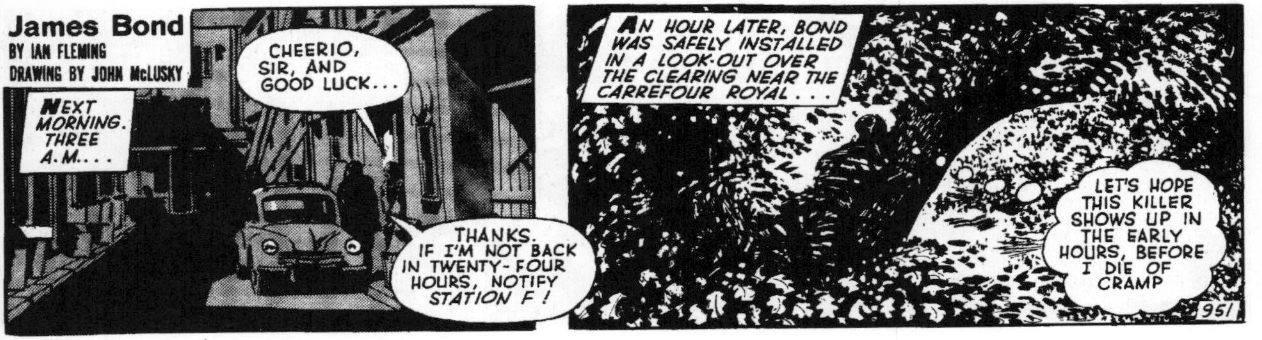
James Bond
BY IAN FLEMING
DRAWING BY JOHN McLUSKY
NEXT MORNING. THREE A.M. . . .
CHEERIO, SIR, AND GOOD LUCK . . .
THANKS. IF I'M NOT BACK IN TWENTY-FOUR HOURS, NOTIFY STATION F !
AN HOUR LATER, BOND WAS SAFELY INSTALLED IN A LOOK-OUT OVER THE CLEARING NEAR THE CARREFOUR ROYAL . . .
LET'S HOPE THIS KILLER SHOWS UP IN THE EARLY HOURS, BEFORE I DIE OF CRAMP
951

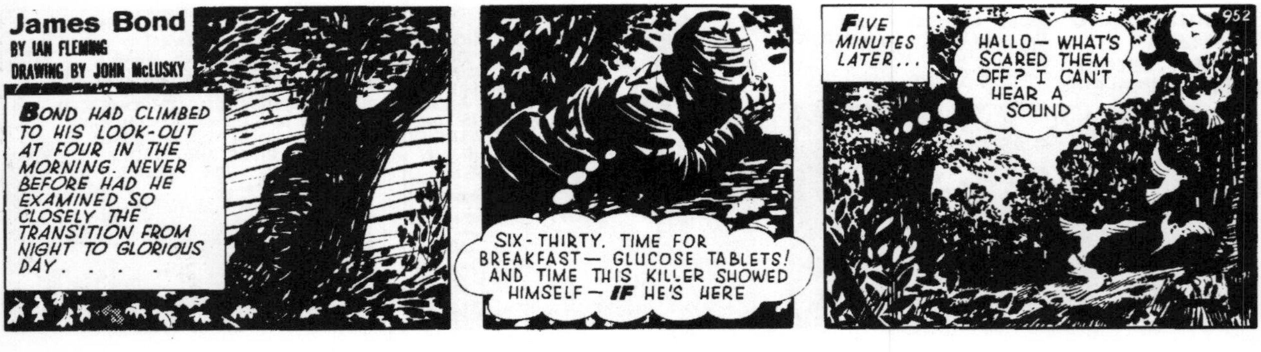
James Bond
BY IAN FLEMING
DRAWING BY JOHN McLUSKY
BOND HAD CLIMBED TO HIS LOOK-OUT AT FOUR IN THE MORNING. NEVER BEFORE HAD HE EXAMINED SO CLOSELY THE TRANSITION FROM NIGHT TO GLORIOUS DAY . . . .
SIX-THIRTY. TIME FOR BREAKFAST — GLUCOSE TABLETS! AND TIME THIS KILLER SHOWED HIMSELF — IF HE'S HERE
FIVE MINUTES LATER . . .
952
HALLO — WHAT'S SCARED THEM OFF? I CAN'T HEAR A SOUND

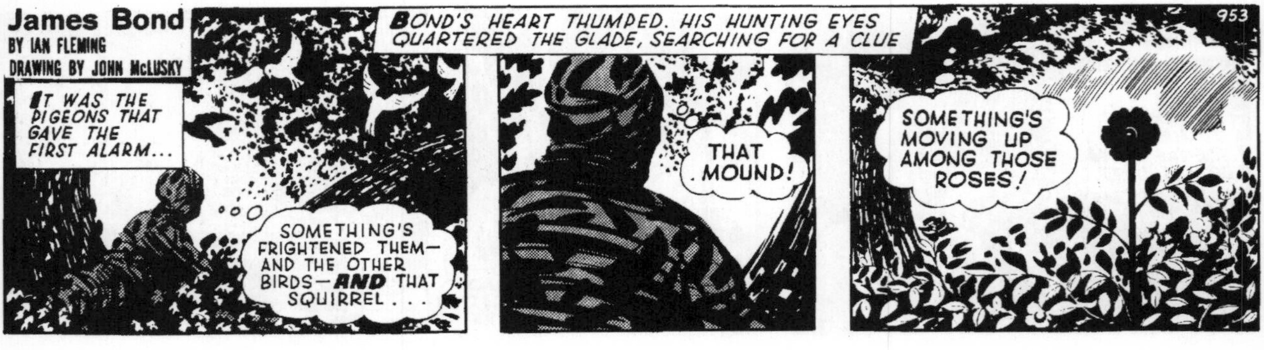
James Bond
BY IAN FLEMING
DRAWING BY JOHN McLUSKY
BOND'S HEART THUMPED. HIS HUNTING EYES QUARTERED THE GLADE, SEARCHING FOR A CLUE
IT WAS THE PIGEONS THAT GAVE THE FIRST ALARM . . .
SOMETHING'S FRIGHTENED THEM — AND THE OTHER BIRDS — AND THAT SQUIRREL . . .
THAT MOUND!
953
SOMETHING'S MOVING UP AMONG THOSE ROSES!

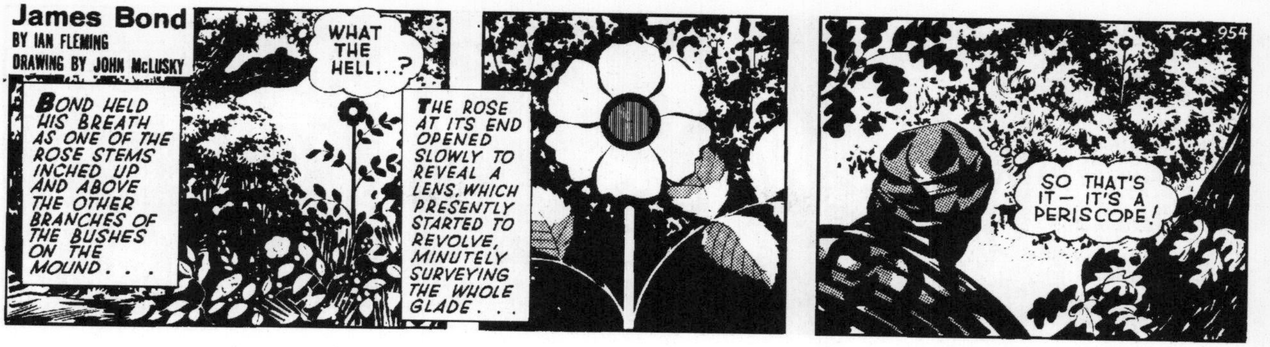
James Bond
BY IAN FLEMING
DRAWING BY JOHN McLUSKY
BOND HELD HIS BREATH AS ONE OF THE ROSE STEMS INCHED UP AND ABOVE THE OTHER BRANCHES OF THE BUSHES ON THE MOUND . . .
WHAT THE HELL...?
THE ROSE AT ITS END OPENED SLOWLY TO REVEAL A LENS, WHICH PRESENTLY STARTED TO REVOLVE, MINUTELY SURVEYING THE WHOLE GLADE . . .
954
SO THAT'S IT– IT'S A PERISCOPE!

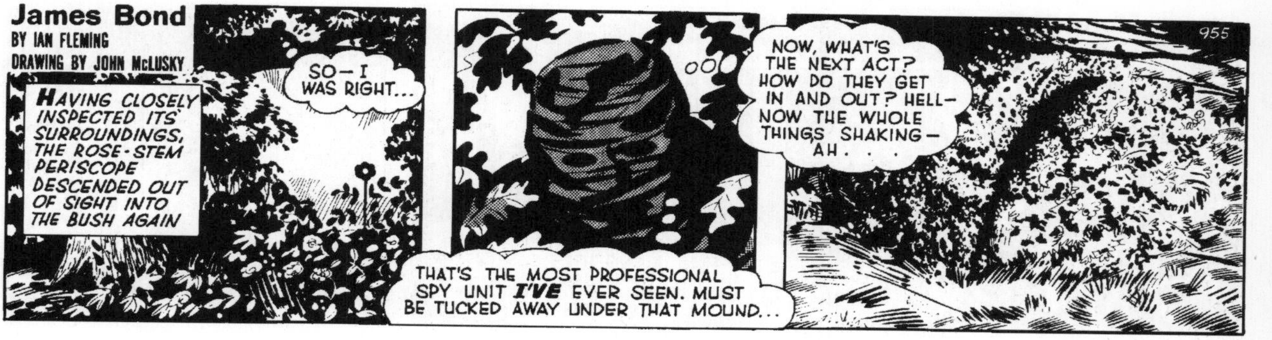
James Bond
BY IAN FLEMING
DRAWING BY JOHN McLUSKY
HAVING CLOSELY INSPECTED ITS SURROUNDINGS, THE ROSE-STEM PERISCOPE DESCENDED OUT OF SIGHT INTO THE BUSH AGAIN
SO– I WAS RIGHT...
THAT'S THE MOST PROFESSIONAL SPY UNIT I'VE EVER SEEN. MUST BE TUCKED AWAY UNDER THAT MOUND...
955
NOW, WHAT'S THE NEXT ACT? HOW DO THEY GET IN AND OUT? HELL– NOW THE WHOLE THING'S SHAKING– AH . . .

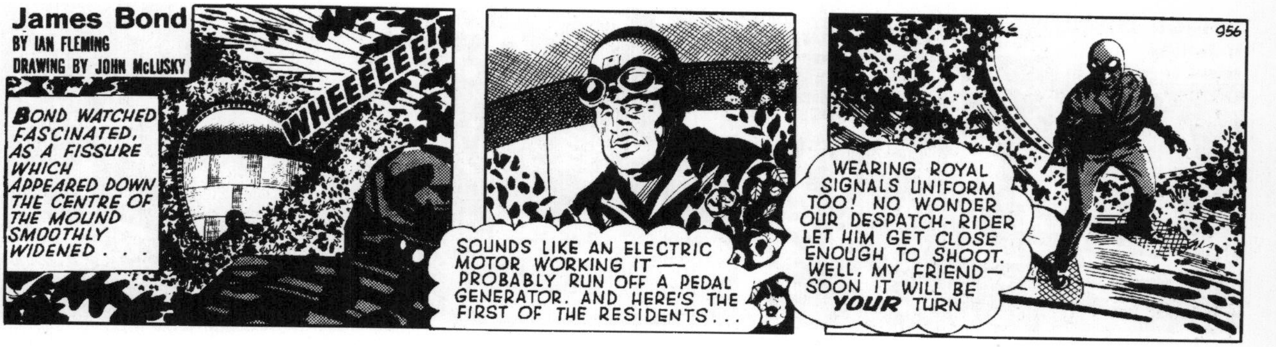
James Bond
BY IAN FLEMING
DRAWING BY JOHN McLUSKY
BOND WATCHED FASCINATED, AS A FISSURE WHICH APPEARED DOWN THE CENTRE OF THE MOUND SMOOTHLY WIDENED . . .
WHEEEEEE!
SOUNDS LIKE AN ELECTRIC MOTOR WORKING IT— PROBABLY RUN OFF A PEDAL GENERATOR. AND HERE'S THE FIRST OF THE RESIDENTS...
956
WEARING ROYAL SIGNALS UNIFORM TOO! NO WONDER OUR DESPATCH-RIDER LET HIM GET CLOSE ENOUGH TO SHOOT. WELL, MY FRIEND– SOON IT WILL BE YOUR TURN

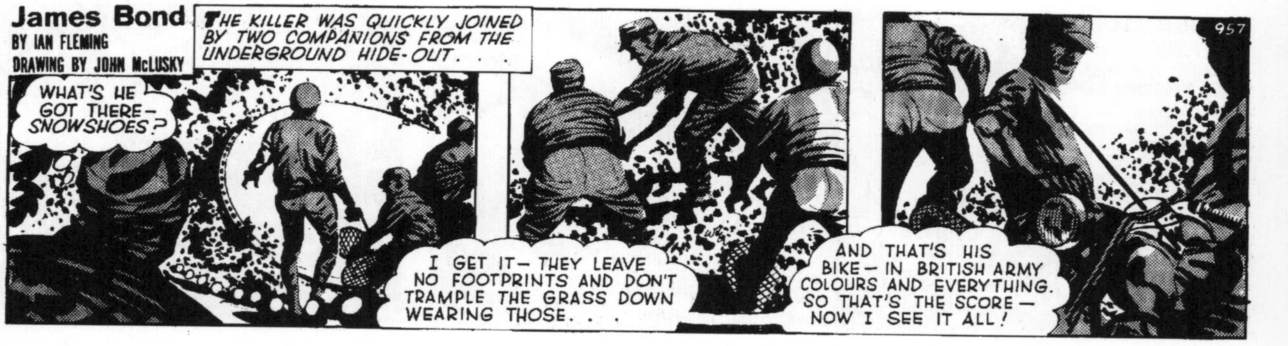
James Bond
BY IAN FLEMING
DRAWING BY JOHN McLUSKY
THE KILLER WAS QUICKLY JOINED BY TWO COMPANIONS FROM THE UNDERGROUND HIDE-OUT . . .
WHAT'S HE GOT THERE– SNOWSHOES?
I GET IT– THEY LEAVE NO FOOTPRINTS AND DON'T TRAMPLE THE GRASS DOWN WEARING THOSE. . .
957
AND THAT'S HIS BIKE– IN BRITISH ARMY COLOURS AND EVERYTHING. SO THAT'S THE SCORE— NOW I SEE IT ALL!

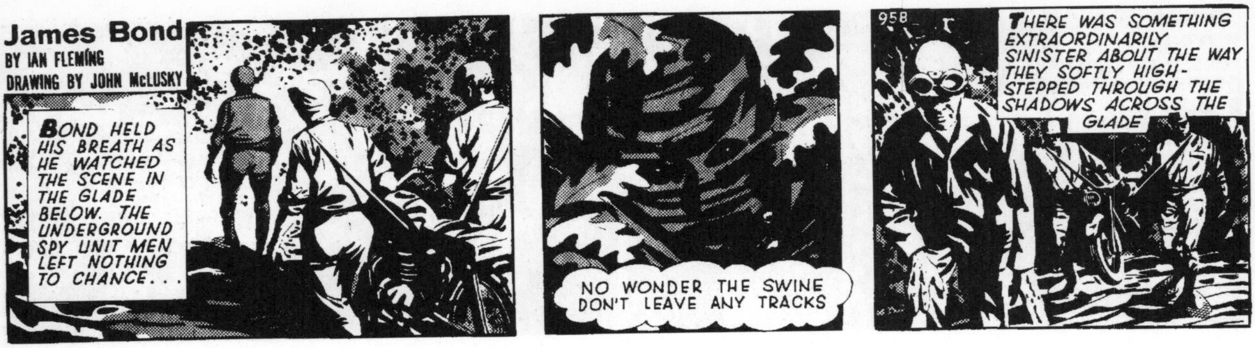

James Bond
BY IAN FLEMING
DRAWING BY JOHN McLUSKY
BOND HELD HIS BREATH AS HE WATCHED THE SCENE IN THE GLADE BELOW. THE UNDERGROUND SPY UNIT MEN LEFT NOTHING TO CHANCE...
NO WONDER THE SWINE DON'T LEAVE ANY TRACKS
958
THERE WAS SOMETHING EXTRAORDINARILY SINISTER ABOUT THE WAY THEY SOFTLY HIGH-STEPPED THROUGH THE SHADOWS ACROSS THE GLADE

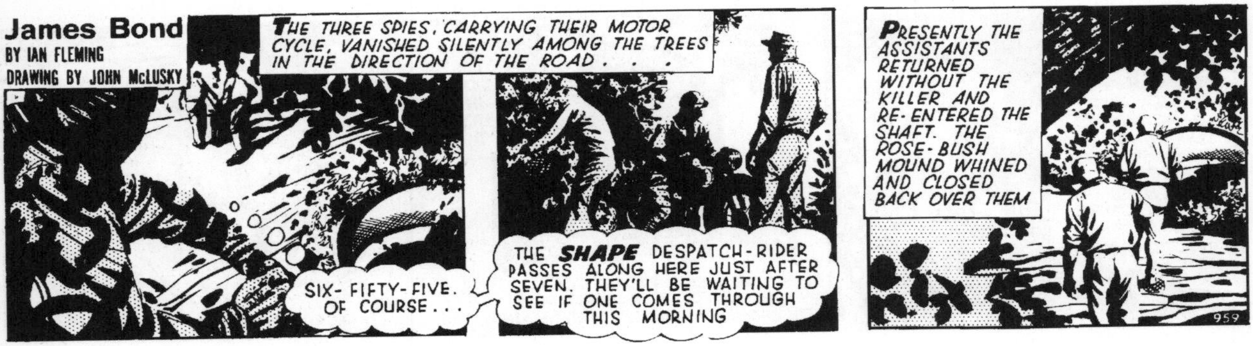

James Bond
BY IAN FLEMING
DRAWING BY JOHN McLUSKY
THE THREE SPIES, CARRYING THEIR MOTOR CYCLE, VANISHED SILENTLY AMONG THE TREES IN THE DIRECTION OF THE ROAD....
SIX-FIFTY-FIVE. OF COURSE...
THE SHAPE DESPATCH-RIDER PASSES ALONG HERE JUST AFTER SEVEN. THEY'LL BE WAITING TO SEE IF ONE COMES THROUGH THIS MORNING
PRESENTLY THE ASSISTANTS RETURNED WITHOUT THE KILLER AND RE-ENTERED THE SHAFT. THE ROSE-BUSH MOUND WHINED AND CLOSED BACK OVER THEM
959

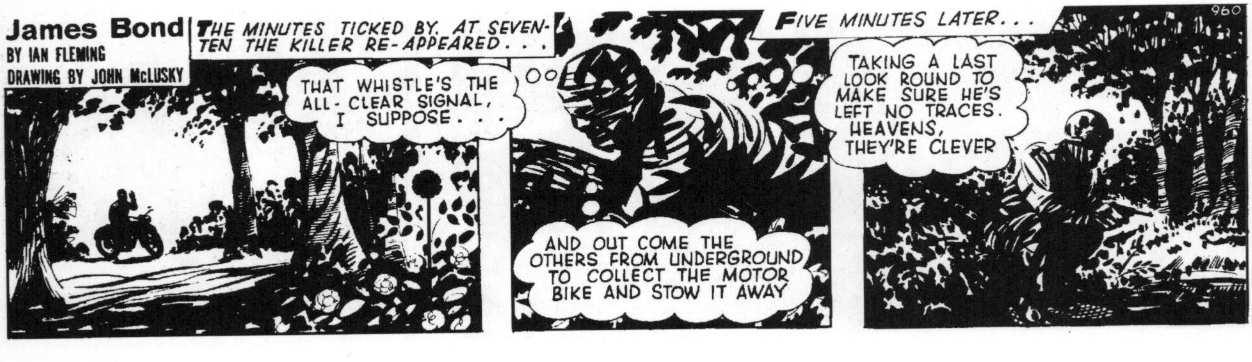

James Bond
BY IAN FLEMING
DRAWING BY JOHN McLUSKY
THE MINUTES TICKED BY. AT SEVEN-TEN THE KILLER RE-APPEARED...
THAT WHISTLE'S THE ALL-CLEAR SIGNAL, I SUPPOSE...
AND OUT COME THE OTHERS FROM UNDERGROUND TO COLLECT THE MOTOR BIKE AND STOW IT AWAY
FIVE MINUTES LATER...
960
TAKING A LAST LOOK ROUND TO MAKE SURE HE'S LEFT NO TRACES. HEAVENS, THEY'RE CLEVER

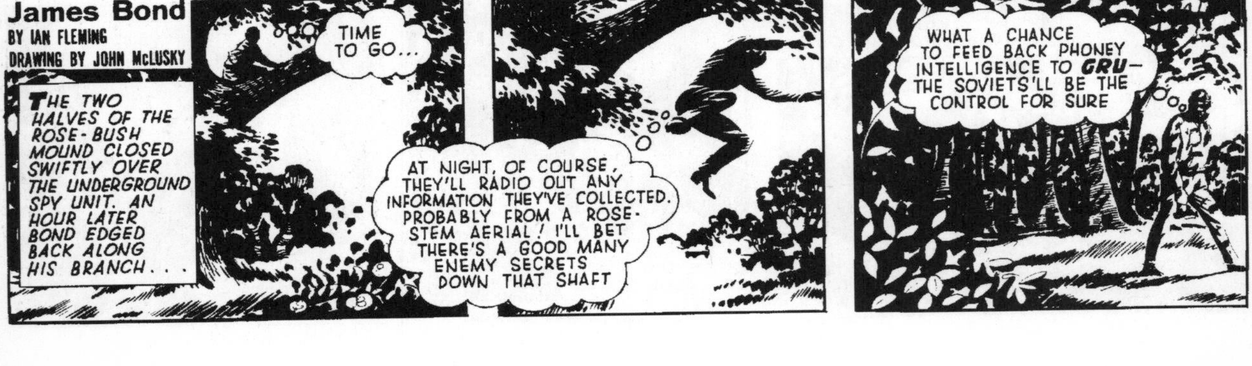

James Bond
BY IAN FLEMING
DRAWING BY JOHN McLUSKY
THE TWO HALVES OF THE ROSE-BUSH MOUND CLOSED SWIFTLY OVER THE UNDERGROUND SPY UNIT. AN HOUR LATER BOND EDGED BACK ALONG HIS BRANCH...
TIME TO GO...
AT NIGHT, OF COURSE, THEY'LL RADIO OUT ANY INFORMATION THEY'VE COLLECTED. PROBABLY FROM A ROSE-STEM AERIAL! I'LL BET THERE'S A GOOD MANY ENEMY SECRETS DOWN THAT SHAFT
961
WHAT A CHANCE TO FEED BACK PHONEY INTELLIGENCE TO GRU — THE SOVIETS'LL BE THE CONTROL FOR SURE

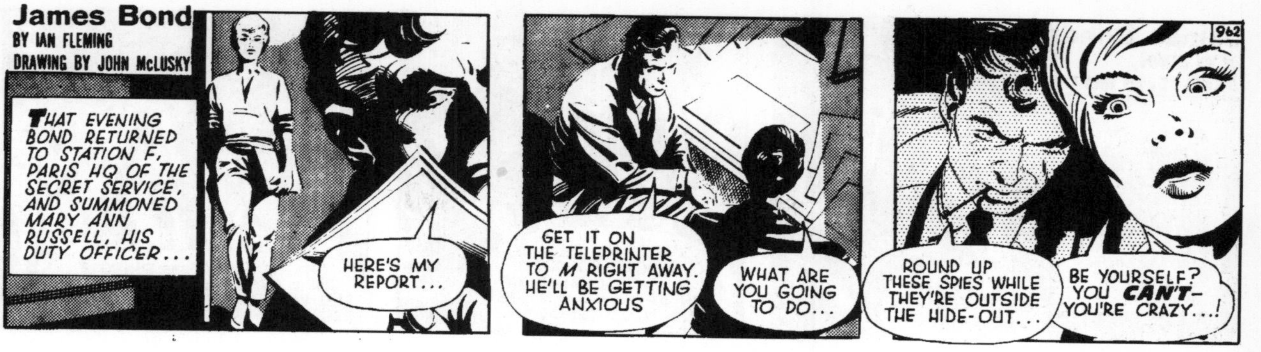
James Bond
BY IAN FLEMING
DRAWING BY JOHN McLUSKY
THAT EVENING BOND RETURNED TO STATION F, PARIS HQ OF THE SECRET SERVICE, AND SUMMONED MARY ANN RUSSELL, HIS DUTY OFFICER...
HERE'S MY REPORT...
GET IT ON THE TELEPRINTER TO M RIGHT AWAY. HE'LL BE GETTING ANXIOUS
WHAT ARE YOU GOING TO DO...
962
ROUND UP THESE SPIES WHILE THEY'RE OUTSIDE THE HIDE-OUT...
BE YOURSELF? YOU CAN'T– YOU'RE CRAZY...!

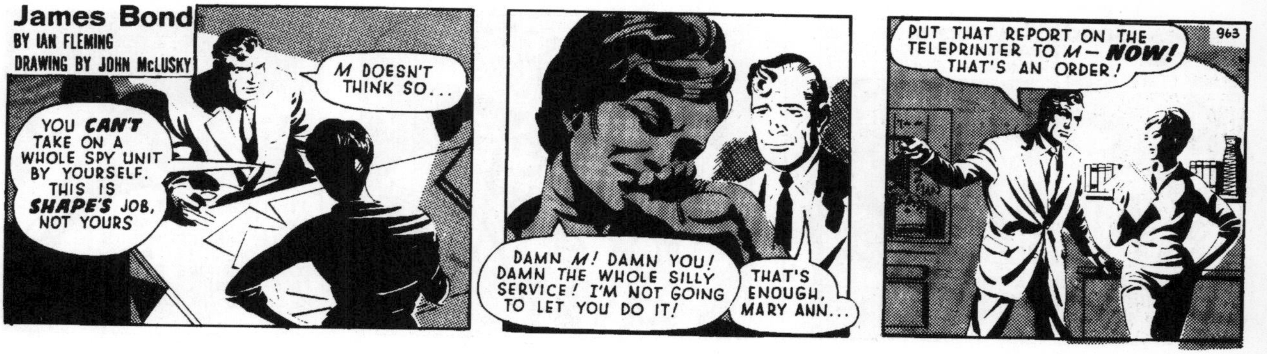
James Bond
BY IAN FLEMING
DRAWING BY JOHN McLUSKY
M DOESN'T THINK SO...
YOU CAN'T TAKE ON A WHOLE SPY UNIT BY YOURSELF. THIS IS SHAPE'S JOB, NOT YOURS
DAMN M! DAMN YOU! DAMN THE WHOLE SILLY SERVICE! I'M NOT GOING TO LET YOU DO IT!
THAT'S ENOUGH, MARY ANN...
963
PUT THAT REPORT ON THE TELEPRINTER TO M– NOW! THAT'S AN ORDER!

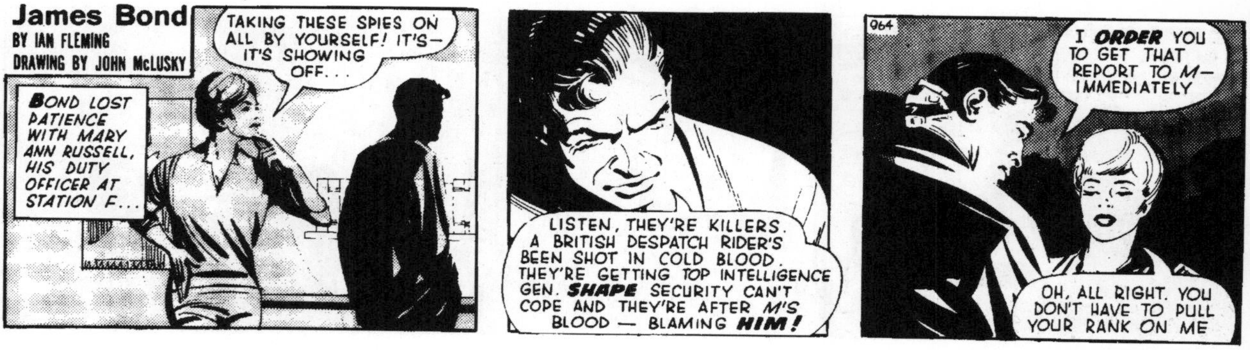
James Bond
BY IAN FLEMING
DRAWING BY JOHN McLUSKY
TAKING THESE SPIES ON ALL BY YOURSELF! IT'S– IT'S SHOWING OFF...
BOND LOST PATIENCE WITH MARY ANN RUSSELL, HIS DUTY OFFICER AT STATION F...
LISTEN, THEY'RE KILLERS. A BRITISH DESPATCH RIDER'S BEEN SHOT IN COLD BLOOD. THEY'RE GETTING TOP INTELLIGENCE GEN. SHAPE SECURITY CAN'T COPE AND THEY'RE AFTER M'S BLOOD — BLAMING HIM!
964
I ORDER YOU TO GET THAT REPORT TO M– IMMEDIATELY
OH, ALL RIGHT. YOU DON'T HAVE TO PULL YOUR RANK ON ME

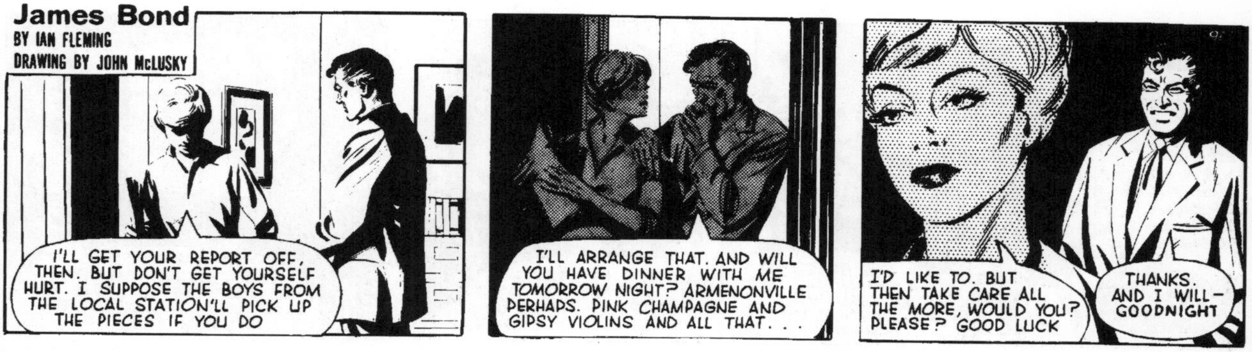
James Bond
BY IAN FLEMING
DRAWING BY JOHN McLUSKY
I'LL GET YOUR REPORT OFF, THEN. BUT DON'T GET YOURSELF HURT. I SUPPOSE THE BOYS FROM THE LOCAL STATION'LL PICK UP THE PIECES IF YOU DO
I'LL ARRANGE THAT. AND WILL YOU HAVE DINNER WITH ME TOMORROW NIGHT? ARMENONVILLE PERHAPS. PINK CHAMPAGNE AND GIPSY VIOLINS AND ALL THAT...
I'D LIKE TO. BUT THEN TAKE CARE ALL THE MORE, WOULD YOU? PLEASE? GOOD LUCK
THANKS. AND I WILL– GOODNIGHT

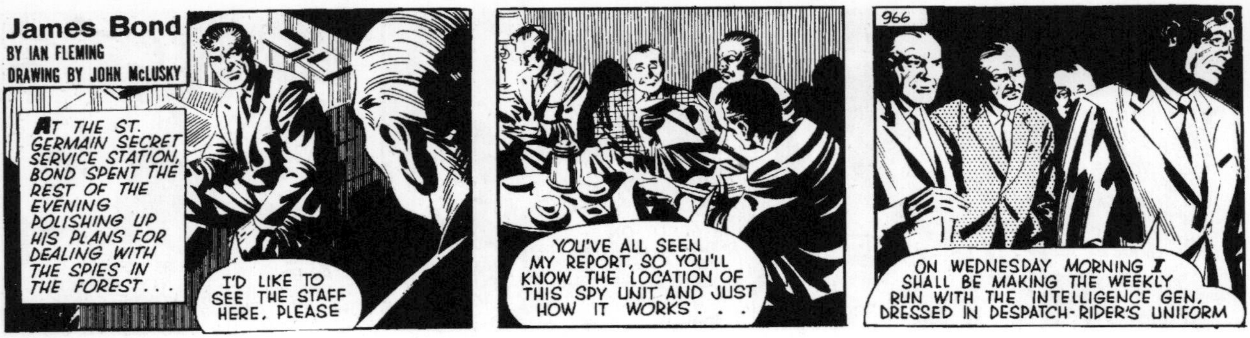
James Bond
BY IAN FLEMING
DRAWING BY JOHN McLUSKY
AT THE ST. GERMAIN SECRET SERVICE STATION, BOND SPENT THE REST OF THE EVENING POLISHING UP HIS PLANS FOR DEALING WITH THE SPIES IN THE FOREST . . .
I'D LIKE TO SEE THE STAFF HERE, PLEASE
YOU'VE ALL SEEN MY REPORT, SO YOU'LL KNOW THE LOCATION OF THIS SPY UNIT AND JUST HOW IT WORKS . . .
966
ON WEDNESDAY MORNING I SHALL BE MAKING THE WEEKLY RUN WITH THE INTELLIGENCE GEN, DRESSED IN DESPATCH-RIDER'S UNIFORM

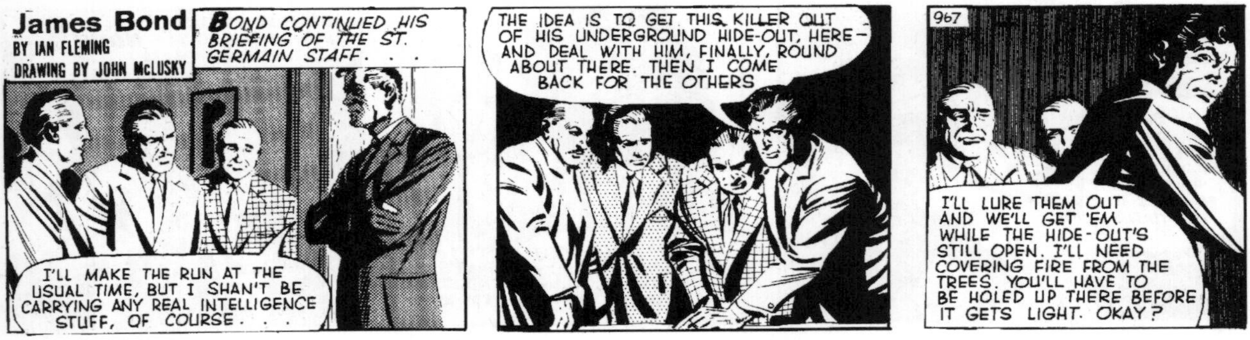
James Bond
BY IAN FLEMING
DRAWING BY JOHN McLUSKY
BOND CONTINUED HIS BRIEFING OF THE ST. GERMAIN STAFF . . .
I'LL MAKE THE RUN AT THE USUAL TIME, BUT I SHAN'T BE CARRYING ANY REAL INTELLIGENCE STUFF, OF COURSE . . .
THE IDEA IS TO GET THIS KILLER OUT OF HIS UNDERGROUND HIDE-OUT, HERE— AND DEAL WITH HIM, FINALLY, ROUND ABOUT THERE. THEN I COME BACK FOR THE OTHERS
967
I'LL LURE THEM OUT AND WE'LL GET 'EM WHILE THE HIDE-OUT'S STILL OPEN. I'LL NEED COVERING FIRE FROM THE TREES. YOU'LL HAVE TO BE HOLED UP THERE BEFORE IT GETS LIGHT. OKAY?

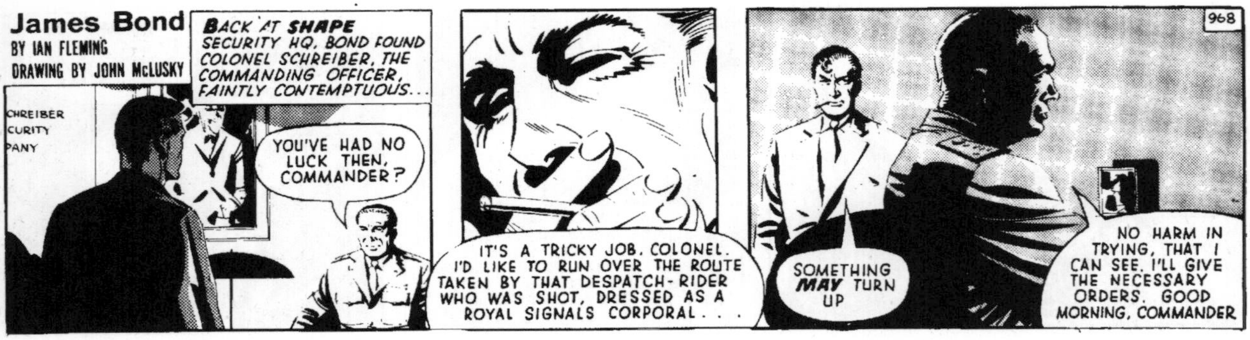
James Bond
BY IAN FLEMING
DRAWING BY JOHN McLUSKY
BACK AT SHAPE SECURITY HQ, BOND FOUND COLONEL SCHREIBER, THE COMMANDING OFFICER, FAINTLY CONTEMPTUOUS . . .
CHREIBER
CURITY
PANY
YOU'VE HAD NO LUCK THEN, COMMANDER?
IT'S A TRICKY JOB, COLONEL. I'D LIKE TO RUN OVER THE ROUTE TAKEN BY THAT DESPATCH-RIDER WHO WAS SHOT, DRESSED AS A ROYAL SIGNALS CORPORAL . . .
968
SOMETHING MAY TURN UP
NO HARM IN TRYING, THAT I CAN SEE. I'LL GIVE THE NECESSARY ORDERS. GOOD MORNING, COMMANDER

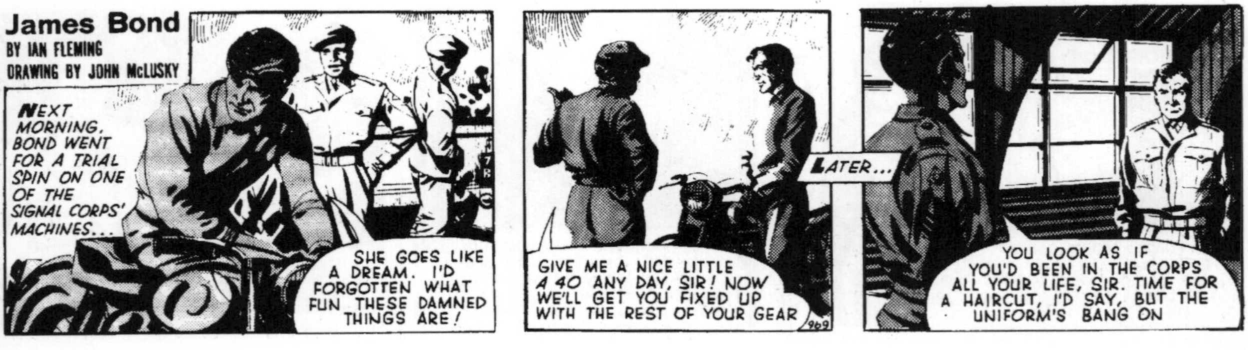
James Bond
BY IAN FLEMING
DRAWING BY JOHN McLUSKY
NEXT MORNING, BOND WENT FOR A TRIAL SPIN ON ONE OF THE SIGNAL CORPS' MACHINES . . .
SHE GOES LIKE A DREAM. I'D FORGOTTEN WHAT FUN THESE DAMNED THINGS ARE!
GIVE ME A NICE LITTLE A 40 ANY DAY, SIR! NOW WE'LL GET YOU FIXED UP WITH THE REST OF YOUR GEAR
969
LATER . . .
YOU LOOK AS IF YOU'D BEEN IN THE CORPS ALL YOUR LIFE, SIR. TIME FOR A HAIRCUT, I'D SAY, BUT THE UNIFORM'S BANG ON

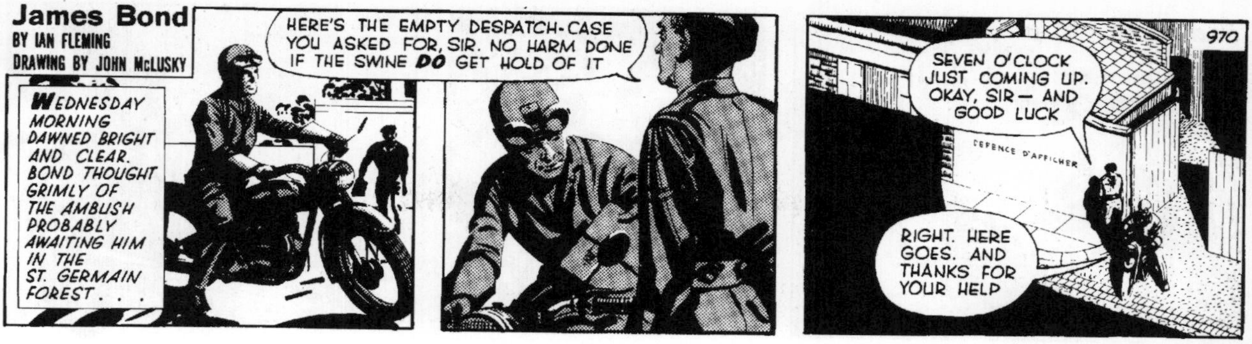
James Bond
BY IAN FLEMING
DRAWING BY JOHN McLUSKY
WEDNESDAY MORNING DAWNED BRIGHT AND CLEAR. BOND THOUGHT GRIMLY OF THE AMBUSH PROBABLY AWAITING HIM IN THE ST. GERMAIN FOREST . . .
HERE'S THE EMPTY DESPATCH-CASE YOU ASKED FOR, SIR. NO HARM DONE IF THE SWINE DO GET HOLD OF IT
970
SEVEN O'CLOCK JUST COMING UP. OKAY, SIR— AND GOOD LUCK
DEFENCE D'AFFICHER
RIGHT. HERE GOES. AND THANKS FOR YOUR HELP

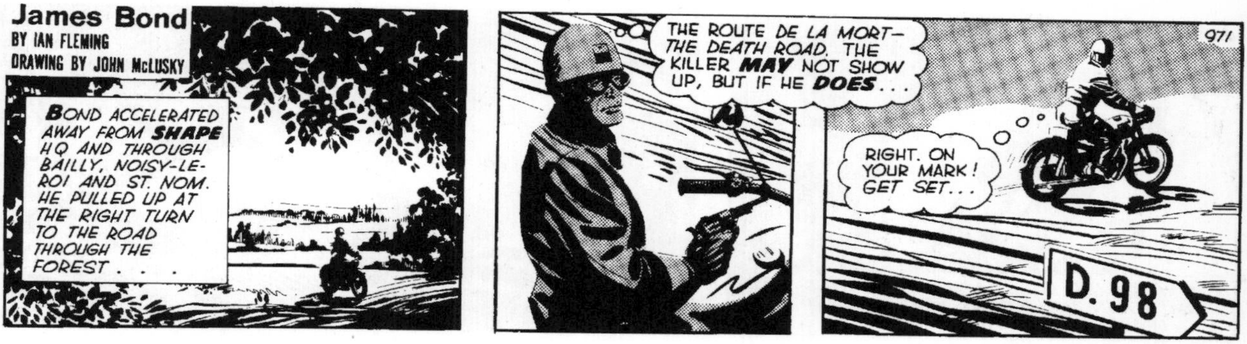
James Bond
BY IAN FLEMING
DRAWING BY JOHN McLUSKY
BOND ACCELERATED AWAY FROM SHAPE HQ AND THROUGH BAILLY, NOISY-LE-ROI AND ST. NOM. HE PULLED UP AT THE RIGHT TURN TO THE ROAD THROUGH THE FOREST . . . .
THE ROUTE DE LA MORT— THE DEATH ROAD. THE KILLER MAY NOT SHOW UP, BUT IF HE DOES . . .
971
RIGHT. ON YOUR MARK! GET SET . . .
D. 98

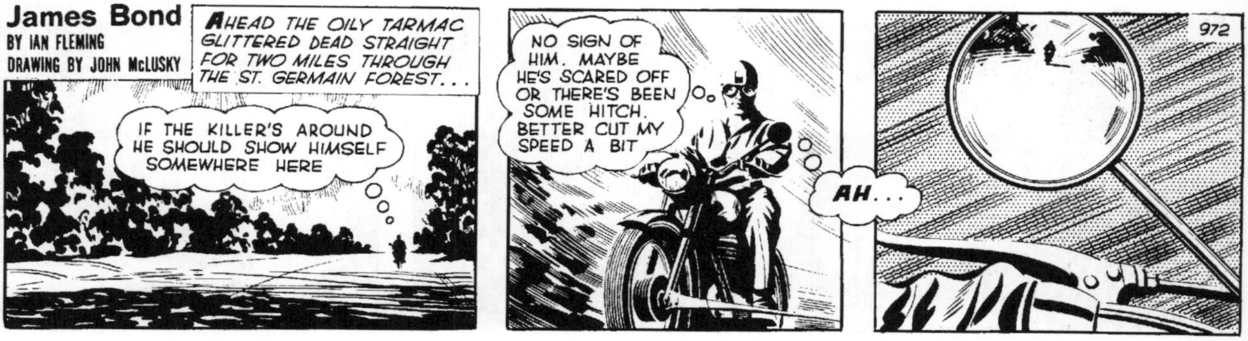
James Bond
BY IAN FLEMING
DRAWING BY JOHN McLUSKY
AHEAD THE OILY TARMAC GLITTERED DEAD STRAIGHT FOR TWO MILES THROUGH THE ST. GERMAIN FOREST . . .
IF THE KILLER'S AROUND HE SHOULD SHOW HIMSELF SOMEWHERE HERE
NO SIGN OF HIM. MAYBE HE'S SCARED OFF OR THERE'S BEEN SOME HITCH. BETTER CUT MY SPEED A BIT
AH . . .
972

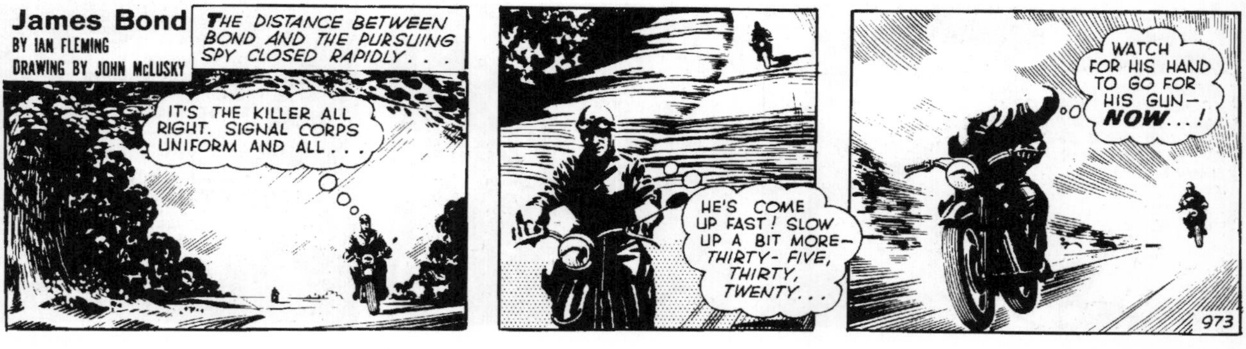
James Bond
BY IAN FLEMING
DRAWING BY JOHN McLUSKY
THE DISTANCE BETWEEN BOND AND THE PURSUING SPY CLOSED RAPIDLY . . .
IT'S THE KILLER ALL RIGHT. SIGNAL CORPS UNIFORM AND ALL . . .
HE'S COME UP FAST! SLOW UP A BIT MORE— THIRTY-FIVE, THIRTY, TWENTY . . .
WATCH FOR HIS HAND TO GO FOR HIS GUN— NOW . . .!
973

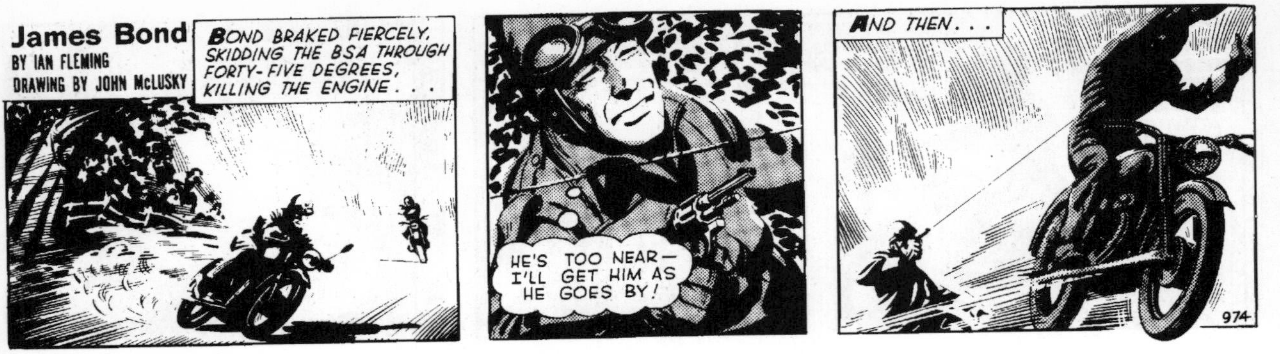
James Bond
BY IAN FLEMING
DRAWING BY JOHN McLUSKY
BOND BRAKED FIERCELY, SKIDDING THE BSA THROUGH FORTY-FIVE DEGREES, KILLING THE ENGINE . . .
HE'S TOO NEAR— I'LL GET HIM AS HE GOES BY!
AND THEN . . .
974

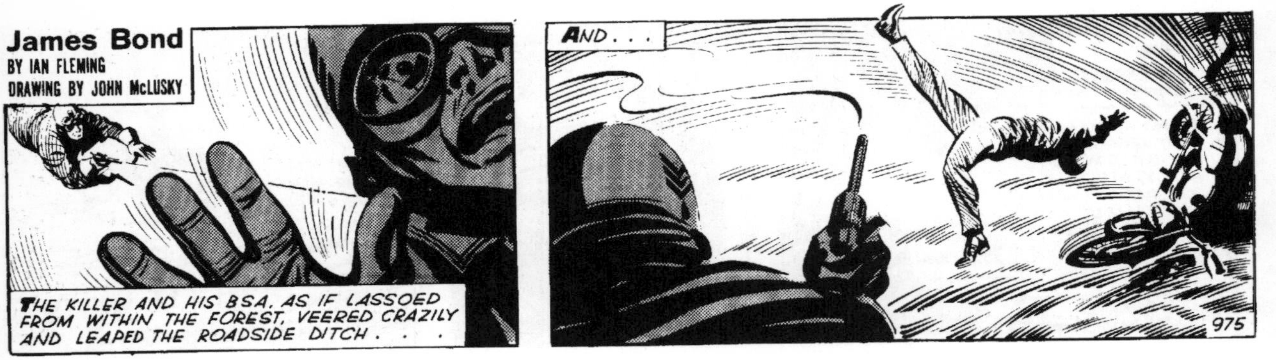
James Bond
BY IAN FLEMING
DRAWING BY JOHN McLUSKY
THE KILLER AND HIS BSA, AS IF LASSOED FROM WITHIN THE FOREST, VEERED CRAZILY AND LEAPED THE ROADSIDE DITCH . . .
AND . . .
975

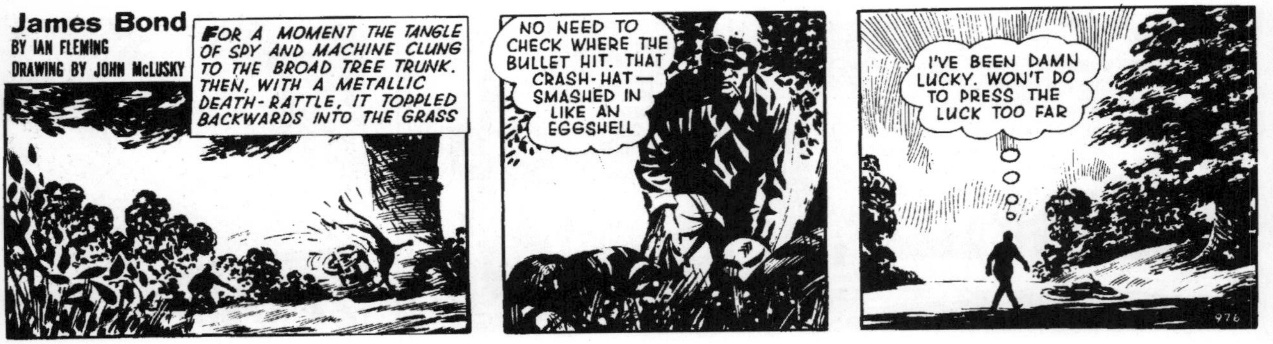
James Bond
BY IAN FLEMING
DRAWING BY JOHN McLUSKY
FOR A MOMENT THE TANGLE OF SPY AND MACHINE CLUNG TO THE BROAD TREE TRUNK. THEN, WITH A METALLIC DEATH-RATTLE, IT TOPPLED BACKWARDS INTO THE GRASS
NO NEED TO CHECK WHERE THE BULLET HIT. THAT CRASH-HAT— SMASHED IN LIKE AN EGGSHELL
I'VE BEEN DAMN LUCKY. WON'T DO TO PRESS THE LUCK TOO FAR
976

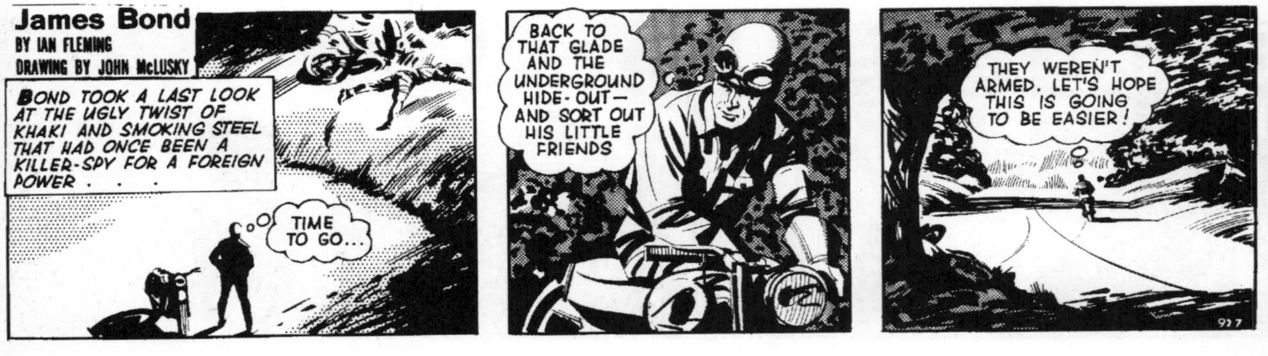
James Bond
BY IAN FLEMING
DRAWING BY JOHN McLUSKY
BOND TOOK A LAST LOOK AT THE UGLY TWIST OF KHAKI AND SMOKING STEEL THAT HAD ONCE BEEN A KILLER-SPY FOR A FOREIGN POWER . . .
TIME TO GO...
BACK TO THAT GLADE AND THE UNDERGROUND HIDE-OUT— AND SORT OUT HIS LITTLE FRIENDS
THEY WEREN'T ARMED. LET'S HOPE THIS IS GOING TO BE EASIER!
977

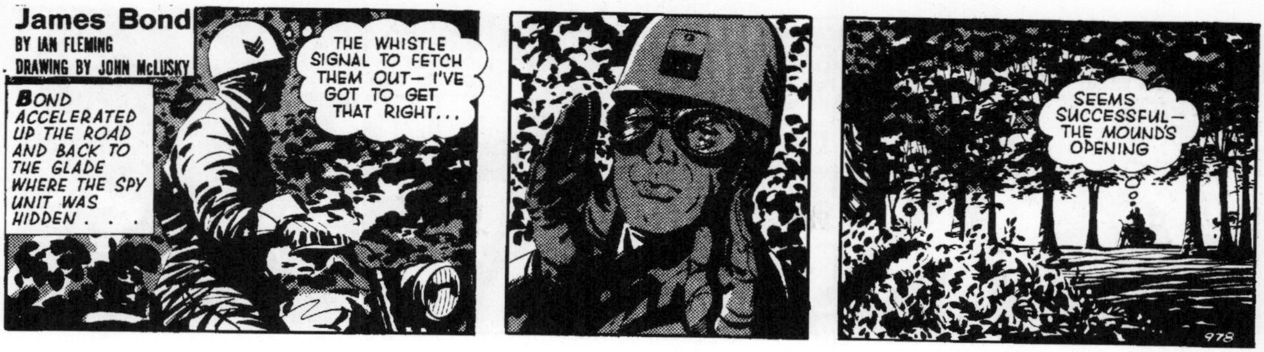
James Bond
BY IAN FLEMING
DRAWING BY JOHN McLUSKY
BOND ACCELERATED UP THE ROAD AND BACK TO THE GLADE WHERE THE SPY UNIT WAS HIDDEN . . .
THE WHISTLE SIGNAL TO FETCH THEM OUT— I'VE GOT TO GET THAT RIGHT...
SEEMS SUCCESSFUL— THE MOUND'S OPENING
978

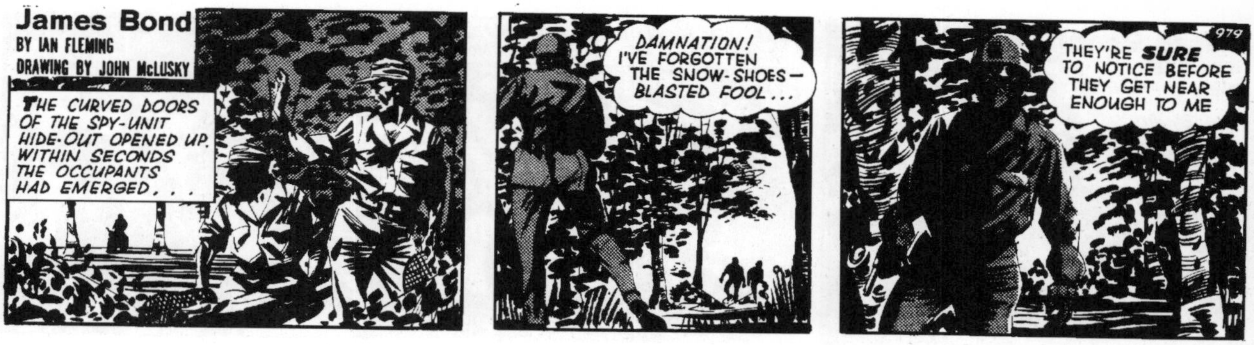
James Bond
BY IAN FLEMING
DRAWING BY JOHN McLUSKY
THE CURVED DOORS OF THE SPY-UNIT HIDE-OUT OPENED UP. WITHIN SECONDS THE OCCUPANTS HAD EMERGED . . .
DAMNATION! I'VE FORGOTTEN THE SNOW-SHOES— BLASTED FOOL...
979
THEY'RE SURE TO NOTICE BEFORE THEY GET NEAR ENOUGH TO ME

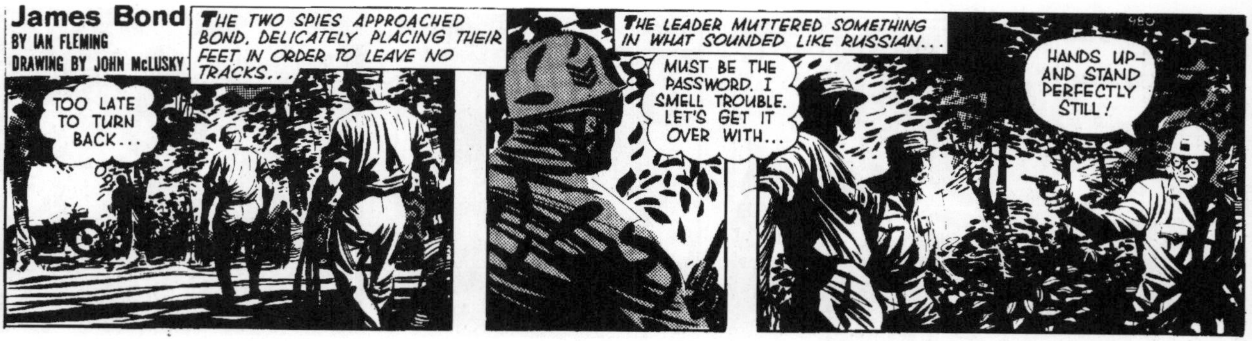
James Bond
BY IAN FLEMING
DRAWING BY JOHN McLUSKY
THE TWO SPIES APPROACHED BOND, DELICATELY PLACING THEIR FEET IN ORDER TO LEAVE NO TRACKS...
TOO LATE TO TURN BACK...
THE LEADER MUTTERED SOMETHING IN WHAT SOUNDED LIKE RUSSIAN...
MUST BE THE PASSWORD. I SMELL TROUBLE. LET'S GET IT OVER WITH...
HANDS UP— AND STAND PERFECTLY STILL!

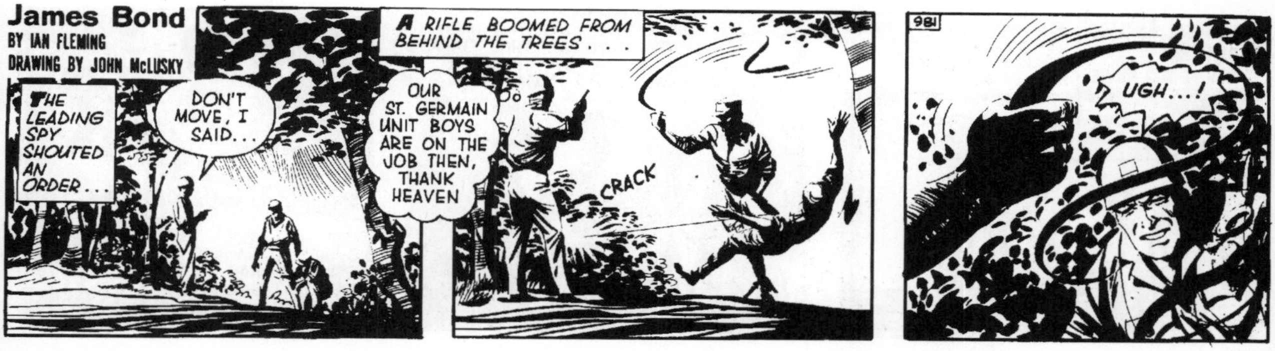
James Bond
BY IAN FLEMING
DRAWING BY JOHN McLUSKY
THE LEADING SPY SHOUTED AN ORDER...
DON'T MOVE, I SAID...
A RIFLE BOOMED FROM BEHIND THE TREES . . .
OUR ST. GERMAIN UNIT BOYS ARE ON THE JOB THEN, THANK HEAVEN
CRACK
981
UGH...!

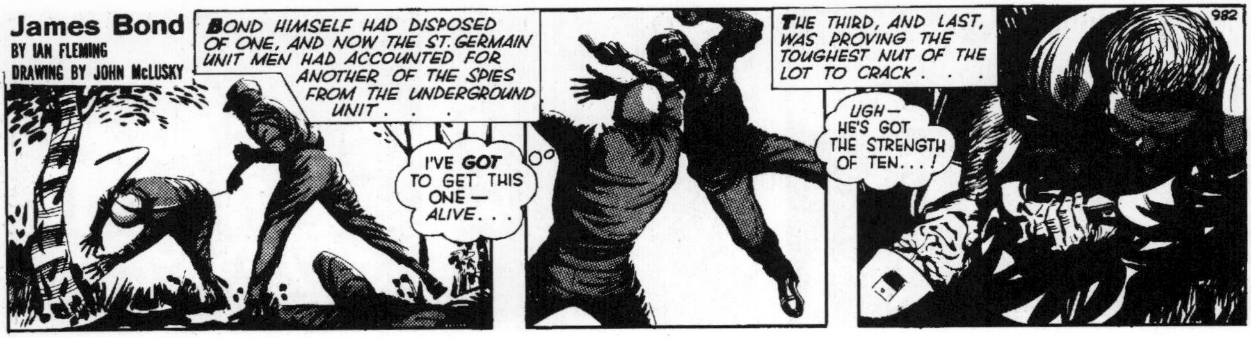
James Bond
BY IAN FLEMING
DRAWING BY JOHN McLUSKY
BOND HIMSELF HAD DISPOSED OF ONE, AND NOW THE ST. GERMAIN UNIT MEN HAD ACCOUNTED FOR ANOTHER OF THE SPIES FROM THE UNDERGROUND UNIT . . .
I'VE GOT TO GET THIS ONE — ALIVE . . .
THE THIRD, AND LAST, WAS PROVING THE TOUGHEST NUT OF THE LOT TO CRACK . . .
UGH — HE'S GOT THE STRENGTH OF TEN . . . !
982

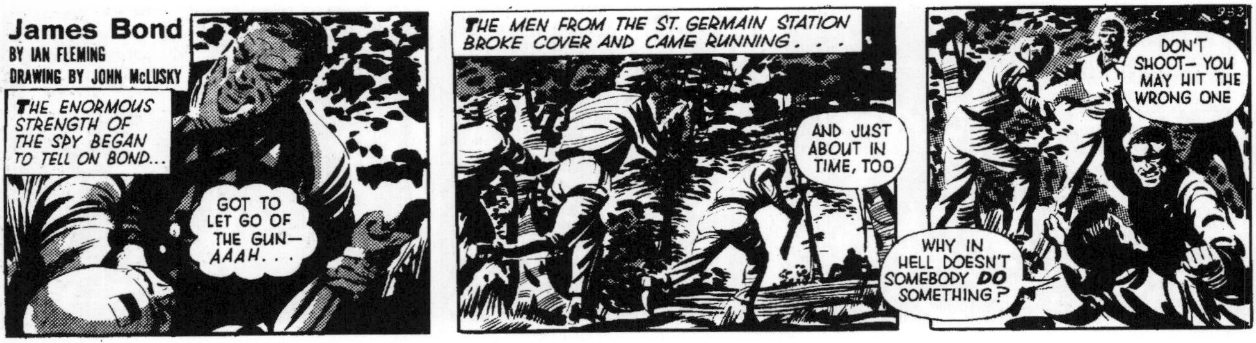
James Bond
BY IAN FLEMING
DRAWING BY JOHN McLUSKY
THE ENORMOUS STRENGTH OF THE SPY BEGAN TO TELL ON BOND . . .
GOT TO LET GO OF THE GUN — AAAH . . .
THE MEN FROM THE ST. GERMAIN STATION BROKE COVER AND CAME RUNNING . . .
AND JUST ABOUT IN TIME, TOO
DON'T SHOOT — YOU MAY HIT THE WRONG ONE
WHY IN HELL DOESN'T SOMEBODY DO SOMETHING?
983

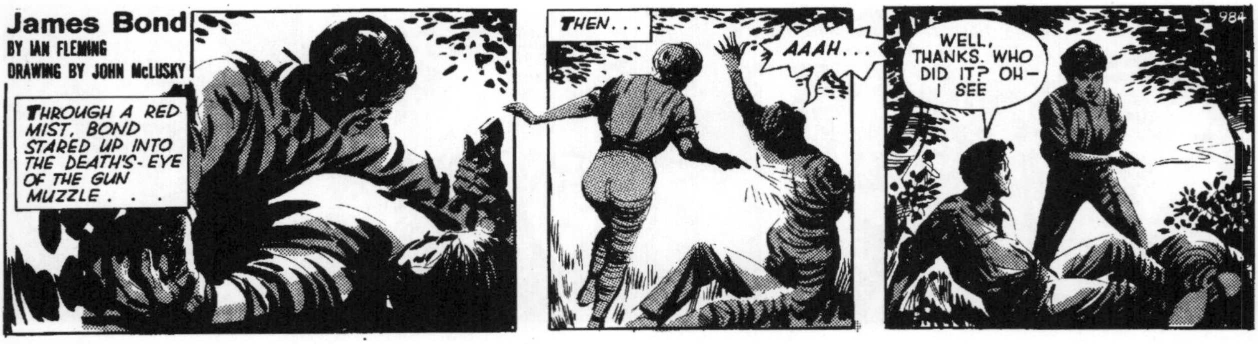
James Bond
BY IAN FLEMING
DRAWING BY JOHN McLUSKY
THROUGH A RED MIST, BOND STARED UP INTO THE DEATH'S-EYE OF THE GUN MUZZLE . . .
THEN . . .
AAAH . . .
WELL, THANKS. WHO DID IT? OH — I SEE
984

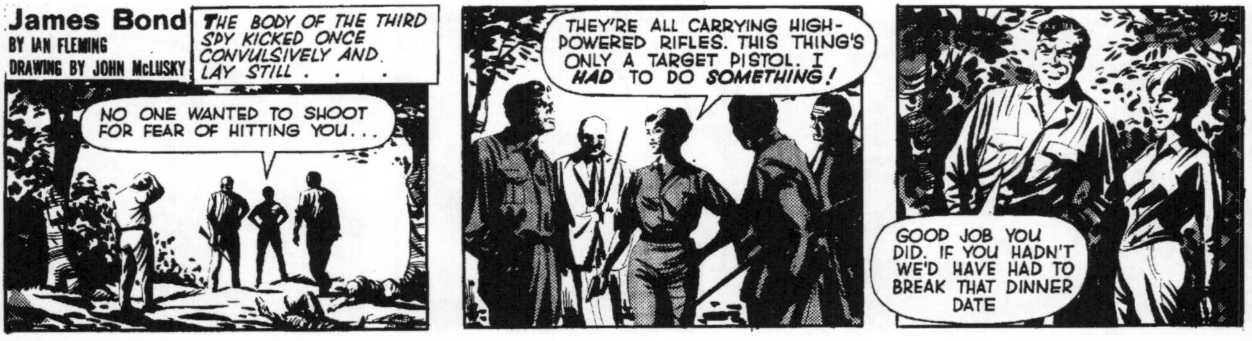
James Bond
BY IAN FLEMING
DRAWING BY JOHN McLUSKY
THE BODY OF THE THIRD SPY KICKED ONCE CONVULSIVELY AND LAY STILL . . .
NO ONE WANTED TO SHOOT FOR FEAR OF HITTING YOU . . .
THEY'RE ALL CARRYING HIGH-POWERED RIFLES. THIS THING'S ONLY A TARGET PISTOL. I HAD TO DO SOMETHING!
GOOD JOB YOU DID. IF YOU HADN'T WE'D HAVE HAD TO BREAK THAT DINNER DATE

James Bond
BY IAN FLEMING
DRAWING BY JOHN McLUSKY

BOND BECAME BUSINESS-LIKE. THE SPIES WERE DEAD. THEIR UNDERGROUND HIDE-OUT WAS OPEN, INVITING INSPECTION...

I'D LIKE TO GO DOWN THERE...

ONE OF YOU MEN TAKE THE MOTOR-BIKE AND REPORT THE GIST OF THIS TO COLONEL SCHREIBER AT *SHAPE* SECURITY HQ...

AND TELL HIM TO SEND AN ANTI-SABOTAGE SQUAD. THAT SHAFT MAY BE BOOBY-TRAPPED

986

James Bond
BY IAN FLEMING
DRAWING BY JOHN McLUSKY

BOND FELT THE TENSION INSIDE HIM UNWINDING. THE BUSINESS OF THE HIDDEN SPY UNIT WAS FINISHED. M WOULD BE HAPPY...

987

COME OVER HERE, MARY ANN RUSSELL, NUMBER 765 OF THE SECRET SERVICE...

I WANT TO SHOW YOU A BIRD'S NEST — IN THERE

IS THAT AN ORDER?

YES!

End of story

007

FOR YOUR EYES ONLY

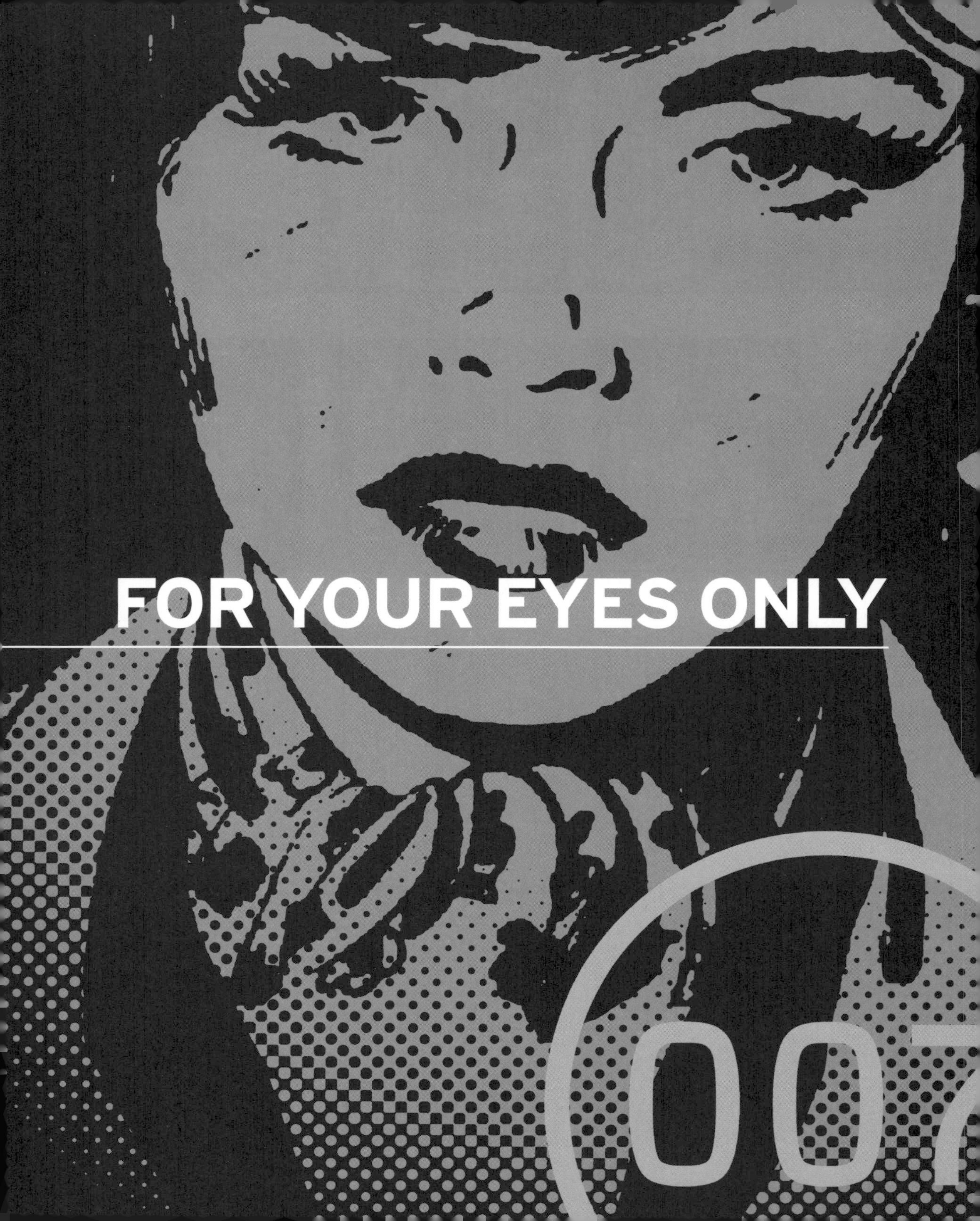
007

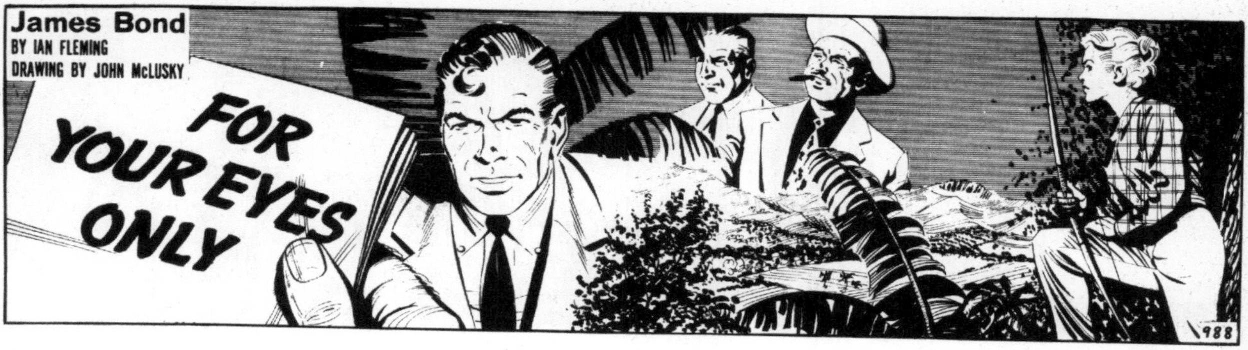
James Bond
BY IAN FLEMING
DRAWING BY JOHN McLUSKY
FOR YOUR EYES ONLY
988

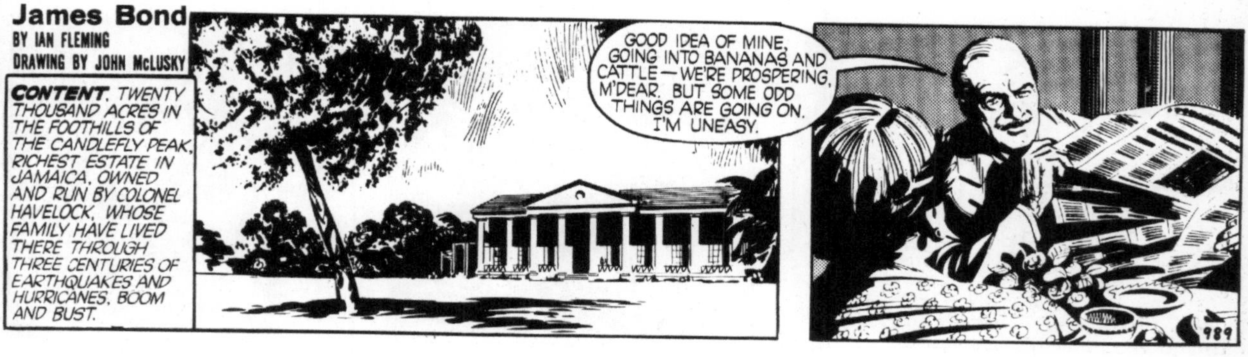
James Bond
BY IAN FLEMING
DRAWING BY JOHN McLUSKY
CONTENT. TWENTY THOUSAND ACRES IN THE FOOTHILLS OF THE CANDLEFLY PEAK, RICHEST ESTATE IN JAMAICA, OWNED AND RUN BY COLONEL HAVELOCK, WHOSE FAMILY HAVE LIVED THERE THROUGH THREE CENTURIES OF EARTHQUAKES AND HURRICANES, BOOM AND BUST.
GOOD IDEA OF MINE, GOING INTO BANANAS AND CATTLE—WE'RE PROSPERING, M'DEAR. BUT SOME ODD THINGS ARE GOING ON. I'M UNEASY.
989

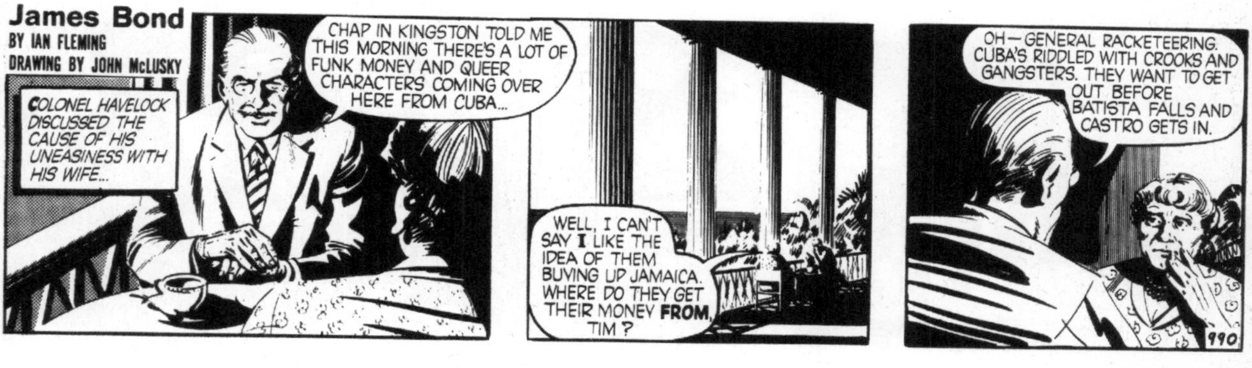
James Bond
BY IAN FLEMING
DRAWING BY JOHN McLUSKY
COLONEL HAVELOCK DISCUSSED THE CAUSE OF HIS UNEASINESS WITH HIS WIFE...
CHAP IN KINGSTON TOLD ME THIS MORNING THERE'S A LOT OF FUNK MONEY AND QUEER CHARACTERS COMING OVER HERE FROM CUBA...
WELL, I CAN'T SAY I LIKE THE IDEA OF THEM BUYING UP JAMAICA. WHERE DO THEY GET THEIR MONEY FROM, TIM?
OH—GENERAL RACKETEERING. CUBA'S RIDDLED WITH CROOKS AND GANGSTERS. THEY WANT TO GET OUT BEFORE BATISTA FALLS AND CASTRO GETS IN.
990

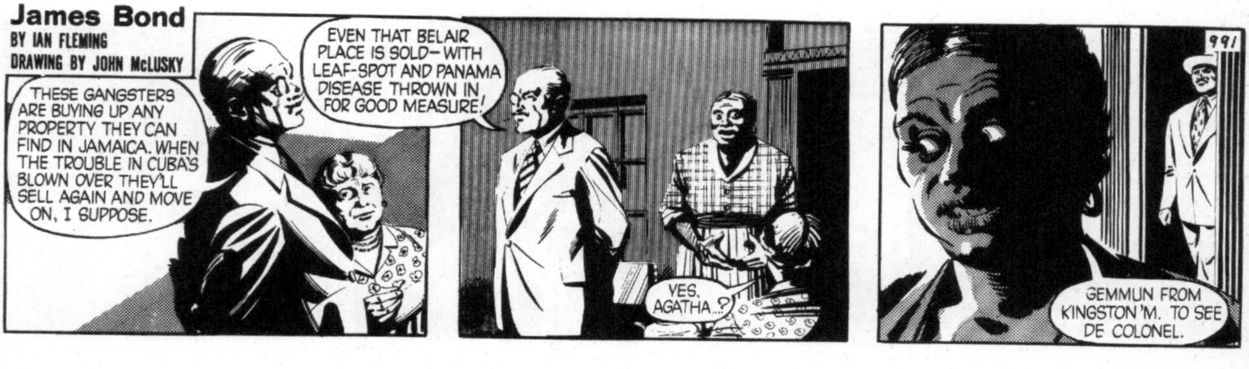
James Bond
BY IAN FLEMING
DRAWING BY JOHN McLUSKY
THESE GANGSTERS ARE BUYING UP ANY PROPERTY THEY CAN FIND IN JAMAICA. WHEN THE TROUBLE IN CUBA'S BLOWN OVER THEY'LL SELL AGAIN AND MOVE ON, I SUPPOSE.
EVEN THAT BELAIR PLACE IS SOLD—WITH LEAF-SPOT AND PANAMA DISEASE THROWN IN FOR GOOD MEASURE!
YES, AGATHA...?
991
GEMMUN FROM KINGSTON 'M. TO SEE DE COLONEL.

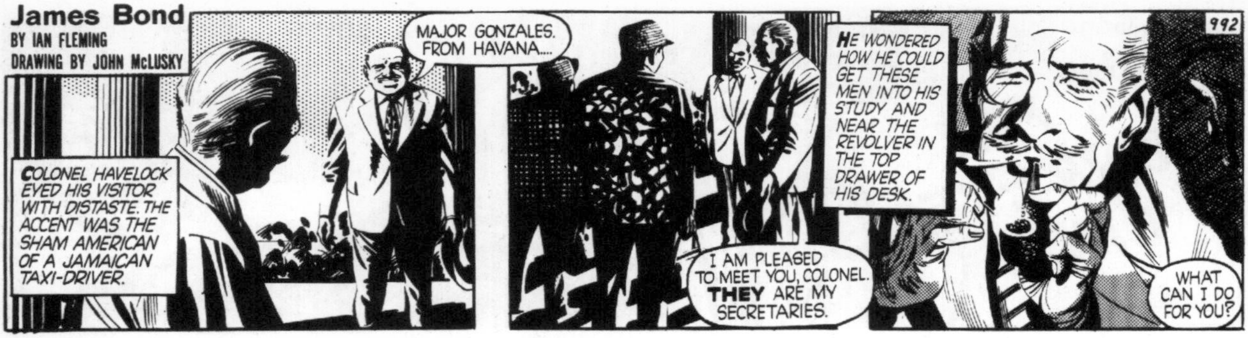
James Bond
BY IAN FLEMING
DRAWING BY JOHN McLUSKY
COLONEL HAVELOCK EYED HIS VISITOR WITH DISTASTE. THE ACCENT WAS THE SHAM AMERICAN OF A JAMAICAN TAXI-DRIVER.
MAJOR GONZALES. FROM HAVANA....
I AM PLEASED TO MEET YOU, COLONEL. THEY ARE MY SECRETARIES.
992
HE WONDERED HOW HE COULD GET THESE MEN INTO HIS STUDY AND NEAR THE REVOLVER IN THE TOP DRAWER OF HIS DESK.
WHAT CAN I DO FOR YOU?

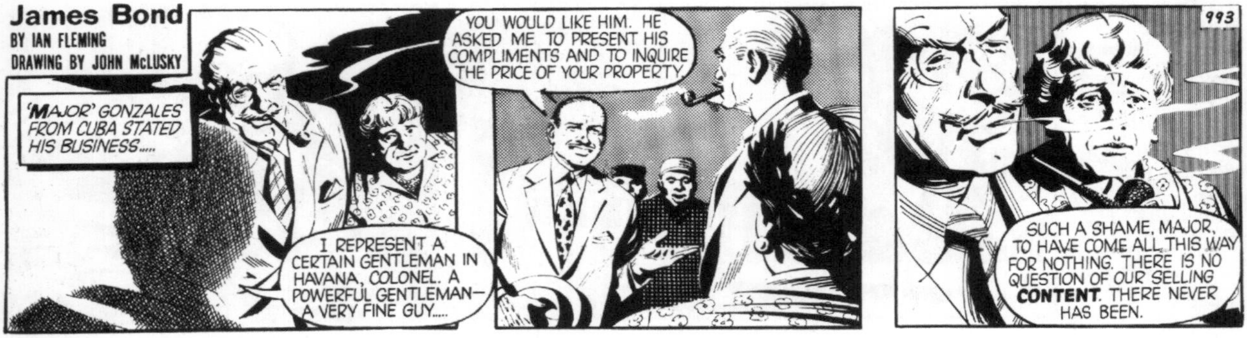
James Bond
BY IAN FLEMING
DRAWING BY JOHN McLUSKY
'MAJOR' GONZALES FROM CUBA STATED HIS BUSINESS.....
I REPRESENT A CERTAIN GENTLEMAN IN HAVANA, COLONEL. A POWERFUL GENTLEMAN— A VERY FINE GUY.....
YOU WOULD LIKE HIM. HE ASKED ME TO PRESENT HIS COMPLIMENTS AND TO INQUIRE THE PRICE OF YOUR PROPERTY.
993
SUCH A SHAME, MAJOR, TO HAVE COME ALL THIS WAY FOR NOTHING. THERE IS NO QUESTION OF OUR SELLING CONTENT. THERE NEVER HAS BEEN.

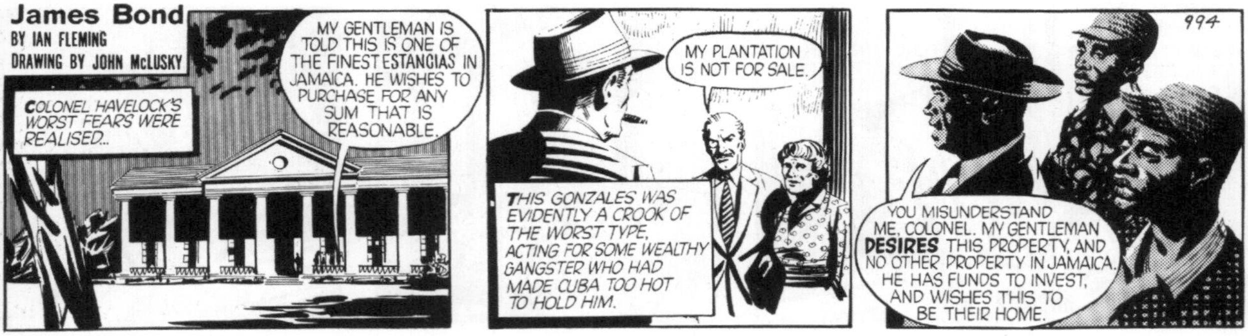
James Bond
BY IAN FLEMING
DRAWING BY JOHN McLUSKY
COLONEL HAVELOCK'S WORST FEARS WERE REALISED...
MY GENTLEMAN IS TOLD THIS IS ONE OF THE FINEST ESTANGIAS IN JAMAICA. HE WISHES TO PURCHASE FOR ANY SUM THAT IS REASONABLE.
MY PLANTATION IS NOT FOR SALE.
THIS GONZALES WAS EVIDENTLY A CROOK OF THE WORST TYPE, ACTING FOR SOME WEALTHY GANGSTER WHO HAD MADE CUBA TOO HOT TO HOLD HIM.
994
YOU MISUNDERSTAND ME, COLONEL. MY GENTLEMAN DESIRES THIS PROPERTY, AND NO OTHER PROPERTY IN JAMAICA. HE HAS FUNDS TO INVEST, AND WISHES THIS TO BE THEIR HOME.

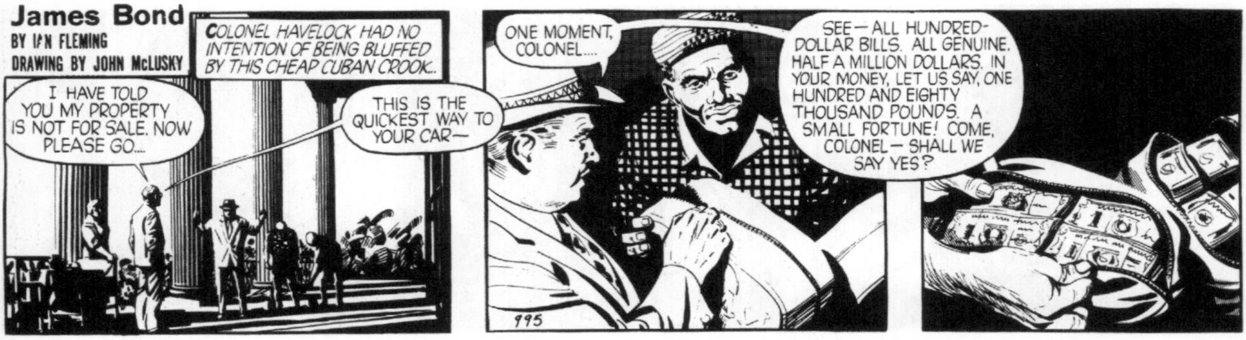
James Bond
BY IAN FLEMING
DRAWING BY JOHN McLUSKY
COLONEL HAVELOCK HAD NO INTENTION OF BEING BLUFFED BY THIS CHEAP CUBAN CROOK..
I HAVE TOLD YOU MY PROPERTY IS NOT FOR SALE. NOW PLEASE GO...
THIS IS THE QUICKEST WAY TO YOUR CAR—
ONE MOMENT, COLONEL....
SEE— ALL HUNDRED-DOLLAR BILLS. ALL GENUINE. HALF A MILLION DOLLARS. IN YOUR MONEY, LET US SAY, ONE HUNDRED AND EIGHTY THOUSAND POUNDS. A SMALL FORTUNE! COME, COLONEL— SHALL WE SAY YES?
995

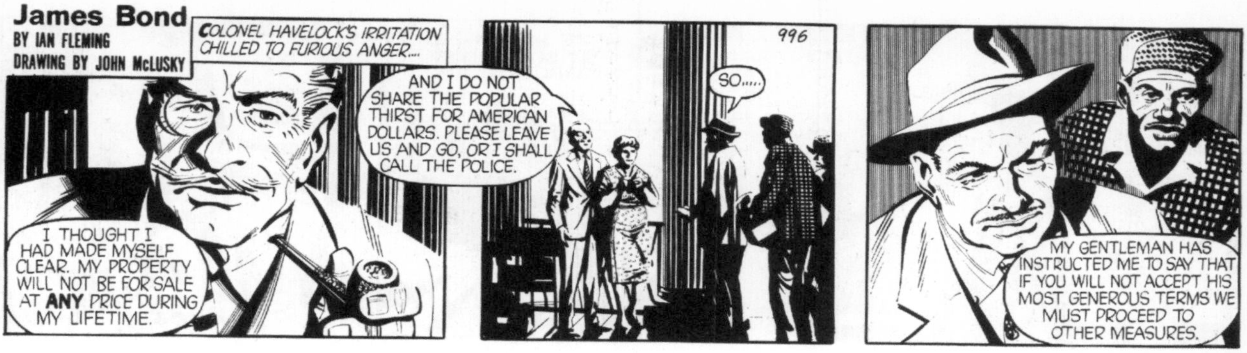
James Bond
BY IAN FLEMING
DRAWING BY JOHN McLUSKY
996
COLONEL HAVELOCK'S IRRITATION CHILLED TO FURIOUS ANGER....
I THOUGHT I HAD MADE MYSELF CLEAR. MY PROPERTY WILL NOT BE FOR SALE AT ANY PRICE DURING MY LIFETIME.
AND I DO NOT SHARE THE POPULAR THIRST FOR AMERICAN DOLLARS. PLEASE LEAVE US AND GO, OR I SHALL CALL THE POLICE.
SO.....
MY GENTLEMAN HAS INSTRUCTED ME TO SAY THAT IF YOU WILL NOT ACCEPT HIS MOST GENEROUS TERMS WE MUST PROCEED TO OTHER MEASURES.

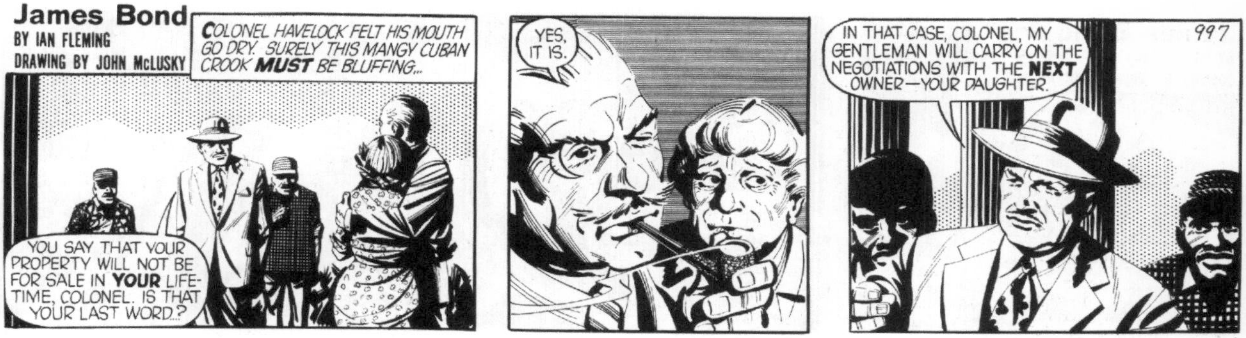
James Bond
BY IAN FLEMING
DRAWING BY JOHN McLUSKY
997
COLONEL HAVELOCK FELT HIS MOUTH GO DRY. SURELY THIS MANGY CUBAN CROOK MUST BE BLUFFING...
YOU SAY THAT YOUR PROPERTY WILL NOT BE FOR SALE IN YOUR LIFE-TIME, COLONEL. IS THAT YOUR LAST WORD..?
YES, IT IS.
IN THAT CASE, COLONEL, MY GENTLEMAN WILL CARRY ON THE NEGOTIATIONS WITH THE NEXT OWNER—YOUR DAUGHTER.

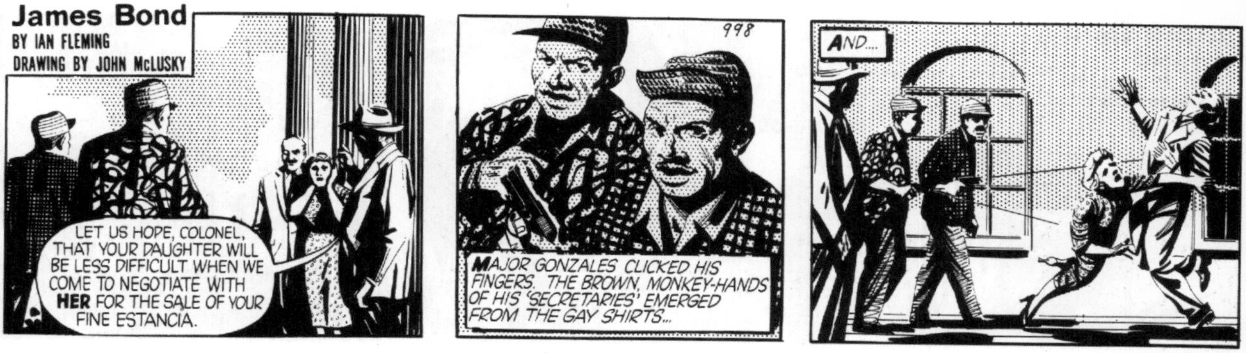
James Bond
BY IAN FLEMING
DRAWING BY JOHN McLUSKY
998
LET US HOPE, COLONEL, THAT YOUR DAUGHTER WILL BE LESS DIFFICULT WHEN WE COME TO NEGOTIATE WITH HER FOR THE SALE OF YOUR FINE ESTANCIA.
MAJOR GONZALES CLICKED HIS FINGERS. THE BROWN, MONKEY-HANDS OF HIS 'SECRETARIES' EMERGED FROM THE GAY SHIRTS...
AND...

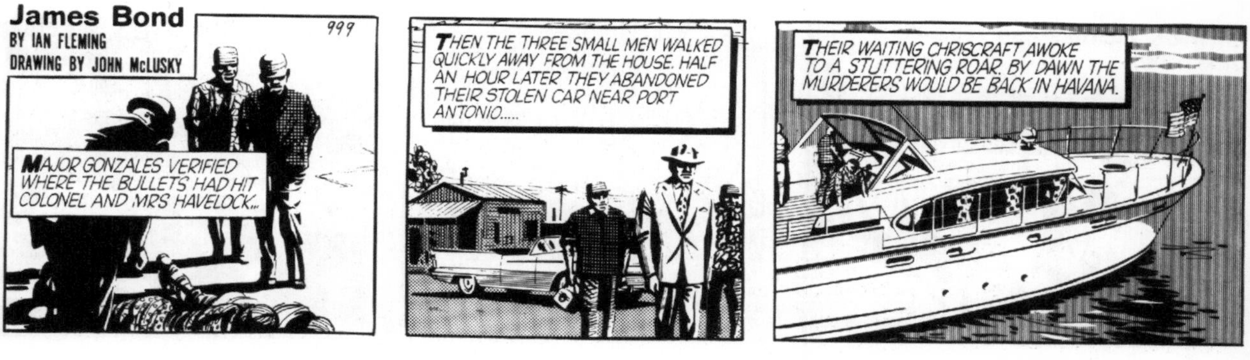
James Bond
BY IAN FLEMING
DRAWING BY JOHN McLUSKY
999
MAJOR GONZALES VERIFIED WHERE THE BULLETS HAD HIT COLONEL AND MRS HAVELOCK...
THEN THE THREE SMALL MEN WALKED QUICKLY AWAY FROM THE HOUSE. HALF AN HOUR LATER THEY ABANDONED THEIR STOLEN CAR NEAR PORT ANTONIO.....
THEIR WAITING CHRISCRAFT AWOKE TO A STUTTERING ROAR. BY DAWN THE MURDERERS WOULD BE BACK IN HAVANA.

James Bond
BY IAN FLEMING
DRAWING BY JOHN McLUSKY

A MONTH AFTER THE BRUTAL KILLING OF THE HAVELOCKS IN JAMAICA, JAMES BOND, ON ROUTINE DUTY IN LONDON, WAS SUMMONED BY M, HIS CHIEF...

BOND FOUND THE HEAD OF THE SECRET SERVICE UNUSUALLY HESITANT THAT MORNING...

WHAT'S HOLDING HIM? COULD BE SOMETHING PERSONAL ABOUT THIS

THEN...

REMEMBER THE HAVELOCK CASE, JAMES?

DOUBLE-DEATH

MYSTERY

ONLY WHAT I READ IN THE PAPERS, SIR

1000

James Bond
BY IAN FLEMING
DRAWING BY JOHN McLUSKY

DAILY... COLONEL AND WIFE FOUND SHOT
MURDER of the...

NOW BOND KNEW WHAT WAS TROUBLING M. THE HAVELOCK CASE WAS NO CONCERN OF THE SECRET SERVICE

ELDERLY COUPLE IN JAMAICA...

DAUGHTER CAME HOME ONE EVENING AND FOUND THEM FULL OF BULLETS. GANGSTERS FROM HAVANA, OR SOMETHING, SO PEOPLE SAID...

I KNEW THE HAVELOCKS. NICE PEOPLE. I WAS BEST MAN AT THEIR WEDDING. MALTA, NINETEEN TWENTY-FIVE

I SEE, SIR. ANYTHING I CAN DO TO HELP?

1,001

James Bond
BY IAN FLEMING
DRAWING BY JOHN McLUSKY

I TOLD STATION C IN CUBA TO LOOK INTO THE HAVELOCK KILLING IN JAMAICA. GOT NOWHERE WITH BATISTA'S PEOPLE, BUT WE CONTACTED ONE OF CASTRO'S INTELLIGENCE MEN...

GOT THE WHOLE STORY A FORTNIGHT AGO. MAN CALLED VON HAMMERSTEIN HAD THE COUPLE KILLED. THIS IS HIM— A NAZI, EX-GESTAPO...

GOT HIMSELF A JOB AS HEAD OF BATISTA'S COUNTER-INTELLIGENCE. MADE A PACKET OUT OF EXTORTION, BLACKMAIL AND PROTECTION, THEN HE STARTED EASING OUT AS CASTRO GOT NEARER

I SEE...

1002

James Bond
BY IAN FLEMING
DRAWING BY JOHN McLUSKY

ONCE CASTRO STARTED MAKING HEADWAY, THIS KILLER VON HAMMERSTEIN BEGAN SALTING HIS MONEY AWAY READY TO GET OUT OF CUBA...

HOW, SIR?

HE SENT A TOUGH CALLED GONZALES ALL OVER THE CARIBBEAN BUYING UP THE BEST ESTATES, BANANA PLANTATIONS AND SO ON, AT TOP PRICES. IF THE OWNERS OBJECTED HE USED FORCE

U.S.A. | Bahamas | 0 400 MILES
Cuba | Atlantic Ocean
Central | Dominica | Puerto Rico
America | Jamaica | Haiti
Panama | CARIBBEAN SEA

THAT'S HOW THE HAVELOCKS WERE MURDERED. NOW THEY'RE PUTTING PRESSURE ON THE DAUGHTER – GIRL OF ABOUT TWENTY-FIVE. VON HAMMERSTEIN GOT AWAY FROM CUBA RECENTLY

WHERE IS HE NOW?

1003

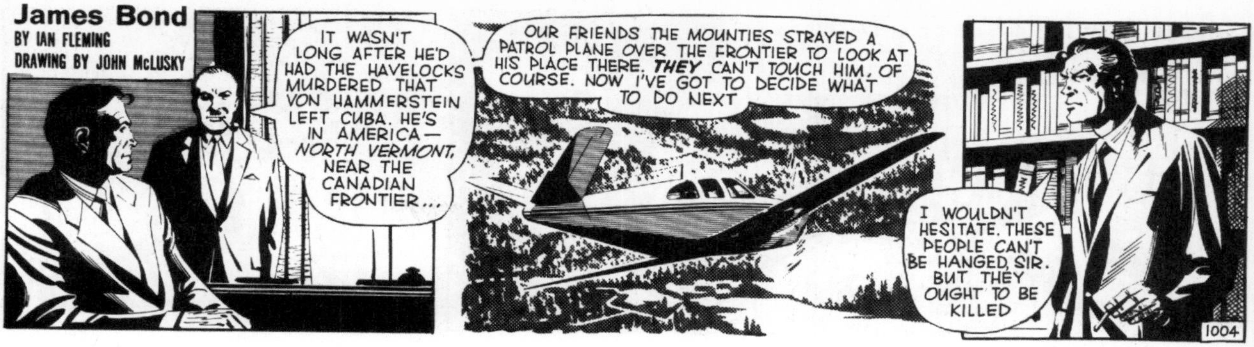
James Bond
BY IAN FLEMING
DRAWING BY JOHN McLUSKY
IT WASN'T LONG AFTER HE'D HAD THE HAVELOCKS MURDERED THAT VON HAMMERSTEIN LEFT CUBA. HE'S IN AMERICA— NORTH VERMONT, NEAR THE CANADIAN FRONTIER...
OUR FRIENDS THE MOUNTIES STRAYED A PATROL PLANE OVER THE FRONTIER TO LOOK AT HIS PLACE THERE. THEY CAN'T TOUCH HIM, OF COURSE. NOW I'VE GOT TO DECIDE WHAT TO DO NEXT
I WOULDN'T HESITATE. THESE PEOPLE CAN'T BE HANGED, SIR. BUT THEY OUGHT TO BE KILLED
1004

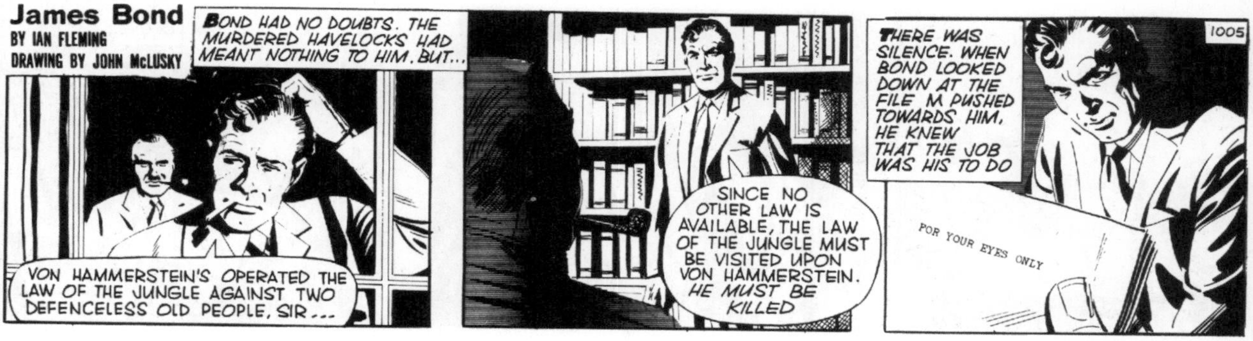
James Bond
BY IAN FLEMING
DRAWING BY JOHN McLUSKY
BOND HAD NO DOUBTS. THE MURDERED HAVELOCKS HAD MEANT NOTHING TO HIM. BUT...
VON HAMMERSTEIN'S OPERATED THE LAW OF THE JUNGLE AGAINST TWO DEFENCELESS OLD PEOPLE, SIR...
SINCE NO OTHER LAW IS AVAILABLE, THE LAW OF THE JUNGLE MUST BE VISITED UPON VON HAMMERSTEIN. HE MUST BE KILLED
1005
THERE WAS SILENCE. WHEN BOND LOOKED DOWN AT THE FILE M PUSHED TOWARDS HIM, HE KNEW THAT THE JOB WAS HIS TO DO
FOR YOUR EYES ONLY

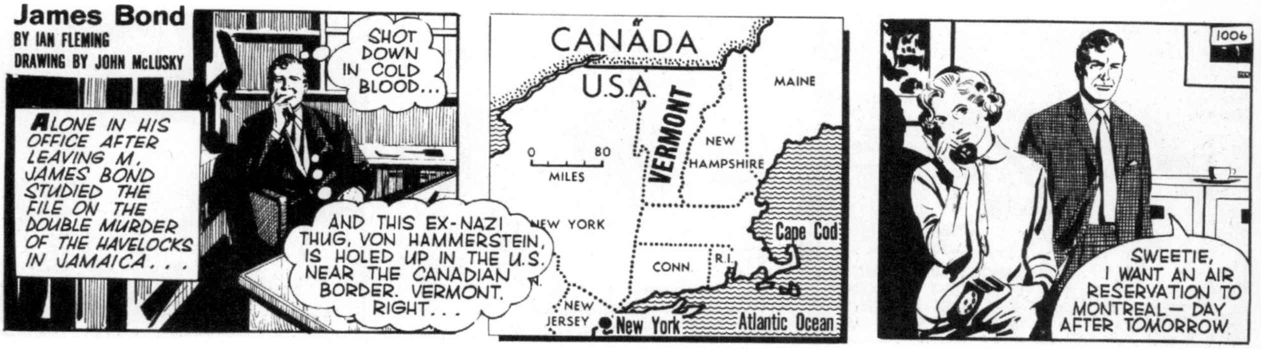
James Bond
BY IAN FLEMING
DRAWING BY JOHN McLUSKY
ALONE IN HIS OFFICE AFTER LEAVING M, JAMES BOND STUDIED THE FILE ON THE DOUBLE MURDER OF THE HAVELOCKS IN JAMAICA...
SHOT DOWN IN COLD BLOOD...
CANADA
U.S.A.
MAINE
VERMONT
NEW HAMPSHIRE
0 80
MILES
NEW YORK
Cape Cod
CONN.
R.I.
NEW JERSEY
New York
Atlantic Ocean
AND THIS EX-NAZI THUG, VON HAMMERSTEIN, IS HOLED UP IN THE U.S. NEAR THE CANADIAN BORDER. VERMONT. RIGHT...
1006
SWEETIE, I WANT AN AIR RESERVATION TO MONTREAL— DAY AFTER TOMORROW

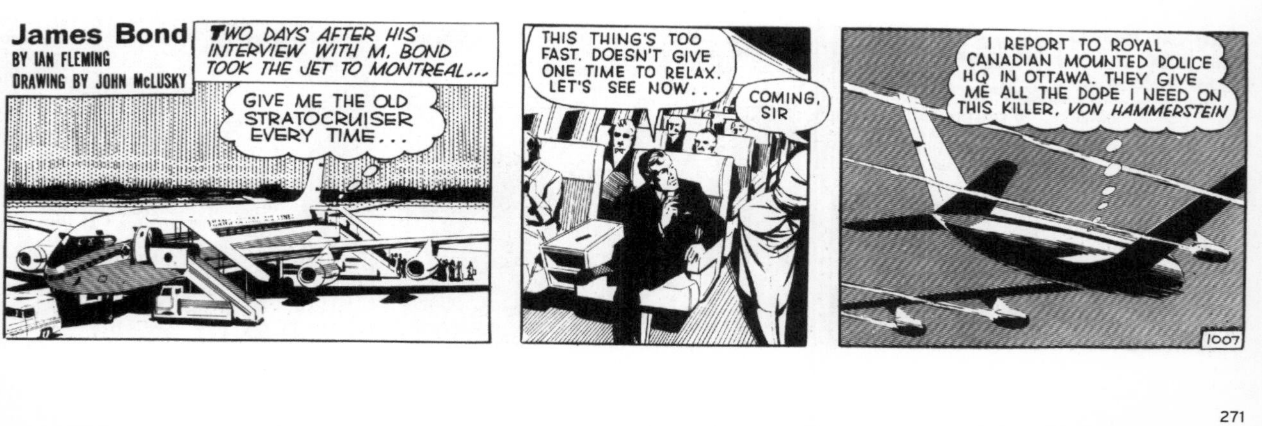
James Bond
BY IAN FLEMING
DRAWING BY JOHN McLUSKY
TWO DAYS AFTER HIS INTERVIEW WITH M, BOND TOOK THE JET TO MONTREAL...
GIVE ME THE OLD STRATOCRUISER EVERY TIME...
THIS THING'S TOO FAST. DOESN'T GIVE ONE TIME TO RELAX. LET'S SEE NOW...
COMING, SIR
I REPORT TO ROYAL CANADIAN MOUNTED POLICE HQ IN OTTAWA. THEY GIVE ME ALL THE DOPE I NEED ON THIS KILLER, VON HAMMERSTEIN
1007

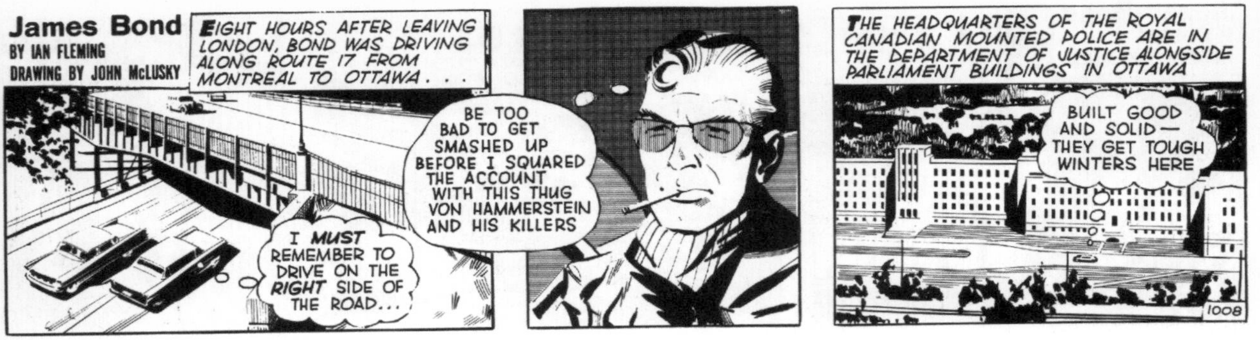
James Bond
BY IAN FLEMING
DRAWING BY JOHN McLUSKY
EIGHT HOURS AFTER LEAVING LONDON, BOND WAS DRIVING ALONG ROUTE 17 FROM MONTREAL TO OTTAWA . . .
I MUST REMEMBER TO DRIVE ON THE RIGHT SIDE OF THE ROAD...
BE TOO BAD TO GET SMASHED UP BEFORE I SQUARED THE ACCOUNT WITH THIS THUG VON HAMMERSTEIN AND HIS KILLERS
THE HEADQUARTERS OF THE ROYAL CANADIAN MOUNTED POLICE ARE IN THE DEPARTMENT OF JUSTICE ALONGSIDE PARLIAMENT BUILDINGS IN OTTAWA
BUILT GOOD AND SOLID— THEY GET TOUGH WINTERS HERE
1008

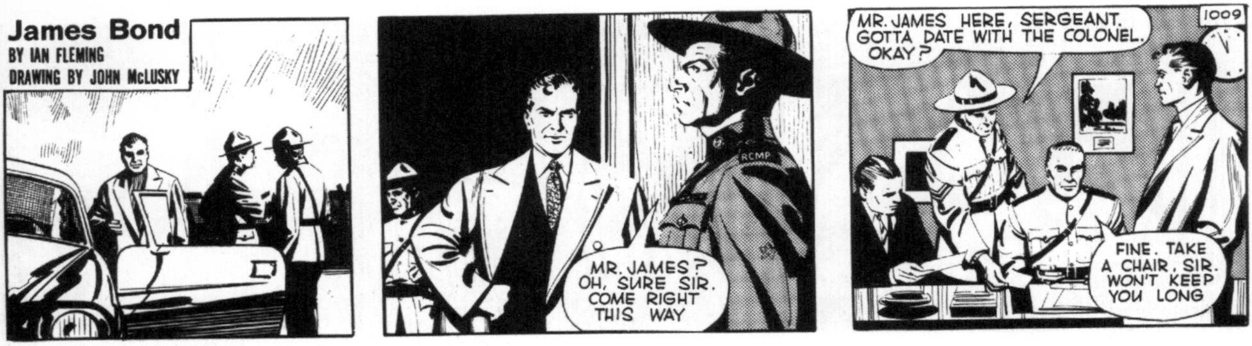
James Bond
BY IAN FLEMING
DRAWING BY JOHN McLUSKY
RCMP
MR. JAMES? OH, SURE SIR. COME RIGHT THIS WAY
1009
MR. JAMES HERE, SERGEANT. GOTTA DATE WITH THE COLONEL. OKAY?
FINE. TAKE A CHAIR, SIR. WON'T KEEP YOU LONG

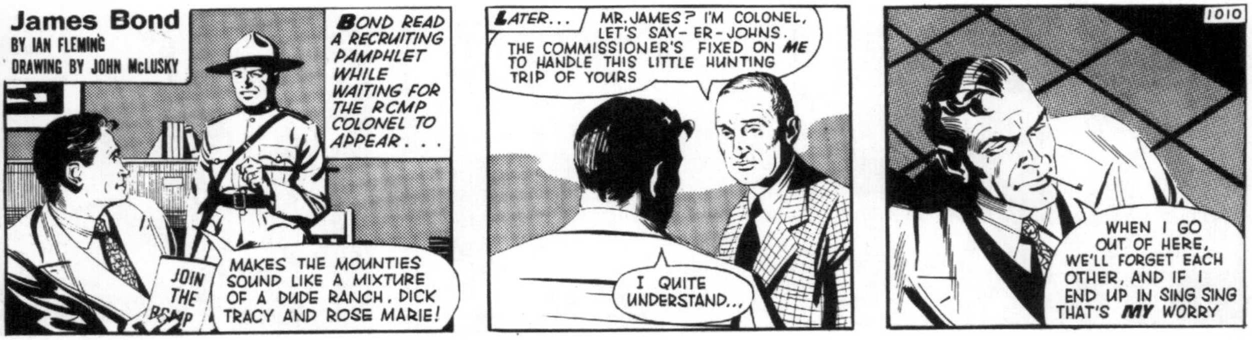
James Bond
BY IAN FLEMING
DRAWING BY JOHN McLUSKY
BOND READ A RECRUITING PAMPHLET WHILE WAITING FOR THE RCMP COLONEL TO APPEAR . . .
JOIN THE RCMP
MAKES THE MOUNTIES SOUND LIKE A MIXTURE OF A DUDE RANCH, DICK TRACY AND ROSE MARIE!
LATER...
MR. JAMES? I'M COLONEL, LET'S SAY- ER- JOHNS. THE COMMISSIONER'S FIXED ON ME TO HANDLE THIS LITTLE HUNTING TRIP OF YOURS
I QUITE UNDERSTAND...
1010
WHEN I GO OUT OF HERE, WE'LL FORGET EACH OTHER, AND IF I END UP IN SING SING THAT'S MY WORRY

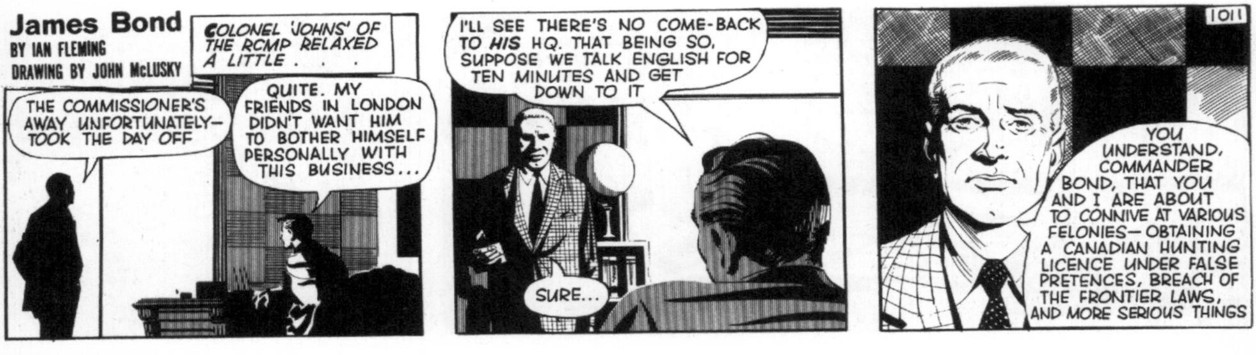
James Bond
BY IAN FLEMING
DRAWING BY JOHN McLUSKY
COLONEL 'JOHNS' OF THE RCMP RELAXED A LITTLE . . .
THE COMMISSIONER'S AWAY UNFORTUNATELY— TOOK THE DAY OFF
QUITE. MY FRIENDS IN LONDON DIDN'T WANT HIM TO BOTHER HIMSELF PERSONALLY WITH THIS BUSINESS...
I'LL SEE THERE'S NO COME-BACK TO HIS HQ. THAT BEING SO, SUPPOSE WE TALK ENGLISH FOR TEN MINUTES AND GET DOWN TO IT
SURE...
1011
YOU UNDERSTAND, COMMANDER BOND, THAT YOU AND I ARE ABOUT TO CONNIVE AT VARIOUS FELONIES— OBTAINING A CANADIAN HUNTING LICENCE UNDER FALSE PRETENCES, BREACH OF THE FRONTIER LAWS, AND MORE SERIOUS THINGS

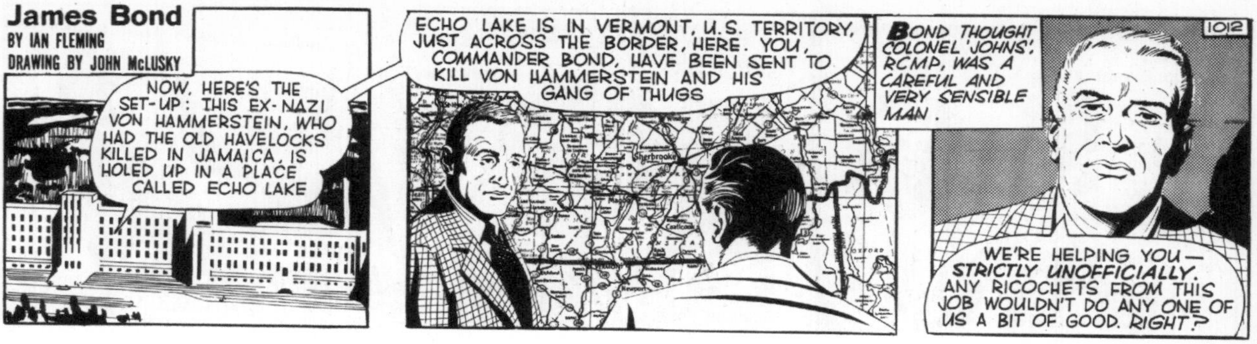
James Bond
BY IAN FLEMING
DRAWING BY JOHN McLUSKY
NOW, HERE'S THE SET-UP: THIS EX-NAZI VON HAMMERSTEIN, WHO HAD THE OLD HAVELOCKS KILLED IN JAMAICA, IS HOLED UP IN A PLACE CALLED ECHO LAKE
ECHO LAKE IS IN VERMONT, U.S. TERRITORY, JUST ACROSS THE BORDER, HERE. YOU, COMMANDER BOND, HAVE BEEN SENT TO KILL VON HAMMERSTEIN AND HIS GANG OF THUGS
1012
BOND THOUGHT COLONEL 'JOHNS', RCMP, WAS A CAREFUL AND VERY SENSIBLE MAN.
WE'RE HELPING YOU— STRICTLY UNOFFICIALLY. ANY RICOCHETS FROM THIS JOB WOULDN'T DO ANY ONE OF US A BIT OF GOOD. RIGHT?

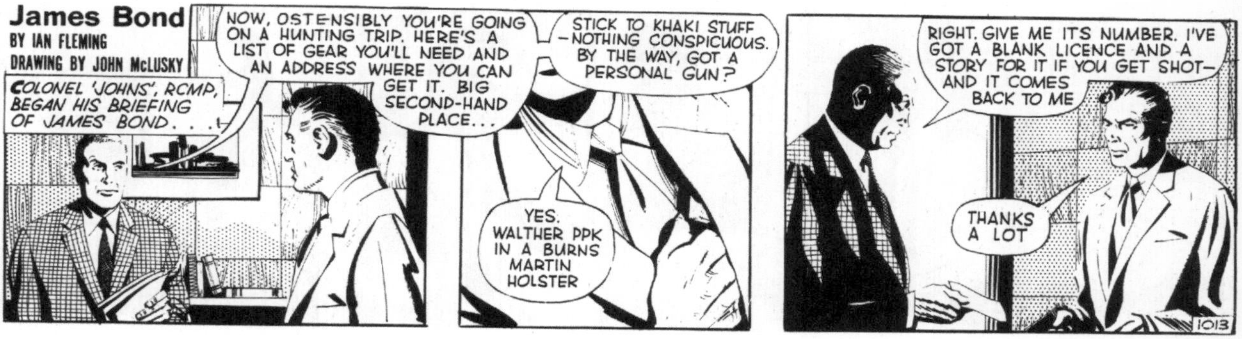
James Bond
BY IAN FLEMING
DRAWING BY JOHN McLUSKY
COLONEL 'JOHNS', RCMP, BEGAN HIS BRIEFING OF JAMES BOND . . .
NOW, OSTENSIBLY YOU'RE GOING ON A HUNTING TRIP. HERE'S A LIST OF GEAR YOU'LL NEED AND AN ADDRESS WHERE YOU CAN GET IT. BIG SECOND-HAND PLACE...
STICK TO KHAKI STUFF —NOTHING CONSPICUOUS. BY THE WAY, GOT A PERSONAL GUN?
YES. WALTHER PPK IN A BURNS MARTIN HOLSTER
RIGHT. GIVE ME ITS NUMBER. I'VE GOT A BLANK LICENCE AND A STORY FOR IT IF YOU GET SHOT— AND IT COMES BACK TO ME
THANKS A LOT
1013

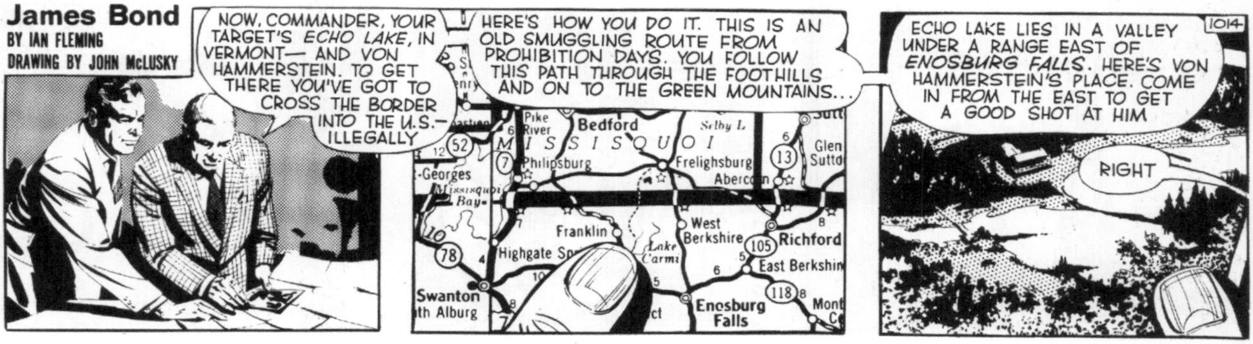
James Bond
BY IAN FLEMING
DRAWING BY JOHN McLUSKY
NOW, COMMANDER, YOUR TARGET'S ECHO LAKE, IN VERMONT— AND VON HAMMERSTEIN. TO GET THERE YOU'VE GOT TO CROSS THE BORDER INTO THE U.S.— ILLEGALLY
HERE'S HOW YOU DO IT. THIS IS AN OLD SMUGGLING ROUTE FROM PROHIBITION DAYS. YOU FOLLOW THIS PATH THROUGH THE FOOTHILLS AND ON TO THE GREEN MOUNTAINS...
Bedford
MISSISQUOI
Philipsburg
Frelighsburg
Franklin
West Berkshire
Richford
East Berkshire
Swanton
Enosburg Falls
1014
ECHO LAKE LIES IN A VALLEY UNDER A RANGE EAST OF ENOSBURG FALLS. HERE'S VON HAMMERSTEIN'S PLACE. COME IN FROM THE EAST TO GET A GOOD SHOT AT HIM
RIGHT

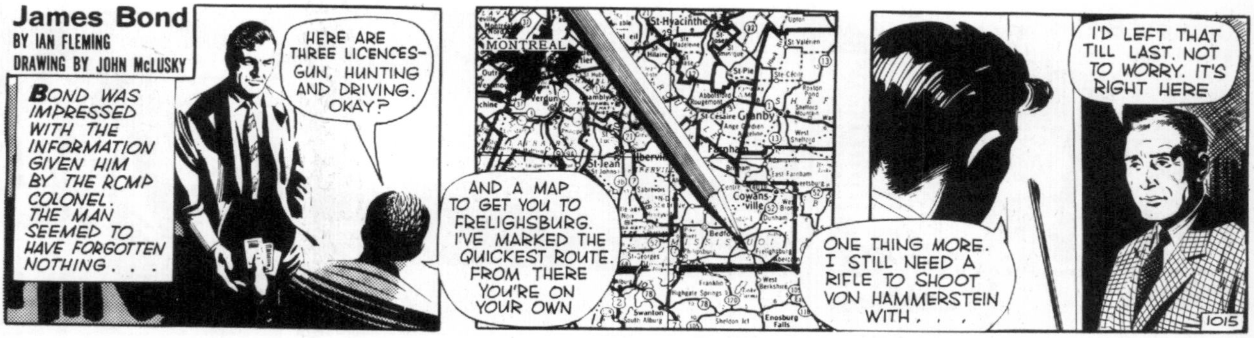
James Bond
BY IAN FLEMING
DRAWING BY JOHN McLUSKY
BOND WAS IMPRESSED WITH THE INFORMATION GIVEN HIM BY THE RCMP COLONEL. THE MAN SEEMED TO HAVE FORGOTTEN NOTHING . . .
HERE ARE THREE LICENCES— GUN, HUNTING AND DRIVING. OKAY?
MONTREAL
AND A MAP TO GET YOU TO FRELIGHSBURG. I'VE MARKED THE QUICKEST ROUTE. FROM THERE YOU'RE ON YOUR OWN
ONE THING MORE. I STILL NEED A RIFLE TO SHOOT VON HAMMERSTEIN WITH . . .
I'D LEFT THAT TILL LAST. NOT TO WORRY. IT'S RIGHT HERE
1015

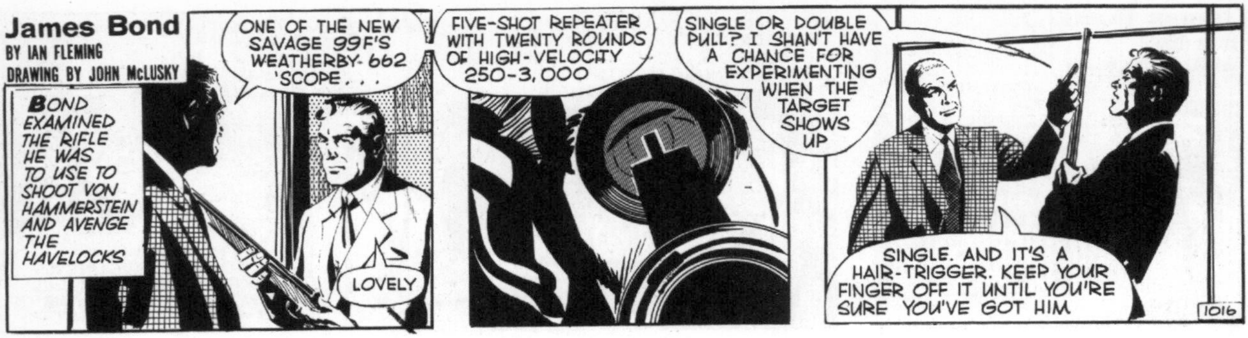
James Bond
BY IAN FLEMING
DRAWING BY JOHN McLUSKY
BOND EXAMINED THE RIFLE HE WAS TO USE TO SHOOT VON HAMMERSTEIN AND AVENGE THE HAVELOCKS
ONE OF THE NEW SAVAGE 99F'S WEATHERBY-662 'SCOPE . . .
LOVELY
FIVE-SHOT REPEATER WITH TWENTY ROUNDS OF HIGH-VELOCITY 250-3,000
SINGLE OR DOUBLE PULL? I SHAN'T HAVE A CHANCE FOR EXPERIMENTING WHEN THE TARGET SHOWS UP
SINGLE. AND IT'S A HAIR-TRIGGER. KEEP YOUR FINGER OFF IT UNTIL YOU'RE SURE YOU'VE GOT HIM
1016

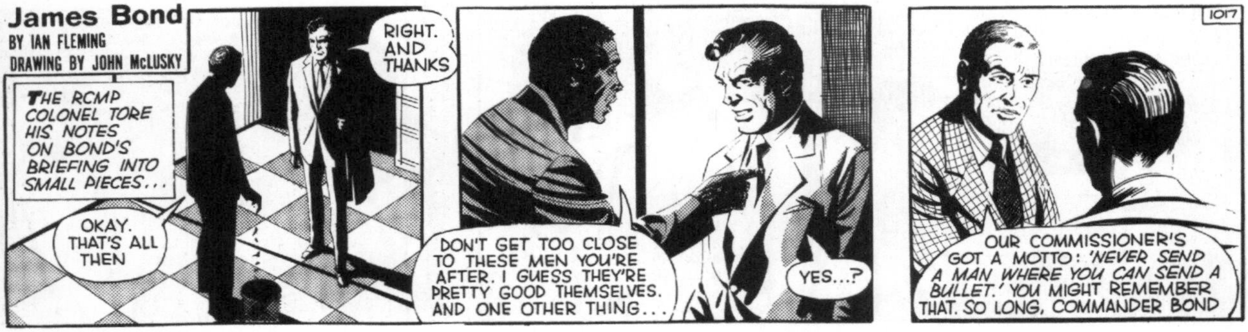
James Bond
BY IAN FLEMING
DRAWING BY JOHN McLUSKY
THE RCMP COLONEL TORE HIS NOTES ON BOND'S BRIEFING INTO SMALL PIECES . . .
OKAY. THAT'S ALL THEN
RIGHT. AND THANKS
DON'T GET TOO CLOSE TO THESE MEN YOU'RE AFTER. I GUESS THEY'RE PRETTY GOOD THEMSELVES. AND ONE OTHER THING . . .
YES...?
1017
OUR COMMISSIONER'S GOT A MOTTO: 'NEVER SEND A MAN WHERE YOU CAN SEND A BULLET.' YOU MIGHT REMEMBER THAT. SO LONG, COMMANDER BOND

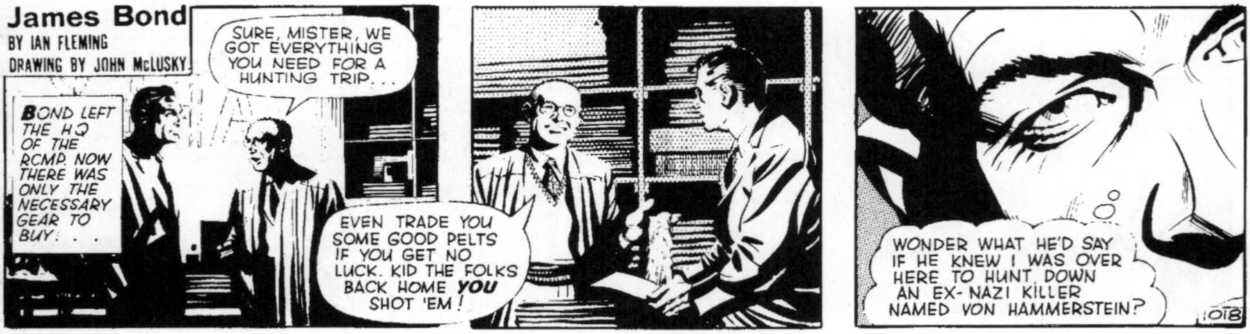
James Bond
BY IAN FLEMING
DRAWING BY JOHN McLUSKY
BOND LEFT THE HQ OF THE RCMP. NOW THERE WAS ONLY THE NECESSARY GEAR TO BUY . . .
SURE, MISTER, WE GOT EVERYTHING YOU NEED FOR A HUNTING TRIP . . .
EVEN TRADE YOU SOME GOOD PELTS IF YOU GET NO LUCK. KID THE FOLKS BACK HOME YOU SHOT 'EM!
WONDER WHAT HE'D SAY IF HE KNEW I WAS OVER HERE TO HUNT DOWN AN EX-NAZI KILLER NAMED VON HAMMERSTEIN?
1018

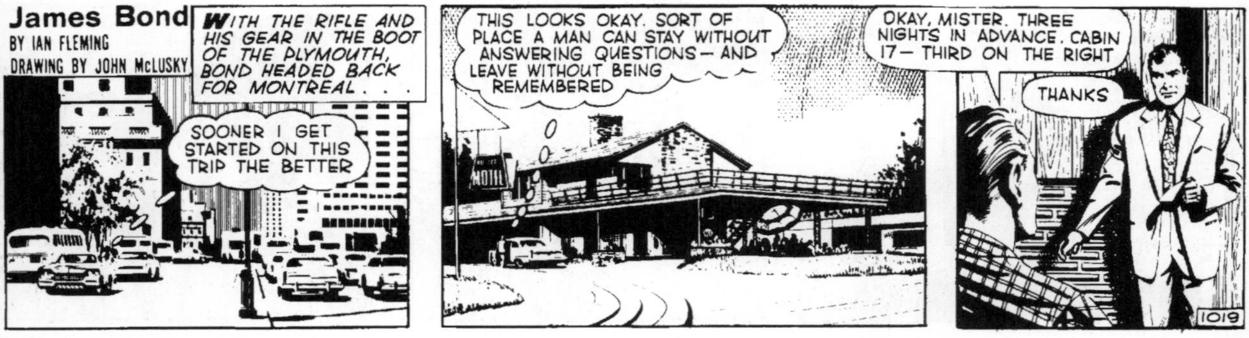
James Bond
BY IAN FLEMING
DRAWING BY JOHN McLUSKY
WITH THE RIFLE AND HIS GEAR IN THE BOOT OF THE PLYMOUTH, BOND HEADED BACK FOR MONTREAL . . .
SOONER I GET STARTED ON THIS TRIP THE BETTER
THIS LOOKS OKAY. SORT OF PLACE A MAN CAN STAY WITHOUT ANSWERING QUESTIONS — AND LEAVE WITHOUT BEING REMEMBERED
MOTEL
OKAY, MISTER. THREE NIGHTS IN ADVANCE. CABIN 17 — THIRD ON THE RIGHT
THANKS
1019

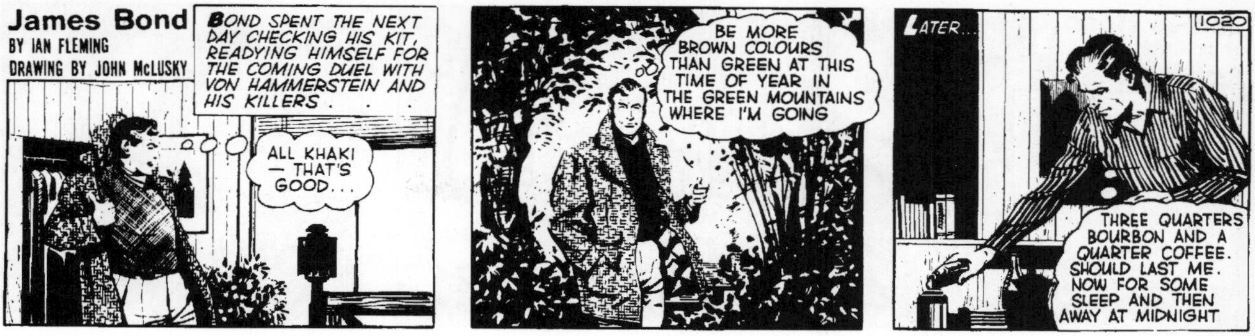
James Bond
BY IAN FLEMING
DRAWING BY JOHN McLUSKY
BOND SPENT THE NEXT DAY CHECKING HIS KIT, READYING HIMSELF FOR THE COMING DUEL WITH VON HAMMERSTEIN AND HIS KILLERS . . .
ALL KHAKI — THAT'S GOOD...
BE MORE BROWN COLOURS THAN GREEN AT THIS TIME OF YEAR IN THE GREEN MOUNTAINS WHERE I'M GOING
LATER...
1020
THREE QUARTERS BOURBON AND A QUARTER COFFEE. SHOULD LAST ME. NOW FOR SOME SLEEP AND THEN AWAY AT MIDNIGHT

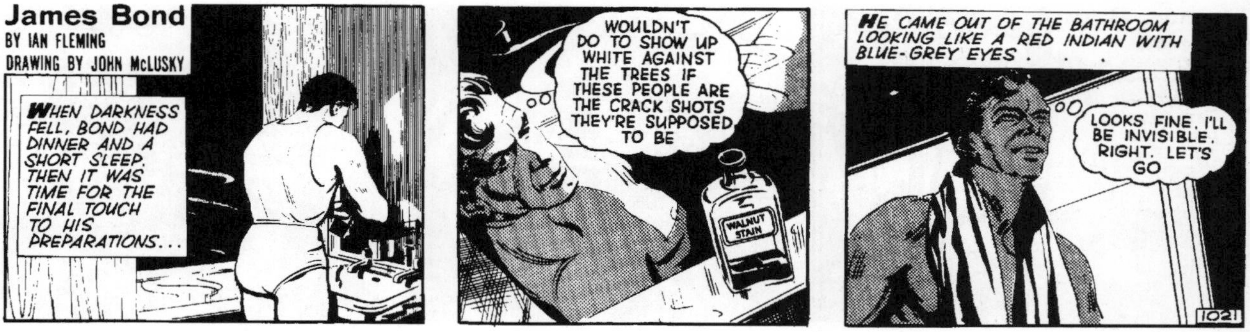
James Bond
BY IAN FLEMING
DRAWING BY JOHN McLUSKY
WHEN DARKNESS FELL, BOND HAD DINNER AND A SHORT SLEEP. THEN IT WAS TIME FOR THE FINAL TOUCH TO HIS PREPARATIONS...
WOULDN'T DO TO SHOW UP WHITE AGAINST THE TREES IF THESE PEOPLE ARE THE CRACK SHOTS THEY'RE SUPPOSED TO BE
WALNUT STAIN
HE CAME OUT OF THE BATHROOM LOOKING LIKE A RED INDIAN WITH BLUE-GREY EYES . . .
LOOKS FINE. I'LL BE INVISIBLE. RIGHT. LET'S GO
1021

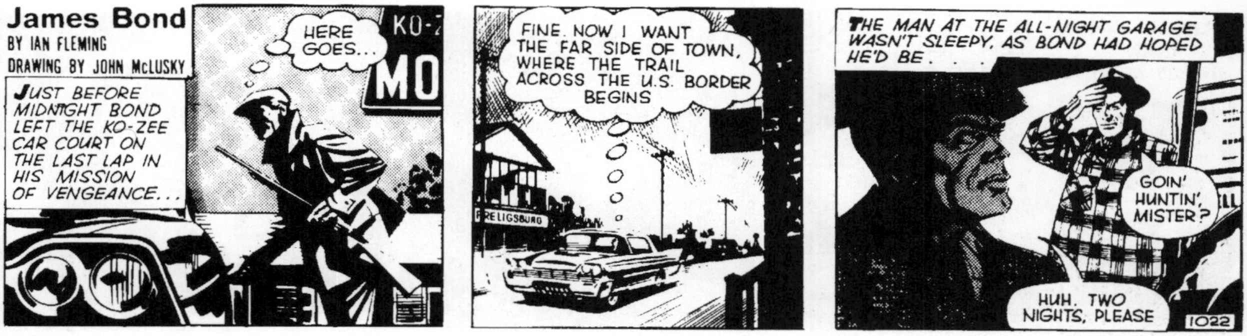
James Bond
BY IAN FLEMING
DRAWING BY JOHN McLUSKY
JUST BEFORE MIDNIGHT BOND LEFT THE KO-ZEE CAR COURT ON THE LAST LAP IN HIS MISSION OF VENGEANCE...
HERE GOES...
MO
FINE. NOW I WANT THE FAR SIDE OF TOWN, WHERE THE TRAIL ACROSS THE U.S. BORDER BEGINS
THE MAN AT THE ALL-NIGHT GARAGE WASN'T SLEEPY, AS BOND HAD HOPED HE'D BE . . .
GOIN' HUNTIN', MISTER?
HUH. TWO NIGHTS, PLEASE
1022

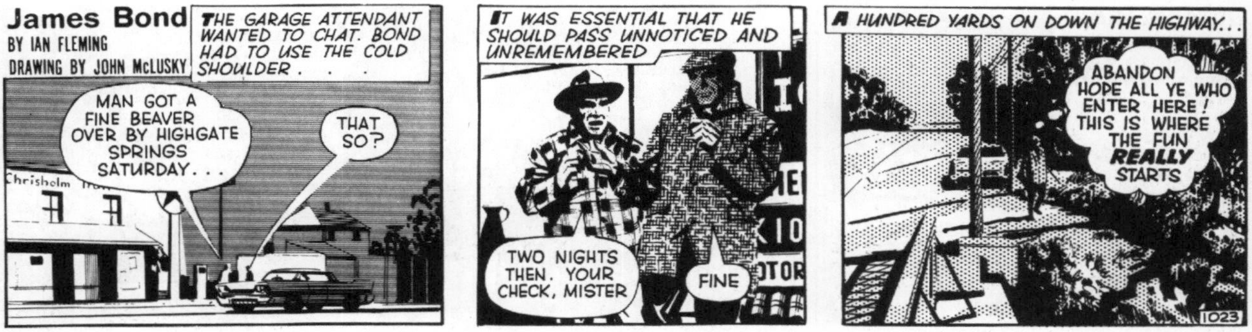
James Bond
BY IAN FLEMING
DRAWING BY JOHN McLUSKY
THE GARAGE ATTENDANT WANTED TO CHAT. BOND HAD TO USE THE COLD SHOULDER . . .
MAN GOT A FINE BEAVER OVER BY HIGHGATE SPRINGS SATURDAY...
THAT SO?
IT WAS ESSENTIAL THAT HE SHOULD PASS UNNOTICED AND UNREMEMBERED
TWO NIGHTS THEN. YOUR CHECK, MISTER
FINE
A HUNDRED YARDS ON DOWN THE HIGHWAY...
ABANDON HOPE ALL YE WHO ENTER HERE! THIS IS WHERE THE FUN REALLY STARTS
1023

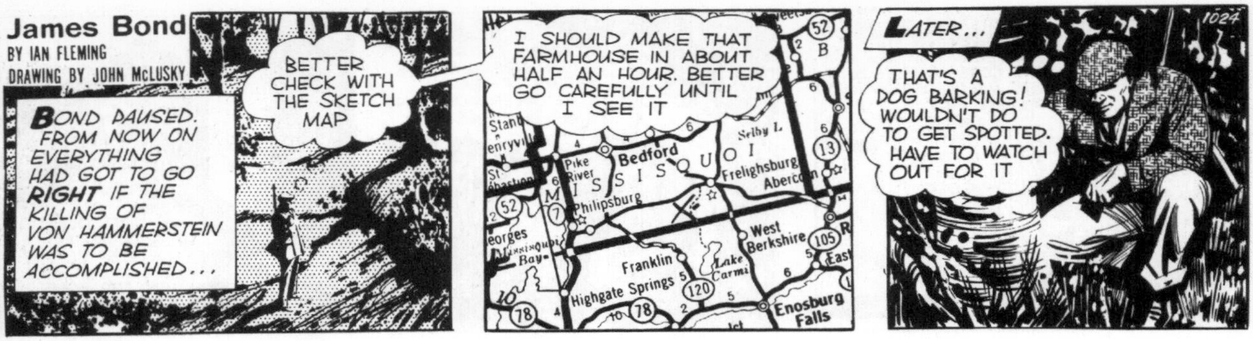

James Bond
BY IAN FLEMING
DRAWING BY JOHN McLUSKY
BOND PAUSED. FROM NOW ON EVERYTHING HAD GOT TO GO RIGHT IF THE KILLING OF VON HAMMERSTEIN WAS TO BE ACCOMPLISHED...
BETTER CHECK WITH THE SKETCH MAP
I SHOULD MAKE THAT FARMHOUSE IN ABOUT HALF AN HOUR. BETTER GO CAREFULLY UNTIL I SEE IT
Pike River
Bedford
Selby L.
Frelighsburg
Philipsburg
West Berkshire
Franklin
Lake Carmi
Highgate Springs
Enosburg Falls
LATER...
1024
THAT'S A DOG BARKING! WOULDN'T DO TO GET SPOTTED. HAVE TO WATCH OUT FOR IT

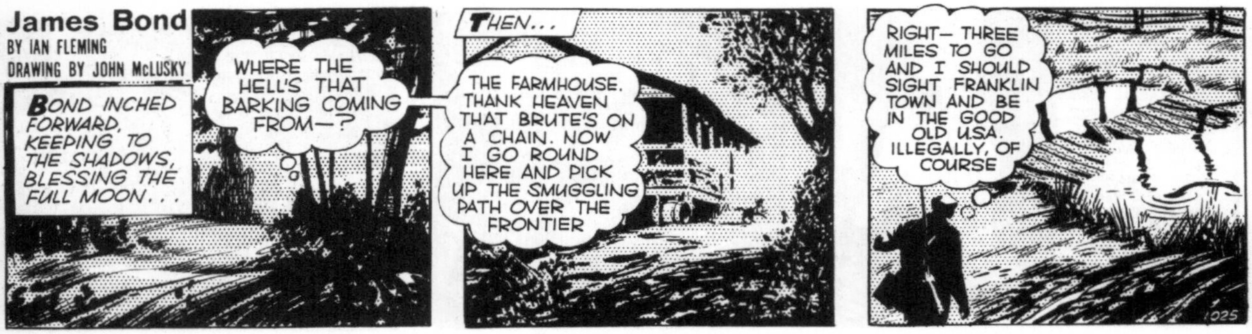

James Bond
BY IAN FLEMING
DRAWING BY JOHN McLUSKY
BOND INCHED FORWARD, KEEPING TO THE SHADOWS, BLESSING THE FULL MOON...
WHERE THE HELL'S THAT BARKING COMING FROM—?
THEN...
THE FARMHOUSE. THANK HEAVEN THAT BRUTE'S ON A CHAIN. NOW I GO ROUND HERE AND PICK UP THE SMUGGLING PATH OVER THE FRONTIER
RIGHT— THREE MILES TO GO AND I SHOULD SIGHT FRANKLIN TOWN AND BE IN THE GOOD OLD U.S.A. ILLEGALLY, OF COURSE
1025

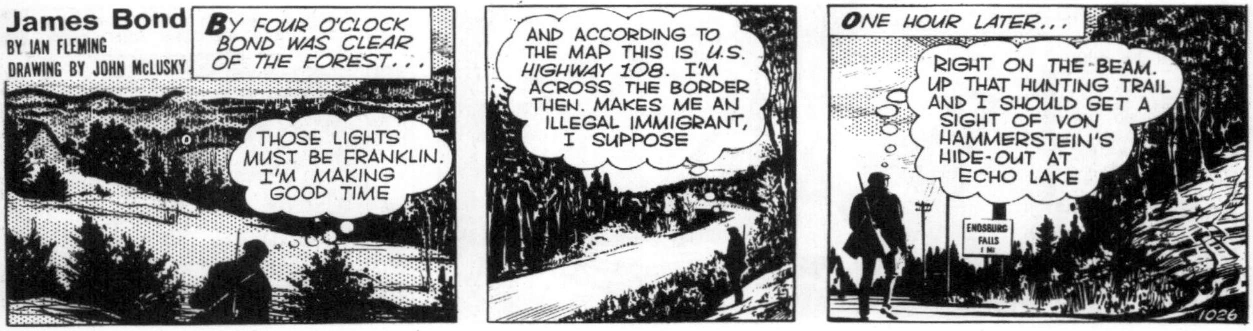

James Bond
BY IAN FLEMING
DRAWING BY JOHN McLUSKY
BY FOUR O'CLOCK BOND WAS CLEAR OF THE FOREST...
THOSE LIGHTS MUST BE FRANKLIN. I'M MAKING GOOD TIME
AND ACCORDING TO THE MAP THIS IS U.S. HIGHWAY 108. I'M ACROSS THE BORDER THEN. MAKES ME AN ILLEGAL IMMIGRANT, I SUPPOSE
ONE HOUR LATER...
RIGHT ON THE BEAM. UP THAT HUNTING TRAIL AND I SHOULD GET A SIGHT OF VON HAMMERSTEIN'S HIDE-OUT AT ECHO LAKE
ENOSBURG FALLS
1026

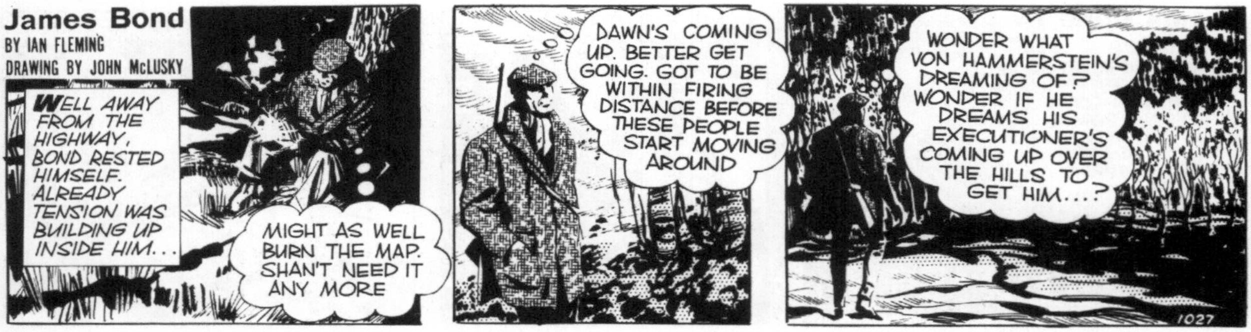

James Bond
BY IAN FLEMING
DRAWING BY JOHN McLUSKY
WELL AWAY FROM THE HIGHWAY, BOND RESTED HIMSELF. ALREADY TENSION WAS BUILDING UP INSIDE HIM...
MIGHT AS WELL BURN THE MAP. SHAN'T NEED IT ANY MORE
DAWN'S COMING UP. BETTER GET GOING. GOT TO BE WITHIN FIRING DISTANCE BEFORE THESE PEOPLE START MOVING AROUND
WONDER WHAT VON HAMMERSTEIN'S DREAMING OF? WONDER IF HE DREAMS HIS EXECUTIONER'S COMING UP OVER THE HILLS TO GET HIM...?
1027

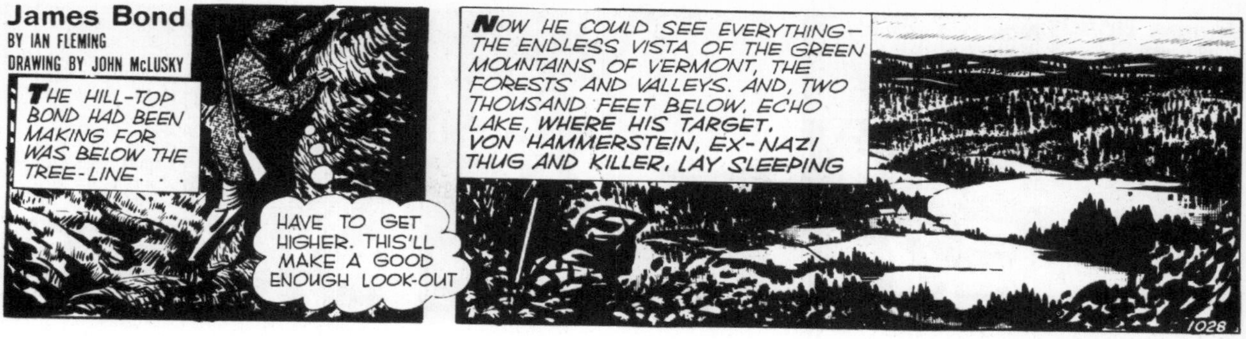
James Bond
BY IAN FLEMING
DRAWING BY JOHN McLUSKY
THE HILL-TOP BOND HAD BEEN MAKING FOR WAS BELOW THE TREE-LINE . . .
HAVE TO GET HIGHER. THIS'LL MAKE A GOOD ENOUGH LOOK-OUT
NOW HE COULD SEE EVERYTHING– THE ENDLESS VISTA OF THE GREEN MOUNTAINS OF VERMONT, THE FORESTS AND VALLEYS. AND, TWO THOUSAND FEET BELOW, ECHO LAKE, WHERE HIS TARGET, VON HAMMERSTEIN, EX-NAZI THUG AND KILLER, LAY SLEEPING
1028

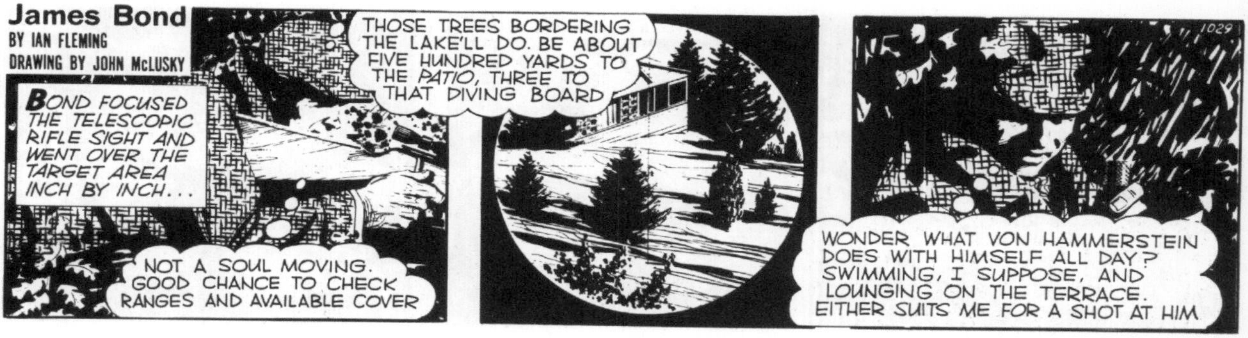
James Bond
BY IAN FLEMING
DRAWING BY JOHN McLUSKY
BOND FOCUSED THE TELESCOPIC RIFLE SIGHT AND WENT OVER THE TARGET AREA INCH BY INCH . . .
NOT A SOUL MOVING. GOOD CHANCE TO CHECK RANGES AND AVAILABLE COVER
THOSE TREES BORDERING THE LAKE'LL DO. BE ABOUT FIVE HUNDRED YARDS TO THE PATIO, THREE TO THAT DIVING BOARD
1029
WONDER WHAT VON HAMMERSTEIN DOES WITH HIMSELF ALL DAY? SWIMMING, I SUPPOSE, AND LOUNGING ON THE TERRACE. EITHER SUITS ME FOR A SHOT AT HIM

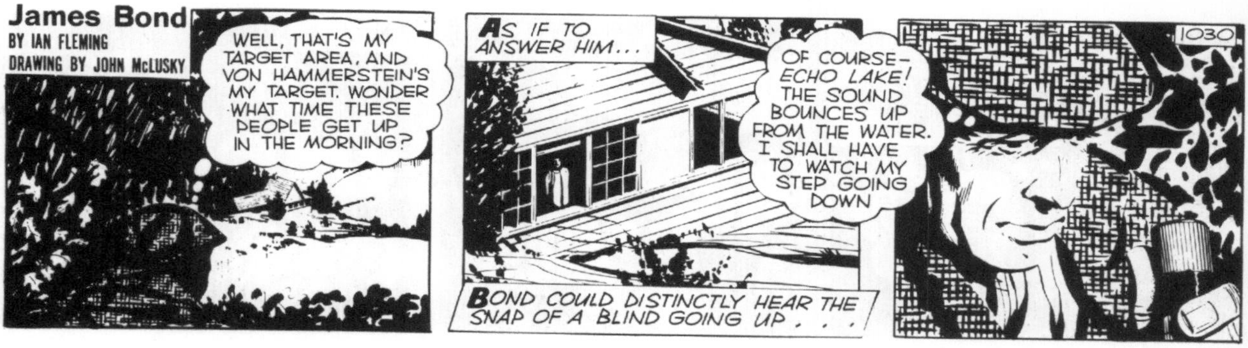
James Bond
BY IAN FLEMING
DRAWING BY JOHN McLUSKY
WELL, THAT'S MY TARGET AREA, AND VON HAMMERSTEIN'S MY TARGET. WONDER WHAT TIME THESE PEOPLE GET UP IN THE MORNING?
AS IF TO ANSWER HIM . . .
BOND COULD DISTINCTLY HEAR THE SNAP OF A BLIND GOING UP . . .
OF COURSE– ECHO LAKE! THE SOUND BOUNCES UP FROM THE WATER. I SHALL HAVE TO WATCH MY STEP GOING DOWN
1030

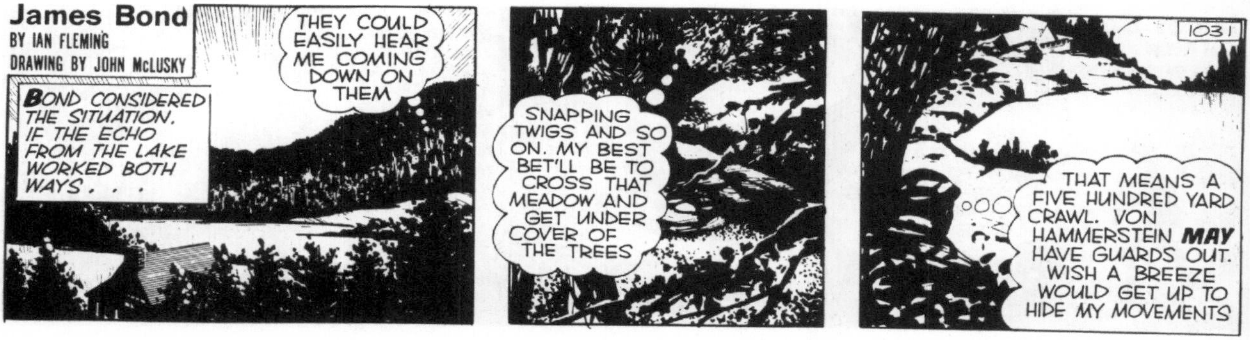
James Bond
BY IAN FLEMING
DRAWING BY JOHN McLUSKY
BOND CONSIDERED THE SITUATION. IF THE ECHO FROM THE LAKE WORKED BOTH WAYS . . .
THEY COULD EASILY HEAR ME COMING DOWN ON THEM
SNAPPING TWIGS AND SO ON. MY BEST BET'LL BE TO CROSS THAT MEADOW AND GET UNDER COVER OF THE TREES
1031
THAT MEANS A FIVE HUNDRED YARD CRAWL. VON HAMMERSTEIN MAY HAVE GUARDS OUT. WISH A BREEZE WOULD GET UP TO HIDE MY MOVEMENTS

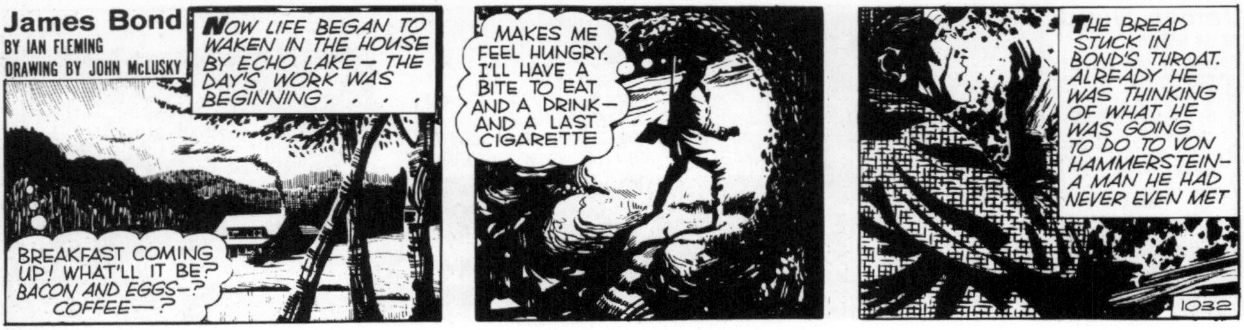
James Bond
BY IAN FLEMING
DRAWING BY JOHN McLUSKY
NOW LIFE BEGAN TO WAKEN IN THE HOUSE BY ECHO LAKE — THE DAY'S WORK WAS BEGINNING . . . .
BREAKFAST COMING UP! WHAT'LL IT BE? BACON AND EGGS—? COFFEE—?
MAKES ME FEEL HUNGRY. I'LL HAVE A BITE TO EAT AND A DRINK—AND A LAST CIGARETTE
THE BREAD STUCK IN BOND'S THROAT. ALREADY HE WAS THINKING OF WHAT HE WAS GOING TO DO TO VON HAMMERSTEIN—A MAN HE HAD NEVER EVEN MET
1032

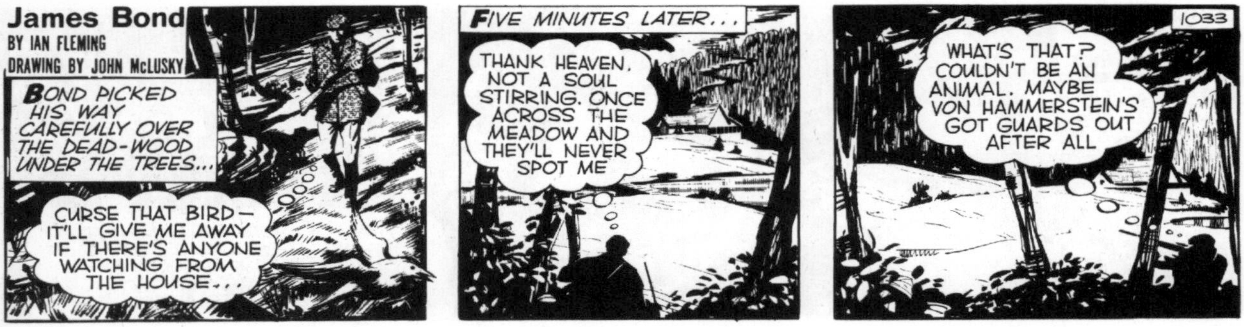
James Bond
BY IAN FLEMING
DRAWING BY JOHN McLUSKY
BOND PICKED HIS WAY CAREFULLY OVER THE DEAD-WOOD UNDER THE TREES...
CURSE THAT BIRD—IT'LL GIVE ME AWAY IF THERE'S ANYONE WATCHING FROM THE HOUSE...
FIVE MINUTES LATER...
THANK HEAVEN, NOT A SOUL STIRRING. ONCE ACROSS THE MEADOW AND THEY'LL NEVER SPOT ME
1033
WHAT'S THAT? COULDN'T BE AN ANIMAL. MAYBE VON HAMMERSTEIN'S GOT GUARDS OUT AFTER ALL

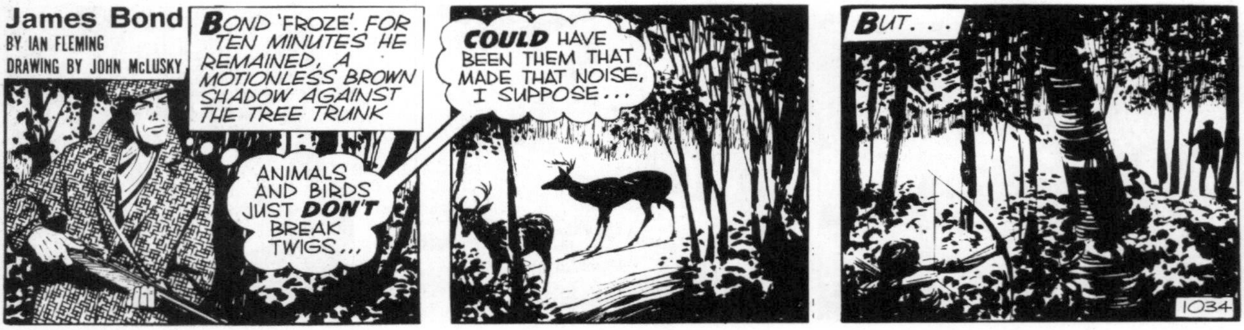
James Bond
BY IAN FLEMING
DRAWING BY JOHN McLUSKY
BOND 'FROZE'. FOR TEN MINUTES HE REMAINED, A MOTIONLESS BROWN SHADOW AGAINST THE TREE TRUNK
ANIMALS AND BIRDS JUST DON'T BREAK TWIGS...
COULD HAVE BEEN THEM THAT MADE THAT NOISE, I SUPPOSE...
BUT. . .
1034

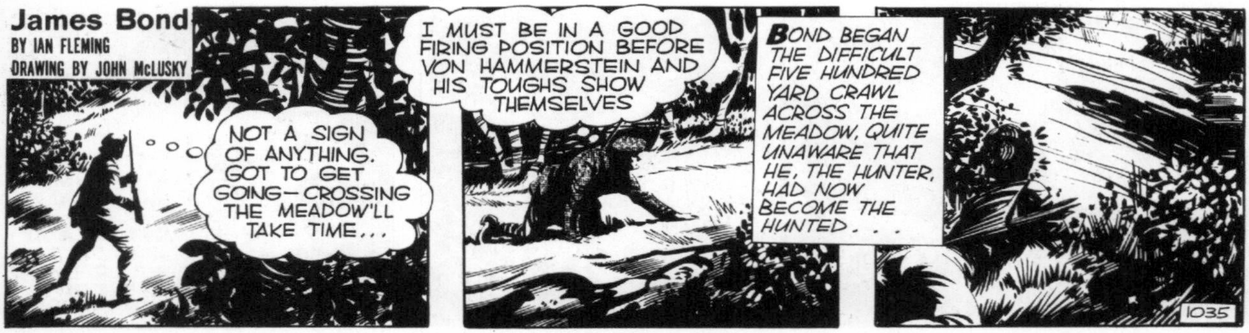
James Bond
BY IAN FLEMING
DRAWING BY JOHN McLUSKY
NOT A SIGN OF ANYTHING. GOT TO GET GOING—CROSSING THE MEADOW'LL TAKE TIME...
I MUST BE IN A GOOD FIRING POSITION BEFORE VON HAMMERSTEIN AND HIS TOUGHS SHOW THEMSELVES
BOND BEGAN THE DIFFICULT FIVE HUNDRED YARD CRAWL ACROSS THE MEADOW, QUITE UNAWARE THAT HE, THE HUNTER, HAD NOW BECOME THE HUNTED . . .
1035

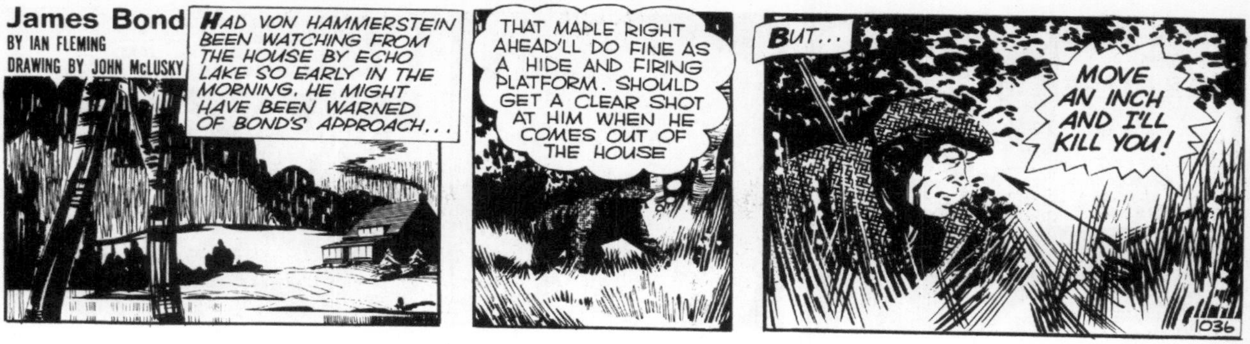
James Bond
BY IAN FLEMING
DRAWING BY JOHN McLUSKY
HAD VON HAMMERSTEIN BEEN WATCHING FROM THE HOUSE BY ECHO LAKE SO EARLY IN THE MORNING, HE MIGHT HAVE BEEN WARNED OF BOND'S APPROACH...
THAT MAPLE RIGHT AHEAD'LL DO FINE AS A HIDE AND FIRING PLATFORM. SHOULD GET A CLEAR SHOT AT HIM WHEN HE COMES OUT OF THE HOUSE
BUT...
MOVE AN INCH AND I'LL KILL YOU!
1036

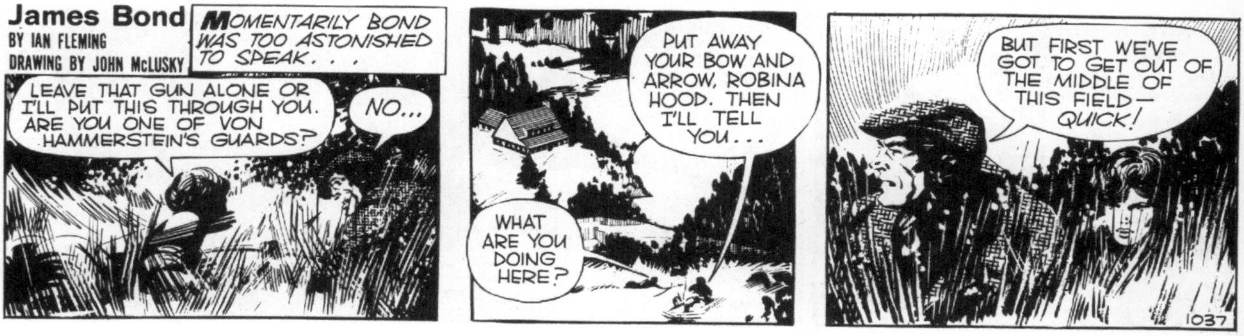
James Bond
BY IAN FLEMING
DRAWING BY JOHN McLUSKY
MOMENTARILY BOND WAS TOO ASTONISHED TO SPEAK...
LEAVE THAT GUN ALONE OR I'LL PUT THIS THROUGH YOU. ARE YOU ONE OF VON HAMMERSTEIN'S GUARDS?
NO...
PUT AWAY YOUR BOW AND ARROW, ROBINA HOOD. THEN I'LL TELL YOU...
WHAT ARE YOU DOING HERE?
BUT FIRST WE'VE GOT TO GET OUT OF THE MIDDLE OF THIS FIELD—QUICK!
1037

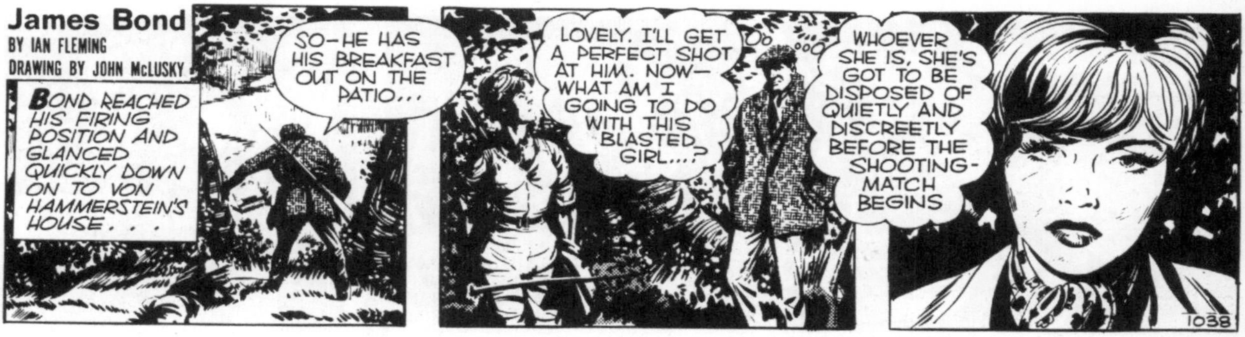
James Bond
BY IAN FLEMING
DRAWING BY JOHN McLUSKY
BOND REACHED HIS FIRING POSITION AND GLANCED QUICKLY DOWN ON TO VON HAMMERSTEIN'S HOUSE...
SO—HE HAS HIS BREAKFAST OUT ON THE PATIO...
LOVELY. I'LL GET A PERFECT SHOT AT HIM. NOW—WHAT AM I GOING TO DO WITH THIS BLASTED GIRL...?
WHOEVER SHE IS, SHE'S GOT TO BE DISPOSED OF QUIETLY AND DISCREETLY BEFORE THE SHOOTING-MATCH BEGINS
1038

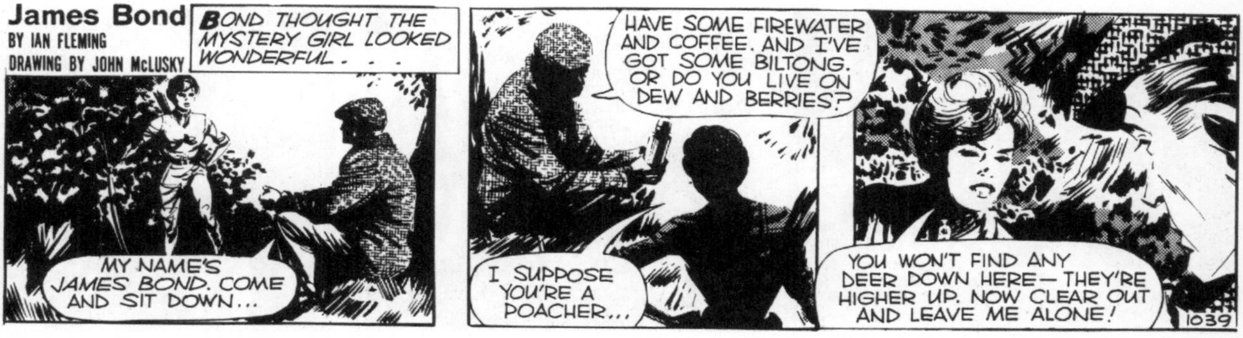
James Bond
BY IAN FLEMING
DRAWING BY JOHN McLUSKY
BOND THOUGHT THE MYSTERY GIRL LOOKED WONDERFUL...
MY NAME'S JAMES BOND. COME AND SIT DOWN...
HAVE SOME FIREWATER AND COFFEE. AND I'VE GOT SOME BILTONG. OR DO YOU LIVE ON DEW AND BERRIES?
I SUPPOSE YOU'RE A POACHER...
YOU WON'T FIND ANY DEER DOWN HERE—THEY'RE HIGHER UP. NOW CLEAR OUT AND LEAVE ME ALONE!
1039

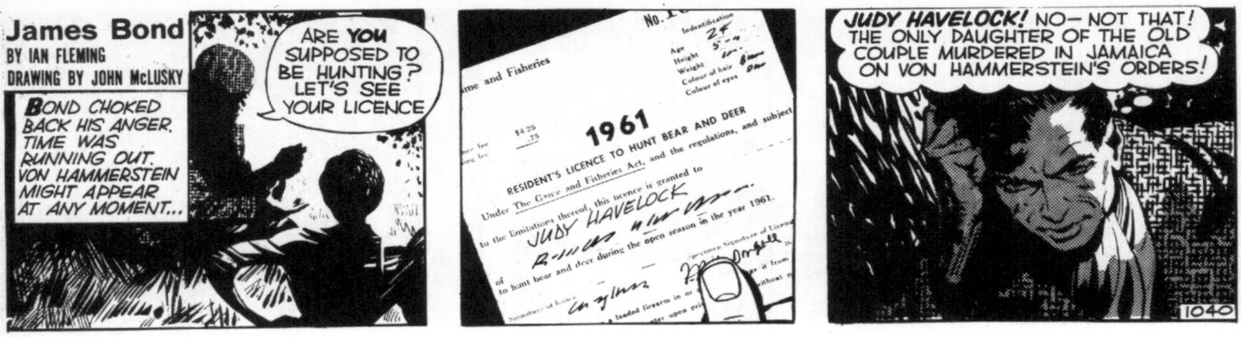
James Bond
BY IAN FLEMING
DRAWING BY JOHN McLUSKY
BOND CHOKED BACK HIS ANGER. TIME WAS RUNNING OUT. VON HAMMERSTEIN MIGHT APPEAR AT ANY MOMENT...
ARE YOU SUPPOSED TO BE HUNTING? LET'S SEE YOUR LICENCE
1961
RESIDENT'S LICENCE TO HUNT BEAR AND DEER
JUDY HAVELOCK
JUDY HAVELOCK! NO— NOT THAT! THE ONLY DAUGHTER OF THE OLD COUPLE MURDERED IN JAMAICA ON VON HAMMERSTEIN'S ORDERS!
1040

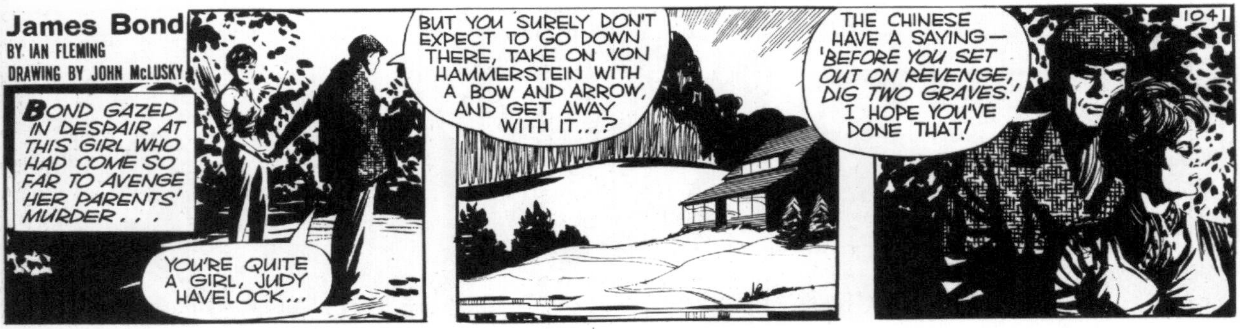
James Bond
BY IAN FLEMING
DRAWING BY JOHN McLUSKY
BOND GAZED IN DESPAIR AT THIS GIRL WHO HAD COME SO FAR TO AVENGE HER PARENTS' MURDER . . .
YOU'RE QUITE A GIRL, JUDY HAVELOCK...
BUT YOU SURELY DON'T EXPECT TO GO DOWN THERE, TAKE ON VON HAMMERSTEIN WITH A BOW AND ARROW, AND GET AWAY WITH IT...?
THE CHINESE HAVE A SAYING— 'BEFORE YOU SET OUT ON REVENGE, DIG TWO GRAVES.' I HOPE YOU'VE DONE THAT!
1041

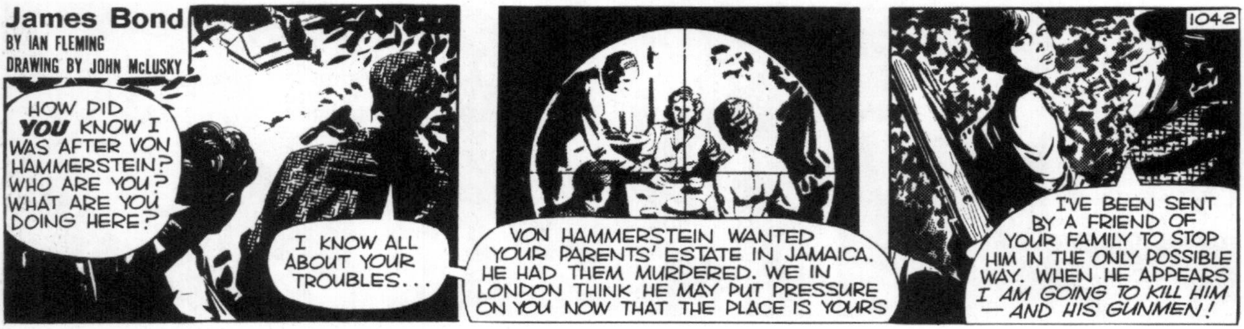
James Bond
BY IAN FLEMING
DRAWING BY JOHN McLUSKY
HOW DID YOU KNOW I WAS AFTER VON HAMMERSTEIN? WHO ARE YOU? WHAT ARE YOU DOING HERE?
I KNOW ALL ABOUT YOUR TROUBLES . . .
VON HAMMERSTEIN WANTED YOUR PARENTS' ESTATE IN JAMAICA. HE HAD THEM MURDERED. WE IN LONDON THINK HE MAY PUT PRESSURE ON YOU NOW THAT THE PLACE IS YOURS
1042
I'VE BEEN SENT BY A FRIEND OF YOUR FAMILY TO STOP HIM IN THE ONLY POSSIBLE WAY. WHEN HE APPEARS I AM GOING TO KILL HIM — AND HIS GUNMEN!

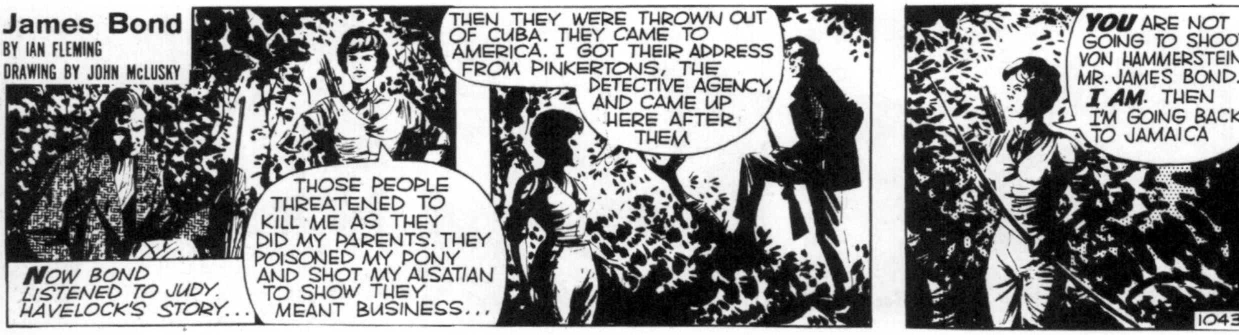
James Bond
BY IAN FLEMING
DRAWING BY JOHN McLUSKY
NOW BOND LISTENED TO JUDY HAVELOCK'S STORY...
THOSE PEOPLE THREATENED TO KILL ME AS THEY DID MY PARENTS. THEY POISONED MY PONY AND SHOT MY ALSATIAN TO SHOW THEY MEANT BUSINESS...
THEN THEY WERE THROWN OUT OF CUBA. THEY CAME TO AMERICA. I GOT THEIR ADDRESS FROM PINKERTONS, THE DETECTIVE AGENCY, AND CAME UP HERE AFTER THEM
YOU ARE NOT GOING TO SHOOT VON HAMMERSTEIN, MR. JAMES BOND. I AM. THEN I'M GOING BACK TO JAMAICA
1043

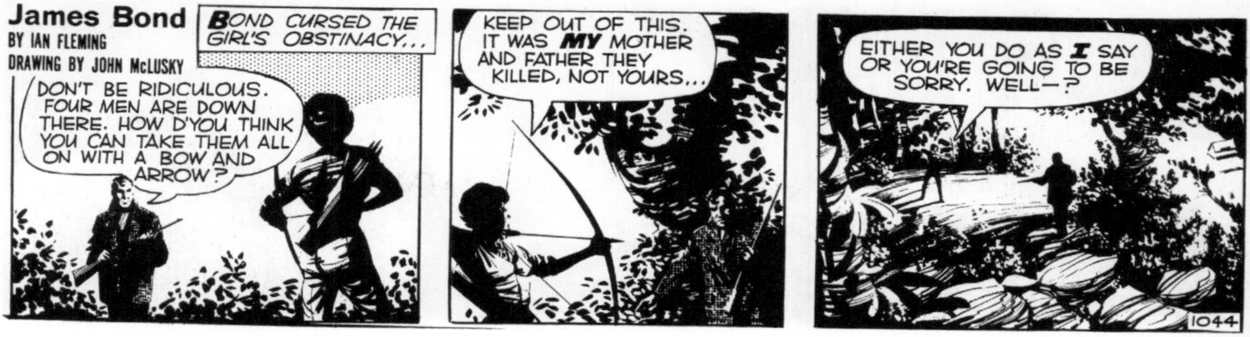
James Bond
BY IAN FLEMING
DRAWING BY JOHN McLUSKY
BOND CURSED THE GIRL'S OBSTINACY...
DON'T BE RIDICULOUS. FOUR MEN ARE DOWN THERE. HOW D'YOU THINK YOU CAN TAKE THEM ALL ON WITH A BOW AND ARROW?
KEEP OUT OF THIS. IT WAS MY MOTHER AND FATHER THEY KILLED, NOT YOURS...
EITHER YOU DO AS I SAY OR YOU'RE GOING TO BE SORRY. WELL—?
1044

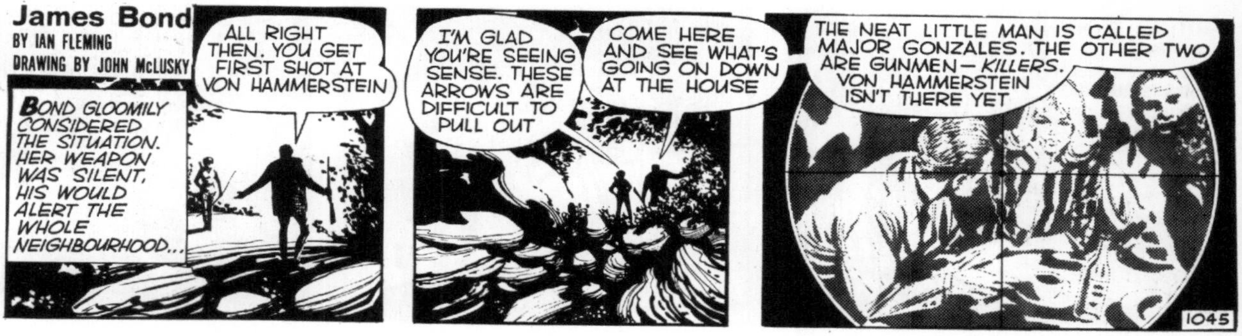
James Bond
BY IAN FLEMING
DRAWING BY JOHN McLUSKY
BOND GLOOMILY CONSIDERED THE SITUATION. HER WEAPON WAS SILENT, HIS WOULD ALERT THE WHOLE NEIGHBOURHOOD...
ALL RIGHT THEN. YOU GET FIRST SHOT AT VON HAMMERSTEIN
I'M GLAD YOU'RE SEEING SENSE. THESE ARROWS ARE DIFFICULT TO PULL OUT
COME HERE AND SEE WHAT'S GOING ON DOWN AT THE HOUSE
THE NEAT LITTLE MAN IS CALLED MAJOR GONZALES. THE OTHER TWO ARE GUNMEN—KILLERS. VON HAMMERSTEIN ISN'T THERE YET
1045

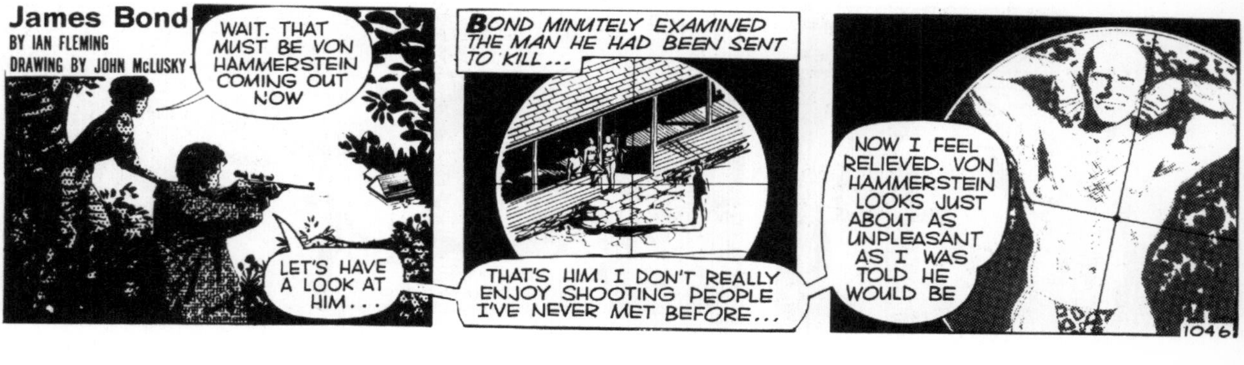
James Bond
BY IAN FLEMING
DRAWING BY JOHN McLUSKY
WAIT. THAT MUST BE VON HAMMERSTEIN COMING OUT NOW
LET'S HAVE A LOOK AT HIM...
BOND MINUTELY EXAMINED THE MAN HE HAD BEEN SENT TO KILL...
THAT'S HIM. I DON'T REALLY ENJOY SHOOTING PEOPLE I'VE NEVER MET BEFORE...
NOW I FEEL RELIEVED. VON HAMMERSTEIN LOOKS JUST ABOUT AS UNPLEASANT AS I WAS TOLD HE WOULD BE
1046

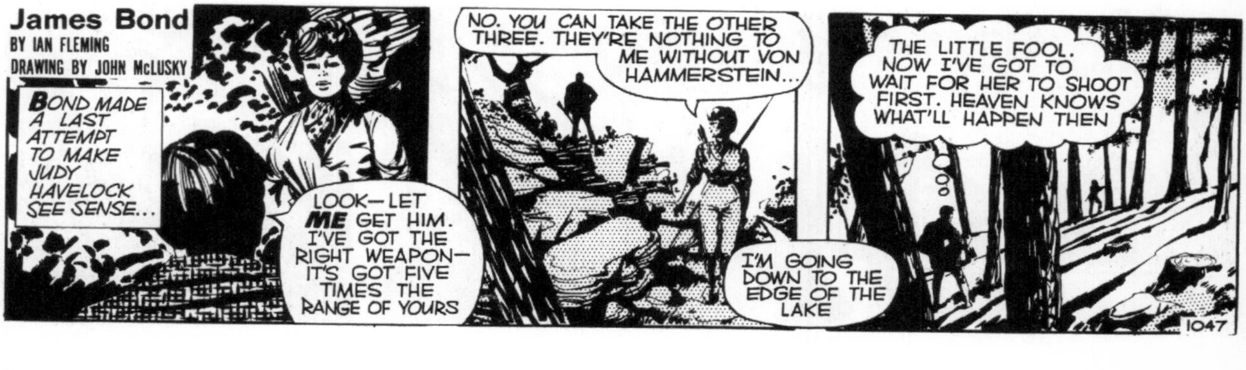
James Bond
BY IAN FLEMING
DRAWING BY JOHN McLUSKY
BOND MADE A LAST ATTEMPT TO MAKE JUDY HAVELOCK SEE SENSE...
LOOK—LET ME GET HIM. I'VE GOT THE RIGHT WEAPON—IT'S GOT FIVE TIMES THE RANGE OF YOURS
NO. YOU CAN TAKE THE OTHER THREE. THEY'RE NOTHING TO ME WITHOUT VON HAMMERSTEIN...
I'M GOING DOWN TO THE EDGE OF THE LAKE
THE LITTLE FOOL. NOW I'VE GOT TO WAIT FOR HER TO SHOOT FIRST. HEAVEN KNOWS WHAT'LL HAPPEN THEN
1047

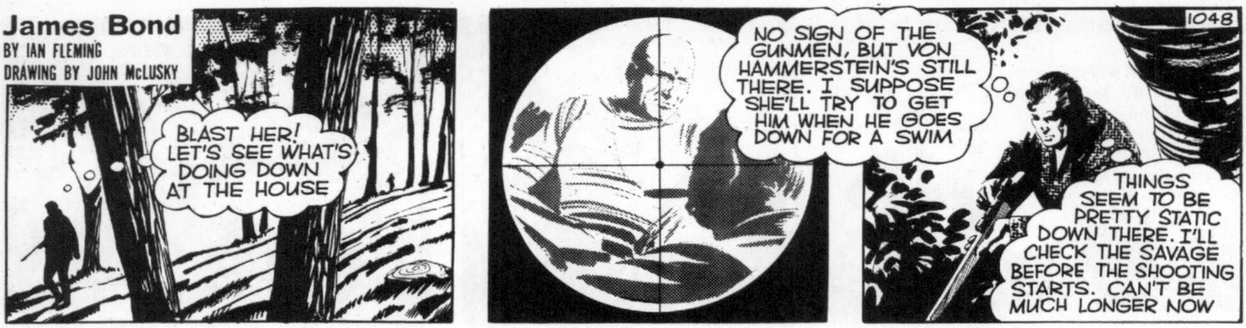
James Bond
BY IAN FLEMING
DRAWING BY JOHN McLUSKY
BLAST HER! LET'S SEE WHAT'S DOING DOWN AT THE HOUSE
NO SIGN OF THE GUNMEN, BUT VON HAMMERSTEIN'S STILL THERE. I SUPPOSE SHE'LL TRY TO GET HIM WHEN HE GOES DOWN FOR A SWIM
1048
THINGS SEEM TO BE PRETTY STATIC DOWN THERE. I'LL CHECK THE SAVAGE BEFORE THE SHOOTING STARTS. CAN'T BE MUCH LONGER NOW

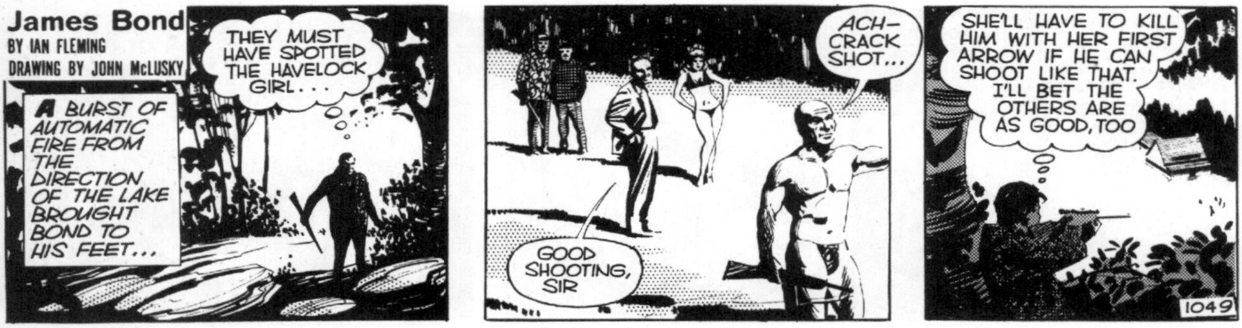
James Bond
BY IAN FLEMING
DRAWING BY JOHN McLUSKY
A BURST OF AUTOMATIC FIRE FROM THE DIRECTION OF THE LAKE BROUGHT BOND TO HIS FEET...
THEY MUST HAVE SPOTTED THE HAVELOCK GIRL...
ACH-CRACK SHOT...
GOOD SHOOTING, SIR
SHE'LL HAVE TO KILL HIM WITH HER FIRST ARROW IF HE CAN SHOOT LIKE THAT. I'LL BET THE OTHERS ARE AS GOOD, TOO
1049

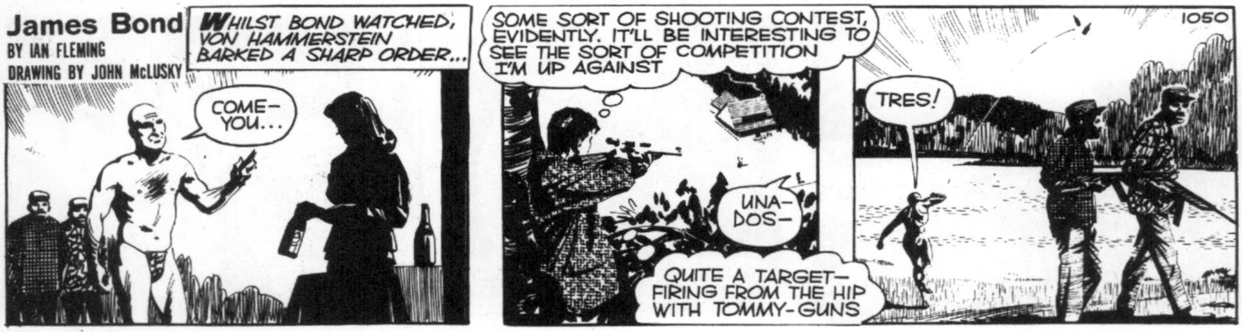
James Bond
BY IAN FLEMING
DRAWING BY JOHN McLUSKY
WHILST BOND WATCHED, VON HAMMERSTEIN BARKED A SHARP ORDER...
COME-YOU...
SOME SORT OF SHOOTING CONTEST, EVIDENTLY. IT'LL BE INTERESTING TO SEE THE SORT OF COMPETITION I'M UP AGAINST
UNA-DOS-
QUITE A TARGET-FIRING FROM THE HIP WITH TOMMY-GUNS
1050
TRES!

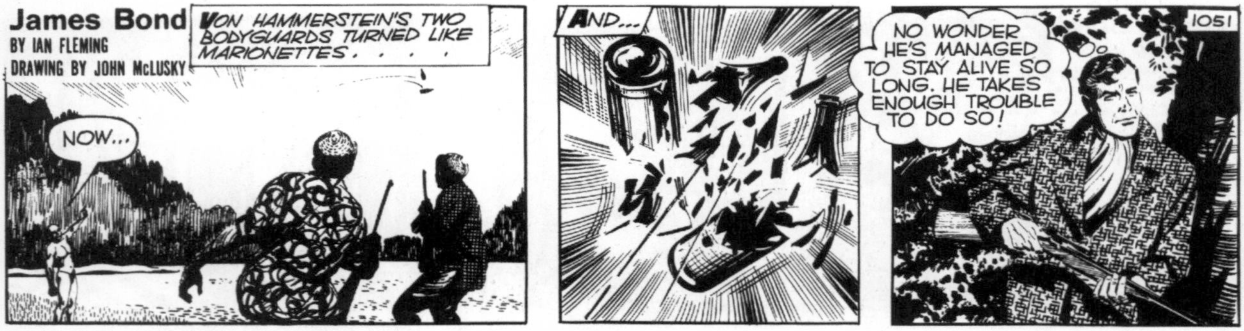
James Bond
BY IAN FLEMING
DRAWING BY JOHN McLUSKY
VON HAMMERSTEIN'S TWO BODYGUARDS TURNED LIKE MARIONETTES . . . .
NOW...
AND...
1051
NO WONDER HE'S MANAGED TO STAY ALIVE SO LONG. HE TAKES ENOUGH TROUBLE TO DO SO!

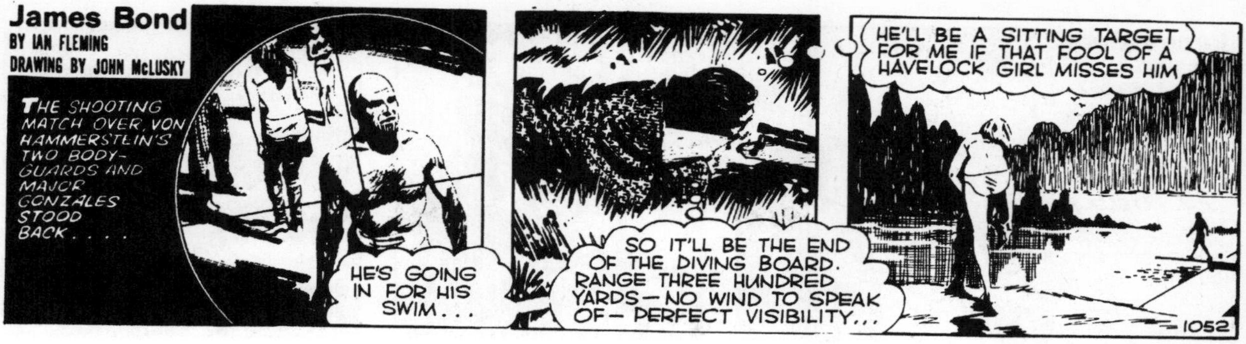
James Bond
BY IAN FLEMING
DRAWING BY JOHN McLUSKY
THE SHOOTING MATCH OVER, VON HAMMERSTEIN'S TWO BODY-GUARDS AND MAJOR GONZALES STOOD BACK . . . .
HE'S GOING IN FOR HIS SWIM . . .
SO IT'LL BE THE END OF THE DIVING BOARD. RANGE THREE HUNDRED YARDS—NO WIND TO SPEAK OF— PERFECT VISIBILITY . . .
HE'LL BE A SITTING TARGET FOR ME IF THAT FOOL OF A HAVELOCK GIRL MISSES HIM
1052

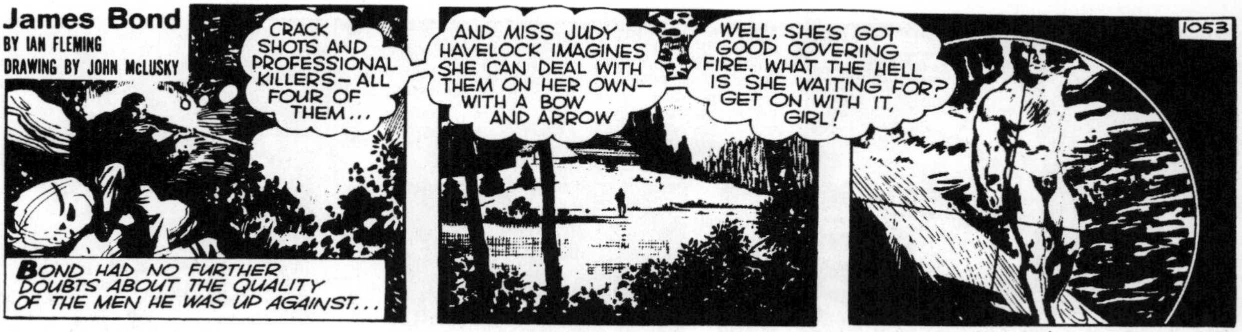
James Bond
BY IAN FLEMING
DRAWING BY JOHN McLUSKY
CRACK SHOTS AND PROFESSIONAL KILLERS— ALL FOUR OF THEM . . .
BOND HAD NO FURTHER DOUBTS ABOUT THE QUALITY OF THE MEN HE WAS UP AGAINST . . .
AND MISS JUDY HAVELOCK IMAGINES SHE CAN DEAL WITH THEM ON HER OWN— WITH A BOW AND ARROW
WELL, SHE'S GOT GOOD COVERING FIRE. WHAT THE HELL IS SHE WAITING FOR? GET ON WITH IT, GIRL!
1053

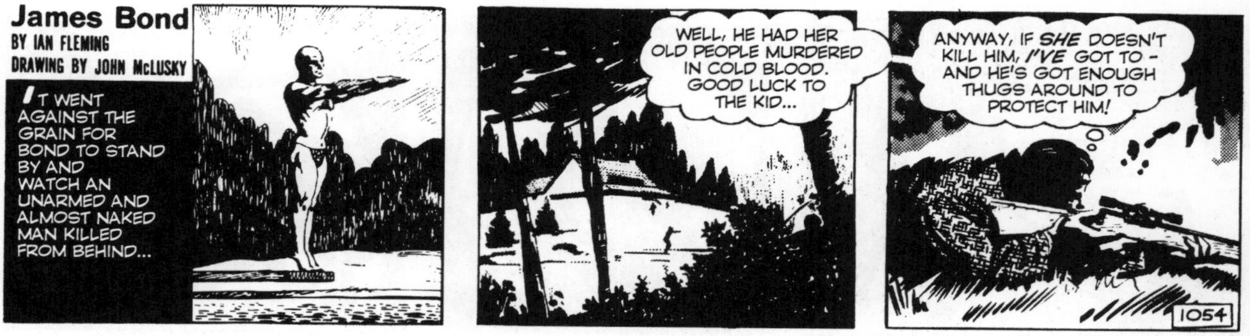
James Bond
BY IAN FLEMING
DRAWING BY JOHN McLUSKY
IT WENT AGAINST THE GRAIN FOR BOND TO STAND BY AND WATCH AN UNARMED AND ALMOST NAKED MAN KILLED FROM BEHIND...
WELL, HE HAD HER OLD PEOPLE MURDERED IN COLD BLOOD. GOOD LUCK TO THE KID...
ANYWAY, IF SHE DOESN'T KILL HIM, I'VE GOT TO - AND HE'S GOT ENOUGH THUGS AROUND TO PROTECT HIM!
1054

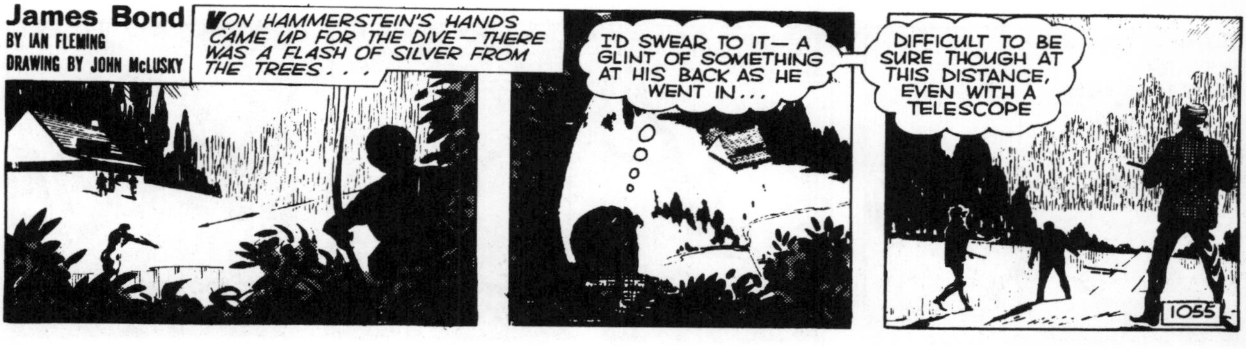
James Bond
BY IAN FLEMING
DRAWING BY JOHN McLUSKY
VON HAMMERSTEIN'S HANDS CAME UP FOR THE DIVE— THERE WAS A FLASH OF SILVER FROM THE TREES . . .
I'D SWEAR TO IT— A GLINT OF SOMETHING AT HIS BACK AS HE WENT IN . . .
DIFFICULT TO BE SURE THOUGH AT THIS DISTANCE, EVEN WITH A TELESCOPE
1055

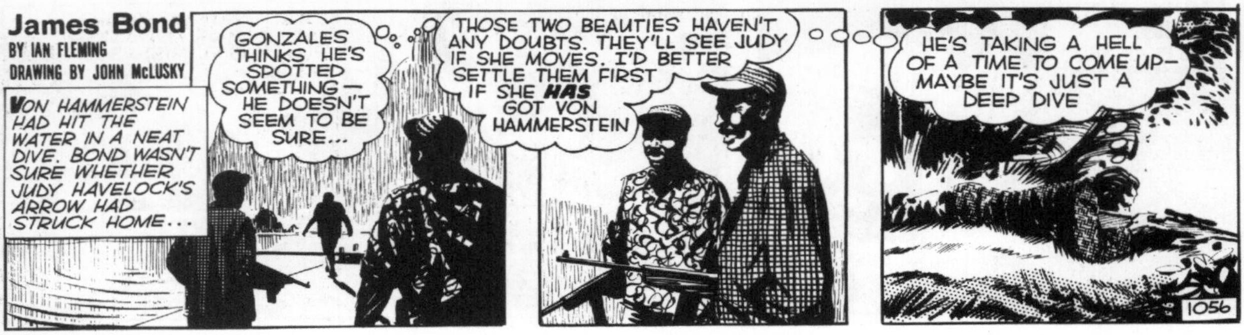
James Bond
BY IAN FLEMING
DRAWING BY JOHN McLUSKY
VON HAMMERSTEIN HAD HIT THE WATER IN A NEAT DIVE. BOND WASN'T SURE WHETHER JUDY HAVELOCK'S ARROW HAD STRUCK HOME...
GONZALES THINKS HE'S SPOTTED SOMETHING—HE DOESN'T SEEM TO BE SURE...
THOSE TWO BEAUTIES HAVEN'T ANY DOUBTS. THEY'LL SEE JUDY IF SHE MOVES. I'D BETTER SETTLE THEM FIRST IF SHE HAS GOT VON HAMMERSTEIN
HE'S TAKING A HELL OF A TIME TO COME UP—MAYBE IT'S JUST A DEEP DIVE
1056

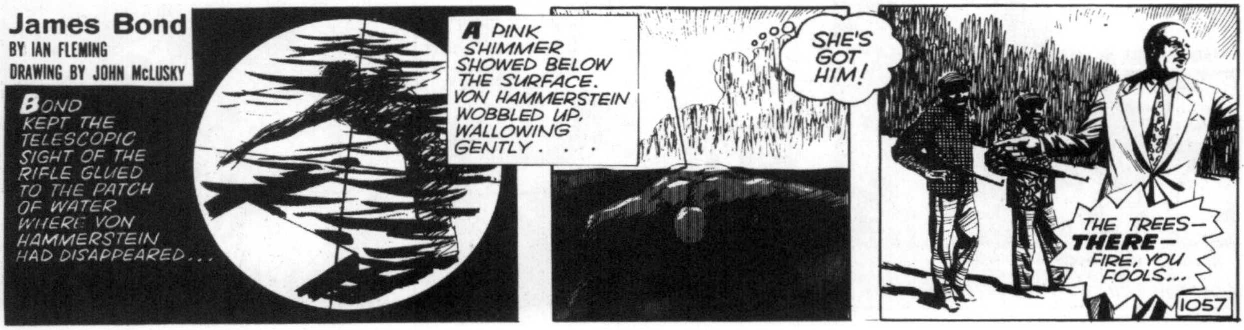
James Bond
BY IAN FLEMING
DRAWING BY JOHN McLUSKY
BOND KEPT THE TELESCOPIC SIGHT OF THE RIFLE GLUED TO THE PATCH OF WATER WHERE VON HAMMERSTEIN HAD DISAPPEARED...
A PINK SHIMMER SHOWED BELOW THE SURFACE. VON HAMMERSTEIN WOBBLED UP, WALLOWING GENTLY....
SHE'S GOT HIM!
THE TREES—THERE—FIRE, YOU FOOLS...
1057

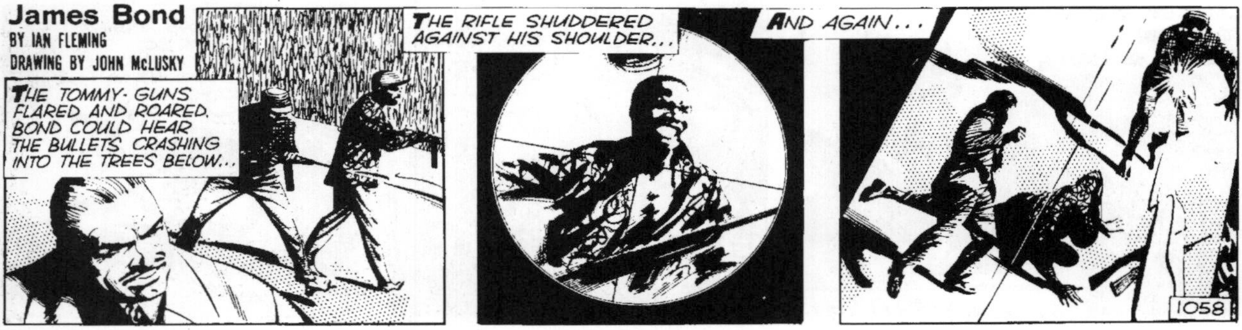
James Bond
BY IAN FLEMING
DRAWING BY JOHN McLUSKY
THE TOMMY-GUNS FLARED AND ROARED. BOND COULD HEAR THE BULLETS CRASHING INTO THE TREES BELOW...
THE RIFLE SHUDDERED AGAINST HIS SHOULDER...
AND AGAIN...
1058

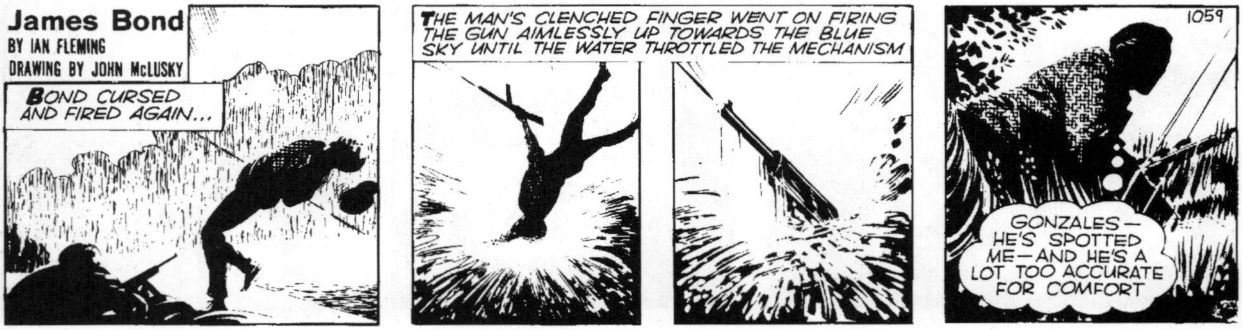
James Bond
BY IAN FLEMING
DRAWING BY JOHN McLUSKY
BOND CURSED AND FIRED AGAIN...
THE MAN'S CLENCHED FINGER WENT ON FIRING THE GUN AIMLESSLY UP TOWARDS THE BLUE SKY UNTIL THE WATER THROTTLED THE MECHANISM
1059
GONZALES—HE'S SPOTTED ME—AND HE'S A LOT TOO ACCURATE FOR COMFORT

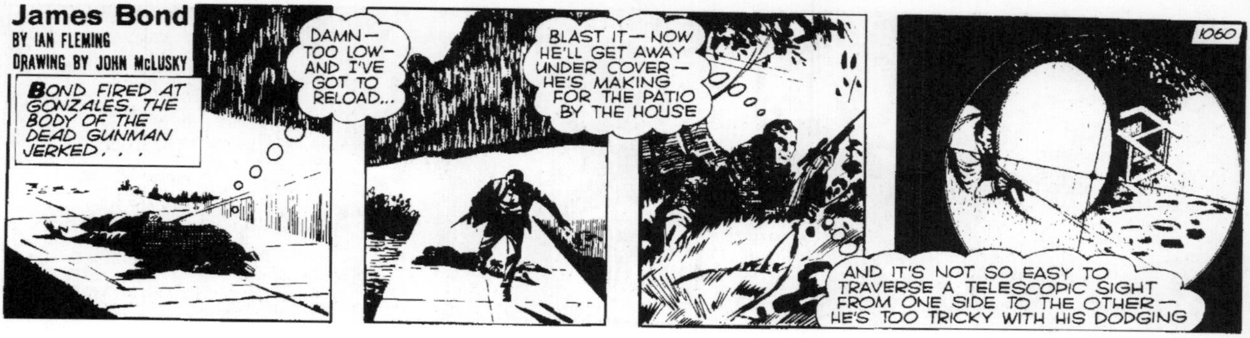
James Bond
BY IAN FLEMING
DRAWING BY JOHN McLUSKY
BOND FIRED AT GONZALES. THE BODY OF THE DEAD GUNMAN JERKED . . .
DAMN— TOO LOW— AND I'VE GOT TO RELOAD...
BLAST IT— NOW HE'LL GET AWAY UNDER COVER— HE'S MAKING FOR THE PATIO BY THE HOUSE
1060
AND IT'S NOT SO EASY TO TRAVERSE A TELESCOPIC SIGHT FROM ONE SIDE TO THE OTHER— HE'S TOO TRICKY WITH HIS DODGING

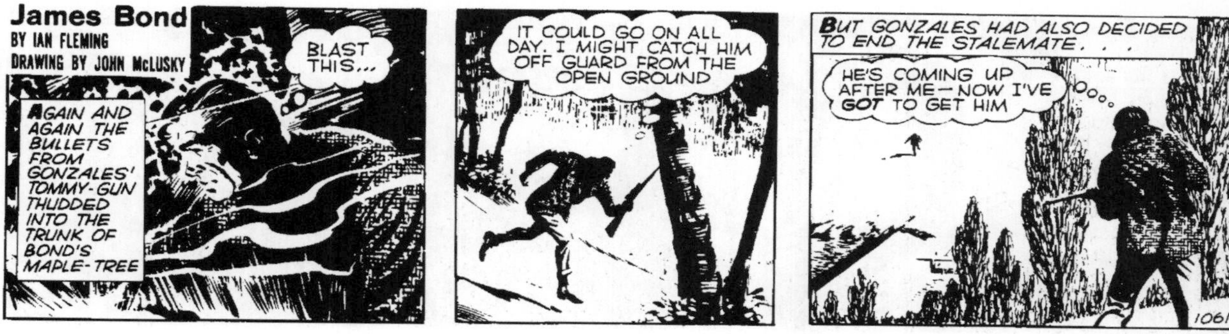
James Bond
BY IAN FLEMING
DRAWING BY JOHN McLUSKY
AGAIN AND AGAIN THE BULLETS FROM GONZALES' TOMMY-GUN THUDDED INTO THE TRUNK OF BOND'S MAPLE-TREE
BLAST THIS...
IT COULD GO ON ALL DAY. I MIGHT CATCH HIM OFF GUARD FROM THE OPEN GROUND
BUT GONZALES HAD ALSO DECIDED TO END THE STALEMATE. . .
HE'S COMING UP AFTER ME— NOW I'VE GOT TO GET HIM
1061

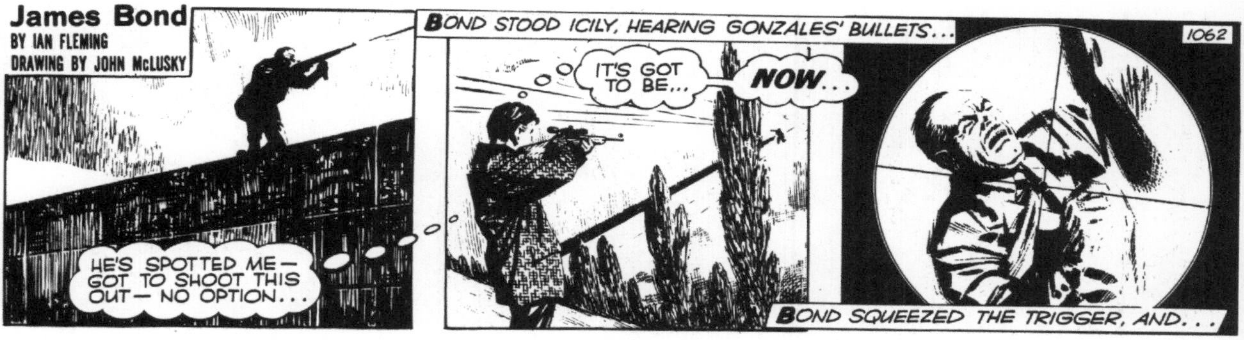
James Bond
BY IAN FLEMING
DRAWING BY JOHN McLUSKY
HE'S SPOTTED ME— GOT TO SHOOT THIS OUT— NO OPTION...
BOND STOOD ICILY, HEARING GONZALES' BULLETS...
IT'S GOT TO BE...
NOW...
1062
BOND SQUEEZED THE TRIGGER, AND...

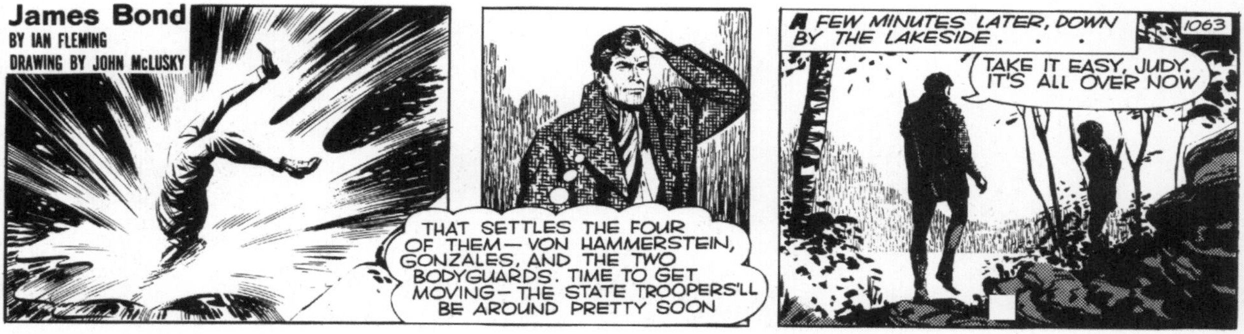
James Bond
BY IAN FLEMING
DRAWING BY JOHN McLUSKY
THAT SETTLES THE FOUR OF THEM— VON HAMMERSTEIN, GONZALES, AND THE TWO BODYGUARDS. TIME TO GET MOVING— THE STATE TROOPERS'LL BE AROUND PRETTY SOON
A FEW MINUTES LATER, DOWN BY THE LAKESIDE . . .
1063
TAKE IT EASY, JUDY. IT'S ALL OVER NOW

James Bond
BY IAN FLEMING
DRAWING BY JOHN McLUSKY
YOUR PARENTS' KILLERS ARE DEAD– THERE'S NOTHING MORE TO WORRY ABOUT. NOW, LET'S HAVE A LOOK AT THAT ARM
YOU WERE ALL WOUND UP. . .
IT'S NOTHING– SOMETHING– A BULLET, HIT ME. IT'S NICE OF YOU TO BE LIKE THIS. AFTER I WAS– SO AWFUL. . .
1064
I DIDN'T KNOW IT WOULD BE LIKE THAT– THE SHOOTING– THE KILLING–
IT HAD TO BE DONE. THEY'D HAVE GOT YOU OTHERWISE. THEY WERE PRO KILLERS, THE WORST. I TOLD YOU THIS WAS MAN'S WORK

James Bond
BY IAN FLEMING
DRAWING BY JOHN McLUSKY
NOW YOU'RE COMING BACK WITH ME– ACROSS THE CANADIAN BORDER AND BACK TO LONDON
ALL RIGHT
I'LL GET YOUR PASSPORT STRAIGHTENED OUT. AND YOU'LL NEED SOME CLOTHES. IT'LL TAKE TIME
WHERE ARE YOU TAKING ME TO. . . ?
1065
WE'LL BE STAYING TOGETHER IN A PLACE CALLED THE KO-ZEE MOTEL. . .
I'VE NEVER STAYED IN A MOTEL. IT'LL BE NICE– WITH YOU. I'M COMING. . .
END OF STORY

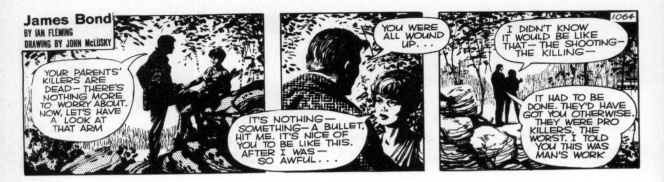

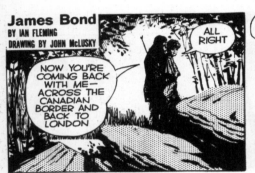

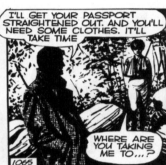

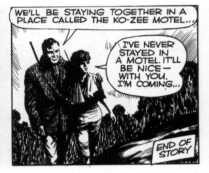

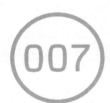

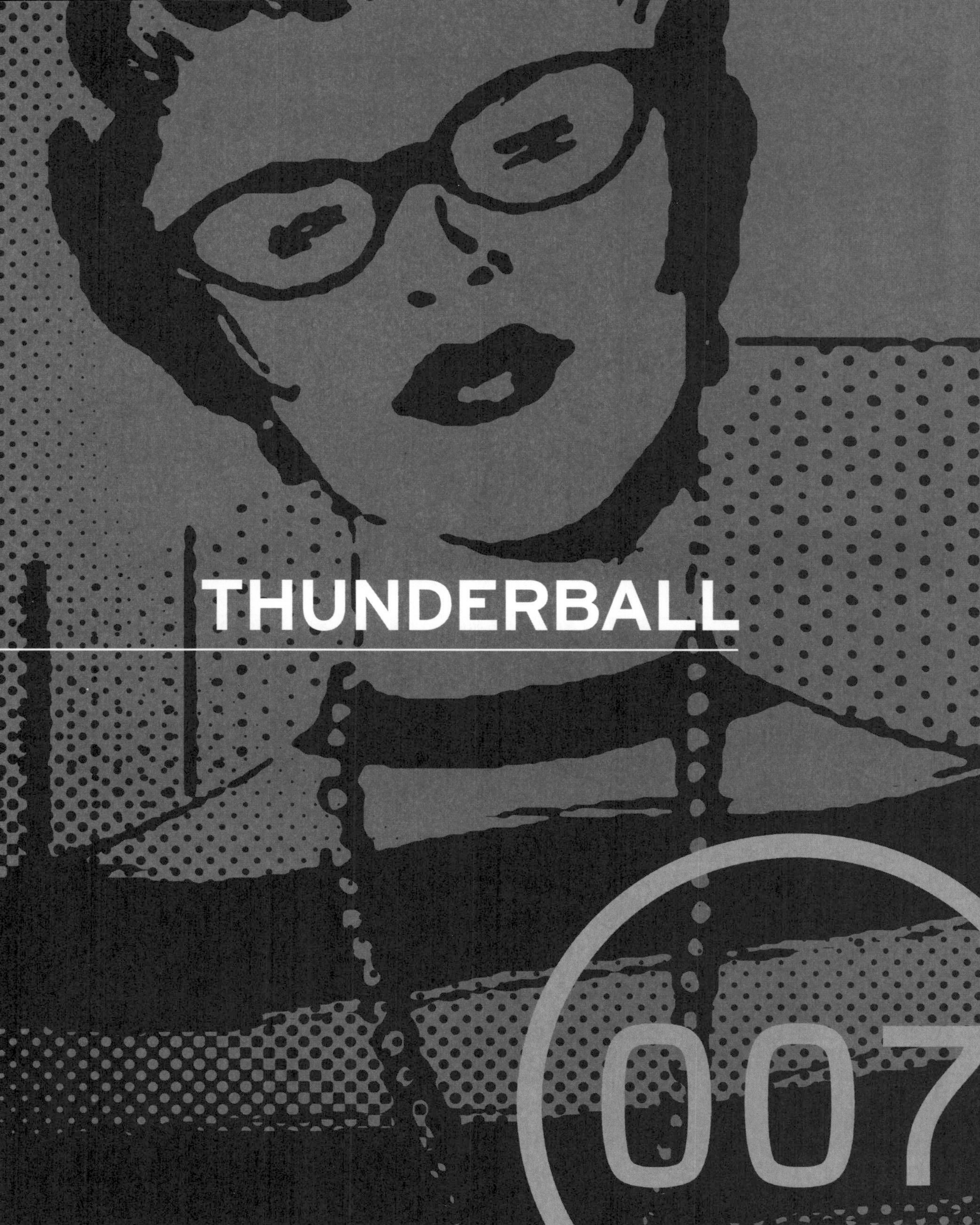
THUNDERBALL
007

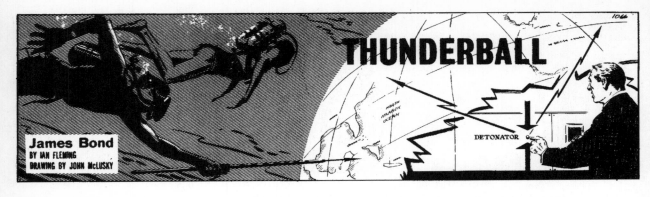

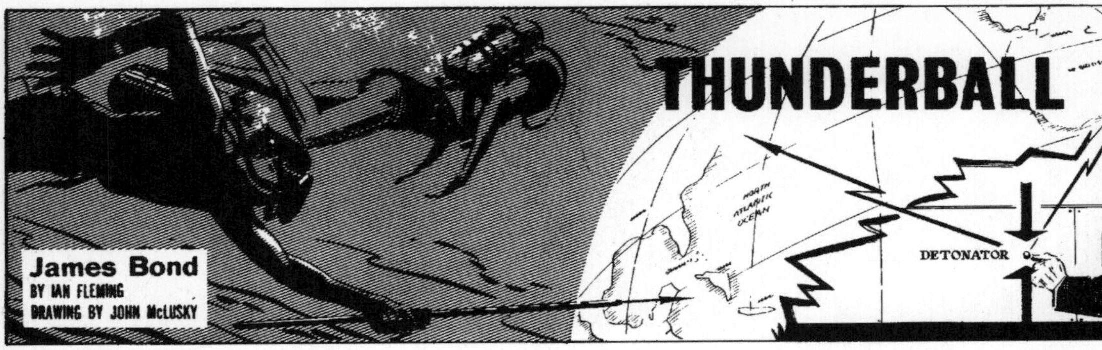
1066
THUNDERBALL
James Bond
BY IAN FLEMING
DRAWING BY JOHN McLUSKY
DETONATOR

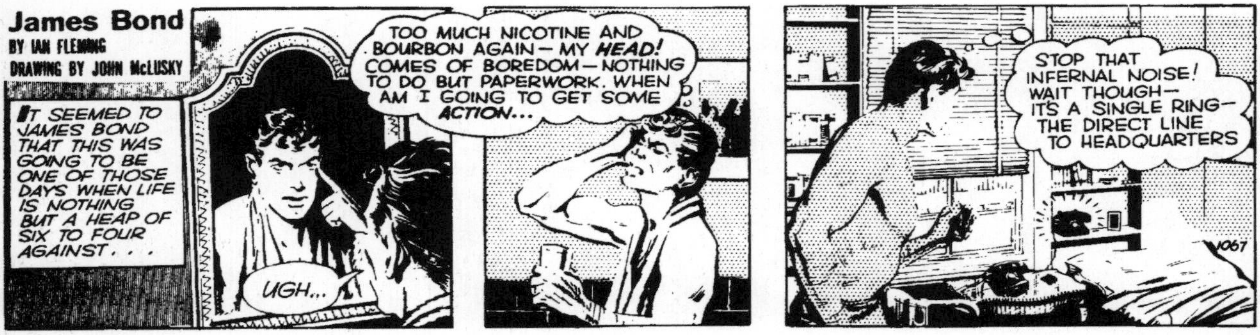
James Bond
BY IAN FLEMING
DRAWING BY JOHN McLUSKY
IT SEEMED TO JAMES BOND THAT THIS WAS GOING TO BE ONE OF THOSE DAYS WHEN LIFE IS NOTHING BUT A HEAP OF SIX TO FOUR AGAINST . . .
UGH...
TOO MUCH NICOTINE AND BOURBON AGAIN— MY HEAD! COMES OF BOREDOM—NOTHING TO DO BUT PAPERWORK. WHEN AM I GOING TO GET SOME ACTION...
STOP THAT INFERNAL NOISE! WAIT THOUGH— IT'S A SINGLE RING— THE DIRECT LINE TO HEADQUARTERS
1067

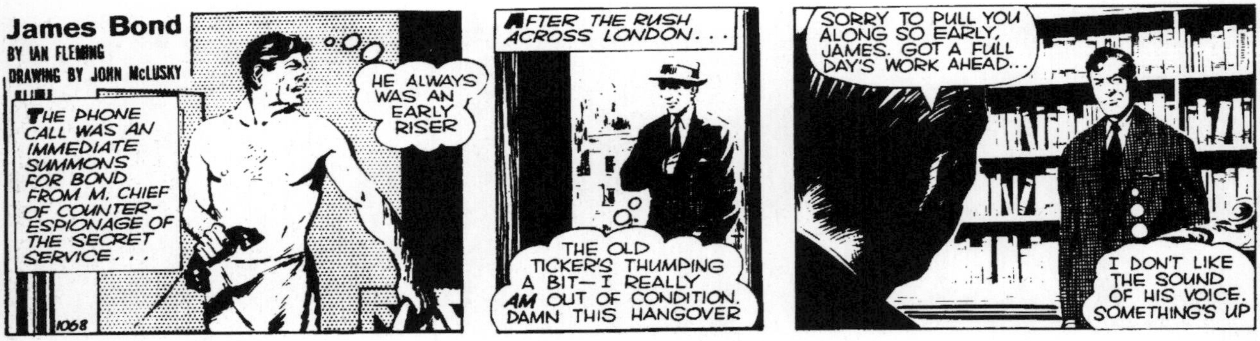
James Bond
BY IAN FLEMING
DRAWING BY JOHN McLUSKY
THE PHONE CALL WAS AN IMMEDIATE SUMMONS FOR BOND FROM M. CHIEF OF COUNTER-ESPIONAGE OF THE SECRET SERVICE . . .
HE ALWAYS WAS AN EARLY RISER
1068
AFTER THE RUSH ACROSS LONDON . . .
THE OLD TICKER'S THUMPING A BIT— I REALLY AM OUT OF CONDITION. DAMN THIS HANGOVER
SORRY TO PULL YOU ALONG SO EARLY, JAMES. GOT A FULL DAY'S WORK AHEAD...
I DON'T LIKE THE SOUND OF HIS VOICE. SOMETHING'S UP

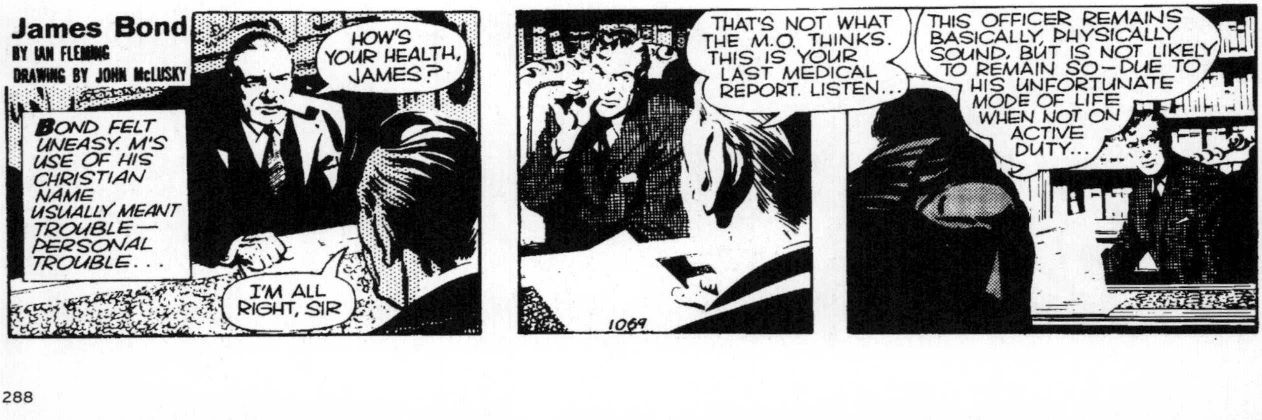
James Bond
BY IAN FLEMING
DRAWING BY JOHN McLUSKY
BOND FELT UNEASY. M'S USE OF HIS CHRISTIAN NAME USUALLY MEANT TROUBLE— PERSONAL TROUBLE . . .
HOW'S YOUR HEALTH, JAMES?
I'M ALL RIGHT, SIR
THAT'S NOT WHAT THE M.O. THINKS. THIS IS YOUR LAST MEDICAL REPORT. LISTEN...
THIS OFFICER REMAINS BASICALLY, PHYSICALLY SOUND, BUT IS NOT LIKELY TO REMAIN SO—DUE TO HIS UNFORTUNATE MODE OF LIFE WHEN NOT ON ACTIVE DUTY...
1069

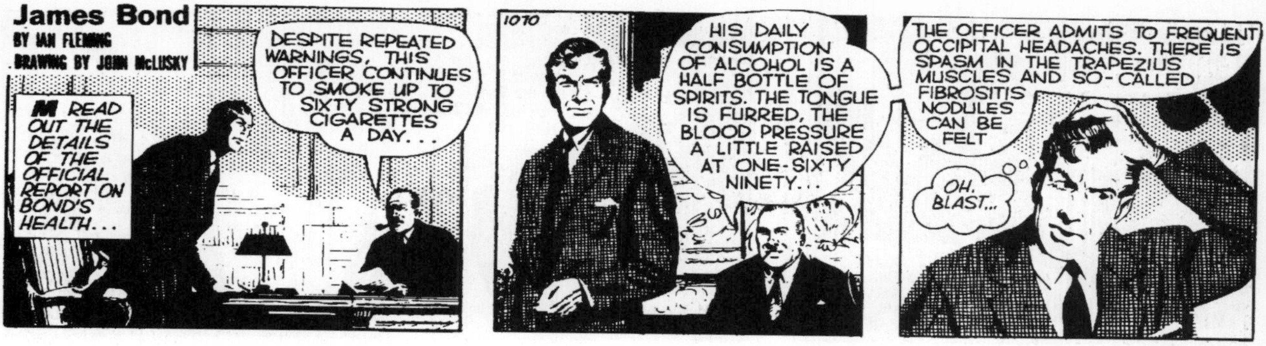
James Bond
BY IAN FLEMING
DRAWING BY JOHN McLUSKY
M READ OUT THE DETAILS OF THE OFFICIAL REPORT ON BOND'S HEALTH...
DESPITE REPEATED WARNINGS, THIS OFFICER CONTINUES TO SMOKE UP TO SIXTY STRONG CIGARETTES A DAY...
1070
HIS DAILY CONSUMPTION OF ALCOHOL IS A HALF BOTTLE OF SPIRITS. THE TONGUE IS FURRED, THE BLOOD PRESSURE A LITTLE RAISED AT ONE-SIXTY NINETY...
THE OFFICER ADMITS TO FREQUENT OCCIPITAL HEADACHES. THERE IS SPASM IN THE TRAPEZIUS MUSCLES AND SO-CALLED FIBROSITIS NODULES CAN BE FELT
OH, BLAST...

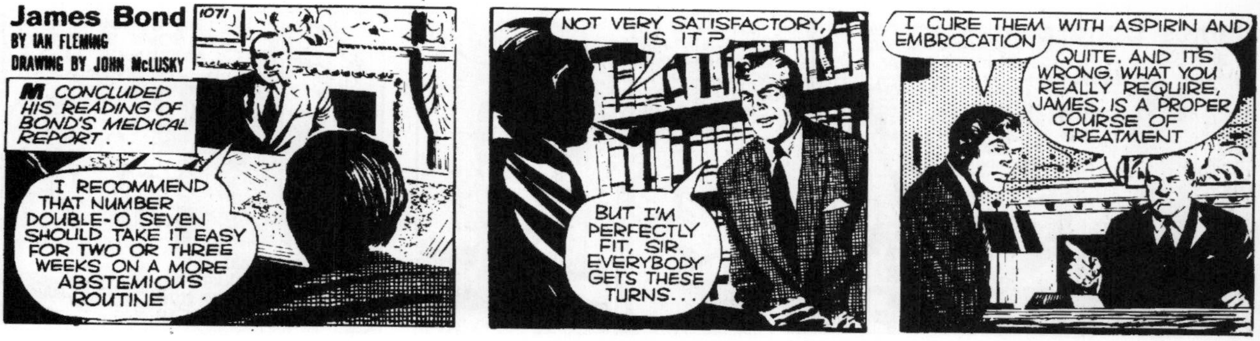
James Bond
BY IAN FLEMING
DRAWING BY JOHN McLUSKY
1071
M CONCLUDED HIS READING OF BOND'S MEDICAL REPORT...
I RECOMMEND THAT NUMBER DOUBLE-O SEVEN SHOULD TAKE IT EASY FOR TWO OR THREE WEEKS ON A MORE ABSTEMIOUS ROUTINE
NOT VERY SATISFACTORY, IS IT?
BUT I'M PERFECTLY FIT, SIR. EVERYBODY GETS THESE TURNS...
I CURE THEM WITH ASPIRIN AND EMBROCATION
QUITE. AND IT'S WRONG. WHAT YOU REALLY REQUIRE, JAMES, IS A PROPER COURSE OF TREATMENT

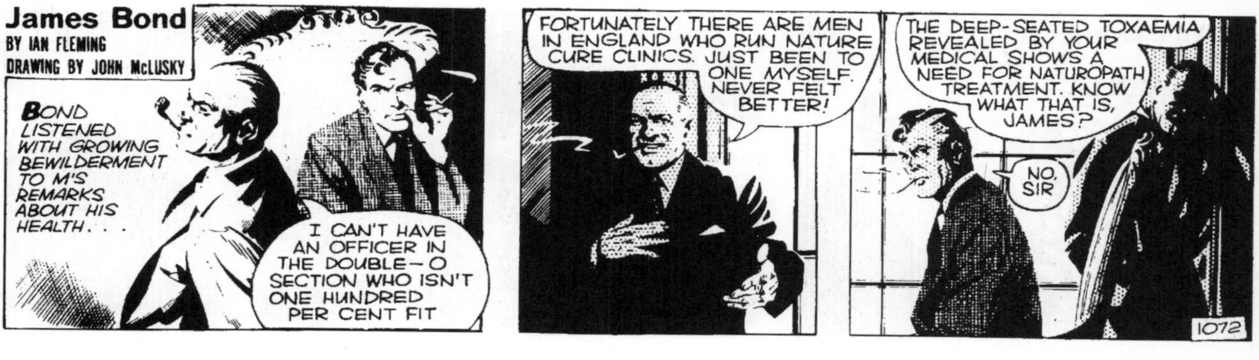
James Bond
BY IAN FLEMING
DRAWING BY JOHN McLUSKY
BOND LISTENED WITH GROWING BEWILDERMENT TO M'S REMARKS ABOUT HIS HEALTH...
I CAN'T HAVE AN OFFICER IN THE DOUBLE-O SECTION WHO ISN'T ONE HUNDRED PER CENT FIT
FORTUNATELY THERE ARE MEN IN ENGLAND WHO RUN NATURE CURE CLINICS. JUST BEEN TO ONE MYSELF. NEVER FELT BETTER!
THE DEEP-SEATED TOXAEMIA REVEALED BY YOUR MEDICAL SHOWS A NEED FOR NATUROPATH TREATMENT. KNOW WHAT THAT IS, JAMES?
NO, SIR
1072

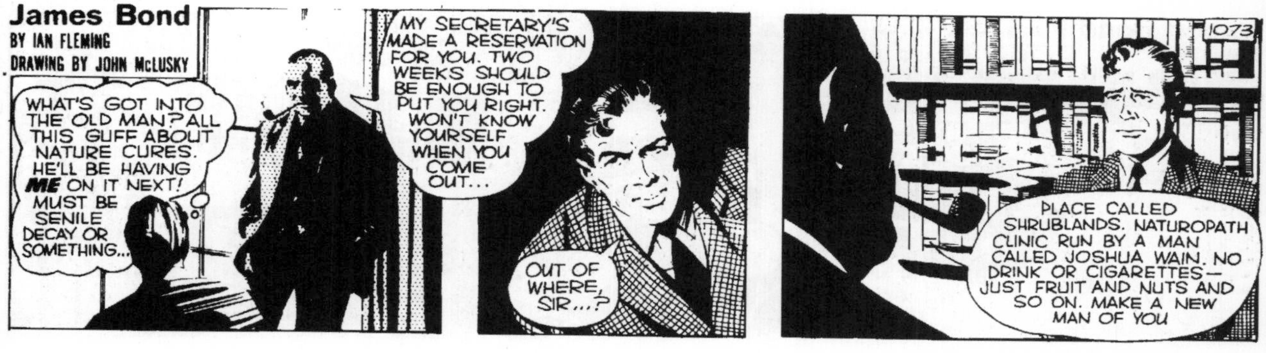
James Bond
BY IAN FLEMING
DRAWING BY JOHN McLUSKY
WHAT'S GOT INTO THE OLD MAN? ALL THIS GUFF ABOUT NATURE CURES. HE'LL BE HAVING ME ON IT NEXT! MUST BE SENILE DECAY OR SOMETHING...
MY SECRETARY'S MADE A RESERVATION FOR YOU. TWO WEEKS SHOULD BE ENOUGH TO PUT YOU RIGHT. WON'T KNOW YOURSELF WHEN YOU COME OUT...
OUT OF WHERE, SIR...?
1073
PLACE CALLED SHRUBLANDS. NATUROPATH CLINIC RUN BY A MAN CALLED JOSHUA WAIN. NO DRINK OR CIGARETTES— JUST FRUIT AND NUTS AND SO ON. MAKE A NEW MAN OF YOU

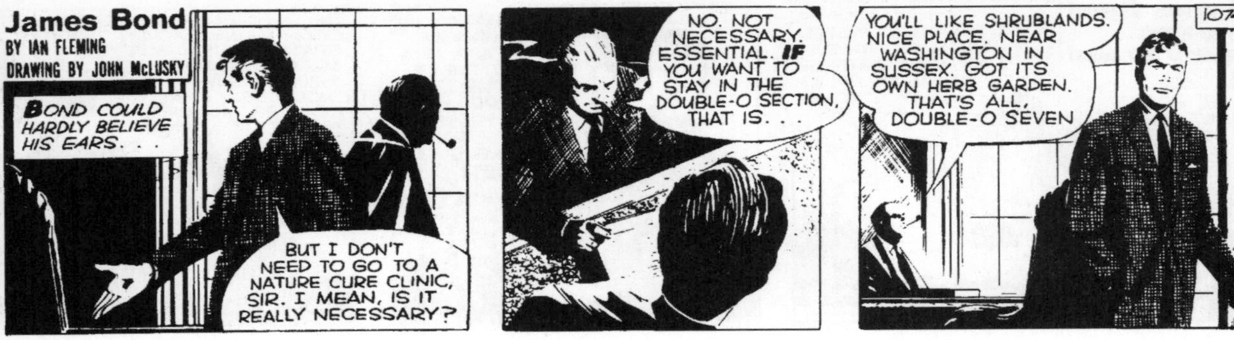
James Bond
BY IAN FLEMING
DRAWING BY JOHN McLUSKY
BOND COULD HARDLY BELIEVE HIS EARS. . .
BUT I DON'T NEED TO GO TO A NATURE CURE CLINIC, SIR. I MEAN, IS IT REALLY NECESSARY?
NO. NOT NECESSARY. ESSENTIAL. IF YOU WANT TO STAY IN THE DOUBLE-O SECTION, THAT IS. . .
YOU'LL LIKE SHRUBLANDS. NICE PLACE. NEAR WASHINGTON IN SUSSEX. GOT ITS OWN HERB GARDEN. THAT'S ALL, DOUBLE-O SEVEN
1074

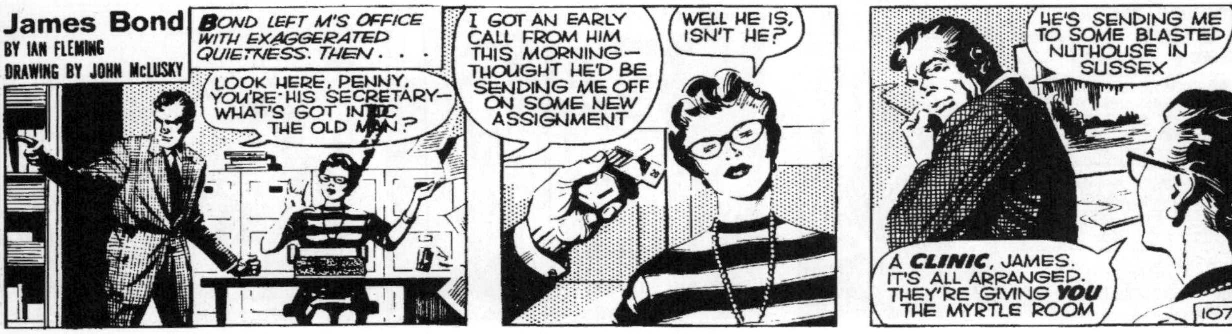
James Bond
BY IAN FLEMING
DRAWING BY JOHN McLUSKY
BOND LEFT M'S OFFICE WITH EXAGGERATED QUIETNESS. THEN . . .
LOOK HERE, PENNY, YOU'RE HIS SECRETARY– WHAT'S GOT INTO THE OLD MAN?
I GOT AN EARLY CALL FROM HIM THIS MORNING– THOUGHT HE'D BE SENDING ME OFF ON SOME NEW ASSIGNMENT
WELL HE IS, ISN'T HE?
HE'S SENDING ME TO SOME BLASTED NUTHOUSE IN SUSSEX
A CLINIC, JAMES. IT'S ALL ARRANGED. THEY'RE GIVING YOU THE MYRTLE ROOM
1075

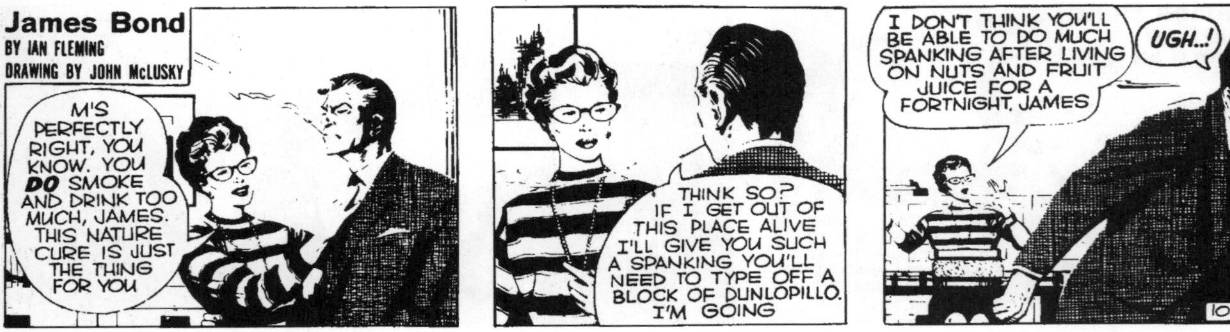
James Bond
BY IAN FLEMING
DRAWING BY JOHN McLUSKY
M'S PERFECTLY RIGHT, YOU KNOW. YOU DO SMOKE AND DRINK TOO MUCH, JAMES. THIS NATURE CURE IS JUST THE THING FOR YOU
THINK SO? IF I GET OUT OF THIS PLACE ALIVE I'LL GIVE YOU SUCH A SPANKING YOU'LL NEED TO TYPE OFF A BLOCK OF DUNLOPILLO. I'M GOING
I DON'T THINK YOU'LL BE ABLE TO DO MUCH SPANKING AFTER LIVING ON NUTS AND FRUIT JUICE FOR A FORTNIGHT, JAMES
UGH..!
1076

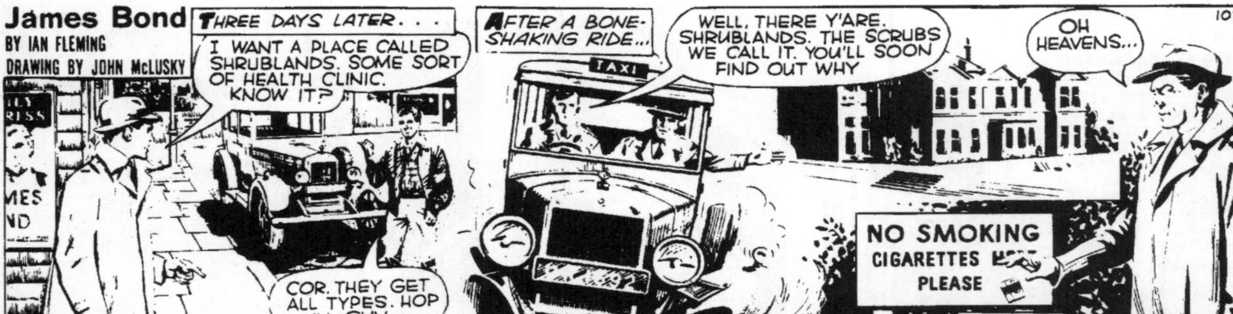
James Bond
BY IAN FLEMING
DRAWING BY JOHN McLUSKY
THREE DAYS LATER. . .
I WANT A PLACE CALLED SHRUBLANDS. SOME SORT OF HEALTH CLINIC. KNOW IT?
COR. THEY GET ALL TYPES. HOP IN, GUV
AFTER A BONE-SHAKING RIDE...
TAXI
WELL, THERE Y'ARE. SHRUBLANDS. THE SCRUBS WE CALL IT. YOU'LL SOON FIND OUT WHY
1077
OH HEAVENS...
NO SMOKING
CIGARETTES
PLEASE

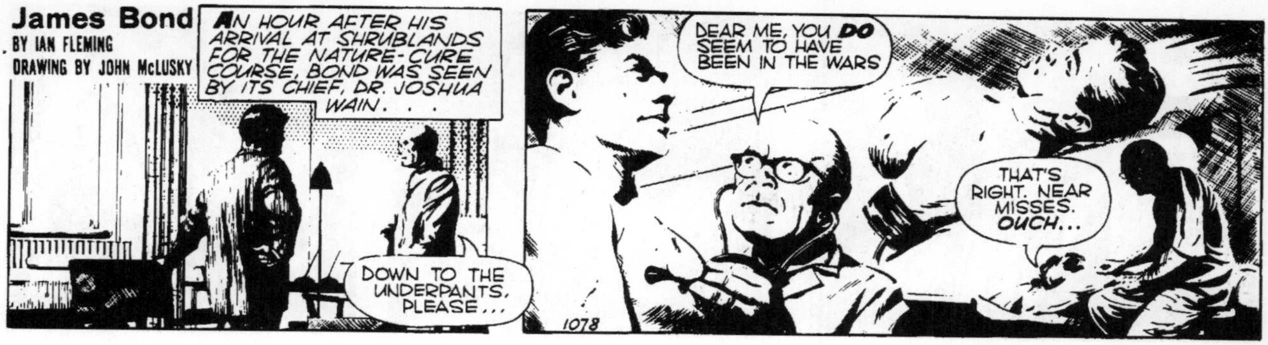
James Bond
BY IAN FLEMING
DRAWING BY JOHN McLUSKY
AN HOUR AFTER HIS ARRIVAL AT SHRUBLANDS FOR THE NATURE-CURE COURSE, BOND WAS SEEN BY ITS CHIEF, DR. JOSHUA WAIN. . .
DOWN TO THE UNDERPANTS, PLEASE...
DEAR ME, YOU DO SEEM TO HAVE BEEN IN THE WARS
THAT'S RIGHT. NEAR MISSES. OUCH...
1078

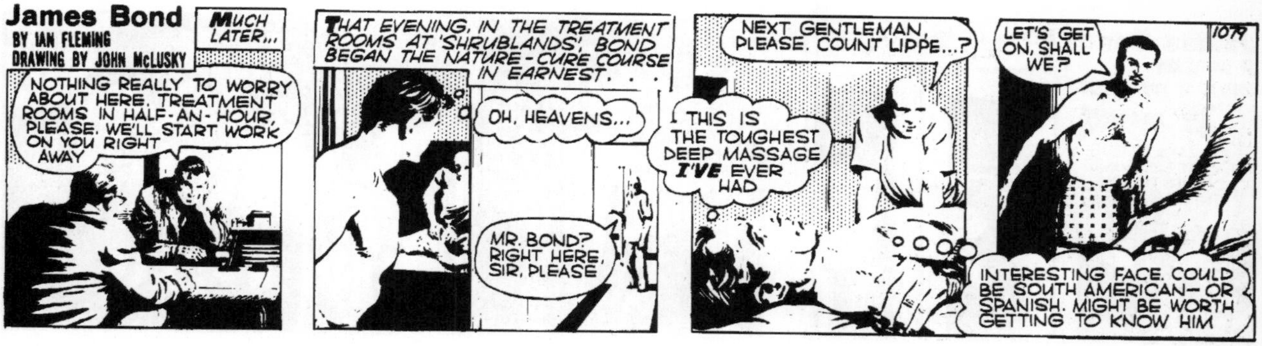
James Bond
BY IAN FLEMING
DRAWING BY JOHN McLUSKY
MUCH LATER...
NOTHING REALLY TO WORRY ABOUT HERE. TREATMENT ROOMS IN HALF-AN-HOUR, PLEASE. WE'LL START WORK ON YOU RIGHT AWAY
THAT EVENING, IN THE TREATMENT ROOMS AT 'SHRUBLANDS', BOND BEGAN THE NATURE-CURE COURSE IN EARNEST. . .
OH, HEAVENS...
MR. BOND? RIGHT HERE, SIR, PLEASE
NEXT GENTLEMAN, PLEASE. COUNT LIPPE...?
THIS IS THE TOUGHEST DEEP MASSAGE I'VE EVER HAD
LET'S GET ON, SHALL WE?
1079
INTERESTING FACE. COULD BE SOUTH AMERICAN—OR SPANISH. MIGHT BE WORTH GETTING TO KNOW HIM

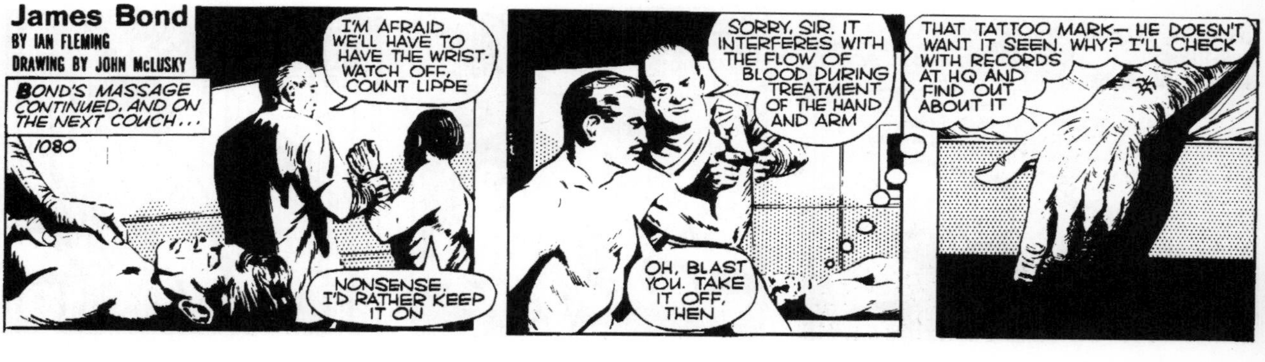
James Bond
BY IAN FLEMING
DRAWING BY JOHN McLUSKY
BOND'S MASSAGE CONTINUED, AND ON THE NEXT COUCH...
1080
I'M AFRAID WE'LL HAVE TO HAVE THE WRIST-WATCH OFF, COUNT LIPPE
NONSENSE. I'D RATHER KEEP IT ON
SORRY, SIR. IT INTERFERES WITH THE FLOW OF BLOOD DURING TREATMENT OF THE HAND AND ARM
OH, BLAST YOU. TAKE IT OFF, THEN
THAT TATTOO MARK— HE DOESN'T WANT IT SEEN. WHY? I'LL CHECK WITH RECORDS AT HQ AND FIND OUT ABOUT IT

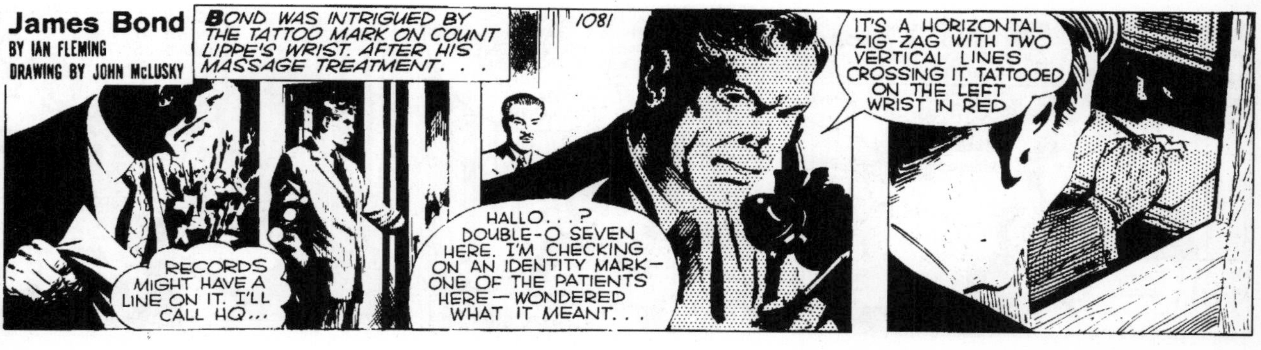
James Bond
BY IAN FLEMING
DRAWING BY JOHN McLUSKY
BOND WAS INTRIGUED BY THE TATTOO MARK ON COUNT LIPPE'S WRIST. AFTER HIS MASSAGE TREATMENT. . .
RECORDS MIGHT HAVE A LINE ON IT. I'LL CALL HQ...
1081
HALLO. . .? DOUBLE-O SEVEN HERE. I'M CHECKING ON AN IDENTITY MARK— ONE OF THE PATIENTS HERE—WONDERED WHAT IT MEANT. . .
IT'S A HORIZONTAL ZIG-ZAG WITH TWO VERTICAL LINES CROSSING IT. TATTOOED ON THE LEFT WRIST IN RED

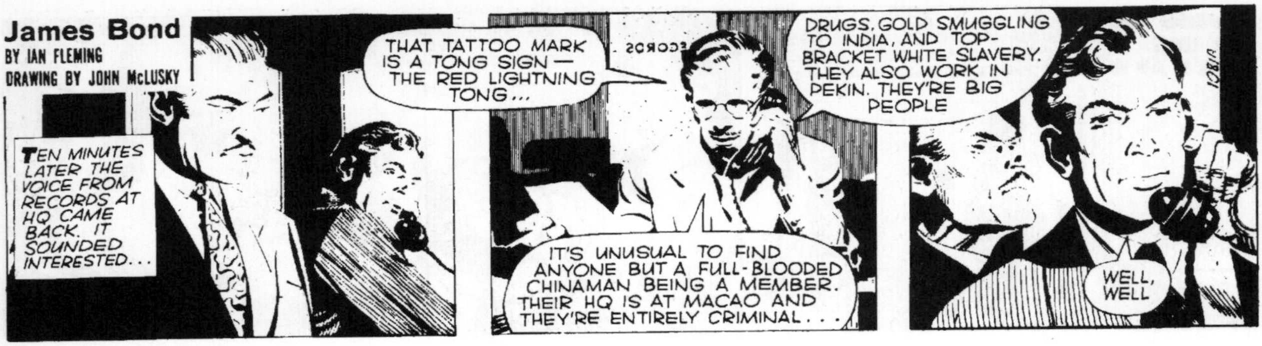
James Bond
BY IAN FLEMING
DRAWING BY JOHN McLUSKY
TEN MINUTES LATER THE VOICE FROM RECORDS AT HQ CAME BACK. IT SOUNDED INTERESTED...
THAT TATTOO MARK IS A TONG SIGN — THE RED LIGHTNING TONG...
IT'S UNUSUAL TO FIND ANYONE BUT A FULL-BLOODED CHINAMAN BEING A MEMBER. THEIR HQ IS AT MACAO AND THEY'RE ENTIRELY CRIMINAL...
DRUGS, GOLD SMUGGLING TO INDIA, AND TOP-BRACKET WHITE SLAVERY. THEY ALSO WORK IN PEKIN. THEY'RE BIG PEOPLE
WELL, WELL

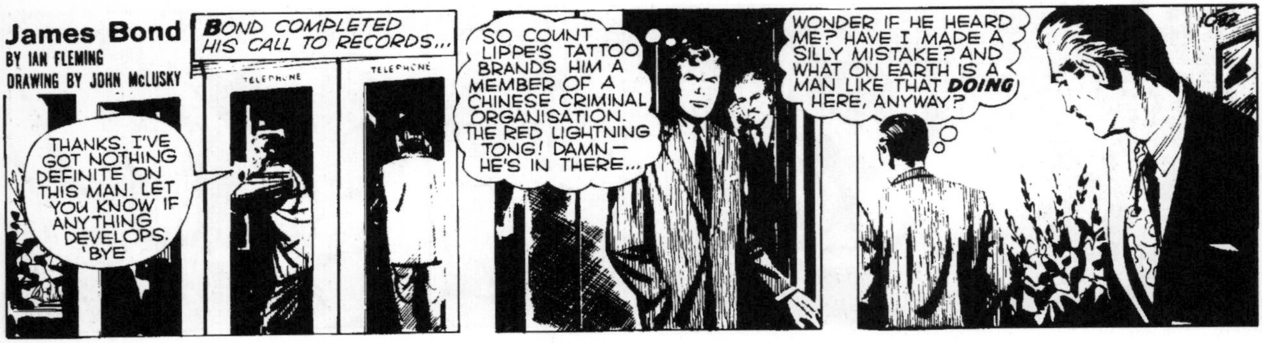
James Bond
BY IAN FLEMING
DRAWING BY JOHN McLUSKY
BOND COMPLETED HIS CALL TO RECORDS...
TELEPHONE
TELEPHONE
THANKS. I'VE GOT NOTHING DEFINITE ON THIS MAN. LET YOU KNOW IF ANYTHING DEVELOPS. 'BYE
SO COUNT LIPPE'S TATTOO BRANDS HIM A MEMBER OF A CHINESE CRIMINAL ORGANISATION. THE RED LIGHTNING TONG! DAMN— HE'S IN THERE...
WONDER IF HE HEARD ME? HAVE I MADE A SILLY MISTAKE? AND WHAT ON EARTH IS A MAN LIKE THAT DOING HERE, ANYWAY?
1082

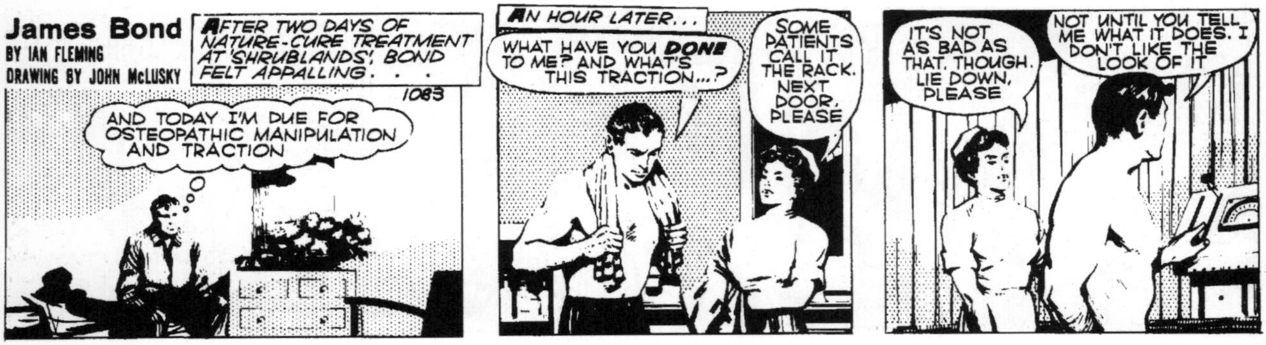
James Bond
BY IAN FLEMING
DRAWING BY JOHN McLUSKY
AFTER TWO DAYS OF NATURE-CURE TREATMENT AT 'SHRUBLANDS', BOND FELT APPALLING . . .
1083
AND TODAY I'M DUE FOR OSTEOPATHIC MANIPULATION AND TRACTION
AN HOUR LATER...
WHAT HAVE YOU DONE TO ME? AND WHAT'S THIS TRACTION...?
SOME PATIENTS CALL IT THE RACK. NEXT DOOR, PLEASE
IT'S NOT AS BAD AS THAT, THOUGH. LIE DOWN, PLEASE
NOT UNTIL YOU TELL ME WHAT IT DOES. I DON'T LIKE THE LOOK OF IT

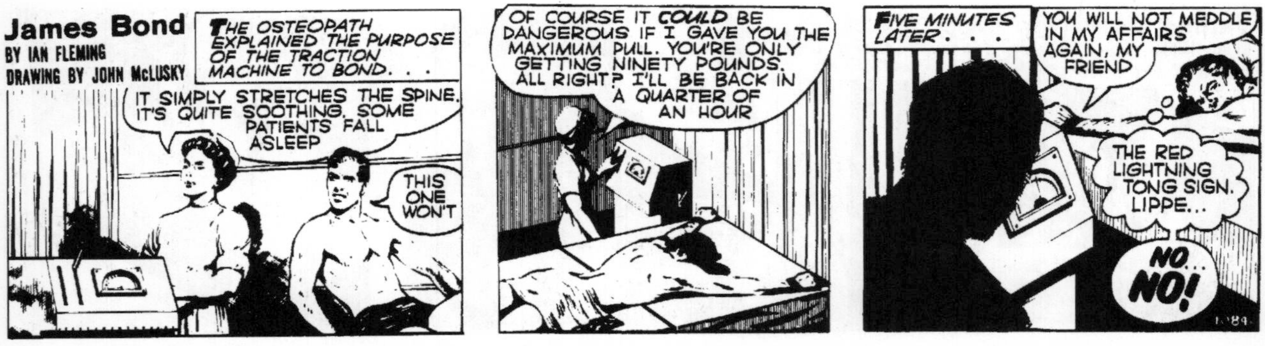
James Bond
BY IAN FLEMING
DRAWING BY JOHN McLUSKY
THE OSTEOPATH EXPLAINED THE PURPOSE OF THE TRACTION MACHINE TO BOND...
IT SIMPLY STRETCHES THE SPINE. IT'S QUITE SOOTHING. SOME PATIENTS FALL ASLEEP
THIS ONE WON'T
OF COURSE IT COULD BE DANGEROUS IF I GAVE YOU THE MAXIMUM PULL. YOU'RE ONLY GETTING NINETY POUNDS. ALL RIGHT? I'LL BE BACK IN A QUARTER OF AN HOUR
FIVE MINUTES LATER . . .
YOU WILL NOT MEDDLE IN MY AFFAIRS AGAIN, MY FRIEND
THE RED LIGHTNING TONG SIGN. LIPPE...
NO... NO!

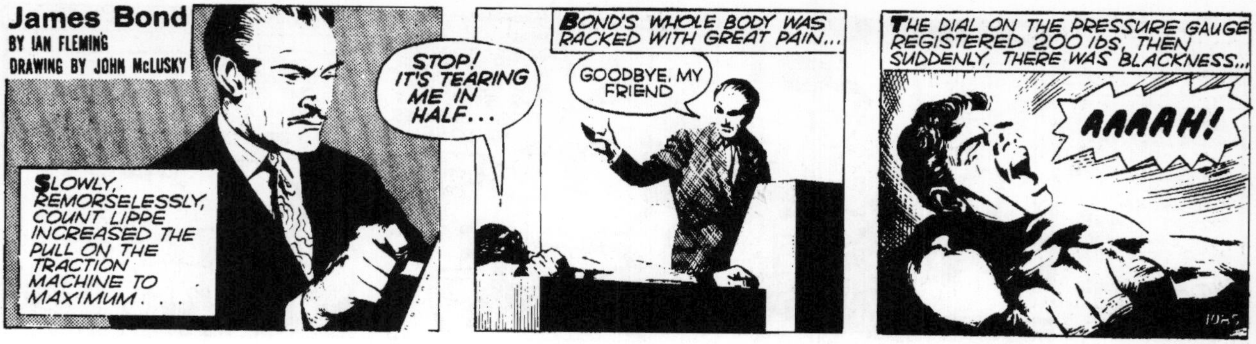
James Bond
BY IAN FLEMING
DRAWING BY JOHN McLUSKY
SLOWLY, REMORSELESSLY, COUNT LIPPE INCREASED THE PULL ON THE TRACTION MACHINE TO MAXIMUM . . .
STOP! IT'S TEARING ME IN HALF...
BOND'S WHOLE BODY WAS RACKED WITH GREAT PAIN...
GOODBYE, MY FRIEND
THE DIAL ON THE PRESSURE GAUGE REGISTERED 200 lbs, THEN SUDDENLY, THERE WAS BLACKNESS...
AAAAH!

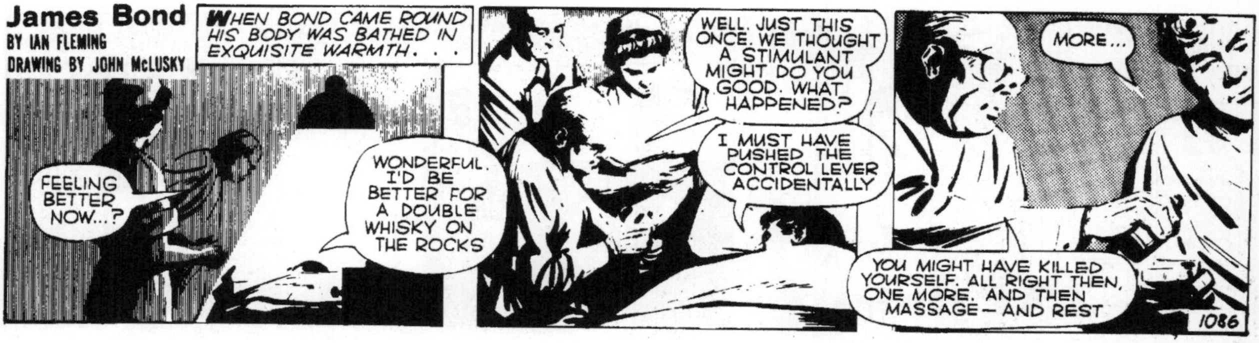
James Bond
BY IAN FLEMING
DRAWING BY JOHN McLUSKY
WHEN BOND CAME ROUND HIS BODY WAS BATHED IN EXQUISITE WARMTH . . .
FEELING BETTER NOW...?
WONDERFUL. I'D BE BETTER FOR A DOUBLE WHISKY ON THE ROCKS
WELL. JUST THIS ONCE. WE THOUGHT A STIMULANT MIGHT DO YOU GOOD. WHAT HAPPENED?
I MUST HAVE PUSHED THE CONTROL LEVER ACCIDENTALLY
MORE...
YOU MIGHT HAVE KILLED YOURSELF. ALL RIGHT THEN, ONE MORE. AND THEN MASSAGE – AND REST
1086

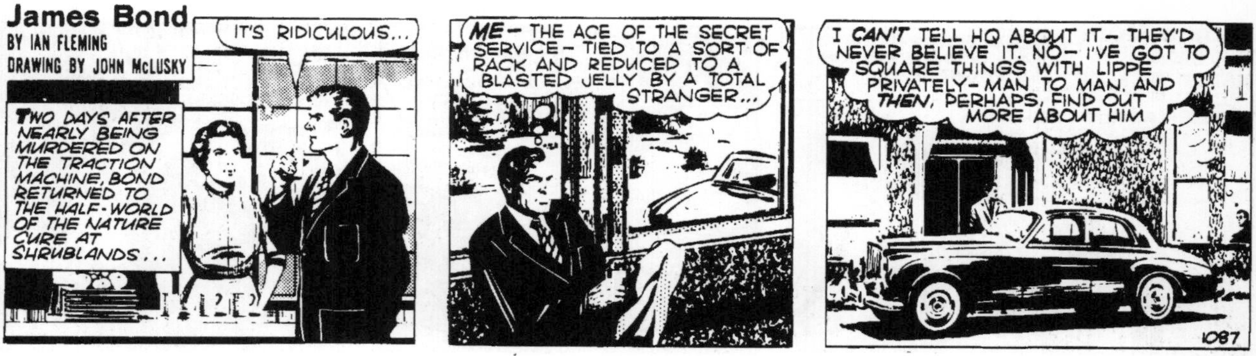
James Bond
BY IAN FLEMING
DRAWING BY JOHN McLUSKY
IT'S RIDICULOUS...
TWO DAYS AFTER NEARLY BEING MURDERED ON THE TRACTION MACHINE, BOND RETURNED TO THE HALF-WORLD OF THE NATURE CURE AT SHRUBLANDS...
ME – THE ACE OF THE SECRET SERVICE – TIED TO A SORT OF RACK AND REDUCED TO A BLASTED JELLY BY A TOTAL STRANGER...
I CAN'T TELL HQ ABOUT IT – THEY'D NEVER BELIEVE IT. NO – I'VE GOT TO SQUARE THINGS WITH LIPPE PRIVATELY – MAN TO MAN, AND THEN, PERHAPS, FIND OUT MORE ABOUT HIM
1087

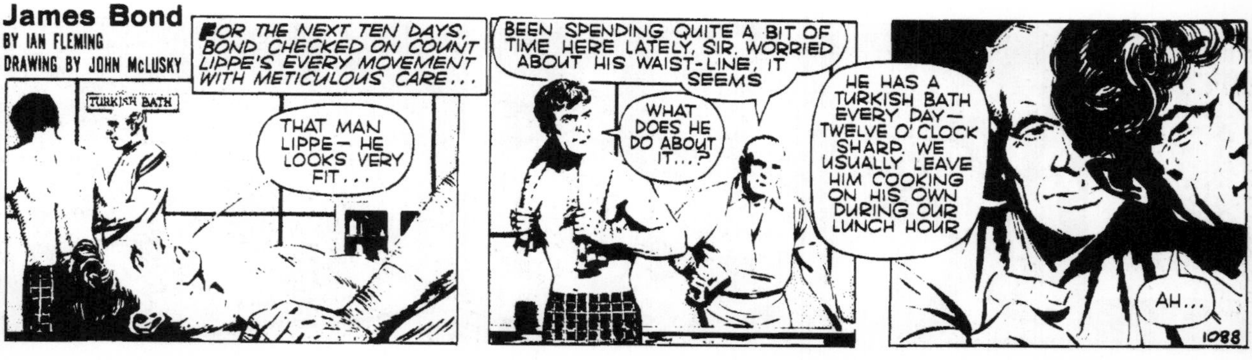
James Bond
BY IAN FLEMING
DRAWING BY JOHN McLUSKY
FOR THE NEXT TEN DAYS, BOND CHECKED ON COUNT LIPPE'S EVERY MOVEMENT WITH METICULOUS CARE...
TURKISH BATH
THAT MAN LIPPE – HE LOOKS VERY FIT...
BEEN SPENDING QUITE A BIT OF TIME HERE LATELY, SIR. WORRIED ABOUT HIS WAIST-LINE, IT SEEMS
WHAT DOES HE DO ABOUT IT...?
HE HAS A TURKISH BATH EVERY DAY – TWELVE O'CLOCK SHARP. WE USUALLY LEAVE HIM COOKING ON HIS OWN DURING OUR LUNCH HOUR
AH...
1088

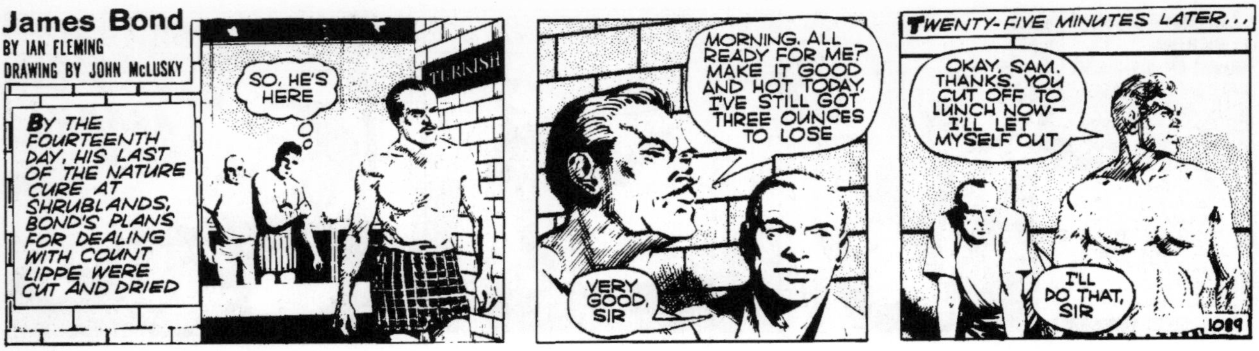
James Bond
BY IAN FLEMING
DRAWING BY JOHN McLUSKY
BY THE FOURTEENTH DAY, HIS LAST OF THE NATURE CURE AT SHRUBLANDS, BOND'S PLANS FOR DEALING WITH COUNT LIPPE WERE CUT AND DRIED
TERKISH
SO, HE'S HERE
MORNING. ALL READY FOR ME? MAKE IT GOOD AND HOT TODAY, I'VE STILL GOT THREE OUNCES TO LOSE
VERY GOOD, SIR
TWENTY-FIVE MINUTES LATER...
OKAY, SAM. THANKS. YOU CUT OFF TO LUNCH NOW— I'LL LET MYSELF OUT
I'LL DO THAT, SIR
1089

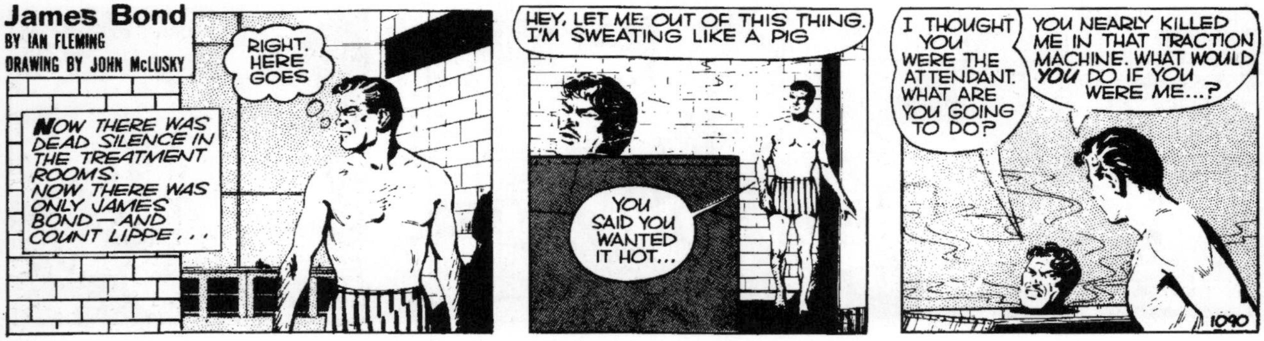
James Bond
BY IAN FLEMING
DRAWING BY JOHN McLUSKY
NOW THERE WAS DEAD SILENCE IN THE TREATMENT ROOMS. NOW THERE WAS ONLY JAMES BOND—AND COUNT LIPPE...
RIGHT. HERE GOES
HEY, LET ME OUT OF THIS THING. I'M SWEATING LIKE A PIG
YOU SAID YOU WANTED IT HOT...
I THOUGHT YOU WERE THE ATTENDANT. WHAT ARE YOU GOING TO DO?
YOU NEARLY KILLED ME IN THAT TRACTION MACHINE. WHAT WOULD YOU DO IF YOU WERE ME...?
1090

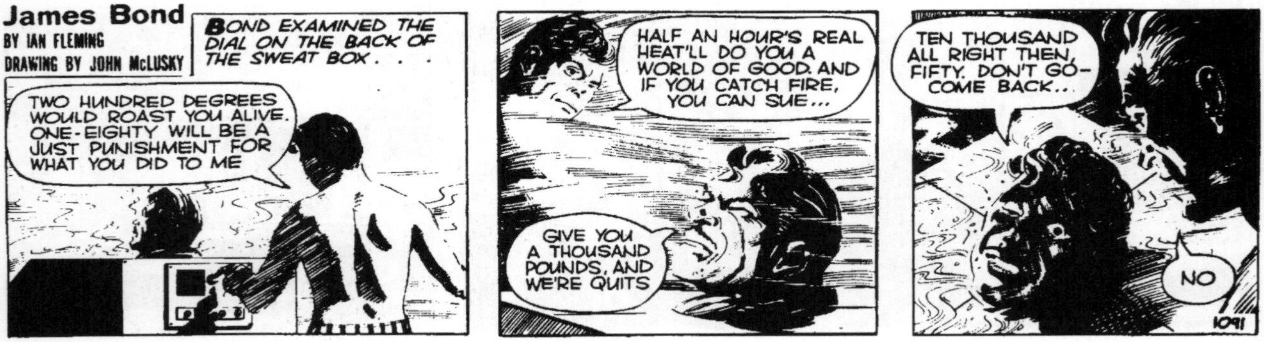
James Bond
BY IAN FLEMING
DRAWING BY JOHN McLUSKY
BOND EXAMINED THE DIAL ON THE BACK OF THE SWEAT BOX...
TWO HUNDRED DEGREES WOULD ROAST YOU ALIVE. ONE-EIGHTY WILL BE A JUST PUNISHMENT FOR WHAT YOU DID TO ME
HALF AN HOUR'S REAL HEAT'LL DO YOU A WORLD OF GOOD. AND IF YOU CATCH FIRE, YOU CAN SUE...
GIVE YOU A THOUSAND POUNDS, AND WE'RE QUITS
TEN THOUSAND ALL RIGHT THEN, FIFTY. DON'T GO— COME BACK...
NO
1091

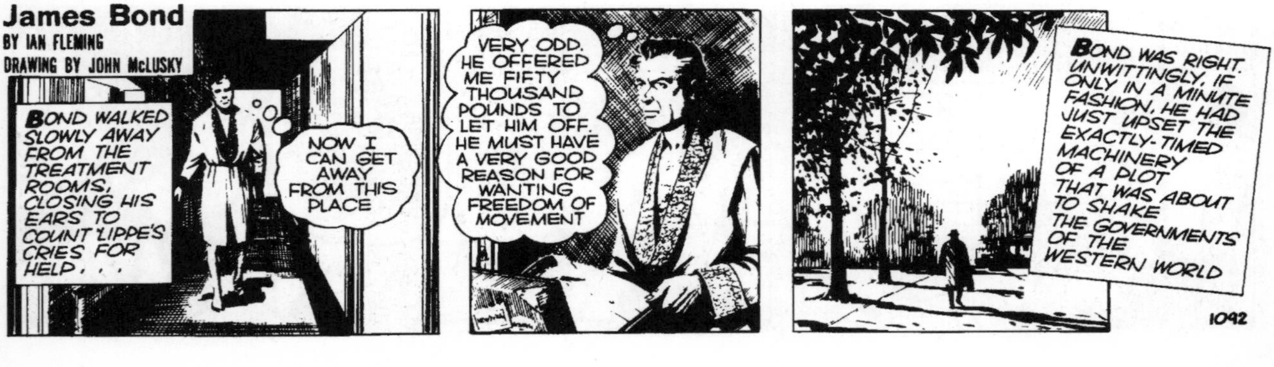
James Bond
BY IAN FLEMING
DRAWING BY JOHN McLUSKY
BOND WALKED SLOWLY AWAY FROM THE TREATMENT ROOMS, CLOSING HIS EARS TO COUNT LIPPE'S CRIES FOR HELP...
NOW I CAN GET AWAY FROM THIS PLACE
VERY ODD. HE OFFERED ME FIFTY THOUSAND POUNDS TO LET HIM OFF. HE MUST HAVE A VERY GOOD REASON FOR WANTING FREEDOM OF MOVEMENT
BOND WAS RIGHT. UNWITTINGLY, IF ONLY IN A MINUTE FASHION, HE HAD JUST UPSET THE EXACTLY-TIMED MACHINERY OF A PLOT THAT WAS ABOUT TO SHAKE THE GOVERNMENTS OF THE WESTERN WORLD
1092

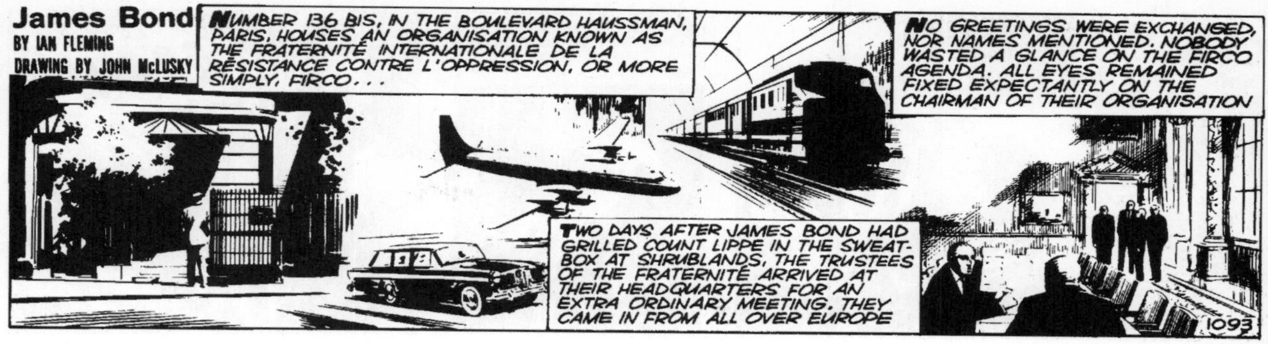
James Bond
BY IAN FLEMING
DRAWING BY JOHN McLUSKY
NUMBER 136 BIS, IN THE BOULEVARD HAUSSMAN, PARIS, HOUSES AN ORGANISATION KNOWN AS THE FRATERNITÉ INTERNATIONALE DE LA RÉSISTANCE CONTRE L'OPPRESSION, OR MORE SIMPLY, FIRCO . . .
TWO DAYS AFTER JAMES BOND HAD GRILLED COUNT LIPPE IN THE SWEAT-BOX AT SHRUBLANDS, THE TRUSTEES OF THE FRATERNITÉ ARRIVED AT THEIR HEADQUARTERS FOR AN EXTRA ORDINARY MEETING. THEY CAME IN FROM ALL OVER EUROPE
NO GREETINGS WERE EXCHANGED, NOR NAMES MENTIONED. NOBODY WASTED A GLANCE ON THE FIRCO AGENDA. ALL EYES REMAINED FIXED EXPECTANTLY ON THE CHAIRMAN OF THEIR ORGANISATION
1093

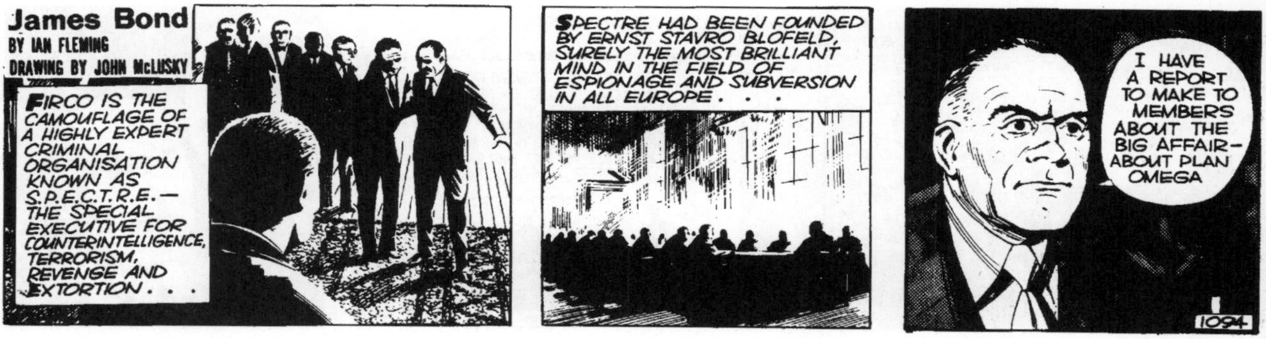
James Bond
BY IAN FLEMING
DRAWING BY JOHN McLUSKY
FIRCO IS THE CAMOUFLAGE OF A HIGHLY EXPERT CRIMINAL ORGANISATION KNOWN AS S.P.E.C.T.R.E.— THE SPECIAL EXECUTIVE FOR COUNTERINTELLIGENCE, TERRORISM, REVENGE AND EXTORTION . . .
SPECTRE HAD BEEN FOUNDED BY ERNST STAVRO BLOFELD, SURELY THE MOST BRILLIANT MIND IN THE FIELD OF ESPIONAGE AND SUBVERSION IN ALL EUROPE . . .
I HAVE A REPORT TO MAKE TO MEMBERS ABOUT THE BIG AFFAIR—ABOUT PLAN OMEGA
1094

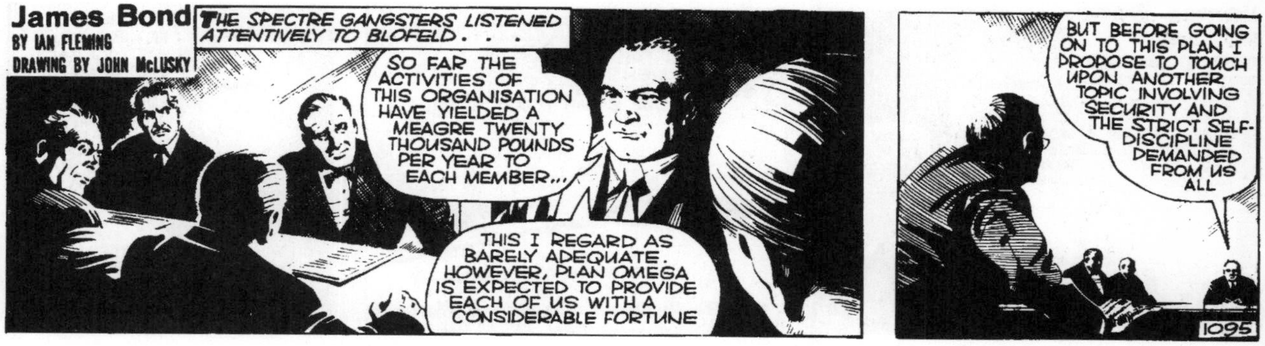
James Bond
BY IAN FLEMING
DRAWING BY JOHN McLUSKY
THE SPECTRE GANGSTERS LISTENED ATTENTIVELY TO BLOFELD . . .
SO FAR THE ACTIVITIES OF THIS ORGANISATION HAVE YIELDED A MEAGRE TWENTY THOUSAND POUNDS PER YEAR TO EACH MEMBER...
THIS I REGARD AS BARELY ADEQUATE. HOWEVER, PLAN OMEGA IS EXPECTED TO PROVIDE EACH OF US WITH A CONSIDERABLE FORTUNE
BUT BEFORE GOING ON TO THIS PLAN I PROPOSE TO TOUCH UPON ANOTHER TOPIC INVOLVING SECURITY AND THE STRICT SELF-DISCIPLINE DEMANDED FROM US ALL
1095

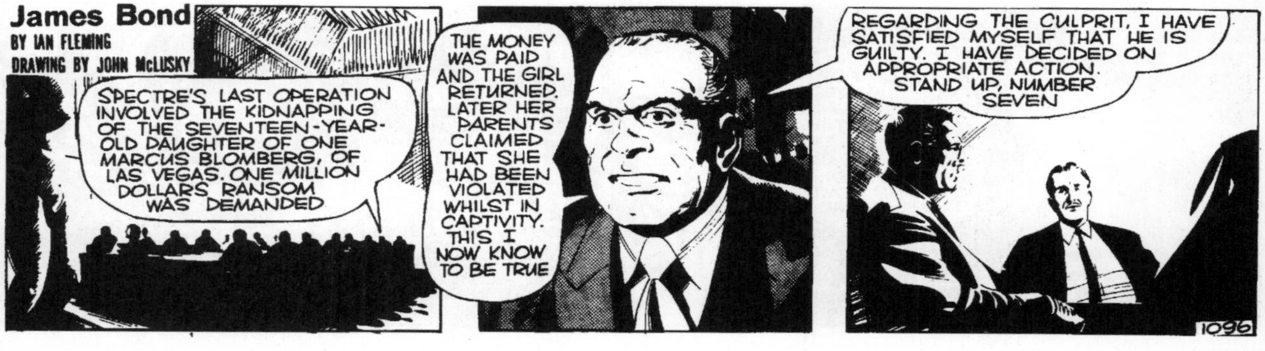
James Bond
BY IAN FLEMING
DRAWING BY JOHN McLUSKY
SPECTRE'S LAST OPERATION INVOLVED THE KIDNAPPING OF THE SEVENTEEN-YEAR-OLD DAUGHTER OF ONE MARCUS BLOMBERG, OF LAS VEGAS. ONE MILLION DOLLARS RANSOM WAS DEMANDED
THE MONEY WAS PAID AND THE GIRL RETURNED. LATER HER PARENTS CLAIMED THAT SHE HAD BEEN VIOLATED WHILST IN CAPTIVITY. THIS I NOW KNOW TO BE TRUE
REGARDING THE CULPRIT, I HAVE SATISFIED MYSELF THAT HE IS GUILTY. I HAVE DECIDED ON APPROPRIATE ACTION. STAND UP, NUMBER SEVEN
1096

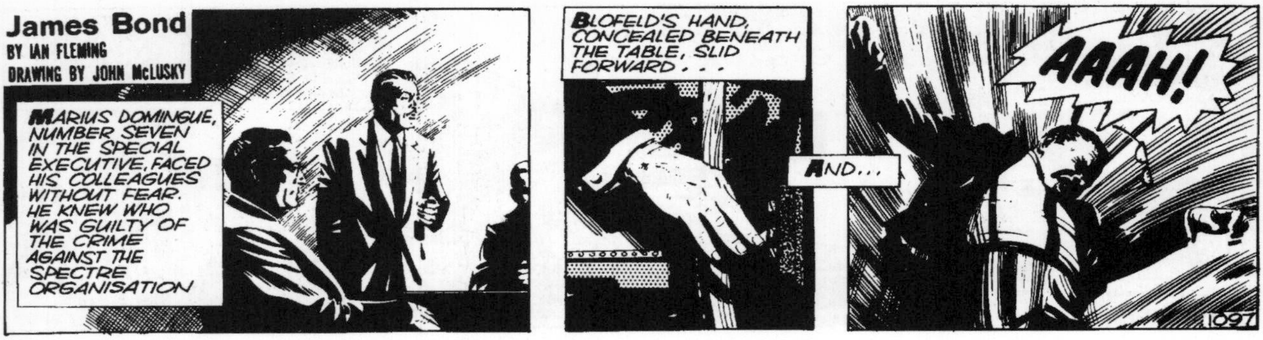
James Bond
BY IAN FLEMING
DRAWING BY JOHN McLUSKY
MARIUS DOMINGUE, NUMBER SEVEN IN THE SPECIAL EXECUTIVE, FACED HIS COLLEAGUES WITHOUT FEAR. HE KNEW WHO WAS GUILTY OF THE CRIME AGAINST THE SPECTRE ORGANISATION
BLOFELD'S HAND, CONCEALED BENEATH THE TABLE, SLID FORWARD . . .
AND...
AAAH!
1097

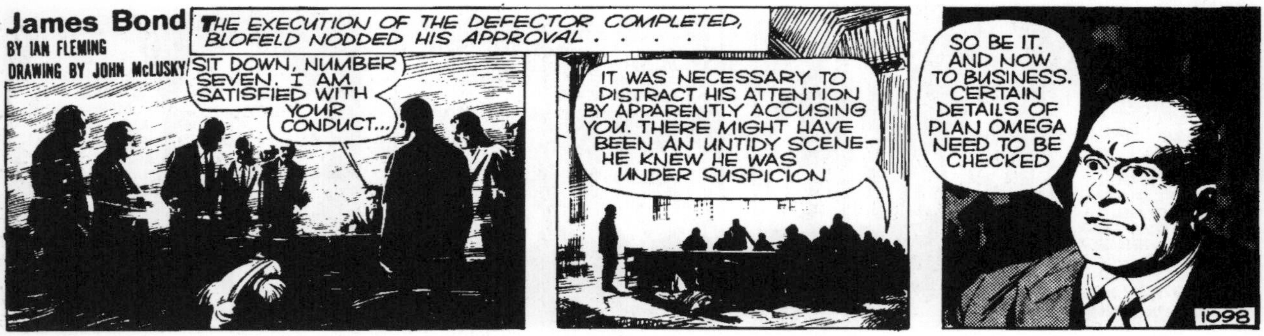
James Bond
BY IAN FLEMING
DRAWING BY JOHN McLUSKY
THE EXECUTION OF THE DEFECTOR COMPLETED, BLOFELD NODDED HIS APPROVAL . . . .
SIT DOWN, NUMBER SEVEN. I AM SATISFIED WITH YOUR CONDUCT...
IT WAS NECESSARY TO DISTRACT HIS ATTENTION BY APPARENTLY ACCUSING YOU. THERE MIGHT HAVE BEEN AN UNTIDY SCENE— HE KNEW HE WAS UNDER SUSPICION
SO BE IT. AND NOW TO BUSINESS. CERTAIN DETAILS OF PLAN OMEGA NEED TO BE CHECKED
1098

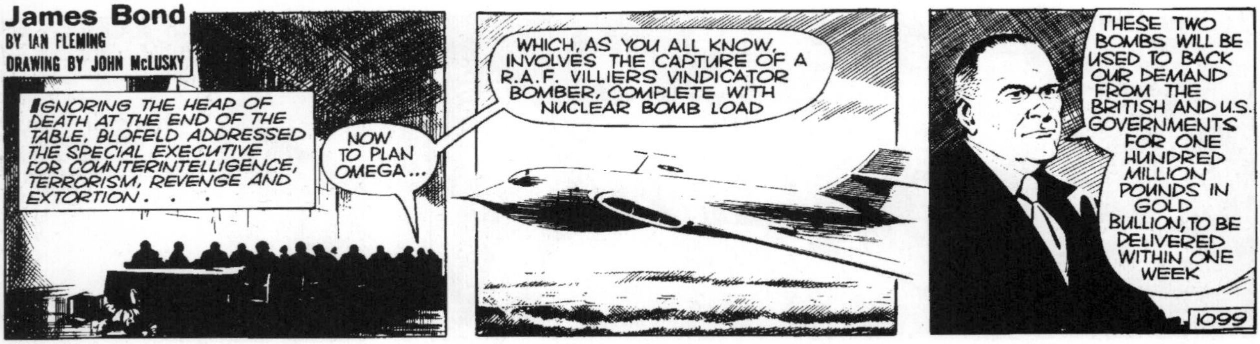
James Bond
BY IAN FLEMING
DRAWING BY JOHN McLUSKY
IGNORING THE HEAP OF DEATH AT THE END OF THE TABLE, BLOFELD ADDRESSED THE SPECIAL EXECUTIVE FOR COUNTERINTELLIGENCE, TERRORISM, REVENGE AND EXTORTION . . .
NOW TO PLAN OMEGA...
WHICH, AS YOU ALL KNOW, INVOLVES THE CAPTURE OF A R.A.F. VILLIERS VINDICATOR BOMBER, COMPLETE WITH NUCLEAR BOMB LOAD
THESE TWO BOMBS WILL BE USED TO BACK OUR DEMAND FROM THE BRITISH AND U.S. GOVERNMENTS FOR ONE HUNDRED MILLION POUNDS IN GOLD BULLION, TO BE DELIVERED WITHIN ONE WEEK
1099

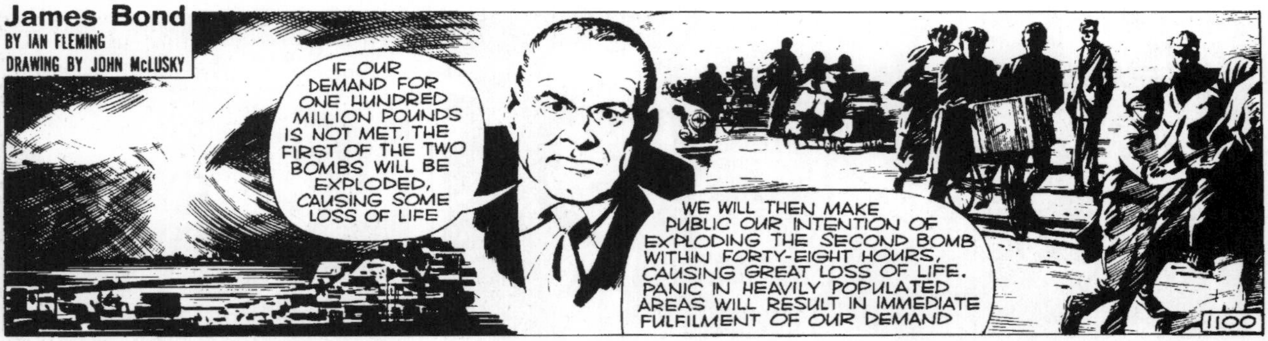
James Bond
BY IAN FLEMING
DRAWING BY JOHN McLUSKY
IF OUR DEMAND FOR ONE HUNDRED MILLION POUNDS IS NOT MET, THE FIRST OF THE TWO BOMBS WILL BE EXPLODED, CAUSING SOME LOSS OF LIFE
WE WILL THEN MAKE PUBLIC OUR INTENTION OF EXPLODING THE SECOND BOMB WITHIN FORTY-EIGHT HOURS, CAUSING GREAT LOSS OF LIFE. PANIC IN HEAVILY POPULATED AREAS WILL RESULT IN IMMEDIATE FULFILMENT OF OUR DEMAND
1100

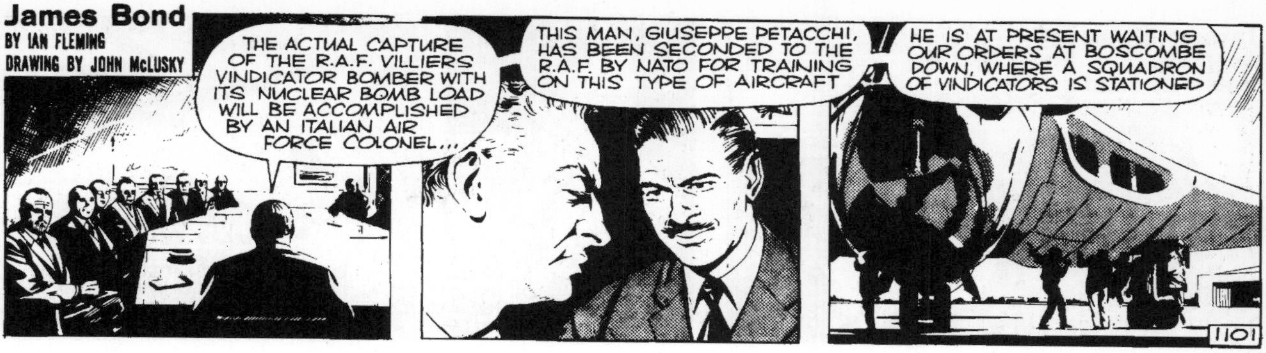
James Bond
BY IAN FLEMING
DRAWING BY JOHN McLUSKY
THE ACTUAL CAPTURE OF THE R.A.F. VILLIERS VINDICATOR BOMBER WITH ITS NUCLEAR BOMB LOAD WILL BE ACCOMPLISHED BY AN ITALIAN AIR FORCE COLONEL...
THIS MAN, GIUSEPPE PETACCHI, HAS BEEN SECONDED TO THE R.A.F. BY NATO FOR TRAINING ON THIS TYPE OF AIRCRAFT
HE IS AT PRESENT WAITING OUR ORDERS AT BOSCOMBE DOWN, WHERE A SQUADRON OF VINDICATORS IS STATIONED
1101

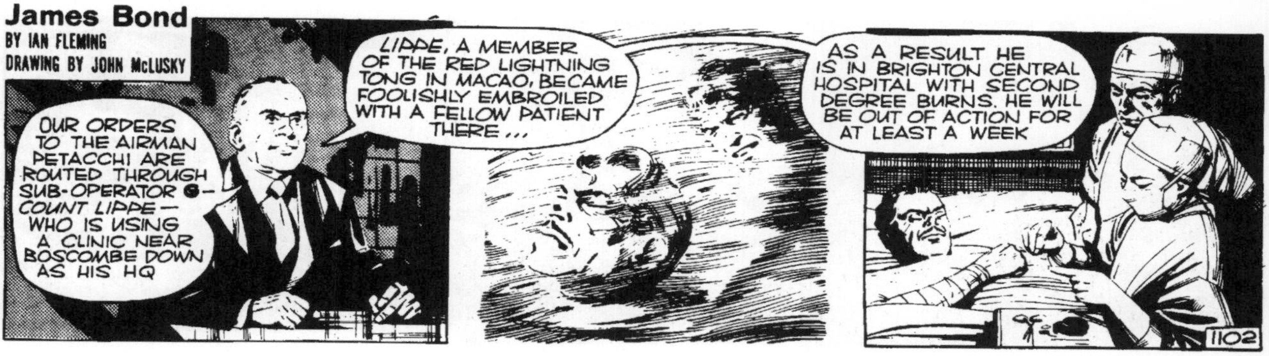
James Bond
BY IAN FLEMING
DRAWING BY JOHN McLUSKY
OUR ORDERS TO THE AIRMAN PETACCHI ARE ROUTED THROUGH SUB-OPERATOR G - COUNT LIPPE - WHO IS USING A CLINIC NEAR BOSCOMBE DOWN AS HIS HQ
LIPPE, A MEMBER OF THE RED LIGHTNING TONG IN MACAO, BECAME FOOLISHLY EMBROILED WITH A FELLOW PATIENT THERE...
AS A RESULT HE IS IN BRIGHTON CENTRAL HOSPITAL WITH SECOND DEGREE BURNS. HE WILL BE OUT OF ACTION FOR AT LEAST A WEEK
1102

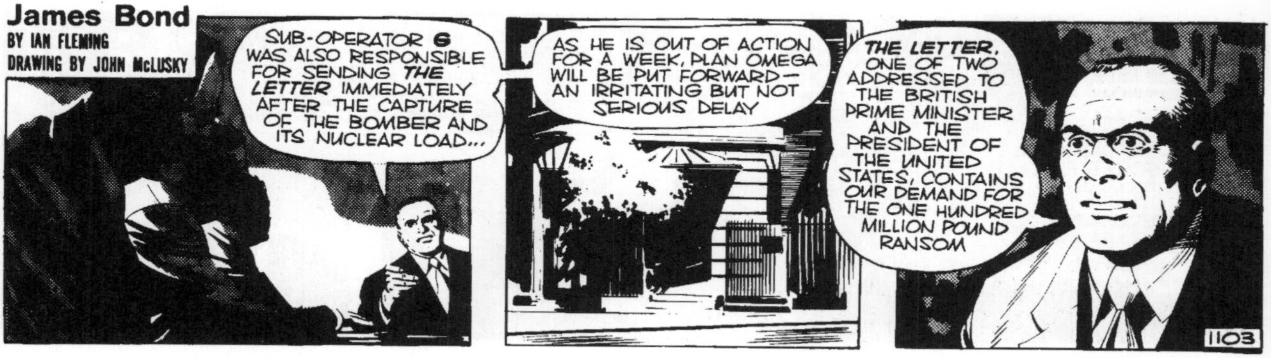
James Bond
BY IAN FLEMING
DRAWING BY JOHN McLUSKY
SUB-OPERATOR G WAS ALSO RESPONSIBLE FOR SENDING THE LETTER IMMEDIATELY AFTER THE CAPTURE OF THE BOMBER AND ITS NUCLEAR LOAD...
AS HE IS OUT OF ACTION FOR A WEEK, PLAN OMEGA WILL BE PUT FORWARD - AN IRRITATING BUT NOT SERIOUS DELAY
THE LETTER, ONE OF TWO ADDRESSED TO THE BRITISH PRIME MINISTER AND THE PRESIDENT OF THE UNITED STATES, CONTAINS OUR DEMAND FOR THE ONE HUNDRED MILLION POUND RANSOM
1103

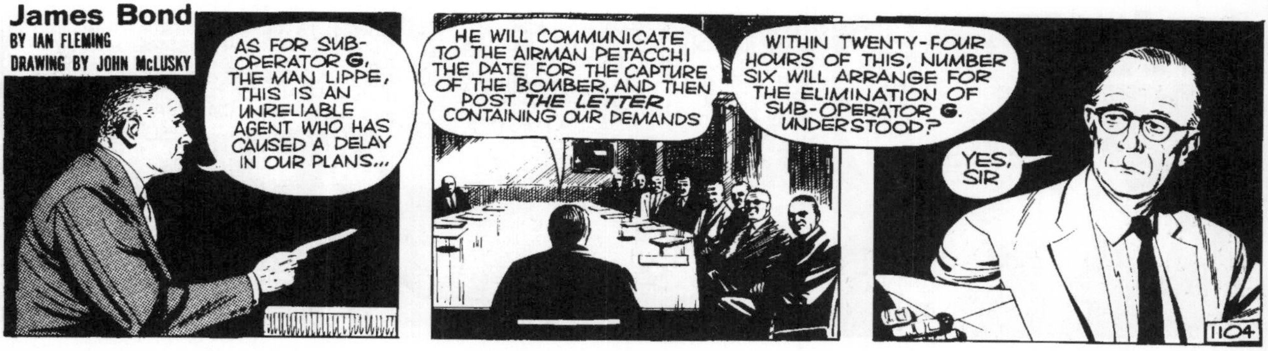
James Bond
BY IAN FLEMING
DRAWING BY JOHN McLUSKY
AS FOR SUB-OPERATOR G, THE MAN LIPPE, THIS IS AN UNRELIABLE AGENT WHO HAS CAUSED A DELAY IN OUR PLANS...
HE WILL COMMUNICATE TO THE AIRMAN PETACCHI THE DATE FOR THE CAPTURE OF THE BOMBER, AND THEN POST THE LETTER CONTAINING OUR DEMANDS
WITHIN TWENTY-FOUR HOURS OF THIS, NUMBER SIX WILL ARRANGE FOR THE ELIMINATION OF SUB-OPERATOR G. UNDERSTOOD?
YES, SIR
1104

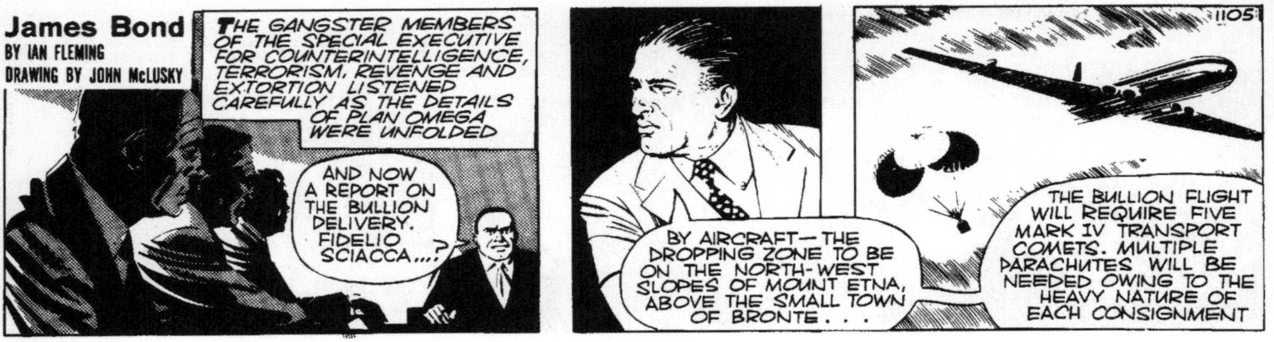
James Bond
BY IAN FLEMING
DRAWING BY JOHN McLUSKY
THE GANGSTER MEMBERS OF THE SPECIAL EXECUTIVE FOR COUNTERINTELLIGENCE, TERRORISM, REVENGE AND EXTORTION LISTENED CAREFULLY AS THE DETAILS OF PLAN OMEGA WERE UNFOLDED
AND NOW A REPORT ON THE BULLION DELIVERY. FIDELIO SCIACCA...?
BY AIRCRAFT—THE DROPPING ZONE TO BE ON THE NORTH-WEST SLOPES OF MOUNT ETNA, ABOVE THE SMALL TOWN OF BRONTE . . .
1105
THE BULLION FLIGHT WILL REQUIRE FIVE MARK IV TRANSPORT COMETS. MULTIPLE PARACHUTES WILL BE NEEDED OWING TO THE HEAVY NATURE OF EACH CONSIGNMENT

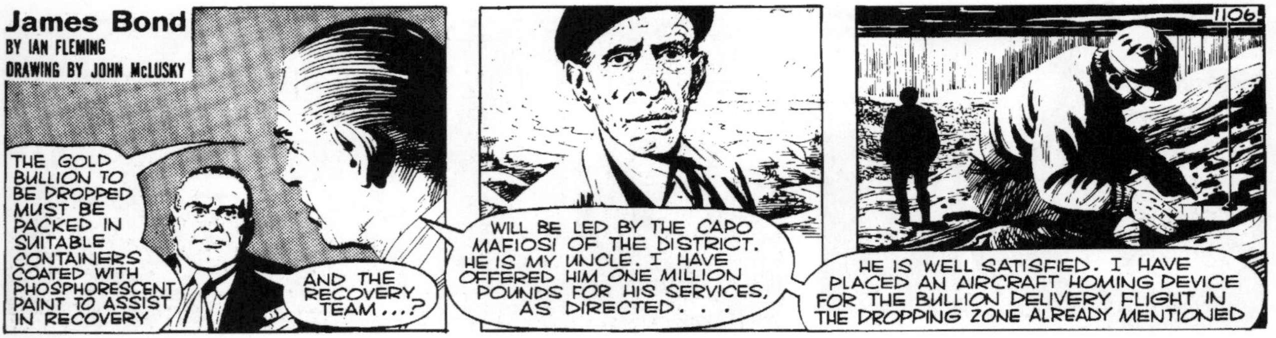
James Bond
BY IAN FLEMING
DRAWING BY JOHN McLUSKY
THE GOLD BULLION TO BE DROPPED MUST BE PACKED IN SUITABLE CONTAINERS COATED WITH PHOSPHORESCENT PAINT TO ASSIST IN RECOVERY
AND THE RECOVERY TEAM...?
WILL BE LED BY THE CAPO MAFIOSI OF THE DISTRICT. HE IS MY UNCLE. I HAVE OFFERED HIM ONE MILLION POUNDS FOR HIS SERVICES, AS DIRECTED . . .
1106
HE IS WELL SATISFIED. I HAVE PLACED AN AIRCRAFT HOMING DEVICE FOR THE BULLION DELIVERY FLIGHT IN THE DROPPING ZONE ALREADY MENTIONED

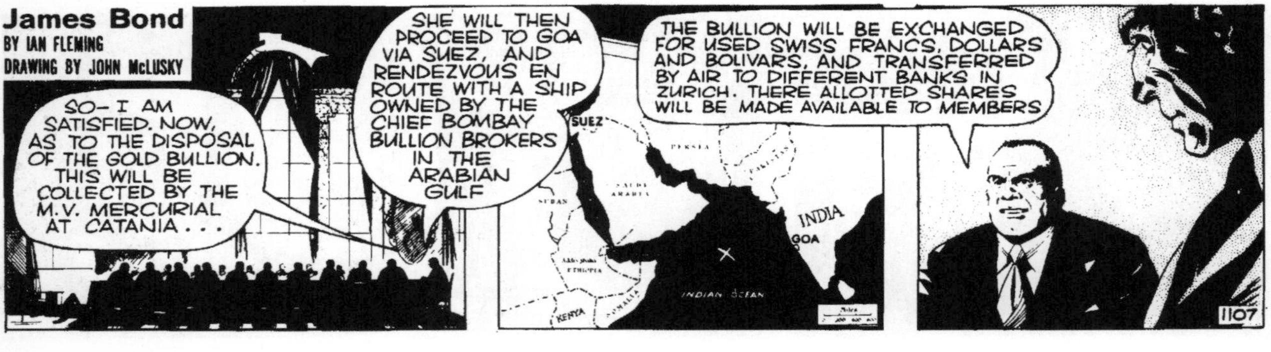
James Bond
BY IAN FLEMING
DRAWING BY JOHN McLUSKY
SO—I AM SATISFIED. NOW, AS TO THE DISPOSAL OF THE GOLD BULLION. THIS WILL BE COLLECTED BY THE M.V. MERCURIAL AT CATANIA . . .
SHE WILL THEN PROCEED TO GOA VIA SUEZ, AND RENDEZVOUS EN ROUTE WITH A SHIP OWNED BY THE CHIEF BOMBAY BULLION BROKERS IN THE ARABIAN GULF
SUEZ
INDIA
GOA
KENYA
THE BULLION WILL BE EXCHANGED FOR USED SWISS FRANCS, DOLLARS AND BOLIVARS, AND TRANSFERRED BY AIR TO DIFFERENT BANKS IN ZURICH. THERE ALLOTTED SHARES WILL BE MADE AVAILABLE TO MEMBERS
1107

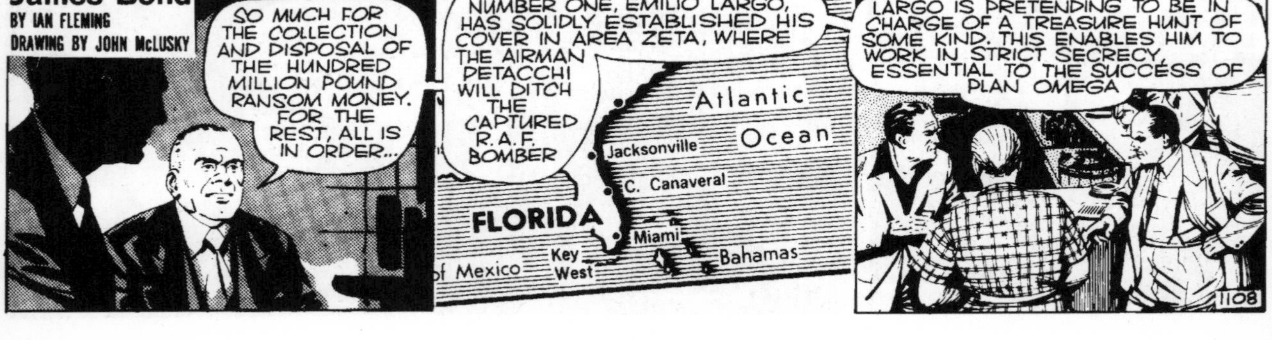
James Bond
BY IAN FLEMING
DRAWING BY JOHN McLUSKY
SO MUCH FOR THE COLLECTION AND DISPOSAL OF THE HUNDRED MILLION POUND RANSOM MONEY. FOR THE REST, ALL IS IN ORDER...
NUMBER ONE, EMILIO LARGO, HAS SOLIDLY ESTABLISHED HIS COVER IN AREA ZETA, WHERE THE AIRMAN PETACCHI WILL DITCH THE CAPTURED R.A.F. BOMBER
Atlantic
Ocean
Jacksonville
C. Canaveral
FLORIDA
Miami
of Mexico
Key West
Bahamas
LARGO IS PRETENDING TO BE IN CHARGE OF A TREASURE HUNT OF SOME KIND. THIS ENABLES HIM TO WORK IN STRICT SECRECY, ESSENTIAL TO THE SUCCESS OF PLAN OMEGA
1108

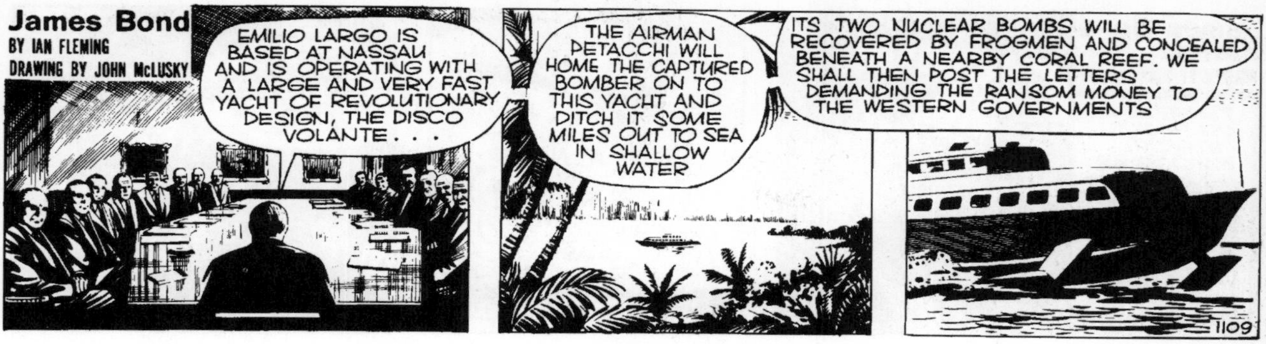
James Bond
BY IAN FLEMING
DRAWING BY JOHN McLUSKY
EMILIO LARGO IS BASED AT NASSAU AND IS OPERATING WITH A LARGE AND VERY FAST YACHT OF REVOLUTIONARY DESIGN, THE DISCO VOLANTE . . .
THE AIRMAN PETACCHI WILL HOME THE CAPTURED BOMBER ON TO THIS YACHT AND DITCH IT SOME MILES OUT TO SEA IN SHALLOW WATER
ITS TWO NUCLEAR BOMBS WILL BE RECOVERED BY FROGMEN AND CONCEALED BENEATH A NEARBY CORAL REEF. WE SHALL THEN POST THE LETTERS DEMANDING THE RANSOM MONEY TO THE WESTERN GOVERNMENTS
1109

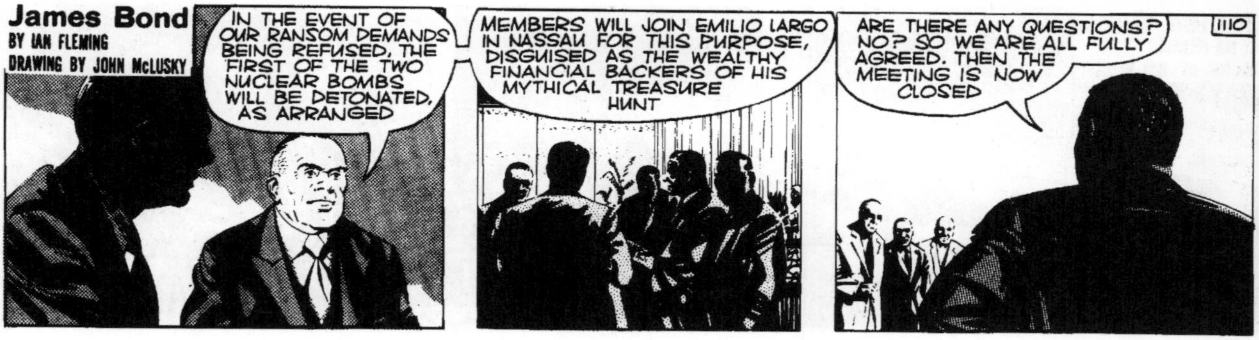
James Bond
BY IAN FLEMING
DRAWING BY JOHN McLUSKY
IN THE EVENT OF OUR RANSOM DEMANDS BEING REFUSED, THE FIRST OF THE TWO NUCLEAR BOMBS WILL BE DETONATED, AS ARRANGED
MEMBERS WILL JOIN EMILIO LARGO IN NASSAU FOR THIS PURPOSE, DISGUISED AS THE WEALTHY FINANCIAL BACKERS OF HIS MYTHICAL TREASURE HUNT
ARE THERE ANY QUESTIONS? NO? SO WE ARE ALL FULLY AGREED. THEN THE MEETING IS NOW CLOSED
1110

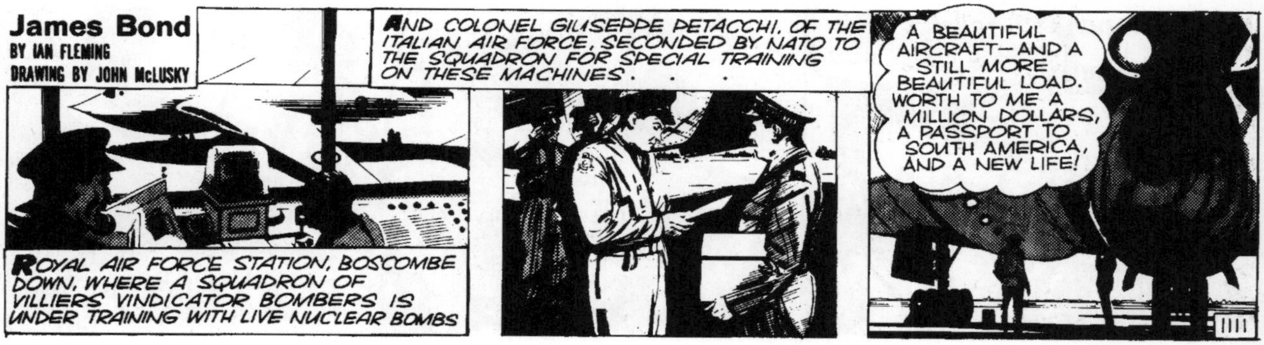
James Bond
BY IAN FLEMING
DRAWING BY JOHN McLUSKY
ROYAL AIR FORCE STATION, BOSCOMBE DOWN, WHERE A SQUADRON OF VILLIERS VINDICATOR BOMBERS IS UNDER TRAINING WITH LIVE NUCLEAR BOMBS
AND COLONEL GIUSEPPE PETACCHI, OF THE ITALIAN AIR FORCE, SECONDED BY NATO TO THE SQUADRON FOR SPECIAL TRAINING ON THESE MACHINES . . .
A BEAUTIFUL AIRCRAFT—AND A STILL MORE BEAUTIFUL LOAD. WORTH TO ME A MILLION DOLLARS, A PASSPORT TO SOUTH AMERICA, AND A NEW LIFE!
1111

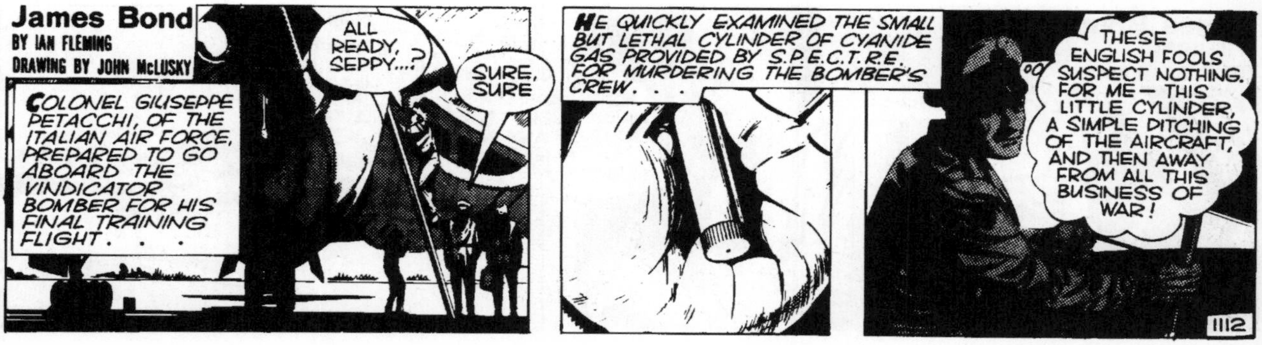
James Bond
BY IAN FLEMING
DRAWING BY JOHN McLUSKY
COLONEL GIUSEPPE PETACCHI, OF THE ITALIAN AIR FORCE, PREPARED TO GO ABOARD THE VINDICATOR BOMBER FOR HIS FINAL TRAINING FLIGHT . . .
ALL READY, SEPPY...?
SURE, SURE
HE QUICKLY EXAMINED THE SMALL BUT LETHAL CYLINDER OF CYANIDE GAS PROVIDED BY S.P.E.C.T.R.E. FOR MURDERING THE BOMBER'S CREW . . .
THESE ENGLISH FOOLS SUSPECT NOTHING. FOR ME— THIS LITTLE CYLINDER, A SIMPLE DITCHING OF THE AIRCRAFT, AND THEN AWAY FROM ALL THIS BUSINESS OF WAR!
1112

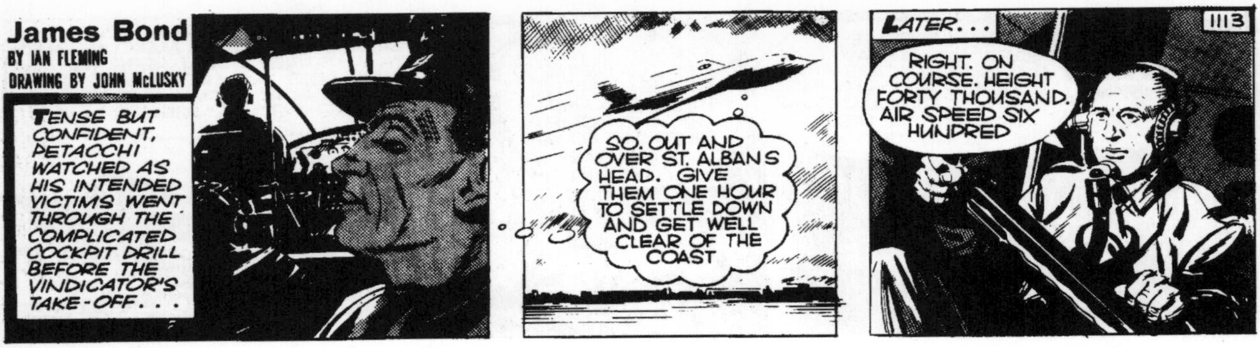
James Bond
BY IAN FLEMING
DRAWING BY JOHN McLUSKY
TENSE BUT CONFIDENT, PETACCHI WATCHED AS HIS INTENDED VICTIMS WENT THROUGH THE COMPLICATED COCKPIT DRILL BEFORE THE VINDICATOR'S TAKE-OFF . . .
SO. OUT AND OVER ST. ALBANS HEAD. GIVE THEM ONE HOUR TO SETTLE DOWN AND GET WELL CLEAR OF THE COAST
LATER . . .
1113
RIGHT. ON COURSE. HEIGHT FORTY THOUSAND. AIR SPEED SIX HUNDRED

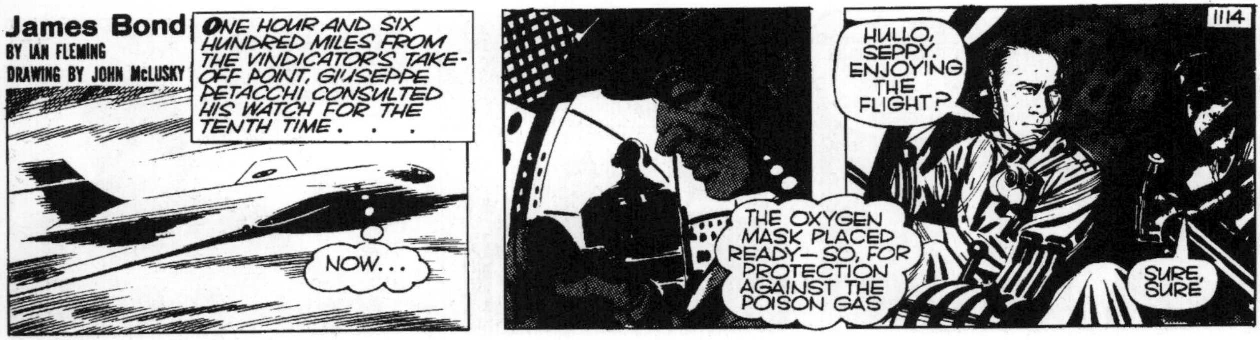
James Bond
BY IAN FLEMING
DRAWING BY JOHN McLUSKY
ONE HOUR AND SIX HUNDRED MILES FROM THE VINDICATOR'S TAKE-OFF POINT, GIUSEPPE PETACCHI CONSULTED HIS WATCH FOR THE TENTH TIME . . .
NOW...
THE OXYGEN MASK PLACED READY— SO, FOR PROTECTION AGAINST THE POISON GAS
1114
HULLO, SEPPY. ENJOYING THE FLIGHT?
SURE, SURE

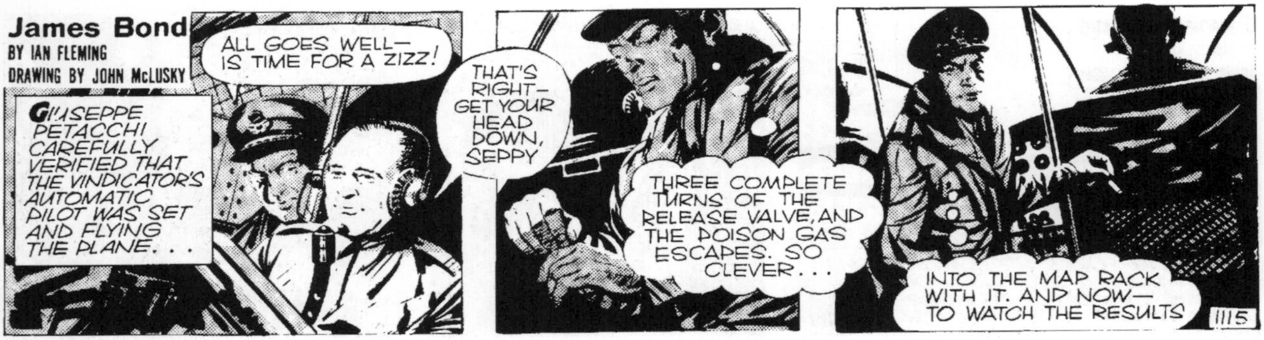
James Bond
BY IAN FLEMING
DRAWING BY JOHN McLUSKY
GIUSEPPE PETACCHI CAREFULLY VERIFIED THAT THE VINDICATOR'S AUTOMATIC PILOT WAS SET AND FLYING THE PLANE . . .
ALL GOES WELL— IS TIME FOR A ZIZZ!
THAT'S RIGHT— GET YOUR HEAD DOWN, SEPPY
THREE COMPLETE TURNS OF THE RELEASE VALVE, AND THE POISON GAS ESCAPES. SO CLEVER . . .
INTO THE MAP RACK WITH IT. AND NOW— TO WATCH THE RESULTS
1115

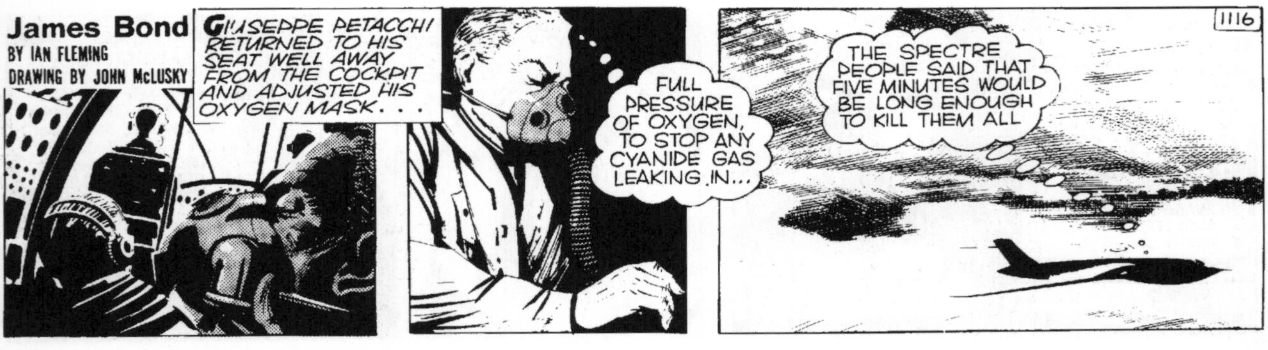
James Bond
BY IAN FLEMING
DRAWING BY JOHN McLUSKY
GIUSEPPE PETACCHI RETURNED TO HIS SEAT WELL AWAY FROM THE COCKPIT AND ADJUSTED HIS OXYGEN MASK . . .
FULL PRESSURE OF OXYGEN, TO STOP ANY CYANIDE GAS LEAKING IN...
1116
THE SPECTRE PEOPLE SAID THAT FIVE MINUTES WOULD BE LONG ENOUGH TO KILL THEM ALL

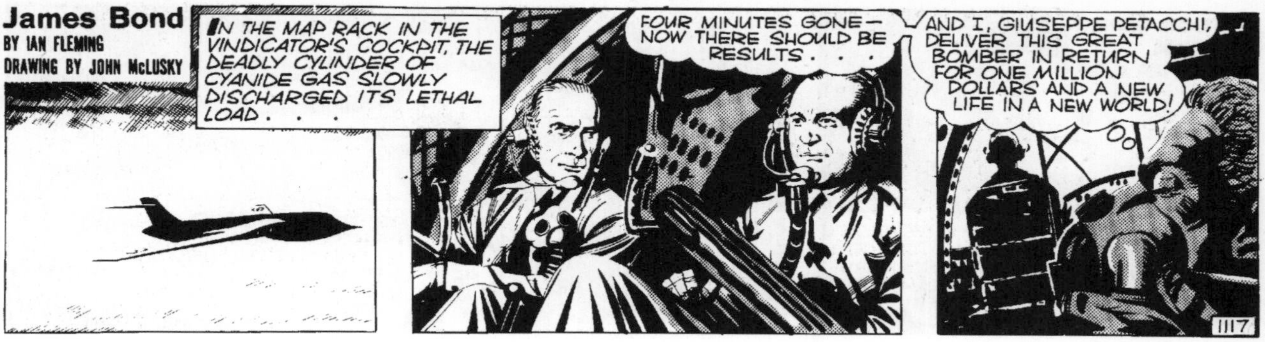
James Bond
BY IAN FLEMING
DRAWING BY JOHN McLUSKY
IN THE MAP RACK IN THE VINDICATOR'S COCKPIT, THE DEADLY CYLINDER OF CYANIDE GAS SLOWLY DISCHARGED ITS LETHAL LOAD . . .
FOUR MINUTES GONE—NOW THERE SHOULD BE RESULTS . . .
AND I, GIUSEPPE PETACCHI, DELIVER THIS GREAT BOMBER IN RETURN FOR ONE MILLION DOLLARS AND A NEW LIFE IN A NEW WORLD!
1117

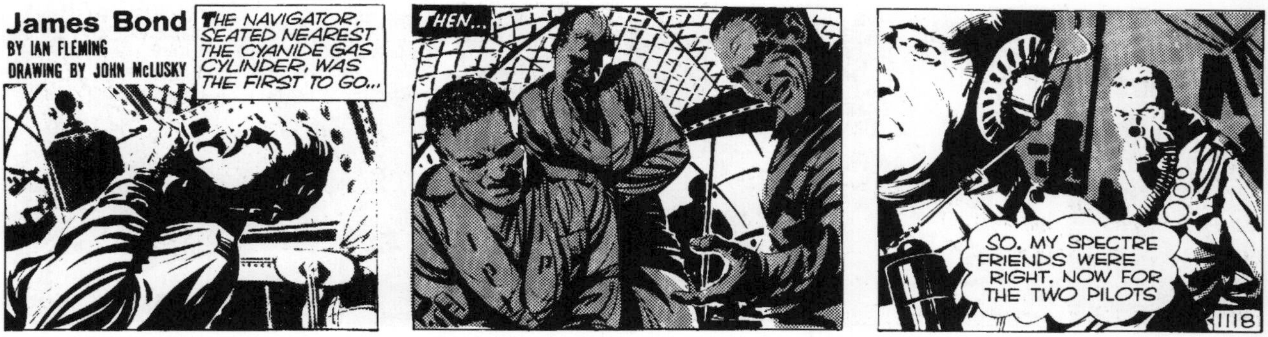
James Bond
BY IAN FLEMING
DRAWING BY JOHN McLUSKY
THE NAVIGATOR, SEATED NEAREST THE CYANIDE GAS CYLINDER, WAS THE FIRST TO GO...
THEN...
SO. MY SPECTRE FRIENDS WERE RIGHT. NOW FOR THE TWO PILOTS
1118

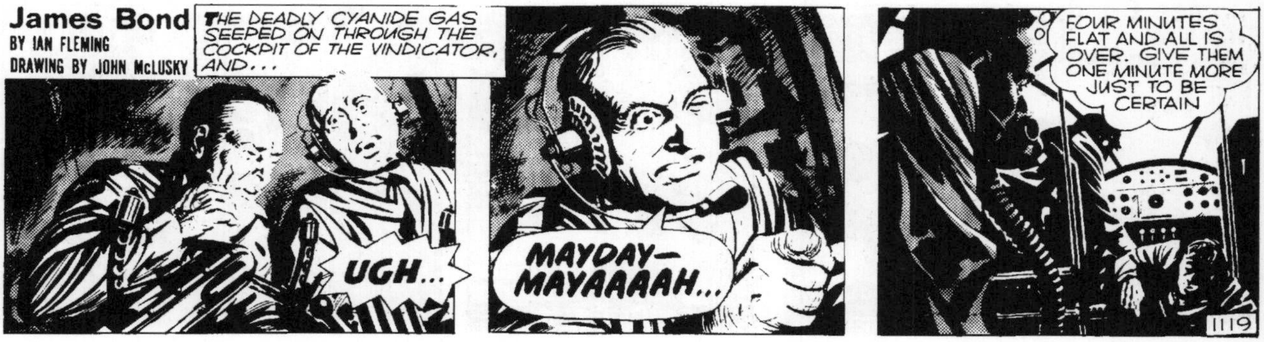
James Bond
BY IAN FLEMING
DRAWING BY JOHN McLUSKY
THE DEADLY CYANIDE GAS SEEPED ON THROUGH THE COCKPIT OF THE VINDICATOR, AND...
UGH...
MAYDAY—MAYAAAAH...
FOUR MINUTES FLAT AND ALL IS OVER. GIVE THEM ONE MINUTE MORE JUST TO BE CERTAIN
1119

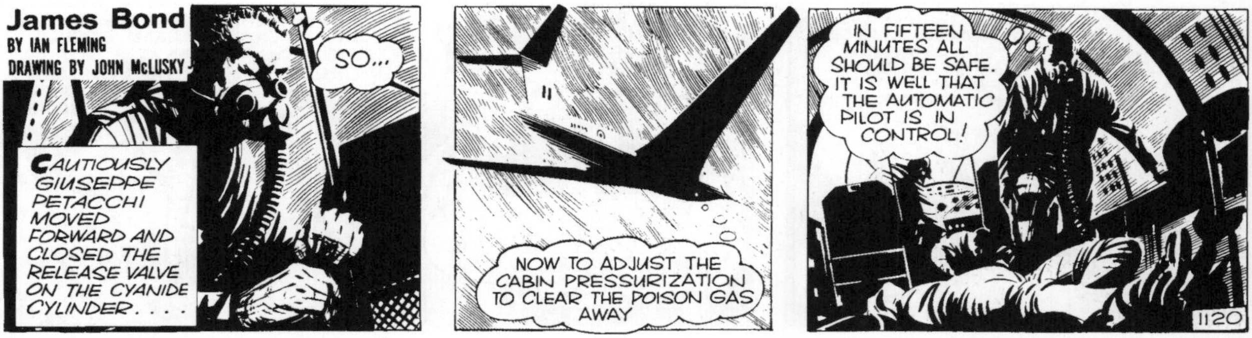
James Bond
BY IAN FLEMING
DRAWING BY JOHN McLUSKY
SO...
CAUTIOUSLY GIUSEPPE PETACCHI MOVED FORWARD AND CLOSED THE RELEASE VALVE ON THE CYANIDE CYLINDER . . .
NOW TO ADJUST THE CABIN PRESSURIZATION TO CLEAR THE POISON GAS AWAY
IN FIFTEEN MINUTES ALL SHOULD BE SAFE. IT IS WELL THAT THE AUTOMATIC PILOT IS IN CONTROL!
1120

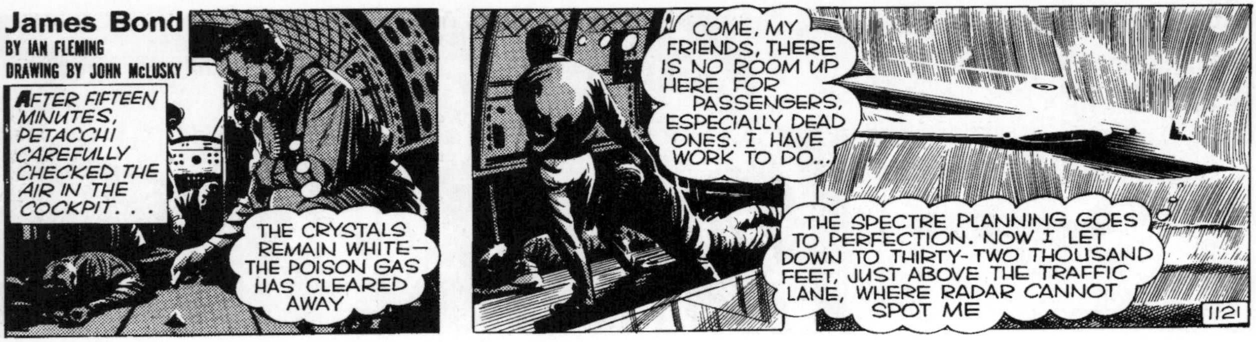
James Bond
BY IAN FLEMING
DRAWING BY JOHN McLUSKY
AFTER FIFTEEN MINUTES, PETACCHI CAREFULLY CHECKED THE AIR IN THE COCKPIT. . .
THE CRYSTALS REMAIN WHITE— THE POISON GAS HAS CLEARED AWAY
COME, MY FRIENDS, THERE IS NO ROOM UP HERE FOR PASSENGERS, ESPECIALLY DEAD ONES. I HAVE WORK TO DO...
THE SPECTRE PLANNING GOES TO PERFECTION. NOW I LET DOWN TO THIRTY-TWO THOUSAND FEET, JUST ABOVE THE TRAFFIC LANE, WHERE RADAR CANNOT SPOT ME
1121

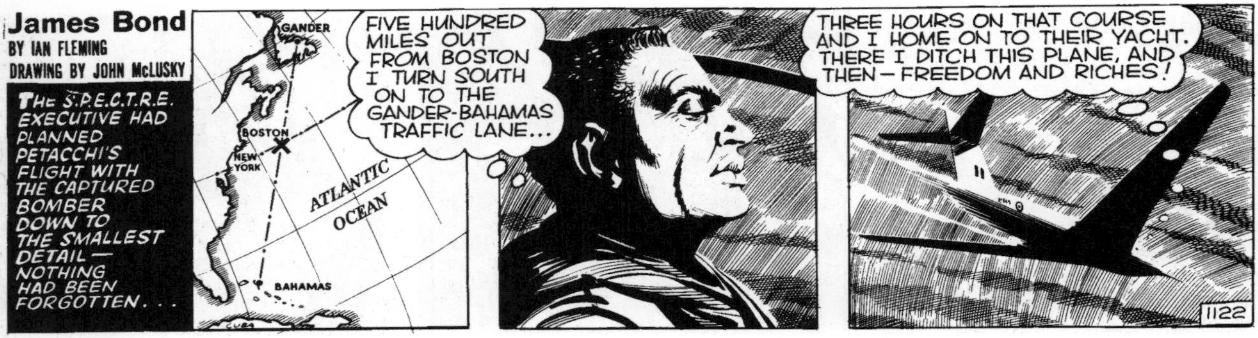
James Bond
BY IAN FLEMING
DRAWING BY JOHN McLUSKY
THE S.P.E.C.T.R.E. EXECUTIVE HAD PLANNED PETACCHI'S FLIGHT WITH THE CAPTURED BOMBER DOWN TO THE SMALLEST DETAIL— NOTHING HAD BEEN FORGOTTEN. . .
GANDER
BOSTON
NEW YORK
ATLANTIC OCEAN
BAHAMAS
FIVE HUNDRED MILES OUT FROM BOSTON I TURN SOUTH ON TO THE GANDER-BAHAMAS TRAFFIC LANE...
THREE HOURS ON THAT COURSE AND I HOME ON TO THEIR YACHT. THERE I DITCH THIS PLANE, AND THEN— FREEDOM AND RICHES!
1122

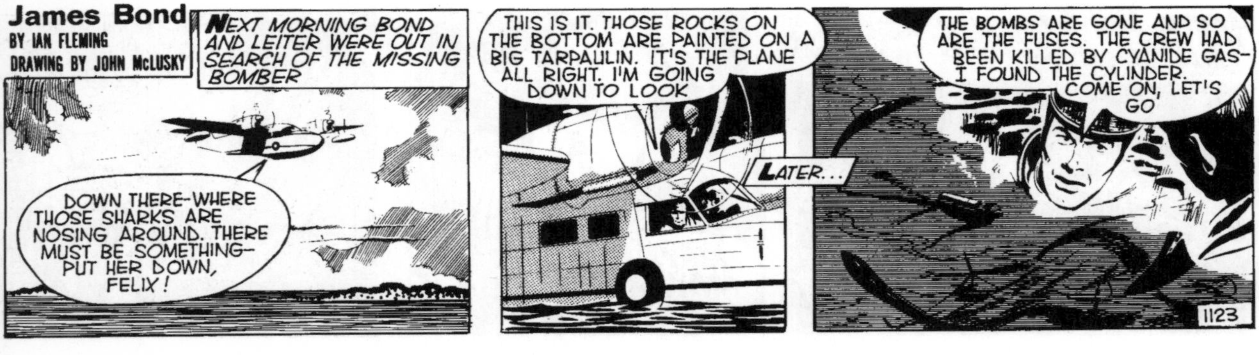
James Bond
BY IAN FLEMING
DRAWING BY JOHN McLUSKY
NEXT MORNING BOND AND LEITER WERE OUT IN SEARCH OF THE MISSING BOMBER
DOWN THERE-WHERE THOSE SHARKS ARE NOSING AROUND. THERE MUST BE SOMETHING- PUT HER DOWN, FELIX!
THIS IS IT. THOSE ROCKS ON THE BOTTOM ARE PAINTED ON A BIG TARPAULIN. IT'S THE PLANE ALL RIGHT. I'M GOING DOWN TO LOOK
LATER...
THE BOMBS ARE GONE AND SO ARE THE FUSES. THE CREW HAD BEEN KILLED BY CYANIDE GAS- I FOUND THE CYLINDER.
COME ON, LET'S GO
1123

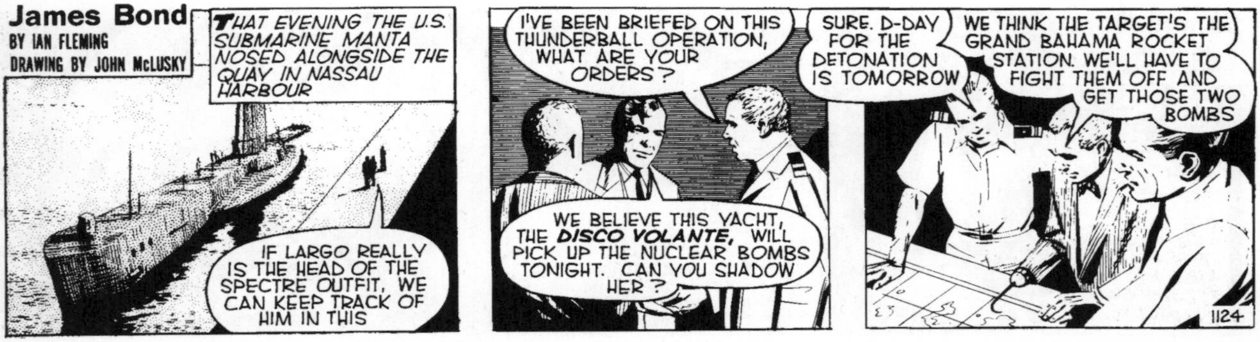
James Bond
BY IAN FLEMING
DRAWING BY JOHN McLUSKY
THAT EVENING THE U.S. SUBMARINE MANTA NOSED ALONGSIDE THE QUAY IN NASSAU HARBOUR
IF LARGO REALLY IS THE HEAD OF THE SPECTRE OUTFIT, WE CAN KEEP TRACK OF HIM IN THIS
I'VE BEEN BRIEFED ON THIS THUNDERBALL OPERATION, WHAT ARE YOUR ORDERS?
WE BELIEVE THIS YACHT, THE DISCO VOLANTE, WILL PICK UP THE NUCLEAR BOMBS TONIGHT. CAN YOU SHADOW HER?
SURE. D-DAY FOR THE DETONATION IS TOMORROW
WE THINK THE TARGET'S THE GRAND BAHAMA ROCKET STATION. WE'LL HAVE TO FIGHT THEM OFF AND GET THOSE TWO BOMBS
1124

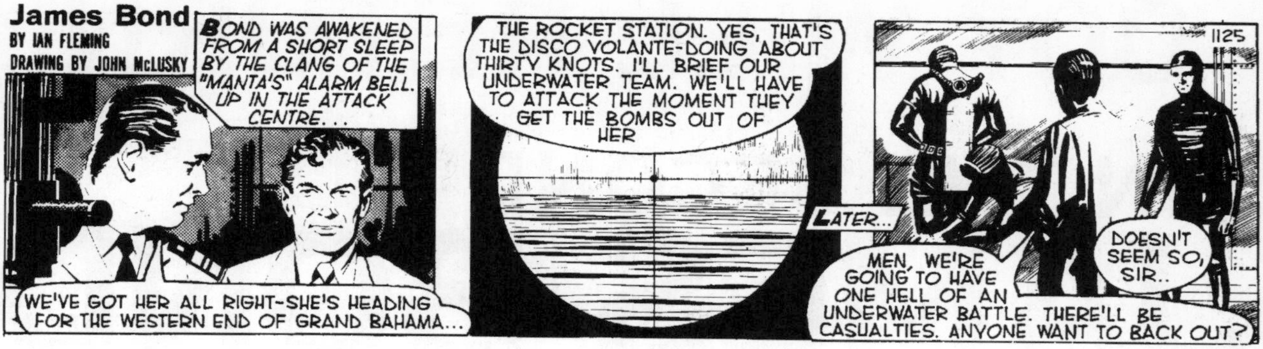
James Bond
BY IAN FLEMING
DRAWING BY JOHN McLUSKY
BOND WAS AWAKENED FROM A SHORT SLEEP BY THE CLANG OF THE "MANTA'S" ALARM BELL. UP IN THE ATTACK CENTRE...
WE'VE GOT HER ALL RIGHT-SHE'S HEADING FOR THE WESTERN END OF GRAND BAHAMA...
THE ROCKET STATION. YES, THAT'S THE DISCO VOLANTE-DOING ABOUT THIRTY KNOTS. I'LL BRIEF OUR UNDERWATER TEAM. WE'LL HAVE TO ATTACK THE MOMENT THEY GET THE BOMBS OUT OF HER
1125
LATER...
MEN, WE'RE GOING TO HAVE ONE HELL OF AN UNDERWATER BATTLE. THERE'LL BE CASUALTIES. ANYONE WANT TO BACK OUT?
DOESN'T SEEM SO, SIR..

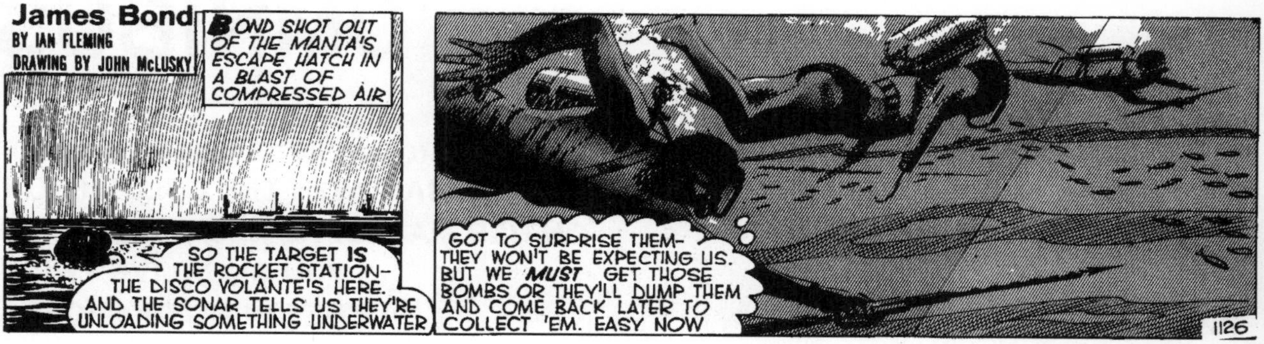
James Bond
BY IAN FLEMING
DRAWING BY JOHN McLUSKY
BOND SHOT OUT OF THE MANTA'S ESCAPE HATCH IN A BLAST OF COMPRESSED AIR
SO THE TARGET IS THE ROCKET STATION- THE DISCO VOLANTE'S HERE. AND THE SONAR TELLS US THEY'RE UNLOADING SOMETHING UNDERWATER
GOT TO SURPRISE THEM- THEY WON'T BE EXPECTING US. BUT WE MUST GET THOSE BOMBS OR THEY'LL DUMP THEM AND COME BACK LATER TO COLLECT 'EM. EASY NOW
1126

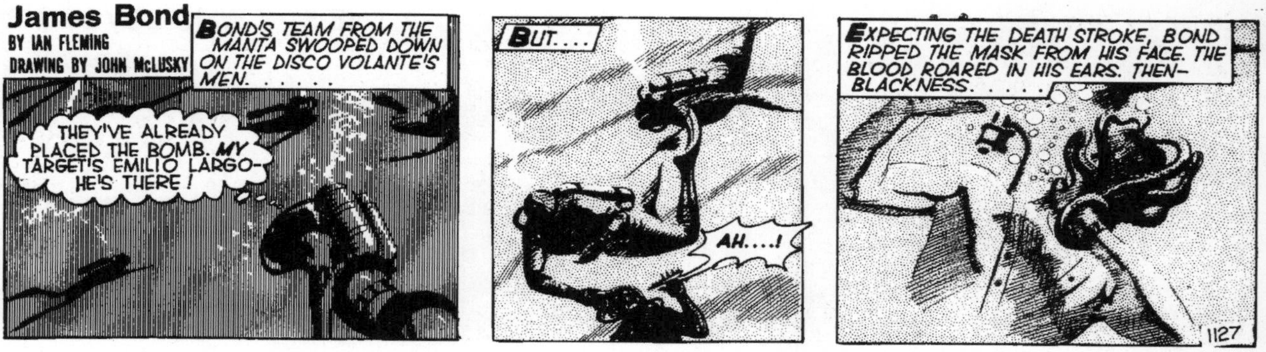
James Bond
BY IAN FLEMING
DRAWING BY JOHN McLUSKY
BOND'S TEAM FROM THE MANTA SWOOPED DOWN ON THE DISCO VOLANTE'S MEN. . . . . .
THEY'VE ALREADY PLACED THE BOMB. MY TARGET'S EMILIO LARGO- HE'S THERE!
BUT. . . .
AH....!
EXPECTING THE DEATH STROKE, BOND RIPPED THE MASK FROM HIS FACE. THE BLOOD ROARED IN HIS EARS. THEN- BLACKNESS. . . .
1127

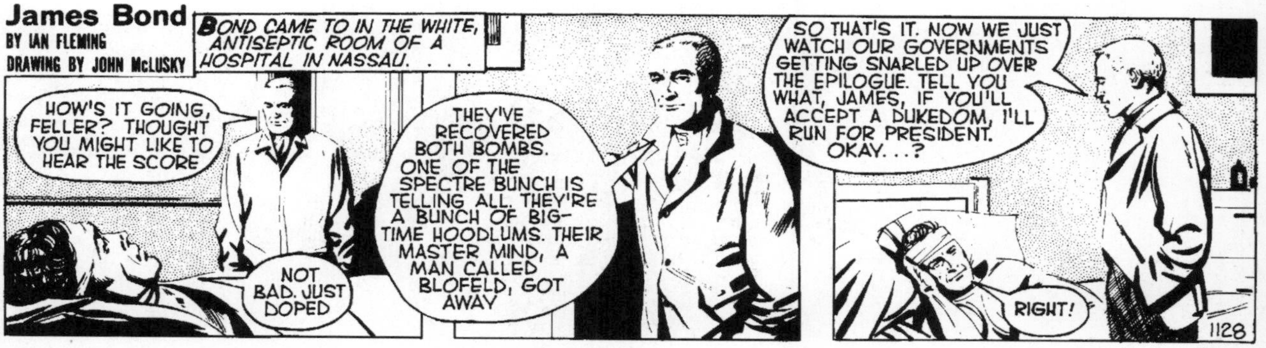
James Bond
BY IAN FLEMING
DRAWING BY JOHN McLUSKY
BOND CAME TO IN THE WHITE, ANTISEPTIC ROOM OF A HOSPITAL IN NASSAU. . . .
HOW'S IT GOING, FELLER? THOUGHT YOU MIGHT LIKE TO HEAR THE SCORE
NOT BAD. JUST DOPED
THEY'VE RECOVERED BOTH BOMBS. ONE OF THE SPECTRE BUNCH IS TELLING ALL. THEY'RE A BUNCH OF BIG-TIME HOODLUMS. THEIR MASTER MIND, A MAN CALLED BLOFELD, GOT AWAY
SO THAT'S IT. NOW WE JUST WATCH OUR GOVERNMENTS GETTING SNARLED UP OVER THE EPILOGUE. TELL YOU WHAT, JAMES, IF YOU'LL ACCEPT A DUKEDOM, I'LL RUN FOR PRESIDENT. OKAY. . .?
RIGHT!
1128

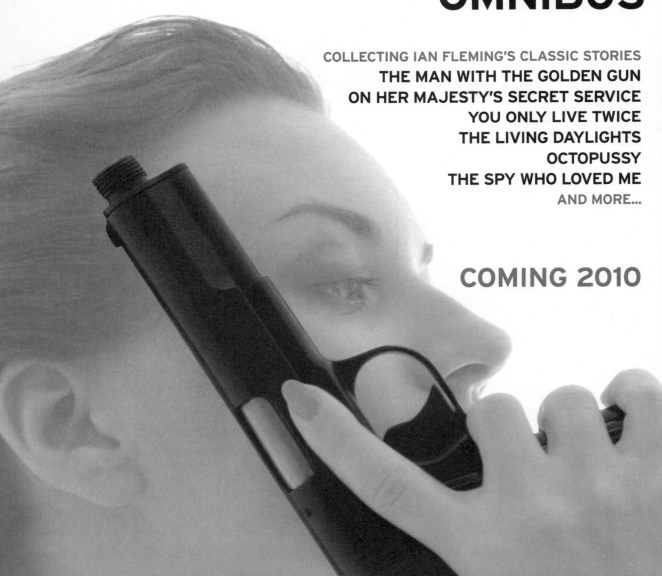

007 WILL RETURN

IN THE SECOND
JAMES BOND
OMNIBUS

COLLECTING IAN FLEMING'S CLASSIC STORIES

THE MAN WITH THE GOLDEN GUN
ON HER MAJESTY'S SECRET SERVICE
YOU ONLY LIVE TWICE
THE LIVING DAYLIGHTS
OCTOPUSSY
THE SPY WHO LOVED ME
AND MORE...

COMING 2010